EPOCH'S END
The Complete Series

By
Mike Kraus

© 2022 Muonic Press Inc

www.muonic.com

* * *

www.MikeKrausBooks.com

hello@mikeKrausBooks.com

www.facebook.com/MikeKrausBooks

Want More Awesome Books?

Find more fantastic tales right here at books.to/readmorepa.

* * *

If you're new to reading Mike Kraus, consider visiting his website at www.mikekrausbooks.com and signing up for his free newsletter. You'll receive several free books and a sample of his audiobooks, too, just for signing up, you can unsubscribe at any time and you will receive absolutely *no* spam.

Book 1: ENDURE

Preface

A remote island off the coast of New England

The wet sand cooled Robert's feet as he pulled the small sailboat a little farther onto the beach and stepped back to ensure the gently lapping waves wouldn't drag it away. Once satisfied the boat was stable, Robert put his hands on his hips and gazed across the beautiful North Atlantic from the island's shore.

The sun glinted off the flat surface, the stark blue horizon line dividing the water and the clear blue sky, birds calling down the shore. Robert took a deep breath of fresh air and let the tension drain from his body, stress from the day job melting away like wax down the side of a candle. He backed up the beach onto the drier sand and wiggled his toes in its warmth.

A pair of wine glasses clinked together, and Robert turned to see Denise kneeling on the beach blanket, auburn hair whipping around her shoulders as she held up the glasses and tapped them together, a sly expression on her face.

Robert couldn't help but grin, his beautiful wife looking like a goddess against the backdrop of the old lighthouse on its grassy rise. Turning his back on the ocean, he grinned and tried to wipe away the mild guilt at drinking so early in the day. But it was their vacation, and the picnic was just the start of things to come.

"Coming, honey," he said, starting over when his daughter called from the lighthouse yard.

"Hey, Dad! Look!"

Robert turned to see Cleo's head sticking up above the tall grass, her golden-brown hair sunbaked as it lay over her shoulders. Her finger was aimed at something in the ocean, and he turned to face the water as a school of flying fish burst from the waves and flitted upward in a spray of dazzling foam.

"Flying fish! *Exocoetidai*!" Robert's smile was wide and a little strained. Being from New Bedford, Rhode Island, he'd heard of the flying fish reaching as far north as Buzzards Bay, though it was strange to see them so far out.

They were beautiful creatures, sunlight glinting off their cylindrical bodies in sparkles of wiggling movement as they soared hundreds of meters through the air. Gulls swooped down and plucked some out of the sky, beaks snapping them up in a frenzy of activity.

Robert turned away from the ocean and trudged through the sand toward his wife, kicking warm "You sure it's not too early for wine?" Robert asked with a smile, already knowing the answer.

"It's never too early for wine! The kids are playing in the lighthouse. Now," she smiled, holding a glass up toward him, "this lady wants to spend some quality time with her husband."

The children's laughter danced down the hill, and Robert glanced up at the lighthouse to watch his son, Brad, chase his sister around. They were running the sand trails between the dunes, the rustic lighthouse and its beach-scrub yard lingering in the background in its deep brown granite face, the iron catwalk spotted with rust where it encircled the octagonal lighthouse on top.

"Stay where we can see you!" Robert called up to them.

"Okay, Dad!" Cleo called back.

Robert started to sit when the feeding birds clambered and squawked excitedly, the burst of activity causing his wife to tick her head to the side.

"The flying fish are beautiful, aren't they?" Robert reached for a wine glass.

"It's not just flying fish anymore," Denise replied, still staring at the ocean, nodding at the water.

Brow furrowed, hand still held out for a glass, Robert half turned and gazed back at a dozen or more dorsal fins cutting through the water, moving south at a high rate of speed, tails churning up the foam as sleek gray forms accelerated like bullets across the surface. Clicks and squeals penetrated his ears above the sounds of rolling surf, drawing him the rest of the way around to face the water.

He squinted. "Those are… dolphins?"

Denise put her hand to her forehead to block the sun. "I think so. And… Oh, look at that!"

Five large humps rose above the water's surface, massive gray backs with hard crescent shapes slipping through the waves and diving hard, sending sea foam splashing up. They drove through the ranks of dolphins and sent them turning and zipping away through the water.

"Those are humpback whales." Jaw hanging open in awe, Robert stared at the whales' barreling, knob-ridden snouts as they pushed through the other animals, knocking them aside, fins smacking the water as whale songs lifted high and strained.

"This is crazy," he said, blinking in amazement as the squarish head of a sperm whale breached the water's surface, its body soaring several meters into the air, trailing salt water, a squid clenched in its mouth. The squid's tentacles still clung to the whale's head, hooked in even as the deep-sea creature was actively being devoured.

"Those two came from deep down. Something must have driven them to the surface." He staggered closer, feet dragging through the sand, hand raised to his eyes in bewilderment. "What the hell's going on to get them running scared like that?"

"Robert?" Nancy's voice rose with an uneasy lilt. "Do you feel that?"

"Feel what?" Robert watched as Denise backed up along the beach, hands held out as if she were trying to get her balance.

A tremor echoed through the ground, a slow, low rumble of tectonic shift that shook the sand, sending his feet vibrating in a wave that moved up and down his legs, setting every hair on end. Eyes darting to Denise, she returned a wide-eyed horrified stare. The ground bucked, lifting Robert off his feet and tossing him into his wife, sending wine glasses flying, the bottle tumbling to the sand, red wine spilling out in a quivering gush. He caught her, turning, eyes darting like a pinball as they stumbled around. Robert held on to her, the two dancing on the balls of their feet to stay upright.

Cleo screamed and Brad cried out, "Mommy! Mommy!"

"The kids," Robert's voice ejected in a panicked grunt, watching as Cleo tried to stand before being violently thrown back to the ground. Brad ran toward his sister, but the grassy yard kicked upward and pitched him into the tall grass, tumbling head over heels.

"No!" Robert cried. Teeth gritting against Nature's fury, he braced himself with his hands on Denise's shoulders, pushing himself to his feet. Denise helped stabilize her husband, gripping his arms until her fingernails made furrows in his skin, pushing and shoving him ahead like a shield. He stumbled forward five yards before losing his balance, and he threw his legs wide just to stay upright. Denise smashed against him then fell away, staggering, hands bent into claws as she strove to cling to him.

Robert craned his neck back toward the beach, mouth falling open at the massive form surging toward them, skimming across the wet sand on a layer of brine like a water demon from the darkest depths of the ocean. At first, Robert couldn't believe his eyes, but the massive black-backed creature slid toward them, its white underbelly plowing through the sand, displacing a thousand pounds of grains in a sweeping wake.

Adrenaline shocked his limbs, and Robert jerked backwards, dragging Denise with him. They stumbled a dozen yards and fell to the side as the killer whale slid past them, six tons of massive bulk throwing a wake of gritty brown sand over their heads, a pungent brine smell washing over them.

Wiping his eyes with one hand, spitting, choking, coughing up sand, Robert grabbed Denise and shouted into her face. "We've got to get to the kids!"

"How?" she called back, straining to be heard over the rumbling.

"Crawl!"

Robert pulled her away from the Orca, falling to all fours and propelling himself forward any way he could. He kicked with his legs and knees, digging his arms into the sand, using them like flippers. Head down, ears honed-in on the screams of his children, he dragged himself across the shivering sand.

After several yards of scrambling, Robert glanced back to see Denise lying sprawled on the beach, face turned up to him, frozen in terror, a silent scream ripping from her throat. Her hair shimmered where it fell across her forehead, arm outstretched and reaching, fingers clutching.

Robert faced forward and dove with his arms spread wide, crawling harder, glaring up toward the rise as the brown granite of the lighthouse burst apart. The stones shook out of the wall, mortar turned to dust, sifting down in a dry cascade. Up in the lighthouse, glass exploded from the massive lantern pane, sending razor sharp shards zipping to the ground. The catwalk buckled and broke away, and the tower split and folded downward in a screech of twisting metal.

The steel cupola rolled off and plunged end over end in a slow-motion free fall toward their children. The rounded bell smacked the ground with an ominous clang, cutting off their screams. A moment of shock and disbelief passed through his system, a dreadful reality gripping him with shock.

"No!" Robert screamed.

Tears and sand stinging his eyes, Robert pounded forward, arm over arm, dragging himself across a ground that had become more ethereal than firm, determined to somehow reach his children. Changing direction, he grunted and shouted unintelligibly as his struggle to crawl grew. He cried out in dismay as a crack ran across the base of the dune, sand sifting into the gap. The ground buckled, dumping the lighthouse into some bottomless underground chasm before a dozen water geysers sprouted up into the sky, the ends flailing outward in a fine mist.

Up the beach, more geysers and cracks sprung open, vomiting up fish, eels, and gelatinous creatures onto the beach, leaving them squirming and flopping around as they died. Rolling onto his back, Robert tried to find Denise, his heart seizing again at the sight of another crack running into the sea, the killer whale floundering half inside the gaping fissure.

Denise was gone, disappeared, swallowed up or taken by the ocean waves. An anguished cry tore from his lips as he closed his eyes and prepared to meet his maker. Powerful forces tore apart the island, split by the violent tides. A chasm cracked the island's bedrock, the yawning maw consuming rock and silt and sand, punctuated by geysers of freshwater stirred up from the ocean floor and shot up from the muck.

The crack continued toward the east shore where it split the island in two. Stone exploded upwards, massive rocks tumbling through the air, cracking together like lightning before exploding into brittle bits, crumbles of sediment raining down, splashing into the spreading waves.

The island slowly slid beneath the churning swell of silt and freshwater soup surging upward from the Earth's crust, bubbles gurgling upward in a final, wet gasp.

The sea fell silent, and it was all gone.

Introduction

The European Science Foundation believes a mini ice-age occurred between 8,000 and 15,000 years ago, starting in North America when Glacial Lake Ojibway reached maximum volume and joined Lake Agassiz. A broken ice dam allowed massive pulses of freshwater to flow into the North Atlantic and Arctic Oceans. The sudden influx of freshwater diluted the circulation of seawater in the North Atlantic, weakening its "conveyor belt" of warm water flowing north and locking the northern hemisphere in freezing temperatures.

Ice sheets formed, throwing humanity into a mini ice-age for 1,300 years. Recent data shows this "Big Freeze" developed over the course of a few months or years, at most. We can assume the icy temperatures drove humankind's ancient ancestors south toward the equator where it was warmer, following herd animals they might hunt. With room to roam and populations at lower levels than today, our ancestors could have adapted to such a harsh environment, using their survival skills to exist in the brutal cold until conditions improved.

But what if, in the near future, a freshwater surge from the bottom of the North Atlantic caused another "Big Freeze," developing over a period of weeks to disrupt the North Atlantic conveyor belt? What if flash-freezing cold fronts swept across the United States and Canada, driving temperatures to well below freezing, causing ice sheets to form, and raining down massive hailstorms? Such a swift climate shift would create the perfect conditions for tornadoes and mass flooding, with rising sea levels devastating coastal cities. Crops, livestock, and flora would be destroyed, bringing countries in the northern hemisphere to their knees.

Imagine a future where most of North America becomes uninhabitable, a crackling, frozen wasteland covered in snow and ice. The United States infrastructure crumbles, vehicles and machines lock up and become useless, and supply chains break down beneath the weight of overpopulation. In this dismal future, survivors fight over essential supplies, rioting and killing each other within the first few weeks. Those unable to find food or shelter huddle in makeshift camps, burning anything they can find, for a single spark of heat.

Desperate for food and fuel, those able to travel flee their worthless homes to head south in endless caravan lines, clinging to the hope of reaching warmer climates. People drop like flies during the trek south, the weakest falling first, whittling down the North American population bit by bit. As tent cities swell along the border of California, Arizona, New Mexico, and Texas, tensions between the United States and Mexico boil over. Mexico closes their border, and the two sides fight violent clashes that leave thousands dead, displacing what humanity remains. The survivors of the collapse pick from the scraps, form alliances, make enemies, and fight for their very existence.

In this bleak and desperate new ice-age, only the most hardened and resourceful individuals will survive.

Chapter 1
Tom McKnight
Portland, Maine

Tom McKnight strode between the long rows of advanced technology on display at the Portland Undersea Expo, eyes roaming over tables filled with micro-tech camera platforms for seafloor mapping, advanced rovers with new engine designs, demonstrations of better skirting materials to be used for oceanic cleanup of plastics, and a wide array of budding technologies.

He looked forward to events like the Undersea Expo to get out from beneath the daily grind of his day-to-day job with Maniford Aquatics Engineering. Spending time with his sixteen-year-old daughter, Samantha, was an added bonus that fit in perfectly at the end of her school's summer break.

"Check it out!" Sam gestured ahead, rushing from his side, trailing a mane of ringlet curls, sand-colored and long past her shoulders.

She stopped before a heavy table where two pieces of machinery rested, each the size of a large dog. The rovers sat on tracks, outfitted with sleek-looking propellers nestled against their beetle-shaped bodies. With all the retractable cameras, clasps, and digging arms spread open, they looked like something off the Battle Robots show.

"They're the new B-Model iCore rovers." A man with *Suresh* on his name tag peered over the display with a smile, glancing between Sam and Tom as he rejoined her side. "These have an improved engine design that makes them twice as maneuverable as the A-Model machines. They can stop on a dime, pivot, and even fit into crevices on the seafloor."

Tom knelt down in front of the glass front of the display. "Looks like they've got the older Series-6 Titan cores in them. Have you put them to use yet? Any big contracts?"

"We signed on with the Oceanic Research Group to do some filming of the seafloor for a television special they're airing next year." Suresh placed a hand on each of the rovers' black casings. "A week from now, these two guys will be down on the seafloor off the coast of California, filming amazing stuff."

"Congratulations," Tom said, and he meant it. "I know how hard it is for young tech startups to gather funding to build delicate and expensive machines. There's a lot of interest in it these days with all the conservation efforts happening."

"I love undersea television shows," Sam spouted, her girlish enthusiasm showing through. "I want to be a marine biologist, sort of like my dad."

"You're a marine biologist?" Suresh asked with a raised eyebrow. "I'll bet you get out on the water a lot."

"Not really a biologist," Tom dismissed the notion. "I'm more of an engineer. I spend most of my time testing and analyzing propulsion systems for the Navy on behalf of Maniford Aquatics. I was part of the Sub-X project a few years back."

Suresh's eyes grew wide and he glanced down at his own rovers self-consciously. "That's amazing! The Sub-X was a beast!"

"It still is," Tom nodded, a slight grin playing at the edges of his mouth.

"I mean, that monster could hover at a depth of thirteen thousand feet for five months." The man's voice rose to a higher pitch, his grin wide. "You guys took samples and videos of places no one had ever seen."

"It was a challenging project." Tom smiled with pride. "I'm glad you enjoyed our work."

"I'll keep following the progress." Suresh held out a card with aqua blue coloring, hand shaking almost imperceptibly. "Here. Take our card. Please."

Tom accepted the man's card and thanked him, then he and Sam turned away from the display.

"Can I have one of those rovers for my birthday instead of a car?" Sam asked, one corner of her mouth lifting in a smart smile.

"That's a lot of weekends working at the ice cream shop," Tom smiled. "Take you a few centuries to save up."

"I was hoping to get a loan," she countered.

Tom laughed as they strolled along, arm thrown over her shoulder. "Ohhh, right. At the First Bank of Dad, I assume?"

The pair continued their Expo tour, stopping by a 3-D model of the sub-oceanic crust. They wowed at dozens of undersea gadgets, advanced breathing apparatuses, and diving suits on display. At the end of the row, a massive, high-definition display hung on the wall beneath a sign that read *Ocean Watch*. Sam rushed forward, leaning up against the table and staring up at the Ultra 8K video of a school of whales cruising through the ocean.

Ocean Watch had grown in popularity since its inception a few years prior, with a goal of providing twenty-four-hour news and livestreams related to the world's oceans. They broadcasted specials on oceanic policing, pollution, and nature shows focused on the magnificent world beneath the vast blue surface.

Tom caught up to Sam, watching her wide eyes with his hands in his pockets. She streamed the channel almost twenty-four hours a day while doing homework or before bed. He couldn't be certain she'd really follow through with becoming a marine biologist, but she certainly had the enthusiasm for it, and her aptitude was off the charts.

A woman approached them with her hands behind her back, wearing a blue Ocean Watch T-shirt. She let them study the screen for a minute before addressing them. "Can I help you with anything?"

"Ocean Watch is my favorite channel," Sam said, her green eyes wide at the massive display.

"Have you signed up for our mailing list?" The employee flashed a pleased smile.

"Absolutely," Sam replied. "I get all your notifications and watch all of your extra content."

"That's a stunning display," Tom said with a nod.

"It's one of the biggest interactive Ultra 8K displays in the world," she said with a smile. "We film all of our oceanic content at that definition, which, as you can see, delivers stunning results."

An in-screen box nestled in the top right corner showed an Ocean Watch reporter with the Ocean Watch logo emblazoned on her shirt. Standing on a windy pier, the woman's black hair gusted around her head as she pressed her hand against her earpiece. Something on the ticker running across the bottom of the screen caught Tom's eye.

"Can you turn that up?" Tom asked the Ocean Watch employee.

"Oh, sure," she replied. She lifted a remote control and pointed it at the screen. A sound bar appeared and inched upward, the reporter's voice growing louder and clearer.

"We've just received a report from our North Atlantic research vessel about a mysterious change in migratory patterns off the New England coast." She turned and glanced over her left shoulder. "Schools of humpback whales, dolphins, and bluefin tuna have turned south, abandoning seasonal feeding grounds for reasons unknown, although a contributing factor could be some unusual seismic activity reported along the continental shelf near New England. Ocean Watch reporters are working with the Oceanic Research Institute and the USGS to find out just what's happening. We're not sure what this will mean to fisheries off the coast, but we'll bring you more information as it arrives."

The in-screen box changed to a woman in a wet suit training a group of whales.

"What does that mean?" Sam peered up at her father. "What she said about the feeding grounds."

"What do you think?" Tom asked her.

Sam twisted her face in thought, eyes lifting. "I'd say it would have to be something massive, dynamic event to drive whales and fish out of their feeding grounds. Could an earthquake do that?"

"I'm… not sure," Tom said, frowning.

"We have reliable monitoring equipment," the Ocean Watch woman said with a smile. "We use pattern-recognition satellite software and have connections to crews in almost every ocean. Only the United States Navy has better equipment."

"I'm sure you're right," Tom gave the woman a polite smile and a nod, a twinge of fear and heat flitting through his stomach. "But if what they're saying is true, it could mean some real problems for the upcoming fishing season." He shrugged, forcing a smile and gave Sam a nudge. They walked away, looking around for another good display. They'd been in Portland since Wednesday but still had almost a quarter of the showroom left to explore.

"What do you want for lunch?" Tom asked, trying to put the thought of the odd report out of his mind.

"I don't know," Sam replied with a shrug. "I liked the place we ate on Thursday."

"I was hoping you would say that." Tom's phone buzzed in his pocket, and he reached to take it out. "Vietnamese it is." Reading the caller ID, he felt his stomach drop. "Sorry, hon, I need to get this call. You go ahead."

Sam nodded and skipped ahead without him, her eye caught by a flashy fishery and aquaculture display.

Tom accepted the call and put his phone to his ear, his greeting tinged with a deep sigh and a hint of suspicion. "What's the emergency, Ray?"

Ray Leeds led the Maniford Aquatics Engineering project team and had a brilliant mind for bringing the right people together to complete a job. Tom held Ray in high regard since they'd started working together over a decade ago, but Ray rarely called on weekends unless he needed a fire put out.

"Hello, Tom!" Ray's voice was unusually chipper. "How's it going in Portland?"

"The weather's been beautiful, and we're having a grand time at the tech convention," Tom said through half-gritted teeth, glancing at Sam where she spoke animatedly with the presenter. "All-in-all, it's been a great mini-vacation. I'll be nice and fresh when I come back to the office on *Monday*."

"That's… heh. That's the problem, Tom." Ray's frown found its way across the line. "I need you today on the *Marin* as soon as possible. She's part of the Navy's North Atlantic Task Force, stationed a few hundred miles off the New England coast. I've got a chopper coming to pick you up now."

Tom winced, stomach sinking farther, and he half-turned away from Samantha, lowering his voice. "I can't do that. I've got Sam with me, and she's looking forward to Vietnamese food for lunch."

"No worries! You can bring her along," Ray said. "I'll have the ship's mess cook up something special for both of you." When Tom didn't immediately reply, Ray pressed on, his tone firm and unyielding. "Look, Tom. It's nothing dangerous. I just need you to double check some data and help us with some detailed seafloor mappings."

"What about Sue Anne? She's as good as me."

"Sue Anne has the coding skills, but she'll need your help to validate the data," Ray went on in that plaintive yet firm way he always did, making it seem like Tom was the only aquatics engineer employed by Maniford Aquatics. "You practically built the Proctor Software from scratch. You know where all the possible glitches and important bits are."

Heat rose from Tom's sinking stomach, and his voice dripped with the dry tone of frustration. "It's not something that can wait until Monday? This is the last day I'll have with my daughter here in Portland, and I'll be home by tomorrow morning."

"This is important. Trust me. It's something you'll want to see." A measure of pleading crept into Ray's tone. "I'll even give you an extended break for Christmas. I'm talking four weeks and an additional three percent bonus on top of what you already get. Whatever you want."

Tom watched Sam grinning at the displays, already planning a way to tell her they had to cut their trip short. The hours he worked under Ray were exhaustive, and his family often suffered for it. Tom apologized at least once a week for missing some teacher's meeting or one of Sam's sports events. But that was the price one payed for joining a cutting-edge startup business that didn't outsource every aspect of the business. No, Maniford did almost everything in-house. And Tom was the best of the best – and Ray knew it.

"Okay, but I want all that in writing. Send over an email. Now. The entire month of December off, with a *five* percent bonus thrown in."

Ray's chair audibly creaked as he sat back and sighed in relief. "Consider it done! There's a chopper due to land in…" Ray spoke to someone off to the side before coming back to Tom. "Three minutes, on the baseball field behind the Portland Exposition Building."

"Wait, what? Right now?"

"See you in two hours."

Ray hung up, and Tom placed the phone back in his pocket, red-faced, chin low. A wave of disappointment lifted his chest, and he let out a breath of frustration. His time with Sam was – was *supposed* to be – sacrosanct, and cutting their trip short was going to cost him some major points. *Not to mention what Barbara's going to think.*

Carefully, lips lengthened into a grimace, he approached the girl and rested his hand on her shoulder. Sam turned, her expression falling as soon as she saw the look on his face.

"We're leaving, aren't we?" Her lips sank in a deep frown, her green eyes already glassing over with moisture.

Tom's heart broke on the spot. Not only was he having a good time at the Expo, but their father-daughter time was important in keeping her on the right track as she approached adulthood and faced real-world problems.

"I'm afraid so, honey. That was Ray, and he needs me to verify some data for him. Right away." Tom rolled his eyes. "It's probably nothing, but he insists that it's *super* important."

Sam only knew Ray as the guy who always took her father away, which had made him her arch nemesis. "Of course, it was Ray." Her voice grew in volume along with her frustration. "Doesn't Ray have a family, too?"

"Hey, take it easy, Sam. I don't think I'd be getting interrupted on the weekend if it wasn't important."

"Just like every other time." Sam made an exasperated noise. "Mom says he's a—"

Tom laughed, interrupting her before she could finish the thought. "Mom's not wrong." His expression grew pained again and he shrugged apologetically. "Sorry, kiddo. Hey – I always make it up to you, right?"

Sam's crossed arms grew looser as she considered his point, before finally dropping them to her sides. "Yeah… but just wait till mom hears about this. She's gonna be—"

"Sam…" Tom chuckled again. "Come on, let's hustle. I think you're going to enjoy this, actually."

They exited the building, and he called for her to take a left, pointing her through the parking lot where they'd parked their Hyundai rental car. Sam stopped at the car, waiting for him, but Tom walked right by, angling for the baseball field, leaving her to trail behind him.

"Uh, Dad? The car's right here."

Tom kept walking as the fast chuffing sounds of helicopter rotors drew near. Sam called to him twice more before he finally heard her sneakers pounding on the pavement after him as she caught up to his side.

Reaching the ballpark fence, Tom opened a gate and stepped through, descending a set of metal stairs to the ball field.

"What are you doing?" Sam traipsed down the steps behind him, her feet making hollow sounds on the metal as her thumb hitched over her shoulder. "The car is back there."

"There's been a change of plans. I told you that you might enjoy this, didn't I?" Tom grinned secretively, giving her a conspiratorial wink before staring upward as the Navy Sea Hawk helicopter swept in over their heads in a wash of wind and noise. Its tail stretched long behind a rectangular body, twin turboshafts whooshing menacingly on either side of the engine. With a receded cockpit, its chin stood out, mounted with an array of sensory equipment.

The aircraft soared close over their heads and angled down toward the outfield. "We're taking a limo."

Sam's curls whipped around her head as she gawked at the light gray chopper settling onto the stretch of short green grass, its blades chopping the air, whipping bending blades of grass to the ground in massive swaths. They reached the bottom of the stairs, and Tom leapt the rail and landed on the soft turf, turning to reach up to his daughter. Sam took his hands and jumped over to stand with him, eyes wide and staring, mouth hanging open.

A woman in a blue digital uniform with a rounded, bulky helmet dropped from the crew area and gestured them over.

"Let's go," Tom shouted over the noise

"Wait!" Sam grabbed a ponytail holder from her pocket, pulling her mane of hair through it. "Okay!"

Tom took her hand, and together they ducked and jogged toward the helicopter. Her shocked expression only grew as the wind cut at them, whipping their light jackets and forcing them to lean forward to keep moving.

"Sorry again, kiddo!" Tom shouted over the whine of the engines as they began to spool back up.

Sam's expression was no longer one of disappointment, but of awe. "Dad, are you serious? This is *awesome!*"

Chapter 2
Barbara McKnight,
Wyndale, Virginia

"Linda, Jack, let's go!" Barbara McKnight called as she turned on the John Deere mower and waited for them to get in the wagon along with their buckets of feed and bales of hay. She'd just finished loading the heavier bales of hay into the trailer, and the heady scents of grass, manure, and mud drifted through the air.

The kids were played over by the pond, wasting time while she itched to get on to the heavier farm chores. Looking down, she flexed her calloused, tanned hands, nails cut short and colorless, fingers strengthened from years of farm work. Still, they were thin and nimble with just a few wrinkles.

She shifted in her seat, taking the pressure off the Smith & Wesson pistol holstered on the back of her right hip, and checked her watch. It was already 11:23 a.m., and they had a lot left to do.

The kids ran around the nursery building, Jack soaking wet and Linda dry except for a big dripping spot on the front of her shirt.

Barbara clicked her tongue. "I leave you guys alone for ten minutes and you end up soaking wet. Linda, you're supposed to be watching him."

Looking guilty, the girl offered an excuse. "He keeps falling in. What should I do about that?"

"She sprayed me with the hose," Jack accused her in return, an innocent look on his face as he pointed to his sister.

"Given the evidence," Barbara frowned, "I'd say there's a bit of truth to both stories. Get in the wagon so we can get moving, please."

"Can we go get changed first?" Linda asked.

"Nope," Barbara shook her head. "Learn to keep dry. Now you can spend the next two hours working in your wet clothes. Hop in."

The kids grumbled as they climbed into the back of the wagon, sitting opposite one another on the benches that ran along the insides, feet propped up on the bales of hay. Linda was fourteen with a light sense of humor, and Jack was six and as inquisitive as a cat. The younger two kids were opposite their older sister Sam, who was in that phase where she took everything way too seriously sometimes.

Foot on the gas, Barbara moved the mower forward, sitting loose in the seat, letting her body sway with the bumps. The McKnight compound was laid out in a circular fashion. If standing on the concrete back patio, looking out toward their woods, she'd see a small duck pond slightly off to the left, able to accommodate a dozen or so animals, its edges covered in finely trimmed grass, the surface mirroring the grey clouds above.

Nestled close to that was the nursery where they kept their baby rabbits, chicks, and goats as soon as they were born. Beyond those structures, and farther left, were the animal pens, an old barn, and a feed yard for the larger animals. Directly ahead was their greenhouse with its clean, shimmering glass, and off to the right was their newest barn and generator shed, both painted a deep red color like something out of a painting.

She'd normally have an hour of Tom's time in the early morning to help with chores before he started working from home or had to drive in to the office, but he and Sam had taken half a week off to go to Portland for an aquatic tech convention. Barbara was counting on her youngest two to backfill, though it was debatable how much they were actually contributing to the cause.

The mower trundled past the pond and nursery into the side yard where the scents of hay and barnyard animals filled the air. The manure was especially pungent, tweaking her nose, its rich scent reminding her of all the life thriving on their small farm.

She turned off the mower, met Linda and Jack at the back of the wagon, grabbed a five-gallon bucket of feed, and stepped toward an approaching herd of animals. Ducks, yard chickens, and sheep pressed toward them, their anxious bleating rising as they anticipated feeding time.

The kids headed north to the chicken coops where they kept a variety of fowl including pure bred brown, orpington, and barnvelder chickens. A single emden goose, spitting mean when he wanted to be, acted as a guard dog for the birds – and an excellent one he was at that.

Barbara had trained the kids how on to feed and water the chickens while checking for abandoned nests and eggs. They'd sort through the lot, place any unattended eggs in another nest, the incubator, or in a basket for eating later. On the days when they weren't goofing around, they did it well.

Barbara faced the approaching beasts as they bleated, clucked, and quacked excitedly, accompanied by their rooster's rousing crow. With a soft, widening smile, she reached into her bucket, grabbed a handful of dry feed, and tossed it in all directions, the flock spinning away to follow the food. Off to the side, their German Shepherd, Smooch, eyed the proceedings with a watchful eye from the edge of the yard, her tail wagging slowly in the dirt.

Barbara kept tossing feed until the kids were done in the chicken pen. Placing the empty feed bucket back on the trailer, grabbing a small bale of hay, they moved to the rabbit pens right next door. The 10-by-15 structure was enclosed by mesh buried a couple feet down into the ground to discourage predators that managed to make it past Smooch into the main yard. Inside, they kept a mix of Netherlands dwarf rabbits and cute mini-rexes for a variety of uses.

"Come on, kids. Make it snappy." Barbara opened the outside pen door and stepped in, checking the mesh for breaks while the kids entered the hutch and checked the feeders, scooping out any dirt the rabbits had thrown inside from their incessant digging.

Barbara's phone buzzed in her pocket, and she fished it out, hoping to see Tom's name on the caller ID. She hadn't heard from him all morning, and she wondered what he and Sam planned for the day's activities. Instead, Marie Everett's name showed on the display. Marie and her husband Darren owned a piece of land down the road, a modest twenty acres and a medium-sized lake. The pair had helped Barbara and Tom get off to a great start when they'd started their farm years ago, alternating between giving them animals and selling them at steep discounts.

Barbara put the phone to her ear. "Morning, Marie."

"Top of the mornin' to ya," the woman replied in a terrible imitation of an Irish accent. "How's it going over there?"

"Oh, you know," Barbara chuckled, shaking her head as the kids' laughter rang out from the hutch, not sounding like they were getting much done at all. "Just behind on chores, *as usual*."

"We just finished with ours and were about to have lunch." Marie's tone dropped an octave, sobering from her friendly disposition. "Have you seen the news?"

"I haven't had a chance," Barbara replied, watching the kids as they ran outside to grab more hay and ducked back in, making some game of it. With a glance up at the clouds, she asked, "Is it the weather? Storms coming in?"

"Just get inside and see for yourself."

"Can it wait thirty minutes?"

"I don't think so," Marie's voice darkened further. "Just go look."

"Okay, Marie. Give me a few, and I'll call you back." Barbara frowned, hanging up the phone and stuffing it back into her pocket. Marie's tone wasn't one she was used to hearing, and something shivered deep in her gut. "Okay, kids. Chores are on hold. Back in the wagon!"

Without question, the pair slammed the hutch door shut and sprinted from the pen, leaping into the trailer in a fit of laughter. Shaking her head, Barbara hopped in the driver's seat, started the mower, and circled around to the house.

At their concrete patio, she killed the mower and got out, dusting her hands off as she unlaced her boots. The kids got their shoes off and beat her to the sliding glass door, pushing their way inside.

"Put on some dry clothes," Barbara called after them, stepping into the kitchen in her socks, padding across the tiles to the living room carpet. "I have to check something out, then we're going right back out to finish our chores!"

The pair grumbled but ran upstairs to get changed as Barbara found the TV remote in the bundle of covers she'd fallen asleep under the previous evening. She turned on the television where it rested on a stand in the room's corner, the screen snapping to life before she switched to the network news channel.

The normal afternoon anchor, Chris Penn, sat behind the news desk, wearing a crisp white shirt and a blue tie, his thick brown hair wavy where he'd combed it back.

"… for those just tuning in, we have a natural disaster developing in the North Atlantic off the coast of New England. The ocean conservation group Ocean Watch just reported an abrupt migration of whales, dolphins, mackerel, and bluefish tuna away from their natural feeding grounds, accompanied by a shift in ocean temperatures. Local fisherman have voiced concerns over their empty nets, dropping from several tons of fish a day to almost nothing overnight. Let's go to Tanya Mocahbee for the latest."

The broadcast changed to a lady reporter standing on a fishing dock somewhere in the North East United States. Dressed in a windbreaker with the CNF logo on the left breast, she nodded as she took the hand off. The wind blew her hair around her shoulders, and she tucked a lock if it behind her ear as she gave the camera a serious look.

"Thanks Chris. I'm here at Max's Fishery on the coast of Rhode Island, and I've been watching some of the trawlers come in. It's disturbing to see dozens of boats docking with nothing in their nets. Fishermen are all telling me the same thing. There's just nothing out there."

The camera switched to a man standing on the edge of his docked boat with one foot up on the side, his yellow parka and hood contrasting with the dismal, grey day.

Tanya lowered a microphone to his lips.

"We brought up our nets this morning, and they were empty," the man said as the camera focused in on his wrinkled, salt-burned face. The man gestured to the deck of his boat, and the camera followed to show a slick wooden deck covered with empty nets, white buoys, and smears of scales and blood. Only a handful of fish floundered around when he should have been ankle deep in squirming bodies.

"What about the other fisherman?" Tanya asked. "How are they doing?"

"It's the same for everyone." The man's head shook with disgust. "They're not bringing in anything. No cod, mackerel, or tuna. Nothing."

"What do you think caused it?"

The man gave a tired and confused shrug. "I couldn't tell you that, ma'am. I'm as baffled as the next person. One thing I can tell you is that this will ruin a lot of people if something doesn't change, and everyone who depends on these fish to survive will have empty freezers this winter unless we can shift our boats south. But the cost of fuel is high these days, so that'll be a tough proposition."

Barbara crossed her arms, watching the report with a twist of her lips, thinking about their own food stores. They purchased fish at a local market and kept it frozen for the long-term, though just in time supply chains meant any sort of disruption could be felt sooner than expected.

Tanya pulled the microphone up and turned to the camera. "You heard it right from the source, Chris. It'll be a rough winter unless the authorities can come up with some answers."

"Thanks, Tanya," Chris said as the broadcast returned to the anchor desk. Chris fixing the camera with a hard look. "While fishermen struggle along the American East Coast, we're receiving new information from Ocean Watch and NOAA Fisheries that suggests a possible clue as to why this is happening. Satellite images show a potential rift along the North Atlantic shelf, deep beneath the waters, possibly contributing to the disruption. While it isn't clear how, we learned the Navy is sending their North Atlantic Task Force to the area to investigate. Stay tuned. We'll keep you posted when we know more."

The news cut to a commercial, and Barbara bit her lower lip with concern. It didn't seem like any of the news would affect her family, though one could never be certain with the world constantly in flux. Her thoughts once again turned to Tom and Sam in Portland, the news report momentarily forgotten. As if by magic, her phone buzzed again, the image on the screen causing a grin to spread across her face as she swiped on the green bubble.

A loud blast of static greeted her, garbled voices and a high-pitched hum cutting through in the background.

"Hi, honey," Barbara said, wincing. "Is that you, Tom?"

"It's me," Tom replied, his voice popping through the static. "Can you hear me okay?"

"I can hear you, honey." Barbara switched the phone to her other ear and walked toward the sliding glass door, staring out toward the woods. "We miss you guys. Having fun?"

"We were, yes. But we, uh… we just finished up at the convention hall."

"What?" Barbara glanced up at the clock. "It's not even noon on Saturday, and you've got a whole day left tomorrow."

"We have to cut the trip short," Tom said, voice raised over the high hum. "Ray called."

She frowned at the mention of Ray's name. While she liked and respected Tom's boss, and certainly appreciated that her husband was gainfully employed, she didn't like the late-night calls and constant overtime. She'd never gotten used to Ray sending her husband on lengthy trips to naval testing sights all across the world.

Barbara frowned at the mention of Ray's name. While she respected Tom's boss – and appreciated the generous benefits that came with his employment – the late night calls and constant overtime were a constant irritation. Plus, seeing Tom sent off on lengthy trips to naval testing sites around the globe had never been her favorite pasttime.

Tom's line cut out again and came back with the high-pitched whine in the background, along with a steady thumping. "I take it you aren't in Maine anymore. He got you in a helicopter again?."

"Good assumption," Tom said in agreement, his voice loud, almost a shout. "We're on our way to the *Marin* which is stationed a little off the coast from our location. Sam is with me, enjoying a helicopter ride."

Barbara closed her eyes, and her stomach turned at the thought of her daughter sitting in the back of a helicopter as it soared hundreds of feet above the ocean.

"I'm not going to lie, Tom. That makes me a little nervous. You've never taken the kids with you before."

"Don't be. This is a Navy Seahawk, and these pilots are top notch. Ray's promised it's a quick checkup of a system, and the bonus'll be more than worth it. And Sam's having a blast, trust me!"

Barbara nodded, though her stomach remained clenched tight, nauseous and heavy. "That's good. I'm glad she's safe and having fun. So, tell me what you're doing out there." Barbara turned back to the television, eyes flashing to the television screen where the story about the fisheries continued to run. "Does it have something to do with investigating that rift on the seafloor?"

Tom paused for a long second.. "How did you know?"

"CNF is running a story on it," Barbara replied stiffly. "They're talking about the mass migration of animals and some other things. I'm not sure I know—"

Tom's static-filled words cut her off, though she couldn't make out what he'd said.

"I'm sorry, honey." She turned and stepped toward the door glass as if that would help the signal. "I'm losing you."

Tom raised his voice as he struggled to project through the bad connection. "We're getting close…ing…stead but…and we'll call…ter we land, okay?"

Barbara raised her own voice. "Okay! Please be careful!"

"We will! Love you."

"Love you, too." The connection died, leaving Barbara standing in the quiet living room with her phone held against her chest, tapping it lightly against her breastbone.

"Who were you yelling at?"

Barbara turned to see her two youngest standing there in a fresh change of clothes, ready to continue their chores.

"Oh, that was your father. He called to say he and Sam were having a great time." It wasn't a lie, but telling them that their big sister was getting to ride in a helicopter would invariably lead to distractions that would keep them from getting their work done.

Linda smiled. "I'll bet Sam is geeking out."

"I'm sure she is," Barbara agreed, gesturing to the door. "Okay. Let's get back to it. We'll finish the rabbit hutch first then move on to the greenhouse. We're going to be getting our hands dirty today."

Chapter 3
Tom McKnight
Research Vessel Marin
US Navy Task Force, North Atlantic

Under blue skies, the Seahawk swept toward the massive aircraft carrier. Its bulky hull was balanced perfectly in the turbulent waters, displacing the lead-gray swells as though it were an immovable object – which it very nearly was. Planes lined the flight deck edge near the catapult lines, wings folded and cables holding them in place. The control towers jutted up with antennae, communications disks sprouting from the framework.

Sam plastered her face and hands to the window, her jaw hanging open in sheer awe of the sight. "That's an aircraft carrier, Dad," she said in a breathless voice. "It's absolutely huge. Look at the planes!"

"She's the USS George Washington." Tom grinned at his daughter's excitement. Sam had only seen such magnificent vessel in movies or on television shows and seeing it up close was an entirely different experience. Tom had worked on an aircraft carrier a time or two during his career, so to see his daughter's exuberance was like going back in time.

The helicopter banked to the left, bending them in their seats, swinging around to approach a spot on the flight deck where a Navy crewman wearing an orange vest waited. Tom's stomach flipped as the chopper's sleek body nosed-up and levelled out to land. In spite of all of his flights, his stomach still couldn't get used to sudden aerial maneuvers.

Sam squeaked as the Seahawk's wheels touched down and their accompanying crewman took the McKnight's headsets before running up and throwing open the door on Sam's side, letting in an explosion of sea wind and engine noise. After getting an all-clear signal from the deckhand, the crewman unbuckled Sam and helped her out of the helicopter before reaching in for Tom. Already unbuckled, Tom waved the man off and jumped down, placing his hand on his daughter's back to make sure she stayed low. The girl's head turned back and forth, hair whipping around like a horse's tail, eyes taking in the sleek-looking jets stretched out around her against the endless blue sky.

The deckhand guided them to another, smaller helicopter with its blades already running. The Sea Ranger bore Navy markings but was brightly colored in red and white instead of the dull grey of the Seahawk. The side door hung open, and he helped his daughter inside before sliding in next to her. Seatbelts snapped and the crackle of the pilot's voice popped into their new headsets.

"Welcome, Tom and Sam McKnight," the pilot said. "I'll be taking you to the research vessel *Marin*, about fifty miles farther out, near the shelf. It won't be too long a ride. Everyone comfortable?"

Tom and Sam both nodded, though he took her hand, giving it a squeeze. "You okay?"

"Are you kidding?" She flashed him a glance, her jade green eyes wide with wonder. "This is amazing! Those are *real* jets. I wonder where the pilots stay?" She pulled her hand away and shifted to the window, nose pressed against the glass once again.

"They quarter the pilots below decks and…" Tom's words trailed off as the smaller chopper lifted off the deck with a sudden blender-like whine. The aircraft teetered a moment before raising higher, bending forward toward the north. They slipped over the carrier's flight deck to career over the frothing ocean in a tilting sweep, bending Tom's stomach as they left what remained of safety behind.

Letting out a deep, slow breath, he wondered if he should have pushed back on Ray a little harder. While he didn't doubt the pilot's skill, their ride on the smaller aircraft was noticeably rougher. The wind slapped at them like a toy, the craft shaking and shuddering in the turbulence, and he swallowed hard and gripped the arms of his chair.

In spite of her greenness, the jarring trip didn't seem to phase Sam one bit. She sat twisted to her left, leaning out as far as she could to peer down at the agitated sea as it made foam kisses beneath them. Her side profile reminded Tom of her mother, with her long, straight nose and full lips, green eyes gleaming like gems. But their personalities couldn't have been more opposite. Sam thought more like Tom, more interested in data, analytics, results and the abject beauty of natural sciences. Barbara had a mind for the practical side of things, with an eye toward organization and hands-on work, and she loved managing their small farm with help from Tom and the kids.

Soon, they spotted a white speck on the horizon which grew into a roughly oblong-shaped object. It was a ship not even a sixth the length of the aircraft carrier, but still impressive in its own right. The *Marin* boasted a heavy front end with three decks with a command center on top surrounded by glass windows angling outward, its top deck filled with communications antennas and circular dishes. The rear of the ship sat flat compared to the rest, with three big submersibles nestled into the deck and a massive crane perched near the rail.

A dozen smaller research ships and trawlers rocked around the larger ship, each arrayed with similar types of antennae, cranes, submersibles, and deep-sea research equipment. As the pilot curved around toward the big ship's landing deck, its bold white color stood out against the water with *Marin* painted in a curvy blue font across the bow.

The ship ripped through the choppy waters at a good clip, carving a circular pattern as its hull sensors blasted signals toward the ocean floor, sucking up the return signals to form topological images and graphs he'd no doubt be poring over.

The wind gusted, causing the chopper to sway, shudder, and groan and the pilot shifted his joystick left, ascended several feet, then banked toward the Marin once more. The entire time, Tom's belly sunk and lifted, palms sweating as he gripped his knees. He half expected them to turn around and head back to the George Washington due to the choppy winds, but the pilot wasn't giving up so easily.

They approached the ship at a side angle, pointing the aircraft's nose perpendicular to the deck and flying sideways to match the ship's speed. Shoulders and arms tense and stomach churning, Tom fought to keep a resolute face as the pilot worked the chopper's joystick sideways and forward, approaching the rising and dipping landing pad with care.

Sam jerked her attention back and forth between her side window and the bubble-shaped front glass with a wide grin plastered on her face.

"You're enjoying this *way* too much," he shouted into the mic.

"Are you kidding? This is awesome!"

They eased over the Marin's deck and landed on the orange pad with enough finesse that he didn't even realize they'd set down until the pilot hit several switches to taper off the high engine whine, throttling it all back.

"Nice landing, man," Tom said, unable to hold back his sigh of relief.

"Thanks, Mr. McKnight," the pilot replied. "Someone should be along to… ah! Here comes the colonel."

A blonde woman stepped up, beige uniform clinging to her form, hair pinned to the sides of her head with aviator sunglasses perched atop her nose. She stooped low and approached the helicopter, reaching Sam's side of the helicopter and popping open the door with a slight wave.

"Mr. McKnight!" she shouted over the noise on deck and the swells crashing around the vessel. "Good to see you again! Step on out, and I'll get you inside."

"Lieutenant Colonel Banks! Likewise." Tom nodded and helped his daughter unbuckle herself before handing her off.

Climbing down after her, they followed the officer across the helipad, down a short staircase, through a deck door and into a small room filled with jackets, life vests and other equipment. Banks slammed the door behind them, cutting off the majority of the wind and ocean noise. Her sunglasses were whipped off and settled in her breast pocket as she turned to face the McKnights, extending a hand in Tom's direction.

"I didn't expect to see you out here, Lieutenant Colonel." Tom held out his hand as his legs adjusted to the ship's rocking.

"It seems fate keeps throwing us together." A faint smile broke through her stoic expression as she shook Tom's hand. "I take it this is your daughter, Samantha? Leeds mentioned you'd be bringing someone along with you." Banks extended a hand to Sam, who took it and nodded.

"Yes ma'am! You can call me Sam."

Then she moved past them, saying, "I'll get the young lady situated in the recreation room and take you downstairs where we need you."

"I'd like to keep Sam with me, if that's okay." Tom followed the officer through another door and down a short hall to a locker room, beckoning Sam to follow.

"It would be better if she settled into the rec room." Banks stopped in the room's center and turned. "They've got video games and a pool table, plenty to do since she's not cleared to view some of the feeds we'll have up."

Tom stepped in front of Sam and faced Banks with his hands planted on his hips, giving her a weary sigh. "Look, I'm here at your request, not the other way around. If it was up to me, we'd be back in Portland eating Vietnamese food and having a pleasant walk through town. My daughter stays with me."

The officer's lips remained perfectly straight, and Tom couldn't read a single real emotion behind the woman's eyes. Banks was a by-the-book kind of officer, especially when it came to getting what she wanted, but he wouldn't be bullied by her again – especially when it came to Sam.

"I can't let uncleared civilians in the control room. I've got protocols to—"

"Get her cleared," Tom said without a hint of ire, stating a simple fact, something the Colonel could accept or not. "Or we can get on that helicopter and go home."

Banks tensed for a moment, judging Tom's resolve, her blue eyes fixed on him with a narrow edge before something inside gave and she shifted her gaze to Sam. "I'll get her cleared to enter ASAP. Until then, she can stay with you." She jerked her chin and moved through another door. "Follow me please."

They moved through a maze of corridors and stairs, descending ever downward into the bowels of the ship. The sounds changed as they traveled, transitioning away from the muffled sounds of the wind, waves and deckhands to the rumble of engines and low conversations between military and civilian crew members as the trio slid past them. While Tom had noticed the ship's movements before, its ceaseless rocking was starting to get to him, and his stomach began swirling with nausea.

"Are you feeling sick?" Tom asked Sam as they continued to descend.

"I'm fine," she replied with a grin. "I'm totally fine."

"Of course, you are," he mumbled. "I guess I should be glad Ray called me before lunch."

"If either of you are feeling queasy," the lieutenant colonel said, "I can bring you something. You do tend to get queasy for the first couple hours on board, if I remember correctly."

"Thanks, Colonel Banks. I'd appreciate that. And yeah, it'll pass… but fixing it sooner is better than later."

"Understandable."

At the bottom of a gray stairwell, Banks led them down a short hallway past a mess hall to a black steel door. The Colonel placed her hand against a hand reader, causing the door to click and pop outward.

"We'll get you both setup in the system so you can come and go freely." The Lt. Colonel pulled the door the rest of the way open, stood back, and gestured for them to enter. "Until then, you'll need my access to go in and out."

"You sure we'll be here long enough to need our own access?"

"Protocol." Banks pointedly ignored the question, and Tom shrugged. *Pick your battles, boy.* It had been one of his father's favorite phrases and it still served him well.

The three stepped into a dark, quiet control center with two rows of computer stations and a walkway down the center facing a large wall of monitors. The three paced along the back of the room as Navy personnel and civilians manning the computer stations focused on their personal screens, typing rapid-fire on their keyboards or speaking to people in their headsets. Occasionally, they glanced up at the larger screens on the wall, whispering to each other.

"Impressive set up," Tom said, looking around agreeably.

"The *Marin* is the pride of the Navy's new research fleet," Banks replied. "She's equipped with single and multi-beam echo sounders to map the seafloor, and an advanced echo sounder to assess fish stock, courtesy of Maniford Aquatics Engineering."

"Yes, I remember that project." He leaned in close to Sam and gave a conspiratorial stage whisper. "Of course, if you read the latest issue of *Science*, you might note that the *Marin* can detect a lot more than just fish with that sounder."

Ignoring him, Banks continued. "And the Marin has a vast array of oceanic and atmospheric sensors to collect ocean data—"

"Merged and extrapolated using the Proctor software," Tom cut in.

"Which is why you're here," Banks nodded, then turned as someone approach from one of the front stations. "Ah, here we are. Mr. McKnight, I think you know Ms. King."

He turned to see a woman in her early thirties approaching, her stout form sporting a blue blouse and a black skirt that fell to her knees. White sneakers adorned her feet, and her red hair hung to her shoulders in an extended bob-style haircut.

"Sue Anne." Tom grinned broadly and held out a hand. "Good to see another familiar face!"

"I didn't expect to see you until our regular Monday conference call," the woman replied, "but here we are." She spoke in her usual clipped but polite tone, accent soft and southern. They exchanged a brief handshake before she turned her attention toward Sam. "And this must be one of your daughters. Sam, I'd say?"

"That's me," the girl replied with a smile.

"Good to meet you." Sue Anne returned the smile before shooting a glance at Banks. "Mind if I get Tom caught up?"

"Please do," Banks replied. "I'll report up the chain that you two have started working on the data."

"Right this way." Sue Anne gestured behind her, turning, slipping between rows to lead the McKnights to a pair of closely placed computer terminals up front, giving them the best view of the wall screens. Each workstation had two monitors, a keyboard and mouse, and a headset to make calls.

Tom pulled up an empty chair for Sam to sit in before settling into an open spot beside her. Sue Anne took up the seat on his right and turned her monitors in his direction. "What do you know so far?"

Tom rested back with an empty hand gesture. "We saw a news report about ocean life fleeing south, caused by possible seismic activity, but that's it. Must be something big; my wife even mentioned it on the phone when I told her we were heading out here."

"It's definitely big. Here's what we're seeing." She nodded, pointing to her screen at a 3D map of the seafloor overlaid with digital contour lines marked with depths and distances. A black disruption in the middle showed what appeared to be a fracture in the seafloor, its shape long and jagged. She pointed to one side of the crack, toward a slight upward indentation. "What we have here is a bit of subterranean volcanic activity around the shelf which we think caused this crack."

"Based on the overlay markings, that's almost a kilometer long." Tom's eyes widened as he scanned her screen.

"Ten football fields long," she nodded, glancing at Sam to help her feel more included in the conversation, "about one football field wide."

"Caused by a tectonic plate shift?"

"Likely, but here's the kicker." Her soft tone took on an unusual intensity and her accent grew deeper as she leaned forward for emphasis. "Instead of seawater rushing into the crack like you might expect, or there being some kind of outflow of magma, our instruments are detecting a freshwater outflow. Ice cold fresh water."

"So, a deep-earth aquifer pushing outward?"

"Yes, and the pressure is so intense that it's chipping away at the crack's edges, widening it with every passing minute and expelling billions of gallons of water per hour."

Tom blinked. "Billions per hour? What does Proctor predict?"

"Based on pressure readings, Proctor expects it to reach one quadrillion gallons of displacement within two weeks."

Tom sat back in his chair, rolling the number around in his brain for a moment. The background hum of equipment and people faded away as he considered estimates and approximations, a slow dark dawning gripping his brain. Lips drawing a thin line across his jaw, he leaned forward with a side glance at his daughter. Sam continued to look across the wall screens, marveling at the data being presented, seemingly oblivious to their conversation. "You do realize that's an astronomical number, right? Borderline impossible?"

The southern accent hardened. "Yes. I still stand by it."

"Then Proctor must be wrong."

"It's not, Tom. I've checked and rechecked it." Sue Anne shrugged. "But that's why you're here. To help make sure there isn't some kind of bug in in the software."

Head shaking, mind working through the possibilities, he thought about something from his past to make the comparison. "I remember having a discussion with a friend of mine from college. I think we had a couple of beers and were talking about what it would take to flood North America. Freshwater-wise.

"After some quick napkin math, we concluded that it would take three quadrillion gallons of water to flood North *and* South America. That's a foot of water over both continents. Then we thought about where we could actually get that much water. A reservoir? An aquifer? Turns out, draining Lake Superior into the continents would do the trick."

"Just one lake?"

"Well, to be fair, a *big* lake." He gestured at her screen. "Three quadrillion gallons big. And Proctor is saying we'll have a quadrillion gallons of water dispersed into the world's oceans in two weeks? I mean, it won't flood the world right away, but it would raise sea levels enough to cause major problems on the coasts almost immediately. And if the pressure remained stable for months, that would mean three or four quadrillion gallons of water forced into the world's oceans in a brief span of time. That would cause *mass* flooding on a scale like we've never seen."

Sue Anne's face turned pale and she opened her mouth to protest, but Tom waved her off, becoming animated enough in his explanation to draw Sam's attention. "That's why I'm saying these numbers have to be off. Something's not right." The tension building inside him eased back and a nervous chuckle escaped, half for his benefit and half to help calm Sam's wide eyes. While he'd spent a lot of time helping develop the Proctor software, it was easier to admit it had a flaw rather than believe the predictions were real. "Give me an hour, and I'll find the problem."

Sue Anne gestured to the keyboard. "Be my guest."

Tom turned to Sam. "I'm going to start running some numbers now, so I'll need to concentrate. You okay to hang out here with me?"

She nodded. "Can I get something to drink, though?"

"I'll take her," Sue Anne said, standing up and brushing off her skirt. "I've been looking at these screens for twelve hours, and I could use a break."

"That's fine," he replied, lifting his eyes. "Keep her close, please. I don't want her roaming the upper decks."

"No problem," Sue Anne said. "We'll be right in the mess area if you need us."

Tom watched them go before leaning over the keyboard and hammering a few keys with his fingers. Pulling up a window, he logged in to the Proctor software using a standard admin ID and password and got to work.

* * *

An hour later, Tom sat glancing back and forth between his computer screens, his heart feeling as though it was in the grip of a vice. He'd begun his data verification with a deep scan of the Proctor software to ensure the program was working properly. When it came back with just a few common front-end errors typical of an improper configuration, he fixed them and re-ran the analysis based on Sue Anne's data. In spite of the slight hope he held that somehow the configurations could have caused such an egregious miscalculation, the prediction results remained the same. It still showed millions of gallons of water being dispersed into the ocean with a prediction of several quadrillions total in less than two weeks time.

After Sue Anne and Sam had returned with soft drinks, snacks, and some coffee for Tom, he and Sue Anne had worked for another 45 minutes, debugging the code while trying to draw out any errors in Proctor's algorithms. When they found three small errors in the back-end logic, Tom relaxed and settled back in his chair with a relieved sigh. Sue Anne grinned, and even some scientists in the room who'd been following their progress gave soft claps of relief and satisfaction.

At some point during their work, Colonel Banks had slid in, standing in the back with her arms folded across her chest, watching the proceedings intently. After Sue Anne made the corrections and Tom re-ran the data analysis the workstation screens refreshed to show that the data had changed, though not for the better.

Stomach churning with unease, insides burning with a primal fear, Tom watched a time-lapse forecast of the one-kilometer crack widening and spreading even farther until the screen couldn't hold it any longer. A freshwater flow rate number ticked up by exponential increments on the right side of the screen, millions and millions of gallons of freshwater flowing into the Atlantic ocean, then billions, then quadrillions. The scientists groaned when the results refreshed to the big screens.

Tom gaped, the words coming out in a whisper. "The previous Proctor predictions underestimated the flow rate, and by a sizeable amount. This shows…" He couldn't find the words, his mind reeling from the implications. His memory from ages ago flashed through his mind, recalling again the napkin math he and his friend had done, trying to somehow fathom the sheer quantity of water it would take to cover North and South America. The room grew small, the crevasse below them morphing in their minds from a benign curiosity into a time bomb.

"We'll have three quadrillion gallons of freshwater less than a month." Sue Anne shook her head, her eyes ticking fearfully across to him. "That's three times more than the previous prediction. It's the same amount of water as in—"

"Lake Superior." Tom was already nodding, fists clenched tight on the desk next to his keyboard, shoulders squeezed so tight he thought they might pop.

"There's always the possibility that there just isn't that much water below the sea bed," Sue Anne offered.

"Maybe. But with these pressures at play I somehow doubt it." Turning, he looked back at Banks. "Tell me the government has a plan to stop the freshwater flow. Some kind of earth fill or drill venting." The Colonel looked at Sue Anne for a long moment before slipping back out of the room without a word.

Sue Anne, in turn, looked around at the bustling people in the room. "We've got a lot of prominent geologists, bathymetrists, naval specialists, and oceanographers in this room, and I've talked to them all." She shook her head, the ends of her red hair flicking. "We don't have a plan, Tom."

Tom swallowed and stared at the screens, remembering yet another piece of his past – one that had helped lead him down his career path. A story told first by his parents, then repeated in Sunday school, then repeated by he and his wife to their own children. As if reading his mind, Sam took his hand, whispering what he was already thinking.

"There wasn't supposed to be another flood."

Chapter 4
Barbara McKnight
Wyndale, Virginia

Barbara swiped a wet cloth across oak kitchen table, sweeping crumbs into her hand before stepping to the garbage can and dropping them in. At the sink, Linda rinsed off dishes and handed them to Jack who then loaded them into the dishwasher with clinks and rattles. Giving her daughter a playful bump of her hip, Barbara placed her rag beneath the flowing water. "Sorry, dear."

"That's okay," Linda smiled, pausing her dish rinsing to grin up at her mother.

The cleanup after dinner had been surprising – if not a bit suspicious – but a welcome change from the reminders that often had to be handed out. With a quiet sigh, she slid to the table and started wiping off the remains when Linda appeared at her side, taking the rag from her hand.

"We've got this," she said with a nod. "Sit down."

Barbara gave her middle child a doubtful but playful frown. "Alright, what are you two trying to sneak past me? You're being awfully nice."

The girl shook her head of thick brown hair. "Nothing. We were just a pain in your butt today, so we wanted to make it up to you. Well, I had to talk Jack into it, but he still wanted to." Linda glanced back at him, rolling her eyes. "Sort of."

The loving look in the girl's eyes sent an unexpected swell of emotions through Barbara's chest, and she abandoned her rag with a sigh and sat heavily in a chair, letting the kids work. Jack took over full dish duty, standing on a booster step as he rinsed off the dishes. He gave each a shake before stepping down and loading them into the dishwasher.

Jack was average height for his age, with the trademark chestnut-colored McKnight hair and brown eyes, just like Linda and Tom. It was Sam who took more after Barbara with the green eyes, though her eldest daughter's hair wasn't sandy blonde like hers, instead varying between dark and light brown depending on how much sun she got, its texture thick and uncharacteristically curly.

The aches that had plagued Barbara all day eased as she watched the pair work, and she settled back and let her shoulders slump. It wasn't easy getting older, and at forty-three she was starting to feel it, particularly in her back and joints. Leaning to the side, grimacing slightly, she pulled her phone out of her pocket, checking to see if Tom had replied to any of her four texts since they had last spoken.

When she didn't see a response, she turned on her news app to get a quick update on the developments in the North Atlantic. She scanned a few headlines, tapping on them to read the first few paragraphs before moving to the next, the articles providing first-hand accounts from fisherman baffled at the complete desertion of marine life in the area.

Maps outlined new exodus and death patterns of several species, from the largest whales to the smallest fish, washed up by the millions along the New England coastline, bloated corpses cooking under the sun. Wrinkling her nose at the imagined stench, Barbara switched to her CNF news app, turning the sound down enough that it wouldn't draw Jack and Linda's attention.

She clicked on the "Go Live" option and watched a CNF round table with the anchorman appearing on the left side of the screen and two other experts' faces filling the frame's right side.

"Welcome, everyone. I'm Chris Penn, and I'm here with expert Tammy Roberts, head of Oceanic Studies at UCLA Berkley, and Janav Singhal from the Oceanic Research Institute." Tammy sat in what appeared to be her home office, while Janav sat in an outdoor location with palm trees waving behind him.

Chris glanced down at his laptop before lifting his eyes to the camera. "Let's start with you, Tammy. We've all seen the alarming reports of marine life fleeing North Atlantic waters. What's your theory on why this is happening?"

Tammy Roberts looked into the camera with dark brown eyes, her sable hair swept over to one side with a brown scarf hanging loose around her neck. "As you know, offshore drilling in the Atlantic was banned until just recently with new drill sites positioned off the coast of Florida and Virginia. It's clear what happened here, Chris, and I think we'll soon see some scientific evidence that backs this up. That these activities of offshore drilling have contributed to a tectonic shift which has opened up a flow of fresh water, severely disrupting the migration and feeding habits of huge numbers of underwater species."

Chris shifted in his seat. "So, drilling caused an earthquake off the New England coast, which then caused a crack in the seafloor and fresh water pouring out of it is driving all the fish mad?"

Tammy nodded with confidence. "A crude way of putting it, but yes. I'm not a geologist, but I know that we're messing with forces we can't begin to understand, and everything is connected; tidal currents, wind, rain, all of it. That's what drives marine patterns all over the world, and the drilling interrupted nature's cycle. I expect it to get worse before it gets better. It's clear we've gotten ourselves into another mess."

"While I agree with some of what my colleague is saying, some of it is absolutely not true," Janav interrupted, scoffing, holding up his hand in protest. "The *anomaly* – please, not 'crack' – is not the result of offshore drilling."

"Go ahead, Janav," Chris said with a nod, eyebrows furrowed with concern. "Tell us your theory about this… anomaly."

Janav brushed curls of hair out of his eyes and made a firm, gripping gesture with his hand. "My colleagues and I have been studying shifts in oceanic temperatures and radiation levels in the Atlantic for some time. What we're seeing is an expansion of low-yield nuclear testing in the deepest parts of the ocean."

"And who's doing this testing?"

"Who has the power, authority, and jurisdiction to do whatever they want in the region without consequence?"

"So you're saying the United States Military is conducting nuclear testing off the New England coast?"

"Not off the coast, but out past the shelf on the edge of US Waters."

Chris lifted one corner of his mouth in a doubtful tick. "You'd think someone might have noticed that. Not to mention the fact that it's against international treaties."

"Someone *has* noticed," Janav insisted. "We've had teams in the area for years, making note of every fluctuation and shift in the Earth's crust, radiation levels, all of it. Some of our research vessels have even spotted nuclear submarines in the region."

"That's ridiculous," Tammy countered. "We'd have seen massive spikes in radiation. We need to engage our senators and congress people and get those drilling operations off the Virginia coast shut down—"

"That drilling isn't even within 300 miles of this new anomaly." Janav made a disgusted face as tensions across the channel grew. "How can you blame it on some butterfly effect spanning over 300 miles?"

The conversation quickly devolved into a near-shouting match between the two guests, and Chris let them argue another few seconds before he jumped in to get them settled down.

"Wait a minute, folks. Just hold up. Can't we just fill in this cra—anomaly?"

Janav jumped in. "Ironically, we may indeed need to use explosives to collapse the fissure upon itself and seal it, thus cutting off the freshwater flow into our world's oceans. We may even need to use nuclear weapons."

Tammy scoffed, her brown hair flipping dramatically. "That would be like jabbing a hot poker into a burn."

Barbara could barely keep her comment to a murmur. "You're all idiots."

"Thanks, Tammy and Janav." Chris cut the pair off, taking a deep breath. "We'll get back to you in a minute." He turned his attention fully on the camera, his face filling up the screen, taking over the report. "We've heard from fishermen who reported massive losses of catches – and thus profits – over the past few days, and many may never recover unless they receive quick and direct federal support. But officials aren't just worried about jobs. It's the disruption to the US food supply chain that has them most concerned.

"The latest numbers from the National Oceanic Atmospheric Administration state that American fisherman landed over 12 billion pounds of seafood last year, a number that has steadily increased over the years and is well over half of the total seafood Americans consume. What happens when that valuable food source becomes depleted?

"Already, we're seeing the first signs of panic at fish markets as people fight over seafood with highly inflated prices, from a supply that could be depleted in a matter of days."

The camera switched to the scene at a local fish market near the shore, where dozens of boats remained docked in the background, bobbing gently on the water, seagulls perched on their deck rails with no deck crews in sight.

Chris continued. "While fisheries in the Mid and South Atlantic can make up for some losses, the effect on dinner tables across the northeast will be seen almost immediately. For more on that we'll switch over to some reporting from our own Tanya Mocahbee, who's been digging into this on the ground level."

The screen swapped views to show a field reporter placing a microphone in front of a middle-aged woman with a scarf wrapped over her head. After a perfunctory introductory question, Tanya asked the woman for her take on what going on, receiving an animated response.

"We usually shop at the market for fresh fish, but a pound of salmon was twenty-five dollars!" The woman shook her head. "I don't know anyone who can afford that. And when we tried to get meat at the store, the shelves were empty!"

The view then switched to a clip of a boy standing near the market entrance looking around with a shy expression as he spoke into Tanya's microphone. "I saw two guys fighting over the last two pounds of mackerel. They beat each other up pretty bad, and one guy went to the hospital in an ambulance."

"Though this crisis is still in its early stages, it's clear that it's having an effect on everyone, from vendors to customers." Tanya spoke from behind the camera as it panned to a montage of people haggling over prices, shoving and pushing the seafood vendor before two policemen rushed in to break it up. Another scene showed a grocery store where a man had his cart half full of meat packages and two other people blocking his way to the checkout aisle. One of the blockers reached in to take a package when the man drew his cart back and rammed them.

Chris Penn's face returned to the screen. "Could this be the start of another panic run where it's not necessary? Or is this the sort of response that *is* necessary given the unique set of circumstances? Are they ready to weather another storm? How will the government respond to the crisis?"

As Linda approached the table with a glass of ice water in her hand, Barbara closed the CNF news app and turned her phone face down on the table.

"Is something wrong with the ocean, Mom?" she asked, placing the water on the table.

"Oh, thanks, honey." Barbara lifted the glass and had a sip. "You didn't have to do that."

"You always say to stay hydrated, right? Plus, you look worried, and your face got real pale."

Barbara stared at her middle child, a slight smile playing at the edges of her mouth. "Okay, just what did you hear?"

"Just the last part, about how bad it could be."

"Well, this is a natural disaster," she replied. "All the fish up in Maine and along the coast? Something happened to them, but that doesn't mean it's a permanent thing or that it will affect us here in Virginia."

"Dad and Sam are up north in Maine." Linda leaned her hip against the table. "Are they in trouble?" The girl's eyes turned inquisitive and a little glassy, her emotions worn boldly on her sleeve.

"I spoke with your father earlier today, and I'm expecting another call any minute. There's no reason to think they won't be all right. And you know we're prepared to handle whatever comes our way here at the house, right?"

"What are we preparing for?" Jack slid into the seat to her right with a half glass of milk in one hand and a single chocolate chip cookie in the other. He started to put the cookie in his mouth when he paused. "Can I have a cookie?"

Barbara tsked and fixed him with a dry look. "Yes, you *may*. And next time, ask first before you take. And as far as what we're prepared for. Well, everything." She stood and ruffled Jack's hair. "You two finish up in the kitchen. I'm going downstairs to check on some things."

Barbara stood and moved to the basement door right off the living room. She tugged it open and hit the wall switch on the right, bathing the stairs and landing below in soft yellow light. At the bottom, she hit a switch on the south wall, and low-watt, high lumen bulbs burst to life on the ceiling, revealing a swirl of dust motes around her head.

"Place needs a little dusting," she admitted to herself, arms folded across her chest in thought. It had been a few days since she'd worked in the basement. With Tom and Sam gone to Maine for the week, they'd focused mainly on yard chores and left things downstairs alone. With news of current events and the potential for food shortages occurring, it might be time for a full inventory and review of everything they had.

The bottom floor was an open configuration with a battery room in the northwest corner. The HVAC unit and water heater rested against the north wall behind the stairs, and against the west wall sat two chest freezers and a double-door refrigerator like the one they had upstairs. In the southwest corner stood three massive gun safes and two smaller ones acting as bookends with a long bench a few feet in front of them and Barbara made a note on her phone to triple check their ammunition stockpile.

They'd saved the entire east side of the basement for food and water stores. Ten tall metal shelving units stood holding canned goods, baking goods, MREs, and other dry stock, all carefully labeled and incorporated in with their normal meals to avoid wasting anything. The end rows held emergency bottled water, liquid goods, assorted juice mixes, toiletries, first aid kits, camping gear, and other necessities.

Barbara noted things they'd need to top off at first glance, circling a reminder at the bottom of her list so she'd be certain to do a thorough, shelf-by-shelf inspection at some point in the near future. Soups and canned fruits the kids had been eating for their lunches were obvious necessities, though there'd likely be more that would need to be cycled through and replaced.

Turning away from the shelves, she opened the door to the battery room that served as the central connection point for all their power needs. A light breeze blew across the banks of batteries from the ventilation system, ensuring that that room didn't overheat. The battery room had been Tom's pet project for an entire summer, adding a second breaker box with a quick switch inverter to make a seamless switch to battery and then generator power should the grid power ever go dead.

Fifteen deep cycle batteries sat on shelves on the west side of the room, wired in a parallel configuration to act as one big, rechargeable battery for their house. 2,400 amp hours worth of storage capacity would keep the key appliances running for a few days, and twelve high-efficiency solar panels were enough to recharge the battery bank each day, if necessary.

Need to do a power test, check for corrosion, make sure I don't need to switch any out. Or just wait for Tom to get home to take care of it.

Barbara winced at the thought, banishing it from her mind. Tom would be home with Sam in tow before she knew it.

After another quick look around she turned off the basement light and headed up the stairs. Jack greeted her at the top, holding out her ringing phone. Barbara reached for it, an excited note kicking up in her voice. "Is it your father?"

"Not sure," Jack shrugged. "I don't recognize the number."

"Thanks." She stepped into the living room, looking down at the glowing screen. He was right. The number wasn't familiar. Still, she'd gotten enough odd calls from Tom when he worked special projects out of town, so it could certainly be him dialing in on a secure company line. She clicked to accept the call and stepped toward the front door, putting the phone to her ear. "Hello, this is Barbara McKnight. Who am I speaking to?"

"Hi, honey. It's me."

Barbara sighed with a deep breath, the weight of pent up tension released from her shoulders. "We were getting worried about you."

"Sorry about that," he apologized in a mysterious, hushed tone. "And I'm sorry, but I can't talk long. I shouldn't be talking to you at all, but I found a side room with a secure line and wanted to call before things… before they fell apart"

"Why? What's wrong?" Barbara opened the front door and stepped out onto the porch, shutting the door behind her to stay isolated from the kids. She drifted to one of their porch chairs and sat on the edge, knees together with her left arm hugged across her stomach.

The sky yawned wide and blue above her head with dark billows of clouds working their way up from the south, stretching, reaching northward on an insistent drift of wind. A pair of birds flitted by, robins banking back and forth against the gray-blue backdrop of Virginia sky. Far below, at the end of their sloping front yard, a car cruised by on the old country road.

"Things have taken a turn for the worse, and you need to prepare yourselves. I mean *prepare* prepare yourselves. Worst case scenario preparations."

"Not joking?"

"Not joking."

"Is it the crack in the ocean floor?" Barbara asked.

"Yes. What's the news been saying?"

"Everything under the sun," she replied. "They're speculating it was caused by offshore drilling or underwater nuclear testing."

"Well, I don't how it happened, but I can confirm the anomaly originates from a seafloor eruption. We're seeing billions of gallons of freshwater flowing into the ocean, and it's getting worse by the second. It's not only going to devastate the fishing industries in the North Atlantic, but also the Mid and South Atlantic. I'm not an expert on supply chain, but I imagine this will devastate other industries." A hesitation caught his voice. "We'll probably see some flooding."

"Flooding? What kind of flooding?"

She heard the sound of Tom shifting the phone to his other ear, his voice growing more hushed. "We're seeing a massive, increasing flow rate as the water eats away at the crack and expands it. We're estimating that water will pour into the Earth's oceans at the rate of about one quadrillion gallons per week. Based on some calculations we've done, severe flooding is inevitable… on a worldwide scale."

She'd heard Sam talk about rising sea levels before, and though the details were vague, they hadn't been fun conversations. "How bad is this going to get?"

Tom's tone grew rushed. "Honey, I'm sorry, but I have to get going. My, uh, boss is looking for me." He slowed down to a more loving tone. "Stay safe, and I'll call you as soon as I can. Don't worry about Sam. She's safe here with me. Sue Anne – you remember her from the work party last year – she gave Sam on a tour of the ship. That girl is so curious." A nervous laugh slipped out. "Just batten down the hatches and wait for us to come home. I love you."

"I love y—" The line died, leaving her words hanging, stomach dropping, leaving her with a hollowed-out emptiness, a dark anxiety like someone had swiped gray paint across her soul. Smooch trotted around the side of the house, ears perked up, quiet and curious, head cocked to side in that sympathetic, "I know something's wrong; how can I help" manner.

"Hey, girl," Barbara dropped her hand down to call the dog over. Smooch hopped up on the porch and placed her nose into Barbara's hand, accepting the attention. With a stroke along the dog's neck, she pulling the animal closer and buried her face in her fur, drying the tears that had settled on her cheeks.

She pulled away and gripped the dog's collar firmly but playfully, locking eyes with the intelligent animal. "Are you ready to work, Smooch? We've got a lot to do."

The dog gave a playful woof, panting, tongue lolling, paws dancing in excitement.

Chapter 5
Tom McKnight
Research Vessel Marin
US Navy Task Force, North Atlantic

Tom hung up the phone at the behest of Sam's incessant hand gesturing and bugged eyes that indicated that Lieutenant Colonel Banks was coming. The girl had been keeping watch so he could make the unauthorized call without anyone knowing. The Marin's work was considered top secret, and breaking protocol would be met with severe reprimands from the naval authorities – doubly so if Banks was involved.

"Thanks." He replaced the phone and stepped from the alcove, angling Sam into the combination recreation and mess area on their level. Grabbing her hand, he pulled her to the soft drink dispenser on the right-hand wall nearby. Lieutenant Colonel Banks entered the room, spotted Tom and Sam, and made a beeline for them.

"There you are," Banks said in her hard-edged tone. "I'd wondered where you'd gotten off to."

"Just getting something to drink," Tom said, waiting for the officer to unload on him. He'd been gone ten minutes without letting Banks know. Tom filled a plastic cup with ice and placed it under the dispenser, choosing Sam's favorite soda and filling it up. He gestured for his daughter to put the specialized ship lid on it so the contents wouldn't spill, while he faced the Colonel. "I needed a break from the debugging." He reached up and dug his fingers into his eyes, only half-faking rubbing weariness from them. "Still trying to wrap my head around it all."

"No problem," Banks nodded with narrowed eyes. "Let me know next time, and I'll let you back in. Come on back. There's something you'll want to see."

"What's going on?" Tom asked.

"We're sending down our rovers to have a look at the site."

"Oh, really?"

"We can only observe so much remotely from the Marin," Banks said. "Sometimes the ship's sensors can misread data from way up here. We need to get some vessels down there to have a closer look."

"I can't argue with that," Tom agreed, though he still hoped their data *was* wrong, somehow, and all this was just an error.

Banks gestured for them to follow and led them back to the control room after re-scanning his hand at the security ID reader. They turned and stared up at the wall screens as Sue Anne joined them from her workstation, grinning at Sam.

Banks stood with her hands on her hips, gesturing at the monitors. "We're sending two remote controlled rovers and our manned submersible, the Sea Bell."

"You're sending a manned vessel down there?" Tom's brow wrinkled. "That seems incredibly dangerous. The turbulence alone could tear—"

"Too late to turn back now," Banks cut him off, pointing to the wall screens, each one with a camera view of the three submersibles, labeled Sea Devils One and Two, and the manned Sea Bell. "They're already on the way."

Tom's eyes scanned all three screens, moving back and forth across the different oceanic views, peering down into the deepening blue depths with an occasional drift of bubbles across the camera lenses. Particulate matter floated in the viewfinder, swirling and racing away as the craft descended in corkscrew patterns toward their destinations. For a moment Tom's mind was taken away by the sight, transported back to the last time he had sat in the driver's seat of such a submersible before snapping back to reality at the sound of someone's voice nearby.

"Sea Devil One is passing through two thousand meters over the trench area." Tom glanced to his right to see a man and woman sitting close together at workstations with several smaller monitors in front of them. In their hands they gripped complex-looking joysticks with buttons and thumb toggles on them and they wore headsets, their necks craned forward, eyes wide and staring, barely blinking, focusing on their smaller screens like it was an intense video game. "Sea Devil One approaching twenty-five hundred meters," the man mumbled, his voice piped over the room's speakers.

The woman driving to his right responded. "Sea Devil Two right behind you."

Tom's eyes shifted to the middle wall monitor as the second remote submersible followed the first one's spinning propellers while it wove through the updraft of current.

"This is Specialist Norton in the Bell," a man's voice piped through the room's speakers. "I've got both submersibles in my sights. Engaging exterior lights."

Tom glanced to the third wall monitor as the Bell descended behind the smaller craft, catching glimpses of them in the murky blue as the Bell's powerful light beams cut through the darkness. His insides instinctively clenched the deeper they sunk, imagining Norton sitting cramped up inside the submersible's hull, working his controls to keep the craft steady despite the strong upward currents.

"How much pressure can the Bell take?" he asked, leaning closer to Banks.

"The Bell is one of the highest-rated deep diving vessels in the world," the officer responded. "She's rated for eight kilometers, and we're only going half that today."

"There are more than just pressure dangers down there," Tom whispered, receiving an emotionless stare from Banks in response.

"I'm having some difficulty controlling my craft," the pilot of Sea Devil One said. "Gauges are going crazy. This turbulence is getting bad."

"Can confirm," Norton said, his voice shaking like he was soaking in a tub of ice water. "I'm coming over the fissure now and experiencing some heavy tidal surges and eddies. Never felt anything like it down this deep." The Bell's camera shook and rattled, bumped around, shivering as they drove through swirling clouds of grey sediment.

"Reaching close to three thousand meters," the pilot said.

Dirt and debris flew at them, the submersibles passing through silty clouds while being whacked with pebble-sized shards, some even rock-sized as the water exploded in a massive swirl of particles that clouded their view. Debris shooting upward smacked into the vessels, rocking them, spinning them about and pushing their noses up before the pilots regained control and pressed them downward again.

"Getting pounded pretty good here." Norton's voice maintained its hyped-up quaking as larger stones the size of fists bounced off side of the Bell, some of them rattling the vessel hard. "I'm altering course to compensate, trying to find calmer pockets of water."

"Approaching four thousand meters," the pilot of Sea Devil one said, holding the joysticks in a steel grip as he worked to keep his rover from flying out of control.

Tom shifted his attention back to the first screen where clear patches showed through the murky water. The edge of the fissure stretched out before them, a dark shadow at first, becoming more defined the closer they raced toward it. It yawned beneath the rovers' spotlights, an impossibly massive scar in the ocean floor, a bottomless pit that threatened to consume them if not for the rovers' powerful beams beating back the darkness.

"There you are," Tom whispered, stomach churning with dread. It was one thing to see the fissure in 3D renderings and sonar scans, but up close and personal was an entirely different matter. A few soft gasps came from around the room and he felt Samantha stepping closer to him, taking his hand in hers.

"I'm hitting calmer pockets." Norton's tone eased down from the nervous panic of a moment ago, and the Bell's view steadied as he approached from an outward angle rather than descending on top of the anomaly. Still, it was nowhere near perfect as the tail end of the Bell whipped around, its pilot cursing to get the vessel under control.

"I'm setting my sea devil down here," the first pilot said, guiding his rover to the seafloor.

Tom watched the Sea Devil One's descent on the screen second screen, watching it from behind as the first rover's tail raised and lowered, flipping side-to-side like a dog's tail as it careened to a slow halt near the edge of the crevice.

"I'm settling a hundred yards north," the woman pilot said, and she broke off Sea Devil Two to find a spot farther along the fissure.

Norton chimed in. "I'll sit right here behind this outcrop and pick up samples. Should be some interesting deep crust pieces mixed in with the expelled material."

"I've got all of you on tracking." A controller sitting at a workstation in front of Ben and Sam called out. "Hulls are holding just fine, nothing was knocked offline sensor-wise. We're green across the board."

The Bell rested on the seafloor, facing the crevice, lights shining out across the deep black emptiness as debris fell around them like a soft rain, pinging on the submersible's roof with light sounds. Motorized arms with claws reached out, picked up loose bits of rock and detritus lying around seafloor, depositing them into bins on the Bell's underbelly.

"Why are we gathering rock samples?" Tom asked.

Colonel Banks kept her eyes on the screens as he answered. "Our geologists want to check the geological makeup and how old they are. Once we know the composition, we can tune our instruments to scan below the seafloor to determine just how deep this thing goes."

"That makes sense," he nodded. "Unless the aquifer just runs itself out."

"Then we can cut our losses and deal with the global ramifications." Banks turned to Tom. "But if it won't stop, we'll need to consider some more drastic options."

"What can we do about it?"

"The pressure is pushing outward, so using conventional explosives and collapsing the crevice is probably not an option, but we're exploring the use of nuclear weapons to create a big enough crater at the edges of the aquifer to reduce some pressure in order to—"

Sam tapped her father's arm, pointing at the screen showing the Bell's camera. "Is that supposed to be happening?"

Tom followed to where his daughter pointed, gaping in shock. The sand from the edge of the crevice settled inward, revealing a slight crack breaking off from the main sore, spreading faster, winding its way toward the Bell like a lightning bolt, tossing up sand and debris in curling eddies. He glanced at the other rover cameras and was alarmed to see several more cracks rippling across the ocean floor in a spiderweb formation, sections of stone falling away like a rotted tooth.

He lurched forward and snatched the controller's headset off their ears, screaming into the microphone. "Norton, get out of there! Get out of there now!"

A grunting sound came over Norton's mic as the seafloor broke into massive chunks. Some fell inward, falling away in brittle chunks, others burst upward with explosive force. A loud crunch echoed from the speakers as Tom was about to shout into the microphone again, a huge piece of the seafloor slamming into the bottom of the Bell like a boxer's uppercut. The impact launched it into a twisting, stomach-turning roll like a corkscrew roller coaster and Norton's horrified scream cut out after a split second along with the video feed.

"We've… we've lost contact with the Bell," a controller said, turning in his seat to look back at Banks with a somber, wide-eyed expression.

On another screen, Sea Devil One was next. The turbulent currents hurled it upward, end over end in a dizzying whirl. Frantic, the pilot wrenched the joystick around, jerking the submersible in a shuddering spin before pitching it forward. It hung in place for a moment before the pilot's massive overcorrection plunged the vessel into the yawning crevice, where unfathomable forces threw it to and fro. Sea Devil One disappeared into the blackness, and the pilot slammed his hands on his desk and cursed.

Sea Devil Two fared better, briefly. Its pilot fought the controls and kept the thing righted, nose pointed down. The camera stared down into the rumbling opening as it vomited huge chunks of basaltic rock up toward the surface at tremendous velocity. A shotgun blast of water and stone zipped toward the rover while, on the screen, an enormous jagged chunk of the seafloor barreled end-over-end directly toward it. The pilot had no time to react and the video feed cut off with a shudder and a blink.

Dead silence filled the room, and Lieutenant Colonel Banks stood with her hands on her head, eyes wide and darting between the screens as if expecting the feeds to come back at any moment. The image of the shooting chunks of rock and earth had seared itself into Tom's head, the debris pushed upward by massive subterranean pressures a thousand times more powerful than a volcanic eruption, a super geyser of destructive power. Tom's eyes moved around the room as calculations for speed and distance slammed through his brain in a fraction of a second.

"Everyone listen to me!" he shouted, adrenaline kicking through his bloodstream. "We've got to get up upstairs. Run for the deck. Get up there now!" He grabbed Sam's hand and jerked her toward the door, throwing it open and dashing into the hall before anyone could stop him.

"McKnight!" Banks shouted after him. "Where are you going? McKnight!"

Chapter 6
Barbara McKnight
Wyndale, Virginia

Linda and Jack sat on opposite ends of the table with Barbara in the middle, facing the kitchen. Her curious and emotional daughter waited patiently, hands folded in front of her, while Jack fiddled with two of his action figures. He posed them in various positions until he found one he liked and then made smashing, punching sounds as he clashed them together.

"What's going on, Mom?" Linda asked, pointedly ignoring her younger brother's antics.

Barbara turned to better face her daughter, gazing across the table. "You know how Sam and your father were at the Portland Undersea Expo?"

"*Were?*"

"Yes, were. Things changed, and your father got called in to work."

"Mr. Ray called, didn't he?" the girl asked, already knowing the answer. The kids had never met Tom's boss, but they understood him as the man who always ruined their plans. "Mr. Ray's always calling and making Dad do stuff."

"Yes. He called, and your father and Sam went out on a boat to investigate the strange things we've been seeing on the news. You know, the fish all going south."

Jack looked up from his action figures, big brown eyes blinking once. "Are the fish going to come back?"

"It's a little more complicated than that," Barbara grimaced as she tried to explain. "It has something to do with an earthquake and a crack in the seafloor. A lot of water is surging into the ocean from an aquifer. That's an underground water source. And this aquifer might cause some flooding, along the coastline and in other places. Does that make sense?"

Both kids nodded, though Jack seemed uncertain, his normal upbeat spirit quickly turning grim. Linda took the news in stride and got to the important question. "When are they coming home?"

"That's a good question, honey, but I don't have the answer. When I talked to your father last, he said…" Barbara's words trailed off, her eyes moving back and forth between the kids. Then she figured it was best to come right out with it and not try to hide it. "Your father thinks this event, this *flooding*, might be dangerous to us. To anyone living near the coasts. And he said we should batten things down here for when him and Sam get home. And that's why I need you guys to help me with that. You know, battening things down. Can you do that?"

"Sure, but I don't understand something." Linda replied, "We're 350 miles from the coast. How could any flooding affect us?"

"Another great question. If a few cities get flooded, it could have a ripple effect across the country, maybe even the world. When bad stuff happens in one part, it can have a ripple effect across a lot of other areas."

"Like when that hurricane destroyed things down south last year," Linda said, her hazel eyes falling to the table, trying to pull vague memories from the time. "We weren't close to it but we couldn't get groceries for a while, right?"

"That's right. A lot of people were hurt and killed. The hospitals were full, they didn't have power for a long time and some people got really hungry, too."

"We didn't go hungry or lose power, did we?"

"No, because we'd prepared ahead of time." Barbara gave the girl a pointed nod. "A lot of people in the cities didn't prepare very well, or didn't have the means to escape. When they ran out of food and water, some of them got violent. It didn't happen everywhere, but enough to make for a scary situation." She left the implication hanging in the air.

"How can we be ready this time?" Jack had put his figures down and stared up at his mother with serious concern in his eyes. "Since Dad's not here, am I the man of the house?"

Barbara worked hard to keep a grin off her face. "You are, buddy, but we all share the responsibilities, and I'm still in charge." She gave him a wink. "We have to keep each other safe. We have to watch each other's backs, okay?" Her eyes drifted back and forth between the kids until both nodded in agreement.

"With our well we've got more than enough water, but we could stand to restock some canned goods and top off our freezers with meat. How does that sound?"

"Sounds easy enough to me," Jack said.

Linda nodded. "We can help with that."

"Okay. Get your shoes on and let's move out. Hopefully we'll beat the rush to the store."

The kids ran for their shoes, and Barbara remembered it had gotten chilly outside earlier after she'd spoken with Tom. She called out, "It's a little cool out, so bring your jackets!"

After changing into her tennis shoes and donning a light jacket, she found her purse and dug out her keys, waiting for the kids on the porch. While she stood there, she adjusted the small pistol on her hip, tucking her shirt neatly over it. Just when her patience had nearly reached its threshold, they came tearing down the stairs to join her. "Settle down, kiddos," she said, leading them out to their old gray Ford F150 in the driveway.

Smooch came around to see them off, and she allowed the kids to pet the German Shepherd a second before getting them inside the truck. She kicked the old engine on and eased down their long gravel driveway where it wound down to Wyndale Road. She took a left and kicked the truck up to 45 , the fresh, crisp scent of country air gusting through the cabin.

They passed the Everetts' farmstead and followed the narrow paved road until it turned into Wallace Pike, big tires crunching on pebbles as they wove through the forested hills and open farms of backwoods Virginia where it bordered with Tennessee. The lights of businesses and homes along I-81 made a glowing line on their left, a strip of civilization in the dusk light, and the city of Bristol came front and center as they approached the north side of town. Barbara swung the truck beneath I-81 and headed south into Bristol proper, the old country roads giving way to pockets of businesses, construction companies, stores, greasy gas stations, and strip malls. Car lights turned and cut across the darkening roads, briefly illuminating the pavement.

Traffic seemed normal, no one panicking, life moving along with typical country ease. While she was concerned with potential unrest in populated areas, there was no sign it had reached Bristol - yet. As her eyes scanned around, hands loosely on the wheel, she doubted anyone had connected the things happening in the North Atlantic with their own little town. That, more than anything else, would give her a distinct advantage.

She took a right on Euclid Avenue and cruised another mile to the Food King on the west side of town. A nearly empty parking lot greeted them, confirming Barbara's suspicions, and she had no problems pulling up to the front row of spots, whipping the old Ford in and killing the engine. Getting the kids out, she marched them to the front and grabbed a cart at the entrance, gesturing for Linda to grab one of the smaller carts and have Jack hold onto it, too.

The Food King had become Tom and Barbara's best kept secret. Smaller than any of the big chains, and without the brand recognition that drew in the masses, the place boasted the best meat in the area and at more than reasonable prices. They had a small-town feel and purchased deer, pheasant, fowl, and other non-standard fare from local farmers and hunters and even did a lot of their own processing, cutting out the middleman.

Barbara pushed her cart past the check-out lines, waving to several of the cashiers she knew, and angled straight for the meat counter on the far-right side. She spotted Matthew Trimboli behind the counter, the wide-shouldered man with a red-stained apron tied around his waist and a huge cutting board behind a display of steaks, fillets, pork chops, and chicken, his cleavers sitting off to the side in a neat row.

The tall, barrel-chested man smiled when he spotted the McKnights.

"Howdy, Barbara." Matthew waved from behind the meat counter and then nodded at her children. "Kids."

"Hey, Matthew," Linda smiled back. "Are you playing Santa again this year?"

The butcher spread his hands wide on the counter, his massive 6-foot, 7-inch frame towering overhead as he gave Linda a broad smile. "You'd better believe it. What can I do for you folks today?"

"Hi, Matthew," Barbara replied with a smile. "Give me a second." She leaned down to the kids and held out a brief list of canned goods for them to pick up. "Can you guys grab me the things off this list with as little fuss as possible." She turned her serious expression onto Jack. "That means Linda calls off what she needs, and you get the *right* things. Nothing extra, and I don't want to see or hear cans rolling down the aisles. Show me you two can be responsible, okay?"

Jack nodded fervently, and her daughter plucked the list from her hand with a reassuring smile. "Got it, Mom. Be right back, no fuss."

Barbara watched them go, not convinced they'd complete a task without *some* fuss, though she remained hopeful and turned back to the meat counter with a sigh.

"How are things here at the store?" she asked. "Busy?"

"A little slow," the butcher admitted. They exchanged more small talk, Barbara asking about Matthew's father, who owned the store, then after his kids and wife. Matthew asked after Tom, and she only mentioned the trip to the Portland Undersea Expo he was attending with their daughter, though she said nothing about his sudden assignment out in the North Atlantic over the mysterious anomaly in the seafloor. Five minutes later, she got to the point.

"I need some meat," she said, scanning her list.

"That's what I'm here for," Matthew agreed, and he leaned over the counter to get her order, holding his hand out.

Barbara handed him the list she'd made, and he stared at it before glancing at the meat he had on hand in the main display case. "Big list you've got here. I'll need to get some pieces from cold storage. Might take a minute."

"That's fine," Barbara agreed. "I can check on the kids while we wait. I'll leave my cart here if you don't mind."

She walked around the edge of the store, glancing from her list to the rows of shelves, trying to remember if she might have missed something. Grabbing a jar of her favorite hot peppers and some snack cakes for the kids, she did an about face and headed for the canned soups and vegetables, idly searching for her kids. In a larger store, she wouldn't have dare dreamed of leaving them to go off on their own, but Food King was different. Every employee – down to the cashiers, baggers and cart-boys – were vetted by Matthew's father, had multiple background checks and knew the McKnight's by sight. It was a safe space of sorts, a place where the kids had practiced doing things on their own in public without any fear of someone "wandering off" with them.

Crossing into the next aisle, Barbara found Linda pushing the smaller cart down the soup section, holding the list in one hand and pointing out things for Jack to pick up. Like an efficient elf, the boy rushed off to grab whatever his sister asked for and placed it into the cart in record time. The smaller basket stood three-quarters full, so they'd made substantial progress and she almost didn't want to interrupt them. Almost.

"Excellent work, kids," Barbara said, placing the jar of peppers and two boxes of snack cakes in the cart.

"Cakes!" Jack's grin grew as wide as his eyes.

"Only one a day, and only after dinner," she said, tempering his enthusiasm.

"I know," he replied in an offended tone. Then he rushed over to a shelf, grabbed two hearty beef stews, and returned to the cart to plop them inside.

"How's it going?" she asked Linda.

"We're almost done," her daughter said with a firm and professional tone, taking her responsibility seriously. "Just three more things."

"You guys are doing great. When you're done, bring the cart and your brother over to the meat aisle. I'll head back to see how Matthew is doing."

"Okay."

Barbara glanced around to see the store remained empty, and she realized it was only 45 minutes to closing time. Returning to the butcher's counter, she found her cart filled with plastic bags full of meat packages. Matthew was bringing the last few packages around the counter when Barbara came up, though she stopped when he placed two packages in her cart and stepped back with his hands on his hips.

"What?" Barbara gave a half-hearted laugh.

"This is double what you normally get." He looked down at her with his soft, gray eyes. "Ya'll having a party or something?"

Barbara hesitated, considering lying to him, but instead opting for a version of the truth accompanied by a shrug. "Tom's out of town on business, said he wanted me to pick up some extra supplies. I'm not entirely certain why, but here we are."

Matthew started to nod but then shook his head instead. "I'm sure you know what you're doing. Good seeing you again, and give my best to Tom."

"Good talking to you, Matthew."

Barbara pushed the cart toward the front of the store, Linda waiting for her with their completed list and Jack hanging onto the side of the cart, staring at everything inside. They moved through the checkout line quickly, the final bill coming up much larger than normal. After a brief wave to the cashier, Barbara marched her kids back to the truck, pushing their carts as Jack ran circles around them.

Before they had a chance to put a single bag away, Barbara's phone buzzed in her purse. She took it out and stared at the screen, eyes tracing over the words and widening slowly in fear. Hand shaking, face flushing pale, she stared at the screen as a ball of dread formed in her stomach.

"What's wrong, Mom?" Linda asked. "You look like you've seen a ghost."

Barbara stuffed the phone back into her purse and jerked the tailgate down, throwing the bags into the back with urgency. "Help me, kids."

Jack sprung into motion, reaching into the smaller cart to grab out grocery bags and hand them to Linda, his eyes never once leaving his mother who stood virtually throwing their bags to Linda, who in turn transferred them into the back of the truck and then helped her mother with the last few meat packages. They secured everything with a tarp and some string, making sure no bags flew out.

After they'd finished, before they got in the truck, Linda stared at her mother in sheer confusion. "Mom?" Her voice quivered. "What's going on?"

"Get in," Barbara circled around to the passenger side door and popped it open, helping Jack into the back of the cab. She squatted and leveled her gaze at her daughter, speaking in a hushed, fearful tone that was foreign to both children. "Keep your brother in the truck and wait for me here. Keep the doors locked and *do not move*. I'll be a few minutes inside. If anything goes wrong, just honk the horn, okay?"

"Okay." Linda's eyes were turning glassy, her voice hanging on the edge of tears. Barbara touched her daughter's cheek and reached back to give Jack's knee a comforting squeeze. Then she slammed the door shut and rushed to the back of the truck, grabbing both cart handles and turning them toward the store. Both children watched as their mother shoved the carts toward the entrance like an offensive lineman driving for the goal line. She jammed the smaller cart into the small cart stack and pushed the larger cart on through. Linda and Jack stared out the front windshield in confusion, and the boy pushed himself between the seats as his mother disappeared from sight.

"What's wrong with Mom?"

"I don't know." A single tear streaked down the girl's face, though she couldn't say why.

Thirty minutes later, Barbara came barreling outside with another cart full of meat and more bags of canned and dry goods, this time overflowing the top of the cart with several packages threatening to spill out. Linda climbed out of the car, turning to tell her brother to stay inside before she shut the door behind her.

They met at the back of the truck, and Barbara began transferring bags from the cart to the truck bed, reaching over the tailgate to add to the already enormous pile they had.

Linda didn't help right away but stared at her mother, looking for an explanation. "What's going on? What did the text say? Why did you get more meat?"

"Help me, please." Barbara nodded at the cart, and her daughter dug some bags out and helped, casting a wary glance around, noting an older couple as they passed by, staring at the pile of meat in the cart like the McKnights were crazy.

"They won't be thinking that soon," Barbara muttered under her breath.

"Won't be thinking *what* soon?" Linda's tone grew plaintive as she put the last of the bags into the back of the truck and stood there with a questioning look.

"Get in the truck please, Linda." Barbara wheeled the empty cart back to the front of the store and jammed it into the cart stack, returning to the truck where her son and daughter waited inside. Climbing in, she settled behind the wheel, feeling her daughter's withering stare and her son's teary confusion. Rather than try to explain or water down the truth, she handed her phone to Linda and let the girl read the text message she'd received 30 minutes earlier. Linda scanned the words with Jack peeking over her shoulder, their faces turning ashen as true fear and worry set in. Linda raised her eyes to her mother, mouth agape as Barbara put the truck in drive and pulled out of the lot, heading for home.

Chapter 7
Tom McKnight
Research Vessel Marin
US Navy Task Force, North Atlantic

Tom pushed Sam up the stairs, forcing her to take two at a time, navigating the thin halls and cramped stairs, asking crewmen for quick directions until they made it onto the deck. Some members of the crew were gathering there, many having heard about the rovers getting smashed to bits, and a pair of sailors stood by the rail, looking down into the waters.

"Someone from central control told everyone to get to the deck," one said. "Wow, would you look at that turbulence!"

"They say it destroyed the rovers," the other replied. "Man, are those rocks bubbling up? What in the world…?"

"We should be safe. Our hull is double plated, several inches of solid steel, man."

"No alarms yet…"

Tom caught bits and pieces of conversations, eyes darting around as the ball of dread in his gut expanded to his chest, an overshot of adrenaline causing his hands to shake. Spotting a rack of life preservers hanging on the deck wall, he strode over and grabbed two of them, tossing one to Sam.

"Put the top part over your neck and then tie it around your waist," he said, fixing his own over his head and tying it up with a fixed look of concentration. Sam stared in disbelief across the rolling deck, holding the life preserver up but not putting it on.

His next words boomed loud, drawing the attention of the sailors at the rail. "Come on, Sam! Put it on! Now!"

Shocked into motion, she threw the preserver over her head and started to tie it around her waist. Tom grabbed his phone out of his pocket, checking it for a signal. The Marin swayed to the port side, edging them forward closer to the rail and he let himself fall forward, going with the tilting deck rather than fighting it. His stomach hit the side harder than he expected, and his phone slipped out of his hand and tumbled. With a panicked gasp, Tom slapped it against his left forearm and pinned it there. Then he brought it to his chest and gripped it tight, a relieved sigh slipping from between his tight lips.

The ocean surface rumbled in a fit of brown froth, drawing his eyes. A sulfuric scent wafted off of it, forming a nauseating scent in the air as muddy waters churned and bubbled around the ship, stones knocking against the hull with thuds and bumps that grew in intensity and violence. Something bigger was roiling beneath the surface, a monstrous creature making itself known as it slowly rose from the depths.

"What's happening?" One of the sailors shouted to his shipmate, gripping the rail as the ship swayed back to starboard.

"I don't know. I'll call down to central control!"

"Stay close, Sam." Tom pulled his daughter by the arm, and they walked back toward the center of the deck as the ship settled into a level position once more.

"What's going on, Dad?"

Ignoring her question, he glanced up to the second deck rail to see the ship's captain staring down at the roiling waves with his hand spread wide. His communication officer held a handheld radio with a six-inch antenna, shouting a message to another ship. Tom's eyes fell back to his phone, a solid five bars worth of signal showing thanks to the ship's satellite connection. He furiously typed out a message to Barbara as muddy ocean spray hit the side of the ship and rained dark drops on his screen. Each word seemed to take an eternity to type with the deck moving beneath him, his hips shifting and moving with the rocking motion.

Barbara, you may not hear from us for a while. The worst has happened. Lock everything down and hold down the fort until we make it home. I'll protect Sam at all costs. Will contact you once we reach shore. Expect the news to report several ships went down, but we will survive. I promise. We love you. Talk soon.

"What do you mean the worst has happened?" Sam had been watching around her father's shoulder as he stood hunched over typing, and her voice thrummed with fear, wide eyes wide staring at him like she could squeeze an answer out of him by force of will alone. "Dad, what do you mean *the worst*?"

Tom took her by the arm, pulling her across the deck to the opposite rail, peering down at the growing maelstrom with a desperate shake of his head. "Look, Sam. The crust holding back that freshwater aquifer was under a lot of pressure, and it just burst. All of these rocks we're seeing come to the surface – not to mention any trapped gases that would affect the ships' buoyancy - are just the tips of the proverbial iceberg."

"There's no way these ships will sink." Sam was shaking her head, though her eyes told a different story. The girl clung to her father's arm as if waiting for him to tell her he was just kidding, and everything would be fine. "We're not directly above the crevice, are we?"

Tom's eyes scanned the deck for a way to get his daughter out of the oncoming danger, his gut feelings growing more intense as the seconds ticked by. "The Marin is near the outer edge of the crevice, but you saw it blow open on the feeds. It's spreading wider, and the debris and gases are launching rocks up at us. Anything that falls back to the ocean floor will come back up, too. You can see it."

Finger pointing out toward the other circling ships, they watched them teeter and rock violently, the muddy expulsion of debris bubbling up on every side. One trawler pitched up and down like a toy, the crew taking evasive action by cranking the engines and turning the boat out of the choppy waters. He pulled Sam along the rail, navigating around sailors and scientists who'd come up from below decks to gawk at the wild and dangerous surface waves.

Colonel Banks, Sue Anne and the rest of the scientists emerged from the door to the lower decks, and the officer spotted him and called for him to stop. Tom ignored her calls, continuing to pull Sam around to the starboard side of the ship, looking for a way off. The Marin had two free fall lifeboats sitting in a nook on the starboard side of the ship, ready for evacuation, but they were massive, twelve-person vessels better reserved for the ship's crew and scientists. He and Sam would need something smaller and, more importantly, faster.

"McKnight!" Banks shouted at him. "McKnight, get back here, damnit!"

"Shouldn't you stop to see what she wants?" Sam asked, running into a sailor rushing past to get to another part of the ship. "It's that officer lady."

"No." A punch to the ship's hull punctuated Tom's terse reply, sending them stumbling and falling against the rail, clutching each other as they tried to stay upright on the slippery deck. A head-sized piece of bedrock shot into the air just past the bow, ascending a hundred feet or more before it tumbled down to splash into the ocean again. Tom imagined the barrel of a shotgun aimed up toward the surface from a thousand meters down, preparing to blast sediment and basaltic chunks the size of compact cars into the Marin's hull with steel-shattering force. His skin ignited with heat and he forced down the panic rising in his gut for both his and Sam's sakes.

"We'll have to be smart if we want to survive this." He spotted a small inflatable boat with an outboard motor hanging from a winch off the side of the Marin, and he pulled his daughter to the rail, gripped her shoulders, and leveled his gaze at her. "I'll lift you over and put you down on the boat."

Sam glanced at the two-foot gap between the slick rail and raft and shook her head madly. "Are you sure we aren't safer staying on the ship?"

"It's not safe." He tried to keep his voice low and firm, though a note of terror slipped through. "This thing is going to sink, honey."

"It won't. It—"

A hand grabbed Tom's shoulder and spun him around. He found himself face-to-face with Colonel Banks, Sue Anne standing behind her with two scientists and a sailor, all of them swaying, staggering, arms out to keep their footing on the Marin's tilting deck.

"What are you doing, Mr. McKnight? You can't just leave the boat!"

Tom took a step toward her, growling. "Get everyone on the lifeboats and off the ship. You don't want to be anywhere near it when it goes down."

Banks nodded to the sailor who headed for Tom, arms outstretched, but fell to the side, knocking over the colonel in the process. Tom grabbed his daughter, lifting her toward the rail. "Climb and jump, Sam. I won't let you fall." Glancing over his shoulder, he called out to Sue Anne who had managed to stay upright, watching him with a horrified expression. "Come on, Sue Anne! You know what's about to happen!"

For a second, Sue Anne looked like she might join Tom and Sam, but a growl from Colonel Banks sent her stumbling backward. Turning his attention back to Sam, Tom watched as she grabbed the edge of the rail, climbed up, crouching, panting, placing one foot on the winch frame. He helped her balance by gripping the waistband of her jeans, then shoved her across the open space. Sam's arms flew wide as she landed in the boat with her face smashed against the soft tubing on the other side with a soft "Umph!"

Tom climbed up onto the rail next, balancing for a precarious moment, leaping just as the boat lurched to the port side. His feet slipped, flying backward, and he hung suspended in the air for a stomach-flipping moment, nothing beneath him but a strip of churning ocean. Then the raft was rising along with the Marin, lifted by the massive force shoving from below. Tom landed on the slick plastic and slid to the edge next to Sam, side of the small craft punching into his thighs, bending him forward to stare down at the froth and foam before Sam grabbed his arm and helped pull him back.

"Thanks!" Tom gulped, turning to grip the control panel, palm pausing over a green button. Banks had finally regained her footing and stood two feet from the rail, glaring furiously, but unable to deny the growing chaos blossoming around them bubbling up from the seafloor. Something massive struck the Marin's hull, sending shockwaves through solid steel ship, bending hull plates and ringing the craft like a bell. Those standing on deck crashed to their knees except for Banks, who clung tenaciously to the rail.

"Get them to the lifeboats!" Tom yelled, voice rising above the sound of churning waves and thudding bedrock against the hull. "Even if it's the last thing you do, get them out of here!"

The colonel's expression shifted, anger giving way to dawning realization. She turned away from the rail and gestured to Sue Anne and the rest of the scientists for them to follow her. "Come on! To the lifeboats! This way!"

Tom hit the button on the controller to make them go down but paused when he locked eyes with Sue Anne, who stood near the rail with her feet spread wide to keep herself from falling. "Come on, Sue Anne!" he shouted, gesturing wildly for her to jump across. "There's room for all of us!"

The woman looked at the space between the ship rail and the swaying raft, and her head shook, eyes wide, bottom lip quivering.

Tom waved her off. "Okay, then go with Banks! Go! Just get off the ship!"

The coder turned away and staggered across the deck as Tom hit the button to lower the raft. The water-slick hull of the Marin passed beside them, and the ship's alarm rang, a loud repeated blaring that cut through the gurgle of water around them.

"Dad, we'll be cut to pieces." Sam peered down at the boiling mess of rock and brownish foam, the seafloor reek smacking them in the face.

"No. No we won't," Tom whispered through clenched teeth. Sliding back and forth across the boat's bottom like he'd been doing it his entire life, veins pounding with adrenaline, he disconnected the lifeboat as soon as they hit the water. He placed his foot on the side of the raft, grabbed the starter cord, and jerked it. The engine growled to life, and Tom grabbed the tiller grip, guiding the boat away from the Marin as waves smacked against the sides. They were lifted and tossed around, foam bursting over the sides, slivers of fist-sized bedrock shooting into the air around them.

"Hang on!" Tom shouted, twisting the tiller grip to give the engine more gas. Sam spread her knees, balancing lower, hands thrown out to hold the rope grips on both sides of the boat, using her weight like a ballast. The raft responded to Tom's control, rocketing forward through the choppy waves, jumping and bouncing over air bursts, wind whipping muddy foam across their faces. They cut through the splashing and gurgling waves, several fist-sized stones bouncing off the sides of the raft or falling inside with them. Using the sinking sun as a guide, Tom angled the raft away from the shore, weaving between two distressed ships to head in a southwesterly course, driving to the edge of the rough waters.

"Isn't the shore that way?" Sam shouted, nodding her head in a more westerly direction.

Tom raised his voice above the engine's high puttering as the raft picked up speed and bounced atop the turbulent swell, hair blowing back from his face. "If the crevice is breaking along the coastal shelf, it'll probably turn inland, so we need to get around it before we head to shore!"

"Do we have enough gas?"

Tom started to reply, but a spine-chilling rend of metal forced him to look back. The vessels they'd just passed wallowed in an explosion of water and air bubbles like a pan of boiling water. The ships rocked forward and backward, side-to-side, crews scrambling across their decks, desperate to pilot them out of danger.

"Too late," Tom murmured, too low for Sam to hear.

One boat's stern dropped while the bow raised, metric tons of water pouring over the back in an instant, the weight of it dragging them downward, causing the stern to sink deeper into the muddy pit, slipping backwards into the hungry waters. A sailor stood on the second ship's bow, leaning over the rail and pointed to the other sinking craft, shouting a command, waving his arm in a circular motion for the driver to turn around and go in for a rescue.

Tom eased back on the throttle as they shot past the edge of the turbulent zone, and Sam turned and joined her father in watching the second craft try to reach the sinking vessel. They almost made it when a burst of debris exploded around them, blasting a spattering of holes in their hull near the bow, sending the ship into a nosedive it never recovered from. Sam gasped, clinging to the side of the raft, staring at the ship as it plunged into the boiling waves, tilting and listing to its starboard side as figures were thrown to and fro. Tom wrapped one arm around his daughter and covered her eyes with his hand, but she grabbed his wrist and jerked it down, her face red with ocean spray and tears.

The second ship followed the first, rolling over, showing the bottom of its hull for a long moment before the voracious sea claimed it. Ships – both Navy and civilian – around the Marin were caught up in the slow, washing machine-like agitation. Bows lifted and crashed violently, snapping hulls, sailors leaping from the sides into the ocean as the boat went under. A clap of water and air gripped the Marin's sides, dragging the massive ship into a downward spiral that deepened with each rotation. Sailors holding inflatable rafts between them leapt into the water, their orange and yellow crafts bouncing between them as they climbed inside, only to pitch and roll before the roiling waters consumed them as well. Others jumped in without life rafts and were instantly dragged under, hands sweeping up once before disappearing into the depths.

High against the side, Tom spotted one of the large steel lifeboats still in its cradle. But on the next rotation it had disappeared, launched into the water with what he hoped were people inside. He narrowed his eyes, peering across the turbulent water, unable to spot it.

"The lifeboat, dad… The Colonel and… the others."

"They're meant to withstand storms way worse than this, sweetie," Tom replied, as much for himself as for her. "They'll be okay. By the Grace of God, please protect them and see them safely home," Tom whispered as they drifted farther away from the turbulence.

"Amen," Sam agreed.

Tom turned the throttle, and the raft shot forward, arcing toward the shore.

Chapter 8
Barbara McKnight
Wyndale, Virginia

As darkness settled over the town of Bristol, the sun's dusky light faded completely, giving way to streetlamps and headlights, lit storefronts and interior lighting casting long shadows across desolate parking lots. They'd hadn't even left the town proper when Linda pointed out the passenger window to a dozen people standing in a gas station parking lot, all gathered around a pickup truck, ears pinned to the open windows. The adjacent mini-mart lights glowed sharply, spreading sallow light over the fuel island.

"What are they doing?" Linda asked, her head turning as they passed.

"I'm not sure, kiddo." Barbara accelerated slightly, noticing a similar setup in a fast-food restaurant parking lot on their right. People had gathered around the open windows of a couple of vehicles, and appeared to be crowded around a television just inside the restaurant as well.

"Mom, look out!" Jack shouted.

Her attention jerked forward as a car cut in front of them, squealing out of a strip mall parking lot and shooting east. Barbara slammed on the brakes, coming to a lurching halt as the offending car tore off down the road with a brief squeal of tires. With an exaggerated sigh, Barbara pulled to the shoulder and brought the truck to a stop.

Linda was holding Jack's hand but staring at her mother. "You okay, Mom?"

"I'm fine," she replied, voice tense and quivering. "Thanks for the warning. I shouldn't have let myself get distracted."

Barbara gazed over at the strip mall off to her right, past the gas station to where a half-dozen people approached a Dollar Saver store as an employee closed and locked the doors. Two people knocked their fists on the glass while the employee pointed to her watch and shook her head. The small crowd of people grew more agitated and hit the glass harder. The employee backed away, pulling out her phone as she withdrew into the depths of the store.

"What's getting into people?" Linda asked, watching the scene unfold. "Is it because of what Dad texted?"

"I'm not sure… let's find out." She reached over and turned on the truck radio, tuning to NGR news where a reporter greeted them in an urgent voice.

"… regular programming to bring you this emergency update from the North Atlantic where researchers were investigating an anomaly that caused a mass exodus of sea life in the area. Several ships have gone missing, including the sonar ship, Gypsy, where NGR reporter Shannon Reese was embedded. Please be warned what you are about to hear might be disturbing."

The broadcast switched from the calm inside of a radio studio to somewhere outdoors with the unmistakable sounds of waves crashing against the side of a boat. Barbara had heard waves crashing before, and the ones being broadcast didn't sound like normal waves at all. They had a frothy edge mixed with a spattering of thuds on what she took to be a deck. A woman grunted, cursed, and gave a muted cry as something clattered nearby.

"On?" Pause. "Okay, I'm ready, Jim." Pause. "This is Shannon Reese reporting for NGR from the deck of the Gypsy, two-hundred miles off the coast of New England. Actually, I just got inside before a rain of rocks and debris fell over us. The ocean appears to be boiling or bubbling up all around us, and I see some ships in distress." A long pause hung in the air followed by a rattling noise. "Jim, where did that ship… oh, no." A voice spoke nearby. "It went under? Are you serious? Are we—"

An alarm rang out on the ship, cutting through the truck cab speakers and startling Barbara back in her seat. She should have turned off the broadcast, because it was frightening the children – hell, it was frightening *her* – but she couldn't bring herself to touch the dial.

Shannon got her voice under control as shouts rang out in the background, loud thuds continuing to strike the deck. "I just learned that two ships have gone under because of the surface turbulence, but our captain is steering us out of the disruption zone, and we should be safe in a just a moment." Something rattled again, and a high, surprised gasp escaped her. "Uh, we're tilting now… something's pushing the bow of the ship upward, and water is coming in. I'm standing in about six inches… What Jim? Yeah."

A violent cacophony of sound burst from the speakers and seemed to go on forever. In reality, it was only about ten seconds, the power of the sound causing Barbara to flinch and grip the wheel. Shannon's voice returned, panic-fueled and strained, breathing into the microphone in brief gasps. "Ship stopped moving. Trying to hang… on. Oh, no. Jim, wait! I don't think… I don't…" A thick crunch burst through the truck speakers like a pickax slamming into ice, followed by Shannon's brief scream before the broadcast cut out.

After a moment of empty space, the NGR studio returned, the reporter's voice low and respectful. "We captured that disturbing audio fifteen minutes ago, and we've not received an update from Shannon since. While it appears we have lost contact with her, we want to assure our audience that every effort is being made…"

Barbara had to remove her tight grip on the steering wheel before she flipped the radio off and sat back in her seat, tightening her grip to keep her hands steady as she accelerated again, resuming their journey home.

"Mom?" Jack whispered, voice shaking. "Is Dad okay?"

* * *

Barbara pulled into their driveway as night deepened around them. The crunch of the tires over gravel stopped, and she put the truck into park and killed the engine. Hands shaking, she swallowed with a dry click, staring down at the phone in her lap. The screen still displayed the five texts and calls she'd sent to Tom, all in desperation, begging for him to pick up or reply so she knew they were okay, and all failing to go through. She squeezed Jack's hand briefly and climbed out of the truck, helping him down. They met Linda at the tailgate, and she directed her daughter to grab some packages as Smooch trotted up. Tail wagging excitedly, she panted pressed up against Jack, but he pushed her away, face turned up to his mother.

"Mom, you didn't answer Jack's question," Linda stopped with her bags in hand. "Is Dad okay? Was he on one of those boats? He practically said so on the text he sent."

Barbara grabbed a couple bags for herself and edged the kids toward the back door with her hip, all four walking around together. The soft sounds of clucking and bleating came from the dimly lit pens as the farm animals settled in for the evening. "I'm not worried," she replied with a wan smile.

"Is that why you called him a million times just now?"

"Okay, first off, twice is not a million. And I admit I was a little panicked at first, but I'm okay now. And your father is fine, as is Sam. He said so in the text. "

In truth, Barbara's insides were turning inside out, her gut sick with worry, but the last thing she wanted to do was frighten the kids "Look, I'll keep trying to call and text, but your father also said they were going to survive, and I trust him on that. I know they're safe. They have to be."

"Are you sure?"

Barbara nodded even as her eyes turned glassy with worry. "I know you're both a little antsy." She stopped at the sliding glass door and set down her packages. Unlocking the door, she slid it aside and ushered the kids through. "But there's no sense in worrying, because why? What do I always tell you?"

"Have faith?" Linda asked hopefully, her eyebrows raised.

"That's right. While we really care about your dad and Sam, there's nothing we can do to help them. We have to believe they're going to be okay. Your job is to keep calm and help me keep things under control here. That means getting the groceries away and getting settled in for the night."

Her son's face was plaintive, eyes round with concern. "But—"

"Maybe *you* could work ahead on some schoolwork before bed while your sister helps me put things away?"

Jack's eyes widened in protest. "But I thought we were on a break from school."

"Yes, you are. But I want you to be ready for when we start things up next week, okay? The next grade is going to be a big step up for you!"

Jack opened his mouth to try and argue, but Barbara skillfully cut him off at the pass. "Would it help if I let Smooch study with you?"

Jack's expression lifted, his tone turning slightly calmer. "I guess that would be cool."

"Okay, I'll go get Smooch, and you get into your PJs and get your books out. Remember where we left off?"

Jack nodded slowly, slouched over shuffling down the hall and up the stairs as Barbara turned to her daughter. "Put the meat bags in the basement next to the freezer. Everything else, on the counter." She put her fingers in her mouth and gave a low whistle, and Smooch came trotting in, head held at an inquisitive tilt as her tail wagged. "Good girl," Barbara said. "You go with Jack, okay?" Barbara pointed up the stairs, repeating his name. "Jack! Got it?" The German Shepherd gave a light bark and nuzzled her hand before darting up the stairs after the youngster.

She hesitated a moment then followed Smooch down the hall and up a short flight of steps. In the upstairs loft, she took an immediate right into a short hall that connected the younger children's bedrooms. A bathroom door stood in the center, dividing the bedrooms without them sharing doors. Their oldest, Sam, had her own bedroom on the left side of the house with her own bathroom and a small walk-in closet. On the short connector hall, Jack's door was on the right side, and Barbara quietly peeked in, greeted by the pleasant sight of her son sitting at his desk, already in his favorite blue pajamas. He pulled his English textbook from its place on a shelf and moved it next to his laptop, powering the machine on before leaning down to rub Smooch's head.

Jack giggled and wrapped his arm around the dog and hugged her, seeming distracted from thoughts of Tom and Sam and the trouble they might be in. Barbara got him started on his English lessons and then left him to work on his own, with Smooch curling up on a dog bed next to him, head on her paws, eyes ticking back and forth between the boy and his mother.

She left the two in Jack's room, returned to the first floor, and joined Linda at the truck where she was still carrying bags. "Great job, you almost got them all," Barbara said, complimenting her daughter as she passed, reaching down to scoop up the last bunch of bags until she could barely lift her arms over the back of the tailgate.

She followed Linda into the house and down the basement where Linda had piled the meat near the two freezers. Barbara threw open the first chest and directed her daughter to hand her the individual meat packages in their white paper wrappings. She placed the first package inside, rearranged some frozen packages around, then placed a second one inside.

Linda stood holding two packages of meat, waiting for her mother to take them. Her eyes were as big and wide as twin moons as she stared upward. "Do you really think they're okay? I mean, they were out there on the ocean, and so was that reporter lady." The girl gulped. "And if her boat sank, Dad's could have, too."

Barbara stopped shifting around the meat and leaned over the freezer with both hands as a wave of emotional exhaustion passed through her. With a shivering sigh, she pushed herself straight and turned to face her daughter.

"You saw the text." Barbara smiled as broadly as she could muster. "You know as much as I do."

"So, they could be dead?" Linda's voice held its quivering tone, eyes bloodshot from crying. "I didn't say anything on the way home because I didn't want to scare Jack, but he knows something's wrong." She shook her head, her frown deepening. "I mean, we have to accept that something could have happened, right?"

Barbara wanted to argue, but couldn't shake the reporter's voice from her head. The gasping, gut-wrenching terror, the deck thuds and crashing sounds as her ship sunk in the middle of the ocean and the woman's last scream cut off like a quick tearing of paper in a quiet room. Barbara had always looked toward her faith to help get through rough patches. Not blind faith, but honest heartfelt belief in herself, in her family, and God when the days grew long, and times got darkest. She held out her chin defiantly and raised her eyes wide to her daughter.

"While there's a possibility your father and Sam might be in trouble, I refuse accept that they're gone, and I won't *believe* it until someone proves it to me. Your father said he would protect Sam. He said we should expect to hear that several ships went down, right?"

Linda nodded.

"Right, so it sounded like he knew what would happen, which makes me think your father had a plan for getting him and Sam out of there. He said they would survive, right?"

"Yeah… yeah, he did." Linda's chin lifted to match her mother. She sniffed and wiped at her eyes, thinking about it and then nodding with more confidence. "He said he would protect Sam, that they would survive, and they'd talk to us soon."

"That's right. And your father always keeps his promises. You know that. So, until I hear different, I'm going to do as your father asked and get things ready for when they get home. I really believe they'll be here, and I'd love it if you believed it, too."

Linda seemed to draw on her mother's strength, her eyes defiant, confident, lifting to meet her mother's gaze as she bent to help with the bags and hand them over. "I do." The voice shook on the edges, but was full of defiance of the odds and faith in her father.

"That's better," Barbara smiled. "Now come on, let's get this done before the meat gets warm, hm?"

The two continued rotating the older meat to the top of the freezer while putting the fresher purchases at the bottom. By the time they'd finished, she had two frozen packages of boneless chuck roast she transferred to the refrigerator to thaw for dinner the following evening, and had already mentally planned out the next week's worth of metals.

"Now what?" Linda asked.

"Let's take the cans over and add those to our stocks, then we'll take a full inventory. How does that sound?"

"Sounds like a great start to me."

They picked up the bags of cans and carried them to the other side of the basement, stopping by the first row of shelves, all packed tight. Linda entered first, fitting between the shelf and wall and walking to the end where she turned around. Barbara handed her cans, which she placed in the backs of the rows as she rotated the older stock forward. Once they completed their stocking, they exited the row and faced each other.

"What now, Mom?"

At the end of each row of shelves hung a clipboard filled with inventory sheets and a small flashlight. Barbara picked the clipboard off the end of the row and nodded for her daughter to take the flashlight. "I'll read off this list of items, and I need you to count them off and verify the amounts I tell you are correct. It's a little tricky because the lower and higher shelves are hard to reach, but I've got a stool if you need it."

"Okay," Linda lifted a flashlight off its hook and flipped it on to ensure it worked. "Starting on the first row, right?"

"That's right."

Linda nodded, turning to head for the back row to get started. Over the next half hour they inventoried hundreds of canned and dry goods. There were the standard items like corn, green beans, and stewed tomatoes to use for soups. They'd placed their heavier stocks on the second row of shelves, including vacuum-sealed rice bags, pinto beans, black and red beans, and rolled oats, all stored in plastic buckets and totes to keep them fresh and vermin-free. The last few rows held dozens of boxes of MREs and buckets of freeze-dried camping food composed of a wide variety of meal types. The packing and expiration dates were printed on the tops and sides in easy-to-read lettering.

"Your father picked these up at a huge discount a few years ago."

"That's why Dad's awesome," Linda said with a grin. The girl had pulled her thick curls back into a ponytail and had a thin sheen of sweat covering her forehead. She worked hard, and it showed. "Are you ready for me to count?"

"Get in there, tiger," Barbara joked, and she started down the list as her daughter counted and verified each box number with the packing date, last inspection date, and menu type.

"We've got ten years' worth of MREs and other long-term survival food packed in this room alone," Barbara said, smartly.

"Ten years? Wow!"

"Yeah, we're not messing around when it comes to our survival." She gave her daughter a light tap on the forehead with her pen, raising a giggle from the girl. Then she looked at her clock and saw it was getting late into the evening. "How do you feel? Do you want to finish up tomorrow, or keep going?"

"I can keep going," Linda said with a hopeful expression. "We've got chores to do tomorrow."

"We might not get much sleep," she replied, raising an eyebrow.

"That's okay, Mom. I want to keep going." Linda paused for a moment. "It keeps my mind off of… you know."

"I'm still feeling restless, too," she agreed. "We might as well exhaust ourselves. I'll check on Jack when we're done."

"Him and Smooch are probably sleeping by now." Linda rolled her eyes. "You know how they get sometimes."

Barbara pushed a lock of sandy hair behind her ear. "You're probably right. Ready?"

A quick inventory of their liquid supplies came next. They counted boxes of powdered fruit juices and jugs of pineapple, cherry, and strawberry juice, along with a few bottles of the same which they'd rotated regularly since they only had a year shelf life, though in all likelihood they'd likely stay fresh for months beyond their expiration date thanks to the cool, dark conditions they were kept in.

Water was not a problem for the McKnights. They had one hundred and fifty cases of emergency canned water, equaling three hundred and thirty-seven gallons which would last the family just under a year. But they stored the bulk of their water in thirty, stackable, fifty-gallon tanks equaling them fifteen hundred gallons of water to provide an additional six hundred days. The fifty-eight-gallon rain catcher tank appeared to be half full the last time Barbara checked it, giving them an extra ten days. With a well on the farm that could be hooked up to a hand pump in emergencies, keeping water stored for long-term use wasn't a requirement, but Tom and Barbara's preparatory decisions were nothing if not thorough.

Linda stopped counting and met her mother at the head of the row. "How long would all this water last?"

"So, just what we have in this basement would give us over nine-hundred days, but we can probably stretch it if we want, though we still have to consider food preparation and sanitation."

"Two and a half years, give or take."

"Yep, but our real saving grace is the well and creek. As long as we can keep the pumps operational, we'll have an unlimited supply of water for us and the animals forever.

"Awesome."

"Agreed. Now, we just have the last section with the energy bars. Those have a five-year shelf life, and we usually rotate through those like we do with meat and canned goods."

"Looks like we're ready for anything," her daughter agreed.

Next came their camping gear, complete with tents, backpacks, sleeping bags, flint and tinder and other fire-making supplies, thermal and wool blankets, ponchos, tarps, and para cord. A pegboard on the wall held multiple stainless-steel survival knives for hunting and defense, lock knives, hatchets, folding shovels and pickaxes, multi-function tools, and collapsible fishing rods. An assortment of NiMH rechargeable batteries stood nearby along with chargers, plus lanterns, lantern batteries, and boxes full of plastic flashlights, penlights, and a half-dozen heavy-duty flashlights that could double as weapons.

There was also an assortment of small and large bandages, boxes of gauze, medical tape, and elastic wrap along with an entire section of shelving dedicated to 15 general use first-aid kits, five trauma bags with splint and tourniquets, five burn kits for skin and eyes, suture kits and suture practice kits, a small box with scalpels, forceps, and clamps, and four boxes of quick clot powder. In a 2.6 cubic foot refrigerator at the end of the row, they stored their antibiotics, both human and animal. Barbara ran down a list of a dozen bottles of Amoxicillin to treat ear, nose, and throat infections with another dozen bottles of clarithromycin as a backup. They had Ciprofloxacin for urinary tract infections and bronchitis, and Metronidazole for bacterial infections of the abdomen. Since the McKnights were not doctors, they'd put an antibiotic guidebook in a plastic baggie and placed it on top of the refrigerator for reference should they need it.

"Most of these still have a shelf life of a year," Linda noted as she read them off to her mother. "Do we rotate these out, too?"

"Usually, but we've been slacking there." Barbara bit her lip. "Replacing some of these older bottles will be on the top of our list of things to do this week, but we might be better off growing our own herbal remedies for the long term. If things get bad, people will raid hospitals for supplies."

The girl stared at her with a worried expression. "Do you think that will really happen?"

"I really don't know, honey," she replied with an uncertain shrug, "but that's why we did all this. Just in case the worst *does* happen."

"Well, that takes care of all the storage shelves." The girl flipped her flashlight off and on, eager to get into more inventory. "What do we check next?"

"We keep our bug-out bags over here." Barbara walked to a shelf near the bottom of the steps. "They'd placed the bags to keep them in a central location to grab and go if they needed.

"Okay, I know a little more about the bugout bags," Linda said. "There's Jack's, mine, and Sam's." She pointed to each of them.

"Do you know what's in them?"

Linda ticked off things on her fingers. "They should have three changes of clothes—"

"I think Jack has already grown out of his clothes," Barbara said, stopping the girl. "And yours may be too small, too."

"So, we need to replace those, right?"

"Yep. What else?"

"Besides the clothes, we should have a change of shoes, a first aid kit, flint and tinder, a knife, and a tin with fold up fishing gear, a flare, string and other stuff. Oh, and a three-day supply of food with water filtration straws."

"Very good," Barbara nodded.

"Not bad," Barbara said after they'd finished with the bags. "There's room for improvement, but these numbers are solid." She turned, facing the other side of the basement. "Now that we've inventoried our general supplies, let's check out our power situation."

They stepped past the freezers and double-door refrigerator to the battery room on the northwest side of the basement. As soon as Barbara opened the door, a breeze of cool, dry wind washed tugged on them, courtesy of the additional ductwork Tom had installed to keep the batteries cool and dry. Barbara stood in the room's center and turned in a full circle. The circuit breakers rested in the north wall, and the west wall held a shelf with three rows of five batteries, each of them weighing upwards of seventy-five pounds each.

A small work bench holding boxes of wires, soldering tools, plugs and connectors sat against the east wall, where Tom did most of his wiring work on the batteries. Three new batteries sat off to the side of the bench, packaging still intact. They were maintenance-free units that Tom had wanted to work into their current battery bank over time, though they'd had to put off purchasing the other twelve considering they ran over twelve-hundred dollars apiece. While Linda knew about the battery room, she didn't know much about the batteries they used or how the system worked, so Barbara walked over and stood next to the batteries. "These are all deep-cycle batteries. That means they provide a steady amount of current over a long time."

"And we use the solar panels to recharge them, right?"

"We can do that, but it wouldn't make a lot of sense to do it until the power goes out. It's much better to use trickle charging off the grid for now to keep them topped up and cycle them, then use solar if we have to. We've got a dozen solar panels that work year around, but your father has three more he wanted to add before the summer was over." Barbara shifted her weight to her right foot. "That's something I'll need your help with."

"Why more solar panels?"

"Well, we have a lot we need to power. We've connected the freezers, refrigerators, the hot water heater, the network, the washer and dryer, and some outlets in the kitchen so we can run small appliances and charge our devices. But we have to be smart in how we maintain it."

Linda glanced toward the southwest corner where they kept their three massive gun safes and two smaller ones sitting off to the sides. "Should we do an inventory on those?"

"I already know what's in the safes."

"What, enough weapons and ammunition to fight off a small army?"

Barbara clicked her tongue, holding back a smile. "Fine, let's have a peek."

She moved between the pair of benches stretched in front of the safes and keyed in the proper number sequences on all three, turning the five-spoked handles and heaving the heavy doors open to release the scents of gun oil and metal before flipping on the interior lights of each.

The first safe held eighteen ARs locked into their holders, including a Ruger Carbine, a Ruger AR-556, and assorted half and fully built out custom configurations. From the top shelf hung a mix of a dozen revolvers and semi-auto pistols along with magazines, quick loaders, and tens of thousands of rounds of ammunition nestled against the right-side wall.

Inside their second safe, they kept shotguns and hunting rifles, including a Beretta A400 shotgun, a Benelli M2 semi-automatic shotgun, a Timber Classic Marling 336C rifle, and a Mossburg 500 along with boxes of shells. Inside the third safe lay four compound bows and three bulky crossbows, and they'd removed the cubbies to store over five hundred arrows and crossbow bolts.

"That's an insane amount of fire power." Linda shook her head.

While Barbara didn't get excited about weapons, the amount of protection they'd afforded themselves provided a feeling of comfort and safety. She very nearly made an offhand quip about the amount of firepower on hand, but she never wanted the kids to boast or joke about the weapons without understanding the responsibility that came with it.

"What are the four rules of gun safety?" Barbara asked, turning the moment into an opportunity for review.

"Every gun is always loaded," Linda started, looking up at the ceiling as she thought. "Never point a gun at anything you aren't going to shoot. Keep your finger off the trigger until you sight your target, and be sure of your target and what's behind it."

"Not bad," Barbara agreed. "And you know how we have to be extra safe around your little brother?"

"He knows all the safety rules, but he's still a kid. He shouldn't be playing with any sort of weapon, not even the knives. That's why we don't let him play down here."

"Right on. Do you remember where all the hidden weapons are in the house?"

Linda nodded enthusiastically. "Revolver in the lock box on the fridge. A pistol with its magazine next to it in the upstairs bathroom above the cabinet mirror. There's also a shotgun in the living room mantle, recess-loaded with alternating slugs and buckshot, safety on."

Barbara smiled. "Sounds like you memorized this from your dad. What else?"

"We've got the AR and magazine, also not loaded, suspended above the barn's side door, and another loaded revolver inside the shed, sealed in a watertight lockbox behind the well pump."

"You remember the code?"

"8-7-2," the girl said smartly.

Barbara hitched her hip out and folded her arms across her chest. "Perfect. And you remember what I'm carrying in my waistband at the small of my back?"

Linda pointed to her mother's back hip. "You've got a Smith & Wesson 380. You let me shoot it last month."

"Good. You'll make a good little trooper." Barbara looked at her watch and saw it was well past midnight. "Hey, I'm pretty tired. How about you?"

"Yeah, I'm pretty tired. But we did good tonight, right?"

"I couldn't have done it without you, kiddo." Barbara wrapped her arm around her daughter and squeezed. They shut the gun safe doors and trudged up the stairs, Barbara collapsing in one of the kitchen chairs, and Linda sitting opposite her. The girl's face was smudged from crawling around on the floor, and her hazel eyes looked less panicked than when they'd arrived.

"Are we all set and ready for… whatever might happen?"

"We're mostly in great shape. We may want to refresh some of our medical supplies, but otherwise we're looking good. I may take a break from chores tomorrow to run out for a few extra things, then we'll get things locked down." She leveled her gaze at her daughter and reached across the table to pat her hand. "You were awesome tonight. Go get ready for bed, and I'll be up to check on you in a minute."

Linda gave her mother a big smile before getting up and leaving the kitchen, leaving Barbara alone with her thoughts. She placed her elbows on the table and rested her chin in her hands, rubbing at her tired eyes. Somehow, she felt, there would be many more long days ahead. She just needed Tom and Sam to come home, though, and everything would be okay.

Chapter 9
Tom McKnight
North Atlantic

The early morning sun spread its rays above the horizon like a gently reaching hand ready to wake up the world, golden hues spreading upward from beyond the sightline. Thin fingers of light drove away the darkness, stretching across the waves as the boat rocked up and down. The light brightened as the minutes passed, the sky turning from a solid color into a gradient of orange, radiating upward in brilliant yellows that cut through the brightening sky. Smudges of gloomy clouds dribbled like spilled coffee across a glass table, sunlight highlighting the edges and turning them soft and glowing.

After getting away from the fleet's destruction, Tom had cut the engine to wait on the rescue vessels he was confident were already on their way to the area. The chances of them reaching shore were less than optimal with just a small tank of gas and a pair of paddles, so waiting on a rescue near the disaster zone looked like a better idea than potentially being adrift at sea. He figured the crew of the Marin had used the small craft as a means of quick transport between research vessels given that it clearly wasn't made to be on the ocean for an extended period of time.

"I'm so cold," Sam said, teeth chattering as she pulled a small thermal blanket up to her chin, huddling against Tom. Huddled together, they sat on the raft bottom, resting back on a wooden seat, leaning to the side against the raft's rigid interior bladder, Tom's arms thrown around his daughter to drive away the chill.

"It's colder than I'd expect," Tom admitted. "It's still spring, but I've never spent the night on a raft in the middle of the ocean." He snorted in bemusement. "How about you?"

Sam shook her head and shivered. "First time for me, too."

"It should warm up in a bit," he said. "The sun's coming out, see?"

His daughter nodded at the beautiful sight, though neither one of them could muster up much awe after witnessing the fast destruction of the fleet followed by a sleepless night rolling on the waves.

"Will we get rescued?"

"We'll get rescued," Tom said, and he meant it. "No way all those ships go missing without someone coming to look. We may have motored too far away from the target area to be picked up right away, but better to take a bit longer than risk getting capsized. They'll search for miles and miles all around."

"That's good," Sam said, not seeming convinced with her father's reassurances. They sat in silence for several minutes, watching the sun creep up over the horizon and waves lap up against the side of the boat. In spite of their tenuous position, the good news was they had a small survival kit stowed in a pocket inside the rigid interior of the boat, and inside Tom had found a thermal blanket, several hand flares, a compass, rope, waterproof tape, a flat-tipped knife, and an emergency first aid kit, two days' worth of energy bars, and some plastic bladders filled with water.

The sky filled with a gradual blend of orange to blue, lighting the bottoms of the coffee-stained clouds with a vibrant white glow. Tom sighed at the sight, the ocean's waves both soothing and agitating, its vastness too deep to comprehend. Even from the deck of a large ship, Tom had always felt a mix of unease and awe toward the ocean. Sitting in their small raft made his unease grow to near panic - they were small and inconsequential, a couple of specks in a vast wet wilderness.

Two hours ticked by as they drifted and swayed endlessly. They shared some water and an energy bar and then took separate seats facing each other as the sun warmed them, settling back once more to wait for help.

"Do you think Mom's worried about us?" Sam asked.

"She's absolutely worried about us, and Linda and Jack are, too. But I don't know what they've heard or if they even got my last text." Tom shifted on the wooden slat and fished his phone from his pocket. He'd turned it off overnight to save battery life, his signal dying after the ships carrying the repeaters went down.

Flipping it on again, he noted the phone signal was still dead, but at least the GPS worked.

"Check it out." He held the phone out for Sam, pointing to their location. "We're right here. Looks like we drifted to the southwest, and still about 200 miles off the coast."

She leaned back with a nod, shedding her thermal blanket as the air grew warmer. The girl offered a faint but hopeful smile. "Should we start paddling to shore?"

"I don't think so," he answered. "We should stay put and wait for help to come to us. If we get too far out—"

"I was just kidding, Dad." Sam gave him a toothy grin and Tom returned the smile.

"Sorry, hon. You know how I get, trying to find a solution to every problem."

"It's okay," she replied. "I'm just giving you a hard time." She noticed him staring off to the south, and she turned to follow where he was looking. "What is it?"

He stiffened in the boat and pointed. "I think that's an airplane. Do you see it?"

Sam shielded her eyes with her hand and furrowed her brows, staring hard. "Yep, that's definitely a plane. And it's coming right for us!"

"Yes it is! Quick, let's not take any chances!"

Sam crouched in the shifting boat and waved her hands wildly while Tom tore off his red windbreaker before diving for the rescue kit. He dug the waterproof smoke flare out and stood in the back of the boat, turning his head to get a sense of which way the slight breeze was blowing. Once the plane drew close enough to make out the individual propellors on the wings, he raised the flare high and pulled the ignition tab. The stick hissed violently as it ignited, vibrating in his hand, and a heavy cloud of smoke spouted from the end, rolling away across the sky. Despite the wind, the smoke kept a compact trail, lifting, floating upward and spreading. They would be impossible to miss, especially from a plane flying directly toward them, and Tom used his right arm to wave his windbreaker off to his side, willing one of the plane's crew to see them.

"Over here!" Sam shouted, gradually starting to stand up, rocking the small craft. "Over here! Come get us! Help HELP!"

"Hey! Settle down or you'll fall in," Tom shouted over his daughter. "Also, you know they can't hear you, right?"

"Oh." Sam abruptly stopped shouting. "Right. Sorry." Sam sheepishly crouched lower to stabilize the boat but kept her hands held high, taking her own windbreaker off to wave it around, mimicking her father's motion.

"That's a C-130," Tom said as he watched the big aircraft approach, flying a hundred feet above the ocean's surface. The thick, bumble bee fuselage buzzed over the waters, driven by four massive propellers creating a loudening drone of sound. They continued waving but the plane held its course, flying toward where the ships had gone under without so much as an acknowledgment it had seen them. Tom's stomach sunk as the massive plane buzzed over their head at a flat angle. Then his spirits shot through the roof when an object spilled out of the open rear door and tumbled downward, a massive orange parachute slowing its descent.

Tom pumped his fist in the air as the package drifted toward the ocean a hundred yards away, Sam giving a yell as she joined her father in a triumphant dance, until she lost her footing and almost spilled into the ocean. The flare went flying as Tom grabbed her arm to steady her, and he laughed as they sat down in their seats, hope flaring in his chest. "Told you they'd be here soon! Hold on, let's see what they dropped for us."

Tom started the outboard motor and turned the boat toward the drifting package, keeping them at a steady pace so they were close when it finally splashed down. Cutting the motor, he moved past Sam to the front of the raft, reaching down for the parachute cords. He wound them in and pulled the parachute material out of the water, laying it across the front of the boat. As he pulled the crate marked with yellow and red stripes alongside the boat, he noted the plastic triangular tabs on each side and flashing yellow lights spaced out at regular intervals that would increase the crate's visibility at night.

The crate was smaller than the width of his shoulders and light enough for the average adult to lift and Tom hauled it into the boat, setting it gingerly down on the bottom in between himself and Sam. The tabs had large arrows emblazoned on them and raised print in multiple languages, including English, instructing the user to "pull to open." Tom popped off the tabs, opening the top of the crate and revealing its contents. A paper sat atop a bundle of supplies, and he took it out by the corner and handed it to Sam so he it didn't get wet.

"Read these, please," Tom said, digging into the crate's contents.

Sam unfolded the papers and shuffled through them. "Looks like they printed this recently. It says, 'For anyone reading this message, please remain calm. We've marked your location for pickup as quickly as possible. The Navy and Coast Guard are responding to calls along the Northeastern Seaboard in response to an undersea disturbance that occurred at twenty-one hundred hours yesterday evening. Please stay calm and maintain your position. Help is on the way. The contents of the supply crate are as follows.' And they list out all the supplies." Sam finished reading and lowered the paper, looking at her father.

"The entire Northeastern Seaboard?" Tom murmured in muted horror, eyes narrowed as he stared into the crate. "There might be residual cracks all the way to the coast."

"Is that bad? It has to be bad, right?"

"It's not good," he agreed, turning back to the crate. "But at least we've got some help." He pulled out a small air tank for inflating an emergency raft complete with folding tent poles and a tarp, emergency rations for three days, four gallons of fresh water, more signal flares and a flare gun, a first aid kit, and an emergency transponder with clear instructions on how to turn it on. Tom sat back and read the instructions, turning the crate around for Sam to look through.

"This isn't a lot of food or water," she commented.

"No, it's not. It was only meant for short-term use. You know, until rescue arrives."

"Are we going to wait to be rescued?"

Tom shook his head. "I don't want to leave the area, since they'll be back to pick us up. But if the anomaly has opened up to the coast, and it continues to spread along the seafloor, the damage would be catastrophic. Rescue operations could get overwhelmed, and they might not come back for us right away." Tom looked at the stretch of water between them and the land that was somewhere over the horizon. "We need to make a break for shore."

"But you said we don't have enough gas to make it." Her green eyes were plaintive.

"No, but we can make it a good distance with the gas we have." He flexed the folding pole pieces in his hands, gauging the material's strength. "When that runs out, we'll get creative."

Chapter 10
Military Central Command
Undisclosed Location

Air circulates through the chilly, conference room, flitting across the bare gray walls and hardwood handrail to swirl around two large coffee urns. A boat-shaped conference table stretches end-to-end across the room, its polished hardwood surface reflecting the faces of those seated in the stiff, leather chairs. A dozen massive screens add color to the stark white overhead lights and give the room some sense of realism. Satellite images rotate on two screens, high-definition satellite images showing a place in the North Atlantic where their research vessels went under, damaged areas along the New England coast, and several small islands cracked in two.

Two screens display overlayed blue and green-tinted depth charts, detailing the shelf off the New England coast which now has a long gash in it, one that curves and cracks its way along the coast in spiderweb fragments like a windshield pegged with a stone. Other ominous-looking screens provide real-time weather projections and ocean current flow tracking for a variety of prediction scenarios, including the worst possible ones. Raw weather data pumps across two screens in a burst of light and information only a few in the room can read. Staffers and advisers lean over the shoulders of key military personnel as they check ever-changing information on their laptops, eyes sometimes widening at what they see while some peck out responses in a clatter of nervous typing.

A mix of designer suits, high-brass military uniforms, staffers and specialists dot the room, though only the four nearest the screens are dressed in blue jeans and t-shirts. Number crunchers, data specialists and PhDs to a one, they're clearly uncomfortable among the cold, calculating officials and government heads. The high brass talk over one another, interjecting and interrupting, theorizing on the fly, and giving the impression of a group of very important people grasping at straws, working to get a handle on an impossible situation. The room smells like cologne, boot polish, and ozone, a combination that might have been suffocating if not for the continual air circulation.

A door near the coffee urns opens, and the chatter dies down as a tall man in a suit strides into the room and to the far end of the table, gives everyone a brief, nod, and sits. He's tall and strong-jawed, with piercing gray eyes and a thick head of dark hair sprinkled with salt.

"I'd like to get an update on the situation." His eyes roam the table before settling on the man directly to his right. The man wears a white Navy button up with muted gold bars marking his shoulders and a plate of colored badges lining his left breast pocket and he appears visibly disturbed. "Let's start with you, Admiral Spencer."

"Thank you, Mr. President," the Admiral says, jowls shaking beneath a pair of wire-framed glasses perched on his nose. "As you're aware, we sent thirteen research vessels to a location near the New England shelf where we detected some unexplainable activity. Our primary concerns were the reports of marine life disturbances, specifically their sudden migration away from their primary feeding grounds, decimating the local fisheries within a forty-eight-hour period.

"Our ships were investigating the event and discovered an anomaly on the seafloor. A crevice from which our instruments detected a massive influx of freshwater from a sub-surface reservoir. We sent three rovers down to investigate, one of them manned." The admiral glances around the room. "The crevice ruptured, and we lost all the rovers, though not before confirming that our instruments and readings had been right."

"And the ships?"

"All thirteen lost, destroyed during the eruption." Murmurs fill the room as the admiral continues. "We estimate a loss of over one hundred and fifty sailors, including some critical technical experts who were on site to help with the data analysis." The admiral's tone lifts. "Some could be in lifeboats, waiting for pickup. The Coast Guard is on the scene helping with rescue efforts, but the nearest Navy support is still hours away because of our recent restructuring of the fleet in response to heightened tensions in the South China Sea. We had no reason to expect this level of destruction or else we would have stationed resources more… strategically."

The president nods, turning to the man on his left, Rick Manglore, his chief scientist who shifts in his chair and clears his throat. The man wears his shirt wrinkled and twisted on his skinny frame, his tie loose. A thick tuft of brown hair lays back against his head, like he's ran his hand through it a hundred times to no avail and his bright blue eyes widen as the president addresses him. "Mr. Manglore, what can you tell us about this anomaly?"

Rick shuffles some dog-eared papers into a stack and pulls one of his two laptops closer, eyes flickering between the screens. "Thank you, Mr. President. My team has, um, pulled together all the data at our disposal, and I'll try to give you a summary. The anomaly the admiral spoke about is difficult to map due to its depth. But based on the force of the sub-floor discharge and surface turbulence recorded before the Marin sunk, in addition to readings taken from various points outside the disaster zone, it's clear that the crevice in the seafloor is expanding." Rick rubs his jaw and gives his head a slow shake. "We've mapped the anomaly, shown on monitor three there on the wall."

The president glances over at the monitor showing the ominous cracks and trenches spidering up the shelf wall and into the shallow part of the crust, digging through it in furrows.

Rick continues. "Fresh water is surging into the ocean at astronomical rates. I'm talking millions of gallons of water over the course of a few hours. More than a quadrillion a week at this rate. It could raise the sea levels or… or worse."

"Explain what 'worse' means."

"As freshwater enters the North Atlantic, it dilutes the salt water. Normally, the ocean could easily absorb a small infusion." The scientist stammers and chuckles to himself. "I-I mean, it *is* the ocean." When no one else even grins, he clears his throat nervously and continues. "But at the rates we're seeing now, it could disrupt the Gulf Stream flow into the North Atlantic, or even stop it entirely."

The president closes his eyes and takes a deep breath. "I'm a politician Mr. Manglore. Explain it to me like I'm a child."

Rick straightens in his chair and uses his hands to emphasize his points. "Well, Mr. President, the Gulf Stream brings warmth and nutrients up from the equator. It's the lifeblood of the Northern Hemisphere. Without it we'll continue to see a disruption of sea life and currents, and we could see a change in precipitation resulting in crop failures. And if water continues to pump in from the aquifer, sea level could rise by several inches, at which point we'd see mass flooding along key coastlines, trillions of dollars in damage, costing tens of millions of lives, and countless other potential disasters I can't even begin to scratch the surface of.

"Long story short, Mr. President, the worst is that North America could become uninhabitable."

A shudder runs through the room. Dr. Manglore folds his hands in front of him and rests them on the table, his body quivering slightly with nervousness. The president leans back in his chair and ponders what the scientist said, the words weigh heavy on his heart, but there's no place to run from his responsibility as protector of the nation's people.

"I'll ask the obvious question," the President asks calmly. "What can we do about it?"

Rick shrugs after a moment, and his eyes lift to the president. "I don't think there's anything we can do to stop the freshwater flow, Mr. President. All we can do is prepare for what's coming."

Chapter 11
Barbara McKnight
Wyndale, Virginia

Barbara shivered as she stepped into the chilly air, stopping on the front porch with a cup of steaming hot coffee in her hand. She sipped the sweetened and creamed brew, enjoying its richness in the cold morning. A glance up showed her a beautiful blue sky with puffs of cottony-white clouds off to the west, giving hope to the new day. A deep breath brought the grassy smells of late summer, honeysuckle drifting across her nose, its sweetness lifting her spirits that much further. She peered down across their pasture which rolled down to the fence along Wyndale Road. The vivid green space held fifteen grazing Barbados sheep and a pair of donkeys, Rosco and Martha, all of which were heading toward the house at the sight of Barbara.

She'd only gotten five and a half hours sleep, though it had been restful despite the emotionally turbulent day. The day's chores, the shopping trip, and the late-night inventory work she'd done with Linda had worn her out, and she'd fallen straight asleep as soon as her head hit the pillow. Jack came out behind her, shrugging on his light jacket and zipping it up. Linda followed on the heels of her little brother with a yawn, her wavy hair pulled back into a ponytail, her normal style for doing chores.

Smooch trotted around the side of the house, tail swinging, tongue lolling. Barbara set her coffee cup down on a small table near the door and greeted the high-spirited dog as she trotted up the three steps to the front porch. The animal walked around Barbara's legs to plant herself in a perfect heel formation at her right hip.

"Braver Hund!" *Good dog.* She pulled the dog's head against her side and rubbed beneath her chin. Sam had named the puppy five years ago, because Smooch was the most licking puppy they'd ever had, and despite Tom's protestations, the name had stuck. But the dog was far from reserved when protecting the family and their property, having received no small amount of professional obedience and protection training.

Linda gave smooch a head rub and walked on by, skipping down the three steps into the yard while Jack threw his arms around the dog's neck, giving her a hug before he chased after his sister.

"Frei!" Barbara snapped the word, German for *free*, in a tone reserved for commanding the Shepherd, and the dog bounded down the steps and chased after the kids, ready for a quick bout of roughhousing with Jack before they got started for the day. The trio went about their morning chores, motoring around the property in their John Deere mower and trailer. When they reached the chicken pens, Linda had a question.

"Hey, Mom," Linda said from where she attended to the mixed-breed farm chickens.

"Yeah, hon."

"You said we should get things locked down. What did you mean by that?"

Barbara brushed aside a pair of light-brown Orprintgon chickens to gather a pair of eggs that would be good candidates for the incubator. Tom hadn't been specific in his text about battening things down. They'd talked about how they might secure their property during a "red alert" event, but they hadn't counted on being separated during such a time, especially not with a fair distance – not to mention part of an ocean – between them.

She put down her basket and drew her phone from her pocket, checking for new messages, a frown tugging down the edges of her mouth when she saw Tom hadn't texted. Putting the phone away, she took her basket to the prep area and opened up the incubator, placing some inside. "First thing, we need to do a walk-around and make sure we lock the windows and gates, so if someone breaks in, we won't be easy pickings. And if they do, we have to make sure they regret it, know what I mean?"

Linda winced. "Sort of… not really."

"It means I might have to shoot someone, Linda."

"Do… do you really think you'll have to do that?"

"As a last resort only." Barbara glanced back to see a strange look on Linda's face. "How does that make you feel? Do you think you could do that, if someone broke in?"

Her daughter swallowed hard, a big gulp that ran slow down her throat. "I guess if someone broke in and was trying to hurt us, we'd have to do something, right? I gotta say, though, that's a little scary, Mom. Would they hurt us?"

"They might try." Barbara winked. "But remember, they've got to get through Smooch and me first."

"Which they probably won't do," Linda said with a confident tone, smile hesitant as she turned with her own basket. Barbara placed two of Linda's eggs into the incubator shelves while reserving the rest for the next day's breakfast.

"They might try," Barbara said, not wanting to frighten her but at least keep her open to the possibility. "They might even knock me down or hurt me. You need to be ready if that happens. We might need your sharpshooting skills." She gave her daughter a playful elbow and led her out of the chicken coop, leaving the rest of the eggs to pick up later.

"I'll do my best," Linda replied, voice steady, just a hint of fear between the words.

They left their baskets in the chicken coop and walked down the long, winding driveway that wound down the shallow rise, stopping at the lane's gate. It stood open, though a chain and padlock rested in the grass nearby. "Grab the chain and lock over there, will you?"

Barbara grabbed the end of the long, aluminum fence and lifted it out of the gravel, dragging it around until it was shut. She threw the latch closed and took the chain from Linda, wrapping it through the gate bars, securing it to a wooden fence post. She then retrieved the key from a small recess in the fence post, then laced the padlock through the chain and snapped it shut.

"Let's check the fencing up to the barn and make sure it's in good shape."

Barbara led her daughter along the fence line at the bottom of the property where it wound up past the fields to the barn, looking for holes or breaks in the field fencing and barbed wire strung along the top. Once they reached the barn, Barbara stepped inside and took a deep breath, relaxing in the comforting scent of old wood, dust, and hard-packed dirt. The barn was an old pegged-style construction from the 1920s built as part of the original farmstead. She and Tom had restored the older sections and added some new things like windows, locks, and additional stability to the loft, and Tom had run an underground electric line to the barn just as he had all the buildings on the property.

Five stalls lined the north and south barn walls. The first stall on the left was a small tool area with hoes, spades, rakes, hay bale hooks, and axes all hanging in their proper pegs. The other four stalls on the left side remained empty through the spring and summer, though they made perfect places to put the larger animals when the weather turned cold. Barbara closed the rear barn doors and latched them closed, using a padlock to secure them. Key in hand, she motioned toward the side of the house. "Let's check the fields and see where we stand on the produce."

They circled the back of the house, coming around toward the side and front where their modest fields stood. Aside from their small cornfield, they grew potatoes, carrots, beets, lettuce, and other assorted vegetables. Barbara inspected the corn rows first, happy to see two ears of corn on most of the stalks, their sprouting silks turning brown.

"These will be ready to harvest next week," she grinned, then moved over to the two smaller fields and examined the rest of their modest crops. "Looks like the potatoes and tomatoes are just about ready, and I see peppers, and several heads of lettuce that are ready. We'll need to harvest all this and get it inside as soon as possible. We can store most of it in the big barn for the short term. Later, we'll preserve it and put it on the shelves. I'm not sure what we can do with the lettuce, though."

"Aren't we going to sell most of what we bring in at the farmer's market?" Linda asked.

"There may be no farmer's market next week, or the week after," Barbara pointed out, glancing up at the sun which had been beating down on them for the last hour, chasing off the chilly morning.

"But how can the farmer's market be affected by no fish in the ocean?" The girl removed her light jacket and tied it around her waist. "I mean, just because we can't buy fish doesn't mean we shouldn't sell our stuff at the market."

Barbara picked a weed out of the garden and stood straight. "Well, there are a lot of reasons. For one, not having fish will make people want other things to eat, like chickens, cows, pigs and vegetables. But farmers haven't accounted for that demand, so they won't have enough food right away to feed everyone."

"But they can just make more, right?"

"It's not that easy," Barbara replied. "It might take months or even years to ramp up farms to feed huge numbers of people."

"So, that means we should be able to ask for more money for our crops, right? I mean, they'll be more in demand with all the meat shortages."

"Smart girl," she chuckled. "Clearly, your father has been telling you all about supply and demand. Most of the time, I would agree that with a higher demand for food, any kind of food, we could make a killing at the market. But…" Barbara drew the word out long, "producing so much on such short notice would be impossible."

"Farmers would need more time to ramp up."

"Right. Like, we couldn't just *suddenly* produce more lettuce. We'd have to make a bigger field, plant more seeds, and wait until the crop had grown to harvest it. But in the meantime, people would be getting pretty hungry." She paused a moment, trying to think of a concrete example. "Have you ever been hungry before? I mean, super hungry."

"Once or twice. Like that time we drove to Florida. Dad drove most of the day without stopping for dinner because he wanted to get to the hotel. But then we got to the hotel too late, and no restaurants were open. We missed dinner and had to have vending machine stuff till the morning. I thought my stomach was going to eat me from the inside out."

"And you and your sister got grumpy and started fighting, remember?"

Linda nodded. "We were *hangry* at each other."

"Imagine that hunger times a hundred. Imagine being hungry and having no way to go to the grocery store to get food, or the farmer's market, and all the restaurants are closed, even McDonald's – not even from a vending machine."

"Sounds like a lot of people will be mad if the food starts running short."

Barbara reached out and placed her palm on the girl's shoulder. "Bingo. And what do you think they'll do when they realize they can't get their food at the grocery or farmer's market?"

Linda's hazel eyes gazed out across their field of crops, something like a light switch turned on in her eyes. She gestured to their crops and nodded. "They'll try to take ours."

"Double bingo."

"Especially if they come from the city, right?" Linda's eyes grew wide with fright. "I mean, they don't have any farms there."

"That's true, but they could come from anywhere, even the suburbs or smaller cities, too."

Linda frowned and swallowed another lump. "And we'd have to stop them. That's what you were trying to tell me before."

Barbara wrapped her arm around her daughter's shoulders and squeezed. "I'm not trying to scare you, dear. I'm just letting you know these things so you can think in three dimensions."

"Three dimensions?"

"Yep. You have to see things from all sides. For example, let's say things go bad in town. We may not want to show our faces at any of the farmer's markets. Why do you think that is?"

The girl's face lit up with the answer. "Because someone could see us there with our food in our truck. They'd wonder if we had more. They might even follow us home."

"That's right, and that's exactly what we have to do – think about everything, and the potential consequences for everything that we do. There are plenty of things that can happen that we might not realize up front unless we train ourselves to do it."

"How do you know all this stuff, Mom?"

"I grew up taking care of all my brothers and sisters," Barbara replied, her eyes drifting out across their abundant field of food, a plentiful bounty that wouldn't have existed if she hadn't met Tom. "I had to learn a lot of things on my own, the hard way. My dad wasn't around to help much, and my mom worked all the time."

"I'm impressed."

Barbara chuckled, though it was a dry, humorless chuckle as she forced down the memories. "I'll tell you more about it later if you're interested. For now, let's keep walking the fence line."

They walked around the barn and continued their inspection of the fence, heading toward arguably the most unique building on their property. The A-frame greenhouse took up 1,000 square feet of their property, long and slender as it stretched from the fence line inward toward the house at an angle. Sunlight glinted off the glass and double-insulated sides and roof as they approached the front door and went inside.

"There's not much we can do if someone wants to break in here," Barbara said. "All they have to do is cut the plastic or break the glass."

She stepped through the entryway around the fan, greeted by the fresh sent of warm plant life and rich soil. They'd laid the greenhouse out into three sections, with plants and herbs in the first two and an aquaponic garden in the third section. Rich green leaves cascaded from hanging baskets on her left and right, placed above grow beds running along the floor and placed three feet from the wall to keep the plants away from the plastic in the deep winter. A small table sat off to the right near the door where they germinated the next crop of corn, strawberries, and watermelon. Peppers, cabbage, and tomatoes grew year-round with a wintertime temperature that stayed well above freezing even in the coldest days with the help of some heat lamps.

They walked through to the middle section where a mixture of basil, thyme, cilantro, garlic, rosemary, oregano, and a dozen other herbs greeted them, growing on small gray trays stacked on cart shelves. The plants received additional light on drab days from the full spectrum LED lights Tom had affixed above each shelf.

"We sell a lot of these herbs year-round, but this may be the last crop for a while." Barbara toyed with some tarragon leaves, putting her fingers to her nose to smell the faint whiff of licorice. "We might need to expand our echinacea, chamomile, and ginger growth. It wouldn't be much, but anything would be helpful if our regular medicines and pain relievers run out."

They moved to the end of the section where a fan in the greenhouse wall provided exhaust, and Barbara opened the door to the closed off aquaponic garden. The grow beds were eight feet long by three feet wide, allowing enough space for them to be placed away from the wall to avoid any creeping chill.

"Your father usually handles things in here," Barbara said, whispering in the delicate balance of the room. "He knows a lot more about the ratios of fish to grow beds and how much to feed them and all that. I just keep the fish fed and clean the filters."

"How does this thing work?"

"We pump in fresh water from that pump box by the well," she walked to the far end of the grow beds where two water lines sprouted from the concrete floor, "which is filtered at the source and pumped through to all the feed troughs, then the pond, then here." She traced the line with her finger as the attached hose circled up and bent down into the water tank below the grow beds. "It enters this regulator and then goes into the fish tank. When we feed the fish, the fish waste fertilizes the water. Then a pump inside the fish tank pushes the fertilized water up to the plants so they can feed."

Linda peered into the fish tank to watch a goldfish dart over to a shadier part of the pool. "Seems easy."

"There's a lot more to it," she replied. "Your father regulates the water and filters the fish's solid waste, but I don't mess with that. Like I said, I feed the fish and tend to the plants."

Linda nodded while Barbara fed the fish and then dusted her hands off. "Let's go."

They exited the greenhouse and made their way around the north section of the property where it enclosed a large swath of woods. Oaks and Virginia pines stood at attention, their bulky branches and leafy canopies providing the perfect playground for the kids and Smooch. Tom had cut a trail through to the center of the woods where he'd built them a small tree house and a covered fire pit surrounded by chairs.

As they walked the rest of the fence line around swaths of trees, the fresh scent of green brushed over them. She marked areas of the fence that needed attention with white ribbons for later repair before heading to the utility building. She picked the loose lock off the latch staple and opened the double doors, the odor of motor oil, freshly cut grass, and gasoline smacking her in the face, the complete opposite of the welcoming animal smells of their two barns.

Inside the 20-by-40 foot building they kept spare five-gallon gas containers, a John Deere riding lawn mower, a John Deere Gator utility vehicle, two small trailers, and two double-walled, 500 gallon fuel tanks, one running alongside each wall. The back wall held several containers of fuel stabilizer for long term storage of their gas preserves. If things deteriorated to the point where gas stations closed up shop, having that long-term fuel for the generators would be essential.

"I know we've been sucking fuel out of the right-hand tank for the past three months, but I'd say it's still at least seventy-five percent full."

"So, it needs a top off?"

Barbara put her hands on her hips. "I can probably pick up 10 or 20 gallons today, assuming things haven't gotten worse since the last time we went out." She pulled out four five-gallon gas containers, then stepped back, closed the doors, and slammed the latch home, dropping the padlock into the staple and locking it tight. Pulling out the key, she dropped it into her top pocket with the ones from the other barns. "I don't know about you, but I could use a sandwich."

"And soup?"

Barbara winked. "I'll make the sandwiches, and you can make the soup."

"Deal!"

They each picked up two empty gas containers and walked past their water well toward the end of their gravel driveway where it turned into pavement. Near the patio, parked in front of the garage doors, was their 2001 Chevy Astro Mini Van and their trusty gray 1975 Ford F150. They threw the gas cans in the back of the F150 and continued on toward the house. Smooch's dog house – sized more like a tiny shed – sat in the rear, complete with vents to allow drafts to come in during the scorching summer months, and a flap over the door to seal in her body heat when the weather got chilly.

She and Jack came tearing around from the side of the house where they'd been playing, and Barbara gestured at the doghouse. "Platz, bitte!" *Lie down, please.* The German Shepherd angled toward her house and stopped at her food and water bowls where she began lapping up water. Then she circled her food dish and curled up next to it on her padded mat.

"Jack you didn't feed Smooch," Barbara glanced at the dog's empty food bowl and scolded the boy with her eyes.

"She didn't look hungry," he complained, stopping at the edge of the patio.

"No lunch for you until you feed her."

"Aw, okay." He slapped his hands against his side and ran back to the feed shed to grab a scoop of dog food.

Linda sighed as they entered the air-conditioned kitchen, holding her arms out to dry off the sweat they'd accumulated through the late morning before sitting down. Barbara crossed to the fridge, grabbed some bread off the top, and dug around inside for the sandwich supplies.

"Mom, rest a minute."

"If I sit down, I won't get back up."

"Is that really a thing?"

"When you get a little older, it becomes a thing."

Linda snickered and got up, pulling two cans of chicken noodle soup from their pantry. She poured them into the pan and switched on the burner. Ten minutes later, they placed three bowls of soup and ham sandwiches topped with homegrown lettuce, tomato, and onions on the table. Jack entered a moment later, pulling off his dirty sweatshirt to air it out.

He started to sit down, but Barbara lifted her hand to stop him. "Ew, no. You go upstairs and change first."

"You guys didn't have to change," Jack protested.

"We got a little sweaty and dirty, but you look like Smooch dragged you through the garden." His shirt was marked with grass stains and mud, and even a little blood. Barbara made an incredulous sound. "Did you cut yourself?"

Jack held up his elbow and showed her a scrape on his elbow that looked swollen and bright red with blood.

"How in the world did you…" Barbara shook her head and stood, grasping the boy's elbow, holding it up to get a better look. "This'll need some work, buddy. Come on."

Barbara left her soup and sandwich behind in search of a wet wipe, some Neosporin, and a bandage. While she was working, her phone buzzed, and she dropped his hand, straightening as she dug the phone from her pocket, hoping to see Tom's face. Instead, it was just a CNF breaking news notification and she clicked on it without thinking, and a page appeared with an ominous title.

Official Statement from the President of the United States

The President of the United States has declared a national state of emergency due to the the emerging threat posed by the undersea anomaly in the North Atlantic. State governments along the coast are being encouraged to deploy National Guard resources for assistance with flooding along the Eastern Seaboard. The Coast Guard is already engaged in rescue efforts, and Navy resources…[Read More]

Barbara's face flushed, fear twisting her heart just when she'd started to gain confidence in Tom and Sam's homecoming and she instinctively dialed her husband again. "Please, please, *please*, pick up, Tom," she whispered, the words fraught with anxiety, skin flashing hot with a sense of doom. "I really, really need you to pick up."

Once again, though, he didn't, her call going straight through to voicemail, leaving her feeling emptier and more worried than ever.

Chapter 12
Tom McKnight
North Atlantic

As the sun dipped low, the top still shone through the undersides of the clouds with intense clarity, the light fading toward the edges, reflecting downward across the waves, a long ray stretching out above from the star's center, a silent finger outstretched toward the opposite horizon. Tom and Sam huddled on the wooden slats of the life raft, feet pressed against the bottom of the craft, wet with ocean spray, cooled by the wind's chill fingers. He used a portion of the parachute to cover his shoulders and left Sam the thermal blanket. A splatter of wetness danced across his neck, and Tom gave an involuntary shiver as he stared past Sam to their outboard engine.

The fuel needle was on the empty mark, and whatever fumes were left he wanted to save for an emergency. After a quick check on his phone, he'd seen they were still 35 miles offshore, drifting south beneath the flat bottomed section of Connecticut. As bad as it was being stranded offshore, things could, he thought, be *much* be worse. The ocean could have been pulling them farther out to sea, but with the anomaly causing a shift in the currents, they were lucky it was instead pushing them in a favorable direction – not exactly toward land, but not exactly away from it, either.

A wave smacked the side of the raft, making it rock back and forth beneath them though they both ignored it, having gotten used to the ocean's playfulness, and their bodies automatically shifted with the water's rough turbulence. The trick was not to fight the motions but to go with them, instead, so he and Sam both tried to keep their muscles and spine loose and flexible as the raft bobbed back and forth, though the effort required was exhausting.

"How are you feeling, Sam?"

"A little cold… but okay."

"Hungry? Thirsty?"

"Nope. I'm good. This ocean is a pain in the butt though."

"No kidding."

"Think we'll drift in toward shore?"

Tom shook his head, cold water dripping from his hair, the scent of the sea fresh and salty, cut with an underlying scent of seaweed and decaying. "We're getting closer, which is good. And I'm saving the last of the gas in case we have an emergency. I think I can safely say we won't be floating off to England. But where it's going to land us, I just don't know."

Sam sighed, shoulders slumping. "I wish there was something we could do besides wait. I'm about to do some jumping jacks out of boredom."

The sun's upper lip finally descended below the horizon, and a stiff breeze whisked across them, blowing slivers of cold water in from the side as waves bounced against the raft. Shivers coursed up Tom's arms and down his back despite the parachute pulled over his shoulders, and he glanced down absent-mindedly at the material, eyes widening as an idea began to form.

"Say… I might have a way to get us ashore faster."

"Oh, yeah?" Sam perked up. "What?"

Gesturing for Sam to move back to the last seat, he searched around in the survival kit and retrieved the square-tipped knife. Once she'd slid off the middle seat, Tom knelt on the floor of the raft.

"I want you to use the knife to dig through the middle seat," he said. "I'll get it started for you, but it's only about an inch of wood to get through and we don't want to break the blade or accidentally drop it over the side. So never hold it out over the water, okay?"

Sam nodded, grinning to have something to do after hours of drifting. Tom gripped the heavy black handle and dug the knife's corner into the center of the wooden seat, carving out little slivers that fell to the floor of the boat. Despite having a square tip, the blade was thick and strong, and the corner easily dug into the wood.

"See?" He looked up at Sam with raised eyebrows. "We want to make the hole no wider than the blade itself. Not much more than an inch."

"Got it, Dad."

As Sam got to work digging on the seat, Tom turned to the front of the boat and sorted through the parachute material he'd dragged on board previously. A small pile of nylon and string, the parachute wasn't very large and didn't provide a ton of material to work with, but it was lightweight, strong, and – most importantly – made for catching the wind. When Sam was done digging the hole, he took the knife back and together they worked to spread out the parachute, pulling it open between them, the bottom part on Tom's end and the top part up by Samantha, some material laying over the edges and washing around in the waves.

"We need to cut out a rough triangle shape," Tom said. "Do you think we can do that?"

Sam turned her head at as if picturing it. "We already have the bottom, so we can cut all the way up the outside of one rib, then diagonally down. The diagonal part will be hard because you'll have to cut through some strings to get back to the bottom."

"I see what you're saying," Tom agreed. "That actually might work."

He used the serrated edge of the knife to cut up one rib all the way to the top, then he cut at an angle back down to the bottom, slicing through the strings to make the shape. Grinning, he held up a roughly triangular piece of material, five feet tall and two feet wide, with pieces of frayed string and nylon hanging off.

"It's rough, but it should work."

"I'll pile the rest of the parachute in the back of the boat in case we need it for something else." She turned to her father. "What now?"

"We'll have to reinforce the shape so it doesn't just flop around in the wind." Tom pulled out the fishing pole pieces and assembled them, leaving one piece out. Using pieces of tape to fix the two pole pieces to the edges of the nylon material, he left about a foot of pole on one end, forming the shape of a sail. With the knife he cut small holes in the sail a half inch from the pole frame and reinforced them with pieces of tape, forming grommets. Weaving string through the holes, winding it around, he reinforced the entire structure, leaving a short length hanging from the corner to use for steerage. By the time he was done, Sam had nearly dug through to the underside of the seat, her hands numb and buzzing.

"I'll finish the hole." Tom picked up the knife and put the blade inside, rotating it to smooth out the rough parts before sticking a few pieces of their remaining tape inside, softening the edges and keeping it from splintering further.

"Let's switch positions," Tom moved to the back of the boat, awkwardly holding the makeshift sail as a stiff breeze tugged at the material before he even put it up. Once they'd traded positions, he shot his daughter a hopeful grin. "Ready? Hold on!"

"Ready!" Sam stepped back and sat on the front seat, holding the edges to keep her balance. Tom hoisted the sail and placed the pole into the hole they'd cut, lifting it straight. He started to sit down when a gust of wind caught it and nearly ripped the steering line out of his hand. Snatching it back he threw his weight backwards, bringing the whipping sail under control as the entire boat shifted and jerked with the wind. The pole wobbled, rattling and jerking inside the hole, but Tom used both hands and pulled harder, leaning back, fighting the wind with a groan, his forearms taut as he wrapped his arm around the string and forced the raft to submit to the wind. After a few long moments of struggle, a full minute of sweating and trying to angle the sail, working the line until his fingers were raw and nearly bleeding, Tom got the boat turned around and straightened out, pointing them toward the setting sun. The small raft leapt forward faster than he had anticipated, the makeshift sail working better than he had hoped.

"Quick, put something between the end of the pole and bottom of the raft," Tom's teeth were clenched, every breath a struggle as the breeze continued to gust from behind. "I don't want the friction to rub a hole in the boat's bottom."

Sam took a piece of tarp, folded it, and taped it under the twisting, grinding pole and Tom glanced down with a nod. "Excellent job, kiddo. Let's get this party started."

Samantha watched as Tom leaned backward, leveraging his weight as he struggled to finish turning them, sputtering in the face of the water kicked up by the bow of the raft as it bounced along the waves. When he finally had the raft heading due west, he tied the line once around the rear seat to hold it taut, using it as a dry pulley to bear most of the strain and make it easier to adjust the sail without further injuring his hands. Satisfied they could hold their course for a good length of time, he wrapped the rope around the seat twice more to lock it in place and let go, flexing his hands, coaxing blood back to his fingertips until the numbness faded.

"You did it, Dad!" Sam beamed from the other side of the raft. "You're so awesome!"

"Aw, shucks," Tom said with a mock bashful grin and a wink. "I'm always happy to help, ma'am."

Sam giggled and crawled across the raft, her ponytail whipping around as she dragged the thermal blanket with her. She sat on Tom's left, leaning against him and covering them both up. Samantha exuded warmth, and Tom closed his eyes and wrapped his arm around her, relishing the peaceful moment in spite of their uncomfortable conditions. As Sam had gotten older, she'd resisted movie nights and cuddling on the couch with her family, trading those times for hanging out by herself or being with friends.

"You should probably get some sleep, kiddo. Hard to tell how long it'll take to get within sight of the shore."

"I can't. I'm too amped up to even think about sleep. I mean, the past two days have been crazy. We saw so much and met so many people. But they all… died…" Sam's words trailed off, her voice falling to a breathless whisper.

"I know," Tom said, swallowing a hard lump as he thought about Lieutenant Colonel Banks, Sue Anne and all of the sailors and civilians on the vessels, hoping beyond hope they'd somehow managed to escape. The pair were quiet for a few moments before Samantha sighed and wrapped her arm tighter around her father.

"I'm just happy we're on our way home."

"Amen to that," Tom agreed.

"What do you think Mom and Linda and Jack are doing?"

"Probably trying to keep up with the farm and getting supplies for whatever will come next. Jack is probably getting in the way, mostly."

"Rough housing with Smooch, no doubt." Sam laughed, but her voice stalled and hitched as a sudden and unexpected sob choked from her throat. She gripped Tom's shirt hard and pressed her face against his arm, quietly crying.

"Hey, hey, what is it?" Tom wrapped both arms around her, squeezing her almost too tight.

"I just…" Sam sniffled, burrowing her face deeper into his arm. "I miss them. I miss Mom and Linda and Smooch, and even stupid Jack."

"Hey, Jack isn't stupid," Tom chuckled, "he tries not to be annoying, but he doesn't always succeed."

Sam snorted and laughed.

"And he's invincible, too," Tom continued. "I've seen him and Smooch goofing around, and that kid comes back with skinned knees and elbows every time. Doesn't even cry."

"Yeah, he feels no pain," the girl agreed, repeating a line Barbara had often said about their youngest. "He plays so much, he forgets about the knocks and bumps."

"If only we could all bear pain so easily, right?"

The raft gently rose and fell, and it seemed they were picking up speed, skipping atop the waves as the sail tension sagged and tightened under the wind's breath.

"So, you think all those ships sunk?" Sam whispered after a moment.

"We only saw about half go down." Tom winced inwardly at his words. "I'm hoping a lot of people escaped on their closed lifeboats."

"Were those the big orange boats in the cradles on the side of the ship?"

"Yeah, the big orange things. They hold twelve to twenty people each, which would be most of those aboard the Marin. And those puppies can take a beating. They're designed to go through the toughest storms and come out without so much as a leak."

"Good," Sam nodded. "I hope they made it. But what about the crack with all the rocks and freshwater shooting out? Is it going to flood everything?"

Tom slowly shook his head, his eyes drifting toward the dwindling sun. "To be honest, hon, I'm not sure. Based on what I saw in the belly of the Marin, confirmed by the rovers and all, some places could definitely get flooded, and it'll cause a lot of disruptions. Supplies will become the biggest problem. You remember what happened the last time a hurricane hit the coast, right?

"Yeah. I remember you and Mom let me watch some news with you guys. People argued about how dangerous things would get, and they started hoarding supplies. But we had plenty of stuff. I mean, we had food and water and electricity, even when the rioters attacked the power company, and Bristol lost power for three days."

"Yes, and remember those weird people who kept driving by the farm?"

"I do," Sam shivered, turning her face up to him with a question in her eyes. "But you didn't seem afraid of them at all."

"Oh we were scared, don't doubt it. Your mom and I both. But we were prepared." Tom nodded. "And we still are." Something stirred in his chest, a hardening of his spirit made his heart thump hard. "There's no way on God's beautiful and wondrous green earth your mother or I would ever, under any circumstances, allow anything to happen to you kids. We'll march through anything for you guys."

"I believe it," Sam nodded and started to say more, but paused, eyes flitting to the sea. "What I'm trying to say is... I guess... Thank you."

Tom's eyes widened, watered, a tear streaking down his weathered cheek.

"Are you crying, Dad?" Sam blinked up at him, half-joking and half-touched.

"I'm not crying," Tom replied in mock defense, wiping the tear away with a swipe of his hand. "I just got some salt water in my eye."

"Right," Sam said, drawing out the word as she lay her cheek against his chest and smiled.

The last bit of sun slipped away over the horizon, leaving them exposed to the sheer blackness of night in a soft exhalation of chilly winds. Their little lifeboat-cum-sailboat cut through the water like a trooper, still heading west as the stars came alive. Tiny pinpricks of light flickered and blinked in a variety of colors, from deep reds to vivacious blues, and solid white pinpricks like holes poked through sheer plastic sheeting. Tom watched the sky intently, its vividness and lack of light pollution in deep contrast top the view from their patio back home.

"Now that the sun set, how do we know we're still heading toward the shore?"

"Well, I was about to grab the compass out of the survival kit, but I'm too comfortable to move. So, I guess we can navigate by the stars." Tom craned his head to the right and stared into the sky, searching for something. "First, you have to find the Big Dipper."

Sam's eyes drifted upward and followed his. "There's seven stars in the Big Dipper, right? I remember that from one of my science lessons you helped me with."

"That's right. Can you find it?"

Sam stretched her arm from beneath the thermal blanket and pointed upward. "There it is."

"Good find," Tom said with a nod.

"You already found it, though."

"I sure did. I always could find the Big Dipper from land easily enough, but it's even brighter out here on the ocean with no city lights to drown out the stars. Now, look around the ladle part of the cluster. See that really bright star to the right of it?"

"Yep."

"That's the North Star, and the Big Dipper will always spin around it. So, if the North Star is over our right shoulder..."

"The coast should be at our feet?"

"That's right. We're generally heading in the right direction, though I can't tell you if we'll land in New Jersey or Delaware or Virginia, but we'll hit land soon."

"Best news all day," Samantha yawned, her voice growing weary as she settled down and pulled the thermal blanket up snug against her chin. She closed her eyes and her breathing deepened until light snores drifted upward to echo among the waves. Tom leaned back and held the taut steering string where he'd tied it to the seat, keeping a guiding hand on it just in case something happened. The boat was cruising along fine for the moment, though, and until they needed to change course, Sam could sleep.

Chapter 13
Barbara McKnight
Wyndale, Virginia

After their brief lunch extended into midafternoon, and Barbara was anxious to get outside and get some things done. She'd phoned Tom multiple times over the last few hours, leaving several messages, and she'd even tried calling the naval and coast guard offices to get some update on the rescue efforts. That avenue had proved fruitless as well, as all her insistent questions had been deflected by agents who took her information and promised a return call when they found anything out.

"Useless bureaucrats!" Barbara slammed her fist on the kitchen table and took a long, steadying breath. "Alright. We can't do anything about this right now, so let's get outside and get some work done."

Linda looked up from where she was lying on the couch, watching TV. "But I'm sleepy," she replied, shifting in her cuddled position. "Can we give it a break?"

"Nope. Now come on. Up!"

"Geez, Mom," the girl replied, still unmoving. "What else could there be to do? We've done *everything* today."

"Not everything." Barbara slipped her boots on. "We can get ready to *get ready* to bring in some crops, if you know what I mean. Come on. Let's go. Just a couple more hours."

"Ugh. Finneeee." Linda swung her legs off the couch and groggily looked for her tennis shoes, calling out. "Come on, Jack! Jack! Where the heck is he?"

When no response came from upstairs, Barbara tied her shoes and moved down the hall, stopping at the foot of the stairs and calling up. "Come on, Jack. Let's go, son. We've got a little more to do today."

A heavy sigh greeted her, a thump of disgruntled feet on the floor, followed by some overexaggerated rustling.

"I'm serious! Get a move on!"

"I'm coming," the boy called down, his voice heavy with sleep.

Barbara stepped through the front door and onto the porch, folding her arms over her chest as she stared out at their modest field which lay off to the right. While the kids were on their way, Barbara walked around to the side of the house and grabbed a big plastic trashcan, pulling it around front. As the kids stepped out, she grabbed off the lid and tossed it aside.

"Let's get the harvesting bags set around the field first," she called. Inside the trashcan lay a stack of neatly folded canvas bags, and she tossed several on the porch as the kids came up to grab them. "Place them in plastic bags to keep them dry and set them around the fields at ten-foot intervals," she told them. "Put a rock on each one so the wind doesn't blow them away, okay?"

"I remember from doing it last spring," Linda nodded, snatching a handful of bags and piling them up in Jack's waiting arms.

"Good. And help make sure your brother does his job right, okay?"

"Okay," Linda sighed. "Come on, Jack. Grab some bags and let's get going."

Linda and Jack took armfuls of bags out toward the fields, and Barbara walked around to the side of the house and made her way to the fuel shed. Her back and legs had grown stiff from overworking herself the last few days, pulling double time with Tom and Sam gone. Moments passed where she wanted to lie down on the couch and forget about everything. After all, they had enough supplies, and anything else they needed could wait until later. But she couldn't let herself stop. She told herself it was for the sake of preparation, working until exhaustion wore her to the bone and sent her into a dreamless black sleep, but in truth it was for worry's sake more than anything else.

"Quit dragging your feet," she told herself in a whisper through clenched teeth. "Tom'll be home soon enough. Then you can relax."

She strode past their trucks, the day's dust drifting by on a cool breeze that was unseasonable even for the end of summer. It was a dry, lifeless thing that caressed her cheek, sending a shiver down her spine. Shrugging it off, she stopped in front of the shed and threw opened the doors, staring across her selection of vehicles. The riding mower and its wagon usually took care of the minor jobs, and they only used the Gator for tougher ones.

The mower was already hitched to the wagon, so it was an easy decision. She climbed onto the mower's seat with a squeak of springs and started it up. The engine came to life with a puttering yawn, jerking and lurching as she pulled out of the shed and turned toward the large barn. Stopping there, she grabbed a pair of wheelbarrows where they hung on the wall and wheeled them, one at a time, out to the trailer. The wagon had just enough room for them to fit, so she stacked them and secured them with bungee cables before driving back to the field. The kids were still hard at work placing all the bags, Jack lying each out and placing a rock on top under Linda's watchful eye.

Barbara stopped and unloaded the wheelbarrows before heading back to gather some smaller tools and gloves. She drove around the side yard, trying not to disturb the animals as they wandered the yard. There were meandering sheep and chickens pecking around in search of stray bits of feed while Smooch snoozed in the chicken coop's shade, its single, gnarled oak tree with branches sweeping off to the sides.

From another shed she grabbed work gloves, shovels, and assorted hoes, driving those to the front of the house where she placed them on the front porch before heading back to double check the kids' work. The late day sun had returned, churning up the cooler air, beating down hard on the back of her neck and shoulders as she walked around the field's edge.

"Looking good, guys," she said, arms folded, eyes searching over the tall cornstalks with their dog ears, the rich-smelling dirt washing over her, the sweet weedy aroma of vegetation circling her head. "Let's wrap this up."

Both Linda and Jack were laughing and jostling each other through the rows, having finished up putting their last bags out. The pair raced toward the wagon, climbing in the back and thumping down on the rail benches. Barbara turned the riding mower around and circled past the house and garage, trundling by the concrete car deck. After letting the kids out, she pulled up to the fuel shed and backed the trailer and mower inside with an expert's practiced touch before everyone piled out.

"Okay, guys. Ready to prep for canning?"

Linda's expression dropped like a stone. "Oh boy."

Her younger brother wrinkled his brow suspiciously. "What's canning?"

Jack wasn't old enough to remember last year when Barbara had gone on the canning-spree-to-end-all-canning-sprees, stocking their shelves full and selling off a lot of their product as well. Sam and Linda had done their best to help during the first part but had quickly lost interest, leaving her to finish up most of it.

"I know you hated doing it last year," she said to Linda, "but give it a shot this time, okay? I really need your help."

"Sure, Mom," Linda replied, sighing like she'd just been given a life sentence.

In the kitchen, the air was arctic cold compared to outside, and Barbara's skin shivered as the sweat dried. Rifling through the kitchen cabinets, she explained to Jack. "Canning is the art of packing food into cans with pressure so we can eat them later. It makes the food last a lot longer."

"And is *super* boring," Linda added with a scowl.

"Too bad you hate it so much," Barbara added with a mockingly sad face. "But it still has to be done."

"I know, I know," Linda said in a resigned tone, eyes watching as her mother pulled items from the cabinets. "I'll help, and Jack will, too."

It was Jack's turn to frown. "I will?"

"Yes, because it will keep you from getting dragged through the garden by Smooch." Linda reached down with clawed hands and attacked Jack's sides. The boy giggled and thrashed, twisting away in a mad storm of laughter as she chased him through the house.

"Much better," Barbara murmured with a smile. Then she called louder. "Hey, can you kids bring in the boxes of cans from the garage?"

"Yes, ma'am!" Linda called back as she caught Jack trying to get through the front door, dragging him back toward the garage, giggling harder, squirming, and – through cackles – calling for Smooch to help him destroy his terrible sister. Barbara couldn't help but grin, their laughter infectious and pure, a soothing salve on her worried soul.

From the low kitchen cabinets she fished out the rest of her tools: a funnel, a de-bubbler, a jar lifter, her jar sealing tool, a rack to place the hot jars on, and several ladles. She also found an enormous pot to boil the water, the perfect size to hold several pint and quart-sized jars. The kids brought in boxes of cans and lids as she washed everything and set it to dry, placing ten boxes' worth in two stacks, side-by-side, on the kitchen table.

"Are we canning food all week?" Linda asked, leaning on the breakfast bar as Jack sat down.

"We might." Barbara shook off some ladles and placed them in the dish holder to drain.

"What about school?" Linda asked. "Shouldn't I be working ahead, too?" A voracious reader, Linda had taken to her school work more than anyone else in the family.

"We were going to," she picked up a towel and dried her hands off, "but we might take an extra break to get things prepared here. By then, your father and Sam will be home, and they can jump in and help." Linda's expression hovered between hopeful and falling flat, and an idea sprung to live in Barbara's head.

"Linda, why don't you pull the grill up and we'll have us a little cook out tonight?"

A grin snapped to life on the girl's face, and she gave an enthusiastic nod. "I could eat."

"I could eat a hamburger," Jack announced. "*And* a hot dog, too."

"Because you *are* a hot dog," Linda made wide eyes at her brother.

"Your *face* is a hot dog," the boy fired back.

"Just go get the grill ready please," Barbara laughed, "Jack – you stay close while we get things rolling."

While her daughter went out and pulled the grill up, Barbara grabbed condiments from the fridge and placed them on the table, along with the buns. Fishing around in the meat tray, she snatched two pounds of ground beef she'd thawed and a pack of hot dogs and placed them on a plate. She got out plates from the cupboard and set them on the counter with a clank, automatically counting out a total of five before she realized her mistake. Suddenly overcome with the emotion she'd locked up all day, she welled up, eyes glassing over with tears. The back door opened, and Linda poked her head in, pausing when she saw her mother's troubled look.

"Mom, are you okay?"

"Yeah, I'm fine." Barbara wiped at her eyes, laughing it off.

Linda was there in a flash, wrapping her arms around her mother's waist, refusing to let go. After a moment's hesitation she relented and wrapped her arms around her daughter, squeezing her tight, curling her head down to bury her teary face in her thick hair, smelling hay and grass.

"No. No, I'm not okay," she admitted.

"What's wrong?"

"I'm a little angry that your father went to help Ray when he should have been home with Sam by now. Mostly I'm sad, though. I don't like not hearing from them for this long."

"You know Dad. He always helps Mr. Ray. It's his job, right?"

"Yes, it is." Barbara sniffled.

"It's scary worrying about them and missing them," the girl said with a solemn frown. "I even miss Sam a little."

Barbara recovered, pushing her daughter away to hold her at arm's length. "That's hard to believe, honey. You actually miss Sam? Well, I… I never thought I'd hear those words come out of your mouth."

Linda blinked with teary eyes as a smile lifted the corner of her mouth. "I know, right? She usually gets on my nerves."

"She dances on your last nerve, constantly."

"Yeah."

The girl's mock exuberance brought a gut laugh out of Barbara, and she hugged her daughter again, squeezing hard and receiving an equal squeeze back. "Thanks for the hugs."

"No problem. Sometimes Moms need help, too."

"Okay, let's get this stuff outside."

"The grill's primed and ready to go," Linda sang, and she grabbed the plate of hamburgers and hot dogs. "Want me to throw them on?"

"Please. I'll grab the condiments and cheese."

Barbara came outside a minute later with wrapped food in her arms, two bags of buns hanging from her fist. She put them down on a side table and took over for Linda on the grill, taking the spatula from where it hung on a hook. Soon meat was sizzling on the grill, hotdogs spitting grease, the rich scent of melting cheese causing her stomach to rumble and her mouth to salivate in anticipation.

While the meat cooked, Barbara and Linda ran inside and returned a moment later with a plate of lettuce, cut tomatoes, pickles, and onion slices, placing them on the side table. They grabbed a bowl of homemade potato salad, cold baked beans, and a jug of iced tea from the fridge, returning it all to the porch.

"Jack! Where are you?" She turned to Linda, taking the hot dogs and burgers off the grill, starting to arrange them all on buns. "Go find your brother, please."

Linda brought Jack downstairs a moment later, and the trio made their plates, Smooch eying them carefully from the edge of the patio, her eyes focused on every motion that was taken. Still, she wouldn't put a single paw on the patio while the family ate unless they called her over. As he made his plate, Jack noticed Smooch and he grabbed a hot dog off the plate, ready to throw it before catching himself. He paused and glanced back at his mother. "Can Smooch have one?"

Barbara smiled, nodding at him with a wink. "I made an extra one just for her. Just one, though. And only because she's been so good."

"Okay!" The boy launched the hotdog at the Shepherd. Smooch tracked the fast-flying projectile, stretching up at the last second to snatch it out of the air and gobble it down in two bites.

They made their plates and took them to a screened-in portion of the patio, sitting at a picnic table to eat in satisfied silence. A splash of pinprick stars gleamed down from the night sky, the moon peeking out from behind the clouds, brightening the edges in a surreal, ruddy light. A cool breeze blew through, sending shivers down Barbara's arms as she watched the trees down the hill and across the distant road sway gently.

"I could do this every day." She reached over to turn up the electric lantern resting in the center of the table. "It's so peaceful out."

"Me, too," Linda declared, throwing her mother a sideways grin as Jack kicked his feet from where he sat on the bench and jammed a pickle into his mouth.

"It makes me glad your father and I picked this place."

"When's Dad and Sam coming home?" Jack asked. "I thought you said they'd be here by now."

"Well, I didn't exactly say *that*," Barbara picked at her beans with her fork, choosing her words cautiously. "If things had gone as planned, they would have been home today. And you know they went to help Ray out on the boats."

"But that thing out in the ocean probably got them like it got the reporter lady."

"I know you're worried – I am too – but there were a lot of boats out there. We don't know the anomaly… thing sank them all." Barbara glanced at Linda, gently shaking her head. Linda nodded, Jack oblivious to the quick exchange as he rearranged the toppings on his burger that had fallen halfway out of the bun.

"What is it, even?"

"I don't know the scientific details," Barbara replied, turning to him, giving him her full attention. "It sounds like a big hole in the ocean's floor, letting in a bunch of freshwater from deep inside the Earth. And I guess it's gushing really fast, probably stirring up a lot of stuff from the bottom, and that's what made the ships sink. But your father said he and Sam would come home."

"But when?"

"I don't know. Maybe they were waiting on a rescue boat to pick them up."

"Maybe…" Jack let his words trail off as he reached for another pickle. "Or maybe they got hurt or something. Maybe…" his eyes lifted, filled with tears, pickle dangling from his fingers. "Maybe Sam drowned, or Dad drowned."

Barbara lowered her chin, took the pickle from his hand, and put it down, taking his arms in her hands, leveling a firm gaze at him. "Hey, bud…" She started, before Linda jumped headfirst into the conversation.

"Are you kidding?" Linda scoffed. "Dad can probably swim that entire ocean, and Sam is so full of hot air she can probably float."

Jack's tearful eyes flitted to his sister, a small grin expanding on his face. His sister grinned back until the boy finally broke out laughing.

"You guys are silly," Barbara smiled at them both, giving Linda a slight nod of appreciation. "But your sister's right. And we're doing exactly what we should be doing here at home. We're sticking to the plan and getting stuff done. And tomorrow we'll get even more done. Why don't you guys get washed up and get settled in for the night?"

Jack and Linda picked up the plates and left the screened-in patio to go inside, leaving Barbara alone on the porch with her thoughts and half a glass of tea, her eyelids growing heavy with sleep. All talk and guesswork aside, she tried to imagine herself with Tom and Sam, guessing where they might be. Whether it was on the deck of a rescue ship, on a lifeboat or somewhere in between, Barbara didn't care, so long as they were safe.

"Come home soon, you two," she whispered. "We need you."

Chapter 14
Tom McKnight
North Atlantic

Ocean winds slammed the small craft, bucking Tom and Samantha where they lay flat along the back, drenching them with salt spray, filling the raft with an inch of water. They flew up waves a meter and a half high and plunged into the troughs, counter waves rising over their heads, towering and dark, threatening to slap down on them in a wash of foam. The ocean had started getting choppy just before noon, deep gray clouds creeping in above them as the wind picked up, forcing them to lean back and forth to keep the raft balanced.

They'd placed all the supplies in the boat's front to act as a ballast, distributing some weight forward so their stern didn't dip down too low and fill with water. The sea's uncanny locomotion disquieted Tom, the up and down of the waves, one second riding a crest where he could see for miles around, the next penned in by walls of green and gray. Still, he'd been on worse seas, they'd be fine as long as they didn't panic – and the waves didn't get much larger. They'd eaten a breakfast of sorts prior to the weather turning, and it seemed a "three-day supply of food" barely lasted two people two days, making the need to quickly reach land even more imperative.

Sam shifted to the middle of the boat, leaning forward with her arms spread wide across their supplies, hair wet and clinging to her face as she acted as Tom's spotter while he kept them on course. Cold water sprayed into their faces every time they landed in a trough, slapping them awake with frigid palms across their cheeks. Tom bared his teeth and grunted as his shoulders strained to hold the makeshift sail straight. He'd covered his hands with strips of parachute material to keep them from blistering, fighting the ever-changing winds, leaning forward and back with the motion of their little craft. The ocean stretched vast all around them, an implacable thing filled with a darkness he felt small and helpless against.

"Keep your head on straight, Tom," he growled to himself, pulled with both hands, arms aching with the effort. "Keep your head on straight and you'll get out of this. Just a few more miles to go." His eyes lifted to Sam where she shifted with the rolling waves and he shouted over the noise of the wind and water. "How's it looking up there?"

They started cresting a wave, Sam edging higher to peer over the front of the boat just as they reached maximum height. The boat rode the crest for a handful of seconds, pausing at the top of the world before plunging like a rollercoaster to the bottom. A squeal burst from her lips as Tom's stomach leapt into his throat and she turned, placed her hands on the sides of the boat, crawling back toward Tom. Locks of hair had long ago come out of their ponytail and lay plastered across her cheeks, but her eyes glowed bright from her salt-drenched face.

"I wasn't sure before," she shouted over the ocean noise, "and I wanted to ride a couple more waves before I said anything." She nodded her head, the faint hint of a smile creasing the corners of her mouth. "There's definitely the outline of land ahead. We're right there. I can see it!"

Tom tied the steering rope around the seat to secure it and dug his cell phone out of his pocket, gripping it tight as he turned it on. The phone signal was still dead, and the battery had drained to twenty-five percent, but the GPS still worked. They were coming in off the coast of Kitty Hawk and Nags Head, near the border of Virginia and North Carolina. He lifted his head, eyes focused across the tops of the waves as they crested once more. Being so close to Norfolk he'd expected to see a lot of shipping traffic, though they'd not seen a single running light through the night nor any sign of any vessels during the day, either.

Another shiver ran through Tom's arms, spreading across his shoulders and down his back, and not even all the work he'd done steering the boat had generated enough heat to ward off the chill.

"Do you want to take a break and get warm?" Sam said. "I can drive for a bit."

"Not when we're this close." Tom adjusted the line around his hands, gritting his teeth against the dull aching pain. "We should be in phone range soon, so I want you to check the signal every fifteen minutes." He handed her his phone, and she nodded and gripped it tightly. "We're down to 25 percent battery life, so keep the screen off until you check, okay? And whatever you do, don't drop it overboard!"

She nodded again and turned in that slow, precise manner required to stay aboard the rocking boat or get tossed into the ocean, making her way back to the middle of the raft to resume her watch.

* * *

Two hours later, Sam turned back to him, holding the phone up. "We're just a mile and a half off now!" she shouted with a grin plastered on her face. The swells had grown, tossing the small craft even higher, dousing them with a constant spray of cold saltwater, emphasizing even further just how small they were in the grand scheme of things.

Soaked to the bone, all the way to his socks, Tom glanced up at the sky, watching it growing darker and wilder before his eyes, streaks of gray clouds racing toward the shore. While wet and miserable, he was thankful for the strong wind pushing them toward land, despite it damaging their makeshift sail, the nylon tattered and frayed along the edges, and at least two grommets having broken and in need of repairs.

On the next swell, Tom glanced up and caught sight of land. He understood Sam's excitement, the thin line along the horizon drawing him in with a sense of impending safety, feeling instinctively driven to reach it. It must be what Noah felt like on his ark when he spotted land for the first time after so many days at sea, a desperate yearning to have his feet on solid ground and escape from the rocking motion of the waves.

Least we don't have to deal with animals on board.

Glancing back at the outboard motor, he was tempted to start it up and accelerate them through their last leg, but with the wind so strong, they could wait a little longer. With each rising swell, with every hundred yards that brought them closer to shore, Tom spotted the tops of homes and buildings making a jagged skyline along the beach. It wasn't until they were less than a mile of the beach that he noticed something off about the shoreline. The homes stood too close together, some looking wilted and shifting, the waves pushing too far up onto the beach and spilling over into the streets. With a new pit of worry blossoming in his belly, Tom tied off the steering line once more and reached to take hold of the mast.

"What are you doing?" Sam shouted back when she noticed him pulling the mast out of its hole.

"I was going to wait a little longer, but I think we'll motor the rest of the way in."

"Awesome!"

The wind tried to pull away the sail as soon as he removed it from its mooring, but he turned it flat and slid the end of the pole beneath the front seat, allowing Sam to put one knee on it to hold it down. Tom started the engine in a puttering snarl, and they rocketed forward over the waves, surging and dipping, leaning and shifting in their seats as the boat pushed swiftly toward the shore.

"I'm getting a signal and voice mail notifications!" Sam cried out a minute later. When she turned to show him, her left hand slipped off the edge of the boat and she fell forward, faceplanting into the soft rubber side. Tom almost dove after her, but Samantha sat up and shook her wet hair out of her face. "I'm fine! I'm okay!"

"Be careful!" he shouted back, his heart pounding inside his chest like a race car's piston.

She frowned as she reset herself in the bow, slipping, clinging with one hand to stay steady. "Sorry, Dad! Just glad your phone's waterproof!"

"It's okay. Just... try to call your mother!"

"I just did." She shook her head, her voice sounding hoarse from all of the shouting they had to do. "I'm getting a weird clicking sound."

"Can you text her?"

"I'll try." Sam's fingers tapped the front of the phone as she typed something out. She stared at the screen for several seconds before she raising her face and shook her head. "Nope, nothing. It's not sending."

"Okay, check voice mail."

Another minute, another shake of her head. "More clicking. I can't load a web page either. The phone shows we have a low signal, but I can't connect."

"Alright, just keep at it while I get us to shore."

Tom turned the throttle up to near-max and they shot over across the waves with skips and bumps, his legs spread out in the bottom of the raft to keep himself balances, body tense as he fought to smoothen the ride. He spotted a neat row of sand banks with homes and condos perched at the top, and he steered straight for them. Kelp and washes of shells and dead fish had washed up onto the dunes, getting caught in wooden staircases that wound down to the beachhead, waves lapping at the slats and covering the bottom of the stairs. High tide markers were visible when the waves receded but were temporarily covered when they returned.

"It shouldn't be close to high tide yet," Tom murmured to himself. "Those waves have washed out people's backyards."

"Ugh." Sam gave the phone a shake. "We've got a stronger signal, but I still can't call or text out."

"I'll take it." One hand out, one on the throttle, Tom reached for his phone, took it and slipped it into his pocket. Eyes pinned forward, he steered straight for a section of dune slightly raised above the other, watching as the waves rolled up over the wet sand for miles, devouring shoreline. "Once we get ashore, we have to bring the raft up as high as possible." He pointed toward where he wanted to land between two staircases. "And we should tie it up if we can."

"Why? Can't we just leave the raft on the beach?"

"I want to keep it handy in case we need it again." His mind drifted back to that crevice in the seafloor, the myriad of cracks discovered running all along the shelf, busting the crust like an eggshell. "This isn't even high tide. When that rolls in, the flooding will only get worse." He pointed and let his finger drift from right to left, showing that he meant the entire beach. "Look behind me. What do you see?"

Sam raised up and squinted east toward the distant horizon. "I see gigantic waves and black clouds. Wow, really black clouds."

"They've been getting darker every hour since before noon, and the wind has picked up a lot. Let's just keep our options open."

Sam nodded and turned back toward the shore, leaving Tom with his ominous thoughts and questions.

Chapter 15
Barbara McKnight
Wyndale, Virginia

Normally a moderately heavy sleeper, Barbara woke to a single beep from her phone. She rolled over, grabbing the device off her nightstand, frowning at the sight of a news alert on the screen. With a sigh she put the phone back and flipped onto her left side, pulling the sheets up tight to her chin. They'd be starting late, already missing their early morning start, her tired mind wanting to squeeze out every minute of sleep more than it wanted to be responsible and get up at the crack of dawn.

She'd stayed up longer than normal the previous night, watching a movie with the kids and munching popcorn. Probably not the smartest decision before a long day of harvesting, but she figured they deserved it after spending the last few days lingering on the hot edge of worry. The hours of distraction had done wonders for her brain and she'd fallen straight to sleep, not waking once the entire night.

Another beep came, swiftly followed by another and another, each time the accompanying vibration rattling the keys she'd left on the nightstand. It was such an irritating sound that a bolt of agitation plucked at the base of her brain, a spike of frustration that pushed her close to full alertness. Barbara snatched up the phone up in frustration and rolled onto her back, hitting the quick dial button for Tom. She placed the phone to her ear but only heard an odd clicking sound and not even a ring or voice mail.

"Weird." She dropped the phone to her side and lay there with her eyes closed for several minutes, caught between going back to sleep and just waking up. 8:30. It never hurt to get an early start on things, but harvest day was hard, and she didn't want to face it. Drifting off again, her breathing deepened, thoughts drifting in a foggy sea, worries transported far away. *A few more minutes, then we'll get started. Just a few more—*

The phone beeped and buzzed once more , followed by six or seven ones in rapid succession that shook her leg, driving her annoyance from zero to a hundred in a fraction of a second. With a frustrated groan she snatched up the phone, scowling at the blinking alerts, muttering under her breath. "What's so damned important?"

She clicked on her notifications and found several from CNF and several other local news apps she received regular information from. Scrolling to the national news site, she read a headline describing dangerously rising tides along the United States Eastern Seaboard, suspected to be both from incoming storms and the North Atlantic anomaly. Barbara sat up and leaned against her headboard with one leg cocked to the side, reading on.

"Authorities from the Coast Guard and Navy are issuing evacuation orders for multiple US coastal cities along the Eastern Seaboard in the wake of intense flooding predicted to occur over the next seventy-two hours. Higher than normal tides and a brewing storm have authorities worried residents will become overwhelmed. Authorities in Florida and South Carolina have declared states of emergency, and we expect others to follow. The FEMA Director stated earlier this morning that the agency is setting up camps inland where people are being encouraged to take shelter should they not have anywhere else to go."

Worry picked at her brain as she scrolled through her other notifications, many of them rehashing what CNF said, except for one local news notification out of Bristol informing local residents of widespread cell phone and internet outages. Barbara looked for some national news on the same topic and found that several major cities were experiencing the same problems.

"What in the world is happening?" Fully awake, she swung her legs off the bed and dressed in her jeans, boots, and a white T-shirt. She slipped her 380 into the waistband behind her right hip, brushed her teeth, and headed downstairs. The kids weren't up, having taken full advantage of her sleeping in, and she had no reason to get them moving quite yet. She put on a fresh pot of coffee and tried to call Tom one more time, but all she got was the same clicking sound as before, and texts were failed to go through as well.

After pouring her coffee, she gave the cup a light hit of cream and sugar before moving to the kitchen table. There, she tried firing off an email to Tom, noting that the internet was slow but usable. In her message, she told him they were okay and hunkering down, then added how much they missed him and Sam and hoped they'd reached safety. Watching the "sending" icon spin for a long moment before the email finally went through, she sipped her coffee, shoulders tense, brain on fire with concern before she realized it was time to get moving. Moving meant distractions which meant less worry about the present and more work put into improving the future. She stood and crossed to the foot of the stairs, yelling up the stairs.

"Linda, Jack! Let's go! Up and at 'em! Be down here in ten minutes!"

Barbara returned to the kitchen and placed her coffee cup on the table, retrieving some bacon, sausage links, eggs, bread and butter to get breakfast started. Soon, a pan on their stove sizzled, sputtering and spitting grease onto the stove and counter until Barbara covered the pans with wire mesh screens.

"I can make the scrambled eggs!" Linda flew in, circled the kitchen table, and stopped to sniff at the coffee maker. She grabbed a mug down from the cupboard and poured herself a cup, Barbara raising her eyebrows questioningly. "Coffee? Since when?"

Linda shrugged, added about the same amount of cream and sugar as her mother, took a sip, made an odd expression and placed the cup down on the table. Then she skipped back to the counter and got a large glass bowl and started cracking eggs into it, whisked them up with a fork, stepped to Barbara's side and dumped them into an empty pan. With a yawn, she started pushing them around with a spatula and after a few minutes the eggs formed up into puffs of yellow and white.

"Eggs are about done, mom."

"Bacon and sausage, too. I'll make the plates if you pour the drinks. I'm thinking OJ and water?"

"Sounds good."

Jack came down just as Barbara put down their loaded plates on the table, late as he typically was. Linda poured them each an orange juice and glass of water, then all three sat to eat. She reviewed the day's plan, going over feeding of the animals and then jumping into the details of harvesting. After a few minutes of explanation, she sat back and gave both children a serious look.

"We'll need every ounce of energy there, so I don't want you guys goofing off too much and wearing yourselves out before the work's all done, got it?" Linda nodded, but Jack only blinked and frowned.

Barbara's eyes lingered on her son. "I know you love mornings playing with Smooch, but I really need you on the ball today, okay?"

"Yes, ma'am."

"Oh, I got a yes ma'am." She raised her eyebrows to Linda and sat back with a bemused expression. "I hardly ever get a yes ma'am without having to remind him!"

"I *never* get a yes ma'am," Linda mock pouted.

"Because you're not a ma'am yet," Jack explained, holding a piece of half-eaten bacon. "You have to be really old for them to call you ma'am."

Barbara snorted, jaw hanging open, shoulders slumped before she couldn't help herself any longer and burst out into laughter.

* * *

Heat bore down on the trio as they attacked the cornrows with a vengeance. Their fields were small enough to harvest by hand, without needing any mechanized assistance, at least until they expanded into the back of their property down the road sometime in the future. Barbara's shirt was already soaked through with sweat as she felt around the stalks for full ears, ones where the silken ends had turned brown, and broke them downward before popping them off. She handed the ears to the kids who piled them in sacks, stuffing them inside. Once full, they took turns loading the sacks into wheelbarrows, and either they or she wheeled them up to the trailer where they tossed them in back.

The yield was plentiful, with very little silk rot and a lot of big, full ears, and she left the smaller ones to grow more before she harvested them over the next week. They wouldn't be growing any more until next season, so they could take their time cutting down the stalks and clearing the fields.

"I think Dad and Sam are lucky," Jack announced as Linda piled several ears of corn in his arms. "They're getting out of all the hard work."

Barbara stood straighter, wiping a heavy sheen of sweat off her brown, taking a deep breath as she looked over at her son.

"Not lucky." Linda came up and held her arms out, fixing a suspicious gaze on the horizon. She wore smudges of dirt on her cheeks, matching her earth-colored eyes. "Maybe they planned it. They knew it was harvest time, so they made up a story to get out of working. And they paid the world to go along with it."

Jack nodded, eyes wide. "Yeah, sneaky."

"I don't think so," Barbara laughed, then she pretended to think hard about it. "Well, maybe…" A mischievous expression flashed across Linda's face. Barbara grinned back, and Jack looked back and forth between the two until he finally figured out the joke, then started grinning, too.

They moved around the field and harvested their green beans, spinach, peppers, and a few ripe tomatoes which the kids ran over to the wagon and put in special plastic containers to keep them from getting smashed and bruised. For their three rows of potatoes, they'd planted both Yukon gold and reds, the stems of which were pulled and to the edge of the field as eventual fodder for the chickens and additives for a small compost pile. Barbara used a pitchfork to loosen the soil as Linda and Jack came through behind her and dug out the knobs of potatoes, putting them in sacks.

She crouched down as she worked, keeping her back straight to try and keep from straining it, but it was still hard work, and she paid attention to the aches and pains of her body to keep from pulling something. Both of the kids had turned their work into a game, having fun competing to see who could fill a sack of potatoes first. Linda stayed ahead by being quick and efficient while Jack mostly stumbled in the loose dirt, fell, and got dirty – losing the game, but being victorious in his own way.

Around noon Barbara signaled a quick break of light sandwiches, some fruit and cold water. The kids sprawled out in the grass, tossing pieces of their bread to Smooch while Barbara stood sweaty in the middle of the field with a glass of water, picking a potato out of the dirt and brushing it off to check the quality of their yield, thumb rubbing over the dark spots. It looked like they were harvesting them before too much rot could set in, and it was nothing that couldn't be cut away.

They used the wheelbarrows as a temporary place to put things until they had them filled enough to wheel up to the wagon. With the back of the wagon bursting with corn ears and potato sacks, they finished with the onions as late afternoon approached and the sun dipped low. Barbara's legs shook with exhaustion, arms caked with dust, sweat turning it to mud on her skin. Linda and Jack had gone mostly mute, transformed into zombie children lugging bins and baskets to the trailer with nary a smile on their faces.

"Come on," she encouraged them. "We're almost there. I'm making brownies for desert tonight!" They both picked up the pace at her words, and despite the exhausting day, her helpers came through with flying colors. They lugged the remaining onions to the wheelbarrows and added a half sack of potatoes that had been lying around before racing back and forth among the rows, grabbing the odd vegetable that had been dropped during the day.

Standing back a few feet from the back of the wagon, Barbara watched Linda and Jack, eyes tracing over the day's bounty. Bins of corn rested at the front of the wagon, ears of green bursting over the top, practically begging to be shucked. Eight sacks of potatoes lay neatly stacked behind them, and Barbara estimated they might have two or three hundred pounds' worth. They'd stacked bulging bins of onions and radishes behind the potatoes, and smaller bins of tomatoes took up the rail seats, their red skins glistening in the dwindling, dusky sunlight. The entire wagon burst with goodness, and Barbara squeezed her children as they came to stand on either side of her.

"We've been blessed this year," she said with a shake of her head, eyes turning glassy with emotion. "All the hard work, planting in early and mid-summer really paid off, and you kids worked so hard today." She held them close, palms cupped on their shoulders. "I wasn't sure we could do it without Dad and Sam, but we did. They'd be mighty proud of the work we did here today."

"Because we're awesome." Jack put his arm around his mother's waist.

"We are extremely awesome," Barbara agreed. "Let's take this around back and start on dinner."

"Good! I'm starving!" Linda added, rubbing her stomach as Jack looked up at Barbara, his eyes stretched open as wide as he could force them.

"Can we have brownies first?"

Barbara nodded twice and then shook her head, teasing him. "No, we cannot."

"Awww, but Mommm..."

"We're having roast and…" she gestured to the back of the wagon, "well, boiled potatoes and green beans with stewed tomatoes. *Then* brownies."

She climbed behind the wheel of the mower and started it up while the kids squeezed in back with the crops. Before pulling away, she scrutinized the field. They'd left their tools and gloves everywhere along with a few small bins and extra sacks and the corn rows remained standing as well, waiting to be cut down and cleared to prepare the field for next spring.

"We've got a lot of cleanup to do over the next week," she called over her shoulder as she climbed into the mower seat.

"And Sam and Dad will be home to help," Linda announced confidently.

Barbara pursed her lips but didn't respond, instead putting the vehicle in gear and driving around to the back patio while the kids kept things from spilling out on the way. Parking, turning the mower off, they climbed down and picked out their dinner from the bins and sacks, leaving the rest tied up till they could get to it the next morning. Once in the house, Barbara turned back to Jack.

"Alright, kiddo, get yourself cleaned up first so you're not a walking pile of dirt waiting to get on everything." Together with Linda she started on dinner, seasoning the small roast and popping it in the oven while Linda cut up potatoes and beans, started them on a rolling boil. By the time they had finished starting on the prep work, Barbara's entire body hurt, and she tossed a piece of raw potato in her mouth and sat at the kitchen table, pulling out her phone letting it clatter onto the table face down.

Linda joined her, falling into a chair with a sigh. "That was the longest day of my life."

Barbara reached out a sore arm, patting her daughter on the shoulder. "It was your and Jack's first genuine test out in the fields without Sam, and you two did amazing."

"Better than Sam?"

"I don't know," Barbara pretended to think about it. "Sam was pretty good."

Linda leveled a hard gaze at her mother, and Barbara lowered her voice to a conspiratorial whisper. "Well… given that kept crazy Jack in line the whole time, I'd say you beat her."

"That's what I thought," the girl crowed, sitting back and folding her arms across her chest with a smug expression.

Barbara turned her phone over and flicked her finger over the screen to bring it to life, checking her voicemail, texts, and emails, much to her disappointment.

"Still no news from Dad?"

"Not a peep." She swiped down to bring up her news alerts and began scrolling through them. "More stuff on the potential flooding and storms. Wow, it sounds bad. They're setting up FEMA camps to accept refugees."

"What does that mean? I know what FEMA is, but I'm not sure about the camps."

"Well, if the coasts get flooded, then it will put a lot of people out of their homes, and that's why they're called refugees. The FEMA people will have to situate them farther inland where there's less flooding."

"When is that supposed to happen?"

"Severe storms hit the coast overnight." Barbara's eyes scanned the news reports. "But it's hard to say exactly how heavy the storms will get down the road."

"More bad things for Dad and Sam to deal with." Linda shook her head, eyes glassy and distant.

Barbara reached across the table and rested her hand on Linda's. "Hey, don't lose hope. I'm not losing hope." It was the truth, though there had been moments when she'd felt despair deep inside her, and there were only so many chores to keep them busy before their bodies fell apart. "What else can we do but pray, hope and wait?"

Linda shook her head. "I guess nothing."

There was a stab deep in Barbara's heart at the sight of her daughter's worry, with hardly a thing she could do to ease it, stuck between a desire to be forthright with Linda while still sheltering young Jack from the worst of the news. "They're going to put up a website so people can check if family members got rescued."

"Or to check if they got killed." Linda spoke matter-of-factly. Barbara nodded slowly at the reality of the statement. The restless feeling akin to a caged animal that had been nagging her for days began its restless pacing, and her chest heaved with a sob, though she held it in check. Moments ticked by as the pair made small talk, Jack came back into the room, Linda ran off to get cleaned up and then came back, and eventually the oven timer dinged and Barbara patted her daughter's shoulder, throwing Jack a smile. "I'll get the food ready if you two set the table."

"Okay, mom."

Barbara's eyelids grew heavy before she'd finished half her plate, ready to fall into bed and crash without so much as brushing her teeth, but her mind wouldn't let her focus on anything without thoughts of Tom and Sam swirling in the background.

Looking at her clock, she saw it was only 8:30, and sighed. "All right, I say we get the dishes done then clean and store some of this food to occupy our time tonight. We should at least get the potatoes into their boxes and put downstairs."

"Aw, Mom." Jack flailed his arms out and slapped them against his legs. "I'm so tired, I could sleep a week!"

"I've got this much energy left." Linda held up her hand and made a tiny space between her thumb and index finger, giving her brother a sideways glance and receiving a stuck-out tongue in response. "So I can help some."

"Just an hour, okay? Then I'll set you both free before bedtime." Both of them nodded wearily in response, and Jack hopped off his chair, heading for the back door. "I'll get the potato boxes."

"Good boy," Barbara said, standing. "Linda and I will bring in some bins."

The last hour of work didn't go as easy as earlier in the day, and they only boxed a quarter of the potatoes, dropping many of them onto the floor and spreading out dirt and debris in the process. At some point, Barbara realized it was pointless; they'd become useless robots, exhausted and weak-willed, their big, heavy dinner weighing them down with the lure of sleep. She dismissed them after thirty minutes, watching them walk off with slumped shoulders, too tired to even complain.

"Oh hey, you two, by the way… aren't you forgetting about something?" The pair stopped and looked back at her, and with a grin, Barbara opened the pantry and pulled out a box of brownie mix.

Chapter 16
Tom McKnight
Outer Banks, North Carolina

High tide swept in along the beaches of the Outer Banks, consuming two-hundred miles of coastline before sweeping in around the sides to nibble at the mainland. Waves washed over the sand dunes to spill into back yards and sweep over pools, pushing lawn furniture, plastic balls, floats, and parts of wooden fencing everywhere in a debris-filled soup. Gusts of wind screamed in from the sea, driven by ominous clouds, the moon's pale luminance drenching the world in an eerie, greenish tint. Shingles and pieces of siding spun through the air, slapping down in the street, sailing hundreds of yards across the stretch of land near Kitty Hawk where Orville and Wilbur Wright had made their first successful flights while the wind tore off the tops of the sand dunes, sending spray and sand grains blasting over the houses.

Tom and Samantha trudged down the lightless street, looking around for anyone or anything to help them reach the mainland. The city lay abandoned, evacuated, the streets devoid of life. No dogs barked, no headlamps gleamed and none of the stores or shops in the vacation town remained open. The place was all shut down, dead, vacant, and empty.

Sea grit blew at them sideways, whipping up and stinging their cheeks, the makeshift ponchos they'd constructed out of the parachute material barely keeping it out. Their legs shook and wobbled, still weary from balancing on the rocking raft, gripping its sides and riding the waves while Tom's hands were bloody and bruised from steering the damn raft – and yet they still had so far to go. Tom had put together a makeshift pack out of the raft's emergency kit plus the things they'd found in the supply box. They had a knife, the emergency first aid kit, rope, flashlights, and the rest of their food and water and he'd also added what remained of their tape and some small strips of sail cloth.

They kept to the middle of the road, away from deep puddles of water growing along the curbs and in the streets as they walked, keeping tight to each other.

"This is scary," Sam said as she walked stiffly, fists at her sides.

"It's terrifying," he replied. "The storm is gaining power and the entire OBX might flood in a matter of hours from the storm surge alone. We need to make sure we find a safe place to shelter before that happens. Hopefully, we'll get close enough to a working cell phone tower and I can tell your mother we're okay. She's probably worried to death."

Ahead lay several blocks of businesses and four-story condominiums - dark, squarish lumps in the dwindling light.

"Let's pick it up," Tom urged, shoulders hunched, head bowing forward. "We need to make it there before the flooding gets worse."

"Where did everyone go?" Sam asked with a glance around, pulling her makeshift raincoat tighter to her shoulders.

"Probably evacuated. It wouldn't surprise me if the entire coastline from Florida to Canada had moved inland."

"That's a lot of people." The girl's hair whipped around her head as another wind gusted in. She turned her face away from the stinging sand. "Is that why you tied the raft to a telephone pole? You expected this to happen?"

"It was just a hunch," Tom admitted. "I don't want us to get too complacent. Every move we make has to be a good one, if that makes sense."

"How could the water rise so much? I mean, I saw the crevice with my own eyes, but how could it flood all the oceans? They cover seventy percent of the earth."

Tom shook his head. "Remember what I said about Lake Superior?"

"Yeah, but I was thinking in *inches*. This seems a lot more than that. How could a few inches cause so much chaos?"

"It would only take about three quadrillion gallons of water to set things in motion. To, um, throw off the currents along the coast. That, coupled with the storms would do it. Storm surge is no joke."

"The crevice must have broken apart more, and the dispersal is worse than we thought. That's the only thing I can think of."

"It's just so crazy." Sam glanced past him toward the ocean where waves and winds beat at the beach front homes. Her tone took a more annoyed tone as she tried to wrap her head around the concept. "Is there really that much water *under* the ocean?"

Tom chuckled. "Yeah, it's really hard to imagine millions and billions of anything much less quadrillions, but yes there's plenty enough water around to do it. The Earth's crust is a mysterious place. Aquifers could be anywhere, with unimaginable pressures forcing things upward."

"Wow," she said, her voice bordering on disbelief.

"We don't fully understand the complex mechanisms that are plate tectonics," Tom added. "Well, we understand the basics, but we've still got a lot to learn."

"Like with volcanoes and earthquakes and stuff?"

"Right. That stuff can do other things – as we're learning now—crap, hold on."

They both put their heads down as a massive gust of wind whipped up, blowing garbage and debris across their path, sand stinging their faces, cold trickles of water snaking beneath their makeshift ponchos.

"We know that volcanoes can spew lava at well over a hundred miles per hour, but we measure that by the distance the molten debris shoots out and the time it takes to get there." Tom made a wincing face and rolled his stiff right shoulder. "Our underwater instruments can be even more accurate. The readings from the Marin clocked the water forced out of the crater at 170 miles per hour in some spots."

"What does that mean?"

"It's coming out fast. Really, really fast." Tom shook his head. "Based on the cracks forming when the Marin sank, it would have to be an unfathomable amount of pressure forcing that thing open. I would even expect to see some volcanic activity around some sections because of the shifting plates, but that likely won't be everywhere. You're right, Sam. It's hard to imagine, but it's happening right now."

They walked in silence for a few blocks, Tom eying the abandoned condos and beach front homes in the path of the storm, contemplating whether he wanted to risk breaking into one and taking shelter. Cars sat abandoned in the streets and driveways, sand blasted and dripping wet with spray, many with surfboards and vacation gear strapped to the top. While the risk of anyone being home was minimalized given the evacuations that had no doubt taken place, he wasn't sure how well the area would fare under the incoming storm.

"And that isn't the only problem."

Sam shot her father a wide-eyed gaze. "What could be worse?"

"The salinity of the water will change in all the oceans. I don't know by how much, but even a small amount—"

"Even I know what would happen then," she interjected. "The sea life that depends on specific salinities to survive could start to die off. And the fish that feed on them will die off, and so on. But won't the aquifer lose pressure after a while?" Sam asked, grasping at straws.

"You would think so, but it wasn't slowing down the last time we checked." He shrugged, eyes scanning the tearing roofs and bending trees all around them, leaning sideways into a particularly nasty blast of wind. "But who knows? I keep thinking there's something I'm missing. Well, hoping, really, more than thinking." Sam stared straight ahead as he talked, her feet squelching in her wet tennis shoes, hair stringy with salt water. "Sorry to bum you out, but I feel like it's important to be honest with you." He pulled her closer and gave her shoulder a squeeze. "You're almost an adult, and it's important you hear the truth, without the candied sugar on top, if you know what I mean."

A brief smile cracked her frown. "Thanks. I appreciate that."

They walked in silence, feet scraping across the pavement.

"What else could happen?" Sam narrowed her eyes. "I mean, if this ruins the oceans, it would have some effect on land."

"A lot of people will be without sea food," Tom said. "I'm not a supply chain expert, but I would expect this would affect things in other markets."

"No more shrimp," she said.

"No more lobster."

"No more tilapia or salmon."

"No more Chilean sea bass," Tom countered with a raised eyebrow.

Sam shot her father an accusing squint. "That's a weird one, but okay. Um, no more megalodon shark steaks."

"Oh, I'll really miss those," he laughed. "How about, no more giant squid sandwiches?"

"Ew! Too chewy for me. How about, no more Pliosaurus soup?"

"How about…"

They ran down the list of things they'd miss about the Earth's oceans, each selection sillier than the last, playing a morbid game that took their minds off their anxiety. Lights ahead caught Tom's attention, and he interrupted the game to poke Sam, pointing at the glow. "Check it out."

She lifted her head, a smile spreading across her face as she spotted the lights spilling out into the roadway ahead. "How far is that?"

"About a mile or so, I'd bet." He half-turned and side-skipped ahead. "Let's go."

She caught up to him and together they hurried forward, eager to find some help. The precious glow radiated from a gas station and two fast-food restaurants, their inside lights still on, a few cars idling in the lots or pulled into the drive-throughs. Tom and Sam slowed down while he took in the scene. In the gas station lot, people were pumping gas or filling up gas containers, working at a frantic pace but not panicking. Families milled around the pumps, standing in close circles; fathers, brothers, and uncles in protective stances, shoulders back, eyes moving over the other travelers. He saw a few mothers and children standing around, eating, or munching on snacks, holding whispered conversations while they waited for the pumping to conclude. Guiding Sam around the pumps, they angled toward the entrance, multiple pairs of eyes lingering on them due to their unique choice of clothing. As they entered, a tall man with a rotund stomach and a Florida Gators baseball perched on his head stepped out, holding the door for them as they passed.

"Thank you!" Tom said.

"No problem," he smirked, "love the rain jackets."

Tom smiled, guiding Sam into the gas station, then took a look around. "Let's get some drinks first. Stay close, okay?"

They took a circuitous route around the edge of the store, squeezing past several people standing in the automotive aisle until they made it to the drink section, Tom edging his way between people crowded around, the refrigerator doors opening and shutting repeatedly, frosting up with moisture. The others in the store weren't panicking or emptying the shelves, but a sense of urgency hung in the air while whispers about the storm and evacuations took place around them. Tom and Sam waited behind a man who took out three waters before they reached for two each for themselves before backing out of the cooler, Tom nudging Sam in the opposite direction as they both cracked open their bottles and took deep gulps.

"Okay, let's get something to eat."

She nodded and he followed her to the snack aisle where they met a similar crowd of people, all of them plucking things off the racks just to have someone else step in and pluck off more, packages disappearing in a ruffle of packaging. Tom figured the racks would be bare in less than an hour. A middle-aged woman met his eyes, appearing troubled until she spotted Sam, then her expression softened and a soft smile played across her lips. "Stinks to have our vacations ruined, right?"

"Uh, yeah," Tom replied. "Mandatory evacuation, eh?"

"Yeah, haven't you been listening to the news?" The woman picked a package of honey cashews off the rack and turned on her heel. "Good luck. Be safe."

With a nod, he exchanged a look with Sam before they dove in for some cheese-flavored chips for him and sour cream and onion chips for her before grabbing four packs of jerky and a handful of energy bars. Laden with food, they made their way to one of two check out aisles, standing in a dense line of people that extended past a pair of ice-filled soft drink barrels.

The line moved slowly, the two register attendants struggling with the credit card readers, frustrated expressions on their faces. Tom shifted his things to one arm and had a peek at his phone again. It was down to ten percent power, and it appeared to have strong signal. He tried texting and calling Barbara again, but received the same response he'd gotten since they'd arrived.

"Anything?"

"I think the local towers are probably done." He nodded toward the front. "And the attendants are having trouble processing credit cards. Luckily, I've still got cash, wet though it may be."

He shoved his phone back into his pocket and retrieved his leather wallet. Salt stains ringed the black leather around the edges, and when he opened it up, a pinch of grit and sand spilled onto the floor. He fished out a soggy twenty-dollar bill out of a row of them and raised it at Sam.

"Oh, I almost forgot," he said. "I wonder if they have a charger for my phone?"

He handed her his pile of food and sidestepped to a small electronics kiosk, poking past the CD players and plug extenders until he found the phone chargers. After a brief search, he found the one he needed and stepped back in line with Sam, glad to see they'd almost reached the counter. They were just about to move ahead with the line when Tom felt a hard tap on his shoulder. He turned to see a man standing in line he hadn't noticed before.

"Can I help you?"

"You're cutting in line," the man said, his eyelids heavy, face slack, a hint of agitation in his eyes.

"I'm not cutting in line," Tom responded, lifting his chin but keeping his tone civil. "I stepped out to grab a phone charger. This is my daughter."

The man's eyes slid to Sam and she glared back at the man as if daring him to challenge them. A queasiness gripped Tom's stomach, fist clenching around the phone charger package, ready to escalate if the man pushed the issue, but he backed off, shoulders lowering easing with a nod. Tom sighed inwardly and turned to face the counter with Sam, whispering in her ear.

"Everyone's on edge right now. We need to get out of here."

"Check it out, Dad," Sam whispered back to him, pointing at a small flat screen TV tucked up in the corner by the cigarettes. The Weather Channel was playing, depicting a massive, spinning super-cell hanging off the North Carolina coast.

"That's why the clouds were so dark," he told Sam, leaning in, swallowing hard, berating himself for not doing something as simple as checking the weather before acquiescing to Ray's request. *Not that it would have mattered... we were out there for, what, two days? If we hadn't put up that sail and instead waited for a rescue...* Tom didn't finish the thought.

"Dad," Sam whispered again, already on his wavelength, "why would they tell people in those emergency drops to stay where they were if a hurricane was on the way?"

"They probably planned to pick them up quickly, but they got overwhelmed with things on shore? I'm not sure."

The television played at a low volume as the weather woman stood in front of a big map of the North Carolina coast, gesturing at the super-cell, making circular motions with her hands over the outer bands before indicating a spot on the map where the meat of the storm would make landfall, her words barely audible above the murmuring people in line.

"... Hurricane Kate is expected to make landfall within twelve hours, hitting the Outer Banks, and driving inland and to the south. Winds of one hundred and sixty miles per hour are expected near the storm's center. Experts say it could be one of the worst storms in 50 years, adding to the nagging issues already plaguing the United States, especially given the storm's rapid strengthening in the last twenty-four hours after nearly hitting the Florida coast earlier in the week. Evacuations are almost complete, and FEMA and state officials are urging anyone still in those coastal areas to get out as soon as possible. They are bracing to receive hundreds of thousands of displaced people in camps further inland." A list of FEMA, state and local shelter locations scrolled down the screen and she continued. "We advise that if you do not have family in the interior regions, or a safe place to stay, make your way to the nearest shelter immediately."

Tom's nostrils flared with a sharp exhale. They didn't have any means of transportation farther inland, nor could they seem to call anyone for help.

"That'll hit us, right?" Sam's expectant green eyes peered up at him. "I mean, if we're not out of here in twelve hours."

Tom stepped up and nodded to the cashier, a young man, eighteen or twenty, with blue eyes and a short crop of black hair, conveying both a hint of impatience and an air of nervousness. Tom and Samantha placed their things on the counter and shoved them forward, one water bottle falling over and rolling back toward them which Tom set upright before holding out his soggy twenty.

"Oh, great. You have cash." The young man flashed a slight smile, relief on his face as he scanned their items as he talked. "Credit cards are taking forever."

"What's up with that? Is it totally down? I noticed cell phone service is out, too."

The attendant shrugged. "It started going downhill yesterday. I heard on the news it's because of some upgrade happening in the area or something, I dunno. Anyway, the upgrade plus a big surge in calls because of the ocean thing that's happening and bam, cell towers are overloaded and down all over the region."

"The 'ocean thing?' You mean the anomaly?"

"Right. But at least the power is still on, for now." The young man shrugged at Tom and took the proffered twenty from his hand. He popped the drawer, counted out their change, handing it over with a sigh of resignation and a half-hearted smile. "Anyway, you have a good day. Try to get inland if you can."

Tom put his change in his pocket as the young man bagged up the food and water, sensing the growing restlessness in the crowd behind him. "Sorry, but do you know where we can rent a car?"

The attendant's jaw worked back and forth, eyes narrowed in thought. "Mm, I don't think so. All the rental places are closed, and anyone with any sense is long gone, which makes me question my sanity. But I promised the boss I'd close up, so here I am." He shrugged. "He's paying me overtime though."

The young man studied Tom's despondent face, offering one more piece of advice. "Maybe someone outside can give you a ride out of here. Otherwise, it's going to be a rough ride. Sorry."

"Not your fault. Thanks, though." Tom nodded and sighed, ignoring the urge to detail what the pair had been through for the past couple of days, gesturing for Sam to step toward the door. Together, they headed outside and sat on the curb near the front door, watching the stream of people begin to dwindle as more cars pulled out. The starkness of the gas station lights seemed harsh and unrelenting as they stared east into Hurricane Kate's face. It was dark out, ripples of lightning flashing across the sky, the wind picking up in gusts that almost blew Sam's chips out of her hand before she snatched them back. A light smattering of rain began to fall, pattering on the awning cover and striking the pavement and a gust of wind blew it sideways at them, sprinkling Tom's cheek with an icy touch, sending a shiver down his spine.

"No way we're going to be able to ride out something like this," he growled. "We need to find a way off this sand bar *now*."

Chapter 17
Military Central Command
Undisclosed Location

The conference room grows warm as two dozen people and their laptops compile data and look for solutions to the ever-shifting problem they commonly refer to as "The North Atlantic anomaly." Those who hadn't known each other two days ago and hesitated to speak due to political concerns now communicate openly, cooperating in every facet of the program. Coffee urns have been drained and refilled a dozen times and stacks of pizza boxes are falling out of black trash bags in a pile outside the door while some of those present fall asleep in their chairs or lie down in the hall on hastily constructed cots.

The mood fluctuates between concern and hope as the country's greatest minds search for a possible solution in what seems like an impossible situation. From the central command room they mobilize the military, FEMA, the scientific community, and other public and private entities to throw the bulk of US might at the situation. Their faces are bathed in artificial light from tablets, laptop screens, and several flatscreen televisions along the wall. Whiteboards are filled with mathematical calculations, scribbles, and bullet points while several screens show simulations being projected and tweaked upon.

The President sits at the head of the conference table, his jacket long ago removed and his tie slightly loosened around his neck while his sleeves are rolled up and his eyes show signs of weariness. Members of the Secret Service sit behind him in a pair of chairs against the wall while another couple stand on the other side of the room by the doors. They wear earpieces and curved mics, their attention unwavering as they constantly scan those gathered in the room.

"Rick, what's the word?" he asks his chief scientist sitting on his left, dispensing with formalities.

Dr. Rick Manglore looks more disheveled than before, if that were possible. Shirt untucked, tie hanging over the back of his chair, he pulls his twin laptops closer and peers back and forth between the screens. The room is now quiet at the sound of the President's voice, eager to hear the latest updates.

"Thank you, Mr. President," Dr. Manglore begins. "We're monitoring the anomaly from a distance, using sensitive equipment carried by unmanned submersibles as well as data fed from a pair of nuclear submarines. They've enabled us to merge our extrapolated data into some predictive models."

"Layman's terms please."

The scientist nods. "We can confirm the water expulsion into the North Atlantic continues at an unprecedented rate. We can now confidently say that sea levels will rise by just under an inch across the globe. While that might not seem like a lot, it will have a disastrous effect on coastal regions and sea life."

"Any good news?"

"Actually, I do have some good news about the temperature drift we'd been looking at." Rick shifts forward in his chair, glancing down at one of his screens as if confirming something. "The worst-case scenario of the anomaly causing a massive temperature drift seems to be unfounded, at least for the moment."

"That's great. I guess we can drop the order for the Ford company to start making winter coats." The President manages a smile as a few chuckles echo from around the room.

"I'm proud of you folks," the president continues. "Despite the significant tasks set before you, you've risen to the challenge. You've crunched data on the anomaly, helped coordinate the FEMA refugee camps, and started relief efforts. All done in record time, I might add. We still have a lot of work to do, but we've got a solid handle on what's happening, all thanks to...." The president trails off as, down the length of the table, a figure fidgets and sighs, muttering to himself.

Dr. Zeke Jarvis has an unshaven but youthful face framed by a scruff of beard. His jeans and T-shirt are well-worn, like he's just come out of some remote jungle somewhere, and a pair of beaded necklaces and bracelets lend him an air of eccentricity. Sensing the President's eyes on him, Zeke shifts with discomfort and looks away.

"Dr. Jarvis," the president says with a nod, "You have something to add to this conversation?"

"You can call me Zeke, Mr. President." The man nods, leans forward, throwing his eyes toward Dr. Manglore. "With all due respect, there's no way to know how the anomaly will affect the world's ecosystems, or the weather. So much damage has already been done and—"

"I don't disagree with you," Dr. Manglore interrupts, "but we've been over the numbers. My team's models are showing—"

"Models are meaningless," Zeke shoots back, expression hot as he turns his attention to the president. "This is an unprecedented event with an unimaginable scope. Every hurricane scenario, every earthquake we try to plan for... this event blows those out of the water, if you'll pardon the expression. For all my esteemed colleague's models, we might as well be pulling wild guesses out of our asses. This kind of scenario has *never* been planned for!"

"With all due respect," Dr. Manglore emphasizes Zeke's own words, "I'm working with the best instruments—"

The President waves for Rick to quiet down, then he folds his hands in front of him, a habit he's taken up to remind him to be patient with people. "What are you getting at, Zeke?"

The scruff-laden man bellies up to the table, emboldened by the President's interest. "If we want to prepare, then we have to imagine the worst-case scenario for every single effect, and damn all the instruments. We have to prepare the population for whatever might come, and pray that we get something less catastrophic. We are talking about a potential disaster that will dwarf anything we've ever experienced. I'm talking extinction level event." Silence fills the room, thick and stuffy for a long moment, until the President responds.

"Okay, Zeke. I get that you think we need to play by the worst-case scenario. What do you suggest?"

The scientist's eyes skip over the table. "First thing's first, I wouldn't stop Ford from making winter jackets."

The President chuckles, glancing around. "I was just kidding about that. They weren't really making winter coats."

"They should start." His voice is dead serious, and a smattering of laugher stops as quickly as it started. All eyes are on Dr. Jarvis as he throws down a stack of notebooks in front of him. Rifling through the stack, he jerks one out and holds it up, a "Top Secret" label stamped across the front in red ink.

"This is a contingency plan for the complete collapse of our crop system because of a foreign biological agent attack." He picks another and holds it up. "This one is for a West Coast earthquake, the 'big one.' And this third one… This is a real doozy. It's a contingency plan in the event the Yellowstone Caldera were to blow." The scientist rifles through a few more, tossing each on the polished surface with smacks.

New Madrid earthquake.

Nuclear attack.

Virus outbreak.

Asteroid impact.

"Emergency teams have been over these plans hundreds of times," the scientist continues. "They know them by heart. But since we don't have a contingency plan for the specific events happening in the North Atlantic, we have to review these plans, take the best parts of them that match conditions we *could* see from this event, and merge them into something new." Finger raised, he points across the table.

"We need Dr. Manglore's team to make estimates on crop destruction and what it might take to build temporary farming establishments in the Midwest. We need to crunch numbers on what it would take get people migrated inland, away from the coasts, maybe even farther south, in case the amount of water that comes through is quadruple what we're expecting. Hell, we need to plan on those temperature abberations, too, no matter how unlikely anyone thinks they are.

"The laundry list is right here in these contingency plans. We need to plug those numbers into your models so we can make predictions on *that* data, not what's coming out of a bunch of instruments on the ocean floor." Zeke's voice lowers as he sinks back into his chair. "Even then, it may not be enough. But if we don't have a single, focused response on the worst case scenario, we may never have a chance."

Dr. Manglore starts to speak, but the President holds up his hand, silencing him. The President remains motionless, eyes fixed on the pile of notebooks in the center of the table, the rest of the table coming to the same conclusions he has now reached. Sitting back in his chair, the President continues with a more determined tone. "All right, Dr. Jarvis. I take your point. Dr. Manglore – you have any objections to projecting worst case scenarios?" He looks over at the scientist, who has gone from looking like he was fit to be tied to being thoroughly deflated, sunken back in his seat, eyes still trained on the pile of notebooks in the center of the table.

"Very well, then." The President nods decisively. "I want all these contingency plans picked apart and the worst case scenario projections from each turned into raw data with updated population, agricultural, and economic numbers. I want those numbers and at least initial model forecasts based on what we know – and assuming the worst about what we *don't* know – on my desk before tonight."

The room explodes into motion, half of the individuals crowding around Dr. Jarvis, gathering up the notebooks and requisitioning copies of other disaster plans from archives. Dr. Manglore, to his credit, is on his feet, already working with his colleagues on updating model projections, the severity of the situation in front of them crystal clear.

A suited figure leans in close to the President, whispering in his ear through the commotion. "Are you sure going with the 'worst case' for *everything* is the best idea, sir?"

The president nods solemnly. "If the worst doesn't happen, we'll be heroes for over-preparing. If the worst does happen…." His eyes flicking down to a small manilla envelope emblazoned with the Presidential seal he has kept covered with folded hands, marked on both sides with 'Eyes Only' in blue ink.

"If the worst *does* happen, we won't be caught sitting on our asses."

Chapter 18
Tom McKnight
Outer Banks, North Carolina

The storm bore down on the North Carolina coast in a hammering of wind gusts reaching speeds of a hundred miles per hour, sending the tops of trees bending down, bowing, creaking, and breaking. A litter of debris sailed through the air, scattering across the roadways and bouncing off cars with loud, metallic thumps. Waves came up and over the beachheads to the east, flooding yards, sweeping through homes, gutting them of furniture and personal belongings as the few remaining streetlamps flickered, flashed, and died.

Tom and Sam watched from the inside the gas station, faces pressed against the glass as the rain rapidly picked up in intensity. Blasts of white lightning attacked the sky, tendrils spiking outward in long flashes. The place had emptied out an hour ago, and there were no cars left in the parking lot, the attendant – Jerry – the only other soul left besides them. Lifting his phone, Tom tried to call Barbara again, but the network was still down and his call failed. He tossed it into their emergency supply pack, standing with his hands on his hips staring out into the darkness, worry gnawing at his gut. They were trapped on the Banks with no safe way back to the mainland.

Jerry, finished with his cleanup work, stepped outside, circling the store while dropping the hurricane shutters into place. When he reached Tom and Sam's window, he shrugged apologetically and lowered the shutter, locking it in place and blocking their view to the outside world. He reentered the store, stepped to the counter to grab a motorcycle helmet and keys from behind it, then turned with a shrug. "Sorry, but I have to close the store. I need to kick you out."

"Is the land line still down?" Tom asked.

"Yeah. I've already tried three times." The attendant leaned against the door, wincing as he held it open an inch. "Again, I'm really sorry, folks. I've got to close up and get home. I suggest you find some shelter."

"Can we stay here?" Sam asked, hopefully.

"Unfortunately, you can't. It's an insurance thing, and my boss would kill me if I left anyone here overnight."

"Thanks for letting us stay here for a bit." Tom nodded at the young man, pushing through the door to step into the cold, intensifying rain.

"No problem." Jerry turned and pressed the doors shut, locking them with his keys before dropping the storm shutters on those.

"I'm guessing you don't have a spare motorcycle around here somewhere?" Tom chuckled grimly, voice raised into the wind. "We asked around, but no one else was willing to give us a ride out."

"I wish I could give you a ride. I'm really, really sorry." he replied, gesturing with his helmet toward a motorcycle sitting in the last parking spot. A gust of howling wind tore through the lot, pushing them around, whipping debris across the parking lot, rippling standing puddles, blasting water everywhere.

"It's starting to get pretty crazy out here," Samantha said, voice creeping upward in a strained note as Jerry threw his leg over the motorcycle, preparing to take off.

"Hey, wait," Tom called out. "What about that over there? Can we stay inside it?"

The attendant buckled his helmet over his head but spared a glance at a medium-sized RV sitting on the side of the lot. "That thing? Someone left it there a week ago and never came back for it." He stared at it, head tilting, lips pursed. "I guess that'd be safer than standing out in the open. I'd say go for it. I won't say a word to anyone about it."

With a hurried glance toward the ocean, Jerry put his riding gloves on and turned the ignition on his bike, raising up and throwing his weight down on the kick starter. The medium-sized, 400cc engine roared to life, spitting fire from its exhaust, smoke clouding up and passing through the pelting rain. The throttle revved, the bike backed up, and fell off its kickstand.

The McKnights backed away, giving him plenty of space to turn around. Jerry flashed a hesitant smile and wave, settling onto the seat, revving the engine while releasing the clutch. The back tire peeled out on the wet pavement before catching and shooting the bike toward the other side of the parking lot before bending south along the main street, speeding off with the high clatter of piston noise and puff of exhaust.

The wind hit Tom and Sam in a screaming gust that caught Tom's pack and spun him a little. It howled, whipped, and slapped at them, threatening to rip their makeshift ponchos right off. The material was already in tatters, barely held together by tape, and the wind chill cut straight through to the bone.

"We're not seriously staying out here all night, are we?" Sam clung to her father's arm like was an anchor. Tom stared at the RV where it rested near the dumpster. It was in good shape with a rounded roof, beige in color with brown trim, the driver's cabin connected to the sleeper unit.

"No, we're not." Stalking across the lot to the trailer, he pounded on the door and shouted above the wind. "Hello! Anyone home? Hello!" He tried again and again, but no one answered. The wind flung fatter droplets of rain at them, sweeping the pavement in sheets, flying in sideways, soaking through their clothes as lightning flashed overhead, illuminating the old RV in vivid hot light.

"I don't think anyone's home," Sam shouted, almost pleading.

"Okay. Okay." He reached out and tried the doorknob but it refused to give, locked from the inside. Removing his backpack he handed it to Sam, gesturing for her to stand back. A pained and reluctant grimace crossed his face before he backed up and slammed his shoulder against the door near the latch, trying to break it. Twice more he tried, each time the door bowing inward a little more, the flimsy lock cracking as it weakened. Finally, he gripped the handle and turned the knob hard, snapping it, allowing him to jerk the door open.

Tom ushered Sam inside and followed behind her up two stairs to stand in the RV's small kitchen, pulling the door shut behind them. To his right was the open door to the driver's cab, the factory seats worn with age, a sleeper bed above them. A kitchen table and bench seats sat against the opposite wall.

The latch on the door still caught, but barely, and he grabbed his pack from Sam, digging out a flashlight and lifting it in his left hand. From his pocket, he removed his titanium pen, holding it in a tight grip in his right hand as his eyes scoured the inside of the RV. The pen was a keepsake gift from Barbara from years ago. When he worked on government jobs, he'd never been able to carry a weapon for protection, but thanks to some contracting work in the past, a self-defense specialist had given him a crash course in how to use a blunt tactical pen to great effect.

"Follow me," Tom whispered to Sam.

Flashlight in hand, he flipped it on and shined it around, the beam playing over the old cracked counter top, the faded cabinets, the stained vinyl flooring and water-stained ceiling. Sheets of rain bore down harder, hissing in waves against the RV's roof, the faint hint of rotting food, salt spray and fresh rain poking at his nostrils. Shoulders tense, he moved farther into the small kitchen section, sweeping the light around, peeking in the open cabinets sparsely filled with plates, bowls, and silverware. The sink was full of dirty dishes, a box of cereal spilled across the counter and the refrigerator lay half open, the flashlight beam revealing plates of rotting food covered with plastic wrap, fetid cheese on the middle shelf, bottles of half-consumed fruit juice at the top.

"Yikes." Tom wrinkled his nose, shutting the door and sliding the latch shut before shining the flashlight down at the kitchen floor where reddish stains marred the vinyl.

"Are those bloodstains?" Sam asked, stepping back.

"I don't think so," he replied. "It looks like someone spilled juice or something. It's just a messy old camper." He gave her a quick wink. "I don't think anyone was murdered here."

They moved toward the back of the RV, sliding past the wardrobe and storage and into the main sleeper section. The previous owners had left the bed folded down, half-made, with a faint odor coming from the unwashed sheets. Tom didn't see any pictures, clothes, shoes, or even a travel bag, but a set of drawers sat recessed into the wall, half open with a few random bits and bobs he couldn't make out. Turning to Sam, he pressed toward the front, the door flying open in the face of a sudden gust of wind that had tugged it off the half-broken latch.

"See if you can keep the door handle closed. Look for a bungee cable, string or something."

"Okay."

Tom strode all the way to the front where the rain washed down the windows in thick layers, making it impossible to see. He sat in the driver's seat and looked around the center console. Popping the lid on one compartment, he rifled through the RV manual, insurance cards, and an invoice. He held the latter up and skimmed it, calling back to Sam. "Hey, I think this is a rental. And whoever had it was behind on their rental payments."

"Is that why they abandoned it here?"

"I'm guessing yes. They didn't want to catch up on the payments." He dug further beneath the papers and found a set of keys inside. With a grin, he held them up and jangled what appeared to be a side door key, a utility box key, and an ignition key, held together on a small key chain with the rental company's logo. Sam poked her head into the cab area with a wide-eyed, dubious expression.

"Are those the keys to the RV?"

"I think so." Tom held the ignition key between his fingers and stuck it in the slot. He gave it a half turn, and the dashboard lights came on, the gas gauge showing it was still half-full. His grin widened and he slapped the steering wheel in excitement. "Looks like we have transportation."

"Let's go," Sam encouraged him. "We can just drive it right out of here."

Tom surveyed the outside as the rain poured down in sheets, lighting tearing across the sky, thunder rattling the windows, the high winds causing the RV to rock on its wheels. Flipping on the windshield wipers, he watched as the blades tossed the rain from side to side, the sheets pouring down faster than they could be wiped clean.

"It's too late to drive out of here now," he shook his head. "Visibility is next to nothing, and if the wind hits us the wrong way, it could send us toppling right over. We should hunker down for a while, try to wait for the storm to let up a bit so we can drive out of here safely." Tom leaned forward, trying to see out toward the water. "We should be safe from any flooding; whoever built this place put it pretty high up. I'll pull over back behind the store. The brick walls should give us some protection and it's even higher up back there. When the storm dies down, we'll drive farther inland. Sound good?"

"Better than nothing, I guess." Samantha shrugged. "But yeah, sounds good."

Tom turned the key fully and the RV started with a clatter, the frame vibrating for a few seconds before it settled into a relatively smooth idle. He drove it over to the north side of the gas station to protect them from the brutal southerly winds, though he still parked several yards away to avoid damage should the building collapse. There was a noticeable reduction in how hard the RV rocked once he got it situated, though he had to admit that it wasn't the most desirable way to ride out a hurricane. Vehicle in park, he turned it off and climbed back into the kitchen to join Sam where she'd just finished fastening the door shut with some shoestrings retrieved from one of the drawers in the bedroom section.

"Great find," Tom said appreciatively, flipping on the primary light switch, being rewarded with a comforting soft glow from a ceiling fixture. "And we have electric!"

"Not bad!" Sam smiled, her eyes looking taking on a sea green color in the light. "Now let's check out the sleeping digs."

Tom grabbed his pack and followed her to the back of the vehicle, flipping on another light, watching as Sam circled around, testing the mattress and sheets. Dust motes floated up into the air, and the musty scent of mildew and body odor blossomed around them.

"Gross." Sam grimaced as she dusted off her hands. "I don't think I want to sleep on those."

"That coming from the girl who slept a night on the open sea."

Sam put her hands on her hips and fixed her father with a mock glare. "It's not like I had a choice."

"I could have thrown you overboard," Tom murmured, grinning as he turned away.

"I heard that," Sam replied.

"Heard what?" He placed his pack on the floor and began opening drawers. In the middle one he found a set of fresh pillowcases, sheets, and even a light comforter. He turned and held them up for Sam. "What if we cover the bed in these? Should be okay, right?"

"Yeah, those are much better."

Tom threw her the pillowcases while he placed a blanket over the musty sheets. He sat on the edge of the bed and took off his shoes, peeling off his soggy socks with a grimace. "Oh, boy," he said, staring down at his pruned feet. They'd been soaking wet for almost a full day between the ocean waves and the rain, and the cool air on his feet felt wondrous.

"Gross," Sam said from the other side. "My feet look like raisins, too."

Tom chuckled, heading to the bathroom, giving the door a gentle tug to open it. He flipped on the light switch to see a foot pedal operated toilet with a roll of toilet paper sitting on the tank. With his foot, he pressed the foot pedal halfway down and grinned when water filled the bowl, then he pressed the pedal to the floor to flush it.

"We have a working toilet!"

"Yay!" Sam called from the other room.

He unlatched the shower and pulled it open. The vinyl floor was stained but appeared clean. "We've got a shower, too. It might be useful to wash the salt water and grit off our skin."

"Awesome!"

Tom rinsed off his arms, head and feet, then returned to the bedroom to find Sam stretched out on the far side of the bed against the wall, her socks and shoes cast aside and her pants rolled up to her knees. Eyes shut, she breathed deeply with her hands folded across her stomach, already fast asleep beneath the constant thrum of rainfall.

Tom picked up the second clean blanket, shook it out and spread it over the bed, going around to tuck his daughter in. A solemn weariness settled onto his shoulders as he picked up their socks and shoes and took them into the bathroom to hang them from the towel racks. Searching through the bathroom cabinets, he found a pair of towels to dry off his feet, wrapping them up before lying back on the bed. After turning all the lights out, Tom reached into his pack and pulled out some snacks, then he settled back against the headboard, munching on jerky, sipping bottled water. The window above his head resonated with the pattering rain, wind tossing it into the glass like a ship on a choppy sea. They were still in danger – a lot of it – but they were still safer than they had been on the open ocean. The wind could get nastier, the winds more brutal, but it would take a lot more to blow them over. If they were lucky, the brunt of the storm would blow over during the night and they could drive away in the morning, finally heading for home.

Chapter 19
Barbara McKnight
Wyndale, Virginia

A familiar buzzing woke Barbara, the incessant sound she'd grown to dread, always filling her with hope at first, but inevitably crushing her with disappointment when it wasn't Tom calling to say that he was almost home. She slid her hand across the sheet and picked up the device where it lay next to her, dragging it closer, a light rain falling outside, drizzling against the window in a light pattering of noise and wind, threatening to put her back to sleep.

The notifications had been silent for almost thirty-six hours, leaving her wondering if she'd ever hear from Tom or her daughter again. She'd saved her tears for those grim moments just before sleep when her loneliness grew deep, and memories of better times haunted her, wanting to protect Jack and Linda from the deep pit of emotions.

Holding the phone in front of her face, she saw it was 2:13 a.m. She swiped the screen with her thumb to load the news notifications drop-down, which showed a string of news items from national and local sources, many of them earlier stories that hadn't made it to her through the slow-moving web.

"Must be some big news," she murmured. "I wouldn't be surprised if someone said the angels were trumpeting from Heaven at the rate things are going."

Scanning through the notifications, she saw nothing from Tom, but she read through the rest of the news items, only concerned if they offered any information about the health of her husband and daughter. Barbara had already tried the FEMA website, searching for Tom and Sam's name, finding nothing. One article in, and she wished she'd never even looked. The headline read, *Atlantic Problems Grow in Intensity*, with the sub-title, *Dozens of ships lost at sea!* She tapped on it to read more, but the news failed to load the article. *Big surprise.*

Backing up to the previous screen, she satisfied herself with reading only the headlines, piecing together the story from bits and pieces of information. In Miami and Myrtle Beach, there were reports of rising waters as high tides swamped beaches, restaurants, and communities. New York reported the same, with the Lower Bay pushing over beaches and driving people inland to safety. Panic was growing along the Mid-Eastern Seaboard as communities braced for an incoming hurricane set to make landfall in the next few hours.

Every state along the US East Coast joined Florida and South Carolina in activating their National Guard units, moving in to coordinate with and assist FEMA and local authorities as they worked to rescue and care for the displaced. There were reports from cities both large and small of people rushing to stores, local chains reporting low supplies of toilet paper, frozen goods, pasta, canned goods and, of course, water.

Multiple headlines told of people walking out of grocery stores with carts full of groceries and not paying for them, confrontations erupting into fist fights and arrests and even a shooting in Virginia Beach that had left one man dead and a child critically wounded. Barbara shook her head, sighing sadly. A hurricane would bring out the best – and worst – in people under normal circumstances. But the hurricane combined with rising waters and the mysterious 'anomaly' in the North Atlantic were a step too far, it seemed.

The situation would bring out the best in people, or the worst, and though Barbara hoped to see more of the former, it was apparent that the worst was winning out by a landslide. She shook her head and placed her phone face down on the bed, already tired of the reports, each day more worrisome than the last. Nothing mattered except locating her husband and daughter, knowing that they were okay and seeing them again. All she cared about – all she needed – was a message from Tom.

Barbara squeezed her eyes shut and tried to put the news behind her, trying to think of good things, like the day she and Tom had purchased the property. Back then, it had been a dilapidated farmstead, the original barn and several other unidentifiable structures laying in ruin. They'd used an excavator to tear it all down and called in a massive truck to haul it all away. She smiled in remembrance of the day they'd poured the home's foundation. She'd been pregnant with Samantha at the time, and they'd been staying at a local motel while the property got built. Tom had just joined Maniford Aquatics Engineering and was working for next to nothing while the business grew. It had been a precarious time, but despite the uncertainty, those had been the days of planning and dreaming, of promises of financial freedom, of breaking away from the grid. Those were the days held together with strong threads of love, devotion, and a sense of duty to one another.

When the house was finished, and Samantha popped out like an angel, their uncertainty had blossomed into joy. Barbara smiled through tears, turning over, pulling the covers tight to her chin. Their room stood in the stillness, a small desk fan circulating air. She needed sleep. The farm – the *kids* – depended on her to be at her best. Yet, try as she might to banish them, her head was filled with waking thoughts. Even the pleasant ones stirred emotions inside her, nagging her awake. At some point, after tossing and turning back and forth, she realized sleep was impossible, threw the covers off and got up.

Sliding into her slippers, she shuffled to the bathroom and relieved herself, then got a drink of water from the tap and stood in front of the mirror with a sigh. She caught sight of her bleary green eyes in the glass, her sandy hair hanging loose on her shoulders. She didn't look so tough, standing there; in fact, she looked frail and just a little bit frightened.

"Not the Amazonian warrior queen you've always aspired to be," she smirked and exited the bathroom, crossing to the window where she fell into a wide, comfortable rocking chair. It was her "sleepy chair," its seat and arms covered with blankets and coverlets. She sometimes had coffee in it, or read a book while gazing out over the southern field where the sheep and donkeys grazed. The darkness and rain hid everything, the porch light barely chasing back the darkness. Barbara contented herself with watching the rain patterns trickle down the window in glistening drops, dreaming of what Tom and Sam might be doing, how they were undoubtedly making their way home, and what Tom would say about all the work she and the kids had gotten done while they were gone.

A flash of lightning popped off, brightening the droplets as they followed distinct paths, gathering into globules of moisture before streaking to the bottom of the pane. Barbara's thoughts drifted, limbs heavy and lethargic, yet her brain refused to let her fall asleep. Tomorrow would be a nightmare, but she couldn't take a sick day, not on a farm when so many animals depended on her for their very survival, and certainly not in the midst of a brewing storm that felt more ominous than any she had faced before. There had been plenty of natural and man-made disasters in her lifetime, and even though she couldn't pin down why the 'anomaly' seemed different, she could feel that it was, deep in her gut. *We need to be ready, no matter what.*

She continued staring at the rain as it pattered against the window and trickled down, down, down.

Chapter 20
Tom McKnight
Outer Banks, North Carolina

Early morning light broke through the curtain of rain, passing through in fractals of light, casting the inside of the trailer in a sheen of gray. The RV creaked and tilted on its springs in the gusting wind, the thinly framed walls bent and stretched to their limits as they groaned, wind and water pitching against the glass.

Tom watched the ceiling warily, half expecting the roof to rip off and fly away like something out of the Wizard of Oz. He hadn't slept well except for a few fifteen-minute spurts, the storm waking him up every few minutes with cracks of lightning and the snapping of branches, pieces of roofing, siding or branches smacking against the RV's sides and roof, rattling and rolling off in clatters of noise. Prolonged blasts of wind had whistled over them like a tornado, sometimes dying down for a minute or two before picking up again, and just when he'd started to fall asleep, a snapping tree branch or piece of debris would hit the vehicle and jolt him awake.

He'd closed his eyes against the battering storm with his fists clenched in his lap, ready to protect Sam – who had slept through the entire thing without a care – at the first sign things were going south. If the RV became compromised, they'd leave it and make a run for the store where he'd somehow tear off a storm shutter and get them inside behind the brick-and-mortar walls. Halfway through the night, Tom had given up on sleep and paced the trailer, checking the blinds, peering out into the storm in case someone tried to barge their way in like they themselves had done. He'd finally settled into the RV's driver's seat, charging his phone off the RV's ample batteries, though the signal remained weak and he still couldn't get any sort of connection. Sipping bottled water and chewing on an energy bar, he tried the radio, but the AM signal sounded like white noise in the storm's interference.

The floor creaked behind him, and Tom turned to see Sam standing in her bare feet with the comforter hanging off her shoulders, watching the storm raging around them.

"I can't believe I slept through all this."

"Have some breakfast with your dad?" Tom offered, gesturing to the passenger seat.

"I *am* hungry," Sam agreed. She bent to their packs and pulled out a bag of chips and bottled water before joining him in the cab, plopping into the passenger seat.

"You must have been super exhausted," he said. "It was a long night at sea."

"I can't believe I spent an entire night at sea, too. Wait till Sandy hears about this. How's the phone signal?"

"Still rotten. My phone is charged to one hundred percent, but I can't reach anyone." He gestured at the dashboard radio. "And the radio signal sounds like scrambled eggs."

"Mm. Scrambled eggs. That sounds great."

"Yeah, it does," Tom agreed with a chuckle. "With sausage and biscuits."

"And sausage gravy."

"And pancakes."

"And Chilean Sea Bass—"

"Not again," he scoffed with a slow shake of his head.

Sam shot him a quirky smile and turned to gaze out the front windshield. "So, what now? Are we leaving?"

Tom squinted into the hard-slamming rain. "Well, there's almost enough visibility to drive by, but we'd have to take it slow. The storm's let up a *tad* but we'll still have to take it easy. I was thinking we could try to head inland and find a car rental place. It's only another four hundred miles to get home. We can drive that in a few hours."

"Let's just drive the RV home. You said yourself that the person who abandoned it was late on their payments. No one's going to miss this old piece of junk."

He made a pained face. "I'm not too keen on holding on to this. It's not ours, and we didn't pay to use it. The rental company might have even listed it as stolen. If we get pulled over trying to get home in it, you might see your old man heading to jail. And I'll wager they've declared the area in an official state of emergency which means the penalties will be that much harsher for anyone caught looting or stealing."

"Okay. I can understand that."

Tom dusted his hands off and stood. "Still, we might be stuck in here another day, so we might as well clean out the refrigerator."

"Seriously?"

"It could be a smelly ride, especially if the fridge pops open."

Sam's nose wrinkled at the faintly repulsive odor hanging in the air. Despite the door being shut, some of the smell had escaped from a small leak or broken seal in the unit.

She relented with a groan, then stood. "Okay, fine. Let's get it over with."

"It'll be like ripping a bandaid off."

They found plastic bags beneath the sink, and Tom grabbed a piece of paper to cup in his palm as a makeshift glove. Spreading the mouth of a bag opened, he swiped the spilled cereal off the counter and into it before moving to the dreaded refrigerator. Sam opened the door and held the bag open while Tom grabbed out the items and tossed them inside.

He let the rotten meat slide off the plate and drop into the bag before taking a second glance at the brown meat juice running down the plate and dropping it in, too. Next went a bag of moldy carrots, a small tub of butter, and the packs of fuzzy cheese. Following that were two bottles of old fruit juice, two bottled waters which neither had been brave enough to sample, and some assorted plates of unrecognizable food items. Sam made a face every time he dropped something in, and she practically crawled out of her skin if anything touched her through the bag.

"Don't be such a baby," he chuckled. "It's just rotten food."

"It's just so gross. Floating on a boat on the ocean was hard, but at least it didn't smell so bad."

Tom's mind staggered at the sixteen-year-old's logic. "You… you realize that you do a *lot* more gross stuff on the farm, right? What with cleaning pens and all."

She tilted her head. "Well, that's true. I hadn't thought of that."

"See, it's all in your head."

He took the bag from her and pulled the drawstrings tight, crossing to the side door and peering out the window. The wind and rain were a whipping cyclone, though he figured he'd be able to get to the dumpster with little trouble if he kept his head down. After fetching his shoes and still slightly soggy socks from the bathroom, he sat on the bench seat at the kitchen table and put them on.

"When I go outside, make sure the door stays shut," he said.

Sam nodded and stood right behind him, ready.

Unwinding the string from the doorknob, he turned the latch and pushed his shoulder against the door. It came open, but the wind shoved it right back with a spray of water. Growling, he pushed again, and the door came open enough for him to slip through, the wind blasting him, whipping the door in the other direction, dragging him outside with his hand still on the latch. Arm jerked stiff, he staggered and lurched forward, Sam yelping in surprise as rain blew into the RV in a gale.

With a lurch, he pulled the door hard in the other direction, knee stuck behind it, using his body weight to shut it against the wind. Reeling, Tom threw all his weight behind the door, teeth clenched as he slammed it in place. He turned back to the storm, head down, trudging through the pounding rain, the garbage bag full of rotten food being thrown around in his hand. He made his way across the front of the store to the dumpster and lifted the lid, tossing the bag inside before staggering back toward shelter.

As he passed the store, arm thrown up in front of his face to protect from flying debris, he noted Jerry's motorcycle wasn't where it had been parked the previous night, though the store hours written on the glass said they should be open. Still, he doubted anyone, including Jerry, would be back any time soon. If Tom had guessed right and there was in fact a state of emergency, it might not be legal to return until the crisis had passed. *Hope that kid made it home safe.*

The storm smacked him around as he angled toward the RV, the howling winds throwing debris everywhere, shingles, tree limbs and trash cutting the air like flying scythes. Ducking, he rushed forward and opened the door just wide enough to slip inside. Sam stood with some extra towels she'd found, tossing one to him and wiped up the puddles that had formed on the kitchen floor. As he dried off his head, he turned and re-latched the door handle and secured it with the shoelaces, clothes dripping on the floor.

"Okay, I'm ready to get driving," he said, shaking off a chill and hopping into the driver's seat, Sam joining him on the passenger side. With a turn of the key the RV started and Tom started up the defroster, waiting for the fog on the windows to dry as the wipers struggled against the onslaught. Heat from up over the dashboard brushed over his cheeks, and his eyes drifted shut, sleep tugging at them as he enjoyed a moment of relevant calm. Shaking himself free of the stupor, he released the emergency brake, put the vehicle into drive, and did a circle in the parking lot, pulling onto the main road and taking a left.

Moving north, the RV's tires cut through sheets of water blowing across the pavement while off to the right he watched the sea pouring over the dunes more ferociously than the night before, grasping and greedy ocean fingers reaching their tendrils onto land, moving around what they could not destroy. The water reached all the way to the road, stretching for their tires, washing sand in front of them, forcing Tom to stay all the way to the left or get caught up in it.

"It looks like the flooding is getting worse," Sam said, staring at the pavement cast in the headlights' gleams as Tom shook his head in dismay. "Or is it more because of the storm?"

"I was just wondering that myself. It's probably a little of both."

"And you mentioned there might be other ramifications, right? From the desalination of the water?"

"Did I say that?"

"You hinted at it."

Tom turned the wheel slowly, eyes flicking back and forth, careful to avoid being washed off the road. "I had been thinking about the fish being driven out of their feeding grounds and the rise in sea levels. But…" His words trailed off with the possibilities.

"Yeah?"

Tom shook his head again. "It's pretty complicated, and I don't want to speculate too much."

"Dad, come on. It's me, not some stranger."

"Well, when pollution or chemicals get into the oceans and rivers, it can cause over-salinity—too much salt in the water. It can be as bad as too little salt."

"Kind of like what's happened with the fish being driven away?"

"That's right. In fact, pollution has gotten so bad in places, they've had to set up desalination plants to keep the water balanced for local fish populations, and for drinking. They're even talking about desalinating ocean water for use for drinking."

"Seems like we'd have an endless supply of water, right?"

"You'd think so," Tom nodded, hands gripping the top of the wheel as he steered them through a massive puddle, spraying water off to the sides in high arcs. "But doing that to the oceans could have an enormous negative impact on them. I mean, it would take desalination on a scale we've never seen before, but some of the plans I've seen from other countries make me wonder if it's not so far-fetched as some people seem to think. And, if it were to happen on a large enough scale, the destruction of micro-organisms vital to biodiversity could—"

"Wipe out the base layer in the food chain, causing a chain reaction of effects that would spread all the way up to the top." She hesitated for a moment. "Us."

He smiled. "Smart girl."

Sam fixed him with a hard look, her eyes roaming his face as she watched the wheels turn inside his head, the same sort of look Barbara gave him when she was digging for information. "So, could there be something *worse* than the long-term destruction to the base food chain?"

Tom nodded slowly, eyes narrowing at the road. "Yeah, I'm thinking more about the…" His thoughts drifted off as he caught sight of something laying off the right side of the road, half-buried in six inches of churning sand and water. "Is… is that Jerry's motorcycle?!"

Sam followed his gaze, and she gasped, pointing and shouting at the sight of a figure curled up near a cluster of rocks fifteen yards further along, off of the road, on their side of a large sand dune. "Yeah, and that's Jerry!"

Chapter 21
Barbara McKnight
Wyndale, Virginia

Despite a long night and almost no sleep, Barbara had attacked the day with a voracity and energy she hadn't expected. After pounding enough coffee to reanimate a corpse, she'd gotten the kids moving and the chores done in record time, tending to the animals and fixing a few spots in the fences she and Linda had tagged as needing attention.

Once they were done, they'd moved back inside, turning the kitchen into a mess of canning equipment, and by the time afternoon arrived she'd already preserved over a dozen jars of tomatoes and beets and was drying out potato slices to make dehydrated potato flakes. After cleaning up, she'd had enough time to start an early dinner and then put the kids upstairs to get cleaned up and finish some schoolwork.

That had been almost an hour ago, and at the rate she was going, dinner would be done just before four thirty. She'd given up on obsessively checking her phone for a message from Tom, opting to stay busy and occupied so she wouldn't dwell on the horrible, looming possibility that tugged at the back of her mind every time she caught sight of the device. Grabbing an oven mitt and pulling open the oven door, the savory flavors of another perfectly-seasoned roast washed over her. She reached in with a long spoon, unwrapped aluminum foil from the top of the pan, pushed aside some carrots and potatoes at the bottom of the pan, pouring juice over the meat.

Her plans for the evening were to give the kids an early dinner and get them back on a bit more schoolwork, hoping to get back to some sense of normalcy. Then, once they were fed and occupied, she figured she would can food until she collapsed into bed around nine or ten o'clock, hoping the physical labor would help her fall into a deep, dreamless sleep.

With everything in the kitchen set, Barbara poured herself yet another cup of coffee, unwilling to let the inevitable crash hit her. Leaning against the kitchen counter, she rolled her weary shoulders, releasing a sigh. Her entire body felt claustrophobic, tired, pent up, agitated, and alert at the same time. It was from lack of sleep and she was no stranger to the feeling, having been there many times before working double and triple shifts to make ends meet before she'd found Tom, so she could deal with it again. All it took was a little focus.

And maybe a little air.

Barbara strolled through the kitchen, turning down the hallway to the front door. As she stepped outside, an older model Oldsmobile caught her eye as it drove slowly down the road, moving eastbound. It was a worn shade of forest green but for a gray front panel and bumper and she idly watched it move, expecting it to continue up the road. Instead, it slowed down near their front gate at the end of the driveway, coming to a shuddering stop, puttering and rumbling as it belched out blue smoke from the exhaust.

With her hand still lingering on the door handle, she squinted and tried to make out the figures inside. It was too great a distance to tell for sure, the gray sunlight glinting off the window glass, making it impossible to see inside. Her eyes moved away from the car and settled on their crop field over to her right. The people in the car had to see the fresh-cut corn stalks, the wheelbarrows, the sacks and tools still lying around. She silently cursed herself for not cleaning up as the handful of sheep out front went about their grazing, the donkeys lifting their heads in vague curiosity as the car's engine backfired with more smoke.

Where the hell is Smooch? Barbara glanced around as the car idled raggedly, clinking like it needed an oil change and a tune up. After a full two minutes of them sitting there, Barbara stepped to the porch edge to make herself more visible, placing her cup on a nearby table, hand resting on her Shield. A split second later, the Oldsmobile tore off in a squeal of tires, dust, and bluish smoke, motoring on down the road. She stared after them until she heard children's voices coming around the side of the house and down the driveway. Barbara leapt off the porch and craned her neck to catch Linda and Jack walking around the house, skipping and talking and laughing.

"Hey!" She snapped, the sound of her voice like a whip crack, the kids stopping mid-stride, heads turning toward her, eyes like saucers at the sound of her voice. "What are you doing out here?" She waved them toward the porch. When they walked toward her, half-strolling in their confusion, she hissed, "I said get your butts over here!"

They broke into a run toward the front porch, and Barbara waved them inside. "You should be upstairs, studying!"

"We got done with our work." Linda glanced worriedly over her shoulder as she high-tailed it through the front door, followed closely by Jack. She crouched next to them, her eyes moving back and forth between her two children, making them aware how serious the situation was. "There was a car out there, and the people inside saw you guys!"

Both kids glanced toward the door, then back at Barbara.

"Was it the one going away?" Jack asked, making a waving gesture with his hand.

"Yes! It sat in front of the house for two minutes. The people inside spotted the sheep and donkeys, and they saw that we'd just harvested some crops, too." She blew out a self-depreciating sigh. "It's my fault. I should have brought the animals around back two days ago, and we should have cleaned up after the harvest."

"We were working so hard though." Linda's voice was almost a whine. "We're not Superman. Supermen? Superpeople!"

"We can't use that as an excuse. And where in the world is Smooch?"

"She was fussing with the chickens, so we put her on her chain."

Barbara folded her arms across her chest and stared at her daughter, her jaw working overtime as she tried to control her response.

"Was that wrong?"

"Look…" Barbara started to speak but shook her head at herself, pausing to check her temper until the combination of motherly fear and anger faded. "Let's go over a few rules. Rule number one. Never lock up Smooch. If she's fussing with the chickens, come get me and I'll set her straight. We need her to keep watch in the yard. Rule two. You two can't go outside alone anymore. You ask me first if you want to step foot outside."

"Why?" Jack asked.

"Because people are about to go crazy?" Linda answered for her.

"That's right," Barbara forced a smile. "You remember what we've been talking about? About people getting mad and desperate when the supplies start running out?"

She nodded. "Yes."

"Well, I think it might be starting to happen soon."

"But it hasn't been on the news," Linda said, looking sheepishly at the floor. "I know you told me not to look at the news because it would scare me, but I checked last night...."

"Well, you didn't see the headlines this morning when I looked." She shook her head and inhaled, trying to dissipate the anxiety coursing through her. "Danger is brewing, I can feel it. The people in the car were scouting our property."

Jack's eyes watered, lip quivering. "Do they want to hurt us?"

Linda noticed her brother's distress, and she dropped an arm over her brother's shoulder to comfort him. "What can we do to help?"

Barbara's heated emotions faded like someone had dipped her in chilly water. Her kids were amazing, and they meant well, and it wasn't their fault Barbara hadn't been clearer about the dangers they faced.

"Excellent question." She smiled warmly at them, patting them both on the back. "Besides the rules I just gave you, I want you to start paying attention to things happening around the property when we're out doing chores. Keep an eye on the road and watch the trees and fields past the fences. Let me know if you see anything weird, okay? Strange cars, people, stuff like that. Can you do that?"

Both children nodded, and Barbara stood and guided them back to the kitchen, turning to sit in one of the chairs.

"Linda, why don't you get some tea for you and your brother?"

Jack watched his sister go to the cabinet and take out two glasses before he turned his face to Barbara as she pulled him close. "Are people going to hurt us?"

"I don't know if they'll hurt us, but they might want want some of our things. Maybe *all* of our things."

Linda got out a bottle of tea from the refrigerator. "Why can't we let them have some? I mean, we have so much. And we help people a lot, giving them things and even money sometimes. Why can't we do that here?"

"That's a tricky question," she replied, choosing her words carefully, hoping to avoid contradicting what she'd said and demonstrated in the past while also adequately explaining a unique situation to a pair of children. "Your father and I have always said to trust people until they give you a reason not to trust them. But times are changing right now, and we have to make sure we protect ourselves first and foremost."

Linda poured her brother a half glass of tea and brought it to the table, putting both glasses down before taking a sip of her own. "They have to give us a reason to trust them?"

"That's right," she replied. "They have to *earn* our trust first. Of course, we might help someone if they really need it, and if they ask nicely. But if they come onto our property without asking, without giving us a reason to trust them – and in doing that giving us a reason to *not* trust them – we can't help them. Do you understand, Jack?"

"I think so," he nodded thoughtfully. "That's why you want us to be on the lookout."

"Exactly." She put her fingers out and lifted his chin. "Can you do that for me? And ask my permission before you go outside each and every time?"

Jack nodded again as he swallowed down his tea and set the empty glass on the table. "I will, Mom. I promise."

"Okay, then. Go on upstairs and get cleaned up for dinner. It'll be ready in a little while."

"Do I have to get cleaned up?" Jack whined. "I just washed my hands a few minutes ago."

"Yes." She rubbed his cheek with her thumb, pinching it with a smile and a wink. "It takes you two seconds to get dirty. You've still got smudges on your face. Go on. Get cleaned up!"

Linda finished her tea and took both glasses to the counter, setting them in the washer before she headed back through the kitchen, following her brother. Barbara grabbed her arm gently, stopping her in her tracks, her daughter's face turned up. "Yeah, Mom?"

"I need you to watch your brother, okay?" Barbara whispered. "When we're out in the yard taking care of chores and even inside, too, if I'm not with him. Don't let him out of your sight."

Linda's eyes widened. "Are you scared, Mom?"

"Not scared, just… wary of strangers coming around the house. But we'll be fine if you help monitor your brother. I mean, you need to stay glued to his hip. You know how slippery he can be."

"You can count on me," Linda agreed, her eyes focused and sincere. "I'll watch that little booger like a hawk."

Barbara fought back unsuccessfully against a chortle, weariness melting away for the moment. "Thank you so much, Linda. I love you."

"Love you, too." The girl's voice lifted with a note of hope. "Want me to get cleaned up, too?"

"Yes, please."

Linda gave her mother a brief embrace and hurried across the hardwood floor. With the kids busy for a moment, Barbara stood and walked to the basement door, descending into their supply room and angling for the gun safes. Opening the one with the rifles and handguns, she grabbed two more .338 magazines and slid them into her pockets. She shut the safe and moved to the middle one which held their shotguns, grabbing the Benelli M2 semi-automatic already loaded with alternating shells of slug and buckshot, slinging it on her shoulder by its strap before shutting the safe and tromping back upstairs on weary feet. Down the hallway, she stepped back onto the front porch, glancing around the property, strolling over to retrieve her coffee cup. Mouth dry, she had a taste, the brew bitter and cold on her lips, sobering her to the dangerous reality they faced.

"So much for sitting on the porch and relaxing," she murmured, placing the coffee cup back down and stepping off the porch, moving around the right side of the house, around to the animal pens and wooden fence line. She traced the same path she and Linda had taken the other day, eyes gazing out at the other properties, eyes drifting into the woods beyond. She paid special attention where the trees pressed up against their fence, places that would provide good cover for anyone entering the property, and considered how much work it might take to clear it back before sighing in resignation. *Too much, at least for right now.*

Swinging across the backyard to Smooch's doghouse, she found the dog lying in the shade. On one knee, Barbara ruffled her fur and unclipped her chain. Smooch made a beeline for the chicken coop, but Barbara growled. "Nein, Smooch!" *No!* "Hier! Fuss!"

The Shepherd turned on a dime and loped back to her, wrapping around her legs to heel in perfect position at her right side, looking up and awaiting her next command. "Komm!"

The afternoon sun beat down as she strode deeper into the yard, marching along the dirt path, surrounded by woods with Smooch glued dutifully to her side. The sweet smells of pine and spruce drifted out of the woods, dirt and pollen a veritable musk riding on a soft breeze, the air cooling her sweaty brow. She continued the fence line patrol out past the barns, knees brushing through the tall grass. Beyond the woods, she walked from post to post, eyes sliding along the wooden rails, the posts all intact, still wrapped with vines and brush.

After forty-five minutes of checking she decided everything looked fine. There were no breaks in the fence or signs that anyone had been on the property and she started to head back to the house when the sound of a car engine reached her, the same unmistakable puttering rhythm that matched the vehicle from an hour ago. Head shaking in disbelief, Barbara walked swiftly along the fence line toward their driveway, half-jogging through the long grass and broken underbrush, leaping a dead tree branch and pumping her legs as her blood surged with a heady rush of adrenaline. Smooch sensed her tension, and the dog trotted at her side with her ears up and her nose pointed straight ahead. Reaching the top of the rise, Barbara moved past their second barn, then the fuel shed, peering down at the road with narrowed eyes. At the end of the driveway was the same green Oldsmobile, approaching from the direction it had last disappeared, its plume of noxious blue smoke belching into the air.

"Nein! Komm!" Barbara growled as Smooch started to take a few steps forward, and the Shepherd swung back toward her and trotted along her left side, keeping herself between the vehicle and her master. Barbara deftly swung her shotgun into a firing position and stalked past their cars and down their gravel driveway. Her boots carried her into the yard, coming even with the vehicle, turning with it as it curved back around in front of their property and slowed. The car was coated with rust spots around the edges of the door, hubcaps long lost, the front right tire an obvious donut spare.

Shotgun barrel lowered, eyes narrowed, cheeks flushing with the heat of anticipation of a potential confrontation, she strolled across the yard in clear view. The three men inside were dressed in ratty T-shirts, hands dirty as they gestured at each other inside the car, one man pointing toward the McKnight property. The man in the back was skinny with a mop of loose brown curls that fell over his eyes. When he caught sight of her his eyes flew wide with fear, hands slapping the seats in front of him to get his accomplices' attention. The other two men craned their heads to look, their faces exploding with surprise. The man in the passenger seat mouthed something and his eyes widened as he caught sight of the German Shepherd and Barbara's bold, shotgun-laden strides along with the scowl stitched across her face.

He pounded the dashboard with his hands, and the driver hit the gas, the car jerking forward in a snap of backfire, shooting off down the road with a sharp squeal of tires. Barbara and Smooch followed the car for another fifteen yards, making sure they saw her watching them until they curved out of sight. She stood there for a few minutes, nerves jangling, head buzzing with aggravation, breaths coming shallow and hard. No one cased a place twice without planning to raid and steal from it.

"Braver Hund, Smooch," Barbara said, giving the Shepherd a pat. *Good dog.* Her hands gripped the shotgun so tight they'd gone numb and she loosened it, allowing her shoulders to relax, clamping down on the anxiety bubbling up in her gut. Whoever they were, they wouldn't strike that evening, or the night after, but they'd undoubtedly come. They'd wait for an opportunity when the McKnight's had their guard down, when her family had a false sense of security, and when the puttering green Oldsmobile was a faint memory – or perhaps they'd be bolder and try to come sooner, expecting her to expect that they'd wait.

She walked over to the fields, placed her shotgun in a wheelbarrow, and began cleaning up the front yard. She kept Smooch close as she gathered the extra sacks and all the tools they'd left lying around, putting loose foliage into garbage bags and setting them in the second wheelbarrow. She glanced out at the road often, half-expecting the Oldsmobile to return.

Barbara had started working up a sweat and was about to push the wheelbarrows around back when a honk drew her attention. She snatched the shotgun up, turned, and stalked toward the road, easing up when she sighted the familiar red Jeep sitting at the end of the driveway. She jogged down to them with a smile on her face, recognizing her older neighbors who lived a couple miles down the road.

"Hey, Darren and Marie!" she called, slinging the rifle back onto her shoulder.

"Hello, Barbara!" Darren called out from the driver's seat while his wife waved vigorously, a big smile plastered on her face. "Hey, Smooch!"

The German Shepherd knew the Everetts, but not very well, her tail wagging ever so slightly as she stared at the older couple, staying glued to Barbara's side. The Everetts were in their sixties, Darren with a round, friendly face and a full head of gray hair on his head, parted on the side and neatly combed. Marie was a robust woman with a thick frame and a head of short-cropped, stylish gray hair, her complementing her husband perfectly and the other way around.

"How are you, Barb?" the woman asked with a beaming smile.

"Oh, boy, are you two a sight for sore eyes," Barbara said with an exhausted sigh, approaching the red Jeep and placing her hand on the door frame. "I'm good, how about you?"

"We're doing great, as always." Marie jerked her thumb back in the direction they'd come. "Just hunkered down at home after the emergency declaration. Can you believe everything that's happening?"

"It's crazy," Barbara nodded. "And Tom's not here, so I've got my hands full with the chores and my two youngest."

Marie's face dropped in concern. "Oh, really? Where's Tom gotten off to?"

She briefly told them about Tom being called off to his job, but kept things vague, not mentioning details beyond being unable to get a hold of him and hadn't spoken to him in a handful of days.

"That's too bad," Darren said. The man's thick mustache danced on his upper lip, giving his face a jolly appearance. "But I'm sure he'll be home soon. I can't imagine anyone can keep that man from getting anywhere he wants to be, and I'm certain he'd rather be home now where you need him."

Barbara nodded and gripped the door frame. "What are you guys doing out this way?"

"We wanted to check on *you* all, actually," Darren said.

"And we were going stir crazy in the house," Marie added. "It's getting tough to not go out and see what's going on, but we aren't about to check in on town, based on the things we've heard."

"You aren't wrong there. Actually, I'm glad you swung by." Barbara bit her lip and glanced to her right where the beat-up car had puttered off down the road. "We had a bit of a scare today. A beat-up green Oldsmobile passed by a couple times… I think they're casing the place. I scared them off, but just be aware they're out there."

"We've seen some trouble, too, on the TV" Darren said with a solemn nod. "I bet that Olds had people from Bristol or some other big city coming out to get their hands on some goods. We'll keep an eye out for them, don't you worry."

Marie winked and offered a perfect smile. "And you aren't the only one armed and ready, after all."

"Don't I know it!" Barbara laughed. "Well, check up as often as you like. In fact, you know what? Come stop over and have dinner with us tomorrow night. We just harvested a ton of fresh vegetables. We could all use some company, and the kids could stand to see some friendly faces. All they've seen is my surly mug the past week, and they're sick of it."

"I doubt that," Maria pooh-poohed her. She glanced at Darren before turning back. "And we'd love to come have dinner tomorrow with you all. Nothing like eating fresh harvest straight out of ground!"

"You got that right," Darren echoed.

"All right," Barbara tapped her hand on the door edge. "It's a date."

"Do we need to bring anything?"

"Up to you, but I think we'll have it all covered. And thank you!"

Darren put the Jeep into drive and pulled away as Barbara backed off. The Everetts waved as Darren swung the vehicle around and cruised back in the direction they'd come. She watched them go, grateful beyond measure they had such good neighbors nearby, certain that the dinner would be the start of an ongoing alliance. Anxiety calming, Barbara took a deep breath and let it out slowly, loosening her jaw, allowing her shoulders to sag before striding back to the field to finish packing up their tools, Smooch trotting along by her side.

Chapter 22
Military Central Command
Undisclosed Location

President John Zimmerman sits back in his chair at the head of the table and thumbs through a data packet he received from his key staffer, Maxine. Cool air blows down from an air duct in the ceiling, the ventilation drying the sheen of sweat on his forehead. Staffers move quietly about the room, distributing coffee and tea and late lunches on plates. The smells of cold cuts, French fries, and bacon fill the air as everyone eats a hurried meal while they work, talking around mouthfuls of food. Smaller tables fill the left side near the wall screens, small groups of scientists and military personnel whispering amongst themselves as they discuss and debate various scenarios.

The big screens still blink and flow with data, one showing the anomaly cracking the ocean floor like an open wound in the Earth's crust while another displays simulations of North Atlantic currents sweeping up from South America and along the United States Eastern Coast, stalling where they meet the anomaly, salt waters dissipating and moving around the fracture. There are wind current models next to them, along with a map of the Eastern Seaboard where a circular storm is landing near Norfolk, Virginia, its tendrils sweeping out to cover the land in rain and wind.

While all of those screens are important and hold valuable information, the President isn't concerned with them. He closes the report in front of him, and the others at the table follow suit. The once chipper faces are sour, their positive moods crushed. President Zimmerman stares off into space for a long moment, stunned with what he's read, unable to wrap his mind around the data summaries and what they could mean to the country.

Out of nowhere, baseball enters his mind. He vaguely remembers years past when a national crisis brought the sport to a halt for two full seasons, though they were able to start back up once it was over. Baseball has never been his favorite sport—he's a football man—but he watches enough to know what it means to the citizens of the United States and it's hard to imagine such simple pleasures going away forever. Concerts, 4th of July Parades, Christmas Festivals, speeches, rallies, and Rose Garden events – everything hangs upon the edge of a razor. If the data in the report is true, the entire world could have to say goodbye to anything that doesn't involve survival, and not just for a season or two.

His eyes fall upon Dr. Zeke Jarvis, the disheveled scientist who pushed them to quantify projected worst-case data from various crisis plans, cross-referencing aspects of said events with the worst-case possibilities from their current situation. The President wishes they could go back in time when they were blessedly ignorant of the truth, but they're at a point where they must address the problem set before them or face utter annihilation. He takes a long, slow breath, steadying himself for the inevitable.

"Dr. Jarvis, how certain are you that these estimates are correct?"

The scientist leans forward. "Nothing is one hundred percent accurate, sir. But based on these scenarios, and after including the extrapolated data from the anomaly, I'm eighty-seven percent certain this is the direction we're headed. Even if we're only fifty percent accurate, we're in for a very dark road ahead."

The president nods and looks to the rest of the logistical experts in the room. "You've seen the plans contained within this report. Do you agree with the suggestions, and does anyone have any thoughts on how we can execute something on this scale?" Phrases like 'extinction-level event,' 'mass migration,' and 'extraordinary death tolls' flash through the president's mind, ones sprinkled liberally throughout the report in a myriad of worst case scenarios and proposed, hypothetical solutions.

Roger Clark, the FEMA Administrator, speaks up. He's a tall, barrel-chested man with a crew cut and a pair of thick-rimmed glasses perch on his nose. He clears his throat and nods to start, giving off a military air of authority despite not being in uniform. "As Dr. Jarvis suggested, we created a preliminary strategy based on combining other emergency response strategies, trying to find synergies between them and the projected worst-cases from our current situation. This will make any disaster we've ever faced look like a walk in the park." Clark leans closer and removes his glasses, using his free hand to rub at his eyes. "Our first concern will be mass rioting, followed by food shortages."

"Not necessarily in that order," Dr. Jarvis interjects. "We'll need to be flexible and ready to alter direction at a second's notice. That will be critical to our survival."

"Survival. Not success?" The President queries.

Director Clark nods. "Survival, sir. We've already seen the first signs of rioting and food shortages in some cities along the East Coast and it will spread if it goes unchecked. The news agencies aren't making things any better – it'll be hard enough to keep peace and order without them riling people up. If we have to course correct at any point, the press will have a field day."

Heat flashed through the President's chest. He has a love-hate relationship with the press, acting as both his greatest ally and worst enemy at the same time. "Leave the press and public to us. You just worry about getting me the plans we need. Thanks." He looks around at the table, his gaze settling on his head assistant, Maxine. "I want to meet with all the governors and mayors listed on the Priority One call list."

"I'll get a conference call set up, sir," Maxine replies.

"No conference call," the president says. "I want them here, in Washington. Direct flights, and don't let them make any excuses. Tell them I'll have marines dragging them here in handcuffs if necessary. This is Code Red, Priority One. They need to know the seriousness of what's happening. Oh, and tell them to bring data related to their local resources. Fire departments, police, anything they have available on state, country, city or whatever levels. Those folks'll be the ones in the trenches executing the plans, and I want their input."

"Yes sir," Maxine says with a grim tone, her eyes dropping as she vigorously taps on a laptop in front of her.

The president turns to the others at the table. "Now, let's talk about how we can get our East Coast internet and cellular providers together and pull our communications infrastructure out of the dark ages before we're plunged right back into them."

Chapter 23

Tom McKnight
Outer Banks, North Carolina

Tom slowed the RV and squinted through the window through the pounding sheets of rain, streaks of wind-blown sand and bits of debris. The man lying on the side of the road was just a blur on the wet glass, the wipers futilely trying to sweep off sheets of water, though he could see him curled up in the brine and sand. It was impossible to make out his condition, how badly he was hurt or any other details about him, and Tom hesitated as he watched, silently willing him to get up or turn out to be some kind of optical illusion.

"Is he alive?" Sam asked impatiently, pulling against her seatbelt as she leaned forward, snapping Tom out of his stupor. "Are we going to get out and help?"

"I… I don't know."

His first inclination was to put the RV into park and rush to help the young man, though the storm was still strong against the side of the vehicle, rocking it, threatening to wash them out or blow them over. Out there alone, the wind could topple him and a storm surge could drag him through a cut in the dune where he'd quickly be drowned and lost forever. A piece of debris shot across the road and smacked off the front windshield with the speed of a fast-pitched baseball, and he shivered involuntarily as the thought of it smacking him in the skull flashed unbidden through his head.

"It doesn't seem like a great idea, but if that's the guy from the gas station…"

"I'm pretty sure it is," Sam said. "That *is* his motorcycle."

Despite the potential danger, Tom couldn't leave Jerry – or whoever it was – lying in the road. He gripped the steering wheel until his knuckles turned white, flicked on the RV's emergency blinkers and pulled to the left side of the road, far away from the briny waves and churning foam. As soon as they stopped, Sam jumped up and grabbed the side door handle, removing the shoelaces and popping it open, wind gusting though the crack, whistling and screaming, rain pouring in to sprinkle Tom where he sat three feet away.

"Wait!" he warned, leaping up, grabbing her arm and pulling her back with one hand while pulling the door closed with the other. "Nuh uh, kiddo. You stay here. I'll go get him."

"But, Dad, I can help! I can—"

"No," he said firmly. "Stay here."

Sam held the door for a moment but relented, backing up and sitting on the edge of her seat up front. "Okay. Fine. Just be careful. If you need me just wave your arms or something, okay?"

"I will," he gave her a smile. "Just hang out here, keep the door closed, and be ready to open it when I bring him inside."

"Will do."

Tom took a deep breath and threw open the side door to the storm's angry squalls. He stepped out, Samantha taking over control behind him, forcing the flimsy door shut as soon as he was clear of it so it didn't blow back and get torn off. He circled to the front of the RV, head up, arms covering his face, eyes focused on the other side of the road. The beach front homes in the distance had taken a beating, portions of their roofs missing, windows punched out by flying debris and debris sticking out of their sides at odd, impossible angles. Yards sat buried under feet of turbulent water, fingers of the salty sea foaming over the beachheads and sand banks to swirl in a briny swamp before retreating into the deep only to be pushed back in by wave after wave.

Tom stopped at the front of the RV, hunkered down against the idling vehicle, using it as protection as pieces of wood and tree branches skittered and rolled across the road. Hand resting on the hood, peering across at Jerry's prone form, trying to form a plan that would give him the best possible chance of emerging unscathed.

*Right… safety in **this** kind of weather? Oh, screw it.* With a deep breath of moist air and a shrugging off of his concerns, Tom left the RV's protection. Hunched down, feet spread for balance, he trudged across the street, angling for the immobile man. Rain sprayed him from every side, blowing upwards and from the sides, salt spray stinging his cheeks and neck. Both arms thrown up in front of him, he tried to protect his face, but he couldn't keep the water, salt and stinging sand out of his eyes no matter how hard he tried. Within twenty seconds, he was soaked through to the skin, shudders running through his limbs. Teeth clenched, feet dragging through six inches of rushing water, he pressed forward through the sand, ever closer, circumventing the motorcycle and angling toward the prone form up against the dune.

The body lay near a cluster of rocks, gray and black and jagged, covered in blowing sand, patches of seaweed scattered all around. Tom glanced between a pair of sand dunes at the vast ocean stretched out to his right, the invading waves charging a hundred yards inland between the mounds. Gray, frothy water surged across the sand, splashing over his shoes and halfway up his legs. When he came close to the body, he splashed out through the deeper water, reaching the prone form after a moment's struggle, realizing straight away it was Jerry based on the helmet, leather jacket, and motorcycle pants all being the same ones Jerry had on when he left the store the previous night.

A foot-high wave rushed in, smashing up against Jerry's form in a spray of water. The young man had clenched up, turned to the side and braced against the rock as the breaker splashed up his legs and frothed upward. It split around him before settling and drawing back sluggishly, the young man's position against the rocks keeping him from being swept away, and Tom got the impression he might have crawled there on purpose.

Coming closer, bending over, Tom reached out and touched Jerry's shoulder. "Jerry!" Tom shouted, his voice thin against the ravaging wind. "Hey, buddy! Are you okay?"

A part of him expected the man to be cold and stiff, dead and gone from injuries sustained in the wreck. But when Jerry groaned and uncurled himself, Tom grimaced with relief. Encouraged, he stepped closer and knelt next to him, gently rolling the young man backwards until he could see into the space where the helmet's visor used to be. Scuffs marked the man's forehead and cheeks, blood caked his mustache and nostrils and his lip was busted open and swollen, trembling in the cold. Worse, the young man's skin had a gray sheen to it and felt cold when Tom put the back of his hand to Jerry's cheek. His jaw chattered at the touch, eyelids fluttering, mouth moving but unable to form words. Tom figured Jerry must've been laying in the chilly waves for hours, and he was likely near the point of hypothermia – if not already well past it. Looking him over before moving him any further, Tom saw that the right arm had taken some nasty-looking damage, the leather sleeve shredded to reveal a rough-looking bloody scrape on his forearm and elbow. No bones were visibly sticking through the skin that he could tell, but out in the elements as they were, he couldn't be certain.

"Hey, man!" Tom shouted, and he reached inside his helmet to place his hand against the young man's cheek again. "Hey, buddy, are you okay?! Talk to me, Jerry!"

The gas station attendant murmured and groaned louder, eyes fluttering open, their color faded to a blanched shade of gray almost matching his skin. He tried to move his right arm, causing his face to twist into a grimace that stretched his busted lip. Jerry drew his wounded arm in closer to his body, voice somewhere between a hoarse whisper and a groan. "It hurts like hell."

"You must have taken a spill!" Tom said, voice raised above the storm. He adjusted the man so he lay on his back with his head elevated above the rushing waves, concern over drowning taking precedence over exacerbating any potential neck or spinal injuries. "Can you remember what happened?"

Jerry shivered, eyes fluttering, voice so thin Tom had to put his ear up next to Jerry's lips. "The wind was blowing hard, debris… everywhere. I was watching the waves coming up to the road, just… not… paying attention. Hit a slick spot… That's all I remember."

"The crash must have tossed you." Tom jerked his chin upward. "You probably hit the rocks. I think your arm is broken!"

Jerry nodded weakly and shut his eyes. "I woke up but… couldn't stand. So, I thought I'd just stay put and hope someone saw my motorcycle."

"Smart man," Tom grinned. "My daughter saw your motorcycle."

"I thought… thought you stayed in the RV?"

"It's a long story, and I'll tell you all about it when after we get you off this beach. How are your legs? Can you feel them? Can you move them?"

Jerry tightened his body, kicking out with his right leg, then his left. He wiggled his feet slightly, voice louder as he spoke. "My legs are sore, and my left ankle feels wrenched."

"Hang on!" Tom shouted, leaning over the man as another wave crashed in, spraying upward, rolling around them, then slowly receding. They weren't strong enough to be an actual problem – yet – but if they stayed where they were, the ocean would undoubtedly claim them. Once the wave receded, Tom put his face close. "Come on! Let's get you to your feet!"

He helped Jerry into a sitting position and turned him so his right side rested against the rocks. The man moved sluggishly, making Tom do most of the work.

"Brace yourself against the rock and push yourself up," Tom urged. "I'll get under your left arm and support you." When Jerry swiped lethargically at the rocks, struggling feebly, Tom shouted at him over the wind and rain, trying to push him to overcome his lethargy. "Come on, Jerry! I can't help you if you don't try! Do you want to die here?!"

The harsh note sparked something in the young man, and he leaned hard against Tom, using the rock as leverage, rising with a surge of energy, his knees wobbly, feet shifting in the sands. Another wave came in, smacking them in their knees and jostling them around and they leaned into it and against one another, their legs spread apart to anchor them.

"Steady as she goes!" Tom strained to bear the Jerry's weight as they left the safety of the rocks and worked their way back to the road. Jerry wasn't heavy by any means, but the weight of his saturated clothes and heavy motorcycle helmet – not to mention Tom's own soaking clothing – didn't help. Their feet sunk in the sand, wind hitting them like a prizefighter throwing unrelenting punches. To his credit, Jerry came more alive with every step, his legs growing steadier, still limping but moving with his rescuer. They reached the edge of the road, closer to safety, and Tom let out a grunt of relief as a pair of headlamps cut through the wall of rain and he squinted as the RV pulled toward them from the opposite curb, coasting up slowly, the glare from the headlights dousing them in light. An enormous grin broke out on Tom's face as the lumbering vehicle pulled to a stop next to them, his daughter's face peering at them from the driver's seat, obscured by the torrents of water spilling over the windshield.

"Sam!" Tom's voice was hoarse from all of his shouting at Jerry. "Door!"

Samantha hopped out from behind the wheel and jumped into the back, the side door flying open a few seconds later, smashing against the side of the RV. She stood with her hand thrown out, gripping the inside handle with her other hand to steady herself against the wind. Tom helped Jerry limp closer while Sam reached for him and together they helped Jerry hop up the two steps and then over to the kitchen table, where they turned him around and let him fall onto the seat.

"Good job." Tom shot his daughter an approving smile as he returned to the door and shut it behind him, throwing the shoestring loop around the handle to bolster it.

"No problem." Sam barely hid her pleased smile as they got Jerry better situated so he rested his wounded arm on the table. Seeing how wet they were, she started toward the back of the RV. "I'll grab some towels."

Tom stooped and tugged around the bottom edge of the helmet. With a slow pull he dragged the piece off in a shower of salt water and sand and placed it on the table.

"Thanks," Jerry said, sputtering and spitting, wiping his uninjured hand across his face, hair plastered to his forehead. Some color had returned to his face, though he was still pale, his shivering shaking his entire body top to bottom.

"No problem," Tom replied, putting the back of his hand to the man's cheek. "We need to get you warm, though."

Turning away, he went to the cab and cranked the heater to full blast, moving around the RV to ensure the vents were open and putting out warm air. Back at Jerry's side, he bent close. "We need to get your jacket off. Okay?"

Jerry nodded, gritting his teeth and held his left arm out, Tom grabbing the sleeve and tugging it off. He pushed Jerry forward and swept the jacket behind him, leaving only his injured right arm encased in ragged leather. He shifted to the other bench seat on the opposite side of the booth as Sam returned with some towels, exchanging a worried look before Tom turned his attention back to their guest and his wounded right arm.

"Can you lift it at all?"

Jerry shook his head, tears filling his eyes as he tried. "Hurts like hell, man."

"Looks like you've got some swelling along your wrist and arm. I'll have to cut the jacket off." He turned back to Samantha. "Can you grab the emergency first aid kit out of my pack? The one we got from the raft?" Sam nodded and stepped to their nearby packs, breaking one open, taking out a hardback-book-sized metal case with a medical cross stamped on top and plunking it on the table in front of him.

"Thanks." Tom opened the case to reveal a set of compartments filled with painkillers of various types, gauze, and antiseptic. A small drawer beneath the row of compartments held a small pair of scissors, forceps, and a needle and thread kept sealed in plastic. Tom broke open the scissor pack and began cutting at the leather jacket, delicately at first, starting at the cuff area and working his way upward. The scissors were remarkably sharp for their size, slicing through the thick leather with relative ease, and soon he'd gotten several inches through the tough material, all the way to the elbow. With a tug, he divided the material aside to reveal more of the wound, all three of them wincing at the sight. The skin on the inside of his arm was scraped in an angry pink mark like a burn and a seven-inch abrasion wound around his elbow in the shape of a lake. Near his wrist, deeper marks punctured his flesh, almost like a dog bite. It looked like he'd tried to break his fall on the rocks, smacking against them before sliding to the sand.

"That's—," Sam started to say, hand thrown over her mouth when Tom interrupted her.

"Going to be just fine." Tom flashed his daughter a quick shake of his head as he grabbed the saline rinse and sterile swab from the kit, Jerry too absorbed in groaning at the sight of his arm to notice the quick back and forth between Tom and his daughter. Tom cleared his throat and addressed Jerry directly.

"I'm not a doctor, but looks worse than it is, I think. You won't need stitches, and it doesn't *appear* fractured, but it is swollen, so I'd expect to see a crack or sprain on an x-ray." His gaze lowered. "Son, that must have been painful as hell lying there all night. Hats off to you for sticking it out."

"I try not to give up," Jerry replied, his teeth chattering as the first waves of warmth sunk into his body.

"I can tell." Tom smiled at him. "Brace yourself, alright? We'll get the jacket off and clean this up as best we can."

Jerry nodded as Tom began cutting off the rest of the jacket, removing the sleeve at the elbow before slipping it off his arm completely. He squirted saline on the sterile pad and cleaned around the still-open wounds, holding the injured arm steady as Jerry winced with the sting. Once he'd wiped away the dirt and grit, he applied an antiseptic cream followed by butterfly bandages to close the puncture wounds around his wrist. He finished it off by wrapping the arm in gauze followed by medical tape to create a soft pad of protection around it.

Jerry lifted his arm to test it out, raising it a few inches and wincing in pain before setting it on the table again. He shook his head. "I can't get it any higher than that."

"You might have a shoulder injury, too," Tom said, standing up. "Maybe even a slight fracture. Give me a second."

He moved to the back of the RV and cut a strip of material from a clean blanket with the scissors. Returning to the kitchen table, he used the strip of cloth to fashion a makeshift sling around the young man's neck. Together, he and Sam set the arm inside the sling, and Jerry relaxed back in his seat with his patched-up limb held close to his chest. "Keep this arm immobile, okay?"

"Thanks a lot," Jerry said, nodding. "I was starting to wonder if the tide would sweep me out. I thought I'd made it to a safe spot."

"The tide is rising by the hour," Tom said assuredly, "and it's cold, obviously. Another few minutes out there and you couldn't have crawled away if you tried."

Jerry shook his head and let out a sigh steeped in appreciation. He raised his eyes and looked around the vehicle, taking in the kitchen cupboards, counters, and cabin. "So… you did break into the RV?"

Tom's face turned red with slight embarrassment. "Not something I'm proud of, but yes. The phones were down, and the storm was getting worse. We broke in to keep ourselves safe and then found the rental papers suggesting the renter had abandoned it. The plan was to drive it farther inland where we could return it then rent a car to get home."

"You did what you had to do, and I don't blame you." Jerry gave a good-natured scoff, the color already returning to his face as the RV's heat took effect. "And hey, you never know, the rental place might give you a reward for returning this heap to them." Jerry continued, his voice taking on a reserved tone. "Anyway, I'm glad you showed up when you did. You saved my life. Thanks. I mean it."

"You're quite welcome," Samantha said primly.

"No problem," Tom added. "What should we do about your motorcycle?"

"There's no place to put it on the RV, and it's a beater, anyway." Jerry shrugged. "I doubt anyone will try to steal it in the storm and I doubt it'll get washed away where it is. But if you can get me up to Virginia Beach to my folks' house, they can help me pick it up once the storm passes. My dad has a truck."

"That shouldn't be an issue for us," Tom agreed. "We're heading up north anyway, so it should work out well. We'd be happy to get you back home – but a hospital should be first on the list."

"Oh, man, I'd really appreciate that." Jerry nodded his thanks. "You folks are real life savers."

Tom patted Jerry's good shoulder and motioned at the front of the RV. "Alright, let's get a move on. It's going to get bumpy, so hold on."

Chapter 24
Barbara McKnight
Wyndale, Virginia

Knives and forks softly clanked against their plates as the family ate, smells of roast, carrots, and potatoes smothered in gravy lingering in the air. They ate quietly, too tired to do much in the way of talking, interrupted only by Jack taking a big, slurping drink of milk.

"Quit slurping, Jack," Barbara reminded him, and he took a regular drink and placed his glass on the table. "Thank you."

Linda sat on her left, and Jack on her right, Barbara's eyes sliding to Sam's empty seat and over to the opposite end of the table where Tom usually looked back at her.

"It's nice you guys put down place settings for your father and Sam."

Linda shrugged, chewing, stabbing a potato with her fork. "It only seemed right to have some silverware ready. They could come through the door at any minute, right?"

"That's right." Barbara's throat squeezed with emotion, and she cleared it with a cough, cutting into her roast to keep the newly formed conversation casual, hiding her nagging fear. "So, Darren and Marie are coming over for dinner tomorrow."

Linda's face it up. "Really? I love seeing them!"

"Yeah, they drove up right when I finished checking the fences earlier today." She took a bite of her roast. "They came to check up on us. They even caught sight of the car that drove by our house, and they agreed we need to be super careful. They're pretty concerned about current events, but they're prepared. Just like us, right?"

Both children nodded, though Linda seemed slightly reserved.

"Let's go over it again. What do you guys do when we're out doing chores?"

"We look around sometimes to check if anyone is spying on us or…" Jack thought for a second "… watch for people sneaking up on us."

"Right. And what if you see a stranger?"

Jack answered again. "We stop what we're doing and sneak away to get you."

"Right. But what if you can't sneak away?"

Jack grinned with a spot of gravy in the corner of his mouth. "We scream our heads off."

"And it doesn't matter what they say," Barbara said. "You come find me, and if they try to stop you—"

"Scream our heads off," Jack interrupted in a gleeful tone.

She shifted her attention to her daughter, one eyebrow arched. "Your brother is killing it here, Linda. Anything to add?"

"We know all this, Mom," Linda said with a sigh. "We went over it twice today."

"I want you to know how important it is, that's all. You need to set a good example for Jack. Or maybe it's the other way around." Barbara raised her eyebrows. "Maybe Jack is the responsible one here."

Jack grinned widely at his sister.

"No, he's not." Linda gave her brother a pointed look, then looked toward her mother. "We always have to be aware of our surroundings. Someone could be waiting in the woods or in the next property over. We have to look around at our surroundings a lot and do it randomly at different times."

"And?" Barbara smiled inwardly.

Linda continued. "If we see someone, we're supposed to drop what we're doing and come find you, quietly. If we can't do that, then we—"

"Scream our heads off!" Jack kicked his feet against his chair legs.

"And even if they have some candy or a cool toy—"

"Or an ice cream cone," the boy added.

"Or a million dollars," Linda finished. "We can't trust them. We're not to speak to them. Just come find you."

"Very good," Barbara nodded. Despite feeling slightly overbearing and repetitive, the situation required diligence on both her and the kids' parts, and she'd keep on pushing until she was certain everyone had the rules imprinted in their minds. "And what else?"

"We don't go outside by ourselves," Linda added. "And we have to ask you first. We have to make ourselves a hard target, not an easy one."

Barbara grinned, her daughter sounding like she was reciting the rules out of a textbook. "Not bad," she said. "I'll be testing you tomorrow when we're out doing chores. Someone's got to keep you kids on your toes." Barbara kept her lips pursed, a playfully tugging at the edges of her lips.

"If you're going to test me," Linda challenged, eyes glaring across at her brother, "then I get to test Jack."

"Perfect."

"Hey!" Jack frowned at the two, unhappy to be the last person in the pecking order.

"And one more thing—" Something began buzzing in the kitchen, interrupting with a sound like a swarm of bees trapped inside a hive. It took Barbara a moment to realize she'd left her phone on the kitchen counter, rattling and shaking so hard it started vibrating toward the edge. She leapt out of her chair to catch it, barely snatching it out of the air before it smashed on the floor.

"Nice catch, Mom!" Jack called with delight.

"Thanks!" she replied, shaking her head at how close she'd come to losing her connection to her missing husband and daughter. Heart hammering with the sudden rush, Barbara leaned her hip against the counter, turning until her back was against it. Holding the phone out, she watched as dozens of news alerts rolled down her screen. It looked like old notifications that had been backed up over the past few days because of the network outages were just hitting her phone all at once.

"Anything from Dad?" Linda spoke around her food.

"Checking. Jeez... There's about a million of them." The messages kept coming faster than she could dismiss them. News alerts, emergency messages, state and county alerts and many she didn't recognize. She flicked through them, clearing the junk quickly, in search of anything from Tom. A series of messages labeled with yellow and red emergency symbols caught her eye and she clicked on the first one.

Presidential Alert: *The president has declared a national state of emergency. More details will be provided at 8 PM Eastern Standard Time. Please remain indoors and near your televisions, radios, phones, and computers for more information.*

"Wow, seems like a lot's been happening." Barbara had never seen a Presidential Alert before that wasn't a test, and its ominous tone was both shocking and expected. She'd preached to the kids about things getting worse, and it was happening right before their eyes. She scrolled through more messages, reading through headlines speculating about the Navy's convergence at the site where the original thirteen ships went down, with one citing anonymous sources saying that they expected them to detonate nuclear weapons to try and seal the crevice at the bottom of the ocean and another calling the story ludicrous. Yet another suggested some tensions were escalating in the South Pacific as the United States and China traded barbs over the cause of the seafloor fracture, as though such an event could be caused by human hands.

Barbara shook her head at the sheer volume of speculation and hearsay and scrolled to her contact list, pulling up Tom's name tapping on it to call him before putting the phone to her ear. The reply was immediate. "Your call cannot be completed as dialed."

"Well, shoot." Another alert hit Barbara's phone, tickling her ear with a message and she looked at the screen. It was a text from their cellular carrier, saying they'd restored partial service to voice and text, but there were still outages they were attempting to resolve. Heart lifting at the thought of progress, she held her phone close and squeezed it. "I'll be back," she said, bumping off the counter. "You guys finish eating."

"Is it Dad?" Linda called after her. "Did he send a message?"

"I'm not sure, yet. I need to check something, though."

Barbara padded into the hall and took a right down a shorter passage leading to their master bedroom suite where she had a small desk near the window with her laptop and a few decorations. The computer had gone into sleep mode early the previous week after Tom and Sam left, and Barbara hadn't had time to get on it. She pulled out the rolling office chair and sat, lifting the lid, clicking a small icon in the bottom right corner to check her internet connection. To her pleasant surprise, it showed a strong connection indicating that their internet service had been restored, in spite of voice and text still being spotty. Barbara pulled up her email and composed something to Tom.

Dear Tom,

First, me and the kids miss you guys so much, and we can't wait for you to return to us. We've got internet back! Still spotty phone service, and I can't reach you on voice or text. I wanted to let you know we're okay and safe at home, holding down the for, like you said. I hope we can talk soon, so please email me back as soon as you can. And get home safely.

Love,
Barbara

She hit "Send" and leaned back in her chair. Typing the words had brought an unexpected surge of emotion bubbling up, beating through the hopeless waves of inner despair that had been plaguing her and as she clutched her hand to her heart, she didn't know whether to be happy or sad. Barbara leaned forward again and used her mouse and keyboard to navigate to the local news site, happy at the fast-loading speed over what she had been experiencing on her phone. She clicked on the live stream, hoping to get some up-to-date news, but the feed froze before it started. With a glance at the connection icon, she saw the internet service was already down, just as quickly as it had been restored.

"Jeez," She bit her lip. "This is nuts."

She put her hand on the laptop lid and slammed it closed, raising her fist and clenching it tight until several lengthy breaths calmed her nerves. Eventually, she lowered her hand and rested it, palm down, on the laptop. Crushing the computer wouldn't help, except maybe for the brief satisfaction of taking her frustration out on a machine. With a sigh of resignation mixed with frustration, she returned to the kitchen and joined the kids in cleaning up. They scrapped their leftovers into plastic containers and set them in the refrigerator then rinsed the dishes, placed them into the dishwasher, and wiped off the table.

Barbara put soapy water in the roast pan to let it soak in the sink, completing each task like a lifeless zombie, mechanical movements as she numbed her emotions that had gone from sad to elated to crushed again, her chest heavy with a constant weight. Shaking it off for the sake of Jack

"You kiddos want to watch a movie?"

"Yeah!" Jack said. "Can we watch Call of the Wild?"

"That sounds perfect to me. Linda?"

"I'm good with that," she replied, adopting a posh English accent. "Shall I put on the popcorn?"

"If you can fit more in your belly, sure," Barbara chimed, giggling at Linda's rounded abdomen on her skinny frame.

They got comfortable on the couch, Barbara leaning against the couch's left arm while Linda took the right, Jack in between them laying on his sister's curled up legs and a pile of pillows. Two big patchwork coverlets stretched between them, and the warmth caused Barbara's eyes to grow heavy with sleep. She pulled out her phone and scrolled through the news, getting pieces of headlines and graphics as the data connection sputtered along. Finding any helpful nugget of information had become a compulsion in her sleep-deprived mind and her thumb refreshed and re-refreshed, and she closed all her applications and restarted her phone three times to see if it would help, but the connection never improved.

"Mom, put your phone down and watch with us."

Barbara glanced up to see Linda staring at her across the couch, smiling. "Dad and Sam will be fine. You have to have faith."

"Faith," Barbara whispered. "By the grace of God."

She placed her phone face-down on the end table, reached beneath the covers, and pulled them tight to her chin. Jack kicked his legs against hers as she settled into the warmth, letting it soak in, turning her attention to the television where a dog named Buck began a grand adventure. Outside, the sky darkened with streaks of dark clouds sweeping in, a covering of gray that spread above them like a curse, blotting out the sun and sky. Along with it came chilly gusts of air, the whipping winds stirring the trees out back as thunder crashed in the distance, grumbling like an old man, crackling and fading in waves of sound.

The sheep bleated and began a slow procession toward the side yard, followed by the donkeys, seeking the cover of the trees and fowl pens, their primal instincts driving them together, squeezed tight for comfort and safety. Smooch sat in the side yard as the animals approached, her eyes lifted to the menacing storm, a plaintive whine wiggled up from her chest. The patches of dark streaked fast across the sky, curved and stretching, marking the outer bands of the massive storm already pounding the Eastern Seaboard.

Chapter 25
Tom McKnight
Outer Banks, North Carolina

Tom crept the RV along Highway 12 at a snail's pace as they were rocked by the concussive force of hurricane winds striking in from the south like a hammer. Shingles, roofing, garbage and deck furniture sailed across their path along with, the larger pieces striking the side of the RV with bone-shuddering force. Some larger trees lay on their sides, their gnarled roots sticking up in surrender as they captured slivers of siding and debris gusting along the ground in their clawed fingers.

Smaller trees had been tossed like spears, the wind hurling them through vinyl siding and windows while older buildings had partially toppled over, brick and glass and storm boards scattered across parking lots. Light vehicles sat skewed on the road, knocked against each other by storm surge, clogging the path ahead, making Tom take detours around them. The ocean waters lapped far up the beach and over the dunes, spilling up to the road and around the beach homes that lay washed out, stretched thin and drowned in sand and brine. Those still standing remained half-buried in the rolling waves, their insides gutted of furniture, bedding, and toys.

A rush of water swept in and covered the road, causing Tom to slow down. As the wave receded, a storm door flew through the air, flipping end over end like a wounded butterfly to land on the opposite side of the road and career out of sight behind a building. He lifted his foot off the brake and allowed the RV to roll forward once more, keeping to the left, eyes pinned forward and to their right to watch for any incoming waves and debris.

Jerry sat between Tom and Sam on a flipped-up cleaning bucket he'd found in a cabinet. The young man's cheeks were growing rosier by the hour, and he clung to Tom's chair arm with a firm grip, no longer wanting to be stuck in the back at the small kitchen table. He appeared to be in good spirits after eating a few snacks, then guzzling down a bottle of tepid water. The young man's eyes were wide as he stared out at the raging storm with a shake of his head. "I have to thank you two again. I would have been fish food if you two hadn't come along. Seriously, thank you."

Tom kept his eyes on the road and gave a firm nod. "The storm is moving slow," he said, the headlights fighting back against the bitter dark storm. "It's not just blowing over like you'd expect. That's what's causing some of these buildings to wash out, I bet. And it'll cause similar damage across hundreds of miles of coastline. We can only hope the storm eases as we get closer to Virginia Beach."

"How do you plan on us getting there?" Jerry asked. "I mean, we could divert west across the Highway 158 bridge into Point Harbor or stay on Highway 12 and shoot straight through the wildlife refuge."

Tom wrinkled his forehead in confusion. "The highway goes right through the wildlife refuge?"

"Not exactly. It goes through the new tunnel they just completed," Jerry explained. "You know, beneath the refuge."

"Oh, I didn't realize that," Tom replied. "I'd heard of the tunnel being built near the reserve but was too busy to keep up, I guess. What's it called again?"

"It's called the Currituck Banks Tunnel. I ride through it every day. It's amazing. Super low footprint. State-of-the-art. I read they built it using the best Japanese automated tunnel boring machines and US-made drill heads and venting techniques. It's supposed to give folks an alternate route to Virginia Beach."

"I saw a documentary on it last year," Sam chimed in.

Tom raised an eyebrow "Really?"

"Like Jerry said, they built it to have minimal effect on the area's wildlife. There was a big hoopla over it, because some activists didn't want it built, but they did it anyway. The construction people used ground-penetrating radar to pinpoint the route to the millimeter, and they didn't need any explosives because of the advanced boring techniques."

Jerry nodded at Sam. "Hey, you know what? You're pretty smart."

"Thanks," Sam grinned modestly.

"So, it got completed, obviously," Tom said. "It probably made the activists pretty mad."

"There were some protests." Sam shrugged. "But they stopped after a while when they realized nothing was really happening that they *could* protest. Kind of hard to protest something underground."

"I used to have a crazy long commute to get home, but the tunnel cut that almost in half." Jerry grinned. "Plus, it's cool to drive through."

Tom gave his daughter a dubious but impressed glance. "I didn't realize you were so interested in construction projects."

Sam shrugged. "I only knew about it from the Ocean Watch Newsletter. The story was interesting, so I followed it." Her voice took on a tone. "I guess I'm an expert on the matter."

"Okay, Miss Expert." Tom chuckled. "Which route should we take? The bridge into Point Harbor or the tunnel?"

"The tunnel would be faster, for sure," Sam remarked, running the back of her hand along the window. "Plus the storm might have damaged the bridge into Point Harbor. Then again, the tunnel could be flooded despite having a dozen fail-safes built in. I guess we've got to pick our poison."

"Have you gone through the tunnel when it was storming?" Tom asked Jerry.

He nodded but winced. "Yeah, but not when it was this bad. Still, it stayed open through two hurricanes last year."

"I'm sure the tunnel is okay." Tom took one hand off the steering wheel and rubbed the side of his face. "But this is a powerful storm, and the world is… changing rapidly."

Jerry frowned. "What do you mean, changing rapidly?"

Staring through the flapping wipers, listening as debris smacked their vehicle, considering his words carefully. "It's… hard to explain, he said. "Maybe I'll try after I've had some time to think. I'd rather hear about you. Are you full time at the gas station?"

"Only until I can find something better. It's not like I have to pay for school anymore."

"You had to quit?"

"Yep. I dropped out when my mom and dad got sick." Jerry's tone dropped a notch. "Cancer, both of them around the same time. Lung cancer for dad, breast cancer for mom. My dad passed away, but Mom came through with flying colors. Well, she still has some issues, but we're pulling through it."

Tom's tone took on a somber note. "I'm sorry to hear about your parents, Jerry. What kinds of problems is your mother having?"

"She's still tired all the time, plus the mental stuff from going through so much chemo and losing all her hair. It's been rough on her."

Tom glanced at the young man with admiration. "I'm impressed you put them above your personal interests and took care of them. Few people would have done that. Couldn't have been easy."

"It wasn't. It still isn't." He sighed. "But my mom always says your situation is what you make of it, so I'll keep plugging away."

Tom's chin furrowed, lips turning down. "You've got the right idea. When do you think you'll get back in school?"

"I might not go back. I'm thinking more about trade schools now. Maybe I'll get an electrician apprenticeship."

"That's not a terrible idea. You can make good money that way, and you'd be learning a trade."

Jerry lowered his eyes, a slight smile creasing his face before lifting his gaze to Tom. "What about you? What do you do for a living?"

"Oh, you know. I do a little of this, a little of that."

"My dad is an engineer," Sam butted in. "He's super smart, but he'd never admit it."

"I'm not super smart," Tom said, cheeks reddening. "I just help people solve problems, that's all."

"So, you're a genius," Jerry said.

"No." He chuckled. "I do have a PhD in Marine Biology and double master's in mechanical engineering and fluid mechanics. But it's just a fancy way of saying I fix things. I diagnose and solve problems on expensive pieces of marine hardware and software. It's mostly contract work for private companies and the Navy."

"That sounds incredible."

"It has its perks. You get to travel a lot on cool boats."

"And aircraft carriers," Sam added.

"In fact, we were just out on a flotilla in the North Atlantic, investigating—"

"That thing they were talking about on the news? The seafloor anomaly thing?" Jerry's eyes grew wide, and he looked back and forth between Tom and Sam as his words rushed from his lips. "You guys were on the Navy ships? No way!"

"Yes, we were on those ships." Tom shot a glance at Sam. "What's wrong?"

"You guys don't know?! That entire group of ships sunk! Totally gone. They just up and vanished into the ocean without a trace!"

A gust of wind kicked up and rocked the RV back and forth, a piece of debris thudding off the roof as Tom swallowed hard. "Sam and I were there, but we managed to get away on a life raft as things were… happening. I'm not sure if the others made it. Are you sure all the ships went down?"

"I'm positive. It was all over the news just before the storm started getting worse. Like, a while before you guys came in."

A somber silence descended over the cabin as Jerry's eyes moved back and forth between the two. "Wow, man. So, like, you know what caused all those ships to go down?"

Tom nodded.

"You saw it?"

"Yeah. It's a crevice on the seafloor. A gigantic crack that's worked its way up into the shelf, and it might have even reached the mainland or spread farther out to sea."

"But how could that cause so many ships to sink?"

Tom slowed down as he waited for another wash of sand and salt water to shoot across the highway, white foam dancing over tree limbs and debris as he wove through it, almost like the beach was eating its way inward on a course to consume the mainland.

"Water is surging up from an underground aquifer." Tom pressed the gas and pushed the RV forward as the wave receded. "It's fresh water, which is causing major problems."

"I heard something about the migration changes in the fish. Like, they're swimming south, or something. One person said it might change how commercial fishing works, and we'll see food shortages."

"I can't say I disagree with that, but I think fisherman can make up for that in the southern regions, and we've got a strong agricultural supply chain to take up some slack." Tom forced his explanation in an effort not to sound too alarming. But, in fact, he was growing more concerned by the hour. "Other things worry me, though."

"Like what?"

"The rising sea levels, for one. Those will cause coastal flooding and drive people inland." Tom shook his head as he imagined the chaos. The housing market would take a major hit. People would lose their homes and fortunes. "Boy, that'll be a mess."

"When do you think the major flooding will happen?"

He shrugged. "I don't know. I'm not sure it *will* happen, but at the rate the water was pouring out… well, anyway. It's difficult to tell anything with the storm raging like this. I've got some special software that helps me predict things and extrapolate data, but without access to the internet and a computer, I couldn't begin to work it out. Plus, I'd have to see some normal conditions first."

Tom gripped the steering wheel as another wave washed across the road, breaking over the RV's tires and splashing up the sides like a boat plowing through a heavy storm. He could dance around the topic as much as he wanted, downplaying the anomaly's effects on the world, convincing himself that nature and human ingenuity was robust enough to absorb the changes the fresh water surge could cause and shrug off the loss of fishing. But he couldn't downplay the danger caused by the disruption in the North Atlantic currents.; the flow of warm water north was crucial to sustain sea life and life on the land.

A nagging worry resurfaced, tapping at the back of his brain, and while he didn't want to alarm Sam or Jerry, it was time he admitted something might be seriously wrong.

"I… I think we're facing something that could change the course of human history."

Chapter 26
Barbara McKnight
Wyndale, Virginia

The chesty *woof* of Smooch's barking woke Barbara from a dead sleep. It wasn't the casual, slow barking at a squirrel or the cat in the next yard over. It was insistent and gruff, interspersed with high, urgent yips that sent a shiver across her skin. Someone had to be on the property for the Shepherd to bark so viciously; none of the barnyard animals causing a stir would get her so worked up. Barbara rolled out of bed and into her slippers, then she kicked them off and grabbed her boots instead.

Once they were on her feet and laced up, Barbara knelt next to the night stand and retrieved her pistol out of the biometric safe on the bottom shelf. She clipped the holster to the waistband of her pajamas before striding to the closet. Throwing open the door, she grabbed the Benelli M2 semi-automatic shotgun where she'd tucked it behind the hanging clothes, loading it up with shells from her top bureau drawer. Barbara alternated rounds of buckshot and slugs, and then chambered a round with a loud, satisfying clack.

She moved to the window and peered out at the yard, watching Smooch where she stood off to the side, looking west across the property. Three minutes passed, and Barbara saw nothing. Squinting, leaning her forehead against the smudged glass, she peered outside until a glint of yellow caught her eye down by the barn at the edge of their property. It was a flashlight, and a pair of shadowed legs and feet walking around the light as the beam darted back and forth over the grass. The shadows seemed to be moving around the shed, looking for a way in. They didn't seem concerned about the barking, though she caught the shadowy forms throwing glances up at the house.

Her rising anger flushed adrenaline through her system. The idea that someone was on their property, without their permission, pissed her off more than it scared her, the two emotions clashing inside, her shotgun shaking in her steel grip.

"Take a deep breath and take care of business," she whispered to herself.

Barbara turned and strode into the hallway, swinging right toward the foot of the stairs. She darted around the banister post and flew up the stairs, taking them two at a time, hissing Linda's name. Her daughter lumbered out of her room, hair messed up, eyes wide with surprise in the hall night light.

"Someone's outside," Barbara stated in a flat tone. "Get the pistol from the bathroom and go wait in your brother's room."

"But, Mom—"

"Go!" Barbara's tone brooked no argument.

"Okay." Linda turned to do her mother's bidding, until Barbara stopped her with another loud whisper.

"Wait!" Barbara snapped, and Linda whirled back. "Remember what we talked about. Protect your brother and yourself. If anyone comes through his bedroom door but me, you know what to do. You squeeze the trigger until it clicks."

Linda's eyes turned glassy with fearful emotion, but she nodded that she understood.

"Good girl. I'll shout out when the coast is clear."

Barbara descended the stairs and made her way back to the master bedroom suite where they had a side door off of Tom's office. She unlocked the deadbolts, grasped the doorknob, and quietly opened it. Holding her breath, she stepped outside into the warm summer air, still moist from the rains. The grounds were quiet but for the soft bleating of sheep and clucking of fowl, Smooch's incessant barking having spooked them along with the sheep, some of them drifting across the yard toward the woods, acting as perfect cover for what she needed to do. Barbara sneaked to the edge of the house where Smooch was barking, calling, gesturing for the animal to come without telling her to be quiet.

"Fuss!" *Heel*.

Smooch tossed her head toward Barbara, mouth clamping shut as she trotted over. Without stopping, Barbara strode into the yard toward where the flashlight bobbed, ducking behind the meandering sheep, moving from one animal to the next, keeping the animals between her and the moving light. Smooch trotted and danced by her side, head thrown up and barking as she glared across the space at shadowed figures.

When she came within two hundred feet of them, she gave the dog a slap on the chest and pointed out to her left. "Veraus!" *Go out*. She hissed the word, and the dog instantly obeyed, loping off to the left, still barking her head off, froth flying from her lips. As Barbara watched from amongst the herd, the people messing around by the barn wheeled and crouched in surprise, noticing a change in the barking.

The full moon peeked from behind the streaking clouds, illuminating them for Barbara to see – the same men from the green Oldsmobile. Barbara hadn't expected them so soon, but they'd apparently wasted no time in going to town on the McKnight's property. They wore dark, shabby, oversized coveralls, and each carried a crowbar, at least one holding a small dark shape resembling a pistol, all of them tracking Smooch racing across the field, one of them pointing at the flying beast. One of the men said something to the others with a nod, then he started walking with halting steps toward the house, pointing in Barbara's general direction but clearly not seeing her, gesturing for the others to follow him.

Barbara flipped the safety off the M2, lifted it to her shoulder, stood up amongst the herd like a demon rising from hell, and fired. The gun slammed against her shoulder, buckshot spraying out and peppering the nearest man and the one behind him before rattling against the side of the barn. Both men howled as they danced, holding their shoulders and legs as the sheep bolted in every direction, their panicked bleating a herald to Barbara's fury.

She fired again, a slug splitting between the two men standing farthest away and blasting a massive hole in the barn's side, splintering the wood to pieces. Two of the men shot her panicked glances, while the one nearest her simply dashed toward the fence line as she sent another hail of buckshot at their backs, shredding fabric and flesh, their screams piercing the night. Limping, dropping their tools and weapons everywhere, they all made a beeline toward the fence. They cut their clothing and skin on the barbed fencing along the top, crying as they clambered over and fell into the next property over.

Barbara stalked behind them, long gun at the ready, her expression full of rage, prepared to end the first man who turned to challenge her. Stopping at the fence, she watched the men flee through the tall grass, disappearing into the shadows in a haze of smoke and mist. Smooch's barking died down as she rejoined Barbara's side, smoking shotgun in her hands, ears ringing above the low din of crickets and still-panicked sheep.

She took a deep, quivering breath and released it in a whisper. "And stay out."

A part of her initially regretted shooting at the men, but she'd been far enough away for the buckshot to spread, and – most importantly – they'd chosen to step onto the McKnight's property uninvited with ill intentions. Plus, if Smooch's barking hadn't been enough of a warning, then nothing she said would have deterred them. No, they'd come to steal – or worse – from her family. The thought brought back a swell of anger, her hands going rigid around the cold steel, making her wish she'd have fired just one more time. After a minute, her adrenaline waned, and Smooch sensed the change, panting and wagging her tail, eyes staring up at Barbara for approval. She knelt next to the dog and rubbed her head, both of them watching the tall grass where the men had disappeared. The minutes passed slowly, but the men didn't come back. Finally, with a heavy sigh, Barbara stood and shouldered her shotgun, brushing her hands on her pajama pants.

With one last look at the grass, she turned and headed back toward the house. "Komm, Smooch," she commanded, the Shepherd popping up and trotting obediently by her side. While most of the sheep still lingered around the animal pens, a few had shot off to a far part of the yard, frightened by the shotgun blasts and smoke. She didn't bother with them; they weren't going anywhere, and would most likely make their way back to where they belonged by morning.

Near the side of the house, Barbara released Smooch, and the dog loped off around back toward her doghouse to resume her guard duty. Stepping into Tom's office through the side door, she walked through the master suite and into the foyer. At the bottom of the stairs, Barbara looked up and called out. "Coast is clear, Linda and Jack! You kids can come out!"

The pair appeared at the top of the stairs, Linda holding the pistol pointed down away from her brother, finger off the trigger and lying flat along the gun's frame. While only fourteen years old, she looked much older standing holding the gun, her eyes glassy with emotion, but holding a stoic resolve.

"Linda, would you please secure your weapon and come downstairs?"

She nodded and walked off with the pistol to remove the magazine, eject the chambered round and store them safely where they belonged while Jack trounced down the stairs, staring at the shotgun in his mother's hand. He wrinkled his nose, nostrils flaring, eyes wide with a mixture of fear and curiosity. "Did you have to shoot someone?"

"Come on." She jerked her chin in the kitchen's direction, and they moved down the hall and past the kitchen table. Barbara rested the shotgun on the counter next to a plate of chocolate chip cookies and gestured to a chair. "Sit down. I'll get you some milk and cookies in a minute."

"All right!"

While she waited for Linda to come down, Barbara stepped to one of the high cabinets near the sink and opened the door. Reaching up, she brought down a box of shotgun shells, loading three shells into the shotgun to replace the ones she'd fired and then returned the box of shells to the top shelf. When Linda came down a few minutes later, she gave her mother a businesslike nod and sat across from her brother. Barbara grinned, pleased she took the weapon seriously, reminding herself to double check the gun later after the kids went to bed just to be absolutely certain things were in order.

"What happened?" Linda asked, sliding into a chair across from her brother. "We heard you fire the shotgun. We thought…" The girl's voice hitched, and she turned her face away from her brother, trying to protect Jack from trauma just like Barbara protected them.

"Some bad men came to the house and were poking around the yard and the barn," she confirmed, pouring each of the kids a glass of milk.

"Was it the men from the car?" Jack asked.

"Yep, the same ones." Barbara placed the glasses on the table and went back for the plate of fat, chocolate chip cookies next to the shotgun.

"You were right," Linda said, shaking her head. "You knew they'd be back."

Barbara brought the cookies to the table and set them down, hands still shaky from discharging the weapon multiple times. It had been a while since she practiced with the Benelli, and it had a kick that had shaken her through her ribcage. "True, but I didn't think they'd come back so fast. They must be desperate. I figured they would give us time to get comfortable."

"Do you think they'll be back?" Jack asked as he grabbed a cookie off the plate.

Barbara snorted. "I don't think they will, but we have to be prepared in case they do or in case others like them do."

"Did we do good?" Linda asked.

"You did amazing," Barbara nodded and winked. Then she took a cookie off the plate and held it out to her daughter. "Here, have a cookie."

Linda looked back and forth between the cookie and her mother, a smile replacing the tear-filled eyes. Barbara smiled with her, and in a few moments both of them were back to their bubbly selves, joining Jack's semi-oblivious-to-danger excitement for the late-night snack. After a few minutes of jokes and meandering conversation, Barbara glanced over at the clock. *Ten after three? Seriously?* It was too early for coffee, but there was no way she'd be able to get back to sleep, so staying busy while her body and mind settled seemed like the best solution.

"Okay, finish up and get back up to bed."

"Can I have one more?" Jack asked, eyes pleading.

"Absolutely not. I want both of you back in bed ASAP. I'll be up to check on you as soon as I can."

Jack downed the rest of his milk, hopped off his chair, and ran to Barbara, throwing his arms around her waist. "Thanks for protecting us, Mom! And for the cookie." He squeezed hard once and then ran off to get back into bed, Linda smiling as she stood up and walked over.

"Same here, Mom. Thanks."

"No, thank *you*." She pushed the girl's wild locks off her shoulder and gave her a warm embrace, whispering to her daughter. "I couldn't do any of this without you. You've been such a blessing to have around, and your father will be so proud of you when he gets home."

They broke the embrace, Linda stared at her mother with wide eyes. "Do you really think he'll be proud of me?"

Barbara tilted her head, the question causing her heart to stir. Ever since Linda had gotten big enough to challenge Sam at most physical activities, they'd developed a healthy bit of competition. But, unlike her sister who could be aloof and uncaring, Linda always sought validation from her parents, wearing her heart on her sleeve, her strength coming from working with others.

"Of course he will. He already is." Barbara nodded. "You're becoming a great leader by helping your brother and taking over all these projects. Your father is going to *super* impressed."

Linda pursed her lips. "Yeah, but Sam has always been his favorite."

"Now, that's *not* true." She stared at her daughter's stoic expression before it broke, revealing the slightest grin on Linda's face. "Uh huh, I knew it." She playfully turned a hand towel from the counter into a whip, snapping it at Linda's legs as the two giggled. "You almost had me there!"

Linda laughed as she danced around the table. "I *totally* had you going!"

Barbara grinned as she grabbed Linda, wrapping her in a final embrace, whispering in her ear. "Good work today, kiddo. Now get back in bed, alright? Another long day tomorrow."

A grin creased the girl's face. "Okay," she whispered. "Thanks, Mom." Then she turned on her heel and went up to her room. Barbara stared after her for a moment and allowed a slow smile to play across her lips. Linda would be fine, she just needed little more encouragement to get her confidence built up.

Barbara bent and took off her shoes, standing, padding to the coffee machine in her socks, giving in to the temptation, preparing a fresh pot. After a dash of cream and sugar and a quick stir, she returned to the table and sat in her dirty pajamas with the coffee steaming beneath her nose. Another sleepless night and there'd be no time to rest tomorrow, either. Haggard and worn out, stretched to the edge of her limits, she released a quivering sigh, before she pulled out her phone from her pajama pants, looking for a message from Tom, unsurprised but still disappointed at the result.

She sipped her coffee, swallowed, and closed her eyes, willing the adrenaline to disperse from her body as the shakes came back, reminding her of the events of the evening. The world was changing fast – far faster than she'd thought possible. And while she wanted to believe things would get better, her gut told her the worst was yet to come.

Chapter 27
Tom McKnight
Outer Banks, North Carolina

Kitty Hawk was a dead town, lightning waltzing across the sky like camera flashes taking pictures of the destruction. There were no cars, no lights, and not a single soul anywhere along the highway. Homes built to withstand fierce storms dotted the road on both sides, mostly holding up but still showing signs of wear. Parts of roofs were missing, entire sections disintegrated and spun up into the windy mix swirling over their heads. Broken trees and heavy limbs lay everywhere, serving as tools of destruction, wind tossing them into the sides of houses, sloughing off slabs of siding and smashing decks. Stripped tree trunks had punched through windows and brick walls, leaving indentions in the deteriorating brick and mortar and giving the town a deathly feel, like a ghostly city filled with shadows of a lost civilization.

To Tom's right, the ocean had devoured Highway 12, sinking the pavement multiple feet and shifting pieces around like a puzzle. Most everything else along the shoreline lay in clutters of junk, broken apart by frothing waves and carried out with the storm's fury.

Tom spotted a large slab of roof several meters out in the water, floating along and undulating as the waves passed beneath it while an RV park lay beaten to a pulp nearby, vehicles piled up to create a reef of fiberglass, metal, and rubber. He had abandoned Highway 12 to the storm, rerouting to Croatan Highway where they continued their journey north. Thanks to the wind and waves, though, the going was still excruciatingly slow. Debris and obstacles littered the road, making it impassable in places while chunks of light metal, bricks, and wood lay scattered everywhere, nails, glass, and other sharp objects waiting to shred their tires.

Tom turned down side streets and squeezed through parking lots, focusing hard on the light given off by his headlamps to keep them moving. No matter what the detour, he always found his way back to Croatan Highway, usually with Jerry's help.

The young man shook his head as they passed a home with its roof blown off. "It's a good thing we didn't take the southern bridge."

Tom took his eyes off the road and shot Jerry an incredulous look. "There's a southern bridge?"

"Yeah, but it floods too easy during storms, so no one uses it anyway."

Tom nodded and turned his attention back to the road, watching as the wind blew sideways rain in a gray spray across their path. The road swept them briefly westward then north again, the landscape turning from quaint beachside homes to more commercial properties. Retail stores stood like black monoliths in the distance, surrounded by empty parking lots swept with rain. A John's Shrimp Joint off to the right had its front caved in from a crashed delivery van that had been tossed into it while a Trailman's Sporting Goods store sat off to their left, its front glass blown out, everything dark inside. Several hotels sat clustered together, havens for Outer Banks tourists and Tom caught sight of lights on one of the upper floors of a Travel Master Hotel, but when he blinked they were gone.

"Wow, this place is a mess," Jerry said. "Breaks my heart."

"I'm sorry to see it," Tom replied, feeling like he was offering condolences at a funeral.

"There's so many boating and surfing shops," Sam remarked, staring out her window at the hobby shops lining the side of the road. "I'll bet it would have been great for a vacation."

Jerry pointed at a lone structure with blue trim, its sign long ago blown off, facing ravished by the wind. "I worked there a few years back. Bottlenose Surf and Sport."

"What happened?" Sam asked.

"A new owner took over and brought in his family to work the store, pushed the rest of us out." He shook his head, gazing wistfully at the passing shop. "I loved working there, man. I got to repair surfboards and motors. The people were cool, and I got to try out the new gear."

Sam raised an eyebrow. "Wow, that sounds cool."

"I wish I could find another place like it, but jobs have been hard to come by lately. I'm just lucky to have my job at the gas station."

"What were you going to college for?" Tom asked. "I mean, what classes were you taking?"

Jerry pursed his lips and shifted his head side-to-side as if putting some guesswork into his answer. "I guess I drifted for the first semester, though I took a lot of general science classes, mainly math and engineering. But I enjoy working with my hands, building things, and fixing them. That's why I miss the old Bottlenose shop." He turned his attention to Sam. "What do you want to go to school for?"

Sam shrugged. "I'm not sure, but something like my dad does. Maybe not working with equipment but on boats working with ocean and marine life somehow."

"Sam loves the ocean," Tom offered. "She's always been interested in marine biology, and she watches Ocean Watch nonstop."

"That's true," she agreed, grinning.

"That's my favorite channel, too," Jerry said with a light chuckle. He held his fist up for Sam to bump. Sam knocked her knuckles against his, and the two spread their fingers in an explosion gesture.

Tom pulled the RV to a stop in front of a leaning road sign, the only one he'd seen at least partially standing for miles. One arrow pointed straight ahead for the Wright Memorial Bridge heading west toward the mainland, while the other arrow angled toward the exit ramp for the Currituck Banks Tunnel, going north.

"Okay, Jerry. Decision time. Which way? Tunnel or bridge?"

Jerry stared straight ahead for a moment before his eyes shifted off to the right. He gave a thoughtful wince as he turned his attention back to the road leading to the bridge. "I'd say we try the bridge first, since it's closest. If it's out, we can backtrack and make for the tunnel. It's a crap shoot at this point."

"Sounds like a plan to me," Tom said. "We'll try the bridge, then go for the tunnel as a last resort."

"Keep following this road along the curve." The young man made a sweeping motion with his arm. "It should swing us west."

Shoulders tense, eyes focused on the pavement at the edge of their headlights, Tom let off the RV's brake and gave it some gas. They swung around the bend in a northwesterly direction, moving against the southern winds, the vehicle bending to the right as Tom wove between the overturned trees when a splintered branch smacked the side of the RV.

Jerry gave a low whistle. "Geez. One of those could punch right through."

Nodding, Tom urgently pushed the RV up to thirty miles per hour and then slowed again as they approached another scattering of debris. A gas station sign had spun end-over-end to smash in the middle of the road, forcing him to cut through a strip mall parking lot before rejoining Croatan Road. The RV rocked harder, water beating at them in violent sheets, wind whistling through small gaps worn in the siding. Even more rain and debris hit the side of the vehicle, rattling them, causing them all to jump with every impact. Still, the wheels stayed on the ground, the warm defrost continued to pump, and the three remained warm – if not exactly cozy – inside the cabin.

"It's pretty ironic they named the road 'North Croatan Highway'," Sam said, looking around. "The place is a ghost town, just like the abandoned Roanoke settlement they found."

"Creepy," Jerry agreed.

Sam laughed nervously. "Maybe we'll find an old rock with "FEMA" engraved on it."

Jerry cocked his head to the side for a moment before bursting out laughing, Tom cracking a smile as well before he glanced down at the gas gauge and frowned. "We're running a little low on diesel, so we'll need to stop somewhere soon. I hope we can find someplace open. Maybe after we get closer inland."

The young man grunted in reply as he peered doubtfully out the window. "There are probably a couple of places after the bridge. Or, we could siphon some from another vehicle if we have to."

Tom raised his eyebrow at the young man. "You siphon gas often?"

Jerry shook his head emphatically. "My Dad taught me how in case of emergencies only. He needed to transfer some from one of his broken-down cars into one that worked. That's when he taught me."

"I can see where it would be a valuable skill." Tom agreed. "Let's try to resort to theft only as last resort, though, all right?"

They finished the big left turn and straightened out, heading directly west, fully exposed to the howling wind. Long, growling gusts shook the RV, rattling the dishes in the cabinets, causing Tom's head to hurt, sweat breaking out on his brow.

"Are those taillights?" he asked, leaning forward to stare. He swore he saw a pair of red lights through the haze, though he didn't fully trust his eyes. The rain made shapes on the glass, bending light, distorting distant objects. The wind played tricks with his ears, vibrating the vehicle through to steering column, throwing his sense of touch off. Tom could swear he felt the tires slewing across the road twice only to blink and realize they hadn't moved at all.

"Actually, they are." Jerry confirmed.

"I see them, too," Sam added.

"It's the first sign of people we've seen." An overwhelming feeling of relief flooded through him, knowing they weren't the only people struggling through the storm. "It looks like they've stopped. I think I'll pull up and have a quick chat, if they're willing."

Tom blinked his headlights on and off three times he pulled up next to the newer white sedan. The RV sat several inches higher than the car, so as soon as Tom rolled down the window, a wash of rain from the car's roof sloughed off and splashed him in the face. He wiped his hand down his face and ducked below the constant sheet of rain, pleased when the person in the car's passenger side cracked their window, too. They were a middle-aged couple, the man wearing a gray T-shirt and the woman a blouse with a flower design. Their faces glowed with a vibrant tan, the skin around their eyes lighter from wearing glasses out in the sun.

"Hi, there!" Tom called to them, screaming over the wind. "How are you folks doing?"

"You're looking at it!" the woman yelled back, wincing as water pelted her, gesturing around with her hand. "The storm caught us. Thought we could get inland this morning, but we had to stop."

"I understand," Tom nodded as he hollered over the wind. "On vacation, I presume?"

The woman nodded vigorously.

"Were you headed for the Wright Memorial Bridge?"

They both nodded.

Tom glanced in the bridge's direction through sheets of grayness, then nodded at their idling car. "What's the problem?"

The woman's lips turned down into a frown. "The bridge is covered in water."

"How do you know?"

"Some state police officers came by earlier and headed out to the bridge, but they never came back." She gave a worried glance out the front window. "We never found out for sure. We don't want to drive closer until the weather clears."

"What about the tunnel? Is that open?"

The woman shrugged. "No idea. We were just trying to get to Elizabeth City a short way inland."

Tom followed her gaze and nodded, still determined to get across the bridge if he could. "Thanks, a lot," he hollered, waving his thanks before rolling up his window. With the cabin sealed, he sat half-soaked from the waist up, glancing at Jerry to see him wiping his face from the residual spray.

"Well, I guess we just keep going." Tom pulled the RV forward another fifty yards and stopped.

He rested his arms on top of the steering wheel, blinking at the road ahead. It was a wall of bleak grayness with nothing in sight beyond the safety of their headlights. The wind died for a moment, the shrill wails lessening. Unbuckling his belt, he gestured to his daughter.

"Sam, switch with me."

Jerry scooted back so Tom could get out and once they'd stepped back into the kitchen, Sam stepped across and plopped down in the driver's position.

"Here," Tom leaned down and whispered, giving her his titanium pen. "Keep your eyes open. Remember how I told you to use this, right?"

Sam rolled her eyes. "Yeah, but Jerry won't try anything."

"Not what I meant," he said. "It's in case someone approaches the RV. We're sitting out here with our lights on. Anyone watching from a building might try to take it."

Her chin ducked in a nod. "Ohhh, I see. Got it."

He moved back and gestured for Jerry to take the passenger seat and once they were situated, Tom leaned forward. "I'll go down the road a bit and see if the bridge is passable. If not, I'll see if the officers know about the tunnel and if it's safe to drive."

"What?" Sam said, both eyebrows raised in surprise. "No, Dad. You can't go that far by yourself."

Jerry's worried look matched Sam's. "She's right, Mr. McKnight. It doesn't seem like a good idea, no offense."

"None taken," Tom said as he moved farther into the kitchen. "But I'll be fine. I want to do some simple scouting. It'll keep us from running into trouble if we keep pressing forward."

He opened a cabinet door beneath the sink and pulled out a garbage bag, punching three holes into the thin plastic, pulling it over his head to use as a rain poncho. Sam shook her head, looking back and forth between her father and the storm outside.

"Please don't do this, Dad. Can't we wait like those other people?"

"That could be forty-eight hours or more at the rate this hurricane is moving, and who knows how bad it'll get before it eases up." Tom shook his head. "You really want to sit out here that long, then have to go find gas to get us through the tunnel?"

"Then let me go," Jerry insisted.

Tom dug the remaining tape from his pack and started sealing the plastic around his arms. "Jerry, you have a busted arm, and I'm definitely not sending my daughter out. That leaves me. I'll go out, see what's what, and come right back."

"You'll get yourself hurt, or worse," Sam frowned.

"No, I won't." Tom fixed her with a firm expression. "We don't have enough gas to waste driving up and down the roads. If I can find out which path is passable by getting a little wet, we'll save a lot of time and effort. Trust me, okay?"

Samantha twisted her lips, realizing her father was right. "Just be super careful."

"Tie the door shut behind me," Tom said, edging toward the side door. "If I'm not back in thirty minutes, pull forward and see if you can find me. And here, take this." He dug his phone out of his pocket and handed it to her. "Keep trying to reach Mom. We haven't gotten service so far, but you never know. It might come back."

"Okay. Please be careful."

"You already said that."

"It deserves repeating."

Tom gave his daughter a loving look and offered her a reassuring smile before turning, untying the string around the latch, flipping it, and shoving the door open. The wind gusted, whipping the door back, but he was ready for it, gripping the edge tight, turning his body and leveraging his weight to slam it shut. With one last look back, he crouched and charged forward, disappearing into the harrowing storm of dismal gray.

Sam wrapped the shoestring around the doorknob and returned to the driver's seat just as her father passed from the reach of their headlight beams. She settled back, heart thudding in her chest as she gripped the titanium pen in her hand.

"He'll be okay," Jerry offered, wincing as he shifted his arm against the passenger side armrest. "He seems tough."

Sam flashed him a smile, but her frown returned just as fast. "True, but this storm is intense." Her eyes rolled upward at the clouds before peering all around and a glance in her side mirror showed the other couple fifty yards back, their vehicle idling silently in the darkness.

They sat for a good minute before Jerry coughed to clear his throat. "So, um, what did he mean when he said we were facing something that could fundamentally change the course of human history?"

Sam shrugged. "Not sure. Something he's been thinking about for the past couple of days. Something about the anomaly on the seafloor and all that freshwater pumping into the ocean."

"He mentioned all that," Jerry nodded. "But he implied something else. Like, something catastrophic."

"No clue," Sam said, glancing at him. "But my dad hardly ever says something until he's absolutely sure about it. I'd listen if I were you, if he ever says what it is."

They lapsed into silence once more, nothing but the wind's fury and the ceaseless slamming of rain against the thin walls of the RV to disturb them.

Chapter 28

President John Zimmerman
Oval Office
Washington, D.C.

President Zimmerman stands alone before one of the bulletproof windows, staring at the south lawn beyond the glass. The grass is trimmed to perfection, the bushes shaped with expert care. Marine One, the President's helicopter, squats pristine and shining in the yard, waiting to whisk him to any destination at a moment's notice.

The door behind him opens, and Vice President Craig Pickering steps in and trots over to a small oaken table on the far side of the room where a globe of whiskey sits on a stand. He pops the top, pours himself a finger's worth, leaves it neat, and puts the decanter back. He lifts the glass and rotates the whiskey around to let it breathe while he joins the president at the window.

The pair stare at the garden grounds and the East Wing, Pickering taking a sip of whiskey, welcoming the numbing sting on his lips and the burn as it travels down his throat and lands in his stomach like liquid fire. The president is halfway through a glass already, and Pickering nods at it.

"Drinking early today, Mr. President?"

The president chuckles humorlessly. "Looks like I'm not the only one."

"Drastic times call for drastic measures," Pickering replies with a cordial nod.

They sip their whiskey, soaking in the sight of the open grounds like they'll never see them again. President Zimmerman turns abruptly, steps to his desk, and places his glass down. Resting his hands on the back of his chair, he allows his eyes to linger on the presidential seal in the center of the floor before lifting his eyes to the walls. "Is this my legacy, Craig? Is this all I've done?"

Pickering turns to the president, tilting his head. "What do you mean?"

"All this… *disaster*. All the changes that are coming. Is this what they'll remember me for?"

The Vice President understands his worry, already having thought the same thing himself. With a slow nod, he replies. "More than likely, sir. You said it yourself. The world will change in a fundamental way. Nothing will work the same. This'll affect every coastline and leave no country untouched. We're all in this together, and many world leaders are doing the same damned thing. We're all being forced to do take similar actions."

"Exactly." John shakes his head. "This country has lost some luster over the last few decades, but we have a chance to show our leadership and pull the world through. I'm proud of that.

"I've taken three dozen calls today, one from the Russian Prime Minister, the other from the President of China. The state department is going twenty-four-seven, and it's all hands-on deck. I can't screw this up."

"You won't screw this up," The VP assures him. "Look at what you did when that earthquake hit Los Angeles. We saved thousands of lives, all thanks to your leadership."

Zimmerman nods but remains quiet and doubtful. "This will be millions, Craig. Millions of lives in the palm of my hand. I mean, I've always felt that responsibility, but not as keenly as today. It's humbling as hell. And it frightens me to my core."

Pickering speaks carefully but with more urgency. "Just follow the advice of your experts, John, and we'll be fine. Share information with other countries as much as you can, like we agreed. Keep their trust. You never know, it could bring a new age of peace and cooperation unlike anything the world has ever seen. It's all you *can* do."

The president lifts his glass and swirls the amber liquid inside, appreciating the sharp bourbon smell that rises from the glass. "And what about what I didn't tell them?"

Pickering lowers his head and shifts nervously. "You mean about the biggest threat?"

"That's the one. It seems impossible that could happen, but if our experts are right…"

The Vice President lowers his head and walks around to the front of the desk, turning to face the man he's worked for the past three years. "The Joint Chiefs are in agreement here, sir. You made the right call. If we have to do what we think we will, tipping our hand to the world would be suicide."

"What if they find out before we make our move? They won't want to work with us. Hell, some might even see it as an implicit declaration of war." The President shakes his head. "It's bad enough our country might not stand a chance, but to have the entire world resenting us…"

The President pauses for a long moment, eyes glued to his glass. "Half the population, Craig. That's the best-case scenario they could give me. Half the United States population dead, maybe more." He downs the rest of his whiskey and slams the glass down hard enough to cause Pickering to flinch. "And there's not a damn thing we can do about it except cause a conflict like the world has never seen."

Craig shakes his head. "But we *must* do it, sir. For the good of the country. For the good of the people."

"What's good about it if we betray our morals to accomplish it?" Spittle flies across the desk as the President hisses the words, his chest rising and falling with anguished breaths. "What good are we if we only think about ourselves?"

Pickering remains silent as the President's frustration fades like heat from an overworked computer and they stand in quiet silence, contemplating the oval-shaped room, the walls adorned with the president's personal selection of images. Several highly detailed photos of outer space and space equipment; ships, capsules, and engines; images of the country's most famous pilots. Portraits of John F Kennedy, George Washington, and Abraham Lincoln rest on a table behind his desk.

President Zimmerman purses his lips, a low growl coming from the depths of his chest, a primal expression of frustration with no way to release it.

Chapter 29
Barbara McKnight
Wyndale, Virginia

Barbara startled awake, the chair rocking forward as she shifted her feet on the hardwood. Her head rolled back and forth, eyes blinking away the confusion as the dawn's light greeted her and she sat forward, feet settling back on the floor, panicked briefly by the strange place she'd woken up in. Her racing heart slowed as she realized she was in her rocking chair by the window, the weight of her movements causing the chair to shift and cause her to stir. Shutting her eyes, sighing, she allowed the events of the previous night flood back into her mind. Smooch's fevered barking. The men sneaking around the barn. Barbara stalking them through the yard, using a herd of sheep as cover. Surprising them and chasing them off in a hail of buckshot.

She'd not killed anyone, and her conscience rested easy as a result, and the men must be recovering somewhere, picking out pieces of buckshot from their backs and shoulders in agony. Barbara wasn't happy with what she had to do, though she wouldn't have changed her actions if she could. Protecting her family and their property was essential, especially in a time of crisis, and to do anything else was antithetical to what she believed in.

After the kids had gone to bed, she'd gone back to her room, blinds open, watching the road from her seat, rocking back and forth until the motion put her to sleep. She shifted in the chair and winced, shoulders and back stiff from sleeping in the chair all night. Her nose wrinkled at the waft of gunpowder residue that rose off her clothes and she rubbed at her face, pushing away sleep and exhaustion, grateful for the light of day but wishing she had a few more hours to recover.

The Bellini shotgun rested against the wall nearby by the window, and her phone sat on a small end table. She picked up the device, her fingers moving over the screen instinctively to check for messages and alerts. It took her two seconds to figure out the phone service was still screwed up, and the internet was still spotty, at best. A dry chuckle escaped her lips, mocking all the talk about how it was getting restored soon.

Barbara stood, stretched her arms above her head, and moved down the hall and into the kitchen where she washed the old coffee out of the coffee pot, threw the filter out and started herself a fresh pot brewing. With a warm mug in hand, Barbara stepped into the living room and flipped on the television, looking for something to help distract her from her thoughts about the previous night.

Feeling out of the loop, whatever the "loop" might be, she began flipping through the channels, eyes drifting over the static and sputtering coverage, catching enough to know that she'd missed a lot over the past several hours. She'd missed the President's speech the evening before, and several news stations and an army of talking heads were breaking it down, summing it up, rehashing, and analyzing it. She turned to CNF and watched as her favorite news anchor, Chris Penn, talked through some highlights with a pair of guests. The anchorman appeared on the left side with his guest on the right, a woman with black hair cut sharply to her shoulders, her dark brown eyes staring into the camera. The banner beneath her name read "Carla Sims" and beneath that, "Former US Secretary of State."

"What do you think he meant by that?" Chris asked, his steel-gray eyes pinned hard on the camera, his thin face tense, jaw set. "When the President said we're in an unprecedented time. That we're experiencing a fundamental change in how the world works. Do you agree with that?"

The former secretary of state pursed her lips. "Coming from anyone else, I would say that statement was hyperbolic. But we've never known the President to mince words or make exaggerated claims about anything." Carla shook her head. "I think his entire speech will take some time to digest. The claims of the freshwater surge are being verified by independent scientists. And the fish and wildlife agencies across the world are understandably concerned about the President's statement surrounding our oceans and fisheries being destroyed. I mean, if half of what the president said is true, we're in for a rough ride. Possibly even the roughest ride the world has ever seen."

A liquid chill trickled down Barbara's spine, and she shook off the shiver, taking a sip of her coffee. She didn't understand what any of what they were saying meant, realizing she needed to watch the entire speech from the start if she wanted to understand it. She left CNF and scanned through the channels until she found the speech playing on a loop on one of the capitol programming stations. Based on the time stamp beneath the headline, it appeared she'd caught the speech near the beginning and she grabbed the remote and turned the volume up.

The president was a handsome man in his sixties with an honest face and an unassuming disposition, though his face was dark, his eyes betraying the telltale signs of sleeplessness that Barbara was all too familiar with.

"… this time of great need. Make no mistake, what is happening in the North Atlantic will change us all. Not only those who live in the coastal towns and cities but also those who move inland. It's important that we pull together and help our fellow citizens in whatever way we can." The President paused, shifting his attention around the room, lifting a hand with a slight gesture of explanation.

"The anomaly you've all been hearing about is real. It began as a crack in the seafloor, ten kilometers long and a kilometer wide. The first ships to arrive on the scene sent rovers to investigate, and what they found was that a sub-surface aquifer appears to have burst, sending unprecedented amounts of fresh water into the oceans. The pressure intensified and widened the original anomaly, sending cracks and fissures all along the shelf off the coastal United States. We're still mapping the extent of the damage, and we'll make the raw data available to the scientific community at large to encourage information sharing and cooperation."

The president worked his jaw back and forth for a moment, and his eyes flashed with that familiar steadfastness the country's citizens had grown used to. "What does this damage mean? It means the undersea currents have been disrupted, and the salinity of the oceans, to a great extent, is changing. In the immediate area around the anomaly, marine wildlife is already dead or has migrated to other parts of the ocean. What it will do to the rest of the oceans, only time will tell. We're just understanding the forces at work here, but for now, we need to come to terms with the fact that there isn't a way to stop the freshwater surge.

"In addition," he fixed the camera with a grim expression, subtly reposition his body to brace himself more against the lectern, "we expect sea levels to rise as much as two inches over the next three weeks to a month."

The reporters in the room turned their heads to one another and murmured in shock, and the President held his hands out to ask for calm in the room.

"You may be asking yourselves what's next, and I wholeheartedly understand." The president glanced down at the podium. "As of this moment, I'm declaring a federal state of emergency. We'll be working with the country's emergency response teams and the governors and mayors of every state and city to work through contingency and response plans. We'll be implementing evacuation orders within the next week for any coastal regions affected by the sea level rise which itself builds heavily on the evacuations that were already in place from FEMA to handle hurricane Kate. We're taking precautions to secure our ports and working to solve the intense logistical issues surrounding this unprecedented crisis. Make no mistake – this situation is one unlike any the country has ever faced."

Barbara had gotten some information about the anomaly from Tom, but to hear the news from the president gave it an ominous connotation. Evacuations meant they would force people to move inland from the coast and everything Tom and Barbara had been preparing for would come true. The evacuations hadn't started yet, and already she'd had to chase three men off her property. The implications of what could happen next were staggering.

As if answering her concern, the president continued. "Let me make something clear. While we struggle through this difficult time, looting and rioting will not be tolerated. I'm prepared to bring the full weight of the United States armed forces to bear to ensure our citizens remain safe. National Guard troops will be on point from the onset, but we will be augmenting their deployment with active-duty troops in non-combatant roles, in accordance with state and federal guidelines. I want to be clear one more time: The disaster we face does not give anyone permission to break the law or make things more difficult than they already are. We're all in this together, and we owe it to our family, friends and fellow Americans to keep level heads through this crisis."

Barbara chortled, appreciating the sentiment, but not believing it was a promise the President or local law enforcement could keep. He lifted his chin and addressed the forum in a resolute voice. "I know this is a phrase you're hearing a lot right now, but it's true. This is an unprecedented time, leading to a fundamental change in how our world works. It's frightening, but we'll survive and come out the other side more prosperous than before…"

She heard the kids rustling around upstairs, the familiar bumps and knocks as they brushed their teeth and changed from pajamas to chore clothes. Grabbing the remote from her lap, she snapped off the television and sat back on the couch, stunned by the president's address. Jack tromped down the stairs and Linda's quieter steps followed him as they entered the kitchen, Jack heading straight for the refrigerator while her daughter angled for the coffee.

"Morning, Mom," Linda called.

"Morning, Mommy!" Jack exclaimed, opening the fridge and reaching to get a bottle of orange juice from the door. He paused. "Can I have some orange juice?"

"Morning, kids." Barbara's voice was rough and full of emotion, and she coughed to clear it. "And, yes, you *may* have some orange juice. Pour me a glass, too, please."

"Okay!"

"Want some oatmeal?" Linda asked. "I'm having oatmeal."

"That sounds great," Barbara nodded absentmindedly. "A little sugar and cinnamon for me, please."

"You got it."

The President's words ran circles through her mind. While it didn't alter her fundamental plan to keep the homestead safe, it added some urgency to the situation and she struggled to think about how they could improve things. They would have to keep a close eye on the animals, possibly even rounding them up at night and putting them into the animal barn. They could make better use of Tom's camera system, and she could set a guard shift with Linda which would give Barbara some much needed rest while ensuring someone was awake at all times. Smooch was an amazing first line of defense, but they needed more layers. Keeping a sense of normalcy was important, but by far the most important thing was to keep everyone safe, no matter the cost.

She shook her head, dismissing the thoughts. *One step at a time, Barbara. One step at a time.* She stood and walked into the kitchen, taking a piping hot bowl of oatmeal from Linda with a smile and ruffle of her daughter's hair.

"Thanks, dear."

"You're welcome."

She took her oatmeal and coffee to the table, grabbing a spoon along the way, and sat in her usual seat. Her daughter had not only heaped sugar and cinnamon atop the bowl, but a dollop of butter, too, the hearty aroma of cooked oats and buttery sweet spices caressing her nose, causing her stomach to rumble with hunger. With a deep breath, she dug in with her spoon, mixing the contents of the bowl before taking two large bites. Jack placed her glass of orange juice in front of her, and Barbara gave him a wide smile around her bulging cheeks.

"You guys are amazing."

Jack grinned and grabbed his own glass of juice and a minute later they were all seated. Barbara gave them a few minutes to eat before she began to share some of what she'd heard and read. "So… I heard some things on the news today. They're starting mass evacuations of people inland from the coast."

"I thought they were already doing that," Linda said.

"That was for Hurricane Kate," Barbara nodded, "but now they're doing it for the whole coast, from New York to the tip of Florida."

Linda didn't look surprised as she took another bite. "That's a lot of people."

"A staggering amount," she conceded.

"So, more people will come on our farm?" Jack asked, his eyes wide and innocent. "You'll have to defend ourselves more?"

Barbara laughed. "Not necessarily. The President has called for everyone to keep their cool during all this. He said looting and lawlessness will not be tolerated. He even said he'd use the military to keep everyone safe." Barbara shrugged, her attempt at making things sound better than they were falling flat to her own ears. "I know he means well, but I can't see how they can keep tabs on everyone. Maybe things will be fine, but Bristol could fall victim to looting soon. And then you'd be right, Jack. We could have more problems like we had last night where I have to shoot at people."

"When you say you shot, what do you mean?" A darkness passed over Linda's face. "I mean, Smooch woke us up with her barking, you went to see who it was."

"Well, after Smooch woke me up, I went to the window and saw some flashlights down by the barn." Barbara shrugged at the simple explanation. "I went outside to get a better look and saw three men snooping around with crowbars. So, I crept up on them and shot at them to make them go away."

"Did they try to hurt you?" Jack asked, Barbara immediately sensing where the question was going.

"I didn't give them the chance," she replied plainly, meeting him eye for eye. "Three people making a beeline for our house in the middle of the night carrying crowbars aren't here to give us cookies and milk."

"Did you…" Linda studied her mother's face carefully.

"I didn't kill anyone," Barbara said. "I was pretty far away, so the buckshot was spread out. I sent them running with their butts on fire, though."

Jack giggled. "Mom shot them in their butts."

A slow smile spread on Linda's lips as she focused back to her oatmeal, and Barbara chuckled even though it wasn't really funny.

"What's the plan for today, Mom?"

"I want to make a quick run to the store after breakfast to fill the spare jerry cans we have with gasoline in case we need it for the generator later. Then we can drive by the grocery store and see how crowded it is."

"The stores will be packed, right?" Linda asked. "I mean, if everyone is thinking like we are, they're probably going nuts stocking up."

"Maybe. But if it is really busy, we'll skip it. We've got plenty for when the Everetts come over. Are you guys excited?"

"Yes!" Jack exclaimed. "Is Mr. Darren going to bring over his baseball card collection again?"

"I don't know, but I'm sure he'll have some cool stuff to show you." Darren always brought over something to wow the kids, whether it was an old sports card, an ancient coin, or some other oddity he'd picked up at an antique auction or garage sale. Sometimes he found old arrowheads on their property and brought them over for the kids to have.

Barbara finished her last bite and collected all the bowls, rinsed them in the sink and placed them in the dishwasher while the kids went outside to feed Smooch and throw some feed out in the yard. She saw to the Benelli shotgun, temporarily ejecting the shells and putting it back in her closet. Once she'd secured it and double-checked that Linda had secured her pistol from the night before, she stepped outside and collected Linda, the two of them hitching their cargo trailer to the back of the F150 before placing ten five-gallon jerry cans into the back and lashing them down with bungee cords.

"Okay, you kids ready to go?"

"Ready!" Jack called, running up through the yard with Smooch close on his heels.

"Smooch," she called, and the dog's ears perked up at sound of her name spoken in a sharp tone. Barbara patted her leg, and the dog sprinted over. When she got there, Barbara rubbed the Shepherd's head and scratched behind her ears. "You were such a good girl last night. We're so lucky to have you." The dog gave a playful yip before Barbara released her and the three climbed into the F150 and were soon back on the road toward town.

For the first time all week, her stomach knotted up at the thought of leaving their home unprotected. There might soon come a time when she might need to leave Linda home to watch over things in the event she had to go into town. She frowned, the pit of dread in her stomach swelling, trying to keep from falling into negative thoughts about Tom and Sam still not being home.

"What's wrong, Mom?" Linda asked, blinking up at her with concern.

"Oh, nothing," she replied, wiping her arm across her forehead. "It's just a warm morning."

Instead of bypassing the retail parts of town, Barbara took Clear Creek Road and purposefully drove by the Walgoods Supercenter outside of Bristol. The parking lot was busy, and traffic bustling back and forth along the roads, vehicles whipping through the parking lots, bunching up at the Highway 19 intersection, speeding through to beat yellow lights, one car narrowly missing another turning left. Horns honked and tires squealed, Barbara's shoulders tense as they went, driving defensively, eyes focused on the road. She hopped on I-81 west toward Bristol and then took I-381 south into town. From there, she took a right on Euclid Avenue, noting restaurant parking lots were empty while the grocery store lots were packed. Bypassing all the big-name stores, she returned to the Food King on the west side of town. The lot was half full, people pushing their carts briskly, yet not in a panicked rush.

"Okay, let's give this a try," Barbara said, parking in an empty area toward the back of the lot. It was a longer walk, but she wanted to ensure they could get out quickly if necessary. She took Jack's hand as they approached the front doors. "Stay close to me."

"Want me to get a cart?" Linda asked, skipping ahead.

"A small one, please."

The three formed a tight group as they pushed through the door. The aisles were crowded, most people shopping or talking quietly while a few others darted through the rows, dropping things into carts or baskets in a rush. People seemed more conscious of those around them, throwing dark looks aside without making direct eye contact. Barbara couldn't be completely sure, but she thought she noticed the waistline bulges of several people carrying, far more than she saw on an average day. She angled toward the meat counter and, for the first time she could remember, took a number from the dust-covered ticket dispenser on the far side of the counter. Several older couples, two mothers, and an old, bearded man stood among those waiting to pick up meat.

Big Matthew Trimboli was working behind the counter, sweating as he packaged steaks, chuck roasts and ground beef in white paper packaging, tying them up, stamping them with a price tag, and handing them over. He had an assistant with him, a tall young man in his early twenties with a similar build to his father—Matthew's son, Todd. The younger man wore a red-stained apron, hands bloody as he fetched cuts of meat from the back for his father. Matthew Trimboli worked fast, cutting the line in half in just a few minutes. People took their packages, nodded to the butcher, and moved on while people piled up behind Barbara and the kids. When it came her turn, Matthew's eyes grew wide and Barbara chuckled, throwing her hands up playfully.

"Easy, Matthew. I'm just here for some chickens. Three please."

"That's good to know." His shoulders sagged in relief. "It's been insane here today."

"Good for business, right?" She tried to sound hopeful.

The big man leaned forward over the meat display and kept his voice low. "I'm not complaining, but I'm running low on everything. You're getting the last of the chickens. If this keeps up, I'll have to shut down until I can restock."

"That's not good." Barbara shook her head, mouth twisted down in a frown. "It's probably just a knee jerk reaction to the President's address. You saw it, right?"

"I watched it with the wife last night," Matthew said. "Really frightening stuff. Are you folks prepared?"

"As much as we can be," she replied with a glance around. "I just hope people remain civil."

"Let's hope so." Matthew drew back from the display and moved to fill her order. With the chickens settled in the cart, they moved through the aisles, gathering a few things on her list before heading to check out. It was an older type of market, and the self-serve kiosks hadn't yet arrived so lines were lengthy, credit card transactions exacerbating the delays, though everyone remained patient and polite despite the underlying tension in the air. She assumed everyone standing in line had seen the President's address and were making preparations for the worst. A lot of folks might not be prepared like the McKnights, but they knew what they needed. It was the ones who didn't – who weren't prepared in any shape or form – that worried her the most.

Those without more than a couple days' worth of food in the pantry would tick down their list of options, first figuring the stores would restock the following day, or the government would have food banks and FEMA camps, too. When those failed to be sufficient, or started to run out of supplies, it would be easy enough to move to taking from their neighbors, especially if they had a large enough group, one that was organized and took matters into their own hands.

Barbara shook off the image of the three men stalking toward the house the previous night as they reached the end of the line, the kids stacking food on the conveyor. A few minutes later they were wheeling out of the store, heading for the truck and loading everything up. The flow of cars into the parking lot had increased substantially since they arrived, and Barbara

"It was kinda weird in there," Linda commented as Barbara pulled the truck and trailer out of the lot.

"Definitely a little tense," she agreed. "Now you see what I mean about things going south in a hurry."

The girl nodded. "And it's just the morning. Wait until tonight."

"That's what I was just thinking." Barbara drove off and pulled into the nearest gas station where they waited in line for one of the ten rows of pumps to be freed up. Dozens of vehicles crowded the pumps and parking spaces in front of the gas station, many of them with luggage carriers on top, the owners looking haggard like they'd driven through the night. Surprisingly, in spite of the chaos, they were able to fill their cans relatively quickly, Barbara paying inside to avoid any delays with credit card readers at the pumps. She pulled out of the gas station once they finished and got back on Euclid Avenue, heading east through Bristol. Business had picked up even more since they'd first entered town, and the horns had taken a life of their own. The air was full of them, bleating and blatting like a herd of sheep penned in tight as cars vied for position on the roads. They bypassed several traffic jams – including a fender bender where those involved were red-faced, shouting at each other – forcing Barbara onto a tree-lined back road that led them away from the traffic and into more rural surroundings where farms and hills stretched for miles.

Relief washed over her as she pulled up the gravel driveway and shut the gate behind them. Driving up the gravel lane, she scanned the yard for any signs of trouble, relaxing when Smooch trotted around the back of the house with her tail wagging. Barbara took a wide turn to the right, pulling the trailer in next to the fuel shed. Enlisting Linda's help, they lugged the five-gallon cans inside and stacked them on shelves before checking the generator to see it was full, easily able to power the hydroponics, freezers, refrigerators, and a small window air conditioning unit for several months with the fuel they had on hand.

Locking up the shed, they grabbed the groceries from the back of the truck and lugged them inside. Barbara started prepping the chickens for dinner and had Linda help cut vegetables while Jack took care of some simple chores in the yard that they'd not been able to get to earlier, Smooch staying close to his side and Barbara watching him out through the window, vigilant for any signs of trouble. Once done with the food preparations, Barbara put the chickens in the oven to prepare for Darren and Marie coming over later, then she released the kids with the instruction to continue with their studies.

"I'll take a look at the work you've been doing," she said, "and if you've been doing well, I'll give you a couple days off before we get serious again."

"Outstanding," Linda said with a grin.

"Can I play some video games when I'm done?" Jack asked.

"As long as you don't rush and do the work right."

Jack grinned and took off up the stairs, Barbara steeling herself for what sort of results she'd be faced with when checking them over later. Jack was flighty at the best of times, mind bouncing from subject to subject, focusing on anything serious taking an extraordinary amount of energy and effort. It had gotten better in the last year, but he still required more attention when it came to his schoolwork than Samantha or Linda ever had.

With the kids situated and dinner in the oven, Barbara took her phone out of her pocket and retired to the couch. She turned on the television and browsed through some news channels to find them still spotty, sometimes freezing completely. It didn't matter, though, given that they were just rehashing the president's statement, anyway, the "experts" on heavy display. Everyone had a hot take or a theory on what was happening, and they excelled at stoking the flames of controversy while providing very little in the way of clear direction and calming influences.

The internet and data services remained down, so it didn't surprise her to find nothing from Tom. The nagging sense of numbness had returned but she'd normalized it, pushing the emotion down for the tenth time that day, casting aside the negative thoughts swirling in her mind. Technology was falling apart, but it didn't mean Tom and Sam were injured or dead and it didn't mean they wouldn't walk through the front door at any moment. She closed her eyes tight against the drone of the television, lips barely moving, saying yet another prayer for her family.

Please, God, see them home safe. See them home soon.

She repeated it over and over, but the words hardly made a dent in the wall of doubt plaguing her mind.

Chapter 30
Tom McKnight
Outer Banks, North Carolina

Tom took long, plodding steps through the waves of rain, growing familiar with the storm's cadence, going along with the ebbs and flows of cyclonic rhythms, adjusting his body to brace against the high winds. He staggered forward when they dissipated, using vehicles for cover, marking one after the other, fifty yards at a time, on his way to determine the status of the bridge. Blue flashing police lights came as a surprise when he stumbled upon them, squinting through layers of rain, wondering if he was seeing things. Two police cruisers sat side-by-side, blocking the lanes to go across the bridge, the gray storm consuming their headlights and taillights like a black hole until they were only several feet away.

Tom waved through the back window of the right-hand car, but he doubted the officer saw him. So, he approached between the idling vehicles, hunching down to avoid the most ferocious winds, being careful not to startle them. Stepping up to the driver's side window, he waved to get the officer's attention. The man jerked around in his seat at the sight of Tom, rolling down his window and resting his arm on the edge of the door. He wore a clear rain poncho over his uniform and sat sideways with his right hand down by his hip.

The officer gave Tom a once over and shouted over the crackling of his police radio and blistering winds. "What can I do for you, sir?"

"I'm wondering if the bridge is clear!" Tom shouted back. "We're trying to get inland from the storm."

"That's a negative on that." The officer's voice was loud and overbearing. "A wave came over the bridge and struck a truck. Overturned it. Until we can get a crew out here to clear the vehicle, the lanes must remain closed."

Tom half-turned his body toward the bridge, peering across at the inbound lanes. He couldn't see more than fifteen feet in front of him, though he was certain no police cruisers sat on the other side. He turned back to the officer. "How about the other side? The inbound lanes?"

"We haven't gotten clearance to open those yet, but we're working on it." A sheet of water rolled off the top of the cruiser and splashed down over his arm and into his lap. The man shook his arm and made an annoyed sound.

The radio inside the vehicle crackled, and a voice broke through the static. "… flooding in the <inaudible>… 64 bridge washed out… proceed to Whalebone Junction…"

Tom raised his voice, trying to keep the officer's attention. "Can we cross on the other side, officer? I know you said it's shut down, but—"

"Negative on that, *sir*!" The officer blinked at the rain in annoyance, then at Tom. His partner leaned forward in the passenger seat, re-emphasizing what the first one had said. "We can't allow anyone to cross. We're in the middle of two national emergencies here."

Tom peered in with confusion written on his face. "Two?"

"Yeah, we've got this one," the officer looked all around at the storm. "And the President's declaration—"

The radio crackle interrupted the officer. "… maintain position… guidance from Washington… east coast evacuation…"

Water crawled down Tom's neck and soaked his shirt, the plastic starting to stretch and tear and the tape starting to pull away from his jacket. "What about the Currituck Banks Tunnel? Can we pass through there?"

"I wouldn't advise it, sir," the officer said. He dropped his arm and hit the button to roll up his window a few inches. "You should have gotten out when they governor called for the evacuation. Your best bet is to sit in your car until the storm abates. Once the weather clears, we'll work on getting you inland."

Tom started to say something more, but the window rolled up and sealed shut. He nodded and turned, trudging back the way he'd come, slogging through the wind and rain, pulling the tattered remainder of his poncho around him. But rather than return to the RV, Tom waited until he got out of the policemen's eyesight and dashed across a swampy strip of grass to the other side of the road. He turned west and pushed his way toward the bridge once more, his tattered poncho fluttering before it snapped, ripped from the tape, his armpits, shoulders, and chest soaked.

After five minutes of battling his way through the wind and rain, he finally came to the part of the structure that spanned the water. Legs apart, dragging one foot after the other, he staggered to the edge and looked down at the roiling waters. The waves were a deep shade of gray as they slammed against the moorings and sprayed upward like foamy, gnarled hands. Every few seconds, one hit the side of the bridge and sent spray over the barrier to land with a tremendous splash on the bridge. Several inches of water raced across to the other side, hit the opposite barrier and sprayed upward again.

Tom tried to imagine crossing it in the RV and quickly decided it was too risky of a proposition. They could get flipped, rolled over, or washed over the side and there was no way would he risk putting Sam and Jerry in such obvious danger. The choice was clear: they'd have to try the tunnel. He'd approach it with the same strategy as the bridge, getting close enough for Tom to get out and scout, making sure it was okay to drive through before committing them.

Lightning cracked nearby, so close the hairs on his arms raised with the static charge, the air scented with ozone. With a last glance at the bridge, he turned and trudged back toward the RV, peering ahead into the gloom for what seemed like forever until he finally spotted the headlights. They seemed paltry in the storm's rage, but the inside promised a dry haven. Waving at Sam and Jerry where they sat in the front, he circled to the side door and hammered his fist on it until it flew open and he staggered up the stairs, tearing off the bits of plastic still clinging to him and drenching the floor with water. Sam slammed the door shut behind him and wrapped the door handle shut tight.

"Hey, you made it!" Jerry chuckled as he took the loose plastic and held it up with a shake of his head, putting the useless garment in the kitchen sink. "But your poncho is shredded."

"No kidding," Tom laughed with the young man, relishing in the dry heat wafting over him from the vents. He marched back to the bathroom and stripped off his wet coat and shirt, leaving him with just a soggy T-shirt. Sam handed him a towel and he dried off as best he could before making his way to the front where Sam had thrown down two more towels to soak up the water on the floor, Jerry placing his foot on one and sweeping it across the kitchen floor.

"I put a towel down in the driver's seat for you." His daughter gestured.

"Thanks." Tom stepped between the seats and plopped down with a heavy sigh.

"It's the last dry one we have," she reminded him. "No more drying out."

"Too bad we don't have a machine dryer," he frowned. "We'll just have to hang them up in the bathroom and hope they dry."

"Wait, there's a small, clip-on fan in the bedroom." Sam gestured toward the back of the vehicle. "We could probably use that to help dry things out."

"Great idea," Tom agreed. "Make it happen."

Sam went back to get the clothes and towels drying while Tom had a drink of water and rested until she got back. They took up their positions with Sam in the passenger seat, Jerry seated between them on the cleaning bucket, the two of them staring at Tom, waiting for the detailed report on what he'd seen.

"I found the police," he said. "And I walked out to the bridge."

"What did the cops say?" Sam said, her words full of hopeful excitement. "Is it safe to cross?"

Tom shook his head. "I don't think so. The weather is insane out there. Water is washing onto the bridge and sweeping over it, and the police said a truck overturned which is blocking the outbound lanes. No one can cross. I went out and stood at the edge, but the visibility is terrible. All I can tell you is that it looks extremely dangerous to cross. We'd be lucky to make it halfway before we got tossed into the bay."

"So, that's a no-go." Jerry shook his head.

"I'm afraid so." Tom agreed.

"Why don't we just stay here?" Jerry offered. "We could sit tight for a few hours until the storm passes, then drive out in the morning."

"No way," Sam said. "I want to be home. Like, yesterday."

Tom recalled the garbled talk on the cops' radio. "I don't think that's a good idea either. While I was talking to the officers, I heard their radio dispatcher calling out. They mentioned flooding, and the 64 bridge had washed out. I caught something about an east coast evacuation, but I don't know what that meant. Plus we have no idea how long it'll be before the storm actually passes."

Jerry's gasped, eyebrows raised in bewilderment. "Wow, the 64 bridge washed out? I *never* heard of that before, man. If that bridge got washed out, then…" He let his words trail off, but the fear in his eyes spoke volumes.

Tom stared rigidly between the two. "That's why I have a bad feeling about staying here. If the entire Outer Banks flood, we'll be in big trouble. This RV doesn't float as far as I'm aware."

"Pretty sure it doesn't," Jerry gave a nervous laugh.

"So, it's the tunnel?" Sam gripped the arm of her chair, her fingers digging into the cloth.

"I think it's our only option." Tom nodded with grim confidence. "We can check it out first, and if we see any issues, we won't go in."

Sam and Jerry both nodded, though the young man still looked shaken. Tom put the RV into gear, backed up, and turned the vehicle around, heading back the way they'd come. They approached the older couple who still sat there with their hazard lights on. Hand raised, he waved to them as they passed, though he doubted they saw him through the storm. As they eased down the highway, they passed the same dark retail outlets, squatting like shadowy monoliths of some past age. He wove around more debris, the RV shivering and shaking as the air-currents whistled and shrieked through its many gaps.

"I can't wait to be out of this wind," Sam said, a shudder passing down her spine as she sat in the passenger seat. "The roof feels like it'll blow off any second."

"Knock on wood," Jerry said, rapping his knuckles beneath the cabin bunk over their heads.

"I'm trying to find the exit for the tunnel." Tom squinted into the rain, straining his eyes. "I thought it was around here somewhere. Jerry, do you… Ah, there it is!"

He came to an exit ramp branching off to their left, and he turned the vehicle onto it in a slow turn to keep them from tilting, not giving the wind enough of a finger hold to flip them over. As they slowly turned north, the rattling and shaking eased, and even the windshield wipers worked better.

"The wind is hitting us in the back instead of the side now," Tom said, as if they needed an explanation. "Should be easier on us from here on out."

They transitioned out of the commercial sector of town and passed through more neighborhoods with one-lane side streets and thin byways between houses, places for sand and debris to wash through in an endless flood. The same sort of destruction they had seen to the beachfront homes when driving north from the gas station presented itself again, though many of the homes they passed by had suffered even more than the first ones.

"The town looks old," he said. "I mean, it looks strange butting up against the highway."

"Yeah, they upgraded the main road when the tunnel went in. People weren't happy about it since it brought a ton more traffic through."

"I'd be pissed off to have a big highway running through my quaint little neighborhood, too," Tom agreed. "I guess that was part of the debate Sam was talking about when they were first building the place."

Their headlamps cut through the sideways drizzle, providing a gloomy view of the houses crowded the road on both sides, absorbing the wind's abuse while shielding the RV from the weather's worst. Parts of their roofs hung off, and great swaths of wooden siding fluttered and flapped in the wind. Debris skittered across the pavement, skimming over a thin layer of water. Off to the right, the waves pushed up between the homes, eating away at them big-by-bit, the black abyss of the sea closing over the shoreline. Tom worried they might be too late, and the tunnel might have already flooded, but he pressed forward, making good time and reached the edge of the wildlife preserve just after midnight. A sign to the right read *Currituck Banks Tunnel* and Tom pulled the RV to a stop where the road started dipping down into the wide, four-lane tunnel entrance.

He stood up in his seat, scanning down into the misty-wet blackness. Water drained down into the tunnel, though there weren't any standing pools like he had expected. "Seems safe enough," he said with a glance over at Jerry. "I don't see any stalled or broken-down vehicles piled around the entrance." He smirked, trying to sound humorous. "It's just a simple drive deep underground in the middle of a hurricane, right?"

"Looks scary to me." Sam's wide, green eyes peered down.

"I think they have good built-in drainage and electric pumps with backup generators," Jerry added.

Tom put the RV into park, stood, and prepared to go down. "Only one way to find out."

Something rustled by his side, and he turned to see Jerry holding out his shredded plastic poncho from earlier, a wide grin plastered on his face. "I thought you might need this, Mr. McKnight. It worked pretty well before."

Tom laughed and rolled his eyes, and Sam covered her mouth to stifle a laugh. Pushing past the young man, Tom stood at the side door, turning to Sam.

"We'll lock the door behind you," she said before he could ask. "Be super careful, Dad."

"I will." With a brief nod, he swiped the flashlight off the kitchen counter, unhooked the string from the door latch, and stepped out. The door whipped around viciously, but he wrestled it closed and trudged the last thirty yards to the tunnel entrance.

The area around the tunnel entrance trapped the wind in a mini vortex, and it smacked him and tossed him off balance as water rushed past his shoes, drenching his already wet socks down to the skin, rain roaring in his ears. As he reached the entrance, he raised his flashlight but was surprised to find the emergency lights in tunnel's ceiling still on. They illuminated the road as it stretched off into the distance, a sheen of water flowing past him, spreading across the pavement, though it appeared to be draining off somewhere. Whatever mechanisms the engineers had built to keep it from flooding were clearly still functioning despite the massive amounts of water and loss of power around the area.

"Hats off to the people who built this," he mumbled to himself. "This is really brilliant." He glanced down the tunnel one more time and then sprinted back through slapping wind to the RV, knocking on the door for Sam to let him inside. Once in, he towel-dried his face, neck, and arms.

"How's it look?" Jerry asked.

"Not bad, actually," Tom replied, unable to hide his excitement at the possibility of reaching real safety. "The water is draining fine, and the tunnel lights are still on."

"When they built it, they said it was a marvel of modern engineering." The young man agreed. "Looks like they were right."

"That means it's home sweet home for us," Sam said with satisfied assuredness.

Tom hopped into the driver's seat and rested his arms over the wheel. "Let's do this."

Chapter 31
President John Zimmerman
Oval Office
Washington, D.C.

The President sits behind his desk in the Oval Office, hands folded in front of him as he focuses on what Senior Advisor Rita Cortez is saying. She sits across from him, her round face bronze-toned with a dash of freckles splashed across her nose and cheeks, going over banking information and statistics. His lead staffer, Maxine, looks tired but sharp after several nerve-wracking days assembling an exhaustive string of meetings with local and foreign leaders, heads of business and agriculture, and even the Director of the CDC.

Others linger in the room – cabinet members, staffers and scientists, some taking notes on their computers while others are in the queue to present the President with his next issue to address. Maxine sits on Rita's left, and the key staffer is his saving grace. The young thirty-three-year-old watches over him like a hawk, keeps his schedule rolling, and shields him from unnecessary distractions. She's become as much a trusted staff member as Rita.

"Mr. President? Are you hearing me?"

His eyes slide back to Rita, inhaling sharply as he sits up slightly in his chair. "Sorry. I was distracted."

She nods and continues. "The First United States Bank and others, while encouraged by your transparency and leadership, are looking for more concrete answers. They want to know how we'll control interest rates and lending in the short-term and long-term."

John nods. "We can only do that after we've seen the overall plan. Can they give us another two weeks?"

Rita shakes her head. "I'll try to get us some more time, but they're getting anxious."

"I understand that, but a lot of what we need to plan for will depend on where the resettlements put us. There will be miles of irretrievable coastline, and the insurance companies will want bailouts."

"They're already barking," Rita agrees.

Zimmerman nods. "They'll get their time to speak. Once we outline the restructuring layout for the effected states, we'll see what kind of land grants and transferable loan options are available. All subsidized by us, where needed."

"People won't be happy about assuming new loans with higher interest rates," she reminds him.

"We'll take into consideration what they had left to pay on their homes," he shoots back. "They'll get a new home with the same, or lower, interest rate, and we'll boost construction jobs almost five-hundred percent. It's a win-win for everyone."

"But they won't enjoy moving from their beach front homes to the Arizona desert." Rita gives him a sideways smirk.

"It won't be quite that bad," he scoffs and waves his hand. "Most will only have to move a few miles inland. Believe me, when all this is said and done, no one will want anything to do with the water."

Maxine raises her hand to her earpiece and then touches her temple, a sign someone important is on the phone. He breaks off his conversation with Rita and nods to the staffer. "What do you have for me, Max?"

"Canada's prime minister is on the phone. Line two."

The president shifts in his chair and loosens his collar, eyes darting once around the room before he lifts his voice to get their attention. "Folks, I need some privacy. Can you clear the room, please?"

Everyone filters toward the doors except for Rita and Maxine, both required to stay, monitor, and record the president's call. With everyone gone, John takes a drink of water from a nearby glass and gives Maxine a nod. A laptop rests on the woman's knees, and she taps some keys to start the White House recording. Then she hits one last button to activate the president's speaker phone and complete the connection.

With a last look at Zimmerman, she addresses the person on the line. "Hello, sir. You are on the line with the President."

"Prime Minister," John starts off warm and cordial. "Good to hear from—"

"Let's cut through the crap, John." The Canadian Prime Minister's gruff French accent berates him through the phone speaker, causing Zimmerman to wince inwardly. "Why are your teams holding back critical information about the unfolding disaster at our collective doorsteps?"

"I'm not sure what you're talking about," Zimmerman says, his voice surprised and a bit too innocent. "You've got access to the same raw data we have, and my people have been updating your teams daily."

"We have access to the data, but you've not passed along your predictions on the rising sea levels and how you expect to handle things on your end. And we can't do anything ourselves without knowing what you plan to do. We've asked for your contingency plans a dozen times."

"We've provided you with our short-term plans," the President replies, his tone slightly more forceful. "The long-term solutions will soon follow. We'll know more by the end of the week, and I'd be happy to share that with you then."

"Allow us to come to those meetings," the Prime Minister insists. "We can make decisions together."

"I'm afraid I can't do that," Zimmerman says. "It's a matter of national—"

"You say you're our partner and friend," the Prime Minister interrupts, "yet you're holding back critical information about the unfolding disaster. And you fail to invite us to high-level, shared sessions to understand our collective problems and determine a collective response. This is not like you, John." The Canadian prime minister pauses, lending an ominous tone to his voice. "I hear our friends to your south are also concerned about your guarded approach."

The President closes his eyes and allows his frustration to wash over him and then off so he doesn't bite back too hard. "One week, Pierre," the President says. "We'll know more by then, and we'll *share* it."

"I don't want to see a list of evacuation locations and interest rate adjustments." The Prime Minister's tone sharpens once more, almost to the point of a threat. "I want all the data on the anomaly you have, and I want your cooperation. If you don't share all your information with us, then we'll share to the world what our own sources tell us. Think hard on this, John. We'll not stand by and let hundreds of millions of people die."

Zimmerman swallows hard and grinds his jaw. "One week, Pierre. One week." The Canadian ends the connection wordlessly with a single click.

"Well, he's pissed," he says, staring at the phone.

"Just a little." Rita takes a deep breath and holds it, shaking her head at the sting of the Prime Minister's words.

"I can't say I blame him. We'd been on good terms ever since he took office three years ago, and we always worked together to improve trade agreements. I know Pierre, and there's no doubt he's already putting things in place to prepare his people for an American collapse, or worse. They might even move troops to their border to protect themselves against incursions – fat lot of good that'll do, though."

"You think they'd go that far?"

"I don't want it to come to that, but it could."

Rita shakes her head. "Do you think we're approaching this correctly? We can't have the world mistrusting us now."

"I don't see any other course of action but to keep this under wraps." The President leans forward and rubs his forehead between his index finger and thumb, Rita looking down at her lap, not seeming convinced anymore.

There's a knock on the door, and John calls for them to enter. Vice President Craig Pickering steps in and shuts the door behind him, giving Maxine and Rita a nod.

"I take it Pierre isn't happy?" the Vice President asks.

"Not in the least," he replies. "He didn't come out and say it, but he clearly knows *something*. He senses we're not being honest with him at the very least."

"Which we're not." Pickering shakes his head. "How did they find out? Did someone leak it?"

"Maybe one of the scientists…" Zimmerman lowers his hand to his chin and spreads his fingers wide to rub along his jawline. "It's just as likely they have their own people taking measurements. It wouldn't be too difficult to figure out from there."

"Just what we feared the most." Rita glances back and forth between the President and Vice President, and she seems suddenly anxious to change course. "Maybe we should reconsider—"

"I'll inform the CoS to gather the cabinet," Pickering says, stiffening. "We'll provide some recommendations within the hour." The Vice President gives them all a nod and exits the room.

John lifts his eyes. "Ladies, can I have a few minutes alone, please?"

"Of course," Rita says, and she gets up to leave.

"Do you need anything?" Maxine asks.

"No, thanks. I just want a few minutes of quiet. I need to think."

"Of course, sir." Maxine gives him a curt nod before following Chief Advisor from the room. The door shuts quietly, leaving the President alone with his thoughts, his mind drifting to his family, as it often does. His wife, Heather, has been a rock for him, and their two kids are his pride and joy, both growing up to be outstanding citizens.

He decides that he'll have to sit them down and tell them the full truth as soon as he gets a chance - he might even call them all home so he can do it face-to-face. It will be a sobering conversation, but necessary. He doesn't want to scare anyone, but they'll need to prepare for the worst. Everyone will need to prepare for the worst, but for his family he decides to exercise some executive privilege and ensure they're among the first to know.

Chapter 32
Barbara McKnight
Wyndale, Virginia

Smooch's intense barking spiked Barbara's senses, the yipping and chesty coughs as her fangs snapped the air clearly audible even inside. Barbara clamped her lips together and strode from the kitchen into the dining room, moving aside the sheer curtain with one hand to peer out the enormous front window, her other hand resting on the gun nestled against her back hip.

Out the window, pulling up in their red Jeep, were Darren and Marie leaving a trail of dust as they soared up the gravel driveway and parked behind the McKnight's old minivan. With a smile on her face, Barbara went out on the porch to meet them, lifting her hand and waving as the pair climbed from the Jeep and approached. Marie wore her usual jean shorts, loose blouse, and tennis shoes while Darren wore sandals, khaki shorts, and an American flag button-up shirt. Their smiles were warm, though reserved, almost worried in appearance, but even still, Barbara grinned from ear to ear as she descended the porch stairs and met them on the stone walkway, giving each a hug. "It's great to see you guys," she said, her voice quivering with bubbling emotion. Turning, she gestured for them to follow her inside. "Come on in. Dinner is just about ready."

"Great!" Marie replied, following fast on Barbara's heels in a quick shuffle of her feet. "It's good to see you, too. It seems forever since we got caught up."

Darren snatched the sunglasses off his face and crossed the threshold behind them. His eyes searched down the hall and then up the stairwell as he kicked off his shoes. "Where are those little ones of yours?"

Footsteps came running from Jack's room to fly across the upstairs floor and he was suddenly at the top step, beaming down at them, Linda appearing behind her big brother and waving down.

"Hey, there, Jack of All Trades. And Linda." The old man chuckled. "How's it going, you two?"

"Great, Darren!" Jack burst out.

Linda nodded.

"Hey, I've got something for you two, if your mother will allow it." The man shot Barbara a reserved glance, his usual jovial expression reduced as Barbara gave a mock serious nod.

Marie kicked off her shoes, took Barbara's arm, and turned her back down the hall. "In the meantime, I'll help Barbara with whatever smells amazing in the kitchen."

Barbara allowed the older woman to turn and guide her down the hall where they entered the kitchen and began setting the table. Marie seemed distracted, trying to remember where Barbara put her plates, silverware, and glasses and Barbara shot Marie a frown. "Why don't you sit down, Marie? Let me get this."

"Nonsense." The woman was trying to sound cheerful, but not doing a convincing job of it. "I still remember where most everything is, and I'm more than happy to help. It's the least I can do for you feeding us."

"I appreciate it, Marie, truly," Barbara said, pointing to the drawers and cupboards where the dishes lay. Darren, Jack, and Linda wandered into the kitchen a moment later, the kids turning objects over in their fingers and Barbara grinned at them. "What do you have there, kids?"

Jack held up an inch-and-a-half long object, grinning broadly. "Mr. Darren found this on his property. It's a shark tooth fossil!"

"He finds them all over the yard," Marie waved. "He's always digging around in the dirt like a little kid."

"That is *very* cool." Barbara acted impressed.

"We're not sure what kind it is," Linda glanced at the object before looking up at her mother. "Can I go look it up? I mean, if the internet will connect?"

"Knock yourselves out," she nodded. "Let me know if it works."

The kids raced upstairs, and she gestured for Darren to sit. "Take a load off."

"Don't mind if I do," the man said, pulling out Tom's chair and dropping into it, his extra weight shifting as he sat. "How have you all been? Have you heard anything from Tom and Samantha?"

Barbara moved to the stove, checking on the boiling potatoes while Marie stirred the stuffing on the back burner. "We've been doing okay. Had to drive some unwanted guests off the property last night, but nothing I couldn't handle. Still nothing from Tom, though. The phones and internet are still sketchy, but they promised to restore service soon. You know how it is."

"We do," Marie nodded. "As soon as we heard the President's emergency declaration, we hit the store and stocked up on a few things."

"Us, too," Barbara confirmed. "The Food King on the other side of Bristol wasn't too crowded, but there's a tension in town…" She let her words trail off as she recalled all the beeping horns and aggressive drivers from earlier, along with the fender-bender that looked like it was about to devolve into blows.

"We felt it, too," Marie said, putting her hand on Barbara's back before she turned and grabbed the pile of plates to carry to the table. "People starting to show their impatience with each other."

"In any case," Barbara continued, "we should be good on supplies for a while."

"We know how you and Tom like to stay prepared," Marie laughed, setting the plates down with a *clink*. "You've come a long way from when you first moved out here."

"Tell me about it." Memories flashed through her head, remembering work they'd done on the place over the years between the rebuilding projects, the animal care and the gardens, all work to make their farm functional and closer to being self-sufficient. "And you two helped us so much, especially with the garden. We made some mistakes at first."

"But you took to it fast," Marie pointed out as she spread the plates around.

Darren leaned forward and tapped his fingers on the table conspiratorially. "So, tell us. Have you been able to get any new information on the anomaly? Our communication services are down, too."

"All I've gotten are some updates from CNF and some local channels," she said. "But it's all repeated, rehashed, and filled with speculation. And our internet and data are still spotty, like I said. Actually, I'd say it's been almost nonexistent."

"Oh, for sure." Darren settled back. "All the same, could we turn on the news? I'd like to check if there's anything new happening."

"Of course!" Barbara replied. "Go ahead."

"I can't believe you." Marie made a shushing noise. "Watching the news at our host's house."

"She said it was okay!" Darren shot Marie a guilty look as he got up and walked into the living room.

"It would be good to catch up," Barbara eased Marie's mind before calling into the living room. "The remote should be on the end table on the left."

"Thanks. Found it!"

"Do me a favor, though. Not too loud, okay?"

"No problem."

As Barbara drained the potatoes, the television snapped on, and Darren began flipping through the news channels.

"What about these uninvited guests you were talking about?" Marie picked up the pile of silverware and placed it on napkins on the table. "You said you had to run them off?"

Barbara piled the drained potatoes back into the boiling pot, added a few dollops of butter, salt, pepper, sour cream and garlic, and grabbed the potato masher out of a drawer, working the mixture into a creamy delight. "Yeah, those three guys in the green Oldsmobile you saw the other day? They came back."

"Are you serious?" Marie gasped. "What happened?"

Barbara launched into the story, starting with how Smooch had woken her up in the middle of the night barking at something out by the barn, how she'd seen the flashlights flickering and grabbed her shotgun and got the kids up and about Linda's initial alarm when she'd told her to fetch one of their spare weapons and lock herself in with her brother.

"Oh, those poor kids." Marie shook her head as she delivered glasses of water to the table, one for each place setting. "I can't imagine going through that at their age. To deal with that danger." Marie's face grew remorseful.

"They did great, though." Barbara got out the remaining lumpy bits of potato, then she used a spoon to taste it, adding a pinch more salt to the mix. "And they're going to have to get used to it. I just told them about what the President said, and how things were going to get tough soon."

"I think you'd have to," Marie agreed. "They have to be prepared, too."

"But I filter it, you know?" she said. "I don't want them to listen to a bunch of conjecture and fear mongering."

"I couldn't agree more."

Barbara finished her story, telling about how she'd gone outside with the semi-automatic shotgun and stalked the three men all the way to the side yard. In a rushed tone, she told Marie how she'd fired at the men, peppering them at a distance with buckshot, firing one slug into the side of the barn, leaving an unfortunate hole she'd have to patch later. Marie stopped working on dinner and stood in rapt awe, listening to Barbara finish her story, grinning when she told the part about hitting the men with the first round of buckshot, then she flat out laughed when Barbara described chasing them over the fence and how they'd fallen into the next yard like a scene from keystone cops. Barbara ended by emphasizing how she was glad she hadn't seriously injured anyone – at least as far as she knew.

"They would have deserved it." Marie waved her hand at her face to cool herself off, then she fixed Barbara with a serious stare. "If everything they're saying is true, it will only get worse. We'll see more people from Bristol coming out here to scout the area, if you know what I mean. They'll get bolder with every passing day. It's good to show strength right off the bat. Let them know you won't be easy pickings."

Barbara cocked her hip and looked at the other woman with a thoughtful expression. "I just can't believe it's already happening. I mean, it's like something you'd see in a movie or on television. Hard to believe a worldwide disaster is happening in our lifetime, but here it is. I mean, I thought plain old hurricanes and earthquakes were bad."

The older woman nodded absently, lost in her thoughts. Then she tilted her head as something struck her. "You may not have hurt those men last night, but it may eventually come to that. You know, hurting someone badly. Maybe even killing them."

"I'll do what I have to do," Barbara replied. "No question about that."

"Good," Marie agreed with a terse nod. "Now, let's get those chickens out of the oven."

They each grabbed a pair of potholders, and Barbara threw open the oven, allowing a wave of heat-roasted chicken to flow past them before they reached for the pans.

"Ladies, can you come in here?" Darren called from the living room, his voice tinged with a hint of panic. The two women exchanged a look before taking the three chickens out of the oven, the fat popping, broth bubbling in the pan. Setting the steaming pans on the counter to rest, they whipped off their oven mitts, tossed them next to the chickens, and marched out to the living room.

"What are you fussing about, Darren?" Marie asked, her head cocked sideways at the television mounted above their fireplace.

"That right there." The man pointed.

Barbara stopped beside the couch with her hands on her hips, focusing on the screen. President John Zimmerman sat behind his desk in the oval office, microphones from all the major news networks pointed up into his face. His blue-gray eyes held that firm confidence that so many had come to love, though a heavy burden lingered in his eyes, the creases of the man's face deeper somehow.

"Good evening, my fellow Americans. I come to you tonight with critical information that's vital to the survival of our nation."

Chapter 33
Tom McKnight
Outer Banks, North Carolina

Tom gazed out the front window at the water pouring down into the tunnel, and his vision blurred for a second. He blinked, shook his head, and rubbed his eyes with his fingers. They still hadn't moved from the spot near the tunnel's entrance, and he was starting to doubt his ability to drive them safely through it despite how encouraging the inside of the tunnel had been. Hours of squinting into the pouring rain had given him serious eyestrain, and a headache had formed at the base of his skull.

"What's wrong?" Sam asked with a concerned look.

"I was just about to drive, then I realized how tired I am. I can't remember the last time I got a good rest." He blinked down at the tunnel once more before shaking his head. "I think it's been at least two or three nights."

"I can drive," Jerry offered, raising his right hand slightly and squeezing it into a fist, wincing in pain before lowering it back down.

"Not with one hand," Tom said. "And not with my daughter's life at stake. Sorry, son."

"Then let me drive," Sam said, her tone insistent.

Tom stared hard at his daughter then looked down at the water sliding into the tunnel, the deluge leaping over rocks and debris on the pavement. "No, you just got your license a few months ago. Besides, your mother would kill me if she found out."

Sam nodded knowingly. "So, what do you want to do?"

"I'm thinking we can chill out for thirty minutes. You know, a half an hour of rest to give my eyes a break. I'll wake up ready to drive through the tunnel and get us the rest of the way home."

"Sounds good," Sam said, slapping her hand on her knee. "I'm tired, too."

"You guys can do what you want," Tom climbed from behind the wheel and slid past Jerry. "But no one gets behind the driver's seat. Understand?"

They both nodded while Tom grabbed his pack and staggered toward the RV's bed on wobbly legs. The lack of sleep, constant driving, and trudging through the ferocious storm had taken their toll on him, and the pull of sleep drew him to the bed like a magnet. In the back, he turned and dropped on the edge of the mattress, pulling a strip of beef jerky from his pack. Tearing off the wrapper, happily munching, Tom allowed his body to relax and when he finished with the jerky stick, he fished out a bottle of water and drank half of it. He capped the bottle and placed it on the nightstand next to the bed, then he kicked off his boots and swung his legs up where they relaxed, the tension draining from his body like water pouring from a bucket. He set his watch alarm to thirty minutes and rested his head back with a quiet sigh.

Eyes closed, he listened to the sounds of the storm. Rain sprayed the thin camper walls in a pattering of small and large droplets, like the purring of a great feline. They sat in the storm's belly, their tiny RV, small and inconsequential in the grand scheme of things. Debris rattled the roof in soft prattles and tumbles. He trusted the RV though, confident it wouldn't just blow away at the first stiff wind. Feeling safe and warm, a weariness grasped his mind and pulled him ever deeper into a welcoming black. Within two minutes, Tom was fast asleep.

* * *

He awoke with a start, head and shoulders coming off the pillow like a bomb had gone off. But the RV remained still, rainfall gusting against the vehicle's sides, causing it to sway, the sounds crisp in his ears, his vision sharp, all senses alive and alert. It seemed doubtful that a thirty-minute nap would leave him feeling so well-rested and he raised his watch, looked at the time, a sinking feeling tugging at his insides.

"Oh, man. It's been three hours! My alarm must not have gone off." He stretched his arms high over his head and yawned, trying to wake up. And as the minutes passed, he realized the long rest might have been a boon—he felt great. Provided they hadn't wasted too much fuel idling in the rain, they should be able to make good time through the tunnel.

Tom put his soggy shoes back on, grabbed his pack and made his way to the front where Jerry had fallen asleep at the kitchen table, back laying in the seat with his feet flat on the floor. Sam lay where he'd left her in the passenger seat, though she'd lowered the seat back and lay curled up with her jacket thrown over her like a blanket. A sheet of rain poured down the front windshield, lightning cracking in the distance, thunder following in low, fading growls. The storm, as he had hoped, hadn't worsened, and looked like it might be weakening as it stalled out over the coast, dropping torrents of rain on the OBX.

"Hey, guys." Tom gave Jerry's leg a light tap with his toe and shook Samantha by her shoulders. "Come on, Sam, Jerry. Time to get up."

Jerry moaned and rose onto his elbows, Sam uncurling and stretching her legs up over the dashboard, her dirty socks crooked on her feet, shivering and rubbing her arms as she turned the heater up.

"What time is it?" Sam asked. "How long have we been—"

"Three hours," Tom replied.

"Whoa! Three hours?" Jerry sat on the edge of the bench and rubbed his face. "That's longer than we wanted, right?"

"Yep," Tom said with a glance out the front window. "But I'm not complaining. At least my brain isn't covered in fog anymore."

Tom passed around some snacks and then climbed into the driver's seat. Sam got up to stretch her legs, and Jerry hopped into the passenger side. They chewed jerky sticks and drank water and sweet tea in silence, listening to and watching the storm raging outside. The sky remained gray, fed with layers of continual rain, and everything flowed down into the tunnel to drain off to some mysterious place. Tom glanced down at the gas gauge to see they'd used a decent amount of fuel but figured they'd have enough to make it through the tunnel.

Placing his unfinished bottled water into a cup holder, he put the RV in gear, and eased down the road toward the tunnel. They approached the entrance and crept inside at a conservative twenty miles per hour. The lights running along the tunnel's ceiling remained on, but they flickered slightly, never loosing total power but never reaching their full brightness, the flickers coming seemingly at random, not with the crashes of thunder. The RV's tires sent shallow waves of water surging away to splash against the center barrier and white painted brick walls and Tom's eyes fell back to it, estimating its depth. "Looks like the water has gone up a few inches already." He kept his voice steady, not letting on to the hint of worry gnawing on his gut. "But I think it's still okay to drive through."

"I drove through it before when the water was this deep," Jerry agreed. "I made it through okay."

With a slow nod, Tom pushed onward, leaving the tunnel entrance and the open world behind. Almost immediately, claustrophobia settled its hands on his shoulders and pressed down. He pushed the trapped feeling from his mind and glanced over at Jerry, striking up a conversation to distract himself from their surroundings.

"So, you liked your work at Bottlenose Surf and Sport?"

"Absolutely," Jerry nodded. "Best job I ever had."

"What was so great about it?"

"Well, like I was telling Sam, I could take out their new surfboards and try some of the latest diving gear." Jerry smiled, thinking back. "I'm not a professional or anything, but I'd go out with the boss's son. They had a boat, and I qualified to dive at some shallow depths."

"I used to dive a long time ago, after I quit my government job and started working for Maniford." Tom's tone turned reflective as he recalled some of the first jobs Maniford had landed, doing scuba diving to inspect the hulls of ships and submersibles and provide recommendations on their structural integrity. "But I was a much younger man. I guess I just never had time to keep up on my training, but I sure do miss those days."

"The underwater world is amazing," Jerry agreed, eyes falling reflective and distant. "I probably wouldn't have minded working in that field, but my dad always pushed me toward finance or business." The young man frowned. "I guess he's gone now, so I can do whatever I want." His expression brightened as he thought of something else. "Oh, man. We used to get remote control submersibles in at the Bottlenose. They were awesome. Me and the boss's son used to take them out by the coral reefs when his dad was out of town."

Tom smiled, his interest piqued. "Like the Zephyr models they used to sell?"

"That's right. The latest model we had in the shop was the Zephyr Five. What a beauty. Unfortunately, it cost three grand. Not something I could afford." Jerry shook his head in appreciation. "It took amazing video and pictures. I got good with it, too. I could stand it on its head and sneak up on the jumpiest of fish." He patted his cell phone in his pocket. "I could show you some amazing pictures, but it's all in the cloud, and with cell service out…" He let his words trail off.

Tom turned the wheel slightly to the left as Jerry talked, noting the front of the RV starting to sluice around a bit in the rising waters. It was nothing he couldn't handle, and he swung the front-end back in line with little problem, giving Jerry a fond look. Opportunities to work on ships and with million-dollar submersibles didn't come easy. It had taken Tom years of contracts with equipment manufacturers and research teams before they'd offered him a ride on one of the big submersibles like the Sea Bell, the sub that had gone down with the Marin. It had been a once-in-a-lifetime experience and he understood Jerry and Sam's fascination with the oceans.

"I've got an idea," Tom said. "After we get out of this, I'll arrange for us to take a sub tour." He glanced back at Sam. "All three of us."

Jerry gave him an incredulous look, lips blowing air in a scoff. "What do you mean? Like, a Disney World ride?"

"No, I mean on a real submersible. Maybe a Sub-X Project vehicle." Tom grinned, wondering why he hadn't thought of it sooner. "We service those subs every two months, and I can assign myself to the project team."

The young man's face lit up. "You mean like the *Mothra?*"

"Yep." Tom slowed as they hit a patch of water that half-covered the tires, sending waves sloughing off in both directions to splash against the walls. Spray streaked across the windshield, and Tom hit the windshield wipers once to clear the glass.

"What about the *Goliath?*"

"We just serviced that one," Tom replied. "She'll be scheduled for another service in two months, and we can hop aboard then."

Jerry fell back in his seat and shook his head, jaw hanging open. "You're not kidding, are you?"

Tom laughed. "I'm not kidding. I'd like to take you guys out one day. Soon. I can't promise when, right now. But write it down as a promise."

Sam shook her head and fixed her father with a doubtful gaze. "I thought you had to get special access for that?"

"I do," Tom said, watching her in his rearview mirror. "I'm sure I can get it, though. I'll pull a few favors. Heavens knows I have enough of them saved up. I— Whoa, this water is getting high."

The RV plowed through another big patch of water and the bottom bumper caught a wave, sending spray flowing over the vehicle's hood, creeping up to the window like it might go right up the glass and cover them. Panic tweaked Tom's brain, hands shaking on the wheel, and he took a nervous breath to settle himself down.

"That's about as high as I've ever seen it," Jerry exclaimed. "I wonder if the drainage system is broken?"

"Or maybe the drains simply can't handle it," Tom added.

The young man didn't reply right away, suddenly uncertain about the danger of the rising waters. "Well, it *should* be able to handle rainfall into the tunnel. Unless there's something else going on."

Tom absently turned on his windshield wipers to clear a bit of spray off from the glass, then turned them off. The spray continued to fall from above.

"Wait, why is it coming from above?" Jerry asked.

"I hope that's not what I think it is." Tom turned the windshield wipers back on and peered upward. More trickles fell from the tunnel's roof, hitting the windshield and rattling across the top of the RV in fat droplets. He flicked his wipers to the next highest speed to keep up with the growing trickles.

"That is *definitely* coming from the roof," Jerry confirmed. "And it's getting worse."

Tom kept his eyes focused on the flooded road, but he kept glancing up to discern the source of the water, the lights flickering but remaining on, though the constant splashing made it almost impossible to see. One time, the wipers cleared the glass, and he spotted something he had been expecting but praying not to see.

"There it is." Tom pointed upward at a crack running jaggedly down the center of the tunnel to the left of the lights, spreading out, thin fissures stretching to the walls. He sat back, shaking his head in frustration. "A big crack."

"Yep, I see it." Jerry stared upward with a wincing expression. "That's a good inch or two wide. It's—"

A small chunk of something broke from the ceiling and hit the window in a splatter of sand before it bounced over the roof. The wipers cleared the particles off, but more continued to fall, mixed with pieces of root and grass.

Tom twisted his hands on the wheel and focused on the road as his gut twisted. The crushing weight above them—stone and sand and water—pressed down ominously, threatening to collapse at any moment. He swallowed hard as he plowed through another deep puddle, realizing the water level wasn't receding at all. A tire hit a rock, bouncing them all in their seats, rattling his teeth together.

"Something must have happened to the tunnel from above," he stated flatly. "It's compromised."

"There's no way," Jerry stammered, eyes darting at the ceiling and walls as he gripped the arm of his seat. "It's withstood other storms—."

"Doesn't matter," Tom said. "We need to get out of here. But do we turn around or go forward?" He shook his head as indecision warred inside his head. If they turned around, they knew how far it would take them to get back. But he'd have to stop and back up, and that might give the water time to travel down the tailpipe and stall them out. "Do you know how far we have left to go?"

"I'm not sure," Jerry said, his voice rising. "I never paid attention to that. There's no markers or—"

"We're going forward," Tom growled, gripping the wheel, shoulders pressed forward, foot pushing the gas pedal down. The RV plowed ahead, hitting pools of water interspersed with shallow stretches, but the shallows grew deeper and deeper the farther they progressed.

"It's halfway up the tires, Dad" Sam called out. He glanced back to see his daughter standing by the door, looking out the side window, then she turned and rushed toward the RV's rear, calling, "I'll check behind us."

"It's a total collapse," Tom said, more to himself than anyone else, his mind racing with the single thought. *Keep the gas pedal down and the engine RPMs up.* If water got into the tailpipe, they were done, and they'd be forced to get out and wade to safety.

Tom kept his foot on the accelerator, increasing their speed to thirty-five miles per hour, their front end sliding around in the muck. The frame rattled as they hit more obstacles hidden below the murky surface and Tom's shoulders tensed in expectation of hitting something sharp enough to flatten their tires. A glance upward showed the crack spreading and rippling ahead of them even as they drove, visible through the splatters of wet debris on the windshield. Jagged offshoots split from the main fissure and marked the walls with jagged slashes all the way to the water line, a deep, chest-rattling rumbling coming from all sides.

Sam ran from the back of the RV in a stomp of feet. "The ceiling, Dad! It's collapsing behind us! It's all coming down!" He glanced back to see her slack-jawed expression, eyes wide, chest heaving with terror. Adrenaline lanced through his bloodstream, and he pressed himself forward, foot pushing gradually on the accelerator, the RV pushing stubbornly through the rising water like a boat through ocean waves.

"Go, man! Drive!" Jerry clutched his seat arms, his good hand raised as if he could shield himself from the falling debris. "I think I saw a sign back there. We've got a quarter mile to go!"

"I'm driving, I'm driving!" Tom shouted through gritting teeth, pushing the words from deep in his chest. He glanced left into his side mirror and watched pieces of the tunnel fall free and smack the water behind them, red taillights showing hints of a total collapse. Sand was spraying down into the wake they left behind, chasing them through the flooded tunnel, threatening to bury them if they stopped.

He watched his speedometer rise. Forty. Forty-five. Fifty. The water broke over the sides of the RV, the water reaching halfway up the grill, steam rising off the hot engine block. Chunks fell on the RV's roof like hammers, leaving dents in the thin material, the tunnel closing in on them like a fist, trapping them with water in front and the weight of a mountain collapsing from behind.

Sam fell to her knees between the seats, one hand gripping Tom's chair and her other hand grasping Jerry's arm. "Dad, what'll we do? It'll collapse on us. It's going to—"

"If we stall, we may have to exit the RV." Tom's half-snarl cut through his daughter's panic. He kept his voice calm and tight despite his rising desperation. "If that happens, don't open the door. Just roll down the windows, climb out, and run or swim to the exit. Sam, do you have your flashlight?"

Samantha patted her sides before turning to retrieve the emergency flashlight out of Tom's makeshift pack. "I've got one for me and the one we found in the RV."

"Give the extra one to Jerry," Tom said, his voice sounding small in the hail of debris raining down, pounding stones and thick chunks of mud thwacking the windshield and hood, the wipers unable to clear it fast enough. His shoulders clenched tight as something that sounded like a basketball thudded on the RV's roof. The tunnel lights died a few seconds after the impact, leaving only their headlamps to cut through the darkness, their glow casting odd shadows across the ceiling, dim caricatures that danced and capered above them.

Something bigger smashed against the RV's roof, and a chunk of the ceiling splashed in the water off to their right, followed by a piece of reinforced steel. The RV's front end slid to the left, then right, and Tom whipped the wheel to compensate. Their speed had reached almost fifty miles per hour and the water had receded from washing over the hood, creeping lower the farther they traveled. Hope crept into his mind, just a faint glimmer that they might fly out of the tunnel to safety. Something heavy smacked the windshield near the bottom center, spiderweb cracks branching out and spreading across the glass.

Sam and Jerry cried out and Tom bore down harder, determined to drive around or through anything that lay in their path. Ahead of them, a gigantic section of ceiling was hanging from the quivering rebar and a piece cracked off and plummeted toward them. Tom jerked the wheel left, and the concrete smashed down on the RV's right front corner and bounced off, instantly killing the headlamp in a shower of sparks, glass and metal. The vehicle slid hard to the right and Tom whipped the wheel the other way, overcorrecting and driving their front end toward the center divider.

They crashed into the steel and cement barrier at a sharp angle, metal and plastic exploding in a crunch. The impact threw Sam and Jerry forward, and Tom popped out of his seat, head cracking against the window. The vehicle bounced off and kept going, though, sliding along the concrete divider, engine sputtering, the left headlamp winking like a dying soldier in the tunnel's darkness.

Head swimming, Tom silently cursed himself for not strapping on his seatbelt, but there wasn't time to worry about it. He straightened the RV's wheel and hit the gas, trying to keep the engine alive, pushing through the molasses-like churn of water and falling debris. More pieces struck the RV's hood, denting it, cracking it, steam bursting through the crevices carved through to the radiator. Water dripped on his hands from the windshield cracks and the RV's axle on the right side was grinding, causing the steering wheel to shake. Sam shouted for them to keep going as Jerry slammed his palm on the dashboard, encouraging the vehicle to keep fighting.

But despite their pleas, despite Tom coaxing the gas pedal and doing his best to keep them moving, the engine puttered, coughed and finally died, their remaining headlight winking out with it, plunging them into total darkness.

Chapter 34
President John Zimmerman
Oval Office
Washington, D.C.

"My fellow Americans… Dammit. The screen isn't scrolling at all. Fix it!"

President Zimmerman shakes his head and clenches his hands in front of him, turning them over, tapping his fingers impatiently on the desktop as his eyes shoot across the room, the film crew behaving like amateurs, his patience wearing thin.

"Working on it," Maxine assures him, and she turns and ducks behind the lights to work with the people in charge of the teleprompter.

Around him, he can feel the exhaustion and tension in the air as people circle their wagons, fight amongst each other and quibble about the smallest things, including his own staff and cabinet. His upcoming address is intended to lift the shroud of mystery surrounding the anomaly and establish a renewed trust between the United States and Canada, and the people he's depending on to keep it together. Part of him wants to believe it, but part of him thinks it'll be more like pulling off a band-aid as slowly as humanly possible.

He waits, staring at the people behind the cameras and lights, glancing at the teleprompter screen as it resets itself, scrolls, then resets itself again.

Maxine leans out of the blare of lights with a nod. "Should be good now. Ready?"

He nods, straightens in his chair, and clears his throat. Once ready, he nods once to the camera and allows a reassuring smile to spread on his lips. It's not a fake smile; he genuinely feels a connection to the American people, and he wants to be honest with them. He wants them to feel secure. There's nothing fake about it, and nothing fake about the fear that grips him behind the smile.

"My fellow Americans. For the first time in our history, we're faced with an existential crisis…"

Behind the cameras and lights, one staffer leans closer to Maxine, whispering, "Hey, he pronounced existential right this time."

Maxine glares as the man before turning her attention back to the President.

"As you are all aware, the undersea anomaly off the United States Eastern Seaboard has brought us to a national state of emergency. Our experts have confirmed sea levels have already risen, and there is no sign of it stopping anytime soon. It has devastated sea life, and it has crippled our fishing and shipping industries beyond belief." His voice took a grim note. "Still, the worst has yet to be realized."

The President pauses, contemplating the enormity of his next words as the teleprompter waits. After gathering himself, he continues.

"We've reason to believe the amount of freshwater expelled from the aquifer is several times more than Lake Superior, which itself contains enough water to raise global ocean levels by roughly a centimeter. While that's concerning, it's not the worst effect. Because the water expelling from the aquifer is fresh water, it is diluting the saline levels in our oceans to a severe degree. Not only has this caused the destruction of sea life and sea life habitats in the North Atlantic, but it's affecting the ocean's currents, too. These are the lifeblood of our planet." He pauses for a moment, trying to strike the right balance as he shifts from a professional demeanor to a more conversational one.

"I didn't even realize how important these oceanic rivers are to keeping a balanced ecosystem. The North Atlantic Drift moderates the temperature in the northern hemisphere by bringing warm water up from the southern tropics. Sea life migrates to spawning and feeding grounds based on the warm water flow. It all plays a vital role in the cycle of life."

The President shifts in his seat and looks at the camera from a slight side angle. "You're probably asking yourself why this is important." Zimmerman allows the suggestion to linger for a moment before he continues.

"Scientists monitoring the situation have detected temperature aberrations in the North Atlantic that are spreading. We believe these temperature changes are a direct result of the desalination of the waters near the anomalous zone. With the flow of warm water being carried up from the south disrupted, significant temperature changes throughout the Northern Hemisphere will occur.

"In other words, we expect to see temperatures dropping rapidly in our country and beyond. This will become clearer as the days pass, particularly as we enter the fall and winter months. While we cannot predict how drastic these temperature drops will be, or how fast they will occur, we suspect they will be… devastating.

"We could see a reduction in crop yields over the next two years along with housing shortages as we shift the population farther inland. These are not simple problems, and the solutions will not only be complex, but require that we come together as a country, united in survival. But the biggest threat of all, the thing that threatens our future as a nation, is the degeneration of our society into panic. Again, I want to reiterate that those wishing to take advantage of the situation will find themselves outmatched, both physically and psychologically. We will not tolerate criminal behavior, and I will utilize the full extent of my executive powers to ensure the rule of law is followed. Local law enforcement and state agencies are standing by to keep our citizens safe. We will stand together as a nation, united as one, ready to take on the greatest challenge we've ever faced."

John's chest lifts as he takes a deep breath, chin raised with slight defiance, ready to take a metaphorical punch.

"I want to assure you that the people who serve your interests – your government representatives, health care workers, scientists, and law enforcement agencies – have the full support of the Federal Government, and we will do everything within our power to ensure we meet this challenge head on. We have the best people in the country working on this, the top minds from every institution. I feel it is of the utmost importance that we help each other during these trying times. Remain calm, use caution—but please, do not panic—and continue about your lives as normally as you can.

"The situation won't change overnight, and we have every reason to believe the temperature shifts I mentioned will appear gradually, allowing us to adapt and overcome them. We will make more information available as soon as we're able.

"God bless us, and God bless these United States of America."

"Cut!" someone calls from behind the cameras and lights, and the room erupts in a bustle of studio professionals as the Chief of Staff and others in the President's cabinet review the video for broadcasting.

Maxine approaches with a bottled water and hands it to him. "That was good, sir. Impressive."

"Thanks, Max," he says with a nod. "It felt good. Well, as good as an announcement like that can be."

"Are you okay?"

He nods but in reality, he's far from it, his stomach filling with, the nausea making him downright sick.

"You'll keep the country unified," she assures him. "The citizens will follow you through the valley of death if it comes to it."

"I know they will." His eyes turn up to the producer. "Got everything you need?"

The producer stares at a smaller screen, watching Zimmerman finish the speech on a delayed recording. The man gives him a thumbs up and flashes him a grin. "Got it in three takes. Not bad, Mr. President."

Zimmerman slumps back in his chair as the crew packs things up. Maxine stands by, intercepting other aids and staffers and directing them away from the President. The crew wheels out the last of the lights, leaving him with just Maxine and a lone figure who stands near the door with two glasses in his hand.

"Maxine, can you give us a minute?"

"Of course, sir." The woman marches past him with a nod before exiting the room.

The vice president approaches and hands one glass to Zimmerman who accepts it before relaxing back into his seat.

"Was it convincing?" he asks.

"If I didn't know the truth myself, I'd believe every word you said."

"It's only a half-truth, technically." John swirls the amber whiskey in his glass before sipping some down. "Think it's enough to get the Pierre off our asses?"

The VP stands near the edge of the President's desk. "The guy has some high morals, but he's still a politician. He knows tough choices need to be made. Yours most of all. If he wants our help, he'll back off."

Zimmerman takes one more sip of whiskey, stares at the glass, then tosses down the rest, lighting a fire in his belly. He sets the glass on his desk with a solid clank as a range of emotions spin inside his head. "Maybe. I still wonder if I should have told them the complete truth."

"About the true rate of speed this nightmare is descending on our heads?"

"They deserve to know. They're our fellow countrymen, Craig." Emotion grips his chest, pulling, twisting, and tearing at him as a deep helplessness sets in. He stands and walks around the desk with his glass in hand.

"Not a good idea," he says with a sigh, turning as the President makes a direct line to the decanter. "You'd have more riots than you could shake a stick at. Violence sweeping the nation like we've never seen. It'll be hard enough to control the panic once we broadcast your announcement. At least this way, you're giving a few people a chance to prepare before the real trouble hits. At least for those who can read between the lines."

"What will we give them? A paltry month?" He pours himself another drink and sips this time, forcing himself to slow down. "That's not much time to prepare. For them, or for us."

"Everyone's working on it, pulling sixteen-hour shifts. I had to order Rick to get some sleep last night. The guy looks like the walking dead, and he's in charge of a dozen task forces. But he's good. The entire staff is good. We're ready for it."

"What if word leaks out?"

"We'll burn that bridge when we come to it. Until then, all we can do is keep working, and keep praying."

Chapter 35
Barbara McKnight
Wyndale, Virginia

The three sat in shock as the President's address ended and the news returned. The CNF anchor appeared flabbergasted and sent the broadcast to an immediate commercial break, leaving Barbara, Darren, and Marie staring at each other as a furniture jingle played in the background.

"Good thing we stocked up," Marie said, lips pursed as she broke the silence. "The stores will be a nightmare tomorrow."

Darren shook his head in amazement. "How could… I mean, this has to be a joke, right? I'm not sure I understood all that about the desalination of the oceans, but I caught the temperature change part. How much will temperatures change? And how fast? Are we talking about Christmas in September?"

Barbara shook her head, her thoughts returning to Tom and some things he said the last time they spoke. "Tom guessed all this, and he tried to tell me about it the last time we talked before we lost contact. I don't understand it all, either, but it's real. I just hope Tom and Samantha can get back to us before things get bad."

Marie came over and wrapped her arms around Barbara's shoulders. The shorter woman had to reach high, but she had a grip of steel, pulling Barbara close and squeezing. "It'll be fine. Tom will find his way back. In fact, I'll bet he's on the road right now."

While Barbara appreciated the sentiment, she had trouble believing it. Despite her faith and every bit of trust she had in her husband, the days were growing longer and the nights lonelier. She'd never be remiss in her duties as a mother, farmer, and wife, but the grim reality of the situation loomed over her like a guillotine waiting to fall.

"Thanks," she said, patting Marie on the shoulder and breaking from the embrace. Marie sat on the couch while Barbara fell into Tom's recliner, her mind racing with the implications. She thought about the farm, the animals, and the plants that fed them, trying to imagine a major freeze hitting them and what it would mean to the farm.

"We've got vast supplies of feed," she said, expression falling from glum to destitute, "but we'd need to have more for the long term—months' or years' worth of it. The fields might be all but useless in the cold, so we'd have to expand those and guard our hydroponic system and greenhouse full time. I'll have to rethink a lot of things."

"And we'll be here to help with that," Marie assured her, leaning forward on the cushion.

"Well, ain't that something?" Darren scoffed from the couch. "Frigid temperatures are coming, but we just don't know how bad or fast." He looked at Marie. "We've got some things to do around the farm if we're going to be ready, too."

Marie nodded knowingly. "All this talk of weather changes ups the whole game. Here we thought we were preparing for grocery and meat shortages, but now we have to deal with our own crops freezing."

"I was just thinking the same thing," Barbara agreed. "If you two need any help at your place, I've got a small but powerful labor force on hand, and we'd be glad to do what we can." The truth was, Barbara didn't think she could spare much time or effort, given everything they still had to do. Still, she'd help the Everetts if they asked.

"It's nothing we can't handle ourselves," Marie assured her, "but we'll be sure to let you know if we need some helping hands."

"Please do."

The kids tromped downstairs and stormed into the living room area, and Barbara turned and greeted them. "Did you guys find out what kind of shark tooth that was?"

"Nope." Linda shook her head. "Internet is still being dumb."

"Are we going to eat?" Jack asked. He looked at the kitchen and then at the adults, scratching his head in confusion.

"Of course, we're going to eat," Barbara said with a glance at Marie, both women standing and heading into the adjoining kitchen.

"Oh, yes, yes," the older woman patted the boy's shoulder as she went by. "We were watching something on the news and forgot about dinner. You kids have a seat and we'll get it served right up to you."

"Good, because I'm starving!" Jack announced.

"The place settings are already down," Linda said, and she moved to her usual chair, pulled it out, and leaned against it.

"I already got them," Marie chimed. "You just sit yourself down, child. Your mom and I've got this."

"Okay," Linda replied, plopping into a seat across from her brother. Darren ambled over and joined the kids, looking like one himself, talking about his theories on the shark tooth and what animal it might have come from. Barbara appreciated him keeping his happy-go-lucky expression up for the kids, suspecting it wasn't entirely a farce.

After dividing up the chickens, reheating the mashed potatoes and buttering up several ears of corn, the family and friends started eating. It was a somber ordeal, with the adults lost deep in their thoughts while the kids prattled on about random things, Jack worrying over his school lessons and Linda scoffing at how far behind Samantha was.

"Sam can get caught up once she gets home," Barbara assured her, adding with a sarcastic frown. "You know how much she loves catch up work."

"Oh, she'll hate it." Linda gnawed down her corn cob like a rabbit all the way to the end, leaving greasy little kernels in the corners of her mouth.

Jack giggled uncontrollably at the sight and Linda giggled, too, the sound filling the room and lifting Barbara's spirits from the bottomless pit they'd fallen into. It must have done something for Marie, because the older woman smiled at the young pair with a glassy-eyed expression.

"This is quite a spread," Darren said, nodding at the gigantic bowl of mashed potatoes, ears of corn, and chicken breasts split open. "You ladies really outdid yourselves. We'll have to up our game when you folks visit."

"Thanks," Barbara replied, feeling sheepish at the compliment. "You all are always welcome over here."

After finishing with their meals, she asked the kids to clean up while the adults moved back into the living room to stretch their legs.

"You know you're more than welcome to stay over." Barbara continued the good will offerings as she plopped back into the recliner. "Anytime. We need to stick together more than ever. If anything happens, or you feel threatened, our door is always open."

"Same goes for you and the kids," Darren told her with a grim nod. "With our kids all moved out, we've got more than enough room and supplies for you and yours."

"I echo Darren's sentiment," Marie beamed. "If you and the kids feel threatened, you pack up and head over to our place. You got that?"

"I do," Barbara nodded. "And we will."

"Good."

Darren fidgeted, standing in front of the couch, clearly anxious to get back home and get started on the prep work that none of them had realized would be needed so quickly.

"I guess we better get going then," Darren said, shooting his wife a look.

Marie slapped her hands on her knees and glared back. "What? And not help clean up? Get your butt in there and help those kids, Darren Everett."

The man gave a sheepish grin before he joined the kids in the kitchen. The room was a mess, counters covered with food that needed to be covered and put away, scraps needing to be thrown away, and dishes to be washed. Jack lifted his arms high and cheered when he saw the older man coming to help, and Linda grinned and redirected him to the kitchen table where they began swiping up dirty plates and dishes.

"What's first on your to do list?" Barbara turned to Marie.

Usually, their visits extended long into the night with Darren and Tom talking about their hydroponic gardens, comparing notes, and challenging each other to do better, Darren amusing Jack with his stories while the ladies sat talking around the table.

"We've got a couple places on our fence to secure," Marie replied, "so it'll be an early wake up call. And it is *hell* getting Darren out of bed at a decent time. He likes to hit snooze a dozen times before I can get him moving, then it takes him some more time to get serious."

Barbara crossed her arms, chuckling. "I understand because I'm more that way than Tom. But I guess I picked up the slack after he and Sam left. I'm not sure how, but…" Her words trailed off behind a wall of growing emotion.

"Because you've got another gear," the older woman said.

"A what?"

"You've got another gear. Like in a car. Some people only have three gears and others have four. Some have five gears, or even eighteen."

"Like a semi-trailer truck?"

"Exactly!" Marie chuckled. "Seriously, Barb. You're a good woman, and that's why I consider you my friend."

A genuine smile spread across Barbara's face, warmth filling her chest. "You too. Thank you, Marie."

With Darren's help, the kids whipped the kitchen into shape, and soon Darren joined the women in the hallway where they'd been edging toward the door.

"We'll stay longer next time," Marie said as the two began putting on their shoes. Barbara fixed the Everetts with a sad look, unable to keep the frown off her face and they embraced, the kids waving their goodbyes as Darren and Marie moved down the stone walkway to their Jeep, started it up, turned around, and rolled away down the gravel driveway. Barbara meandered back to the kitchen with the kids, giving Jack's shoulders a squeeze.

"Really great job, kids," she said, looking around at the spotless table, freshly wiped counters, and sparkling stove. They'd even dimmed the lights like she often did when closing things down for the night, giving the kitchen a warm, well-used aura. "It looks great in here. All we need now is a candle."

"I'll light one," Linda said.

Barbara started to protest, but a wave of weariness passed over her, and she took a seat at the kitchen table instead. It was early evening, and she still had time to unwind before laying down for the night. She pulled her phone out of her pocket and checked for a message from Tom, not surprised when she found nothing.

"Why didn't Mr. Darren and Mrs. Marie stay longer?" Jack hung near her right arm, leaning half on the table, raising and lowering himself with impatience. "And why did we eat so late?"

"You're just full of questions tonight, aren't you?" she replied, ruffling his hair. "Sit down."

Jack shrugged and fell into his chair, and Linda joined them after lighting the candle. With the room embraced in a cozy light, they sat quietly, her daughter picking at her fingernails while Jack fiddled with his place mat and kicked his feet under the table.

"So, the reason the Everetts left early is because they have to prepare."

"Prepare for what?" Jack asked. "Bad people? Like we're preparing?"

"Sort of. It's something we heard about on the news while you kids were upstairs trying to find out what kind of shark tooth you had."

"Is that why we started dinner late?" Jack asked.

Barbara nodded.

"Must be something new," Linda added with a raised eyebrow. "Something bad?"

"Well, it was the President. And he gave us some new information about the anomaly thing in the ocean. And what he told us makes us think the trouble we've been talking about will get bad faster than we thought."

Jack's mouth formed an O as he thought about it. "Like, more people coming to our farm? More people trying to take things?"

Barbara reached over and placed her hand over his to offer comfort. "I can't say for sure, but I don't want to sugarcoat anything. I think things will get very tough from here on out. And, realistically, more people will probably come to the farm, meaning us harm."

"Will Dad and Sam be okay?" Jack's legs had gone limp from his previous kicking, and his face sunk. "I'm worried about them."

"I know, honey. I am, too. It's not the best situation to be in, and I wish I could just talk to them. But with phones and the internet down, and no idea where to look…" She let her words trail off, then she hardened her expression, for herself and for her son. "But I would never doubt a promise from your father. And his text said they'd be home. Linda saw the message, too." She shifted her eyes back to her daughter. "So, I'll keep believing it to infinity. Even if it sounds silly. You know what I mean?"

"I think so."

Linda had stopped fiddling with her fingernails and stared at her mother with glassy eyes. Anger and frustration circled in the depths like a restless animal and Linda started to say something but clamped her mouth shut.

"And no matter what," Barbara continued, "we can make it, as long as we keep our faith in God and keep loving each other. Focus on the good things and not the bad. Do you understand me?"

Jack nodded immediately, but Linda hesitated a moment, blinking slowly. "We'll be strong," she finally said with a sigh. "We'll stick together and believe in Dad and Sam no matter what." She reached across the table and took her mother's hand, squeezing it, the simple yet mature gesture filling Barbara's heart with love and pride.

"You kids go on." She lifted their hands in mock playfulness. "I'm setting you free for the night!"

Jack cheered and sprinted upstairs while Linda got up, gave Barbara a kiss on the cheek, and followed her younger brother. Barbara stood and picked up her phone, carrying it with her to the living room, standing behind the couch, twisting her lips in doubt as she checked her data connection, her jaw dropping open at the sight of several full bars of signal strength. She flipped to the text application and typed out a message to Tom before the service could die again. She stated that they were fine, and that everyone missed them, then she encouraged them to get their butts home ASAP but to keep safe doing it. With a click, she sent the message and watched as it went through. That taken care of, she clicked "Call," hoping beyond hope that she might reach him on the phone.

Clutching the phone, ear pressed to the speaker, she dared hope someone would pick up, anything to reassure her they were alive and safe. But the line rang once and gave the same tired response she had grown to loathe.

"Your call cannot be completed as dialed."

She tried calling again, but the call failed a second time, and the screen showed a broken connection, the signal having faded away to nothingness. Barbara's eyes squeezed and she gripped the phone and held it up, ready to throw it across the room and smash it to bits. She held on to the device, took a deep breath, and opened her eyes instead, though, walking to the charger on the end table before plugging it in.

Stepping to the kitchen, she imagined what the world would look like the next day. People were probably already panicking, taking stock of their meager stores and planning to get up early for a morning store run. Some might even start looting that night, striking before business owners had time to set their defenses.

They had radios and plenty of batteries, so they could stay up to date on AM and FM broadcasts, even shortwave ones, but they had no way to broadcast anything themselves. Tom had considered looking into a HAM radio but hadn't gotten around to it, and she cursed herself for not having pushed him to invest more time and effort in that. Creating an off-the-grid home was a lifelong endeavor, though, not something they'd accomplish overnight. The familiar twinges of doubt pierced her mind. It was a comforting thing to have a massive backup system in place in case the world fell apart, though it was quite another to have finally reached the point they needed it.

"You're ready for this, Barbara," she told herself. "You've been preparing your entire life for this. Don't sell yourself short. You need to have confidence and faith."

She looked up as heavy raindrops fell on the roof, hammering the shingles with authority, lightning blinking through the blinds. Adjusting herself in her chair, Barbara folded her arms across her chest, soaking in the warm candlelight, lulled by the storm's pattering sounds. It might be her last moment of peace, and she wanted to enjoy it before the world threw everything it had at her – before it forced her to defend her children and home with her very life.

* * *

Outside, the darkness grew thick, the sky a black curtain, cloud edges highlighted by the moon's eerie glow. The rain fell harder, fat droplets falling onto the sheep's woolen coats and hitting the dry dirt yard in tiny puffs of dust. The farm animals made exaggerated bleats and pushed toward the house, crowding between it and the chicken coops, using the big tree for shelter.

The Everetts' Jeep curled down the lanes on their way home, Darren taking his time to ensure they got there safely. They passed by several lonesome homesteads on the way, lighted windows winking at them through the trees as they drove past. Some were black, either unoccupied or the residents having gone to bed, thinking about the President's announcement, staring at the ceiling, wondering what they would do in the next morning.

The Everetts passed a driveway with a medium-sized sedan sitting in it, tucked back out of sight where the driveway wound up through the property. The three men inside watched the Jeep pass with focused attention, eyes narrowed and calculating. Mack, Pedro, and Ricky watched closely, all three nursing injuries in the forms of bandaged arms, legs, and backs from where the buckshot had struck them. The wounds were painful, but not serious, and certainly nothing that would keep them from paying a visit to the woman who'd hurt them.

Pedro shifted uncomfortably in the passenger seat, glaring at the Everetts' Jeep until it passed out of sight around the bend. He'd gotten the worst of it, with one pellet buried deep in the back of his leg. It had taken Mack's girlfriend, a registered nurse, almost thirty minutes to dig the thing out, Pedro yowling the entire time despite being dosed up with pain medication.

Mack gripped the wheel as the three turned their heads in the other direction, back toward the McKnight's home where it sat upon the distant hill, lights barely visible through the growing mist. A sneer formed on Mack's face as he fantasized about what he would do when they returned.

Chapter 36
Tom McKnight
Outer Banks, North Carolina

"Dad?"

Sam crawled across the floor in the pitch dark, feeling her way around, touching a wall, bumping her knees on things that had flown from cabinets. She didn't remember much, only the sideways whip of the RV's front end and an impact that sent her tumbling. She thought she might have hit her father's chair, then bounced backward, staggering and windmilling, to land near the bathroom, but her memory was fuzzy, clouded with pain and confusion.

As she crawled, her body thrummed from the crash, the crunch of metal and concrete resounding deep inside her bones. Water was cascading on the RV's roof like a waterfall, pieces of debris thudding on the roof right above her head, concrete and mud rolling off the sides. She winced with every impact, gasping and shutting her eyes to focus more on her sense of touch. As she groped blindly, she felt something warm, realizing with a start that it was a hand.

"Hey!" she hissed, fingers feeling along the arm to the elbow, then a shoulder, finally reaching a scraggly haired face. "Jerry, is that you?" She gave his face a light slap, but he didn't respond and Sam leaned forward and put her ear to his nose. The young man was still breathing, but given that he'd already hurt his arm and leg in the motorcycle crash, there was no telling how much more he could actually take.

She lifted her chin and called out in a shaky voice. "Dad? *Dad?*" She was about to give up and search around for her flashlight when a noise cut through the silence.

"Sam?" His voice hung weak and raspy in the silence, like he'd been eating sand. A tiny spot of light appeared ahead of her, and she crawled over Jerry toward it.

"Dad?"

"I'm here. I'm okay."

She crawled toward the light, and in three more paces made it to where he lay between the seats, halfway in the kitchen. The light came from a key ring he held up, some glow-in-the-dark thing that cast frightening, reedy-thin shadows across his features. With a gasp, she reached up and touched his face, fingers finding something warm and wet near his temple.

"You're bleeding," she said. "That's not good."

"My head hurts like hell." He hissed and sucked his teeth. "Sorry. Don't tell your mom."

"Are you okay? Is anything broken?"

"I don't think so." Tom coughed, then groaned. "Just my head."

"We need to find the flashlights."

He nodded in the faint light. "It probably got knocked out of your hand when we crashed. Sorry about that, kiddo."

"It's fine. Let me find it, and we'll get you off the floor."

"How's Jerry?"

"He's back by the bathroom, on the floor." Sam's voice shuddered with exasperation, her head swirling and dizzy. "He's breathing but non-responsive."

"Okay. Look around for your flashlight." He handed her the keyring. "Use this to see by. Once you find your flashlight, check on Jerry."

Sam took the keyring out of her father's hand and turned back to the RV's interior. Crawling around, hands slapping in a half-inch of water, she held the keyring close to the floor, squinting in the dim illumination for any sign of a flashlight. She checked all around the cabinet area and over by Jerry before returning to the other side, checking around the refrigerator until she reached the side door.

The bottom of the stairwell was flooded with water to the first step, but she stuck her hand down in the cold water and gasped when her hand closed around the flashlight shaft. Jerking it out of the water, she found the power switch and it snapped to life, bathing the RV's inside with a yellow glow..

"Yes!" she squeaked, then turned and crawled back to Jerry to check on him. He lay on his back, head toward the back of the bus, arm thrown to the side. His wounded limb had fallen out of the sling, and Sam went to work putting it back inside and when she'd finished securing his arm, she tried to wake him up again, but his eyes remained shut, his breathing shallow.

With Jerry stabilized to the best of her ability, Sam crawled back to her father, who'd found his way back into the driver's seat. She knelt next to him between the seats, shining the flashlight at the nasty gash on his right temple. The skin was scraped badly on his forehead, ending in a centimeter gash of puckered skin that ran from his temple to his ear.

"How did you get that?"

"No idea," Tom said as he tried to start the RV.

When he turned the key, the engine coughed and choked, doing its best to come to life but it barely turned over, much less started, so he reached to the center console and flipped a few switches.

"Try the lights."

Sam found the light switch near the door and turned it on, bathing the RV's interior in a brighter, though still soft, glow. She flipped her flashlight off and joined him up front, falling into the passenger seat with her arms crossed on her chest. She peered ahead into the gloom. "What if the tunnel caves in around us, Dad?" she asked. "What if we're trapped down here?"

"The interior lights are running on spare batteries," Tom replied. "But the battery should still have juice. Let's see where we are."

He reached up to the steering column and turned it to the manual setting, illuminating the tunnel before them, though "illuminate" was hardly the right term to use. The single remaining headlamp cast a paltry glow about thirty yards farther into the tunnel, water and grime covering the light, giving it a dirty tint as it showed huge slabs of fallen concrete and globs of mud four feet high, sandy drips splashing in the murky water all around them.

"So much for that," Tom said. "Hey, at least the tunnel didn't completely collapse on us."

"But we can't drive out." Sam nodded at the knee-high pieces of concrete blocking their way. "Even if we could get the engine started, we're not getting through that."

"Dead in the water," Tom agreed.

"Was that a dad joke?" Sam shot him a sour glance. "Because if that was a joke, it wasn't funny."

He held up his hands in an appeasing manner. "Nothing about this situation is funny. We'll have to walk the rest of the way. In a hurry, too." He winced as a piece of ceiling hit the RV's roof and bounced off. Water had leaked into the vehicle ten minutes prior, and the floor was slick and wet.

"Well, we're not leaving without Jerry."

Tom gave her a confused look, almost like he was shaking off some mental fog. He shook his head. "No, honey. We won't. We're not leaving anyone behind."

"So, we wait for him to wake up?"

"Unless we can float him out of here." Tom looked around. "I could probably carry him over my shoulder, but that water out there is bound to be freezing. I can't promise I can make it."

Sam rubbed her arms with her hands, hugging herself close as Tom's gaze wandered to the cracked windshield, covered in mud and water, flecked with small stones. He leaned forward, squinting, eyes narrowed at a spot in the corner.

"What is it, Dad?" Sam shook her head and leaned forward.

Tom's jaw tightened at the sight of the bit of frost forming in the bottom left corner of the windshield. It was spreading across the glass like a bacteria, consuming the clear glass and plastic composite with frozen crystals. His heart hammered a little harder, and he flipped off the headlamps off before Sam could see it, leaving just the rear cabin lights on. "It's nothing," he said. "We need to save battery life if we'll be here awhile. Otherwise, we might not have any lights at all."

Sam shook her head, arms hugging herself tighter, staring at him as frosted breath escaped from between her lips. "Dad? Is... Is it getting colder in here?"

Book 2: SHATTER

Chapter 1
United States Air Force Base
Somewhere in Alaska

A freezing cold wind gusts in from the bay, brushing the backs of humpback whales as it dances across the waves and heads inland. It strikes the shore, flitting up the rocky banks covered with driftwood, cutting low through the pines, spruces, and hemlocks like a low-whistling scythe. Snow shakes from tree boughs, cascading down in a white powder that hits the ground and explodes into dust. A bald eagle clings to a branch high in a Red Alder, crouched against the abrasive air currents with its feathers clenched tight to its body, eyes half shut in the gusts.

The wind whips and twists through the forest before bursting across an open airfield. Crosswinds from airplanes landing at the base create a dusting of snow that hovers a foot above the pavement, the sounds of propeller engines and jets vibrate the solid gray sky as maintenance crews work stiffly in their orange coveralls.

Storage buildings and hangars squat at the northern end of the runway while clusters of radar stations lie to the east with huge dishes sticking up from their roofs, rotating back and forth, monitoring for incoming ICBMs or submarine missiles from Russia. A nondescript watch building squats on the eastern edge of the runway behind a six-foot snow drift. Inside, two men sit at a shared computer desk, staring at a bank of monitors stretched before them, occasionally pecking at their keyboards. The watch leader sits in the back of the room with his own desk and displays, a dead silence hangs in the air except for the low hum of two space heaters.

The three men are pensive as they study their screens, bundled up in jackets and parkas despite being inside with the heat turned to high. The door opens and a fourth man enters along with a sweep of cold air that chills the room. Clint – according to his nametag - carries a cardboard carrier with several foam cups resting in the grooves. He quickly shuts the door behind him and stomps his boots before bringing his burden over to the computer desk, setting it down at his empty station.

"The mess hall is busier than hell," he passes the beverages around, tendrils of hot steam drift up from the tiny holes in the lids. The men mumble thanks and reach for sugar packets and creamers. They remove the tops, break open the additives, and stir in the contents.

"A lot of stuff happening, huh?" a man with curly black hair, Jed, replies. Clint sits with his own coffee held between his gloved hands, snow-dusted hat still on his head as he takes an experimental sip of the dark brew. "Yeah. You'd almost think we're a regular airport with all the maintenance folks coming in."

"We're packed to the hilt these days," Jed agrees. "I heard they had to bunk some in the control tower!"

"Poor planning, for sure. Anything happen on the radar while I was gone?"

"Nope. Skies are clear."

"Good to hear." Clint switches back to the original topic with a shake of his head. "It's not just more people arriving on base. I've never seen them bring in so much equipment."

"Any idea what it's for?" The youngest of them, DeShane, finishes stirring in five packets of sugar and three creamers. The rest of the men consider him 'one of *those* guys', the least experienced and the most easily excitable – possibly due to all the sugar in his coffee.

"I have no idea," Clint says. "It looks like they're renovating the radar buildings. They must be in a hurry, because they already finished the ones they started this morning."

Jed stretches a beanie over his head, stands, and crosses to the door. He pulls it open and quickly steps outside, dragging it shut behind him to keep the cold from lowering the inside temperature too much. He walks to the edge of a snowbank created by the plows and climbs the hardened ice. Hand thrown up to shield his eyes from the bright sun, he peers across the runway. A weighty C-130 descends to the tarmac, propellers rumbling like thunder as its rear wheels touch down with a low squeal of rubber, the front dropping with another squelch of sound. A dusting of snow swirls around the massive plane as it trundles by, passing a dozen parked aircraft in every available spot.

Jed's eyes shift to the control tower where workers raise a large piece of insulation and plastic to the top and a second group bolts it over the watchtower glass. They refit the doors with short tunnels that extend out several yards - *no, not tunnels*, he muses. *Chambers, maybe.*

The massive C-130 slows down at the end of the runway, and flag crews guide it toward the hangar where it will be unloaded. A truck hauls materials along a service road, weaving between radar stations and dropping off supplies. Workers bustle, adding insulation layers and chambers around the doorways to all the buildings.

The wind snaps up and blows down his coveralls, chills skittering across his chest and shoulders and he decides he's had enough. Jed turns, waddles back to the watch building and enters, letting in a brief punch of cold air as his companions grumble. He retakes his seat and sips his coffee, trying to get his head around what he's seen.

"It's weird. It's like they're weatherproofing the entire place."

"Could it be related to the president's speech yesterday?" DeShane asks. "You know, what he said about upcoming temperature drops?"

"Nah, that's all BS," Jed replies, still shivering from the cold, trying to cut DeShane off from one of his usual lectures about climate change. "They're just making a show for the *Rooskies* since they've been rattling their sabers so much lately."

"Budem Zdorovy!" Clint raises his cup.

"To your health!" Jed repeats the toast in English, going along with his friend, trying to keep the spirit light. They all lift their steaming drinks high and sip, lost in their thoughts for a moment.

"I don't know." Clint settles in his seat. "We haven't seen this much traffic since tensions were real high a few years ago. And since when do they double-staff us?" He shivers and shakes his head at the monitors. "There's literally nothing to look at."

"Maybe they're taking climate change seriously," DeShane offers. "I mean, why else would they be double-insulating the buildings?"

"Oh, here comes the climate change BS again," Clint scoffs.

"There's only one climate up here," Jed agrees with his friend, "and that's cold as hell."

The kid held firm. "The average temperature has dropped five degrees already this week."

"Which is next to nothing."

DeShane shakes his head. "It's actually a lot. And we've had some high waters, too. My friend down in Port Graham radioed to say the streets are flooded. That's just a few miles from here." The young man furrows his eyebrows. "I wish the cable and phones weren't down so we could get through to someone."

Clint stares at the screens, eyes flitting from the first to the third and back again. "And still the Russians aren't even running any drills. Nobody is."

Someone clears their throat in the back of the room, and Jed turns to see the most senior member of the team stare at them from his desk, the watch leader, Peter, someone Jed's known and come to trust over the years. He's dressed in a pair of sharp-looking, all-weather coveralls, yellow with black trim. A grizzled beard clings to his cheeks, and his ice-blue eyes seem somehow colder than the environment outside. His longish hair is pressed back from his forehead from running his fingers through it continually.

Peter's the oldest of them and has more experience than all three combined. His legs are crossed, and he leans forward with a knowing expression written on his wise face. "Nobody will launch anything...yet. But my bones tell me something's afoot, and it ain't good. Something really bad's on the horizon. Something cold."

Jed looks around as silence grips the room, a chill tingling his shoulders and causing him to shiver as he considers the man's words, driven to discomfort by the cryptic warning. He's heard the old man make predictions before, claiming to feel upcoming storms in his bones. Most of the time, he's right.

"Sounds like we could use a little global warming right about now," Jed says, chuckling at his own bad joke, his voice trailing off into silence. No one else laughs as wind whistles through the base, hammers bang, and rattling space heaters underline his thoughts. Jed turns to a small window and watches white powder whip against the glass.

Chapter 2
Tom McKnight
Outer Banks, North Carolina

"Dad? Is...Is it getting colder in here?"

"It feels like it," Tom replied. He shined his flashlight at the windshield, narrowing his eyes at the bit of frosty glass. "But *that's* not a good sign."

"I should go back and check on Jerry." Sam got up and made her way to where the young man was lying on the floor in the kitchen area, propped up on his side to help him breathe. Tom attempted to stand but fell back in his seat, still dizzy from hitting his head in the crash. He put his fingers to his right temple and winced at the lump before bringing his hand around, noting a small bit of blood. *Don't need* stitches, he thought. *I hope.* Trying again, he rose slowly and managed to stay on his feet, stepping between the seats to join Sam where she knelt by the young man where he rested against the bench seat on his back, half slouched.

She lifted her ear from his nose and gave Tom a relieved smile. "He's breathing okay, at least."

"Great," Tom said. "I'll get us some blankets."

He went to the back and checked the covers on the bed. Holes in the roof had allowed water in and soaked all the bedding, so he turned to the blankets they'd originally stripped off. Piled in a corner, the sheets had stayed mostly dry and were only a little wet on the edges. Holding them out and re-folding them a little, Tom carried them up front.

Sam sat cross-legged next to Jerry with her flashlight sitting on its end so the light hit the roof and dispersed somewhat, giving a sort of inverted lamp effect to the place. Tom laid a blanket on her shoulders and draped another over Jerry, adding a throw pillow from a storage compartment, which he placed under his head. He gently felt Jerry's scalp for signs of a deeper injury, his fingers working their way around his hairline until he found a raised lump just above the base of his neck.

"He's got a nasty bump on the back of his head," Tom said. "That's probably what knocked him out. I'm a little worried he might have a concussion, but at least there's no blood and he's breathing." Tom took the last blanket for himself and knelt next to his daughter where they huddled for warmth.

"How's your head?" Sam looked at him, face aglow in the stark light and shadows.

"Hurts like the dickens."

"The dickens, Dad? Really?" Sam's expression was a mix of exhaustion and amusement. "That's such a *dad* thing to say."

"Is *heck* better? It hurts like heck?"

"That's almost as bad."

"Sorry." He reached up and touched his fingers to the spot again. "I want an ice pack."

"Careful what you wish for." Sam's eyes flicked to the front of the RV and the ice-flecked windows. Water dripped around them, plunking on the counters with wet smacks, splashing in a puddle by the door. Tom ignored the closed-in, anxious feeling growing inside his chest and tightened his grip on the blanket as he pulled Sam in closer to his side.

"Do you think he'll wake up?" Sam asked, glancing down at Jerry, pressing her finger into his side to rouse him.

"I doubt he's going to just spring up and be fine." Tom clicked his tongue. "That only happens in movies. In the real world, a hard hit like that usually results in a concussion or severe brain damage."

"Oh." With a worried expression, Sam nudged him again, harder and more pointedly. "Come on, Jerry. Wake up." Her eyes shifted to her dad and then up at the drips smacking on the roof. "I hope he wakes up soon. I don't want to leave him here."

"We won't abandon him," Tom assured her. "We'll carry him out if we have to."

"If we're able to." Sam bit her lip. "Is there anything else you can do to wake him up?"

Tom shook his head. "I'm an engineer, not a doctor."

Sam snorted, poking him in the side. "Thanks a lot, Bones."

"Wouldn't that make me Scotty?"

Sam rolled her eyes, chuckling in spite of their severe situation. She sat for a moment then straightened, pulling her blanket tighter around her shoulders. "You probably could have been a doctor, though."

"Never crossed my mind. Not that I wouldn't want to help people. I guess I always enjoyed mechanical systems, not bodies. Machine stuff, you know?"

"But isn't the human body like a machine?" Sam raised an eyebrow. "It has the respiratory, muscular, pulmonary, and nervous systems. They all have to work together for a person to live."

"Yes, in that way it is very much like a machine." Tom blinked. "I see your point."

"Well, maybe you should have gotten a degree in medicine, too. You know, along with your other ones." Sam lightly gripped Jerry's shoulder and gave him a little shake. "Come on, dude."

"I think two is more than enough..." He gestured, tugging at her arm. "Hey, hey, honey, you're going to aggravate his injuries if you keep that up."

Sam pulled back, eyes wide as she watched Jerry. "Sorry."

The dripping continued, almost incessant in the half-darkness and Tom sighed, a glint of amusement in his eyes. "I can see how Jerry might be cute to a teenage girl," Tom suggested with a mockingly matter-of-fact tone. "It's only natural you'd really care about the guy."

Sam raised her eyebrows in warning.

"He's a handsome kid," he went on. "I'll bet he has a lot of girls after him. I guess I shouldn't be surprised when my own daughter--"

Sam grabbed a wet pillow from the floor and whacked him with it, splattering water across the RV floor. They glared at each other until the girl broke down in a fit of giggles as Tom laughed, too, teeth chattering in the cold.

A low moan rose from Jerry's lips, and Tom jerked his eyes downward as the young man shifted and tried to sit up. Sam put her hands on him, gently pushing him back down to the floor.

"You took a nasty hit to the head," she explained, holding him as he struggled. "Take it easy."

Tom helped adjust the pillow beneath the young man's head. "What's your name? Do you remember it?"

"Jerry." His eyes slipped from Sam to Tom.

"What about the day? Do you know what day it is?"

"Tuesday or Wednesday." His speech was slightly slurred. "I lost track after the storm hit. Then I fell off my motorcycle." Lifting his hand, he felt around in the back. "Ow, that hurts."

"That's where the bump is," Tom said. "You should avoid touching that area."

Jerry nodded and shifted onto his side so he wouldn't brush the back of his head against the pillow. "What happened?"

"We crashed," Sam replied. "We're still in the RV inside the tunnel."

Jerry's eyes widened slightly as he glanced around, drawn by the dripping sounds. "The tunnel! We need to get out of here. This whole thing could collapse on us!"

Tom took out his key chain light and held it up in front of the young man's eyes. "Can you follow this without turning your head?" As the light moved slowly back and forth, Tom watched carefully as Jerry's eyes tracked it accurately, both pupils the same size, dilating in response to the beam.

"What do you think?" Sam asked. "Can we make it with both you guys hurt, and the RV broken down?"

Tom rested back on his heels. "Well… he knows where he is, and his eyes work, so he might not have that bad of a concussion. But we have to get him to a hospital. And he's right about the tunnel. This thing will eventually come down on us." He looked down at Jerry. "Think you can walk?"

Jerry propped himself up on his left elbow. "My head feels like a cracked egg, but I don't want to stay here another minute if we can help it."

Tom stood. "It's settled, then."

The two got Jerry to his feet and watched as he wobbled and straightened, nodding to the pair. "I'm good."

Tom fished out some pain killers from his medical kit and handed them to the young man along with a bottled water and an energy bar. Jerry popped the pills down and sat on the bench seat to eat his snack. They occasionally tossed out a question to test him, and his speech grew stronger and less slurred with every passing moment.

Tom threw glances out the front window, watching water and sand slowly drip on the window and hood. "I think the risks of staying here outweigh the risks of leaving the RV at this point. We need to get moving."

Sam and Jerry both nodded, though the young man winced every time he moved his head.

"Let's grab everything we can use out of the RV," Tom turned to Sam. "Not just our stuff, but *everything*."

Jerry gingerly stood and helped where he could as Tom and Samantha gathered blankets, a pillow each, plastic bags, cups, silverware, and the RV rental papers and keys. Once gathered on the kitchen table, they strategically arranged the items into their makeshift backpacks to get the best fit, trading things between them if one pack had more or less room.

"Why do we need all this stuff?" Sam asked as she squeezed a small pillow down to make it fit.

"You never know when it might come in handy," Tom replied. "As long as it's not too heavy, we'll take it."

"Tell me we can find a working car and drive out of here," she continued with an exasperated sigh. "Then we drop Jerry off and get our butts home."

"At this point, we don't know what's out there in the tunnel or what we'll have to do to break free." Tom shined his flashlight at the front windshield, noting that the ice crystals had spread halfway up the glass, freezing in places where there the moisture was thin. "What's happening out there isn't likely to go away."

"It looks really bad," she agreed with a whisper as she followed his flashlight beam. "We could freeze before we make it out of here."

Jerry gave Sam a playful slap on the back with his good hand. "I don't know how I managed to hook up with you guys, but I wouldn't want to be down here in the cold darkness with anyone else." He laughed and then winced, holding his hand to his head.

"I hope that hurt," Sam sneered playfully.

"That's not nice," Jerry murmured. "Remind me not to crack jokes or even smile, at least until the pain meds kick in."

"You can goof around when we get out of here." Sam lifted her backpack to her shoulder. "Until then, no messing around."

Tom grinned, listening to them go back and forth.

"What are you worried about? Your dad is an awesome dude. I mean, look how far we've come already. He'll make sure we're prepared for anything. We have a great chance of getting out of here, as long as we do what he says."

"I appreciate the sentiment," Tom laughed uneasily as he stuffed the rest of the plastic bags inside his backpack and shrugged it over a shoulder. "I don't think any of us are ready for what's coming."

"What do you mean?" Jerry crouched a little, testing his legs. "It is what you were talking about before? The fundamental change in human history?"

Tom slowly nodded.

"Yeah, I didn't know what you meant, so I asked Sam. She didn't get it, either."

One hand on his hip, Tom levelled his gaze at Jerry, shifted it to Sam, and glanced at the windshield one last time. The forming ice crystals weren't daunting, but it was proof his theory was coming true right before their eyes.

"Grab the rest of the blankets," he said. "We're going to want them later. Let's get out of the RV and start walking. I'll explain along the way."

They gathered up all their things and bundled themselves tight with as many layers as they could. Sam stood by the door, staring at the foot of water lapping up to the second step. She shook her head and started to put her boot in it, but Tom clutched her arm as an idea struck him. "Wait, wait, wait. Come here."

He moved to the driver's seat and knelt on it, rolling down the window to see the median next to them. The concrete barrier stood a foot above the waterline as the gentle flow of dirty floodwaters continued south into the tunnel's depths. "If we can climb out there," he nodded at the median, "we should be able to stay dry."

"That's a great idea," Jerry said, peering around him where the median stretched into the darkness.

"Can you reach?" Sam asked.

"I'll give it a try." Tom pulled off his backpack and put it through the window, dropping it on the median. He raised his arms and leaned out, slumping forward until his palms rested next to his pack, wiggling through, putting one foot on the door frame while bringing the other to the concrete. Once steady, he hopped down, slipping on the slick surface and banging his shin on the median's edge. Tom clamped his lips on a curse as he quickly stood and bounced in place while sucking air through his teeth.

"Are you okay?" Sam said, poking her head out.

"Hnnngggg. Mm. Yeah. I'm fine. Just slipped a little." He grimaced, settling his hopping down. "Go ahead and hand Jerry out."

"You're up," she said, backing into the cabin to give him room.

Jerry knelt in the seat and put his one good arm through the window. "I'm not sure how I'm going to do this."

"Lean on your left side," Tom said. "I'll support your upper half." He grasped Jerry's good arm and grabbed his shirt with his right hand. "Get one foot on the door frame and bring the other down to the median."

It was awkward at first, but Jerry managed to wiggle and bounce on his side, pushing against Tom as he squirmed from the truck cab. Wedging his right foot into the corner of the door frame, he pressed Tom backward, drawing a gasp from the man.

Tom glanced behind him as his heels settled on the edge of the median. Another inch, and he'd slide off the side into the water flow. Not a deadly fall – at least not immediately – but one that would have left him soaked and very cold.

"Sorry," Jerry grunted as he tried to get his left leg under his right. Using Tom as leverage, he rolled out and landed in an awkward, stretched way, but Tom held on, backing up along the median to keep his injured companion from smashing his face on the concrete. Clutching Jerry hard by his shirt, he held him up until he got his feet beneath him. The young man swayed groggily, forehead resting against Tom's shoulder.

"You okay?"

"I think so," Jerry nodded. "Just give me a second. My head feels like I'm walking down a rolling clown tunnel."

Sam winced. "That doesn't sound fun." Jerry held on for several more seconds before straightening slowly and taking a step back.

"Okay, honey," Tom gestured to Samantha. "Your turn."

Sam tossed her pack on the median, climbed from the cab, and jumped down easily before grabbing the backpack and swinging it onto her shoulder. "I'm ready. You guys good?"

Jerry swooned a bit and Tom put an arm around him to take more of the weight. "Throw your arm around my neck. There you go." Once Jerry was stabilized, Tom nodded to his pack. "Sam, can you hand me that?"

"I can take it." The girl grabbed the heavy backpack and shouldered it along with her own. She swayed slightly but leaned forward to balance them. "No problem."

Tom nodded his thanks. "You guys ready?"

"Yup." Jerry's eyes lifted to the dripping ceiling. "Let's get out of here. This place is creeping me out."

"Me, too," Sam added, stepping to the edge so they could move past her. "How long do you think it will take us?"

"No clue." Tom focused forward, bringing Jerry alongside him and falling into a steady rhythm. He peered ahead through the gloom cast off by the RV's single headlamp, the water rippling as though serpents were swimming beneath the surface. "Could be two miles. Could be ten. Any thoughts, Jerry?"

The young man shook his head glumly. "No idea. Keep shining the light on the walls and maybe we'll see a sign."

There was a low snap, and Sam's flashlight came on, illuminating the wall to their left before she swung the light back to the right, searching for markers Jerry might recognize. Tom placed his right foot down carefully and bore the young man's weight, then he swept his left foot forward, falling into a hunched rhythm. While his back felt strong, his stooping posture caused his spine to be uncomfortably bent, and he didn't know how long he could walk like Quasimodo.

When Sam's light hit a marker on the wall that read, *Sandbridge Beach, Two Miles*, Tom's hopes soared.

"Hey, two miles isn't bad," he stepped faster. "At this rate, I'd say it'll take us a little over ninety minutes."

"A creepy, wet, long walk." Sam 's light pierced the gloom. "Just what I always wanted to do."

"Don't forget the cold," Tom chuckled dryly. In spite of their situation, they were still alive and moving. At the moment, that was all that mattered.

Chapter 3
Barbara McKnight
Wyndale, Virginia

The mid-morning sun pushed at the layer of gray clouds that stretched across the horizon, but it could not punch through. Wind blew in heavy gusts over the treetops in the yard, bending the branches in undulating ripples of rustling leaves as grass waved in the wide fields that rose from both sides of the road. Debris whipped through the air, paper and broad-leafed fronds turning and flipping in the wind, their forms slapping against tree and fencepost alike before vanishing into the distance.

Rain fell on the old, gray Ford F150's windshield before the wiper swiped it away. The truck sped down the road a little too fast, going ten or twenty miles per hour over the speed limit, swerving into the center lane and whipping back to the right, slowing as it drew closer to a gravel driveway. The truck turned in and trundled up toward the house, wheels crunching, suspension shaking as it passed the recently harvested field wet from rain storms and circled around to the right of the house, pulling in behind a blue Astro van. Barbara put the truck into park and killed the engine, her trembling hands tapping nervously on the steering wheel as she released a quivering sigh.

"Are you okay, Mom?" Linda leveled a stare at her mother from the passenger side.

"I'm fine," she said, flashing her middle child a hesitant smile. Then she reached for the door handle and popped it open. "You ready to help get all this stuff inside?"

"Yep!" Linda got out, Jack hopping down behind her. Barbara shoved the door the rest of the way open and met them at the back, lowering the tailgate to reveal three dozen bags of goods. Two bags rolled from atop the pile, but her daughter caught them before everything could spill out. One orange escaped and rumbled toward the edge and Barbara reached to snag it before it fell, but her clumsy grab only knocked it to the gravel.

She bit back a curse and turned to pick it up, but Jack was already there. He bent and snapped up the fruit, lifting it to show its unblemished peel. "It's okay," he smiled. "It's okay, Mom."

The one thing they didn't have much of on the farm was fresh fruit, and she'd wanted to pick up some before the stores ran out. That was the reason they'd braved town again – and it was truly the *last* time they'd be going back.

"Thanks, kiddo." Barbara took the orange from the boy and returned it to the bag. "Hands please."

Jack held out his hands and made fists, and she slipped some of the lighter bags on his wrists. She and Linda lifted the heavier ones, and the trio walked toward the back of the house. Barbara glanced down at the pickup's front end as they passed it, shaking her head at a large dent on the fender where the truck's faded blue paint was stripped away, leaving bare metal and the streaks of white from the other car. As she turned around the corner of the house, the bags bounced off her legs. Smooch greeted them with a low woof and a wagging tail, ears up and head tilted curiously to the side. Jack's gleeful cry at the sight of the dog broke through her surliness, and Barbara grinned at his ability to go from zero to happy simply at the sight of his animal friend.

She set her bags down by the sliding glass door. Drawing the key from her purse with her still-shaking hands, she struggled to fit it into the lock. She took a deep breath to calm herself, then unlocked the door and shoved it aside.

"On the table, please," she called out after them as Jack plowed through with his bags smacking against the door frame. "Easy, buddy. Don't bruise the fruit."

The boy placed his burden on the table, followed by Linda. Barbara took her bags to the counter and set them down before removing food items and grouping them to be more easily put away. Glancing over, she saw her son trying to slip outside to play with Smooch.

"Hold up, Jack. I loaded some new lessons into your school application." She gave him a pointed look. "Why don't you get started on that?"

"Aw, Mom. Do I have to do schoolwork now?"

"No time--"

"Like the present," Linda finished for her mother as she dropped bags on the table.

Barbara flashed her daughter a pleased look before doubling back on the boy. "You can play with Smooch later. Get upstairs and open your lessons."

"Okay, fine." Jack turned and slapped his legs, moping dejectedly through the kitchen.

"The door, please."

Jack spun on his heel, marched back to the door, and slid it shut before dragging his feet all the way to the stairs.

"Attitude adjustment!" she called out, getting a half-hearted "yes, ma'am" mumbled back in response. With Jack sorted, Barbara and Linda began to work in earnest on putting away the groceries.

"Bristol was insane, Mom. Right?"

"Insane doesn't properly describe it," Barbara said. She gathered the plastic bags into a bundle and placed them under the sink to save for later. "Dangerous, stupid, and greedy would probably describe it better."

Her heart rate kicked up and sweat beaded on her forehead as she recalled the day's shopping trip – one where she'd almost killed a man. When she woke up that morning, her hope had been to beat the crowds by hitting the stores before anyone else, but she'd been terribly wrong. By the time they arrived in Bristol, people were out and about, speeding everywhere, horns beeping as she'd witnessed a half-dozen near collisions. The grocery store and mini mart lots were packed, folks jostling at the entrances and shoving huge cartloads of food to their vehicles.

Sirens had wailed the entire time, and she'd occasionally caught sight of flashing lights as police cruisers and ambulances rushed through town.

"It was a bad idea going there in the first place." She opened a cabinet and stacked soup cans inside.

"Well, you couldn't have known everyone would be acting so weird." Linda brought over a handful of matching items.

"I disagree," Barbara replied. "I *knew* people would be acting weird. I just didn't listen to my instincts. Do you believe those two at the Market Saver?"

"Not at all."

The first sign that returning to Bristol had been a bad idea happened when they drove past the Market Saver on the north edge of town. While sitting in a short line of traffic, Barbara had glanced into the parking lot to see a man and woman approaching another smaller woman putting groceries in the back of her car. The newcomers had stood inches over her, looking predatory and fearless.

"When I saw those standing over her like that, I almost jumped out of my skin." Barbara shook her head.

"Me, too. That was *super* creepy. Do you think they would have hurt her?"

"Who knows? Maybe if those two guys hadn't come along."

"When the lady tried to slam her trunk shut and the guy stuck out his hand and caught it?" Linda's voice held a mixture of fear and uncertainty. "I knew there'd be trouble. Then when he started yelling at her…" Her brow furrowed. "Do you think they've done that routine a lot?"

"Probably. It was pretty effective," Barbara admitted.

"I can't believe she didn't notice. The grocery bags must have made noise when the guy's…accomplice started yanking them out of the trunk."

Linda grabbed a net of tangerines and put them in the bottom drawer of the fridge. "Is that why we went to the Meat King? Because you knew the other places would be bad?"

"That was my intention," Barbara replied. She turned and leaning against the counter. "But that didn't turn out so well either, did it?"

"No. The Meat King was *stuffed* with people. And the shelves were totaled." People had nearly picked the store clean by the time she'd parked and got the kids inside and they'd pushed their cart past two dozen people surrounding the meat counter where Matthew Trimboli worked feverishly to fulfill orders.

"We still got mostly what we needed," Barbara said, biting her lip, remembering the mad dash through the store where people were grabbing anything and everything. She stepped to the table and lined up the five first aid kits they'd found pushed to the rear of a bottom shelf though in truth it was Jack who'd actually discovered them, bending low to the ground where no one else could see.

"Can you believe the Meat King ran out of actual meat?" Linda leaned against the wall of breakfast nook.

"I've never seen that happen." Barbara folded her arms over her chest. "People weren't happy when Matthew announced it."

"Especially that old guy. He said it was bullsh--"

"Language…" She cut her daughter off with an exasperated look.

"Just kidding, Mom," the girl grinned. "I wasn't going to say it."

Barbara rolled her eyes at Linda and went back to organizing and putting away the groceries. They'd stood in line with three dozen shoppers as four cashiers tried to check them out and while Barbara had kept her cool on the outside, watching everyone carefully and making sure Jack didn't wander off, she'd grown more tense with each passing second. Some impatient people simply left the line and shoved their carts toward the door without paying and two managers stood at the exit, stopping dashers before they could escape with hundreds of dollars of items, but for every two they caught, one got through, emboldening the attempts of more.

She'd spotted a young couple with ratty hair staring at Linda and the contents of her cart, and she'd glowered at the pair until they saw her looking and cast their eyes aside. Barbara wanted to avoid confrontation at any cost, but that didn't mean she'd be an easy target. Forty-five minutes after that, they'd finally left the store, and she and Linda pushed the cart up a slight incline to the pickup truck.

Remembering what had happened to the lady at Market Saver, Barbara made the kids load the groceries in the truck bed while she kept an eye on their surroundings. By then, cars were packing the lot, and folks were hurrying toward the store in loose groups. An older couple tossed the McKnight's a furtive look, glancing over their cart and groceries before moving on, Barbara's gaze following them the entire way until they reached the store. Linda and Jack had picked up the pace and soon had the truck filled. Barbara hadn't bothered putting the cart back in its corral but left it sitting in the open off to the side before getting the kids loaded up and climbing behind the wheel.

As she pulled out of the lot, she'd watched in her mirrors as the Meat King managers tried to turn people away. Frustrated shoppers filed out of the store like angry zombies, heads down and gesturing to their friends and families before turning their eyes on recent customers loading bags into their cars. The turned-away people flowed back through the parking lot, eyeing open trunks and picking easy targets out of the crowd. Not wanting to become another victim, Barbara had quickly put the truck in gear and pulled toward the access road leading from the store when a vehicle flew out of nowhere and clipped her left front bumper.

She'd slammed her foot on the brake, causing them to lurch forward, the kids crying out in surprise as the offending car had stopped in front of them, angled so it blocked her from leaving. She'd rolled down her window to address the driver when an unsettling feeling twisted in her gut. A woman sat in the passenger seat, looking back at her with a fearful and guilty expression. The way their cars were positioned, the lady couldn't get out, and Barbara couldn't drive forward. The driver's side door flew open, drawing attention to a tall, red-haired man circling around the car who had pointed at her as he shouted, stalking forward. "I'm not going to hurt you! We just need the stuff in your truck!"

With a gasp, Barbara had thrown the truck in reverse and squealed away from the wreck, retreating into the lot until another vehicle pulled out behind her and laid on their horn, causing her to slam on her brakes again. The red-haired man had continued approaching, hands raised, face drawn with anger. She'd hit the gas, and the F150 jerked forward with a bark of tires. Eyes flying wide, the man spun away and slapped the side of her truck with the flat of his hand, cursing Barbara as she wove around him and his car and got the McKnights back on the road.

"Mom, are you okay?"

Linda's voice tore her back to reality. Barbara reached behind her head and removed her ponytail holder. She'd pulled it so tight it was giving her a headache.

With a smile at her daughter, she said, "I was just thinking of the guy who tried to stop us."

"He was *super* scary," Linda agreed. "Do you think he would have hurt us?"

"I don't think so. Well, maybe." She blinked. "Actually, I have no clue, and I didn't want to find out. That's why I took off so fast."

"You did good." Linda stepped over and wrapped her arms around Barbara's waist. "I guess we won't be going out again for a while."

She hugged her daughter back and gave a dry, humorless laugh. "You've got that right. We're staying home for a very, very long time."

"Good. I feel safer here."

Barbara broke the embrace and held Linda at arm's length. "Thank you."

"For what?"

"For calming me down."

"What do you mean? I didn't do anything."

Barbara didn't expect her to understand, because she'd always tried to keep a calm demeanor in front of the kids, but just being able to talk about what happened had eased her nerves considerably and her hands and fingers had even stopped shaking.

"I like talking to you, that's all."

"I guess you're okay to talk to, too," Linda replied with an uncertain smile, then she looked at the remaining items stacked on the table. "We don't have any room in the basement or in the cupboards for this stuff."

"Let's move it into the dining room."

"Okay."

They carried several stacks of cans and the first aid kits to the adjacent room where she'd already cleared off space in the near corner for extra supplies.

Linda straightened and pretended to dust off her hands. "What next?"

"Next is coffee."

Barbara marched into the kitchen, dumped the old swill in the sink, and started a fresh pot brewing. As the rich aroma leaked into the air, she turned and leaned against the counter with her arms folded across her chest. Linda took a seat at the kitchen table and removed her shoes, placing them neatly next to her chair before she finally spoke up.

"What would you have done if you'd hit him?"

"The man who tried to take our stuff?"

"Yeah." Linda's eyebrows scrunched as she reframed the question. "What I mean is, would you have helped the guy or called an ambulance?"

Barbara's expression turned cold, eyes staring straight ahead. "I would have kept driving."

"Seriously?"

"Remember what we talked about with situational awareness?"

"Yeah, but what's that got to do with helping a guy you just hit?"

"We heard the ambulances when we arrived in town, remember?"

"Yeah. They were all over the place."

"And the woman we just talked about," Barbara said, pointedly. "The one who almost got robbed."

"Right, yeah."

"Well, keeping all that in mind. If I'd hit the guy, and we got out to help, do you really think the police or an ambulance would have come right away?"

Linda paused before responding. "It was pretty crazy out there, so I guess they would have been busy with other people. No, I guess they wouldn't have come right away."

"I'd take it a step farther. My bet is that if we'd helped the guy, someone else would have tried to rob us, or worse."

"That's… kind of a good point, Mom."

"While I would have stopped for an injured person a week ago, I won't be taking any unnecessary chances from now on. Not if it puts us in danger. "

The coffee maker sputtered as the last bit of coffee steamed out and Barbara took a big blue mug from the cabinet and filled it close to the brim. Adding a little cream and sugar, she put the cup to her lips and breathed in the rich aroma before sipping. "I'll defend our property, vehicles, and animals at all costs. Because without them, we won't survive. You understand what I'm saying?"

"I think so." Linda gave a slow nod. "It means..."

"If anyone messes with us, I'm going to take them out. That means fight, kick, shoot, or run over them to protect you guys."

A dark look crossed Linda's face, and her eyes fell to the table.

"Don't worry," Barbara grinned. "I'll try to give them a warning. But sometimes, like today, there might not be time to do that. If someone comes out of their car and challenges me like that, I'm not going to play nice. It's their fault if they get hurt."

"No holds barred."

"What?"

"No holds barred," Linda repeated. "That's what the wrestlers say when there're no rules in a match. I learned that from Jack and Dad."

Barbara narrowed her eyes. "They watch wrestling?"

Linda nodded. "Late at night sometimes after you and Sam fall asleep."

"I didn't know that." She smiled at the revelation, then her expression sobered and she gave her daughter an appreciative nod. "That's actually a good way of putting it, though. When it comes to defending the McKnight family and our house, it's no holds barred from now on."

"Sounds like we're on the same page." Linda grinned.

"I guess we are." Barbara smiled back. "By the way, I loaded some more lessons into your school app, too." She fixed her daughter with an apologetic look. "I couldn't let Jack have all the fun."

"No, that's great since I already finished my other ones." Linda tilted her head pointedly. "Waiting for you to grade them."

She smiled at Sam's scholastic voracity. She never complained about doing schoolwork and, in fact, she seemed to enjoy it a great deal – at least compared to Jack.

"I have one favor to ask." Linda gave her a sheepish look. "Can I take a cup of coffee up with me?"

Barbara sighed, shook her head with a look of mock disapproval and raised her index finger. "Just one cup."

"Awesome!" Linda came to the counter and poured herself a short cup, adding a little cream and a half teaspoon of sugar. "Thanks, Mom!"

Barbara watched her daughter pad out of the kitchen and down the hall, looking uncomfortably grown-up with the steaming coffee mug in her hand. She took a sip of her own coffee, the bittersweet brew clearing her head and soothing her nerves. Turning, she strolled to the sliding glass door and stared out across the property at their fuel shed and barn off to the right. Beyond that was their camping spot and the stretch of woods half circling the farmstead, with Smooch lying out in the grass, ears up, watching over everything.

"How am I going to protect all of it?" she murmured to herself. The dangers she and the kids had talked about since the start of the anomaly were turning into reality faster than she imagined possible. The official announcements had been prescient - there was, indeed, looting, rioting, and desperate people willing to do anything to feed themselves and their families no matter the cost to others. And, according to the president's announcement, looters might soon be the least of their troubles, what with the weather predicted to start changing, too.

We believe these temperature changes directly result from the desalination of the waters near the anomalous zone. This will disrupt the flow of warm water being carried up from the south... In other words, we expect to see temperatures dropping rapidly in the United States.

She thought about where Virginia was in relation to everything else in the Northern Hemisphere. They weren't so far north that they'd experience the colder temperatures right away, but they definitely weren't in the south, either, so she couldn't count on it staying warm for all that long.

"Weeks? Months? Days?" Barbara mumbled to herself in quiet frustration. Not one who enjoyed not knowing when things would happen or not having a solid, step-by-step thorough plan, she was out of her depth. Still, it seemed that erring on the side of moderation would be the most prudent course of action. "Okay, so we probably have some time to focus on defense," she said with a more confident nod. "After that, we'll kick our winter preparations into high gear."

That meant she needed to fortify the house or, at a minimum, the bottom floor, just in case things got really bad. The good news was that the crops were harvested and mostly put away and the only vegetables left in the garden were the winter squash, which could be picked in two weeks. Between the grocery runs and their stockpiles, they had enough food and water for the entire family for a very, very long time.

But she had the animals to think about, and the green house. Her mind started going down that path when a horn honked outside. Ticking her head to the side, Barbara set her coffee cup on the counter and crossed into the dining room. She stood at the window and peeked through the blinds to see Darren and Marie's Jeep parked at the end of the walkway and, concerned that they weren't exiting the vehicle right away, she stepped outside and hurried to the end of the walk.

Darren sat behind the wheel, watching Barbara approach with a pensive expression, his white-gray hair uncombed and sticking out on the sides, his shirt hanging loose off his shoulders like someone had pulled it around the neck. Marie wore the same frazzled look as her husband, concerned and tired, her lips drawn tight and her hair messed up. A glance in the back showed several grocery bags piled up, though half of their contents appeared to have been scattered about and strewn in the back of the vehicle.

"Hey, you two!" Barbara called out, waving and huffing. "You look frightful. What happened?"

Marie's expression soured. "Have you been out to the stores yet today?"

"We went out earlier," Barbara confirmed, placing her hand on the door frame near Darren's arm. "It's a madhouse, but we managed to pick up some supplies. I'm guessing you did, too."

"That's right." Darren chuffed. "We braved Crazy Town."

Marie gave a pained grin. "That's what he calls Bristol now."

"And the name fits," he growled back.

Barbara's eyes lingered on the man's stretched shirt and a red mark on his neck. "Looks like you saw some trouble."

"Nothing we couldn't handle," Darrin gave her a grim nod. "A couple of guys tried to steal our stuff. Two months' worth of food. They scared the hell out of us, I tell you."

"Oh, no. What did you do?"

He smirked. "What we always planned to do in such a situation. I got their attention while Marie drew her pistol."

"The big boy didn't like me jamming my gun in his back," she winked.

Barbara gave an approving nod to the feisty older couple and chuckled. "Remind me not to mess with you two."

Marie smiled mischievously and grabbed her husband's arm. "That's right!"

"And I'm assuming you didn't believe the president was being totally truthful about the cold temperatures?" Barbara asked. "That's why you were out today, right?"

Darrin raised his finger and pointed at her, growling not at her, but at the general state of the world. "Another true statement. We figured we'd get the jump on people and top off our supplies. No jump, but at least we got some supplies."

"You want to come in and talk about it over a cup of coffee?"

"Thanks, but we need to get home and put this stuff away," Marie said, nodding to the Jeep's back seat.

"I understand."

"Hey, now that things are heating up around town, we should stay in touch," Darren said, pointedly. "I have a HAM radio back at the house. Does Tom have anything like that?"

"No, sadly not. We'd thought about getting one but never got around to it." Barbara wrinkled her brow. "But we do have some handheld radios in the basement. Would those work?"

"Those would work great." Darren fished around in the small console between their seats until he found a pen and scrap of paper. He scribbled something on it and handed it over with a smile. "That's the frequency I'm on. Try tonight at 7PM, and we'll see if we can talk."

"Great." Barbara took the note and held it up. "It'll be a relief having a direct connection to you guys."

"Sometime later I'll bring my old HAM set over and get you set up so you can receive the same broadcasts I do."

"That sounds like fun, and it'll put my mind at ease with Tom and Sam being gone."

Marie's expression deepened. "You still haven't heard anything?"

"Not yet." Barbara shook her head, the sadness resurfacing for a moment before she pushed it back down again. "But we're not giving up hope."

"You absolutely must not." The older woman reached across her husband and placed her hand on the door frame, palm up. "Tom's going to make it home. I can feel it."

"I know." Barbara rested her hand in Marie's and closed her eyes at the comforting squeeze the woman gave her. "I just wish he would hurry up."

"Well, we're going to head out now." Darren started the Jeep and put it in gear "You be safe, and we'll talk later."

Barbara bade them farewell and stepped away from the Jeep as they did a circle at the top of the driveway and pulled away in a spin of tires and spit of gravel. She raised her hand and waved as they rolled down to the main road and turned left, headed for home.

"I'm so glad we have some friends around here," Barbara said in a breathless whisper before trudging back up the driveway to the house where she headed inside, found her coffee cup and refilled it. She grabbed a notebook from her drawer and sat at the kitchen table, looking around as she tapped her pen on the notepad. *Time to make a list… hmmm.*

The first, easiest thing would be to cover the windows to make it harder for someone to break in. *There was some plywood in the barns from some project of Tom's, wasn't there? I'm sure I can dig up a few spare padlocks, too.* While the locks wouldn't keep someone determined from getting into the house, having a bit of extra security would be better than nothing. The true defense would have been steel core doors with properly anchored frames that couldn't be broken, though something like that would be next to impossible to come by on short notice. *We'll do what we can with what we've got.*

After jotting down a few notes she expanded her thinking around defending the herd and flocks. Smooch was the perfect watch dog, but she couldn't be everywhere at once, so Barbara wrote out *barbed wire, improved corral,* and *double check the signs.* The No Trespassing signs wouldn't keep anyone off the property, but on the off-chance that things returned to normal faster than it seemed they would, they'd at least provide a valid legal defense. *If only they'd have passed that purple paint law last year.*

She and Tom had talked about setting up alarms, tripwire hooks, and trail cameras around the property, but she wasn't sure they had all the equipment on hand. Barbara wrote *tripwire* and *noisemakers* on her notepad and sat back again, the scope of what she had to protect settling on her. Their property was massive, and anyone could approach from the woods or sneak up on them from any side.

"I swore Tom had some notes on this stuff." She muttered to herself as she stood and made her way to the basement to Tom's battery room. She flipped on the light and crossed to his workbench, the surface of which was covered with an assortment of small batteries, wires, tools, and a pile of spiral notebooks. She opened the first one and read through his tree stand designs, sheds, and other structures they'd planned on building.

The second notebook held battery room designs with various current and wattage notes written in the columns, arrows showing the direction of electrical flow through the circuits. He'd scribbled the names of connectors and wire gauges in the margins with question marks next to them and while Barbara wasn't clueless on basic wiring, what Tom had written might as well have been Chinese.

Hoping there was something in the notebooks she could use, she tucked them under her arm, flipped the light off and went back upstairs where she piled them onto the kitchen table and sat down in front of them. Choosing a notebook that looked like something she could read, she pulled it in front of her. Lifting her coffee cup, she took a slow sip and then opened to the first page, silently praying that Tom could give her some ideas without actually being there.

Chapter 4
Tom McKnight
Outer Banks, North Carolina

Tom McKnight walked along the median with Jerry's arm thrown over his shoulder, keeping the injured young man upright. He'd handed Sam his flashlight and she kept to his left, training the beam on the concrete barrier, though it occasionally slipped across the murky water to show the surface bouncing in agitated waves. Heavy drips echoed in the dark chamber, stones plopping as a mist of seawater clung to their faces, the flooding having leveled off with no signs of draining.

"I wasn't sure at first," Tom said, "but I kept thinking about the Atlantic Drift. Much of our warm temperatures are brought up from more temperate oceans by currents."

Jerry adjusted his grip on Tom's arm with a grunt as he replied. "And if the saltwater infusion is screwing up those currents, that would cause major temperature shifts in the United States?"

"Probably the world. At least in the Northern Hemisphere. The sun would continue to warm the more temperate zones but even those temperatures would drop over time."

Sam clicked her tongue. "But earlier, on the, um, boat, you said it would take weeks to see any significant changes, remember? It's only been a few days."

"That's what worries me," Tom lifted his chin. "This thing is accelerating way faster than any of us – well, probably anyone at all – predicted."

"How long will it take for things to get *really* cold?"

Tom gave a mental shrug. "It just depends on how much water we're talking about. At this point, it's incalculable. Beyond quadrillions, certainly. And the surge pressures being exerted must be insane. Plus, there are the regular atmospheric conditions to consider. And what do you mean by *'really cold'*? There are so many factors I'm not an expert at."

"You're not an expert?" Jerry scoffed. "You sure sound like one."

Tom chuckled. "No, I'm a glorified technician who picked up some oceanic and biological tidbits over the years from people I've worked with. I'd never profess to be an expert on any of it. Especially not on something so esoteric as a possible shift in the North Atlantic current."

"If it's so esoteric," Jerry grunted, "how do you even know about it? Has anyone theorized this before? I mean, I've watched documentaries on climate change theories and all that stuff but none that predicted this."

"That's just it," Tom blinked into the swirling mist as droplets spun in the flashlight beam. "It's bits of theories I heard over the years. No one ever came right out and said, 'ice age.' Most people I've talked to tend to agree that an ice age occurs when summer temperatures in northern hemispheres fall below freezing. But it usually takes place over thousands of years and lasts even longer."

"What normally causes it?"

"Again, most agree that it's related to the Milankovitch cycles."

"What are those?" Sam asked.

"Well, it explains how changes in the Earth's tilt and orbit combine to disperse solar radiation differently," Tom clarified as he shifted beneath the young man's weight, jaw clenching with the strain.

Jerry nodded. "I've heard of that. It has to do with how the environment reacts to the heating of the planet."

"Exactly," Tom nodded. "The Earth tilts and shifts continuously, but the currents are usually there to balance things out. Now, the anomaly is there, disrupting the currents by messing with the temperature and salinity of the water. If they're not bringing that precious warmth up from the south..."

"Ice age," Sam finished for him.

Tom nodded. "Of course, scientists love to speculate and play the 'what if' game, asking questions about things that may or may not happen." Sam shivered, pulling her blanket tighter around her shoulders, hand shaking as she held the flashlight pointed forward. "Well, what they *thought* might happen," Tom corrected himself, teeth chattering momentarily. "No one has ever proved a theory either way. We're still taking shots in the dark."

"You sure it's still a theory, dad?" Sam chuckled half-heartedly, though Tom had no good response.

They fell into silence, their heavy breathing keeping them company as Sam played her flashlight all around the tunnel. The air had turned frigid and their breaths puffed in the dim light like a trio of gusting steam pipes. The drips were heavy and slow, like molasses plopping into the brackishness on either side of them. Sometimes, droplets landed on his head and neck, sending deep shivers through his body.

Ice and small pieces of debris crunched beneath their feet and whenever Sam swung the flashlight upward, Tom noted cracks and fissures in the stones, though they didn't seem deep enough to cause a cave-in. Then again, collapses often happened in the blink of an eye and without warning. With a grimace of urgency, Tom picked up the pace, shuffling them forward faster.

The median stretched wide enough for two people to stand side-by-side, though Jerry's right foot occasionally slipped off the edge, sending concrete dust and ice chips into the water. Grabbing an extra flashlight from his jacket, Tom flipped it on and shone the light across the murky surface to his left, moving back and forth as he looked for a vehicle or other mode of transportation. So far, the tunnel was almost empty of wrecks and stalled cars. Anything they spotted was stuck in the flood, seawater no doubt having gotten in the engines, the occupants having long since gotten out – or worse.

Tom suddenly stopped and flipped off his light. "Sam, turn off your flashlight." She did, leaving them in complete darkness. Eyes squinted, Tom peered ahead, searching for a sliver of light that might mark the end of the tunnel.

"Okay, Dad, this is creepy," Sam whispered. "What are you doing?"

"Sorry, I was just trying to see some daylight ahead." He flipped the light back on. "Looks like nothing yet."

Sam turned her light on, too, and they continued walking.

"It's getting steeper," Jerry noted with a weak voice. "Could that mean we're closer to the exit?"

"Probably," Tom replied, watching the water beginning to rush past them, surging in a gush of grayish foam as it licked the sides of the median just beneath them. His energy surged as their chances of escaping the oppressive tunnel grew real. "Let's pick it up. We've got to be almost there!"

Encouraged, Tom urged them even faster, lifting Jerry up and practically carrying him to the end. After another fifty yards of limping and shuffling, he spotted the soft pale light of day beckoning them from the tunnel's end.

"Is it morning?" he asked, more to himself than anyone. "Or afternoon?"

"Who cares?" Jerry replied with a grin. "As long as it's *outside*!"

"I'll second that," Sam said, shuffling up behind them.

They approached the tunnel's entrance, and Tom stared out at what remained of the storm. The tunnel sat back off the ocean, hidden in brush and bending trees, giving them a wide view of the beach as waves rushed in and flowed over the road. The seawater swept in low toward the houses on their left, crashing against them in massive sprays of foam. Boats lay stranded or gently rocking in people's yards, piled up along with the cars like toys—hulls shattered, stripped clean, a wasteland of detritus mixed up and scattered by the hurricane.

Sam came to stand on Tom's left, wrapping her arm around his. The wind buffeted them, blowing sideways rain inside the tunnel to sting their faces. "I'll take this over being in stuck back there any day."

"Agreed," Tom nodded firmly.

"Sandbridge Beach is ahead," Jerry breathed. "I used to come here a lot. We're getting close."

Tom glanced down at his ward. "You hanging in there, buddy?"

"I am. Literally."

"Okay, let's keep going," Tom gave a shivery chuckle.

He trudged another fifteen yards with Sam on one side and Jerry clinging to his other. Eventually, they ran out of median and had to climb down, Tom wincing as water rushed over his shoes as wind blew their wet pants against their legs. They had about thirty yards to the median's end and Tom stopped, hesitant to leave the protection of the tunnel and re-enter the storm, but something caught his attention in the distance. A light - several lights - winked and flickered through the haze. He pointed and raised his voice to be heard above the din. "It looks like something up ahead."

"What are they, houses?" Sam asked.

"Not sure," he replied. "I guess we'll find out soon enough. It's a good sign if the power's still on."

"That means heat!" Sam's teeth chattered next to him.

"And shelter," Jerry added tiredly.

Tom scanned along the beachfront homes then switched to the left side of the road where the North Bay sandwiched them in. The houses on that side were built on land strips that wove out into the water and every other foundation had been swept out, leaving piles of wreckage floating in the shallows. It looked like a giant child had dragged their hand along the bay shore, spreading brick and wood framing like jam across a tabletop. Boats had floated up onto roads with the rest of the flotsam, smashing their hulls against street signs and trees and the wind, while still volatile, didn't hold a candle to the RV-rattling gusts from the day before.

"Maybe it's not all that bad anymore." Tom cocked his head as he listened. "In fact, I think the storm is letting up a bit. Sam, can you turn on the phone and check it?"

"Oh, yeah," she said, pulling the phone from her pocket and powering it on. After a moment, she shook her head. "Nothing yet."

"Keep it handy. We have to get a connection sometime."

They increased their pace, shuffling the last few yards to the exit. Tom remained aware of Jerry's fragile state, though the young man was stabilizing. He carried most of his own weight but still leaned on Tom's shoulder as they fell into a good rhythm, Tom stomping one boot in front of the other, half bent under the strain while Jerry shuffled beside him, stepping strong with his left foot but swinging his right in a wide arc. They plodded forward in the same manner, trudging stiffly against the water rushing past them into the tunnel.

"Good job," Tom said, encouraging him. "Hang on and lift your feet. If you trip, we're both going--"

"Dad!" Sam screamed.

He half turned to his left, trying not to unbalance Jerry as his daughter stood with his phone in her hand, eyes wide. The screen was lit up, and it buzzed repeatedly, causing it to slip from Sam's slick grasp. With quick reflexes, she caught it and gripped it tight, then held it up for him to see. "Look!"

Tom watched as a flood of notifications and messages poured through, the phone continuing to ding and buzz as even more rolled in. There were news alerts, texts, and emails and Sam wisely pulled up the messaging app and scrolled through the text messages. Tom spotted some from his boss, Ray, at Maniford Aquatics Engineering, but Barbara had sent him at least a half dozen.

"Pull up your mom's messages," he spoke through tight lips. "Hurry."

Sam leapt off the median and landed with a splash while Tom guided Jerry back toward it and lowered him down so he could sit on the edge. Then, Tom hopped down and huddled over the screen with Sam, reading the texts while continually wiped water droplets away.

"They're okay, but they're worried about us," she grinned. "Mom wants us to get our butts home safely."

Tom glanced up at the sky and murmured sarcastically. "Be home soon, honey. As soon as Mother Nature lets us." He turned back to his daughter. "Call her now. Please."

Sam clicked her mother's name and put the phone to her ear. A pause followed as the girl sniffed and stared out into the grayness until, finally, she shook her head. "It won't ring through."

"Let me try."

He took the phone from her, used his thumb to redial, and put the device to his ear. He waited as it rang and rang, finally breaking to a message stating that "All circuits are busy. Please hang up and dial again. If you--"

He ended the call and pursed his lips, pulling up the text app. Then he replied to Barbara's message, going back and forth repeatedly with his shivering thumbs after making several cold-induced errors.

We're safe. Got to shore. Heading north. Almost to VA Beach. Will find a ride home. Don't worry about us. Stay safe!

Hitting the "Send" button, he stared at the spinning status icon in the center of the screen. It churned for a good thirty seconds before the message finally showed as sent and he offered Sam a hopeful smile. "Well, that's all we can do for now."

"What about all the other notifications? What do they say?"

Tom held the phone in front of his face and began scrolling through them. His jaw slowly dropped as he read the most prominent headline; an emergency announcement from the president. While several news sources offered a full replay of the video, Tom wasn't foolish enough to think it would actually load with him standing in the middle of the storm and very low reception. Focusing on the headlines, he mouthed the words as he scrolled.

"A surge of water from the anomaly...suspected freshwater aquifer... flooding... destruction of sea life habitats..." He stopped and looked at Sam. "Nothing new there, right?"

"That's what we saw on the ship," she agreed with a nod. "The rift in the sea floor, and those rovers getting wrecked."

Tom continued to scroll. "Massive destruction of sea life... desalination of ocean waters... currents disrupted... temperature changes..." Tom squeezed the phone and looked up, blinking into the cold mist as fear gripped his heart. A different kind of fear than the claustrophobia of the tunnel, but constricting all the same. After taking a deep breath, he reluctantly resumed, shaking his head. "They expect it to get colder over the coming months."

"Things are *already* colder," Sam observed.

"No kidding." Tom reached the end of the president's announcement, which amounted to the usual platitudes. The American people had nothing to fear. He would bring the might of the Federal Government to bear. Looting would not be tolerated.

"Looting," Tom murmured with a shake of his head.

"You think it's going to be bad?"

"I don't know." Tom shook his head. Their family lived well outside the Bristol city limits but could certainly be one of the first targets of people raiding in the surrounding countryside.

Digging deeper into the notifications, he chose an alert from his weather app, opening it to reveal more notices about record low temperatures and ice advisories along the East Coast. Maine was posting chilly numbers in the coming week, and Virginia was looking like early fall.

"It's the end of summer," he shook his head. "We shouldn't be seeing temperatures in the forties and fifties yet."

"Jeez, Dad." Sam stood on her toes, reading around his shoulder. "That doesn't look good at all."

"No, it doesn't," he agreed.

"What should we do?"

"We focus on what we can control," he replied easily. "We'll take Jerry to a hospital and then get our butts home, like your mother said. Once we get back, we'll worry about whatever else is happening."

Tom put the phone in his pocket and moved over to where Jerry crouched.

"How you feeling?"

The young man lifted his head. "Pretty good. You know, hanging in there. Terrible, if I'm being honest."

"Ready to travel?" Tom smiled.

"Yeah, man. I can't wait to get soaking wet again. Highlight of my life."

Tom laughed, came over and squatted, letting Jerry wrap his left arm over his shoulder. He heaved the young man to his feet and turned them toward the storm. The trio left the tunnel's protection, leaning into howling gusts with saltwater whipping around them. Tom sniffed brine and sometimes swallowed it, making him want to gag while the wind brought cold like a scythe to cut across them. The collective noise roared in his ears, whipping against his cheeks, but he kept his head down and focused ahead through the grayness.

It only took twenty minutes of slogging to feel miserable again and, at some point, Tom realized he'd allowed his chin to drop to his chest, eyes tracing the concrete and swirling waters instead of keeping an eye out ahead. Waves sometimes washed across the road, dragging sand and dirt from beneath the foundation to leave it cracked and breaking apart and they had to step over the rough patches or circle around if the cracks were too wide. After fifteen minutes of slogging along Sam suddenly broke away.

"Wait here, guys!"

Tom looked up to see his daughter ditching her backpacks on the side of the road and picking her way down the sunken shoulder toward a large fishing boat that sat in six inches of water. The hull bore a gaping, jagged hole, and seawater poured out as it tilted to port.

"Wait, wha-what are you doing?" Tom called out, too tired to physically stop her. "Be careful!"

Leaning in, hands on the edges, Sam peered into the broken hull before sticking one foot in, sidestepping, and vanishing from sight. Panic surged through Tom's body and he nearly dropped Jerry on the road in lieu of slogging down and dragging her back out. "Okay, Sam! Get back here, now!"

The girl emerged from the busted hull, obeying her father but not without her prize: in her hand was a yellow, heavy-grade parka, still freshly vacuum-sealed in spite of the boat's condition. Smiling, Sam removed it from its plastic packaging and draped garment over her Tom and Jerry's shoulders, the thick, water resistant material settling on them to keep them dry and, hopefully, slightly warmer.

"How'd you know that would be in there?" Tom asked.

"Standard emergency gear. I saw spots for more and some discarded packaging, but no more parkas. I'm good though," she replied with a wink, adjusting the backpacks as she put them back on. "These things trap a lot of heat."

"Nicely done. Remind me to *not* curb your TV watching time in the future." Tom gave Sam a thankful nod, and they trudged on.

"How long until we reach your neighborhood?" he asked as Jerry gazed ahead at the distant lights flickering through the grayness, eyes moving left and then right as if looking for landmarks to identify.

"I don't know," he shook his head. "Everything is messed up. I don't recognize anything around here."

"How will you know when to turn into your neighborhood?"

"I guess I just will," Jerry shrugged his good shoulder sheepishly. When Tom leveled a hard stare at him, the young man answered more directly. "Seriously, I'll know when we get there. I really will."

Tom stymied his doubts, raised his chin, and kept going.

* * *

"Dad, is that what I think it is?"

They'd been walking for forty-five minutes when her excited tone drew his attention. Lifting his head, he saw his daughter standing near the right side of the road, looking toward the flooded beachfront homes as the water gently lapped at her shoes.

"What is what?"

Sam pointed her flashlight. "Over there."

Tom squinted and directed his own light after hers, seeing only washed-out yards and foaming ocean. "Sorry, Sam. You'll have to--" Tom stopped as he saw its eyes in the reflection of her flashlight pointed into the shadows under a large, bending tree. The middle house sitting beneath the bowed branches was a gray beach home with most of its roof missing. On a small section of the remaining shingles crouched an orange tabby cat, its fur wet and sticking out in all directions, tucked into a recess, presumably to protect itself from the rain and cold. It had wrapped its tail tightly around its body and was staring down at the gently sloshing waves with wide, frightened eyes.

"See it now, Dad?"

"Yeah, I see the cat." A frown creased his features. "But we need to keep going, Sam."

"Seriously?" The girl stared back at him. "We can't just leave it there."

"C'mon, Sam. We've got more to worry about than a cat. The water will probably recede, and it'll jump down and be fine."

"Probably?" Sam started walking out toward the edge of the road. "What if the house washes out, or the waves keep rising?"

"Believe me, honey." Tom shook his head. "Cats can survive almost anything. I'm sure the critter will be fine."

"Just a quick minute, okay, Dad? I can just prop up a board up there for it to climb down on!" Without waiting for his go-ahead, Sam ran off of the road through the sand and water, heading for the house.

"Sam! Hey!" Tom shouted and clenched his jaw in frustration. He started to release Jerry but realized as soon as he did, the young man would collapse to the pavement. Tom took a deep breath to calm himself before quickly scanned around. When he found what he was looking for, he turned to Jerry.

"Can you stand for a second?"

"Yeah. I'm good."

Tom got out from beneath the young man's arm and held him in place for a moment to make sure he didn't topple over. He ran a dozen yards to a crumpled lawn chair, snatched it up, and brought it back. The furniture was mostly intact except for a twist in the frame that made it sit lopsided. Tom straightened it as best he could before helping Jerry sit down on it and, once he got him settled, Tom looked him in the eye. "You good?"

"Oh, yeah. This is actually nice." The young man settled back and pulled the parka to his chin as rain beat against the plastic, chuckling as he watched Sam. "I'm fine sitting right here. You guys save the poor kitty cat."

"Right." Tom rolled his eyes, nodded and jogged over to Sam where she walked back and forth along the shoreline. The house with the cat stood forty yards away in the middle of a seawater lake, the waves rolling in and swirling together to foam up to their boots.

"How deep do you think it is by the house?" Sam asked.

"Judging by where the water is rising, probably eight or ten feet at most."

"So, four to six feet when it's out?"

"Sounds about right." Tom pointed to the turbulent swirling. "We can't just wade out there because we don't know what the cross currents are like. They might not look strong from here, but they could easily drag us under."

"What can we do?"

"Look for something we can float out to it."

"Like a raft?"

"Yeah."

They walked up and down the shoreline, searching for something they could ride. Tons of floating debris had washed up on shore, but nothing that could hold either of them and the wooden fishing boat they found wrecked in the yard was far too large and damaged to maneuver into the water. Tom spotted a telescoping pool skimmer, picked it up, and tossed it over near the road.

"Pile up anything useful there."

"Okay."

Sam threw herself into the work, dashing for objects, gathering everything she could find. Tom's weariness kicked in, and he was still somewhat upset with her, but one of Samantha's soft spots included animals, and taking a short break from their perilous journey to indulge her wouldn't hurt. Ten minutes later, Tom stood in front of the pile of rescue items with his hands on his hips.

"All we have is this super long heavy-duty pool skimmer, two cushions, and a bunch of junk," Sam said, blowing a gust of air that was swallowed up by the wind.

"And none of it is stable enough to float us to the cat." Tom glanced over his shoulder at the animal still hunkered at the corner, staring at them with big, yellow eyes. He sorted through the pile of stuff and held up a small plastic bin without holes in it, one cushion and the pool skimmer. "Hey, I think I have an idea."

"Oh, yeah?"

Tom slipped off his backpack and placed it on the side of the road, digging out some rope, tape, and a small serrated knife from the RV's kitchen. He flipped the bin over and rested the pool skimmer's end on the bottom. With thick layers of duct tape, he firmly affixed the two pieces together so the bin rested on the skimmer like a basket, bringing the tape high up on the bin's sides. He turned it over and set it down near the shoreline before removing the cushion cover and holding up a soggy slab of foam. Squeezing the seawater out, he cut it to fit the bin and pressed it down inside to act as a landing pad for the animal - if it would jump. Tom took off his jacket, shirt, socks and shoes, and pants, handing them to Sam to keep as dry as possible and leaving him in just his boxer briefs.

"Dad, are you going to be okay?" Sam sounded worried and slightly regretful that she'd put her father down this path. "You don't have to do this if you don't want to. I understand we can't save every animal."

"I'll be fine," Tom shivered. "It'll be cold for a minute, but I'll get over it. Not sure if you'll get over seeing your old man in his skivvies, though." Rope looped around his waist, he tied it tight and handed the other end to Sam.

"I see what you're doing," she said, taking the end and wrapping it around her arm to get a good grip.

"I'll walk out until the water is past my knees," Tom explained, "then I'll push the bin out to the cat. If he jumps in, great. If not..."

Sam nodded.

"Just make sure to pull me back if a wave snags me."

Sam wasn't likely to have the strength to haul a full-grown man from an ocean current if it caught him, but it was better than nothing. Grabbing up the pole, Tom took a deep breath and pushed the bin into the water with the handle. It floated on its own, so he waded out toward the house, pushing it ahead of him.

"Keep your flashlight trained on the cat please."

The beam glinted off the water as Sam switched it to her right hand before settling on the wet, scrawny animal on the edge of the roof. The waves were tame at first, surging past his shins and throwing him slightly off balance as debris swirled around his legs, banging into him but not threateningly. As the waves receded, though, they pulled hard, forcing him to brace himself on the sandy bottom with each step.

A cresting wave hit his knees and rolled past, and Tom stopped to check on the cat. It gazed at him, wet and miserable, but with a hint of curiosity and hope. With a shake of his head, Tom held the pole against his side and loosened the extender part of the handle until it stretched almost twenty feet. He locked them in place, and pushed the bin toward the cat once again. The house stood in the middle of the water, the only solid object between himself and limitless ocean. If a cross current grabbed him, and Sam couldn't hold on, there would be nothing to keep him from being dragged out to sea.

The small waves were astonishingly strong, and he fought to balance in the push and pull, positioning the bin as close as possible, still ten feet too short. Cursing silently, he edged out farther into the waves, wincing as the water rode up his thighs to wet his boxers. Legs spread, Tom pushed the bin closer to the half-submerged structure, reaching and stretching, hanging on to the very end of the pole with his fingertips, but still three or four feet short. Inch-by-inch he scooted out farther, pushing the bin out, stepping on debris beneath the water, something sharp pricking his heel, but he ignored it and shifted his foot to the side. Eventually the bin floated and bobbed just three feet below the house's eaves, close enough that the feline could easily leap into it.

"Come on, buddy," Tom called to the cat. "Hop in!"

The cat stared down at the bin and then lifted its head, blinking at Tom slowly, and not even kissing noises or shaking the bin slightly got the animal to jump in. Tom's legs had been cold for several minutes, but the chill had climbed up his spine and caused his teeth to chatter. Still, he remained focused, edging out another half foot until the water ran straight up his thighs and into his groin.

"Come on, little guy!" he called through clenched teeth over the crashing ocean waves and tight, swirling winds. "Don't just sit there. I'm trying to save your butt."

Suddenly, the cat raised from its crouch and crawled to the roof's very edge, staring intently down at the bin.

"That's it, buddy," Tom said in a gentle tone. "Come on, now. Hop on it there."

The cat glanced at him and then at the bin again as Tom tried to hold it steady. The animal's backside shifted, and it seemed to tense itself to leap. Then it settled back into a laying position once more, licking its front paws. Tom shook his head, blowing air, feeling his frustration rise.

"Don't be afraid." Tom tried to sound soothing through frustration and clenched teeth, barely holding the handle with his fingertips. "Just jump on down. Don't make me swim out there to get you."

At first, he thought the cat would stay put, but at the last second it tensed and leaned forward, its head tilted as it looked between the person and strange object in front of it. Finally, the cat leapt forward, landing softly and silently in the bin. A moment later, two paws clutched the bin's edge, and the cat's face peered over at him, meowing loudly before lowering itself out of sight.

"Good kitty," Tom whispered. "Good, good cat."

He started to draw the animal to him when a receding wave yanked the pool skimmer from his grip. The handle smacked the brine, and the entire thing began drifting away. Tom lunged forward, reaching and grasping for the handle, but it had already strayed several feet, the waves dragging it inexorably out to sea, taking the cat with it. Gritting his teeth, Tom bit down against the inevitable cold and leapt fully into the water. The chilly brine clapped against the sides of his head, filling his ears with noise as the sand beneath his feet suddenly dropped out.

With clenched, shivering jaws, he surged forward, taking two full strokes before snagging the pole handle. Sam call out to him, but her voice was distant and Tom tried to lunge backward, but his toes barely skimmed the sand. Swinging his feet beneath him, he kicked himself backward, dragging the bin toward shore the rope growing taut around his waist as Sam added her strength to the rescue.

A wave swept up and smacked him in the face, saltwater rushing into his mouth. Tom sputtered and spit it out, feeling the burn in his throat as the ocean suddenly did him a favor and shoved him toward the road. Tom's feet touched the sand, and he gained traction. Leaning backwards, dragging the handle backward and the cat and basket with it, he kicked himself away from the gray house and the limitless sea. Back straining, teeth chattering, he fought the waves until the water only reached his thighs.

"Hang tight, kitty," he growled as he surged backwards, exiting the dangerous waves into the lazy, shin-deep wash. Tossing the handle behind him, he splashed forward and reached into the bin, scooped out the animal, clutching it to his chest before turning and trudging the rest of the way to shore, dripping and cold as the wind whipped against him.

Once on dry ground, the cat squirmed and twisted in his arms until Tom let it go, the animal hitting the sand on all four paws before sprinting away with its tail straight up.

"That's gratitude for you," Tom gasped as he stood in the wind and rain, dripping and cold. His numb fingers plucked at the rope around his waist until his daughter leaned in and loosened the knot.

"Sorry, Dad," Sam apologized as she coiled the rope. "I didn't want you to do all that. I… I shouldn't have guilted you into it."

"It's okay," Tom sighed. "I think the kitty will be fine now. No more animal rescuing until we're safe though, okay?" Sam nodded wordlessly, her face still ashen from her father's close call. Tom turned and picked up his clothes, marching back to Jerry with his arms hanging wide, water still dripping off him.

"We need to get you warm," Sam said, following behind him.

"That's probably a good idea," Tom agreed through chattering teeth, his breath coming in ragged puffs of air. He looked around for shelter from the wind and sprinkling rain, but the landscape offered nothing.

"I have some extra things in the backpack," he said, already pulling out towels they'd brought from the RV. After drying himself as best as he could in the rain, he stood behind Jerry and Sam, stripped off his soaking boxers and pulled on his dry jeans and shirt. When he was done, Samantha helped Jerry out of the lawn chair and onto the ground, and Tom plopped into it with a shivering sigh, examining his right heel. The cut was sharp and appeared fairly deep, and when he wiped it clean, his hand came back bloody.

"Oh, no," Sam exclaimed, already reaching for the first aid kit in his backpack. "That looks nasty. Stay there. Raise your foot. I've got this."

With no choice, Tom leaned back and allowed her to work. Sam knelt on one knee and lifted his injured foot to rest on her leg. She cleaned the area with an alcohol swab, applied an overly generous amount of antibacterial ointment, and covered the wound with a bandage. Once patched up, she grabbed his socks and pulled them on, following with his boots. Tom closed his eyes as heat slowly returned to his body. All laced up, Tom stood and applied some pressure to his right foot. The bandage was squishy from the ointment, but otherwise gave him very little pain.

"Good work," he said with a nod, then Sam stepped in front of him and clutched his arm.

"Thanks for saving the cat, Dad." She nuzzled her forehead against him before turning to help pick Jerry up.

With a chattering grin, Tom stepped over to the young man's good side and bent to let him latch on, blown slightly sideways by a gust of wind. Together, he and his daughter lifted Jerry to his feet with Sam slinging his backpack over her shoulder. They rejoined the road and continued walking north, hobbling toward the distant lights shining through the stormy night. While they didn't have much to show for saving the cat, Tom's heart was light. It was one small life spared, and his daughter both appreciated him for it and – hopefully – had some newfound respect for the hazards they would soon be facing.

Chapter 5
President John Zimmerman
Military Central Command
Undisclosed Location

Staffers surge through the conference room double doors and into the hallway beyond, carrying white boxes filled with notebooks and documents as a young man staggers by with his arms around the pair of coffee urns they'd been swilling from the past several days in their caffeine-fueled meetings. A woman in jeans and a tucked-in shirt stacks the last of the staff laptops into a secure bin, slams the top closed, and locks it. With the help of another IT staffer, she lifts it onto a cart and wheels it away toward the entrance doors which form a choke point where clusters of workers bang past each other with terse apologies at first and then soon just silence.

Three members of the facility staff remove the wall decorations; portraits of former presidents, pictures of shuttle launches from the Kennedy Space Center, and grand images of Navy ships are brought down. There's even a small painting of George Washington crossing the Delaware River that makes its way out the door in the hands of a rushing staffer. A woman lifts the presidential seal from the wall and follows the facility staff out of the room while others remove chairs, office supplies, printers, and projectors. More IT people crawl beneath the long table, unhooking cables and routers and throwing them into a rat's nest of gear.

An aide transporting a stack of notebooks feints sideways to avoid someone coming the other way and they miss colliding, but his load destabilizes and slides from his arms to hit the floor with a bang.

"Sorry, Mr. President," the aide glances sidelong at him before falling to his knees to scoop up the documents.

"It's okay," Zimmerman says. He stoops to pick up two notebooks and hands them over, and the aide thanks him and carries the stack from the room. The president stands and steps back to give the facility teams more space, watching as the two flags flanking the presidential seal are delicately lifted from their racks and hurried out of the room.

With a shake of his head, the president turns to the group of uniformed and suited figures behind him. "It's so damn depressing. Is this really necessary?"

"It's absolutely necessary." Chairman of the Joint Chiefs of Staff, General Mark Davidson, nods stiffly. "We need to change locations immediately to ensure the safety of you and your family."

"When will they arrive at Liberty One?"

His key staffer, Maxine, leans in from his left. She's smaller in stature than the general but no less sharp in her jacket and skirt. "They're in route from a conference as we speak and should be there in ten hours."

The president fixes her with a warm look. "Your son?"

"He's with my mother in Cincinnati. They should be okay for now."

"Call them and let them know a chopper will be by to pick them up."

"Really, Mr. President? You don't have to do that."

He levels his gaze at her before drawing her away to a corner of the room where they can talk in private. Once there, he turns to face her, a somber expression on his face as Maxine stares up at him with her smart brown eyes, sharp but relaxed, blinking as she waits for him to start.

"You know I won't take no for an answer, Max. Your boy and your parents are coming with us."

"There's more important people to see to," she protests calmly, "those involved with running the country."

"And who'll keep those people running?" The president gives her a disbelieving look. "Do you think I'll suddenly not need your services anymore?"

Maxine shifts uncertainly, eyes falling to the floor.

"What is it? You can speak freely."

"The memos went out yesterday, sir. Critical personnel and their families *only* allowed at the Liberty One site. I'm not listed as critical personnel. That would be folks like Admiral Spencer, or General Davidson."

"We'll make an exception in your case."

"I'm not sure you can, sir." Maxine's tone remains cool and professional, her eyes flat with finality. "It's NSC policy, sir. When you leave this bunker, I'll be assigned somewhere else for the length of the crisis."

Jaw fixed, he tries to imagine making it through the next months without Maxine's sharp skills. In truth, he's probably allowed her more access than she had any right to have, yet she was pivotal in keeping him on track.

"Look, I'll pull a few strings. You're coming to Liberty One with us. There's plenty of room."

"You don't need to--"

"That's the end of the conversation, Max. You've been critical to me staying on point with meetings and notes. You understand what I need to see and when I need to see it. And I know you've been assisting the vice president, secretary of state, and joint chiefs. Quite a few people depend on you."

"Sir, I only help them when I can," Maxine stammers, for the first time seeming uncertain. "You've always been my top priority."

The president grins. "You're damn right I am, but if you think these people aren't going to fight to get you onboard, you're crazy. You're the best staffer we've ever had, and we'll need that at Liberty One."

Maxine's chin lifts. "Yes, sir."

"Now, as soon as we're done with this meeting, I want you to prep your family for travel. Let me know what authorizations or signatures or ass-kickings you need to make things happen. Understood?"

"Yes, sir. Thank you, sir."

The pair return to the group of suits and uniforms, Maxine with a slight hop in her step as she gestures toward the door. "Let's move into Conference Room B so these folks can work."

The president, his advisors, staff, and bodyguards exit the main conference room and jam into a smaller one at the end of the hall, half the size of the first one with none of the amenities. The president takes a seat as a pair of low-level staffers make their rounds, taking requests for beverages or food if anyone needs it. He orders a black coffee and settles back, loosening his tie as his eyes trace around the room and General Davidson tosses a notebook down in front of him.

"Details of the latest operation."

He stares at the words "Top Secret" stamped across the cover. He doesn't want to open it. *Dreads* opening it. But he finally does, flipping through the laminated pages slowly as he studies each one. His eyes wander over photos of the compound the SEAL unit is about to hit. There's a command center, a small landing field, and several other munitions buildings and key structures. The president takes note of the guard towers, fence, and naked desert stretching between the target and hills where the team will insert, tasked with infiltrating hostile territory to secure targets and vital information.

He turns to his right where Admiral Spencer sits. "Do you have an update on the operation?"

The heavyset man lowers his phone and gives a terse nod. "The SEAL team is on target, sir. They'll insert in an hour."

"Remember, they're not to use lethal force," he reminds the admiral, fixing him with a stern look. "They're our allies, after all."

"For now," one of the suits at the back of the room says.

"I've made my lieutenant aware," the admiral's jowls shake as he ignores the suit, "but that'll be a tall order. Things could get tense out there."

The president nods and sighs. "It's too late to second guess ourselves. I hope we remain allies after this, but I don't see how it'll be possible."

He continues flipping through the pages, studying phases, decision points, and contingency strategies. His eyes fall across the potential casualty numbers and his breath locks in his lungs.

"What's the earliest time for an annexation?"

"That depends on the information we gather from the operation. We could have our forces in place within two weeks."

"What about international blowback?"

"It will be fierce," Davidson nods stoically.

The president is amazed that the general can keep up his hard exterior even as the brittle threads of the government are beginning to come apart at the seams, though that's precisely why he made the man a personal advisor years ago. Steadfastness in the heat of battle is worth more than gold these days.

"We expect strong objections from the UK, Canada and France," Mark continues, "and outright condemnation from Russia and China. We're hoping by that time everyone else will have their own problems to deal with, though. They'll be fighting for every ounce of warmth they can muster, doing whatever they have to in order to survive. They'll have their own insurrections to deal with and anything that's been simmering in these countries for years will end up boiling over. They'll have to redraw new borders, secure them, and quell coups. Soon, what we're doing will be the norm, not the exception."

"If we're lucky," Navy Admiral Spencer adds, "someone else will jump the gun and take the attention off us being first."

"And where will that lead us?" The president shakes his head. "Outright war with the victors?"

The suits and uniforms don't have an answer for him, so he presses on in a stoic tone, borrowing a page from General Davidson's book. "We're entering a new phase of the operation, and things are about to get extremely difficult. There's no going back and no way to spin off what we're doing. If the mission fails, the mask will be thrown off and our intentions exposed. The White House Press Secretary has her orders, and she'll do the best she can to deny and disavow. The international community will come down on us hard no matter what, though."

"We'll succeed," Admiral Spencer spits the words, his heavy jowls jiggling. "I have the utmost confidence in my SEALS. They're the best we have. If they can't do it, no one can."

"I'm sure they are, Ben." The president nods. Then he shifts gears, his mind already on other things beyond the special ops mission and move to Liberty One. "And what about Iran, the EU's, and Russia's nuclear arsenals? With things falling apart like this, someone's going to try to steal those key codes, arm the weapons, and start World War Three."

"That's a genuine concern, sir," Davidson agrees, rolling with the president as easy as grease. "But as you know, we have operations on standby if we must intervene. Our people on the inside will raise the alarms if they think those codes are in danger of falling into the wrong hands."

The president nods, satisfied with the answer, though it's not like he has much of a choice. A staffer sticks her head through the door and calls Maxine over. The woman stands and goes over, listening, bobbing her swan-like neck before turning back to the room.

"Attention everyone; it's time to transport the president to Liberty One."

Zimmerman stands and addresses the group. "You all have your jobs. Godspeed to you, and above all, I want open communication and transparency from everyone in this room. We're going to be dealing with hell on earth here soon – let's try to stay together on this." Those in the room nod with certainty, their eyes locked on the leader of the free world.

"Please, Mr. President." Maxine holds out her hand to him to indicate it's time to go.

He gives them one last look before he exits the room with Davidson, Spencer, Maxine, and his guards in tow. They traverse a long, pristine hallway and enter an elevator. Standing aside, the staff waits for the president to put his hand against the security palm reader until the light clicks green, then he presses a button, and the car rises.

At the top, the doors slide open, exposing them to roaring winds, Zimmerman stepping onto an air pad surrounded by craggy mountains. Marine One, the big Sikorsky VH-3D Sea King, squats in the center, a whale of an aircraft, shaking and shivering with power as it waits for the president to board. They approach the chopper as it churns wind around their heads, the president ducking aside as particles of dirt and detritus whisk against his skin. Spencer and Davidson climb the stairs and enter the aircraft while Maxine stands off to the side. The president turns and gestures for her to step aboard, but a secret service man quickly strides over and blocks her entry.

"Sir, the staff at Liberty One will see to you once you arrive."

"Maxine's coming with us," the president insists. "She's holding the critical mission information we'll need at the new site."

"We can have that information transferred for you."

"But Maxine understands it better than anyone. She's been in all the meetings, and she knows the players. We need her at Liberty One."

"Let her come aboard," Spencer shouts from inside the crew quarters, his gruff voice barely audible over Marine One's rising turbine whine.

The secret service man levels an uncertain gaze at the president. "Sir, this is highly irregular."

"We're dealing with a lot of highly irregular things lately," he grumbles loudly into the man's ear as his hair whips in every direction. "Step aside. *Now.*"

The man puts his finger to his earpiece and listens to someone speaking. After three seconds, he nods and moves out of the way. "Yes, sir. Sorry, sir."

"Thank you." The president gestures for Maxine to board and she approaches the stairwell slowly, staring up at the massive aircraft.

"Come on, Max. We don't have all day."

The staffer flashes him a wonderous grin as she boards the aircraft, dropping her emotional wall. The president takes one look around the air pad at the military personnel and staffers he's leaving behind, certain it's the last time he'll see them. As he turns and enters the cabin, the door rises and shuts with a thud and click of locks. Three minutes later, Marine One lifts off and heads southward toward the Liberty One site.

Chapter 6
Tom McKnight
Virginia Beach, Virginia

They walked for an hour or more, slogging along the windswept road as the wind and rain pummeled them like a tireless prize fighter. Their waterlogged clothes hung off them and weighed them down, hair dangling into their faces, water dripping beyond annoyance. Jerry had kept up but was growing noticeably weaker, sometimes slipping and slumping to the point that Tom had to heave him up hard, the young man groaning as his injured right arm swung around, the bandages soaked through with saltwater and rain. Aches gripped Tom's back, his foot throbbed and his legs felt like rubber, but still he gritted his teeth and cinched Jerry against him, body bent with cramps as he put one foot in front of the other, taking it one, two, three steps at a time.

They passed through residential neighborhoods where the storm had wrought astounding damage, stripping every other house of its roof, wood and vinyl skins taken down to the bare wood framing. Swing sets and fences had blown over, some carried across to neighbors' yards or tossed haphazardly into the street, and a few had impaled themselves into the sides of homes, smashing windows and gouging deep holes.

Driveways sat mostly abandoned, the few vehicles still left sitting alone on the side of the road, their windows broken, hoods dented. One vehicle sat on the street, roof crushed by a fallen limb, looking like something out of a movie set rather than reality.

"Looks like everyone bolted after the first hurricane warnings," Tom mumbled, receiving a grunt from Jerry in return.

As they walked, they watched for pieces of wood with nails sticking out or other sharp objects hidden beneath the undulating floodwaters that sometimes crossed their path. Sudden wind gusts blew stinging rain into their faces, forcing them to look down or turn away. Tom stiffened as a wave rolled over the road and hit their knees, Samantha latching onto his arm as Tom became the anchor, holding the trio steady. They leaned left as the water receded, feet planted to keep from being dragged down to the asphalt. Once it had passed, they continued on, eyes scouring the roadways and skies for more surprises. Tom saw no signs of life, and the closest houses remained powerless as the wind howled and whistled through the eaves, leaving them feeling more isolated and alone than he had felt in a very long time.

"Still with me, Jerry?"

"I'm here. Just so tired."

"Do you want to rest?"

"No." Jerry picked himself up as if Tom had woken him from a snooze, lifting his feet higher and renewing his lurching gait. "I keep looking up at those lights, hoping they're from Virginia Beach. If so, my house should be close." He stared at the array of destruction all around them. "I'm not going to lie, though, all this's got me a little worried."

"Is your house close to the street?"

"No, it's set back from the road, so it should be okay… I hope."

"That's good news." Tom shared Jerry's worry about what they might find, but tried to keep the conversation relatively positive. "We'll keep walking until you want take a break."

The main road thinned to two lanes, and the houses squeezed closer together, but the change didn't stop the storm. Swirling dervishes whipped up miniature funnels that spun across the concrete and hit them, bursting into mist as pieces of siding and shingles drifted lazily through the air, debris twirling by and glancing off them.

"I know this is exhausting," Tom tried to sound hopeful, "but things seem to be calming down. The wind has definitely backed off since I stood at the bridge earlier."

"Oh, that's great news, Dad." Sam shivered next to him, her arms clenched in front of her, shoulders hunched over with cold. "Glad to know the storm is letting up. Could you please tell the *storm* that?"

Jerry scoffed weakly. "Yeah, Tom. This is like a walk in the park. If the park had a hurricane in it."

The pair laughed, and Tom chuckled softly at his own expense before sobering quickly in the chilly wind and rain. Ten minutes passed, and Sam drew his attention off to their left.

"Whoa."

They slowly shuffled past an overturned car smashed into a power pole, then slowed to a stop and stared at it. A mid-sized, black sedan with its front end weighed down and its tires sticking up in the air, the taillights were shattered, and the rear passenger wheel spun lazily in the wind.

"How'd it get like that?" Jerry wondered aloud.

"I'd say a wave caught it, flipped it, and shoved it into the pole." Tom shook his head. "Must have happened when the hurricane made landfall."

"I feel sorry for the people inside," Sam said, squinting.

"Are… are they still in there?" Jerry voiced what they were all thinking.

Tom squinted at the vehicle's rain-slicked and dirt-covered windows, unable to determine if the shadows in the seats were actually dead bodies.

"Wait here." He slipped from beneath Jerry's arm, leaving the young man standing on his own, and ambled toward the road, half crouching to get a better view. When he reached the window, he bent and wiped his hand across it, sending droplets flying. As he squatted and looked inside, he spotted a pair of heads dangling upside down, hair and heads swirling six inches under the water, hands and forearms swaying against the roof of the vehicle as the water lapped back and forth. Tom's chest deflated with a pang of dread. The wave must have caught them off guard, submerging them before they could escape their seat belts, leaving them trapped, drowning in less than a foot of brine.

Heart heavy, he stood and ambled back to the others, both of them wearing expressions of trepidation as they watched him approach.

"They're still in there." He wiped dripping moisture from his mouth and chin, swallowing back an uneasy nauseousness that was rising in his stomach, "but they didn't make it."

Sam hugged herself, and Jerry swayed on his feet, staring at the wrecked vehicle, Tom leaning in so the man could throw his arm over his shoulder and continue down the road. With the pall of death looming fresh in their minds, Tom focused on staying positive. It was hard while in a crouched posture, but he forced himself to pat Sam on her shoulder with his free hand and shoot her a smile. She responded with a miserable stare, though a faint smile tugged at the corners of her mouth as she, too, tried to focus on the positives over the negatives.

They were passing through an intersection when Jerry suddenly shifted his weight and drew Tom to a stop, standing for a long moment as he panted for breath, swallowing and looking around.

"You need a break?" Tom shifted Jerry's weight with concern.

"No... No break." He gasped and winced between his words. "W... we need to go left here. House is...is right down the street."

Tom turned toward the street in question, and the trio shambled along with slightly more energy in their lurching steps, though as they entered the neighborhood, they slowed once again at the sight of the houses, somehow in worse shape than the ones closer to the waterfronts. Almost every roof had been skimmed off, bare two-by-fours stuck up from frames, insulation hung over the edges in wet tufts and parts of the brick and siding walls had collapsed, some smashed by heavy limbs or toppled by saturated foundations.

Nearly every window in every house lay shattered, only one or two here and there still intact and, like out on the main thoroughfare, the streets were nearly empty of cars and trucks. Those remaining had their windshields broken with dents and scraped paint on almost every surface while some had been pushed out of driveways into the middle of the road by the storm surges. The remnants of larger trees dotted the landscape, their once-proud forms reduced to splintered stumps and scattered branches and bodies.

"This way," Jerry was somber as they hobbled toward an intersection, nodding toward the right-hand street, Tom gladly obliging as he angled them in the right direction. A few homes on the block had escaped damage, but one had been hit especially hard, a ranch-style home off to the right, cracked open like an egg. A massive tree had fallen and split the frame longways, the sides bulging outward in a displacement of brick and wood.

Without warning, Jerry jerked away from Tom's grip, crying out in anguish, tripping, and stumbling toward the home. He got his feet beneath him and sprint-limped full-on while clutching his wounded arm to his side. Tom shot a glance at his daughter before sprinting after Jerry, his legs heavier than lead, his foot throbbing and his lower back feeling like stretched taffy as he tried to catch up.

"Jerry, wait!" he called, catching his elbow at the bottom of the driveway as gently as he could, drawing him to a halt as Sam ran up beside them, gasping clouds of mist. Jerry jerked out of Tom's grip, hysterical as he touched his hand to his head and then pointed up the driveway at a maroon Toyota SUV, eyes wide, mouth opening and closing like a fish out of water.

"What is it, Jerry?"

"T-that's my mom's car." His voice ticked up to a frantic pitch, his expression a mix of dread and terror. "Her *only* car. She didn't evacuate... so where is she?!"

Tom put his hand on Jerry's shoulder and stared at the vehicle. Judging by the debris that had settled on the roof, it didn't appear to have been driven in a while.

"I'll check it out," Tom said firmly, giving a knowing nod in his daughter's direction. "You stay here. Sam, watch him."

"Got it," Samantha replied as she took Jerry's elbow with one hand and wrapped her arm around his waist. The young man's expression hovered between curiosity and terror, cooperating only because he didn't want to face what was inside.

Tom walked up the driveway, tapering off to a light shower, though the sky still loomed gray and angry above, wind tousling his hair as he surveyed the damage. Approaching slowly, watching each step for any dangers, he approached the front door, moving up the pathway to the porch as he looked for a way in. The home was an older model ranch-style with a long profile and flat-shaped roof. Because it didn't have a second floor, the tree hadn't been slowed, making the impact to the first floor that much more catastrophic.

The massive oak had fallen from right to left across the entire length of the house, leaving the place in shambles, the front entryway having collapsed longways, bulging into a sideways U-shape. The door remained on two hinges, though the wood was twisted and splintered and over the garage and bedrooms, the oak's crushing weight had squeezed out pieces of the roof framing. Curtains lay draped over two-by-fours and drywall slabs and insulation hung wet and droopy from the eaves, like the insides of squished doughnut, bits of it scattered on the ground amidst the bricks that had broken free and landed in the shrubs and flowerbeds.

Tom stepped off the path and moved left into the yard, searching for a safer entry point than the perilous-looking front entrance. The living room seemed to have suffered the least amount of damage, where a tree branch had punched through the window, but otherwise the area around it looked relatively intact. He bent and picked up a loose brick from the flowerbed and approached the glass-jagged frame, carefully smashing out the larger shards and running the brick along the edges, clearing the rest. He took off his jacket and placed it across the windowsill, pulling himself up and lying with his stomach on the framework, face buried in the dripping leaves and offshoots. He slid inside, reached out, and grabbed a branch to avoid touching the floor and raking his fingers through broken glass.

Using the branch for leverage, Tom wiggled his body inch-by-inch into the room. Shimmying forward, arms straining to keep himself upright, he cocked one knee and dragged his foot inside to place it on the floor, then he pulled the other leg through and stood in what remained of a living room. The massive tree trunk rested a few feet off the ground and the only way past it was to crawl. Grabbing his jacket off the sill, he placed it on the floor and ducked into the wet, dripping leaves once more.

Even on his hands and knees, there wasn't much room, so he laid down and wiggled beneath the trunk. A mossy smell mingled with the rich bark scent, and several fat drops of rain fell cold on his neck as the tree creaked and groaned above him, sending his pulse racing at the thought of it collapsing on him and snapping his spine.

Tom quickened his pace, inching forward on his elbows, using his knees to help propel himself through as he kept his shoulders hunched and face turned away to avoid the still-settling debris. Finally, he crept free of the hulking presence and stood in a middle of the living room, beneath what had been a vaulted ceiling. Taking out his flashlight, Tom flicked it around at the ramshackle surroundings. The old-style, flower-print wallpaper hung in swaths, shredded by branches and collapsed framework. The tree had fallen just left of the fireplace, but the force of its impact had crumbled the mantle and surrounding bricks, sending old picture frames flying to the floor where they rested on the filthy hardwood in a soup of rain, mud, and sand.

Tom's shoes crunched through the glass and debris as he stooped and picked up one of the pictures, turning it over to let the busted shards fall to the floor, then flipping it back. A man and woman in their forties stood on the side of a forest trail in some remote woodsy setting, a stone bridge looming in the background, a famous archway in what Tom thought might be Kentucky. A teenage Jerry stood atop the bridge, wearing a superman shirt with his hands raised into the air.

Tom smiled and returned the picture to the cracked mantle, then he bent and retrieved more. They mostly featured Jerry over the years, the older couple prominent in them as well, the family resemblance uncanny. The young man had inherited his mother's eyes and hair, but his smile matched his father's. There were pictures of him with what Tom assumed to be cousins, all taken at amusement parks or vacations and he returned the last photo and turned a circle in the room.

Debris covered a wood-framed couch to his right, its dirt-encrusted cloth cushions depicting a home style scene with wagon wheels and fall foliage. To his left stood the open dining room, a table with a floral tablecloth leaning at an awkward angle due to the partially caved-in floor. End tables had tumbled over, old lampshades resting in the puddles and a curio cabinet had fallen onto the table, its precious glassware spilled out and shattered, shards mixed with the dirty water and sand on the floor.

"Hello?" Tom called out timidly, "Is anyone here?" Nothing made a sound but for the wind outside and the dripping of water on the rugs and hardwood, so he continued on, preparing to venture farther into the house. After retrieving his jacket from the floor and shaking off the debris, he slung it over his shoulder and circled the couch, half-limping as his spine loosened, entering a hallway that ran parallel to the fallen tree. The top right corner of the passage was ruptured, branches and wood having broken through to soften the drywall and send pieces of it to the floor. Ducking as he proceeded, Tom shined his flashlight at the floor to avoid stepping on anything sharp. He started to shout louder, about to use Jerry's mother's name, but shook his head when he realized he'd never gotten it.

"Hello? My name is Tom. I'm looking for Jerry's mother! Hello?!" No one responded, so he moved deeper.

The tree had demolished the rooms on the right side of the hallway, making them impossible to open. Doors lay crushed, their frames splintered, the trunk's bulk blocking any chance of entry. The rooms on the left had avoided the worst of the damage, though the ceilings had partially collapsed, leaving gaps for rain to drip down the walls. He found a ruined sewing room with soggy floors and drooping plaster, an old-style sewing machine resting in the center with a rack of wet clothes leaning against it, felt, fleece, and flannel materials lying piled in bins full of water.

He backed into the hall again and moved forward, calling out, "Hello? My name is Tom McKnight. I'm looking for Jerry's mother. Is anyone here?"

Again, no reply.

He swallowed as the prospects of finding her alive grew dimmer, though he gripped the handle of the next door down and pushed it in, watching the frame to make sure it wasn't about to collapse in on him. The flashlight beam danced across a massive table that occupied most of the space where, on its surface, a set of miniature train tracks made a loop. A small town hugged the train line, complete with a general store, farmsteads, a municipal building, and a passenger station while in the far corner stood a hillside, its face dotted with cabins and homes. Rain dribbled through the sewing room's partially collapsed ceiling, drenching the tiny town in a deluge, flooding the tracks and dripping down the hill like a river. If the temperature continued to grow colder, it would soon become a wintry scene with everything covered in frost and ice.

Farther along the hall, he found an empty bathroom and guest bedroom before reaching the end of the passage, Tom's stomach giving a twist as his eyes tried to penetrate the gloom. His flashlight beam fell on three suitcases scattered in the hall, one of them shut with clothes sticking out. The door lay open, but when he guided his light inside, all he saw was the bulk of the tree's body and more branches and leaves.

Must be the master bedroom. Tom bent forward and brushed away offshoots and dangling leafage as he passed through the doorway, guiding his light around, poking into the darkest spots. The room had taken some of the worst damage of the entire house, and it was difficult to make out anything.

"Hello? Jerry's mother? Hello?"

Falling to his hands and knees, Tom moved deeper into the room, peering directly beneath the massive trunk where it breached the floor. His beam abruptly caught a pale, wet arm in the darkness where it lay trapped beneath the tree's bulk and Tom jerked back, slamming so hard against the wall that he knocked the wind from his lungs. Gasping, eyes wide, he stared at the shaking foliage he'd just disturbed, hoping what he had seen was some kind of optical illusion, his mind playing tricks on him in the darkened, cold house.

After catching his breath, he fell forward again, crawling back to the same spot, reluctantly guiding his light to where he had seen the arm, forcing himself to look. It was, indeed, a human arm, moist with deep bruising around the elbow where the blood had pooled, sticking up and outward, as if the full body lay beneath the tree trunk. The hand was opened wide, a silver band on the ring finger and the nails were painted pink. Bile rising in his throat, Tom swallowed again and whipped the flashlight beam from the arm down the length of the trunk.

He regretted it instantly. Ten feet along the tree's girth, near the wall to his right, his light fell on a leg sticking out of the rubble. It was horribly twisted, positioned like the person had taken a direct hit from behind and was pushed through the drywall, ending up roughly on their belly. The leg wore a pair of jeans and men's size eleven sneaker, the number printed large on the rubber sole, bloodstains still on the wall and pooled around the body, only partially washed away by the incoming rain and seawater.

Tom's gut churned, and he turned away, reeling backwards, crawling and then staggering to his feet, scrambling along the hallway, diving into a bathroom where he crouched over the toilet and heaved his stomach contents into the bowl. Why he'd felt the urge to get to the bathroom before voiding the contents of his stomach, he didn't know, but he knelt gasping and panting, eyes shut as the acrid stench of what he'd produced threatened to trigger another flood. Falling backwards against the tub, he caught his breath, spitting water, blood racing in his temples. The sight of Jerry's mother and the unknown dead man stuck to the backs of his eyelids, and he shook his head to try and cast off the thoughts.

After a moment he gazed up at the half-collapsed ceiling and dripping walls and he shifted, gathering himself, wiping the saliva from his chin. With his wits gathered, Tom rose to his feet and walked back to the bedroom, crouching inside, looking for Jerry's mother without shining the light directly on her. Tom caught a glimpse of the pale arm and delicate hands and he closed his eyes, remembering the smiling woman in the living room photos.

"You have to do this," he growled to himself. "You *have* to."

He slowly reached up and put his fingers on the wedding band, giving a gentle tug, but it didn't immediately come off. He tried again, squeezing the ring a little harder and he brushed her cold, clammy skin, an involuntary grimace stretching his face. Water dripped down the discolored flesh to flow over his hand as he shook and jerked the wedding band, but it seemed stuck in a deep groove on her finger, partially due to bloat and partially because it had probably been years since she had last taken it off.

Twisting and tugging, the ring suddenly slipped free and Tom grasped it in his fist as he backed up, saying a silent prayer for the two deceased. Then he retreated from the tangle of leaves and branches and stood in the bedroom entryway, bracing himself for what was to come next.

Chapter 7
USS South Carolina
North Atlantic

"Dive to three thousand," Captain Arkin says, watching the screens on the control panel wall.

Deck Officer Stanski echoes the captain's command. "Pilot, make your depth three thousand, twenty degree down bubble, two-thirds."

Arkin watches the gauges as they descend through the murky depths, twisting down toward the anomaly in a corkscrew fashion. Water and a thin trail of bubbles zip past the high-definition cameras mounted on the bow's photonic masts, their external lights penetrating a few hundred yards into the encroaching darkness, enough to capture detailed images. External lights and cameras are not normal equipment on a military submarine, and the thick wads of hastily-laid wires are a testament to the unusual nature of their situation.

"What's our approach?"

"Coming in from the south, Captain," Stanski says.

"What's it like out there?"

The Chief Engineer, Melissa Trent, replies. "We're picking up mild turbulence as we approach the anomaly. Hull integrity remains stable. All systems green."

Arkin frowns, thinking of what happened to the research ships when the anomaly burst open earlier that week. While he's confident his Virginia Class submarine can motor through without batting an eye, he doesn't want to take any chances.

"Let's flatten out and take her in easy."

"Aye, sir," Stanski says. "Pilot, bear due north, zero bubble, one-quarter."

The line of bubbles and flying debris slows considerably as the boat plows through the waters at a more deliberate, even pace, the hull vibrations shifting ever so slightly.

Arkin stares hard at the screen as if his mind could extend from the cameras and see far ahead to the anomaly.

"Can we clean up the visuals?" he asks.

"Aye, sir," Stanski replies. The deck officer plays with some controls on the panel in front of him, and the image clears and lightens. Still, all they see is a deep darkness beneath them, an impenetrable, unsettling nothingness.

"What's our depth?"

"Three-thousand eighty feet, sir."

"And they say this anomaly is at five-thousand feet?"

"Correct."

"That's pushing our maximum depth."

While the Navy publicly claimed Arkin's sub could reach eight hundred feet, test missions had attained nearly six thousand. Testing their limits in an area where dozens of vessels have succumbed to one of the strangest underwater events would never be first on his priority list, but orders are orders.

"Take us to four thousand."

"Aye, sir." Stanski repeats the command to the pilot.

The nose of the sub dips further into the darkness, and Arkin instinctively grips the closest handrail. He watches as the depth meter ticks downward fifty feet at a time, eyes flicking between it and the large monitors that have been hastily bolted to the far walls that show a visual of the exterior environment. As they pass thirty-five hundred feet, a rush of turbulence shakes the entire sub like a gentle earthquake.

"I felt that," he murmurs, gazing at the screens.

"Incoming," Stanski announces calmly as a rock roughly the shape and size of a human head glances the top of the hull, zipping past the mast at about sixty miles an hour.

Arkin jerks back slightly. "A little more warning next time."

"Sorry sir. The turbulence is throwing off the sonar. Everything's moving around down there like a boiling pot of soup. I'll have to filter for objects greater than two meters."

The steady thrum of the engine and air circulation units calm Arkin's nerves even as they pass through more clouds of debris, rocks and dirt pinging against the ship's hull, but none are large enough for them to cause damage.

"Where are we in relation to the anomaly?"

"This is the last known mapping from the Marin." Stanski gestures to a side screen displaying a three-dimensional view of the continental shelf. The anomaly crevice stretches ten football fields long from north to south with spider-web cracks branching throughout the earth's crust. He points to a green dot slipping along the shelf wall, indicating their current location. "We're approaching the thickest part of the anomaly between these two branches, as we planned in the briefing."

"Good," Arkin nods. "Start the advanced scan of the ocean floor. I want to throw everything we've got at it. Get me something I can use."

"Initiating scan using BQQ active sonar and engaging hull panels. Give me fifteen minutes, sir."

"We've reached four thousand feet, sir," Stanski announces.

"Full stop. Let's settle in and wait for the scans."

* * *

Down in the engine room, Chief Petty Officer Lane Nelson shakes his head and adjusts his earpiece. He felt the abnormal turbulence from a minute ago, and though alarming, there are very few things short of a direct collision with another ship that could displace the 7,800-ton South Carolina. He maneuvers expertly through the cramped engine room with its rows of high-tech gear, leaving only two feet of space to slide by. Squeezing between compression systems with digital gauges, pump regulators, and turbine casings, he observes his crews' actions.

Six petty officers and specialists stand at workstations, monitoring the ship's balance and speed, watch engine health and pipe the information to Chief Engineer Trent up in the control center with the captain. Nelson walks behind the sailors, inspecting their screens and pointing where he wants adjustments made. During the briefing, Captain Arkin mentioned the nature of the mission and the inherent danger of approaching the volatile crevice. But Nelson was skeptical until he felt the ship's hull shimmy and shook like an airplane cabin in low altitude turbulence.

He relays the most recent command to his sailors. "We're going to four thousand feet. Be ready for more turbulence. We may need a throttle adjustment to handle the heavier currents. Keep an eye on the power ratios."

"Can we take that kind of pressure, Chief?" Smith asks. "The most I've been is two thousand on my previous assignment."

"Not officially," Nelson grins. "But I know for a fact we can dive past five thousand. We did it before the last scheduled maintenance."

"Good to know." She appears relieved.

"I'm not worried about the depth." His grin falters as he looks at a feed from engineering that shows the ocean crosscurrents rising from the floor in strange patterns. "But I don't like those. Not one bit."

* * *

The submarine rattles again, causing Captain Arkin to snatch the rail. "Can someone let us know when these waves of turbulence are about to hit us?"

"We're getting a lot of noise," Trent replies. "I've never seen thermohaline currents like this. And the mixture of debris is only adding to the force."

The ship shakes again, tilting ten degrees before stabilizing.

"Depth?"

"Three thousand eight hundred and twenty-two."

"I said I want us at four thousand."

Stanski works the controls on his panel. "We were, sir, but it's almost impossible to maintain our depth with the freshwater surge coming up from the bottom."

"I understand there's a surge," Arkin takes his eyes off the screen and leans over the deck officer's shoulder, "but how can it be pumping out with that much force still?"

Trent calls from the port where she and her sonar specialists work. "Can you look at this, sir?"

Arkin lets go of his rail and steps over to her side, gripping an overhead handle to steady himself, peering at a screen that depicts a model of the South Carolina and its position. Digital lines flow over the hull, representing the forces surrounding them. The surge is clearly coming from the ocean floor, separating around the ship before drifting upward and the digital lines turn yellow and red whenever an especially strong current hits them.

"After I apply these two filters," she adjusts some knobs, "this is what I'm seeing."

He watches as the radar range increases so they can see water rising a hundred feet below them. Not only does it surge upward, but it's rife with dangerous cross currents. A sudden swell rises in a burst of red lines, and Arkin clenches the handle as the submarine takes another hit of turbulence, rattling his thermos where it rests in a nearby cup holder.

"Those will only get stronger the farther we descend," the engineer says. "If we want to see the anomaly from this position, we'll have to dive through them. It'll be like plunging into a blender."

"Can we handle those pressures?"

"Technically speaking, yes. But it might not be a fun ride."

Stanski gets the captain's attention, pointing at a side screen once again. "Rather than dive straight down, we can back off to here, dip beneath the current, and approach along the sea floor."

"What's the depth on that?"

"Five thousand two hundred, sir."

The captain releases the handle and makes a grab for another handrail, swinging around to his chair. The USS South Carolina is a three-billion-dollar submarine, one of the best-equipped in the country's arsenal. Not only is it of significant dollar value, but it remains a major military deterrent to anyone threatening American shores. A hundred and seventeen crew members and fifteen officers are onboard and going deeper would put the ship and all those lives at risk. His mission is to get a visual on the anomaly and re-map the ocean floor around it, though, and the depth is within known operating parameters, and the turbulence – though annoying – has been minimal so far.

With a grim expression, he nods to Deck Officer Stanski. "Take us on that course to a depth of five thousand two hundred feet. And I want eyes on that floor as soon as we have it."

"Aye, sir. Pilot, reverse to the heading on your screen, then descend to five two zero zero. Fifteen degree down bubble. Full speed."

* * *

"We're diving to fifty-two hundred feet," Nelson tells his sailors, Smith visibly paling at the news.

"Jeez."

"It's not our job to question the depth," he says as he passes behind her, "just get us there. Now increase the throttle sensitivity so we can power through that mess of currents down there."

"Yes, sir," she replies, making the adjustments on their screen.

The mysterious elevator-like motions of the ship cause his stomach to flutter and sink. "No matter how many years I spend in a sub's belly, I'll never get used to descents." Smith gives him a half-smile before returning to her task.

"How's the pressurizer look?" he asks another sailor.

"No adjustments required, sir. It's handling the ask for more power just fine."

"Good. This will be our girl's first big test in a while," Nelson muses. "Let's keep her humming people--"

The sub tilts forward, and his feet slide from beneath him, forcing him to snatch a rail as they begin a rapid descent. While he can't see a single thing outside the ship, he feels the weight of billions of gallons of water pressing down on their heads, a small part of him wanting – and resisting the urge – to scream. His training kicks in and he shuts down the claustrophobic feeling, focusing on the task at hand.

"You're sweating on me, sir," Smith says.

"What?"

"You're sweating on me." The sailor reaches down and swipes her finger on a screen, lifting it to show him a bead of moisture she'd picked up.

"Sorry." Nelson shifts his position so he's not hovering over her and draws his arm along his sweaty forehead. "It's damn hot in here. Can we cool it down?"

"Got it," a sailor calls. The air circulation unit kicks up, driving a gust of cool air across his face.

"Thank you," he murmurs, moving quickly down three stations where a man monitors the primary circuit of the nuclear-powered engine. The diagram and overlay show the reactor, pressurizer, main coolant system, and steam generator, the latter of which is operating at fifty percent capacity and inching upward.

The chief petty officer starts back to Smith when the submarine jerks like it hit a wall. Nelson barely snatches a rail before he slides toward the front of the engine room, grabbing at air while several sailors grumble and groan as they hang on against the tilting vessel. Something grips the submarine and shakes it, and he bangs his knee on a pipe before he can brace himself. Half hanging from the rail, feet spread on the floor, Nelson grabs the tether on his belt and looks for a hook. He spots one next to a stabilization pump behind him and takes a swipe at it, missing badly, falling so that he hangs by one arm. They're pointed downward at a forty-five-degree angle, and if he lets go, he'll tumble over Smith and slam into the front of the engine room.

"A little help!" he calls.

Smith turns and puts her foot against Nelson's hip. He counts to three and lunges for the hook while Smith shoves, their combined effort giving him the momentum he needs to reach the hook and snap his tether in place. He holds on and waits for the tumultuous shaking to stop, the hull groaning as the HY 100 steel absorbs the massive pressures squeezing it. Shoulders drawing tense, Nelson's stomach and legs lock tight as he presses his feet down. Craning his neck, he sees the other sailors clinging to rails or interlocking their feet around pipes, keeping their faces on the screens.

The turbines whine powerfully in the next compartment over, the submarine jerking and wobbling as it remains on course. Nelson can't begin to guess the amount of force gripping and squeezing them and a warning note rings out in the back of his mind. At fifty-two hundred feet, with the convulsions and juddering, the hull could certainly crack open like an eggshell, the pressure crushing them to death before they have a chance to blink.

At least it would be fast.

"You okay, sir?" Smith calls over the rattling, squalling ship. "You look pale."

"I'm fine. You look a little pale yourself."

Smith looks at him with a calm expression, but fear dances behind her eyes. "That's because I'm holding in a scream."

The pair stare at each other, and Nelson grins, spitting out the first part of a phrase that's all too common aboard the USS South Carolina, one of their crew mantras.

"I have faith in my maker!"

"And I have faith in this magnificent machine!" she fires back.

Nodding, grinning, his stress tenuously under control, Nelson's eyes search the surrounding screens for warning lights or a sign something is wrong. No alarms blare and none of his sailors shout and blessedly, finally, the boat levels out, the turbulence fades and his body uncurls, relaxing.

"Smith, I'd have a general report."

"Everything is stable," she glances over her shoulder. "I made some adjustments to the generator, topping it out at sixty-five percent capacity. The pressurizer was barely taxed. They had all the power they needed up top."

"That's what I like to hear. Send that up to Trent." Nelson releases a sigh of relief, then he unhooks himself and moves down the line to do a quick review of the gauges. "Stay sharp. We've still got a return journey to make."

* * *

"Report!" Arkin calls out from his chair in the control room.

"Engines are stable," Trent reports calmly. "Minor leaks but nothing major. We have some damage to one high frequency sonar mast. Communications remain up."

"Good work." Arkin nods, then he glances at the deck officer. "Are we where we should be?"

"The undercurrents shoved us about three hundred yards south," Stanski says, "but otherwise, we're looking good."

The captain nods and folds his arms across his chest. "Okay, good. Now give me a visual of the ocean floor."

"Screen one," Stanski points.

Arkin shifts his eyes to the leftmost screen, watching as the panorama ahead of them changes to an angle beneath the boat. They hover forty feet above the ocean floor. Spotlights illuminate a sandy bottom covered with debris and massive basaltic stones. He marvels at the sight, in awe that they've come through the intense pressures to reach what seems like an alien world.

"I'll never get used to a visual like this. Those stones looked like they were freshly cracked off," he says. "See how the sharp color contrasts? They haven't been sitting there long."

"Could they have been thrown up by the anomaly?"

Arkin shakes his head. "I don't think regular currents could do that, but based on what we just experienced, I'd say yes. How are you coming on that advanced scan?"

There's a pause, then Trent replies, "Eighty percent done, sir. The filters we applied are taking some additional time."

"Let's move ahead while we wait. One quarter."

"Aye, sir. Pilot, ahead one quarter."

The submarine eases forward, and the seafloor slips by beneath them as they approach a cluster of boulders the size of cars, one as long as a bus, appearing both on the jerry-rigged monitors and on the sonar scans.

"Those are big," Stanski whispers.

Trent cranes her neck to see. "They must have been part of the original blow out."

Sprinkles of debris filter down from above like a dark rain as particulates swirl and gust in the quieter currents, swishing back and forth in front of the camera lens. Stones the size of fists smack the top of the hull and bounce harmlessly off.

"It seems to have stabilized," Arkin says. "Point the bow lights down. I'd like to see out ahead of us."

Stanski reaches across his console and uses a joystick to angle the powerful bow spotlights at the ocean floor. The bright glow illuminates a debris field that stretches ahead as far as they can see.

Arkin glances to the map on his left and sees their green dot approaching the anomaly's edge. "We're getting close to the original mapping."

"It's a little less than a quarter of a mile."

"One tenth."

"Aye, sir. Pilot, take us to one tenth."

They slow to a crawl, cruising along the sea floor like the silent killer the sub was built to be. They aren't killers today, though, instead merely observers in a dangerous, alien world. A bead of sweat trickles down Arkin's temple, and he quickly wipes it off in annoyance. A dark line creases the horizon as the submarine shudders through more turbulence, though this time the rumblings are tight and intense.

"We're running into surge-currents from being so close," Trent says.

"Are we in danger?"

"These are green currents, according to my feedback. Gentle compared to what we saw at higher depths." Trent taps on her keyboard. "I wouldn't recommend hovering above the opening, though... wow, that's incredible."

Arkin turns his attention to the screens and watches as they approach a scene that defies all imagination. The anomaly extends as far as he can see, its edge made up of jagged rocks. Parts of the crust of the earth have punched upward a hundred feet while other sections have fallen away, lending a raw, untamed look to the place. His eyes dance over the rugged cliffs and gullies it left as water shoots through a hundred gaps, blasting silt and stones directly at the camera. The endless, yawning darkness beyond devours the spotlights, wordlessly threatening to devour the South Carolina as well.

"All stop."

"Aye, Captain. Pilot, all stop."

"We can't even see to the other side of it," Arkin says. "I think the original mapping showed it was a single football field across. The spotlights they rigged should reach that far at this depth, or so the techs said."

"It does appear to have changed in size." Trent types something before looking up. "I just grabbed a snippet of the data being compiled. It's definitely expanded... looks to be twice as wide it had been originally."

"It's doubled in width?" Arkin stares at the massive fissure, knowing what it did to the Marin and a dozen other ships up at the surface. He looks into those black depths, and a chill runs up his spine. "How far are we away from finishing the mapping? The faster we can send that upstairs, the faster we can bug out."

"Less than two minutes now, sir."

The ship shakes again, quickly followed by a side current that sweeps the bow ten degrees to starboard.

"Pilot, hold position." Stanski sounds annoyed as more debris blasts from the gullies, bigger stones tumbling out amidst a cloud of dust that momentarily blinds the camera.

"I've got the advanced scan done," Trent finally announces, jabbing the keys with her fingers.

"Put it up on screen three," Arkin says, turning to the right-hand monitor.

"Yes, sir."

Arkin watches as a three-dimensional map of the anomaly takes shape, eyes darting back and forth between screens one and three, confusion and alarm twisting his face. "The crevice has… changed. Substantially."

"Yes, sir."

"Superimpose the new layout over the original and put it on screen one."

"On it."

A second later, the images merge. The second one overlays the original in light blue colors.

"There are another dozen, no, *two* dozen new fractures." Trent turns toward the captain with a horrified expression. "Sir, this thing is not only still surging, but it's expanding."

"Send the information upstairs. Now."

"Yes, sir."

* * *

"It's so quiet now," Smith says. Her dark eyes lift and roll from port to starboard like she can see the ocean through the hull. "I wonder if we're above the anomaly."

"That's not something we need to worry about," Nelson replies. "Just keep an eye on the engine and run that diagnostic."

"Yes, Chief." Smith goes back to her screens, knobs, and levers.

The ship rumbles and shakes again, and the boat shifts enough to make Nelson lose his balance. He throws his hands against a cluster of pipes running from floor to ceiling next to Smith until the ship rights itself and settles down.

"Stay frosty!" he calls to the others. "We don't know how long we'll be here. Could be ten minutes or ten hours."

"The briefing said we were just gathering data." Smith shoots over her shoulder.

Another sailor, Jergins, steps to one of three passages leading to the back of the ship. "Sir, I'm going to check on the generator. I'm detecting a small pressure loss. It's minor, but we might need to change a coupling or hose."

"Negative," Nelson shakes his head. "Switch to auxiliary pumps. I don't want you making repairs while we're climbing through those currents again."

"But, Chief, I can have the part changed out in less than ten minutes."

The chief petty officer thinks about it before agreeing. "Switch to auxiliary pumps *first*, then repair the primaries if you can. Either way, I want you back here at your station in ten minutes. No excuses."

"Yes, Chief!"

Jergins returns to his post and makes the switch to auxiliary, a hiss of air and steam from the next compartment over confirming it's done. The sailor then dashes down the passage between the long row of machinery to check the pressure loss. Nelson's attention is on Smith's screen when something cracks against the hull with a leaden crunch he feels through his guts and spine, the submarine rolling to starboard before jerking back to port.

Unbalanced and unprepared for the impact and lurching boat, Nelson's hand slips from the rail, and he flies into the aisle. His head smacks an engine casing before his tether jerks him taut and bends him backwards. Bouncing back with a pained cry, he slams against the pipes next to Smith, grabbing her arm to steady himself.

"Are you okay?" Her eyes fly wide as the ship continues its jostling.

"Fine," Nelson growls. "Sounds like--"

Alarms ring out, and someone cries out from the engine room. "Nelson, help!"

The chief petty officer levels a hard look at Smith. "Keep an eye on that pressure loss Jergins was talking about. We should be on auxiliary pumps. Let me know if it becomes a problem!"

Smith nods fervently. "Yes, Chief!"

Nelson untethers himself and staggers across the chamber, his feet doing a weird dance as he tries to balance on the shifting deck. Reaching the end of the row, he grabs a sailor named Callahan where he clings to his station, the sailor's eyes glued to the hatch ladder. Nelson's stomach lurches as he sees Pendleton leaning on the ladder with her left elbow locked over a rung. Her right arm hangs at an odd angle against her side, her face a mask of anguish, eyes pleading.

"She was heading for the ladder when the ship bucked her," Callahan explains.

"I'm coming!" Nelson squeezes the words through clenched teeth.

He pitches himself to the floor and crawls over the steel grating to Pendleton. When he gets there, he clutches the ladder above her head and positions himself so he's not leaning against her injured arm. Looking down, he sees her forearm is bent sharply below the elbow.

"What happened?"

"I was moving between the auxiliary array panels when the ship rocked. I got thrown around..."

Kneeling by her side, he sees her dazed expression, eyes unable to focus on much but the pain and he places his hand on her good arm.

"Hang on. We're going to get you out to medical."

Neslon turns toward Callahan to ask for her assistance when something strikes the ship with jarring force. It isn't the usual rumbling and shaking from crosscurrents or turbulence, but a direct strike from a massive object that causes Nelson to sink to his knees, still clinging to the ladder.

A wail goes up from Pendleton, and when he looks down, he sees that he's fallen against her injured arm, blood soaking through her crew outfit and dripping on the metal grating as a pipe splits and sprays water into the chamber, alarms blaring in the passage.

* * *

"What the hell was that?" Arkin growls and pushes himself off the main control panel. Alarms ring out on every deck, sending unsettling spikes through his head. Next to him, two sonar officers pick themselves up off the floor and stagger back to their seats.

"Not turbulence, Captain." The deck officer says from where he clutches a rail, eyes stuck to the console screens.

"We must have drifted above one of the new cracks," Trent calls sternly from her station, her feet spread on the floor to balance herself as she pokes at her touchscreens. "We didn't know it was there."

"Full reverse. Get us away from that rift," Arkin orders as he slips over to Trent, staring at the screens casting the room in blinking red lights.

"Damage?"

"We've lost fifty percent power to the main turbine. Leaks detected in multiple locations – here, here, and here." She points to the screen with a model of the USS South Carolina, lights pulsing along her bottom where the worst of the damage occurred.

"The reactor?"

"Twenty percent pressure loss to the main turbine."

"She's got plenty of power," Arkin murmurs. "Get us all the juice you can. Stanski?"

"Pulling out. Way too slow."

The captain lunges to his post and turns his attention to the screen. Sand and debris swirl around the camera lens in a cloud of haze as stones and rocks zip across his vision in a dizzying display. Something strikes the ship again, quickly followed by a second, bone-rattling blow. Their direction shifts, and Arkin's stomach lurches.

"What's happening?"

"We're being pushed upward," Stanski says with disbelief. "The surge is shoving us to the surface."

"The surge is definitely increasing," Trent agrees as she cranes her neck toward the captain. "The crack is expanding."

"What's that mean?"

"The crust is breaking apart," she explains, her voice tense, "and the pieces are shooting to the surface. If we end up above it..."

"It'll be like a shotgun blast," Arkin whispers as horror spreads across his face. A pipe bursts above his head, steam exploding downward and sparks fly as water shoots through cracks in the compartment wall, taking out all but one of their monitors.

"Hemorrhaging turbine pressure," Trent shouts. "Hull is cracking in multiple sections!"

"Put the reactor on standby! Switch to auxiliary diesel," he orders, cursing himself for not deciding sooner. "Get us out of here, Stanski!"

"Aye sir! Pilot, we're switching to diesel--"

A geyser of water strikes the deck officer in the face and chest, blasting him off the panel and into the sonar controllers. Hands reach down to help him up, but the control center is already flooding. The damaged hull groans, steel ticking and knocking under the massive pressures exerted by the surge, but still the submarine goes up and up and *up*.

* * *

Nelson staggers through the engine room with one arm wrapped around Pendleton as water drips and sprays from the cracked hull and split pipes, groans reverberating along the twisting metal with ominous implications.

"What's going on?" Smith shouts as they approach her station.

"I don't know," Nelson shakes his head at the submarine's groans. He instinctively knows virtually every sound the sub can make, but he's never heard it so sick before. Something shifts in the floor's vibration. "The reactor just went offline."

Smith is already nodding. "They've switched to diesel. There's nothing more we can do here." She spins from her station and gets on Pendleton's opposite side, taking the woman by her belt loop to help hold her up.

Nelson grabs the comm microphone, puts it near his lips, and speaks to everyone under his immediate command.

"All engine room personnel. Fix that pressure leak and seal the lower chambers! Callahan, Jergins, Smith. With me!"

Five of them meet at the hatch ladder, Nelson handing the injured Pendleton to the others, descending to the deck below.

"What are we doing?" Smith asks, sputtering water.

"We're going to drop Pendleton off by the crew quarters and then head to the diesel room to make sure that engine keeps running."

"Yes, sir!"

Nelson hits the deck below as Pendleton climbs down, holding her arm against her side. He wraps his arm around her waist and turns her toward the forward compartments, not waiting for the others to join them. They push through the hatch into a room filled with pipes and electrical systems used in support of the nuclear reactor positioned on the deck above. The ship takes another hard knock along its bottom, one that travels through the ship's frame and up his legs to his hips. Pendleton starts to collapse, but Nelson grabs her waist harder and lifts her tighter against him.

"Come on!" he urges.

They stagger through the mess hall, bumping together as they stumble beneath the blinking lights, shouting sailors flying past them, heading for the front or rear of the ship as emergency alarms blare repeatedly. Someone knocks into Pendleton, causing her to cry out and Nelson angles her to the middle of the compartment, shoving aside a table and chairs until they reach the hatch to the crew bunks. He sits her down, well out of the way of any rushing sailors.

"Stay here. When we get out of this, we'll have the medic take a look at that arm. Until then, you'll have to deal with the pain."

Pendleton nods, biting her lip, tears streaking down her face, remaining strong and falling back on her training. Nelson turns back toward the mess and sprints across the compartment, jostling between two sailors and shoving his way to the hatch where Smith, Callahan, and Jergins wait. He nods, leaps on the ladder, and slides down to the auxiliary engine room with a splash. Looking down, he sees he's standing in two feet of water, the big diesel engine slamming away, pistons pounding amidst the groaning of the hull. He gets out of the way as the others land beside him, all of them spreading out around the new heart of the ship.

"Turn on the bilge pumps!" Nelson shouts as he trudges through the water to the control panel. "I want this water out of here. We've got to--"

A spattering of thuds slam the submarine's hull with massive booms, causing the ship to roll hard to port. Nelson slips, falls to one knee, and tries to right himself, but the sub continues to roll, and he has nothing to hold on to. He slides across the chamber, smacks his head on something, and gets pinned between the two diesel fuel tanks. Smith cries out from somewhere, and Jergins shouts to Callahan.

"Get those pumps on," Nelson mutters as the sub tips at a funny angle. He tries to raise his voice as his head swims and stars blaze behind his eyelids.

"Nelson! Grab my hand. Nelson!"

His eyes snap open to find himself on his knees against the port wall of the boat, the water rising fast around him, already almost reaching his chest. Lifting his face, he sees Smith standing on the edge of the fuel tank with her hand stretched down to him.

"Grab my hand. Come on!"

Grimacing, Nelson reaches up and clasps her hand, allowing her to lift him as he leverages himself against the side of the tank. Once standing, he hops up and grabs the edge and between them, they swing him up where they collapse against each other. The stubborn diesel engine sputters and backfires as electrical systems short out all around them, smoke filling the room along with the stench of leaking fuel. The knocks stop, but the hull still groans, the submarine having given up all attempts at righting itself.

"I think this is it," Nelson says, looking around helplessly as an eerie silence settles over them.

Smith turns her horrified face up to him, her dark eyes searching his face for a ray of hope. When the sailor doesn't find what she's looking for, she nods and takes a defeated breath. A strange sense of calm comes over Nelson. He often wondered if he would die aboard a submarine, but his idle thoughts had never come to fruition. An image flashes through his mind of a time when he was a boy playing in the bathtub with U boat models. He remembers how much he loved the sleek, militaristic design, knowing from an early age that he would one day serve aboard one.

He grips Smith's chin in his hand and speaks calmly and deliberately. "It's okay. We've all got to go sometime. At least we're doing it five-thousand feet below the surface of the ocean in service to our country."

Smith's expression relaxes. She nods and takes a long, sputtering breath. Her eyes focus on him with a sense of understanding and gratitude. She brushes seawater out of her face. "I'm honored to have served with you, sir."

"Me, too, Smith." He nods. "You're an amazing sailor."

They hold each other, eyes locked as the floor buckles, brine and diesel fuel spraying all over them. Something catches fire, and the auxiliary engine room explodes in a burst of flames. The USS South Carolina drifts free of the debris field, leveling out as the forces pushing it toward the surface diminish. It travels in a long arc before slowly descending to the ocean floor, three-billion-dollars' worth of electronics and steel bending and warping beneath astronomical pressures. Somewhere around 5,500 feet, the submarine implodes in a snap of light and sound, a candle snuffed out by the storm.

Chapter 8
Tom McKnight
Virginia Beach, Virginia

Tom worked his way along the hallway with the wedding ring in his fist, guiding his flashlight back and forth to avoid stepping on sharp objects. In the living room he placed his jacket on the floor and crawled beneath the tree, keeping his palms raised so he didn't cut his exposed skin on fallen glass. After getting through, he dragged his jacket out, shook it, and covered the bottom of the window frame, then put his feet through until he sat on the sill, feeling around with his toes, dropping quietly to the loamy flowerbed where he originally entered.

Steadying himself, he turned and retrieved his jacket before looking for Sam and Jerry. The pair had come up the driveway and stood beside the SUV, Sam's arm still wrapped around Jerry's waist. Tom approached reluctantly, eyes downcast as his heart hammered in his chest. He stepped on the sidewalk and shuffled up to them, shaking his head slowly as he looked at Jerry.

The young man already appeared distressed with tears streaming down his cheeks, but when he saw Tom his face morphed into shocked reality. His jaw dropped, and his eyes widened as he clenched his good hand into a fist and heaved a big, gasping breath. Jerry turned to the house, staring with wide eyes and shaking his head in disbelief, seemingly wanting to both sprint away and collapse into a sobbing ball at the same time.

Tom held out his fist, and Jerry blinked before realizing Tom was trying to give him something. The young man put his hand out, palm up, and Tom dropped the ring into it. Jerry's mouth hung open as he stared at the wedding band with instant recognition. A single tear raced down his cheek.

Tom gave him an apologetic look. "I don't know what to say. I--"

Jerry shot toward the house in a ball of frustrated energy, face twisting into a grimace. Tom had been expecting it, and he stepped in his way, partially blocking him and grabbing his good arm.

"No, let me go!" Jerry squirmed, nearly jerking from his grasp. "You can't stop me. I want to see. I have to see!"

"No!" Tom growled as he hugged him, leaning his weight on him to sap his energy. "The house is destroyed! You'll just hurt yourself trying to climb in. And you can't get to where she is, anyway."

Jerry jerked and fought, but his strength was quickly dwindling. "Are you.. sure?"

Tom nodded and guided the young man down the driveway toward the street, wind and occasional droplets of rain thrashing them. "There was another man in there with her. It looked like they were getting ready to evacuate when the tree fell. Do you know who he was?"

"It could have been one of her friends from church," Jerry replied with a sad shake of his head. "She knew people from there. They… they helped each other out. He was probably helping her pack when…."

"That makes sense," Tom nodded, keeping the young man locked in an embrace to keep him from running foolishly back to the house.

"I can't believe it." Jerry shook his head, falling against Tom, squeezing him with his good arm, fist digging into the small of Tom's back. Tom absorbed the pain, soaking in the frustration and sorrow as he patted Jerry's shoulders comfortingly. "Let it out, buddy. I know it's hard, but we're here. Just let it go."

Jerry sobbed for another minute, shaking in Tom's grasp, the emotion draining from his body until finally he let go and stood back, blinking at his house.

Sam came up softly behind him. "Hey, Dad. What should we do now?"

Tom lifted a set of keys and jangled them. "I found these laying on the floor on the way out. I think we should take Jerry's mother's car and get him to a hospital."

Jerry sniffed and wiped the water and tears from his face. He blinked at Tom once and shook his head like a man coming out of a dream. "You can just take it."

"What?"

"After you get me to the hospital. Take the Toyota. You two need to make it home."

Tom shook his head. "You'll need transportation, too ."

"I'll figure out something."

"Do you have any relatives around?"

Jerry gave a dejected shrug, all sense of hope and energy drained from his being. "Nope. No one."

Tom grimaced at the young man's pain. "Look, we're not going to just leave you at the hospital and take your car. We'll wait until you get patched up."

"But that could take a lot of time," Sam was nearly whispering. "Don't we want to get home?"

Tom shushed her with a sharp look before. "We'd be happy to take you with us if you want."

"I appreciate the offer." Jerry shrugged, pained eyes staring at his house. "I don't care either way. I just… I just want to get out of here now."

Tom nodded. "Okay, let's get moving. We'll decide everything else later."

It was an older Toyota pickup, not especially rugged or large, and Tom used the key to unlock the door and stuck his head inside. The vehicle had an old car smell topped off with a fruity air freshener, but it was spotless. Jerry started to clamber into the back, but Sam insisted he take the front passenger seat and he obliged with a half-hearted shrug.

"Hey, Sam," Tom asked as he climbed in. "Can you watch me pull out and make sure I don't hit something that will flatten the tires?"

"Sure." Sam strode down the driveway and waited.

After Jerry climbed in, Tom started the engine. The Toyota sputtered to life, and he clipped his seatbelt on and adjusted his seat and mirrors. Reversing down the driveway, he kept Sam centered in his side mirror as she waved him back. Once in the street, he straightened the vehicle and gestured for her to come inside. Sam hopped in, shutting the door against the gray, hazy cold, and Tom put the Toyota in drive and eased ahead, turning his wipers and brights on and focusing on the road. Tom sighed. Despite the tragedy of discovering Jerry's deceased mother, finding moving shelter once again was a huge relief.

He made it one block before his daughter leaned between the seats.

"Dad. Heat."

"Right. Sorry about that." His fingers adjusted the controls on the console and warm air blasted through the cabin. The window immediately fogged up, and he turned on the defrosters to clear it. Even though he'd angled the middle vents toward the back seat, Sam stayed leaning forward, eyes shut as her hair blew back.

"My face is so numb," she said. "I can barely feel it."

Tom put his hands up and wiggled his fingers in front of a vent, the warm air sting his cold skin. A minute later, his body responded to the heat by shaking off chill in several long shivers that coursed from his shoulders down through his back. Tom looked sidelong at Jerry to see him leaning against the window with his head in his hand, staring out at the storm, seemingly uninterested in the heat even though his teeth were still chattering.

"Hey, why don't you guys take off your shoes and socks and dry your feet."

"Good idea," Sam said. She immediately shifted in her seat, put her feet up, and started untying her shoes. When Jerry didn't move, Tom leaned closer.

"Hey, man. I know you're hurting, but you should warm up your feet, okay? At least get them dried off."

Wordlessly, Jerry bent forward and reached for his shoelaces with much less enthusiasm than Sam.

"Thanks. Maybe hang them over the vents when you get everything off." Tom started to settle in but then remembered something. "Jerry, one more thing. Where's the nearest hospital? Do you have one close?"

"There's a small one in Virginia Beach." His voice sounded muffled from his bent position.

"Perfect."

Tom found his way back to the main road and headed north, moving slowly, pushing on through the residential neighborhoods, weaving between trashcans and pieces of housing in the road. There wasn't a shoulder to drive on, but the front yards lay flat on both sides of him, and he navigated swampy lawns to bypass poles and other debris that were too big to drive over. One downed pole came with a tangle of wires lying in the street and he angled right into a driveway, knocking over a mailbox to get past the mess. When the mailbox wouldn't immediately fall, Tom gunned the engine and smashed over it, the cement base grinding along the truck's underside before he could straighten it out in a slosh of tires.

"Whoa," Sam said, clinging to Jerry's seat. "We almost got stuck."

"I didn't know if those wires were live," he said. "If there's power running through them, they could pack a pretty big punch."

"Could they have hurt us?"

"Absolutely. Us or the car."

By the time he reached a commercial area, it was 3:27, and the storm had largely let up. The sky still loomed ominous and gray and a light rain fell, but the wind had tapered off considerably, revealing the devastation that lay thick around them. Entire sections of homes had washed out as seawater picked apart the structures piece-by-piece, while bedding and bits of furniture drifted in ponds of brine. Three-family condominiums sat stripped of their roofing, their shingles and parts of gutters floating in backyard pools.

Cars and minivans parked in driveways were covered in debris, windows shattered, shells dented. A copse of privacy trees had come down on top of a condo, the massive back deck on the south side collapsing under the weight of fallen oaks and pines, limbs having smashed through the windowpanes and knocking down entire sections. A swath of three single-story bungalows had washed out and merged into an impossible pile of wood and mangled materials and any palm trees still standing were wilted and bent.

They passed a seafood takeout restaurant on their left, the big red shrimp sign hanging off and slapping back against the storefront. The beach shops and lots were filled with ocean overflow, lakes of brackish water holding slewed vehicles half-buried in wet sand. Tom ticked off insurance costs in his head but lost track after a few blocks – just the area they were in would constitute millions, and overall, it would undoubtedly be in the multiple billions of dollars.

They stopped at a T-shaped junction in the road. Across from them, a six-story condominium complex stood against the gray backdrop of clouds. A large swath of its roof had blown forward and hung over the front of the building like a man with a flipped toupee. The right side of the structure had partially collapsed, the topmost balconies slouching as the wind whistled through them and two telephone poles had blown over and lay across the street, their wires twisted and jumbled. Tom turned the truck into the Sandridge Market parking lot, coming out on the other side to reenter the road.

"Should we take a left here or keep skirting the beach?"

"The hospital is farther north." Jerry glanced toward the ocean. "It's up to you."

"There's still flooding along the beaches," Tom continued, "but I don't think we're in direct danger anymore. I think staying straight will get us there faster." No one argued, so he took a quick right and then an immediate left, joining the beachfront road approaching Virginia Beach. After another thirty minutes of silence, left alone in his thoughts, Tom turned to them. "You guys want to put your shoes and socks back on?"

Sam plucked hers from a pair of rear vents and put them on. "Toasty," she smiled. Then she frowned as she held up a shoe. "My sneakers are still a little soggy." With his injury, Jerry struggled to put on a single sock, so Sam leaned in between the seats and helped him get it on.

"Thanks," the young man mumbled.

"No problem." She wrapped her arm around his shoulders and gave him a squeeze. "That's what friends are for."

Jerry smiled as she collapsed back in her seat, his eyes curious and darting in all directions. "Where to now?"

"I see lights coming up," Tom said. "I think they were the ones we spotted way back there."

"And people, too," Sam pointed out. "Do you think we can pull in and talk to someone? Maybe they're even open."

Tom looked around. A seafood restaurant sat off to the right, its busted windows glowing like the face of a Jack-o'-lantern. The siding had been stripped away to reveal the underlying insulation, and rubbish lay strewn across the parking lot. Two trucks sat out front and shadows shifted inside, indicating someone was there. A beach supply store squatted off to the right with a single car in the lot, the back half of the building fully collapsed beneath the weight of a tall light pole.

"There's caution tape up everywhere," Tom pointed out the strings of yellow blocking off the entrances. "They're not open, so it's probably just the owners salvaging what they can."

"Oh," Sam replied with disappointment.

"That's okay," he assured them. "The fact that people are coming back is a good sign." He turned to Jerry. "How's your head?"

"It's still hurts a little, but it's not raging like it was before."

"Good. Do you know where the hospital is from here?"

"Let me see." Jerry raised in his seat and gazed around. "Wow, it all looks so different. It's hard to tell where we are." His head swiveled, eyes scanning the destruction for something familiar. "Wait, I see where we are. Take a left and then another right. That'll get us over the inlet. After that, we'll head inland a bit more."

"Thanks," Tom said.

They crossed a bridge spanning the inlet which was almost too flooded to cross, the waves slapping up the pillars and spraying over the sides, splashing their windshields with foam and brine. Once across, they drove through blocks of bungalows and condos, all of them victims of the ocean and winds.

"It's like driving on another planet." Tom marveled at the destruction.

"No kidding," Jerry whispered. He seemed to have temporarily put aside his mother's passing, the scale of the destruction around them taking his mind off of his immediate grief. They approached a large commercial square with upscale restaurants and delicatessens, a beach-themed shopping center sitting off to the right with a grocery store and pharmacy on the corner.

"What's going on with those stores?" Sam called from the backseat.

Tom glanced back to see her peering out the right rear window, following her gaze to see what she was looking at. Trash and scraps of shingles had blown across the store lots, but he noticed at least six cars parked, skewed in their spaces as if someone had hastily pulled in without worrying about the lines. Flashlight beams bounced around behind the grocery store glass from deep inside the structure and Tom's focus shifted to a gas station on the next corner where a group of people had gathered around the mini mart's front entrance. The crowd was seven or eight strong, pushing and shoving each other, pointing and yelling at a man standing behind the shattered storefront who waved a long metal pole at them, feigning threats with wild eyes, shouting as if daring them to try and enter. The crowd pressed in and retreated in waves, seeming to test their own courage, their arms raised, fists swinging back and forth.

"They want to rob him." Tom said as dread tickled his stomach. "They're just bucking up the courage to do it."

"Seeing which one of them wants to get bashed first," Jerry added, observing the scene warily.

Tom craned his neck as they passed, staring as long as he could, secretly rooting for the store owner. At the last second, he turned his attention forward with a squeamish twist in his belly.

Sam moved across the seat and looked out the left-hand window. "There's more looting over here. It's everywhere." A group of people carried armfuls of cans and snacks from another mini mart, waddling out to their vehicles, dropping packs of chips and peanuts on the wet concrete before dumping their hauls in the backs of trunks.

"Don't stop," Sam urged. "They look mean."

"And desperate," Jerry added.

"I'm not stopping," Tom assured them, though he'd briefly considered going back to help the store owner before quashing the idea. He couldn't risk throwing himself into a violent confrontation like that – it wasn't anywhere close to the same as rescuing a cat off a roof.

"Ah! Shi—oot!" Tom slapped his palm against the steering wheel.

"What, Dad?" Sam exclaimed, leaning forward.

"I forgot the radio!" He slammed the power button, expecting to hear classic rock come blaring through the speakers, or even talk radio, but instead what greeted them was a man's robotic drone as he recited a pre-recorded message.

"… evacuation is mandatory. All coastal residents are required to move inland. Carry only necessary items. If you do not have a vehicle, proceed to your nearest emergency shelter with one bag or suitcase per person. Warm clothing is strongly advised, especially for the young and elderly. Shelters are being erected farther inland where you will be safe from the rising waters. If you have loved ones who…"

Tom turned down the radio and stared ahead as the recording played in the background, blinking with apprehension as his predictions materialized right before his eyes.

"That sounds great," Sam piped from the back. "They've got shelters setup farther inland. That means people are getting help. Everything will be okay."

"Oh yeah, sure, but even if you believe that, keep in mind that they said 'rising waters.'" Jerry shook his head. "That doesn't sound like the end of the flooding."

"And they said to dress warm," Tom whispered at the grayness stretching before them. "It's happening."

Chapter 9
Tom McKnight
Virginia Beach, Virginia

"Dad, you were right," Sam said. "The cold..."

He'd tied the Atlantic Drift disruption to the chilling temperatures they were experiencing two together days ago, wanting his theory to be wrong. Yet, there it was, right in front of them, and when mixed with the general reactions of the populace and the oddly worded message on the radio, he couldn't help but wonder what information was being kept from the citizens of the country.

He pursed his lips, gripped the wheel, and focused on what he could control. Getting Jerry medical attention and then transporting himself and Sam home were the big priorities and were his only focus at the moment, lest he allow himself to become too distracted by the forest to see the trees.

"Okay, let's get to that hospital," Tom said.

"Just keep going straight." Jerry raised in his seat and peered ahead along with Tom. "We'll take a left in another mile and a half."

He drove them along a track of scenic Virginia Beach, the ocean-smothered sands oozing between the oceanside condos and resorts, brackish water carrying debris through the commercial district. Waves swept across US-60 and poured into Lake Holly on their left where the lake's surface kicked up frothy waves. Cars sulked on the grassy shore and lay dumped in the lake, a pair of headlamps pointing up at the sky, cutting through the gloom. The hurricane had abated, but the ocean had claimed its ground and held it.

Jerry shook his head in awe as he stared out the window to his right. "Turtle Bay Resort is wrecked."

Tom looked away from Lake Holly and took in the wind-beaten building. It was a massive structure, taking up the entire block and the tide had moved through the first floor with a strong ebb and flow, gutting its contents to leave swirling pools behind. Resorts and condos gave way to restaurants and bars, and those farther inland had suffered less damage than the beachfront ones. Miraculously, a few still looked operational, though feebly. The wind and rain had wiped storefronts clean and shaved shingles from roofs, but some owners appeared to be inside, lights glowing, a handful of cars in the lots.

The Toyota was the only vehicle on the road, a lonely car hugging the center lane to avoid the reaching grasp of waves that swept around their tires. A pair of power lines lay across their path once again and Tom angled right, planning on cutting through a patch of swampy grass to get by when Jerry shifted in his seat, pointing in the direction they were headed.

"There's a wave coming up."

Sam slid across the backseat. "Uh, Dad? He's not kidding."

"Yeah, I see it." Tom watched the sea race through the parking lot, raising the six inches of brine to a foot or more as it gained momentum. It was thirty yards out, then twenty, then ten, its speed faster than any of them would have imagined.

"Hang on!" Tom angled hard into the rising swell as water smacked the truck's side, rocking them on their shocks as it sprayed up over the roof. The floorboard shivered, and the steering wheel suddenly jerked loose, Tom grabbing it hard and whipping it back and forth, hitting the gas but still unable to control their movements.

"We're sliding," he murmured, glancing left as the wave pushed them toward the power lines. Desperately, he spun the wheel harder, pressing the gas until the wheels grabbed the concrete with a jolt and the Toyota rocketed forward, fishtailing past the potentially dangerous leads. Tom didn't realize he'd been holding his breath and he let it out in a gush as he brought the truck under control, easing his speed down to ten miles an hour as they pulled out of the wave's grasp.

"Jeez, Dad." Sam deflated.

"Yeah, I know." He wiped the sweat off his brow, scanning the deceptively dangerous road. "There's a reason you don't drive through moving water."

Shoulders unclenching, Tom settled back and noticed one or two vehicles on the road ahead of them, another handful cruising the store and restaurant lots, mostly where the flooding was low and the lights welcoming.

"Look at these geniuses." Jerry nodded out the passenger window.

An SUV cut slowly through a parking lot in front of a strip mall, braving the tidal flow. Their tires left a wake behind them, headlamps reflecting off the murky water that flooded over their fenders as they cruised through it.

"They're casing the place," Tom ground his teeth together. "Looking for easy loot."

Jerry nodded. "I'd put my money on that electronics store right there..."

On cue, the SUV stopped and backed into a spot in front, sending water up to smack against the glass. Seawater rose and swirled around the truck tires, receding and rising dangerously.

"If they get water in their tailpipe," Tom said, "they'll be swimming home with wet cell televisions. I wonder how much those will be worth?"

"Idiots." Jerry shook his head.

Tom looked across at a motorcycle shop and a few beachfront inns as a small motorboat driven by two scrubby-looking men puttered alongside a flooded nightclub, dragging a floating trailer behind them, disappearing around the back corner of the building in a swirl of sea foam.

"They're up to no good, too," Jerry said.

"Probably wanting to get at the liquor." Tom nodded. "It would be easy enough to get in, but if the water rises too high, they'll be trapped."

Sam remained in the rear seat behind him, gazing farther inland. "Things are looking a little better that way."

Tom grunted, shifting his attention back to the left where the flooding had been minimal. Small groups of people gathered outside fast-food restaurants and tourist stops, some with open signs glowing brightly in the windows. They left their vehicles and crossed the lots, stooped over with umbrellas whipping back and forth as if hurricane shopping was a completely normal thing to do.

"The power is still on," Tom mused, "which makes me even happier we avoided hitting those power lines earlier."

"Quick thinking," Jerry agreed. "I would have figured they were dead and ran right over them."

"I'm surprised they haven't killed power to the entire city," Tom said, "though I guess that'll happen once the repair teams get here." He nodded toward the road. "Okay, which way now?"

"You'll want to take the next left," Jerry pointed vaguely with his good arm. "That'll be 30th Street. It'll get us to US-58. Then it's just one more right at First Colonial, and another mile to Sentara-Virginia Hospital."

"Sounds good."

Tom pulled up to the 30th Street intersection and slowed. The building on the left-hand corner was a nondescript condo and across the street squatted a strip mall-style structure, partially hidden from the road by four windblown elms set fifteen feet apart.

As wind whistled across the windshield, blowing rain droplets sideways across the glass, he took the left, circling so the trees and stores lay on his right. Glancing over, he saw a hardware store and ABC Liquors between the elms, their windows and glass doors smashed, though not by any obvious flying debris. They cruised past the third elm when Jerry jerked back in his seat.

"Hey!"

Tom shifted his attention slightly left to see three people rushing toward them from the direction of the liquor store, coming out from behind the trees and a parked vehicle that had blocked them from view. They were twenty-somethings, two men and a woman, dressed in jeans and dark jackets that clung wet to their bodies, each with a heavy backpack weighing down their shoulders. They shouted and waved at the Toyota, the men carrying blunt objects in their hands, their voices muffled by the distance and the wind.

"What do they want?" Sam asked, her voice rising in panic as she slouched back in her seat.

"No idea," Tom replied, studying them warily, pressing down on the gas, accelerating down the lane.

"Who cares?" Jerry pressed himself back in his seat. "They look like trouble."

Judging by their clothes, they weren't gang members but their expressions were eager, hungry, and wild with abandon, the backpacks hanging from their shoulders bulging, a few bottles of liquor poking out of the edge of one of them. One of the men raised his bat and shouted for them to pull over, his expression hard and fierce.

Sam leaned forward. "We're not stopping, are we?"

"No!" Jerry pushed away from the door as the trio came within ten yards of them. "Keep going, man! Get us out of here."

"I'm with Jerry on this one." Tom growled the words with a pinch of tension.

He kept cruising past and sped up a little, turning his eyes back to the road. Shouts and curses followed them, and Tom glanced in his rearview mirror as the woman hurled a glass bottle at them, spinning end-over-end before it fell short to smash in the street behind them. Tom glanced back at Sam as she straightened in her seat, her expression hung slack, eyes wide with panic while Jerry sighed with relief and sat back in his seat.

"And that's why you don't stop for people." Tom focused back on the road, his hammering heart slowing slightly. "Especially not a group of them. Not in a crisis like this."

"I won't argue with that." Jerry settled back in his seat. "But it makes me wonder why you stopped for me on the beach."

"Every situation is different," Tom explained as he drove. "You have to use your head. You were a good guy when we showed up at the gas station, you helped us when you didn't have to, and when we found you, you were injured and in obvious need of aid. Those people back there? We have no idea who they were, they were healthy looking, from what I could tell. And they had their choice of working vehicles. Their bags were heavy with goods, probably stolen. Now, what would a group like that want with us? No one knows for sure, but their actions didn't exactly spell good intentions. You, on the other hand, were alone and injured on a beach. Big difference, right?"

"I see what you mean." Jerry nodded his agreement. "Where did you learn how to think like that?"

Tom glanced back where his daughter had pulled herself forward between the seats again. "Sam, tell him."

She smiled knowingly and turned to Jerry. "It's all about being prepared. In this particular case, situational awareness. Mom and Dad have drilled it into us since we were little. Paying attention to people's actions, not just their words. Doing what you have to do to survive. You know, stuff like that."

Jerry shot a look backward. "I'm glad we didn't stop for *that* group."

"I hate to interrupt Sam's seminar," Tom quipped, "but are we getting close to the hospital?"

"Take a right up here on First Colonial."

Tom did as Jerry directed, swinging them right at the next intersection to put them on another heavily commercialized road. Having gone a half mile inland, the stores and restaurants were brighter with lights, and though the wind and rain damage was still significant, it was still much less than it had been at the outskirts. Less than a quarter mile later, they approached a squat, five-story brick building that took up the entire city block, a parking lot broken by swaths of grass islands separating it from other structures in the surrounding area.

"Is that it?" Tom pointed.

Jerry had taken to staring out his window but raised in his seat, eyes going wide when he saw the building. The grassy areas were a mess, trees lying bent or ripped out of the ground, and mulch covered the lot along with debris carried in from the oceanfront, floating in a half inch of water that sluiced across the lot beneath an ink stain of clouds. He took a right to skirt around the building's south side where the worst of the hospital's damage had occurred. Windows were blown out, brick ripped away in huge swaths to reveal the blue insulation beneath. A section of the fourth-floor wall looked punched in, a massive tree trunk lying at the base of the building along with crumbling debris. The emergency entrance was just a shell of its former self, the wind having stripped the awning clean, leaving just the columns and a partial roof while the hospital sign lay a hundred feet away in a contortion of metal and glass.

Tom stopped at the base of the lot and gaped at the number of cars parked near the emergency and front entrances. Some vehicles appeared beat up, but they fit perfectly in their spots, a sign that people had driven them in after the storm. Around the hospital doors stood a veritable swarm; a woman stood on her toes looking over the taller heads while her friend held an injured person by the arm, one lone man sat in the grass away from the crowd, bandaged head hanging low as he stared at his lap and two women in blue scrubs climbed upon a table near the emergency entrance, gesturing at those assembled and back at the building.

Someone tossed their hands up at the women in scrubs, yelling something while a small group sheltering a limping woman shoved their way through the crowd, many reacting poorly to the intrusion, pushing back with equal aggression, the crowd swaying and boiling like a cauldron. Tom swallowed a lump in his throat at the thought of trying to get Jerry past the gauntlet and into the hospital proper.

"That doesn't look good."

"No, it doesn't," the young man agreed.

Tom pointed to an elderly couple walking away from the hospital along the entrance lane. "Hey, maybe they can tell us what's going on."

The woman wore high-water slacks with a jacket and tennis shoes and she kept to the man's right, closer to the road, with her arm locked in his as he limped ahead, clutching him in the steadily growing cold. A red-stained bandage was taped to his wispy-haired skull, leaking blood down his temple as he cowered inside his coat against the knife-like winds and temperatures. Tom eased up next to them as Jerry rolled down his window, leaning across his injured companion's lap to get their attention.

"Hey, folks!" he called, waving. "Hey there!"

The old man kept shuffling along, boots scuffling on the pavement, not seeming to see or hear him, but the old woman's piercing blue eyes raised, judging the trio in the space of a second, smiling pleasantly when she finished her assessment. She tapped on her husband's arm so that he stopped and lifted his chin toward the truck.

"Hello there!" she called. "Strange turn of weather, huh?"

"You're telling us." Tom grinned. "It feels like God shook the whole Eastern Seaboard."

"That it does." The woman's smile grew. "What can a couple of old folks help you with?"

"Well, we were wondering what's going on at the hospital." Tom moved his head in the direction of the entrance. "My friend here has a badly injured arm, and we need to get him seen to."

"Damn fools turned us away!" the husband blurted in a gruff tone, lifting his head in indignation.

His wife chuckled tiredly and patted his arm. "It's true. They said his wound wasn't serious enough to have him admitted. They're just too swamped right now."

Tom squinted in confusion. "I don't understand. Do all those people have injuries from the storm?"

She nodded. "Most of them, yes."

"Why didn't folks evacuate when they had the chance?"

"They tried, I think." The woman's eyes turned worried. "Most were heading south from Cape Charles. Someone said it had flooded higher than they'd ever seen it, all around the area. But when they tried to cross the Chesapeake Bay Bridge, waves washed a lot of them off. The ones who made it came here."

Tom shook his head with the tragic news. "Are you two going to be okay?"

"We'll be fine." She glanced at her stooped husband. "We live close by, and his injury isn't bad. But he's on blood thinners, and I just can't get the bleeding to stop."

"Damn fools wouldn't let me in!" the old man blurted again, flexing his fist and shaking it.

"Can we help?"

"Oh, no," she smiled. "That's okay. I'll get it to stop. You just see to your friend."

"Thanks," Tom called, Sam and Jerry echoing the sentiment as the elderly couple continued down the walkway.

Tom eased back in his seat as Jerry rolled up his window. The crowd in front of the hospital was swarming the doors, splinter groups trying to break through to gain access inside, largely failing in their attempts. Two large men stood in a stare-off confrontation on the edge of the circle to their left, looking like they might come to blows, while a handful of new cars pulled into the lot from another entrance, searching for parking spots. A group of eight people rounded the building's eastern corner, carrying wounded between them, stopping at the sight of the crowd, looking like they were trying to figure out some alternative way of getting through.

"I don't like the looks of this at all." Tom breathed a heavy sigh, his hopes of getting Jerry some help dwindling by the second.

"What are we going to do?" Sam asked, leaning forward in her seat.

"I'm not sure." Tom rested his hands on the steering wheel, gripping the worn plastic, settling back to give it thought. He glanced at Jerry. The young man's arm hung in the makeshift sling, his eyelids half closed – not on the verge of death, but too fragile to just drop off and leave, especially with the growing angst of the crowd at large.

"We really need to get him *inside* that hospital."

Jerry scoffed. "Nah, seriously, Tom. I'm *fine*. Well, mostly fine." The young man tried to sound chipper, but his words lost their energy, and his face fell slack again. "I'll be okay. Just get me close to the entrance and I'll take care of myself."

"I don't think so, son. I can't drop you off here to deal with that." Tom gestured at the boiling crowd in front of the hospital entrance. "And I'm hesitant to leave you in the car. You could black out or worse."

Jerry continued to shake his head, shifting to face Tom. "Look, you two have to get home. You can't be staying around here babysitting me."

"It's not about babysitting you." Tom bumped his palm lightly on the steering wheel in frustration. "It's about leaving you in good hands. There's no way I'm making you deal with that crowd up there."

"I'm a big boy, Tom. I can handle myself--"

"Guys, wait," Sam interjected with a hand on both of their seats. "This arguing isn't going to work. Is there another hospital we can drive to? Somewhere farther inland, maybe?"

"Well yeah. There's one between Norfolk and Virginia Beach. Sentara-Leigh Hospital. But I've never been there."

"We have to give it a try," Tom agreed. "At the very least, you need a CAT scan on that arm, and maybe your head, too. It's not much farther out of our way, and hopefully they don't have a crazy crowd like they have here."

Jerry looked at them with a grin. "I guess you're stuck with me for a little longer."

Tom winked. "We'll do what it takes to find you help. Plus, you've helped us just as much as we've helped you."

"I disagree with that. But thank you."

Jerry smiled as Tom put the Toyota in reverse, half turning to peer over his shoulder to look behind him, his eyes flying wide.

"Get down, Sam!" he screamed, his voice cracking, shoving her sideways into the backseat, turning and grabbing the gear shift to jam it in drive. Something heavy smacked the back window, shattering the glass, drawing a squeal of surprise from Sam as the truck shook on its springs. Safety glass exploded everywhere, and a cold gust of air whipped through the vehicle's interior as Tom slammed on the gas pedal, shooting them forward.

Chapter 10
Somewhere in Mexico

The cracked ground bleeds its warmth into the evening sky, the night winds lifting to circulate it across the great body of desert that spreads all around them. A cloudless sky looms above, a scattering of pink, red, and cerulean stars shining on black-clad forms. The seven-soldier SEAL team jogs quietly over the uneven desert floor, weaving between scrub, cacti, and clusters of Mesquite trees with rifles cradled in their arms, visors pulled down to provide a preternatural sense of sight. They pound up a scree-covered rise and pour over the crest to descend into a rock-strewn gully, following the weaving course west, shoulders brushing against the gully walls that grow shallower with every step. At the end, they climb out and sprint north across the open ground toward a distant, saddleback rise.

Head on a swivel, Lieutenant Scott picks his way up the rocky, scrub-choked hillside, choosing his steps carefully, fleet-footed as his boots carry him to the top where he raises a fist and calls a halt, the team automatically spreading out and taking up defensive positions. He taps some buttons on his helmet's temple, magnifying his view, seeing wide across the desert floor, blinking at the landscape's greenish tint that reveals the fenced-in military complex spread out over a quarter mile of parched earth. Guard houses dot the fence line every hundred yards and the complex itself is lit up like a Christmas tree, bright against the dark desert sky.

"Objective Night Wish in sight," his voice is inaudible as he mouths the words through the secure comms system, the black band around his neck picking up the intentions of his speech and turning them into a transmission.

The lieutenant scans the complex, confirming that the layout is consistent with his briefing maps and training facilities. A command center and a tight cluster of munitions sheds lie to the east, storage structures and a motor pool rest on the west side of the facility and the airfield with a helicopter pad sit directly in front of them on the south side of the encampment. An occasional patrol vehicle cruises the road that encircles the site and there are guards posted and on patrol, but there does not appear to be a readiness level consistent with their presence being detected.

"Prepare to move. Our first priority is to secure the command center and intel," the lieutenant reminds them, "then extract ourselves no matter what the cost. The admiral would like to keep casualties low."

"How low, sir?" McCarthy asks.

"Preferably zero."

A few on the team scoff, two whispering to each other where they squat behind a rock, the desert winds whipping at their backs.

"Are we sure this a good idea?" McCarthy asks.

"Are we supposed to care?" Gilliam replies.

"Not really, but I thought they were our allies."

Someone snorts, and Lieutenant Scott snaps. "Knock off the chatter. Keep your minds on the job."

The team quiets down and waits for his command to move out while he performs one more survey, picking apart the base's defenses.

"It's hotter than what they told us in the briefing," he murmurs, "but more than tolerable. There's a clear insertion point along the south fence line. We cut across the road, disable the watch tower, and we're in."

He taps a button on his helmet, and the magnification instantly snaps back to normal view. Scott breaks cover, rising from his position behind the rock, and starts down the hill.

"Fall in," he commands the team, and they descend the rugged trail to the desert floor. He jogs ahead, picking up speed, not concerned about being seen quite yet. They're still a quarter mile from the insertion point, their combat outfits made of a specialized heat-reducing material that covers every inch of their bodies. They will be almost impossible to detect until they're right on top of the base but still, they exhibit caution, using the desert brush and defilades to pick their way closer, avoiding the watchful eyes of the guards in the south tower.

They reach the road in two minutes, easing into a ditch so they don't kick up dust. The tower is twenty yards ahead of them, Scott's night vision showing two guards stationed atop the steel-framed construction. One stands at the glassless observation window, looking slightly west while the other lingers at the back of the guardhouse, their spotlight off, tilted upward to the night sky.

Scott starts to rise when the sound of a light vehicle roars in from his right and he hits the ground, holding his rifle ready. The vehicle rumbles past them, washing them in a wave of oil-scented heat before moving down the road. Once the Jeep passes, Scott checks the guard tower one more time and streaks across the road, the SEAL team on his heels. They lean against the base of the scaffold, huddled around the ladder, no sign of detection or alarm from above.

"McCarthy, Gilliam. You're up."

The pair wordlessly and silently scale the scaffolding toward the platform and Gilliam is the first to reach the top. He grabs the soldier overlooking the grounds and pulls his head down, applying a front choke hold. The man fights and punches Gilliam's shoulders, but the lack of oxygen overwhelms him.

McCarthy appears next, heading through the window to grab the second guard when the sounds of a struggle ensue. Something slams against the wall, rattling the structure and a pair of dark forms hit the observation rail, leaning out over thirty feet of open air. McCarthy grunts in his earpiece, stabs, and makes a twisting move that sends the soldier flying. The body plummets thirty-five feet to thud on the ground and Scott creeps forward, noting the blossoming circle of blood on the soldier's fatigues, a gaping wound across his throat.

"Dead," Scott says with a disappointed shake of his head. "So much for no casualties."

"Sorry, sir," the tone is cold, devoid of emotion and apology.

"Tie up the other one and get down here. Someone split the fence."

Another pair of SEALS takes clippers to the chain linkage, snipping it wide open. The team files through the gap like liquid darkness, racing toward the airfield. They fall-in behind a pair of long maintenance trucks, the troops crouched as the lieutenant creeps past his men to a front fender, peering around it at the aircraft hangar.

The lights are on and the three bay doors all stand open, but while there's some activity happening inside, Scott can't see what it is. He looks farther north toward the command center and adjoining roads, watching as a dozen figures from a nearby building run out and leap into the back of a troop transport. A soldier slams the gate closed, and the truck pulls onto a side road and heads for a junction. Another platoon jogs in formation in front of the command center and takes a left to disappear around the other side.

"Things are definitely heating up," Scott says. "I wonder if they're on to us."

"It couldn't have been the guard tower, sir," McCarthy says in his ear. "We bundled the soldier up good and disabled the comm."

"They could have been tipped off by someone else," Scott muses. "Maybe they detected the helicopter."

"Or maybe they have really good instincts."

Scott scoffs and turns his attention back to the plane hangar. A pair of aircraft roll out, surrounded by a half-dozen men in orange coats. The aircraft are shaped like jets but only a quarter of the size with rounded domes where the cockpits should be.

"I've got my eyes on a pair of drones," he tells the team. "They're launching them. Could be trouble for us."

He waits patiently as the aircraft taxi onto the runway, propeller noise whining up, the maintenance crew's full attention on the spy craft. The drones gain speed and start to lift off. Two maintenance workers raise their arms and wave while others jostle and joke, clearly enjoying the takeoff show.

"Stay on me," the lieutenant orders.

Without waiting for a reply, he breaks cover, half-crouched and leaning forward, sprinting toward storage sheds sitting on the hangar's south side. The propeller noise drowns out the sound of their running boots, though it seems to take an eternity to cover the distance. Scott reaches the buildings first, ducking behind a wall in a rush of breath, heart slamming blood through his veins. He creeps between the structures, staying away from exterior lights that shine poorly from above the shed doors and a glance back toward the runway shows the drone team still occupied with the aircraft lifting into the sky.

"Now."

The lieutenant sprints toward the massive hangar, staying within the shadows, knees pumping until his chest presses against the wall. Flattening himself, he waits beneath the glow of exterior lights while his team flows silently up beside him, their forms like liquid filling the corner where the wall meets the ground. Scott creeps to the southwest corner of the building and peeks around. In back, fuel trucks sit side-by-side, and supply crates are stacked in rows three high and five wide. Glancing back the way they came, he sees spotlights shining down across the desert as if searching for someone.

"They're waking up." A discomforting feeling settles in his belly. "It's just a matter of time until they discover the insertion point."

"Then let's shake and bake," McCarthy says, the rest of the SEALS in agreement.

With a silent nod, Scott creeps along the rear wall past steel doors, maintenance vehicles, and crates. At the northwest corner of the building, he taps his temple and uses his magnification to scan the north grounds again. Platoons jog along the service roads, and three groups of six soldiers each break off and stand at intersections. He identifies at least two VCR-TT armored trucks in position in front of the command center with .50 caliber guns mounted on top.

"This is going to be--"

Something clicks behind a bay door behind them. The SEAL team snaps into action, forming a semi-circle around the entrance, rifles raised to their shoulders. There comes a pop and a rummaging sound as the metal door rolls upward, slamming against the top of the frame. A man strolls out, wearing a gray maintenance outfit while he stares at a clipboard in his hand, completely absorbed by its contents. It's only when he smacks his head on a rifle barrel that he stops, raising his eyes, jaw dropping when he sees the black-clad soldier on the rifle's other end.

Before he can so much as grunt in surprise, a gloved hand slides around his mouth, choking off any sounds. The SEALS converge on him, binding him and placing him in a heavy, but breathable, sack. Two men drag him to the supply crates, open an empty one, and drop him inside, while another pair quietly shuts the steel door he came out of. The lieutenant returns to the corner of the building and looks out across the grounds.

"Stevenson and Taggart, you're up."

The pair sprint past him, heading north to the armory.

"Rose and Holloway. Go."

The next pair spring from cover, following Stevenson and Taggart but angling slightly to the right. Scott gives them thirty seconds before gripping his weapon tightly against his chest.

"McCarthy and Gilliam, with me."

The pair gathers behind him as he stares out at the spotlights now crisscrossing over the grounds. He takes note of the parked vehicles, sheds, and dark buildings where they might seek cover, forming a path in his mind before he gives a breathless whisper.

"Let's go."

He darts from cover and sprints across the open field with his men tight on his heels, their dark forms weaving a course, crossing access roads and dancing around search beams. They avoid a foot patrol by silently scaling a supply building, retrieving their ropes, and creeping to the other side before dropping to the ground, and the lieutenant notes a marked increase in vehicles rumbling to life and shouts from prowling troops. What should have been a quiet base has come fully alive.

They cross to a power station, fall to their bellies, and crawl to the command center's western side. Removing their climbing gear, they toss sleek hooks thirty feet to the roof and scale the wall like shadows, drawing themselves up over the edge and rolling to their feet. At the top, Gilliam and McCarthy slip away to take out a pair of gunners stationed in the corners while Scott slinks toward a set of stairs leading down. An enemy soldier jogs to the top just as he arrives and Scott whips the butt of his rifle around and strikes the soldier in the jaw before grabbing the man by his fatigues and jerking him forward to hit the roof face first.

After a quick check to ensure the man is unconscious, Scott creeps to the edge of the stairs and makes sure no one else is coming. He glances back to see Gilliam and McCarthy have successfully disabled the two gunners, and they lay bound on the hot tar roof. His men join him at the stairs, and they tie up and drag his man to the side.

Scott addresses his men. "Team, we are entering the command center. Stand by."

"Roger that," Stevenson says.

"Standing by," Rose replies.

Scott gestures for Gilliam and McCarthy to lead them down the stairs. Before he follows them, the lieutenant glances up at the white, green and red flag waving from a pole out front, its strips flapping in the cooling desert wind. He shakes his head, doubt creeping into his mind, agreeing with Smith and McCarthy's earlier sentiment. They are invading a sovereign nation's base – one of their closest allies, no less – performing an act of war. Keeping the casualties low won't make a difference when the bill comes due.

Quick-stepping it, he follows his men down the stairs and into the belly of the command center, disabling two more guards with soft grunts and groans before navigating a block of steps that corkscrews downward. At the bottom, they face a long hallway that stretches fifty yards underground. Scott knows the passage is filled with monitoring gear, cameras and motion detection systems.

He nods to Gilliam and the man removes a baseball-sized sphere from his jacket and rolls it down the hall like a bowling ball. As it moves, it emits a strong electromagnetic pulse that temporarily disables any delicate electronic equipment in the walls. The SEALS sprint along the passage directly behind the sphere, reaching the end in less than ten seconds, a steel door separating them from their goal. Gilliam uses a coded transponder to disable the lock and pop the door and as it flies open, the sound of gunfire erupts, catching the trio off-guard.

The control center is a large room with three rows of computer stations lined up with gaps on the sides and down the middle. Scott rolls to his right, rises with his weapon, and squeezes off a burst at a soldier coming around the edge, sending his feet flying up, rifle jerking reflexively to fire at the ceiling. McCarthy and Gilliam combine to take down two more, any pretense of civility ended, their momentary surprise overridden by their years of carefully-trained instincts.

The lieutenant sees a man typing vigorously at a console across the room, shouts for him to stop, but when he doesn't, he targets him and fires, putting a bullet through his left temple, blood and brains spraying the far wall in an elliptical shape. By the time they're done, three Mexican soldiers and two officers are dead. Scott jogs over to the console the man was typing at and sits. Still logged in, he uses the man's access to pull up the data he needs. As he works, he makes contact with his men outside the control center.

"Stevenson. Rose. Do you read me?"

"Yes, sir," replies Stevenson.

"Loud and clear." Rose's voice cuts through static.

"Be advised, it's about to get hot up there."

"Are we still keeping casualties low, sir?" Stevenson asks.

"Negative. That bird flew the coop."

"Standing by."

Scott removes a USB stick from his pocket and pushes it into a slot on the computer. Fingers flying over the keyboard, he types a few commands and begins loading the data, watching a meter on the screen as it measures the data upload progress.

"They're looking for us hard now," Rose says in his ear. "Lights are sweeping everywhere."

"Hang tight," Scott glanced at the monitor. "We're at fifty percent."

"They're moving on the command center," Rose said. "Be advised."

"Noted. Sixty-two percent." Scott stands and addresses his teammates next to the door. "McCarty and Gilliam. You two advance and make sure the stairwell remains clear. Seventy-five percent."

The pair exit the command center and stalk down the hallway, leaving Scott alone in the room.

"Moving in to support," Rose said.

"Same here," Stevenson adds.

"I hear boots on the stairs," McCarthy murmurs. "Engaging."

A close rattle of gunfire goes off like a snare drum through his earpiece, quickly followed by another nearby.

"Two down." Gilliam states. "I'm smoking the stairs. Be advised."

Scott grabs the bottom of his visor and lowers it, locking it in place, sealing his mask and activating an air filtration unit in the side. "Ninety-three percent," he says. Almost there. "Rose, are you in position to disable those armored vehicles sitting out front?"

"On it."

The gunfire and explosions continue, intensifying in a rising press of sound, the signature rifle bursts of his men laying a cover that's impossible to defend against. He can almost feel the enemy's fears as his soldiers rise from the shadows, more resembling monsters of legend than actual blood-and-flesh men.

"Ninety-eight percent," he says. A moment later, he jerks the stick free and places it inside a pocket in his vest. "Got it. On my way. Prepare for evac."

He steps over dead bodies as he strides toward the door, the battle escalating through his earpiece; bursts of rounds, shouts and cries, and a distant boom. Scott grips his rifle tight to his chest and prepares to charge into the fray. A soft groan draws his attention, and he spins to the right, snapping his rifle up to fire. A Mexican soldier lies on the floor in a pool of his own blood, trying to lift a pistol to shoot Lieutenant Scott, but he doesn't have the strength. At the last second, his shoulders shiver, and the weapon clatters useless to the floor.

The man glares at the lieutenant before his eyes glaze over, and he dies. Scott stares at him a moment and then exits the room, slipping into the approaching smoke like an apparition.

Chapter 11
Tom McKnight
Virginia Beach, Virginia

The sounds of shattering glass stung his ears, and Tom twisted and glared out the foot-wide crater someone had made in it, the safety glass spiderweb-cracking all the way to its edges but not bursting completely. Standing slightly behind and to the side of the Toyota were a man and woman from the ABC Liquor parking lot, both holding bats, the man lifting his to swing it again, face twisted into a grimace.

Tom jammed the truck in reverse and slammed his foot on the gas, tires squealing as they shot backward, splitting the pair and sending them dodging off to the sides. The man's bat flew down as they roared past, smacking the front windshield and causing the glass to spiderweb like the back window.

"Seatbelts!" Tom yelled over his shoulder as he continued careening toward the main road. "And hang on!"

He couldn't see much out the rear window, most of it just a white mesh of jagged, puzzle-piece lines. A glance forward showed him the pair of attackers running after them, but Tom didn't slow down, pressing the pedal harder, gripping the steering wheel as the Toyota twisted back and forth in retreat. His rear tires ground hard against the curb before they leapt onto the sidewalk and weaved into the grass. Tom tried to overcorrect, but the truck slewed and slid, ignoring his commands.

He slammed his foot on the brake, locking them up to send them hydroplaning across the swampy ground, a thick tree trunk centering itself in his rear window. He had a fraction of a second to clench his shoulders before they smashed into the tree in an explosion of airbags and flying glass. Tom rocked back in his seat and fell forward over the deflating balloon, sucking air between his teeth and groaning, staring through the cracked front windshield at the figures slogging through the grass toward them.

He turned to Jerry, the young man gripping his right shoulder, his expression caught in a pained daze. Releasing his arm, he reached for the door handle, mumbling something about getting someone to help them when Tom growled, grabbing his arm back from the handle.

"No!"

A bat smashed against his driver's side window, jerking his attention back, a woman glaring down at him through the cracked glass, teeth bared.

"It's those people from the liquor store! They're trying to bash our windows in!"

A thick, shadowy figure stood at the front of the car, arms spread in a masculine, dominating pose. "Get out of the car!" he screamed, raising a baseball bat and smashing it on the Toyota's hood.

"Come on! Get out!" the woman screeched. She brought her bat down to smack Sam's window just behind him, cracking it from center to edge before lowering her aim and whacked the door with a heavy thud.

"Leave your shit and get out of the car!" the man shouted, clobbering the hood again.

Tom looked around for something to defend themselves with, but he only had his titanium pen and his bare fists. Another slam to the doorframe shook off the last of his momentary confusion, and he realized with a start that, in spite of a collision that should have automatically cut the engine off, the Toyota was still idling.

Eyes wide with hope, he grabbed the gear shift and tugged it to the drive position, then slammed his foot on the gas, sending the engine into a rattling uproar. The wheels spun on the slick grass, spitting up grass and mud from the Toyota's rear, the vibrations causing the vehicle to slip down off the tree, the tires biting deeper and deeper.

The rear end swerved, the wheels grabbing earth, propelling the truck forward in a surge. The front bumper clipped the man, spinning him to the ground, a pained wail exploding from his mouth as the Toyota slammed over him. The woman gave them a parting shot as they passed by, her bat harmlessly smacking the frame, flying out of her hand to the wet ground.

Adrenaline coursing through his veins, Tom tried to straighten the vehicle, but only ended up fishtailing, swerving through the wet grass. He glanced back to see if Sam was okay before Jerry gave a warning grunt and pointed with his good arm.

Tom jerked his attention forward, lowering his head enough to see through a small patch of solidified glass. The Toyota curved to the right and was careening down a shallow slope, picking up a dangerous amount of speed. Before he could stop them, they hit the sidewalk and bounced into the street in a squeal of tires, the wheel jerking from his hands as they skidded and raced toward a small row of shops. Grabbing at the wheel, Tom tried to get control of the truck, but it was like trying to wrestle a wild animal that bucked and twisted beneath his grip, the storefronts rushing at them at breakneck speed, the writing on the windows exploding in size.

The Toyota jumped the opposite curb with a violent shudder, completely out of control as it plowed through a storefront in a storm of shattering glass. The front bumper drove deep into the store, smashing product displays and boxes, sliding across the carpeted showroom before hitting the checkout counter with a jarring shudder before the engine coughed, choked and finally, inevitably, died.

Tom shook his head, blinking in the swirling dust. The windshield had burst completely, revealing a sign on the wall that read *Adonis Mobile*. Lowering his eyes, he saw his lap filled with pieces of safety glass atop the deflated airbag, and through the haze and confusion, a warning tapped at the back of his brain.

Get moving. Someone is still after you.

He grabbed his door handle and popped it open, shoving it outward with a rough squeal and the grind of bent metal on metal. Tom swung his legs out of the truck and stood, holding his head as he swooned. With the airbags already burst from the first crash, they'd not been as protected on the second. Head ringing with pain, he shuffled through the debris and whipped open the rear door, reaching in to snatch his pack from the floorboard before his dizzy head caught up with him and he saw Sam lying slumped to the side, hands out on the seat as she stared dazedly up at her father.

"Are you okay?" he grunted fumbling to unsnap her seatbelt.

She shook her head. "Yeah. Maybe. I don't know."

"Come on, Sam. Help me get you out."

She came to her senses, unbuckled herself, and started to climb out, dragging her own pack behind her when the shouts of the woman echoed down the hill, the man they'd run over still screaming to high Heaven. Tom's eyes lighted on a door in the back of the store and he gripped Sam's upper right arm and guided her around the debris until she saw it.

"Go there."

Samantha slung her pack onto her shoulder and shuffled over towards the door, legs wobbly and uncertain while Tom turned back for Jerry, the young man sitting dumbfounded in the passenger seat, shoulders slumped, blood trickling from his nose and lips. There was no room for Tom to circle the front of the Toyota so he climbed onto the hood and slid to the other side, settling on wobbly feet, turning, shuffling, pulling the passenger door open.

"Come on, Jerry," he leaned in, reaching to unbuckle the seatbelt. When Jerry didn't move or make any attempt to exit the vehicle, Tom leaned in and gave him a hard slap on the cheek. "I said come on, man. We need to go."

"Hey, Rick!" the woman shouted from outside. "They're over here! They smashed into the store!"

Tom glanced up to see a trio of shadows crossing the street with the outlines of weapons in their hand. One appeared to be limping, but he didn't wait to find out how badly the person was injured.

He gave Jerry's cheek another hard slap and hissed, "Hear that? They're right outside the store. Let's *go*."

Jerry pushed Tom's hands away, his eyes glazed over, his words barely audible as he slurred them out. "Just leave me here. I'll only get you hurt."

"No way." Tom snatched the Jerry's forearm and pulled him half out of the seat. "You can either come willingly, or I can drag you." He tugged again, rolling Jerry onto his injured arm, causing him to jerk straight, sucking air with a grimace as the pain spurred him on to action.

"Okay. Jeez! I'm coming."

Half-dragging him out of the seat, Tom roughly guided him toward the hood and helped him slide to the other side before jumping on and scooting across, more gracefully than before. Feet down, he pushed Jerry toward the back door where Sam held it open, the trio entering a stockroom full of cell phone boxes, display signs, and a pair of stepladders.

"I think this is the way out," Sam said in a strained whisper, pointing to another door on the opposite side.

Tom nodded and kept his hand on Jerry's back, shutting the door to the sales floor behind him as he guided the still-dazed Jerry through. Sam unbolted the other door's locks, pushed it open, and stepped outside, Tom shoving Jerry behind her. When they exited the back of the building, they found themselves standing in the strip mall's dirty back ally. Garbage cans lined the passage, and soggy trash, cardboard boxes and pieces of debris lined the ground. Tom checked inside the nearest trashcan, a big plastic one with the lid thrown back and three-quarters filled with water. Gripping the handle, he leaned back and dragged it over to the door , parking it against it the metal as a makeshift barricade.

"Where to now?" Sam asked, her head swiveling in both directions.

"There." Tom pointed right to the end of the row where another door stood open.

Sam turned and guided Jerry down the ally's length with Tom skittering behind them. Something slammed the door behind them, and he shot a glance back to see the door being shoved against the heavy garbage can. They hit it again and the can began to budge, sliding outward a full inch. The door handle was on the other side, so their pursuers couldn't simply peer through the crack to see them, but once they spread it a foot, they could easily slide through.

"Hurry, guys," Tom said, urging them forward. "I don't know why these a-holes want us so badly, but we need to hustle! Just slip inside that there, and we'll lock it behind us!"

Fists pounded on the door behind them followed by curses and shouts of rage as Sam strode on Jerry's left, holding his arm and half-pulling him toward the open door. Jerry picked up the pace, shuffling faster until he staggered through the entrance, then Sam went next and Tom followed right behind them. Once in, he turned and grabbed the doorknob, swinging the door shut as quietly as possible, then locked the knob and deadbolt. As he did so, he heard the heavy garbage can skid across the concrete and out in the alley.

Taking Jerry from Sam, Tom raised a finger to his lips, then held the young man with one arm while pulling out his flashlight with the other, flipping it on, looking around at a rectangular storage room with shelving that stretched end-to-end. Spotting a shadowy area, he guided them toward it.

"Sit down," he whispered, snapping off his light.

The trio sunk to the floor behind a shelf, Tom leaning forward, ears perked up and listening for the sounds coming from the ally. A thin sliver of light leaked in beneath the door, shadows snaking past as sneakers shuffled and shouts rang out, their pursuers making their way down the ally, thumping on every door and testing to see which were locked. Someone stopped just outside theirs and beat on the metal, throwing a shoulder against it several times before finally giving up with a curse, then the footsteps and shadows moved off to the next target.

With a slow sigh of relief, he snapped on his flashlight and pointed it at the floor. Jerry sat beside him, shoulders slumped forward, head hanging low with Sam sitting cross-legged next to him, rubbing her hand up and down his back.

"He's cold," she whispered, eyes leveled at her father. "But at least it's warmer in here."

A rich scent filled Tom's nostrils, tweaking it in a Pavlovian response and he raised the flashlight beam at the metal shelves across from him, seeing boxes of roasted coffee everywhere. After days of travel across the open ocean, decimated waterfronts and being assaulted, the sight and smell of so much coffee was a welcome distraction.

"It's a Coffee Town." Tom gave a faint smile as he whispered the familiar jingle. "It ain't coff-ee, unless it's Coffee Town coff-ee..."

Sam joined in with him on the last two words, helping him finish the popular song. "Best coffee in the world," she added.

Tom grinned as he followed the shelves with his beam, leaning forward so he could see to the end. Old brewing machines sat side by side along with cleaning equipment and bottles of descaling agent. There were brushes, filters, and deliming springs and at the far end of the storeroom, separate from everything else, sat boxes of pastries and other confectionaries.

"You... guys should... just... leave me." Jerry's words were slurred and weary. "I'm sorry, I... should have... recognized the car."

Tom exchanged a confused look with his daughter. She shrugged, so he turned back to the pastry boxes and squinted to read what was printed on the sides, his stomach rumbling, helpfully reminding him that they hadn't eaten much of anything since leaving the tunnel.

"You guys are... just going to get... hurt around me." Jerry shook his head and gave a shaky sigh, convulsing slightly with a full-body shiver. "I did... best I could. Worked sixty...hour weeks..."

Tom glanced back, eying Jerry carefully, the young man's face a picture of disappointment and sadness.

"Does he have a concussion, Dad?"

"I'm not sure," he replied.

"Here, have a drink of water." Sam produced a bottled water, unscrewed the cap, and stuck it in front of his face.

"Oh, thanks." Jerry allowed her to put it against his lips and tilt it up. He took two swallows before jerking away and spilling some down his chin. "Ouch, my lip."

"Oh, that *does* look bad." Sam leaned closer, removing a piece of cloth from her pack before tipping the bottle to wet the rag and dabbing lightly at the blood beneath Jerry's nose and lips.

"Is it broken?" He raised his chin and winced slightly at her touch, his head shaky, eyes seemingly unable to focus on her face.

"I don't think so," the girl said, craning her neck to get a straight-ahead view. "It doesn't look crooked or anything."

Jerry deflated once more, his speech growing slightly less slurred. "I guess it doesn't matter. If it isn't busted now, it will be soon. And you guys will be, too."

Tom narrowed his eyes and shined his light at the young man's chest. "What are you talking about, son?"

"I can't let that happen," Jerry mumbled, delirious as he shook his head. "Not... not after you helped me."

Tom leaned over, gripped Jerry's jaw, and lifted his face. "Hey, buddy. It's me. Do you know those people who attacked us?"

Jerry pulled out of Tom's grasp, face twisted in disgust. "Just a couple of lowlifes who I... I had to borrow some money from a few months back."

"You borrowed money from them?"

"Yeah."

"But they're not your friends?"

"Hell no."

"So, they're loan sharks?"

The young man drew his knees to his chest and wrapped his arms around them, trapped beneath Tom's stern gaze. "Sort of. Well, not exactly." He winced and tried to bury his face.

"Are you kidding me right now?!" Tom's face turned red, his voice still low, but filled with anger. "Spill it, Jerry. Are they loan sharks?"

Jerry raised his head, eyes filled with pain. "Yes, they're loan sharks, more or less. My mom was... in pretty deep debt after my dad died. And I needed a ride to keep working. You know, to help my mom out. I borrowed the money to buy my motorcycle from them. I had bad credit and couldn't get it any other way. When I missed a payment, they started harassing me. I've been avoiding them for weeks, but they must've recognized me in my mom's car today." He looked Tom in the eye, body shrunken, voice timid. "Now, I guess you're on their shit list, too."

Tom's feelings of growing discomfort grew until he exploded, grabbing Jerry by the front of his coat, jerking him closer, hissing through clenched teeth.

"Did you seriously just get my *daughter* and I targeted by an organized gang? What the hell were you thinking?!"

Chapter 12
Tom McKnight
Virginia Beach, Virginia

"I can't believe you." Tom paced back and forth along the shelf of French Roast and Columbian blends, hands on his hips, staring holes in Jerry as he muttered under his breath, still aware enough of their situation to not completely give their location away to anyone passing by outside. "You got us injured. You got my *daughter* injured. Could have gotten us *killed*. Now we're being hunted by people we don't even know."

Tom's right fist clenched and unclenched as thoughts of Sam bouncing around in the backseat of the wrecked Toyota played on repeat.

"I'm so sorry, Tom." Jerry's head practically vibrated on his shoulders. Half-sobbing, half-terrified, he shook it back and forth, eyes lifted imploringly, tears streaming down his cheeks.

"If you'd just told us that when we first saw them," Tom seethed, "we could have driven right past Sentara-Virginia Hospital and went on to Sentara-Leigh."

"I *know*." Jerry's pitch raised, vocal cords stretched tight. He tried to stand, hand out and explaining, but he lost his balance and fell back against the wall, Sam catching him, putting her hand on his good shoulder, glancing between him and her father.

"Why didn't you tell us until now?" Tom came to stand directly in front of him, planting his feet apart with his fists resting on his hips. "All you had to do was be honest with us when you realized what was going on. We trusted you."

"I... I don't know," Jerry smashed his hand against his forehead, pinching his skin between his palm and fingers. "I just didn't think of it. My brain was all mixed up. I still can't think straight."

"Dad, c'mon." Sam's voice was quiet, her eyes lifted imploringly.

"We could have been killed back there." Tom pointed in the general direction of the hospital. "We almost got our heads bashed in. Don't you see it?"

"I do see it. I do." She nodded and stood, shifting between him and Jerry, her face falling slack in a firm but neutral expression - not that of the child he'd raised for years, but of a young woman who recognized on her own the mature thing to do. What she had been taught to do.

"It's okay, dad. We're here. Maybe a little beat up, but we're safe. All of us."

Tom's anger deflated in an instant, rushing out of him with the breath he'd been holding onto. His chest shrunk down, his shoulders sagged and he leaned back against the wall, all the fight and bluster gone as quickly as it had come.

"He's knocked his head about three times in the past day. And..." Samantha hesitated, glancing down at Jerry, motioning at him to her father, mouthing the words *his mom*.

Tom took a deep breath and relaxed. "You're right," he nodded. "You're absolutely right. We've all taken some hard knocks over the past couple of days." Easing himself down, he sat next to Jerry, patting the young man's good arm. "Hey, I'm sorry. I shouldn't have flown off the handle like that. You didn't do anything wrong, and definitely nothing intentional toward us."

Jerry sniffed and looked up. "S... Seriously? You forgive me."

Tom sighed. "There's nothing to forgive, son. You just made a mistake. You've been in and out of it since we picked you up off that beach and even if you'd thought to warn us about these a-holes when we first saw them, you couldn't have known they'd follow us all the way to the hospital. I should be getting us out of here instead of berating you. It's me who needs the forgiving. I apologize, Jerry. Can you forgive *me*?"

Tom held out his hand and Jerry's lips widened into a half smile, taking the proffered hand. "I appreciate that. I promise, I don't have any other weird secrets or anything. That's probably the worst thing I've ever--"

Shouts from outside the back of the shop jolted Tom, his head jerking up as footsteps thundered down the alley, stopping at the coffee house door. A fist pounded heavily and repeatedly against it, rattling it in its frame.

"I *told* you I heard them in there!" a woman called out, cackling with demented delight. Raising her voice, she called out in a singsong rhythm. "Heeeyyy, Jerrrryyy, you in there, little budddddyyy?" The door shuddered under a fresh barrage of pounding, the steel and wood groaning but refusing to budge.

"We should break it down," another voice said.

"You two find our people and circle to the front." Tom recognized the gruff voice of the man with the injured foot, his words filled with pain and frustration. "I'll stay here. I can barely friggin' walk anyway."

The voices mumbled and feet ran away down the alley, though the man outside the door continued hitting it, the long barred handle rattling with every impact.

"You in there, Jerry?" he shouted. "You might as well come out! All this chasing is just pissing us off more, plus we want to meet these new friends of yours!"

Tom raised Jerry from the floor, rotating his body toward the rattling door with a grim expression as he aimed his flashlight beam into every corner of the room in search of a weapon. There were a mop and bucket tucked behind the ice cooler and hundreds of pounds' worth of coffee beans, but nothing that would stand up to baseball bats.

"I'm sorry for putting you guys in danger," Jerry's voice fell to a pained whisper. "Turn me over to them. If you do that, they'll let you walk out of here. They don't want you... Just me."

Tom opened his mouth to answer when the shop's front door banged open with a ringing of bells and shuffling of feet, causing his stomach to sink. He looked over at Samantha standing next to Jerry, a pained expression on his face as he considered their options. Sam started to say something, but he cut her off with a raised finger. Turning to the shelves, he grabbed an aerosol can and placed it in her hand. From his pocket, he produced one of the lighters they'd found in the camper, handing it over along with the can and a whisper. "Remember what happened in the barn when you were eight?"

She stared at the can and lighter, shaking her head slightly. "I'm not—"

"Think back. Do what we did then, okay?" Tom turned to address Jerry next.

"Let's get this over with." He put his hand on Jerry's neck, forcing him through the kitchen-style doors and into the café. They entered the service area where fancy coffee brewers squatted on the counters and Tom tucked his hand behind the young man's back as if hiding a weapon, shoving Jerry around the massive cappuccino machine, facing the group who'd come in together.

The woman from before stood in the middle of the room, her dark hair swept to one side over her forehead, though she'd removed her jacket, leaving her in a dirty white tank top and jeans. In her hands she held the same wooden baseball bat that had smashed up Jerry's mother's truck, gently raising and lowering the fat end in one hand, a devilish grin on her face. Fog gusted from her breath as her eyes dropped warily to Tom's waist, her smile sinking when she noticed that looked like he clutched a weapon to the young man's back.

One thick, burly man stood off to the left, edging around toward the counter, a long tire iron dangling from his hand, its sharp end brushing the floor. Four others were spread out behind the lead pair, each holding some type of blunt weapon, smiling when they saw Jerry sniveling in Tom's grasp with his arm in a sling.

"I'm going to give you what you want," Tom said, keeping his voice calm. "But you have to let me and my daughter go. Okay?"

"No way," the woman snickered, head shaking, voice raspy from yelling. "You hurt one of our people."

"You could have asked for Jerry nicely instead of destroying the car," Tom's voice remained cool even though his heart felt like it might break a rib if it beat any harder.

"It doesn't matter," the circling man snarled. "You screwed up. You pay the tab. Jerry understands that, don't you Jerry?"

Tom glanced back, spotting a shadow of Sam's face in the swinging doors' square window as he silently prayed that she had figured out what his cryptic message meant.

"Look, my daughter and I are just trying to get home. We've got nothing valuable on us. You don't need to hurt us, right?" He tilted his head, trying to sound reasonable. "I can just give you Jerry, without a fight, as a show of good faith. You take him and do whatever you want with him and let us go so we can get home. Deal?" Tom felt Jerry's body sag at his words, a soft whimper escaping his lips as the two leaders exchanged an amused glance.

The man scoffed. "He thinks this is an episode of CSI or something. Next thing you know, he'll be asking for a bag full of money."

The woman clicked her tongue, the bemused grin spreading once again. "No deal. This is what's going to happen. You'll give us that shit-heel. Then you and your little girl will stay put while we decide what to do with you."

"That doesn't sound fair," Tom shook his head, drawing it out. "It's not like I'm asking for much here--"

The man jumped onto the counter and slid across to the other side, landing deftly on his feet. Tom jerked Jerry back to the storeroom door, turning his body left and right, threatening with his supposed hidden weapon.

"You don't have anything in your hand, do you?" The woman stepped to where Tom had been standing a second before and shook her head.

"I'll slice his spine and he won't be worth a damned thing to you, so help me!" He growled the words so convincingly it gave the pair a pause.

"Let's see it," the woman jerked her chin up, though she stayed put, the man at her side, both of them considering whether his threat was real.

Rapidly running out of options, Tom began thinking up another bluster when he heard someone stirring behind the storeroom door and the clink of metal against aluminum. He grinned and retreated another foot, pulling the sniffling Jerry along with him. Glancing back, he saw Sam's curly head blending with the shadows in the smallish window. The door edged open six inches, and he saw her standing just inside the entryway, holding the aerosol and lighter up, finger resting on the nozzle, the whites of her eyes glinting with fear and determination in the darkness. Exactly the look he wanted to see.

The man behind the counter stepped toward them, coming within a few feet, feigning a swing of his tire iron.

"You're right," Tom quickly shifted his position and his words rushed out. "I'm asking *way* too much. But this little ass has been nothing but trouble for us, too. I mean, just look at him." Tom scoffed, manhandling Jerry again, who merely went limp in response, all sense of hope gone from him. "He's pathetic. Just take him and let us go, alright? We never wanted to step into this business between you and him."

The woman considered Tom's words for a long moment, holding up a hand to stop her companion from advancing any farther. "Alright, man. We can do that. We're bored with you, anyway." Her gaze slid to Jerry, a grin stretching her lips wide. "Time to pay the piper, shit-heel. I'm sure we'll find some way for you to work off your debt. Plenty of stores to loot thanks to the storm."

Tom shifted his feet, putting his back foot against the storeroom door frame as a defeated whine grew in Jerry's chest, edging up to his throat. Tom cringed, leaning forward, whispering quietly in Jerry's ear. "Sorry for this, man. But I have to do it. Just try to keep your body loose, okay?"

Tom gripped Jerry's neck tight and held it tight, then, throwing his whole body into the motion, he shoved off against the door frame, launching Jerry at the woman like a battering ram. With a strangled cry, the young man bowled into the woman, knocking her over a table, her legs flying up as she toppled off to crash on the floor. Tom kept moving, driving Jerry like he was steering a wild animal, using their combined weight to overwhelm their attackers. One of the men swung a bat at them, but by the time he managed to even start pulling back on the weapon Tom had already steered Jerry into the man's body, plowing him over, sending the bat sailing across the room. Just as quickly as he had pushed forward, Tom yanked Jerry backwards, dragging him in a staggering retreat toward the storeroom.

"Do it!" Tom yelled as they tripped and staggered backward, tumbling to the floor in a heap.

Sam pushed through the swinging doors, stepping over Tom and Jerry as she pressed the aerosol nozzle down, spraying flammable chemicals at the lighter. The emerging spray blossomed with heat and flame, coating the air with a choking chemical smell as a roiling, living flame emerged. She turned the makeshift flamethrower on the flanking man, setting him on fire before shifting toward the others, forcing them to scatter back as Sam rushed forward, sending a gout of fire in every direction.

The leader had just gotten to her feet when her dark locks caught fire and went up in a roar. Screaming, eyes slammed shut, she shook her head like a wet dog, tossing soot and flames off her, the scent of burning hair, scorched flesh and smoke mingled with the rich bean flavor of the room, causing Tom's stomach to wretch.

Sam feigned left and right, chased the woman toward the door before making a huge sweep to the left that caught two more members on fire. They stomped and danced and flung their arms wide, screams winding upward into wails of agony as they tried to extinguish themselves but only ended up fanning the inferno.

The men launched themselves past Sam to get to the door and she retreated, but still delivered another burst of flame as they flew by, lighting their clothes on fire, sending them rolling and crashing out of the shop. Turning, guiding the hellish geyser in every direction, Sam spotted a woman hiding behind a table and bore down on her with the nozzle pressed. The woman's eyes shot wide as she crawled and scrambled to the entrance, staggering outside with Sam hot on her heels.

"Sam!" Tom shouted after her, worried that her youthful exuberance would lead to missteps and overextending.

His daughter heard him and backed through the door, letting her finger off the nozzle as the flame died, shaking her hot left hand, though still not giving up her responsibility as she stayed near the door, can and lighter poised for further use.

"Are you two okay?" Sam glanced back at Jerry and her father as the two slowly began to sit up.

"I think so," Tom forced a thin smile through his pain. "Nice work. Jerry, you okay?"

Like Tom, the young man had fallen as well, though he had gone face down and was just starting to sit up, holding his injured arm with his head down. Tom pivoted on his backside and rose to his knees, circling to look him over.

"Sorry about using you as a battering ram," he apologized, hesitating to touch the sling-bound arm. "Did you land on it?"

"Yeah, but it's okay." Jerry sucked air through his teeth, face twisted in a dazed grimace. "Just give me a minute."

Tom mirrored his expression. "I should have at least warned you. We were kind of running out of time and I had to come up with something to stall them."

Jerry was already shaking his head. "Don't worry about it. I'm always up for new experiences." A chuckle escaped him as he released a gasp of pain and sucked it back in. "I'm grateful you drove them off. Thank you so much. I--"

"I couldn't give you over to them." Tom patted Jerry's good shoulder and gave him a coy wink. "Much as I might have wanted to." After helping Jerry to his feet, Tom joined his daughter peering through the front glass of the store. The gang had scattered and Samantha handed him the lighter and can and he examined the faint soot marks on the lighter hood and her hand. "Seriously. Nice work."

"Thanks," she grinned, putting her finger in her mouth.

"Where'd you get that idea?" Jerry got slowly to his feet, still holding his shoulder but no longer wincing in pain.

"I watched a little too much TV once when I was a kid."

"'When I was a kid'" Tom rolled his eyes. "You're *still* a kid, kiddo."

Samantha laughed, "Yeah, well, anyway, I saw a movie where someone used a can and a lighter and I tried it out in the barn and... yeah. Good thing Dad smelled the smoke, otherwise the place would have gone up."

"Smart thinking. Dangerous, though." Jerry replied.

Sam shrugged. "Remember what we were talking about, about being ready to survive? You gotta do whatever you gotta do. This was... well, *is* one of those situations."

"I guess so."

"I don't think the owner is going to appreciate the damage." Tom looked over the flipped tables and chairs that lay broken around them. Sam's fireball had scorched three of the walls, curling the paint and leaving a sooty circle over a set of booths, and the smell of burning chemicals hung heavy in the air.

"Hopefully they have insurance." Jerry said, then he gestured toward the street. "But the fire damage is probably the least of their worries."

Tom and Sam followed where Jerry was pointing to the front of the hospital where it appeared an all-out fight was taking place. Far across the street to their right, another row of shops was in the process of being ravaged, people lugging goods out in armfuls, dropping stolen items as they carried them to waiting car trunks. Two women fought in front of a beauty store, locked in a hair-gripping brawl that left them swinging in circles, a few people cheering them on while others carried off food with furtive glances at the fight. At least a half dozen other altercations had broken out on the sidewalk and in the streets, with swinging fists and shouted curses appearing to become the norm rather than the exception.

Groups of hoodie-wearing bike riders roved the edges of the crowds, watching the rising chaos like a flock of so many vultures. A car tried to drive through the crowd, apparently heading for the hospital and a group of the bikers immediately surrounded the vehicle, bats and crowbars smashing the glass and denting the doors. Someone threw themselves on the hood and splayed out, blocking the driver's view of the road, causing them to slam on their brakes and jerk to a halt.

"No, no no… don't stop," Tom murmured. "Do *not* stop."

The crowd swarmed the vehicle, one person slamming their hands on the driver's side glass, ripping open the door and reaching in, grasping the man from behind the wheel. The pair fought for a moment before someone else shoved their boot in and kicked the driver in the side of the face, causing him to go limp.

"Oh, no." Sam slapped her hand to her mouth as the crowd pulled the driver out and dragged him into the hungry crowd where he disappeared in a sea of swinging arms and legs.

Tom gently took Sam's arm and guided her away from the window, motioning for Jerry to follow. A group of five sprinted by outside the coffee shop, carrying bags bearing the label from the cellphone store they had crashed into. At the same time, a man and woman in two separate vehicles drove up, colliding with each other on the opposite curb, and judging by their wild gestures and aggressive positions, they were in the middle of an argument that was about to turn very ugly.

"I think it's time to go," Tom said, continuing to guide Samantha and Jerry toward the back of the shop. "Let's grab our backpacks and bug out."

Chapter 13

Barbara McKnight
Wyndale, Virginia

A thousand thrumming fingertips pounded against the siding, driven by the wind in a furious, desperate gust, water gushing from the corner spouts into their drainage system along the sides of the house. The storm had been losing steam over the past forty-eight hours, burning itself out like a child trying hard not to fall to sleep, but still packing enough of a punch to wake the dead. Continued, repeated gusts struck the sliding glass door, but each was weaker than the previous ones, the child slowly succumbing to the inevitable.

"The storm is dying down," Linda licked her lips as she finished the last few bites of her green pepper soup. It was one of her favorites, with stewed tomatoes, rice, chopped steak, and big chunks of green peppers and onions tossed in. Barbara had served it with pieces of butter bread and milk, and the kids were devouring it, some part of their hunger no doubt driven by the ferocity of the storm outside.

Barbara got up from the table and walked to the sliding glass door, gazing out at the pole lights, raising her eyes to the dark clouds above their heads. The sky hung above them in a shade of deep gray, its edges pale and bright as the fading sun threatened to break the morosity of the storm.

"It's a lot weaker now." Barbara agreed. "Hopefully we'll see sunshine again tomorrow."

She placed her fingers against the glass, feeling the tendrils of cold seeping through. "Is it me, or is it getting colder out?"

"I was hot carrying in groceries," Linda pointed out with a shrug.

Barbara slid open the glass door and put her hand out, the light rain kissing her skin followed by the gusty breeze. "It definitely *feels* colder." She stepped onto the patio and gazed toward the big thermometer on the chicken coop. The light barely reached it, and she had to squint to read the number. With a frown, she returned to the kitchen and shut the door behind her. "I think it says forty-nine degrees."

The girl stopped eating, tilting her head up with a questioning expression. "It was sixty-seven when we got back from the store."

"It's nighttime now," she countered, lip caught between her teeth. "It's always a little cooler at night."

"True," Linda said.

Barbara returned to her seat to finish her soup.

"Do you think Dad and Sam will have a hard time getting through town?" Linda asked, her voice chipper, though her skittish glances betrayed the doubts clouding her mind.

"I think your father is smart enough not to go directly through crowded places." Barbara shook her head. "He'll know people are dangerous."

"I hope they get here soon."

"They will. I'm sure of it." Like her daughter, Barbara sought to keep her words and attitude positive, though her inner thoughts were as dark and gloomy as the storm outside.

"Can I play games after dinner tonight?" Jack's expression lifted as he tilted up his bowl to show he'd finished.

"I'm thinking we should go downstairs and put away the food we canned. We've got to rotate the inventory, so we eat the oldest stuff first."

"We need to build more shelves," Linda said, taking two big gulps of her milk. She set her glass on the table, leaving a line of white liquid on her upper lip.

"You've got a mustache," Jack laughed and pointed.

"Big deal." The girl licked off the milk and made a face at him.

Barbara smiled, her thoughts turning to her daughter's earlier comment. It was true that they had an overabundance of canned goods and even some fresh vegetables. "You've got a good point, Linda. We should have more shelving materials out in the old barn. Your father and I put them away after we set up the basement."

Linda thought about it. "We can use the Gator to bring them up."

"That's right."

"Can we do it in the morning?" Jack sounded whiny.

"I know you want to play games," Barbara replied firmly, "but we need to at least get something done today. After we bring some materials in, you can take the night off after that, okay?"

"Okay!" Jack agreed.

"And we still have a lot of potatoes to process, too."

"Crates of them." Linda finished her soup and took her bowl to the sink.

"I'm thinking we can start the potatoes boiling and bake two crates tonight. Then we'll grind them up. That should give us one jar of flakes with a shelf life of two years, maybe more. We'll do a few jars a day, working around our other chores and defensive plans until all the potatoes are gone. We can make potato chips, too."

"I *love* potatoes chips," Jack said, almost singing the words. "And French fries. Can we make those, too, Mom?"

"We sure can." Barbara finished her bowl and leaned back.

"That's because you're a potato head," Linda smirked.

"Am not!"

Satisfied that she'd gotten a rise out of her brother, Linda crossed one arm over her chest and faced her mother, going over the list of things to do, ticking things off on her fingers. "So, we need to bring up building materials and rotate the inventory, right?"

Barbra nodded. "We'll haul materials tonight, including extra plywood to cover the windows. After that, we'll see how we feel. We don't have to rush the shelving. Like I was saying earlier, I want to bolster our defenses first. Once that's taken care of, we'll--"

The lights flickered and died, leaving just the pattering of rain in the quiet darkness.

"There they go again," Jack announced from the table.

"I'm betting it'll be back in one minute." Linda held up her watch and hit the stopwatch function.

"Minute and a half!" the boy replied.

Barbara stood and returned to her spot at the back door, breathing quietly, holding her fingers against the glass, the icy tendrils caressing her fingertips once more. Grid power had been spotty all day, and they'd been playing a game to guess when it would come back on. Ten seconds passed, then twenty. After a minute and a half, she removed her chilly fingertips from the glass and shook her head.

"Okay, this is annoying. I was hoping it would stay on at least two more days. I still haven't activated the battery bank or generator." She frowned, thinking of how the storms must be affecting the power along the coastal states. "Well, it's not like it was a surprise. I should have gotten to it earlier."

Linda stood. "Do you want me to help you?"

Barbara unclipped a thin flashlight from her belt, flipped it on, and shined it toward her daughter. "Nope. Light a pair of candles and start cleaning up the kitchen, please. I'll have the power back on in less than fifteen minutes."

"Okay, Mom."

Barbara unlocked the sliding glass door and pulled it open an inch before she had second thoughts and shut it. Crossing to the closet, she grabbed a thin hooded sweatshirt and shrugged it on. It seemed crazy to have to wear one prior to fall's official start, but the air had a bone-chilling feel to it. Back in the kitchen, Linda had gotten the candles going while Jack brought their bowls to the sink. With a quick smile, Barbara pulled open the door, stepped out, and slid it shut behind her.

She pointed the flashlight out at the yard, the light drizzle falling through the light beam, pattering on the roof and grill cover. The scent of wet honeysuckle wafted through the air, the strong odor of manure and wet wool almost canceling it out. With her breath coming out in gusts of mist, Barbara took five steps away from the house and guided the beam toward the chicken coops and beyond. The sheep huddled around the structures with the wide oak branches providing shelter, their wool coats wet and wilted as the donkeys stood in their midst and Chuck, their rooster, clucked somewhere nearby, voicing his displeasure at so much rain.

"I'll get you guys some space inside soon," Barbara promised.

The barn they usually sheltered the animals in sat down along the west side of the property where the men had intruded. It was farther away from the house than she liked, and she'd been wondering if she shouldn't move them to the newer barn where they'd be easier to keep an eye on. Head shaking with indecision, she took a breath of moist air, angled right, and strode toward the fuel shed as Smooch came trotting up. Barbara bent and took the dog's head in both hands, giving her furry cheeks a good rub.

"C'mon, girl. Foos." She patted her own hip as she walked, causing the animal to heel alongside her in an excited trot, the dog's eyes never leaving her as they made their way to the smaller building on the east side of the property. At the entrance, she gave the dog a sharp hand gesture, saying, "pass auf!" Guard! Smooch did a turn, sat, and looked out at the property with her ears standing straight up.

Barbara went inside and primed the generator before topping it off with fuel and hitting the start button, listening as the engine rumbled to life. With a glance toward the door, she saw the exterior lights pop on and bleed in through the doorway. She glanced at her watch and saw it was 6:47 PM, almost time for her to turn on her radio and try to pick up Darren's call. She exited the building, her intention to head straight for the basement, activate the power and grab the radio in one trip.

Outside, she slammed the door behind her and locked it. With the yard lights back on, she headed back to the house but took a sharper angle toward the driveway, distracted by the sight of the truck, wanting to take another look at the dent.

"Foos!" she called to Smooch. The dog broke from her sitting position and ran along Barbara's side. When she got there, she aimed her flashlight beam at the dent with its blended smudge of white and gray paint, grunting with displeasure. There'd be no insurance claim, and they wouldn't be having the damage repaired – at least not right away. With things in town starting to turn sour, it was unlikely that mechanics would be serving customers, let alone even open.

"Let's go, Smooch," Barbara said, starting to turn toward the back yard when movement caught her eye at the end of the driveway. Eyes narrowed, she pivoted and strode to the corner of the garage as a vehicle cruised slowly past their home and driveway. It was too dark to determine the color, but it had a similar shape to the green Oldsmobile from the other day and the loud, sputtering engine was unmistakable.

"It's them again," she said, lips tightening to a scowl.

Smooch picked up on her tension, emitting a low growl from her chest as she followed the car with her alert eyes. The vehicle drove around the corner where it disappeared behind a line of trees and Barbara expected the engine to fade as it kept going, but its brakes squealed gently, the motor idling away with the same soft, puttering misfires.

As she stood and waited, her chest swelled with a mixture of anger and fear. Aggravation gnawed at her belly, her breathing picked up, and she fought to control it by grabbing her Smith & Wesson from its holster, feeling its comforting weight in her hand as she waited a long minute, listening, hoping that the engine sound would die away

"They're not leaving." She whispered as she backed toward the house, snapping "Foos!" at the dog.

The intruders had returned despite being shot at, so they were undoubtedly prepared for Barbara being armed. Forcing down her fears, she backed around the corner of the house, certain she had plenty of time to get inside before they came up the hill. Smooch's head whipped to the left, ears pinned back, body frozen as a deep growl swelled from her chest and grew into a fit of vicious barks.

Two men stepped from behind the fuel shed and trotted toward them and Smooch lowered her head, creeping forward to meet them, but Barbara snatched the dog's collar, hissing, "*Foos, Smooch. Foos!*" The dog obeyed her command and retreated, fore paws dancing on the ground like she wanted to tear the men apart as Barbara pulled her toward the sliding glass door less than twenty yards away.

"Get off my property," she shouted, holding her weapon up, hearing the crunch of footsteps behind her a second too late. Barbara reeled to see a shadow creeping up behind her, arms reaching in a stretch of shadows across the house siding. Her fingers slipped from the dog's collar, Smooch launching herself at him in a snarl and flash of teeth, hitting him hard, snapping and biting, forcing the man to swat at her with a canine catch-pole in his hands. He jabbed the noose at Smooch's head, missing, giving her jaws a chance to snatch his jacket and clamp tight, swinging him into the backyard.

Barbara took aim at him for a few seconds, looking for an opening that would keep Smooch safe, but with none presenting itself and Smooch clearly in control, she spun to see that the men from the barn were fifteen yards away, sprinting at her with grim expressions on their faces. Her weapon spat a round at the man on the right, but he dove around the corner of the house, her panic throwing off her aim.

The second man launched directly at her, reaching for her gun, hitting it, almost knocking it from her hands. Barbara danced back, shoes scuffling across the concrete patio as she pulled the pistol to her chest and squeezed off two rounds, point blank, the gun recoiling, the sharp cracks slapping her ears. She swore she hit him, but he didn't slow down, didn't stop his grimacing, pawing charge. Panic spiking in her brain, her feet continued their delicate retreat, almost tripping over a dog bowl and garden hose. Eyes slammed open, face twisted in blind terror, she popped off another round even as she was turning to run. The man grunted in pain, his voice cut off in a pinch of sound, one hand clutching his chest, stumbling toward her, grimacing in a mask of pain as he crashed to the patio, remaining still and silent.

Smooch's yelp snapped Barbara's attention. Man and dog were in a tug-of-war beneath the light pole, Smooch with the man's right wrist in her mouth and the man trying to get it back. The dog snarled and whipped her head back and forth with the catcher's noose wrapped around her neck but the man had lost control and was punching at the animal's head with a closed fist.

Barbara stalked toward them, jaw set, blood pounding through her veins. Weapon raised, ticking the sights left and right, she rested her finger on the trigger. The man squatted, trying to gain leverage and jerk his hand from the dog's shaking maw, his foot slipping from beneath him and he fell hard on his back with a pained grunt. Smooch let go of his wrist and dove toward his face, bloody fangs snapping when he swung his wounded right fist at her, the blow glancing off her back, sending a knife clattering to the dirt, its blade stained with blood and fur.

The German Shepherd danced back and then dove in, grabbing at his other arm and pulling it away. The man ripped himself free, but Smooch lunged, ravenous with rage, snapping and grabbing, locking her jaws on his ankle, dragging his leg straight. He kicked out, but the dog let go and darted at him from a different angle to seize his upper arm. Holding his shredded hand against his chest, the man spun on his backside, swinging and kicking at the enraged animal.

Barbara lowered her weapon as she crept closer, voice barely above a hiss. "Smooch, foos! *Foos!*" At first, the dog didn't respond, so she took firm hold of her collar with her left hand and leaned backward, repeating the command. "Foos, Smooch!"

She released the man and allowed herself to be drawn toward the house, looking back and barking the whole time. Rolling on to his side, the man glared at the animal and then at the knife lying in the dirt a few feet away. He raised to his knees, crawled over, and scooped it up.

"Drop it!" Barbara shouted, lifting her gun one-handed, her aim drifting and jerking as she tried to hang on to the Shepherd.

Either the man didn't hear her, or purposefully ignored her, but either way he stood with his ripped-up right hand held against his chest, bloody weapon tight in his left. His glare shifted from Smooch to Barbara, his already pained grimace stretching wide as his eyes narrowed with indecision. Steadying her arm, Barbara made good on her threat, firing four successive shots at the man's center of mass. He jerked each time, twisting, raising his good hand to protect himself. The first three shots were like punches to his chest while the last one clipped off his index finger before pounding him in the sternum. The man fell backwards into the dirt where he groaned and keened and curled into a ball.

Barbara called for Smooch again and they finally arrived at the sliding glass door, and she jerked it open and ordered the dog inside as a bullet smacked the door frame near her head, drawing her shoulders up tight as she slammed it shut. Once inside, Barbara let Smooch go and pointed at the kids where they stood wide-eyed in the candlelit hallway.

"Linda! Jack! Upstairs! Now! Defensive positions."

As the pair fled to the stairwell, she dashed across to the basement door with Smooch in tow, the sliding glass door shattering behind her in a crash of glass across the kitchen tiles. Wincing, she yanked open the basement door and ordered Smooch down. Right behind the dog, she turned and slammed the door shut behind her, locking it before descending the stairs two at a time. As soon as her boots hit the floor, she dashed to the gun safes.

Pistol back in its holster, she raised her shaking hand to the first safe's keypad, pecking in the code until the digital lock blinked green before spinning the spiked wheel and pulled the heavy door open with a grunt. Heart hammering in her chest, she quickly selected a Colt M4 Carbine, grabbed a magazine from the shelf, and jammed it into the receiver. She charged the weapon with a clack, snatched two spare magazines, and stuffed them in her waistband. With a glance at the stairs, she strode to the battery room where Tom kept all the electronic equipment.

She flipped on the light and moved to her husband's workbench. Resting her rifle on top, she searched through the loose parts, tossing wrenches and screwdrivers aside. There were boxes of circuit boards and several coils of thick battery wires, but no radios. She bent and checked the open bins on the next shelf down, relieved to discover five handhelds resting in the middle bin. Barbara removed all five and set them in a row on the bench, eyes lifting to the living room above her where the floorboards creaked beneath heavy boots.

She turned on the first radio, but it didn't even give a burst of static to indicate it had power.

"Come on. Please say one of these has some battery life left."

She flipped on the second radio, then the third and fourth. None of them offered her any luck. The last was a newer model, one she remembered her husband had purchased prior to leaving on his trip with Sam and when she turned it on, it emitted a low squelching sound, the light on top glowing green.

"Yes," she hissed, glancing at her watch to see it was just past seven. "You'd better still be on, Darren…"

Taking the paper from her pocket with the channel and frequency information he'd given her, she tuned the radio to the right settings and put it to her mouth, hitting the talk button.

"Darren, are you there? This is Barbara. Please come in."

A brief pause followed where she held the radio with both hands, staring down at it and mentally forcing the man's voice to come through. Just when she was ready to put the radio down and deal with the strangers on her own, Darren's jovial tone came across the air, startling her.

"Hello there, Barbara. Nice to hear you got it on the first try. How are things at the McKnight homestead? Over."

"I'm in trouble," she replied with a low hiss. "There are men in the house, and I'm down in the basement. Over."

When he came through again, his voice had sobered from jovial to deadly serious. "Where are the kids?"

"Upstairs in the bedroom. Defensive positions, which means Linda should have a gun."

"How many men are in the house?"

"At least one," Barbara stammered. "Maybe more. I shot two."

"We're on our way. Hang tight."

She left the radio on low volume and clipped it to her belt before grabbing her rifle and exiting the battery room. Smooch was pacing near the foot of the steps, restless and limping on her left front leg as she stared upward with a low growl. Rifle cradled in her arms, Barbara went to the dog and knelt, holding out her hand for Smooch to sit. She whined, turning to lick her wound but unable to reach her blood-soaked side.

"Good girl." She ruffled the dog's head and moved it aside to get a better look. A deep gash bled from Smooch's shoulder, and Barbara found at least two more stab marks along her side, just above the ribs. Jaw grinding, she gripped the carbine and took an angry breath as the floor squeaked overhead, Smooch's head jerking up, her chest whine growing into a low growl, pain forgotten.

Barbara put her lips next to the dog's ear. "Nein. Bleib!" *No. Stay.*

She rose and crept to the stairs with her eyes lifted, barrel raised, the weapon's stock pressed up against her shoulder. Foot-after-foot she moved up the stairwell, pausing as the doorknob jiggled, freezing in place. Aiming to the right of the rattling knob, Barbara slid her finger onto the trigger, then stopped. Without knowing for certain who was behind the door, she couldn't risk shooting Jack or Linda if they were trying to get down into the basement. Barbara released a steady breath and ascended two more stairs, uncertainty burning in her heart as she moved the barrel to the right and up the door frame, waiting for a sign.

The doorknob jiggled again, then something heavy slammed against it, rattling the door from other side before striking a second time with a deep thud against the wood. Barbara's finger slid back to the trigger; neither of her children had that much weight to throw around. The intruder thumped the door a third time, splitting the wood frame with a tearing sound, two screws holding the deadbolt flying out and bouncing down the stairs, though the bolt itself still held firm.

Barbara settled the stock against her shoulder and drew a breath, swallowed, and released it in a smooth exhale. With a clenched jaw, she ascended two more steps so she wouldn't be firing up into the second floor and shot four successive rounds through the door. The pops were deafening as holes exploded through the wood in a loose grouping. Someone screamed in pain and fired back, two smaller dots punching through but missing her as she ducked away. Barbara surged up the stairs, unlocked the deadbolt, and flung the door open, falling back as it slammed against the wall. Head even with the floor, her barrel swept back and forth across the kitchen and living room.

Everything remained quiet, agitated dust motes swirling in the candlelight's glow as rain pattered outside on the patio. The smell of gun smoke and blood filled her nostrils, stinging her sinuses with a coppery, acidic reek. A glance down showed splatters of red on the kitchen tile, a trail of crimson curving through the living room, staining the carpet. Barbara pressed against the left-hand wall, exposing herself to the kitchen. Based on the blood trail, the man had retreated in the other direction, and Darren was on his way, so she just had to hold on a little longer.

Something hit the front door, and she heard the unmistakable sound of a door ripping open. Feet pounded up the stairs, causing her heart rate to spike, and she rose and peeked into the living room, spotting a man's forehead and eyes above the back of the couch, a gun resting on the cushion. The muzzle flashed as she jerked backwards, a round ripping into the stairwell wall in a puff of drywall dust.

Jostling and shouts came from upstairs, and a gun fired from Jack's room. Throwing caution to the wind, Barbara ducked and leaned forward with her rifle barrel pointed upward at the couch. The intruder could shoot at her through it, but her Colt M4 carbine could shoot through cushions and flimsy wood, too.

She fired six rounds into the back of the couch just below where the man's pistol rested, foam and dust exploding in puffs. The gun and the arm holding it flew backward out of sight, accompanied by a harrowing, anguished howl of pain. Barbara grunted and rose to her feet, swinging the rifle toward the living room as she came into the open. Realizing she was aiming too high, she dropped the barrel just as the man came into view, then paused as she saw him lying splayed on floor before the mantle, blood draining into the carpet, eyes open, all life gone out of them.

A shot from the hall brought Barbara back to reality, and a bullet stung the back of her left arm, but she was already spinning and returning fire with a desperate cry of rage and fury. She sent three wildly aimed rounds at the front door, the bullets punching through the sidelights in a shatter of glass, catching sight of a shadow as her target dashed into the dining room.

Barbara swept her gun left and fired a handful of times through the dining room entrance, hoping to hit him as he flanked her. She almost got lucky as he appeared beneath the archway just as her bullets shaved off pieces of the decorative trim to send wood chips flying off, but the man jerked back and disappeared before she could get another shot off.

"Hold up, everyone!" Someone shouted from the foot of the stairs. "Hold up! Let's settle down!"

Barbara retreated to the busted sliding glass door, glancing outside into the rain make sure no one was lying in wait for her. The man in the backyard still lay where she'd shot him, but no one else crept across their property, at least that she could tell.

Wind whipped inside the kitchen, whistling across the jagged shards of glass remaining in the door frame.

Crouching, she returned her attention to the front of the house, rifle barrel jerking back and forth between the dining room and hallway, uncertain where her target would pop his head out next.

"You hear me, lady? Stop shooting!"

"Get out of my house," Barbara growled between panting breaths. "Or I'll take the rest of you out just like I did your friends."

"That was good shooting," the man called back. "But you'll need to stop! Especially if you want your son back alive!"

Barbara's blood ran cold, hands frozen to her rifle grip. She glanced to the basement door to see Smooch padding up the stairs and gave a sharp shake of her head, whispering harshly.

"*Nein. Bleib!*" The dog whined and sat on the top step, waiting.

"You hear me, lady? I said I've got your son, and I'm pointing a pistol at his head. Say something, little boy."

"Um, Mom? It's me... Jack." His voice quavered with fear.

"Hey, baby." Barbara spoke through a growing well of tears, eyes blurring, voice shaking. "Everything is going to be okay. Just... don't move. Do what the man says until Mommy can get you free."

"Okay, Mom," came her son's withering reply.

Wiping her eyes quickly, she put every ounce of anger and wrath into her tone. "Let him *go*."

"That's not going to happen. What *will* happen is this. You're going to put down your rifle and play nice."

Barbra grimaced and set her jaw. "What do you want?"

"We want your guns and supplies."

"I don't have much," Barbara said in a halting tone. "Just enough for me and my kids for a few months. It wouldn't do you any good."

The man scoffed. "Nice try. But we know you harvested a bunch of vegetables. And we saw you come back from the store at least twice with truckloads of groceries."

"Right. But that's all I've got. It might last us a month or--"

"And I know you have a pistol, a shotgun, and what seems like a pretty decent rifle. You have solar panels on your roof. Who knows what else you've got stored in your basement?"

Barbara bit her lip and inhaled sharply, a fresh wave of panic welling up in her chest, summoning all her will to quash it, as she couldn't go on the offensive for fear of getting Jack hurt. If, on the other hand, she put her rifle down, they'd all be at the intruder's mercy. Given she'd killed three of his friends, she doubted they'd let her go without extracting some kind of revenge.

"I'll give you some supplies," she said in a desperate gambit. "Let my son go and I'll give you as much as you can carry. You can even take my truck. I'll give you some guns and ammo, too. But you have to let my boy go and leave."

"Sorry, lady. We're not going anywhere for a while." His tone took on a grim, sinister note. "Now, I'm not going to say it again. Drop the rifle and put your hands in the air."

Chapter 14
TomMcKnight
Virginia Beach, Virginia

The trio made their way down the sidewalk, Sam and Jerry walking on Tom's right, bunched together for protection. From their new angle, he saw the opposite corner held a gas station and a mini mart and in front the largest fight they'd witnessed had broken out, with packages of food scattered on the concrete and plastic soft drink bottles rolling between people's feet.

Cars and trucks had come out of the woodwork, and while some slid past the milling crowds, others stopped to avoid hitting bystanders or for other, more nefarious purposes. Those that got caught in a sea of agitated onlookers were attacked with flailing weapons, windows busted out as people were dragged from their vehicles, no distinction made between the innocent and guilty. Tom turned away with a sick feeling as sirens wailed in the distance, the sound no comfort amid the growing disarray.

"This place is a magnet for crazy," he said as they approached the cell phone store they'd originally crashed into. "I'm not sure if it's because the hospital's so close or what."

Jerry nodded as he watched the fights. "It's the only medical facility for a few miles, unless you count some urgent care centers around."

Tom glanced up at the hospital where he could no longer see the front doors or any of the people crowding the area. "I hope the staff got things under control."

"What if they didn't?"

"If the rioters get inside, they'll probably tear it up." A disappointed crease formed in his forehead. "And the people who really need help won't get it."

Sam had been hugging herself as she walked, but she started shivering, teeth chattering under the intense cold that Tom hadn't noticed previously.

"Is it getting colder?" she asked.

"I think so," he replied, finally noting the sobering chill against his cheeks. It was the late afternoon, early enough in the year to still be warm enough for a t-shirt and shorts, yet it felt like a day smack-dab in the middle of fall. "The temperature is definitely dropping."

"Is it because of what you were talking about earlier?" Jerry asked.

"I hope not. Maybe it's just an unusually cool day." Tom's response sounded about as convincing to himself as he figured it did to Jerry and Sam, neither of whom responded.

They reached the cell phone store, and Tom peeked in through the smashed storefront to see the place empty. The Toyota still sat inside, its front end pressed against the counter, dust and ceiling tiles scattered on the roof. Almost every window was busted in from the beating it had taken except for one of the small rear ones. Glancing around at the brawling groups across the street, he gestured for the others to go ahead of him and, with a lingering look at the rising anarchy, he entered the store behind them and stepped over broken glass and debris to circle to the driver's door.

"Think it'll start?" Jerry asked, moving to the passenger's side and slipping into the seat.

"I'm going to find out." Tom got in, mildly surprised to find the keys still in the ignition and the gear shift in the drive position. Sam remained outside the truck, standing by the storeroom door, looking in as her father put the vehicle in park and turned the key. The engine coughed and sputtered but didn't turn over and he touched the gas pedal and tried again to the same effect.

"Third time's the charm." He flipped the key again and gave a little more gas until the smell of fuel permeated the air.

"Oops, I think you flooded it," Jerry said.

"Yep," Tom agreed, but he still wasn't ready to give up.

He popped the hood release, got out of the car, and circled to the front. Shoving aside the collapsed service counter, he stood by the bumper and reached beneath the hood to slide the release latch with his fingers. Then he raised the hood and lifted the prop rod in place.

One look at the engine block told him what the problem was.

"This pretty much explains it," he said as Sam and Jerry stepped closer for a better view. "There's a piece of metal stuck in the front." Tom leaned back and pointed at the shard. "It passed right through the grill and radiator, cutting several hoses and at least one belt, too." He addressed his daughter. "Looks like we're walking."

Samantha's expression turned dejected, but Jerry only blinked at the engine, eyes hollow, and Tom shifted his focus to the young man, sensing they needed to decide something soon. "I'm really sorry I couldn't get you to a hospital like we promised. I really wanted a doctor to look at your arm." He glanced at his daughter. "But Sam and I need to get moving if we're going to make it home this century."

"That's okay about the arm," Jerry shrugged. "Honestly, it's doing okay, considering you used me as a battering ram."

Tom drew a pained look. "Again, sorry for that, too. But you were a really great ram..."

"We all have to be good at something," Jerry scoffed dryly, a slight smile flashing across his face. "But if it's all the same to you, I'd like to keep going with you guys."

"It's a long way from here, son." Tom's pained look changed into one of concern. "I mean, you're more than welcome to come, but I can't promise the journey will be smooth, and I can't guarantee you won't be hurt."

"No, I know," Jerry agreed with a vigorous nod. "But I don't care. My parents are dead, and I have no family or friends here. I might as well start my life completely over somewhere new." He glanced toward the front of the store. "And, let's face it, I doubt I'll fare too good in this town on my own. Especially after today."

Sam kicked at the glass on the floor, watching Jerry with a mixture of sympathy and hope, the young man's voice growing firmer, eyes clearing from their daze. "I'd be happy just to be around people *not* out to get me. After we reach your place, I'll decide where I want to go."

"We can't just kick him out, Dad. Not even after we get home."

Tom started to respond when Jerry cut him off. "I completely understand you might not want to keep me around, Mr. McKnight. I mean, it's my fault we're in this current mess. You two would probably be halfway home by now if we'd not run into those jerks. And me not telling you about them almost got you killed. I'm sorry, again, and I promise not to be a burden, even with my arm."

Tom gave Jerry a pat on his good shoulder, smiling. "Thanks for taking responsibility for yourself, and for the apology. But you haven't been a burden. In fact, we wouldn't be this far if not for your Mom's car." Tom gestured toward the street. "You see what it's like out there now. Sam and I could have fallen victim to your buddies at any point, regardless if you were with us or not." Tom shook his head sympathetically as he glanced at his daughter, then he caught Jerry's eyes again. "We'd be happy to have someone with a solid head on their shoulders to keep us company on the way back. And we won't kick you out once we get home. We'll figure something out."

Sam flashed her father a smile that was worth all the gold in the world, and Jerry's expression perked up with the news. "Thanks a lot." His voice was halted, and he choked on the words, holding back the emotions flooding through him. "That's... that's great. I really appreciate it."

"All right. Let's check out the situation." Tom stepped from the front of the car and cautiously stood by the driver's door while the other two went the opposite direction to stand on the passenger side. Outside, the chaos was feeding on itself, gaining momentum as the rowdy crowd swelled to over two hundred. Tom moved to the rear of the Toyota and leaned forward, peering out the store entrance. The car the couple had been arguing in sat around the block at the far end of the strip mall, the front hugging a telephone pole, engine hissing radiator fluid, doors thrown wide open. The driver and passenger were both gone, and bodies lay sprawled on the street behind the vehicle, unmoving, their limbs and necks twisted at unnatural angles.

"Note to self," he murmured. "Don't drive through rabid crowds of people wielding baseball bats."

Sirens wailed and squelched in the distance and the crowd's din grew louder, punctuated by raucous shouts and screams.

"Let's grab our packs and get moving," Tom said, returning to the driver side door. They pulled out their spare jackets and backpacks, slinging them on their shoulders as Tom gestured to the front of the store, leading the way with the younger pair trailing close behind.

"Shouldn't we take the alley again?" Jerry asked.

"I want to go back to the coffee shop for a minute. I saw a case of bottled water and some other snacks we might need. Plus, we locked the alley door, remember? We won't be able to get back inside it from there."

"Oh. Yeah. Right," Jerry replied.

Exiting through the front of the store, Tom sent the pair ahead of him and stayed in the rear as a guard. They stuck close to the wall, hurrying along, glancing back repeatedly to keep tabs on the unruly mobs while moving in a way to attract the least attention possible. The numbers were growing, though some of the chaos had spread north toward stores he couldn't see and more fights continued to break out around the strip mall, though many dissipated as quickly as they started with victors looting their spoils only to become the victims of other, larger groups themselves.

Furtive glances were thrown in their direction as they reached the coffee shop and slipped inside the lingering stench of burnt hair and leather, and Tom hovered around the front door, not meeting anyone's eyes directly. Satisfied they wouldn't be followed, he backed into the store.

"I hope it doesn't get much colder than it already is." Sam adjusted her backpack with a shiver. "Otherwise, it's going to be a long, miserable walk home."

"I hope not, too," Tom agreed, then he nodded to the coolers resting beneath the counters. "You two grab the bottled waters and pick up any snacks you see. Load Sam up with stuff."

"Where are you going?" The girl slid her pack off and set it on the floor near the cooler.

"I'm heading to the back." Tom flashed a grin, pushing through the swinging doors to the storeroom. The smell of singed hair and flesh in the air couldn't keep him from salivating over the table full of pastry boxes that were still untouched. He opened a box of glazed donuts sitting on top, grabbed one out, and stuffed it in his mouth, swallowing the entire thing in two bites before taking the box out front and tossing it on the counter near Sam and Jerry with a grin.

"Help yourself," he said. "Not exactly good for us, but it's calories, and we need those more than anything right now."

"Oh, man! Nice find!" Jerry looked at the box with wide, hungry eyes, shoving it closer to Sam as she came up. "Ladies first."

"Thanks," she smiled, picking a donut and chomping into it.

"I'm going to load up on some," Tom said. "Might come in handy for a little pick-me-up later."

"Sounds good." Jerry spoke around a mouthful of pastry with a smile.

Back in the storeroom, Tom put his pack on the floor and found an empty hard plastic bin on a shelf. He loaded it with more donuts and pastries, then sealed the lid, putting the treasure box at the top of his pack and drawing the strings tight around it. It barely fit, but already he was in a much better spirits after the sugar surge, jamming a vanilla cream donut in his mouth for good measure as the pair came in. Sam's pack hung heavier on her shoulders, and even Jerry carried a bag full of bottled water.

"Have a couple more," Tom indicated the endless supply of boxes. "Just don't get so sick you can't walk."

Sam reached for an icing-covered pastry, taking a bite out of it and chewing happily. "Too bad we can't brew up some coffee."

"If we had power, I would," Tom assured her with a chuckle.

Jerry slipped onto a stool near the wall while he ate, swooning slightly

"Are you okay?"

"Just your average day on the road," he quipped. "Bruises, beatings, and treats."

"I know how you feel," Tom said, touching his hand to his temple. "I've got a low-level headache that won't quit." He looked around, and an idea struck him. "You know what? I wonder... hang on, wait here."

Tom went back out front to the ice cooler and threw open the top, grinning at the large mound of ice that was still frozen inside the machine. He found two clean rags and placed them on the counter before scooping out some ice and pilin it in the middle of the rags. Pulling up the ends, he formed two ice packs, then placed one on his right temple and grabbed the other, taking it into the storeroom to present to Jerry.

"Here, this should help with the swelling."

"Good idea, Mr. McKnight." The young man accepted the ice pack with his free hand and placed it against the back of his head, then closed his eyes and sighed with relief before taking another bite of his donut.

Tom pulled up his own stool and took a break while Sam climbed on a service table and allowed her shoulders to slump forward, the trio enjoying a sweet-tooth lunch and cool water as the sounds of chaos reigned outside.

"Is the ice helping, guys?" Sam's eyes shifted between the pair.

"My headache is already a lot better." Jerry was leaning against the wall with his head holding the pack in place.

"I have to admit." Tom jiggled the ice around in the wet rag, some of it dripping down his neck. "My pain is almost gone."

Sam smiled. "Awesome. When should we get moving again?"

"In a minute."

"Where are we going to go?"

Tom shrugged. "West. We head west."

"Think we'll find another car?"

"We're definitely not walking all the way to Bristol." Tom lifted his eyebrows momentarily. "So, I'd say finding a vehicle is a priority. I don't want to steal something, but I'm beyond the point of worrying about the police. I'll get us home first and deal with the consequences later."

"I can't imagine they'd consider us criminals for that," Jerry said in an agreeable tone. "Do you think we'll--"

The coffee shop's front doors pushed open, and feet crunched on the glass and debris inside. Tom threw his finger to his lips, ordering Sam and Jerry to keep their mouths shut and he slid from his stool, placed his ice pack down, and crept toward the swinging doors, peering through the window.

A handful of people had entered the café, and while the smears on the glass made it impossible to get a good look at them, they seemed focused on the counter and the remaining drinks in the coolers.

He turned away and motioned for Sam and Jerry to follow him to the back door, gently unbolting the lock to pull it open. It squealed as it dragged along the tile floor, Tom's shoulders tightening in a cringe. Behind them, footsteps shifted and shuffled out on the floor as several people made their way toward the back. Tom stepped outside, looked both ways to make sure they were in the clear, and gestured for the other two to hurry through. Not bothering to hide their movements, the trio half-jogged, half-lurched along the alley as the door slammed shut.

"Take a left at the end," Tom growled, anxiety nipping at his heels.

They reached the end of the alley and came to a sidewalk, slipping under the weight of their packs, bumping against each other, stumbling and holding themselves up to keep from falling. Soon, the trio were running as fast as they could along the sidewalk, leaving the chaos behind.

"I think we're away," Tom huffed and puffed, glancing back to see no signs of pursuit. He slowed down and led them across a street, getting his bearings. "Any idea which way is west?"

Jerry looked around, gasping from the run, at first seeming confused until his sense of direction kicked in. "We need to go back the other way." He turned and led them one block south before limping west again, his spine bent sideways, arm still hanging in his sling.

"Will this get us to the hospital?" Tom asked.

"Yes. A hundred percent."

"How far?"

"About five miles."

"Great," Sam sighed in dismay.

"Glad you found those donuts," Jerry quipped, still panting as he tried to catch his breath. "Talk about a burst of energy!"

The young man wasn't far off in his statement. Tom had gotten a massive surge from the sweet pastries, but he already felt the big crash coming on. A siren made a swooping, penetrating sound from two streets over, and more crowd noise swelled from an upcoming corner store. Distant gunfire popped off in a back-and-forth exchange in the language of violence as someone shouted and a chorus of people screamed and shrieked.

"Let's avoid that mess," Tom suggested with a dark look in that direction.

"I couldn't agree more." Jerry led them north a block and then turned west yet again. The young man swallowed hard. "This city's one big nightmare."

"Yeah, no kidding." Tom glanced around, eyes searching the shadows. "But I have a feeling it's going to get a lot worse before it gets better."

Chapter 15
Tom McKnight
Virginia Beach, Virginia

The night beat down on them, cold and relentless while the moon loomed big and bold behind the thinning clouds, casting a pallid glow across the heavens. The road stretched out long and winding through North Virginia Beach as thousands fled the hurricane ravaged area in trucks, cars, or on foot. Families rolled suitcases along the pavement, looking exhausted and weak as they trudged along in the ever deepening cold. Bodies were not uncommon, scattered mostly among the alleys, offering silent proof of the violence being meted out.

Jerry, Sam, and Tom often stumbled across abandoned luggage filled with apparel and toys, and each time they did, Tom ordered Sam and Jerry to pick through the clothing and layer up to keep warm. Vehicles by the dozens sped by, sometimes dangerously, whipping up the wind and stopping for no one. A family of four had passed them on bicycles, happily pedaling along in a perfect row. Later, they found the same family sitting on the side of the road against the guardrail, the wife dabbing at her husband's bruised face as the kids looked on in horror.

"What happened to them?" Sam asked, her face its own mask of uncertainty and fear.

"Looks like someone robbed them," Tom said. "Those bikes drew attention to them, and we need to avoid that."

While he felt sorry for the family, they had to press on. Tom had to keep his wards on their feet until they reached... something. What it was, he wasn't exactly sure, but they'd been walking for hours, and his enthusiasm was waning. He shivered and grumbled, cold even after finding an extra sweatshirt and jacket to wear from the discarded cases.

They trudged past blacked-out commercial buildings where crowds of young people gathered, Tom assuming they must be looking for easy loot the way they scoped out every passing stranger. Tom had quickly learned how to scope out the dangerous types and keep an eye on them until they passed. Some groups of travelers outpaced the trio, and Tom made sure to pull Sam and Jerry aside to let everyone pass who wanted to. There were families and couples as well, tourists based on their styles of clothing, probably trying to get home.

Jerry slogged along next to him, carrying his own weight but slowly, while Sam remained steady, lagging behind slightly so she could stay away from the street.

She called up with chattering teeth. "Do you think we'll reach the hospital tonight?"

Tom shook his head, shuddering as a chill ran across his shoulders. "I doubt it. We're not making good time, and Jerry mentioned earlier that we still have several miles to go. We should probably find a place to rest for the night."

"Like in one of those," Sam asked, pointing past him to a pair of hotels just off the road. One was a medium-scale, travel-style hotel, but the windows were dark and roughly a dozen people milled around the parking lot as three guards in flannel shirts stood at the entrance, all with shotguns in hand.

"Who are the people with the guns?" Sam asked.

"Probably the owners," Tom replied, tersely. "I'd bet they're trying to keep looters out of the hotel."

"What about the other place?"

Tom shifted his attention to a dingy motel squatting next to the nicer one. It was a single-story affair with grungy walls and busted screens on the windows. Its power was on, but the place didn't have any customers and a half-dead neon sign stood atop a tall pole with the words, "The Château," scrawled in fancy letters, a few of them dark and a few flickering ominously.

"It's only forty bucks for the night," Tom said. "I don't have the cash, but I do have my credit cards."

"If they still work," Sam added.

"The power's on." Tom's tone was doubtful, but he couldn't ignore their sheer exhaustion and the ache in his shoulders. "I say we give it a try." He started down the exit ramp, gesturing for the other two to keep up.

Sam frowned as they drew near. "It looks like something from a horror movie."

"Beggars can't be choosers," Tom replied over his shoulder. "You good with this, Jerry?"

"Only if it has Free HBO," he quipped tiredly. "Seriously, I'm more than fine with it. I could pass out right where I'm standing."

Tom chuckled but moved faster down the ramp and soon he and Sam had left the young man behind and had to stop and wait for him.

"I'm not a huge horror movie fan," Tom mumbled, "but I've seen zombies move faster than you."

"That's a good one." Jerry chuckled, his grin sluggish.

"You're definitely not winning the Zombie Olympics," Sam snorted.

"Oh, great. You guys are teaming up on me now."

"Just kidding." Tom leaned down, offering his shoulder.

"I know, me too." Jerry threw his arm around Tom's neck, and they made faster time to the end of the ramp. At the intersection, he looked both ways out of habit before crossing diagonally to the other corner, trudging warily past the folks in the commercial hotel lot who appeared to be setting up camp. They sat on suitcases and the pavement with light blankets thrown over them, seeming more tired than threatening, so the trio continued down the sidewalk, angling into the Château Motel toward its front desk.

Beneath a bent and dripping awning, Tom allowed Jerry to stand on his own while he peered in through the glass. While the lights remained on, no one stood at the front desk. He knocked on the glass door and waited, but no one came, then he tried pushing it open, but it was locked.

"This isn't good," he mumbled.

"Maybe it's an omen," Jerry said. "Fate is telling us not to stay here."

"Or maybe they just don't want zombies," Sam fired back.

"Very funny."

Tom ignored the two and pulled out his cell phone. He dialed the number written below the address on the door, but the phone didn't ring inside the office. He stuck the device back in his pocket when he realized service was down, anyway.

"Why don't we just break in?" Jerry asked.

"Because I don't want to destroy their property." Tom shook his head as he turned to the young man. "Plus, I don't want to get arrested."

"You're right," the young man replied. "But is it okay if I sit here for a minute?" He didn't wait for Tom's answer but put his back against the glass and slid down.

Tom took a good look at the pair beneath the awning lights. Sam's shoulders slumped as she bore the burden of her backpack and Jerry's bag, dirt smudged her face, and her clothes were soggy and dingy, her tennis shoes looking like they had a hole developing on top. And, while they'd been making zombie jokes all night, the young man really did appear dead where he sat on the concrete, his back against the lobby glass and his head in his arms. For his part, Tom's feet throbbed, and his back felt strained and weak on the lower left side, stretched thin like beaten leather.

"You know what?" He shook his head. "Breaking in isn't such a bad idea. I'll leave the owners a note on how to get hold of me for payment, and I'll cover any damage we do."

"You don't have to explain to us, Dad." Sam's greenish eyes looked drained in the dirty yellow light. "I mean, look at us. We all need to rest. We know you'll make good."

"Okay." Tom nodded and gestured. "Let's walk around and see if there's an easy way in… and one that's a bit less out in the open for folks to see us if we end up having to break something to get in. Jerry, do you want to stay here?"

"As much as that appeals to me, I'd rather stick with you guys." Leveraging himself against the glass, he wiggled upward until he was standing once more. "Oh man, I have blisters on my blisters."

"We all do," Tom acknowledged, glancing at his dirty shoes.

With the decision made, he stepped away from the entrance and walked along the row of rooms while Sam and Jerry dragged their feet behind him. He tried a few of the door handles and found them all locked, and the curtains drawn. Two cars sat in front of a pair of rooms, and Tom didn't try those for fear of disturbing someone. As they went, he glanced out toward the street, on guard for anyone who might try to challenge them, and when they reached the end of the row with no clear way in, Tom guided them around to the back where they stepped into a mushy yard of soaked grass.

"What are we looking for?" Jerry asked as they splashed through the wetness.

"There." Tom pulled out his flashlight, flipped it on, and pointed it at a rectangular window about eye level. "The glass is opaque, so it's probably for the bathroom. I figure someone might have left one open. If so, maybe Sam can crawl through. That way, we don't have to break any doors or windows."

Jerry nodded. "Good thinking."

Tom walked along the building's rear, stepping around trash, small branches, and other garbage left by the storm, the water squelching in his shoes, pouring into the shoestring eyelets, chilling his feet to the bone. As they went, he reached out and pushed against all the windows, but none opened. He tried a back door that likely led to a storage room, but found it locked and when they reached the back of the lobby, Tom saw the back door standing open. His eyes traced the doorframe and pavement, his chest clenching, arm thrown out to keep Sam and Jerry from moving any farther.

Sam bristled at her father's sudden caution, her eyes settling on the open door, searching the area to see what he saw. "What's wrong?"

He shushed her softly and crept forward with the pair sticking close behind him. Light poured out of the open doorway to illuminate the pried frame, a short, round-nosed shovel leaning off to the side. Shining his flashlight at the ground, bright red splashes leapt out in the blossoming beam.

"That's blood," he hissed, immediately gesturing for the pair to move away. "Stay back."

Sam took hold of Jerry's arm and guided him backwards. Tom tossed his daughter his flashlight and bent to snatch the shovel off the ground, leveling the blade like a spear, moving cautiously toward the door, head ticking sideways as he listened. He stepped inside an office storeroom with an old desk backed into the corner and several chairs stacked three high next to it, file cabinets lining the right-hand wall and messily folded linens sitting on the left.

The door on the room's opposite side hung open, and light poured through as Tom snuck across the floor and stepped into a short hallway that smelled of dust and mildew. The main office and lobby lay off to the right, but the blood trail continued to a second door opposite him. It hung open a foot. Nothing stirred, nothing made a sound, yet the hairs on the back of Tom's neck lifted on their own, followed by a chill running down his spine. He shook off the fearful cold feeling and crept across the hall to listen at the threshold. When no sound reached him, he put his left hand against the door and gave it a gentle shove, quickly re-gripping the shovel, holding the pointed end forward in case someone came at him.

It was a quiet hotel office with a metal desk sitting near the opposite wall, papers scattered across its surface and on the floor. A pair of chairs had toppled over, and the air was heavy with the coppery smell of blood. Tom stepped farther into the room, crouched with a white-knuckled grip on his weapon, ready to thrust it at the first sign of a threat. Something tickled his stomach, instincts kicking up and he wheeled and slammed the door shut, bringing the shovel up to strike.

No one was there and he sidestepped to the right, peering around the desk, instantly wincing at the scene of carnage in the back corner of the room. A man and woman wearing staff uniforms lay next to a partially opened safe. The man rested with his back against the wall, slumped over a lap full of blood while the woman lay face down on the other side of the safe, one arm thrown up, a wicked gash on the back of her skull.

Bile rose in Tom's throat as he placed the shovel on the desk and knelt next to the man, touching his cold arm before squatting and twisting, moving to the woman and putting his fingers on her bloody neck. Like the man, her skin was as frigid as the weather outside, and he felt no pulse.

Standing up, Tom retreated two steps and placed his hands on his hips, shaking his head in revulsion and sadness. His eyes slid to the safe, noting the door was cracked. Whoever had hurt the poor souls had gotten what they wanted, and a version of the probable events formed in his mind like a movie reel.

He imagined the criminals breaking in through the back door, using the shovel to wedge the door open. He pictured the frightened employees cowering in the office as the intruder rifled through the place. In the process of searching the premises, the intruder had found their safe and the two hiding there. They'd commanded the employees to open the safe before the deadly scuffle broke out, and then managed to open it anyway, with or without the employees' help. Tom imagined a hundred similar robberies all around the city - maybe even thousands of them along the coast. The storm was like Christmas for opportunistic criminals everywhere, and when mixed with the other, more serious threats, it was a wonder things weren't worse than they already were.

The scent of blood filled his stomach with disgust, and though his stomach protested, he performed a quick search of the desk drawers, turning up a master keycard to all the rooms. Grabbing the shovel, he exited the room, closing the door quietly behind him.

"Dad, are you okay in there?" That was Sam, calling from outside.

"I'm fine, honey. Coming out now."

He moved across the hall and through the messy storeroom, stepping out into the chilly night once more. Sam and Jerry both looked miserable and cold, though it was better than the fate of the employees inside.

"What's in there?" the young man asked.

"You don't want to know," Tom replied grimly, holding the card up. "I've got a master key and we have a place to rest. That's the most important thing."

"Score," Jerry said, falling in behind him as they moved around to the front of the hotel.

"Why don't we want to know what happened in there?" Sam asked, tagging along.

"Because it's bad."

"Like, *bad* bad?"

"Exactly like that," Tom agreed. "Someone robbed the place and killed two employees inside. It's an ugly scene, trust me."

Sam clamped her mouth shut, her expression grim, her face unreadable. Back in front, Tom looked along the row of rooms to see which one would be best. They were all pretty much the same, though a few near the office appeared to be larger suites. They wouldn't be fancy, but the more space the better, particularly since splitting up would put them at a disadvantage. He chose #7, putting the key against the reader and listening to the satisfying click as the bolt popped before pushing the door open and squeezing inside, flipping on a light.

"Welcome to the presidential suite," Tom announced with a flourish at the good-sized room with two queen-sized beds, a couch, a desk, a vanity sink, and a small kitchen-style table with a pair of chairs.

He let the others in and shut the door behind them, throwing the deadbolt and letting his backpack slide to the floor. He immediately went to the blinds and separated them with his fingers, looking out in the parking lot to see if anyone had noticed their intrusion.

Sam shuffled to the table and slung Jerry's bag of snacks on it before letting her own backpack slide off with a sigh. She wobbled backwards, trying to shrug off her coat but failing before her legs hit the bed. Collapsing back, she hit the mattress hard, arms spread wide, a gust of air bursting from her lungs, and less than twenty seconds later her light snores filled the room. Tom turned and saw her lying with her jacket half-on, mouth hanging open and strands of wet hair across her face.

"Out cold," Jerry said, looking over. "That's about how I feel."

Tom moved to the nightstand between the beds, flipped on the light, and went back to turn off the main switch, satisfied with the much dimmer room. "Better." *And safer*, he thought.

"I wonder how the power is on here but not in the other hotel?" Jerry eased himself down onto the edge of the second bed.

"I'm not a hundred percent sure." Tom circled over to Sam and helped get her jacket the rest of the way off. The girl groaned as he removed one arm, then the other, shifting her body so he could pull the coat from beneath her. "I don't think this place would have a generator, so it might just be the luck of the grid. You know how sometimes one subdivision block can have electricity but everything around it is dead?"

"We go through it every hurricane season." Jerry nodded.

He held up Sam's soggy jacket and hung it on the back of a chair to dry, then he bent down to remove her shoes and socks.

"I'll see if we've got hot water." Jerry stood and walked into the bathroom.

"Hey, check and make sure there's a window back there," Tom called, placing Sam's shoes aside and peeling her wet socks from her feet.

"Roger that," came the reply.

Wet socks and shoes in hand, he crossed over to the air conditioning unit by the window and, flipping up the control panel hood, Tom pressed the button for the heat, setting it for low to get started. Despite the power being on, their streak of bad luck refused to let him believe that it would turn on until it finally did. Reaching out, he held up his hands to the vent until warm air flowed, then he increased the power to medium and draped Sam's socks over the top. A nearby chair was placed in front of the heater next, shoes arranged in the seat to warm them up and dry them off.

The sound of water bursting from a nozzle came from the bathroom, and five seconds later, Jerry gave a pleased whoop.

The young man's head poked out. "We've got hot water!"

"And the window?"

"Yep, just like all the other rooms. Sam can definitely fit through. It'll be a tight fit for us, though."

"That's good enough." Tom gave a satisfied nod. "Why don't you take a shower and get warmed up. Throw your shoes and socks over here and I'll start them drying."

"That's the best part." Jerry grinned. "There's a mini washer and dryer in here, too."

"Oh, that is *great*." Tom closed his eyes in relief. "We'll still use the air conditioner to dry our shoes, but the rest of our clothes can go in the washers."

"Are you sure you don't want to go first?" Jerry sat in a chair, reached down, and untied his laces with his good hand.

"No, you go ahead." Tom sat on the edge of the second bed and removed his own socks and shoes. "Do you need help?"

"I got it," Jerry said. A burst of excited adrenaline fueled the young man, and his shoes and socks were on the floor in less than a minute. Tom chuckled, glad to finally be in a safe, warm room for the first time all day. Jerry tried to scoop up his wet articles when Tom waved him off. "Leave them there. I'll get them."

"Thanks." Jerry turned and walked gingerly into the bathroom where steam was already leaking out.

"Make sure you take off your sling," Tom called in as he collected his things. "And be careful with your head. Let me know if you need any help."

"Yes, sir," Jerry called back just before the door shut.

Tom placed the young man's socks and shoes on the chair and vents to dry. There wasn't quite enough room for them all to sit in front of the warm air flow at the same time, but he could easily rotate them and make sure they got equal time in the heat.

He stood with a groan, luxuriating in the feel of his bare feet on the dry, prickly carpet. Back aching, shoulders sore from carrying the backpack all day, Tom rolled his shoulders and went to check on Sam. He hated letting her sleep in damp clothes, but they didn't have anything else to wear until they could take stock and dry out. Lifting her legs, he straightened her out and then put his arms beneath her to reposition her so her head lay on the pillow. She groaned and mumbled weakly in protest, her body shivering as a throw cover from the couch went over her shoulders, then she curled up on her side with a contented sigh.

Moving back to the air unit, he turned the heat to high, readjusted their shoes, and peered between the blinds once more. The lot was quiet except for an occasional passing car on the expressway and the sounds of voices from the next hotel over; if anyone had noticed them entering their room, they either didn't care or had bigger fish to fry. Tom rolled his shoulders again and allowed some built-up tension to escape. Despite feeling safer, his mind wouldn't rest. Taking his backpack to the table, he put two chairs side-by-side and moved Sam and Jerry's packs over to make room, then he opened them up and began unpacking the contents into organized stacks on the table.

He pulled out three ragged boxes of donuts and placed them in a row, followed by fifteen pure-protein energy bars, twenty-two bottled waters, seven caffeinated energy drinks, a box of meat sticks, and a smaller pack of spicy jerky plus a small plastic bin of scones from the coffee shop.

"Coffee."

Tom stepped to the long bureau with the TV and complimentary coffee maker. Filling up the pot from the vanity sink, he tore open a pack of coffee and started a fresh brew, then he found the TV remote and took it with him back to the table, flipping on the TV to white noise while he continued with their inventory.

There were four flashlights, some rope, tape, and scissors, three pillows from the RV, his first aid kit, phone charger, and an assortment of clothing harvested from suitcases. While they were wearing most of what they'd found to keep themselves warm, they still had some extra T-shirts and socks in their packs. Tom placed the garments over the back of a chair and went to fetch his coffee, stirring in some powdered cream and sugar. He stepped away from the TV with his beverage in one hand and the remote in the other. Pointing it at the screen, he flipped through channels not expecting to find anything, though in two clicks, a distorted image of a news broadcast with broken audio bled through.

"Must be picking up a local station on the antennae," he said to himself as he took the first sip of coffee, the cheap, bitter brew warming his throat and stomach, tasting like it had come from heaven itself. Tom backed up and sat on the bed near Sam's feet, lifting the remote and turning up the volume.

"...the president is backing a statewide of emergency for all East Coast cities as floodwaters continue to rise. Experts say the freshwater surge from the anomaly hasn't slowed down and is still spewing billions of gallons of freshwater into the ocean. Emergency services are urging residents to remain calm and report any incidents of looting to the local police..."

"There's more than looting going on, lady." Tom shook his head. "There's murder. Plus, how can we call if our cell phones aren't working?"

The thought of his cellphone reminded him that he'd actually been able to receive and send texts at one point, so he placed the remote on a table and pulled his phone from his pocket. A quick check revealed no new messages from Barbara, though, and he still couldn't reach the internet through a browser app. With a sigh, Tom retrieved the phone charger and plugged his device into the wall, listening as the news broadcast continued.

"... Canada's Prime Minister praised President John Zimmerman for putting a bold face on a difficult situation. The US President's speech is on replay around the world as countries cope with the ramifications of rising waters and cooling temperatures. Mexico's President, Juan Carlos Esposito re-iterated their alliance with the United States, though we have no word yet on whether the two countries are actively developing a plan to..."

The sound turned garbled, voices warbling and drowned out by static before clearing five seconds later, though Tom had heard enough. He lowered the volume and shivered as the hot coffee worked through his veins, throwing off the chill, feeling more energized than he had in days in spite of his exhaustion. The bathroom door opened behind him and he turned to see Jerry peeking out in a burst of warm steam, wearing a big, fluffy robe, his hair hung damp on his forehead, and his cheeks a rosy color.

"That was amazing." The young man spoke in a whisper.

"How's the arm?" Tom asked, waving him out. "Let's see."

Jerry stepped into the room and slowly flexed his limb. "It doesn't feel bad, actually. I can move it, at least."

"I want to see the skin." Tom gestured and Jerry came over and gently tugged up the robe's sleeve. Tom could barely see in the shadowy light, and he set his coffee cup down, turning the young man toward a lamp resting on the bureau, flipping it on and raising the wounded arm and its pinkish flesh.

"It doesn't look too bad," Tom said, inspecting the scuffs. "I think the bandage kept the infection out. Here, let's redress it."

They moved over to their supplies, Jerry taking a chair. Tom opened his first aid kit, kneeling next to the young man, removing the tube of antiseptic and the rest of his gauze and bandages, placing them in a row at the table's edge.

"Do you think whoever broke in the place is still around?"

Tom shrugged. "I'm honestly not sure, but I hope not."

"I mean, how bad were the people--"

"Killed?" Tom raised his eyebrows. "Pretty much all the way. Dead as doornails, as the saying goes."

"I mean, how did it happen?"

"Does it really matter?"

The young man shrugged as Tom applied ointment to the skinned parts of his arm.

"Blunt force, from the looks of things. But I think we should drop the subject," he sighed. "It'll only make you nervous. We need to stay vigilant, but we also need to stay focused on what we can control."

"Right."

Jerry sat quietly for a minute as Tom used a cotton swab to spread the ointment over his skin. The young man winced a time or two, but otherwise handled the discomfort well.

"Where are you from?" Jerry asked. "I mean, I know you live in Virginia now, but originally?"

"Ah. Well, I was a military brat, son of an Army Colonel. We moved around a lot as a kid. It was tough making friends, but I had my books. I mean, they traveled with me, you know?"

"I know," Jerry responded with a nod.

"It was a blessing in disguise. It kept me out of trouble and got me into MIT."

"I didn't realize you went to school there, but it doesn't surprise me. Not after you figured out the whole temperature thing."

"I just put two and two together."

"Two plus two is surprisingly hard for a lot of people, if you know what I mean."

Tom glanced up. Jerry's eyelids lay half shut, his previous burst of energy waning in light of the soothing shower and medical treatment.

Jerry continued. "Do you think people understand it's going to get *way* cold? Like, not just a few degrees."

"We don't know that for sure."

"We kind of do. It's still the end of summer, and I shouldn't be able to step outside and see my breath. And the RV window back in the tunnel. It had a layer of ice on it."

"Two valid points," Tom admitted with a wry smile. "Hopefully, things level off and it doesn't get much worse. At least not until people are able to prepare."

"Do you think..." Jerry let his words trail off.

"What?"

"Do you think people will be forced to move south? I mean, if it gets really bad up north, how long could they stay in the northern latitudes?"

"That's a question I don't think anyone can answer." Tom forced a thin smile. "At least not until some time passes."

"Let's hope that doesn't happen," Jerry finished.

"I agree with you there."

Tom finished bandaging Jerry's arm and let his robe sleeve fall. "All done. Why don't you take the second bed and get some sleep?"

"Best thing I've heard all day."

Jerry stood and shuffled over to the other bed, throwing back a corner of covers, climbing in and crawling beneath them. He rested his head gently on the pillow with a sigh. Smiling wanly, Tom sipped his coffee and moved to the blinds. Fingers pressed between the slats, he separated them and peered into the dark parking lot yet again. The lights from the Château's sign and building glinted off the puddles, raindrops falling in a light drizzle, but no one appeared to be watching from the shadows and no groups of people gathered in the lot. They were, it would seem, safe.

Tom grabbed one of the unused chairs, turned it around, and wedged it beneath the door handle before killing the television and both lamps, leaving him with a sliver of light from the bathroom to see by. He picked a dry pair of jeans, a T-shirt, and socks from the pile of things and laid them out on the table, then he gathered all the dirty clothes and took them into the bathroom. Shutting the door, he stripped down and threw everything in the washing machine. With laundry soap from the cabinet, Tom started their first load, the thought of clean, dry clothes boosting his mood through the weariness and aches coursing through his body.

He turned on the shower and held his hand beneath the steaming hot spray, a shiver running up the back of his legs as he stepped in and got beneath the piping hot spray. He'd originally wanted to get in and out as quickly as possible but ended up staying in for an extended length of time, washing up and standing beneath the spigot's hard spray as it pounded down on his shoulders, the steaming water washing away both dirt and the aches from his sore muscles.

Ten minutes later, he felt like a regular human being again and once dressed, he found his way to the couch, taking his coffee with him, his thoughts drifting to Barbara and the kids back home. Tom and Sam being gone had undoubtedly been hard on them, especially as they would have seen the news and started preparing for the diminishing temperatures, particularly if they had worked on getting any remaining crops harvested. Even with Tom and Sam's help it was a multi-day project just to get them gathered, nevermind the processing and storage. *We'll be there soon enough*, he thought, *just hold out a little while longer*.

Tom's thoughts were interrupted by the ding of the washer, and after he flipped the clean laundry to the dryer he returned to the couch, laid down and stuffed a throw pillow behind his head, relaxing with a sigh. He closed his eyes, his mind returning to his family as he imagined Barbara standing by the field, directing the youngsters on what to harvest while Smooch ran around barking like crazy. The dog would try to distract Jack and keep him from his duties, but the boy's mother would get control of that situation quick. She'd order the German Shepherd away and get their son back to picking, ruling over the activities like a fair but ruthless dictator, ensuring that no matter what happened, the family would be kept safe and secure.

Tom allowed himself a tentative smile as weariness forced him to shut down. He finally surrendered to it, drifting into a peaceful sleep devoid of screaming wind and rain and murderous people, filled with thoughts of seeing his family once again.

Chapter 16
Barbara McKnight
Wyndale, Virginia

"I won't tell you again," the man snarled. "Drop the rifle and put your hands in the air."

"Let me see my son," Barbara demanded, trying to keep the quake out of her voice. "I want to see a show of good faith."

She heard a shuffling sound from the foot of the stairwell. A moment later, a short man with a crop of dark hair shoved Jack around the banister and squared to face her. His left hand gripped the boy's neck, his right hand holding a pistol to the back of his head. Jack blinked at her with big brown eyes, fear written across his face and Barbara quelled the instinctual urge to take the man's head off, as she'd risk hitting her son or cause the man to fire his gun. She turned the barrel to the side, keeping it pinned on the dining room entrance as the man took two steps into the hall and stood beneath the second-floor landing, using Jack as a shield.

"Here's your son." His eyes ticked to Barbara's rifle. "Now, put it down."

"If I put down my gun, you'll kill us."

"Not true." The man shook his head, brow pinched in the middle. "Me and my buddy just want your stuff. We'll fill your pickup with supplies and guns then be on our way. I want to be in Kentucky by morning."

The short guy's partner stepped into the foyer behind the leader, holding a pistol at his side. He was one of the men she'd hit with buckshot the other day and his work shirt seemed puffier on his left torso, likely bulging due to a thick bandage.

Keeping her face hidden, Barbara looked at the man's injury, "But I killed three of your friends and hurt another."

"Not friends. I recruited them from one of the markets earlier. Told them I knew someone who had tons of supplies. I've only known them a few hours." He smiled cruelly. "Why do you think I sent them in first? You sure did a number on them, I'll give you that."

"So, you don't want revenge?"

"I want to get the hell out of Virginia," the man growled. "And I don't want to shoot a kid, for real. It's not something I want on my conscience. Just lay down your weapon, let us load up, and we'll go."

Barbara weighed her options, finding none that were good given Jack's predicament. "Okay. Fine." The words had to be forced out, like the last bit of toothpaste from an empty tube. "I'll... I'll put my gun down."

"Good decision." The man looked visibly relieved.

Barbara held her weapon horizontally and stooped, bending at the knees, placing it on the floor while shooting Smooch a quick warning glance. The dog sat obediently on the top step, her left paw slightly raised and head low, her snout pointed toward the hallway, lips drawn back to expose her fangs.

Free of her weapon, Barbara stood and raised her hands, and the man shifted the gun from Jack's head to aim it at her stomach. Relief washed over her, glad to have Jack in slightly less danger despite her own peril.

"Now, where's that mutt of yours?" The man pushed Jack forward another foot.

"She's at the top of the stairs." Barbara's eyes flicked to the door. "Injured."

"Call her over. I can't have her running around while we're trying to complete our business."

Smooch's lips were still drawn in a half snarl, and while Barbara had no doubt she'd throw herself into harm's way if given the opportunity, the dog was as much of a weapon as her rifle. If used at the wrong moment, she could end up causing more harm than good.

"I can take her downstairs and lock her in a room," she offered.

"You can take her outside and chain her up," the man commanded, squeezing Jack's neck.

"Ouch," the boy said, whining, tears at the edges of his eyes.

Smooch growled deep in her chest, her lips curled up to reveal the full extent of her polished white fangs.

"If you can't get control of the animal," the man waved his weapon at the basement stairs, "I swear I'll put it down!"

"No!" Barbara's eyes watered at the thought of it. She'd been holding back feelings of anger and desperation for the past ten minutes, struggling to stay strong for Jack's sake, and the dam suddenly broke, hot tears streaking down her cheeks, her breath coming in gasps. "I'll just shut the door, okay? Just don't hurt my son, please!"

Jack's lips quivered at the sight of his mother crying. "It's okay, Mom..."

"Let's go," the man waved his gun. "Get the dog. I'm starting to lose pati--"

A vehicle flew up the driveway in a rumble of gravel and the man stepped away from Jack, peering out the sidelight. He still held the boy's neck, but there was space between them, his gun sliding to the side so the weapon was pointed at the wall. Barbara made a break for her rifle, but there wasn't enough time to guarantee a kill shot. If she made a single mistake then she – or worse, her son – would pay the price. The man turned back, adjusting his grip on Jack's neck and giving the boy a little shake.

"Who is that?!"

"Oww!" Jack yelped and squirmed. "You're hurting me!"

"Why don't you shut up?" The man redoubled his grip, drawing a high-pitched squeal from the boy. Barbara held out her hand as if to intervene, as though she could reach out with an invisible hand and grab her son back, but Linda got to him first.

"Get off my brother!" The cry went out from the top of the stairs a split second before shots rained down from the landing above, transforming the tense scene into a whirlwind of light and noise. Two rounds shattered the hardwood but at least one struck the man as he dove ahead, shoving Jack in front of him, eliciting a pained howl as he moved.

Body surging into motion, Barbara launched herself at the man, slamming into him as her son tumbled past them and they went down in a tangle of arms and legs, Barbara clawing at his face, biting and scratching at any exposed skin. The man raised his pistol to shoot her, but Smooch was already beside her master, clamping down with her fangs onto his wrist and jerking his hand up so his two shots struck the ceiling, gun flying away to clatter across the floor.

The man screamed and swung his free fist, hitting Barbara with a glancing blow across her head, though instead of disabling her it empowered her, an instinctual rage blossoming in her chest as chills streaked up her back. She would end the man. Death was no longer an option. Only victory.

Face buried in his neck, teeth clamping on the soft, hot flesh of his throat, she bit down, her jaw clenching tight, the muscles and tendons beneath the skin of his neck stretched taut as she gnawed. His flesh broke, and she tasted blood as it gushed between her lips, the man letting out a guttural, panicked cry as he panicked, shoving her away, punching, striking her with three glancing blows across her cheeks and chin.

Stars exploded in Barbara's head as her hold loosened but she shrugged off the pain, shifting her hold, grabbing the bite wound with her fingers and digging her nails into the broken flesh. The man thrashed and bucked, but he only had one free hand as Smooch tore and ripped at his forearm and wrist, rending them to shreds. Warm liquid sprayed across Barbara's face, followed by a hot, salty, penny-rich taste on her lips. A major artery had been torn based on the amount of blood on herself and the floor – but by which one of them, Smooch or herself, she didn't know.

His attempts to hit her turned into a flailing escape, screaming as he tried to fight off the tenacious, blood-soaked woman and her dog. But Barbara had latched on to him, using her weight to keep him pinned, Smooch's tugging keeping his one arm out of the fight. The man grunted and spat, bucking once more before a sudden weakness took him and he fell back against the tiles.

Finally, as the last of his life drained out of him, Barbara let go of his throat, blood dripping from her lips and chin as she slowly stood, a crimson avenging spirit, locking eyes with the last intruder at the end of the hall. While he still held his gun, it shook in his hand, his face a mask of horror at the sight before him, Barbara and Smooch both slowly stepping over the shredded corpse at their feet, beginning to make their way down the hall.

Caught in a vengeful bloodlust, Barbara flinched as her own name found its way through to her still-ringing ears, realizing after a long moment that it was Darren, calling out to her, his voice sounding small and far-off, echoing from a different world altogether.

"Barbara!"

She snapped back to reality at Darren's bellow, glancing down at her red-stained hands, then back up at the man in front of her who was backing away, gun hand shaking even worse than before.

"Be careful, Darren!" Barbara yelled as she searched around for her rifle, the man giving her a final terrified expression, eyes ticking between her, her dog and the second-floor landing before he threw open the front door and lunged outside, his gun raised. As soon as he stepped out, several rounds of incoming fire peppered his body and he stumbled and crashed in the yard.

"Mom!"

"Oh, baby," Barbara cried as she grabbed Jack, squeezing him tightly to her chest, red transferring from her soaking clothing onto his arms and skin as she held him, kissing his cheeks, wanting nothing more than to hold him and never let go. "Where's your sister? Linda? Linda!"

Without waiting for his reply, Barbara pulled Jack along beside her, staggering along the hallway as she called up. "Linda! Linda! Are you up there?"

She reached the bottom of the stairwell, eyes cast upward as her stomach twisted with dread, not wanting to see what had become of her daughter but forcing herself to look, anyway.

To her deep relief, Linda flew down the stairs taking two at a time. "Mom! Mom!"

"Baby!"

Barbara caught her on the way down, the girl's weight driving her to her knees. She gripped Jack in her right arm, Linda in her left, squeezing her children tight.

Darren was visible through the open doorway, standing in the yard, rifle pointed at the man he'd shot while he nudged the body with the toe of his boot. Marie was moving fast up the walkway, holding her AR-15 with the barrel pointed upward, rushing to the front stoop where she took one look at the blood covering Barbara's face, hands, and chest, gasping in shock.

"Are you okay?" the woman asked with breathless concern. "Is there anyone else in the house?"

Barbara nodded slowly, then shook her head with indecision. "I think there were only five, but I'm not certain."

Marie gave a terse nod and marched down the hallway only to be met by a limping Smooch. Blood smeared the German Shepherd's face and chest, her fur a wet, ruddy brown color. She whined painfully but still pushed forward, intent on making her way back to her master.

"Smooch!" Jack cried, seeing the wounded animal, breaking from Barbara's grasp to run to her. The boy skidded to his knees, throwing his arms around her neck, her nuzzling him with her bloody muzzle, whining and whimpering the whole while.

"Careful," she warned. "Poor girl is hurt bad."

195

"Smooch, no!" Jack cried, releasing the dog and gently touching at the fur surrounding her injured neck. "What did they do to her?"

"I think she'll be okay, honey," Barbara assured him, more a side thought than anything else. "Just be careful with her, okay?"

"Okay." Jack nodded, his bottom lip sticking out.

Barbara wrapped both arms around Linda, squeezing her once before holding her away. "What happened? Where did you go? Why weren't you with your brother?"

Linda's cheeks were wet, her eyes swollen from crying. "I'm so sorry, Mom. Really, I am. We heard the gunshots. I got the gun from Sam's bathroom, just like last time. Then I ran to Jack's bedroom like I was supposed to, but he wasn't there. That's when the man came up and found him in the *other* bathroom. He shot his gun, and I got scared. I hid under the bed and waited. I'm so sorry."

"That was a good decision," Barbara dismissed her apology, "You did amazing, sweetie."

"I snuck out when I heard your voice," Linda continued. "I watched the whole time until I found my chance."

"That was a good shot," Barbara smiled, holding Linda out at arm's length, wiping a bit of red from her daughter's cheek. "Weren't you worried about hitting your brother?"

Linda was already shaking her head. "No way, mom. The men got distracted by Darren coming. I watched the guy who had Jack. His gun was moving around. I knew I could hit him! I just knew I could!"

Linda's expression was so fierce and full of fire that Barbara didn't doubt her for a second.

"Did I do bad?" Linda's expression began to droop, and Barbara gripped Linda's arm, staring hard into her eyes as relief and pride coursed through her body, filling her heart and chest.

"No, baby. You didn't do bad. You did so good. And I love you more than I can even explain right now. You did so, so good." Linda's smile returned, shining like a gift of gold.

Shoes shuffled on the porch and stepped into the foyer, and Barbara glanced up to see Darren watching them with a drawn expression, his face going pale when he saw the blood spattered across most of Barbara's body.

"Why don't you two run some warm water in a pan for Smooch," she said, standing and addressing her children. "We need to get her cleaned up and see how bad she's hurt. Go through the dining room. The hallway is..."

She glanced at the intruder lying near the kitchen table in a massive pool of blood. There were corpses in the house, her children had witnessed – and taken part in – the slaughter, and there was no use in trying to hide it from them. That small sliver of innocence was forever gone, and no matter how much it bothered her, she'd have to learn to give it up.

Barbara sighed and shook her head, watching as Linda and Jack hustled through the dining room and entered the kitchen, going for the pots and pans below the sink, Smooch trailing behind as Jack talked to her.

Watching her children alongside her, Darren spoke in a low, grim voice. "I'd ask if I killed that asshole outside for a good reason, but after seeing this…." He trailed off, looking at the bodies, letting out a low whistle. "Are you okay?"

"You did," she nodded, sniffling as she turned to face him, throwing her arms around the man's wide, round shoulders. "And I am. Emotionally, anyway."

"Sorry if I got here a little late." Darren patted her on the back, giving her a gentle squeeze.

"You were right on time." The tears flowed from Barbara's eyes, carving out paths of white among the red.

"Well, that'd be a first," Darren chuckled. "Make sure you tell Marie that. She's always complaining how late I am."

Marie marched up the front path on cue, stepping inside, eyes narrow slivers as she glanced in the corners of the room.

"I checked all around the house and didn't see anyone," Marie said, breathlessly. "I think we're clear."

Barbara nodded, her emotions on the edge of breaking, expression slack as she started wiping the blood and tears off her face with a conflicting sense of horror and relief.

Marie rested her rifle against the door and threw her arms wide. "Come here, darling. It looks like you could use another hug."

"I could use about a hundred hugs," she replied with trembling lips.

Barbara fell into Marie's embrace as Darren patted her gently on the shoulder, crying on her friend's shirt, smearing her with blood as distant thunder boomed and rumbled across the evening sky.

Chapter 17
Tom McKnight
Virginia Beach, Virginia

Tom woke shivering on the couch, shoulders shot through with a chill. He turned onto his side and curled into a ball, bringing his knees tight against his chest, but even that didn't help, and he continued to feel the deep cold settling into his bones. With the temperature too much to ignore, he opened his eyes, greeted by a silent, relatively dark room, lit only by the shades of pale light entering from the bathroom window and around the blinds.

Sitting up with a grumble, Tom yawned and smacked his lips, checking his watch to see it was 10:17 AM. He leaned forward, snatching a bottled water he'd been drinking from off the table. Top off, he tilted it back and took a mouthful, swishing it around before standing to spit it in the vanity sink before moving to Samantha's bedside. Sometime during the night, she'd tossed off the throw cover and climbed beneath the sheets and comforter to bury herself in piles of warmth. Lifting one corner, he saw she was clutching a pillow to her chest, holding another tucked between her knees.

He leaned down and gave her shoulder a shake. "Hey, Sam. It's time to get up. We need to get moving again."

"What time is it?" she asked with a stir.

"Almost ten thirty in the morning. I think we got some pretty good sleep last night, but the power went out."

Samantha put her arm outside the covers for a moment before grabbing the corner and throwing it back over her head. "Too cold!" she cried.

"Not too cold," Tom replied and flipped it back down.

"Bad dad," Sam said, snatching the blankets and diving beneath them once more. "Too cold. Sleep."

"You've got two minutes to get up and moving." Tom circled around to the other bed. "We need to get back on the road pronto."

He did the same to Jerry, pulling the covers down and giving him a gentle shake on the shoulder, careful not to touch his wounded arm.

"What time is it?" The young man moaned as he stretched his legs beneath the blankets.

"Time to get up," Tom muttered. He gave the young man's foot a wag as he went by. "We need to pack up and get moving. With the power out this is no longer a safe harbor."

Tom went to the dryer and retrieved his and Jerry's clothes, bringing them out and tossing them at the foot of the bed.

"Sorry, Sam," he shrugged at her. "You wore your clothes to bed."

"Did she get a shower?" Jerry suddenly sprang from beneath the covers and sorted through his clothes, still favoring his injured arm, tucking it close to his chest. "Did she already have coffee?"

"No, and *no*." Samantha finally tossed off the blankets with a wistful smile. "But I slept so good."

"You might want to try the shower anyway," Tom said. "The water heaters are insulated and if it's a gas water heater, it might still work depending on how it's lit." Tom motioned at the chair where he'd hung fresh garments. "You should be able to find some dry clothes in here, too."

Sam climbed out of bed and disappeared into the bathroom. Door shut behind her, she began rummaging around and soon, water burst from the shower spigot, then ten seconds later, Sam gave a happy cheer.

"Must be working," Tom smiled.

Jerry and Tom changed into freshly washed clothes, the soft material brushing wonderfully against their skin. Tom pulled on two pairs of socks and an extra sweatshirt over his T-shirt, grunting as he forced the garments over each other.

"Hopefully, we can stay dry this time." Tom smoothed out the wrinkles in his shirt. "Last thing we need is to get wet and cold all over again."

"What's the plan for today?"

"I'd like to salvage a few things from the hotel," Tom said, "then hit the road. How's your arm?"

"Much better, surprisingly." Jerry lifted it straight out, almost able to get it over his head before wincing with pain and withdrawing it.

"That's great. Come here, let me check the bandages."

They met at the table where Jerry sat opposite him with his arm stretched across the surface. Tom peeled back a corner of tape to see the scraped skin still moist with antiseptic.

"This is still okay, I think." He pressed the tape back in place. "I've only got enough supplies for two more dressings, so we should conserve it."

"I'm good with that," Jerry agreed, taking his arm back and testing it.

Tom crossed to inspect their shoes. Despite the power being out, the heat had been on long enough to dry them and he put Jerry's on the floor at the foot of the bed, then slipped his own boots on, tying them up tightly. Standing, he raised on his tiptoes a few times to loosen them up.

"Just like new," Tom grinned.

"Hardly," Jerry laughed as he sat on the edge of the bed and pushed his feet into his tennis shoes, "but much better than last night. I'll take warped and dry over wet and soggy *any* day."

"Agreed," Tom knelt to help Jerry tie his shoes, then stood to look at their supplies spread out across the room. "Let's start packing."

He stepped to the table and loaded their backpacks, putting the bottled waters and drinks on the bottom before adding the jerky and energy bars, followed by the first aid kit, miscellaneous supplies, and clothing. He left the bulky pillows behind but took the sheets off the bed, folded them tight, and crammed them on top.

"We still have a little room." Tom gestured at both his and Sam's backpacks where they rested on a pair of chairs "I'll save it for stuff we find in the hotel. Donut?" He flipped the top of a pastry box open.

"Don't mind if I do," Jerry said.

"I hate to eat them again." Tom sighed and reached for one himself. "But the sugar crash will be worth it."

"Definitely." Jerry spoke around a mouthful of sweet cake.

Sam popped out of the bathroom ten minutes later in a robe with a towel wrapped around her head. She trailed a huge waft of steam, which was exaggerated in the chilly room.

"That was amazing." The girl stepped to the chair with the clothes. "But it's freezing out here."

"I left you two pairs of socks and a sweatshirt."

"Thanks, Dad." Sam frowned as she sorted the clothes. "I'll have to wear my old jeans, but they're dry enough."

After selecting what she wanted, the girl took her things into the bathroom to change. She appeared a few minutes later fully dressed in a baggy gray sweatshirt hanging off her girlish shoulders. The towel came down next, her wet hair falling out in curls and she ran her hair through the towel, trying to get it as dried as possible.

Tom stood at the window, peeking between the blinds for the third time since waking, still seeing no signs of any danger in their immediate vicinity. "Keep drying that hair of yours, kiddo. We want to make sure you're completely dry before we go outside."

"I'll run a brush through it," she replied, returning to the bathroom. "That might help."

Tom nodded absently as he stared into the morning sunlight shining across the parking lot, blinking in pleasant surprise. "Huh. The sun's out."

"No way," Jerry rose from the edge of the bed and joined him at the window, parting the blinds with his finger. "Wow. Seems like forever since I've seen that beautiful orange ball. It's so bright."

"It's about to get brighter." Tom gestured for him to step back, tugging the cord to raise the blinds all the way to the top, allowing in a wash of light. Jerry raised his arm to cover his face and Tom narrowed his eyes at the brightness. The sunlight shined through the glass to cut sharply across the carpet, warming the air instantly, bringing with it a sense of hope in spite of their situation.

Sam appeared, made a happy noise, and dashed over to brush her hair out in the sun's warmth. The room filled with the smell of her shampoo, and Tom smiled, remembering how the house back home used to smell some mornings with three girls around, all of them using some slightly perfumy product on their hair or skin.

"Make sure you both take a leak before we go," Tom strode over to the bathroom. "We might not have many places to stop once we're on the road and I, for one, don't want to use the bushes."

They each took care of their business and stood by the front door, Sam donning a black beanie they'd found in a suitcase and tucked her hair up into it before they threw on their jackets and shouldered their packs.

"Ready?" Tom asked.

They nodded, so he moved the chair aside, unbolted the lock, and opened the door, stepping out in the chilly air. While the sun beat down warm across the lot, their breath puffed out in small gusts of mist, puddles on the ground already looking half-frozen and the nearby power lines starting to ice over.

"Let's go check the lobby for something we can use."

Tom guided them to the rear, and they entered through the same pried-open door as the evening before. Following the blood trail inside, they crossed the old storage room and into the hall.

"Stay out of there." Tom pointed to the closed office door and gestured for them to go the other way toward the lobby.

"Is that where the..." Sam swallowed, unable to finish her sentence.

"Yes. And you don't want to see it."

They filed into the lobby area, Tom angling straight for the front desk, rifling through the shelves and drawers. He started from the bottom drawers and went upward, leaving them open after rifling through each one, moving swiftly and with purpose.

"What are we looking for?" Sam circled inside.

"Food. First aid kits. Like this." Tom drew out a compact plastic square with a red cross emblazoned on the front from beneath the desk. He handed it to Jerry and turned so the young man could place it inside Tom's pack.

"Got it," Sam said, glancing around. "It looks like there's a dining room over there. I'll go check it out."

Tom finished with the desk and circled to stand in front of the window where they'd first knocked the evening before. Two cars passed by on the road, and at least a dozen people walked along US-58, one family bundled up against the chilly morning air, a few others dressed in vacation clothing, shivering as they huddled together for warmth. Puffs of steam trailed behind each person, betraying the chill in the air even as the sun still shone bright overhead.

"Score!" Sam called out from the other side of the lobby. Tom turned and saw her pointing into a storeroom next to a buffet-style counter where they likely used to serve complimentary breakfasts. He crossed to where Sam grinned at him and stepped past her into a compact kitchen area. To their right were industrial-sized jars of peanut butter and jelly, biscuit gravy, freeze-dried eggs, dessert snacks, and packs of chocolate chip and oatmeal cookies and a basket of fresh fruit still sat on a prep table.

"Oh, this *is* a score, Sam. Great job." Tom shed his pack and placed it on the floor. "Grab all the fruit you can carry."

They loaded up with a bunch of bananas, a half dozen apples, and four oranges, then they threw in some cookies and small boxes of dry cereal to top it off. It was a lot of sugar to be carrying around, but it would provide them with much-needed calories and it was a good balance to the protein from the jerky sticks they had.

"Look at this." Jerry had slipped in behind them and strode to the other side of the room. Tom followed him and found the young man pointing to a stack of bottled water cases.

"We should find a cart and load it up," Jerry suggested. "We could take turns pushing it."

Tom shook his head. "No. We need to be as discreet as possible, and these backpacks we're carrying are already going to make us stand out like sore thumbs. Pushing along a cart filled with water will just slow us down and make us easy targets."

"Like that family that had their bikes stolen," Sam pointed out.

"Exactly. We don't want to draw too much attention to ourselves. We're just a trio of refugees with meager supplies trying to find our way back home."

"Low profile. Got it." Jerry bent and pulled three bottles from a case that was already open, handing them around. "Still, we should each take one for the road."

Tom thanked him, popped the top on his, and took three big swallows before looking around the room. "Okay, guys. I think we're loaded up with as much as we can carry. Let's hit the road."

They shouldered their packs and crossed the lobby to the front door, Tom turned the deadbolt, and they stepped into the sunlight, walking up the ramp to join the other travelers on US-58, heading west on the right side of the road. The trio kept at least twenty yards between themselves and those walking in front and behind them, Jerry walking on Tom's right, and Sam on his left.

"How are you guys feeling?" he asked, rolling his shoulders beneath his backpack. The aches that had been taken away by the hot shower had returned thanks to sleeping on the couch, and the backpack was ensuring that he wouldn't soon forget them.

"My head feels a little better," Jerry replied. "But my neck aches. I think it's from the crash. Or maybe it's sore from when you used me as a battering ram." Jerry chuckled. "Actually, it's hard to tell."

"I know what you mean," Samantha agreed. "My left knee hurts, and my neck is sore, too. I can't decide if it's from the wreck or when I was lighting those people on fire."

"Sorry you guys had to go through all that. There's a lot about this whole experience that I'd change if I could."

"You did great, Dad." Sam gave him a playful elbow in his ribs. "I mean, if it wasn't for you, we wouldn't have even made it off that research boat. We might still be out there floating in the ocean... or worse." Tom shuddered at the reminder of all the vessels and lives that had been lost due to the anomaly.

"How do *you* feel, Tom?" Jerry asked, patting him on the shoulder. "You've been through all of this, too, and barely said a word about yourself."

"A lot like you guys," he replied. "I'm sore. My knees and feet hurt. I'm not the young man I used to be."

"Yeah, but you've got old man strength."

Tom chuckled dryly and shot Jerry a mock sour look. "I'm not *that* old."

The trio lapsed into silence, devoting their energy toward making better time and soon they were passing people on the highway, giving each group a wide berth, keeping their words and gazes to themselves to avoid attention. A twenty-something woman with two younger kids in tow marched ahead of them, the mother wearing her sandy blonde hair back in a disheveled ponytail, a heavy backpack hanging from her shoulders, suitcase in one hand. Her son pulled a red wagon behind him with a small cooler and stack of bottled waters in the bed while the little girl wore a pink backpack with a dolphin on the back pocket as she gripped her mother's hand, constantly shifting the pack's position. It was stuffed to bursting with belongings, and her shoulders bowed forward with the weight, causing her – and her brother and mother – to look more like a trio of zombies than people as they trudged westward to no end.

Tom winced inwardly at how vulnerable they'd be to anyone wanting an easy score. Sam flashed her father a sad glance and he sighed, nodded and slowed, drawing closer to the woman.

"Excuse me, ma'am," Tom said. "Ma'am?"

The woman slowly raised her head, her tired blue eyes blinking at Tom like he was a ghost.

"Do you need some help?"

"W-what?" Her response was confused, like she was having trouble processing what Tom was saying.

"We can help you carry something if you want," Tom offered.

Fear flashed in the woman's eyes, and she stopped and turned to wrap her arm protectively around her daughter. The little girl watched Tom and his companions with big, fearful blue eyes.

"We're fine," the woman snapped, pulling both children closer. "We don't need any help!"

Tom changed tactics. "How about some food? Are you hungry?"

She blinked, a frown mixed with disbelief. "Are… you serious?"

"We're totally serious." Sam walked up, wearing a grin, already holding out three bananas, offering them to the mother. The woman stared at the fruit and then up at Sam.

"Well, okay," she said with fading reluctance. "Yes, I think the kids are a little hungry. We've been walking all night and didn't eat breakfast." She accepted the three bananas and handed them out to the kids, whose faces lit up as they eagerly peeled them and took big bites. Seeing her children enjoying the fruit, a smile spread on the woman's face, and she turned her grateful expression upon Tom. "Thank you so much. I'm… sorry I was rude before. It's just so dangerous out here." She lowered her voice. "I saw three people get beat up last night. It was ugly."

"We know." Tom nodded. "No apologies needed. Go ahead and eat. We'll wait with you. The more the better when it comes to staying safe out here."

When they finished their bananas, Sam offered the mother two energy bars and gave the kids some prepackaged rice treats from the hotel. Tom and Jerry stood guard as other groups passed them, some shooting them side glances to measure them up, receiving the pair's scowls and furrowed brows in return.

The mother took a long drink of water from a bottled water Sam had given her and her whole body visibly relaxed, clearly refreshed from whatever hell she had been going through. "I can't thank you enough," she said, all trace of her former hostility gone.

"Where are you headed?" Tom asked.

The woman's eyes ticked westward. "That way. My parents live in Windsor. It's not terribly far, but my car broke down. What about you guys?"

"We're headed in the same direction." Tom turned and glanced at the red wagon. "Jerry, can you carry that cooler?"

The young man walked over and took the cooler out from the wagon bed. Sam knew what her father was about to suggest, and she removed the stack of waters and put them in her backpack.

"Wait, w-what are you doing?" The woman's voice rose with renewed tension until Tom walked over and took the wagon handle from the little boy with a smile.

"Kids, get inside. I'll pull you."

The children looked up at their mother expectantly, her fearful eyes fading as she flashed Tom and Sam a grin. "Yes, go ahead, kids. Get in and let the nice man pull you."

The pair's faces lit up as the girl climbed in back with her legs crossed and her brother sat in front of her with his feet hanging over the edge.

"Let's go," Tom nodded and pulled the kids along, their mother falling in close beside him, relaxed again but still staying close to her progeny.

"I'm Jean," the mother said, falling in beside him. "And you have no idea how grateful I am for this."

"Actually, I do. I have kids myself, and I'd want a stranger to do the same for them if they were in trouble."

"Do unto others..." Jean said.

"Exactly. I'm Tom."

"Nice to meet you, Tom. Are both of those yours?" She nodded at Sam and Jerry who'd fallen in behind them.

"Just the girl. That's Samantha – Sam for short. The other guy is Jerry. He's a stray we picked up on the side of the road."

"Hey!" Jerry laughed.

Jean chuckled. "I guess we're strays, too."

"Maybe we all are."

As they walked, they chatted briefly between periods of silence, Tom telling Jean where they were from near Bristol, and her replying that she knew of the place but had never been there. Tom's eyelids eventually fell half shut as the talk died down, the kids fussing in their tired boredom as the adults redirected their energy into walking. The mother and her children were a burden, but that was okay with him; there was no way he could live with himself if he allowed the small family to travel alone, unprotected in a world becoming more violent by the minute.

The flow of refugees around the group grew, and soon they weren't able to keep much space between themselves and others as the convoy of bodies grew more crowded. Tom kept them close to the side of the road, using the sidewalk where they could, allowing unencumbered people to pass them without much trouble.

Cars sped by down the middle of the road, all of them heading west through the endless sea of storm blasted buildings, loose shingles fluttering in the gusting breezes, parts of roofs hanging free, pieces falling to the road. Rain dribbled on them from the sky and dripped from the eaves, carried sideways at them by the wind. Garbage and debris were scattered everywhere from the storm, and he'd only seen two emergency vehicles the entire time, both of them bearing markings that seemed uncomfortably like impacts from weapons. A few stores on the north side of the highway were open, but the owners stood at the doors with guns, only letting in a few people at a time, watching over both their customers and their wares with an intense gaze.

The group crossed bridges over river inlets choked with debris, bloated fish and skiffs with smashed hulls floating aimlessly, torn into driftwood, half-sunk and useless. As they crossed one concrete span, Jerry caught up with Tom and stared down at the mess below them, gesturing at the swaths of dead fish.

"Is that from the anomaly?"

Tom kept his voice low but nodded. "The desalination killed the fish, and the rising waters pushed junk upriver in a massive surge." Tom's expression darkened. "I think every coastal city in the United States is going to look like this soon, especially on the northeastern seaboard. It'll spread beyond that, too, and fast."

They walked for another mile beneath a sky dotted with patches of light gray clouds, the sun sometimes peeking through, casting a warming light on their shoulders. But, more often than not, they travelled in chilly shadows with a merciless breeze that swept in to nip at their cheeks, bringing reminders of the hurricane and the near-death experiences that had accompanied it.

"It feels like football season," Jerry whispered.

Tom blinked. "You're absolutely right. It's like October or November."

"This seems bad. Is it?"

Tom gave the younger man a look and nodded once.

They continued along US-58 until they reached a cluster of a hundred people gathered in the road, the flow of refugees stopped, new groups melding with the flock before the entire line turned south. Jean stood tall, raising herself up on her toes to see over their heads.

"Is it blocked ahead?"

"Not sure," Tom said. He tried to peer over the crowd, but he couldn't see anything but a sea of people. Jerry stepped toward a burly older man with a child under one arm and his wife in the other.

"What's going on?"

The man nodded west. "The bridge is out, but they say there's another a little ways south of here. People are crossing there."

Jerry thanked the man and looked to Tom, who nodded and looked west with a pained expression. "I guess we don't have much choice but to follow these people for a spell. Anyone have any objections to that?"

No one did, so they turned south with the flow of foot traffic. Tom did his best to keep them out of the thick of it, skirting the edges of the crowd to the left, crossing a grassy median and stepping into the eastbound lane to join another road heading south. Small groups not unlike Jerry's loan shark friends stood idly on corners in clusters of half a dozen or more, watching the flocks of refugees with hungry eyes.

"They're like a pack of wolves," Tom said. "Keep your back straight, eyes ahead and expression angry. They'll go after the ones they think are the most vulnerable, first."

Jean gazed at them with pursed lips and fearful eyes. "The stores are all looted, so I guess they're looking for stragglers to pick off."

The wolf packs crowded the storefronts, standing in a sea of broken glass from the overnight robberies. Tom spotted a shoe store with its shelves stripped bare next to an electronics store and a clothing consignment shop that had both been ravaged, the windows busted out and goods dropped in the lot.

"No wonder the crowd is packing in." The stream of refugees had begun clustering tighter together, fathers and mothers stared at the roaming groups on the outskirts, offering up their own challenges to the groups' implied threats. After an hour of marching, the retail stores and groups of miscreants thinned out, giving way to a string of fast-food restaurants. Tom glanced at Jean to see her shoulders slouched again. Her kids were half asleep in the wagon, and their little group wasn't making headway like before, any energy they'd gotten from the bananas and snacks having long since worn off.

Tom picked out a burger joint and angled toward it. "Let's take a break in this fast-food lot."

They moved around to the takeout window where they could sit and watch the people walking south without being too obvious of a target, removing their packs placing them against the wall. Sam and Jerry dug out jerky sticks, snacks, and a pair of unsweetened iced teas which they all shared. Tom took a few steps away from the building and sat on the curb beneath the ordering kiosk, watching the flow of refugees, partially out of curiosity and partially to act as a lookout for any danger that might come their way.

Families of four or five staggered along haggard and exhausted, feet dragging on the concrete, a young couple guided their elderly parents down the road and several other groups had bonded together, the strong gathered around the weaker members for protection and safety. He spotted more bicycles, but the sounds of vehicles had grown distant several blocks back as people were likely moving off US-58 and onto I-264, which was bound to be a mess.

Sam and Jerry kept Jean's kids occupied and entertained, plucking their minds out of the stressful situation for a few moments. Jean, meanwhile, approached Tom, sitting next to him, arms wrapped around her knees. Gone was the false bravado and fierce protecting attitude from when they had first met, peeled back by the McKnights' and Jerry's collective kindness to reveal her soft, demure core.

"Did you say your wife and youngest are back in Bristol?"

"That's right. I haven't been able to reach them since all this started. Well, no, I take that back. Cell phone service came on for a bit, and I got a bunch of messages from Barbara. I sent her a reply, but I'm not sure if she got it."

"I hope she did," Jean smiled, giving him a pat on the arm.

"What about you? Do you have a spouse to get to?"

"Newly divorced here." Jean raised her hands with a guilty look.

"Oh, I'm sorry."

"Don't be. It was long overdue. At least we got a couple little angels out of it."

"Yes, you did." Tom glanced back. "They're cute kids."

"Thanks."

"Hey, I heard you whispering to Jerry back there. I mean, I know you're out here like the rest of us, but you seem to have an idea of what's going on."

"What do you mean?" Tom glanced at his hands. "It's pretty simple. We just got run over by a hurricane."

"Come on, now," Jean prodded as she stared out at the marching crowd. "You know it's more than that. I'm not *that* stupid."

Tom nodded reluctantly. "Obviously I'm not directly in touch with anyone from the government or any science agencies, but my background is in engineering, and I have my theories."

"Do tell."

He pulled a face. "I don't want to give you any false information, or dash your hopes, or raise them or anything else."

"I'm a big girl. Tell me what you think and I'll be the judge for myself."

"Fair enough," he nodded. "There's a lot of moving parts to what's going on."

"It's not just the hurricane, is it?" Jean fixed him with a firm look. "It's that thing the news people were talking about right before the storms hit, isn't it? The anomaly, or whatever."

"Yeah."

"I wasn't paying much attention between my two jobs and taking care of my little monsters." She gestured back toward her kids. "But I heard what they were saying about the freshwater hurting the oceans. Then I caught part of the president's emergency announcement before I had to leave for my waitress shift."

"I only saw the headlines on my phone," Tom admitted. "I didn't watch it myself. Are you concerned about something specifically?"

Jean's expression turned troubled. "Well, he mentioned something about the temperatures dropping but that it wasn't going to happen for months." She lifted her chin and blew a breath of moist air into the sky. "I've got news for them, though. This is Halloween weather."

"We were just saying that." Tom jerked his head toward Jerry. "But we used the term 'football weather.'"

"So, what do you think? Did they feed us a bunch of crap?"

"I wouldn't say that." Tom tilted his head, still trying to remain evasive while satisfying at least some of the woman's curiosity. "But they may have mis-calculated. Or, hey, this could be an unexpected cold spell. They've happened before."

Jean sighed. "Yeah, you sound real convinced of that. Come on, Tom. What's really going on?"

"Nothing good. Nothing good at all." He replied, his tone darker than he intended. For a moment Jean sat in silence, mind churning through the possibilities before she spoke again.

"Any advice on what we should do?"

"Get home to your parents. Then think about…"

"Bundling up?"

Tom looked her directly in the eyes, meeting her gaze fully, lowering his voice to a whisper. "Think about *moving* south. For good."

Jean's jaw fell open and she sat, staring at Tom, struggling to find the words to respond. "Move south? For good?" She let out a half-laugh. "Come on, you've got to be kidding around. Right?"

Tom stared at the ground between his feet, then shrugged. "Just think about it, okay?" Without waiting for a response, he stood, calling back to the others. "Come on, Sam. Jerry. Put the little ones back in the wagon. We've got to get going."

They shouldered their packs, got the kids situated, and rejoined the flow of traffic heading south. In spite of the glum subject matter during the talk between Tom and Jean, their group as a whole was re-energized and rested, and then soon surged ahead, passing others in the crowd.

"It looks like we're turning again." Jean pointed.

Tom followed her finger to where the flock made a sharp turn, heading west along a set of railroad tracks moving inland. Just as they reached it, he stopped them and went to the wagon.

"Looks like you'll have to leave your ride behind," he said, glancing over his shoulder. "We can't take it on the tracks."

The girl hopped out right away, but the little boy's face twisted up in stubbornness born of anxiety and fear.

"Come on, buddy." Tom knelt next to the wagon to coax him out. "We need you to be like your sister and get out. I'll even carry you if you want."

The boy clenched the sides and shook his head. Losing the battle, Tom gave Jean a helpless look and she leaned down, reaching for the boy. "Hey, Grandpa has a wagon, remember? You really liked that one. Don't you want to get there so you can ride in it?"

He nodded but still wouldn't budge.

"What kind is it?" Tom asked.

"Oh, it's a Haul Master," she said. "Looks like a big farm trailer."

"Wow!" Tom raised his eyebrows at the boy. "Those are awesome. Don't you want to get to your grandpa's and play with the Haul Master?"

The little boy nodded.

"Okay, then. Let's go, buddy!"

He held out his hands, and the boy finally grabbed hold, allowing Tom to pull him out of the wagon and into his arms. Fully laden with a backpack and small child, he turned and led the group on, leaving the red wagon behind. Jean took her daughter's hand, walking next to Tom with Sam and Jerry bringing up the rear as they crossed the tracks and marched along the embankment on the left.

"Good job," Jean whispered with a smile, no trace of their prior conversation in her tone. "Thanks for that."

"No problem," Tom replied.

They walked for a solid half hour before the crowd slowed and grew thicker, with those standing directly on the tracks pressing ahead while people on the sides climbed the bank to fall in line.

"Looks like a choke point," Tom said, placing the little boy down.

"A traffic jam," Jean added. "Like those times they shut down everything to one lane and funnel cars into it."

They edged forward slowly, yard-by-yard, until they were standing on the tracks with everyone else. The crowd pressed together, and Tom brushed shoulders with a man on his left.

"Sorry," Tom said, trying to give the man room.

"No problem," the man replied with a friendly chuckle. "Getting a little cozy around here, wouldn't you say?"

"Yep."

"It won't be long, and we'll be on the other side."

Tom nodded. "And hopefully to a better situation."

"Well, it's the military who's waiting for us."

"What?"

"This is a military checkpoint." The man shrugged apologetically. "At least that's what I heard. I could be wrong."

Tom's eyebrows raised, and he shot Jean a hopeful glance. "No, it makes sense. That's probably why the line is moving so slowly. They're probably checking IDs or distributing aide or something. If it's true, it's great news."

"Honestly, it's about time," the man said. "They should have been here two days ago."

"I won't argue with you there." Tom recalled the lawlessness they'd experienced over the past forty-eight hours. Between the mob at the hospital, the looting, and the gang who'd chased them halfway through the city and tried to kill them, he welcomed some semblance of law and order. They marched in silence as the tracks straightened out and Tom got his first look at the other bank. Over the shuffling crowd, were clusters of white tents spread over a wide area, dozens of military vehicles, and personnel wearing jackets with FEMA emblazoned on them. Soldiers of some sort – whether they were national guard or active duty he couldn't tell – milled about amongst the feds, mostly keeping to themselves or performing menial tasks to help support FEMA's work.

"I see the soldiers." Jean nudged Tom's shoulder excitedly. "I can't believe we finally reached safety."

Tom nodded, glancing back at Sam and Jerry. His daughter bit her lip and pumped her fist in the air, while the young man nodded his head enthusiastically. Tom, on the other hand, remained muted. The sight of law and order was welcome, to be sure, but he had a natural distrust of state and federal levels of enforcement. What might sound like a noble-sounding effort could quickly degenerate into a nightmare that could dwarf the initial event they were responding to.

Enough of the paranoia, Tom. He shook himself out of the thought spiral. *This is a national disaster. It'd be crazy for them to not be out here.*

The foul reek of dead fish announced their arrival to the bridge, and a moment later their boots were shuffling across the span, hollow sounds echoing on the old wood. Pressed against the rail, he looked down at waters bloated with garbage, boat scraps and even a clammy-skinned dolphin that was floating amidst a group of dead fish. More dead marine life flowed upriver, pressed along in a slow surge, pushed by unrelenting forces hundreds of miles away. The stench assaulted his nose, smacking him in the face, forcing him to turn his face away and swallow his rising bile.

"That's a yucky smell, Mommy," one of Jean's kids said.

"It's *very* yucky." The mother turned and wrinkled their nose.

After twenty minutes of tired shuffling, Tom saw soldiers and FEMA personnel on the opposite bank separating refugees into lines. Staffers stood at a little farther in, appearing to be checking people in on computer tablets.

"This is it," Tom said to the others. "Let's try to stay in the same line, okay?"

Jean, Sam, and Jerry all nodded, huddling closer together, caught up in the excited murmuring of the crowd. The press grew more stifling toward the edge of the bridge as the people behind them pushed forward. Standing at the rear of his group, Tom shoved backward a few inches, feeling trapped against the rail. He quelled his claustrophobia by pinning his eyes forward and taking baby steps until they reached the other side as a staffer directed all of them into a single line angling off to the left and, finally, the space around them cleared, and Tom found he could breathe again.

They approached a soldier holding a computer tablet, checking people through using a stylus. The man addressed Tom in a stiff, cold manner. "Name?"

"Tom McKnight." He gestured behind him. "This is my daughter, Samantha McKnight. And this is Jerry..." Tom realized he didn't know Jerry's last name."

"Sikes," the young man offered. "Jerry Sikes."

"Is anyone hurt?"

"Jerry had an arm and head injury," Tom answered. Then he remembered his own bump from wrecking the RV in the tunnel. "And I took a knock on the head, too."

The soldier stared at him, stylus poised over the screen.

"But nothing serious," Tom hurriedly added. "We're fine, obviously."

"Destination?"

"We're trying to reach Bristol, Virginia. Are there any busses ferrying people farther inland?"

"Not yet, but we should have those set up in a day or two."

"What about rentals?" Desperation crept in at the edges of his voice. "Can I rent a car?"

"Unfortunately, most car rental agencies are east in the storm zone." The soldier pointed back to the west. "There are two that way, but I guarantee those are out of vehicles."

"Damn," Tom murmured, running one hand through his hair, looking back at the people waiting behind him. "What are we going to do?"

The soldier's eyes flashed with impatience. "You'll have to walk or hitch a ride until you get out of the area. The highways from here to Suffolk are jammed."

"Thanks," Tom said with a shake of his head. He led the others through the checkpoint and waited for Jean and her kids. The soldier checked the three in and the small group reformed, gathering away from the throng in an uncertain circle.

"That wasn't very helpful." Jean shot a confused expression around the camp.

"Yeah, I was hoping for a little more direction." Tom's eyes darted through the center of camp, tracing over the fluttering tents and groups of people standing around, looking just as confused as they were. "They've got things set up for the injured, but no shelters for regular refugees."

"Or a ride," Sam added.

"Right." Tom chuckled humorously. "But hey, it wasn't as bad as it could have been. At least they're not detaining people."

The camp spread out all around them, folks wandering through, soldiers patrolling on groups of two or three, armed but bearing casual demeanors, giving the impression that serious trouble had yet to reach them. Strolling through the crowd, Tom's group reached some ration tables where FEMA personnel were handing out bottled water and snacks and Jerry snagged a pack of cheddar cheese chips, Sam grabbed an apple and Jean picked up a bite for her kids.

"Where to now?" the woman asked.

Tom angled them across a soggy grass field toward a row of apartments. Beyond them was the edge of the camp, a motor pool off to the left with massive ATVs and other light armored vehicles and Humvees. "Well, I guess we're going to keep heading west. Maybe if we hang out along I-264 long enough, we'll find a ride. There must be thousands of people leaving. You're more than welcome to--"

"Sir! Mr. McKnight!"

The sound of bootsteps thundered behind them, and Tom turned as the soldier who'd checked them in sprinted along the embankment and into the grassy field where they were milling about. Tom shot Sam and Jerry a doubtful glance as he eyed the approaching uniformed man.

"Sir, wait!" He rushed up and skidded to a halt, almost slipping and falling as he sprayed water everywhere.

"What is it?"

"Are you the same Tom McKnight who works for Maniford Aquatics Engineering?" The words came out in gasps as the man caught his breath after his run.

With narrowed eyes, Tom responded. "That's me."

"I need you to come with me, sir."

Tom's eyebrows pinched together. "Why?"

"The Navy has been looking for you." The soldier pointed his stylus at his tablet. "You're on their watch list."

"The only thing I want from the Navy is a ride home," he replied. "Is that what they're offering?"

"I don't know what their business is with you, sir. Your name came up on this list here. Anyone on the list is considered top priority. I'm supposed to keep the top people on site until they can be picked up."

"Well, I'm trying to get home," Tom replied. "That's *my* top priority."

"Sir, I've got my orders." He shrugged sympathetically. "If you don't come follow me right now, though..." The man left the implications hang.

Tom balked at the hard-edged display, Sam tugging at his jacket.

"We're not going with him, are we?" she asked. "I thought we were going home. Plus, they made us get on the Marin, too. Remember what happened there."

Tom nodded and turned back to the soldier. "Sorry, but my daughter's right. We already put in our time with the Navy boys, and it nearly got us killed. And we're stuck here *because* of that."

"So, you're not coming with me?"

"Affirmative," Tom nodded.

The soldier plucked a radio off his belt and raised it. "This is Private Packar. I need a pair of MPs out near the south side of camp."

"Roger that, Packar," another voice replied. "I've got a couple heading your way. Is it an emergency?"

The soldier leveled his gaze at Tom. "Is it going to turn into an emergency, sir?"

Tom glanced up and spotted two big MPs making their way through the camp. They weren't running or tensed for a fight, but one was on his radio, his eyes scanning across the grounds until they found the soldier Tom was talking to. With a nod, the pair picked up their pace, weaving toward them.

"Nope." He sighed and half turned, adjusting his pack on his shoulder. "Okay, guys. Looks like we're going with the nice soldier."

"Just you, sir." Packar held his tablet at his waist and stood firmly with his boots spread apart.

Tom crossed his arms and matched his hard expression. "No, it's your turn to listen. This is my daughter, and these are my friends. If you think I'm going to leave them behind while the Navy takes me off on some grand adventure, you'd better think again. I *will* fight you on that. And after the shit day I've had, you don't want to make that happen."

Tom stared him down for ten seconds until the soldier finally relented. "We can… keep them in a side tent while you speak with the Lieutenant Colonel."

"All right," Tom gestured. "Good enough. Lead the way, Private Packar."

Chapter 18
The Thibedeau Family
Baffin Bay, Greenland

The Ocean Explorer is smaller than most cruise liners, only one hundred meters long with enough cabin space for just over a hundred and thirty-two guests. Designed for smaller, more intimate ocean adventures, the current course has her motoring south along the magnificent Greenland Coast, carving a path close enough to land for her passengers to see every feature in detail.

Her amenities are modest, with sixty-five exterior cabins, five decks, window dining, a library, bar, an exercise room, massage therapy salon, and gift shop. Her hull is specially strengthened to break through ice – a necessity given her usual routes – though her captain is experienced enough to avoid the worst patches, preferring to avoid alarming the guests if at all possible.

Nathan Thibedeau leans over the observation deck rail, taking in the beautiful sights as the coast slips by off the port bow. He gazes across the turbulent waters as a handful of kittiwakes and other seabirds soar south, diving below the surface, looking for fish, bursting upward again with morsels in their mouths. The birds skim from island to island, alighting upon the barren fjords cutting deep gashes into the crust.

Walls of snow pack the coastline, jagged and cracked, restless as they shift with a sound that resembles sleeping thunder. Sometimes a section breaks off and slides into the sea, moving as if in slow motion, sending up a plume of seawater. Beyond the fjords, crooked mountain ranges stretch far inland, appearing endless, their far reaches and corners disappearing in a blanket of mist that lays over the land, hugging the rugged, snow-covered landscape.

"It's so cold." Nathan's wife, Joan, slides in beside him and hands him a hot cup of cocoa as he stands, mouth agape at the majestic wonder and natural beauty. He accepts the cup and slips his right arm around her waist, drawing her closer.

"Not cold," he counters. "Cozy."

"*Cold*," she insists, but snuggles against him anyway.

"Well, didn't you say you wanted something different? You know, something besides margaritas on the beach? You said, and I quote, 'We do the same thing every year. Can't we be a little more creative?'"

She smirks. "I didn't know you'd take me so seriously."

He chuckles and plants a kiss on her forehead. "It's a breath of fresh air compared to those massive cruise trips we went on the past few years. We're on a great boat with just a hundred other people, not a thousand. A cozy environment with a wild world all around us the likes of which we've never seen before. I tell you, babe. It doesn't get much better than this."

"I will admit, the bar is quaint." Joan smiles pleasantly and takes a sip of her cocoa.

"And everyone is so friendly."

"Except the captain," she quips. "He's got a hard edge to him."

"I think he's awesome," Nathan laughs. "Right out of a movie. You know, the grizzled, hardened seaman?"

"I guess so."

They watch the land slip slowly by in a mash of gray and white snow, foamy seawaters breaking against rocky beaches. Lines of jagged peaks colored a hundred shades of brown stand stiffly, their serrated ridges cutting against the sky. The pair hold each other like they haven't in years, transfixed by the sight.

"Those inlets are called fjords, right?" Joan says.

"That's right?"

"They're amazing. It's like someone just carved up the land. Makes me wonder how they even got there."

"Greenland is mostly a massive ice shelf. Ice covers almost eighty-five percent of the country, so parts of it are constantly shifting and changing."

"Wow."

"When parts of it melt, icebergs break off and cut out those fjords. Over thousands of years, of course."

Joan gives him another impressed look. "Seems like you've been studying up on things."

"Well, I wanted to know what we were getting into." Nathan hides a smug smile, trying not to sound overly confident. He nods out toward the water. "Speaking of icebergs."

As they watch, two massive wedges of ice bob in the distance, their dark white tips knifing into both water and sky.

"It's so beautiful." The tone of her voice says she's very happy, and that's all he needs.

"Mom, Dad!" A young girl's voice carries across the cold air like a dancing snowflake, and he turns to see his nine-year-old daughter, Adda, stroll up wearing a big coat with the strings pulled so tight only her face shows, green eyes above rosy cheeks and button nose, thick mittens adorning her hands as she places them on the rail.

"The princess has awakened," Nathan quips.

"I'm not a princess," she complains. "I'm an explorer."

"Well, no kidding. That's why I brought you here."

The girl stares out at the wondrous scenery spread before her.

"What do you think? Pretty amazing, huh?"

His daughter makes a noncommittal noise as her eyes trace over the icebergs and fjords and mountains, more like her mother than she'll ever want to admit. The sound of approaching feet draws his attention, and Nathan turns to see his fourteen-year-old son, Logan, walk up with two steaming cups of his own.

"Here's your cocoa, doofus," the dark-haired boy extends a cup to his sister.

"Thanks, doofus supreme." Adda takes the beverage and lifts it to her lips for a tentative sip from the steaming surface.

"Easy on the doofus stuff," Joan warns them, but she doesn't take her eyes off the scenery.

Logan joins them at the rail, and they all stand there, watching the wide-open landscape, the ship's twin diesel engines chugging along, the smokestack leaving behind a wisp of steam. More families come up from below, bundled against the cold with warm beverages in their hands. While the sea is rough, it's not pitching and tossing them half as badly as Nathan expected, and he looks for things to point out to the kids.

"It's totally boring," Logan says, though his voice holds a slight hint of awe. The boy had a major growth spurt over the summer, and he stands almost a foot taller than his sister with his cocoa sitting on the rail.

"There are some birds right there," Nathan points out.

"Okay, a few cheesy birds, but no polar bears or anything like that."

"It's not all about the vicious hunters. Can't you see how beautiful it is?" Nathan pulls out his phone to check the GPS. "There should be some cities around here somewhere." When nothing comes up, though, he shakes the device in frustration.

"I've been trying to get on the internet all morning," the boy scoffs, "the ship's wireless sucks. Someone said we're connected on a ship-to-shore satellite link. We won't be streaming any movies, that's for sure."

"I'd be happy to just get the GPS u—ah! There it is!"

The app loads to show him a detailed image of the fjords and nearby cities and Nathan straightens, pointing to the east. "You can't see it but the small town of Sisimiut is right over there."

"Whoop-dee-doo." Logan rolls his eyes.

For the first time on the trip, his son's pessimism starts to get to him. "Maybe you should learn to appreciate nature a little more. Look at that wall of ice, man. That's *insane*." He points to a tall ice barrier on the coastline coming up on their right. Its surface appears flat but patchy, a piece of drywall smothered with plaster, not yet finished by its installers. Its top edge is tinted a deep blue-white color, blueberries and cream, and its core cracks like thunder beneath its own weight.

"That's pretty, Daddy," Adda agrees.

"It's incredibly beautiful," he agrees, latching on to the girl's enthusiasm. "Look, down to the right. There's an ice cave."

Along the sheet's bottom edge yawns an opening that cuts deep inside, wormed through with smaller passages that branch in every direction.

"Can we ask the captain if we can take a boat in there?" His daughter looks up at him hopefully.

Nathan tries not to laugh, not wanting to discourage her curiosity. "The captain would never let us. Those caves could collapse at any moment, and we'd be trapped forever in the cold. Brrrrr!"

He can almost feel his son about to say something smart, when a low crack shakes the air and a huge slab of the top portion suddenly drops free. Tons of ice plunge slowly, precariously into the water, throwing off powder-white snow and mist. It takes the cave with it as it throws up a splash that flattens in a lazy wave.

"Whoa!" Adda cries. "You're right, Dad. We would have been smashed."

"Breathtaking," his wife whispers.

"Okay, *that* was pretty cool," Logan admits.

In another stroke of luck, Nathan spots something just off one of the inlets. He lifts a pair of binoculars to his eyes and, sure enough, there's a pack of long-toothed walruses lounging on a strip of land, the massive creatures watching idly as the ship motors by.

"Look at that." He points. "Oh, wow!"

Adda grabs at the binoculars. "Oh, I wanna see. I wanna see."

He hands the lenses to her, and she lifts them to her eyes, fiddling with the focus knob before *oohing* and *ahhing* at the animals.

"It's a whole family," she says, excitedly.

"I think it's technically called a herd," Nathan corrects her. "Can you see their tusks?"

"Oh, yeah! They look mean."

"They can be."

"They'll tear your head off if you go out there," Logan warns in a creepy tone.

Adda smirks. "Shut up, doofus."

"Your brother's right," Nathan says. "They could really come after you. And the big males weigh about two thousand pounds."

"Wow."

"My turn," Logan reaches for the binoculars, but Adda jerks them away.

"Let your brother have a try," Joan gently chides her daughter.

The girl snorts but gives up the lenses. Logan lowers the strap over his head and walks off, peering through them at more than just the bulky animals sunbathing on the rocks.

A gruff voice pipes through the speakers at the top of the masts, interrupting the family's nature-watching. "Attention. This is your captain speaking. Breakfast is now being served in the dining area. Please make your way down at your convenience."

"Anyone hungry?" Nathan asks, though he already knows the answer as the entire family throws up their hands enthusiastically.

* * *

Nathan saws at his sausage and drags the piece through his egg yolk before stuffing it in his mouth. The family sits around the table, jackets thrown over chairs as they wolf down their food. The selection is mostly that of a standard Canadian breakfast except for the American sausage gravy and fluffy biscuits. Logan and Adda happily scarf down their food while Nathan and Joan sit in the chairs closest to the windows, watching out at the scenery as they eat.

"I love this dining room," his wife says, shrugging her shoulders cozily, grinning at him, eyes flickering with a hint of romance. She's finished her breakfast and holds a cup of hot tea between her hands, her eyes roaming over the wood paneling and old nautical decorations. A ship's wheels, black and white fishing pictures, anchors and bookshelves with seashell bookends trapping old books adorn the floor and walls, giving the modern vessel the look of an ancient sea-faring ship.

"Me, too," Nathan nods. "It's like something out of Jules Verne."

"I was just thinking that." Joan smiles fondly and wistfully. "I have to admit, Nathan Thibedeau, you did a great job on this vacation."

"Wait till we land in Kangerlussuaq. We can get out and do some shopping before we fly back to Ottawa."

"Maybe take a walk through town?"

"Absolutely," Nathan grins.

"Attention folks. This is your captain again. Sorry to interrupt your breakfast, but we've spotted some whales off the starboard side you may want to have a gander at."

"Hey, we're on the starboard side," Nathan says, and he turns to peer through the wide window at the sea.

His eyes scan the horizon as a massive gray hump curves and rolls forward before sliding back below the surface. A smaller one, and then another, breaks through the waves. Adda leaps from her seat and slams her palms against the window to look out, then she immediately jerks her hands back.

"Whoa, that's cold!"

"It's below freezing out there, honey," Nathan reminds her, his eyes still fixed on the pod of whales.

"What kind are those, Dad?"

He narrows his eyes at the gray backs with the single small dorsal. "Humpback, I think."

"Those are humpback whales," comes a gruff voice, "or I'll die lying."

Nathan turns to see a man standing at the end of the table with his hands on his hips. He wears dark slacks and a white turtleneck over his skinny shoulders, and carries with him an air of intensity that Nathan has rarely seen before.

"Morning, Captain," Nathan gives the man a respectful nod.

Captain Mains is a tall, rangy man with a thick tuft of dark hair shocked through with gray. His eyes are grey, his gaze steely and stoic, with a hint of sadness and loss hidden behind the rough exterior.

"Morning folks," he says gruffly. His shoulders are slightly stooped as he lifts a hand and rubs his clean-shaven chin. His eyes drift past Nathan and narrow at the whales, as if troubled by something. "You can see them better from the observation deck. I was about to head up myself."

"Oh, we're going up right now," he assures him with a glance at his wife.

"That's right, sir," Joan nods. "We'll be up there in a few minutes."

"You folks dress warm, now," Mains reminds them. His gaze ticks across the ocean, seeming more distracted than the last few times Nathan's interacted with him. "The temperature's been dropping to abnormal levels."

"We will," she assures him. "We'll make sure the kids are bundled good."

The captain nods and walks away, leaving Nathan and his family to hastily finish their meals. Once done, they slip on their coats, gloves, and scarves with eager excitement and leave the dining room, heading up the stairs to the observation deck. Up top, they move to the starboard rail along with another two-dozen people trying to see the whales and Nathan passes around the binoculars, giving deference to the kids.

"This is so cool," Adda whispers, awe-struck as the ship slides past the whale pod. Fifty yards from the animals, Nathan stops worrying about the binoculars and leans over the rail, smiling as the gray backs roll on right beneath them. Joan clutches his arm and pulls herself close and he glances down, seeing her face buried deep behind her scarf.

"It's getting *super* cold out," she says.

"*Cozy.*"

"No, I'm serious." The look in Joan's eyes gives him pause. "I'm thinking about going back to the room."

Nathan starts to reply when a ponderous humpback breaches the water, body half-lifted out of the sea before it slams down hard. Adda hoots, and Logan claps delightedly while Joan's eyes go wide at the massive splash, a smile stretching on her lips. Still, she clutches Nathan's arm even harder before Adda shouts that there're dolphins, too. He grins as the sea mammals streak like silver bullets through the water, maneuvering around and between the larger humpbacks while his son circles to his mother's side, pointing back toward the bow of the ship.

"Are those what I think they are?"

Nathan follows his son's outstretched arm, jaw dropping at the dark dorsal fins cutting through the water. "I can't believe it. Those are killer whales. Actual killer whales."

"Wow, they're moving pretty fast," Logan comments.

"Aye, they are," a gruff voice says. "And that's not a natural occurrence."

Nathan jerks his attention back to see Captain Mains standing just behind them, arms crossed as he stares down at the cavorting sea mammals.

"What do you mean? Aren't all the tours like this?"

"We might get a pod of dolphins or whales," the captain's words are chosen deliberately, and there's a hint of confusion to them, too, "but it's usually a more casual affair. Sometimes they play across the bow of the ship, dipping and breaching left and right. Putting on a show for the tourists. Not like this though. Not like this." He shakes his head, expression turning grim.

"What's different?"

Mains steps closer to the rail, one hand raised to frame the animals in the water. "We never get schools like this all together, all different species. And look at their direction."

"Moving south, fast."

"That's right. Almost like they're in a panic of sorts."

Nathan chuckles. "They just look beautiful to me."

"I wouldn't expect you to know what I mean," Mains scoffs gruffly. "You're not out here every day."

"No, I believe you. You're the guy with the experience."

"That I am," the captain lets out a ragged sigh.

Nathan glances at the thermometer hanging near the stairwell going down. It showed 2°C, 35.6°F earlier that morning, but it now reads as -3°C, 26.6F. While the Thibedeaus are no strangers to the cold, it's a bit on the cool side for the end of summer, even for Greenland, and especially for the late morning. Nathan dismisses the fluctuation and hugs Joan, determined to enjoy the show despite the dropping temperature.

Captain Mains turns from the rail and walks toward the stairwell, descending to the floor below, his lanky legs carrying him quickly along the hallway toward the front of the ship where he enters the bridge. Approaching the observation window that runs around the entire deck, he stands beside Krucknick and Tart where they keep the ship motoring alongside the whales. He stares through the glass, eyes scanning the foamy, choppy waves, lifting a pair of binoculars from where they hang around his neck to gaze southward.

"Temperature's dropping, captain," Tart says quietly from where he stands at the steering column.

"Aye. I've seen it," Mains replies. "It's not completely out of the ordinary."

"Think it has something to do with the Prime Minister's announcement?"

"More likely it's just us being paranoid, Tart. Someone tells us there's going to be a dangerous drop in temperature in the Northern Hemisphere, and we quake in our shoes every time we lose a degree."

"I don't mean we should quake, sir."

"I know what you mean." The captain's voice takes on an ominous tone. "The temperature drops aren't what scares me. It's the way the whales are moving that does. They shouldn't be in such an agitated state. The killers aren't even hunting. They're just swimming scared. Now, if you ask me, *that's* a direct relation to the anomaly our glorious government officials are speaking of."

Tart nods, seeming satisfied the captain at least partially agrees with him.

"And there's something else." Mains narrows his eyes behind the binocular lenses.

"What's that, sir?"

"Krucknick take the wheel. Tart, with me."

They make the switch, and the deck officer follows the captain out to the bridge wing on the port side below the tourists. Mains strolls past the ship's remote control panel and stands at the rail. He raises his binoculars and scans the coastline farther south, heart skipping as he watches the ice sheets floating toward them. Larger, squarish chunks bob among them, appearing to have broken off the shelves.

"What do you make of the ice?" Mains hands the binoculars to his deck officer. "To the south, if you please."

Tart takes the lenses and raises them to his eyes, scanning as directed, his eyes widening as he confirms what the captain sees. "Aye. Those are sheets of ice. Blocks, even."

"There's no considerable current," Mains whispers. "So, they're sitting there, floating, waiting for us to cut through them. How long until we reach the inlet for Kangerlussuq?"

"A few hours if we steam fast."

"No, I'll not hit that ice running full steam." Mains shakes his head. "Our hull might be built for ice, but I'll not take that chance. Half speed, Tart. Hold course."

"The tourists aren't going to like it."

"I don't care. Once they see the ice flow we're about to hit, they'll understand." Tart stands there for a full thirty seconds, unmoving as the wind gently buffets him, its scent as sterile as cold steel until the captain looks over at him. "Is there any reason you're not seeing to my orders, Tart?"

The deck officer winces into the sunlight glinting off the waters, and finally Tart acknowledges the order. "No, sir. Half speed. Hold course."

He turns on his heel to see it done and the captain lifts the binoculars to his eyes once more, glaring at the ice blocks with his cold, gray eyes, a color that almost matches the chill of the sea.

* * *

An hour later, Nathan lays across the bed in their quarters, warming up as he watches the small TV positioned on the wall next to the windows, following the repeated news feeds that are reporting events along the US and Canadian coastlines. The anomaly. The flooding. And, in some cases, chaos as refugees flee inland in a confused rush of humanity.

He surfs between three stations, two from the United States and one from Canada, wincing at the sweeping views of coastal destruction from Hurricane Kate from when she bombarded her way up the Eastern Seaboard. Beachfront homes in Nags Head lay demolished in piles of wood, shingles, and garbage, siding of every color lays in the mix, peppered with furniture and mattresses. Boats have been dragged off their moorings only to be shoved through shopfronts and homes, hulls crushed like matchsticks. It's a stew of debris that keeps Nathan shaking his head for a full ten minutes. His jaw drops open when he sees a helicopter view showing the tide receding to reveal cars, trucks, and RVs half-buried in wet sand, the juxtaposition both startling and confusing to the eye, causing his brain to hurt.

More disturbing are the reports of floods plaguing cities along the Atlantic Coast and eyewitness testimonies from reporters following the mass evacuation of people inland. From Myrtle Beach to Miami, lines of cars, trucks, and motorcycles clog the highways. Broken down vehicles cause choke points and one helicopter view shows a two-mile-long line of people trekking from Quebec City to Montreal with suitcases in their hands.

Adding to the ominous tone is the speech given by the American president, followed by similar remarks by the Canada's own Prime Minister. They warn that the freshwater surge from the anomaly is causing temperatures to drop slowly, all across the Northern Hemisphere, and it will only get worse over the next few months. It had all started a week ago, but the Thibedeaus were too preoccupied with their vacation to notice. The cruise cost three times as much as a standard trip to Florida, and Nathan had wanted to get his money's worth but by the time they'd arrived in Qausuittuq by charter plane and boarded the Ocean Explorer, the damage was done.

He recalls Joan's complaint about the cold just a short time ago, the figures on the observation deck thermometer sticking in his mind. It all coincides with what the authorities said would happen, only the reality seems more drastic, and panic taps out an icy message up his spine. He sends a text to the house sitter back in Ottawa to get a report on their two dogs and cat but the message doesn't go through, and he sets his phone on the bed as worry nags at him until Joan steps out of the shower. She stands with a towel wrapped around her chest and another bundling her hair, glancing at the screen before rolling her eyes.

"Can we turn something else on? The news is so depressing."

"I'm afraid there isn't much else." Nathan lowers the volume and fixes her with a frown. "They're evacuating Quebec City."

She bends and enters the room, her eyes on the screen, words rushed, dismissive attitude completely gone. "Are you serious?"

"Dead serious. I'll bet Montreal is going to be overrun."

The woman shifts her attention between the television and her husband. "Ottawa is less than a hundred miles away, and we live on the east side."

"Directly in line of anyone moving west."

Joan's eyes grow wide with worry. "You should text Samantha."

"I already have." Nathan raised his phone and dropped it on the mattress. "Like Logan said. The internet is terrible here. It'll probably take an hour to get through."

"Did you try email, too?"

"I did," Nathan nods. His wife's worry only makes his grow that much more.

She stares at the line of refugees on the screen. "Those poor people."

"And you were right about the cold."

"What do you mean?"

"It *was* getting colder outside this morning." He sits up. "Normally, at this time of year, it's a brisk four or five degrees Celsius. I mean, I checked that repeatedly before we came. I *planned* the trip for a time when the weather wouldn't be so bad."

"What is it now?"

"Minus seven."

"That's a huge drop," Joan admits as she moves to the window to peer out.

When Nathan planned the trip, he bumped them to deluxe accommodations, so their room has a big square window rather than a tiny portal. Joan gazes out at the passing sea and the increasingly gray sky.

"I wonder if the captain's decision to slow down has anything to do with the flooding and weather?" Nathan muses out loud. "I mean, if someone had ordered ships back to port, we'd be going *faster.*" He pauses as a horrifying thought strikes him. "Unless Kangerlussuaq is flooded, too. That could mean--"

"I know the reason he slowed down," Joan's voice is quiet as she leans her towel-covered forehead against the window. "You've got to see this, Nathan."

He hops off the bed and pads over in his socks, leaning in next to his wife, absorbing the warmth radiating off her skin, captivated by what's in the water.

"What in the hell...?" His words trail off as his eyes rake over the thick slabs of ice floating past them. Their forms are monstrous, jutting meters out of the water, their submerged forms barely visible but still present, visible occasionally as a streak of grey or white beneath the waves.

"This ship can handle that, right?" Joan suddenly sounds worried.

"It can break through ice," Nathan assures her. "I mean, it's not an official ice-breaker, but it has a modified hull to protect against stuff like this specifically for trips like the one we're on."

"That's good," Joan says with a shiver, turning toward the bathroom. "I'm going to put some clothes on. It's chilly in here."

Nathan nods and watches the ice drift past for another ten minutes as his wife's blow-dryer works on her hair before she exits the bathroom, throws off her towel and puts on a pair of leggings and a long sleeve shirt before adding jeans and winter vest. Due to the supposed mild temperatures for this time of year, his family hasn't brought extra long johns or serious winter attire. He tilts his head and listens to the rattling ventilation system circulate air through the ship. The Ocean Explorer is a great boat, but it's old – very old – and doubt nags at the back of his mind yet again.

* * *

As the hours pass, Captain Mains maneuvers the Ocean Explorer through the worst of the ice patches, expertly navigating between the iceberg-sized chunks with Tart and Krucknick's help. They smack smaller slabs aside and punch through larger ones, knocking the pieces about with crunchy impacts that vibrate the hull. A dozen passengers come up to the observation deck to see what's causing the noise and soon those who hadn't known about the ice flow are chattering nervously about it.

Three men come to the bridge to check on the status of the ship and ask what the captain's plan is. The friendly one named Nathan is especially concerned and a little agitated. He says their cabin is excruciatingly cold, approaching freezing temperatures *inside*. This doesn't surprise the captain, considering it's close to -15°C, 5F outside and Mains assures the men that they're still on track to make Kangerlussuaq by the following morning. He leaves off the fact that the town isn't responding to radio calls since it's not uncommon to have spotty signals, but not so close to shore. The first niggling tick of dread climbs up his spine and wraps around his neck.

"It's only going to get colder, captain," Tart says as if reading his mind.

"I know. I've never seen a temperature swing like this. Let's just hope we can enter the fjord to Kangerlussuaq."

"But they're not responding. Could they have been flooded?"

"Hard to tell. Maybe they weren't ready for the cold. They could be having communication issues. It happens. No sense in panicking just yet."

As the ice thickens, he's forced to plow over slushy chunks and snap through the flat, jagged disks of stubborn frost. It's all-hands-on-deck as he keeps sailors manning the engine room, navigation, and pumps in case the unthinkable happens and the thick steel hull is compromised. An hour later there's a break in the ice and Captain Mains tells Tart to give them full power. The diesel engine roars to life in the ship's belly, driving them across the deceptively calm sea until more ice packs start to form. They bump and knock against them, sending gut-wrenching shudders up and down the Ocean Explorer's sides.

The captain orders them back to half speed and glares out the port side window, watching and waiting for the coastline to appear. He's chilly beneath his heavy coat as the onboard heaters try to keep up with the mist-frozen air, the temperature having stabilized at -17°C, 1.4F. Frighteningly cold and more than enough to lock up the ship.

"We're almost there," he tells anyone who will listen, and all eyes are on the big GPS screen that hangs above the glass as they approach the tip of the fjord leading up the long, narrow strait to Kangerlussuaq.

The hull grumbles and shakes as they make their way around the tip of the fjord. All they have to do is drive up through the calm waters until they reach Kangerlussuaq with its airfield perched up on the rocks. From there, he can release his passengers and let them be someone else's responsibility. In the night, he can barely see the outline of the shore, their GPS and sonar acting as their eyes and ears. As they round the bend and head east toward the inlet, the ice packs tighten around them, big chunks pressing against the hull and squeezing with emotionless force. The ship slows, grinding through packs of hoarfrost as a crunching sound permeates the cabin.

"Full power," Captain Mains orders as it becomes a slog. He briefly considers turning away from the shore and seeking the open ocean where they can at least be free of the ice and sail farther south. Fuel is a consideration, though, as they only have three days' worth of diesel in the tanks, so they must press on.

Again, Tart reads his mind, voice strained as he speaks. "Let's keep going toward shore." The deck officer's eyes dart around at the darkness. "We might not make Kangerlussuaq, but if we get stuck in the ice, we can wait for it to freeze and trek to the small town of Itivdleq on foot. It's only three miles from our current position."

The captain turns, steps away from the window, and reluctantly throws open the door to the port wing, slamming the door shut behind him as he walks into the cutting wind, jerking his coat tighter and moving stiffly to the wing's edge. It's pitch dark out, but the exterior lights illuminate the endless ice field. It still has cracks and fissures that make it passable in the boat, but those are shrinking by the minute, their collapse actually discernable to the naked eye.

His gaze turns northeast toward Itivdleq, hoping to see a glimmer of light through the pitch black. When nothing is visible, he moves to the mounted telescope and points it at the Greenland coastline. Even if rocks obscure his vision, he should still see the glow of Itivdleq's lights. He looks for several moments but finds no trace of a living town. With a frustrated growl, he enters the bridge and notifies his men.

"I don't see Itivdleq. They're gone. Either they've flooded or lost all power. In either case, it does us no good to go there."

"Can we try farther south to Maniitsoq?" Tart asks. "We could shelter there."

"In this ice? It'll take us a full day, if we're lucky." The captain grumbles the words beneath a sheen of genuine panic and fear. Maniitsoq is eighty miles from their current position, but the southern waters might have less ice. "But... I don't see that we have a choice. Change course for Maniitsoq. Maintain full speed."

"Aye, Captain," Tart says. The man punches in the new coordinates and turns the ship away from the inlet, heading farther down the coast. The Ocean Explorer jostles and shakes as it grinds against the ice, the friction felt through every deck. While she'll gamely try to cut through it, every minute locks them in tighter and soon they'll be at its mercy.

* * *

Nathan awakens to a deep tremor, his groan in harmony with the ship's hull as something cracks against the bow with a dull thud, knocking him farther from his slumber, jostling him awake. It's been hours since the first sounds of the ship breaking through ice terrified him, and he's since grown used to them. He understands that this is what a sturdy ship breaking through ice sounds like – or at least that's what he tells himself.

He sits up and looks around to get his bearings, the bathroom light spilling into the cabin giving him enough to see by. The curtains are locked tight against the outside and the lump on his left is his wife buried beneath the covers. Nathan made the mistake of falling asleep on top of the comforter, and now his hands feel like ice and his feet are slightly numb even with his thick socks and boots on. He exhales a sigh of frigid air and realizes he's in the grasp of a deathly cold. The only reason he's not frozen stiff is because he seeped some heat off Joan's covered form.

She stirs next to him. "Nathan?"

"I'm awake, babe. When did we fall asleep?"

Light glows faintly beneath the covers as she checks her watch. "About three hours ago."

A brief spike of panic gut-punches him. "Where are the kids?"

The cover flips down to reveal Adda snuggled beneath the blankets with her mother, and Nathan breathes a sigh of relief. "Where's Logan?" he asks.

"He said he was fine in his room by himself," Joan says. "But it wasn't this cold before. What's the temperature in here?"

"I don't know." Nathan shakes his head, then addresses Adda. "*Cold.* How come you didn't bring Logan with you, honey?"

Adda raised her head two inches and stared at him. "He told us to go away, so we did."

"Yeah, but this is *crazy* cold." He stood, hugged himself, and hopped to get his circulation flowing. After a few seconds of that, he nodded at the pair. "Stay here and keep bundled up."

"Wait." Jean raised from the covers. "Where are you going?"

"I'm going to check on Logan. Then I'm going to have a chat with the captain."

Joan nods and pulls the covers over her daughter, up to her own chin as Nathan dashes to the window and pulls aside the curtains. The grinding is almost constant now, the ice field having completely encircled them. The cracks between the chunks and slabs are slim, just inches at best, and in some places they're melded into one big mass, slowly cutting off the ship's progress, forcing it to go through them rather than around.

Nathan grabs his room key off the dresser and heads for the door. In the hallway, he shuts the door quietly behind him and steps one door down to room 104, knocking firmly. When nobody answers, he knocks again, panic creeping into his mind, and he calls out, face up against the door, shouting.

"Logan? *Logan?!*"

The boy doesn't respond, so he backs up a pace, preparing to slam his weight into the door to force it open. Just as he's lunching forward, the door flies open, and his son stands there with a tired expression. Nathan reaches out and grasps the boy's shoulder, feeling that he's warm, maybe even warmer than himself. "Oh, thank God. You're fine."

"Why... why wouldn't I be fine?"

"Because it's freezing on this level, and you have no one to share body heat with."

"I'm fine." The boy narrows his eyes, looking annoyed. "Trust me."

"Trust you?" Nathan stares at his boy quizzically and then smells the faint hint of smoke drifting from his room. "What's that smell?"

"I found a candle in one of the drawers. That's what I'm using to stay warm."

The ship's bow lifts as they slam through what must be a particularly thick ice patch and Nathan grabs the door frame, feeling the engine clanking , vibrating the floorboards beneath the thin carpeted hallway. He's used to hearing it thanks to the repeated impacts, but he's more aware of its strains and groans than ever before, especially since they seem to be growing more strained with each passing moment.

He levels a hard gaze at his son. "Put the candle out."

"Why?"

"Because I said so. Put it *out!*"

"But, Dad--"

"How are you going to feel when the smoke alarms go off and activate the sprinkler system? You'll be soaked in under a minute. We all will."

"This ship is so old, they probably don't even work."

"Son." Nathan clutches Logan's shirt gently but firmly. "Put the damn candle out and go to our room with your mother and sister. Get into bed with them and keep warm."

"Okay, Dad. Jeez." The boy jerks out of his father's grasp, his sneer almost putting Nathan over the edge.

"I'm serious," he snaps, leveling his gaze, leaving no room for questions. "Get your butt in there, find all the extra blankets you can, and help them stay warm."

"Yes, sir. I'm going right now."

"Good kid."

With his family okay for the moment, Nathan turns and strides down the hall to the stairs leading to the upper decks.

"Wait," Logan calls. "Where are you going?"

He half-turns in reply. "I'm having a word with the captain. None of this seems right."

"Be careful!"

Nathan doesn't reply but hits the stairs hard, flying up them two at a time until he pushes through the door to the captain's deck. His breaths come out as mist, the cold instantly tearing at his cheeks, the darkness so complete that the ship's lights seem paltry, barely able to pierce the gloom. The sounds of crunching ice are loud but somehow gentle at the same time, giving off low squeals as it's compressed, pushed aside by thick layers of steel and the propulsion of the ship's diesel engines. There's a spot of open deck before a short passage leads to the bridge and at the entrance, four men jostle one another, held at bay by two big sailors standing guard.

The sailors don't appear threatened by the passengers, who aren't particularly intimidating, either, but the situation is nonetheless tense, Nathan assuming they're mostly fathers and husbands keen on keeping their families warm and fed.

"We just want to know what the hell's going on," one of the larger passengers says. He's got his hood thrown back, cheeks rosy, a bit of frost caught in his mustache, his bundled coat making him look bigger than the sailors.

"The captain will make an announcement shortly," replied the sailor on the left, a red-haired guy wearing denim coveralls beneath a thick jacket and hood.

"It would be better if he made one now," a second man counters.

"What about the ice?" the first civilian asks. "Did the captain accidentally run us into an ice field?"

"No, he didn't." The red-haired sailor responds to the man with flat certainty. "The ice came upon us suddenly. We had no warning from shore."

The bossy civilian's return glare is an expression of vicious anger barely held in check, Nathan recognizing him as a man who's used to getting what he wants and not used to taking no for an answer. A gust of wind kicks up off the ice, freezing air whipping into the gaps in Nathan's coat, forcing an uncontrollable shiver down his back. There's an unnatural pause in the confrontation as they allow the warmth stealing air to punch through, each of them closing their eyes until the gust passes.

"Again," Red Hair says, recovering. "The captain's going to make an announcement very soon."

"When?"

"*Soon.*"

Bossy plants his fists on his hips. "We should be on a flight back to Ottawa by now."

The guards only stare at him.

"Well, I'll tell you one thing. I want my money back. And your company will have to eat the cost for all our return flights. The itinerary expressly stated we'd be back in Kangerlussauq by 10:30 PM."

The other passengers grumble in agreement.

"You can take that up with the company when we reach shore," Red Hair acknowledges. "Until then, the captain needs his--"

The bow of the ship rises abruptly and then lands with a crash, throwing the passengers forward into the guards. Nathan puts his palm against a metal pole, the frozen surface sending a cold ache through his wrist. As the men untangle themselves, Bossy shoves Red Hair, the sailor returning the favor, smashing the big man back so hard he splits the crowd and lands in Nathan's arms. Nathan catches him to keep him from plunging to the deck, hissing in the man's ear as he lifts him to his feet.

"Hey, buddy, no need to be hostile. Settle down and let me talk to these guys."

Bossy is bigger and stronger than Nathan, and he easily twists out of Nathan's grip. Nathan expects the man to charge the sailors and an all-out brawl to ensue, but the passenger holds himself in check and only glowers at the guards.

"Yeah, man," Bossy replies, red-faced but not entirely witless. "See if you can get some answers from these guys."

"Right. Great." Nathan pushes between the other men and faces the guards, keeping his balance on the shifting deck. "I spoke with the captain earlier about a few things, and we're on good terms. I'll bet he'd let me in to ask some questions." Nathan gestured to the bridge and back to the men standing behind him. "I'll bring his answers back to these guys. You know, so the captain isn't bombarded."

The guards share a doubtful look, but Red Hair nods at the idea. "Who should we say is coming aboard the bridge?"

"Just tell him it's Mr. Thibedeau. I'm the guy who watched the whales with him earlier."

The guard nods, turns, and disappears down the hall and into the bridge that stretches the width of the ship. The passengers relax and shoot Nathan thankful looks as a light dusting of snow falls across their shoulders. The guard returns twenty seconds later and gestures for Nathan to come ahead. Questions from the other passengers fly as he follows the guard down the short hallway.

"Ask where we're headed!"

"Find out if we'll arrive at Kangerlussauq by mid-morning! If so, I can still make my flight!"

The sailor leads Nathan along the hall and through the bridge door where several deck officers turn to look. The room is cold, and he expects to find indignation, contempt, or even an apology written on their faces. What he doesn't expect to find is their eyes filled with fear, lips pensive as they steer the ship, clutching the consoles and instruments like men sailing the razor's edge between life and death itself.

"Here he is, captain," the guard says.

The tall, swarthy Captain Mains stands near the port side glass, looking down.

"Come ahead," he calls, gesturing for Nathan to approach.

Nathan circles a navigation table laden with a chart so intricately marked with course headings and it might as well be Chinese. Only when Nathan comes to his side does the man speak, his accent still indeterminate, his seaman's growl drawn back within his chest.

"Mr. Thibedeau. I hear some passengers are restless."

"Yes, sir. We just want to know where we are and how we ended up in such a thick patch of ice." Nathan follows the man's gaze as the ice slides by beneath the ship's lights. He notes there are no more spiderweb cracks between the layers and chunks. All pretenses of an ice field are gone and all that's left is a big sheet of ice that stretches as far as the lights allow him to see. Any new cracks are caused by the Ocean Explorer as she plows and grinds in a helpless crawl through the endless white.

The captain stares down a moment more before his eyes flick to Nathan. "We tried to head up the fjord to Kangerlussauq, but it's blocked up. We thought to land at Itivdleq, but there are no welcoming lights."

"What do you mean no welcoming lights?"

"The town either lost power or has been flooded." Mains shrugs. "Either way, it's no good to us now."

"Have you called them via radio?'

"We've tried, Itivdleq, Kangerlussauq, Sisimiut, Sarfannguit, and Maniitsoq. Only Maniitsoq responded, and that's where we were headed."

A chill streaks up Nathan's spine. It's one thing to imagine the boat being stranded or ice-locked, but it's quite another to think all the towns along the Greenland coast are flooded or locked in a freeze so deep they might as well be dead.

"Well, at least there's Maniitsoq." Nathan starts to feel relieved before he catches himself. "Wait, what do you mean we *were* headed there."

"It's eighty miles down the coast."

"We don't have the fuel?"

Captain Mains nods. "Not enough to plow our way through this ice."

Nathan stares as the ice lazily passes beneath them and he blinks as he realizes that they're moving even slower than when he first stepped onto the bridge mere moments ago.

"What are we going to do?" he asks.

"We're going to wait."

"Wait for what."

The ship fights and grinds for another twenty yards before the bow lifts one last time, coming to rest in the bed of ice. The engine continues churning for another thirty seconds, and Mains raises his hand, reluctantly giving the command he's been dreading for the last hour.

"Kill it, Tart."

The deck officer hits a button, and a deep silence engulfs them as the engines slowly wind down. Without the sound of the engines, they're left with the groaning ice, creaking hull, and the weak air circulation rattling through the vents. The wind and snow pick up, gusting against the glass and Nathan blinks at the captain in terror.

"Sir, what are we going to do? Can we call for help?"

"All the calls have already been made, but Mr. Tart will initiate an emergency positioning beacon as well. Anyone listening will have our location, and we're not terribly far from shore."

"Maybe someone will send a helicopter," Nathan says, hopefully.

"That's what we're hoping." Mains nods as a crewman Nathan presumes is Tart heads through the right-wing door.

"What should we do until then?" Nathan's thinking about his family, how they can keep warm, and if Adda and Joan brought snacks aboard from their last stop.

The captain sighs and reaches up for a microphone. He flips a switch and feedback snaps through the speakers for a moment before he puts it to his lips and speaks.

"Attention, this is Captain Mains. I'm sure most of you are aware we've been plowing through an ice pack for several hours now. You might also be aware that we have just stalled in it. Due to the dropping temperatures, we're asking everyone who has an external cabin to gather their possessions, blankets, and food stores and make their way to the main lounge. We'll direct the ship's heat into that area. I repeat, we'll shut off heat to the outer passenger quarters and focus it into the main lounge.

"Emergency beacons are being placed, and Maniitsoq knows we're out here. Hopefully, we'll see a helicopter and rescue crew by tomorrow afternoon. Rest assured, the Ocean Explorer is rated for ice like this, and her hull will hold. So, until the rescue crews arrive, please make yourselves comfortable and warm and try to be patient."

The captain hangs up the microphone, staring out at the drifting snowflakes for several seconds before turning and marching toward the front of the boat, lifting his binoculars to his face. Nathan follows on his heels, mind racing.

"What if something happens to Maniitsoq, or they can't send a rescue team? We'll need to take stock of the food on board and ration things, right? I mean, we could be out here for two days, or even a week. Don't you think we should—"

"We're at the end of our two-week tour, Mr. Thibedeau. How much food do you think is left on board?"

"Well, I don't know."

"You'd have to ask the head chef, but my guess is that we've got two or three days worth of food for everyone. Maybe enough water for a week. If Maniitsoq can't send a rescue team, we'll need more than a miracle to save us."

Nathan stands in silence, looking down at the ice that locks the ship. It's beautiful and alien, reflecting the lights like something from a fantasy landscape, almost seeming friendly and inviting in its beauty if not for the inevitable death it brings to the unprepared.

The captain turns to him and rests his hand on his shoulder. "Go see to your family. It's about to get very cold and very uncomfortable. And, Mr. Thibedeau?"

"Yes?"

"You need to prepare them for the worst-case scenario."

"Worst-case scenario?"

The captain's look of finality settles on Nathan like a frigid breeze. He gives a solemn nod and rushes from the bridge to see to his family.

Chapter 19
Barbara McKnight
Wyndale, Virginia

Sunlight shone through gaps in the thick, billowy clouds, painting the darkened edges with bright white highlights. The wind had long since fallen from shingle-tearing gusts to sullen swirls, rustling the trees behind the McKnight property that stood as silent guards, watching the macabre funeral unfold. Barbara, Darren, and Marie had used the Gator utility vehicle to transport the five dead men deep into the woods. They'd taken all morning, and many breaks to dig the graves, wearing gloves to minimize the blisters – or so they told each other.

"It would have been easier if we'd buried them a little closer to the house and not all the way across the property." Darren tamped down on a raised mound and leaned on his shovel.

"I didn't want them anywhere near the house," Barbara replied in earnest. "It would have creeped us all out. The kids would have had nightmares, and I couldn't sleep myself with them lying just outside the door."

"A corpse is a corpse," Darren stated, flatly. "They don't dig their way out of graves or give off ghostly visages."

"This coming from the man who can't watch a scary movie without having nightmares." Maria slapped her husband on the arm.

Barbara put her hand against a nearby tree and looked over the grave site. They'd picked a spot at the far end of the trail near the property line, a place that would be impossible to see from the house, the road or anywhere else any people might wander through to see a group of raised dirt mounds standing side-by-side in neat order.

"I should have given the cops a call," Barbara shook her head nervously. "Hell, I still should. I mean, there's five dead men on my property. That's something right off a crime show."

"I wouldn't worry too much about it," replied Darren. He stepped away from the graves, sliding on some loose dirt. "The way things are deteriorating, I doubt the police will spare time to investigate the deaths of some intruders who broke in on multiple occasions and tried to cause harm to your family."

"You're probably right." She bit her lip. "It's not like I can call them with the phone lines down, anyway. And I'm not driving into town again."

"That's what I'm saying. And Marie and I won't speak to anyone about it."

Marie wiped the beads of sweat from her brow as she stood back from the four graves, looking them over. "Nothing to speak of, is there?"

Darren shook his head. "I can't imagine a thing."

Marie gave Barbara a comforting look. "I think the best thing to do is take stock of your situation and stay prepared. You can't control the rest."

"You're right about that," her husband agreed and Barbara nodded absentmindedly, still transfixed by the mounds of earth. "You want us to say a few words for them?"

"Fu—I mean hell no." Barbara's reply was immediate, both in words and body, jolting from her stock-still position as she looked over at Darren. "No. There's no words worth saying over scum like these."

Together they gathered the shovels and picks and placed them in the basket of her Gator next to Barbara's Colt carbine, then tossed their gloves on top as Barbara climbed behind the wheel. Marie got in the passenger side while Darren took the rear seat, turning sideways so he could fit his knees into the small seating area. She started the vehicle and pulled toward the house with a growl of tires on the gravel and dirt path. The sheep and mules had drifted closer to the woods and when they saw the Gator emerge they crowded around with expectant bleats and mewls, hungry for their breakfast and steadfastly refusing to accept any excuses – including ones that involved cleaning dead bodies out of the house.

"I appreciate the help, folks," she told the Everetts as she parked the Gator near the back patio and climbed out, preparing to go for the feed. "I'll call you if I need you."

Darren remained sitting. "Looks like you've got some hungry beasts to feed."

"Normally, they're fed and happy by now," she replied with a shake of her head, "but we had the bodies to deal with, and now there's the blood and gore to deal with and..." Her words trailed off in a shaky sigh.

"Well, don't expect us to leave without helping you, darling," Marie said. The older woman clutched her arm and gave it a friendly squeeze.

"I shouldn't keep you." Barbara's eyebrows arched. "But it's been one helluva night, and I really don't want you to go."

Without warning, her chin fell, and tears welled up around the bottoms of her eyes. They pooled there for a moment before streaking down her face, chilled by the cold breeze that gusted across her cheeks. Her breath hitched in her chest and finally burst out in a loud and embarrassing sob.

"Now, now." Marie extended her arm around Barbara's shoulders and hugged her. "You've had a rough night, but we're here to help you get through it. And you *will* get through it."

"Thank you. Truly." Barbara allowed herself to be held and then gestured toward the chicken coop, taking Marie up on her offer. "Feed barn is this way."

She got back behind the wheel and carefully drove them through the noisy, roused animals before parking the Gator outside the shed, killing the engine and leading the Everetts inside.

Barbara moved to the feed bench and touched her palm to one small bucket and then another. "These are for the chickens and rabbits and the feed is right there in that trashcan."

"Got it," Marie said. She handed Darren his own pail before turning to peer inside the can. The woman nodded. "We use the same feed mix for our own animals."

Barbara filled her bucket with the usual oat, barley, and wheat mix, then led them outside and gestured at the chicken and rabbit coops.

"We have running water to the troughs," she pointed out. "All you have to do is check them for muck and clear it. The troughs will automatically refill if you scoop enough out." Barbara held her bucket of feed against her stomach and walked toward the animals as they bleated and rushed around her legs. Some of them peeled off and followed the Everetts until she started slinging the mix across the yard.

"There you go." She nodded at the incessantly braying donkeys and clucking chickens. Barbara thought about putting the kids on the feeding chores, but she'd given them the morning off with the express instructions to stay in their rooms. They were to do lessons, play games, watch movies, sleep or basically whatever they wanted, all in an effort to help give their minds some breathing room to help process the previous night's events. There had been crying, hugging, consoling of one another, awkward questions, long bouts of silence, and what the pair needed next was some time alone to just sit and think through things in their own unique ways.

They finished feeding all the animals, then the trio returned to the shed and put the buckets away, Darren dusting his hands off and stepping outside with a smile. "You now have a yard full of happy beasts."

"Thanks again." Barbara smiled at the couple as they watched Chuck the Rooster cluck and crow his way around the chicken yard. "They do all seem pretty happy."

"Anything else we can help you with?"

"I was going to check on the greenhouse, but that'll have to wait until I get the house cleaned up. I don't want to leave that mess there for the kids." She climbed into the Gator and started it up.

"We're right there with you," Marie announced as the couple got inside.

Barbara drove carefully around the animals and parked near their concrete patio. The man who'd died out there with his dog catching noose had done so in the dirt, and his blood had mostly soaked in. Pulling the hose from its carrier, she sprayed over the spot to camouflage it even more. She then headed up to the house and motioned for the Everetts to follow her inside and they stepped through the broken sliding glass door to find Linda on her hands and knees, scrubbing at the red-stained kitchen tiles.

Barbara rested her fists on her hips. "What are you doing?"

Her daughter gave a surprised yelp and quickly stood, pink water dripping from the sponge she held. "Sorry, Mom. Jack fell asleep, and my mind was racing. I just wanted to do something, so I came down and started cleaning. I..." The girl's eyes glossed over with moisture, a mix of fear of her mother's disapproval and the memory of the last night's events.

Barbara crossed the kitchen in two steps and rested her hands on Linda's shoulders. "I know, baby. I can't stop shaking myself. It's okay. What happened last night was terrible, but we did what any rational people would have done."

"We controlled the situation," Linda lifted her face with an imploring expression, looking once again for solace and atonement. "That's what we were supposed to do, right?"

"In this case, absolutely," Barbara nodded. "You were super brave."

"You poor girls." Marie ventured over and reached out with a tentative hand. "You did the right thing. You can't just let someone march in here and threaten you. They sealed their own fate when they decided to step foot on the McKnight property."

Barbara squeezed her daughter's shoulders again and turned to see Darren standing at the line where the kitchen tile met the living room carpet. The man scratched his head as he stared down at the massive bloodstain on the nickel-gray floor.

"We'll have to cut around that stain and rip it out. Padding, too." Darren winced. "Maybe even the wood if we can't get the stains up."

"I figured," Barbara nodded, coming over. "We've got some plywood out back."

"And we've got spare carpet in our garage from our last project," Marie assured her. "It's light blue, so it won't look pretty. But it'll patch this spot up fine."

"Thank you."

They started the cleanup, opening the front door to allow the place to air out while Linda scrubbed the tile and hardwood with bleach while the adults cut a square out of the carpet using a box cutter. They ripped it and the padding out, rolled it up, and handed it to Darren as Linda sat back and admired her work on the hardwood before going after the few droplets that had sprayed out from the main stain, onto the wood, walls and carpet.

"I'll take this out to the fire pit," Darren said. "We'll burn it later."

"Great idea," Marie replied.

He dragged the stained materials outside and loaded it into the Gator, driving it out toward the woods while Linda finished with her scrubbing. She came out of the hall with her bucket and sponges, eying the wood, walls and carpet carefully for any spots she missed before turning to her mother.

"All done. I think. The main patch was on the wood and carpet but there were some droplets I had to go pretty far out to get."

Barbara turned to stare at the gleaming tiles and wood, then looked over at Marie. "It looks great. Do you think we got it all up?"

"Blood is notoriously hard to get off surfaces." Marie frowned. "From what I've heard, anyway. But as far as the tile and hardwood, if it looks as clean as this, then I think we're good. Linda, why don't you get a fresh bucket and let's spot check everything together just to make sure there wasn't anything left. Barbara, do you have a different kind of cleaner? If we keep using bleach, it's going to discolor the carpets."

"At this point, I don't care." Barbara waved her hand. "I just want it disinfected. We'll worry about remodeling later."

When Darren returned, the trio hauled out the destroyed couch and left it on the concrete patio. After a brief conversation about possibly refurbishing the piece of furniture, Barbara shook her head emphatically, insisting that she hated it anyway and just wanted it gone and he promised to disassemble it later and drag it out to the fire pit to be burned along with the rest.

"Let's run and get that replacement carpet," Marie said. The older woman studied Barbara's face, raised her hand and let her thumb drift across Barbara's cheek. "While we're gone, why don't you get cleaned up. You're still covered in blood."

"Good idea," Barbara agreed with a dark chuckle. "I guess I should have done that first thing, but it's not every day we get attacked."

"That might not be true anymore," Marie said. "We need to be ready every minute of the day."

Barbara nodded. "I plan on it. While you guys are away, I'll throw together an early dinner. It's the least I can do for all the help you've given us."

"A home cooked meal sounds wonderful," Darren beamed.

"We'll be right back." Marie assured her before patting her husband's arm and guiding him to the front door.

Barbara saw them out but left the door open, staring out at the property for a few long moments, her thoughts racing but her mind feeling very much blank, a spinning gear without anything to drive. While she wanted nothing more than step into the master bathroom and take a shower, she couldn't – wouldn't – stop working.

She went to the laundry room and opened the door with a gasp, looking in on Smooch where they'd left her to rest. The German Shepherd lay on her dog bed, curled up on her good side. They'd shaved the fur around her stab wounds, disinfected them, and dressed them with gauze and tape and Barbara had even sprayed some nasty-smelling stuff on the bandages to keep the dog from ripping them off.

The biggest puncture was above the Shepherd's right shoulder and, judging from the four-inch knife they'd found in the yard, she could be suffering from internal bleeding, but only time would tell how serious it really was. The lacerations around the ribs had pierced well through her skin and muscle but thankfully hadn't punched too deep as far as Barbara could see.

The sight of her son curled up next to the dog with his face nestled in her fur had elicited Barbara's shock, the exhalation of emotion causing the boy to stir against the animal's back before pulling himself closer to her, tucking his head into her side, careful even in his sleepy stupor to avoid her wounds. Smooch, for her part, barely moved at both Barbara and Jack's motions, merely opening her eyes and whining softly before shutting them again, her breathing deep and labored.

"He snuck down," Linda explained from the kitchen in a quiet voice. "I… didn't have the heart to make him leave."

Barbara put her hand to her mouth, but she had no more tears left to cry, just an undying love for the boy and his dog that would remain etched in her heart forever.

"It's okay," she said and quietly shut the door behind her.

* * *

"Aaaand there we go. That should do it!" Darren ran the last bead of caulk along the inside of the sliding door, sealing the plywood into the pane. They'd cut the piece to fit the door snugly, then used epoxy glue and exterior caulk to seal the gaps. While it negated her ability to see outside, it did make a mostly weatherproof barrier to keep out the occasional drizzles and, most importantly, the cold air.

Barbara set her pot of potatoes on the stove burner and came to inspect his work, nodding in satisfaction. "That's a tight seal. Thank you."

"Not a problem," the broad-shouldered man said, beaming with no small amount of pride.

"Darren can patch anything," Marie called from where she was frying sausages in a pan as a pot of sauerkraut simmered on the back burner, kicking up a strong smell of cabbage. Barbara glanced into the living room at the patched carpet where Darren had replaced the stained carpeting and padding with freshly cut pieces before gluing the carpet in place. Aside from the colors being wildly off, it was a perfect fit, and it was hard to tell that anything had taken place in the home less than twenty-four hours prior.

Barbara clucked and shook her head in admiration as she stood next to Darren. "This is just downright amazing. Where'd you learn how to do all this?"

"That's from a lifetime of doing patches and jerry-rigs on our own house," he admitted. "We were dead broke when we first got married, so we couldn't afford to pay anyone to do the work for us. I did it all myself. Roofs, walls, floors, plumbing… you name it, I figured out how to fix it."

"You even mended my heart," Marie cooed from the kitchen, eliciting a laugh from her husband and Barbara, who smiled and headed back to join her friend.

"Well, let me get back to mashing the potatoes, and we'll patch our bellies next."

"I'll mash them suckers!" Darren shouted, setting his caulk gun down and making his way to the sink to wash his hands before grabbing a potato masher and wagging it at the drained pot. "I make them a little lumpy. Is that okay?"

"Go ahead," Barbara called back.

"Eww," Jack interjected. "Lumpy taters."

"You're going to love them, son," the man scoffed. "Mind if I add a little garlic and onion powder, Barb?"

"Have at it," she replied called with a smile. "Use some butter, too."

"Oh, yes," Darren sang as he sidestepped to the refrigerator, opened the door, and retrieved the butter tub. "Butter is my middle name. And a dash of sour cream!"

"*Heart Attack* is going to be your middle name," Marie murmured, loud enough for everyone to hear. Barbara stifled a snicker then turned to watch as the kids set the table. She came over to help when Linda glanced up, pulling the silverware back from her mother's grasping hands.

"We've got this, Mom. You chill out."

She put her hands on her hips and looked around for something else to do, finding very little that hadn't already been taken care of. In addition to the burials, repairs and cleaning, they'd also brought out Smooch's bed and placed it where the couch had been. The dog rested her head comfortably on her paws with her ears relaxed and her eyes ticking back and forth from person to person, watching the humans work while she breathed slow and hard, still laboring, but her breaths sounded cleaner and less congested than they had a few hours prior.

"I can go out and get the bonfire started." She moved toward the door, but Darren interjected.

"We're saving that for later," he said. "Remember, we're going to cook some snacks on it for the kids." When Barbara made a face, the big man turned and held his hands up. "Hey, it was your idea."

"Go get cleaned up!" Marie called a gentle warning. "I told you to do that before, and you ignored me."

"I *did* clean up," Barbara defended herself.

"You changed your shirt and washed your face a little. You've still got smudges here and there."

She wanted to argue, but Marie's words rung true. Barbara hadn't taken a moment's break since the Everetts had gone home to bring back carpet and padding, busying herself with cleaning the living room walls and doing odd jobs until the couple returned, trying to settle the inner nervousness she couldn't shake no matter how hard she tried. Barbara was sore, exhausted, and anxious and while the prospect of dinner had everyone in high spirits, Barbara couldn't relax. Not without Tom and Sam. Her chest was packed tight with emotion, and she felt like she might break down in tears at any moment – hell, she already had broken down multiple times, her insides feeling hollowed out as hope for her loved ones' return grew more distant with every passing minute.

"I'll just hang around and keep watch." Barbara moved to the three rifles sitting on the counter. The weapons weren't charged, but they had each had full magazines in their magazine wells, ready to be used at a second's notice.

Marie turned the pan heat to low and stomped over to her, snatching Barbara's hand before she could pick up her gun.

"We'll take an occasional peek outside." Marie admonished her with a click of her tongue. "I promise. Now get a hot shower while you can and come back so we can eat."

"Go, Mom!" Linda echoed the older woman's sentiment.

"Yeah, go," Jack called as he dashed to grab the paper towels off the counter.

"Okay, okay!" Barbara said, her reluctant tone coming out more genuinely than she intended. "I'll be right back."

"Take your time." Linda gently shoved her away.

She moved across the living room and stepped into the short hall that led to their master bedroom suite. The room was silent, cut off from the kitchen noise and last evening's violence. With the house cleaned up and the smells of cooking sausages and sauerkraut wafting through the air, the battle and subsequent deaths of four men in her home felt like something from a dream – yet it'd happened.

Stepping into the master bathroom, Barbara sat on the edge of their whirlpool bathtub and untied her shoelaces before removing her boots and placing them in the corner. She peeled off her socks and sighed as the air cooled her feet, still uncomfortable in her clothes that felt painted on, saturated with sweat and blood and tears, her skin tacky beneath the material. She stripped everything off and kicked it to the corner of the bathroom, eyeing it with a sneer. Standing in front of the mirror, she stared at the rat's nest of hair sprouting from her ponytail, then studied the bruises on her shoulders, upper right arm, and thighs. No matter how much she ran through the events of the previous evening in her mind, she couldn't recall how she'd gotten some of them – and she wasn't sure she *wanted* to know, either.

Barbara turned to the shower and started the water, holding her hand beneath the flow, waiting until it got warm. It seemed vaguely wasteful to have the generator running all day, but she'd been too tired to worry about conserving fuel. Her only desire was to wipe away the nightmare and pray for her husband and daughter's safe return.

Barbara opened the door, testing the heat of the water with her foot, about to hop in when something buzzed from a corner of the room. She ignored it first, getting a leg fully into the shower before the buzzing came again and she realized in a flash that it was her phone. Despite a flutter in her belly, Barbara hesitated to step away from the warm embrace of the shower, thinking about all the times it had buzzed only for it to be some random news item she'd already seen a hundred times. Still, though, even if the chances of it being Tom were small, it was still a chance.

She padded over to the pile of bloody clothes, squatted and fished through her jeans pocket until she found her phone. Flipping it around, she saw not a typical news-related notification icon on the home screen, but a text message notification, instead.

Tom?

Her hands shook as she quickly unlocked her phone and read the message.

We're safe. Got to shore. Heading north. Almost to VA Beach. Will find a ride home. Don't worry about us. Stay safe!

Barbara sat stock-still, her body shocked through with numbness. She should be over the moon with emotion, shouting and laughing and crying, but reality wouldn't register even as she read the words over and over again, taking in the information without truly believing it.

"Don't worry about us," she whispered. "Stay safe." She spoke the words again, a trembling smile on her lips. "Stay safe."

Falling to her knees in the stained pile of clothes, she held the phone like it was a bar of gold, a slow swell of tears forming in her eyes. She pressed it to her cheek as if she could feel her husband through it. "Easy for you to say, Tom."

For a moment, it felt like he was standing right next to her, sharing in the dry humor. He wasn't, but he *was* alive. And so was Sam. They'd made if off the Navy vessel and were probably somewhere in Virginia Beach. Eventually, her body caught up to her mind, wrapping around the truth of the message.

Tom and Sam are alive.

Heat blossomed from her belly and slowly radiated through her arms and legs, her head beginning to spin as rays of hope pierced her heart. She read the message again and again, the words becoming blurrier as her eyes traced from the first letter to the last.

"He sent it a day and a half ago. That's not very long." She whispered, then quickly replied to the message, letting him know she'd gotten his text and that everyone was okay, that the Everetts were helping around the house and boy did she have a story to tell him. A laugh of pure relief escaped her, followed by a hitched breath that caught in her throat as she grinned, the news finally striking her like a ton of bricks. Barbara tried to rise but staggered forward, catching herself against the wall with a shivering arm. Her knees were weak, but she fought it, the urge to let Linda and Jack know too strong to fight against.

She walked carefully from the bathroom in a daze of emotion, and only when she'd gotten halfway down the hall did she realize that she was naked. Laughing, she ran back for her robe, shrugged it on and tied it tight, then she picked up her phone and left the bathroom, gaining speed and strength as her emotions rose through her, burning away her exhaustion.

She rushed into the living room, holding the phone up for everyone to see. Sam and Linda were seated at the table, messing around with a tablet game they played against each other on the Wi-Fi while the Everetts were still cooking, gliding around the kitchen with speed born of efficient practice. Linda was the first to notice her mother in the living room, holding up her phone with her wild mess of hair sticking up everywhere.

"Mom, what's wrong?" She kicked her chair back, stood, and circled the table. "What is it?"

Darren and Linda both turned to see, curious and a bit wary.

"Your father and Sam are okay," she said breathlessly. "They're near Virginia Beach! They got our text, and they're okay!"

"Are you serious?" Linda eyes went wide.

"Yes!!" Barbara angled the phone toward Jack and then back to her daughter so they could both read it. Linda came over, narrowed her eyes and scanned the words, her face lighting up with joy when she saw it was true while Jack leapt from his chair and started whooping for joy. For her part, Smooch partially raised herself on her one good leg and woofed, more at the boy's raucous excitement than anything else. Marie and Darren both came out of the kitchen, beaming smiles on their faces, and Marie embraced Barbara, whispering in her ear.

"I'm so happy for you, honey."

Barbara wiped away a tear of joy and nodded in agreement. After a moment, her phone continued to buzz and beep as more new alerts poured in, and she turned it around to look at the screen.

"Is it more from Dad?" Linda asked, beside herself with excitement, though her face dropped as Barbara scrolled through the headlines, slowly shaking her head sadly.

"No, they're not from your father. It's just more phone outages, riots in Raleigh and Richmond, fighting breaking out everywhere. Several cities are locking down and under curfew." She stared at them all in turn. "Everything is getting worse. Much worse."

Darren smiled grimly, looking at Marie who gave a nod of agreement. "Well then. What do you say you go get cleaned up, we finish our dinner, and then we all sit down and come up with a game plan?"

Chapter 20
Tom McKnight
Virginia Beach, Virginia

A cold chill ruffled the tent's flap and walls, thick canvas material keeping out the worst of the cold, but some slivers still slipped through, sharp as knives, finding every patch of exposed skin and reminding all in its path of how deadly it could be. The din of voices grew and fell as refugees streamed past nearby, kept under control by FEMA and the military, disorder and chaos still being kept at bay by the watchful eyes of those in charge.

The trio sat on foldout chairs inside the tent, sipping on bottled water and hot coffee as they waited for a promised "someone" from the Navy to come in. Tom leaned forward with his elbows on his knees and his head in his hands, facing the entrance, drinks at his feet, long since ignored and forgotten.

Private Packar had offered Jean and her kids a cot in another tent, which the woman eagerly accepted, telling Tom her family hadn't slept in more than a day, and they desperately needed to rest before moving on. Tom had encouraged her to get some sleep while they could, and while he wanted to keep the family nearby as potential witnesses in case something went south, they had no responsibility to him, and were likely far safer for leaving sooner rather than later.

"What do you think they want you for?" Jerry asked.

Tom shook his head and gave a knowing sigh. "I bet they flagged us as potential survivors of the research vessel we were on when the anomaly burst open."

"You were on a research vessel?"

"The Marin," Sam added.

"I think you might have mentioned that." Jerry scrunched his eyebrows. "What were you guys doing out there?"

Tom flashed the young man a grim look. "Navy work."

"They took us from our vacation," Sam added. "They wanted my dad to check out the anomaly."

Jerry turned on his stool to face Tom. "So, you're saying you were out there *at* the anomaly. Like, studying it?"

"We might have left that part out," he admitted. "Sorry for keeping you in the dark. It didn't seem important while we were dealing with the hurricane, plus parts of it were classified so…" Tom shrugged. "It wasn't intentional, I promise. And it's not like it would have made any difference in the moment."

"No, that's cool. I completely understand. And it makes sense now, that you know so much about what's going on."

"We were only out there for a few hours, but we witnessed the anomaly's power. We measured the pressure spewing out which made it easy to guess the desalination levels of the surrounding ocean. The rest, the part about the cold, was mostly my own theory." They fell quiet, Tom wondering if anyone else had made it off the Marin. The last time he'd seen his co-worker, Sue Anne, and Lieutenant Colonel Rachel Banks, they were heading for a free fall lifeboat.

After what seemed like an eternity, a sergeant with the name tag of Z. Landry stepped inside and stood with his hands clasped in front of him. His eyes slid to Sam and then Jerry before resting on Tom.

"Sir, can I see your identification, please?" the soldier spoke in a clipped tone.

"Yeah, sure." Tom retrieved his ratty wallet, removed his driver's license, and handed it over.

Landry studied the ID while glancing at Tom's face, obviously thrown off by trying to match the clean-shaven man in the picture with the scruffy-looking, weather-ravaged man sitting before him. Satisfied, the soldier returned his ID with a thin smile.

"Thanks, Mr. McKnight. They'll be glad we found you. Your name was at the top of my list. You must be pretty important to be that high. We've had crews out looking for you the past week when you didn't show up among the bodies."

Tom glanced at Sam in confusion before addressing the sergeant. "I appreciate the extra concern, but we just want to get home. My wife and other children are hunkered down at our farm near Bristol. Can you help us get there? I'd take a horse and buggy at this point."

"You can talk to the lieutenant colonel about that," the sergeant stated flatly. "Now, if you'll follow me, I'll take you to see her."

Tom, Sam, and Jerry all started to rise when Landry turned and blocked the exit.

"Just you, sir."

"I'll tell you the same thing I told Private Packar." He gestured to Sam and Jerry. "This is my daughter and a close family friend. We've been through hell to get here, and I'm not letting them out of my sight."

Tom expected the sergeant to put up a fight, but he shrugged and gestured for them all to follow him from the tent. As they crossed the bustling camp, he lifted his eyes and spotted a series of mobile structures set up at the far end of a theater parking lot.

"That must be where we're headed." Tom muttered. The main portion of the camp spread across the theater lot but extended into an apartment complex and department store. Military personnel patrolled the grounds while medical staff guided injured refugees to white tents with red crosses sewn into the roofs. Humvees and Jeeps escorted tractor trailers that hauled heavy construction equipment along the main highway, heading toward Virginia Beach. Glancing back, Tom watched the refugees flood across the railroad track checkpoint they'd recently come through, the line extending as far as east as he could see.

Samantha shook her head as she followed Tom's gaze. "There are thousands of them."

"Looks like a lot of tourists." Jerry added, Tom nodding but not replying.

Sergeant Landry led them out of the grass and into the theater lot where they strode quickly toward the mobile structures which were set up in an X-shaped configuration with the largest room in the center. Several storage sheds and a mess hall lay off to the side, all of it guarded by armed soldiers, each of whom was dressed in cold weather gear.

"Where are we headed, Sergeant?" Tom asked as he stuck to the man's hip pocket.

"Right there." Landry pointed to a section near the crux of the cross. They moved to a set of metal stairs and climbed to a square porch where a guard nodded and opened the door. The sergeant gestured for the trio to go inside and Tom went first, entering a conference room with a long table, several chairs, and a flat-screen monitor resting on the far wall while Samantha and Jerry brought up the rear.

"Have a seat while I set things up."

Tom circled the table and found a chair close to the screen while Sam and Jerry settled on the opposite side. The sergeant worked with a small video control panel on the table, pressing buttons and adjusting things until the screen filled with a bright blue color and he raised a phone to his lips.

"Lieutenant Colonel Banks, are you there, ma'am?"

At the mention of the colonel's name, Tom's heart skipped a beat, and he glanced at Sam, her eyebrows lifted hopefully as well.

Sergeant Landry continued. "Yes, ma'am. We've got Tom McKnight here with his daughter and a family friend. We can patch them through now. Yes. One moment."

The man hit another button and stepped back as Rachel Banks's face appeared on the screen. She sat in a conference room similar to the one they were in, wearing a beige military shirt, slightly stained and wrinkled, the worry lines at the corners of her eyes deepened since they'd last met, the dark circles above her cheeks speaking volumes about how much she'd slept.

The normally stoic officer smiled and nodded. "It's good to see you, Mr. McKnight. You too, Samantha."

"Hello, Lieutenant Colonel Banks." Sam gave a slight wave.

"This is Jerry," Tom introduced the young man.

"Hello, ma'am." Jerry nodded respectfully, his expression awe-struck.

Tom spoke the next words with breathless relief. "I'm glad you made it off the ship."

"It was a rough ride," Banks replied. "We got to the lifeboat and launched with eight people aboard. Hit the water hard and motored out of the danger zone. We drifted for twenty-four hours before they picked us up."

"Sue Anne?"

"She was with us," Banks nodded confidently. "She's fine."

"Thank God," Tom breathed. "Thanks for getting her out of there."

"Not only did we get her out, but Sue Anne's here in Washington with us, working on the project." The colonel arched an eyebrow. "Frankly, I'm surprised you made it. That little raft of yours didn't seem like much."

"It wasn't, but it was fast. We got out of there in a hurry, then we watched the Marin go down."

"That was a good ship." Banks gave a respectful nod before shifting in her seat. "Look, Mr. McKnight. I need to speak with you alone. If you don't mind sending Jerry and Samantha with Sergeant Landry."

Tom gave the pair a nod, and they stood and followed the sergeant through another door at the rear of the room.

Once they'd gone, Tom spread his hands. "I'm all ears," though on the inside he seriously doubted he wanted to hear what the lieutenant had to say.

"I've got a chopper on the way to pick you up. I need you back on the project with Sue Anne and some others."

"The last time you guys picked me up in a helicopter, it almost got me and my daughter killed." He poked his index finger on the table. "It almost killed us *all*."

"This is just a simple ride to Washington. No boats this time."

"What for?"

"We want you back on data analysis. Sue Anne is doing a great job, but the woman needs to sleep, and we've got some people up here who think you can make a real difference."

"There's no more I can do." Exasperation crept into Tom's voice.

"I doubt that. You're one of the best engineers the country has." Her voice took on a more somber tone. "And we lost a lot of good people on the Marin. People with skills that overlap with yours."

"I'm sorry about that," Tom's voice took on a genuine tone. "But I don't have anything else to contribute. You know the anomaly can't be stopped. And I read that the president announced the upcoming temperature shift to the public. Hell, it's already much colder out. I need to get home and prepare my family. Can you have the helicopter take me there instead?"

Banks shook her head and fixed him with a hard look. "I can't do that, Mr. McKnight."

"Then we're done here." He rose and turned, ready to call Sam and Jerry in so they could leave.

"Wait!" Banks held up her hand as if she could physically stop him. "It's much, much worse than what the president alluded to. The temperature changes will be more than a few degrees. Stop, please. You need to listen."

Tom froze with his eyes closed, then he sat, nodding slowly. "I thought as much. How cold do they expect it to get?"

"Very cold."

"The entire Northern Hemisphere?"

"Will become an ice box."

Tom shook his head as the implications circled through his mind. There would be massive death tolls, if not directly from the cold, then from starvation, mass extinctions of thousands of species, migrations of sea and animal life, and a complete upheaval the likes of which hadn't happened in thousands of years.

"If that's true, it means there's even less I can do to help fix it. And it's all the more reason for me to get home to my family."

"I understand how you feel," Banks said. "I haven't seen my family in weeks."

"But you probably sent them south, right? You sent them someplace warm."

The lieutenant colonel shifted sideways in her seat, angling toward Tom as if she could force him to agree. "A lot of people are doing that, and you should, too. We'll let you warn them."

"Gee, thanks." Tom's voice dripped with sarcasm. "Let me warn them how? And when? As they're freezing to death?"

Urgency, and a hint of anger locked Bank's jaw tight. "Look, Mr. McKnight. The country needs you. The whole *world* needs you. I wouldn't have brought you in if I didn't think you could help."

Tom tapped his palm on the table, nervousness tensing his shoulders. "What, exactly, do you expect me to do? At this point, you've got people to calculate death tolls, flood levels, and the temperature shifts. What's my job?"

"Your job will be to fix the anomaly."

Tom blinked at her, not certain he heard what she said. "You're kidding, right?"

"No."

"Either you guys are flat out naïve, or you're *way* too hopeful. You can't *fix* the anomaly. It would be like trying to snuff out the sun with a garden hose." Tom poked the table with his index finger to emphasize each point. "It's going to continue spewing freshwater until the pressure equalizes. That could be in ten months or ten years."

"We know."

"Then we're back to my original point." Tom stood and turned in a huff. "Sam, Jerry! Let's go!"

The back door flew open, and the pair stepped in with curious expressions.

"Everything okay, Dad?" Sam asked.

"No. Let's go." Tom strode to the side door, grabbed the handle, and shoved it open. He stepped out and ran into a six foot four MP who glared down at him, a shorter MP standing off to the side with a level, unmoving gaze.

Tom balked at them and backed into the room, glancing over to see Landry moving along the other side of the table.

"Mr. McKnight, we need you to stay," the sergeant said.

Tom shifted his attention back to Banks. "What's the meaning of this, Colonel?"

"I have an official order to bring you in. Just issued by Central Command."

"You're going to force me to help you?"

"I didn't want to have to. But essentially, yes."

Tom scoffed bitingly. "You have zero jurisdiction over me. I'm a citizen of the United States, not a member of the military or a state or federal employee. You can't order me around."

"We can, and we will." Banks's friendliness had vanished, replaced by her usual hard edge. "We'll keep you, your daughter, and Jerry until you agree to assist."

Tom put his hands on the table and leaned toward the camera, teeth grinding. "If you know we can't fix the anomaly, then what do you need me for?"

"We need your help to *try* to fix things. Or, barring that, to prepare for the end." Banks growled back.

"The end of *what*?" Spittle flew from Tom's mouth as he shouted at Banks. "The world?"

"The end of our epoch, Mr. McKnight." For a brief, split second, all of the fear and uncertainty and doubt that Banks was holding back shone through her expression. "And the beginning of a new one." They were both quiet, staring at each other over the video link for a long moment until Banks glanced over off-screen and nodded, then addressed Tom again.

"I'll give you a night to think about it." She looked at Landry. "Put them in an isolated tent. Bring them back here in the morning."

"Yes, sir," the sergeant said, gesturing for the trio to head outside.

Chapter 21
Barbara McKnight
Wyndale, Virginia

"This is where they got in," Barbara said, pointing at a spot on the west side behind the fuel shed where the men had broken in. The Everetts had since gone home, and Barbara and the kids were looking around the property, partially as a way to burn off nervous energy and partially to try to identify gaps in their defenses so they could shore them up. A section of the field fence had been smashed down where the men had climbed it and pressed it down beneath their boots, causing the old original wooden rails it was haphazardly attached to to fail, the top two having snapped and collapsed onto the bottom one.

"The fence between the rails is folded over," Barbara continued, "but I think we can straighten it out and reuse it."

"What do we do, Mom?" Jack asked.

"Let's jump back in the Gator." She walked over to the vehicle and got behind the wheel as the kids climbed in. Barbara started it up and pulled around to the newer storage barn in the backyard, talking as she went. "Your father pre-cut a stack of rails for just such an event," she called. "We were supposed to use them as replacements until we found time to install a new fence with t-posts and everything."

"That's Dad," Linda said, "always thinking ahead."

Barbara glanced at her daughter where she sat, seemingly happy, in the passenger seat. Yesterday's events had nearly been washed away by Darren and Marie's energy, their massive cleanup effort, and the delicious dinner, plus the news that Tom and Sam were alive had given Barbara and the kids newfound strength that they didn't know even existed. But, despite their high spirits, she couldn't help but notice her daughter's haunted eyes, and for the first time in her life, she couldn't think of a way to address it.

Linda has shot a man. It hadn't been a killing blow, but a shooting it was all the same, and her innocence was draining away faster with every tough choice she made and every challenge she faced. Barbara couldn't imagine what was going through her mind, she could only be patient and wait for the right time to discuss it, if such a time existed.

Pulling up in front of the barn, Barbara climbed out of the Gator, unlocked the doors, and slid them open before hitting the switch to turn on the interior lights as she led the kids all the way to the back wall where the rails were stacked. Together, they hauled two out and laid them across the vehicle's rear storage rack, then Barbara grabbed a hammer, pliers, and a cordless stapler off its charger and put them in the back next to the rails. Carbine slung on her shoulder, she returned to the driver's seat.

"You guys get in and hold the rails in place."

The kids did as they were told, and she drove them back to the broken fence line with Jack giggling the entire way as he tried to hold down the bouncing rails, continually getting knocked around by them. After parking, Barbara got out and looked out across the open field, eyes roaming over the neighbors' property, skirting the tall grasses and clusters of trees in the distance. Leaving her carbine close at hand on the front seat, she used the pliers and hammer to dig the old staples out of the broken rails to release the field fencing, then she pulled the metal fencing aside, picked out pieces of broken wood, and handed them to Jack and Linda to pile out of the way. The kids then held the replacement rails in place as she nailed them to the posts, then she lifted the field fence and stapled it to the new rails.

"Why do we use the field fence?" Jack asked. "Aren't the rails enough?"

"It's to dissuade coyotes from getting onto the property and getting to the chickens," she responded. "But more to the point, field fence is good for keeping most kinds of animals *in*. A proper setup would see it stretched and attached to t-posts, but we took some shortcuts when we were getting the animals setup originally and in some places we just nailed it to the existing posts and rails." She sighed. "It's definitely not the best fencing job in the world, but it'll get the job done for now."

"Maybe we should put some barbed wire around the top," Linda stood next to her, mirroring her stance. "To keep people out."

Barbara shrugged. "That's not a bad idea, but a single strand of barbed wire isn't much a deterrent. Still, it might be better than nothing. I've seen some at the hardware store downtown, but I'm not sure it's going to be open today." She glanced at the sky, murmuring, "Or tomorrow, or any other day."

"Maybe the Everetts have some?"

"I'll ask when I call over there today," she concluded, catching her daughter's worried look. "What's wrong, honey?"

"Nothing," Linda sighed.

Barbara glanced at Jack and watched as he climbed on the fence, goofing around. "Be careful, son." She guided her daughter down the fence line and faced her, speaking more softly. "I'll ask it again. What's wrong, baby?"

Linda's troubled eyes turned up to her mother. "I just don't want any more people to come here. Except for the Everetts, of course."

"Well, I don't either, honey. Are you afraid what happened the other day will happen again?"

Linda sighed, a tear racing down her face. "We probably can't stop them. We can't stop anyone."

"Your barbed wire idea is a good place to start," Barbara insisted, trying to infuse confidence in the girl. "And I've got some other thoughts about fortifying the first floor. And we *did* stop them, in spite of everything that happened. Does that make you feel any better?"

Linda nodded, but she still didn't seem at ease.

"Help me understand, honey." Barbara placed her hand gently on her upper arm and rubbed it, eyes searching her face.

Linda's gaze dropped to her feet, and she shifted to her other leg and pursed her lips in an undecided expression. "I just don't understand why they tried to hurt us." Her words gained steam, turning angry and indignant. "They didn't even ask first, you know? If they'd done that, we could have given them something. But they didn't, and we had to fight with them. They *made* us kill them."

Barbara nodded. "I know. It all seems crazy, and it's so hard to imagine people panicking so much and doing horrible things to each other, but they are. You saw how folks were acting in town, right?"

"Yeah. All weird, trying to steal and hurt each other."

Barbara was nodding. "Those men? They saw us as easy targets. A quick way to get the things they didn't work for. They figured it was just a weak woman, a dog, and a couple of helpless kids." She smiled, giving Linda a light punch in the shoulder. "And they definitely didn't count on *you* being so darn tough."

Linda flashed a grin at the compliment, then her expression sobered again. "I just wish it could have turned out better."

"Like Mr. Everett said, they didn't really leave us any choice." Barbara's conviction rose at her own words. "I don't want you to think that violence is the first and only option in every situation, but understand something - I wasn't going to let those men hurt you or ruin our chances to survive. I was determined to fight or die to keep us alive."

"How did you know what to do?"

Barbara thought about it a second, then shrugged. "I guess it was just instinct. How did you know when to fire at the man holding your brother?"

"I'm not sure," Linda thought hard. "I saw Jack in trouble, and I wanted to help him."

"But you waited until the right moment to fire so you wouldn't hit your brother," Barbara added. "You used your head."

"Yeah, I guess I did."

She seized on the moment. "You didn't *want* to shoot at that man, but you trusted your instincts, and you only fired when the time was right. You helped save Jack."

"I guess I did." Linda's chin lifted with a smile.

She leaned closer and flicked her eyes toward her son as he amused himself with throwing pieces of the old rail as far into the trees as possible. "Just don't rub it in too much, okay?"

"I won't," Linda chuckled.

Barbara took a deep breath let it out with a sobering expression, resting her palm against her daughter's cheek. "Look, I never want you to have to shoot anyone, or even hurt them. I shot all four of those men, and part of me feels terrible about it."

"You do?"

"Of course. Taking a life is serious business, even if they're bad people. They're still human beings. They probably had families and people who loved them. I would have avoided it if I could. But they came on *our* property and tried to hurt us and steal from us. They held a gun to Jack's head, tried to shoot me, nearly shot you in their panic and almost killed Smooch. I don't think we should feel too bad about what happened."

"I'll try not to feel too bad, but it's still a little confusing."

"If you ever have a question or you're not feeling right, come talk to me. Remember, we went through it together. And I'm here for you, always."

"I will." Linda wrapped her arms around her mother's waist. "You can talk to me too."

Barbara draped her arms over her shoulders, drawing her close. "We're a pretty good team, huh?"

"Yeah."

"Your father is going to be so proud when he hears how well you defended us."

"I hope he doesn't get mad that I totally missed the guy."

A laugh burst from Barbara's lips. "Your father won't be mad. Plus, between you and me, you definitely hit him." Barbara winked at her daughter, then looked at the fence one last time. "Let's head back in, okay?"

"Sure."

They loaded the old rails into the back of the Gator and drove them out to the fire pit. After tossing them in with the couch and stained carpet, with plans to burn them later, they returned to the house, Barbara parking the vehicle near the patio before taking the kids inside.

She went to the laundry room and opened the door to find Smooch sitting up, waiting for them, tail wagging weakly, whipping harder when Jack pushed his way in. He knelt next to Smooch and inspected the bandages like Linda had shown him, lifting one and checking the area where Barbara had put five stitches to seal the wound.

Standing over them, she nodded down. "Is the area swollen, like a bump?"

"Nope."

"Do you see any signs of pus leaking out? Or is there any on the bandage?"

Jack peeled the gauze back farther. "I don't think so. It's just a little bloody."

"Does it smell funny at all?"

The boy leaned in without hesitation and gave a sniff. "Nope. Smells okay."

Barbara nodded satisfactorily. "That's what we want to see. A little blood is fine, but an infection will leave yellow or greenish pus. And if it gets infected, we need to take a different approach."

Jack looked up, eyebrows pinched. "What kind of different approach?"

"Well, it might involve lancing the wound to get the puss out," she said with a frown. "That's why you need to make sure she eats her antibiotics with her food."

"I will," Jack nodded vigorously.

"Come here," she said. "I'll show you what I do."

They left the door open, and Smooch limped out with Jack right behind her. Barbara got the dog bowl and put it on the breakfast nook, then she crushed up amoxicillin and clavulanate capsules and mixed them with a can of wet food. Placing it down, she watched as the German Shepherd ate with her tail wagging contentedly.

"Is she going to be okay?" Jack asked.

"Her appetite is good, there're no signs of infection, and we didn't see any blood in her urine." Barbara rubbed her chin. "I'm no vet, but I'd say she's doing pretty well."

"Can we take her to a vet anyway?"

"Our regular vet is in town, honey, and I'm not sure I want to risk the trip again. Remember, it got pretty crazy last time. I think Smooch will be fine. If she starts to get weaker or something, we'll drive in and see if anyone is still operating, okay?"

"Okay."

"What do you say we have a quick lunch and start working on our defenses?"

Both kids agreed, and she and Linda made sandwiches and brought them to the table with a glass of milk for Jack. Barbara brewed a fresh pot of coffee, and soon they were all at the table enjoying a quiet meal as the violent incidents of the previous two days drifted to the backs of their minds. Linda glanced at her mother as she prepared to take a bite of her bologna and cheese sandwich.

"What are you thinking as far as defenses?"

"We have a ton of leftover scrap wood from when we moved in. I say we take measurements of all the windows on the first floor and cut pieces to fit. Then we'll use long screws to fix the slabs on the inside and outside of every possible entry point, except for the doors."

"That sounds like a good start," Linda agreed.

After cleaning up from lunch, they found a tape measure and went around the house taking measurements, writing the figures on a notepad before driving the Gator to the back barn in search of scrap wood. There they found several pieces on the first level and in the loft and got them into the vehicle's cargo tray. Next they retrieved bricks from a stack inside the barn and used them to hold the plywood scraps down while they drove, then Barbara brought out Tom's circular saw from the barn along with two small sawhorses.

At first, she wasn't sure she should use the saw since they were still relying on generator power. After considering how long it would take her to do it by hand, though, the fuel consumption made much more sense. Plus, it would save her a lot of work and blisters, a welcome relief after the events and bruises from the previous day.

"If we don't have enough wood," Barbara said as she drove them back to the house, "we might have to take apart some barn walls."

Linda's eyes widened. "Won't that leave it wide open?"

"We can take it from the stall walls, I meant," she clarified. "It'll look ugly on the inside, but still be fine on the outside."

"Got it."

They moved the pair of sawhorses into place on the patio and ran an extension cord straight to the outside outlet near to where the large generator continued to hum gently on the side of the house. Barbara tested the saw, holding it up and squeezing the trigger, listening as it sparked to life and jumped in her hand. With goggles over her eyes, she began cutting the scrap wood into perfectly-cut pieces, letting Linda carry them off to lean them against the house beneath each window. Sawdust floated in the air, the scent of cut wood tickling her sinuses with a charred smell, and she soon fell into a steady rhythm of measure, cut, measure, cut, repeated ad nauseum. It took most of the afternoon to get everything cut, and when she was done, she took the rest of the small stack that Linda hadn't already laid out and loaded them into the Gator.

With the sky turning overcast and the wind whipping them with a biting chill, they drove to the first window they wanted to cover. She and Linda held the heavy piece of wood in place while Jack used a pencil to mark the frames with drill spots, then Barbara drilled the pilot holes and stepped back, glancing up at the growing dusk.

"Okay, it's getting dark and cold. Let's pick up the pace so we can get these all done. We're ready to screw this puppy in; can you guys hold it in place?"

The piece was heavy, so Barbara helped them get it in position before letting go to grab the drill. With the kids grunting and groaning, Jack's face pressed against the wood as he leaned his full weight on it, she quickly ran screws and washers in, securing it in place. She'd cut it perfectly to size, giving an inch of space along the sides to peer out of so that they could monitor the backyard and road without compromising the protection and security the boards offered. They applied the rest of the panels all around the house until late afternoon turned into early evening and they could barely see without a flashlight. Exhausted and bruised, they parked the Gator around back and started to go inside, but Barbara slapped her palm against her forehead.

"I think we'll have these up for a long enough time that we should seal them. That way they won't rot from the weather. We should've done it before putting them on but... well, one coat on the outside can only help."

"What's sealer?" Linda asked.

"It's a chemical mixture that we apply to the wood," Barbara touched her chin. "And I think we have some of that out in the barn."

They drove out and picked up a can of sealer, paint pans, and two rollers, then they went to each window and rolled a coating on by the light of electric lanterns. It took them all of thirty minutes to complete, and they did a final inspection, strolling around the house with the petrochemical stench of paint thinner and chemicals hanging heavy in the air.

"It looks like a fortress from out here," Linda commented.

"It kind of does," Barbara admitted. "They'll need an axe to get through that. Even if they do, there'll still be a layer of glass waiting for them – plus a few more surprises."

She glanced at her watch and saw it was 7:23 PM. It was getting cold out, and she was starting to feel it in her bones. "I'll tell you what. It's late. I'll start working on dinner while you guys check the animals. After we eat, we'll figure out something fun to do."

The kids ran off to check the animals for the night, and Barbara went in to start dinner. A quick look in the fridge leftovers from their past three meals, so they'd eat those up before making something new, especially with so much work ahead of her and tomorrow's list of tasks looming large overhead. Finalize a power plan, locate some barbed wire – as a visual deterrent more than anything else – and put up a barrier too, so the animals wouldn't wander into the front yard, the latter of which might involve building a small corral in back.

"Slow down," she reminded herself with a murmur. "Baby steps."

As much as she tried to relax, Barbara couldn't keep her brain from racing. Shredding leftover chicken from the bone, she fixed them sandwiches and re-heated the leftover mashed potatoes, sauerkraut, and sausages from the previous evening as she thought through the immediate tasks, going over what each would entail. By the time the kids were done checking the animals, Barbara had everything on the table and ready to go, the rich sour smell of salt and peppered sauerkraut drifting through the house. They joked while they ate, the kids laughing and feeding Smooch scraps while Barbara glanced at boarded-up back door and kitchen window.

"It's so strange," she murmured. "Feels like we're slowly barricading ourselves inside."

Linda followed her eyes to the back window. "But it's really to keep people out, right?"

"That's right."

Toward the tail end of dinner, Barbara stood, shouldered her carbine, and stepped out onto the back patio, strolling around the house in the darkness, looking back to see if the inside lights were noticeable. The air was frigid and she pulled her light jacket tight to herself as she stepped away from the house, looking back at it every few feet to try and locate any vulnerabilities. Just a faint wink of light seeped out from the kitchen and living room windows, but the master bathroom window was completely dark. They might have to throw blankets or cloths over the blinds to block them totally out, but it wouldn't be a big deal, and she mentally added the task to tomorrow's to-do list.

As she checked and re-checked things in her mind, the sound of car engines caught her attention. It wasn't just one vehicle, like she had grown used to – and weary of – hearing, but several at a time, then more, the noise growing the longer she stood still. Her belly clenched as she unslung her carbine and crept over to their van and pickup and circled the corner of the house, staring down at Wyndale Road.

The two-lane connector road wasn't just a back country road, but it also served to join several major highways and I-81 itself, and whenever the major thoroughfares were shut down, Wyndale would always take the overflow, their little neck of the woods suddenly flooded with headlights and the sounds of engines.

Gazing down at the road, she saw a handful of cars drive by, followed by another group. More joined them, and soon a few grew into a line of ten or twenty. Within fifteen minutes, it was almost bumper-to-bumper traffic, the rumble of car engines filling the air, exhaust fumes riding up the slope. Standing in the driveway, she stared in awe as the headlights washed the surrounding hills in light.

"What in the hell is going on now?"

Static crackled, and Darren's voice came out of nowhere. "Barbara, this is Darren. Are you there? Go ahead."

Startled, she looked around to see if the man had somehow snuck up on her, then she chuckled uneasily, realizing his voice came from the radio on her belt. She snatched it off and put it to her mouth, keeping an eye on the traffic.

"I'm here, Darren. You'll never guess what I'm looking at. Go ahead."

"I'd say it's an endless line of cars."

"That's right. I guess you can see it, too."

"Yep. I'm looking at it now from our bedroom window upstairs." The man didn't sound terribly worried, but the radio had a way of stripping the tone from their voices.

"Think it's overflow from the highway?"

"Yep. I've been monitoring the news all morning on my shortwave receiver. Seems like the traffic is from folks evacuating from the northern states."

"You mean, from everywhere up north?"

"Nail on the head. I'll bet if you went down and looked at all those license plates, you'd see Ohio, Kentucky, West Virginia, and Pennsylvania. You might even catch a few from Canada."

"Wait, what?"

"Rumors are that the feds are actually encouraging people to leave their homes and go south."

"Why?" Barbara asked as she sidestepped to her front porch and sat on the edge, watching the headlights flow past in a slow trickle.

"I've heard it's for a lot of different reasons. Terrorist threats, rioting in coastal cities after the storms, stuff like that. My bet is that I-81 is packed with cars. Folks are exiting at Abingdon and taking alternate routes, one of which happens to pass right through our front yards."

"Oh, no." Barbara bit her lip, eyes following the cars down the road before shifting back to the left to trace the next group going by. "If what you're saying is true, this won't be the usual short detour we're used to seeing. This could last for days."

"That's right. Or weeks."

"Where, exactly, are they telling them to go?"

"Apparently, the feds have set up shelters along the Gulf Coast and Mexican border. They're saying it's just temporary, and people can go back home in a few weeks."

Barbara held the radio with both hands. "Seems strange to be telling people to go south. I mean, folks are starting to panic, but the men who attacked us last night wanted to go west, not south."

"Mhmm. Makes me wonder if there's more to that little temperature story they've been telling us than they're letting on."

Barbara's shoulders clenched as she was reminded of the strange chill in the air, her breath showing up in faint traces of mist. "I tend to agree with that. And I'd bet those folks aren't going back home in a few weeks. It could be months."

"Maybe even years," Darren piled on. "The Northern Hemisphere might become uninhabitable come winter if the temps keep dropping like they are."

She bit her lip. "Should we think about evacuating?"

"Not yet. Between us, we've got good shelter and food stores, and we'd be fools to leave it all behind. Plus, Tom's on his way back, and you need to be here when he arrives."

Crossing one arm on her chest, she stared hard at the cars going by. "So, we just hunker down and try to stay warm?"

"And work on those defenses."

"Like the wood panels we put over the windows tonight," she replied. "Hey, Darren. Would you happen to have any barbed wire around? Maybe razor wire? I want to make folks who don't know better think twice about crossing the fence line."

"I've got a single roll of the stuff, but I've got a friend who might have more. Maybe we can pay him a visit soon."

"That sounds good, Darren. Thanks for the information, and the help."

"No problem. Happy to assist. You stay safe tonight. Keep an eye on the road. If any trouble comes your way, don't hesitate to radio."

"You too," Barbara said. "Talk to you later."

"Bye."

She held the radio in her hands for a minute, staring down at the endless caravan of vehicles. Sedans, vans, and big rigs packed with people and belongings cruised by, engines revving, horns honking, creating a din of noise that was sure to only get worse. All it would take was one of them breaking down or deciding to park in their driveway to put her family in danger yet again.

She'd already locked the front door, so Barbara stood and walked hurriedly around to the back of the house. Embraced by the warmth of the house, she was pleased to find the kids already cleaning up. From the key rack in the hallway, she grabbed the Astro van keys and started to go back outside.

"Wait, Mom!" Linda called, coming in from the kitchen. "Is something wrong?"

"Not yet," she replied. A frightened look appeared on the girl's face, and Barbara quickly put her mind at ease. "It's nothing serious, I promise. There are just some cars on the road, heading south. It's a traffic jam and I want to pull the van down to block our driveway."

"Want me to come?"

"Nope. I want you to stay here and keep cleaning up. I'll be right back."

Barbara exited the house, jangling the keys in her hand as she opened the van door, unslung her carbine, and placed it in the passenger seat. After climbing in and starting it up, she pulled slowly down the gravel driveway, approaching the line of traffic in a light cloud of dust. Narrowing her eyes at the cars rumbling along at ten miles per hour, her headlights reflected off windows, masking the shadowy faces watching her from inside.

When she reached the end of her driveway, Barbara pulled sideways and parked so no one could drive right up to their house, flicking the lights off and killing the engine. There were ditches and partial fencing on either side, so the only way anyone could bring a vehicle up was if it was a large four-wheel-drive one. Satisfied she'd blocked any immediate, easy entry, Barbara got out with her carbine and stood by the van car, cradling the weapon loosely. Headlights off, doors locked, she watched folks glancing at her and the rifle before averting their eyes, choosing to mind their own business over risking raising the ire of a strange woman bearing a rifle and a sour expression.

People didn't seem to be looking for trouble, and after a few minutes of watching she made her way back up to the house, turning to watch the passing traffic when she reached the top. After the events of the last day, she wasn't looking for another sleepless night, waiting for someone to knock down their fence or try to get onto the property, though with Smooch injured and locked inside, she wouldn't have much warning until someone was at their doorstep. While she felt a little better about having some ground floor defenses up, they still had a lot to do the following morning.

Barbara circled to the back and entered the house through the kitchen to find the kids weren't there. They'd left the place in perfect condition with just the breakfast nook light on as well as a candle burning on the table, the scent of cinnamon permeating the house, helping to extinguish the lingering traces of sauerkraut.

"Kids, where are you?"

"In here, Mom!"

Barbara moved down the hallway and took a left into the dining room where Linda and Jack stood by the front window, peering through the gap they'd left to watch outside, both of them carefully monitoring the road.

"We watched you come up, Mom. There's a lot of cars down there." Jack intoned, pointing out the obvious.

"Darren said they're part of an evacuation."

"What's an evacu...vacu..." The boy's eyes scrunched up as he tried pronouncing the word.

Linda scoffed. "An evacuation is when people have to leave one place and move to another."

"Very good."

"But why are all those people leaving?" She continued. "Did someone make them?"

"Is it because of the storm?" Jack piled his question on top.

"Darren and I think it might be because of the temperature change the president talked about."

"Everything's getting colder?"

"Yep, especially up north of us. So, the government is asking people to drive south. And there are so many people doing it at the same time that they're clogging the main roads, so people are driving on the smaller ones, like ours."

"Are they going to hurt us like those bad men?"

"I hope not," Barbara admitted.

"Smooch can't protect us now," the boy said. "She's hurt."

"That's true." She rested her hand on the boy's head as the reality of the task loomed before her. Remaining vigilant for a few hours or a day was easy – keeping watch all the time would take a lot of work. "But at least we have protection on our windows now, right? And I'll stay up a little later tonight and keep watch."

"Can I help?" Linda asked.

"Maybe."

Linda must have heard the doubt in her mother's voice, as her face took on a hurt look. "I can do it, Mom. I won't fall asleep on watch or anything."

Barbara smiled, doing her best to avoid muting her daughter's enthusiasm. "I'll tell you what. I'll take first shift and wake you up for the late morning shift. If you still want to do it then, you can."

Linda nodded enthusiastically.

"And your job will be to come get me if you see anything strange or if Smooch starts barking."

"Okay," Linda said, voice rising with excitement, head still nodding. "No problem. I can do it."

"What are we going to do tonight?" Jack asked, stepping away from the blinds, the cars rolling by forgotten. "You said we were going to do something fun."

Barbara rested her hand on her hip. "Popcorn and a movie?" *While I look out the window every few minutes.*

The kids both nodded enthusiastically.

"Can we watch up in Sam's room?" Jack glanced down the hall where the men had died.

"I was thinking we could pull the love seat over where the couch used to be and pile on." Barbara looked at her children hopefully. When neither of them responded, she shrugged. "What?"

"He calls it the dead guy room now," Linda dipped her head at her brother.

Barbara winced, patting Jack sympathetically. "I understand you don't want to hang out where those guys died." An assuring smile flashed across her face. "Sure, we can watch a movie upstairs tonight. It'll be easier for me to keep an eye on the road anyway."

Jack gave a happy jump and spun in his socks. "Can Smooch watch with us?"

"Of course," Barbara laughed. "You guys get everything set up. Make sure we have lots of pillows."

"Done!" Linda shouted, and the pair bolted upstairs, leaving her alone in the dining room. Barbara turned back to the window and peered through the gap, leaning, watching as the cars and trucks rolled by, an endless river of humanity flowing ever southward.

She slung the carbine over her shoulder and went to make popcorn.

Chapter 22
Barbara McKnight
Wyndale, Virginia

The blaring of a car horn startled her from a deep sleep. Her eyes flew open to near darkness and a soft material brushing her cheeks, stifling her breath, and holding her down. Panic hit Barbara square in the jaw as she pushed against whatever was covering her, rolling her shoulders and twisting, but still unable to untangle herself.

Someone moaned in the bed next to her, and she realized the weight on her leg was her son, jack. Jerking, she freed one foot, shifted, and dragged her other leg out from beneath him before raising her hand and breaking free of the sheets pinning her down, sticking her head out, seeing Linda had fallen asleep on top of the sheets and had trapped Barbara under them.

"Baby, scoot over. I need to get up."

"Was that a horn?" Linda asked, rolling to her right and freeing Barbara from the tangle of blankets.

"I think so." Knees drawn up, she kicked her feet from beneath the covers. The thirty-inch television was still on, the screen blue after their movie had ended hours prior.

She made a disgusted sound. "I can't believe I fell asleep."

The car horn blared again, and she swung her legs off the bed, holding onto Jack to make sure he didn't fall off. Taking up her carbine where she'd leaned it against the wall, Barbara crept to the window, opening the blinds to let in the morning sunlight, much to her son's continual, louder groans.

The line of cars still moved along the road, though a sedan had pulled into the opposite lane and appeared to have stalled.

"That's not good," she mumbled, watching as two men got out of the car and opened the trunk, digging out something inside. Barbara turned away from the window to see Linda sitting on the edge of the bed. "Stay here," she said as she walked past.

She quickly descended the stairs and unbolted the front door, throwing it open, stepping onto the porch, gazing down at the road. She watched as one man knelt by the car's tire, using a tire iron to loosen the lug nuts while another man stood nearby. The pair exchanged the flat tire with a smaller spare, climbed back in the car, and rejoined the flow of traffic heading south, much to Barbara's relief. Aside from the brief delay, the general pace of the vehicles remained in the twenty-mile-per-hour range, but Barbara could imagine a moment when some jam down the road might bring everything to a grinding halt. While she watched, at least two vehicles used the northbound lane to pass others, driving like bullies to skip ahead in the line. With a shake of her head, she headed to the kitchen where Linda had already started brewing a pot of coffee.

"Oh, bless you, child." She kissed her daughter on the head as she passed, placing her carbine on the counter and turning toward the refrigerator.

"Can I have some cereal?" Jack asked as he padded in in his pajamas and slippers.

"I'm making eggs and bacon for myself and Linda. Sure you don't want some?"

"Cereal is fine," the boy said. Then he looked for Smooch's food bowl.

"Have it your way," Barbara shrugged. "And remember to smash up a pill for Smooch. They're in the top right drawer." She watched as the boy emptied a can of wet food into a bowl, smashed up the pill, and mixed it in. Satisfied he'd done a good job, she retrieved the bacon and eggs from the refrigerator and pulled out a pan from the cabinet. She placed down eight strips and kicked the heat to medium-high, then she followed behind Linda, poured herself a coffee and the pair leaned against the counter, sipping their hot beverages as the bacon sizzled behind them.

"I'm worried about those cars out there," her daughter said.

"I am, too."

"What should we do about them?"

"There's nothing we can do. Not directly." Barbara blinked as her mind worked through the to-do list she'd started the night before. We should keep a low profile and continue working on our defenses."

"What's next on the list?"

"We'll feed the animals first." Barbara placed her coffee cup on the counter, took a fork from the utensil drawer, and went to flip the bacon. "Then I think we need to put up additional covering for the windows. I'll talk to Darren a little later and see if we can make a trip for that barbed wire. We should also start gathering and cutting wood in case we need it for fires."

"That' sounds like a full day."

Barbara winked. "Dress warm. And in layers."

Linda finished making breakfast while Barbara crossed into the dining room and rested her carbine against the wall. She peered outside, watching the flow of traffic on its way south. A half mile up the road, she saw two cars pulled off to the side, one parked in her neighbor's driveway, making her glad she'd blocked her driveway with the Astro van. After returning to the kitchen, Barbara toasted some bread, then they plated their bacon and eggs and took everything to the table to fuel up for the day's work.

After breakfast, the kids went upstairs to get changed while she got dressed in the master bedroom. The temperatures weren't close to freezing, but the recent nip in the air told her an extra T-shirt beneath her flannel shirt and work jacket would go a long way. She threw on a pair of thick socks and her work boots, then checked her phone. There were no new messages from Tom, just news headlines that had filtered in through the spotty cellular connection. Glancing over two articles about flooding in the Virginia Beach area, she reminded herself that Tom had texted her, so he and Sam were fine. They'd gotten out of the worst of it. They hadn't been caught in the flooding.

"I just wish you guys would get home." She gave a frustrated sigh before she donned her work jacket, shouldered her carbine, and returned to the kitchen. Before the kids got there, she took a detour to the basement where she unlocked the first gun safe. Along with her Smith & Wesson at her back hip, she added a holster for a .45 caliber Springfield XDS on her front-right hip and tucked the pistol into it. She grabbed an extra magazine for it – loaded with hollow points – and stuff it into her pocket as well. She wasn't normally a big fan of the more expensive ammunition, but after their encounter with the intruders, hollow points were, in her opinion, a must-carry.

She removed her trusty Benelli M2 semi-automatic shotgun next and set it aside, then from the second safe she chose a Mossburg 500 and several boxes of shells. Closing the safes, she grabbed the weapons and carried them upstairs, placing the Mossburg in the dining room on top of a tall cabinet along with three boxes of shells, then she took the Benelli into the kitchen where the kids waited, Smooch standing by the door, wagging her tail but still not able to do much.

"Ready, guys?"

"Ready," Linda said.

"Yep." Jack nodded enthusiastically.

Barbara paused to pull up a small stool to the kitchen cabinets, climbing up, placing the shotgun on the very top cabinet along with three boxes of shells. She talked to the kids as she worked. "I realize I'm putting these weapons in plain sight, but it's only because I want to have something handy in case we're attacked again. You're not to mess with any of the guns. They're loaded. I'm serious, okay?"

The kids both nodded solemnly and followed her as she stepped down, unlocked the back door, and walked out onto the patio, Smooch limping outside behind them, her tail wagging even harder as she found a spot to do her business while Barbara had a quick look around the yard. The animals were gathered where they usually were, close to the chicken and rabbit coops, ready to eat.

"Go ahead to the feed shed. I'm going to do a quick walk around the house."

The kids ran off while Barbara unslung her rifle and cradled it in her arms, circling to the east side of the property past their pickup truck to the front of the house. She focused on the passing cars, their numbers still strong, before settling on some stray sheep lingering in plain sight on the slope. When they saw her, they meandered in her direction, following her around the west side of the house to the feed shed.

"Like a piper," she murmured to herself, smiling. "If I wanted to eat you guys, you wouldn't object, would you?"

Slinging her rifle once more, she filled a bucket with the regular mix, then guided the hungry animals toward the back of the house, hoping they'd linger in the area throughout the day until she could erect a makeshift corral. She slung feed into the yard as the animals congregated about, frequently glancing up at the woods or the fence line, or even at the house, half expecting people to walk around the side at any moment.

The constant flow of cars was a low drone, broken only by a periodic horn beep or tire squeal. There were enough 18 wheelers in the mix that clouds of exhaust occasionally washed over the property, turning her stomach as she wondered how many vehicles had passed them through the night. Given how many had passed since she had gone outside, she estimated it must be in the thousands – perhaps even more. After finishing with the animals, they did a quick look around the house, Barbara coming to stand on their concrete patio, arms crossed as she mentally measured part of the back yard.

"What next, Mom?" Linda asked, mimicking her mother's pose.

She gestured for them to load up into the Gator. "Kids, come with me."

They climbed in and drove out to the barn. Once inside, they grabbed several rolls of black weed barrier and loaded them into the cargo tray, then after they arrived back at the patio, they grabbed the rolls and carried them into the kitchen.

"What's this for?" Linda asked.

"There're too many people passing by. I want to make sure this house doesn't give off a shred of light at night. We'll tack the barrier over the windows before we put the blinds back."

"Great idea, Mom," Linda patted her shoulder enthusiastically.

"Let's get started," Barbara nodded.

They measured and cut weed barrier, then stapled it tight around the windows. She cut small flaps in the sides and used Velcro strips to seal them shut.

Once finished, they put the blinds back in place to form a double barrier against leaking light. She stepped back from the last window they'd completed, admiring their work.

"There's no way anyone can see inside from the road or even the yard," she said.

"It looks like Halloween decorations." Linda ran her hand over the felt-like surface. "Kind of cool and dark and creepy."

"Can we eat lunch now, Mom?"

Barbara looked at the clock and saw they'd gone well into the afternoon. "I think that's a great idea. First, Linda and I are going to do a quick patrol. Can you feed Smooch, Jack?"

"Sure, Mom," he called, already heading for the dog food.

She retrieved her carbine from the Gator's seat and took her daughter on a quick patrol around the house. Like the previous night, vehicles still packed the road, moving at ten miles per hour, some driving in the northbound lane in a rude attempt to pass everyone else, car horn bleats increasing as tension grew along the route. The pair crunched over the gravel driveway, Barbara staring at the traffic. "Once this traffic slows to a crawl, people are going to be tempted to pull over."

"Probably to get some rest or use the bathroom," Linda added.

"That's right. And even though we're keeping a low profile, some folks might see our house as a fine spot to roost for the evening. We need to guard the place twenty-four hours a day."

"You won't even be able to sleep," Linda replied, trying to sound unafraid, but Barbara heard the tension in her voice.

"I know."

"What if people come and try to take the farm? I mean, there are so many. They could do that, right?"

"I guess they could if they joined forces."

"What would we do?"

Barbara swallowed her fear. "I don't know, honey."

They hadn't really discussed a bug-out plan, and with all their food and weapons inside the farmhouse, their entire livelihoods were there, and Tom and Sam would be coming home soon. If she allowed someone to drive them out, there'd be no one to greet her family when they arrived. An image of the raised dirt mounds at the back of the property rose unbidden, and she latched onto it, using it to fuel her determination. *I'll fill the whole damned place with corpses if that's what it takes to keep us safe.*

Jaw clenched, a thought that had been at the back of her mind since the conclusion of the home invasion pushed its way forward. "I was thinking…"

"Yeah?"

"I want you to start carrying the emergency pistol with you at all times."

Linda's eyes went wide. "Really?"

Barbara nodded. "I don't want you to have to do it, but I can't be everywhere at once." She raised her chin. "You're fourteen years old, and you've shown proficiency and safety with the weapon. In fact, you've stepped it up a lot lately. I'm really proud of you."

"Thanks, Mom." Linda's voice filled the quiet space beneath the sound of passing cars.

"And young, eighteen-year-old women join the army and go off to fight all the time." Barbara sighed. "You're not quite that old, but we've trained you well enough."

Linda grinned with uncertainty. "It sounds like you're trying to convince yourself."

"No. You'll do a great job." Barbara smiled sadly. "It's just that I'm your mother, and I don't like seeing you grow up so fast. I don't want you to get hurt."

"I won't."

"You have to do me one favor."

"Anything."

"Your brother. He might think because you're carrying a weapon, that means he can, too."

"I won't let him touch it," the girl promised, shaking her loose hair around her shoulders. "I won't leave it out where he can find it."

"All right. Next time I see you, I want to see the pistol properly holstered at your hip like I have mine."

"That's where I like to wear it." Linda nodded as she tried to hide a grin.

Mother and daughter stared at the line of traffic for five minutes before Barbara turned back. "C'mon. Let's go inside. We'll rustle something up for lunch, then we'll talk about how we're going to do this." She stifled a yawn, her own exhaustion rising to the surface. "You'll be on second shift tonight."

Linda leapt to her mother's side, practically shaking with excitement. "Really?"

"Yes, and we need to be serious about it this time. I'll be on from now until three-thirty in the morning. Then, you're up."

"Okay, Mom. I won't let you down."

Barbara put her arm around her daughter's shoulders and gave a brief squeeze. "I know you won't, baby. I know you won't."

Chapter 23
Tom McKnight
Virginia Beach, Virginia

"This Army food isn't so bad," Jerry said. He lifted a forkful of the so-called scrambled eggs with his injured arm and bent to shovel it in his mouth. Then he raised a piece of buttered toast and snapped off a bite. "I mean, these eggs don't have much of a taste except for grit. And the toast's been sitting out for a week. Maybe two. But at least it's hot!"

"I'll give you that much." Tom chuckled as he sipped his coffee. They'd not slept much all night, despite the comfortable cots Sergeant Landry had provided, Tom wrestling with the answer he'd have to give Banks when the woman called them back. He was still flabbergasted by her response, unable or unwilling to comprehend the magnitude of the situation at large that would cause the normally level-headed Banks to snap like she had. Their own personal issues were long in the past, and while she'd always been gruff and to-the-point, that was just a facet of her personality. To go as far as she had in keeping him under lock and key was unusual to say the least.

Outside the tent, people talked and called out and trucks rumbled by, the endless line of refugees coating the air in a constant drone of sound. They'd come in by the thousands overnight and had continued through the day, moving through camp, some stopping, some being stopped and most of them passing through. True to Bank's promise, Tom, Sam, and Jerry had only been allowed out on a pair of short walks the previous evening, and were otherwise confined to their tent, prohibited from leaving under implied threat of duress.

His daughter raised a sausage link with her fork and gave it a suspicious look before taking a bite, talking around the food. "When do you think they'll come for us?"

"No idea," Tom glanced at his watch. "It's already nine-thirty. That's practically the middle of the day for some military personnel."

"Are you still going to tell them no?" Jerry asked.

"That is a definitive yes."

"Even though you could save the world?"

"One should always do what it takes to save the world." Tom gestured at Jerry with his fork. "But you also have to know when to quit. This anomaly is going to keep spewing no matter what, and the weather will continue getting colder no matter what and the government will use a heavy hand to blunder their way through no matter what. I'd like to avoid all that and spend my time back home with my family, no offense to the world."

"Banks promised to send someone to take care of them."

Tom shook his head. "I'm sure she has good intentions, but I doubt she could live up to that promise. They need all the people they can get right now. They're not going to send a troop of soldiers to stand around protecting the McKnights. If Sam and I don't get home, Barbara and the kids will be left to fend for themselves. I can't agree to that."

"Take it easy," Jerry held up his hands. "I'm just playing devil's advocate here. I'm still fully on your side."

"Sorry, I didn't mean to sound so harsh. I'm just tired of being held up by things outside my control."

"Can we just, like, escape?" Sam asked in a conspiratorial whisper.

Tom stared at his daughter, but she only raised a questioning eyebrow at him. "The thought had crossed my mind," he admitted. "But I want to make sure we have no other choice. I think--"

A bustle outside their tent stopped Tom from speaking and the tent flap flew to the side as Sergeant Landry stepped in, nodding to each of them in turn.

"Glad to see you had breakfast. I was going to take you to see Banks now, but if you want to finish--"

"No, let's go now." Tom put down his fork and dusted off his hands. Then he looked at Sam and Jerry. "You two are staying here."

Tom rose and followed the sergeant outside, sticking close behind him as they wove through the bustling parking lot. Their tent was directly south of the prefab military buildings where he'd spoken with Banks the previous day, and Landry took him to the same building, they climbed the same stairs, moved past the guards, and stepped inside the conference room. Tom took a seat up front, facing the screens, and Landry circled around to sit opposite him. Wasting no time, he raised a remote control and powered on the network device to connect them to the lieutenant, the screen immediately turning blue.

"The call is in," Landry said, eyes shifting from Tom to the screen. "We'll just wait for them to accept the call."

Tom nodded and leaned back, studying the sergeant's stoic features. "You have family around here?"

"No, sir." The sergeant turned his dark eyes on Tom. "They're in Florida."

"Hopefully not near the beach."

Landry shook his head with a dark chuckle. "They're just outside Kissimmee."

"Ah, good. They should be safe from the initial flooding, then. Have you spoken to them recently?"

"I spoke to them two days ago."

"What are their plans?"

"They're going to circle the Gulf and meet up with our relatives in Alabama. I told them to go sooner than later, before the roads get too bad."

Tom mulled that last part over. "The roads'll be packed with cars as people flooded inland. Eventually they'd turn south, chased by the cold Banks was talking about." He sighed. "At least you got to talk to them. I haven't spoken to my wife and kids for a while. I guess going on a week."

Landry's hard expression softened and he lowered his voice. "I just want you to know, I understand your concern. I felt the same way when my dad first insisted on staying in Florida. I had to convince him it would be safer in Alabama. Of course, I'm stuck here, so I can't help them do anything. I really do sympathize with you."

Tom's expression flattened as he stared at the pressboard table, summoning the faces of his wife and children into his mind. "I guess everyone is going through something right now."

The screen blinked from the blue to a view of Banks's conference room. The lieutenant colonel was seated in the same chair as the previous day, buttoned up tighter, her hair pulled into a bun so tight it was hard to tell where her forehead stopped and the hair began. The woman appeared rested, but no less hard-edged, all pretense of her initial good nature having fallen by the wayside.

"Mr. McKnight."

"Lieutenant Colonel Banks," he nodded cordially, setting his jaw in preparation for a verbal joust.

"I hope you had some time to think about what we discussed."

"I have. And I can't say--"

"Before you go on." Banks raised a finger. "I just want to reiterate my dedication to your family's safety."

"I appreciate that, ma'am, but--"

"And we've got a great team working at a top-secret location. You'll be sitting with the greatest minds." The officer lowered her voice. "Along with the president's own top advisors."

Tom shook his head and spoke the next part with a growl. "The last place I want to be right now is in a top-secret location. Where I *need* to be is home with my family. I know they're alive, but that's all I know. Based on what I've read and heard, Bristol could soon be overwhelmed with refugees. That puts them in the direct line of looting and lawlessness, and you know it."

Banks folded her hands on the table. "The president has staunchly come out against that sort of thing. He won't let it happen, especially not to your family."

Tom laughed, raising his hands and looking around the empty room in disbelief. "He can't stop it. I don't think anyone can. At least not all of it."

Banks shifted in her seat. "We can take you to your wife and kids before you set off. We can even—"

"You only have one gear, don't you?" Tom leaned back, shaking his head. "Your plan is always to just throw people or money or equipment at a problem, figuring it will solve things. You'll send a platoon of soldiers to my farmstead, but would even one of them know how to take care of animals or work a greenhouse? Can any of them farm? Can they maintain a hydroponic garden so they have food for the coming freeze? I don't think so."

"We can bring them to us."

"So, you have a camp for all government employees and military families? You'll just pick up my wife, kids, and dog and transport them to some camp where they'll live happily ever after?"

Banks nodded.

"Where's that?"

"Fort Campbell, Kentucky. That's where most of our families are."

Tom was already shaking his head. "Sorry, Banks, but that's not good enough. If we go anywhere, it'll be south. We need to get away from the cold." Leaning forward, he spread his hands on the table, summoning a pleasant tone. "I'm begging you, ma'am. Let us go so we can get home and prepare for what's coming."

Banks sat in mute silence for ten full seconds, her face turning slightly red, her hands clenching tighter on the table. The woman seemed to want to say something, working on the angle, the gears grinding in her head.

She finally shook her head, pointing at the camera. "Look, McKnight. I need you to get on board with this. The Joint Chiefs of Staff are counting on you joining the team. Hell, the *president* is counting on it. This is an all-hands-on-deck event, You can't stand on the sidelines being selfish. Especially not after…"

Tom leaned forward with a hard glare, cutting the woman off before she could finish. "That's water under a very old, very burned bridge, Banks. You're damned lucky I'm even still choosing to *speak* with you anymore. And now you're calling me selfish for wanting to go home to my family?"

"It's not just about you and yours." Banks spoke quietly, her own voice simmering with anger. "It's about the country and the millions of lives at stake."

"Where do you find the gall, Banks? After I took my daughter aboard the Marin, risking our lives to help with the data. Then, when the ship was being torn apart and you ignored my initial warning? Who was being selfish then?"

Banks dropped her eyes to the table, jaw grinding.

"Let me remind you that I had to scream at you to get people aboard the lifeboat." Tom's voice remained level, but his shoulders shook with anger, his palms pressed to the table to keep himself under control. "If you had done you're your damned job and listened to me, you could have gotten more people off that boat. Same story as before, Banks. You don't listen and people die."

"You will *not* put that on me. Not then and not now." Banks' face turned beet red and she stiffened and gave an indignant shake of her head. "No one could have predicted what the anomaly was going to do."

Tom shook his head. "I'm not blaming you for that. What I'm saying is, I don't trust you. I've tried, for the sake of everyone, to leave the past in the past, but the fact is you're still as untrustworthy now as you've always been." Tom slammed his fist on the table. "You don't have my family's best interests at heart. Moving them to Kentucky is a terrible idea! They'll be better off on the farmstead with me and Samantha and Jerry there."

As Tom spoke, Banks' eyes grew haunted, and she followed with a tone of rising anger. "I don't think you understand, Tom. The president will eventually declare martial law. That means you'll need to follow orders. It won't be up to you, so you might as well--"

"You'll let us go," Tom glared. "Until martial law is announced, you'll let us go."

Banks rose slowly, both hands pressed to the table, the corner of her mouth twitching below narrowed eyes. "You don't give me orders, McKnight. You take orders from me."

"I'm a *citizen*, Banks!" Tom stood up to match her stance, slamming both fists on the table. "You can't keep me here locked up because you want me to piss into the wind with the rest of you! I'm at least going to save my family or die trying." Tom shot Sergeant Landry a warning look before he turned and grabbed the doorknob.

"Sit your ass down, McKnight!" Banks shouted through the conference room speakers. With a grimace, Tom threw open the door and came face-to-face with the two MPs who'd barred his way the day before, the taller man standing with his fists balled up, ready to fight, while the woman held her hand poised near the taser at her belt.

"Let me through," he growled, stepping forward and turning his shoulders to the side.

The big MP stepped back, his eyes flicking past Tom to Sergeant Landry for a moment before the pair closed ranks, shoulder-to-shoulder as they blocked his way through. The MP caught Tom's arm and shoved him back inside the room, and the female guard drew her taser, raising it, ready to fire.

"Don't make me," she warned, giving her head a brief shake.

"Sergeant, take Mr. McKnight, his daughter, and their friend to general population," Banks snapped. "They can stew with the low-lives if they want to."

"General population?" Tom turned to glare at the screen. "What the hell do you mean, *general population*? What do you mean *low-lives*?!"

"That will be all." Banks pounded a button on her side of the screen, and the display flicked to blue once more.

"Let's go, sir." Sergeant Landry had come around the table and was gesturing at the door. "Follow the MPs, please. They'll take you back to your tent to collect your daughter and friend. And just to make sure we're clear, I've been given authorization to use force if necessary. Please don't resist."

Tom scowled at the man, and it took every ounce of strength just to keep from hitting the guy, or giving him a piece of his mind.

"Please, sir." Landry's head cocked to the side, eyes imploring. With a look between the three people standing before him, Tom allowed his shoulders to sag and he nodded, wearily, allowing himself to be guided back to the tent.

* * *

"We fought tooth and nail for that crap!" Jerry yelled, glaring at the army staffer who threw their backpacks on a cart and wheeled them out the door. The young man turned to Tom. "Maybe you should have gone along with them."

Tom stood there with his hands on his hips as he looked on angrily, Landry and his two soldiers keeping watch, making sure they didn't interfere or try to flee.

"That's all our stuff, Dad." Sam sat on her cot, watching wide-eyed as soldiers hauled their supplies away. "Are they going to throw us out into the street with nothing?"

"We're taking you to general population," Landry replied. "You'll get three squares a day and have a place to sleep. Follow us, please." The two soldiers stepped outside while the sergeant gestured for the trio to exit behind them.

"At least you left his sling," Tom pointed out dryly as he passed the sergeant. "Or do you need that, too?"

Landry only shook his head and followed them from the tent. Outside, they turned and walked north across a huge parking lot, fenced off between a big square of stores.

"Is this a prison camp?" Jerry asked, his eyes narrow as he squinted ahead.

Tom twisted his lips in doubt, eyes narrowed. The fencing was standard chain link with a round layer of razor wire on top, the corners guarded by armed soldiers who walked the perimeter in pairs, cradling their rifles as they talked softly. About two hundred people milled around in the fenced-in area that they could see, gathering in groups by picnic benches or army tents. Old lawn furniture and chairs lay everywhere, some pulled up to metal burn barrels with flames licking over their edges, residents standing next to them, rubbing their hands above the heat while others held sticks with food stuck to the ends, turning them slowing above the barrels.

Landry guided them to the main gate protected by three armed guards. Two stood on either side of the entrance while an officer sat at a table, staring at a computer tablet with her hair tucked up in her military cap. As they approached she slapped the tablet down on the table, her dark eyes studying the trio intently. Landry motioned for them to wait while he had a word with the officer, presumably relaying Banks's orders and, after a moment of nodding, the woman tapped on her tablet screen before looking up with a raised voice.

"Got them all checked in. Go ahead."

One guard turned to the gate and punched in a code on the keypad, and while Tom tried his best, he couldn't see what was being punched in. There came a beep a second later, and the guard pulled the door open, gesturing for the trio to enter. The refugees inside turned their eyes to the gate, their stares like heat on his skin. Tom turned to Landry, expression, burning with the accusation that needed no words.

The sergeant's expression softened but didn't waiver. "Sorry, Mr. McKnight, but you need to go on in. Don't make me force you."

With a nod, Tom led Sam and Jerry inside, the gate slamming shut behind them, lock snapping closed. He turned to watch as the trio of soldiers marched away, Landry casting a final, sorrowful glance back at them before they vanished before a tent.

"What do we do now?" Sam hugged herself as she glanced around at the prying eyes.

"I guess we find a place to settle in and wait," Tom replied.

"This is crazy," Jerry looked nervously around. "I can't believe we're in an actual prison camp."

"Relax," Tom said. "Banks wants me for something, or she would have let us go."

"Yeah, but she could have kept us in the tent." Jerry stuck close to Sam and Tom. "Why did they stuff us in here?"

"That's Banks's ego talking. She's a control freak. She… she can't stand the thought of someone not following her orders right away. Sam, you saw how he was on the Marin." The girl nodded. "Yeah, well, I've worked with her before. She can be worse than that. Way worse."

"I'd hate to catch her on a bad day," Jerry groaned.

Tom scratched his head and looked around. "Right now, all we need to worry about is getting out of here and back home before things get worse." He gestured to an older man and a younger woman seated at a picnic bench. "They look like nice people. Come on, let's go make friends."

Eyes casting furtively around, shoulders tensed for confrontation, Tom led them through the pressing crowd, ignoring stares and murmurs and outright sneers. Reaching the table, he studied the pair. The man was skinny, in his mid-sixties, with a shag of thin gray hair poking out from beneath his blue hat. The woman looked to be in her early thirties, wearing a gas station jacket over her overalls. The man hunkered down as the trio approached, though the woman peered at them with a degree of curiosity.

Tom held up his hands in an unassuming manner, offering a smile he hoped didn't make him look like a maniac.

"Hi, folks," he said. "We mean you no harm. I'm Tom."

"What do you want?" the man asked with narrowed eyes, voice gruff with a congestion from years of smoking.

Tom tried to scoff good-naturedly. "Sorry, I just thought I'd get to know my fellow inmates. You know, since we're all prisoners here."

"We shouldn't be," the man snapped back. "I was doing just fine when the feds came."

The woman offered a tentative smile and her hand. "I'm Betty, and this is my father, Timothy. Good to meet you."

Tom reached out and shook her hand before stepping back. "This is my daughter, Samantha and our friend, Jerry. Good to meet you, too. Mind if we sit?"

"Not at all." The woman gestured at the free space on the picnic table. "Please do. And don't mind my dad, he's a little grumpy today."

"They should have just left us alone," Timothy continued grumbling under his breath. He held a foam cup of coffee in front of him, half filled with some suspicious-looking black swill.

"Go ahead, guys," Tom told Sam and Jerry. "Have a seat."

The two sat opposite Timothy and Betty, looking uncomfortable and a little cold. Tom stood straight and glanced around before turning his attention back to Betty, his expression flat and pleasant, desperate for information but not wanting to press her too hard.

"Have you been here long?" he asked.

"Just came in yesterday. Slept in one of the tents with another family last night."

"Did the troops assign you to it?"

Betty glanced toward the tents and chuckled. "It's first come, first serve. Just hope you find someone nice to bunk up with or you'll be out here sleeping on a bench."

"In this cold?"

"They gave us these." Betty reached between them and lifted a small pillow roll and a shiny thermal blanket.

"Inadequate," Tom said with a head shake. "Looks like we'll be fighting for a spot tonight." He pursed his lips. "So, what are you two in for?"

"Minding our damn business," Timothy grumbled.

Betty gave her father a warning look. "Be nice, Dad."

"Well, I ain't wrong."

She shook her head and raised her eyes to Tom. "We're from just south of Salisbury. Dad owns a small farm around there. I was checking in on him after the storm and helping clean up when the word came down for the evacuation."

"Evacuation?"

"That's right. We couldn't figure out why they wanted us out *after* the storm. I guessed it was for the flooding they talked about on the news. Still, Daddy's farm is up on a rise, so we opted to stay."

Tom gave her a quizzical expression. "How'd you end up here?"

"The feds came around and ordered us out."

"Are you serious?"

"Yep." The woman nodded and had a sip of her coffee, her lips twisting slightly in disgust. "They sent trucks and vans around, making people pack up their things and go south in droves."

"You refused, I assume."

"Well, Daddy did."

The old man raised in his seat, expression filled with indignation. "I've been on that farm my whole life. It was my own father's. The government comes along and acts like we don't have rights! Maybe we *never* had 'em."

Tom's jaw dropped, a deeper sense of foreboding growing in his gut, thoughts of Barbara, Jack, Linda and the farm surfacing. "They physically forced you to leave?"

"A fed pulled up in a van and told us we had to go." Timothy glared with disgust at a pair of guards patrolling the fence line. "I left ten head of cattle, three horses, and a pen full of pigs."

The sick feeling grew in his intestines, twisting them, turning them to water. "How did they justify leaving your animals to fend for themselves?"

"They didn't say a damn word," Timothy spat. "They just forced us into the van. At gunpoint, mind you!"

"I'll bet they want to take the animals for themselves." Jerry spoke up for the first time. "I mean, that would be the easiest way to do it, right? Tell people they have to evacuate because of the flooding, then sweep in and take all their crops and cattle."

Betty's father turned his glare on the young man, eyes narrowed, lips quivering in fury as the realization struck true. "I'll bet that's *exactly* what they did. Thieving bastards."

Jerry turned to Tom. "That makes sense, right? I mean, if it's going to get as cold as they say, the value of livestock is going to skyrocket. Meat will be worth more than gold. They'd need to have some control over that on a massive scale."

"But they said we could go back, eventually." Betty's looked between Tom and her father. "They can't keep us here forever, can they?"

Tom shrugged, a ball of tar rising in his chest. "The officer we dealt with mentioned the president was going to declare martial law. I think *they* think that they can do whatever they want."

"I told you they were up to no good." Timothy turned his wrinkled gaze on his daughter, the lines in his face chiseled from decades of hard work, worry and tobacco.

"What about the rest of your family?" Tom asked. "Do you have a husband or children anywhere?"

"I've got two kids who are grown up," Betty explained. "One lives in Tennessee and the other in Phoenix."

"They should be okay," Tom's expression lifted. "I don't think people in the interior of the country are feeling the effects like we are just yet."

Betty nodded and gave a weak shrug. "I spoke to my kids just before the storm hit. They were fine then, but I haven't been able to reach them since. Seems like the entire east coast is in a blackout."

Tom took a deep breath and let it out slowly, trying to loosen his rising tension before raising his eyebrows. "You two seem like nice folks. Do you care if I leave my friend and daughter while I walk around and talk to some people?"

"Not at all," Betty replied with enthusiasm. "We could use the company."

"Thanks," Tom said. "What about you two? Are you okay with me having a look around?"

"Sure, Dad," Samantha replied. "We'll hang tight."

"No problem," Jerry agreed.

Tom glanced at Betty. "What kind of facilities do they have? I noticed some larger buildings on the other side of the lot."

"They've got portable toilets in the back corner," she replied. "Mess tent is in the near one."

"Only good thing they have is coffee." Timothy held out his empty foam cup. "And it's not Morning Rise, I'll tell you that."

"I'll see if I can score some for you while I'm over there," Tom grinned.

The older man nodded his deference, gruff face softening slightly. "Much appreciated."

Tom turned in a half circle before strolling across the lot, hands in his pockets as he searched for more friendly faces. Most folks seemed on the up-and-up while a few sat in furtive groups, scoping the other refugees while occasionally glancing back at the guard patrols, looking about as trustworthy as Jerry's loan shark friends.

With a hunched and protective posture, he lapped the enclosure, checking out the restroom facilities. They were a better-than-standard portable kind found at festivals or county fairs, the structure looking more like a trailer, divided for men and woman, with fully heated stalls and basins. The mess hall was in the left-hand corner of the place, like Betty had said, and Tom poked his head inside and saw it was a large, rectangular tent with tables, a buffet line, and boxes of snacks and bottled waters. The buffet promised hot meals, though it had no food at the moment, and the coffee machine had an "Out of Order" sign hanging from it with camo-colored duct tape.

"Looking for someone?"

Tom turned to see a pair of men in their mid-twenties stroll up. They were both short, not particularly athletic but with a certain street toughness about them. The first man had a row of light, spiked hair, wearing a thick jacket while the other had short, tight curls and wore a Tennessee Titan's jersey with layers of long johns beneath them. The pair looked like they hadn't suffered at all during the storm, their clothes clean and dry, and they didn't look tired or beaten down like most everyone else. The only signs that life might had changed for them were the patches of facial hair on their chins and cheeks and slight bags under their eyes.

Tom shrugged. "I'm just looking around."

"I get it," the one with spiked hair said. "You're new to the camp, and you want to get the lay of the land."

"Something like that," Tom agreed. "Just looking for information. Where you guys from?"

"We're from Richmond," the other one replied.

"How'd you guys get here?"

"We were in the middle of a video game tournament when they started evacuating our town."

Tom's jaw fell open slightly, clashing with his lowered brows. "A video game tournament? In the middle of a hurricane? Are you serious?"

"The hurricane barely touched us," the second man snorted, "and we don't watch the news, so we had no idea about the anomaly thing until later."

The one with spiked hair jumped in excitedly. "Anyway, that's what we were doing when the feds started going door-to-door at our apartment complex. Had my headphones on the entire time. When they stormed in, I freaked out and drew my gun on them. Didn't fire though."

"Lucky you," Tom said with a dry grimace. "Could have gotten yourself killed."

"Hey, *they* busted down *my* door," he gaped. "And I own my gun legally. I've even got my concealed carry."

"Okay, I believe you." Tom pulled his hands out of his pockets.

The one in the jersey glanced around and leaned in with a whisper. "We just wanted you to know that we've got things to trade if you need anything."

Tom gave him a bewildered look. "Why are you whispering? There's not a guard within twenty-five yards of us."

"We just like to keep things on the down low, you know?" he replied. "We aren't doing anything illegal, but you never know when Sergeant Landry will get a stick up his ass and give this place an enema."

Tom folded his arms across his chest. "And what, exactly, is the racket?"

"Not a racket." The first one ran his fingers through his spiked hair, giving an offended scoff. "We're taking rations as trade for other things folks might want."

Tom gave a doubtful laugh. "You're in a military prison camp. What could you possibly have to trade?"

"They're not searching *everyone*," Spike Hair said. "Some people got in with bags and suitcases. Where do you think we got these clothes?"

"How long have you been here?" Tom's eyes moved between the two.

"Three days," Titan Jersey replied. "We've got clothes, food, and even information if you're willing to give up your meal rations."

With a sense of foreboding, Tom nodded and started to back away. "I'll keep that in mind if I need anything. Hopefully, we'll be out of here and back on the road soon."

Titan Jersey chuckled. "Shoot, you're not going anywhere. None of us are."

Tom stopped. "What do you mean? How long do they usually hold people here?"

The two shared a look before the first one shook his head like Tom was fresh off the boat. "Word is, they're taking us to a FEMA camp tomorrow or the next day."

"Where?"

"Who knows." The young man shrugged. "Wherever they want, I guess."

Tom took a deep breath, his jaw working back and forth as he stewed over the idea of being relocated. "Thanks guys," he said, turning toward a small hut where FEMA workers were handing out coffee in paper cups.

"That bit of information was free," Ryan said, coolly. "Next one will cost you a meal ticket."

"Yeah, yeah. See you around." Tom waved them off and they disappeared around a corner, leaving him in peace. After standing in line and listening to the quiet murmurs of people all around him, he got a tray of four coffees from the sour-faced worker and returned to their picnic bench with worry gnawing at his gut. Jerry, Sam, Betty, and even Timothy had grown more talkative, chattering away happily as Tom returned with the warm beverages.

"Hey, guys," he nodded to Sam and Jerry. "Can I talk to you two for a minute? Over here."

Casting side glances at each other, excusing themselves from the table, the pair reluctantly got up from their warm spots and followed Tom to an unoccupied burn barrel nearby, flames licking upward to toast their cheeks.

"What is it, Dad?" Samantha asked, concern etched in her face.

"Yeah, we were just getting comfortable." Jerry, holding the warm paper cup with one hand, took a sip from his cup and immediately pulled a face at its bitterness. "Timothy and Betty are pretty cool. We could have made worse friends."

"No kidding," Tom nodded. "I just met a couple questionable dudes over by the coffee hut. Among other things, they were talking about the military moving this camp in a few days."

Sam's jaw dropped in alarm. "Seriously?"

"Yeah."

"Where would they take us?"

Tom looked between the two, his breaths coming shallow, heart thudding as he imagined them falling into a bottomless pit of military control, stuck in guarded camp after guarded camp as the world crumbled around them. "No idea. Could be anywhere. I'd have to guess someplace south. Away from home, for sure."

Sam's eyes widened and darted toward the gate and guards standing with their rifles and thick winter fatigues, her voice rising in a muted squeal. "Crap, Dad. We have to do something. We have to get out of here!"

"Yeah, I know." His brief nod triggered a sharp intake of breath. He looked around the camp once more, the bleakness of the place hammering home, the realization of how utterly trapped they were finally sinking in. Helplessness, resignation, and fear swirled around them like the cold air itself, erupting off the prisoners in the camp, permeating the air like a physical fog, sinking into their flesh and bones. Tom shook his head at the thought, shaking off the mental despair, hardening his gaze and focusing on the task at hand.

"We're getting out of here, guys, one way or another. There's no choice."

"We're with you, dad." Samantha slid her arm around his waist, giving him a squeeze.

"All the way, Mr. McKnight." Jerry straightened up, giving Tom a hard smile.

"Then it's settled. We're getting out of here, and fast."

"Without getting captured." Sam replied.

"Without getting captured, yes." Tom smirked.

"Or shot," Jerry added.

"Or shot," Tom gave the young man a wry smile, then put his arms around both Samantha and Jerry, pulling them close around the burn barrel, mind already racing with possibilities.

Book 3: RETREAT

Chapter 1

Tom McKnight

Pocahontas Village, Virginia

A gust of cold blew through the chain-link fence, ice-cold daggers slicing through the air, no respecters of person as they chilled all in their path to the bone. Everyone standing in the holding facility's yard groaned and hugged themselves tighter as the wind whipped up, flurries of snow on the ground being picked up and flung into faces, hissing as they crossed over hot burn barrels, their cold fingers not enough to quench the flames.

Hunching over steaming cups of warm coffee or cocoa, the only things the military seemed to have endless supplies of, most of the camp stood around said barrels, clustering to the warmth like moths to a light, their clothing and a few provided rough blankets pulled tight to their shoulders, desperate to absorb and hold the heat from the licking flames.

Soldiers fed the fires pallets of wood scraps, though the fuel supply had come less often as the scraps ran low, leaving a desperate pall hanging over those in the holding area. Wood char drifted in the air, barely keeping the throat-gagging stench of overflowing sewage at bay while outside the fence the military camp bustled, but in a different way than at the start. Instead of adding to their supplies and personnel, the surrounding strip malls and storage buildings were being emptied of goods. Officers shouted orders as groups of soldiers loaded crates and storage bins into the backs of trucks eight to ten hours a day, and once filled the trucks tore out of camp toward the expressways, buzzing off to some unknown destination. Fewer and fewer of the endless lines of refugees were brought into camp, some of them ordered aboard troop transports and driven directly south without a moment to rest. All the while the air turned colder, gaining teeth, the wind biting at exposed ears, fingers and cheeks as it slipped through the holding area, finding its way into every open crack and crevice, reminding everyone of just how much had changed.

"It's got to be in the low twenties." Tom McKnight sat on a picnic bench on the east side of the holding area, one hand wrapped around a foam cup, the other resting in his lap. He exhaled a breath of fog and pulled his jacket tighter around his shoulders, automatically shivering at the action. "Layer up" had been the motto of the past ten days as the cold crept lower and lower, but no amount of layering seemed to help.

"It's *never* this bad in September," Jerry agreed, his teeth chattering as he peered up at the steel gray sky, watching hard streaks of clouds ripping from east to west, suffocating the sun's warmth, masking all of its power and glory.

"Everything you said about the bad weather was true." Sam spoke in a flat, heartless tone from Tom's right. She'd been looking glum for the past few days, and Tom couldn't tell if she was sick or just depressed from being locked up.

"They should have let us out of here by now." Jerry was on the other side of Sam, the two men warming her with their body heat.

"None of the officers have been around," Tom said. "Not Landry or even Packar."

"Landry kept tabs on us every hour for a minute there," Jerry added, "but he's AWOL now."

"And he was my connection to Banks," Tom raised an eyebrow.

"Well, who's in charge of the holding area?" Jerry glanced at the gate.

Tom shrugged. "The only time we see anyone is if they're transferring prisoners."

The prisoners in the holding facility had been a revolving door of characters of all types, ranging from those caught carrying illegal weapons or drugs to straight up fugitives from justice, caught up in the sweeps and sent into holding until someone could eventually figure out what to do with them.

Tom had kept an eye on the gate's goings-on, accounting for every newcomer mostly out of concern for Sam. They'd set up their own tent area on the east side with a complete view of the majority of the camp, with all the soldiers' tents and officers' quarters to the south while the refugees inhabited wide white tents farther east. Even the refugee's numbers were starting to dwindle, though, the tents folded up and tossed in the backs of trucks, the people guided into transports with perplexed, slack-jawed expressions, children clinging to their parents with blank, thousand-yard stares on their faces.

Jerry's eyes narrowed in suspicion. "Do you think they're abandoning us?"

"What do you mean?"

"If they aren't coming to see you anymore, maybe they think it's a lost cause. Maybe they're not worried about saving anyone."

"Well, as we've seen, shouting at the guards certainly isn't bringing the officers." Tom had been shouting to see Landry a few days prior, only to be told by the gate guards to shut up. Further attempts to garner information were met with implications of violence, and he had held his tongue after that. "You might be right."

"Either that or they don't need your help and are leaving us to rot out of spite." Sam's green eyes peered out from beneath the fur hat Tom had traded canned goods for and he shrugged, pulling his coat tighter.

The fur hat had been garnered as part of an aggressive trading scheme Tom and Jerry had taken part in, moving all through the camp to find people who had extra of something and trading those things on the opposite side of the camp with people who had an excess of something else. Next to where they sat was a small tent that held all their possessions, filled with the things he'd traded for over the past ten days, acquiring their tent, extra clothing, gloves, and long johns. His original two contacts, Ryan and Todd, had been mysteriously relocated to an undisclosed location to the south and a new man had filled the void, soon doing ten times the business of the previous two, running a veritable market in the holding area and providing ample opportunities for Tom to ensure that the trio had what they needed – for the moment.

Jerry shivered, inching closer to the fire barrel, practically pressing his body up against it. "I don't know about you guys, but our windbreakers won't cut it if it gets any colder. Once it hits the low teens, we'll be in trouble."

Tom agreed. "Yeah, *layering up* doesn't seem to be working so well anymore."

"Maybe we can score some more thermal underwear?" Jerry suggested hopefully.

"I don't think I can put another layer on," Sam replied, flexing her arms. "My arms and legs feel like sausages."

A shout drew Tom's attention before he could respond and he looked around, watching as a pair of detainees argued with a guard on the other side of the fence. The people in the holding area had been growing angry as attention to their basic needs waned, cursing the guards and sometimes openly threatening them. The soldiers snapped back, withholding food or handling people roughly, once going so far as to drag a man outside the holding area for the express purpose of "teaching him a lesson," bloodying his nose, giving him a black eye and tearing his jacket to ribbons before throwing him back in.

A day after that, a young yuppie couple had complained for hours they weren't getting the proper food and housing, walking the fence line, yelling about their rights and freedoms, berating the guards and hurling insults. After a while, two guards had stormed in and took the couple away, angrily shoving them toward the railroad bridge. That was the last time anyone had seen them and while Tom had no proof they'd been harmed, the implication had been clear, and the rest of the detainees had mostly given up on trying to rebel.

"It's getting dangerous." He shook his head. "It feels like we're standing on the edge of a knife."

"What should we do?" Sam asked with a shiver.

"It might be time we bust out of here," Tom looked around.

"Won't we get into trouble?" Her voice rose. "I mean, we can't fight the military, right? You see what they did to the others."

"No, I think they've forgotten about us." Tom absorbed the area with his eyes for the tenth time that hour. The tent positions, the number of guards standing around. "As long as we don't cause a ruckus, they probably wouldn't even notice that we're gone."

"Are you sure?" Samantha motioned off to the side. Two guards were positioned at each of the four enclosure sides with an officer occasionally looking in while the gate was manned by one person, and even he was frequently called away from his post.

"They used to have double or triple the number of guards. When they get low enough on resources, they'll move us. I don't want to be here when that happens."

"I'm on board with whatever you've got in mind." Jerry patted Tom on the shoulder. "We can do better on our own out there."

"I don't disagree." Tom's frown deepened, body tense though he tried to take on a relaxed, slouched posture. "I've just got a few small details to work out."

Jerry straightened, mimicking Tom's intensity. "When should we go?"

"It'll have to be at night. Maybe we can sneak over the fence and steal a transport."

"They'll have the keys for those in a central location, right? Like, a motor pool or something."

"Most of them don't use keys. There's a chance we could slip away with a vehicle that way, but I'm not counting on it. Motor pool's bound to be heavily guarded, more than we are. Walking's probably the smarter solution and it'll attract less attention. We can find a ride in the nearest subdivision."

"Hey there, folks," a smooth voice cut through their conversation. "Did I overhear you talk about taking a joy ride?" A man stepped out from between their tent and their neighbor's, his light blue eyes regarding them with flat indifference, a faint and curious smile playing across his face.

"Sneaking up on people again, Keith?" Tom didn't bother to turn around or mask his annoyance. "One day, you'll sneak up on the wrong person and lose a tooth or three."

"Sorry about that." Keith edged closer, shoving his hands in his pockets as he stepped into the light. "I didn't mean it to seem sneaky. I was just walking the fence line like I always do. Saw you folks gathered around your comfy burn barrel and thought I'd invite myself over."

"Making deals with the guards," Tom replied. "Spying on people."

Keith gave Tom a hurt expression. "That's cold, man. You know I'm the camp *market man* now. I'm just doing my job – you can trust me, you know that. Plus, I like the exercise."

"I don't trust anyone," Tom finally turned to face Keith, sizing him up. "Even less if they're eavesdropping."

"I'll try to remember that next time." Keith gave Sam and Jerry a lingering look before sidling up to the table and pulling a flask from an inner pocket. He held it out to Tom who merely stared him down, then he shrugged, took a drink, and put the flask back where it had come from. "Did I hear someone mention something about climbing a fence and tracking down some transportation?"

Tom's expression remained neutral, while Jerry leaned closer to Samantha and rubbed his hands together while she sipped her hot chocolate in silence, eyes rolling upward.

Keith spread his hands. "Oh, come on, guys. If you're thinking about getting out of here, you can tell me. It's not like I'm going to tell the guards."

Tom gestured at their surroundings. "Are you kidding? We love it here."

"Probably stay here forever," Jerry added with a terse nod. "Best vacation I ever had."

Keith scoffed before grinning with an easy smile that belied the sub-freezing temperatures around them. "Look, guys. If you're going, I want to go, too. Hell, I'll help you."

Tom chortled. "You deal in coats, long johns, and canned soup. How could you possibly help someone escape, much less find them transportation?"

"Because I know where the motor pool is." Keith's grin turned smug. "And I know how many guards they have, and how to get in. That alone is worth its weight in gold."

Tom's frown deepened, and he shuddered inside his coat. Aside from a drafty tent with weak kerosene heaters and standing in front of a burn barrel in the open air, they'd not had any real warmth since being ushered into the detainment camp. The trio were chilled to the bone, and the idea of sitting in a nice warm vehicle that was driving in the direction of home sent shivers up and down his arms. The risk, though, especially with someone like Keith, was enormous.

As if he was reading Tom's mind, Keith acknowledged Tom's uncertainty, lowering his voice and growing more sincere in tone. "Hey, I know what some people think of me. And it's true, I've taken advantage of a few folks. Never you three, though, and even you have to admit that, Tom. But I'll tell you what, I'll even throw in some chocolate."

Sam's voice raised. "Chocolate? Did you say, *chocolate?*"

"That's right." Keith grinned proudly. "Let's see, I think I have a box of assorted truffles and a Kirk's Limited-Edition gift box of chocolate cookies. Good stuff."

"Mom got those once." Samantha's stoic expression broke, and her eyes grew to the size of saucers. "They're amazing."

"They're okay," Jerry added with a dip in his tone. "Belgian chocolates are the best."

Sam rolled her eyes. "We're not in Belgium. Maybe next time we'll hold out for some, okay?"

"Fine." Jerry shrugged. "We'll settle for the assorted gift box and truffles."

Tom looked sidelong at his daughter. It was the most enthusiastic he'd seen her in days. He faced Keith again, sizing up the man. "You just want a ride out of here?"

"That's right." Keith nodded. "I'll give you the chocolates and a way out of here. You take me with you."

"Just until we get outside camp."

"Once we're away from this place," Keith gestured, "we'll go our separate ways."

"Why?"

"What do you mean?"

"Why do you need us?" Tom nodded back at Samantha and Jerry. "If you know where and how to get a vehicle, why would you risk blowing your cover by taking us along?"

Keith met Tom's critical gaze head-on, eye-to-eye. "You're resourceful, all three of you, but especially you." He glanced back at the ramshackle tent and collection of goods. "I've seen how you've been able to keep your little group here fed, clothed and relatively warm in spite of everything. Someone like that is going to be crucial in case things go wrong and, frankly, there's strength in numbers. In short, Tom, I need you. And you need me. Sounds like a winning combination."

Tom met Keith's gaze for a long moment before turning to Samantha and Jerry. The pair were dirty and cold, the growing chill starting to wear on them mentally and physically. Sam's face was thinning, and Jerry wore a haunted look in his eyes. If they waited in the holding area any longer, they'd be too weak to even attempt a getaway.

"Well?" He addressed them. "Thoughts?"

"Let's do it, Dad," Sam said with an enthusiastic nod. "I'm so worried about Mom and Linda and Jack. I want to get home."

"And I'd rather not die here in a tent, if that's okay," Jerry added with dark, humorless chuckle.

With a growled sigh, Tom turned back to Keith. "All right. We're in."

"You won't regret it, Tom."

"I hope not."

Keith kicked at the ground. "So, what were you thinking as far as getting out?"

"We can catch the guards between shifts." Tom glanced at two soldiers standing close together outside the western wall as they talked, almost on top of each other, more interested in what each other had to say than paying attention to their responsibilities. "Those two always end their shift fifteen minutes early. I think they might be romantically involved given that plus how handsy they are."

"Involved?" Sam wrinkled her eyebrows. "You mean, like… *involved* involved?"

"That's right. I never see them apart."

"Good eye," Keith affirmed. "I've heard similar rumors. And it doesn't look like they're worried about us sheep in here."

"They're not." Tom nodded. "I say we wait for them to walk away just before their shift ends. Then we'll roll some barrels up to the fence, climb them, and drop over to the other side."

"Someone in the enclosure might spot us and raise the alarm," Keith warned.

"They won't." Tom shook his head. "If they do anything, they'll try to come with us."

"That would be bad, too. A few hundred refugees running through a military camp won't go unnoticed."

"If that happens, all the better." Tom shrugged. "We'll get away in the chaos." Keith stared at the guards, then looked at the barrels lined up along the fence. They had once all been filled with water for drinking and bathing, but they were mostly empty or getting emptier by the day. "Once we're over the fence," Tom continued, "it's up to you to get us to the motor pool."

"We can hide in the bushes by the strip mall in the back," Keith explained, gesturing to the stores on the west side of the encampment. "And then circle around to the motor pool once we're sure we're in the clear. After that we'll have to wing it a bit."

Tom raised an eyebrow. "Do you know where we can find some weapons?"

"I... might have a key to a locker. But it's in a side building and heavily guarded. I wouldn't recommend trying to steal them."

"It's getting hostile out there." Tom's gaze drifted upward across the camp toward the south. "We're going to need weapons at some point. And not just baseball bats or tire irons."

"Fine. But don't complain to me when you get your heads blown off." He gave an apologetic shrug. "Sorry, Sam."

"It's okay."

"All right." Tom searched the man's face for any sign that he couldn't trust him. The last several days in holding had hardened him toward trusting other people, and putting trust in someone who was effectively a scrounger was difficult to say the least.

Keith put his hands on his hips. "You think I have ulterior motives?"

"It's crossed my mind."

"I swear it's nothing nefarious!" Keith laughed. "I like you guys!"

"Right... the only thing you like is your own skin." Keith started to protest and Tom held up a finger. "But I don't hold it against you. In fact, I'd be worried if that wasn't the case."

"I hardly charged you for Sam's hat, right?" Keith pointed to the furry beanie hugging the girl's head. "What was the final cost? A can of soup and some spam?"

"It was super chunky soup, though," Jerry jumped in.

"I wondered when that would come back to haunt me," Tom snorted. "I figured I'd still owe you something as soon as we made the deal."

"You don't *owe* me," Keith insisted, pointing to a similar hat on his own head with flaps that dropped down over his ears. "I had five already. No real loss for me. And look at your daughter. Her head is nice and warm now!"

"It's true, Dad." Sam put both hands on her head, then cut a look in Keith's direction. "But that doesn't mean you're trustworthy."

"Seriously, Tom." Keith's easygoing smile vanished, his expression turning hard as he looked between the three standing before him. "If we're going to do this, you have to trust me, at least somewhat. We're not getting married – we're just helping each other get out of a shitty situation."

Tom held his peace for what felt like an eternity. Wind, snowflakes and wisps of smoke whipped around the small group as Tom eyed Keith carefully, weighing the pros and cons of their situation and potential escape from it before, finally, letting out a long exhale. "Fine. Be here at 10:30. We'll make our move then."

Keith grinned. "Perfect. That'll give me a little time to tie up a few loose ends. I need to—"

Tom held up a hand. "No-I don't want to know. Just go take care of your business, Keith."

"No problem. I'll see you back here in a couple of hours." Keith backed away, flashing a grin and a thumbs up to the group before slipping away between the tents, quickly disappearing out of sight.

"Okay, now I'm nervous." Sam bit her lip.

"Too late," her father replied, with a raised eyebrow and barely concealed mocking tone. "It's your fault. You committed us to it. That's what you get for having a chocolate addiction."

"Curses," Sam gave a stage whisper, trying and failing to snap her gloved fingers.

"I just hope you get to eat them," Jerry added with a shivery chuckle. "That guy seems okay one minute, then the next he's weird as all get-out."

"That he is. Which is why we're going to watch each other's backs, right?"

"Right." Samantha and Jerry both replied in unison, then Tom stood and gestured for them to follow.

"Come on, guys. Let's warm up and see if we can chat anyone up before we leave and get some more intel, too."

Tom led them to a corner of the yard where a burn barrel sat with a few glowing coals at the bottom. He picked up a scrap of wood from a pallet and tossed it on top, then used a long stick to stir everything around, sending a wave of heat upward. The three of them held their hands near the open end, rubbing them together as they chased away the chill. Tom's upper body grew hot while his lower half stayed cold, the uneven heat annoying him more than he thought possible.

Turning around in an attempt to warm his backside, he watched the pair of lovebird guards outside the fence, their arms locked as they stood facing away from the prisoners. The baked-in military discipline was slipping with them, just like it was slipping with the other guards. Too much cold, too little command oversight and too much trauma from recent events were a boon to their escape.

"Hey guys!" Betty, the first person they'd met in the holding area ten days ago, came up to the barrel, rubbing her hands together and yawning, shivering and sighing with pleasure as the heat washed over her.

"Evening, Betty." Tom flashed her a quick smile.

"Getting colder by the minute out here." Her eyes shifted to him. "Think it's going to hit zero soon?"

"No idea."

"I hope not," she said. "Our livestock back on the farm would suffer terribly if that happened. I'm sure they are already, poor things. Unless, like Jerry said, the government has been, um, looking out for them."

"Stealing them." The young man corrected her.

"Right." Betty laughed. "I guess in this case, I hope they do take them. You know, put them someplace safe if it's going to stay this cold."

"We were just talking about it being too cold for September." Jerry blew in his hands and rubbed them together. "Tom and Sam really need to get home. And I don't want to stay here much longer..."

Betty looked back and forth between them. "Okay, what's going on?"

Sam and Jerry stared into the fire without saying a word while Samantha coughed awkwardly in between them, looking at her father with a pleading expression.

"We're getting out of here," Tom finally answered for them, his voice low in a conspiratorial tone.

"Escaping?" Betty's eyes went wide. "How?"

"We're going over the fence during the guard shift change tonight. Then we'll find some transportation and drive away."

"That easy, huh?"

"That's the plan." Tom shrugged. "But I can't promise it'll be easy."

"I've noticed the officers stopped coming around." Betty clutched her gloved hands to her chest and shivered. "They're not paying attention to us much anymore. Is that why you're going now?"

Tom nodded. "Do you want to come with us?"

The woman turned her face toward the heat, blinking as she contemplated the question. After a moment, she shook her head. "I... I don't think so. I want to, don't get me wrong. My dad hates being here, and he hates the Feds even more. But he's got some health issues, and I can't see him climbing fences and stealing cars." Betty gave Tom's arm a pat and smiled at Samantha and Jerry. "I wish you guys the best of luck. Truly."

"And I hope they find you a good place to settle."

Betty snorted, rolling her eyes. "Ha! I'd be happy if they'd let us go home to our ranch. Dad and I could do just fine on our own, even in this cold." Betty looked around at them each in turn, a hopeful expression rising on her face. "Hey, got time for one last hot chocolate before you go?"

Tom smiled and nodded. "Sure."

Chapter 2
Barbara McKnight
Wyndale, Virginia

"Do you think Mom's going to… shoot them?" Jack's voice quivered, barely above a whisper as he stood by Linda at the second-floor bedroom window, the corners frosted with humidity, the glass cold to the touch.

His sister shrugged, pressing her nose against the glass in spite of the cold. "I don't know. She might, if they don't take no for an answer."

"But there're kids down there, too." Jack's voice was almost a whine, grimacing with discomfort.

"Well, you know the rules." Linda put her hand on her brother's shoulder. "We do what we have to do, bottom line." That's what her father and mother always said, *bottom line.*

"I know. I just don't want anyone to get hurt."

"Me neither." She patted his shoulder and then let her hand drop to the pistol holstered at her hip. The motion brought forth memories, recent ones, ones she had tried to push back into the swirling darkness as she struggled to make sense of them at her young age. The same choices that her mother could soon be forced to make – again – were no stranger to Linda, given that she had been forced to make the exact same one. In theory, protecting oneself with deadly force was as easy to do as it was to talk about. In practice, though, it was an entirely different manner to point a weapon at a human being, no matter who they might be, and squeeze the trigger for the very first time.

The shooting had nagged at her conscience for days, and though she told herself she was just protecting Jack, she played the scene on repeat in her mind, watching the bullet hit the man, the blood spattering their hardwood, her mother's screams, the man's cries of agony. She saw it when she was awake. She saw it when she dreamed. As each day passed, the nagging diminished until it was just a whisper in her mind, a voice telling her that shooting someone was *always* a bad thing… but sometimes it was a good thing, too.

"Mom will make the right decision," Linda said with a confident nod. "She always does."

Down by the road, the wind howled across the McKnight property, blowing wisps of hair into Barbara's face. The fierceness of the creeping cold over the past week had startled her with the way it had gripped the Virginia hillsides, frosting everything in a crisp layer of white, sent warning bells ringing in her head. The puddles in their driveway were frozen, the air biting, far colder than it had any right to be.

She ignored the strands of hair streaking across her cheeks as she held her Benelli M2 semi-automatic shotgun against her chest, pointing it slightly downward as she faced off against the man standing in front of her. His family stood behind him next to their car at the edge of the driveway, blocked from coming up to the house by Barbara's pickup truck. He was younger than her, probably in his 30s, wearing jeans, tennis shoes, and a long-sleeve turtleneck. His haircut might have been fancy at one point, but it had grown out in a tousle and several days' worth of beard growth darkened his jaw.

"Please, ma'am," the man begged. "We just need a night or two of rest then we'll get right back on the road."

His wife stood behind him, small in her coat. Even smaller was their little girl, standing against her mother's legs with pale locks blowing on her shoulders. Smudges stained the girl's face, like she'd been rummaging through garbage and she had a haunted, distant look in her eyes. Their car was a newer model BMW, but its fenders and hood looked like someone had taken a baseball bat to them, the passenger side window cracked in a spiderweb pattern, frost gathered in the corners.

Barbara slowly shook her head, eyes watering with tears and resolution. "I can't do that, sir. I've got my own family to look after. Now, get back in your car and go on up the road. There are probably a dozen or more houses along this stretch of road. A few might be abandoned, and they've all got furnaces. You can get one working."

"Every house we try has already been looted." His voice sunk low. "There's not much left out there."

"That's not my problem."

"We don't have any supplies! Can't you share anything?"

Barbara pointedly ignored the question. "I need you to leave now, or we're going to have a problem."

"I bet you're loaded down up there, living way out here away from people," he took a step forward, tone laced with accusations. Barbara adjusted her stance, planting the stock of the Benelli into her shoulder and he stopped, still fuming. "Stocking up won't do anyone any good! You know that, right?"

"What do you mean?"

"If you're still here when the military comes, they'll kick you out and take all your stuff, anyway. Might as well give some away."

"My concern. Not yours." Barbara replied.

"They have ways of doing it." The man glanced up at the McKnight house, a hint of eagerness in his eyes. "So, everything you've stockpiled won't mean anything. They'll take it all, lady. You might as well give it away now while you can. Help some weary travelers on the road."

"You need to move along."

The man glanced back at his wife before fixing Barbara with a hard stare. He took two steps up the driveway, starting to come around the truck, pointing at the house. "Look, we don't have to be friends, but—"

Barbara raised the weapon and took a step toward the man, causing the little girl to yelp as the woman clutched her daughter to her legs.

"Don't get shot, Daddy," the girl squirmed. "Please, Daddy. Don't get shot."

"I'm not going to get shot," he said, trying to sound cool. Yet, he'd stopped, his gray eyes locked on Barbara. "This woman is nice, and she's going to give us a few things before we get back on the road. Maybe some canned soup, or some bread." He stepped forward again, hands up as he tried to get around her. "Maybe some blankets? Or a weapon?"

Faster than the man could process, Barbara redirected the barrel to just above his head and squeezed the trigger, firing a spread of buckshot with a crack that shook the sky, stopping the man in his tracks, forcing his shoulders to bend forward, face wincing. She snapped the shotgun back to the man's chest as the little girl wailed, her mother dragging her back to the car, both of their eyes wide, panic on their faces as Barbara growled at the man.

"Next round's a slug, and I don't miss twice. You'll be dead before you hit the ground if you don't get your asses *off* my property!"

"You're serious, aren't you?" His voice shook as he took a timid step backwards, hands shaking as he slowly raised them to chest level.

"Five men have already tried to take what wasn't theirs." She narrowed her gaze. "You want to be in grave number six?"

The man backed away, mouth agape, trying to process what had just taken place. When he bumped up against his vehicle, he turned and clambered in, joining his teary-eyed wife and daughter before making a multi-point turn in the driveway, aiming to rejoin the flow of traffic.

Barbara kept the rifle raised, tracking the man in the driver's seat through every movement, only lowering it when he rejoined the flow of traffic, his bitter voice barely carrying back to her over the sounds of horns and engines.

"Karma's going to bite you in the ass, lady!"

Barbara lowered her weapon, glaring at the nearby group of drivers as they passed, watching as each driver's gaze widened as they moved from her face to her hands and then back to the vehicles in front of them, not wishing to involve themselves with the crazy-eyed woman wielding a shotgun. After a few minutes, she turned and marched up the driveway, grumbling to herself.

"Karma already bit us, and we bit back."

The same scene had played out repeatedly over the past ten days. While the overall traffic on Highway 11 had decreased, it increased in clusters as some road down south was jammed or closed down, and with each cluster came someone inevitably stopping for help. They varied in number and sob story. Some were families, some were loners, and once it was even a van load of a dozen nuns, their habits stained with dirt and blood. Some begged, some appealed to her humanity and a select few even tried threats. Most told horror stories about the military coming through and terrorizing families, uprooting them and making them leave their supplies and homes behind. Still, Barbara had turned them all away, sometimes with her scowl alone, though a few times it had taken a warning shot – and once it had even required discouraging a few unsavory sorts with a direct barrage of buckshot. The refugees were getting more aggressive with each stopping, though, and she had a feeling she'd have to start shooting with more than buckshot first - and not bothering with the questions afterward.

Her boots scrunched on three inches of snow, the air holding a dangerous crispness that promised even lower temperatures to come. She'd done all she could for the animals, keeping them in the barns at night and letting them out to roam during the day, but there was only so much she could do. They had enough feed in the barns for several months, but if the cold kept up its brutal barrage, she'd have to consider slaughtering a chicken or sheep if it looked like they might starve anyway. Either that, or she'd have to make some supply runs for more feed, if it was even something that could still be bought, that is.

Where are you, Tom? It's been ten days. Ten days since you texted us. You said you were going to be home. Where are you?

The kids caught her attention before she grew too lost in thought, standing side-by-side in the upstairs window as they gazed down at their mother. Barbara forced a smile that felt more like a grimace, waving, and the kids waved back, turning away to come greet her at the back door, undoing the locks and latches she'd installed and pulling the sliding door aside.

"That was scary, Mom." Jack threw his arms around her.

"I know." Barbara stepped inside as Linda slid the door shut and re-locked everything. "But I made them go away."

The pair ran ahead of her to a table where Linda took her shotgun and Jack brought her glass of unsweetened tea before sitting next to her, each with a drink in front of them, Smooch coming up afterward with a slight limp, resting her snout on Barbara's leg. The German Shepherd hadn't fully healed from her stab wounds, but she was getting better, often begging at the back door to be let out, but Barbara only let her out for potty breaks. The animal wasn't well enough to freely roam the yard where she could potentially re-injure herself or serve as a visual point of potential weakness to any ne'er-do-wells.

"You're my saving grace." She smiled genuinely at the kids while patting Smooch's head.

"You look tired, Mom," Linda said.

"That's funny." Barbara made a quirky face. "I *feel* tired." The goofy expression dropped, not wanting to spend some of her meager reserve of energy joking around.

"Maybe you should let us go outside so we can help with the animals."

"You're already doing enough by keeping watch."

"From our windows upstairs," Linda scoffed. "That's not helping."

"It's giving me time to rest," she countered, placing the coffee cup down.

"Yeah, but you're not really sleeping at all," her daughter pointed out. "You just walk around the house, taking notes and drinking coffee."

"You're not wrong," Barbara stared at the cold cup next to her water, the black liquid a constant reminder of just how exhausted she truly was.

"You need help in the yard. Why don't you let me and Jack put the animals away tonight?"

"I can't let you outside. Not after everything that's happened. We could have trespassers at any moment."

"I'm armed," Linda countered, touching the weapon on her hip. "And we have the air horns with us if we see anyone in the yard. You just need a day or two off, Mom."

Barbara stared at her daughter. The girl's eyes were red-rimmed and glassy with worry. "I don't know..." her words trailed off with indecision.

"We can't go on like this." Linda gave a resigned huff. "One day, you'll get so tired that you'll make a mistake. Then what will we do?"

Loathe as she was to admit it, her daughter made a solid point and a strong argument. Barbara's mental and physical exhaustion surpassed anything she'd ever felt, even beyond the double shifts working as a waitress years ago. Worrying about Tom and Samantha made it hard to sleep, and she'd only felt comfortable with the kids locked inside. They had years of supplies piled beneath them, and plenty of guns to defend themselves, but that safety and security came with a price – constant vigilance.

She nodded reluctantly. "Okay, maybe Linda can help me with the animals tonight and feeding them in the morning. Jack will need to stay inside the whole time, though."

"Aw, Mom," the boy whined. "It's boring in here. I want to go run around."

"That's my final word. We'll see how it goes from there."

"If it goes okay, can I help the day after tomorrow?"

"I said, we'll see." Barbara raised both eyebrows to let him know she was done with the topic. "I don't want to let our guard down one second and having you out there with us complicates things more than I'm comfortable with right now, air horn or not. We'll just... see."

"Okay, Mom."

Barbara took a sip of her cold coffee and put it down. "Okay, Linda. Let's go put the animals inside now. It's getting way too cold to leave them in the yard."

"All right!"

They went to the closet and pulled out Linda's heavy jackets, hats, and work gloves. After layering her up, Barbara inspected her daughter's bundled form. She added a scarf to her ensemble, wrapping it around her neck and tucking it into her coat, then added one for herself, remembering how nippy it had just been when dealing with the recalcitrant family outside.

Thus dressed, they moved to the back door, threw the locks, and stepped out. Barbara had equipped her Bellini shotgun with a strap, making it easy to slide the weapon on her shoulder while walking. The frozen blades of grass crunched under their feet as they walked, Barbara keeping a watch on the cars passing by on the road until they reached the chicken coop where she turned the thermometer on the outside of the coop around.

"Five?" Linda whistled as she looked at the gauge. "How's it just five degrees, mom?"

"That... that is something else." Barbara did a double take, rubbing her thickly-jacketed arms. "It's like deep winter for this part of the state, and we haven't even seen this level of cold in years."

The sheep and goats huddled near the chicken coops, not even bothering to spread out across the yard like they usually did. Their donkeys stood side-by-side in the center, their collective breaths puffing into the air, over a dozen pairs of eyes fixed on Barbara and Linda as they made their way to the feed shed, though none of the animals broke ranks and followed.

"Could they die if we leave them out here?" her daughter asked as they grabbed a pair of buckets.

"Probably not," Barbara exhaled into her scarf, "but if the wind chill sends the temperature below zero, they'd struggle. We should get them inside and make them comfortable while we can."

"How will they stay warm during the day?"

"For now, we'll let the animals gather around the coops during the day and put them away at night. They can huddle together for warmth, and it'll be easier for us because we won't have to chase them down when they wander the yard." They filled their buckets and went outside, Barbara reaching in and grabbing a handful of feed before turning toward the herd and backing away, holding out her hand to coax them.

"Come on, guys!" she called. "Get some food. Mmmm. Yummy feed. Oh, boy! Come on. You know you want some."

At first, the animals resisted breaking ranks, the warmth of their collective bodies too good to leave. But Linda joined in, and Barbara tossed a small bit on the ground and their resolve began to break, first with one sheep, then two. They nibbled at the ground and lifted their heads, bleating at Barbara for more.

"Come on!" She kept retreating, cooing and coaxing them, pretending to throw more feed to get them to follow.

Another sheep broke ranks, and then several more. Soon, the entire herd left the warmth of the chicken coops and trotted after them, bleating with eagerness. The mother and daughter team led the animals to the old barn where Linda handed her mother her bucket and unlocked the doors, throwing them aside. Barbara entered, backing all the way to the far end where she spread the feed in a pair of troughs before twisting her nose and backing away from the troughs in disgust. The place was a mess from the previous night, animal droppings everywhere, the air filled with the scent of manure and mildew. They'd cleared the floor of feed and tools, thankfully, carrying everything to the loft days ago or else it would have been worse, but it was still annoying to deal with.

"Phew, it smells pooey in here." Linda wrinkled her nose as her mother took her arm, guiding her to the doors as the animals eagerly filed around them and went for the troughs.

"Yeah, it's getting bad. We'll come and clean things up soon. For now I just want to get them fed and warm. The mess can wait a bit longer." She glanced at the patched-up hole she'd shot in the wall and walked to the corner where she'd hung an outdoor space heater and plugged it into one of the two electrical sockets in the barn, reaching for the switch but resisting at the last second.

"We're not putting on the heat for them?" Linda asked.

"I think we should wait," Barbara took a deep breath and let it out with a thoughtful sigh. "They'll be fine inside for now. If it gets any colder, we'll hit the switch. For now, it'll be in standby. We need to be careful not to drain the batteries, and we don't want the generator going twenty-four seven."

"Because that'll run us out of fuel, right?"

"Right. We've got enough to get us through the winter, but we still need to ration ourselves to make it that long."

Linda looked over the animals as they eagerly ate and did their business inside the barn. "I'm worried about them, but if you say they'll be okay, I believe you."

"I know it seems mean keeping them locked up in here," Barbara said, stroking the back of Linda's head, "but it's for their own good."

They left the barn and started to shut the doors when Linda pointed back toward the coops and made a plaintive sound. "Oh, no, Mom!"

Barbara spun around with a sharp exhale, smoothly slipping the shotgun off her shoulder and swinging it up at the impending danger. Finger on the trigger guard she kept the weapon raised for a few seconds before lowering it, laughing as a solitary sheep came trotting in. Her expression sobered as she realized it was wounded, limping along and bleating sorrowfully.

Barbara knelt as the animal came up, stopping him from heading to the troughs. He nuzzled her in response as she inspected its left foreleg, pulling back the wet and dirty wool to reveal a small but deep open sore on one knee, just below the joint.

"Hm. He must have clipped on something or caught a hoof from one of the donkeys." The donkeys were gentle animals, for the most part, but quick to show their displeasure when aggravated. "I'll get this tended to when we're done today. For now, we'll let him in to eat." She guided the sheep inside where it happily squeezed between two others and got to the feed.

"They'll get used to us putting them away at night." Barbara threw the doors shut and locked them. "Pretty soon we won't even have to lead them over. They'll just be waiting for us."

They strolled back to the chicken coops and rabbit hutches with the night closing in, bringing a sharp breeze that whipped against her face like a flurry of soft punches. Hands jammed into her pockets, chin lowered, she drew her arms closer to her body as they crunched back across the frozen ground. The coops and hutches already had built-in heating systems that drew a little energy from the batteries and while they wouldn't keep humans particularly comfortable, they would take the edge off the chill for the more sensitive animals. Inside, Barbara noted the temperature was a comfortable forty-seven degrees, which was even a little warm for them. She reduced the heat just a bit, turning the thermostat down, not wanting to stress them too badly, but also trying to save on energy.

"That should be good for now," she explained to Linda. "Chickens have a high metabolism. They can easily tolerate temperatures in the teens."

"Really?"

"Yep! They'll stick together and their body heat will be enough to keep the coop's temperature stable."

"So the whole coop will stay warm?"

"Exactly."

"Oh, and I checked the nursery earlier, and everything's fine in there. Better than fine, actually - we got a new bunny today." Barbara grinned.

"Oh, I want to play with it!" Linda exclaimed.

"Maybe tomorrow," Barbara chuckled, before the pair left the coop, closing and locking the door behind them. She spared a glance at the greenhouse, with its small amount of already-melting snow that had accumulated on the glass roof. She'd gone in earlier and moved the grow beds and baby plants in toward the center and placed a couple of low-watt space heaters inside. While the main purpose of the heaters was to keep the plants from freezing, they doubled as a convenient way to keep the roof clear of snow and ice, ensuring that enough sunlight reached the plants to keep them healthy and growing. If she played her cards right – and the weather cooperated – she could keep the food production up all through the winter.

"Let's go." She snagged Linda's coat arm and gestured toward the house, the pair strolling through the snow to the back door, their footsteps soft and crunchy in the surreal quiet. She started to knock for Jack to let them in when a car beeped at the end of the driveway and Barbara let out a loud groan, her chin slumping to her chest.

"Ugh. Not again…" She swung her shotgun into position and ticked her head at the door. "You know the drill."

Linda nodded. "Go inside and watch from the window."

"Yep. You'll know if I need your help."

With a huff, Barbara stomped around the side of the house while Linda knocked on the back door. "Jack, let me in."

Barbara rounded the corner and went around their pickup, putting on her game face, setting her jaw, narrowing her eyes in a well-practiced glare. Cars had piled up again, moving by on the road like a slow-moving snake, headlamps bleary as they puttered along with occasional honks and squealing tires. It was only when she was twenty yards down the driveway that she recognized the Everett's red Jeep sitting at the end of the driveway, pulled in next to the Astro van.

Marie waved out the passenger window, smiling and calling out as Barbara lowered her Benelli and smiled at the pleasant surprise. "Hey, Barbara! How's it going?"

Barbara stopped and returned the wave. "Come on up!"

Marie nodded and ducked back inside the Jeep, saying something to Darren before she parked next to the van and turned it off. The pair got out and slogged up the snow-covered driveway to greet her, casting a couple of wary glances at the traffic behind them.

"I'm *so* glad it's you two." Barbara slung the shotgun on her shoulder and gripped their hands.

Marie's expression turned worried, pulling her friend into a warm embrace. "Oh, Barbara. You look absolutely tuckered."

"That's what I hear," she scoffed darkly. "It's been hell here the past week, I don't mind telling you." She noticed the Everett's tired eyes beneath their hats and hoods. "And you two don't look so hot, either."

"It's been rough on us the past few days, too," Darren admitted with a slow nod. "That's actually what we're here to talk to you about. Sorry for dropping in on you without calling first. Do you mind?"

"Are you kidding? I welcome the company!"

The three trudged up the walkway to the house, and Linda let them in. The Everetts hung their coats on the coat rack in the foyer and took off their boots, leaving them to melt off the ice and snow onto a towel.

"Oh, it's toasty," Marie beamed. She reached out and rubbed Barbara's arm. "The house looks great. You'd never know it was a bloodbath in here ten days ago…oh." She glanced at the kids as they helped Darren hang up his coat, already deep in . Marie lowered her voice. "Sorry. I shouldn't say things like that."

"It's okay." Barbara gave a wan smile. "We're all pretty used to it by now. We've accepted that we have to make hard decisions to stay safe." She glanced uneasily at her kids as they played with Darren, seemingly oblivious to the conversation between Marie and herself, seeming as normal as they had before the mess of the last few weeks had started. Regardless of how normal they acted on the outside, though, the occasional haunted looks and thousand-mile stares she caught them in belied the turmoil deep on the inside.

Shoving her worries into a corner, she led the Everetts to the shared living room-kitchen and put her own coat and hat on the back of her chair. She and Linda had done the best they could getting the living room back in shape by pulling the pleather loveseat out from the wall to take up more space and bracketing it with a pair of nightstands with a large candle on each. An old coffee table covered the patched carpet, and they'd done an extra dust and sweep job on top of everything. Tom's recliner remained in place, off to the right of the love seat, a throw blanket lying across the back, and the pine-fresh scent of disinfectant was heavy in the air. She flipped on the Benelli's safety and placed the weapon on the breakfast nook behind her as Marie padded to the coffee maker and put on a fresh pot of brew.

"Can you two take guard shift, Linda?" Barbara asked. "Just while us adults are talking?"

"Sure, Mom." The girl turned to the Everetts. "Don't leave without saying goodbye, okay."

Darren patted her shoulder. "We wouldn't even think of it."

Linda gave a smile all around before flying upstairs to position herself at the window. Barbara raised her chin to her son, who clung on Darren's arm, laughing with the older man over a joke the latter had regaled him with. "Jack, why don't you get back on your lessons?"

"I'm *so* caught up on all my lessons," he replied with a sour face. "And I've played most of my games, too. I beat all my high scores."

"Well, go up and put on some nature shows while us adults talk. Just for a bit, okay?" She gave him a wink. "Then you and Mr. Darren can get back to your important work."

Jack reluctantly let Darren go with a sigh. "Okay, Mom. I seriously can't wait until I grow up so I can hang out with everyone."

"It'll be sooner than you think" she muttered to herself, watching Jack go until he had vanished around the corner upstairs before settling in a chair at the kitchen table with an exhausted sigh. Marie brought her a fresh cup of coffee and rubbed Barbara's shoulders.

"So, you did it, huh?" Darren asked, sliding into a chair opposite her. "You let the girl wear a weapon."

"Absolutely," she replied, rolling her head as Marie massaged her. "She handles it well enough."

Marie leaned down. "We have no doubt about your judgement, dear." The woman went back to the coffee maker to pour two more cups. "With only the three of you here, you can't be doing everything yourself."

"She's been a godsend, helping me keep watch." Barbara wrapped her hands around the warm mug. "And she helped me with the animals today."

"That's what we came to talk to you about." Darren glanced at his wife.

Barbara sipped from her coffee, leaning back in her chair. "Go on."

"Based on what you've told us, I think it's safe to say the past ten days have been rough on all of us. People are pestering us. Threatening us. It's getting colder. It feels like things are… unraveling."

Another sip, and she nodded in agreement.

Darren glanced at his wife again. "We… we thought it might be smart to join forces."

"You mean resources?"

"I mean, share a camp. A house *and* resources. And work."

"That's right." Marie brought two coffees over, placed one down in front of her husband, and sat at the table between them with the second mug. The woman's short, steel-colored hair was clipped up, her light-colored eyes settling on Barbara. "Now, being something of preppers ourselves, we know what it means to have worked hard to stock and plan."

"And we understand it's hard to trust outsiders," Darren added with a gesture around at all of them. "We're like-minded people."

"I won't disagree with that," Barbara smiled. "Though you're hardly outsiders. The farthest thing from it, in fact. But do you think it's come to that, then? We're being pushed to that point where we need to team up?"

"We're struggling just to keep an eye on our property. Even with the camera system..." Darren's trailed off in exasperation, raising his hands and letting them flop uselessly on the table.

"We're barely getting any sleep," Marie finished for him. "And even though I love my Big D, it gets lonely for the both of us. It might be nice to have some company. Of course, we would help with everything here. Keeping watch and doing chores, cooking and cleaning, everything that's needed. You know we're not freeloaders."

A part of Barbara resisted, the part that had worked with Tom for so many years to become self-sufficient, and in the first instant she wanted nothing more than to find a way to politely decline. Joining forces with the Everetts, while not a bad idea, almost felt like giving up. Still, the more she thought about it, the more it made sense. There were few people she trusted in the world outside of her family, and the Everetts were two of those few.

"Are you sure?" she asked with a pointed yet pained look. "You've dedicated a huge part of your lives to becoming self-sufficient..."

"We're sure," Darren sputtered. "And even though we've got our pride, we're practically begging you to take us in. I don't know how much longer we can hold out. My joints are killing me from the cold, and Marie keeps making me eat MREs."

"His jokes are really bad, too" Marie snickered.

"Obviously if you say no, there's no hard feelings," Darren continued. "I feel like crap, putting you on the spot like this." He looked over at Marie and she nodded woefully. "We've been hanging in there and we'll keep hanging in there, just like you guys are. It's just an idea. Maybe… think it over for the night? Or however long you need?"

Barbara put her hand over her mouth at the broad-shouldered man's stammering and laughed as a feeling of warm relief flooded over her. "Well, I don't need that long. And I appreciate the out… but I think it's a great idea."

"Are you sure? We can use our place," Marie offered. "It's smaller but it'd be pretty easy to make it cozy for everyone."

Barbara waved her hand. "No, no, no. We've got more room here and our place is easier to defend, too."

"We've got some food stores to contribute." Marie sounded apologetic. "I hope it's not too much. Well, I mean, I hope it's enough *and* not too much."

"We've got more than enough space here," Barbara assured her, patting the older woman on the arm, gripping her hand tight. "We'll have to pack the basement tight, but I think it can be done."

"We also have some chickens and goats," Darren added. "Not a lot of them, mind you, but enough to keep us supplied with milk and eggs. Plenty of feed, too, for them and for your flock."

"That should fit right in with what I've got going on here," Barbara agreed, the full implications of teaming up invigorating her, making her feel more alive than she had in weeks. "With you two helping with the regular work, I can spend more time securing the greenhouse and working on defensive measures."

"Absolutely," Marie grinned, voice rising with enthusiasm, the uncertainty she'd had before vanishing. "Myself, Darren, and Linda on guard duty. Three easy shifts, allowing plenty of sleep time for everyone. We can keep up on the other chores in between. Of course, it would give you a much-needed break, too."

Barbara nodded. "I think this is going to be amazing. Thank you both for suggesting it."

Both Darren and Marie's shoulders sagged in relief at her words. "Thank you so much," Marie beamed. "We were hoping you would agree. You won't regret it."

"I should have come to you days ago." Barbara pursed her lips. "I was too focused on locking things down and doing things on my own. I should have put my pride aside and asked you to come sooner." She scoffed softly, the weight in her chest suddenly lifting. "You'll be helping us a lot more than we'll be helping you. It's me who should be thanking you – so… thank you. Seriously."

Marie half got out of her chair, grinning with tears in her eyes as she gave Barbara an impromptu hug. "You're too kind, Barbara. Thank you again."

"It's settled then," Barbara returned the embrace, patting Marie on the back as the older woman sat back in her seat and wiped her eyes. "You guys can have dinner here and stay the night. We'll get your things brought over in the morning."

Marie clutched her hands together. "And you'll let me take care of the cooking while you take a nap. I'll wake you up in about an hour. Come on..." The older woman made her stand and shooed Barbara from the kitchen, practically pushing her over to the love seat. Barbara chuckled as she turned and watched the Everetts bustle in the kitchen, grabbing pots and pans and digging around in the refrigerator, taking to it with real enthusiasm, the house feeling more like a home with two more people present.

As for Barbara herself, after so long without a physical or mental break, it seemed strange not having anything to do for even a few minutes, let alone an hour. With a wistful smile, she grabbed the throw cover off the recliner and collapsed into it, throwing the footrest out and kicking back. She placed the cover over her legs and wrapped her arms around her pillow, staring at the ceiling, thinking about Tom and Sam, wondering where they were.

"Mind if I start a fire?"

She looked up to find Darren standing over her, nodding toward the fireplace. The stack of wood next to it had remained untouched since she'd been leery of lighting one in the daytime where people could see the smoke.

"It's getting dark out," Barbara said, brow furrowed as she mused. "I don't think anyone will notice. So, yeah, I don't see why not."

"Great!" He smiled enthusiastically and ambled over to the fireplace in his socks. Ten minutes later, as the fire crackled merrily away and the smells of Marie's cooking filled the air, a thought popped into Barbara's head that she hadn't realized she once took for granted. They were safe. Momentary safety, to be sure, and nothing like the safety they enjoyed before the world went to hell on a bobsled, but still, they were safe. A grin tugged at the corners of her mouth at the thought before her eyelids fell shut and she finally, mercifully, slept.

Chapter 3
Tom McKnight
Pocahontas Village, Virginia

"I had a bad feeling about him," Sam said, looking around in disappointment.

"You and me both." Tom huffed with frustration.

"He did say he'd meet us here at 10:30, right?"

"Yep. Now I'm wondering if he'll show at all."

Tom scanned the area for Keith as Jerry and Sam stood nearby, the trio doing their best to look as nonchalant as possible. They'd found an area of fence along the northeast side of the holding facility where the tall camp lights didn't quite reach. Snowflakes blinked to life under the glare only to fade to nothing as they tumbled back into the darkness. A cluster of tents mostly hid the group from view, and the cold had driven most of the refugees inside, so while it wasn't a lot of cover, it would have to do. Between the three of them, they'd moved three barrels into position along the fence line, and all that was left was to finish stacking them and climb over the circle of barbed wire.

The camp was quiet, everyone huddled inside to shelter from the cold night, even the lovebird guards who had left early, as predicted, with their replacements had yet to show. Sam stood in her layers of clothing and furry hat, hands stuffed into a pair of fingerless gloves while Jerry was dressed similarly except for an old baseball cap perched on his head, pressing down his short, dark hair. If the group could get over the fence within the next few minutes, they'd have a clear path to the strip mall across the lot, and from there it was anyone's guess as to where they could go or what would happen.

"Should we go now anyway?" Sam asked, nervously. "I don't think he's coming."

Tom growled. "It doesn't look like it, does it? And I'm not going looking for him. We've got a short window to do this."

"Maybe we should wait until tomorrow?" Jerry's eyes darted around uncertainly.

"No." Tom deflated the suggestion before it could gain any traction. "We've already been here far too long. We're going. Now. With or without Keith." He glanced out into the night one final time, checking for any stray guards before turning to the others. "And it looks like it'll be without. Come on, help me get these barrels stacked."

They pushed two barrels against the other three and lifted them up, pushing them flush with the fence. Tom climbed to the top, turning to take a blanket from Sam. The razor wire at the top of the fence had been a concern for him, especially with Jerry's arm still giving him trouble, but when the thick blanket was placed over it and pressed down, his fears were allayed, and he felt a hopeful tumble of butterflies in his stomach for the first time in well over a week.

"We're good to go. I'll head over first," Tom whispered down. "Then we'll help Jerry over next. Sam, you'll be last once we make sure the coast is clear."

"Got it," Sam replied, her gaze a mixture of determination and nervousness, Jerry looking much the same next to her in the dim light.

Tom turned back to the fence, lifted one boot and rested it on the blanket, testing to see how much pressure he could put on it before the wire started to slice through when a voice cut through the darkness.

"Hey," the voice hissed. "What are you doing?"

Tom pulled his boot back, nearly tumbling off the barrels as he turned to see a thin figure approaching between the tents, arms laden with bundles too hard to see in the dark.

"Keith!" Jerry exclaimed quietly as he turned. "We didn't think you'd show."

"Yeah, we were about to leave without you." Sam folded her arms, helping her father down off the barrels.

"Sorry about that. I just wanted to try to get these for you." The man dropped three packs on the ground, teetering sideways as he released the weight before putting his hands on his hips and giving the trio a cocky grin.

Tom squinted. "Are those… our backpacks?"

"Yep." Keith nodded, beaming with delight.

"No way," Jerry said, walking over and pulling his aside.

"How'd you get them?" Sam asked.

"If I told you, I'd have to kill you," Keith scoffed softly. "Your chocolates are inside, Sam."

As Sam picked up her backpack, Tom eyed Keith carefully, watching him look between Sam and Jerry as the pair rifled through the bags. "How'd you manage to pull this off, Keith?"

"Hey, like I said, if I told you—"

"I'm serious." Tom growled. "How'd you do it?"

Keith's grin faded and he held his hands up. "Easy there big guy. Guard owed me a favor for some stuff I secured for them. Figured that since we're busting out, I'd call that favor back in. I thought you'd be grateful, but, I mean…"

Tom stood for a long moment, studying Keith's face, looking for any traces of dishonesty. When he could find nothing to pin his suspicions on, he gave up, gave a disgruntled harrumph, and muttered a quiet "thanks." Dragging his backpack aside, ignoring Keith's lingering stare, Tom kneeled down, opened the top and thrust his hand deep inside, fishing around, pulling up a wrapped package tied with string before untying the bundle and spreading it out on the ground. The tool pack held scissors, knives, forks, and other implements they'd taken from the hotel kitchen and RV, though what he was aiming for was the small pair of wire cutters he'd found in the hotel storeroom.

He held up the cutters, wrapped the rest, and put the bundle away then sidled wordlessly over to the fence, snipping at the cold steel, twisting and bending the tool to cut all the way through the chain-link. Bit-by-bit, he cut a line down the fence to the ground, then peeled one end back and held it open so they could slide through.

"Okay, guys," he whispered, voice straining slightly. "Squeeze through."

The trio put their packs through first, then Sam, Jerry, and Keith slipped between the sharp edges, going slowly to avoid tearing their clothes. Once on the other side, Keith turned and held the fence open while Tom pushed through, dragging his backpack behind him. He shouldered it and crouched in the lot, feeling suddenly exposed.

"Nice job," Keith said, nodding to the wire cutters as Tom put them away.

"Let's get to the strip mall." Tom urged. "We need to hurry. The guards could swing by any second."

"Right. This way."

Keith went first, leading them across the lot, sticking to the darkest spots where the lights couldn't reach. Glancing around, Tom saw the flashlights of soldier groups casually patrolling the parking lot between refugee tents, many of them gathered in small groups, appearing to be doing more talking than actual guarding. A few broke off from the main group as someone emerged from a tent, heading back to their patrol route before their superior officer noticed their laxity.

"It won't be long before they realize someone's escaped," he murmured to Keith, the cold of the night bringing snowflakes to brush against his face. "We need to speed this up." Keith nodded and pointed ahead of them as they entered a small strip mall area, keeping close to the shadowy storefronts, moving south toward the railroad tracks they'd used to come across into the camp several days prior.

"Stay down," Keith said, pulling them through the strip mall parking lot where the camp light's barely reached, the darkened storefronts dead and lifeless, the lot itself containing a variety of vehicles that were covered with ice and snow. The snowfall and wind were growing thicker, their shoes leaving tracks that were quickly washed away. The trio hunkered down behind an abandoned blue sedan parked in the corner "Look south," he told Tom. "They commandeered that doctors' office building for the military headquarters. The motor pool is in that lot."

Tom peeked over the sedan's hood, watching along a road that crossed the railroad tracks and continued south where a condominium building sat on the right, and the doctors' office building on the left. Privacy trees circled the office building's lot, making it hard to see, though the grounds were well lit with tall halogen lights. On the left-hand side, behind the privacy trees, was a section encircled by fencing and between gaps in the trees, he spotted several large APCs, some light transport vehicles, and two Humvees behind the fence. Signs hung everywhere around the perimeter, warning off trespassers with threats of fines, imprisonment and lethal force. Guards patrolled the area around the pool in groups of twos and fours, one pair stepping from between the privacy trees, climbing a grassy rise and crossing the railroad tracks, heading north past them.

Tom lowered himself back behind the sedan, looking at Sam and Jerry. "That's the motor pool for sure."

"C'mon, let's work our way around to the lot," Keith said.

Following him, the group left the cover provided by the blue sedan and hustled across the street, heading south. They crossed the railroad tracks and angled left into the privacy trees, following them around, shoes crunching on the frozen grass, all staying alert for signs of nearby guards. They moved eastward and stopped near a side gate to the motor pool, in one of the few areas where the halogen lights didn't quite reach. After ensuring no guards were going to walk up from behind them, Tom peered between the trees and studied the fencing.

Double-stranded and twelve feet tall with extra razor wire at the top, the fence was a formidable opponent, putting the fence around their former compound to shame. The gate was similarly constructed, with a card reader and keypad on the near side of it, and a guardhouse sat a short ways inside the gate nestled in between a pair of APCs.

"That fence is much thicker than the stuff we just cut through," Tom commented. "These wire cutters barely managed last time – no way will they work on this stuff."

"What about the guards?" Jerry squatted next to Tom, Sam just on his other side. "Shouldn't there be guards at a gate?"

"It's just a side gate," Keith said, "They're probably in the guardhouse keeping warm. It's not like anyone expects someone to come through here anyway."

"Hey, look," Tom shuffled a few feet through the trees, pointing. "There's a Humvee *outside* the fencing. I say we go for that one."

Tom rose from cover and began squat-walking toward the vehicle until Keith grabbed his backpack, stopping him in his tracks. Tom turned to give the man a dirty look, but Keith merely pushed in the opposite direction, whispering to him. "No, this way."

Keith immediately began making a beeline through the edge of the trees toward the gate while Sam and Jerry stood in the grass, looking back and forth between the two, uncertain of whom to follow. Cursing under his breath, Tom turned and followed Keith to the gate where the man stood by the security swipe pad. Tom was about to ask how they would bypass it when Keith flashed a plastic white card along with a sly grin, sliding the card through the reader. A green light flashed on the side of the reader and the gate popped open, Keith gesturing to it with a dramatic flourish.

The trio followed Keith inside and stopped at the massive APCs, staring up at them. While Tom wasn't an expert in military vehicles, he knew a bit about them thanks to his past contracting work, and recognized the vehicle called a Stryker along with the two other APCs that were of similar size and make, though they appeared slightly older. Keith directed them to one of the older models, a twelve ton, eight-wheeled vehicle squatting next to them with an angular profile, looking menacing in the blaring lights. It didn't have a gun turret like the Stryker but instead had two access hatches in the top.

"I couldn't get a security card for the Stryker," he said, stepping to the rear. "But I found one for this fine LAV-25."

"Light armored vehicle, model twenty-five," Tom said with a nod, standing back to put his hand against the cold steel, the surface feeling more like a block of ice than metal, the structure itself massive and weighty. It was almost the size of half-sized school bus, if the school bus had been compressed, stretched out to the side and painted dark green.

At the rear door, Keith passed the card over the reader and it clicked green, snapping the locks. He grabbed the two handles, turned them, and pulled the double doors open, revealing a small crew section in the back. "Upgrades, huh?" Tom motioned to the card reader as Keith slipped the card back into his pocket. "Part of the extended service life program?"

"Uhh, I guess? I dunno. Not a military guy." Keith shrugged, flashing him a quick smile, and Tom gestured for Jerry and Sam to go inside. They removed their backpacks, ducked, and clambered into the vehicle, then tossed their things in one seat and planted themselves in two others. Tom followed behind them, setting his pack on top of theirs and finding a spot of his own to settle in when Keith's hand fell on Tom's shoulder. "Hey, your seat is up there." Keith pointed to the front of the vehicle.

"Up there?"

"Yeah, I can't drive this thing."

Tom scoffed. "What makes you think I can?"

"Didn't you say you worked for the Navy? You drove some of their boats?"

"Yeah, but those were rides in manned rover subs. Heavily supervised, too."

"See. That's twice as much experience as me already."

Tom shook his head, "There's a big difference between a rover and an LAV, Keith. I've seen guys drive these things before and they're nothing to joke about. Plus, this one is different from the couple I've seen before. It's had a bunch of changes or upgrades or something."

"You've seen people drive them? That's three times as much experience as me!" Tom groaned, but when Keith made no move to get behind the wheel, he stood and made his way to the front, while Keith elicited Jerry's help to close the rear doors. Pulling himself forward with the help of handholds and rails, Tom reached the front of the vehicle. The driver's seat was elevated so the driver could stand and peer through an open portal in the front armor or stick their head through the roof hatch, and Tom stepped into position, shoving open the roof hatch, resting his backside on the seat. Poking his head through the frosted rim, he looked across at the doctors' building, listening to faint voices coming from the guardhouse just thirty yards away.

He backed up and looked down at the controls, a series of buttons, switches and gauges illuminated by lights set into a console. Three small computer screens were placed just behind the steering wheel, though he had no idea what they were for.

"Do you think you can do it?" Keith asked from below.

"It doesn't look much harder than a car or truck. I just have to find the right switches. Half of them don't have labels and I don't know what the rest do. Just give me a minute."

After studying the array, Tom pressed a button, and the front and rear lights came to life with a loud snap, illuminating the parking lot. His heart leapt into his throat, pulse kicking up as he slammed the button to shut them off, listening to see if anyone noticed. When no alarms were raised and no one came out of the guardhouse, he released a shaky sigh of relief and pressed another switch that illuminated the vehicle's interior. He glanced back at Sam and Jerry with a shrug, his daughter nodding while Jerry gave him a thumbs up.

Turning back to the console and inspecting the controls again, he found what looked like the ignition switch, flipped it and pressed a large red button next to it. The Detroit Diesel engine growled to life, turning over with a few coughs before settling into a throaty, deep purr.

"Step one sorted," Tom mumbled to himself, putting his feet on the pedals and relaxing into what felt was a good driving position as he continued examining the controls. Outside, there were shouts from the guard shack which he ignored, fingers playing over the switches and knobs as he tried to decipher the acronyms and abbreviations that plagued them all.

"Hey, quit fooling around," Keith's voice strained with urgency. "We need to get out of here!"

"I'm not fooling around," Tom growled back. "I'm trying to put the damn thing in gear."

Two soldiers circled to the front of the vehicle with their rifles pointed at Tom's head poking out the top, looking confused and angry over having to step out into the cold. "Shut down that truck, *now*!" one soldier shouted, ticking his rifle barrel up.

Tom ducked slightly, trying to keep the armor between himself and the weapons. He hit what he thought was a gear release, and the LAV-25 hitched forward. Just as quickly he jammed his foot on the brake to bring them to a jarring stop.

Red-faced, the guard screamed at him. "I said shut it down right now!"

Tom ducked farther so he could barely see over the rim, slapping his hands on the wheel as someone fired a burst from their rifle, a handful of rounds smacking harmlessly off the heavy armor with a flurry of sparks.

"Jeez!" Tom yelped, releasing the brake and clutch while simultaneously punching the gas pedal. "Hold on, everyone!" The LAV jerked forward, slamming through the fencing, Tom staying low as the chain link flew over his head to rolled off the back of the vehicle, the soldiers scattering to the sides with grunts and curses. Tom jerked the wheel to the left in a squeal of tires before they could ram the office building, alternating his foot between the brake, clutch and gas pedals, trying to straighten the heavy vehicle with its sensitive controls.

Once pointed south, the steering under control, he hit the gas again and launched them forward. Before he could get a head of steam, a pair of hands slammed on the roof, gripping it tight, white knuckles pulling a soldier's angry face into view, screaming at Tom.

"I said stop the vehicle or else—"

Tom jerked the wheel to the right, throwing the soldier off with a wild cry, grimacing as the man tumbled away. He twisted the wheel straight again just as a line of trees materialized in front of him, the LAV bouncing over a curb and slamming into the treeline. The armored vehicle swept smaller trees aside with ease and glanced off a thick trunk covered with frost, throwing up surprised squeals and grunts from his passengers, the impact surprisingly mild thanks to the massive weight of the vehicle. He banked them hard left again as they plunged into the next parking lot over, rifle fire pinging off the rear armor just as uselessly as the initial shots had been.

"You okay, Dad?!" Sam called from the back.

"Yeah," Tom shouted back. "Just getting the feel of-"

The LAV shook as it left the grass, hopped the curb and slammed onto the pavement, racing toward a nearby parked van. Tom yanked the wheel around, glancing off the van's fender and spinning the smaller vehicles completely around in a crush of metal and glass, crystalline shards and polymer pieces sailing off to scatter across the concrete. Inside, meanwhile, Tom felt nothing from the impact, only hearing the screech of metal on metal as proof positive that they had, in fact, hit something.

"This thing is so damn sensitive!" Tom hissed as the vehicle lurched and shook, not in response to the impact, but to his continued corrections and overcorrections as he tried to keep them from hitting anything else. In the clear, he let the LAV coast, straightening it out down the center of the lot toward the road before pulling onto the thoroughfare and turning left, driving another two blocks to the next intersection.

After searching the dashboard while the vehicle slowed to a crawl, he finally flipped on the headlamps to read the street sign. "I'm coming up on Bonney Road," he announced, "Where do I go from here?"

"Take a right!" Jerry called up.

"Roger that!"

Tom turned right, cutting off an oncoming pickup truck, and got the LAV moving west. After getting a better feel for the gas pedal, he pushed the speed up to a comfortable forty-five miles per hour, cold wind whipping around his head through the upturned hatch. They passed signs for I-264, and Tom took another right, putting them on a wide entry ramp, and soon they were buzzing their way westward on the expressway along with a thin line of civilian traffic. Every vehicle they passed slowed instinctively as the larger vehicle roared past, the drivers and passengers alike gawking out their windows at the green camouflaged behemoth.

There were no rearview or side mirrors to check for pursuers, but after fiddling with the console controls a bit more, Tom brought up a rear camera view on one of the video screens mounted in front of him, just below the open hatch. Glancing between the screens, controls and the road, he was able to get a full view of his surroundings.

"I don't think they're following us," he sighed to himself, the tension in his shoulders and chest easing back a notch.

Arms spread wide against the LAV's sides, Keith came to the front and threw open another roof portal. The lid banged back with a clang, letting in more cold wind and he stuck his head out, looking back down the expressway.

"Looking good, Tom! They probably don't have the resources to chase after us," he shouted over the whistling wind and roar of the diesel engine. "They must have bigger fish to fry. I'd say we made it!"

"Hell, yeah, Mr. McKnight!" Jerry called. "You broke us the hell out of there!"

"Good driving, Dad!" Sam shouted alongside Jerry.

Not completely convinced they were home-free – especially after stealing a piece of military equipment – Tom nonetheless relaxed even more, realizing that his hands were shaking on the wheel. He took several deep breaths, calming his frayed nerves, and it slowly dawned on him that they were at least both free of the confines of the camp and on their way west toward home.

Home. Never thought that could sound so sweet. Just keep holding on, Barbara... we'll be there before you know it.

As the traffic lightened up, Tom slowed down slightly, pulling into the right-hand lane and settling the LAV into steady cruising speed, keeping just below the speed limit on the off chance he might have to pull off or, heaven forbid, figure out how to deal with police or military checkpoints. The thought of checkpoints brought back an annoying niggle in the back of his mind that had started up back when Keith had emerged out of the shadows and inserted him into their escape plan. It had grown with each subsequent miracle Keith had performed, and while there hadn't been a chance to question it at the time, it was bothering him more and more with each passing mile.

Settling down into his seat, Tom changed the view on one of the screens to the forward-facing camera. It lacked the depth perception and field of view offered by poking his head out of the top of the vehicle, but had the distinct advantage of his face not feeling like he was kissing the rear end of a glacier, too. Once comfortable with the camera angle, he closed his hatch most of the way down and flicked on the interior heating unit's switch, casting a casual glance over at Keith. "Hey, how did you get a hold of the security cards to enter the motor pool? And the LAV, too?"

"I knew the camp was getting ready for some changes." Keith pulled his own hatch back in place and locked it tight with a clang, sitting heavily in a second seat in front of a communication console. He shrugged. "I got to be friends with one of the guards. Supplied him with a few hard to find things and he gave me your packs and the security cards. That was two days ago."

"He gave you some security cards to access an armored vehicle in the motor pool? Tom raised a skeptical eyebrow. "Seriously?"

"It's desperate times, man." Keith gave a conspiratorial look around and lowered his voice a notch in spite of their private surroundings. "The grunts are getting desperate. And if the grunts start doing stuff like this, you *know* it's getting bad."

"I suppose that makes sense." Tom drove in silence for a moment before changing the subject. "So, you had our stuff two days ago, and you didn't give it to us?"

"Well, technically, it was mine." Keith grinned. "And I didn't owe you anything at the time."

"Right," Tom shook his head, almost impressed with the man's boldness. "But you still don't owe us anything, and you clearly would have been fine doing this all on your own. So, like I asked before, why didn't you just escape on your own?"

Keith released a resigned sigh. "While I am a loner, I also couldn't do it alone. A guy like me needs allies. Friends. People who can do things."

"Like drive a LAV-25?"

"Exactly."

Tom focused on the road, the annoyance still tickling the back of his brain. "So, you just saw the perfect opportunity to get away?"

"I'd been waiting for days. When I overheard you talking about leaving, the pieces fell together in my mind and I realized it was time to make my move. I figured you could probably drive the LAV, if push came to shove." He gestured at Tom and the controls. "Looks like I was right."

"Fair enough," Tom nodded.

"Plus, I like you guys." The man's shrugged off Tom's doubt. "You're good people. Trustworthy. You always dealt with me fairly, and that's more than I can say for others I've met. Honestly, I think we make a pretty good team."

Tom's conversation with Sam about Jerry back when they'd rescued him on the side of the road sprung to mind as he recalled his daughter's willingness to trust the young man despite Tom's reluctance. With Jerry, things had worked out, and he'd proven himself to be trustworthy – hell, he'd proven to be just about as good as family. Keith, though, wasn't Jerry. Not by a long shot.

"First, we appreciate the help," Tom chose his words carefully. "True to your word, you got us out of that camp. Now we're on our way home."

Sam piped up from the back. "Yeah, thanks for that. I just really, *really* want to get home."

"You can travel with us a little longer," Tom ground his teeth at Sam's interjection. "But as soon we find another vehicle, I think it'd be best if we parted ways. We have a home to get to and I'm sure you have people you want to get back to as well."

"I get what you're saying," Keith smiled confidently, giving Tom a wink. "But I think I'll surprise you. You'll appreciate me being around, eventually. Just wait and see."

Pulling himself out of his seat, Keith patted Tom on the shoulder and moved past Jerry and Sam with another smile and bob of his head before he grabbed something to snack on from his pack and made himself a comfortable spot to rest.

Chapter 4
Lieutenant Colonel Rachel Banks
Norfolk, Virginia

"This so-called plan is sheer insanity." General Heller glowers over a large glass table, fingers white as they grip the sides, staring at a three-dimensional strategy map displayed on the table itself. On the map sits the underwater shelf off the North Atlantic coast, the most up-to-date shape of the anomaly included, the entire display slowly rotating to offer a holistic view of the situation.

"Do you have something better in mind, sir?" Lieutenant Colonel Banks stands across from the four-star general, watching him closely. In the background, groups of scientists, civilian contractors and military personnel argue amongst themselves about the anomaly, how much water is flowing from it and what they could possibly do to stop it. The conversation grows more strained by the moment, going from calm discussion to raised voices to threats and shouting.

"It's not my job to have a better idea," the general snaps, knuckles growing whiter as he squeezes the table edges even tighter than before, looking at the group of assembled scientists. "It's my job to make sure your people aren't screwing everything up!"

Banks grinds her teeth together before responding. "With all due respect, *sir*, this is an unknown situation filled with unknown unknowns. We're all doing our best."

"Your best? Losers whine about doing their best. Winners go home and-"

"Ladies and gentlemen, please!" A smooth southern voice settles between them as a stout woman with short red hair steps in. "If y'all can ease down, I can explain how this is going to work."

Despite the thick tension in the room, the men and women quiet, a few turning away in anger while others wait to see what the red-haired woman has to say.

"Now let's look at the map again." Sue Anne Wilkes brushes a lock of her red hair aside and nods to an assistant on the far side of the table, who pushes a few buttons. "Based on the last readings taken, if we place charges deeper along the crevice walls, we should be able to collapse the entire thing and slow down the flow."

"That's what I'm worried about," Colonel Banks says, her military fatigues clinging to her tall, rigid frame. "We don't know how much the anomaly has changed since the last time you took readings."

Sue Anne nods her agreement. "That's true, but we'll retake them once we're back over the spot. From there, we'll adjust our placement." She gestures at the map. "This is just a, um, rough draft, I guess you'd call it."

"A rough draft?" The general growls from across the table. "Sheer. Insanity."

"It's definitely not a perfect plan, sir," the scientist answers. "We'll need to be flexible and course correct on the fly."

"And I expect you'll require the deep-sea assets we have here on base?" Banks steps in and Sue Anne glances at her.

"Yes. Three boats and several unmanned submersibles. I emailed you the full list."

"And Admiral Spencer has authorized you to do this?"

"That's right," Sue Anne confirmed. "You should receive the formal documentation within the hour."

"Thank you, Sue Anne." Banks leans over the table to address the general. "Now, we've got a few options on how to get down there—"

"Listen, Banks." Heller's expression remains taut with barely controlled fury. "We've already lost three submersibles, one with a crew, and several research ships worth billions. Not to mention the USS South Carolina along with a top-notch crew and Captain Arkin. Hundreds of people are dead. There's a limit to the resources we can keep sinking into this effort."

"Bottom line – it's foolish. Besides," the general points across the room, "One of your own people produced a report that shows the pressure has slowed some. It's bound to equalize soon."

"We don't know that." Banks tilts her head. "It's foolish to do nothing."

Another Colonel, one who's been lying in wait near Heller's side, springs forward as the general looks over at him, jumping into the conversation. "If we screw things up down there, we could make matters worse. Far worse. In fact, there's a thirty percent chance of that, based on your own numbers. Isn't that right?"

Banks acknowledges the truth of Colonel Booth's words with a nod.

"And then what?" Booth presses in.

"I'd say it won't matter much what we do or don't do by that time anyway. It'll be too late." Banks waits for the tension in the room to fade before she turns back to the map. "And besides, the president has authorized this plan, so that's what we're going to do."

Colonel Booth levels a cold stare at her. "Have you gotten any help from your asset? The big brain who's supposed to be helping us figure all this out?"

"No, but I'm working on it. I should have his cooperation very soon."

"Shouldn't we wait until we've secured him before we launch this hair-brained scheme?" Heller asks.

"We'll wait as long as we can," Banks agrees. "But no longer than a few days. Then we have to execute the plan. Meanwhile, we'll move whatever ships and subs we need into position."

"I hope you know what you're doing." Heller's contempt for Banks is palpable, his eyes a pair of coals. The general turns back to Colonel Booth and the remaining military people assembled, patently ignoring Banks. "Booth, give me a rundown on the situation on the ground."

Booth turns from the table and moves to a large digital touch screen depicting a digital map of the United States. The entire group switches their attention away from the table and focuses on the screen. All except for Banks, Sue Anne, and the rest of the scientific team.

"I'll start with the power situation," Booth says. "As you know, we've declared martial law and have taken over power stations from Michigan to Virginia." She points to various spots on the map as she speaks, and wherever she touches, the screen brightens. "As the evacuation completes, we'll begin shutting down the plants and moving all fuel and resources south, out of the hands of the incoming Canadians."

"Their incursion," Heller growls.

"To be fair, General." Booth addresses his concern. "We no longer care about the territory. It's the assets we want to salvage. Fuel, weapons, resources."

"Will we be able to hold them off until we get everything out?"

"You mean with the expected skirmishes along the border?"

Heller nods.

"The president is directing the military effort along with General Davidson and his staff. They're working with the Canadian Prime Minister to buy time, but Canadians citizens are slipping across the border by the thousands. Not much we can do to stop that, nor do they want to start shooting our closest allies just because they're fleeing a natural disaster. Communication networks are still down, but that's mostly a resource issue. We're dismantling radio towers in the north and consolidating them in the southern states. It's possible we could re-network the grid in a year or two."

"A year or two." Heller's gruff exterior shows some of its first cracks as his shoulders slump. "How about our evacuations? How are those going?"

"The evacuations are going as well as can be expected." Booth touches the screen to create a long, waving blue line through the Midwest and pulls the line down to a place midway in Georgia. "We're ninety percent complete. It's not hard convincing everyone about the upcoming cold. They can feel it. Using children to encourage the holdouts to comply is working well, too, and only a few are resisting our attempts to bring them in."

"Understood," Heller says. "Thank you, Colonel Booth. Now, let's review the secondary special project."

Banks barely listens to the rest as she returns to the map on the table, her gaze drifting over the three-dimensional model's rises, clefts and deep grooves that cut across the ocean floor.

The anomaly.

Its massive, unbelievable presence is like a stab to the heart of the world, causing them all to do things they wouldn't normally do and make decisions they wouldn't normally make both personally and as a country. Banks is confident she will beat it, though. She'll collapse the bastard in on itself and end the freshwater surge once and for all, effectively saving the world and bringing along all the benefits – both for others and for herself – that will come along with it. The meeting ends, and she quickly grabs her coat and hat, aiming to be the first one out, angling away from Sue Anne and the other scientists, avoiding lingering questions and requests for additional meetings. The time for discussion is over. The plan is in place, and all that matters is getting the asset on board.

A pair of MPs guide her to a black SUV stationed at the military base which will take her back to her sparse accommodations. The wind is brutal, and snowflakes bank in every direction, cutting through her jacket even as she pulls it tighter around herself. She opens the door and climbs in and, once alone in the warm interior, she reaches for the satellite phone, dialing a familiar number.

"Sergeant Landry. This is Banks.

"Yes, thank you. Where are you now?

"Yes.

"Very good.

"Have you heard from Arrowhead? Is phase two complete as planned?

"Excellent. Arrowhead should be able to get the asset to turn willingly. Tell him to look for some leverage first, by any means possible. Have him stay on task until that happens.

"No, we don't have the new home address. With the networks in shambles, we can't just pull it up.

"Yes. Very good, Sergeant Landry. I'll expect an update very soon."

Chapter 5
Tom McKnight
Somewhere in Virginia

A light snow fell as the LAV-25 motored along I-264 through moderate traffic, eliciting looks from drivers that ranged from awe to fear. Each of the vehicles they passed was packed with families and personal possessions, luggage racks strapped to overflowing, trailers stuffed to the gills. The wind was quiet as it flowed over Tom's goggled face, his head stuck up through the hatch, heaters blasting as he struggled to remain warm with the sharp bite of the wind across his face. While the screens and periscope system built-in to the LAV-25 were functional, he hadn't yet figured out how the periscope worked and the camera field of view was too restrictive for nimble driving, leading to a few near misses when changing lanes.

They passed a car with a shaggy dog's head hanging out the window, the animal watching the armored vehicle go by, tongue lolling from its mouth, looking happy to be on an adventure while its owners gave Tom a quick wide-eyed glance. Most of the electronic road signs that dotted the entirety of I-264 were dark, as were the streetlamps, though a few of the signs whose battery backups hadn't yet died still blinked with partially snow-obscured emergency messages.

"The signs are directing people to evacuate to southern cities," Tom called down. "They say not to stop for anything but fuel or rest."

"That fits with what Betty told us," Samantha shouted back up. "You know, about the government kicking people out of their houses and sending them south."

"Yeah," Tom whispered, nodding to himself. Things had seemed bad at the camp, but getting on the road had put it all in stark perspective. He shook his head as he remembered the days upon days of wasted time at the lockup, pressing the gas pedal harder, the desire to get home consuming every fiber of his being. "At least everyone's moving along nice and orderly."

"No Mad-Maxxing?" Jerry yelled from the back of the LAV.

"Not as far as I can see." Tom blinked as his hair whipped around his head. "People are giving us plenty of room. They must think we're part of the military."

"Too bad this thing doesn't have a mounted gun on top," Jerry said. "They'd get out of the way even faster."

"No kidding," Tom scoffed as he wove around a slow-moving semi, pulling in front of it.

They worked their way through Norfolk, hitting pockets of tighter traffic before it lightened up once more. Occasionally he would spot red and blue lights on the side roads and off-ramps, but the police appeared to be staying clear of the main highways. In downtown Norfolk the I-64 traffic got so bad he turned south on I-464 and tried to make some headway. Thanks to less traffic and the snowfall being light, they were able to bypass a large swath of traffic and make decent time. After a while they came across the expressway junction and switched yet again, heading west once more. It had been years since Tom had driven the highways of Virginia without a GPS and audio cues to tell him when and where to turn off, though his memory was decent enough to recall that I-64 connected with another state route that would eventually take them directly home.

"Just keep heading west," he whispered to himself. "Westward, my son."

As they passed by Bower's Hill, he called back down into the LAV, the cold wind picking up, blasting him in the side of the face. "There it is! Highway 58. That should get us straight home. It won't be long!"

"Awesome!" Sam shouted back, the words slurred around a piece of chocolate.

They crossed Lake Drummond next, the massive body of turbulent water peppered with rocking boats, most tied to their docks, though a few brave souls appeared to be traversing the water. Traffic had grown thick, the shoulders clogged with cars trying to go around the main lanes, and it took them a full thirty minutes to span the waterway. Suffolk waited for them on the other side, the city's lights winking, a soft glow pushing upward against the night sky. Tom kept on Highway 58, skirting north around the city, avoiding the crowded clusters of refugees, cold, sterile air whipping against his cheeks, wafts of diesel from the engine occasionally leaking through, burning his nose. Once past Suffolk, they rejoined the main highway, bouncing westward under a bright feral moon.

Lowering himself so he could just peek over the hatch, Tom glanced down at Keith where the man sat in the side radio seat, settled in with a bottle of water between his knees, chewing on a snack from his backpack. The cabin air at the front of the vehicle was all aflutter, a swirling combination of heat from the vents and cold air thrashing down through the hatch, everyone's hair rustled by the gusts.

"I'll bet you guys can't wait to get home," Keith spoke through a mouthful.

"Absolutely," Tom answered with a grin. "That's *all* we've been thinking about since before Virginia Beach. Right, Sam?"

"One hundred percent correct, Dad."

"Where's home for you guys, anyway?"

"Just a nice little farmstead right off the road. A big red barn. More sheep and chickens than you can count. Probably stuff you'd hate."

"Hey that doesn't sound bad, actually," Keith quipped. "I could live off the land."

Tom chuckled. "I'll bet you could. But it's a lot harder than you think."

Keith looked as though he was going to ask another question, but Tom frowned, raising his head back up out of the LAV. "You've got to be kidding me."

"What is it?" Keith asked from the back.

"I think it's a wreck," Tom craned his neck, searching for a way around. "I can see emergency lights flashing ahead." He tried to raise himself to see over the cars ahead, the relative low-set body of the LAV working against him. Keith put his water and snack aside and flipped up the other hatch, hands on the rim, grunting as he pulled up and through to stand on the roof where he balanced himself, snowy wind whipping his tousled brown hair around.

"It's definitely a wreck." he called down and pointed off to the right. "But you can go around."

Tom looked out over a flat field split by driveways and clusters of trees where several cars had already pulled off and tried to go around, but ended up getting stuck in the wet, swampy grass left by the storm, tires spinning and spraying mud from beneath the rear fenders. Under any other circumstance, Tom wouldn't dream of trying to ford such an obstacle, but given that they were in an amphibious assault craft, he was willing to take his chances.

"Get back down here, Keith." Tom called to them. "We're going to do some off-roading."

Keith lowered himself back inside but kept his head poking out higher than Tom was able, watching for obstacles and danger spots in their path ahead. Tom braced himself against the seat and pulled them out of the line of traffic, angling right, rolling over the shoulder and down into a slight ditch. They hit it at an odd angle, nearly jerking the wheel out of his hand though he snatched it back and got the vehicle straightened out before they plowed into a stuck BMW, weaving around it in a slosh of tires and throwing a wake of water against the doors. The driver - wise as he had been to try and go off-road in a wet, swampy mess in his luxury car - cursed them as Tom hit the gas, revving up Detroit Diesel engine to power through the icy-wet grass.

He took a wide, circular path around the stuck cars and trucks, the owners standing outside their vehicles or sitting on the hoods, watching the big LAV roll by with dour expressions. The big wheels churned up a wake like a boat through shallow water as they crossed driveways and side roads, crashing through landscaped gardens and knee-high fences with abandon, throwing Samantha and Jerry around in back. Keith clung doggedly to the hatch rim, looking around as Tom blew by the rest of the traffic, plowing over brush and shrub alike as though they weren't even there.

They quickly approached the front of the line where several police cars sat around an enormous tow truck built for towing 18-wheelers. A tractor trailer appeared to have jackknifed sideways across the road, clogging traffic for miles, and the tow truck was attempting to sort out the mess. The officers standing around their vehicles stared at the LAV as it passed, as if deciding whether or not to try and pursue the lone military vehicle. Tom only glanced in their direction, keeping his eyes pinned forward as he steered closer to the road.

"Think they'll come after us?" Keith asked.

"They can try," Tom shook his head. "I wish them luck if they do, though. What are they going to do, pull us over?"

"I guess not," Keith agreed with a satisfied grin. "Ride on, cowboy."

The LAV angled left, slammed over a ditch, and rejoined the road in a spray of mud and water. With the road clear ahead of them, he kicked their speed up to fifty miles per hour, Tom bullying slower moving cars, cutting them off, whipping around them as the drivers hit their brakes and stared up at the hunk of steel flying by. Cheeks red and numb, goggles strapped tight to his face, he pushed the LAV faster, the diesel's exhaust trailing behind them in a light breath of smoke.

"What's it look like out there?" Sam called up.

"It's totally clear." Tom laughed into the wind. "A straight shot all the way home."

"Best news I've heard in weeks!"

"Great job, Mr. McKnight!" Jerry kicked up his feet. "We've got a sweet ride for the trip home. And here we thought it was going to get harder."

"Well, we're not there yet." Tom tempered their enthusiasm. "Don't take anything for granted."

* * *

A few hours later, as the wind and snow picked up, Tom began to see signs for Emporia, Virginia appear, the green metal partially obscured by snow and ice sticking to it. He slowed as they approached the small town, sporadic lights dotting squares of subdivisions, some of which had power, though others had fallen completely dark. The LAV's headlamps and spotlights cut through the increasing flurry of snow, gusts of powder white thrashing along the top and sides, adding to Tom's increasing discomfort and chilled face.

"Man, this thing's a real gas hog," he yelled down after peeking in to see the fuel gauge. "We're getting low on fuel already."

"Eight or nine miles to the gallon," Keith chimed. "Do we need to stop?"

"We do," he replied. "Not only to refuel, but I need to get my head out of this wind. Pretty sure my cheeks have frozen solid by now."

The highway skirted them north around town, and they passed several exits along the way, each with gas stations whose signs were dark and parking lots were devoid of life. Each time they drove by an exit, Tom shook his head, tempted to get off and attempt to refuel at an abandoned one. While most would probably have backup generators to work the pumps, there was no telling what sort of resistance they might encounter that they weren't fully prepared for. After multiple dark exits, he finally spotted lights off to the right up ahead and straightened in his seat.

"There's a station up ahead with lights on," he told them, "Which means there'll be people. If it looks safe, we'll stop there. That reminds me, are there any weapons in here?"

"I already checked," Keith said flatly. "Not a rifle or pistol to be found. How much gas do we have left?"

Tom glanced at the gauge. "We're right on empty. I'd say we have two, maybe three miles before we stall out based on how it's been guzzling so far."

"Definitely pull off," Keith agreed.

Tom got off at the exit, cruising past a semi parked on the shoulder along with several other cars, swinging the LAV around it to the right and cruising toward a truck stop. The fuel pumps were packed with vehicles, many with trailers hitched to them and roof racks filled with unbalanced luggage and plastic bags, piles of clothing, stereos, and televisions all strapped down with bungee cords.

People stood around protecting their possessions as they waited to get gas and two attendants dealt with customers at the doors, gesturing and holding up fingers, looking to both be taking cash and bartering.

Tom shook his head. "I don't think we're going to have much luck at the regular pumps. I'll pull around to the truck stop part."

The LAV cruised past the pumps and a mini mart, drawing stares and grimaces from the waiting refugees. From there, they circled around a long row of parked eighteen-wheelers to the fueling station at the end of the lot. It looked abandoned, likely because it was hidden from the road next to a rig repair shop, out of sight from the average family passing through in search of fuel.

"I have no idea where the gas tank is on this thing," Tom shook his head as he pulled up to an empty fuel pump, put the LAV in park, and killed the engine. Lowering himself into the crew cabin, he took a breath and shivered as Sam crouch-walked inside the low vehicle up next to him, removing her gloves and placing her warm palms against his windburned cheeks.

"Gosh, Dad. You're so cold."

"I should have stopped sooner," Tom admitted, sniffing through his stuffed-up nose before giving Sam a closer once-over.

"What?" Sam shook her head.

"You look worn out." He put the back of his hand to her forehead. "And you've got bags under your eyes. You're not feverish or anything, though."

"My throat feels a little sore," she said, swallowing hard, "but that could be from sleeping in tents in the cold for the past ten days."

"Yeah, that'd do it," Tom gave a half-hearted laugh, secretly promising himself – and not for the first time – that if he ever saw Banks again, he'd punch her square in the nose for making his daughter sleep outside. "I want you stay in here and rest, okay?"

"I need to use the restroom, though."

Tom nodded hesitantly. "Okay, but I want you and Jerry to stick close together while I work on the fuel situation. No going off by yourself. After that, I want you back in here and lying down. If I bring you home to your mother sick, she'll knock me out."

Sam laughed. "Okay. I promise I'll get some rest."

"Ready to go out?" Keith asked from beside Tom.

"Yeah. Let's do this."

Keith shuffled past the trio and opened the back doors, letting them swing outward so that Sam and Jerry could step out first, followed by Keith and Tom. Stretching his aching muscles, Tom looked toward the repair shop with its tall bay doors shut tight, a mini mart next to it, snow accumulating along the walls.

A regular-sized door between the garage and store opened, and a man with a mechanic's outfit stepped outside, looked both ways, pulled his jacket tighter, and jogged over. He started to wave but lowered his hand and slowed to a walk after getting a better look at the LAV's passengers.

"You're not military," he said suspiciously, coming up to the group.

"No we're not..." Tom squinted at the man's name tag. "Rich. We figured our truck wouldn't fit in with the rest of the cars, so we brought it out here to this pump."

"Normally, that would be fine," Rich said with an apologetic wince, "but these aren't normal times."

"What do you mean by that?"

The attendant gestured. "These pumps are strictly for military use now."

"Well, our vehicle is military."

"But *you're* not."

"No. But we can pay for whatever we use. Gas and food both, if you've got it."

"I need to use the restroom," Samantha said, lightly stamping her feet. "Are you saying I can't go inside and use it?"

Rich looked at each of them in turn, his gaze finally settling back on Sam, giving a half-hearted, defeated shrug. "Yeah, you can use the bathroom. It's at the back of the store."

"Thanks," Sam said, and she and Jerry marched past him.

"About the gas…" Tom started.

Rich was already shaking his head. "You can relieve yourselves, but I'm under orders not to release any of the fuel to civilians."

Tom stiffened with a look around. "I don't see any other trucks here, and there's no military. Besides, you're not military. They can't order you around."

"It doesn't matter." Rich lifted his chin in challenge. "I received word five days ago and been on lockdown ever since. I've had three military caravans come through already. If anyone messes with me, they get swatted by the Army boys." The man patted a slight bulge beneath his coat, though his eyes held a hint of uncertainty. "They even gave me a gun to protect it. I don't want to use it, but I will if I have to."

Keith's hand fell on Tom's shoulder, giving his trademark ear-to-ear smile. "Hey, why don't you let me talk to Rich for a minute."

Tom blinked at the attendant and his nervous, twitchy stare, backing off to let Keith by. "Yeah, sure."

Putting his hand on Rich's shoulder and guiding him toward the LAV, Keith spoke softly, pulling his wallet out of his pocket, flipping it open, and revealing what looked like an ID to the attendant, though Tom couldn't read what was on it. The two men spoke for nearly a minute before Rich threw out his hands in frustration. Keith bent his head lower, making a point as he gestured both at the vehicle and back at Tom, explaining something until the attendant finally nodded and relaxed.

Coming to an agreement, Rich turned and approached Tom with a nod. "I'm sorry about all the fuss, Mr. McKnight. You folks can fill up here. And the store is open to you, too. Showers and all, if you want."

"Thank you," Tom gave Keith a questioning look, receiving only a sly grin in response. "We, um, really appreciate it. We'll just fuel up, grab a few snacks, and be on our way."

"I'll gas us up," Keith offered, patting Tom's shoulder before turning to the pumps. "You go inside and get what you guys want to eat. Make sure you pay the man."

"Right," Tom gave Keith a long look before turning to follow Rich inside. Sam and Jerry were just finishing up when he got there, and Sam stopped, staring through the glass doors of a warming oven sitting next to a fountain drink machine and coffee maker.

"They've got pizza slices," Sam nearly drooled as she stared at the oven.

Rich gave the oven a dubious look. "Uhh, miss, those pieces are several hours old. You sure about that?"

"I don't care. I'd kill for a slice."

Tom smiled. "Go ahead. Old pizza never killed anyone."

"Think Keith will want one?"

Her father turned to look at Keith, who was standing next to the LAV. "Oh yes. I'm *positive* he will."

After getting the suspicious-looking slices of pizza, the trio walked through the store, picking snacks, drinks and candy bars.

"We need to get our junk food fix now," Sam explained to Jerry, "before Mom makes us eat nothing but healthy stuff."

At the register, Tom dug some cash from his wallet, dusting off grains of sand still trapped in the creases, and tossed the bundle on the counter in front of Rich. "That should more than cover everything for us."

Tom had taken in a few hundred dollars while bartering with people in the holding area. He doubted his money was worth anything – and if it was, it likely soon wouldn't be – but Rich rang him up nonetheless, took the money, and put it in the till, grunting to him with a nod.

"Good doing business with you fine folks."

"Thanks," Tom replied, then turned to Sam and Jerry, handing them his pile of food and drink. "I need to use the head," he motioned at the back of the store before taking care of his business. When he came out, he met Samantha back at the store window where she was nervously shifting back and forth. "What's going on?"

"Looks like we've gotten someone's attention." Samantha looked out toward the gas station across the lot where a group of people were gathering, staring at the LAV and pointing.

A nervous feeling ticked up in Tom's stomach. "Where's Jerry?"

"He already went back to the LAV with most of our stuff."

"Good. Let's get the rest and go."

Sam gathered a stack of pizza slices divided by paper plates while Tom grabbed a bag full of snacks and a bag of 2-liters and they both headed out. Keith was just finishing at the pump and came out to meet them halfway between their vehicle and the store.

"Looks good," he smiled at the stack of slices. "Smells even better."

"I was just thinking that," Tom agreed. "Ready to go?"

His attention shifted as a half-dozen people from the other store strolled around the rear of the LAV. They were dressed rough, like they'd just come in from doing farm work, the leader an average-sized man with a Farmall hat and a Carhartt work jacket, slapping the LAV's thick armor as he walked past it. A second group of workers strolled around the front of the LAV like they were going to the store, but they stopped when they saw that their first group had successfully cut Tom and his companions off from their vehicle.

"Damn," Tom hissed.

Reaching behind Sam, Keith nudged Tom with his elbow and held his hand partially open, revealing the security card resting in his palm. "I'll go talk to this other group. You guys get the LAV fired up and ready to roll."

Tom slipped the badge from Keith as the man walked toward the second group with a wave and a loud greeting.

"Sneak inside," Tom whispered to Sam from the corner of his mouth. "Get ready to drive. Did you watch how I did it?" Sam nodded stiffly as the men drew closer.

"Pretty standard stuff. Automatic transmission. Think you can handle that?"

"Give me five minutes to figure it out," she whispered back.

"I can do that." Tom switched the security card to his left hand and slipped it under one of Sam's paper plates as he took a slice off the top. Then he turned to nod at the leader in the Farmall hat. "Hey, buddy. Can I help you with something?"

The man tipped his bill with callused fingers. "We just came over to make sure Rich's following the rules he's been making us abide by."

"What's that?"

"We can't get no gas for our trucks because this part of the station is for military use only." The trucker gestured at him. "But ya'll don't look like soldiers."

"We're not," Tom agreed amicably, taking a big bite of his pizza and chewing loudly, smacking his lips around his food, cringing internally at the hours-old congealed taste. "But we're escorting some officers. Big wigs." He shot Sam a stern look. "What are you waiting for, girl? Get the food inside. The Colonel doesn't want to eat a block of ice."

"Yes, sir." Sam quickly sidestepped around the group and headed for the LAV before they could stop her.

A few looked like they might follow her, but Tom raised his voice. "Please tell me we don't have to kick your asses like we did those people back in Franklin."

The workers turned back to Tom, and the de facto leader narrowed his eyes. "*What* did you just say?"

Tom held the pizza slice up defensively. "Oh, not us. The colonel and his men."

"What colonel? And what men?"

"The ones in the back of the LAV," Tom explained. "We're driving them to Nashville. The Army is consolidating their forces at the base there."

The LAV's doors popped open, and Sam climbed inside. The trucker nodded to Tom's pizza and the bags of 2-liters and snacks in his hand. "So, all that gas and food you got is on the military's dime?"

"That's right." Tom folded the rest of his slice and shoved it in his mouth, chewing with a smile, glancing over to see Keith sweet-talking the other group to keep them occupied. "You know what they say. The military runs on its stomach!"

The LAV engine turned over as he swallowed the last bite, rumbling to life, eight tons of steel shaking as the Detroit Diesel began warming back up. *Good girl, Sam.* Tom side-stepped between the workers as they turned to look.

"Now, if you fellas don't mind, we need to get going or the colonel will have my ass."

The trucker turned back and cut him off. "Colonel, huh?" He scratched at the stubble beneath his chin, his drawl growing longer and more drawn-out. "Seems kind of strange that a Colonel and his 'men' have a bunch of civilians driving them and getting them food." Murmurs of agreement came from the men around him, bolstering his confidence. "Yeah I'm thinking we'll be taking a quick peek inside the back there."

Tom backed up a step, shrugged, and sighed. "All right. But don't be surprised when the colonel pulls out a can or three of whup-ass on you guys. His guards are some real nasty soldiers."

"I'll bet," The trucker spat. "Lead the way."

Tom gestured for them to let him through, and when the crowd parted, he strolled back to the LAV with forced confidence in his step, though on the inside his guts were twisting, his breaths coming shallow and quick. When Tom reached the armored vehicle, he gave the side three hard pats with his palm, making soft thudding noises on the steel. Circling to the rear, he stopped at the doors, a soft light spilling from where they were slightly ajar.

Tom raised his voice. "Colonel Pierce? There're some folks out here who want to talk to you."

A deep voice boomed through the crack. "What's the delay, McKnight? We were supposed to be on the road by now! It's bad enough I have to eat cold pizza. Now I have to sit and wait on your sorry ass?"

Tom turned toward the group standing behind him and gave them an apologetic wince. "I told you he wasn't in a good mood."

The trucker took a step back, glancing at the others with a look of uncertainty. Tom grabbed a door handle with his left hand and smiled, then, at the same time, swung the bag of sodas and snacks backward, whipping it at the lead trucker's head. The plastic bottles slammed square into his nose, the thick plastic and heavy liquid causing a sickening crunch of the man's nose and a spray of red. Tom dropped the bag in the recoil from the blow, thought about trying to recover it then abandoned the idea as he shoved two of the other workers back, throwing open the rear doors.

"Go, Sam! Go!"

The LAV's doors slammed against the sides as it unexpectedly lurched into reverse, the bottom edge threatened to cut off his shins. Tom jumped, hitting the floor as it rolled under him, landing half on Jerry where the young man had been playing colonel from one of the seats. The truckers and workers scrambled to get out of the way, diving aside and pinioning as the military vehicle hurtled by.

"Other way, Sam!" Tom grabbed the chair and hung on, shouting. The eight-wheeled vehicle came to a screeching stop, the transmission shifted, and they leapt forward, the rear doors flying back and slamming together in a cacophony of metallic bangs. Tom watched as they passed the leader of the group, the man's face red with blood, shouting incoherently at them with his middle finger raised high.

The LAV hitched and jerked, tires squealing, tossing them back and forth as Sam tried to control it. Tom crawled to the edge of the back doors, searching for Keith, but Sam was angling the vehicle sharply to the right, circling back to the road as people sprinted after the LAV, fists pumping as they tried to catch them, but thoroughly unable to do so. With the LAV and its security card safely in hand, they could easily head directly home, and for a moment Tom was tempted to leave the man behind as he hesitated at the back doors, torn between closing them and leaning out to look for Keith.

"Dammit." Tom growled, sticking half his body out of the back of the LAV. "Turn, Sam! We need to get Keith!" The LAV jerked in response, cutting a sharp angle through the lot, Tom steadying himself with the handles and bars at the back of the vehicle.

Keith suddenly sprinted into view, huffing and puffing as he ran at an angle away from the crowd, springing for the door. "Slow down, Sam! There he is!" Tom clasped Keith's hand as he got close, pulling him into the crew quarters where they landed in a sprawl across the seats. In a flash, Jerry jumped up and pulled the doors closed, then Tom scrambled and lunged for the handles, locking them together with a twist before the LAV shuddered again, throwing them all back into a tumble on the floor.

"Sorry!" Sam called from the front.

"Just keep driving!" Tom shouted back. "We're all inside! Just get us out of here!"

He turned and watched her sitting in the driver's seat, working the foot pedals as she drove. With a gasp of terror, Tom realized she was too short to see through the hatch – or the road. He lurched toward the front, but a sharp turn caused him to fall backwards.

"Sam, stop! You can't see the road!"

"No, she's got it." Keith climbed past him, falling into the seat next to Sam, gesturing at a screen she was staring at. "She figured out how to get the camera working!"

"Just the front view," Samantha said breathlessly, craning her neck forward as she focused on steering the LAV.

"Nice driving, Sam!" Jerry picked up the fallen security card from the floor and threw it on the seat next to him before he picked up a pizza slice, jamming the corner into his mouth.

Tom sat back, reclining, breathing easier as the ride smoothed out, taking a moment to catch his breath and regain his bearings. "Okay," he said. "We're good. Nice work, Sam. Really nice work."

Keith spun in his seat and beamed at everyone, cackling with laughter. "Was that a wild ride, or what?"

Chapter 6
Barbara
Wyndale, Virginia

A cold wind blew through the open front door of the McKnight house, fingers of chill reaching into every crack and crevice, driving out the heat contained therein. A space heater in the living room helped to keep it at bay to some degree, but the constant in and out of the McKnights and the Everetts belied keeping the door closed even intermittently, so they opted to prop it open instead, rushing through their work so they could be back in warmer conditions as quickly as possible.

"Just take these boxes downstairs and put them next to the other MREs," Barbara said, pushing a cart down the hall and handing it off to Linda.

"Okay, Mom. I know right where to put them."

The young girl had been a workhorse all day and even Jack was contributing a great deal, helping his sister carry the Everett's supplies to the basement. Darren waddled in carrying a box of canned goods, his face red and huffing with the effort, the wind blowing his hat off and dropping it on the hardwood, but he only gave it a perturbed glare.

"That should be the last of it."

Barbara scooted by and shut the door behind him to block out the cold wind, the temperature in the hall the same as outside. "Great, Darren. I can take it from here." She started to reach for the box.

"Nonsense. Just tell me where you want it."

She backed off with a grin. "Follow Linda down the hall. She'll show you the spot in the basement."

"Perfect."

He shuffled down the hall after Linda and her cart, the two standing by the door, fussing to get down the stairs while Smooch sat back on her haunches, watching the pair with her tongue lolling out. Marie joined them at the basement door, moving the last bit of their supplies downstairs and Barbara walked over to Smooch and patted the dog's head, watching as the others carried supplies down into the basement. Outside, the sound of disgruntled animals was dampened by the closed door, but still clearly audible. After transporting the chickens and goats using her pickup and the Everett's trailer, the different groups of animals were adjusting to each other out back in the yard.

Once everything was set and settled, they'd make up their watch shifts and get things back to normal around the house. The six hours of sleep she'd gotten the previous evening had been a godsend already, the world seeming more vivid, her energy level soaring through the roof and, best of all, she hadn't yawned once all morning.

Walking to the basement door, she called down after them. "Rows four and five for the cans!" She smiled and listened as Marie nodded and relayed the message.

Shotgun on her shoulder, Barbara moved down the hallway, opened the front door, and stepped onto the porch. Softly shutting it behind her, she pulled her coat tighter around her shoulders and peered down at the road across their milky-white field. The snow had kept up steadily overnight. Nothing too frightening except that it had come so early in the year, settling on them like an ill omen, a blanket of bite and frost instead of warmth and comfort. Across the street, the land lifted to a tree-covered rise, branches laden with snow, frost and icicles forming beneath them.

They'd parked the Everett's Jeep and trailer at the house but left her pickup down at the end of the driveway, keeping the way up to the house blocked off from the road. The door popped open behind her, and Darren stepped outside to join her, shuffling over the ice-covered wooden planks and followed her gaze across the snowy landscape.

"It's incredible how much the weather has changed." She shook her head. "It's gone from warm to abysmal in a blink."

"I've never seen anything like it," he agreed. "It's frightening, and it makes me wonder if it's going to stop."

She shifted the shotgun on her shoulder, burying her hands deeper in her pockets. "What do you mean?"

Darren pulled his hat down tight and stuffed his own hands into his coat, rocking back on his heels. "I'm no scientist, but I can read a temperature gauge. Even now, it's creeping down, getting close to zero. That's cold enough for these parts in the dead of winter, but it might get colder."

Barbara pursed her lips and breathed the chilled air. "How low do you think it will get?"

"I can't say. But we should be prepared for it to get as cold as it is in Canada."

"And how cold does Canada get?"

Darren shrugged. "It's -10 or -20 Fahrenheit in some places."

"That's cold," Barbara swallowed hard as the awful truth settled on her shoulders. "We can keep ourselves alive at that temperature, and even the animals. But the greenhouse won't make it. There's no way I can keep it warm enough in there without a massive drain on our fuel and solar power." She shook her head. "How long do you think the winter will last?"

"What do you mean?"

"Well, if what the president says is true, and the North Atlantic Drift has been disrupted..." She shook her head harder. "We probably won't get warm air up here for a long time."

Darren's eyes narrowed, and his jaw worked back and forth. "A winter that lasts years?"

"Maybe decades."

"Well, we'd have to consider going south at some point if that's the case." Darren shifted. "You know, joining the evacuation efforts?"

Barbara pursed her lips. "Tom would only want us to go south as a last resort. Plus, he and Sam aren't home yet, and I'm not going anywhere without them."

"The last time you heard from him was when we were here for dinner, right?"

"Days ago," she admitted with a nod. "There's absolutely no cellphone or internet service anymore. It's all down. Gone. Not even a trickle."

Darren shrugged. "Going South isn't something we need to do anytime soon. It's just something to think about, that's all."

Barbara raised her chin. "I don't want to talk about it anymore."

"Sorry," he patted her shoulder. "You know I'd never do anything to hurt you or Tom. I'm mostly thinking of the kids."

She swallowed down a lump and peered back along the road north where a line of vehicles idled between the trees. Barbara's eyes suddenly narrowed, jaw tightening as she watched several armor-plated vehicles rumble between the frost-covered branches. She nudged Darren hard with her elbow. "Let's get inside. Like, right now."

"Oh, hell." Darren exclaimed as he saw the sources of the massive diesel engines rolling in their direction.

Barbara threw open the door, and the two ducked inside. Slamming it shut behind her, the pair crossed to the dining room windows and peered through the gaps between the frames and the protective plywood. A line of Growlers, Humvees and armored personnel carriers rumbled by, vibrating the air and ground alike. Behind the group of smaller vehicles came a tractor trailer hauling a flatbed trailer with a tank sitting atop it, its gun turret tied down with thick ropes and chains. Another pair of trucks rumbled by after it, satellite dishes and deconstructed radio towers loaded on their beds.

"Main highway must be blocked again for them to risk taking such heavy equipment down a narrow road like ours," Darren murmured.

"The ground is shaking beneath my feet." Barbara's voice dripped with awe and worry. "Do you think they saw us?"

"Not sure." Darren glanced toward the living room. "The fire is out, so no smoke."

Barbara recalled the family she'd run off the other day, his words ringing in her ears. "The guy with the family I made leave off said there'd be troops by soon to force us to evacuate."

"They could be a simple transport convoy, based on all the gear their hauling."

"I hope so."

The end of the convoy came into view and passed in front of the house, ending with a line of seven Humvees with mounted guns and loudspeakers. The helmeted soldiers inside stared ahead, hardly sparing the McKnight property a single glance.

Barbara drew a deep breath and sighed with relief. "It looks like they--"

Her stomach sank and twisted as a lone Humvee fell behind the others, rolling to a stop and slowly backing up until it came to a stop next to her pickup.

"Damn, my truck," she hissed. "That's a dead giveaway."

"Maybe not," Darren tried to console her. But when the Humvee's passenger door opened and a soldier got out, he cursed softly. "Shit. Or maybe *definitely*."

They watched another soldier follow the first, both with rifles slung over their shoulders as they strolled up to her pickup, talking amongst themselves. One of them gestured at the vehicle, then up at the house, the soldiers conferring for a moment more before returning to the Humvee and climbing back inside.

Barbara's gut stayed clenched, eyes squinting as she waited. "Did we dodge a bullet?"

"I'm not sure yet."

She willed the men to leave, but her dread only increased when a massive armored vehicle trundled down the road in reverse and switched positions with the Humvee. Towering over the Humvee with a huge metal grate affixed to the front, the APC backed toward the opposite shoulder and turned toward the pickup truck, suddenly accelerating, ramming her truck, smashing it aside in a crunch of metal and shattered glass. The pickup spun violently to the side and came to rest in a ditch while the APC showed no signs that it had hit anything at all.

"Oh, crap!" Barbara drew back.

The APC reversed to make room, and the Humvee turned into the driveway, trundling up the gravel lane.

Barbara immediately turned and stalked down the hallway. "Kids! Marie! Get up here!" Feet pounded up, and soon everyone was gathered in the kitchen.

"What is it, Mom?" Linda asked, panting, eyes wide with worry.

Barbara knelt and took her daughter's hands, imploring both her and Marie. "Some soldiers are coming up the driveway. I need you to--"

A booming, bullhorn-powered voice penetrated the walls, causing everyone to flinch.

"Attention to anyone inside! My name is Sergeant Sawyer with the United States Army Special Recon Unit charged with the evacuation of this area. Please disarm yourselves and step outside. Anyone carrying a weapon may be treated as hostile. I repeat, if anyone is inside, please step outside right now!"

Barbara put her finger over her lips to keep the kids shushed and motioned for Marie to take them to the back. Then she let her shotgun slide off her shoulder and approached the door with Darren close beside her.

The soldiers shuffled up the steps in a scuffle of boots on the wooden slats. Barbara leaned forward, straining her ears to follow their movements as they came to stand on the other side of the door.

"That's a lot of locks," one solder scoffed.

"No kidding," Sawyer replied. "Shoot them off so we can search the place for stragglers." Barbara shot a wide-eyed look at Darren, and the pair backed up as she heard the clack of a shotgun loading from the other side, and a short pause followed.

Barbara squeezed her eyes shut and tilted her head. "Wait!" she called, wincing at having to give themselves up.

"Who is that?" Sawyer yelled as their boots shuffled off the porch, leaping into the yard in retreat. "Is someone in there? Exit the house with your hands up! Do it now!" Barbara kept quiet, trying to think of something to tell them that would make them go away. "I repeat, exit the house unarmed with your hands up!"

"My name is Barbara," she called back. "I'm the owner of the house. What do you want?" Darren gave her a bewildered look, and she shrugged back.

"Do you have any others with you, ma'am?" The soldier shouted, ignoring her question. "Are there any others in the house?"

"My family is inside..." She shook her head. "What do you want? We don't need any help if that's what you're here for. Please go away!"

"Come out, ma'am!"

"No—"

"Exit the home, ma'am. Do it now!" The soldier demanded, unforgiveness in his tone, unwilling to tolerate anything but compliance. "I won't repeat myself. If you don't exit, we will be forced to shoot the door off. It would be much easier if you just came out."

Barbara looked aside to Darren. He held his rifle at the ready, staring at her, waiting for an order. "It's your home," he spoke softly through clenched teeth, though his weapon shook in his hand. "We'll defend it to the death if we have to. Just give the word."

"They're soldiers." Barbara tilted her head, chin low as her eyes darted back and forth. "We can't stand up to that kind of armor and weaponry. Maybe I can get them to leave."

"Lady? This is your last warning!"

She pressed her lips together and gave a frustrated grunt. "Okay, okay! I'm coming out."

Darren reached for the locks but hesitated. Barbara nodded, and he started turning the deadbolts. She gave one look back at Marie and the kids standing between the kitchen and dining rooms, the older woman's arms wrapped around the children, her expression protective and grim.

"Okay, I'm coming out. Don't shoot!"

Darren opened the door, letting in a gust of cold wind. Barbara stepped outside and kept her eyes firmly on the sergeant, a man with dark eyes staring at her from his tightly tied hood.

"Ma'am, put the weapon down." His voice was hard but not violent or unhinged.

Barbara raised her chin, shaking inside but determined to stay strong despite the fear coursing through her blood. "You're on *my* property, telling me what to do? How about you lower *your* weapons and move to the end of the driveway. We can talk down there."

"Not gonna happen," Sawyer argued, his partner keeping his rifle at the ready. "Are you aware of what's going on? Martial law's been declared. We need you to exit your home and prepare to evacuate south."

"You're evacuating people by threatening them? That doesn't make sense."

"It doesn't have to make sense, lady. But those are our orders. Get your people to lay down their weapons and come out with your things packed. We'll allow you one suitcase per person. You'll have fifteen minutes to—"

"No. I didn't hear anything about mandatory evacuations." Barbara lied, shaking her head, pinning him with hot accusation. "And how am I supposed to trust you're from the military? You could be anyone, for all I know."

The pair shared a look before the soldier shot back, "Would just *anyone* be driving Humvees and transporting tanks?"

"You could have stolen them, and be masquerading as soldiers to try and steal from people like us."

The pair of soldiers glanced at each other in confusion. "Seriously, lady?"

Barbara changed tack, trying to stay on top of the evolving situation. "You might be real soldiers, but we're still not leaving our house."

The man must have heard the finality in Barbara's voice, because his expression hardened, and he gave a quick shake of his head. "Lady, you need to do what I'm asking. I have my orders."

"And you need to get off my property." Barbara raised her shotgun.

Sawyer let go of his weapon with one hand and pressed the button on the radio mic clipped to his chest, whispering something into it before gripping his rifle once more. With two guns on her, Barbara kept her Benelli on the leader, trying not to think about how one-way the fight would be if it got started.

"I didn't want to do it, but you made me." His expression lengthened, teeth grinding together as he gripped his rifle.

"Made you do what, exactly?"

In an explosion of violence and noise, the wood covering the sliding glass door crashed in, causing the children to scream as a weapon fired, then another answered in return. Gasping, Barbara retreated up the porch and into the house, keeping her shotgun trained on the two soldiers who were slowly stepping back, keeping their own weapons glued to her center of mass. Inside, Darren was pointing his rifle down the hall with one hand, his other gripping Smooch's collar, his face a mask of rage as the dog jerked against his hold, head snapping as she barked.

Once inside, out of sight of the pair of soldiers, he spun and lined up her weapon alongside his, trying to figure out what was going on. Marie lay in the kitchen, curled up and holding her knee, grimacing, struggling to reach the pistol she'd dropped. Barbara caught sight of the children being carried away through the sliding back door, Jack's feet kicking and both of them screaming as he was taken out of sight.

"Dammit!" she hissed.

"I'm sorry, Barbara." Darren's face was ashen, fear mixed with an uncontainable rage smattered across his features. "I couldn't shoot because I didn't want to hit Marie or the kids," Darren spat as he let Smooch drag him down the hall. "I'll follow them, see if I can get a clear shot."

"No! See to Marie. I'll get the kids back."

She turned and put her shoulder to the door frame, peeking outside, leading with her shotgun barrel. A round zipped past, slamming into the stairs behind her, splintering the wood, memories flashing unbidden of the invasion they had sustained. Barbara waited half a second, held her breath and pushed forward a step, aiming her shotgun out the door, squeezing the trigger and firing blindly at Sawyer. Her wrists burned with fire as the Benelli bucked in her awkward grasp, her muscles and bones screeching in protest as the lead soldier yowled in pain and hit the ground, clutching his leg.

"You bitch!" he screamed, firing two shots back at her from his sitting position, though they went wild, one soaring off into the sky and the other striking one of the bricks on the chimney. Pain laced his words as he tried to scramble to his feet. "I'm going to kill you!"

"No, come on!" The second soldier shouted. "You know our orders! We've got the kids. Let's go!" Barbara peered around the door frame to see one soldier helping Sawyer, half-dragging him to the Humvee. His camos were shredded on his thigh, the buckshot having done its work. Jack's cry drew her the rest of the way outside, glaring with hot rage, her face twisted into a snarl.

"Mom! Mom!" The boy's voice rose in a fear-fueled cry. "No! Let me go, you *jerk*! *Mom!!*"

Two soldiers were hauling her kids across the driveway toward the APC, Jack's feet kicking and dragging through the snow while Linda punched and screamed, but the soldiers held them tight. She ticked her gun in their direction, but they lifted the children off the ground, using them as shields as they reached the armored truck. Seething, she swung the rifle the other way, intent on taking out the two original men, but another soldier circled the Humvee, drawing down on her. Barbara jerked back as more rounds smacked the door frame, wood flying in a burst of sharp fragments where she'd just been standing.

The Humvee doors slammed shut, and the vehicle started up. Sawyer screamed out the window with a pained cry. "You'll get your kids back when you comply!"

Barbara waited a moment before taking another look. The soldiers had gotten in the Humvee and were tearing off down the driveway. Sucking air through her teeth, she charged onto the porch and leapt into the yard, running three steps, raising her shotgun to fire, aiming at the tires. She squeezed the trigger, sending a slug slamming into the Humvee's fender, then fired a spread of buckshot that merely scratched the rear window. A third shot hit the tire, but the run-flats shrugged off the shot, and the vehicle was already down the driveway, heading out behind the APC by the time she had lined up for a fourth.

"No!" Barbara cried as the Humvee hit the road and turned right. "Jack! Linda!" She sobbed as the vehicle trundled along the icy lane until it was out of sight. Glancing at the Everett's Jeep, she thought about grabbing the keys and following them, firing at them out the window like something out of a movie, her grief threatening to overwhelm all sense of caution and rationality.

"Shit!" Barbara turned, about to run for the keys when she saw Smooch standing on the porch, her head ticked to the side in a curious, worried way. She still held her paw gingerly on the ground, not ready for any hard running or fighting. Darren had been right to hold her back; she would have likely been shot and killed otherwise.

The fight evaporated from Barbara's body at the sight. Face twisted in agony, tears stinging her eyes, Barbara climbed the steps, patting her dog's head with a shaking hand. "Come on, girl."

Smooch stared down the road and whined before turning and following Barbara back inside. Darren had his wife sitting up in the hall with blood streaking the hardwood, tightening a tourniquet around her upper thigh after cutting away her jeans with a knife. Marie's face was flushed of color and twisted with pain. She sucked air through her teeth repeatedly, like she'd stubbed her toe and was waiting for the pain to quickly fade away.

"Holy…" Barbara knelt down next to Darren. "How bad is it?" she grimaced, caught between the anguish in her heart and her friend's suffering.

"She just got winged," Darren responded with a clipped tone as he pressed on the wound with paper towels he'd gotten from the kitchen. "The bullet went through the side, but it didn't hit an artery."

"I missed the asshole," the older woman scowled. "I should have hit him. Should have stopped them from taking the children."

"Well, they were professional soldiers, honey," Darren replied lovingly. "We're lucky to still be alive." He looked up. "Do you have a first aid kit?"

"Many. Be right back."

Barbara leaned her shotgun against the wall and flew downstairs, grabbing one of their first aid kits and bringing it up along with a bottled water. She placed the kit down next to Marie and opened it.

"I'm not a medic," Darren mumbled, "but I think I can clean this out well enough. Not sure about stitching her up though."

"I can sew her up," Barbara said. "I did Smooch the other day when she got her stab wounds. She'll want a couple of these, first, though." She raised a pair of pills in her hand. "Non-opioid, but strong."

"Yes, please," Marie agreed, holding out her hands for the pills and the bottle.

Barbara handed them over and then opened the stitch kit as Darren cleaned and prepped the site. After sanitizing her hands, Barbara sat down next to Marie, a flashlight in her mouth, trying her best to focus on the task at hand, and not what had happened to her children moments prior. *Put your oxygen mask on first, then help your neighbor. You can't help someone else if you're unconscious, can you?* The lesson from a flight years prior popped into her mind and she breathed the tension away, forcing herself to relax as she bent in to see the wound.

"Ugh, it's still bleeding too much." Barbara tried to thread a needle with hospital-grade surgical thread, but her hands were still shaking. With another deep breath she relaxed and tried again, finally threading the needle's eye, holding it up, fixing Darren with a firm look. "You'll need to help soak up that blood sew this up."

"Oh, dear." Marie tensed her arms and scowled in anticipation of the pain.

"Rub some of this topical anesthetic on it." Barbara nodded at the kit and Darren removed a pair of anesthetic swabs, ripped the packets open, and rubbed them on the skin around the wound, then he dabbed at it with gauze to clear the blood.

After thirty seconds, Barbara leaned over and gently pressed her finger on the area. "Do you feel that?"

Marie shook her head. "No."

"That's good, but you're still going to feel more than a prick once I start."

The older woman nodded vigorously. "Just do it. I'm ready."

Barbara leaned over the wound, fighting back the urge to scream. To take her mind off the kids being taken, she didn't waste any time and went right to the chore, piercing Marie's skin and pulling the thread through, ignoring the woman's whimpers.

"The kids?" Darren asked as she worked. "What happened out there?"

"They took them," Barbara replied with a stiff shake of her head, lip quivering, eyes watering so badly with tears that she had to wipe them before continuing. When Marie moved beneath the needle, she snapped at the older woman, though immediately regretted it. "Quit squirming! Sorry… I just…" Then, to Darren. "Dab, please. Keep the area clear."

He dove in with the gauze and soaked up the oozing blood as Barbara concentrated, continuing with shaking fingers, placing five more stitches, pulling the final one tight and snipping it with a pair of scissors.

"I've got to get them, D."

"I know." He spoke low and somberly as she packed gauze around the wound and applied a bandage.

"There you go." She gave her friend a pained grin. "Now for the other side."

They flipped Marie over and worked on the back of her leg and, when they were done, they carried her to the living room and rested her on blankets on the floor before elevating her foot on a stack of couch cushions. Emotionally shot, mind racing, Barbara shut the front and back doors and found a comforter for Marie to chase the chill off her skin. The house was freezing, and it would take an hour or two to warm back up. Marie nodded her thanks before closing her eyes, and Darren shooed Barbara off into the kitchen while he tended to her, the two holding a whispered conversation as he spread the blanket out over her body.

They took the kids. The bastards took my kids. With nothing more to do for her friend, Barbara paced in the kitchen with her bloody hands on her hips, silently repeating the words over and over. She retrieved her shotgun from where she'd leaned it against the wall, put it on the counter, and paced more until Darren shuffled in and put his hands on the table, leaning in with a tired sigh.

"She's warm and resting now. She's shaken up, but she'll be fine. You did good, in spite of it all. Thank you."

Barbara nodded, gnawing on her nail, trying to pay attention to his words but entirely focused on the only thing in the world that mattered to her.

"What are you thinking, Barb?" Darren probed gently. "Talk to me."

"I'm thinking I want to scream." Barbara pushed the words through pressed lips, her body shaking with anger as her barely controlled emotions began to surface.

"I know. It would be better to stay calm and think it through before you act."

She whirled on him with bloodshot eyes. "I have to get them back, Darren."

"I know."

"They're using them against me." She clenched her fist and rested it on the back of a chair, shifting back and forth from one leg to the other. "I didn't want to believe that guy the other day when he told me. Or maybe I just didn't think it would happen to me." She looked at Darren, eyes stained red, emotion surging in her chest, voice rising to near panic as she edged around him toward the door. "I need to borrow your Jeep keys. If they're still on the road, I can follow them."

Darren left his spot at the table and reached out to block her path, receiving a hard, hot glare in response. Putting his hands up in the air, he spoke swiftly before she could keep going. "You do that, and you'll be turned into pink mist by one of those mounted weapons they've got. That won't help the kids at all. So before you go off all half-cocked, why don't we plan a little recon mission?"

"They could be anywhere." Barbara protested in rising exasperation. "They could be taking my kids to North Carolina, or even Florida! Who knows where they're going?"

"No. They wouldn't do that right away," he assured her. "If they're doing this to make people evacuate, then they'll have localized holding areas for both children and their families. That means they must be nearby." He finally felt brave enough to rest his hands on her shoulders, feeling her stiffen beneath his palms. "I heard on the short wave that they had standby camps in Kingsport, Bluff City, and Johnson City. Also, there's one in Bristol. It's part of their supply chain. They have to ensure they can keep their operation tight, especially in this kind of weather. So, let's just take a moment to formulate a plan, okay?"

Barbara nodded reluctantly, shoulders relaxing slightly. Darren smiled at her and looked around the kitchen, talking at a rapid-fire, stream-of-consciousness pace. "Let's pack a few supplies, like the soldiers asked. The three of us will drive into town and let the military folks know it was all a big misunderstanding. We'll get the kids back and stay in their camp. See how it shakes out. Maybe it won't be so bad. Or maybe we can plan an escape. They can't hold us forever."

Chills ran up and down Barbara's spine and she stepped away from Darren, shaking her head. "What are you talking about, D? I'm not packing things up. I'm not surrendering." An image of Tom sitting in his seat at the head of the table flashed through her mind, him smiling at the kids as they carried on and competed for their father's attention, everyone overjoyed to have him and Samantha back. "Hell no. We're not leaving. And I'm not going to leave Tom with an empty house to come home to."

Darren sputtered. "I didn't mean… I just… well, I mean, we're not going to live in the camp, Barbara. Not really. But what else are you going to do to get them back?"

A croaking, reedy voice came from the living room floor, cutting through Darren's stuttering. "These are her kids we're talking about," Marie croaked. "Her husband. This is her home, and she's waiting for her Tom to come through that door. If you think she's just going to give up and go off to live in some military camp, you better think again. I'd feel the same way, you big numbskull."

Bolstered by Marie's interjection, Barbara turned back to Darren. "I appreciate the advice, but no, we're not going to live there. What we *are* going to do is go there and take my children back."

Darren half-turned and looked back and forth between the two women, sighing in half-mocking resignation. "All right, all right. You've made your point. In that case, though, we'll need a map of Bristol that shows all possible roads leading into the city. Because what you're talking about is an assault."

She nodded firmly. "I don't want to ask you this, because it's not your fight. But… will you help me?"

"That shouldn't even be a question, hon," Marie croaked. "I might not be able to walk so good, but we're not letting you do this on your own."

"You're not going anywhere." Darren stared at his wife, his normally round, shaking jowls firming as he took on a determined expression, then turned to Barbara. "Wild horses and all the forces of hell itself couldn't stop me from helping you, Barbara. Now, find me that map and let's see what we have to work with."

Chapter 7
Tom McKnight
South Boston, Virginia

"There's a rest stop at the next exit," Tom ducked down from the hatch and eased into a seat behind Sam. "Let's pull over there. We can stretch our legs, then I'll take a turn driving."

"Good, because I'm getting pretty tired." Sam released the wheel and flexed her right fist. "It's a lot harder than driving our pickup."

Tom wrinkled his eyebrows. "Wait, when did you drive the pickup?"

"Mom let me sometimes..." Sam glanced over with a guilty expression. "Oh, never mind."

"No, please, Samantha." Tom grinned with mock parental disapproval. "Go on."

"You did an awesome job, Sam." Keith cut him off with a wink. "Better than I could have done."

Tom settled back, nodding. "Yep. Great job, Sam."

"Thanks." Sam beamed, turning her focus back to the road. After their initial getaway, she had shown enough aptitude with the hulking machine that Tom opted to let her keep driving, taking advantage of the break to lie down on the seats and get a few minutes of shuteye and refuel with some food and water that had survived their encounter at the gas station. As angry as the truckers and workers had been, Tom figured that they would pursue the LAV, but miles down the road there was still just the usual traffic with no sign of anyone chasing them.

The LAV pulled off the exit ramp and Tom got up, poking his head through the hatch, watching as they approached the main building, head on a swivel as he surveyed the area. A pair of empty cars sat at the end of the lot, but the place seemed abandoned otherwise, the midday sun seeping between the clouds, the air holding a brisk chill that tousled his hair.

"Park at the near end of the lot near the vending machines."

"Okay." Sam pulled the LAV smoothly along the curb, the behemoth too big for a regular spot. She parked the vehicle and shut it off, then she stepped away from the seat, shoulders slumped, giving in to exhaustion.

"Are you okay?" Tom ducked forward and gripped her hand. "Oh, wow, honey. Your hands are really cold."

"Yeah… I don't feel so good. I'm really tired."

He guided her to the back, weaving between the seats and their backpacks where Keith and Jerry had already opened the doors. They stepped to the pavement, and Samantha turned and looked up at him with red-rimmed eyes as Tom put his hand to her forehead.

"You're warm. I wish you would have said something earlier." He shook his head. "It's probably nothing, but after we get done inside, I want you to get that rest we were talking about. We'll make a place for you to lay down."

"I'm okay, Dad, really. But yeah… that sounds nice. Thanks."

He turned to Keith and Jerry. "We're heading to the bathrooms. Are you coming?"

"I'm good," Jerry said. "I went back at the last stop. I'll just stretch my legs here."

"Me, too," Keith put his hands on his hips and bent backward, grunting and groaning as he looked up at the sky. "You two go ahead."

Tom nodded and gestured for Sam to follow him. Up ahead were three buildings; one main structure held the restroom and travel kiosks and the other two were simple shelters for coffee and snack vending machines. Constructed of brick and concrete, they were simple but clean, much like the landscaping around them, clearly designed to handle mass amounts of people with minimal upkeep.

They pushed through the front entrance, and Tom looked around, the quiet scuffling of their own shoes and Sam's shallow breathing the only sounds. He stepped over to the women's bathroom and put his ear to the door, knocking, waiting for a response. When none came, he pointed inside. "I'll go check it out first. Wait here."

"Okay."

Tom stepped in lightly, head swiveling to look across the sinks and soap dispensers then crouching and shuffling along the tiled floors to peer beneath the stalls. No shadows moved, no feet scuffled and the sinks were dry. The restroom appeared to have been unused for some time, but he walked down the length of stalls nonetheless and nudged the doors open to double-check. Each swung inward, revealing black toilet seats and paper dispensers. At the end, the supply closet was fully stocked with cleaning products, a mop, and a bucket. Satisfied, he exited the bathroom and held the door open, smiling at Sam.

"All clear," he said. "No crazy people inside."

"Thanks, Dad. I'll just be a minute." Sam started to go in, but Tom stopped her, wrapping an arm around her, pulling her in tight.

"Hey."

"Yeah?"

"You drove great today. I'm super proud of you."

"Thanks." Sam grinned. "It wasn't too hard."

"But you figured out the camera part." He gave her an impressed nod.

"I just hit all the buttons until something came up," she replied with a shrug. "It was just luck."

Tom laughed. "Well, you're *way* luckier than me." She gave a little laugh, followed by a slight cough. "Okay, I'll be right outside." Tom watched her go in and let the door swing shut behind her.

Putting his hands on his hips, Tom sighed and meandered over to a table filled with brochures. Curious, he began sorting through them until he found what he was looking for and, with a smile, he unfolded a local highway map, spreading it out on the table.

* * *

Jerry smiled as he turned his face up toward the sky, basking in the brief break in cloud cover that allowed patches of sunlight to warm the lot. As the one immediately atop him closed, he walked over to another one, closing his eyes as the rays struck his cheeks, chills of pleasure rolling down his back.

After a moment, he turned to Keith where the man lingered near the LAV doors. "You don't need to pee?"

"Nah. I'll hang out and wait for everyone here."

"So, where you from, originally?" Jerry turned his hands over as he spoke, the cold wind nearly perfectly countered by the sun's warmth.

"Oh, just up north." Keith glanced into the LAV. "Small town in New Hampshire you've probably never heard of."

"How'd you get all the way down here?"

Keith shrugged. "Same as everyone else. Herded in like cattle."

"Such a BS thing that's going on." Jerry shoved his hands in his pockets and stared across the grassy field to where the sun cut a swath through the wet grass leading to a woody grove off to the side of the rest stop buildings. "Well, I think I'm going to take a little walk. You know, stretch my legs."

Keith gave a single nod as he looked back into the LAV. "All right. Yeah. That sounds like a good idea. I'll be here."

Jerry stepped up on the sidewalk, strolling through the grass, following the beams of light, kicking at the wetness with his boots, sending sprays of dew everywhere. His head and arm were feeling much better, and his dizzy spells had all but ended. He didn't need anyone's help to walk anymore and, in spite of everything going on, with a full belly and a place to go to, things could be far worse.

His elation dampened as his thoughts shifted to the past, specifically to that of his mother. She'd always been there for him, encouraging him no matter how badly he screwed up, supporting him in purchasing his motorcycle and the hundreds of other endeavors he'd undertaken in his young life. He missed her dearly, though he couldn't complain about his new company, and she would have thought them a great deal better than most of the people he used to hang out with.

The air grew cooler, and Jerry looked up to see he stood in the shade of the grove. The trees stretched out in front of him, wide and wet and in some parts covered in a thin dusting of frost. He peered into the brush and spotted what appeared to be a trail cutting through the trees.

"I wonder where this leads?" Jerry murmured as he stepped onto the path, following the winding way deeper into the woods. Forty yards in, he came across a clearing, in the center of which stood a dark gray tent with a campfire burning in front of it. Hanging from a spit was a pot of steaming food, and Jerry caught the faint scent of beef stew.

"Hello?" he called, stepping forward carefully. "Anyone here? Hello?"

Moving close to the campfire, leaning in, eyes shifting, he nudged a nearby can with the tip of his boot, turning the label up. Sure enough, it was chunky beef stew with brown gravy. Unable to resist taking a peek, he reached out and raised the pot lid as steam billowed around the edges, wafting around his face in a glorious cloud of aroma, the heat of the fire warming his hands and face.

"That's our food, mister!"

Jerry dropped the lid with a clank and spun to face two men standing at the trail's entrance. Their clothes were disheveled, greasy hair sticking out from beneath old hats, one of them skinny with quiet, wide eyes, the other shorter than his companion, a scruff of gray beard lining his jaws. The shorter one's lips worked nonsensically beneath his dancing mustache, eyes darted up and down Jerry's frightened form, coming to rest on his boots.

"B... Boots," the shorter man said in a lisping, mumbling tone. "Coat. New skin for Juan. Give Juan a new skin."

Jerry squinted, confused, and looked down at his own boots. "What? Boots? Skin?"

The shorter man shuffled forward, pointing repeatedly at Jerry's feet like he was pressing an elevator button.

Understanding dawned on Jerry's face. "Oh, you want my boots?" He gave the man an incredulous look, scoffing. "Sorry, man. I can't give up my boots. It's cold out here."

"My friend needs the shoes." The taller, quieter, more articulate man edged closer, around to the side. "He needs them for his feet."

"Yeah, I know what they're for." Jerry put his hands out and took two steps backwards, feeling the fire's heat on the back of his legs. "But he can't have them. I have to stay warm, too." He eyed the trail, then the two men slowly approaching him, gauging his chances of getting away. "Look, I need to get back to my friends. They're looking for me. Just step out of the way, please."

"You can go, after you give the shoes." The taller one's eyes grew wide and threatening, his scabbed lips grimacing.

"And the coat! Need the skin. Need it!"

With surprising speed, and almost in perfect sync, the men rushed in as the shorter one shouted, snatching at Jerry's wrist. Jerry swatted his hands away and backed around the fire, glowering at the pair, stomach twisting in fear. "You'd better back off, dude, seriously! My friends are right around the corn--"

The taller man whipped a short knife from his jacket and charged, cutting Jerry off with a yelp as he leapt backwards, trying to ward off the small blade as it cut back and forth at his head. The blade was too fast to stop, though, and he couldn't block the man's maniacal movements, feeling two jarring stabs to his chest, then another pair in his left shoulder.

He screamed at the fire from the wounds and gave the man a furious shove in return, knocking the man away from him with his reflexive, panicked strength. The man's face twisted in psychopathic rage, and he lunged in low, the knife blade ripping across Jerry's belly. With a desperate cry, Jerry snatched the taller man's shoulders, gripping his jacket and throwing him behind him and he tumbled, falling face-first into the dirt.

With a gasp, warm blood seeping into his clothing, Jerry sprinted toward the trail, but the shorter man slammed into him, knocking him off balance to send him dancing backwards. Crying out, chest aflame with pain, Jerry kept on his feet as the man charged again, his mouth mumbling fast, eyes twitching and blinking as he reached with his grubby hands.

Jerry feinted left, causing the man to fly by and crash to his knees, then Jerry dashed around him, incredible pain and bloody-red warmth blossoming in his shoulder and chest. He kept his eyes on the trail, leaning forward, stumbling and gasping as waves of agony coursed through him. Staggering on, he struggled to breathe, his lungs going soggy and heavy. Shouts and growls chased him along the trail, sending panic shooting through his limbs, and he forced his legs to move despite wanting to just lay down and rest. After far too long he broke from the woods and ran toward the LAV, staggering more and growing more out of breath with each step.

"Guys!" he tried to shout, but his voice came out in a wet rasp, a second attempt at a shout even weaker than the first. Instead of yelling, he focused on running. He had to outdistance the men, beat them to the LAV before they caught him and… *they're trying to kill me. They're trying to kill me!*

The thought was delayed, buried beneath the surprise and pain and impossibility of the fast-moving situation, but true nonetheless. His boots pounded on the wet grass, slipping and sliding as he gasped and he clutched at his chest with his left hand against the cramping and weakening muscles. Still, even in his weakened state, Jerry's legs were strong enough to reach the lot, outdistancing his pursuers before he fell against the armored vehicle with a weak sigh, resting his palms and cheek against the cold metal, catching his breath, summoning his last ounce of strength.

A voice came through the LAV's open rear door. It was Keith, speaking to someone inside, though no voice answered back to him. Jerry slapped his palm twice on the steel armor, but it barely made a sound. Strength waning, he inched toward the back doors, sliding along the green metal, leaving a dark, bloody trail behind. Legs buckling, Jerry collapsed against the armored transport, his breath coming in shallow gasps as a spasm threatened to squeeze the life out of him. Keith continued to speak inside, his voice clear, though Jerry was still unable to summon the willpower to cry out and draw his attention.

Looking back at the woods, he saw the two men who'd attacked him walking quickly across the grass, not acting intimidated by the armored vehicle, still pointing at him and his damn boots. With a wet gasp, Jerry lifted a loose rock from the ground and slammed it hard against the truck's side, sending a deep thud through the armored frame. The conversation inside promptly stopped, Keith's words seeming to turn into a sharp whisper as Jerry's head spun with dizziness. The pain in his chest turned into a nagging ache as the air wheezed from chest, every breath he took a sharp stab of agony. He gripped his sliced shirt, holding the cuts together. "Oh, damn," he whispered, eyes watering with tears, the breaths coming harder, shorter, more desperate as his body tried to fill his lungs with oxygen and displace the blood rapidly filling them.

Keith jumped from the LAV's rear and swung around the doors, taking one look at Jerry and lunging forward, falling to his knees. "What happened, man?"

"Help me," Jerry pleaded, but his words were barely audible. "They…. they want…."

* * *

Tom and Sam were walking down from the main building when Tom heard the two men shout and he put his arm instinctively in front of his daughter, holding her back as he watched the two rough-looking men lumbering across the grass. Keith was kneeling next to Jerry, who appeared to have blood on his hands and chest, trying to help the younger man before he heard the two strangers shout, and he glanced at them before looking up at Tom and Sam.

"Who the hell…?" Tom's heart pounded in his chest.

"These guys hurt Jerry!" Keith shouted as he rose and met the pair at the edge of the grass.

Tom pointed Sam toward the LAV. "Go see to Jerry! Keith and I will handle these two."

The pair faced the two men, squaring off, Tom's fists gathered tight, mind racing with worry. There was a tall one and a short one, both dressed in threadbare clothes, hair sticking out from beneath their hats, both mumbling and goading each other on, focused on Jerry but stopped in their tracks by the appearance of Tom and Keith.

"Back off, you two!" Tom took the lead, putting himself squarely between the pair and Jerry – and his daughter – behind him. The taller of the two men pointed at Jerry with wide eyes, shouting in response.

"He tried to take our soup!"

"And he's gotta pay!" the short one's mumbling was almost too fast for Tom to understand. "Pay with his shoes. Juan needs his shoes. Needs the coat. New coat, new skin."

"What the hell…" Tom looked over at Keith, who stood a few feet away, helping to keep the men from advancing.

"You're not getting his shoes." Keith lowered his voice dangerously, both he and Tom following the men's furtive, skittering movements, solidifying a defensive perimeter around Jerry and Sam.

"I don't think they're going to stop, man." Keith whispered to Tom, who nodded in agreement.

"I don't think so, either."

The taller man suddenly flashed his knife, the blade's red wetness glinting in a ray of sunshine. "I'll slash you too! Gonna slash slash..." He whipped the blade in Keith's direction, his movements shockingly agile, hopping back and forth on the balls of his feet. Tom started to try and grab the taller man's knife hand when the stockier one charged him. Tom shifted his angle, batting away the man's punches, but unable to back up any farther, Tom grabbed him, wrapped his arm around shoulders, and whipped him to the ground, landing hard on the asphalt.

Tom had hoped the blow might knock the fight out of him, but shorter man only croaked and kept swinging his fists, struggling and shouting about boots and coats and skin. He elbowed Tom in the chest, then reached in and grabbed Tom's stomach, pinching and twisting his flesh in a vice-like grip. Teeth clamped shut, Tom shifted his weight to keep the man pinned as he struggled and growled.

"Lemme up! Need boots! Lemme the hell up!"

"Stay down!" Tom pressed the man's greasy head into the ground, using his knee to kick away the man's arms, then twisted him around and held him. "Just stay down!"

A gunshot snapped in the air, followed by an insane howl, and Tom looked up in horror, expecting Keith or perhaps Sam or Jerry to have been shot. Instead, the taller vagrant danced back in a puff of gun smoke, Keith standing nearby, a smoking pistol in his hand. The tall man tumbled to the grass, writhing, clutching his leg as he yowled.

"Dad! Jerry's hurt bad," Sam cried, and Tom shifted his weight atop the captured man and glanced over to see Sam with her hand on Jerry's chest. Her face was twisted with horror, her eyes pleading for someone to help.

Tom pressed his hands on the pinned man's shoulders and leapt up before he could take a blow. The vagrant kicked at him, but Tom had already jumped out of range and the man scrambled to his feet with a glowering sneer, acting like he might rush back in.

"Get out of here, or you'll get what your friend got!" Keith drew down on the man, shouting at him, and the shorter man stared at his prone companion where he moaned and writhed on the ground. He started to help his friend but had second thoughts, spinning and sprinting across the grass in a mad dash, still talking to himself about his favorite three subjects in the world.

Tom turned back to where Keith was carefully ripping off a part of his shirt. With a snap of his hands, he tied a tourniquet on the wounded man's leg with almost professional efficiency, then looked up at Tom. "Go help Jerry. I'll make sure this scumbag doesn't bleed out."

Hearing Sam's sob from behind him, Tom turned and sprang to Jerry's side, falling to his knees opposite his daughter. She'd positioned Jerry so he leaned back against the LAV with his legs splayed, eyelids fluttering. Tom took one look at the amount of blood soaking his clothes and shook his head.

"Grab some rags out of our packs. We have to stop the bleeding."

Sam nodded and ran off.

"Can't breathe," Jerry whispered, blood on his lips and running down his trembling chin.

"Punctured lung – or worse." Tom forced a smile, trying to sound half-convincing. "You'll be okay, Jerry. We just need to get pressure on these wounds." Tom wasn't a doctor, but his time in the field had served him well. Jerry stared into Tom's face, determination flashing in his eyes as he coughed and gripped Tom's shirt, pulling him close with unexpected strength.

"Tom," he whispered, his words barely audible.

"Shhh. Don't talk. Save your energy."

"No. Listen." He pulled Tom even closer, pressing his lips to his ear, mumbling so softly that Tom could barely understand him. As Jerry spoke, Tom watched Keith who was following the tall man as he crawled across the grass, unwilling to receive more help, cursing Keith in every way possible for shooting him. Jerry finally finished, his strength nearly gone, sagging backward and Tom forced a smile at him.

"Okay, man. Just hang in there." Tom parted Jerry's jacket and found the jagged holes cut in his T-shirt, tearing the material apart, gaping at the amount of blood. "You'll be fine, Jerry. We're here." Memories long buried surfaced unbidden, swirling in Toms gut, a tidal force of nausea pushing upward, forcing him to take a few seconds to center himself, practicing what he had been taught to recover.

"Sam!" He called hoarsely, "Where--"

"Right here!" She straddled Jerry's legs, taking some rags and pressing them to his chest wounds, her father joining in, desperately trying to stem the flow of blood. "He has a couple of really bad cuts in his chest, dad. The bleeding won't stop." Tears welled in her eyes as she looked to him kneeling beside her. "What do we do, dad?"

Jerry coughed a gob of blood in Sam's lap, his gaze shifting between them, his breaths shallower than before, barely taking in any air.

"I'll grab some gauze out of our pack and get those holes plugged." Tom guided Samantha's hands to the rags he was holding. "Just keep the pressure on the wounds."

He started to get up, but Jerry grabbed him by the wrist like a vice, knuckles white, leaning his head on Tom's arm. "No." The young man shivered and swallowed, coughing blood again. "Stay. Please." More coughs, less forceful than before, came, his chest barely moving. "So cold. Cold."

Tom eased back down, hand on the side of Jerry's face, watching his skin turn paler shades of white, his breathing coming in panicked, wet hitches. Tom felt his own panic returning in response, the desire to help overwhelming but the ability to affect any changes completely beyond him. He closed his eyes for a few seconds and breathed deep, centering himself again, trying to retain control of his racing thoughts, for Jerry's sake if no one else's. All he could do was wrap his arm around Jerry's shoulders and hold him tighter. He leaned in close as Jerry's fingers dug into his wrist, not fighting the pain, allowing the young man to draw whatever comfort and strength he could.

"I know, it's cold, son." Tears welled and fell, pinpricks of ice on Tom's skin, streaks of salt staining his cheeks. "I'm here with you. We're both here." Jerry gave an uncontrollable shiver, his grip on Tom's shirt weakening like snow melting in his palm.

"D-dad?"

Tom looked at Samantha, her cheeks stained with Jerry's blood, her expression desperate and shocked. Jerry released his grip on Tom's shirt, and a final breath slid from his lips, and he was gone.

In a stupor, Tom held Jerry tight, rubbing his shoulder, heart twisting behind his ribcage.

"Dad?" Sam's voice teetered on the edge of hysterics. "I think Jerry's dead."

Tom stared off into nothingness for a moment, then he reached up and touched his fingers to Jerry's neck, looking for a pulse. He and Samantha looked at each other for a long moment, and Tom slowly shook his head as Sam's tears fell like a waterfall, still holding the rags to Jerry's chest, her breath coming in ragged sobs as she cried for Jerry, begging him to wake up.

Keith jogged up, panting. "I ran those losers off. Can you believe that guy tried to…" His words trailed off as he saw Jerry's condition. "Whoa. Is he…?"

Tom looked up with red-rimmed eyes, his emotions a roiling pit of magma threatening to spew forth, but he held it back, still kneeling on the pavement, holding Jerry in his arms, rocking him back and forth as if putting a child to sleep.

"Yeah." Tom finally managed to speak between his own tears. "He's gone."

* * *

Several exits down the road, Tom, Sam, and Keith stood on a grassy knoll, looking out over rolling fields of frosty white, forest trees swaying in a crisp breeze. Evergreens were mixed with bare-limbed branches, much of the leaves having already fallen off due to the extreme cold, buried under the constant ebb and flow of snow.

A pile of rocks marked the highest point on the knoll. Most of the stones were regular and gray, but they'd taken a few decorative ones in various shapes and colors with them from the rest stop. Sam leaned against her father, sniffling into his shoulder and gripping his arm fiercely while Keith stood off to the side, looking at the LAV where they'd parked it on the side of the road, keeping to himself. Whether it was out of some sense of guilt for not being able to help Jerry, or out of respect for the bond formed between Tom, Samantha and Jerry, Tom didn't know, but neither did he care.

Staring at the pile of rocks covering their friend, Tom spoke haltingly, trying to keep his emotions in check. "We met you in the middle of a storm when things looked grim. We didn't get off to the greatest of starts, but Sam and I saw something good in you. And you must have seen the same in us—"

"You made us laugh," Sam interjected with a soft, choking sob.

Tom nodded. "You had a great sense of humor, and a great attitude, despite not having the best life. You lost your dad at a young age, and the storm claimed your mother, and I felt awful for being the one to tell you about her. I'm sorry for all the times you got hurt while we were traveling."

"Dad's also sorry he used you as a battering ram," Sam quickly added with a sniff.

"That's true," Tom laughed, his heart strained against his ribcage, tears coming once again. "But you were so good at it, seriously."

He waited, half-hoping to hear Jerry's sarcastic chuckle, but the young man's voice was no longer there to fill the silence, no longer there to interject with a joke or some positive, uplifting thing to say.

Tom sighed, pulling Samantha close. "We're honored you trusted us and traveled with us with an open heart. We're honored to have called you our friend. And… and we would have—"

Keith shifted and leaned closer, coughing slightly as he interjected. "Ahh, I hate to interrupt, but it's getting late in the day. I was thinking we should get moving here soon."

Tom and Samantha both looked at Keith, their expressions a mix of scorn and bewilderment.

Keith backed off, raising his hands apologetically. "I mean, I know you folks want to get going, right? You want to get home? Probably sooner than later, right?"

"Right." Tom's reply was colder than he intended, though no apology followed. "How about just another minute or two, so we can say goodbye to our dead friend?"

Keith grimaced and nodded. "Yeah, sure. My-my bad. Take your time."

Tom turned back to the brightly marked grave. "I was saying, we would have enjoyed having you in our home."

"You would have loved meeting Linda and Jack. Smooch, too." Sam touched her trembling bottom lip. "And I know my mother would have loved you."

Tom nodded. "It would have been nice having you around, son." A breath drew deep into his lungs, and his chin fell with regret. "Well, that's about it, buddy." Tom turned to go but then remembered something. "Oh, and we left you with your mother's ring. I know she would have wanted you to have it."

"I was going to take it with us," Sam said, quickly adding, "I just didn't want someone to steal it."

Tom glanced up at the sky. "I had to remind her that your boots are probably worth more than the ring at this point."

He and Samantha both stood in silence at the cairn, watching out over the cloudy skies, lost in their private thoughts until Keith's light cough cut through again. Tom rolled his eyes and let out a deep breath as he turned around, Sam still glued to his arm.

"All right, I get the point. We can go now."

"Cool," Keith said as they walked down to the LAV. "Hey, I'll drive if you want me to. I still haven't had a turn yet, and it's not fair for you to do it all."

"Sounds good." Tom flashed a smile. "We'd appreciate it. I could definitely use some rest, and I know Sam hasn't been feeling so hot, either."

"Perfect!" Keith climbed into the back of the armored vehicle and went straight to the driver's seat while Sam took the communication chair next to it. Bringing up the rear, Tom closed the rear doors and latched them.

"Why don't you take the back, Sam," he suggested, arranging several packs between the crew chairs and tossing a blanket on top. "Lay down here. Get some rest."

"Sure." Sam traded places with him and stretched out on the lumpy bundle he'd made.

"Is that okay?"

"It should be fine." She shifted and moved, fluffing up the pack behind her head before reclining back with a comfortable smile. Tom turned to take the communication seat, and as Keith settled in, he took his pistol from his holster and placed in the center console between them.

"You sure you can drive this thing?" Tom asked, sliding into the chair. "I thought you were worried about that back at the camp."

"I think I watched you guys enough." Keith grinned at Tom, then started the LAV and put his feet on the pedals. Tom nodded and eased back, watching the camera screens pop to life. "It's a lot easier than it looks. Just focus on the screen and start slow." Keith pulled away from the curb and got back on the road, driving them away from the scenic rise, leaving Jerry's final resting place to the wind and snow.

They cruised in silence while the miles passed behind them, Keith sticking to the right-hand lane while he got used to the LAV's controls, taking things relatively slowly. With the hatches all shut to block out the increasingly cold wind, he was forced to focus intently at the screen showing the forward camera, trying to keep the massive vehicle on the road and in between the lines with limited vision and field of view.

Tom stared idly at the radio panel, all the knobs and switches and gauges, all the hand-written notes left by the last crew who'd used the vehicle, none of which he understood. While he couldn't be a hundred percent sure, he thought some of the lights had changed since when they'd started. There were more of them on, and one of the digital tuners had a number on the screen where he could have sworn it was blank before.

"This is insane." Keith white-knuckled the wheel, keeping them moving at thirty miles-per-hour along the old country highway. "I don't know how you two did it and made it look so daggum easy."

"Is the screen too small for you?" Sam mumbled dryly from the back. "I can take over if you want."

"No, it's fine," he laughed. "I just need to get used to it. My kid plays video games all day. I'll bet he'd have no problems driving this thing."

"Right." Tom returned to staring at the radio panel, glancing at the gun sitting in the center console, an uncomfortable silence settling over the cabin.

"I'm, uh, really sorry about Jerry," Keith said, turning the wheel back and forth, craning his neck forward as the pavement flashed beneath them on the screen. "He seemed like a good guy."

"He was." Tom's jaw worked back and forth.

"How long did you travel with him before you ended up in the camp?"

"Just a few days. He was there when we…" Tom started to say 'when we came off the life raft in Kitty Hawk' but stopped himself, clamping down on the words. When he resumed speaking, it sounded forced. "We found him crashed on the side of the road near Virginia Beach." Keith glanced over, a troubled look on his face as Tom continued, his voice stiff. "Everything was looking better." Tom went on, injecting some life into his tone. "Until today."

"It's unfortunate." Keith gave a low whistle, eyes turned back to the screen. "And, hey. Good thing I was there, right? I mean, that guy with the knife could have hurt you or Sam."

"Yeah, good thing." Tom shifted his gaze away, stifling a sharp intake of air. "I just wish you could have helped Jerry, too."

"I know," Keith's voice sunk. "To be honest, I didn't even realize he'd walked off. I was resting inside the LAV when I heard all the commotion."

"He didn't call out for help?"

"No, he didn't," Keith shook his head. "He probably couldn't with those penetrating chest wounds. And, I mean, it's hard to treat those in the field, especially if they're deep. Poor guy."

"Where'd you get the gun, Keith?"

The question was a bolt of lighting on a clear spring day. Keith's whole body seized up for a split second at the sound of Tom's question, hands freezing on the wheel, then he relaxed, giving a confident smile.

"I actually found it in the LAV while you guys were up in the main building. Sheer luck, really."

"Where'd you find it, exactly?" Tom kept staring at the radio knobs as he spoke, his voice calm and level.

"Well, um..." Keith's troubled look deepened for a split second before it grew friendly again and he shrugged. "I found it in the rear locker. The one on the driver's side."

"Interesting." Tom nodded slowly, fiddling with a few of the controls in front of him. "Very interesting considering we searched those lockers, and every inch of the vehicle, after we left the gas station." He gave a soulless chuckle. "There were no weapons on board. I remember checking that specific locker myself. Nothing in it."

"Well, maybe you just missed it," Keith suggested. "Don't be too hard on yourself. Mistakes happen and—"

"Did you have the gun on you this whole time?" Tom's tone grew sharp and hard-edged and Keith sputtered and laughed, trying to play it off, adjusting his grip on the wheel and shifting uncomfortably in his seat.

"*No*. Of course I didn't have it. I would have told you—"

"See, here's what I think happened." Tom interrupted dryly. He shifted his whole body away from the radio controls and angled toward the center console, the weapon less than a foot away from him in the cramped quarters, staring down Keith. "I think you had the pistol the whole time. Even back in the camp."

Keith shook his head, chuckling doubtfully, turning the wheel shakily to the left to avoid an abandoned car left on the road. The screens in front of him showed a snow-covered rural Virginia landscape of passing trees and sweeping backroads, hills and valleys, farmhouses plopped into a picturesque landscapes like paintings on a doctor's office wall.

With Keith watching out of the corner of his eye, Tom gently plucked the pistol from the console, turning it over as he examined it, his voice growing harder. "That's right, isn't it? You had the gun the whole time."

"N-no way, man." Keith tried to shake it off, but his shoulders had grown stiff, his good-natured façade rapidly fading. "How could that be true? I-I was with you the entire time in camp. If I'd had a weapon before that, the soldiers would have searched me and taken it away."

"You weren't in camp when we got there," Tom replied coldly. "You could have been picked up just like you said, or you could have conveniently slipped in later, after she knew I wouldn't work with her."

"S-she? Who—"

Tom cut him off again. "You could be a criminal, wanted for larceny. Or, you could be working for *Banks*." Tom ejected the pistol's magazine and racked the slide, catching the ejected round and slipping it into the magazine, the metallic clacks uncomfortably loud in the confines of the small cabin.

"No, Keith." Tom slammed the magazine home. "I don't think you've been honest with us. And honesty is everything these days."

Keith glanced over and caught Tom's hard expression, a cold, dead stare accompanied by the pistol pointed at his own chest.

"Hey, man," Keith sputtered in disbelief, edging away from the weapon, trying to split his focus between Tom and the road. "What are you doing? You can't be serious!? You think I'm some kind of secret agent?"

"How long have you been working for the government, Keith? How long have you been working for *her*?"

Keith tried to summon the same charm he'd been exuding since they first met in camp, a light chuckle followed by a friendly smile. "That's a good one, man. You think I work for the government?"

"Yes. Yes, I do." The pistol remained leveled at Keith's chest, Tom's grip unwavering.

Keith's amusement faded, eyes turning toward the gun again, jerking the wheel to avoid something else in the road. "That's just stupid. If I worked for the government, why would we have had to steal this LAV? And why would I have helped you break out?"

"Those are good questions, Keith." Tom shook his head, adjusting his grip on the pistol. "And that's exactly what you're going to tell me."

"Dad?" Tom glanced back at Samantha sitting up in her seat, watching them with tired and worried eyes. The circles beneath them had grown darker, and she coughed several times, her face pale but her cheeks red, flushed and sweaty.

"What do you mean, it'll go poorly for me?"

"We've been out here a few weeks on our own," Tom lowered his voice, adjusting his body so Sam couldn't see the pistol or hear him over the LAV's diesel grind. "We've done what it takes to survive. Stolen. Fought. Burned people alive."

Keith swallowed hard. "Look, I don't work for the government, man. I *swear*. Even if I did, what could I possibly gain?"

Tom's cold smile returned. "If Banks told you anything about me, you'll know I've worked government projects before. They're never forthcoming with their true intentions. You have to hold a gun to their heads to get information, and even then it's usually half-truths."

"Tom, seriously, you sound like some kind of paranoid—"

"Why did you kill Jerry, Keith?" Sam gasped from the back of the truck, hearing her father's question while Keith laughed openly in response, sobering quickly as Tom watched him closely.

"I didn't kill him! You saw the guy with the knife, you saw the stab wounds on Jerry's chest! I don't even have a knife on me!"

"Letting someone die is the same thing, Keith. Inaction is as culpable as action."

"No! Not true! I-I'd never let anyone die, especially someone as cool as Jerry!"

"Where were you when Jerry was getting stabbed?"

"Like I said, I was in here, resting! Jerry said he wanted to walk around. I didn't hear him again until he knocked on the LAV a few minutes later. I was—"

"Distracted by someone?" Tom smiled coolly. "Someone at military central command, perhaps?"

Keith's jaw tensed. "You've got me all wrong! The military paid me off, told me to shadow you guys, but I didn't kill Jerry, and I didn't *get* him killed either. I was in the LAV resting, I swear!."

"Quit lying." Tom's voice ground with grit and anger. "Jerry told me the whole thing."

"What?" Keith's façade cracked again, a look of disbelief washing across him.

"When he was outside the LAV, dying, you were inside talking with your buddies. He said you gave them our location. It was Banks, wasn't it?"

Keith's eyes stuck to the screen, the LAV sliding through the rustic Virginia landscape.

"And she helped *you* help us escape," Tom growled. "You made sure the guards weren't there so we could get over the gate. And at the motor pool, you had the security keys." Tom snorted. "The guards didn't try very hard to stop us. They were shit shots, too." Keith's nostrils flared, teeth grinding, and Tom's hand remained steady as he gripped the gun. "Your mission is over. You're done. Pull over. You can walk from here."

Keith shifted uncomfortably. "You can't make me walk, man. It's freezing and getting colder."

"I *can* make you. We've been through hell to get this far. If you don't think I'll use this… If you don't think I won't do it in front of my daughter, you're seriously underestimating me."

"You can't kill an officer. They'll hunt you down."

"Oh, an officer, are we?" Tom raised an eyebrow in mock surprise, then his expression dropped like a rock. "Of course I'll kill you. Did Banks not tell you *anything* about me? If I have a choice between you and my daughter, Sam's going to win every time. Anyone who thinks differently is a fool."

Sam raised up on her elbows, a sick weariness in her eyes, trying to follow the muted conversation. "Dad? Is everything okay?"

"Everything is fine, sweetheart. Keith's going to pull the LAV over or I'll shoot him."

Keith winced, his expression souring. "You sure you'd do it in front of your daughter?"

Tom didn't hesitate. "In a heartbeat."

Keith wagged his head, his tone turning snide. "Regardless of what you think, I helped you get out of that camp. I'm the reason you're heading back to your family. You won't make it the rest of the way without me."

"Pull. It. Over."

"Come on, man," Keith argued, almost whining. "Just because I had a job to do doesn't mean I don't care about you or your family. I thought we made a great team, right?"

Tom pushed the gun roughly into Keith's side, eliciting a grunt of pain. "Shut your damned mouth and pull over. Now!"

Keith leaned away from the weapon, glancing down at the cold steel, then back at Tom, gauging him, measuring up the tired, ragged father and the cold, emotionless face. "You know what, man?" Keith sagged in his seat. "You can go to hell!" In a sudden move, Keith twisted fast and snatched the top of the weapon with his right hand, shoving it forward and out of the way.

Tom squeezed the trigger, firing into the wall, the sound a lightning crack in the closed space. Ears ringing, he jerked the gun back, trying to free it, but Keith hung on, yanking the weapon in the other direction with a grunt, his grip keeping the slide locked, not letting Tom fire a second time. Balling his left hand into a fist, Tom struck Keith in a glancing blow to the jaw, clacking his teeth together with impact then he punched again, ripping his pistol free and pointing it at the man's chest, the slide snapping back into place.

Keith swatted at the weapon, letting go of the wheel and twisting to avoid being shot. Elbows flew and hands grappled between the two men, and with a forceful grunt, Tom stood and shoved Keith out of the seat as he tried to get a shot in, forcing him sideways as the LAV swung back and forth on the road. Faces just inches apart, growling and grunting, they fell against the wheel, forcing it to spin hard to the right, the LAV's sensitive controls responding instantly, pitching them over as it turned in response, tires screeching, Sam crying out as she was tossed to the side in a rough pitch.

The heavy steel chassis groaned as they shot off the road and pounded down an incline, tires hammering against logs and deadfall in the way. Foliage stripped off spare diesel cans and accessories, sending them clattering away and in the cabin, compartment doors flew open, throwing equipment everywhere. Tom flew forward as the vehicle rolled hard, face-planting into a wall as Keith landed on top of him with a heavy yelp of pain, and Tom flipped him toward the hatch as his gun flew loose and joined the other items tumbling around the makeshift clothes dryer.

In the back, Samantha screamed as the LAV continued its roll, tossing them head over heels in a dizzying spin. Their backpacks bounced off the walls, smacking them as the contents spilled out and canteens, fire extinguishers, ropes, and tools rattled over them. Tom's elbow struck something hard, and he gave up on Keith, throwing his hands over his head to protect it from the flying gear.

Tom landed sideways on a soldier's helmet, the rounded metal punching into his upper ribcage, knocking the air from his lungs in an instant. With a gasp, his arms flew out in free fall, unable to control his body inside the twelve-ton monstrosity. After several gut-turning rolls, the LAV finally came to rest on its top corner and hung there for a moment before crashing onto its roof, the armor plates squealing as they settled into place. Tom gasped and coughed as the internal emergency lights blinked on, thin wisps of smoke filling the cabin revealing everything in a pale, red glow.

"Sam," he croaked, his vision swimming in darkness. "Sam?!" he asked again, his voice harder, panic growing when she didn't answer. He shoved off a pile of rope and blankets that had come from somewhere, digging his way up to where a gust of cold air kissed his cheeks. The back of his head ached, and something warm and wet trickled from his scalp. Head on a swivel, eyes searching the gloom, Tom reached out to oblivion as darkness won the tug of war with his mind, and the world spun away.

Chapter 8

Tom McKnight

Brodnax, Virginia

Consciousness returned in a sudden, uncomfortable wave of cold air and congestion. Tom's chest seized as he coughed, struggling to get up off of his side, failing, then rolling off of the helmet he'd landed on. On his hands and knees, Tom drew in long, ragged gasps of air, looking around at the interior of the LAV, struggling to make sense of what he was seeing. The internal lights gave off a dim glow that fell across the messy interior, and after a few seconds of staring, it, like his consciousness, returned. There was the lingering suspicion he'd had about Keith since they'd met him, then Jerry's death, then the confrontation, the argument, the fight for the pistol and... *the crash.*

Tom stiffened, pain coursing through his chest, and he gasped softly, getting to his knees. *Keith. The gun.* Next to him, the driver's seat was empty, but the rim around the open hatch had blood smeared across it. He looked to his left and shifted a backpack to the side, then he shoved off a tarp covering the steering wheel and driving console, but Keith wasn't under there either.

Tom turned and peered toward the back of the LAV, his eyes straining in the dimness, searching for his daughter. The jumble of their supplies at the rear of the truck repositioned itself, moving slightly at first, then gathering strength as something fought its way out, first a boot that kicked up, then an arm. He staggered up on his feet, his sense of direction thrown off in the sideways- flipped vehicle, trying to move toward the back.

"Sam? Are you okay, hon?"

Samantha's warm cough puffed up from the pile, and she shoved the remaining debris off her with a clatter. "I think I'm okay. Oh, my head..."

"Don't move!" Tom said. "Just hang on while I get to you."

He crawled through the mess, tossing things aside as he went; backpacks, boots and helmets that had fallen from the overhead storage were all equally moved with abandon. Flashlights, jackets and tarps were shifted next, then he moved a box of MREs and finally found her bright green eyes staring up at him.

"There you are," he grinned, leaning down, Samantha reaching out and taking his hand, lifting herself from the mess before she squeezed him tight.

"Thanks, Dad."

"That's what dads are for." He rubbed his aching head before looking around. "We need to get out of here."

"Where's Keith?"

"No clue. Keep your eyes and ears open, though."

Tom crawled over the debris to the rear doors and carefully unlatched them, shoving them open. The bottom one slipped from his grip and fell against something outside, not making much of a clatter while the upper one simply fell back against his arm with a dull thwack. Grunting in annoyance, Tom ducked through the open sideways door, stepping carefully out and hopping down into a big, snow-covered grove. A creek's trickle reached his ears, and the surrounding area was moist with dark brown dirt and mud that had been revealed thanks to their rolling tumble.

The LAV had come to rest on a rotted log, crushing its pulpy insides into dust, giving off a thick, woodsy smell. There was a slight tick in the engine compartment of the vehicle as it cooled, but aside from that and the nearby water source, the area was nearly silent, a sanctuary of peace and beauty disrupted by the thirteen ton vehicle. Tom walked around the LAV, leaving Samantha standing at the back, taking in the damage wrought by their crash. Two of the tires were gone while another was bent into the frame, leaving the axle snapped. The armor looked like it had barely been dented, but the catastrophic damage done to the drivetrain was enough to ensure that it would never drive again.

Backwards, up the hill they had descended, the damage was even more impressive. Entire trees had been ripped out of the ground or simply crushed by the LAV, vines and branches hanging from where they had been snapped or broken, flurries of leaves and twigs mixed in with mud, dirt and snow.

"Wow." Sam slowly eased around to where Tom stood, stopping next to him. "I can't believe we survived *that.*"

"It might have been worse if the trees hadn't slowed us down."

"No kidding." She looked around, hands on hips. "What happened to Keith?"

"I think he got tossed in the wreck. Or maybe he crawled out after. Haven't seen him yet regardless."

Sam nodded and put her hand to her temple. "I can't tell if my head hurts from the wreck, or if I'm sick."

"Probably both." Tom turned and felt her forehead, a sinking feeling swelling in his gut. "Oh, you're really hot, kiddo. Here." He guided her to a nearby fallen log. "Sit down for a minute."

Sam, head in her hand as Tom climbed back inside the LAV. "Hang on, let me get you something."

Inside the cluttered interior, he gathered up what he could of their packs and supplies, dragging them outside and placing them upright next to his daughter. He quickly dug out the emergency kit from his backpack, found a package of aspirin, ripped it open, and tapped two into his palm.

"Take these," he said, handing them to her with a bottled water. "And stay here. I'm going to look for Keith. Last thing we need is him sneaking up on us with you not feeling good."

"Sounds good." Samantha swallowed the tablets and guzzled the water, Tom watching her cautiously as he started to back away. She waved him off, wiping a dribble of water from her bottom lip. "I'll be fine, seriously. Go find that ass…jerk."

Tom snorted, a genuine smile spreading across his face, then he turned and started at the bottom of the hill where they had crashed, working his way toward the top, stepping through the slick, frosty vegetation, picking his way carefully upslope while testing his body for further injury. His wrist was a little sore, and his head ached from being knocked around, but everything else seemed to be intact.

About halfway up the hill, standing unbalanced on the incline, he spotted a form lying fifteen yards in the bushes. He carefully picked his way over, taking big steps over logs and stones, finally drawing close enough to the body to see that it was Keith's, lying twisted in the bushes, his light brown hair caked with blood.

Adrenaline fading, Tom shivered in the cold as he quickly bent and searched the body, finding a couple of extra magazines for the pistol and, in his right front pocket, a white key card that looked like the one Keith had originally used to get inside the motor pool and LAV. It was a simple slab of plastic with no name or picture, though it had a faint serial number embossed on one side.

Pocketing the card, Tom next found Keith's wallet and his federal ID inside his jacket. A chill running through from his head to his feet, Tom stepped back from Keith's body, shook his head slightly and turned, leaving it where it lay as he started back down the hill. By the time he reached Sam again, she had already consolidated their three packs into two, transferring the water and light snacks from Jerry's to theirs. She handed her father a bottled water as he came up, and he unscrewed the top and took a swig.

"Thanks. How you doing?"

"Meh. Not the worst. Not the best."

Tom reached out and lifted Sam's chin. "You've got a cut on your forehead."

"And some bruises, too," Sam said with a wince, her green eyes looking tired and numb. "I'll be fine."

Tom nodded and pocketed the water bottle, climbing back into the LAV to search for the pistol.

"Did you find him?" Sam called, peering after her father as he pushed his way up front, rifling through the mess.

"Yeah."

"Is he okay?"

"No."

After several minutes of searching, Tom found the weapon lodged near the floorboards near his head, and he carefully freed it and stuffed it in his waistband before climbing out of the LAV and hopping down next to Sam.

Sam bit her lip and glanced up the hill. "He's dead?"

"It seems that way."

"If… if we hadn't wrecked, would you have really killed him? You know, shot him?"

Tom fixed her with a grim look. "You know the answer to that, Sam."

"Yeah." Sam opened her mouth to continue but stopped.

"What?" Tom prompted her. "What's up, kiddo?"

"This just…" Samantha shifted nervously on her feet, rubbing a shoulder, looking away from her father. "I remember stuff kinda like this. Stories you and Mom would talk about when you thought we couldn't hear. Whispers."

That old gut-turning nausea returned, and Tom forced it down yet again. "I don't know what you heard, but it's not like that here, hon. Not nearly that bad. But I'll do whatever it takes to protect us. You know that."

Sam nodded, wordlessly accepting his reply, then turned back to the packs, changing the subject. "I figured, since we're getting close to home, we can ditch the heavier stuff. I dumped some canned goods and replaced them with MREs from the LAV. I also threw in some thermal blankets and a pup tent."

"Good thinking." Tom rifled through the backpacks, pleased with what he found. "Are you ready to go? Do you feel up to some climbing?"

"Yeah, I'm just ready to get out of here."

"Okay. Let's get to the top of the hill."

They shouldered their packs and climbed through the path of destruction left by the LAV, up through the slick, frosty vegetation, their breath coming in thick puffs of steam. The going was rough with the loaded packs, and Sam slipped several times, but Tom held her steady, keeping her from tumbling backwards. Two weeks prior, Samantha would have danced up the hill like a fairy, but she'd grown as weak as a newborn foal. Twice they were forced to rest so Sam could catch her breath and by the time they reached the top, she was panting heavily, her eyes half-lidded, her legs wobbly as she stumbled along.

"Back when we were on the road, I saw a sign for an upcoming town," Tom said. "It's not far. We can walk to it and find a place to rest. Maybe even scrounge up some medicine for you. We don't have much in these first aid kits to help with a fever, unfortunately."

"Sounds good, Dad."

"Okay, put down your backpack. I'll take it."

Sam let her pack slide from her shoulder, and Tom hoisted both with a grunt. The old Sam would have protested making her father carry everything, insisting that she carry her fair share, but the fight had gone out of her and she submitted willingly to all the help Tom could provide.

"Here, take my arm and hang on." Sam locked her arm around his, and together they shuffled along the highway, their feet kicking up a dusting of snowfall, wisps of white dust pushed around them by the whipping winds.

"I figure we can find a warm place to spend the night, then start fresh and rested in the morning." Tom kept his tone hopeful despite the strain on his back, the burden of their travels once more resting squarely on his shoulders. "If we're lucky, we'll get a car and drive the rest of the way."

"Sounds good, Dad," Sam sniffled again, her voice weak and distant. "I'd love a nice warm bed. Maybe some hot chocolate."

"I can't promise anything, honey. But I'll do my best. I swear, I'll do my very best."

* * *

The sun was on its way down, late afternoon turning into early evening as they approached Broadnax at a snail's pace. The air's remaining warmth had long since evaporated into a crispness that nipped at Tom's cheeks, piercing through their coats and pants, reminding them with every step that things truly had changed. Sam had caught her breath and could walk on her own, but Tom stayed close, keeping an arm around her in case her legs got wobbly. They slogged along, Tom gently urging her to move faster, hating himself for having to push her, but night was coming fast, and getting caught outside in the darkness and cold would be a death sentence, the pup tent a last resort.

A half dozen vehicles passed in the flitting snow, but no one bothered them, and Tom didn't even try to flag them down, instead glowering at each one as it passed, hand firmly on the pistol until they were out of sight. The chances of anyone friendly picking them up was remote, and taking chances on someone's good will when they were at a severe disadvantage was not on his to-do list.

The countryside and farmsteads transformed into small stretches of homes lined up side-by-side along the road, indicating they'd reached the town's outskirts. They were quaint domiciles, one-or-two-family structures with fences and sad front gardens, lightless and lonely in the cold early evening.

"I wonder if people are hunkered down inside," Tom asked out loud. "Though I don't see any smoke coming from their pipes and chimneys. Maybe they evacuated already?"

Sam whispered something he could barely hear.

"What, honey?"

"No dogs," she repeated, tiredly. "Usually, a neighborhood like this would have tons of dogs barking their heads off."

"You're right." Tom scratched his head. "The owners must have taken them when they left."

"The government probably kicked them out, like with Betty and Timothy."

"It certainly looks that way. I just can't believe they moved so many people so quickly. It's only been a few weeks since they detected the anomaly. This place is like a ghost town."

"Yeah, but the weather is getting worse, fast." Sam pulled her jacket tighter, tucking her chin and nose down into the jacket so she could breathe her own warm exhalations.

"We'll look for a scarf for you," Tom assured her. "I should have traded for one back at the camp."

"It's okay. You couldn't have known it would freeze so fast." After a couple more steps, her eyebrows pinched together, a question on her lips.

"Remember when we were back on the Marin, and we were talking about how much water it would take to interfere with the North Atlantic Drift?"

"Yep," Tom nodded. "Billions of gallons over several months."

"Then you revised that to one month."

"That's right."

"Could it be that even more water is coming out than we thought? And that's why it's getting cold faster?"

"I've been running numbers in my head, and you might be right. It could be that the fissure has opened even wider than before."

"And that'd explain why things are getting colder, right?"

"Yes. I mean, it's a pretty direct correlation. With warm waters stuck in the south since the current's been disrupted, there's nothing coming up to warm the air. The stagnation of air currents have let cold, high-pressure systems take over."

"That's unreal. Did you even imagine something like this could really happen?"

"Not in my wildest imagination." They plodded on in silence for a while, Tom's theory given an exclamation point by a stiff wind that hit their backs.

"Maybe some food will warm us up," Tom suggested.

Sam shrugged. "I'm not super hungry, but I probably need to eat."

"Okay, I'll stop for a second. Dig something out."

As he stood there, Sam rummaged around and retrieved a beef jerky snack and a pack of barbecue chips for Tom and some sour cream and onion chips for her. For dessert, they had two packages of apple slices that looked only slightly brown inside their packaging. They munched as they walked, washing everything down with bottled water as they studied their dismal surroundings.

Many of the homes were dilapidated, siding falling off and front doors standing open, sitting off the road with their front doors left wide open, screen doors flapping in the cold breeze. Vehicles were missing from driveways, and articles of clothing and other belongings lay scattered in the yards, poking up among the small drifts of snow. Back in a rust-stained trailer park, several cars had been left abandoned along with a lawncare trailer laden with mowers and other equipment.

By the time they reached the town's main intersection, the sun had dipped below the horizon, blanketing them in near complete darkness but for a shallow pall of moonlight glowing through the clouds' cracks. A gas station sat on their right with a sign that read, "Mike's" and a big rig repair shop sat opposite on the left with junked-out eighteen-wheelers and large tractors in the side lots. All around, bright white signs had been plastered with the words "EVAC NOTICE" printed on them in red capital letters. Tom stepped up to one, reading the lettering beneath the bold print.

"Notice of mandatory evacuations. The Department of Homeland Security is issuing orders for an immediate and mandatory evacuation of US citizens to Florida, Alabama, Mississippi, and Louisiana. Please take only what you can carry. Prioritize food, water, and warm clothing. Proceed to the nearest FEMA check-ins at Jacksonville, Tallahassee, Pensacola, Mobile, and Lafayette. Be kind to your fellow neighbor. Remember, we're in this together!"

Following the message were various numbers to call for assistance. Tom snickered. "Those phone lines are going to be tied up for a while."

"Should we evacuate, too?" Sam asked as she looked around. "Once we get back home, I mean."

"I don't think so." Tom shook his head. "I can't imagine joining millions of people fleeing south. Sounds like a nightmare to me."

"What about supplies?" Sam pointed to a corner sign that indicated a fast-food restaurant and a grocery up ahead.

"We have enough food for a few days. I was thinking we should find a warm, dry place to rest, but I don't see a single hotel in sight."

"What about one of the houses?" Sam gestured to a set of homes on the other side of the street past the gas station and Tom saw one with the front door wide open and a few personal possessions lying on the porch. He nodded toward it.

"I'd say no under any other circumstances, but this whole town's abandoned, and I'd say that place is as good as any to settle in for the night. I'll see if I can get the furnace going and we can crank the heat. If they didn't turn the power off, we can charge the phone and try to give your mom a call. They might even have some snacks inside..."

Tom's words trailed off when Sam stopped listening to him, her head cocked to the side. "Do you hear that?"

He turned in a circle, straining his ears. At first there was nothing, then the buzz of an engine was just barely audible, though not one from a standard car or truck.

"It sounds like a diesel engine," he said. "Maybe a military truck."

"Like the LAV?"

Tom nodded. Doing another turn, he faced the direction he thought the sound was coming from. "This way."

Next to the rig repair shop was a normal country street, angled slightly downward with homes placed spacious distances apart. He crossed the street and fast-walked through the service station lot with Sam keeping up. Together, they slid between two big trucks and stepped into an adjoining backyard, stopping near a tool shed. A little father down the road sat a recessed house, its driveway filled with an idling military Humvee with a massive, unmanned gun on top. Three soldiers stood around the vehicle, shouting at the house and a man shouted back at them, but Tom couldn't see him from their current position.

"This way." Tom grabbed Samantha's arm, pulling her through the back yard to the house whose property they were standing on. "If we circle to the front, we'll have a better view."

"Are you sure it's safe to get closer?" Sam intoned, stifling a cough.

"Nothing is entirely safe anymore, but I want to find out what's going on."

They circled the house, crept through the front yard, and hid behind a bush on the corner. Tom peeked over the top and saw the Humvee parked thirty yards from them, and beyond it was a clear view of the recessed home's front porch where the man was yelling and waving a pistol.

An older man, likely in his late sixties, he was standing behind a waist-high, wooden barricade, his light gray hair brushed back from his temples, wearing layers of outdoor clothing. In his right hand he held a long-barreled revolver, a .357 or something even more potent, keeping it aimed in the general direction of the three uniformed men in front of his home.

"Get out of here!" he glowered at the soldiers. "I don't want no one from the government in my yard or my driveway." With a sneer, he fired his pistol in the air, the crack echoing through the valley. Two soldiers retreated to the Humvee while the third stayed in place, holding up his hands, trying to negotiate.

"Come on, old man. We've got orders to get you out of here. You're the last person in town and it's for your own good."

"You can't force me out of my home!" The old man lowered his pistol so it pointed just over the soldiers' heads, in Tom and Sam's general direction, and Tom sank lower behind cover, pulling Sam down with him.

The soldier softened his tone. "It's going to be a long winter, sir. Don't you want to be someplace warm with people to talk to?"

"I've got plenty of warmth right here. Dual furnace. Plenty of firewood and food. Believe me, you'll be dead from cold long before I will. Besides, I definitely don't want to be around people. Can't stand them."

He fired the weapon over their heads again, driving the last soldier back until the three huddled behind one of the Humvee's open doors where they conferred about their next course of action, their position offering Tom a chance to catch most of their conversation.

"What are we going to do?" one soldier asked.

"We might have to rush him," the sergeant replied.

The third soldier scoffed. "You want to rush *him*?"

Tom watched the old man staring out from his porch, his twisted brow and snarling lips offering up a challenge, daring them to try their luck.

"I hate to remind you," the second soldier said, "but they told us to bring everyone in alive. No more of the rough bullshit after that incident yesterday. If we try to take him by force, someone's going to get hurt. Just throw him on the list and let him freeze to death."

"You're probably right," the lead soldier sighed, then scowled at the man on the porch, lifting his head and shouting past the door. "Okay, old man. Have it your way. But you are now officially on a blacklist for aid. Don't come begging when things get worse."

"You bet I won't!" He yelled back. "Your help isn't the kind I want!"

Heads shaking, the soldiers climbed back in the Humvee and slammed the doors, the man on the porch remaining safely behind cover, watching them intently while covering them with his revolver. Tom drew Sam closer to the bushes, watching as the Humvee roared to life, backed out of the driveway, and growled past them toward the main road, the soldiers still gesturing to one another and the man's house in frustration.

Once the Humvee had turned the corner, Tom drew her from the bushes. "Okay. Let's get away from this guy. He seems like the dangerous type."

They snuck back the way they'd come, crossing back in front of the house and past the porch covered with child's toys scattered in a dusting of snow. They stood near the back corner of the house, looking toward the shed, waiting for the Humvee's engine to fade into the distance before they left cover.

Crouched down, Sam coughed lightly into her fist. "I guess we don't have to worry about any soldiers for a little while."

"Looks that way," Tom said. "But I still don't want to stay here very long." After a moment, he plucked her jacket sleeve and pulled her north toward the next yard. "Okay, come on, honey. We'll go up to the next street and find a place to hunker down."

They left cover, jogging lightly through frosted grass past the next couple houses before Tom slowed them to a walk. Sam stumbled against him, but Tom caught her by the arm, throwing her a worried look.

"Hey, are you okay?"

"Yeah. Sorry, Dad. I'm just a little...dizzy."

Cursing himself for the sidetracking – in spite of the information it had provided them with – he held her tight. "I'm sorry, Sam. Let's find you a place to rest."

"Hold it right there."

Tom froze beneath the weight of a gravelly, familiar voice, his boots locked in place as he gripped Sam's arm.

"Don't try anything funny." The old man's tone was sharp. "Else it'll be the last thing you two do. Just turn around nice and slow."

"Don't shoot," Tom pleaded, still looking but not seeing anyone. "Please. I've got my daughter with me."

"I've got two eyes. I can see who's in front of me. Turn around nice and slow and nobody has to get hurt."

Tom turned slowly, pushing Sam behind him while half holding her as she coughed hard, nearly doubling over. Before them stood the old, scruffy man from the porch, his piercing eyes wild but keen, taking in every detail at a glance as he examined the pair, his revolver aimed squarely at Tom's chest.

Chapter 9
Lieutenant Colonel Rachel Banks
Norfolk, Virginia

"We'll bring in the rovers here." Sue Anne Wilkes points to spots on the three-dimensional model using an extendable pointer. The specific markers are dots of red on the North Atlantic shelf map, some sitting right on the edge of the anomaly while others are farther back. "We've used advanced mapping techniques to identify weak spots in the crust," Sue Anne continues, "and we plan on taking advantage of those."

"To create a landslide effect," Banks adds, making a sliding motion with her hand. Across from her, the President watches the briefing through a video screen, the crowd around the table smaller than before, composed of Banks's scientists, Colonel Booth, and General Heller. The audience on the other end of the video feed is comprised of President John Zimmerman, General Mark Davidson, Navy Admiral Ben Spencer, and Secretary of State Rita Cortez. Others linger behind the President, though their faces remain hidden in the shadows.

"Do you really think you can get the rovers that close?" the President asks.

Sue Anne nods. "Based on readings from USS South Carolina before it went down, we can estimate the cross-currents and enter at the soft spots, using natural formations as a buffer."

"And you're certain you can update the data quickly and make adjustments for a safe insertion?"

"We won't know until we get there," Sue Anne says. "But the Proctor software should be able to crunch the data quickly enough for us to make adjustments on the fly."

"Should be?"

Sue Anne looks down. "I've tweaked the program to the best of my ability, sir."

The president puts his hand to his chin in thought. "Do you see any other high-level drawbacks to the plan?"

Sue Anne doesn't even look to Banks. "Right now, we have more rovers than we do qualified people to drive them. Given the depth we're working with, and the cross-currents involved, it's a tricky environment."

"The few test operations we've carried out over the past few days have utterly failed," Banks further explains.

"Why is that?"

"Lack of piloting experience, sir."

The president blinks at Banks. "Would this be rectified by having your asset on board?"

"Much of it, yes," Banks acknowledges. "He could validate the Proctor software and probably help train some rover drivers. Hell, he could pilot two at once himself."

"Then why isn't he sitting here in this room with us?"

"While the evacuation is going well enough, there have been some hitches."

"That's to be expected." The president nods. "But we're just talking about one man here."

"He's smart and resourceful." Banks nearly growls as she speaks. "He's been hard to convince. Stubborn."

"What's his problem?"

"He's determined to get home to his family," Banks says. "Apparently, that's where he's headed."

"That should be easy enough to find."

"Not so easy with all the networks down," Banks reminds him. "But we're working on getting that home address now and beating him there. He doesn't seem to want to stop until he's back with them."

The president's hand turns into a fist that rests against his chin. "Well, that gives me some confidence he's actually worth a damn. I respect his need to get home, but this isn't about one family. This is about saving the entire Northern Hemisphere from a thousand-year-long ice age. Surely, he can see the sense in that."

Banks glances at Sue Anne. "He's not entirely trusting of me or the military. He and I have a… history. Plus the incident on the Marin scared him off."

"Well, make him see the light." The president's expression is heavy through the video feed. "You're to use any means necessary to bring him in. Do you understand that?"

"Of course, sir. I just need a little more time."

"We're launching the operation in just over a week. I'll give you about half that time to bring him in. Don't make me regret keeping you on my staff, Banks."

"No, sir. I won't."

The president pivots to another subject, leaving Banks to remain straight-backed at her position on the table. Heller and Booth turn and face the video screen hanging above the model of the anomaly while Banks and Sue Anne back away and engage in their own separate conversation.

"You did the best you could," Sue Anne whispers.

"Mm." Banks retains her trademark flat expression and aloofness in the face of Sue Anne's encouragement, ignoring the red-haired woman's attempt to be friendly. Admonishment from the President is not taken lightly, and though she appears calm on the surface, a fire burns inside, anger and resentment over Tom McKnight threatening to boil over.

"I'll give an update on the Mexican annexation," General Davidson says from the president's side of the video conference, the slightest hint of uncomfortableness in his voice. "It's going to plan, and things are proceeding smoother than we expected. We had anticipated President Esposito putting a more organized force on the border, strike divisions of tanks and armored vehicles. Intelligence is showing that they're placed too sporadically, though. The lines are thin, and we should be able to punch through with no problems."

"A few days of aerial strikes should send them running," Heller tacks on. Then his brow wrinkles in confusion. "That's all well and good, but why aren't they more organized?"

"We think the collapsing markets and general breakdown in our country has caused a panic in theirs," Davidson answers. "Esposito has bigger problems than even us. He's facing his own civil war. Pro-American forces – helped by our intelligence community, as I understand it – are trying to get him to agree to a peaceful annexation before a single bullet is fired."

"So, they haven't agreed to come to the table and accept this willingly?" That was Booth, curious.

"Not yet," President Zimmerman shakes his head. "But we're hoping these pro-American rebels will push him toward that eventuality."

"We shouldn't be doing it at all," someone pipes up from the president's side. Someone Banks can't see. "We should be extending an olive branch and insisting on talks."

"Agreed," Booth says. "No offense, Mr. President, we should be exploring more options. It doesn't feel like we are."

"That's why we're not forcing the issue for the moment," Davidson continues in the president's defense. "It's important we keep our heads about us and establish ourselves in the Southern United States before we make our incursion into Mexico. There's still time for us to do that while the temperatures remain tolerable."

One of the scientific advisors standing behind the president receives a piece of paper from an aide. He reads the paper, then steps forward and whispers something in the President's ear. The President listens for a few moments, then clears his throat and speaks up.

"Things here might not be tolerable for much longer. I'm being told we'll have prolonged arctic temperatures as far south as Virginia within a month. It'll get worse from there, and they could last upwards of ten or twenty years. Maybe longer."

Sue Anne covers her mouth, stifling an involuntary cry of shock. Beside her, the usually stoic Banks shudders at the revelation of the entire Midwestern United States turning into a tundra. Crops destroyed, farm animals by the millions perishing in the cold, migrating wildlife decimated as people grow more desperate for food.

"But it all comes down to whoever keeps their cool." The President looks around his own table, snorting at himself. "No pun intended."

"What about Canada?" Heller asks.

The President lifts his finger and gestures to the scientist he'd spoken to before. The man steps forward, and Zimmerman introduces him. "This is Rick Manglor, my lead scientist. Rick, tell them what we're seeing in Canada, temperature-wise."

The man steps into the light, his tousled hair swept back from his temples, tired blue eyes addressing them through the video feed. "Not surprisingly, Canada has experienced less effects from temperature swing – relatively speaking – because it's cold there already. However, it *is* getting much colder, forcing people from the northern regions to flee south."

"People are slipping through the cracks along the border," General Davidson explains, "and the skirmishes are getting worse. We're not just fighting with the Canadian forces. It's the regular citizens who are coming across and scavenging on their way south."

"I fear Prime Minister Clark was a little too transparent," the president says, "and it has caused unnecessary panic, driving people to the border."

"Don't you think it's warranted?" Booth exclaims, eyebrows raised.

"Like I said," Zimmerman meets her gaze. "We all have to keep our heads, top to bottom. From the citizen on the street to the people in this room." The President focuses in on Banks, and she straightens slightly, meeting his gaze head-on as he continues.

"That's why it's important for us to locate Tom McKnight. He needs to help us stop this, or things will unravel even faster. Find Arrowhead and put out an APB on McKnight with all the other agencies, even those engaged in evacuation activities. We need all eyes on this. We'll stop at nothing to bring him in. That means using every bit of leverage at your disposal. Is that clear?"

Banks nods and gestures for Sue Anne to follow him out of the room and into the hall.

* * *

They leave the meeting and find a small huddle room in another part of the command facility. Banks steps inside and asks Sue Anne to sit while she pours them both a glass of water from a nearby pitcher and delivers them to the table. Sue Anne takes a glass and sips, Banks studying her intently. The Colonel already knows of Banks' loyalty to the McKnights, and must tread carefully lest she become spooked.

With a soft tone, Banks picks up where the president left off. "So, you can see how badly we need to find Tom. Even President Zimmerman wants him to come in. So—"

Sue Anne heads her off with her firm accent, waving her hand absently. "I have no idea where he is. We didn't have a secret meeting place or bug out location for when the shit hit the fan."

"I believe you. But do you know where Tom's family lives? I'm pretty sure that's where we're going to find him."

Sue Anne shrugs. "You're the ones with high-tech communication systems and records and databases. It's not like the regular internet is working."

"True, but we've only got his previous three addresses in our records. Nothing about his current residence. We just know it's somewhere in Virginia."

Sue Anne remains stoic, sipping her water again.

"Look, I know you're concerned about Tom and his family, but this is for the best. We need to get his help to stop this thing. You know that."

"Tom won't be caught if he doesn't want to be."

"Leave that up to us." Banks forces a warm smile.

"It doesn't matter. I don't know where he lives. We never talked about that stuff."

"All the same. Try to think about where his family might be. Believe me, no one is going to be hurt."

"I know what I heard. The president said to spare no expense to bring him in. I think he even mentioned the word, 'leverage.'"

"It's regretful he put it that way," Banks concedes. "We certainly don't want to see Tom, or his family, hurt. What good would that do us?"

"I don't know," she shrugs. "I'm not a government agent."

Colonel Banks glances toward the closed door, making a show of ensuring they're speaking in confidence. Then she turns back to the red-haired woman and leans forward in her seat, turning up the pressure.

"Look, it could get dangerous for you if someone thinks you're holding out on us." Banks twirls her finger in the ring of condensation left on the table from her glass. "With things changing so much, you won't have the protections you once had. You can't just hide away from your responsibilities. You'll need friends. I can be that friend, but you've got to help me."

Sue Anne stares at the Colonel for a long moment, a glint of resentment in her eyes tinged with a hint of anger. The look quickly vanishes behind her professional face.

"All I know is that his family has a home in Wyndale, Virginia," she says stiffly. "Somewhere north of Bristol. Whenever we had a break, he always talked about living off the grid. You know, prepper stuff."

"Prepper stuff?"

"Yeah. He mentioned their house was stocked with food, and they had a few barns and livestock. They even had an aquaponic garden and crops they harvested every year." Sue Anne snorts. "Oh, and they have loads of guns."

Banks leans back, rubbing the bridge of her nose, a headache starting to form behind her eyes. "So he's turned them into *those* kind of people. Hell."

"That's what I'm trying to tell you." Sue Anne pokes her finger on the huddle room table. "He's not going to come very easily, if at all."

The lieutenant colonel sits back in her chair, pondering Sue Anne's words. McKnight's history with Banks is long and somewhat sordid – on the Colonel's part – and she's not terribly surprised to hear that the family has gone all-in on their lifestyle, especially after one of McKnight's last times working with her.

"Thank you for the information," she nods, giving Sue Anne a quick, thin smile. "That'll be all."

Sue Anne's eyes linger, the harsh glint flashing for an instant, then the woman draws a sharp breath, stands, and leaves the room. Banks sits in silence for some time, dwelling on her options. Arrowhead hasn't checked in since the stop at the rest area, and that was almost a full day ago. The lack of updates is concerning, considering he's supposed to check in every twelve hours and has managed to do so in some capacity so far.

All she can do is hope Arrowhead contacts her directly. Either way, it's a waiting game, and there's nothing Lieutenant Colonel Banks hates more than waiting.

Chapter 10
Tom McKnight
Brodnax, Virginia

"I thought we could get out of here before you caught us."

"I'm faster than I look," the old man nodded knowingly. "And just because I'm old doesn't mean my eyes don't work. Spotted you behind those soldiers the minute you wandered in. No surprise they didn't see you, though, friggin' idjits." He grunted and waved the .357, Tom tracking the barrel's movements relentlessly. "Now, tell me where you're from and what you're doing here."

Tom held up his hand like he could push the gun barrel down. "Look, we just came in from out of town and are trying to get warm."

"So, you're just passing through?"

"My daughter, she's sick." Tom stepped aside to let him see Sam's hallowed eyes and pale face. "We would have kept walking past the town to get home, but I need to get her inside where it's warm."

"Should've spent more time doing that and less time snooping around."

"Yeah, I know. We heard the commotion and wanted to see what was going on, though. It was nothing to do with you personally, I promise." Tom stood straighter. "Look, if you lower your weapon, we'll just move along."

The older man had shifty, brown eyes, and a dirt-smudged face, but his gaze was sharp and his body sprier than it appeared beneath his baggy clothing. Tom got the distinct impression that the old man was largely putting on an act, and trying to deceive him wouldn't go well for them.

"Well, that could be a problem. You know what they say about a town not being big enough for two people. Three makes it worse."

Tom nodded in understanding. "I completely agree. We don't plan on staying. We just need a night's rest, then we'll be off in the morning."

"You're not agents from the government?" The man gestured pointedly with the weapon. "I heard they were doing that in some towns. Sending in civilians like hall monitors to snitch on people staying behind."

"No way." Tom shook his head. "We're not here to snitch. And we're definitely not working for the government. I'm... well, I'm not exactly on their good side these days."

The old man threw his head back and laughed. "Ha! What'd you do to piss them off?"

"I was on one of the ships off the coast when this all went down. They think I can help them with some project they're doing, so they threw us in a detainment camp, then let us go with one of their agents to try and make me go back and help them. We... didn't let him succeed." The summary was succinct, and had the desired effect of widening the old man's gaze as he listened to Tom.

"Sounds too fantastical to be made up, I suppose." The .357 dropped a few inches as he sized up Tom and Samantha again, scratching his scruff-covered chin. "Where are you headed then?"

"Just outside Bristol. We've got a farmstead there, and my wife and youngsters are waiting for us." He chuckled darkly. "The missus won't like it too much if I bring her a sick little girl. I'm sure you understand."

The man's expression held firm for a long moment, almost long enough that Tom was starting to get worried, but it finally softened and he let the .357 fall to his side. "Well, I might have used to know at one point, but I don't anymore. I suppose you folks can stay in one of the houses on the *other* side of town from—"

Sam coughed in a fit of convulsions, interrupting the man as she bent forward, clutching her chest, clenching her shoulders as the fit grew into a series of dry croaks. Tom turned instinctively and watched his daughter sway, grabbing her and holding her up.

"I appreciate it," Tom nodded gratefully to the man, starting to guide Samantha away. "We'll get as far down from you as possible."

"No, no." The old man holstered his pistol, sighing heavily as he approached the pair, motioning for them to follow him. "Come on," he said, waving for them to follow. "I've got a few things at the house that might be helpful."

"I don't want to impose. We can just go to an abandoned house up the street. I can put her in a bed and kick on the furnace."

"Nonsense. My house is warm and toasty, I've got food and medicine, and, well... call me a soft old man, but I feel bad for holding you up. You two aren't like most of the rest I've seen, so let me do what I can for you and your daughter. It's the least I can do. And I promise, my bark is worse than my bite."

Tom's first instinct was to decline the man's offer again, but Sam's cough returned, her entire body shaking, her knees wobbling as she nearly collapsed from the strain. Even if they found a house with a working gas or electric furnace, it would take hours for the entire house to warm up. She needed warmth sooner than that, and the promise of medicine was too good to pass up.

Biting down the gnawing worry, he turned to the man and nodded. "We'd appreciate it. Thanks."

"That's good." He slid by and gestured for them to follow. "Right this way."

They followed behind the man as he strode boldly through the other yards to his house, hopping fences to open gates for the pair and keeping a careful watch in all directions. While he looked old, he carried himself well, neither overweight nor weak, about Tom's height but moving like he could arm wrestle a gorilla and come out on top.

"My name's Guy Richards," he shot over his shoulder.

"I'm Tom McKnight, and this is my daughter, Samantha."

"Good to meet you both, Mr. Tom."

Guy's house was a ranch-style home with an immaculately kept garden in front, clean siding, and a stone path that wound around to the back. He led them to the porch and up the steps, stopping at the wooden barricade he'd erected where he turned and fixed Tom with a hard look.

"You carrying?"

"I have a pistol and two magazines," Tom nodded. "For our protection."

Guy let his stare linger a handful of seconds, looking both of them up and down yet again before he turned to the front door. "Fair enough, but I don't expect to see it while we're inside."

"Also fair enough," Tom agreed, stepping aside to allow his daughter through first.

"Oh, wow," Sam breathed a sigh of relief as she walked into a wave of warmth in the foyer, her shoulders relaxing as she trembled with a shiver. Tom closed his eyes as the heat hit his cheeks and slipped down his neck, immediately aware of the sweat layering his skin. After sleeping in a tent for a week and then riding in the LAV for hours on end, he was ready to sit back, strip off his thick winter clothing and let the heat soak into his bones.

He stopped and took in the foyer, noticing immediately how crowded it was. Above his head on the right was a coat rack filled with windbreakers, winter jackets, scarves, beanies, caps, and even a pair of hazmat suits. Beneath that sat a rack of boots, tennis shoes, and galoshes. To his left was a medium-sized, locked safe with a biometric reader, and next to that rested a large backpack, stuffed to bursting with a bedroll, flashlight, and knife hanging from the straps. A long wood rack finished the side of the hall, stuffed with freshly split logs that gave the house a pleasant, woodsy aroma.

"Nice bugout bag." Tom pointed at the backpack. "We keep something similar around our house, too."

"Good man," Guy nodded. "I've got one at the back door, too. In case I need to sneak out that way."

"Smart thinking."

"This way." The older man gestured for them to follow.

The main hallway separated the house down the middle. Tom glanced into the dining room and saw three more wood racks and five huge plastic containers connected with hoses and tubing, the words "POTABLE" written in capital letters with a permanent marker on the side of each container. He and Sam stepped into the living room where Guy removed his jacket and placed it gently over the back of a recliner before gesturing to a small couch sitting in front of a large, empty fireplace.

"Go ahead and sit. Make yourselves at home." The man gave them a half smile as he stepped back and waited. "Sorry for the crowded mess. I don't usually have company."

The pair squeezed past the recliner and sat, Tom perching on the edge, looking over his shoulder at their host while Sam slumped back immediately.

"Take your shoes off," Guy suggested. "Get comfortable. I'll put on some tea for us. I hope you like green."

"That sounds great," Tom replied.

After Guy disappeared into the kitchen, he looked around at the room's claustrophobic confinement. Bins, boxes, and packages filled the entire space, stacked nearly to the ceiling. Granted, they were arranged in neat rows with enough room to walk between them, but they still made the place feel more like a storeroom than a cozy living room. Pictures that looked to be years old were hung sporadically on the walls, and a small radio sat on a stand in front of the boarded-up bay window, a small notebook and pen atop the controls, looking recently used.

Sam bent forward and swiped at her boots, trying to untie them and Tom slid to his knees, loosening her laces before slipping the boots off her feet.

"Ahhh," Sam released a luxurious sigh. "I wouldn't be mad if you rubbed them, too."

Tom laughed, but then he felt how cold they were and he briskly rubbed them through her socks, Sam breathing deeply, wiggling her toes and smiling through occasional fits of coughing.

"Here's a blanket for the young miss," Guy reached over the couch, surprising Tom with his stealth before returning to the kitchen. Tom helped Sam get her jacket off and unfolded the blanket, placing it over her and she grabbed the cover's edge and pulled it to her chin, her long, curly hair bunched up around her fists.

"This is nice," she said, kicking her feet a bit.

"Do you want to lie down?"

"Maybe after I have some tea?"

"Yeah, sure."

Tom sat by his daughter's side, angled so he could see Guy moving around in the kitchen behind them. The man hummed a tune as he clinked glasses and ran water. Five minutes later, Guy walked in carrying a long tray with handles and three cups of tea with generic tea tags hanging over the rims.

"I microwaved the water," he said. "I hope you don't mind."

"Not at all." Tom shook his head. "Why would we?"

"Some people are particular, that's all. They like it boiled and steeped and yada yada yada. Me, I'll take microwaved water and generic green tea bags any day."

"Same here," Tom agreed. "Hell, I'd settle for Lipton Classic blend."

Guy chuckled and brought the tray around. There wasn't a coffee table, so the man bent down and allowed Tom and Sam to take their cups before he backed up and sat in his recliner, placing the tray on his lap. He shifted and removed his .357 from its holster, setting it next to his cup, then, with a heavy sigh, the man lifted his cup and took a hearty sip.

Sam raised her cup with both hands and brought it to her nose, closing her eyes and breathing in the steam. Tom returned to his spot next to Sam, keeping between his daughter and their host as he allowed himself to settle back, relaxing for the first time in Guy's presence. He sipped at the tea, sobering at its strong, bitter taste.

"Seriously, thanks for the tea, and the warmth. I know it's hard to trust people these days, and we greatly appreciate your hospitality."

"No problem." Guy nodded stiffly, kicking his feet out. "And you're right about trust. Help me out a bit with that."

"How so?" Tom sipped at the tea again, already sensing where things were going.

"You say you're on your way to Bristol from out in the Atlantic. How in the world did you manage to get involved with all that?"

Tom chuckled, thinking of where they'd been and what they'd done since being on vacation. "It all started when me and Sam were at an ocean technology convention in Maine..." Tom delved into their story, beginning with the call from his boss and working quickly to the part where they were transported aboard the Marin via helicopter. Guy's eyes went wide as Tom recounted his experience with the Navy, how they'd watched the remote submersibles engage with the anomaly deep below the ocean's surface, and how they'd been destroyed.

"That's the thing they were talking about on the news, right? They said it was the root of the cold weather."

"Yep," Tom nodded. "It's severely disrupted the North Atlantic Drift, and it's blocking any warm water from reaching us up here in the north."

"Any chance we can kick-start the drift back up?"

Tom shrugged. "If the freshwater surge peters out and the currents can start flowing again, we might be okay. But it's hard to say how long it would take to thaw things out. Could be a few years. Could be a century."

Guy nodded his head dismally, a resigned look on his face as he stared into his lap. "So, you're some kind of scientist or something?"

"Not a scientist. An engineer. I've worked on naval contracts with my parent company. That's why the Navy asked me to help them with the anomaly. Since I had Sam with me and it was an urgent emergency situation, she came, too."

Guy nodded. "Got it. Go on, please."

Tom covered the destruction of the ships and their subsequent getaway on the motorboat. Guy gripped the arms of his chair as Tom explained how they'd made shore ahead of the storm and met Jerry at the gas station. Next came the drive to Virginia Beach, the trouble in town, and their time at the military camp. He ended with Jerry's death, Keith's betrayal, and their wreck just a few hours prior.

"That's it." Tom drained the last of a second cup of tea Guy had gotten him mid-story. "Now you know everything."

"I'm really sorry about your friend," Guy said with a disappointed shake of his head. "He sounds like a nice young man."

"Thanks," Tom felt that old twisting in his guts, forcing it back down before it could regain control. "He was incredible."

"I have to say, that's just about the craziest story I've ever heard." Guy laughed again, like he had when they had first met him. "But you aren't lying, that's the craziest part. You could be, but your daughter?" Guy's dark eyes flashed over to Samantha. "The innocence of youth betrays deception. And I can see she's been through hell. Both of you have."

"What about you?" Tom leaned back. "Seems like you've had a little excitement around here as well. Namely, an evacuation." Tom gestured toward the outside. "We saw the signs all over town."

"Right," Guy nodded. "That's been the story of the week. Evacuations. Forced and voluntary."

"From what we saw, things looked pretty damn forced."

"They were for most of the town. But I heard about them way ahead of everyone else." Guy stretched his legs and crossed his feet, taking another sip of tea. "On my short-wave radio. I had friends up north broadcasting about it when all this started around ten days ago. Detroit, Chicago, New York, and Cincinnati. Every town in between. It was voluntary at first. The military went door-to-door, offering incentives and aid to coax people out. Of course, some folks resisted, and that's when things got nasty."

Tom shook his head, thinking of their treatment at the camp. "I can only imagine."

"They started getting tough about a week ago. Forcing people from their homes by the hundreds of thousands."

"How did they manage that? I mean, we only have a quarter-million standing troops in the military, don't we?"

Guy chuckled. "Well, they've grown recently. They're recruiting every able-bodied fighter they can. Promising them incentives if they join up. Plus they have the local police forces, national guardsmen, the works. Any protests get shut down by their sound weapons."

"LRADs?"

"Yep. Long-Range Acoustic Devices. Powerful as hell, too. Make your eardrums scream at a hundred yards."

"I thought those were banned."

"They were, but I guess they're pulling out all the stops."

Tom slid his fingers through his greasy hair, letting out a deep sigh. "We must have missed the worst part of the evacuation. Things had already progressed by the time we escaped."

"The military boys passed through here about a week ago, but I was ready for it. I stayed hunkered down until they came to my door. Steel core, eighteen inch lag bolts going into the walls." Guy winked, a grin stretching from ear to ear. "They weren't expecting that. Then they tried the sonic cannons, but I've got special earphones that protected me against every frequency they can throw at me. They even tried pumping gas in here, but I was ready for that, too."

"So, they gave up?"

"They stopped just short of shooting me," Guy sighed resignedly. "I've got some friends up north who avoided being evacuated, too. They're still up there, and they say it's getting cold. Damn cold. Most days are in the low tens. Sometimes below zero."

"That's unbelievable for this time of year."

Guy looked slightly perplexed. "Do you have any idea how cold it might eventually get?"

Tom shrugged. "Well, they figure the average temperature around the globe was around forty-six degrees Fahrenheit during the last ice age. That sounds warm, but it's quite low for an average. For what we're facing, I'd guess Northern Canada and the Arctic wouldn't see much difference than what they're seeing now." Tom shook his head, trying to think. "Southern Canada and the Northern United States might see average temperatures of around minus eighteen or twenty. Possibly lower than that."

"Even here, in Virginia?"

Tom nodded. "They were right to evacuate people. Vehicles and machines start to struggle at those temperatures, and it would be hard for people to keep warm. The only blessing we'd really have is the summer sunlight. Winter will be absolutely brutal."

Guy nodded and gave a low whistle between his teeth. "And that's not all we have to worry about."

"What else have you heard?"

"I'm hearing reports of Canucks migrating south in droves. I'm talking the entire country. We've got military positioned along the border, stemming the flow. That's why the flow of refugees, and subsequent traffic, has slowed to a trickle, but I fear the dam will burst. We'll be skirmishing hard with them soon."

"Americans fighting Canadians," Tom twisted his lips. "I never thought I'd live to see the day. You'd figure we could work something out, make it possible for them to evac along with us."

"Me, too. But who knows what's going on up top with the big brass. At least the temperatures are more stable down south. Cool, but stable."

"Things will get pretty crowded before long."

"People are saying the President has moved all three branches of government from DC to Texas." Guy tipped back his teacup and finished off what he had. "We've got troops all along the US-Mexico border, and so do the Mexicans."

"Oh, man." Tom already knew what he was going to say.

"I think we're going to try to and annex Mexico."

Tom shook his head. "That's going to be bloody."

"Quick and bloody," Guy agreed. "I've got buddies down there who say the tension is getting thick, but the Mexicans aren't in a solid position to even pretend to hold us off. Dealing with their own internal issues."

"Have you heard of any place that's safe?"

"Florida seems okay, but they've got refugees sleeping on flooding beaches. Tens of thousands of them, and government assistance is barely keeping up. Wait until food stores get low and people begin to starve."

Tom's eyes widened, and was his turn to whistle low. "Those people on the beach won't last long. The rising sea levels will sweep them out to sea. Oh, man. I don't even want to think about it. It might get cold up here in Virginia, but at least we won't have to worry about raiders so much."

"The government is commandeering farms and livestock after they drive folks out." The old man made a show of turning and acting like he was spitting over the side of his seat. "Tossing your property rights out the window."

"Even more reason to stay north if you can bear the cold."

"That's what I'm thinking." Guy tipped his empty cup toward Tom. "I guess the only consolation is that the rest of the world is having issues, too. I heard Russia is in a good position with their natural gas reserves. They've jacked up the premiums so high the EU is having to pay through the nose to keep themselves warm, and of course there's talk of war brewing fast. China's in rough shape. But you know them, they're closing their borders and locking down for the long haul."

"I'd imagine Africa is looking pretty good right about now."

"The fighting has already started there. Millions of refugees from Europe and the Middle East heading south." Guy chuckled. "Makes for quite the change from how things used to be, doesn't it?

Tom sighed heavily. "What a nightmare."

"Yeah, you don't even want to know about it."

Samantha, who'd been quiet the entire time as she sipped on her tea, was struck with another coughing fit and Tom glanced over. Her nose was running, her eyes were closed and she absently lifted her forearm, wiping her sleeve across her face.

Tom was looking around for a tissue when Guy sprung into action, quickly switching the tray from his lap to a small table next to his recliner.

"Let me get you something." He circled the couch with a glance down at Sam. "I've got some medicine as well. Just some over-the-counter decongestants and fever reducers."

"That's too kind of you," Tom nodded. "Thanks."

Guy stepped into the kitchen where the sounds of cabinets opening and closing echoed, feet shuffling around, the old man muttering to himself as he searched through his supplies. Tom's eyes lingered in the .357 the man had seemingly absent-mindedly left on the table, temptation reaching up from the dark to grasp at his mind. Rationalizations flooded in before he realized it, ways of justifying doing just about anything in response to the kindness they'd been shown. The old memories reared their ugly heads again alongside the darkness, his gut swirling as Samantha noticed him watching the revolver, her green eyes studying her father, wondering what he was thinking.

It's a survival situation. The dark coaxed him, glinting off the edge of the revolver's cylinder. *Anything is justified. Anything at all.*

"This should help clear the little miss right up," Guy called from the kitchen.

The voice broke Tom from his trance. He blinked rapidly and exhaled hard, realizing that he had been holding his breath since laying his eyes on the weapon. Closing his eyes, he cleared his throat, regaining his composure as the temptation faded as quickly as it had surfaced, leaving only guilt in its wake. "Oh, ah… oh, yeah? What is it?"

"It's extra strength Cough Aid, and not past its expired date." Guy chuckled. "This and a couple super strength cold and flu tablets should set her straight."

The man came back in the room with a bottle of purple liquid, the pills, and a bottled water. Handing Tom the water, he ticked out two pills and gave them over, Tom turning to Sam and nodding for her to take them, and she willingly did so. Guy poured an ounce of the liquid medicine into its measuring cup and started to hand that over, too.

"This might make her drowsy. Hell, I think it's supposed to."

Tom nodded and took the small cup, passing it along to Sam.

"Bottoms up," she croaked and turned the tiny cup up, swallowing all the medicine down. She made a disgusted face. "Oh, that tastes terrible."

"Yes, it does," Guy responded, "but it should help with any congestion and sniffles you might have."

"Thank you," Sam said. She pulled off her hat and set it aside, then she slipped sideways on the couch, curling up and putting her head on a cushion at the end. Feet resting against Tom's leg, she wiggled her toes with a sigh.

"You're welcome." Guy looked at her for a moment, a warm smile on his face, then he took the medicine to the kitchen while Tom took the bottom of the blanket and covered Sam's feet.

When Guy returned, he held a bottle of amber liquid and two small whiskey glasses.

"Have a drink with me, Tom."

Tom waved his hand. "Oh, no. I couldn't."

"I won't force you to, but you really should. This is 12-year-old Pappy Van Winkle bourbon. I don't share this lightly, and I doubt you'll ever see another bottle of it for the rest of your life."

Tom looked at the old-fashioned label and the amber liquid sloshing around inside. While he wasn't a drinker by any means, Sam was resting and it'd be impolite to turn down his host, so, reaching for a glass, he nodded. "Sure. Why not?"

Guy poured a rough ounce for Tom and another for himself, then they clinked them in a toast and leaned back in their seats. Tom took a sip, wincing as the whiskey burned his lips and rolled over his tongue with a distinctive sting. When he exhaled, his breath was tinged with alcohol. "I'm not a big bourbon drinker, but this tastes smooth. Yeah, it's good."

Guy grinned. "Nothing like a stiff drink to wash away the trials and tribulations of the road."

"You've got that right," Tom agreed wholeheartedly. He looked around at all the neatly stacked bins and boxes in the room. "So, all this stuff. I take it you're a prepper."

"I started prepping a long time ago when Erin was alive, but she didn't like it too much." Guy gave a sad chuckle as he gestured around the room. "She said it was a waste of money. She said nothing bad was going to happen in the world, and we'd be better off spending our time and money traveling."

The man fell into quiet remembrance with his whiskey glass on his knee.

"So, did you?"

Guy snapped his head up with a snort. "Did we what?"

"Did you do any traveling?"

"Yessir, we did." A smile crossed his face. "At first, I wasn't much for it. Then we went to Utah and looked out over those magnificent canyons. I saw the effect it had on Erin, and I couldn't resist doing it again and again just to make her happy. We worked overtime to get the money for each trip. Ended up hitting almost every state in the Union. But our crowning achievement was Ireland. Our last night there, we sat in a hundred-and-fifty-year-old pub and drank with some local folks. I couldn't understand half of what they were saying, but it was a great time."

Tom grinned wide at Guy's tales of adventure. "Barbara and I have never been to Ireland. We never got a chance to go much of anywhere." He shook his head with a pang of longing. "I'm really worried about things at home. If the military has been through the rest of Virginia like you said, then we need to get going. I need to know Barbara and the kids are safe."

"Well, you won't be getting there tonight, not with that little girl and her cough. You'll stay the night. I've got an air mattress for you in here, or you can share the spare bedroom, if you can stand the bins and boxes."

Tom spread his hands. "We don't want to be a burden on you. You've already done enough with getting us warmed up. Plus the medicine and whiskey."

Guy gestured with his glass. "So you're telling me you're going to wake your sick daughter, make her put her boots on, and walk back out into the cold at this time of day?"

Tom turned and looked at Sam. Her chest was moving up and down with languid ease and she'd buried her face in the throw pillow with her hair bunched around her face, a light snore coming out of the recesses of the soft fabric. Guilt overwhelmed him as he realized it was the first real rest she'd had since before they'd gone to the conference what felt like years ago.

"Guy," Tom chuckled, "has anyone told you that you're a conniving old coot?"

Guy stifled an uproarious belly laugh. "Words not dissimilar to those may have crossed Erin's lips at one point or another, yes."

"Well, thank you. Again. I don't know what we did to deserve your hospitality, but I accept."

"Then have another pour and sit with me awhile."

Tom nodded and held out his glass, and Guy poured them each another ounce. The two men sat quietly and drank their whiskey as a pleasant hum filled Tom's head.

They talked more about Guy's wife, Erin, who'd passed away three years ago. She had two kids from a previous marriage, but they lived in New Mexico, and Guy hadn't talked to them in a while. Tom told him about Barbara, Jack, and Linda, and his jobs working with the Navy, along with his family's own experiences in farming and preparedness. The two men shared in their commiseration over their lost loved ones – Guy's might have been more permanent, but Tom's was more raw, fed by the constant worry of the unknown.

Sometime around midnight, Guy announced he was going to bed, and left Tom the air mattress and some extra blankets. He blew up the mattress with a portable air pump, worried Sam would wake up from the noise, but she slept right through it, so he left her on the couch where she looked comfortable, Tom stretching out on the big bouncy cushion, staring up at the painted ceiling with a smooth buzz thrumming through his bloodstream. While he wasn't a big drinker, he had to admit a few ounces of whiskey had buffered his overactive brain against the tragedy of Jerry's death and it kept him from worrying as much about Barbara and the kids for just long enough to fall into a deep, relaxing sleep.

* * *

"Hey, Tom. *Tom.* Time to get up. We've got company."

The gruff voice pulled him from a dark dream where he was fighting to get home. He'd been slogging through ice storms and snow, dragging Sam along behind him on a sled packed with all their possessions. Barbara and his other children were somewhere up ahead, but he could barely see them through the ice and sleet. Head down and jaw clenched tight, he pumped his legs to catch up with them, slogging through an endless array of opposition.

"Tom, man. Wake up!" The gruff voice hissed. "They're back. Those damn Guardsmen." Someone pounded on the door, followed by shouts demanding that they come out, fulling awakening Tom, who opened his eyes and bolted upright. Guy stood over him with his .357 strapped to his right hip and a long Bowie knife on the other. He held a rifle cradled in his arms, and his face had regained his disgruntled expression.

"Rise and shine, buddy. Get Samantha up and moving." The man turned and rushed toward the door, yelling to the soldier outside. "You break down this door, you'll get more than you bargained for! Just try it and find out!"

Tom turned to see Sam raising on her elbows, blinking in the sunlight peeking around the edges of the boarded-up windows.

"What's going on?" She rubbed her eyes with her knuckles and looked at him from behind locks of sweaty, greasy hair.

"The soldiers are back. We need to go unless we want to be put on a truck heading south."

"Right," Sam squeaked. She automatically swung her feet off the couch and slipped them into her boots.

Tom felt her forehead as she laced them and tied them tight.

"You're still a little clammy, but cooler."

"I feel a little better," she confirmed.

Tom sat next to her and put on his own boots, lacing them up quickly before looking for their packs as Guy traded choice words with the soldiers at the door.

"You've got thirty seconds to come out, old man," one shouted, "then we're coming for you."

"On what authority?" Guy shouted back. As he argued with the soldiers, he was connecting wires and pieces of thread around the door frame. The wires led to small boxes and bundles positioned on the floor and ceiling. Tom hadn't noticed them when they'd come in, but they were obvious now; explosive traps, and dangerous-looking ones at that. Slipping his backpack on one shoulder, he gestured for Sam to do the same as Guy returned to the living room and pulled them toward the kitchen.

"Look, I parked a vehicle four doors down at my neighbor's house. It's a Honda Civic. Used to be Erin's. The keys are on the floor on the driver's side floorboard. It's not the best in the snow, but stick to the cleared roads and you'll be fine." He moved to the sink and gripped a handle on the wood covering the window, pulling it open, peering outside, squinting in the reflected sunlight off the snow. "I don't see anyone out back. I guess they don't figure I'll try to get away." He slid to the back door, unlocked three deadbolts, and whipped it open. "Now go. Get out of here while I deal with these assholes. I threw some extra things in your packs for you."

Tom pushed Sam through to stand on the patio while he turned in the doorway. "You can't face them alone, Guy. I can help. Just let me get Sam somewhere safe and—"

"No time, Tom. And it's not your fight." Guy put a hand on Tom's shoulder, his normally clear, piercing eyes misting over. "You need to get home to your family. And besides, you gave me something special last night that I haven't had in a very long time."

"What?"

"A friend."

Indecision tore at Tom's gut, but a look at Samantha solved his conundrum. He reached out, grabbing Guy in a quick bear hug, receiving one in return.

"Thanks for the night's rest. And the car. And everything else."

Guy grinned, rough and wiry. "You're welcome. And thanks for having a drink with me. It's been a while since I've found anyone worthy of the whiskey." The soldiers pounded on the door again, shouting their final warning with booming voices. "Now, go, get the hell out of here and get your little girl home."

Tom nodded and pushed outside, turning Sam through the backyard and toward the next house over. They heard Guy arguing a few seconds more before gunfire erupted. It wasn't the .50 mounted on the Humvee, thankfully, just small arms fire, sounding like it was coming from both outside and inside the house.

Tom ran with clenched shoulders, feet shuffling through the thin layer of snowy frost on the grass, fleeing through a gray dawn that wasn't much more than a haze. As soon as they reached the neighbor's driveway, a muffled thud shook the air, vibrating the hairs in his ears, causing them both to grunt and duck in surprise.

"That must have been his front door," Tom said as he shoved Sam around the last house toward the Honda Civic.

"Why are they shooting at him?" Her tone was distraught, voice caught tight in her throat as they pounded to a stop at the vehicle. Sam jerked open the back door and threw her backpack inside and Tom circled to the other side, doing the same. As he tossed his pack in, he glanced up toward the house where sparks of gunfire lit up the morning haze, smoke drifting through the air.

He could barely see what was happening, though through the smoke he could vaguely make out the bulk of two Humvees sitting in the yard with shadow soldiers shifting and moving in clouds of grey and black. One soldier flinched and twisted, pitching backwards as his rifle flew to the ground, another ducking behind cover and returning fire toward the front of the house. Tom had seen enough, and he dropped into the driver's seat and felt the floorboard for the keys, desperate to escape before the soldiers spotted them.

"Jeez, they're really going after him," Sam squealed, her voice tense with dread and fear as she sunk in her seat. "They're trying to kill him!"

Tom found the keys but didn't look up, focused on steadying his shaking hands long enough to push the key into the ignition. He turned it over, and the car puttered to life just as a massive explosion rocked the street, shaking the compact car on its springs, the pressure cracking Sam's window in a blink, though the glass held. He looked past Sam and up to Guy's house where debris had exploded from his garage, flaming shrapnel raining down through the gray haze, lighting up the yard. Three shadows lay flat on the ground, unmoving, while two others had flopped down face-first, arms over their heads to avoid the flying debris.

From the cloud of smoke, a white-paneled van with sheets of metal welded over the sides blasted out of the garage, nearly hitting one of the fallen soldiers before whipping left in a screech of tires. The vehicle straightened, roared, and flew past Tom and Sam, the windows tinted pitch black, the driver's identity unmistakable.

"Should we follow him?"

Tom started to say no, but the two surviving guardsmen had gotten to their feet and were running down the street, pointing and shouting at a new target – the Civic.

"Son of a... yeah, get down!"

Sam slunk farther into her seat as Tom punched the gas, shooting them into the road. Bullets peppered their trunk with metallic thuds, a pair of rounds piercing the back window and shattering glass all over the back seat. Sam cried out as Tom gripped the wheel and angled them down the thin road, spotting Guy's van whipping around a bend ahead, keeping the Civic tight to the turn, pressing right up against the brush crowding in, swinging free and catapulting into a straightaway. Tom hit the gas and launched them after the slower van, hoping to catch it before it turned. As they got closer, the van eased up and allowed Tom to follow, but even as he pulled the trembling Civic closer, the van shot forward again.

"He's not slowing down." Tom ended his sentence with a growl.

"Because they're chasing us!" Sam leaned over the seat, craning her neck to look back.

Tom glanced in his rearview and cursed as the two Humvees bore down on them. The big, durable vehicles took up most of the crowded road, clipping brush and tree branches as they flew by. Tom hit the gas and put some distance between them, but the loud, belching explosions of the .50 echoed from behind as the rounds peppered the trees next to them and clipped the rear fender with a horrendous, chewing sound. Tom whipped them around a curve, putting trees and dirt between them, gaining a moment's reprieve. "Those rounds will tear us apart!"

Tom worked the gas and steering wheel dangerously, pushing them to their limits, falling almost into a trance similar to when he would execute complicated dive maneuvers in a rover. Fear melted away in the face of focus, his tires squealing around bends as he barely kept the white van in front of him. The rolling Virginia plains and hills were tough to tackle at speed but perfect for evasion, providing just enough curve to keep the .50 from turning them into Swiss cheese. They came to a branch in the road, forcing Tom to slow for an instant, the Civic's brakes squealing in protest. The van was nowhere in sight.

"Which way?"

"There! To the right!" Sam pointed as a flash of white rounded a bend in the right fork.

Tom whipped the wheel to the right, dipping them downward as rounds pounded a gnarled oak trunk on the corner. His stomach dropped and then shifted as he took the next bend at almost sixty. The Honda's tires hugged the inner curve, taking out bushes and saplings in an explosion of forest debris, the snow on the road mercifully thin enough to keep the Civic from sliding off.

The white van screeched to a halt, and made a sharp left, tipping dangerously on its frame before righting itself and grinding up a steep hill. In response, Tom slowed to a near stop to make the turn in a squeal of tires and a spray of gravel, then he was pushing them up the hill, the 4-cylinder engine groaning as he pressed the gas pedal to the floor, a pouring of lead clipping the back of the Honda like a loud, metallic rainstorm.

Shoulders clenched, chest pressed against the wheel, Tom kept the gas pedal pinned to the floor, fully expecting his rear end to fall off or the tires to blow, but they kept climbing fast, grinding up the hill and over, dropping them down the other side like a roller coaster.

"Hang on!" he told Sam as they picked up speed and wove through an S-shaped valley doing sixty-five miles per hour, flying past farmsteads sitting off the road, guarded by woods, and once again, the van was gone, nowhere to be seen.

"Where the hell did he go this time?" Tom growled and smashed his palm on the wheel, eyes pinned way ahead to the next curve. Sam raised in her seat and pointed at a flash of white as it skittered up another left-hand turn.

"There he goes!"

"But that's a driveway!" Tom was already slowing hard, turning the wheel as the g-forces pushed them forward. He clenched his teeth as the Honda's wheels skidded across the loose gravel and piles of snow and ice in the road, caught, then swung them onto up the dirt driveway. The back end of the vehicle smacked the mailbox aside, knocking it into the brush with a clatter. Letting go of the wheel so it snapped straight, Tom raced them up a steep lane to the house at the top.

At the top, the driveway levelled out, and he spotted the white van parked next to the house, but Guy was walking past them, charging his rifle with a clack. Tom slammed the brakes, put the car in park, and got out, jogging to meet Guy as he pulled his pistol free, for all the good it would do them.

"I hope they don't see that I knocked over that mailbox."

"Me, too," Guy remarked.

A moment later, the first Humvee flew by in a grind of tires, the second one right behind it. Tom stared, waiting for them to realize they'd been tricked or follow the tracks in the shallow snow and return with a vengeance, but they never did. Five minutes passed before Tom finally let out the breath he'd been holding, still staring down at the road as he shook his head.

"Well, they almost had us."

"That they did," Guy acknowledged.

Tom winced, realizing all the supplies Guy had stashed in his home were forfeit. "Sorry about your house. I doubt you'll be able to go back."

"Well, they'll haul away everything they can carry, assuming the explosion didn't set the place on fire." His frown turned into a grin. "But they won't find the hidden storeroom. I'll give it a few days, or a week, then return for the rest."

"You're more than welcome to come to our place until then," Tom patted the older man on the shoulder. "We could use a trustworthy friend to help hold things down."

"I appreciate the offer, but no thanks." Guy pursed his lips and relaxed the gun in his arms. "I've had my fill of government standoffs, and if people the likes of that Keith fellow are after you, then I'd rather keep my distance. No offense."

Tom laughed. "I don't blame you. Luckily, he's dead and gone, and he won't bother us anymore. But I can't guarantee there won't be more." He glanced back toward the car to make sure Sam was okay, her staring back at him through the glass, her expression flat. "What are you going to do, then?"

"I'll hang around for a bit and collect my supplies." Guy shrugged. "Then I may go in search of my wife's son. We never got along very well, but Erin always wanted us to."

"Sounds like a worthy endeavor. I'll give you my address, anyway. That way, if you're ever in our area, you can swing in and see us."

Guy turned to him with a rugged smile, the lines in the corners of his eyes wrinkling deep. "I appreciate that, Tom. It would be good to have friends... around."

Tom gave him the information and returned to the Honda. Sitting in the driver's seat, he waited for Guy to pull out. When he did, he followed him to the end of the driveway where they took a right, moving in the opposite direction of the Humvees, in search of the main road. Once they reached Highway 58. Guy turned right, and Tom turned left, heading toward what he hoped was home.

"I really liked him," Sam stared in her side mirror as the white van drove away from them and disappeared around a bend. "I listened a little while you guys were talking, before I fell asleep. I could tell he liked us, too."

"He has a good heart," Tom agreed. "Not many people would help out folks like us in need."

"We help out people in need." Sam's voice fell to a whisper. "People like Jerry."

"I guess that makes us good people too, then." Tom held his daughter's hand for a moment, squeezing it tight. "He was a bit rough around the edges, but I wish Guy all the luck in this new world."

"Me too."

Chapter 11
Barbara McKnight
Bristol, Virginia

Snow whipped across the ground, driven by new and angry winds coming in from the west, soaring over the tops of hills to rustle the still-green pines and barren oaks, then whipping down into the valleys. Atop one such hill, Barbara winced against the icy flakes hitting her cheeks as she lay next to Darren, both of them decked out in full winter apparel from head to toe, even their eyes protected by ski goggles dug out of the basement.

"Is this where they're keeping the kids?" They stayed prone to keep out of sight on a rise just north of the military camp near Bristol, their vehicle parked a fair distance away amongst an abandoned cluster of farmhouses set into the backside of the hill, their tracks long since obscured by the wind and snow. Between the time the soldiers had taken the kids to the time she and Darren had prepared and driven into town, a half-inch of white powder had accumulated on the ground, both a hindrance to their progress and an ally in remaining hidden.

Belly down in the snowy grass, Barbara held her binoculars up and scanned the military camp, moving from east to west and then back again. Soldiers had erected large temporary buildings everywhere, most of them fenced in and topped with rolls of barbed wire. Trees encircled the fencing, providing some cover for anyone wanting to approach though patrols walked loosely around the camp on no clear schedule, moving in twos and threes. A single larger building sat on the north side, antennae and a satellite dishes jutting from the top, its bulk blocking smaller storage buildings and sheds they couldn't fully see, the snowy mix adding to their limited visibility.

"I see plenty of people, but no kids." Darren was looking with his own pair of binoculars toward a fenced-in area with burn barrels sending up plumes of smoke. "I see about forty or fifty people milling around in there, but I don't see a single child."

"That many people doesn't seem like a lot," Barbara commented thoughtfully. "Seems they'd have a lot more if they were going around forcing folks out of their homes."

Darren grimaced as a cold wind snapped up the hill, whipping around their faces. "Those are just the people who resisted, like us. The troublemakers. I'd say most everyone else in town has already headed south."

"The camp seems almost deserted," Barbara added, her binoculars moving across the spattering of guards walking the grounds and fence lines, huddling in their coats. "Maybe they're the last ones to go and this is just a skeleton crew. If the kids aren't there with the general population, though, then where are they holding them?"

"No clue," Darren grimaced. "Let's keep looking."

Barbara scanned toward the east, barely able to see through a treeline to Wallace Pike. Eight semis lined the road, some of them still idling, leaving just enough room for military traffic to and from Bristol. Humvees, Jeeps, and APCs were positioned at the front and back of the line, the entire thing stretching almost a mile long. She slowly moved the binoculars to her right again, scanning over houses and backyards, until the military buildings in the field returned to view. Then she raised them, looking south past the holding area to a very small parking lot on the far side.

"What are those blue busses?" She was referring to a half-dozen long, blue school busses parked side-by-side.

"Where?"

"Look past the holding area with the burn barrels."

There was a pause, then Darren exclaimed. "Ah-ha! Those are definitely transports. And, look, people are being loaded onto one as we speak."

"With children!" Barbara exclaimed, watching a couple get on board with a little girl between them.

"So the kids must be nearby."

"Maybe in one of the buildings we can't see."

"Yep."

A cold wind blasted in, blowing snow into Barbra's face. She lowered her binoculars and shrunk into her coat, tensing up against the burst while Darren put down his binoculars and rolled on his side, wincing against the wind. He wore a hunter's hat, fur-lined and buckled beneath his chin, but the wind was a thousand needles, finding every small crack and crevice and exploiting them mercilessly. "First order of business. We need to get a definite location on the kids. That means moving much closer and doing some scouting. Are you ready for that?"

Barbara nodded before looking up to the pale white sky, gray clouds mingling with white ones, the air a solid sheet of drifting snow.

"Let me clarify," Darren said. "If they catch us sneaking around with weapons, they're not going to be thrilled. They most definitely shoot first and ask questions later. Are you ready for *that*?"

"The patrols look loose," she pointed out. "I think we can slip past them."

"They might have snipers around."

"In this weather? Maybe. I doubt it though." Barbara glanced at the sky again. "Regardless, let's hope the storm can mask our movements."

"If you ask me," Darren rolled back to his stomach and gave the camp a second look. "We should go west and use the tree line and snow for cover. We'll see what there is to see and go from there."

"That sounds like a plan."

They stood, retrieved their rifles and moved down off the ridge, heading west, keeping the hill between themselves and the camp. The grass was slick with new snow, and the wind kicked up to blow it all around in furious gusts, knocking Barbara off balance once or twice, forcing her to crouch over to lower her center of gravity.

"It seems to be going from zero to blizzard in no time!" she called up to Darren, who was leading the way with his big shoulders bowed forward. He nodded but didn't say anything, too focused on keeping his footing. At the end of the ridge, they moved south, crossing an open yard with an old flatbed trailer packed with snow-covered bales of hay. Then they stepped over a fractured section of ranch-style fence and kept moving against the intensifying gusts.

"The treeline is just over there!" Darren shouted over the wind. He turned and took off at a run, stiff-legged in his gait. Barbara followed him at a good pace, struggling to see since the visibility had dropped off so drastically. She could make things out about fifty yards along the treeline, but that's where the view ended. She caught up with Darren at the woods, and together they crept a little farther south, stepping carefully over deadfall and fallen shrubs, Barbara constantly watching eastward in case any soldiers encroached from the snow-dusted forest. Sometimes she spotted the fence through the woods, but the wind churned the powder like they were in a snow globe, making the barrier appear and vanish repeatedly as though by magic.

Brush and ice crunched under her feet, tree branches swayed and swished with the frozen hiss of winter winds and the uncut grass reached her knees, so thick that Barbara couldn't see where she was walking. She picked her way carefully, stepping gently to avoid turning her ankle on an ill-placed stone or hole.

A walk that might have taken ten minutes in normal weather was taking them a lot longer and a solid thirty minutes passed before they reached a spot in the trees they could cross. Somewhere in that time, the sky fully disappeared, a solid wall of white and gray settling on top of them like a pillow.

Darren turned to her, his eyes narrowed behind the thick plastic goggles. "I see a path through to the fences, but I can't tell if there are guards on the other side. Want to give it a try?"

She nodded. "Want me to go first?"

Darren shook his head. "I can take us through. Stay with me."

She kept right behind him as the big man barreled headlong along a deer trail, stepping over a fallen log and pushing through sticker bushes. Thorns snatched at her coat, leaving tiny tears and the cold seeped through her clothing, sapping her strength as her body shivered in response. After picking their way to the other side, they stood staring at the fence twenty yards way. The few dozen people in the holding area were gathered next to a pair of buildings or around the burn barrels, trying to stay warm.

Darren started to move. "Let's circle the fence line and find a way in."

"Wait. Can't we ask someone here?" Barbara countered. "Maybe someone here has some information."

"What if they raise the alarm?"

"They won't." She shook her head. "They're in the same boat as us. Troublemakers, like us. I doubt they'd turn us in, especially if they think we're here to help them out."

Darren looked at the shadowy groups with a doubtful eye. "Well, you were right about the storm masking our movements. Maybe you're right about the people, too. Why don't you lead us from here on in? I'll keep a lookout for guards."

Barbara nodded and stepped in front of him, squatting, running for the fence. She could barely see the people standing inside, and no one was facing in their direction, instead bundled against the cold, heads bowed, shoulders hunched, not paying attention to much around them. One woman said something to the others before turning and walking briskly south across the yard with her hands jammed into her pockets and Barbara saw an opportunity and walked along the fence line, matching her pace. When the woman had gotten far enough away from the others, Barbara tapped lightly against the fence with her palm. When she didn't turn, Barbara slapped it harder, causing the steel fabric to make crisp, jangling sounds as the snow and ice fell off.

The woman stopped and glanced to her left. Seeing no one, she turned to her right and spotted the two strangers standing at the fence line, Barbara waving frantically, swallowing a nervous lump in her throat. The wind was blowing hard and the woman stood stock-still staring, so she called out.

"Hey there! Come here... *please*."

The woman hesitated, tossing a glance over her shoulder. Seeing no guards, she strode cautiously over, stopping eight yards from the fence, her dark eyes staring from a face framed in curly, brown hair.

"Hi. My name is Barbara. I..." She couldn't think of what to say, then settled on the simplest possible explanation. "I'm looking for my son and daughter. The soldiers took them."

The suspicion in the woman's eyes broke as she heard Barbara's pleas, and she glanced over her shoulder before approaching the fence.

"They have my son, too," she said, her words coming out in a hiss. "They came for us two days ago in White Mill. Now we're waiting to be moved again."

"But your kids are here, on site?"

"Yes," the woman nodded.

"Why aren't you with them?" Barbara asked, looking around. "If you came along with them willingly, shouldn't they have allowed you to stay with your kids?"

"They're using them to keep us compliant." The woman shook her head, a cold tear streaking down her cheek, the trail starting to crystalize in the freezing temperatures. "They know we won't try to escape if they have our kids."

"Where are they?"

"In a prefab unit a little north of us, in the camp center near the headquarters. It's heavily guarded, though."

Barbara nodded. "Is there a way in?"

"Around by the busses," the woman swung her head around, motioning. "There's a way in. But I doubt you'll just stroll right through."

"I didn't plan on this being easy." Barbara gripped her rifle and raised it. "But I'm getting my kids out." She fixed the woman with a sympathetic look. "Do you want me to get yours out, too? It's the least I can do for helping us."

The woman shook her head. "No, please don't."

"What do you mean?"

"The soldiers are going to transport us south to a warmer location. At first we weren't so sure, but more people are getting on board with the idea. Sure beats freezing up here." She shrugged. "We figure we'll have it okay once we get out of here."

"And you believe the relocation will go smooth? What about when you get there? Won't it be crowded? What about resources?"

The woman nodded, but her eyes were hesitant. "They promised that if we volunteered for processing, we'd get first dibs on a new settlement."

"Did you really volunteer, though, if your kids are being used to hold you here?" The woman opened her mouth to respond, but froze, realizing the truth in Barbara's words as she continued. "Even if they did promise you the world, I can't see them being able to fulfill that promise." Barbara's sighed. "Well, we don't want to leave, but I understand why you'd want to. Can you and the others just promise you won't raise the alarm if I try to get my kids back?"

The woman nodded again. "If you promise not to get any of *ours* hurt. Just take yours and go."

"We'll be very careful. I promise. If everything goes right, we won't have to fire a single round. Hell, they won't even know we were here if things go well enough."

The woman stared at Barbara for a handful of seconds before she gave a reluctant nod of agreement. "Good luck," she said. Then she sighed, turned, and walked away into the fluttering snow.

"Can we trust her?" Darren slipped closer.

"I don't see that we have a choice. She added to your point, though."

"What's that?"

"If we start firing our weapons in there, the soldiers are going to fire back. There's a chance one of the kids could get hurt."

"We'd be fools to go in unarmed."

Barbara dismissed the notion. "No, of course we're going in armed. We just need to be sneaky about this. Pick our battles. Fight only if absolutely necessary."

"I couldn't agree more," Darren nodded. "Let's keep our profiles low and tight and imagine we're just part of the storm. Once we get inside, we'll take the path of least resistance to the kids. Hopefully,we can sneak them away."

"Let's move out."

Barbara led the way, walking south along the fence line with the trees on her right, continually glancing into the camp. All she could see were the dark forms of prefab buildings and the occasional shadow of a person striding stiffly through the storm with their heads down, hands jammed into their pockets. Not a single one looked up to see Barbara and Darren creeping in the cold, the exterior of the camp not even existing in their minds as they went about their tasks and routines. As the pair approached the southeast corner of the camp, Barbara spotted a faint light winking between snow gusts about thirty yards away. She stopped, and Darren almost ran her over before crouching down beside her.

"What is it?"

"A guardhouse, I think."

"Can we get around it?"

Barbara lowered her head. "We're going to try."

She crept ahead through the whipping wind and approached the ten-by-fifteen-foot shack. The plastic window on the near side was frosted, a soft orange glow leaking out. The building faced out from the corner toward Bristol, and there wasn't enough space between the fence and back wall to sneak behind it, so they'd have to go around the front, past the shack door.

She turned to Darren and gestured to show him what she wanted to do, and he nodded his understanding. Barbara crouch-walked to the shed, staying beneath the window as the flimsy prefab structure shook in the wind, boots shuffling across the floor inside.

Moving to the corner, she peeked around. The front door was shut tight, and a number six was stenciled on it. With a glance back at Darren, she crept past the door, hesitating when something brushed against the wood, handle jiggling like someone was coming through.

Voices spoke on the other side.

"...wait a minute... both go," someone said.

"Sure... save on heat," another replied.

Footsteps moved away from the door, and Barbara jumped past it with Darren following fast behind her. Before going around the far corner, she looked back and frowned at the footprints they'd left. She could only hope the guards didn't notice, or the snow would quickly fill them in. Moving on, they crept along the south side of the camp, the fence on their left. She glanced up at the three buses remaining in the parking lot, older in style, painted a flat blue color, puffs of snow collecting in the hubcaps and knobby tire treads.

The skies had grown darker, the storm picking up, the drab atmosphere dropping her visibility to around ten yards. Another guardhouse rose from the gloom, its single window dimmer than the previous one and she crept up and put her back to the wall, unable to resist rising and looking inside. The two guards sat huddled around a kerosene heater, its warm glow casting shadows on their faces like a pair of Halloween figures in a frozen wasteland, the pair not paying any attention to what was going on outside their shelter.

Darren tugged at her jacket sleeve and Barbara crouched and circled the small building. On the other side was a chain link passage leading farther into the camp and the pair continued along, hands tense around their rifles, expecting a guard to emerge from the darkness at any second.

Twenty-five yards in, they passed a gate on the left, likely leading to the holding area with the adults based on how far they had traveled. A keypad and security card reader kept it locked tight and, with no way to open it, she continued, creeping past more gates and security entrances, all of them shut, their contents hidden by the blustering storm.

Darren leaned closer, whispering harshly in the gusting winds. "Is the kids' building in one of those areas?"

"I hope not, because I don't know how we'd get through." She glanced up at the barbed wire. "We sure as hell can't climb them."

Barbara kept on moving until the fencing bent away to either side to wrap the enclosures on either side. Directly ahead, it was a wide-open courtyard with the prefab structures they'd seen from the hill. The woman had mentioned the children's building was on the north side of the complex, in the center near the headquarters, so she guided Darren that way. Two steps in, a voice piped over the camp intercom system, halting the pair in their tracks.

"Attention, camp personnel. Be advised, the snow flurries have been upgraded to a heavy ice storm. Remaining guards, guests, and members of staff should stay indoors to avoid exposure."

"That makes things even easier," Barbara mumbled to herself, chin tucked low, eyes up as they moved through the whipping flurries.

"What's with the 'guests' talk?" Darren whispered to her.

"Trying to make kidnapping sound more palatable to everyone involved, maybe? I don't know."

The gun had long since grown cold in her hands, the chill bleeding through her thick gloves, icy gusts still cutting through her hood and down her neck. The chill seeped in, but her heart hammered, keeping her from noticing the cold as adrenaline continued to surge through her body every few minutes. A blast of wind hit her from behind, causing her to stumble forward, though she maintained her balance and kept moving, and when Barbara looked up again, a guard house stood ten yards away with a number four written on it.

Without warning, the door flew open, and a soldier stepped outside, leaning into the wind, striding ahead as the door slammed shut behind him. He lit a cigarette, stopped, shrugged his shoulders, and took a long draw, then he raised his eyes and gaped when he saw the two rifles pointed at him.

"Keep your mouth shut and drop your weapons," Barbara hissed.

The cigarette fell from his lips and his rifle slipped from his shoulder and hit the pavement. Darren approached the soldier, grabbing his rifle and relieving him of his sidearm, then he pulled a roll of duct tape from his jacket and bound the man's hands behind him.

"Get around to the side," Barbara commanded, jerking her gun the direction she wanted the man to move. After they stepped around the shack's side, she pointed her weapon at the ground. "Sit."

"Are you serious, lady?" The man's initial confusion was being replaced by incredulity, a situation Barbara quickly rectified by jamming her rifle into his side.

"Your people came to my house and kidnapped my kids." Barbara felt herself snarling at the soldier, holding nothing back. "What do *you* think?"

The man's expression dropped, as did his rear in the snow, and Darren bound his ankles so there was no chance he could stand back up.

"How many more are inside the shack?" she asked him.

"Just one."

"Keep quiet, and no one will get hurt. You have my word on that."

"Best make sure that happens ourselves," Darren said, tearing off a strip of duct tape and sealing up the man's mouth. Muzzled, the man only blinked up at them with swirling snowflakes bouncing off his cheeks, eyes burning with fear and frustration in light of Barbara's anger. With a nod to Darren, Barbara left the man sitting on the cold ground and circled to the guardhouse entrance where she grabbed the door handle and waited for Darren to get into position. Darren raised his rifle and nodded, then she ripped the door open, and Darren pushed his way in, shouting in an authoritative tone, his voice masked by the ferocious winds outside.

"Drop your weapons and get your hands up!"

It turned out that the remaining guard was in the same position as the other they'd seen, sitting in a chair in front of a heater with his hands up to warm them, face close to the heat. He wasn't prepared for the big, blustering sixty-something man charging in on him and they soon had the new guard trussed up and soon dragged the first one inside as well, ripping the tape off of his mouth in a quick motion.

Once they had both men sitting harmlessly against the wall, Barbara rounded on them, moving her rifle barrel back and forth as if deciding which would get her wrath.

"Where are they keeping the kids?" she asked.

The guards exchanged glances, both clamping their mouths shut tight.

"I guess you didn't hear me," Barbara's sneer came naturally as she leveled the weapon at the soldier she thought might be more apt to spill the information. "Where. Are you keeping. The children?"

The man stared at the end of the rifle, blinking at the cold steel. He swallowed. "Why do you want to know?"

"I'm going to get my kids and take them out of here, that's why."

The soldier jerked his chin. "They're in the building behind this one."

"Are there any guards in it?"

"*We* were the guards."

The second guard glared at the first. "Tilly, you're not putting up much of a fight."

"I hated us taking kids to begin with," Tilly said with a glance up at Barbara. "It's wrong, and it's not worth getting shot over." He shifted his eyes to Barbara. "Key is on the desk."

She turned and checked a small desk against the wall, grabbing a pair of silver keys strung together on a thin ring, tossing them up triumphantly then snatching them out of mid-air.

"Thanks, Tilly," she said. "What about the adults?"

"Lieutenant Briggs has the door code."

"What building?"

"Come on, lady," Tilly fixed her with a hard look. "Giving you that key was bad enough. If you want the lieutenant, you'll have to find her yourself."

Anger did not come easily to Barbara, and neither did intimidation. Even when faced with invaders in her own home, it had taken a conscious, willful effort for her to draw herself up and face them head-on. Since her children had been taken away, kicking and screaming, though, Barbara's only struggle was how to keep from going *too* hard and *too* fast. Anger came unbidden, her built-up frustrations an ever-erupting volcano with no end in sight.

Barbara watched the soldier for a long moment, then slowly smiled, raised the rifle and placed the barrel against his forehead. "I already shot one of your buddies when they took my kids." Her voice was calm, almost passive, though her eyes blazed with the fury of hellfire. "You'll tell us where the lieutenant is, right now, or you'll die where you sit."

The soldier's eyes went wide and his jaw went slack, stumbling over the words as he realized that the woman in front of him was incredibly, deadly serious. "Y-you're the crazy lady! From Wyndale!"

Barbara nodded, unwavering. "Sounds like me."

The man sucked in a breath and nodded, the rifle bouncing slightly in Barbara's grip. "Lieutenant Briggs is in the headquarters north of here. Biggest building on site. It has a satellite dish on top. You can't miss it."

Pam nodded. "How many are in there?"

"The lieutenant and two guards."

Barbara removed the gun from his forehead and gave a broad, almost deranged smile. "Thanks, again, Tilly. Darren, make sure they don't make any noise."

After Darren had taped over both of the men's mouths, the pair left the guard house and made a beeline for a large dormitory-style structure just north and a little east of the guard shack. She used the silver key to unlock the door and quietly slid it open, stepping into a short foyer with a dozen pairs of small shoes sitting on the floor on her left. A soft light glowed from the next room over, distorted through a set of plastic flaps. Stomach swirling with nervousness, she pressed through the flimsy plastic and looked in on a small dormitory with cots lining both walls. A dim light hung in the center of the room, casting a ring of luminance that barely reached the foot of the beds, tiny, huddled lumps beneath the covers.

"Linda? Jack?" Barbara whispered in the shadows.

"Mom!" Her daughter's unmistakable voice called from her right as sheets flew up and both her children sprung from a single cot. Barbara lowered her rifle and knelt in time to catch them as they slammed into her, grabbing her in enthusiastic hugs. Tears burst from her eyes, she used her free arm to squeeze them back, nuzzling them, smelling the familiar scent of their clothes, and the faint scent of home.

"Barbara..." Darren's warning tone jerked her back to reality as a woman in civilian clothing strode down the center of the room between the rows of beds. She let her kids go and rose, flipping her rifle up and resting the stock on her hip. The woman stopped, face draining of blood when she saw the gun pointed at her chest.

"Who are you?" Barbara snapped.

"I was just--"

"It's okay, Mom." Linda stepped between them with her hands up and Barbara dropped the barrel of her rifle in response, shifting positions. "It's just Ruth. She was looking after us."

"I was just reading her a book." Ruth gestured behind her to a cot where a girl sat up with the covers tossed aside. A picture book lay on the bed next to her, flipped open to the middle.

"Okay." Barbara nodded. She turned back to Linda and Jack. "Guys, get your shoes on. We're taking you home."

"Can you find my mom?" one little girl asked. She'd gotten out of bed and stood there in a denim dress and black leggings, a look of desperation on her face. "I haven't seen her in three days. Please, they won't let me see her."

"Mine, too," pleaded a little boy. "I want my mom and dad. They put them somewhere, and I don't know if they're okay."

"And mine," voiced a pair of sisters.

Barbara glanced around at the sad, frightened faces, all of whom had no clue if their parents were alive or dead, all to keep everyone in line and cooperative. The cruelty of it caused her skin to itch madly beneath her coat, a slow rage building in her gut. She shared a look with Darren before turning back to the kids.

"Your parents are okay, kids. But they're in another part of the camp. Everything is going to be fine."

"Thank you so much," one of the sisters said. "Please, if you find them, tell them where we are."

Lips drawn tight, Barbara turned to face the childrens' guardian, Ruth. The woman was plain looking, her brown hair cut in a bob, wearing jeans and a T-shirt with long underwear covering her arms.

"We're going to find the lieutenant and get their security card," Barbara told her. "Then we're going to free the parents. Do you have a problem with that?"

"Fine by me." Ruth held up her hands in deference. "But you do know some of them don't want to be set free, right?"

"I'll give them the chance to make that decision," Barbara said. "Don't raise any alarms, Ruth. If you do, we'll be back." She shifted her gaze to Darren and then at Linda and Jack. "Stay here, kids. We'll be right back."

"No, Mom!" the boy shouted, throwing himself at her, grabbing her around the waist. "I want to go *with* you."

To her credit, Linda stepped back and put her hand on her brother's shoulders, pulling him away even as tears glassed her eyes. Barbara knelt in front of her son and fixed him with a sincere look.

"I know we just got here, buddy, but we need to just go see to these kids' parents. It wouldn't be right to just leave without setting them free." She looked up over Jack's head, staring down Ruth. "And you'll be safer here than with us, just for a little while longer." Jack sniffled, clinging to her. "I promise we'll be right back, okay? We just need to go open a door for the other parents, then we'll get out of here, okay?"

Jack's blinked at her, his eyes fearful, nose running from crying and Barbara quickly wiped his nose with the sleeve of her jacket and fixed him with a hopeful expression.

"I *promise*, Jack. Okay? Can you and Linda hold down the fort for a minute longer?"

He blinked again, then reluctantly nodded.

"Thanks, Jack." Barbara kissed him on the top of his head and left him with his sister, then she and Darren exited through the plastic flaps and stood by the door as wind whistled softly through the cracks. Darren looked sidelong at her, his face red from the combination of cold and heat.

"This is going to be dangerous. You've got the kids. Why don't we just go?"

"Because once they realize what we've done, they'll come looking for us." Barbara shook her head. "That's why we need to let them all go. If a few other parents decide to escape, it'll make for a good distraction."

"At least until those two guards spill their guts about the crazy lady from Wyndale."

Barbara shrugged. "I'm kinda making this up as I go along. Never said it was a perfect plan."

Darren took a deep breath and released it in a long sigh. "Okay." He reached for the door, but Barbara grabbed his arm, holding him back.

"Plus, they can't just take families from their parents." She thought about the children back in the holding area. "It's the US military we're talking about here, for heaven's sake. We're supposed to be able to trust them. And when we can't trust them anymore, they become our enemies, and we have to do whatever's required to protect our own. Right?"

"I'm with you, Barbara. It's more than a good enough reason for me." With a firm nod, Darren jerked open the door and allowed in the screaming wind. They stepped back out into the cold, trudging their way toward the large cluster of buildings in the middle of camp, Barbara identifying the headquarters by its wider profile and dish on top, just like they'd seen from the hill. Dim lights hung from the eaves of nearby sheds, spilling light onto the snow swept pathways between the buildings. Almost everything else was dark except for a pair of guardhouses at the edge of their vision. She watched the main structure for a moment before creeping to the window on the left and, once there, she leaned in and peeked through the corner of the glass.

The frosted surface made it difficult to see, but she spotted a woman sitting at a desk in the back of the room, her face illuminated by a laptop terminal. Barbara craned her neck until it hurt, trying to locate the others she'd been told about and was just about to give up when someone stood in the near corner and walked right past her. Gasping, she jerked back, chest panting as she waited for them to rush outside, but no alarms were raised, the only noise the wind as it continued whistling between the buildings.

She glanced at Darren and raised two fingers before lifting her eyebrow in question regarding the third. They crossed to the other window, and Darren peeked in and searched for the last person. After a good thirty seconds of hunting, he crouched back down out of sight.

"I found him," he whispered over the wind. "He's in the back, lying on a cot. I think he's sleeping."

"So, we rush in like we did before," Barbara says. "Take them by surprise and disarm them before they can respond."

Darren grimaced. "I don't think we're going to get so lucky again. We might need another plan."

"What did you have in mind?"

He reached into his coat and removed a radio from his jacket. "I got this off Tilly."

Barbara grinned. "Okay. I'm up for a bit of legerdemain."

"Come on." Darren pulled her away from the headquarters to a shed where the shadows and snow hid them, then lifted the radio to his lips and pressed the talk button, shouting into the wind. "Lieutenant Briggs, this is Tilly. Over."

There was a pause before the officer responded. "I read you, Tilly. Sounds like you're outside. Why?"

"We need some help by the kids' dorm."

"What's the problem?"

"Front door got blown in," Darren winked at Barbara. "Need some tools to secure it. Kids are in here freezing."

There was another pause before the reply came. "I'll send Jenkins over. Hang tight."

Darren put the radio away, and he and Barbara backed around the corner, hanging back in the shadows along the side of the shed. They watched as, minutes later, a heavily bundled soldier pushed open the headquarter's door, shut it behind him, and jogged toward them with a large pack under his arms. When Jenkins reached the storage shed, Barbara stepped out in front of him, halting the man in his tracks. The soldier started to open his mouth and reach for his sidearm, then closed his eyes, grumbling a curse as Darren's rifle pressed against his back. They forced the man to the shack with the others, trussed up and immobile, out of the storm's wrath and incapable of sounding an alarm.

"Now we're down to two," Darren said as they jogged back to the headquarters. "And we have to move now before the lieutenant become suspicious."

"If we do it now, she'll think it's Jenkins returning," Barbara smirked. "Should give us the element of surprise."

Darren put his hand on the doorknob and waited for her word.

"I'll cover the sleeper," she whispered breathlessly, heart hammering blood through her veins, the point of no return upon them. "You come in after me and keep the lieutenant from doing something stupid."

Darren nodded, and on a slow count of three, turned the knob and pulled open the door. Barbara rushed in with the breath of wind, leading with her weapon, eyes flitting past the lieutenant and resting on the guard on his cot, the man shooting bolt straight, hair tousled, a confused look on his face.

"Freeze!" Barbara yelled, and the man jerked his hands in the air at the first sight of her weapon.

"*Hold* it right there, lieutenant," Darren growled as he filed in behind her. "Put the weapon down."

Barbara glanced over to see Lieutenant Briggs had a pistol half drawn. The woman was slightly mousy, with brown hair and a straight, firm expression.

"Put it on the table in front of you and step away."

The woman removed the weapon the rest of the way from its holster and slowly placed it on the desk and, with a scowl, she rolled her chair back to the wall. Darren stalked forward, grabbed the pistol off the desk, and jammed it beneath his belt, then backed up to the door, closing it behind them.

"Restrain this one," Barbara said, forcing the freshly woken officer to stay where he was while Darren slid over and trussed him with duct tape. They then moved to the lieutenant and did her the same way, wrists and ankles taped tight, forgoing the pieces over their mouths for the time being.

"Who the hell are you people?" Briggs scowled, shifting in her chair, eyes expression dark as she stared at the pair.

"Nobody you want to know," Barbara replied.

"You'll go down hard for this," she snarled. "Command won't have mercy on people who raid military encampments."

"What are you going to do, take our kids from us or something?" Barbara snapped back, rewarded by the sight of Briggs averting her eyes, her expression sinking with guilt.

"You're damned lucky I don't put a bullet in your head, in all of your heads, for what you did to my family." Barbara had managed to keep her anger pushed down while they were traversing the camp, but faced with the de facto leader, it proved too much for her, rising through her gullet like fire. She leveled her rifle at the lieutenant's face, the woman's rosy features turning pale as Barbara continued. "And before you even think of using the excuse that you were just 'following orders' I suggest you don't, otherwise your friend over there's going to be cleaning your brain matter off the walls."

The lieutenant audibly gulped, all pretense of holding firm in the face of danger gone. "Now," Barbara said, taking a step back and lowering her rifle, "I'm going to take my children, reunite any parents with their children who want to leave, and we're going to take off. Come after us again and you will suffer the consequences. You get me?"

The lieutenant nodded slowly, and Barbara and Darren pulled two cots together and made the pair sit back-to-back off on the side of the room. They turned to searching the room for the security card next, and it only took Barbara a moment to find it on the desk next to the computer, and she tossed it to Darren. She popped open drawers on the desk until she found one with several sets of similar GMC keys, plucking them out and sliding them over the desk.

"Can you go let everyone out?" she asked him, lowering her voice so only he could hear. "Tell them they're free to go, and they can use these bus keys. Tell them to scatter far and wide and to go north if they have a place to go if they want the best chance of avoiding more military involvement. Those who want to stay are welcome to. And bring my kids on your way back. Take care of them, please."

"Got it," Darren said, grinning at her. "No sweat." With one final look over at the tied-up pair, he snatched the keys off the desk and left the control center, throwing the door shut behind him.

With Barbara left alone with the pair, the lieutenant plucked up some courage, speaking with a voice that only partially cracked with fear.

"You'll never get away with this. You know that, right?"

"Shut up."

"If you give up right now, I promise I won't mistreat you. You can go with the rest of the refu—"

"Are you *trying* to get me to pistol whip you with your own service weapon? Giving in to people who kidnap children as a manipulation tactic isn't something I'll ever do. So shut your mouth before I wrap your face in duct tape."

She'd been leaning on the desk, but she backed away, waiting as the adrenaline rush faded, the lieutenant glowering at her, but remaining blessedly quiet. They'd already spent two hours or more on the mission, and the cold and exhaustion were wearing her down. With shallow breaths, she backed up and sat in Briggs's rolling chair, easing back and resting her shoulders, trying to shake off the tension. Looking down at the floor, she released a soft sigh and let her eyes fall half shut.

A flicker on the computer screen on the desk caught her attention, and she turned to read it, her jaw falling open as she saw an image of Tom on the display, his dark eyes staring back at her from some outdoor location with military tents all around. He wasn't smiling, and looked as though he was in a camp of some sort.

"What the hell…." She whispered to herself as she turned in the office chair and scooted closer to the screen, following the familiar lines of her husband's face, his dark brown eyes and rugged good looks. It *was* Tom, but the man in the picture seemed somehow older than she remembered, a thick growth of beard lining his jaws, his hair more ragged than she recalled.

A caption beneath the image read, "Wanted: Tom McKnight. Please contact Lieutenant Colonel Richard Banks at United States Central Command if you encounter this man."

Barbara backed away from the screen, shaking her head faintly in bewilderment. She could only stare at the image, wondering what he could have possibly done wrong be on the military's *Most Wanted* list. She bent over, leaned in and began clicking on his image and other parts of the screen for more information. When nothing came up, she circled the desk and came around to face the lieutenant.

"So, I was looking at the man on the screen. Tom McKnight."

The woman looked up. "What about him?"

"I didn't realize the military had a Most Wanted list." Barbara narrowed her eyes. "Why's he on it?"

"Why? Do you know him?" Briggs smiled coyly, eagerness in her voice.

"No." She shook her head. "I just figured the military would have better things to do right now than hunt fugitives and take kids from their families."

The lieutenant's jaw clenched, and she stared down Barbara, growing defiant again. "Resources are stretched thin, so we don't have time for policing. That's why we only go after the worst offenders. You know, the people they really need to bring in."

"Worst offenders?" Barbara murmured to herself, then raised her voice. "What do you do with them when you catch them?"

Briggs snorted. "I'm not telling you jack shit. But I will say that if you don't let us go and turn yourself in, you'll find yourself on that list as well."

"You can't possibly scare me more than you already have, so don't bother trying." Barbara stabbed a finger at Briggs. "You raided my house and took my children away. The last people who tried something like that are buried in shallow graves on the back forty." Barbara's voice rose with righteous fury, unshaking, and she spat on the floor. "Pray you don't join them, Briggs. We're done talking."

There came a knock on the door just before it flew open, Darren barging in with a grin on his face and the kids bustling in behind him, bundled up, hopeful looks in their eyes, Linda shutting the door behind them and cutting off the wind.

"Kids!" Barbara went to them, turning them away from the bound soldiers and pushing them to the other side of the room, embracing them yet again. She hadn't fully comprehended how much willpower it had taken to leave them while they assaulted the main building, and a flood of emotions surged through her body as she held the pair tight.

"I unlocked the gates," Darren said. "Everyone's free."

"Good work," she said with the flash of a smile, slowly releasing the pair.

"Over half tried to leave in one of the busses, but they couldn't see five feet in front of them. The storm's too heavy. They're going to wait until the weather clears before they go anywhere, and I suggest we do the same."

Barbara stared at him for a moment and glanced at the window where snow was blasting against the glass.

"Darren, I don't want to stay here—"

"I wouldn't suggest it if it wasn't absolutely necessary, Barbara. You know me better than that. The storm's kicked up quite a bit in the last thirty minutes." He glanced out the window, the wind howling across the squat structure, shaking the dish on top. "We get in that Jeep, we'll end up stuck somewhere on the road, or in a ditch, even with the 4-wheel drive. That happens and we're as good as dead."

Barbara's teeth ground together in frustration as she tried to figure out an alternative, but she finally gave up and sighed. "You're right. I don't like it, but you're right. Getting stuck out there is worse than staying with the garbage in here. Let's get settled in and wait out the storm."

Being the biggest building on site, the headquarters had a long storeroom in back and they found a pair of cots inside and forced the officers to relocate, dragging them across the floor, then redoubling their bonds, including taping over their mouths. Darren did his best to make them as comfortable as possible without giving them an iota of a chance to break free. As he worked, Barbara watched, and in the back of her mind, Barbara knew they'd most definitely be on the military's Most Wanted list, just like Tom. Not that it really mattered, especially since Tom was apparently on there for some unknown reason. But hopefully the military would be stretched too far to want to venture north again as the weather continued to worsen, and they'd be left alone.

With a long night ahead of them, Barbara got the kids situated on the cots in the main room, covering them to their chins with scavenged military coats and blankets. She knelt beside them on Jack's side, holding their hands, smiling as she sat and watched them, the simple act more meaningful than it had been since they were much, much younger.

"I'm so glad you came to get us," Linda whispered as she gripped her blanket, pulling it tight to her chin. Her eyes were glassy with emotion, and her smile quickly turned into a troubled frown. "But they took my gun. Can I get it back?"

"Don't worry about it." Barbara smirked. We have more at home, right?"

"Yeah, but I liked mine."

Barbara smoothed her daughter's hair back. "I know you did. We'll find you one just as good."

Darren was standing at the window, looking outside. "Boy, it's storming terrible out there. I hope Marie is okay."

"She's tough as nails, Darren. She's completely fine and you know it."

"You're right. I shouldn't be worried." He smiled and then chuckled. "If anything, she's back there getting some good rest, hobbling around the kitchen, cooking up a big meal for when we return." Darren turned away from the window and leaned against the wall. "Actually, she's probably worried sick."

"I'd say that's closer to the mark," Barbara agreed. She imagined the woman lying on the couch in the living room, staring at the ceiling as she wondered what had happened to her husband and friend.

"Thank you, by the way," Barbara said, still sitting and holding Jack and Linda's hands.

"For what?"

Barbara stood up and gave Darren a rough, hard embrace before pulling back, eyes welling. "For risking all that you have to help get my babies back. Thank you… it means everything."

"*They* mean everything," Darren smiled, then turned back to the window, staring out at the storm, keeping watch on both the weather and any potential intruders that might try sneaking up on them.

Satisfied they had nothing else to do for the time being, Barbara found some snacks and military rations in a locker and handed them out to everyone, then she tried getting the kids to settle down. They were too fitful and agitated to fall asleep right away, so they whispered things in a darkened corner of the room while she met Darren at the window. With a glance at the kids, she lowered her voice, standing close enough to him so no one else could hear.

"I found something else out."

His gaze didn't leave the window. "What do you mean, something else?"

"I found Tom's picture on Briggs's laptop."

"You *what*?" Darren glanced at the computer like it was cursed.

"Yeah, it says he's on some kind of wanted list, but I couldn't find more of an explanation."

Darren scratched his head, turning toward her. "What could Tom have possibly done to get on a list like that? How do they even know where he is?"

"I don't know. I asked the lieutenant while you were freeing everyone, but she didn't know either." Barbara bit her lip, giving a worried chuckle. "Don't get me wrong. Seeing Tom's face was great, but I didn't expect it to be on a military wanted list."

"Tell me about it." Darren stiffened with a grunt, eyes wide with some new revelation. "Hey, do you think it has something to do with that mission to the North Atlantic he was working on? You told me they put him and Sam on a ship out in the ocean. Some job for the Navy or something?"

"Could be," Barbara glanced at the laptop. "Whatever it is, I'm worried for Tom. I'm worried…" Her words left an emptiness in her heart, a new crevice that slowly filled with dread.

"Don't worry, Barbara," he said, catching her expression. "He'll be fine. They've clearly not found him yet, so there's no reason to believe something's happened to him. Hey, maybe that's why he hasn't come home. Maybe he doesn't want them to follow him back to your place."

Barbara shook her head, perplexed. "I just can't imagine what he could have done."

Darren nodded and gestured at the storm. "As soon as it's safe, we'll go out and get back to the Jeep." He settled his shoulder against the wall, eyes locked on the cold, frosted pane. "Why don't you get a little rest? Lay down with the kids. I'm too anxious to sleep."

"You and me both." Barbara bit her lip, glancing at the laptop. "I'll see if there's anything else I can find out about Tom."

With the howling wind outside and multiple soldiers tied up in the two buildings, she returned to the laptop and sat in the lieutenant's chair, clicking randomly on different parts of the screen. She broke off of Tom's face and found more screens with smaller pictures of people on the Army's wanted list, not recognizing any of them, then clicked on other windows which popped up orders, maps, inventory sheets, personnel files, and logistics forms. After a while, Barbara picked up a bottled water and drank as she browsed, not looking at anything in particular, and not understanding most of it – until she caught sight of Tom's name on project personnel list.

"What the heck is this?"

She clicked on it and a new window popped up containing information for an initiative called *Operation Riptide*. As she scanned the mission objective, a thin layer of sweat broke out on her forehead and she began to feel like she was overheating. Near the end, as she saw what they wanted to do with the anomaly and – more importantly – with Tom, she put a hand to her mouth, sitting back in her chair in horror.

"Oh, no. This is... insane. It'll never work. It *can't*."

Distracted from his sentry duty by her talking, Darren walked over from the window, looking at her with concern. "What is it, Barbara?"

She shook her head slowly, remembering the radio broadcast weeks ago, when she'd been in the truck with the kids, listening as a reporter went down with one of the ships. The anomaly had blasted the ocean surface with a barrage of deep sea debris, destroying an entire fleet like they were kids' toys, and she'd worried for a while that Tom might have been on one, sinking to the bottom of the ocean with her daughter.

"I know what they're trying to do." She looked up at Darren, her face stretched tight with fear. "I know what they want Tom for."

Chapter 12
Specialist Lance Morales
Reynosa, Mexico

The spearhead of the convoy pushed across the bridge into Reynosa in a rush of diesel noise and heavy armor. Apache helicopters thrummed as they darted over the Rio Grande River, providing cover, guns searching the shoreline for any lurking enemy forces. Troops stood in Humvee turrets, gripping their weapon handles, preparing to shoot at the first signs of opposition. Smoke drifted upward from dozens of points in the Mexican city, its clusters of buildings so tightly pressed together that fires caught easily and spread quickly.

An explosion went off somewhere, echoing over the river. Helicopter rotors and machine guns rattled off in the distance as airborne strike units hit clusters of Mexican troops in the city. The sky loomed dark and foreboding, the air bristling with violence and the anticipation of bloodshed.

As part of a fast-attack squad, Morales drove point in an up-armored Mine-Resistant Ambush Protected ATV with an M2 heavy machine gun mounted on its roof. His stomach turned with nervous tension as they crossed the bridge over the Rio Grande, anxiously scanned the opposite shore. A glance in his side mirrors showed the rest of the train coming close behind, almost pushing him across.

"Keep your eyes open," he shouted up to the man in the turret. "I don't want to get ambushed on my first assignment off base."

"I've got your back." Lieutenant Ray Smith grinned down at him. "Just keep rolling steady. Remember your training."

Morales took a deep breath. They were both newbies, assigned to their first combat mission. He'd never imagined being in the military; he didn't figure he had the skill for it. But once the recruiter saw he could drive, they'd trained him and made him a specialist right away. After just two weeks, he'd gained elite status with the MRAP and its *plasan* composite armor, flat-free tires, and turbo diesel engine.

"Once we cross, angle left!" Smith called from above in a cloud of cold dust. "Move two blocks and wait."

Morales nodded and kept driving.

The Army only expected light resistance after days of air strikes had purportedly cleared the area, and the commanders wanted boots on the ground and Reynosa secured within the day. As if to emphasize the point, a pair of jets zipped overhead in a sudden whoosh of air that quickly faded as the military trucks rumbled off the bridge and into the streets of Mexico.

Morales recalled the briefing map in his head and took the left-hand turn as Smith had directed, driving through the border crossing checkpoint and crashing over a thin fence to land on Periférico Luis Echeverría Street. Their squad of twenty-five soldiers were to spearhead a southeast incursion into the city, running recon and clearing any remaining forces ahead of the command units. Aside from the MRAP, they had two Humvees and a Stryker APC bringing up the rear.

After speeding past graffiti-covered brick walls and colorful warehouse buildings, they stopped two hundred yards down the road, waiting for the rest of his unit to settle in behind him. He glanced in his side mirrors to see other fast-attack squads dispersing into the city in various directions, on assignments just like his.

"You boys ready?" Morales asked the four Army grunts waiting nervously in back seat. They didn't look ready, but they nodded all the same.

"We got this, guys," he assured them.

"Okay, Captain says to keep going," Smith called down.

Morales hit the accelerator and trundled along the main thoroughfare. The Rio Grande River flowed by on his left, and the city of Reynosa squatted in ominous shadows on his right. They passed apartments and rental buildings, one of them on fire in a blaze of smoke, though he tried to keep from focusing in on any one particular object for too long, splitting his focus between driving and scanning over every shadow and alleyway for signs of life, though none could be found.

"This place is abandoned." Morales focused back on the road, swerving to avoid a spill of bricks that had blown off a building.

"Captain says they probably got everyone out ahead of our assault," Smith responded. "Shouldn't be anyone home but stay alert just the same."

Morales slowly nodded as he cruised at a steady speed, the diesel rumbling beneath him as he stopped and started the big truck in fits, moving around abandoned cars, garbage, and debris and pushing them aside when there wasn't enough space to go around.

First contact with a Mexican military vehicle occurred at the corner of Periférico Luis Echeverría Street and Calle Guerrero. The side armor had been ripped to shreds, its inside still burning after a missile strike. Morales caught sight of a body within the flames, charred and blackened in the driver's seat.

"Holy smokes," he said, gulping. "No pun intended."

Smith heard him, and gave a dark chuckle from up the Humvee's turret as Morales kept driving, circling the city's eastern side until reaching Portes Gil Street. Turning, facing more west, Morales faced the true destruction caused by the air strikes. Entire buildings had been shaved off, stucco, plaster, and framing smashed down like someone had taken a giant knife and skimmed off the top sections of town. A fine layer of haze blanketed the streets, the dust whipping through the vents like the filters weren't even present, his throat beginning to itch in response.

"Should we put on our masks?"

"Not yet," Smith said. "Let's cross the viaduct first and disperse our guys. Take a left here."

"Got it."

Morales whipped the wheel left and cruised toward a viaduct that separated them from the city proper. A Mexican military vehicle and a pickup truck blocked the road ahead, both minced to pieces by an air strike, their original make and model indiscernible.

Specialist Morales angled his MRAP right at them and hit the gas. "Brace yourselves," he shouted before he slammed the trucks aside in a crash of smoldering plate armor and parts, making a large enough gap for the others to get through. As they trundled across the bridge, Morales noted divots in the pavement made by high-caliber gun rounds that cut a path along the asphalt to another sawed-up Mexican military vehicle. A scorched body lay in the road, mangled by flying lead, and Morales shuddered as he drove by, imagining being on the receiving end of the onslaught.

With a glance in his side mirrors to make sure the others were following, he took a left on Calle Tiburcia Street and drove parallel to the aqueduct. Two miles down, Lieutenant Smith called for a stop and Morales slowed the MRAP in a high squeal of brakes, sitting idle at a 3-way intersection. The rest of his unit halted behind him, and Smith exchanged a few words with the other leaders through his earpiece microphone while Morales kept an eye on the buildings ahead. Garza Zamora Street continued southeast while the other two streets pointed deeper into the city. At their location, Reynosa looked more rundown, with graffiti slung across the brick walls and an old radio tower sitting on the corner, half leaning from a direct hit.

"All right, guys," Smith lowered himself from the turret and stared at the soldiers in back. "Remember, the captain doesn't want any civilians hurt. No civilian casualties. Got it? Great. Now, everyone out. Disperse!"

The four troops inside the MRAP climbed out and joined the other members of the strike team, leaving just Morales and Smith in the truck to watch them assemble around the last two vehicles and fall into a loose tagalong formation.

"Okay, take Toltec," the gunner growled as he climbed back into the turret, putting his hands on the firing handles "We want to move quick, but not too quick, okay? You've got soldiers on foot now."

"Got it."

Morales turned the vehicle right and cruised slowly down the street, the big MaxxPro D9.3I6 diesel engine rumbling beneath his feet, returning to his habit of scanning the streets. Two blocks down, one of the soldiers behind them shouted and pointed.

"Stop," Smith said, then cocked his head as he listened. "They're going to check out that apartment building."

Morales did as he was told, sitting in place high above the road. A small team of soldiers jogged toward a tan house with dark trim, disappearing behind some untrimmed trees that ran along the side. He turned up his own radio earpiece to hear their communication.

"Downstairs is clear," a soldier said.

"Let's move upstairs," the captain replied amidst boot scuffling and bumps. "Keep those lines clean. I want this by the book, guys."

Soldiers grunted positively in response, followed by the usual professional radio chatter as they moved to the second floor and cleared it. When they found no civilians or enemy fighters inside, they quickly left the building and rejoined the armored vehicles.

"Sorry." A soldier spoke with a clipped tone. "I thought I saw someone inside. Must just be the jitters."

"No problem," their captain, Captain Jones, replied over the comm line. "Morales, go."

"Where we headed, captain?"

"We're meeting up with Units 4 and 7. Just keep it moving soldier."

He realized he'd been gripping the steering wheel tight, and he purposefully relaxed his hands and eased the MRAP forward. The column crept slower than before as they moved through the denser parts of the city. They passed parked cars and motorcycles, some of which had been left in the middle of the road as obvious roadblocks and choke points. Morales expertly shoved the MRAP through, spreading the wreckage as much as he could. Sometimes, he backed up and made a second pass just to make the passage bigger.

"You're moving like a turtle, Morales," the captain growled. "We're running late."

"Just making sure you don't get any surprises, sir."

"Don't worry about us. Speed it up."

"Yes sir."

Morales pushed them faster, navigating the streets at Smith's direction, covering blocks in minutes, the troops behind him jogging to keep up. Sweat poured down his face as he stared at each new block as an opportunity to be ambushed, the landscape as alien to him as the moon. The streets grew even more quiet, wafts of smoke drifting across his vision as apartments closed in on both sides. Most of the stores appeared gutted with glass shattered everywhere, garbage littering the sidewalks. A pair of helicopters buzzed by right above them, Morales jumping as the chuffing rotors blew the smokey haze into their windshield.

He muted his helmet mic. "Jeez. I wish they wouldn't buzz us like that," he grumbled.

"Yeah, its eerie enough already," Smith whispered back. "Don't need those choppers blowing by us like that."

"A friggin' ghost town," Morales agreed as he approached another roadblock. A pair of tow trucks were parked fender-to-fender across the road, big enough to haul eighteen-wheelers and other large vehicles. Framing the trucks were concrete barriers someone had dragged sideways, making a shockingly resilient-appearing blockage.

"Hold on, Captain," Morales spoke into his helmet mic. "I've got some big stuff to move."

"You've got one minute, soldier. We're halfway to there. Don't make us late."

He nudged the front right fender of his MRAP against the tow truck, shoving it partially aside, then backed up to take a swipe at the other one. As he worked, he noticed the tow truck boom had caught on something, tracing the truck's hook and chain where it was snagged on a barrier. He gave the MRAP a little more gas, but the chain only wrapped around his grill, making it impossible to separate the truck from the concrete, and if he kept going, he'd drag the whole thing with him down the road.

"I think they bolted the hook to the concrete barrier," Morales said.

"Just punch it." The captain sounded frustrated again. "Punch it and plow through, Morales. That's an order."

"Roger that." With a shrug, he smashed the gas, giving the big diesel something to growl about and they lurched forward. Smashing the tow truck aside, snapping the chain in two, a metallic ricochet echoed out that swiftly turned into an ear-splitting retort as an explosion lifted the MRAP's left front tire off the road, rocking him sideways in his seat, his window blowing inward in a shower of tempered glass. As soon as the tires hit the ground, Morales punched the gas pedal and flew through the obstruction, rocketing ahead until they were fifty yards clear before he skidded to a stop, listening as his dashboard warning alarms bleated incessantly. Above, he heard a groan from Smith and shouted up.

"You okay, man?!"

"Yeah!" The turret swiveled as small arms fire peppered the armored vehicle. Morales ducked instinctively, reaching for his rifle as Smith fired the Browning M2 at something off to their left.

"You assholes are going to pay for that!" the gunner screamed as he rattled off consecutive bursts from the big weapon, the belt-fed machine spitting rounds with an intense burring sound that vibrated the hairs in Morales's ears. The Humvee and Stryker guns went off as well, firing at the same time, sweeping their surroundings with a hail of bullets.

"Can you move, Morales?" the captain shouted in his ear, though he only heard it on the right side. Warnings still blared, and every alarm light was blinking like it was disco night.

"I've got damage to all my systems," he said, quickly checking his gauges, noticing a faraway quality to his voice in his right ear and a complete lack of sound in his left.

"Can you move, though?" the captain shouted over his headset.

"Yes."

"Then do it!"

"Yes, sir!"

Morales punched the gas and shot them forward as a mortar exploded right where they'd been sitting. He checked his side mirror to see the other vehicles weave through the smoke and debris, soldiers running alongside them or hanging off the sides, using the armor as protection. Tracers from their guns lit up the air, the heavy rounds making short work of the shabby structures. Houses toppled, spilling into yards, windows shattering, a cloud of smoke shooting into the air all down the street.

"Watch out!" Smith shouted.

Morales glanced off to the right as they smashed through another cement barrier, rolling over it and dragging a piece for ten yards before it finally fell away.

"Heads up, Captain," the driver said. "Left you some garbage."

"Just keep driving!"

Morales focused on keeping a steady speed, hoping the soldiers had gotten aboard the Humvees and Stryker before he sped away. Gunfire popped against his armor and beneath him the machinery was grinding below the MRAP's left side, growing louder and more ominous the farther they went.

He drove deeper into the city, leaving their attackers behind until they came to a 4-way intersection in the road. A three-story casino lay off to the right, a restaurant sat on the left and a spattering of other businesses and apartments dotted the blocks around them. Ahead, the lane turned into a forested drive with trees packed tight against the roadway.

"Stop here," the captain said. "I need to check something."

Morales slowed down at the wide intersection, checking the shattered casino windows on the right. Bricks had crumbled away from the walls and soot scorched the ground, the result of an earlier air strike. He glanced in his side mirrors and saw that the Humvees were packed full with troops, a few of them bleeding, but most intact, successfully evacuated from the ambush.

"Units 4 and 7 are coming under fire, too," Captain Jones said. His voice faded as he talked to someone on another radio, then he came back to their squad. "Let's secure this area until we get some reinforcements."

"This is turning into a shit show," Smith scowled after muting his line.

Morales shook his head and turned in his seat as the soldier climbed from the turret, arms dusty with powder. The man's expression was dazed and angry as he searched for his pack. "Man, it feels like someone punched me in the side of the head with an aluminum baseball bat."

"Same here," Morales said. "My left ear is ringing like crazy." He noticed something on Smith's face and pointed. "Man, you're bleeding. You must have caught some shrapnel from the explosion."

The soldier reached up and touched his left temple, pulling his fingers away to look at the blood.

"I guess so," he grimaced. "Must not be too serious if I'm still standing." He fished a canteen out of his pack, twisted it open, and splashed water on his face, then tilted it up and took several long swallows before holding it out to Morales, who took a swig and gave it back. Turning back, he looked in his side mirrors as the squad dispersed along the road, a handful of soldiers crouch-walking toward the casinos with their gun barrels flicking from window to window. After wiping his eyes with his fingers, Smith climbed back into his cockpit and manned his weapon.

Morales un-muted his line. "Captain, permission to get out and check my truck for damage."

"Affirmative, Morales. Just be ready to roll when we need to go."

"Roger that."

With a glance around, he grabbed the door handle and shoved with his shoulder, climbing down from the MRAP, pulling his rifle out with him. He then pushed his door open with a resounding squeal and began a visual inspection of the armored vehicle. There was heavy scoring on the left front fender and wheel well, and the tire had a metal pipe the diameter of his thumb stuck in it. It was a flat-free tire, though, so he could run on it for a while before changing it.

The steps to the driver's side door were twisted and bent, and his door panel had a fist-sized dent in it. If the armor hadn't been there, he would have been ripped in two by whatever had hit it.

"You did your job, baby." He patted the side. "Now, let's see what you've got going on below."

Bending low, he leaned and peered beneath the wheel well. Past the tire, the lower part of the engine looked like a mess of spaghetti wiring and belts, the MRAP's multiple backup systems the only thing keeping it running. The tie-rod was slightly bent, which was likely causing the grinding noise when he drove. Annoying, yes, but not critical, and nothing that would keep them from getting to a secure location.

"Captain, this is Morales. I've got some damage here, but nothing to keep me off the road."

"Great, soldier. I'm talking to central command now. We'll be--"

The air grew loud, hot and bright as an explosion rocked his vehicle sideways, sending Morales flying onto his backside. Another boom shook the ground, then another, small arms fire pinging against the heavy armor as a wash of smoke poured over him. A nest of bees buzzed in his head as he looked up from his position on the ground, his ears ringing as he rolled and tried to stand. He stumbled to his feet and saw the other side of his truck was burning, yet Smith was still up in the turret, shooting through the smoke at the casino and screaming incoherently.

Members of his unit began returning fire at the casino, and Morales turned in a full circle in search of his rifle. A bullet snapped at his jacket's edge, coming from the restaurant on his side and another smacked his driver's side door. He winced and ducked, spotting his gun ten feet away lying in the dirt. Stumbling over, he snatched it up and spun toward the restaurant, catching movement in an alley as men took up positions. Some wore military fatigues, others wore jeans and dark T-shirts and a pair stood at the corners, taking pot shots at him as the rest sprinted by.

Morales snapped the rifle to his shoulder and fired back at the two men on the corner, stitching three rounds up one's chest, splattering the surrounding restaurant brick with red. The other cursed and took a wild shot at Morales before the soldier sunk two rounds into the man's belly, doubling him over in agony.

The militia men reached a nearby parked car and set up to fire at him while he stood there in the open. Whirling, he sprinted to the MRAP, climbed the warped steps, and slammed the door shut behind him as rounds smacked it. Smith swung his M2 around and fired on the car in response to the assault, the heavy bullets tearing it to shreds, passing right through the frame and finding flesh. The enemy forces howled and screamed, bodies dancing as the bullets ravaged them.

The captain's voice wailed over the radio. "Morales! Saddle up!"

"Saddled, sir!"

"Take the next left in front of you. Head back to the aqueduct. Let's go!"

The truck's engine was still running, though he had no idea how. It had taken two direct hits, the last likely from a rocket-propelled grenade. Flames licked up the right side, and the engine clacked and pinged, threatening to refuse to move. He put the vehicle in drive and hit the gas, the MRAP blessedly responding, lurching forward and clanking around the bend.

"Go, go, go!" Smith screamed, firing at enemy forces on the rooftops.

Morales focused on keeping them on the road, the smacking of rounds against his armor only a distant din through his half-destroyed hearing. By the time he'd made it three blocks, the firing on both sides had stopped, but he couldn't relax, damage reports rolling in across the radio.

Two soldiers had died in the crossfire, and all the trucks had been hit by rocket-propelled grenades or some form of explosive. Luckily, the enemy aim hadn't been the best and all of their vehicles were still road worthy. Their teams had dealt out plenty of punishment in return, Captain Jones estimating a dozen enemy dead and several more wounded.

"That was a double ambush," the captain mused over the radio.

"I saw some of them," Morales added. "It was a mix of soldiers and para-military."

"Guerillas," someone replied

He glanced over his right shoulder where the lieutenant was holding his hand. "You okay up there, Smith?"

"It got a little hot," he yelled down, shaking his fingers out before gripping the firing handles again, "but I'm good."

Whatever ailed the wounded MRAP was beginning to take its toll. The clanking sounds grew more pronounced, and the big truck was drifting to the right. Morales spotted more wreckage on the road, and he slowed the vehicle as they approached.

"Captain, there's another roadblock up ahead, and I don't think my girl can take much more."

"Can you see a way around?"

"Yeah."

"Take it."

Morales jerked the wheel and took them down a tight side street. Buildings pressed closer, some of them looking freshly hit from the air strikes. Bodies lay in the road, and more than just soldiers, at least two women and one small body in the mix.

"So much for avoiding civilian casualties," he murmured, the first faint waft of the rotting flesh tickling his nose.

Signs dangled from storefronts and at least two buildings ahead had collapsed, leaving a wash of bricks in the streets. Morales worked around them, weaving carefully to avoid damaging his truck more than it already was. He took a hard left, then a right, the truck lurching, searching for a path to safety. A cloud drifted past them, obscuring his vision and, coughing and squinting, he careened through the darkness at forty miles-per-hour, avoiding lumps of wreckage and shadowy obstacles, though once he hit a soft bump in the road he suspected was a body. Eyes burning, ears ringing and whole body shaking as the adrenaline started to wear off, he guided them into light, through to a clear path.

"Nice driving, Morales," Smith said.

"Thanks, I—" At that point the engine clanked uncontrollably, and the wheel shuddered in his hands.

"You just jinxed us, soldier." Morales pulled the armored vehicle to the side of the road and brought it to a jarring halt. Then he turned his mic on and spoke to the captain. "Captain, this is Morales. The MRAP is wrecked. We need to hitch a ride."

"My truck's done, too," another soldier added. Morales recognized him as the driver of the Humvee right behind him.

He killed the engine, and he and Smith got out, rifles held casually as he gazed in all directions. Once they thought it was clear, Morales returned to the MRAP, retrieved his pack, and slung it on his shoulders. The pair turned to watch their surroundings as the captain figured out what to do.

They appeared to be at another of the strange, crooked intersections that sprouted everywhere in the city. It was a 4-way with an odd-shaped triangular building on one corner and all the buildings were abandoned, beat to hell, brick and stone falling down like fat raindrops to smack the pavement in splatters of dust. Gunfire rattled off in the distance, explosions echoing like thunder across the ravaged city.

Smith joined him next to the MRAP, lighting a cigarette with shaking hands, the man's eyes flicking back and forth nervously. His face was black and sooty, hair frazzled on one side. But the flames hadn't burned his skin too badly except for a couple of red spots around his temple. The strong scent of burned hair wrinkled Morales's nose, overpowering the cigarette smoke.

"What do you make of it?" Smith asked, standing with his feet shoulder-width apart.

"Make of what?"

"The ambush. They were ready for us."

"You think?" Morales replied with a spatter of sarcasm. "I mean, we're the invaders. We should have expected stronger resistance."

"Yeah, I guess so," Smith shrugged. "Not like we had a choice though."

"Maybe." Morales didn't feel like speculating. He just wanted to keep them from getting ambushed again. And he had other things tugging on his mind. He closed his eyes, struggling to steady his own hands. "I killed two men."

"Say what?" Smith cupped a hand over a soot-coated ear.

"I killed two men back there when we stopped."

When Smith didn't respond, he glanced over to see the lieutenant staring straight ahead with cigarette smoke trailing from his mouth and nose.

"I guess you got some too, huh?" Morales's eyes fell.

"Yeah. A lot." Smith kicked at the ground, voice fading. "I just tried to remember my training, but it wasn't like hitting targets at all. It was like... melting butter with a hot fork."

Morales turned away as the bile rose in his throat. He swallowed it, closing his eyes against the nausea. His training had supposedly prepared him for everything he would have to face – physically, at least. Emotionally, though, he was deep in uncharted waters, feeling the conflict in his mind as he turned the bodies of the two men over and over, examining and re-examining the situation until he wasn't sure what was right and wrong.

The word finally came down from the captain, snapping him out of his trance. "All right, men. We don't have enough room to haul everyone. So, some will walk patrol as others ride. Let's make sure to strip everything useful from the broken down trucks before we move out. We'll take them with us."

The soldiers swarmed onto the dead vehicles and detached the machine guns, strapping them to the other truck roofs, then they grabbed the extra ammunition and valuables and stored them in the Stryker. The team moved with efficiency and completed with the tasks in less than ten minutes, then the captain stood outside his vehicle, talking to his officers and pointing out which direction to go. Once a course was set, the captain stepped back to his vehicle and climbed inside.

"All right, people," he said over the comm. "Let's move out. Morales. Smith. You've got point again."

* * *

They reached the aqueduct twenty minutes later, exiting on a street several blocks down from Tolteco Street. The big gray structure was the most solid thing around them, a massive block of concrete spanning the gray-green waters trickling below. Morales felt a little better with his sense of direction returned and his ears ringing slightly less, though the biggest boost to his mood came from the bulk of the US forces that were just north of the aqueduct and coming south imminently.

"Let's hold our position here." The captain spoke low over the headset. "Hang tight, people. Waiting for new orders from central command."

A sergeant gave the order to form a perimeter around their vehicles and a group of six jogged to one corner and cleared a building. Another group moved to the opposite corner and entered an apartment complex, calling back that it was clear a few moments later.

Morales and Smith stayed back, using a Humvee for protection as they took a breather. Sweat dripped from Morales' helmet, and his neck itched as he peered warily down the street, feeling like an intruder in an alien world. The idea of moving millions – no, tens of millions – of American citizens into another country and expecting them to figure out how to cope was ludicrous. Yet, there they were, paving the road for those to come.

"It took my family generations to establish themselves in the States." He shook his head. "Looks like I'm getting back to my roots."

Smith scoffed. "And not under the best of circumstances."

"Squad, form up," the captain announced. "We're not heading back to base. It looks like Units 4 and 7 have recovered and are converging on the area we were ambushed in. We'll be heading southeast on a new course, following the aqueduct."

Morales turned to Smith. "We're not waiting for reinforcements?"

"I guess not."

"Come on, Smith and Morales. You're back on point. Up front and center, boys. Let's do this!"

The troops were recalled from the buildings and corners, and the pair moved to the head of the convoy and started walking. They kept a steady pace, moving southwest toward the center of town. With the water on their left, and buildings on the right, it made searching for enemies much easier, lessening the directions a surprise attack could originate from.

Morales's boots scrunched on the pavement as distant cracks of battle played out, small microcosms of fights he hoped they were winning, yet also felt guilty for participating in. Their immediate block, thankfully, lay in a blanket of dusty quiet, the wind as still as a final breath.

"Dead silence," Morales whispered.

"Yeah, but the volume can turn up real fast," Smith countered, looking skyward.

Morales nodded, and they kept walking.

The houses on the right weren't much more than shacks, the walls barely standing, no windows to speak of. Power lines sagged on crooked poles and the yards were nothing but dirt and scrub, walled or fenced in, most of it buckled after years of disrepair.

"All right, people," the captain ordered. "Turn right up here. Stay sharp."

Morales and Smith did as they were ordered, putting the aqueduct to their backs as they jogged to the center of an intersection with the armor right behind them.

The ramshackle houses gave way to small businesses and warehouses. They were unremarkable, single-story structures, dilapidated before the invasion and made even worse afterward. Some smoldered, though Morales couldn't tell if it was because of an air strike, or if the owners had taken a scorched earth policy.

"I'd burn my home down too, if we had been on the receiving end of an invasion." Morales mumbled to himself, catching a sideways look from Smith, then a resigned nod of understanding.

"Take another right up here," the captain ordered after they had walked a mile. They completed the same maneuver, entering a wide street made of hard-packed dirt, and Morales felt his sense of direction start to slip again, unable to remember if the aqueduct was off to his right or behind them. The way the streets were oddly angled, he couldn't be sure, and the more turns they took, the worse the feeling got. Running his tongue over his lips, Morales narrowed his eyes and tried to stay focused, but his body was finally starting to complain about being blown up, shot at, and tossed around like a rag doll.

They passed more hut-like structures, some of them collapsing just from the rumble of their armored trucks. "This place needs a facelift," Smith remarked, spitting to the side. "Not sure why we'd invade here."

"Annex, remember," Morales countered him with a derisive snort. "We're totally not invaders. And the weather is what matters. It's warm."

Though Morales was of Hispanic descent, he'd been born and raised in the States, just like his parents. He was a born and bred American, and a soldier, but to be invading his original homeland was a surreal experience, to say the least.

"I doubt we'll see any ambushes here," Smith remarked. "Our guns would tear this stuff apart like paper."

"Los muertos al cajón y los vivos al fiestón," Morales said, head swiveling left and right.

"Your accent is terrible, brother. And what the hell does that even mean?"

"Bite me. I grew up speaking English. It means 'The dead to the coffin and the living to the party,'" he replied. "It's something my grandmother used to say during Día de Muertos, the Mexican Day of the Dead. I think it means that death is inevitable, but we should not fear it. We should live well, and we will live on in the afterlife."

"In other words… Life is a party, then you die?"

"Then you live again," Morales tacked on.

"Interesting." Smith sniffed. "I think I'll just try to stay alive the first time."

They walked by an abandoned school bus, riddled with bullet holes, the frame sunken on one side, the engine smoking, blood splashed across the windows.

"Oh, no," Morales choked out, spotting a body lying half outside the door of the bus. His first thought was that it was a child, but with a second glance he realized it was a man wearing fatigues, a rifle lying nearby. He sighed with relief, then immediately felt guilty.

Smith, meanwhile, scoffed at the body, shaking his head. "They must have been transporting troops in this piece of shit when our guys took them out."

They continued walking, boots scraping through the dirt, finding gruesome surprises on every block. There was a string of cars that had been taken out by the Apaches, the vehicles lying in smoking heaps. A pair of them had been cut down the middle, the .50 caliber penetrating rounds chewing up the metal and people inside. Another group of Mexican soldiers appeared to have been caught in a bombing run, their bodies charred beyond recognition, scattered around several deep craters in an open area next to a building.

"Let's go, people." Captain Jones growled over the comm line. "Keep it moving and keep it tight."

Morales and Smith peeled their eyes from the destruction and kept walking, picking up the pace. They were surrounded by hovels and flimsy, brightly colored, two-story structures. The captain had them turn right at some point, then left again, where they entered an area of small brick homes that seemed more upscale than the previous buildings. Many boasted chain-link fences or brick walls around the yards. Covered decks had grills and lawn chairs, gardens with trees pressing close. There were even decent cars and trucks mixed in with the junkers, all of them abandoned on the side of the road or in the driveways, the space tight and crowded.

"This is the perfect place to hide if you're a guerilla," Morales commented, eyes flitting around.

He glanced up to see a dark face peering at him from a second-floor window. He brought his rifle up, ready to fire, but it was a just a middle-aged woman, her curious expression quickly turning to terror when she spotted the gun, and she dropped the blinds and disappeared from sight.

"You have something, Morales?" The captain's voice was urgent.

"Just a woman. A citizen."

They approached a congested spot with a hovel on one side and a decent, two-story home on the right. The hovel had a corrugated tin fence and a custom van parked out front while a pickup was parked on the opposite side of the street in front of a garage. The road was so thin the Humvees would have to shove something aside to get through, though without the MRAP, the job would be exponentially more difficult.

"Captain, we've got some congestion up here. The armor will need to squeeze by."

"Roger that, Morales."

He and Smith moved to their left to stand near the hovel. They turned away from the street, peering hard at the house and any possible dangers lurking inside. Morales caught a fluttering of movement behind a fence to his right, the sliding glass door in the back sliding open and then cracking shut.

"Captain, I've got movement in the house here." Morales tensed his shoulders. "Want us to check it out while you get the vehicles moved?"

"Affirmative."

He looked at Smith and jerked his head toward the house.

The pair jogged to the makeshift gate which turned out to be a piece of chain link barely hanging from its hinges. Morales shoved it aside where it scraped across a cracked concrete sidewalk, then he pushed through and approached the back patio, the sliding glass reflecting their movements. The soldiers threw their backs against the house on either side of the sliding glass door.

Morales lifted his boot, put it against the door handle, and kicked it open. Then he put his ear close to the opening, straining to hear.

"United States Military," he called in, "We're coming in."

He flashed a look to Smith and gave a nod, then the man spun and entered the house, leading with his rifle barrel. Morales was right on his heels, fanning out and staying low as his eyes adjusted to the dimness.

His gun swept across a living room with a small television and piles of laundry on the couch, and Morales stuck his barrel into the clothing mounds to make sure no one was hiding inside before he gave Smith a nod.

His partner angled off to his left and moved down a long hallway and Morales took the same hallway and followed him for three steps before slamming his shoulder into a door and entering a room with a quick rifle sweep.

He froze when he saw a mother and three kids sitting on the bed. The mother had her arms around her children, holding them tight against her, four sets of deep brown eyes stared at him, their faces drawn up in terror. He felt sudden compassion at seeing the innocent faces staring at him. If his grandparents hadn't found a way to come to the United States, he could have been one of the children, eking out a living in a run-down city with very little prospects for the future.

"Is there anyone else in the house?"

The woman shook her head and furrowed her brow.

"Soldiers? Any soldiers in the house?"

She still looked confused, so Morales called up what little Spanish he knew. "Um, soldado? El soldado?" He gestured around with his rifle barrel.

The woman shook her head vigorously. "No."

"Okay. Thank you. *Gracias.*"

Smith peeked his head in, eyes falling on the family before flipping to Morales. "They okay?"

"Yeah. Just scared."

He tried to smile despite the grave situation, waving as he backed from the room. "Gracias," he said, "grac--"

Someone shouted a second before a massive explosion rocked the house, the walls shaking as dust trailed from the ceiling. The woman and her children screamed and fell forward on the mattress as the noise and vibration shook the place to its core, and the two soldiers spun around, looking at each other with wide expressions.

"Stay here," Morales shouted at them, using his hand to make a downward-pushing gesture. "Um... *Quédate aquí.*"

The woman nodded, her face an agonized expression of fear. Smith and Morales exited the open sliding glass door and instantly drew back as bullets peppered the house, one zipping right by their faces as rounds punctured the corrugated steel fencing.

"Come on!" Smith ducked and dashed out the door, angling toward a part of the fence with the custom van parked on the other side.

In the road, the lead Humvee was stuck, sandwiched between two vehicles and pinned down by guerrillas who had hit right as it was trying to squeeze through. Through the windows, he saw the garage door on the other side had flown up, and fighters were firing at the armored vehicle from inside, the rounds flying in their direction popping the tin fencing.

Neither he nor Smith could get a shot at the people in the garage without shooting through the Humvee, but their unit was giving back as good as it was getting, the driver and passengers fired from their windows in a gangster-style shootout with smoke and brass casing bouncing off the roof and out the windows. Morales was about to tell Smith to circle with him when he heard a loud fizzle and whoosh, and he glanced left just in time to see a rocket-propelled grenade zip up the street in a trail of smoke to slam the lead Humvee. The rocket hit the windshield and burst through the cabin, blowing the remaining reinforced windows out along with bits of flesh and smoke, sending a shock wave reverberating through the street.

Morales caught something sharp to the face and stumbled backward as the tin fencing crashed in and he hit the ground hard, splayed out but still holding onto his weapon, dazed but not out.

"Get suppressing fire on that garage and down the street!" the captain was screaming, a stream of obscenities following his order. Soldiers shouted, but Morales couldn't tell if they were bad guys or good guys, and he couldn't even make sense of any direction. He rolled his head to the left, watching Smith on his hands and knees, starting to rise as a bullet puckered the lieutenant's jacket in a mist of pink and red, then another punched him on his right side, and he fell forward, his cry of pain cut short.

Voices called from the other side of the smoking Humvee where soldiers' arms hung from the shattered windows. Eyes wide, heart pumping adrenaline through his veins, Morales rolled over and staggered to his knees, gripping one of the grenades on his belt and yanking it free. He pulled the pin as he pitched himself forward and with a short hop, he carefully, but forcefully, hurled the explosive over the Humvee and into the garage beyond.

Someone shouted in Spanish just before the grenade ignited, and he was so dazed he almost forgot to duck as shrapnel flew at him in a spray. Morales dropped, almost too late, face down in the dirt, breathing the cool scent of earth, his body sagging in exhaustion. The sound of bootsteps approached, and he rolled over to swing his rifle up, ready to face the enemy head on when he saw it was a pair of soldiers from his unit, and he lowered his weapon, gesturing at his friend.

"Smith's hurt. He needs help."

The soldiers eased the wounded man onto his back with him gasping and groaning in pain. As they helped him up, Morales climbed to his feet and peered through the Humvee wreckage, looking for targets, still stumbling and trying to find his balance. With everyone inside the Humvee dead, he fired through the windows toward the garage, side-stepping to a fallen piece of corrugated steel, shooting down the street where the rocket propelled grenade was firing from.

It was impossible to see through the wafting smoke, but he glimpsed figures moving in the breaks, and he picked at them with small bursts until his weapon clicked empty. He ejected the spent magazine and slammed a loaded one home, snatching the charging handle back and slamming a round into the upper chamber, his movements sheer instinct. He had to keep firing. He had to keep his people covered. There was no other choice.

One of the soldiers working on Smith grabbed Morales' shoulder. "We're ready to go, Morales! Let's get out of here!"

Nodding, he backpedaled, following them through the wreckage. Jagged fencing stuck up everywhere, and bricks littered the ground. Something snagged his pant leg and bit into his knee, but he swung his leg away from the jab and put his boot down on the uneven footing. He was firing the entire time, liberal with his disbursement of rounds, twisting and shooting at anything that moved, ejecting spent magazines and slamming in new ones, laying down enough suppressing fire to keep a small army at bay.

They finally reached the street, and he glanced back to see the remaining Humvee and Stryker squatting on the other side of a wall of smoke. Once clear, he stood between the enemy and his unit members as more wounded were carried out of the smoke. One man was missing his helmet, his head wrapped with a bloody bandage, another was being carried by two of his comrades, a chest wound already covered with an expanding sealing spray designed to temporarily seal off massive injuries.

Five soldiers joined him, providing cover for the wounded, then the .50's from the Humvee and Stryker joined in with their booming song, clearing the streets with bright tracer streaks zipping just over their heads, brass tinkling out among the cacophony as it fell to the street in a hailstorm. Captain Jones stood by the Humvee, face sooty, his rifle in one hand and his radio in the other, screaming orders amid the din. "We've got blockage in the road ahead! Route is broken, repeat, our route is broken!"

The captain listened for a reply, squawked an acknowledgment, then put his radio away and swung his fist over his head. "Everyone to me! Form up to pull back! Let's go!"

Calls in the affirmative rang out and the Stryker and Humvee turned around in the cramped street and started moving back the way they'd come. Orphaned soldiers strode briskly beside the vehicles on ultra-high alert, leaning close to the hard armor, depending on it with their lives to give them some protection from the next salvo of incoming fire.

Morales swept his weapon left and right as he staggered backward, kicking up road dust with his boots. His brain burned as he picked targets almost as fast as he could squeeze the trigger operating purely off of instinct. There was no more thinking, only his training, the weeks of boot camp the dividing line between survival and dying on a filthy backwater street. Bullets smacked the Humvee, and the turret gunner fired back, a few rounds flying past his head, seeming to come from the other direction, the one they were fleeing toward. At first he thought it was friendly fire that had zipped by his ear, but when he glanced back, he saw a dozen Mexican soldiers moving through the streets toward them, setting up a deadly amount of crossfire.

"What the hell? Captain!" Morales pointed and stepped away from the Humvee's armor to shoot past his unit. The captain caught on quick, and the Stryker's big gun spun and delivered a brutal onslaught of tracer-laced fire. Still, the enemy came, slipping through shadows and edging closer, trapping them between two Mexican guerilla units. A grenade flew in and exploded nearby, though Morales' ears were long past the point of caring about the noise, and the Army soldiers pressed their retreat, outnumbered three to one, by Morales's reckoning.

"Hold it, men," the captain shouted. "We're trapped. Take cover! I want men in both of those corner buildings. Find firing positions, on the double! Let's go you lousy bullet-catchers!"

They were sandwiched between two tall brick structures that would provide what they needed and Morales nodded to four of his teammates, leaving the Humvee cover and sprinting for one corner building. He curled his shoulders as he ran, half-crouched, mouth full of dust and gun smoke, eyes stinging with sweat and soot, then followed his team inside, clearing the first floor in ten seconds, moving fast and furious.

Then they flew up the stairs, taking two at a time.

"Spread out!" Morales shouted to the others as he spun into a room, pounding across the weak wooden flooring to the window that overlooked the street before falling to one knee beside it, a clear view of the approaching enemy available over the smoke. Rifle raised, he immediately opened fire, sending them scattering in all directions, breaking off their advance and giving the rest of the soldiers time to get into cover.

"We're set up here captain." He squeezed out the words between controlled bursts. "I've got eyes on the enemy!"

"Good work, Morales! Make 'em pay!"

He fell silent as the radio lit up, soldiers firing from windows and calling out enemy positions, moving and relocating inside the building as they supported each other. Rounds peppered the brick next to him, and he jerked back in a spray of sharp dust, then immediately darted out, firing of a three-round burst that stitched up the attacker's chest.

"Gunner in the Humvee," he called, "Check out the group of three coming down the left-hand side of the road, using the houses for cover. See them?"

"Yeah, on it!"

Morales smiled as the M2 rattled off, then heard boots stomping across the upper floor with a staggered gait, and he raised his rifle barrel, then immediately dropped it. "Geez, Smith! What the hell, man? I thought you were injured. You should be in the Stryker!"

The lieutenant had given up his flak jacket and shirt and had replaced it with a thick bandage wrapped over his shoulder to cover his ribs on the right side, a small dot of blood leaking through in the center.

"You think I want to die in one of those tin cans?" Smith staggered over to the other window and fell to his knees, shooting Morales a crooked smile as he dropped his ammunition pack. He removed two fresh magazines and slid one cross the floor. "Hell with that. I'll die out here with the rest of you lug heads."

Morales dragged the fresh magazine closer and turned to face the window again. He edged up and looked out, spotting more of the enemy running toward them from the center of the city. Several older-model armored vehicles bore down on them, anchoring the assault as the first grenades poured in, slamming the street, rounds flashing and sparking like angry bees. Morales rested his rifle on the frame and kept working, doing his job, hoping their remaining firepower could stop them. He flashed a grin at Smith.

"The living have come to the party, my friend. Let's send them to their next life."

"That's what I'm talking about," Smith replied with a grin and a whoop as Morales took aim and squeezed the trigger.

Chapter 13
Keith
Norlina, North Carolina

He awoke with stinging fingers and toes and tears streaming down his face, his side pinched every time he took a breath and sharp stabs of pain stung him at the base of his neck. But at least he was lying on something soft – and he was awake, free of the nightmarish dreams that had been plaguing him. As his head cleared into wakefulness, he assumed he must have been lying on a mattress or a camping pad, but the soft substance vibrated beneath him like he was moving somewhere.

Opening his eyes, he winced at the light shining in through a crack in some curtains. It was a confined space, probably five by seven feet or so, more or less. A small television was mounted on the wall, and the place smelled like oil and antifreeze, but a comfortable hum of heated ventilation warmed the room, making it comfortable and relaxing.

Keith tried to say something, but all that emerged was a rough groan, his tongue sticking in his mouth, pain lancing down his throat. It hurt to even try to make a sound, and he squeezed his eyes shut as he tried to get his brain moving, to figure out what was going on, to remember-

It came back in a flash. The fake breakout from the holding area. Traveling with Tom and his daughter. Driving the LAV halfway across Virginia. Then he'd made a crucial mistake, letting Tom see him throw his weight around with the gas station attendant. It didn't help matters that he followed that up by screwing up with pulling a gun. Being up front about it from the start might have salvaged things – but then, how was he to prevent Jerry from overhearing him talking to Central Command? The boy should have died faster, should have bled out at the hobos' camp instead of fighting through it back to the LAV.

Worst of all, the chief, cardinal sin, he shouldn't have assumed Tom would just go along with things. The man was a certified genius, and he could put clues together fast. He also put his money where his mouth was, prepared to protect his daughter at any cost, no matter who stood in his way. Keith had made the mistake of underestimating him once – he wouldn't do so again.

A hand parted the curtains as Keith lay still jogging his memory, and a woman's rugged face looked in on him, blue eyes raking him up and down in a matter-of-fact manner. "He's awake, Tex."

"Am I..." Keith's voice came out as a croak and he swallowed a bit of saliva that had accumulated, clearing his throat and trying again, still with a croak, but loud enough to hear. "Are we in a truck? A semi?"

"That's exactly right," the woman said. "They call me Marge, and this is my husband, Tex."

The man in the driver's seat turned and flashed him a dark-eyed glance and a nod, a thick mustache laying on his upper lip, a California Angels ball cap pulled down over his head.

"I'm Keith." He licked his lips, finding them covered in grease, a disgusted look crossing his face.

"Sorry about that," the woman spoke without a hint of an apology. "Your lips were frozen dry and bleeding when we found you on the side of that hill. I put some petroleum jelly on them. Hope you don't mind."

Keith nodded absently, impressed she'd even thought of it. "No, thank you," he nodded. "You said I was on the side of a hill?"

"That's right, young man. Tex and I rolled up to the crash site, saw the busted barrier and torn up trees. We thought someone might be hurt. Imagine our surprise when we saw a full-on *mil-i-tary* armored vehicle smashed up at the bottom of the hill. On our way down to check it out, we found you." She clicked her tongue, turning to her husband, every word spoken straight and to the point. "Who knows how long you were out there? Must have been hours. We saw frostbite setting in on your extremeties and we got you in the truck quick-like. Figured if you were near a truck like that, you were probably important. "

Keith held his hands up and saw his fingers were bound in big white bandages. He could move them, but when he did, a white-hot fire shocked him, the same one he'd felt as he was waking up from his feverish dreams.

Panic struck him from nowhere, and he blurted, "Are they going to cut my fingers off?"

Marge laughed, rolling her head back as she cackled. "I don't think so, hon. They'll be a little tender for a while. We caught you just in time. What in the tarnation happened, though? What were you doing out there?"

The man squeezed his eyes with embarrassment. "Nothing important."

"Nothing important?" Tex was incredulous. "I'd say if you're riding in a military truck like that, it must be pretty important. Come on, now. You can tell us."

Keith nodded, realizing he'd have to mix the truth in with the lies to get anything past the pair. Plain and outspoken as they might be, there was a keen-eyed nature to them as they worked him over with their gazes, sizing him up. "I work for the FBI, and I was on as special op."

"You work for the FBI? Got any ID?"

Raising up, he patted his pants pockets with his palm, unable to feel the piece of plastic, or his wallet, anywhere. "Sorry, but I don't. I was actually working undercover to bring some real rough people in. But if I can use your radio, I'll make a call to my superiors, and they'll confirm everything for you."

"Not necessary," Marge said. "Makes no difference to us either way. We're just happy to help someone. Want some water?"

"Yes, please. Feels like my throat's on fire."

She handed back a canteen, and Keith cupped it between his palms and tilted it up. The cool water went down smooth, wetting his raw throat and settling in his stomach. After a few small sips he handed the canteen back with a smile.

"Thank you. That was good. Hey, where are you headed?"

Marge answered. "We're on our way south. Coming up on Airlie, North Carolina at the moment."

Keith racked his brain to figure out where they were, but either way, it wasn't Virginia. Certainly not where he wanted to be.

"We're just about to pull into an abandoned gas station." She lowered her voice and winked. "Hoping to skim a little diesel for the rest of the trip."

"Rest of the trip?"

"Yeah, son. For the evacuation south."

Keith shook his head like he didn't know what they were talking about.

Tex blew a raspberry. "You work for the government, and you don't know about the evacuations?"

He took on a blank look and shook his head. "Sorry, sometimes us field agents get caught up in our assignments and get a little behind on news. I just knew I had to get the convicts back to base." A disappointed expression fell across on his face. "Looks like I won't be getting them there after all."

"That's too bad, son." Marge sympathized.

Tex pulled off the road and took a couple short turns before slowing to a stop, then engaged the emergency brake with a hiss. "It'll take us a few minutes to get the fuel pumped. Be right back." He pushed open the door and got out and Keith nodded and sat back, desperately trying to figure out how he, in his injured state, could get himself back on track and heading north.

Tex slammed his passenger door shut, and Marge watched after her husband. "I should probably help him. Make yourself comfortable?"

"Can I use your radio to get in touch with my superiors?"

Marge smiled broadly. "Well, sure, honey. That's fine by us. You just come up here in my seat and make your call. Do you know how the CB works?"

He blinked innocently, trying not to ham it up too much, and nodded. "I think so."

"Okay, then. Have at it."

Marge got out and slammed the door behind her and Keith stood and hauled himself up to the front seat, wincing when pain shot up his sides and legs, forcing him to sit back down. He sucked air through his teeth and tried again, placing his palms against the sleeper mattress and shoving himself up, parting the curtain, staggering up to Marge's seat, body on fire in more places than he cared to think about. He took the CB radio from its clip and switched to the designated military channel, then spoke his code.

"Military band, this is 3-ECHO-DANNY-APPLE-4-1. I need authorization on secure band 2-4-7-9-2. I need to reach Colonel Rachel Banks of the United States Navy. Please acknowledge."

Three seconds passed before the reply came through the CB speaker. "Acknowledged, Arrowhead. This is the switchboard. Please provide the security response."

Keith closed his eyes, recalling the numbered sequence. He had to get it right the first time or his secure access would be shut down until he could find another military base and speak to a Colonel, in person, to clear him. He opened his eyes and repeated the numbers for the operator, speaking slowly and precisely with each one. A pregnant pause hung in the air before she came back.

"That's the correct code. Please hold for Lieutenant Colonel Banks."

"Thank you," Keith sighed.

He turned and looked outside at Marge and Tex standing around the front of the store, peering inside the windows. They hadn't even started pumping diesel yet, so he had some time. After a handful of seconds that seemed like a lifetime, the Colonel came on the other line.

"This is Banks."

"Lieutenant Colonel Banks. This is Arrowhead."

"Where are you?"

"I'm outside Airlie, North Carolina."

Banks paused. "That's not where we expected you to be. You called in yesterday to say you were still with the McKnights. Has something changed?"

"It has." He explained what had happened, from the moment he'd been overheard by Jerry, to the young man's death, then he described the crash in detail, though he didn't remember much of it, and ended the story with being left for dead on the side of a hill. "I was picked up by a passing couple who put me in their truck and drove me south. That's why I'm in North Carolina."

"That's shit work, Arrowhead," Banks chastised him. "When can you be back on track?"

"I've got some injuries. Possible frostbite, contusions. No broken bones or—"

"Can you talk the couple into driving you back north? We can offer them some incentives. A place in the National Workforce. Guaranteed rations. Grade-2 housing."

"I'll try."

"If you can't sweet-talk them, do whatever it takes to secure transport and get there yourself, if necessary."

Keith closed his eyes against the sting in his fingers, trying to think of how to phrase his next update without having Banks blow her top. "Unfortunately, ma'am, I wasn't able to secure a specific location of the McKnight home before I lost him."

Banks paused, and Keith cringed, waiting for the verbal assault, though what came next was a pleasant surprise.

"Like I said, shit work. Luckily for you, I picked up a few clues. The McKnight home is in a small town north of Bristol. We checked a few maps and think it's probably on Wyndale Road, in the town of Wyndale."

Keith straightened, absorbing the information, weighing it, and deeming it more precious than gold. "That's perfect, ma'am. Good enough to go on. More than good enough."

"We need Tom McKnight at all costs," Banks sounded anxious, like she was turning away from the microphone. "Report back to me when you're with him again."

"I will. I'll take it from here. You can count on--"

"Just get it done. Banks out." There was a loud click at the other end of the line, and Keith hung up the CB mic, sitting in Marge's seat for a full minute with his head low, flexing his painful fingers. Eventually, the doors popped open, and Marge looked up at him with a big smile.

"Scooch it over, Keith," she said. "Make room for Large Marge."

He retreated to his spot in the sleeper cab and turned as the pair climbed into their respective seats. Tex pulled his seatbelt on and snapped it in place before starting up the truck, as did Marge.

"Did you reach your boss?" Marge asked.

"I did, actually." Keith stomped down the pain in preparation to mix his story up good and somehow convince them to drive him back north. "That's what I wanted to talk to you about."

"Okay, go on."

"My boss is Colonel Rachel Banks with the United States Navy."

"Oh, she sounds pretty important," the woman said.

"She is important. I told her what happened and where we are, and she's asked me to enlist your help in finding the fugitives I was transporting." Before either of the pair could answer, he plunged onward. "It would mean driving back north and catching up with a man named Tom McKnight and his accomplice. I know it's way off course, but we can offer you some incentives that'll make life a *lot* easier. Things won't be the same once the evacuations are complete..." He let his words trail off as he gauged their response.

The pair looked at each other across the seats, and for the first time Marge's usual positive expression turned down in a frown.

"I'm not sure what you're getting at," she said, "but go on."

"If you help transport me where I need to go, I can guarantee you a job with the National Workforce. Grade-2 housing. Rations. Maybe more."

Marge reached to her dashboard and picked up a thin book. "Like the stuff in this pamphlet they gave us at one of the evacuation checkpoints?"

Keith nodded and pointed to the government issued handbook. "Exactly. It's all explained in there. Grade-2 housing is an apartment or better. Probably something new, too. Solar panels. Double insulated walls. You might even qualify for a pet."

"You think they'll really build all that stuff?" Tex scoffed. "Seems like a lot to do in a short amount of time."

He shrugged. "Like I said, I haven't been down to the camps. But I'm sure the Army Corps of Engineers are working on it now. I mean, our lives depend on it, right?" Keith looked back and forth between them. "What do you say?"

"Nothing dangerous, right?"

"Absolutely not. You'd just be driving me around, helping me track down the man I'm looking for."

"Is he bad, this man?" Tex asked. "Is he dangerous?"

"Both." Keith pursed his lips and nodded. "He's both."

Tex and Marge shared a worried look.

"Besides being wanted for crimes against the military," he added, trying not to sound too eager. "He's got a kid with him, too. That's the accomplice."

Marge's jaw dropped.

"Yeah, a young lady," Keith went on, lying through his teeth. "He claims she's his daughter, but we've got reason to believe he took her from one of the camps."

"Kidnapped?"

"Possibly. We're pretty sure, anyway. But we want him for those other reasons, too."

Tex tensed in his seat, seeming especially rankled. "Well, danger or not, we can't just stand by and let a man like that get away."

"I agree," Marge said with an enthusiastic nod. "I'd go crazy if it was my daughter someone had taken. I'd be livid as hell, and I'd want someone to go after her if they could."

"That's how I feel, too," Keith agreed, scooting up closer, putting his arms on the backs of their seats. "See, I've got kids of my own, and I couldn't sleep if someone took them."

Tex bristled even more. "Where do you think they went?"

Keith shook his head and narrowed his eyes, pretending to think hard about the question. "I imagine they were hurt in the wreck, at least a little bit. They wouldn't have any transportation, so they'd have to walk to the next town past where you found me."

"Brodnax," Tex nodded. "We know it well."

"I think we should start there. We might catch them holed up in town or something. You guys can hang back while I deal with him, though. I don't want you two getting anywhere close to danger."

Marge reached across and took her husband's hand and Keith studied the dashboard where a Statue of Liberty bobble head perched. An American flag sticker was stuck over the old ashtray, blocking it from use, and a folded up corner of blue and white stuck out of an overhead compartment.

"You'd be doing your country a great service," he added with a note of sincerity. "We need people like you more than ever."

Appealing to their patriotism got him over the last leg and sealed the deal. The pair nodded to each other, and Tex put the truck in gear and pulled out of the abandoned station, grinning and winking broadly at Keith as he pulled the cord for the airhorns.

"Next stop, Brodnax!"

* * *

An hour later, they rolled into the deserted town, coasting slowly off the exit. Homes were left abandoned, front doors sprung wide open, driveways empty, and large white signs hung on every telephone pole and building.

"I didn't realize they'd made it this far south with the evacuations," Keith was sitting so far forward in the cab that he was nearly parallel with Tex and Marge, the three of them watching the scenery roll by.

"Oh, yeah," Tex said. "With things getting colder, the military boys have really been on top of it."

"I guess I was *really* out of the loop." For once, Keith was being honest when he spoke. Banks hadn't indicated they were so far along with the evacuation, and he couldn't imagine the chaos at the camps down south, though none of it was his concern.

Leaning forward, he looked outside at the passing homes which gradually turned into small shops and businesses. At the biggest intersection in town were a gas station and a truck garage. "Pull into the truck service center, please."

"Will do." Tex drove his rig into the left-hand lot and parked alongside the repair shop. They all got out, Keith climbing down gingerly, favoring his stinging fingers and bumps and bruises. It became quickly apparent he had more injuries than he'd noted sitting inside the sleeper cab as he hobbled around the lot, stretching his legs, his right hip and knee tweaked with pain.

"You're not walking so well." Marge came over with a worried look, resting her hand on Keith's back.

"I'll be fine." He limped along, drawing away from her touch. "I'm just a little sore and beat up. I'll loosen up." Quickly changing his tone, he smiled at her, patting her on the arm. "But I appreciate your concern, Marge."

Turning around, he put on a bit of a show, acting slightly bewildered as he searched their surroundings, all the while picking up bits of clues everywhere. Tex, meanwhile, stood in the middle of the lot and placed his hands on his hips, rotating around a few times before shrugging his shoulders. "I don't see how we can find them unless they come out waving at us."

Keith meandered over to where a couple food wrappers lay scattered on the ground and he crouched down carefully and picked up one, turning it over to see that it didn't have frost on it like everything else.

"You recognize that?" Marge waddled up.

"It looks like an energy bar wrapper from the last place we ate when I was with them. You know, that truck stop several miles back?" Keith nodded vigorously, then stopped, putting a finger to his temple as the headache flared back to life. "Yes, I'm sure of it."

Swiveling to the left, he peered through a series of backyards of houses on the adjoining street, spotting a trail of smoke from something smoldering off in the distance.

Gesturing, he started off toward it. "They must have come this way."

Keith led them through the yards, his limp gradually growing less pronounced, following a pair of footprints in the cold-stomped grass, tracking them to where they circled to the front of another house, ending at a big bush on the corner where his eyes went wide as he stared over the frosted green shrubbery.

Tex walked past him, hands on his hips again, giving a low whistle. "Well daggum. Would you look at this. Keith, what the heck happened here?"

Keith hobbled after him with Marge hovering close at his heels, still concerned for his well-being. A recessed house sat thirty yards off the road, defaced, the porch in two pieces, the front entrance and garage blown out in a blast. Debris and garbage had exploded like confetti across the yard, the grass churned up with big tire tracks, likely created by something like a Humvee or similar that left grooves of mud that were half-frozen with ice and snow.

"What in the bejesus happened here?" Marge scratched her head.

Keith got over his surprise and hobbled forward. "Looks like a fight of some sort. There're shell casings everywhere."

"Were the soldiers raiding someone's home?" Marge asked, her voice heavy with concern.

"Hard to tell." Keith shook his head, acting unsure, though the story came together with relative ease. The military had come by to evacuate the homeowner, likely after the rest of the town had already been evacuated, and found him more prepared than they expected. He'd been more than willing to put up a fight, one that ended in bloodshed judging by the red spatters across the grass.

He stood in the driveway and hobbled in a circle. "Looks like someone escaped from the garage and went left down that road, followed by some others. You can tell by the mud tracks and debris in the street, two sets of them."

"Clear as day to me," Tex chuckled dryly. "Do you think it was your man?"

"Probably," Keith replied. Deep down, in the part of him that had spent years going on similar missions and tracking people for the military and other, more covert agencies, he was certain the McKnights had been through the area. "Think we can get back in the truck and follow this road for a bit?"

"We're on your dime now." Tex gestured helplessly. "Wherever you want us to take you, we'll go."

The trio returned to the truck and pulled around to the side road with the blown-up house. Marge moved to the sleeper cabin and allowed Keith to take the passenger seat so he could guide Tex on where to go, watching out one of the side back windows as they got started again. They cruised by the home's wreckage, Keith giving it one more glance before they continued following the muddy tracks around a downward bend. When the tracks ran out, Keith searched the road for more clues, eventually spotting more tire tracks in the soft dirt, hugging the inside curve, occasionally vanishing and then reappearing as the vehicle left the mud and hit the snow, then went back again. They stuck with the subtle marks until they arrived at a fork with no visible leads. Tex was about to bring the semi to a stop when Keith suddenly called out and pointed.

"Take a right."

"How in the world do you know that?" Marge asked from the back as Tex guided the heavy truck.

"Pretty obvious. There were fresh skid marks in the road. One of my specialties with the bureau is tracking vehicles."

Marge nodded in understanding. "Gotcha."

A few curves later, they approached a road on the left that wound up a steep hill. Thick trees lined the roads and Tex slowed down as Keith leaned forward, studying the road. The trees and leaves on the corner were shredded and scattered across the pavement, clipped not from something hitting them, but almost as though they were trimmed with clippers. *Or heavy gunfire.* As if to prove him right, he spotted chips of metal and pieces of plastic mixed in with the foliage along with bits of brass that had been scattered across the road surface and ground into the dirt.

"Left," Keith patted the center console. "Left here, please."

"Is it all the debris in the road?"

"Yep. I think someone shot at them and hit their car. It seems like someone was pursuing them."

"Oh, my." Marge put her fingers to her mouth. "Are we safe?"

"Oh, absolutely," Keith said, turning to her with a smile. "Whatever happened here is *way* over."

They turned up the steep incline, the big diesel engine growling, Tex shifting appropriately to get it to respond. The truck took the hill easily, bending them over the top until they plunged into a coaster-like drop, weaving through a valley, moving slow in a lower gear, cruising, searching every driveway and ditch. For all of his troubles, Keith couldn't help but wonder if the end of his long road of trials and tribulations would lead to Tom and Sam's corpses. It was a real possibility, but not one he was prepared to deal with – especially given the potential ramifications for himself and the country.

He pushed aside the distracting thoughts as he continued searching for some sign of where the vehicles had gone, passing driveways and roads, Keith's stomach twisting with each curve they took, unsure which way his quarry might have taken.

"What now?" Marge asked. She had both of her pudgy hands on the seats and had pulled herself forward to see between them. "How can you possibly tell where they went? It all looks the same to me--"

"Shh," Keith hissed. His head swiveled back and forth, eyes focused on every tree, branch, and brush.

"Well, you don't have to be that way about it," Marge said. "I was just asking a question."

Keith resisted the urge to elbow the woman in the jaw and instead focused even more. It wasn't until they were almost upon it that he noticed, shouting and grabbing Tex by the arm.

"Here! Stop!" He eased up on his tone. "Sorry, *please.* Please stop." Tex hit the brake and shifted down. "There. The driveway on the left. See the mailbox? It looks like someone knocked it down."

"Well, I'll be doggoned." Marge peered over the dashboard. "It *is* knocked down."

Tex turned the big rig up the driveway over a crunch of debris, the massive truck barely fitting as it smashed through a thin veil of foliage, smacking tree branches and knocking off sprays of snow until they reached the top of the lane. The driveway forked around to a squat, single-story home with dark windows and no other vehicles present.

"Stop here at the top," Keith said, already pawing at the door handle to get out. He finally popped it open and stepped carefully down as Tex parked, then hobbled in a circle, looking at the marks on the concrete until he found what he was looking for, pointing at it. "I see traces of two vehicles here."

"How can you tell?" Marge asked, climbing down behind him.

"On certain pavement, just turning the wheel can leave a rubber mark," he said. "The fresher it is, the darker the mark."

"I see," Marge said, but her confused expression told him she didn't see at all.

"Yes, two cars were here. And look." He walked over to the edge of the driveway and picked up a piece of plastic with a yellow tint. "This is probably a taillight. I bet if we went back to the bottom of the hill, we could match it up with the debris down there. This was the car that hit the mailbox."

Tex had climbed from the driver's seat and stood behind him with his arms folded. "What does it mean?"

Keith looked back the way they'd come, eyes turning wistful as he pieced it together. "I think someone chased a pair of vehicles all the way to this point and then drove on by." He gestured. "The two cars up here waited for them to pass, jumped back on the road, and drove the other way. Hey, do you have a map?"

"Sure thing." Tex climbed into his rig and pulled down a paper road map. Spreading it open, he held it up against the truck's grill as Keith hobbled over and located Highway 58 in Virginia. While Brodnax was too small a city to list, Bristol wasn't, and he soon found the highway that led there via Wyndale Road. If the intel given to him by Banks was accurate, then it would be reasonable to assume that the McKnights had gotten back on track and were moving in that direction.

"I think we need to get on Highway 58 and head west," Keith said. "Is that okay with you folks?"

"Sounds good to me," Tex agreed.

"Sure, Keith." Marge looked gloomy as she waddled to the passenger side door and held it open for him.

Before climbing in, he caught up with her and rested his hand on her shoulder, turning her, giving her his best fake smile. "Sorry I was so snippy before. Sometimes I'm so into my work I get aggravated when someone interrupts me."

"It's okay." The woman hesitated, but eventually broke into her usual cheery smile. "Oh, I can't be mad at you. You're a trained government agent or something. You need to focus and can't have a simple-minded fool like me bothering you."

Keith squeezed her shoulder harder. "You're *not* simple-minded, Marge. You're just curious, that's all. And that's a good thing. We'll just be more considerate to each other in that regard. Sound good?"

"That sounds great, Keith." Marge grinned at him again.

As he climbed in, Tex nodded at him appreciatively. "I'll have us back on Highway 58 in no time. We'll catch these sons of guns before you know it."

"Thanks, buddy. Colonel Banks is going to be thrilled when she finds out how much you folks have helped. You're heroes, as far as I'm concerned."

"Anything for the good old U S of A," Marge sat proudly in her seat.

Keith took his spot in the sleeper cab and laid down gently, trying to avoid aggravating his aches and pains. With his transportation set, all he could do was lay back, rest, and prepare to close a snare around Tom McKnight.

Chapter 14

Tom McKnight

Independence, Virginia

"This piece of junk isn't going to make it much farther," Tom growled as snow wafted across his window. He hugged the winding Virginia back roads like a race car driver, on watch for black ice forming patches on the pavement. The engine and heater were performing fine, but the Honda's rear suspension was finally complaining after being shot up by the Humvee. Something had come loose and was rattling and knocking around, and the vehicle felt looser, like it was spongier than it should be.

"Maybe you shouldn't be pushing it that hard," Sam suggested.

"I just want to get us home."

"I know, and I want to get home, too."

"How far do we have left to go?" Tom eased up on the gas as they rounded a bend, but he punched it again to get them up a slight rise, the little four-cylinder engine puttering and spitting to get the job done.

Sam glanced down at the paper map spread in her lap. "I'd say about fifty miles or so."

"Ugh! So close. So *freaking* close!" Tom hit the wheel in frustration, listening as the heater rattled and kicked out a sudden gust of warm air as the speed of the car changed, betraying just how much of it was held together with spit and baling wire. Despite its condition, though, they'd been driving for an hour, taking the back roads to avoid pursuit on the main highway, trying to stay warm as best as they could.

He no longer had any illusions about the quality of the cold. "Nippy" was no longer the operative word. "Frosty" wasn't even adequate. "Frozen" would have to do, and even that definition was beginning to lack the comprehensiveness to describe the conditions. The snow fell fast, and the wind blew it in wild gusts across the road, the windows were freezing to the touch, and frost spotted the far corners of the glass where the defrosters couldn't reach.

Sam shifted under her jacket, tucking her nose down below the collar. "It's getting colder out, isn't it?"

"Dangerously so."

Tom rounded a bend, and the *tonk-tonk-tonk* sound in the suspension repeated itself even louder than before. As he straightened, the entire frame shuddered and something clanked loudly, but he clenched his shoulders and continued pressing the gas pedal.

"What is that noise?" she asked.

"It could be the CV joint or a bend in the axle."

"It sounds like it's getting worse by the minute."

The vehicle would eventually stall, but every mile they squeezed out of it got them closer to home. He stopped at a junction in the road, waiting for Sam's direction, the Honda's engine idling with a strange, hitching cough. "We may need to try to find a new car soon. Do you see any towns nearby?"

"If we take a right here, that'll put us close to Highway 58." Sam pointed at the map. "That's the straightest way home. Or, we could go left and keep following New River."

"New River sounds better for avoiding crowded areas but getting caught out here on the back roads in this storm would be a nightmare."

"Yeah, no kidding."

Tom nodded. "Okay, I'm going to get us back up to 58. If we break down on it, at least there'll be some towns on the way. We can get off these roller coaster roads in any case."

Sam sighed, her voice hoarse with congestion and relief. "Thanks, Dad."

Tom took the right-hand turn and kicked the Honda ahead. It rattled its way up to thirty-five miles per hour when the rear end rattling smoothed out again. Certain speeds seemed to aggravate the suspension, so he tried to keep it in the sweet spot both for the sake of the vehicle and their sanity.

They took a small hill at a good clip, winding up and easing down again in a gentle coast, Tom squinting through the drifting snow, the car's headlamps barely penetrating the wall of white. A patch of ice appeared ahead of them at the next bend and he slowed, pulling the Honda into the next lane to edge around it. On the other side, a pair of bright headlights suddenly appeared out of nowhere, blinding both of them. A horn blared and Sam squealed as Tom whipped the wheel hard to the right, swerving them hard as the frame rattled like mad, tires squealing as the truck blew by, barely avoiding a collision.

While the maneuver successfully kept them from crashing into the truck, it also put them directly in the path of the patch of ice. Their tires hit it at speed, and the vehicle spun. In his panic over the truck, he jerked the wheel back and forth too hard, exacerbating their slide, and the Honda no longer responded as the rear end fishtailed out to their right, sending them sliding toward the edge of the road.

A rusted guardrail appeared out of the snow, the only thing separating them from a dive over the edge of a ravine, and Tom slammed on the brakes, the wheels finally catching on bits of unfrozen pavement, bringing them to a jarring halt against the rail. The engine hitched in response to the impact, then coughed, sputtered and died.

Tom and Sam sat still in their seats for several seconds after the car shut off, both of them gripping whatever they had their hands on when the car started slipping, their hearts throbbing and stomachs twisting in pure fear. Tom finally glanced over to see Sam's wide eyes as she looked out the front window, breathing heavily.

"Are you okay?"

She nodded and gulped. "Yeah… yeah I'm fine. You good?"

"I'm good."

"Cool."

"Let's not do that again?"

A chuckle slipped out and Sam nodded vigorously. "Yeah. Never again."

Tom stared at the oil and transmission lights glowing, then took a deep breath and lowered the heat and fan. Turning the key in the ignition, he tried to start it back up, and at first the engine huffed like someone punching an old heavy bag, but it didn't start, barely even managing to turn over. He turned the key to the neutral position, closed his eyes and tried again, the coughing strong for a moment but eventually petering out until the alternator was barely kicking. Tom flipped the key to the left so all the electronics went out, then he rested back in his seat.

"Is it dead?" Sam asked, her eyebrows raised in question.

"Not totally, but if I keep going, I'll kill it."

"So… we're stuck?"

"It looks that way, kiddo." Tom gazed outside at the white flakes kissing the glass, then off to the right, past Sam to a near vertical hill a hundred feet high. Shrubs and bushes jutted out from the crevices, accumulating the white powder on their branches. Watching the snow accumulate, a sense of urgency gripped him, and he spoke again, shifting in his seat.

"Two things are really bad about this situation. One, without the engine, we don't have any long term heat. That means it'll be freezing in here before long."

"What's the other thing?"

"We're sitting in the wrong lane." Tom glanced in his rearview mirror. "There might not be much traffic on the road, but we know someone could come around the corner at any moment."

"They could slam into us."

"Yep."

Wordlessly, Sam folded the map up and stuck it inside her coat then pulled her hat down tight, tying it around her chin. Tom turned and opened the top of his pack in the back seat, removing some dry socks and stuffing them into his coat beneath the neck area and sleeves and Sam mimicked him, doing the same.

"We have to be careful out there walking in the snow," he talked as he arranged their things. "It's important to keep the blood flowing, but we don't want to go so hard that we sweat, okay? If we sweat, we'll soak our clothes, and the cold winds will freeze us in our tracks."

Sam swallowed hard. "You're asking me to keep you honest."

"Yes, absolutely. If you feel like you're getting too warm and sweaty, we'll have to rest and dry out. Same goes for me."

"We've got the pup tent from the LAV," she reminded him. "We can always put that up if we need it."

"Absolutely. It'll be chilly, but our body heat will keep us from freezing."

With their gear arranged as best as they could in the small vehicle, they pulled their backpacks into their laps, checked what they had, and cinched the tops tight. For a moment they sat in silence, neither one wanting to be the first to open their door as they looking out at the dancing specks of white.

"I wish Jerry was here." Tom broke the silence first, taking Sam's hand in his own. "That kid was pretty great, all things considered."

Sam's breathing hitched as she held back tears, taking a few deep breaths to calm herself down. "He really would have liked it, I bet. It's really pretty." A long silence sank over the cabin of the car until she continued. "I wish we could stay here a while more and just watch it."

"It's beautiful," Tom agreed, "but we've got to get home. We're almost there. I can almost smell your mother's roast in the oven."

Sam put her hand on the door handle. "Okay, I wasn't hungry before, but I definitely am now. Let's get this over with."

"Fifty miles."

"A little less, but yeah."

They nodded to each other and opened the doors, letting in a gently blowing wind as they stepped outside, slung their backpacks on their shoulders, and walked north in the right-hand lane, leaving the bedraggled Honda Civic behind. Boots scrunched in an inch or two of accumulated snow, and the air cradled a muted quietness. With the wind having temporarily died down, the cold wasn't quite so bitingly bitter, though that could change at the drop of a hat.

Tom pulled his coat snug around his neck and shoulders and turned to Sam. "Feeling okay?"

"So far so good," she replied from deep within her coat, coughing lightly. "I think the medicine Guy gave me worked. I don't feel all achy and feverish like I did yesterday."

"That's good," Tom nodded. "Maybe your fever broke."

Sam's head bobbed. "I feel a little weak, but kinda hungry, too."

"It was the mentioning of your mother's roast." He grinned. "And don't forget mashed potatoes and peas. Pie for dessert."

"All of that. Mmmmm."

Tom forced himself to keep a steady pace, plodding along quickly enough to make decent time but not so fast that they'd start sweating profusely. They talked a little more, mostly about Barbara's cooking and what else they were looking forward to about home before settling into a comfortable silence, the only sounds their footsteps and the occasional gust of wind. Around them, the trees shook off piles of snow as the wind above their heads kicked up, the occasional "oomph" of falling powder out among the trees comforting in an odd sort of way.

After thirty minutes, Tom's toes grew cold, but when he wiggled them they didn't feel wet so he kept going, trying to move them around in his boots to generate a bit of warmth. The road wound up and back down again as they walked, twisting and snaking through the hillocks and valleys. A mile passed, then two, then soon they reached a graveyard surrounded by houses and a church, and just beyond was Highway 58.

After climbing a long hill they came to the junction and, standing at the corner, they looked back and forth along the road.

"Okay, we have to head west for another forty-five miles or so," Sam said, breathing heavy after the climb up the hill. "Then we get our roast."

"Easy peasy, right?"

"Yep."

"If we hear a car coming down the road, let's try to get off and hide, okay? No telling who it might be or what their intentions are."

"Agreed. I don't really want to be taken prisoner again, thank you very much."

They crossed the street and stayed on the right-hand side, heads down as the wind cut across them from the south, harder than it had been on the back road. While the highway was easier to traverse than the winding back road it was more open, exposing them to more of the wind, though the fact it was flat and straight helped make up for it.

Tom took the lead, cutting a path through the few inches of snow on the ground for Sam as they passed by white-covered fields, forests, and hills that stretched out on all sides. Innumerable telephone poles slowly marched by, Sam counting them as they went, and houses sat off the road along with churches and markets. Though the pair were desperate, they hadn't yet reached the point where they wanted to break into somewhere again, at least not yet.

They marched on as night slowly descended, the sky becoming dark and bleak, moving from grayness to a blanket of purplish-blue shades within the space of an hour. Sam tripped and stumbled after the third mile, and while she didn't fall or even hurt herself, it was a sure sign of their growing weariness. Three more stumbles happened afterward, then Tom nearly fell two times, and he finally gave in to the obvious, gazing up at the deepening dark, taking his flashlight out to guide their path.

"We should find a place to stop for the night." He looked to either side of the road but didn't see any houses nearby. "Do you remember how far the last place was?" Sam shook her head and coughed into her coat. "Okay, the next one then?"

Her hat bobbed downward, slumped and weak, her energy fading fast. He resisted picking up the pace, not knowing if the next house would be a quarter mile up the road or ten, though the light snowfall was quickly turning into a winter storm. It ended up being a mile and a half before they came upon a broken-down farmhouse, looking ugly and dank in his flashlight beam. Tom didn't hold out much hope as they got near, the two-story home having fallen into disrepair well before the anomaly and evacuations. The roof sagged in the middle like a saddle, part of the rear corner had collapsed inward and the paint had long since peeled away from most of the exterior. Still, for better or for worse, it was shelter from the storm.

"Let's go check it out," Tom said. They walked up to the front porch together and Tom held his hand out for her to wait for him, then he climbed the stairs, using caution on the rotted wood. The door hung open, holes riddled the walls, the windows had shattered long ago and it didn't appear anyone lived inside.

Pushing the front door the rest of the way open, he poked his head into a dark hallway. He hit the light switch, but the power was gone, so he stepped farther in and shone his flashlight around. Old furniture sat forgotten, old drapes billowed, and the rugs lay torn and rotted on the floor. It was frigid inside, and the walls and ceilings ran with water stains. Mold and dust clung to the air, and something groaned deep within in the framework. Still, he searched the first floor all the way back to the kitchen where he found a pipe had burst somewhere behind the sink, the floor covered in ice.

His stomach twisted with the idea of having to stay in such an unstable, unsafe place, without a better option, his best bet would be to see if the place had a furnace he could get going, or a fireplace he could burn some of the furniture in just to generate a bit of heat. Tom stood by the sink and looked through the window to the backyard where the driveway circled the house, went out past a rusted-out swing set, and led to a big white barn fifty yards distant. In the moonlight, as he squinted, it looked surprisingly pristine, white with dark trim, and no signs of disrepair or collapse.

"Well, that might be a better place for us to rest." Turning to get Sam, Tom jerked back when he saw a shadowy figure in the hallway. He started to reach for his weapon when his daughter stepped out from the darkness and into the kitchen, and Tom slammed a hand to his chest.

"Jeez. Don't sneak up on me like that!"

"Sorry, dad." Sam grinned at him from beneath her hood. "Do you think we can stay here?"

MIKE KRAUS

"Not here, no. This place could fall apart in a heartbeat. But back there," He turned and pointed out the back window to the barn. "It looks like it at least has four walls and an intact roof."

Sam stepped to the window and looked out for a moment, the barn's white paint brightening and darkening as fast-moving clouds passed overhead. "It looks way better than in here."

"Let's check it out." Tom guided Sam out the back door and onto a concrete patio where they shuffled through the yard, past the broken-down swing set and out to the barn. A star-shaped design decorated the side, freshly painted within the past few years based on there being hardly any chips in it, and there being no signs of rotted or bowed wood.

"It's practically new," he said with a bewildered expression. "They clearly took way better care of their barn than they did their home."

"Or maybe they live somewhere else, and use this barn with their property?"

"Good point... I find it hard to believe that anyone who lived in that sort of a house could possibly keep a barn looking like this."

He unlatched the door and slid it open, flipping his flashlight back on as he stepped in. The scents of hay and dust hit him in the face, the air several degrees warmer inside. He took a few more steps, casting the beam about, and the surprised snort of a horse greeted them, its eyes reflecting Tom's light.

"Go on," he grinned. "I think it's safe." He ushered Sam in and slammed the door shut behind them, throwing the latch and stepping toward the center of the building. In spite of the well-kept exterior, he'd half-expected the barn to be just as much of a mess inside as the house was. Instead, though, they found the air pleasant and dry, with no scent of mold or mildew – though the smell of manure was pervasive – and every indication that the place was well taken care of and maintained.

Stalls ran along the sides, and a ladder led up to the loft while a near section held bags of feed stacked in one corner, and yard tools in the other. Bridles and tack hung from the woodwork, and a few saddles were thrown over sawhorses in the corner. The sound of snorting and whinnying softly in annoyance over being disturbed echoed off of the wooden walls, drawing Samantha's attention away from her father.

"It'll be warmer higher up. We should head into the loft and—" Tom turned to find Sam walking toward the stalls, already looking for the animal that had greeted them, and her gasp reached him from across the room.

"Hey, Dad. There's *three* horses in here!"

"Well, I'll be...." Tom joined her and shined his light over each one in turn. One was a chestnut with a white spot on its head, the middle one was mottled beast with dark spots on its flanks and the last stood with its head high, its coat a stunning black and white with vivid definition.

"Oh, this one is so pretty," Sam said of the latter, and she reached her hand out tentatively as she approached.

"Be careful." Tom shuffled slowly behind her, not wanting to spook the animals. "We don't know what kind of condition they're in."

"Hi, sweet horse." Sam held a hand to her mouth and coughed into it, but offered the other to the white and black one to sniff and nuzzle. "This one is nice."

"Sure seems that way," Tom smiled and stood next to the stall to greet the animal. The horse nickered and nuzzled his hand, snorting with pleasure as Sam patted his neck at the same time.

"Good boy," Tom chuckled. "At least I think you're a boy." He felt something nudge him in the back, and he turned to find the chestnut right behind him, looking for attention.

"Oh, you're a beauty, too," Tom said, turning to pat the horse's neck.

He felt the pressure of the road lift from his shoulders as they played with the animals, the scent coming off their well-kept coats, the smells of dry hay and manure filling their heads with memories of home, a comforting presence after everything they'd been through.

"I can't believe someone just left them here," Tom shook his head. "Must have been in an awful hurry, or... worse."

"We should check their food before we settle in for the night."

"I'll do it."

Tom took Sam's pack off her shoulders and dropped it next to the ladder leading up to the loft. He dropped his next to it, then he grabbed a bucket of feed and opened the white and black horse's stall. It was curious as he filled the small troughs, though it went right to eating with no problems, ignoring the strange new creature in favor of filling its belly.

Tom looked at its belly and chuckled, patting the animal on his back. "You, my friend, are a gelding." Moving to the next stall, he saw the chestnut was a mare, and he filled her trough the same way. The horses already had plenty of fresh water, and Tom could get them more just by melting snow or taking some from the house or a faucet near the barn if there was still an intact water line.

"That's it." He put down the bucket and waited for Sam, who was still playing and cooing at the horses. "I'm serious. We need to get you warm."

"Okay, okay... I'm coming."

326

She started up the ladder but could barely lift herself up the rungs, slipping on the third one up. Tom caught her and shoved her up by her backside until she disappeared over the top, then he got their packs and dragged them up, handing them up one at a time for her to set to the side. After retrieving some horse blankets from a cabinet he climbed the ladder and hoisted them over, then finally dragged himself up as well. The loft was crowded, bales of hay filling the entire floor and stacked up on the walls as well, and the roof appeared to be well-insulated.

"It must be at least ten degrees warmer up here."

"It's pretty nice," Sam agreed with a cough.

She'd already started smoothing out a couple of piles of hay into something they could sleep on and Tom helped her, placing a horse blanket down on top. They packed extra hay near one end to form a long pillow for their heads and Sam took off her boots and laid down, Tom following suit, taking up a position on her right.

After a few minutes of relaxation, he retrieved a bag of jerky and bottled water from their packs, finding more of the cold and flu medicine and Tylenol in the top of his pack, courtesy of Guy. Tom tapped out two pills and a small cup of the liquid medicine and made Sam take all of it, then she washed it down with bottled water before settling back, hiding in her jacket.

Tom put everything back in the pack, cinched the top, and pulled the other horse blanket over them. With his hands behind his head and his back stretched out on the comfortable padding, he sighed contentedly. While the loft of a horse barn wasn't nearly as pleasant as the overnight stay at Guy's had been, it was still far better than any of their other options. The wind howled outside, and hard bits of ice peppered the metal roof. Downstairs, the horses snorted and nickered softly, and he half-closed his eyes as a pleasant warmth settled on his body.

He rolled his head to the left. "How are you feeling?"

From the depths of her coat, Sam replied in a sleepy tone. "My chest is still really sore, and I feel pretty weak. But, much better than yesterday. Thanks for getting us here, Dad."

"Things could be a lot worse, right?"

"Heck yeah." Sam's face poked from her coat. Her green eyes fell in his direction. "How are *you* feeling?"

Tom shrugged. "Well, I think I'm okay. I'm tired. My feet hurt. My head hurts. I miss your mom and brother and sister."

"I *really* miss Jack and Linda, too. I'd even let Jack beat me at video games and listen to him gloat just to see him again."

"Okay, that's saying a lot, coming from you."

"I know. I'm going to hug that little nerd as soon as I see him, and I'm never letting him go."

"What are me and your mother going to do?" Tom laughed. "We're more used to dragging you two apart so you don't kill each other."

"I know," she chuckled, the sound muffled in her coat. "How's the saying go? Something about the heart growing fonder."

"Absence makes the heart grow fonder."

"Yeah, that's it." She snuggled deeper into her coat, her voice growing softer. "At least for a few days anyway."

They sat in silence for a few minutes and Tom thought she'd fallen asleep, but she surprised him with a question. "Do you think when we get home, our house will be like the one out front? Abandoned with no one in it?"

A chill ran up Tom's spine at the thought, and he lay still for a moment, thinking. "The truth is, I just don't know." Tom stared at the barn rafters, trying to push back the nagging doubts in the back of his head. "I have to believe the military tried to force your mother to leave, but she would have resisted at all costs. We just have to hope she won."

"But what if she didn't?"

"Then we'll have to be prepared for anything. Which we already are."

Sam's hand slid out of her coat and reached over to hold his and he gripped his daughter's fingers and closed his eyes, trying to summon a pleasant memory that might put him to sleep.

He thought back to when he and Barbara had first built the house, when Sam was just a baby, and they didn't have any animals or the new barn. Barbara had stood out on their back patio with her notepad in her hand, pointing with her pen and referencing the drawings on the paper, turning and smiling at him over their big plans, her green eyes bright and happy. Tired— Lord knew they'd put a lot of time and effort into their forever home—but happy.

"It's going to be amazing." Barbara's words had been breathy and hopeful, but that nagging fear still hung around in the back of his brain, refusing to go away no matter how hard he tried.

Be safe, Barbara. Please be safe.

* * *

Tom woke to the light sounds of tapping on the roof as the wind breathed bits of ice across the metal. Sometimes it grew, making a harder-than-rain cacophony before tapering off into a light, relaxing tapping. Between the warmth of the rough blanket and the sound above, he had no interest in getting up, but he had to get up and moving if they wanted to make progress. He looked over to see Sam had rolled on her left side and lay curled up comfortably, breathing heavily in the stillness.

Sitting up, he pushed the covers onto Sam, then he rolled off the flattened hay, got to his knees, and stretched his arms above his head. His body was sore and aching, but felt much better after a good night's rest. Pulling his phone out of his pocket by habit, he flipped it open, sighing at the long-dead screen, then closed it again. The battery had long since given up the ghost, and even if it did work, there'd be no chance of getting a signal.

He stood up with a few grunts and groans and walked to the edge of the loft, looking down at the dirt floor before climbing down, shivering in the dreadful cold on the bottom floor. The horses stamped in their stalls at his approach, chuffing and whinnying in their own disgruntled ways, and he quickly found three more horse blankets and covered the animals before scooping feed into their stalls, turning his nose up at the overwhelming scent of manure.

Exiting the barn, shoving hard to get the door open, he closed it behind him, squinting into the morning sun as he stared across the yard at a foot of snow. It weighed down the tree branches and had completely consumed the swing set, changing it into a marshmallow-covered shape. It was downright frigid outside the barn and his whole body shivered as he looked around at the powder, grumbling to himself.

"This is unreal. But all the more reason to get a fire going quick."

He spotted a shed off to his right, so he made a path to it through the snow, hoping to find something more suitable for starting and sustaining a fire than just hay. The door had a padlock on it, so he felt around in the drifts for a suitable rock for a few moments, found a fist-sized one, and began smacking it against the lock.

After a few hard smashes, the wood around the padlock hasp gave way before the actual lock, and he jerked the door open, the sound of tearing wood echoing across the open yard. He found a snow shovel and gas can in the shed and carried them over to the barn, walking over his existing path so he didn't have to raise his feet so high. He set the gas can near the barn door and used the shovel to clear a large ring down to the mud and grass, then he rested the shovel against the wall and strode to the house. Inside, he found some newspapers, printer paper, and a few pieces of wooden furniture which he carried out to the barn. He broke the latter it into smaller pieces by stomping them or smashing them with a newly acquired hammer from the shed, breaking them up for kindling.

Tom's back twinged at the mere thought of heading back up into the loft, so he trotted back into the house, poking through the kitchen drawers until he found a pack of matches and a lighter. Back at the barn, he swung open the door and put everything inside on the cement floor, making a pyramid of wood well away from any of the walls, stuffing kindling beneath it. Once done he stood, looking at the high window above the barn doors. Unable to delay the inevitable any longer, he slowly climbed back up to the loft, moving quietly past Sam and walked to the end, seeing a big stick with a hooked end on it.

Picking it up, he stretched out and used the hooked end to lift the latch on the large window and push it outward with a soft squeal. He moved to the other end of the loft and did the same thing to a second window. Both of them didn't fly all the way open, but the pair of them were more than enough to pull the smoke out of the barn, ensuring adequate ventilation for them and the horses alike.

Back down at ground level, Tom poured a sparing splash of gasoline on the wood and paper, just to help get things going, then he stood back and tossed in a match, watching the flames blossom up in a loud *whomp*. Once the initial conflagration died down, he squatted closer and used a long stick to stir the kindling, blowing on it hard until the furniture on top began to crackle and smolder. Something creaked above him, and he looked up to see Sam standing with her green eyes poking up over the top of her coat.

"Whoa, that's warm!" she grinned, holding her hands out as the heat rose.

"Yeah, come on down."

She climbed down quickly, much more assuredly than she'd climbed up the day before, stepping closer to the fire and putting her palms up to the flames.

"I'm just trying to make sure it doesn't die," he said. "Once the biggest chunks of wood get hot beneath it, we'll be in good shape."

"I'll try to find us some chairs in the back."

"Good idea."

Tom went to the house for another piece of furniture, grabbing a heavy wooden coffee table, dragging it to the barn where he broke it apart with heavy cracking sounds. Sam came out of the back, pulling two stools behind her, placing them close to the fire, then backed them up to avoid a big cloud of black smoke that occasionally billowed up. Treated with chemicals as it was, the wood from furniture inside the house wasn't anywhere close to the best choice for a fire – especially indoors. But if the choice was between freezing to death and shaving a week or two off of their lives down the road thanks to some smoke inhalation, Tom would make the same choice every day of the week and twice on Sundays.

Tom tossed the coffee table legs on the fire and sat next to his daughter, the pair of them staring at the flames. "This should be good, for now. I just wish we had coffee to go with it."

"That would be amazing."

"Well, maybe I can find some in the pantry. I'll go check."

Tom followed the path he'd cut through the snow and went back into the kitchen. With the sun fully up – albeit partially obscured by cloud cover above - the house appeared different than it had the night before and earlier in the morning. More dilapidated in appearance, but no less scary and strange, it sat like a discarded piece of refuse on the property, some long-forgotten artifact left to rot. He found an old coffee maker in the kitchen, but the can of instant Java Brew in the pantry only had a stale half scoop and was probably months, or years, old.

Shaking his head, he returned to the fire with an apology. "Sorry, no coffee. None that looked remotely drinkable, anyway."

"That's okay." Sam had already removed a bottled water from her pack and was munching on a granola bar, her cheeks rosy red, and her eyes looking more alive and healthy than they had in some time. Tom picked out some snacks for himself and returned to his stool. They ate in silence as he imagined how they'd get home through the knee-high snow with no vehicle.

Samantha took a crunchy bite of her snack. "There's running water in the back of the barn if you need it. A sink and a toilet, too. There's just a curtain for privacy, but it works. I guess it didn't fully freeze in the barn."

"Seriously?"

"Yeah. I used it while you were searching for coffee."

"Good to know." Tom glanced over his shoulder. "Come to think of it, this barn looks like they built it to withstand a tornado."

"Well, why is the barn so awesome, but the house is so crappy?"

Tom shrugged. "I guess the owners don't actually live in the house. They probably just keep the horses out in the barn, or maybe they use it for storage or something. They might be planning on tearing out the old house and building a new one in its place. Who really knows?"

"Hey, we have some ramen in the packs," Sam grinned. "Want to make a real meal later on?"

"They have pots and pans inside, but I wouldn't trust the old stove in there, even if the gas lines or electricity still work. I'll rig up something out here, and we'll do it the old-fashioned way." He pressed the back of his palm against her head, then her neck. "Are you feeling any better? You don't feel like you have a fever."

"Actually, pretty good," Sam nodded. "I'm still coughing a bit, but the congestion is mostly broken up."

Tom grinned with relief. "That's great, honey. Let's see how you feel later. Maybe we can get back on the road if you're up to it."

Sam nodded enthusiastically but they both looked up at the open window with concern as the wind kicked back up, gusts of snow blowing back inside the barn.

Chapter 15
Barbara McKnight
Bristol, Virginia

Winds and driving snow howled outside the small prefab building, shaking the plastic and metal exterior. Occasionally the satellite dish and other equipment on the roof received a nasty slap from the shifting wind, groaning and creaking but holding fast, designed by engineers who might not have anticipated such extreme conditions, but prepared for them regardless. Inside, Barbara lifted a tin cup and sipped the bitter camp coffee, her feet tapping nervously on the floor, bleary eyes glued to the computer screen as she read and re-read the information about Tom.

"They want him for a mission to collapse the anomaly." She shook her head for the hundredth time. "They need Tom's help."

"You think they got the wrong guy?" Darren sat next to her, leaning back in a springy chair with his feet on the lieutenant's desk. He'd seen the same mission breakdown as Barbara, but he had no better idea of what was going on than her.

"No, I can see the Navy being interested in having him as part of their projects. That's what kept him away from coming home, remember? I wonder if he resisted, and that's why they want him?"

"Well, you'd know that better than me."

"I'm just glad they're not after him for some crime." Barbara drew a pointed breath. "Not that Tom would have ever hurt anyone or stolen anything unless it was to protect Samantha."

"You could be right. Maybe he resisted helping them and tried to get away. Given what we've found out about our wonderful military lately, it seems they'll do anything to get what they want, laws and morality be damned."

Darren stretched and yawned, the pair having been up all night, keeping an eye on the storm and occasionally checking on the bound soldiers to ensure they weren't trying to break their bonds. They'd yet to hear from the soldiers they'd tied up in the guard shack, and the occasional check-ins from the guards they'd passed on the way in were handled by a combination of gruff responses from Barbara and a healthy helping of static from the storm.

Barbara yawned in response to Darren, and for the eighth time began re-reading everything she found on Tom, her fear over what might have happened to him verging on overwhelming. Looking over the report log, the last entry showed a call between an agent named Keith Moore and a Lieutenant Colonel Banks. "It says here his last known location was somewhere east of South Hill. That's not too far. There was a wreck, but the subjects – that's Tom and Sam – escaped from this agent guy, this *Keith*. His code name is Arrowhead."

"Now, that really makes me think Tom was on the way home with Sam."

"I just hope they're not hurt." She shook her head, eyes glassing over with worry. "And I don't like this agent assigned to him. This Keith." She pulled up the man's profile yet again, staring down his photograph. His light hair and plain features were deceiving and his blue eyes were small beneath his thin eyebrows, no sign of a smile visible across his face. "He looks shifty to me."

"I agree," Darren said, observing the screen from afar. "A real shithead, as they say."

The weight of everything bore down on Barbara and she wiped away a tear before it had a chance to race down her cheek, summoning up her courage, refusing to give in to the emotions. "Whatever is happening, I think we need to go. I mean, like, now. Tom and Sam could already be home."

Darren stood straight and crossed to the window. He tapped on it and glanced back. "I have to disagree with you there. This storm has barely eased up. If we wait a few more hours, though, it might be passable."

"It'll be fine."

"I'm telling you, the Jeep isn't going to make it very far in this stuff."

Barbara stood and went to the window, staring at the sheets of snow coming down. She tapped her finger on her chin. "Well, maybe one of those big armored trucks will. What do they call them? Armored people carriers, or something?"

"Armored *personnel* carriers, yeah. APCs."

"Okay. So we get the keys to one of those APCs, throw the kids in the back, and head up the road. We come back for the Jeep later."

"You want to steal a million-dollar vehicle and take it for a spin?"

"I think we've already crossed the Rubicon as far as crimes against the feds go, don't you think? I need to get my kids home safe. I need to be there when my husband and daughter get there. They can bill me for the damned vehicle."

Darren chuckled. "I'm sure glad to have you on my side."

"Besides, there are other guards around. As soon as the weather breaks, they'll leave their shacks and come looking for Briggs."

"You're probably right," Darren said, starting to come around. "We're only a few minutes up the road, and the faster we can get out of here, the better."

"I'll talk to the lieutenant and get the keys. Can you see to the men in the guard shack? Take them some MRE's and water. Make sure they won't die anytime soon."

"All right." Darren gathered the supplies in a satchel and plunged into the cold. The sound of his exiting the building, and the gust of wind blasting through woke Linda and she stirred in her cot, sitting up.

"What's going on, mom?"

"We're going home, honey. Can you wake Jack up and get your and his boots and everything on?"

"Sure, Mom."

Barbara took some rations and bottled water into the storeroom where the lieutenant and soldier sat back-to-back on the cot. Shelves full of supplies lined the walls, and a locked rack of weapons sat on the opposite side. She circled around the pair and stood in front of Lieutenant Briggs.

"Are you comfortable?"

The woman glared at Barbara through angry, dark eyes. "What do you think? My wrists are sore, and I have to use the bathroom."

"I'm really sorry about all this." She shrugged. "But you took my kids... You took a lot of people's kids. You didn't think there would be repercussions from someone, eventually?"

Briggs' former icy, professional demeanor had cracked over the last several hours in captivity, and she nodded reluctantly. "In hindsight... yes."

"If you had children, you would've understood that from the start." The younger woman's face grew dark, lowering her head. "Now, here's the deal. We're leaving you here with rations and water. There are three guards tied up in shack four, and they're being brought water and rations, too. The guards from the other shack are still there, and they'll come looking for you all when the storm lifts." Barbara shifted the rifle on her shoulder, squatting down to get eye-to-eye with Briggs. "I suggest you and your people not come after us. You already took my children from me once. There won't be a second time."

To her credit, the woman managed to ignore Barbara's threat, summon up her courage and try digging for information. "Where will you go?"

"North," she lied. "Far away from you people. Maybe Canada, if they'll let us cross."

Briggs sneered. "You'll never survive the cold."

"Watch us," Barbara hissed. "And consider this – how are your superiors going to react when you tell them that you let a couple of country bumpkins overpower you and your men, free people from your detainment camp and get away scot-free? You think you might be in a *bit* of trouble for that?" Briggs' face faltered and she nervously licked her lips as Barbara tried a different tact. "Have you put everyone through processing yet? All those people out there?"

"Not everyone."

Barbara exaggeratedly looked around, then lowered her voice to a conspiratorial whisper so that the guard nearby couldn't hear. "Then let me suggest something to you, young lady. Use the storm as a reason to bug out fast. Get the last load of civilians that remain and hit the road. The rest, including my kids, were just casualties."

"Casualties?"

Barbara tilted her head, motioning to the brutal storm raging on the other side of the structure's thin walls. "Casualties of the wind and cold. Frostbite. Death. Maybe a few got lost in the snow. Cover your ass. Then you keep going south where it's nice and warm."

Briggs stared at her and Barbara shrugged, standing back up. "Your choice. Now then, where would I find the keys to an APC?"

Briggs gawked. "You want one of our APCs?"

"Thought I might take it for a spin."

"You... they don't use—" She shook her head. "No way. You're *not* taking an armored carrier. Absolutely not."

Barbara ignored her protests. "They don't use what now? Keys? Hmmm... I'll bet they use security key cards, right? Like the ones I saw in your top desk drawer, the ones we used to open the gates."

The lieutenant gulped but kept her mouth shut, worry written across her face. Barbara smiled in satisfaction and turned to walk away.

"You be safe, Briggs." She nodded to the lieutenant. "I hope, for your sake, that I don't see you again."

Barbara returned to the control room and helped get the kids finished bundling up in their FEMA-issued jackets, hats, and gloves. None of them were ideal for blizzard conditions, but they'd be fine for the ten or fifteen minutes it would take to reach an APC. Before leaving, she crossed to the desk and rifled through the top drawer. Sure enough, the five security cards she'd seen previously still sat inside attached to lanyards and she slipped all of them around her neck before checking for more in the other drawers. Satisfied she had the ones she needed, Barbara shuffled over to where the kids were waiting and adjusted the rifle on her shoulder.

"Ready?"

"Ready!"

They peered through their tightly bound hoods as she opened the door, a cone of wind blasting her in the chest, knocking her back a full step before she could recover. A drift of snow fell inside, covering the melt left from when Darren had gone out earlier. Bending forward, fighting the wind's rough gusts, she guided the kids outside, then she turned and pulled the door shut behind her before doing an about-face and staring into the wind once more. It was twice as bad as the previous evening, blasting them like an army of banshees and a full two feet of snow on the ground, which would make it hard for Jack to walk without help. The only positive she could identify was that the sun was starting to come up, making it slightly easier to see even through the intense storm.

"Which way?" Linda shouted.

"Follow me!"

Barbara lifted Jack into her arms and followed the path Darren had created to guard shack four, which was already being filled in by the howling winds. The going was rough, and she quickly learned to keep her feet high and legs pumping to push through the snow. Halfway there, Darren lumbered through the drifts back toward them, ramming forward with long, striding shuffles to clear a path.

When he reached them, he put his hands on her shoulders, practically yelling into her face to be heard over the storm. "The guards are fine. Thirty people and their kids left on busses this morning before the accumulation could get worse. The rest are huddled in the children's' holding area. They'll be fine until the storm blows over, but they decided to stay here and get taken south."

"Great! I'm glad some decided to leave!" Barbara shouted back. "Now let's focus on ourselves. Come on!"

Darren led the way, finding another chain link passage through the east side of camp, rifle out and ready in case of any surprises. Barbara held Jack in her arms while gripping Linda's hand, blinking away the snow that blew in her eyes. All she could do was focus on her friend's wide back as he paved a path for them, the four stumbling and trudging along until they came to a gate. Darren passed a security card over the reader and the magnetic locks popped, then he threw his shoulder against it to shove it open enough for them to squeeze through.

What seemed like a continuation of the vast expanse of white stretched ahead and around them, the snowy grasses rising past her knees, and she clutched her son and kept moving, her thighs screaming from the strain. Once, she didn't lift her boots high enough and stumbled into a soft drift, landing on top of Jack. Spitting snow and ice, she struggled to get upright, grunting and lifting him by his jacket and he suddenly rose out of her grasp, almost levitating upward, and looked to see Darren holding him easily in his arms.

"I've got him! Let's keep going, it's not far now!"

She nodded and allowed Linda to help her up, then together they bowed their heads and followed Darren across the rest of the field to end up in someone's backyard. They slogged past a jungle gym, then down a driveway to the road where the massive APCs sat like monoliths covered in white. Darren stopped at the end of the driveway and set Jack down, keeping him close to his legs to protect him from the wind. "Which one?"

Barbara fished the security cards out of her pocket and sorted through them. They each bore a coded number but were otherwise blank and she looked at the long line of armored vehicles, deciding to try the one on the end that faced the direction they wanted to go.

"The first one!" she shouted, pointing off to her left.

Darren nodded and lifted Jack while Barbara marched between two vehicles and onto the road, cutting a path to the first APC. Standing next to the massive truck, Barbara glanced around in confusion.

"They don't have any doors. Do we have to climb in through a hatch or something?" She looked up, imagining how they'd hoist Jack and Linda on top of the slick, snow-covered machine.

"The door's in back!" Darren yelled. He snatched at her coat arm and made a gesture for her to follow. They found a small pair of double doors in the rear of the vehicle, wide enough for a pair of men to duck through, and they both swept snow off the back with their gloves, looking for a slot to stick a badge.

Barbara found a pad on the left side of the frame. She pulled out her security cards and placed one against it. The pad blinked red, so she tried another, and it blinked red, too. The others failed until she held up the last one with a sigh. If it wasn't the right key, they'd have to go down the whole line of vehicles, or she'd have to trek back to the control center and get the correct one from Briggs. Saying a silent prayer, she passed the last card over the reader, shouting with joy as it blinked green and the doors popped open an inch.

"Yes!" she exclaimed, clearing the excess snow away with her feet as Darren worked to spread the doors the rest of the way open.

Barbara poked her head in to see two rows of cramped seats, storage compartments above and below, and the control section up front. She climbed in first and turned to take the kids as Darren handed them up. He then followed her aboard, slamming the doors shut behind them, the barking wind quieting to a dull roar as the interior lights snapped on, bathing them in a yellow glow.

"This is so cool." Jack looked around in wonder.

Barbara bent over as she slowly walked forward, heading for the controls in the front of the vehicle. "Okay, let's see if I can start this and get some heat on."

"You can do it, Mom," Linda said, patting her on the arm.

She shed her backpack and rifle, climbing past the crowded crew chairs to the front. Falling into the lightly padded driver's chair, she placed her hands on the wheel, searching the controls for a way to start it up, a switch and a button next to the gear switch looking like the best place to start. She flipped the switch to the "On" position and pressed the button, and to her surprise, the vehicle shivered to life with a confident, rattling rumble.

"That was too easy." Darren lumbered to the front and sat next to her in a control seat marked with screens and dials and two separate pairs of headphones.

"Piece of cake," she smiled. "Now comes the tricky bit. I have to figure out how to see out of this blasted thing."

She fiddled with some switches until a monitor popped to life in front of her, showing her a high-definition view of the snowy road.

"It must be a remote camera system," Darren said. "You can drive while still protected by the armor."

"Technology is amazing." She studied the snow-dusted camera view. "But I'm not sure how comfortable I'll be driving with this little video screen."

"There's always the port hatch right there." Darren stood and gestured to a sliver in the armor in front of her, covered by a small hatch. "Just flip the lever up and you can see out."

Barbara frowned. "That looks even harder. Not to mention colder."

The street stretched ahead, curving way up and to the left, though the blanket of white was so complete she couldn't see the edges.

"Mom, can you turn on the heat?" Linda asked.

"Oh, yeah, one sec kiddo."

Barbara searched around for the controls and found them farther on the right. They were even simpler than those for driving the APC, with a fan and hot/cold setting, the former of which she turned to high. Warm air began filling the cabin, and Linda sighed contentedly from the back.

"Thanks!"

"You're welcome," she crooned in return, a smile playing at the edges of her lips. Having her children back was better than she could have imagined. If they could all just get back home, things would be almost back to normal. Almost.

She refocused on the road, a blanket of white with no clear path, snow flying into the camera's eye, half-blinding her. Still, it seemed easy enough so long as she took it slow and didn't run into anything.

"Okay. I'll put it in gear and see if I can pull out. Hold on, everyone."

There were only two pedals, so Barbara treated it like it was an automatic, pressing the button on the shifter and moving it into the "Drive" position. The transmission kicked in, and the vehicle growled in eagerness to go, the engine having smoothed out over the few minutes they'd been sitting still. She eased up on the brake and the APC easily rolled forward, the expected resistance from the snow not present as they moved through it like it wasn't even there.

"This thing must be super heavy," she remarked.

"At least a few tons," Darren agreed. "I have to agree with Jack. It's pretty awesome."

Barbara pulled onto the road, eyes glued to the screen, driving carefully up Wallace Pike as the diesel engine rumbled. The road wound through the Virginia hills, raising over ridges and sinking into valleys filled with snow, though the camera's view made distances hard to judge, and more than once she almost ran off the road or hit a fallen tree trunk due to misjudging depth and distance.

The trees along the roadside were caught in a winter wonderland, their branches bent under the snow's weight, ice clinging to the tree trunks, reflecting dull light from the masked sun overhead and the APC's headlights. The gullies and ditches were filled in like someone had taken a paint roller over everything to smooth out the landscape. Drifts piled against fences, stalled vehicles, and farmsteads along the roadsides.

The wind slammed against the APC's side, barely shaking it, and Barbara turned down the heater, the air inside the cabin already warm enough to cause her to feel beads of sweat breaking out on her forehead. She felt like a bully as they plowed along, kicking up a wake of white from the tires, pushing aside any obstacles in her path. She only had to stop once when the wind gusts made it impossible to see, continuing on once the view cleared. They wove up and over a long, curving part of the road easily enough but started to run into trouble on the descent. She was creeping along, careful not to lock the brakes or make any sharp or sudden turns, but the incline was steep, and their speed increased even though she'd not lifted her foot off the brake. Something scraped beneath them, the knobby tires struggling to retain traction on a thick layer of ice, and Barbara let out a soft gasp.

"What is it?" Darren asked, rising in his seat.

"Um. I think we're sliding." She turned the front wheels back and forth, but it didn't affect their direction.

"It's probably black ice beneath the snow. Try to go with it. Let off the brake."

Barbara did as he instructed, but it felt like sitting inside a lead weight with no way to control it. The APC began to shift and turn sideways as it slid down the road, gaining speed, the grinding beneath them growing even more intense. The frame shuddered as they ran through – or over – some unseen object, and all she could do was grip the wheel, whipping it back and forth in a panic. All of her attempts were fruitless, and they slipped along at a steady thirty miles-per-hour, shedding snow everywhere. As they neared the bottom, a spray of icy snow from a low-hanging tree limb obscured the camera, blinding her completely. She released the wheel, gripped the armrests, and called back, "Brace yourselves, kids!"

The APC dipped sideways and slammed into a ditch, landing with a loud bang, the vehicle's tough frame groaning in protest of being roughly bounced around. Barbara had remembered to buckle herself and both of the children in, but Darren fell on top of her as they hit the ditch, apologizing and excusing himself multiple times as he climbed up and stood on the oddly angled floor. The crash, if it could even be called that, had been far from dramatic. No glass had shattered, and nothing seemed to be broken. It felt more like being on a slow-moving amusement park ride that had come to an abrupt halt.

"That didn't hurt at all," Jack remarked, sounding somehow disappointed.

"Well, we might be stuck, but we *are* in a multi-ton armored vehicle," Barbara mumbled as Darren fell back to his seat with a grunt. She gripped the wheel and peered at a tiny spot on her screen where the snow had been shaken off, giving her a pinhole view of the world outside. "Let's see if I can get us out of this."

She turned the wheel to the right and pressed the gas pedal, the wheels churning in response, the front end promising to find purchase, but another deep part of the ditch stymied them as the vehicle slipped, falling a few inches more, ending up at an even more awkward angle. She tried forward and reverse, twisting the wheel in every direction, though nothing she did freed them. Finally, Barbara gave up, letting go of the wheel and sitting back in her seat, feeling like a fool as the engine idled away. "Well, at least we're warm."

"You couldn't have done any better," Darren said, sounding positive. You've never trained on one of these vehicles. It would have happened to anyone, including me."

"The good news is, we're not very far from the house. Maybe a mile or so." She gave him a hopeful look. "We'll have to hoof it."

"Easy peasy," Darren smiled, looking back at the kids. "You guys ready for a cross-country hike?"

"No!" Linda shouted, while Jack shouted, "Yes!" at the same time.

"It doesn't matter if we're ready or not," Barbara pointed out, turning halfway in her seat, an amused expression on her face. "We can't sit here all day. The fuel will eventually run out, it'll get cold, and you'll freeze into kid-sized popsicles for the bears to come munch on. How about those apples?"

"Good point," Linda nodded. "Kind of dramatic, though, but let's go."

They bundled up again, shouldered their backpacks and weapons, and prepared to leave the APC's protection. Barbara popped the back doors and looked down at the ditch where they'd crashed, sitting on the edge of the truck, sticking her toe into the snow. Her foot kept sinking, then her leg, and she ended up never touching the hard ground.

"This is going to be tricky." Barbara winced, then put her other foot down and dropped off the edge, falling until her feet finally hit hard ground. The snow drift came up to her chest, and she had to wade through it to get turned around.

"Hand the kids to me." She lifted her arms and gestured at them with her gloved fingers.

Linda came first, and while Barbara tried not to set her on the ground, she briefly slipped out of her hands, falling into the drift. Barbara caught her up and walked her to the shoulder of the road where she waded out of the snow and stood on the pavement, then turned and waved at her mother from the safety of the road.

Barbara returned to the truck, a gust of wind blew snowflakes into her face, stinging her cheeks as Darren handed down Jack. He was much lighter and didn't slip from her grasp, and she easily lifted him, carrying him like a stack of firewood under her arm to the edge of the road where his sister helped him to climb up out of the ditch. Darren dropped to the ground last, slipping on the odd footing, Barbara reaching out to help steady him with a hand on his shoulder as he slammed the APC's doors shut.

"I'm good," he huffed, pointing to the road. "Go ahead. I'll be right behind you."

Barbara climbed the side of the ditch, holding Linda's hand for support, then the three of them turned to help Darren. Once they all stood in the road, she faced the screaming wind and looked toward home.

"About a mile, you think?" Darren asked.

"Yep. I recognize this road."

"Let's do it. I'll take point."

"And I'll follow up from behind to make sure neither of these rascals get lost in a snowdrift."

With a chuckle, Darren put his head and shoulders down and began heading into the wind, the kids right behind him, walking in his footsteps. Barbara brought up the rear, slogging through thigh-high drifts as the cold seeped into her coat. After a quarter mile, her breaths came in gasps, and her toes tingled ,but she turned her shoulders down and continued plowing ahead.

"I've never seen a storm like this in my life!" Barbara shouted from the back of the group.

"Me neither!" Darren agreed. "Not around these parts, anyway. It's unnatural!"

The wind punched at them like a prize fighter, causing the kids to wobble back and forth, Barbara reaching out to keep them from toppling into the drifts, shoving them forward in Darren's footsteps. An hour of fighting through the tundra-like conditions brought them to the end of their driveway, where they had another uphill battle, though it was bolstered by the sight of familiar surroundings. Darren waded around their wrecked truck and up the sloping lane to the front porch, the group following behind until they stood in the front yard, looking around at their powder-transformed homestead

"We made it!" Barbara shouted, and Linda raised her bundled arms with a whoop of delight. Jack celebrated by throwing a snowball at his sister, which she retaliated with, and the pair lobbed a few more at each other as Darren and Barbara watched them, relaxation flooding over them as the reality of where they were finally struck home.

"We actually made it." Barbara marveled. "Hard to believe."

"Yup. Couldn't have done it without your tenacity, Barbara."

"What are you talking about? You're the whole reason this even worked. Thank you, Darren, sincerely."

He gave the broad-shouldered man a brief hug before turning to the children, who had devolved into rolling around on the ground, wrestling each other to see who could pour more snow into the other one's jacket.

"Okay, kids. Up!" Barbara gave them a brief hug and gestured for them to stand, then she slogged up to the porch with weak legs. Inside, they shed their boots and clothes, hanging their jackets on hooks and leaving their footwear on a long, rubber mat. A moment after they came in, Marie hobbled around the corner on a crutch Barbara didn't remember owning, looking weak but smiling broadly at the sight of everyone. She threw her arms open for Darren and he grabbed her in a bear hug, giving her a kiss and holding her tight before she exchanged hugs with Barbara, Linda and Jack, the story of what happened pouring out of the children's mouths while Barbara lingered, watching their joy with a swelling heart.

They moved the party into the kitchen where Marie announced she was making hot chocolate, to which Darren responded by shushing her and pulling out a chair so she could sit while he took care of things. Marie smiled, easing down with visible difficulty despite doing her best to put on a brave face.

"I'll get you some stronger pain medication," Barbara assured her, heading to a kitchen cabinet and picking through the bottles. "Is it pretty bad?"

"It's a screamer for sure," she nodded, voice shaking with pain. "Probably the worst I've felt since I was a kid. Eight out of ten on the pain scale."

"I'm so sorry, Marie. Were you able to hold things together while we were gone? You didn't hurt yourself further, right?"

"No, no, I was fine. Just laid down for the most part, worried sick out of my mind."

They let Smooch out of the laundry room, and Jack fed her, then the shepherd hobbled from person to person, gifting everyone with vigorous tail wags and licks, ensuring that they were all well and accounted for. Marie got her medicine, and Darren fixed them cups of hot chocolate, the afternoon turning into early evening as they talked and caught up. Barbara and Linda threw together lunch meat sandwiches and chips as they solidified the events of the past day. There was no real sense of the changing time as they spoke, everything beyond their cozy walls was just bleak grayness.

Near the end of the story, Marie gaped in awe as they told her about the military camp and how they'd broken in, amazed that they'd managed to get the kids out without hurting anyone. "Well, I got tired of lying there," Marie said, "so I got up and hopped around." She lifted the crutch slightly off the ground. "I found this in the garage."

"Must have been from a long time ago when Tom hurt his foot or something." Barbara shook her head. "Leave it to you to get up and find a crutch after getting shot. You're a treasure, Marie."

"Thank you," Marie beamed, already looking better after the heavier dose of pain medication, her expression taking on a dreamier quality to it as the chemicals worked their magic.

They stayed up well beyond midnight, playing a little Uno with the wind gusting and blowing snow against the house. The walls creaked and groaned but held firm under the storm's weight. After a few hours of laughing, talking and giggling over terribly played hands, Barbara sobered up.

"Okay, people. I hate to ruin the fun, but we might have some pretty angry military folks visiting us soon, so we need to set up our regular watch again and be back on guard."

"What about the animals, Mom?" Jack asked, ruffling Smooch's fur.

"The yard animals can stay in the barn, so they'll be fine for one day. We'll feed them in the morning. Put Smooch in the laundry room and go up with your sister to get some rest. I guess we don't have to worry about school right now…" Something in the realization that things would *never* be back to normal struck her in the chest, and she paused, fighting back a swell of emotions. Reading the room, Jack got up and put Smooch in her room, then the kids pounded their way down the hall and up the steps to theirs.

Turning to the Everetts, Barbara spoke. "Why don't you two—"

A horn blew from somewhere out front, a loud, bleating sound that blasted repeatedly, cutting through the storm to reach them up on the hill.

"Do we have *more* guests?" Marie asked with a wrinkled brow.

"Sounds like it," Darren growled. "Military already, you think?"

Barbara shook her head. "I doubt it. Not this fast."

The sound came again, an obnoxious snort, insistent and urgent, whoever it was demanding someone come outside. Barbara went to the counter and retrieved her shotgun, then she padded into the foyer and put on her boots, quickly tying them.

"Mom, it's a truck!" Linda called down.

The Everetts beat her to the front window where they peered through the sliver of space they'd left to watch the road.

"The girl's right. Looks like something big down there."

"It's not the military," Darren peered over his wife's shoulder. "Maybe they're just regular folks, stuck in the snow and can't get out."

Barbara raised on her toes and looked between the Everetts. The sliver they'd left for watching the road was slim, and the storm only made it that much harder to see. With the wind gusting furiously, all she could discern were the yellow and white lights that outlined the truck's basic shape down at the end of their driveway. "I can't really see through the snow."

"It could be Tom and Sam," Marie said, a hopeful note in her tone.

"You might be right," Barbara agreed with a sharp breath of panic. "Darren, throw on your shoes. I'm going out the front door. Can you cover me around the side?"

"One-hundred percent." He shuffled to the stairs and grabbed his boots. Plopping down on the third step, he tugged them on and began lacing them up, then he gave Barbara a pointed look. "My rifle's in the kitchen. I'll grab it on the way out and meet you around front."

She nodded and watched him grab his coat, shrugging it on as he trod down the hall. Barbara waited until he stood at the back door with his weapon before she started throwing the deadbolts.

"Be careful, honey!" Marie called from the dining room.

Barbara nodded, smiling, then she grabbed the door handle and whipped it open. Facing the screaming wind with her shotgun barrel pointing into the storm, she shifted left and right, trying to glare through the mess, but the snow had thickened and the winds were screaming banshees, visibility only twenty yards, at best.

Barbara put one boot on the threshold and hesitated, then she took a deep breath and stepped outside.

Chapter 16
Tom McKnight
Somewhere in Virginia

Sometime around lunch, the wind and snow picked up to unbearable levels, blowing through the open window, the cold and warm air combining to blow into their faces, mixing the black smoke and cinders with it. After a half hour of shuffling around back and forth to find a place to both stay warm and out of the smoke, Tom shook his head and stood, looking up at the high window in the barn.

"We need to ventilate this a little better. There's too much smoke in here. It's only about twenty feet to those upper window." He bit his lip and shook his head. "If we can direct the smoke better, it would solve our problem."

"Shouldn't we just pack to get going?"

"Not yet, honey. We've still got a lot more to go, and we're not moving until you're feeling a lot better. That cold will sap your strength even if you're in tip-top shape. No way are we heading out till you're better."

"But…"

"I know. Me too. We've waited this long, though. We can wait a few more hours."

Samantha sighed and nodded, accepting defeat. "Fine, I guess."

"That's my girl," he smiled. "Now come on, let's figure out how to avoid getting suffocated in here."

"But how?" Sam scrunched her brows in thought. "I mean, what can we use to funnel the smoke out?"

Tom grinned. "I've got an idea. You bring in the rest of the wood from outside and stack it in a neat pile inside here. I'll be back in about forty-five minutes."

"Okay." Sam coughed a little, but still sounded more like her old self.

Tom left the barn and walked to the shed, head down against the rising winds. Bits of ice and snow attacked him from all sides, swirling around his face and riding cold drafts inside his coat. It was approaching the low tens and dropping steadily necessitating a quick pace to his work.

In the shed, he found a sledgehammer, a long-handled screwdriver, a roll of wire and a pair of pliers. He plowed his way through the growing snowdrifts to the house, then stomped up the front porch and went inside, standing with his breath making puffs of warm air, looking at the walls and ceilings. He saw one air intake in the hallway, but it didn't leave him enough space to swing the hammer, so he circled to the dining room and estimated the layout of things under the wall, putting his hand against the part where he thought the edge of the duct would be as the wind whistled through cracks in the old structure and the floors creaked.

"Time to heat things up."

He cocked the head of the sledgehammer back and brought it around with a mighty thud against the wall, sending chips of paint and plaster in all directions. The house was easily a hundred years old, constructed of wooden slats and old plaster, which made it more durable and tougher to get through. Still, Tom was up to the task. He whacked and beat at the walls, pulling away sections until he'd laid bare seven feet of ductwork.

Using the screwdriver and wire cutters to separate the pieces, he yanked them out, placed them in the kitchen and went in search of more. He found more ducts in the living room and smashed the wall apart to reach them. Once he had two long pieces, he ascended the rotted steps to the second floor and removed a few more feet of aluminum. By the time he was done, he was sweating beneath his clothes, chest pained from sucking cold air for an hour.

"I hope this works," he said with a shudder.

He left the sledgehammer in the house and carried the ducts and smaller tools out to the barn. Inside, Sam had kept the fire going, though she sat back a ways from it, trying to stay clear of most of the smoke. Tom fitted two sections of ductwork together and leaned it against the wall, seeing it was already almost long enough to reach the high window.

"I just need to find a way to stabilize it. Be right back."

He returned to the house, dug out some curved vents and brought them to the barn. With the final sections in hand, he carried them up to the loft and connected them together so they bent toward the window, then wove the wire beneath the ducts to suspend it from a ceiling beam while Sam held the other end in place above the fire pit.

It looked like a big, unwieldy stove pipe, but it only weighed about fifteen pounds, so it was easy to wire in place. Tom already noticed a lot of the smoke was flowing up through the duct and rolling out the window into the sky. He climbed down and stood back, looking at the improvised chimney, shivering as the cold air seeped through his clothes to cool his sweaty skin.

"Now I need to make something to catch the smoke and funnel it into the open end. Like the vent hood over a restaurant stove."

Sam nodded and looked around for something to use while Tom trudged to the house once more. By then, the wind and snow were almost blinding, and he shivered uncontrollably as he fought his way to the front door.

Down in the basement, it was even colder than upstairs, topped with a chilling mustiness tickled his nasal passages to a near sneeze. Over by the furnace, branching up from the main heating unit, were wide pieces of duct that would be perfect for what they needed. Hands shaking from the cold, Tom disassembled several sections with the screwdriver and hammer and placed them to the side, and once he had assembled the right-sized pieces, he took them back upstairs and out to the barn.

The wind caught the materials and nearly whipped them out of his hands, but he got them there and kicked on the barn doors, holding the metal tight to his torso. Sam opened the doors, holding on against the wind as Tom pushed his way inside. Without hesitation, he assembled the pieces, fixing the wide-ended one into the long piece that ran to the window and let it dangle. It hung there, drifting loosely back and forth. He picked up the roll of wire, unwound a large section, and tried to weave it under the duct but his fingers were numb, and he could barely handle the pieces.

Sam looked worried. "Dad, are you okay?"

"No." Tom clenched and relaxed his hands several times, though they were numb to the bone. He shook his head. "If I feed down some wire from the loft, can you fasten it under the end piece so we can keep it in position?"

Sam nodded, and Tom climbed up to the loft, feeling bone weary and nearing exhaustion. The trek back and forth through the howling winds had left him breathing hard, and his shoulders ached from hammering at the walls.

Just a little more. Keep pushing.

He put the end of the wire over one of the beams and fed it down to Sam who wrapped the wire beneath the bend in the duct, pulled it snug, and twisted the ends together. Tom let go and stepped back to see the wide-open end resting three feet above the fire pit.

"Excellent," he spoke through deep, whole-body shivers. "Now let's get the fire roaring again."

Together, they threw more wood on the fire, Tom poking and prodding at it to raise the flames until they were licking against the duct, sending smoke straight up and outside. When the first burst of warmth blossomed over his cheeks, Tom released a sigh of relief and collapsed back on his haunches, rubbing his hands together in front of the fire. Sam pulled their stools closer, and together they sat and got warm. The cold left Tom in waves, one minute feeling fine, the next overcome by an uncontrollable bout of shivering. Over an hour, he warmed from the brink of freezing, even taking off his socks and shoes to dry them, and Sam took off her jacket, relaxing as she leaned up against him in front of the fire.

After a while, she eyed their already dwindling wood supply. "I hate to say it, but this wood isn't going to last much longer. Do you want me to go out and collect more?"

"Absolutely not," he said. "I might be cold, but you're sick. The last thing we need is for you to get pneumonia. Plus, I've got another idea."

Tom bundled up and braved the cold once more. Another five or six inches of snow had fallen since he'd started out earlier in the day, and it had almost covered his previously made paths. Arms over his head, he fought his way into the house as it creaked and groaned around him. The wind was doing its work on the already weakened structure, the walls shaking and shuddering.

Leaning against the back of the house were a few pieces of loose plywood and he pried one loose, then punched a hole through one corner with the screwdriver he'd found in the shed. After laying it on the porch, he collected several furniture scraps in the kitchen and bashed them into smaller pieces with the sledgehammer.

Almost an hour later, he had a nice pile of smashed drawers, table legs, and end tables from the upstairs. The bed frames had been a treasure trove of fuel, the heavy, Amish structures having taken him extra time to smash, but eventually he added those to the pile.

Body growing numb, he carried a few pieces back to the barn and threw them on the fire. The space had warmed pleasantly in the time he'd been gone, and he stood back and watched as his hastily constructed duct system guided the sooty smoke up through the window.

"Wow, this thing is working great," he said. "It's pretty toasty in here."

"Is that all the wood you could get?" Sam looked at the few pieces he'd brought out with worry. She'd taken off her hat off and put her hair back in a ponytail.

"Nope," Tom grinned. Despite being numb and exhausted, his confidence was soaring through the roof, every little victory an encouragement, and he clung to hope with blind stubbornness. He walked back to the stalls where the horses were pressed against the rails, nickering for attention, and he patted the mare's snout and accepted some affectionate nuzzling in return.

Sam got up and followed him. "What are you doing?"

"I want to use the horses to help me drag stuff back."

"Oh, that's a great idea." She grinned with a minor degree of guilt. "I've been playing with them all morning. The chestnut mare seems the friendliest."

"I can tell," Tom laughed as the restless animal nudged him harder. "Now, we just need to figure out how to get a bridle on her."

"I can do it. I took riding lessons, remember?"

Tom vaguely remembered having paid for something like that, and they certainly didn't have anything to lose by letting her try. "Okay. Let's give it a shot, then."

Sam selected a bridle off a hook next to the mare's stall and turned it over in her hands. "This one should do nicely. Okay, hold the door for me."

Tom held open the stall door, and his daughter entered, being careful not to tangle the bridle.

"Hey, girl. Good girl." She slowly approached the horse, showing the assemblage to make sure she was friendly. The animal danced on her forelegs a moment before settling down, and Sam reached the reins over her head and laid them on her back, then rested her right arm on the horse's head and pressed down, holding everything in place.

Quickly, Sam pushed the bit against the mare's teeth, but she wouldn't easily take it and tried to spit it out, Tom watching in amazement as his daughter worked her thumbs into the animal's rear gums to get it to open its mouth.

"Wow!" Tom grinned. "I had no idea you could do that."

Sam lifted the brow band over the horse's ears and adjusted everything so it fit snugly, then she handed him the reins with a prim smile. "There you go. You should be able to lead her around."

"Amazing," Tom said, accepting control. "Hey, can you hand me that coil of rope on the back wall?"

"Sure, Dad. By the way, I named her."

"Oh?" Tom raised an eyebrow, already jokingly dreading what was coming next.

"Yep! I know how much you and mom loved the name 'Smooch' so I decided that this one's name should be 'Good Girl.'"

"Good Girl. Are you serious?" Tom deadpanned, then chuckled, rolling his eyes as Sam ran to get the rope. She handed it to him with a grin and he led the horse out of the stall and over to the barn door. Sam held it open for him, and Tom guided the animal out into the cold. At first, Good Girl fidgeted and stamped impatiently, seemingly happy to be going outside. But the first gust of wind hit her, and she flinched and tossed her head, nearly ripping the reins from Tom's hands.

"Good Girl." He patted her neck, reassuring her before leading her along the path to the house. She calmed at his touch and voice, and he gave a begrudging nod of approval. "I can see why Sam called you that."

The drifts had accumulated to his waist, snow almost completely covering the swing set. The wind buffeted them, and a white blindness filled his vision, and Tom held his left arm up to protect his face as the cold pecked away at his rejuvenated shell. His thighs burned from stomping his feet through the new snowfall, and the small of his back felt strained and tired.

At the concrete patio, Tom turned Good Girl around and got her pointed back toward the barn, then he threaded the rope through the hole he'd made in the aluminum sheeting and loosely tied it around the horse's reins. As Tom was securing the load, something snapped inside the near corner of the house and it shifted a bit, pieces of siding and shingles falling to the ground along with a massive pile of snow from the roof.

"Sheesh. Glad we weren't standing there." He turned to the mare. "Yah, girl! Come on! Let's get this back to the barn!"

True to her name, Good Girl allowed herself to be led, easily dragging the five-hundred or so pounds of wood over the snow drifts. Tom's ankles and knees screamed over the last few yards, but victory lingered just inches from his grasp.

"Good girl! Nice work!" Tom called as they pulled up to the door. He knocked, and Sam open the door while he guided the mare inside. Triumph surged through his as he stopped the horse so the pile of wood came to rest by their fire. Tom then circled around and fed a few pieces to the flames to keep it going while Sam shut the door, and together they soon had all the wood offloaded.

"We should have enough wood to last a day, maybe two." Sam stood next to the newly woken blaze with a smile on her lips.

Tom put his hands on his hips and looked everything over.

"We need more." He glanced toward the door. "The way it's snowing out there, I can't guarantee I'll be able to do it later."

"Are you sure?" Sam glanced toward the barn doors. "It doesn't seem like a good idea. Plus… when are we leaving? We're so close to home, dad."

"I know, hon, I know. But this storm is *bad*. Leaving now would just vastly increase our chances of dying out there. If we can hang on a while more until it dies down just a bit, then we'll be fine. I promise we'll leave as soon as it's safer, okay?"

"Okay… if you're sure."

"I'm positive," he said with an assured nod. "I'll leave Good Girl here while I bust up some more wood, then I'll bring her back out to pick it up."

"Okay, Dad. But be careful."

"I will."

Tom untied the rope from Good Girl's neck and dragged the thin piece of plywood back across the snow-covered yard, parking it on the concrete patio. He stared up at the unstable house, noting the right corner had fallen a little more, seeming out of alignment with the rest of the house. The brutal wind pushed and pulled at the roof, and the sides were visibly rocking under the stress.

"I'll stay close to the door," he told the wind with a quick shake of his head. "It won't be a problem. In and out. Piece of cake."

He stepped in and picked up the sledgehammer where he'd leaned it against the kitchen wall. Holding the heavy tool in his blistered hands, he glowered at the kitchen cabinets like they owed him money, then raised the hammer and brought it down with a crack on the fiberboard countertop, putting a massive hole in the center. Three strokes later, he'd smashed the entire left side into pieces, then he grabbed what he could and threw it out the door on the plywood sled. A low squeal resounded through the walls as he walked back in, pieces of plaster fallin from the ceiling.

"Just stay up a little longer," Tom whispered to the house. "I've almost got what I need out of you."

He finished smashing the cabinets to pieces and hauled the remnants to the sled, then dragged a curio cabinet from the dining room to the kitchen door and went to town on it. By then, his hands were numb, fingers blistered and cold as he dismantled the furniture. He swung the sledgehammer through sheer will alone, the frigid air stinging his lungs as he heaved and panted. After it was dismantled, he hauled the pile outside, piece-by-piece, legs wobbly with exhaustion. Taking a break for a moment, he leaned against the door frame, staring down the long hallway for something else he could tear apart.

He'd broken down the easy stuff on the first floor, and while the second floor held another bed frame and a big set of drawers, he'd be insane to go up the stairs given the state of the house. The house felt weak and airy beneath the brutal wind, its leaning obvious, the structural integrity long past compromised by the storm.

He glanced toward the barn as the snow filled up the path at an alarming rate, the intense snowfall having turned his visibility to almost nothing. Looking up, his saw white piling on the roof, thick clusters sliding off and falling along the sides.

"That's it," he decided. "I'm done."

He tossed the sledgehammer down and slogged back to the barn, slipping and sliding the entire way. Tom opened the door and took Good Girl's reins, guiding her out into the cold, and realized that he could no longer see the house from the barn. Pushing forward, he tried to find the path he'd trodden from the previous trips, but the drifts had all collapsed. No matter how much he squinted and glared, he couldn't see more than two feet in front of him. Good Girl was nothing but a shadow behind him, superimposed against the larger shadow of the barn.

He hesitated to continue, but the last load of firewood would give them enough wood to last a couple nights, maybe three. There was no way he wanted to stay for that long, but they were at the mercy of the storm, and whether it kept them from continuing for a few hours or a few days, they'd need to be prepared.

The wind spooked the mare, and she fought him, trying to draw back toward the barn and what she knew was shelter. But Tom went to her, soothing her with his words, holding the reins tightly as he wrapped his arm around her neck.

"Come on, girl," he said. "Just twenty more yards. It's right there."

They passed the swing set on his right. It was completely buried, an edifice on the blinding-white landscape, a way to mark their position in relation to the house. He'd gotten off track a little and made the adjustment, angling to the left, the last fifteen steps seeming to take forever, Tom lifting his feet to keep from dragging them through the thick drifts. He didn't see the plywood slab until he was right on top of it, snow piled high on one side and covering it in a thin layer of powder.

The house creaked and groaned louder than before, the wind raising chunks of ice and snow from the roof and scattering them across the yard with swishing sounds. A piece hit Tom's shoulder, but it broke apart easily; the only real danger was catching one in the face.

He turned Good Girl around and picked up the rope buried beneath the deep white powder, dragging it out and slipping, falling to his knees. With a grunt, he stood and continued his slog to the anxious mare, grabbing her reins with his free hand. Tom had just gotten the rope tied to the reins when a sustained wind blew from the southwest, bending the house toward the backyard. A massive groan went up just before the entire back wall peeled off and fell with a cracking sound that resonated in his head and sent spikes of panic and adrenaline surging through his body.

Tom looked skyward as the top floor shifted and bent toward them, a pile of snow slamming into his face, sending him to his knees and momentarily blinding him. He leapt up, and slapped at the horse's flank, shouting, "Go on, girl! Go! Go! Hiya!"

Good Girl jerked forward as the house came down on top of them. Part of a wall slammed the ground on Tom's right, another piece landing next to the mare. The horse fell off balance and tugged against the sled's weight, bumping him with her shoulder, sending him flying into the snow.

Face down in the cold, he heard a sickening thump, then a high, pained whinny as something heavy hit the snow next to him. A weight rolled on his leg but he scrambled from beneath it as the rest of the structure fell all around him in a crash of shingles and wood. Tom threw his arms over his head as he crouched down, cursing himself as images of his daughter flashed through his mind. He pictured her sitting in the barn, probably hearing the house collapse and wondering what happened. She'd wait for a few minutes, hopeful of his return, then, eventually, curiosity would draw her from the barn to wander outside and find him dead in the snow.

Tom waited for the pieces to finish falling, wincing and flinching as debris struck him in the shoulders and arms. Part of a huge section of framing ripped loose, spun, and smashed near his head, throwing up a wave of snow. The collapse stopped almost as soon as it had begun, leaving him with his cheeks pressed into the cold snow as the wind continued to gust, the sound of Good Girl's labored breathing reaching him from a few feet away.

Tom raised on his elbows and looked around. Piles of twisted wood and shingles lay everywhere, already collecting snow, barely visible through the storm. He crawled to the horse where she lay on her side, chest heaving in a labored way, though he couldn't see what was wrong with her. Tom rested one palm on her back and scrambled toward her head, her breathing labored and her chest rumbling with deep distress.

"Hey Good Girl, what's wrong?" Tom edged closer, gently cooing as he looked for an injury in the swirling snow. The horse tried to raise her head at his approach, but quickly dropped it, snuffing again.

"Is it your head, girl? Did something hit you?" Crawling closer, he saw blood pooling from her forehead and upper body into the snow and, nearby, a large section of the house frame lay partially on top of her. "That's what hit you," he murmured. "And if you hadn't been in the way, it would have hit me."

Good Girl snorted and tried to rise again, thrashing her legs, but fell back weakly. Eyes watering, guilt stabbing him in the chest, Tom sat there listening to the whipping wind and the horse's labored breathing. A sick feeling filled his gut and he gave her a little nudge with his shoulder, and when she wouldn't budge, he returned to her wounded head and tried to assess the injury. Squinting and prodding, he felt around until he found a soft spot just above her eyes, the mare shuddering and whinnying in pain.

"Oh, no." Tom's eyes filled with tears. "I'm sorry, girl. I really am. You did such a good job. Such a very, very good job."

He waited with her for a few moments, stroking her nose and speaking softly to her, until her cries of pain became too much. Rising on shaky legs, he pulled his pistol from its holster, patted the horse on the neck, and placed the barrel against her head, squeezed the trigger and delivered her from her suffering with a single crack.

Tom thrust the weapon back in its holster and staggered over to his wood sled, freezing tears running down his cheeks. He cleared some of the wreckage and gathered up a few smaller pieces of wood, tucking them under his arms, looking in the direction of the barn. There was no time to get another horse and drag the rest back, and spending much more time in the storm would just result in getting himself killed, too.

Tom shuffled through the blizzard with a heavy heart, and when he stepped inside the barn and shut the door behind him, he faced Sam, her green eyes piercing and worried in the fire's glow.

"I heard the gunshot. What happened?"

"I'm… I'm sorry, hon. There was an accident."

Samantha's eyes filled with tears and she held onto Tom's side, embracing him. "How?"

"We were just about to pull away with the wood I collected when the house collapsed on us. Storm must have been too much for it. Good Girl took a hit that would have taken me out if she hadn't been there. I…" Tom threw the wood down in frustration with the rest of the pile. "She was suffering. Badly."

Sam's eyes fell to the floor, and her bottom lip trembled.

"I'm sorry," Tom gestured helplessly. "It was my fault."

His daughter quietly walked over and took his hand, leading him to his stool. She pushed on him until he finally sat, almost falling off before balancing himself, shoulders slumped with weariness and defeat. She sat down next to him and held him tight, both of them staring at the fire for a few moments before she spoke again.

"Don't be upset, Dad. I know you had to do it, or she would have suffered, right?"

"Yes. Her head was…" He let his words trail off as he rubbed his hand on his pants, trying to forget the gorier details. "She was hurt very badly. Now she's just another casualty in all this."

Sam shook her head. "As far as I'm concerned, she saved you from dying. And I'm grateful to her for that. Otherwise…" Sam's voice broke down into a sob. "I would have been alone."

Tom turned and gripped his daughter by the wrists, staring her down. "You'll never be alone. I won't let it happen. Do you understand me?"

"I know you won't." She squeezed his shoulders, her eyes glassy with tears. "You've always worked so hard for us."

Tom straightened in his chair. "Well, it's because I love you. I love you and Linda and Jack. And your mother, too."

"We have to get out of this." Sam turned back to the fire, her expression hard, her tone serious. "We have to get home and make sure Mom, Jack, and Linda don't become casualties, too."

"They won't, honey," Tom assured her. "They're probably home right now still waiting for us to get home. It's our job to make sure that happens. And we will."

Tom stared at the fire and the decent-sized pile of wood they had left, then looked up at the ductwork he'd created. The smoke was funneling out properly, leaving them with the life-saving heat against the bitter cold outside. From the mental inventory he'd been keeping, they had enough food to last at least two days, three if they stretched things, and enough wood inside the barn to last at least another full one, with a couple more back by the collapsed house. Beyond that, they'd be forced to get moving again, storm or not.

"I think we're okay for now." He dug his toe into the ground near the fire. "For a few days, anyway."

"Good." Sam nodded. "So, we hang on here and count our blessings. And be grateful that we didn't try to stay in the house, too"

Tom nodded at his daughter, a wash of pride coming over him for the maturity and resolve she showed in the face of their dire situation. "That's exactly what we'll do. Count our blessings. Keep going. Hold on for your mother, Jack, and Linda." He coaxed up a grin. "It's been a long day. How about we rustle up something to eat?"

"That sounds good," Sam smiled.

Together, they dug into their packs and began rummaging for food.

Chapter 17
Specialist Lance Morales
Reynosa, Mexico

Smoke blossomed as the building was rocked hard by a mortar or rocket, parts of the ceiling crashed down, and Morales gripped his helmet to protect himself from the falling debris. By the time the dust had cleared, he looked up to see a massive hole in the wall, and part of the floor had collapsed into the next level down.

Squinting into the drifting cloud, he tried to find Smith. The man hadn't been wearing a flak jacket or helmet when the strike occurred, and the chances of him coming out of it without more scratches was probably zero.

"Smith? Hey, Smith! Are you okay?"

"I'm good!" His partner crawled from the dusty haze and grabbed his shoulder. "What about you?"

"You've got nine lives, man, I swear. Yeah, I'm good," he nodded. "But the place is going to collapse."

They helped each other stand and lurched past the collapsed section of floor, making for the steps.

"Captain?" Morales activated his earpiece and shouted into the mic near his lips to be heard above the intense noise. "Our building is compromised. We're coming down."

He yelled to the other soldiers on the floor to meet him on the stairs, then he got beneath Smith's shoulders and helped him over to the other side of the room. Only two of their team met them on the landing, both reporting squadmates had been KIA.

"Damn," he cursed, "Okay boys. Let's go down." A part of the stairwell had collapsed, leaving only a small portion for them to stand on. "You go first, hurry," Morales commanded the other two men.

They took the stairs carefully, leaping over the collapsed section to land on the floor below. He handed Smith down to them and was prepared to leap down himself when something hit the house again. The resulting explosion knocked him into the wall, and the brick and wood slid above him, precursors of an imminent total collapse. Without thinking, he leapt into midair, landing hard on both feet, feeling the impact jolt him through his hips.

"Go!" he waved the other men out, half-shoving them for the door.

As Morales followed them, stumbling into the street amidst a hail of bullets, the house fell in behind him. Dust and debris blossomed out, completely obscuring his vision, loose pieces of brick and mortar flying up and outward, small bits of which plinked against the back of his helmet and armor plating. Somehow, through the smoke and debris, he managed to find Smith and the other two soldiers and pushed them toward the Humvee.

After making sure Smith was secure against the armor, he leaned on the fender and tried to make himself as small as possible. "Captain, it's getting hot out here!"

Morales raised his rifle and fired into the impossible haze as everything burned around him. His lungs were full of soot, tickling and painful, drawing up a deep cough even as he tried to shoot straight. Somewhere off to his side, a piercing scream echoed out, followed by shouts calling for help, response, then the voices went quiet. The Humvee gunners were still plugging away, shooting into the heart of the enemy even with their chances of survival dwindling by the moment.

"Hang tight, men," the captain said. "I've called in air support. Hold your ground..." The radio crackled, the connection falling to pieces. "... no place to go. Hold...!"

Three dark shapes rushed him through the smoke, the barrels of their weapons blazing, and Smith cried out in warning as did one of the other soldiers. Morales leaned forward and put two figures down with a pair of three-round bursts, but the third guerilla angled in the other direction and ran around the Humvee out of sight. With explosions rattling the air and bullets hemming him in, Morales dropped his rifle in his lap and drew his knees tight, slamming his hands to his ears with a scream.

The sound of rotors cut through the symphony of noise, a cyclonic wind scattering the soot and clouds in every direction. Squinting, he threw an arm upward to shield his vision as the thin profile of an Apache gunship drifted into view, soaring low over the buildings, its wings expelling a pair of rockets while the 30mm cannon twisted in all directions, spitting retribution at every target its gunner could find. The first Apache floated out of view but was quickly replaced by another aircraft, and then a third as the attack craft flooded the area with a cleansing fire, pushing the sounds of battle down the road.

Morales sat in the encroaching silence before leaning back against the armored truck, slowly rising to his feet. The soldiers that had carried out Smith stood nearby, checking the wounded man for injuries.

"I'm *fine*," Smith was saying, standing tall in the haze, swatting at the medic's hands. "What I could really use is a shirt. What do you say?"

"We're taking you back to base, Lieutenant Smith."

"Negative," the lieutenant spat, "and I outrank both of you. Now find me a damned shirt and bring it here."

One medic nodded doubtfully and ran to fetch something for the man to wear, and Smith looked at Morales, giving him a cheerful wink. "Come on, soldier," he said, "we're forming up again and marching our butts out of here."

"Best thing I've heard all day," Morales nodded and moved to the opposite side of the Humvee, looking around at the damage the Apache's had wrought. Huge craters marked the ground where the rockets had struck, and three Mexican light armored vehicles sat smoking in the road. Pieces of metal and polymer lay strewn everywhere, as were bodies stretched in grotesque poses in the dirt or hanging from truck windows, cooked in the fire of combat.

Morales looked up and saw the helicopter attack group spreading out over the ensuing blocks, still dropping fire on their enemy's heads. There were occasional half-hearted attempts to return fire, but each one was quickly squelched by the deadly choppers.

More US troops filtered in on the aqueduct road along with several Humvees and personnel carriers cruising by in a hurry, chasing the helicopters as they finished off the remnants of the Mexican force. He stared at the spotless vehicles and then at the damaged ones they'd driven out of the violent maelstrom, a rolling contradiction if he'd ever seen one. Smith walked up, buttoning a new shirt and tucking it into his dusty, bloody BDUs, Morales watching the man wince whenever his body moved a certain way.

"I know you're a big tough guy and all," he scoffed, "but those medics might have a point. Why don't you chill out?"

"Are you kidding?" Smith looked at him like he was crazy as he strapped a replacement body armor system over the top of his shirt. "We just took the brunt of some serious resistance. Now we get to move on to the next objective. It's not the time to go sitting in some hospital, my friend."

"Okay, but I don't want to hear you pissing and moaning when you start leaking from that hole in your chest again."

Smith patted him hard on the shoulder, grinning wildly, his hair singed on the edges, face smeared with blood and dirt. "Don't count on it."

They found the remainder of their group gathered on a corner in the wreckage of a destroyed schoolhouse. Captain Jones stood in the middle of the troops with his hand and waving, his red hair poking out from the edges of his helmet, a veritable beacon for his men to gather around.

"Settle down, soldiers," he said. "I've got our next orders. You'll be happy to know we'll be leaving this hellhole and moving on to Monterrey." A few cheers rose from the group, and many looked visibly overwhelmed with relief. "We lost ten men and took a handful of casualties." The captain stared at the ground for a moment before raising his eyes again. "They were our friends and comrades, but I can tell you from experience that it won't do any good to mourn them now. We get to the next objective, finish our job, and then mourn later. Worrying and crying now will get you nothing but killed. Do you understand me?"

The men and women nodded, including Morales. He hadn't trained long with their particular unit, and the only one he knew closely was Smith.

"Captain Moon is going to reinforce us," Jones continued. "Fresh faces for fresh fights."

Another captain approached through the crowd, wearing clean fatigues and a wide stare as he looked at their beat-up unit. Morales gave the man a nod as he passed. Moon stepped on a big stone next to Jones and turned to address the group. "Great work, soldiers," he said, resting one fist on his hip. "We didn't expect the kind of resistance we saw today, but you prevailed against some pretty rough odds. You should be proud of yourselves."

Morales nodded just to join in with the rest of the team, but it was hard to feel lucky after getting their rear ends kicked up one side and down the other.

"Saddle up, soldiers," Captain Jones clapped his hands. "We're heading to Monterrey."

* * *

With so many forces converging from across the States and beyond, fresh military equipment was a dime a dozen, the long-bloated military budget finally finding a use as most major repairs and refits were foregone in favor of swapping in new equipment instead. The MRAP Morales drove smelled like someone who hadn't showered in a month, but it handled like a charm, taking each turn smoothly, its engine smooth and steady.

After restocking and taking a short breather to grab an hour of sleep and some food, they'd picked up the pace, leaving the smoking city of Reynosa behind and driving deeper into Mexican territory. The wide-open road stretched ahead of them, bracketed by an endless expanse of scrubland. They passed a massive power station that had been guarded by all sizes of armored fighting vehicles, the field littered with ERC 90 Lynxes and VCR APCs, all smoldering and shredded in the desert around the station. Charred bodies lay sprawled out as well, blackened like pieces of bacon cooked too long in the pan. None of the extensive preparations had stood a chance against US air dominance or their mechanized divisions.

If it hadn't been for the resistance they'd seen in Reynosa, Morales would have almost felt sorry for them. Not a single US strike had hit the power station thanks to their advanced airstrike capabilities, and it was a testament to the United States wanting to keep the infrastructure intact. After all, they'd be moving millions of Americans across the border soon, if it wasn't already happening, and there was no sense in destroying infrastructure that would be used within weeks, on the outside.

Beyond the power station was a wasteland as they left Reynosa behind and traveled southwest on Highway 40D, watching the landscape slip by. The endlessly flat scrub held only rocks, sand, stunted trees and wide blue skies. There were phone towers and corporate buildings on the outskirts of the city, most of them left in one piece except for the occasional military units hit by air strikes, leaving debris and scorch marks everywhere.

They passed one roadblock of destroyed APCs and LAVs, and Morales nudged aside the wreckage with his MRAP to make way for his freshly-reinforced unit. Other US strike forces cut through the side roads on their way to take control of small Mexican towns and to the north he spotted a massive, mechanized division with tanks creating a dust cloud half a mile long.

"Now I know why the captain was pushing us." Morales spoke to the men inside his truck. Along with Smith in his turret, they had six new soldiers in the back.

"We were supposed to be way ahead of them," Smith confirmed. "But you really can't blame us. We got hammered."

"You take a lot of fire?" one soldier asked from the back seat, hesitance marking her voice. She sat in back with the other five, all of them gripping their weapons tightly between their legs, barrels pointed up.

"I'm not sure what I'd call it," Morales said.

"We got ambushed three times," Smith explained. "Walked into a blender. Lost ten of our buddies."

"Wow, that sounds rough." The soldier's voice shook as her wide eyes flitted between Smith and Morales, betraying her newness to the service. Both men were covered in dust and blood, especially Smith, the soldier's pants stained, his shirt and body armor tight around his new bandages. Morales, meanwhile, was covered head to toe in dirt and had scratches and bruises he couldn't account for, and his head hurt like someone had taken a hammer to it.

"Were you scared?" another asked.

Smith jumped on the question. "I'd be an idiot if I wasn't, and you should be, too. Being afraid keeps you alive. Otherwise, being in battle is like being at an end-of-the-world party." The lieutenant's brow wrinkled. "Well, kind a nightmare, too. It's a combination nightmare-party that you're not sure you'll live through."

"Oh," the soldier replied, exchanging uneasy glances with the other fresh faces.

"Los muertos al cajón y los vivos al fiestón," Morales whispered to himself as the landscape slipped by. *The dead to the coffin and the living to the party.*

A dark flurry rose on the horizon, approaching from the south, and Morales leaned forward, trying to get a bead on what it was.

"I think we've got some units in the air," Morales said after a moment. "Check it out."

"Yep, I see it." There was a pause and then Smith continued. "It's an enemy chopper squadron."

Morales listened as the lieutenant immediately called in air support. "Should I keep going?"

"Yes. All they've got in their arsenal are some lightly upgraded Hueys and Sikorskys. We can hold them off until help gets here."

"I'm starting to feel like a pin cushion," Morales shook his head.

"We're not taking cover?" the first woman soldier asked.

"This is about the best cover you're going to find," Morales slapped the MRAP's roof. "We're anything but helpless. We've got some armor, and we can give them some solid ground to air fire. Hold on though. I'll probably be performing evasive maneuvers." He winked at the pale-faced soldiers in the back. "Hold on to your butts." The soldiers were strapped in already, but they shifted and sunk in their seats, grasping for handholds.

"Here they come," Smith growled, staring at the growing dots on the horizon. "I'm locked and loaded."

Six helicopters flew low across the desert flatlands, breaking formation and spreading out, making themselves harder targets. A rocket fired from one wing, setting off an alarm in the MRAP, and Morales punched the accelerator, shooting them forward, slamming a button on the console at the same time. Flares popped from launcher tubes on the side of the massive vehicle, arcing up and away from the convoy, and the missile curved behind him, slipping between his MRAP and the trailing Humvee, its rudimentary targeting systems confused by the white-hot flares before it finally exploded harmlessly off in the ground.

Gunfire rained down, and Morales whipped the wheel left and right to make them a harder target to hit. Smith opened fire with M2 once they were in range, sending a pair of choppers banking away before he could shred their thin fuselages. More vehicles in the convoy opened fire on the helicopters as they turned away, driving them back from the convoy, providing less of an easy target than the pilots had likely originally thought.

Morales looked into his side mirrors to see the rest of their convoy motor through the smoke and explosions with no problems and Smith gave a satisfied whoop from the turret, though the soldiers in back were still looking around with uncertainty. It dawned on Morales that, after a few hours of fighting, he was already a seasoned veteran compared to the men and women he was transporting. Straightening in his seat, he hit the gas and pushed them ahead, but his blood turned to ice when he saw contrails descending on them from about two thousand feet.

"Smith, we've got more company. I think they're Mexican fighters, probably F-5's!"

After a pause, the gunner confirmed it through his scope, and he spun his Browning M2 to aim in their direction, for all the good it would do. Morales gripped the wheel, his body tense in expectation of what was to come, but just when the jets were beginning to take on a firing approach, they took an abrupt turn and circled back south.

"What the hell?"

"It's our boys!" Smith yelled. "F-22s, baby!"

Six jets with the star of the United States on the side roared overhead, a scant five hundred feet above ground, missile trails streaming away from their wings as they fired upon the retreating F-5's. Two of the Raptors broke off, pursuing the fleeing helicopters, one firing upon two with its missiles and another raking a Sikorsky with machine gun fire.

"They aren't going to last long," Smith hooted. "Hell yes!"

Morales glanced over his left shoulder to see the Mexican choppers that had tried to assault them spin from the sky trailing smoke and flames, decimated fuselages smacking the ground in heavy explosions of billowing fire. More Raptors blew through the sooty clouds and passed overhead at low and medium altitudes, their afterburners screaming as they pursued enemy aircraft and prepared to set up for attack runs on ground targets.

"Woooo!" Smith shouted, laughing and coughing as he aggravated his wound, then he lowered his voice in a growl. "Watch where you're going, Morales!"

Morales whipped his attention back to the road to see that he'd wandered off to the left side, tires grinding on the shoulder gravel with a field of debris in front of him. "Sorry," he called, guiding the heavy MRAP back to center.

The convoy continued on through the ever-darkening desert skies, tank battalions and air support keeping pace with them on both sides. Despite Captain Jones's constant urging, the MRAP wasn't a race car, and some of the heavy tanks out in the field could almost match his speed. Still, Morales tried. He kept the gas pedal pinned near to the floor, their pace a solid sixty miles-per-hour and they soon left the tank divisions behind, once more in the lead and once more the spearhead of the incursion into Mexico.

They passed a smoking heap a quarter mile off the side of the road, the strewn wreckage emblazoned with a white star. Smith scowled as they drove past the wreck, shaking his head. "Chalk one up for the bad guys. That won't happen too often, though."

Morales nodded silently. The lieutenant might be right, but it still wasn't the cakewalk they'd anticipated. Their briefings had been full of cowboy enthusiasm, the older soldiers bragging about how easy the invasion would be. Quicker than Iraq, even. He realized it must have been the veteran officers trying to put a bold face on things. Either that, or they'd miscalculated the Mexican forces all together.

Morales coughed. "Clear sailing from here on out, right?"

"That's the spirit, Morales."

* * *

After an hour and a half of grinding through the desert, brash winds blowing dust through the MRAP's cracked windows, they approached the outskirts of Monterrey beyond the Sierra de Papagayos Mountains. Morales drove parallel to long stretches of ranch-style fencing and farmhouses, all in much better shape than they'd found in Reynosa. They were still in the lead, first to arrive in town as reports told of light armored resistance out in the desert that had kept the US tank divisions tied up.

Captain Jones called a halt, and they pulled up next to a massive fuel refinery squatting out Morales' window. The towers and stacks stood tall in the distance, still emitting smoke and steam from refining efforts that would soon be in American hands. The soldiers were allowed to get out and stretch their legs, and Morales took advantage of the time to walk a few yards from the MRAP and kick his boots to loosen himself up. Smith got out and strode to the edge of the road, tapping a cigarette from his pack and lighting up. "That's the *Refinería Cadereyta*," he nodded at the stacks and towers.

"Oh, yeah?"

"Yeah. I think they process natural gas and maybe some oil there."

The smoke from Smith's cigarette mixed with the diesel and oil stench coming off the convoy's hot engines as Morales gazed southwest toward Monterrey. Distant booms resonated in the air along with the whine of aircraft engines and smoke clouds spiraled up from the center of the city, the ominous threat of violence looming on the horizon's edges.

"I wish I felt like the air strikes were working," he said. "They worked well when we were on the road, but now? Seems to be a little less effective."

"You and me both." Smith followed his gaze, arms crossed, one hand tucked over the bulge of his chest bandage.

"Definitely not looking forward to the next assault," Morales winced, feeling his scalp itch. "I doubt they'll have citizens with flowers in their hands, cheering as we blow into town."

"You just keep driving like you did back there, and we'll be fine."

"I stunk it up."

"No way. You killed it, man. For your first time in combat, you did great. I mean, *we* did great."

"Let's just hope the captain thinks so."

"It doesn't matter," Smith patted his shoulder. "We're in this together, and all that matters is achieving the mission objective while keeping us alive. Okay, maybe we lost some good soldiers back there, but we saved a lot, too."

"Including your sorry ass," he grinned.

"That's right," Smith chuckled. "Even my sorry ass."

The captain called everyone to mount up, and they returned to their vehicles. Morales put the MRAP in drive and pulled out and soon, the four-vehicle unit was back on the road. "Next stop, Monterrey," the captain said over the comm line, tweaking the nervous feeling already growing in Morales's gut.

The landscape turned lush over the following miles as the desert lessened and more trees and green grasses lined the three-lane highway. They passed towns that looked like something they would find in the United States, gas stations, restaurants, and truck depots filling every available acre along the road. Traffic picked up as well, or at least the evidence of past traffic, as more vehicles littered the highway. Some appeared abandoned, though others had been dragged out and placed strategically as roadblocks.

The highway barriers looked more hastily constructed than the ones in Reynosa, and they were nothing the big MRAP couldn't handle. Morales shoved sedans, pickups, and vans aside and in some spots, he had to smash through what appeared to be entire junkyards that had been dragged onto the road. Car parts, junked wrecks, stoves, refrigerators, and construction equipment stretched in thick lines to stall the American forces and they'd even passed an abandoned excavator on the side of the road, which explained how the wreckage had been pushed into position.

MIKE KRAUS

"They threw in everything but the kitchen sink," Smith mused from his perch.

"Looks like it."

Before deploying, the soldiers had been warned that IEDs were a possibility, but military intelligence suggested that they were nowhere near the same risk as in the Middle East. Nevertheless, the risk was yet another reason why Morales pushed through the clutter first, the massive MRAP's armor designed to reflect IEDs that could cripple smaller vehicles.

The first IED they encountered blew up on their left side as Morales slammed through an abandoned truck, but it was nowhere powerful enough to do more than scratch the MRAP's armor. It fizzled and popped, no more harmful than a Fourth of July firework, but startled everyone in the vehicle nonetheless, setting them on edge.

They passed through the small town of Cadereyta Jimenez, Morales glimpsing thin streets, sometimes wide enough for only one car. The vast blocks of homes gave off a squat appearance, none of them more than two stories high. Like Reynosa, many were surrounded by steel, brick, or wooden fences. Blocks of homes were in a varied array of construction, older buildings crumbled on their foundations with new structures springing up in their wake, painted with wild, vibrant colors.

Exotic trees sprouted from the ground, none of which Morales could name, and they passed stripped billboards and more frequent signs for Monterrey coming up in the next few miles. The distant booms grew louder, closer as he narrowed his eyes and peered ahead at the long, curved road to their destination. At the end waited a deep bank of dark clouds, and not just from the endless fighting, fires and explosions.

"Looks like rain ahead," he shouted up to the gunner. "Think it will affect our air support?"

"Negative," Smith said, his tone flat and tired. "Those Air Force guys will fly through hurricanes for us, believe me."

"You don't sound very convincing."

"Just trying to keep things on a positive note."

Morales shook his head and kept driving.

As they approached the city, he caught his first glimpse of the Cerro de la Silla Mountain range, a vast stretch of gently sloping green ridges and magnificent pinnacles with white-gray clouds gathered around its tallest peaks.

"You know what I heard?" Smith shouted down.

"Tell me what you heard."

"We had so many international companies based in Monterrey that we pre-planted assault teams to take the city from the inside out."

"Then why is it burning so badly?"

The lieutenant shrugged. "Got me."

He gaped at another string of Mexican light armored vehicles in the middle of the road, trashed by US aircraft. There was such a mess that he had to carefully pick his way through, burning oil, diesel fuel, and smoking flesh burning his nostrils, causing his eyes to water painfully. Captain Jones once again grew perturbed at Morales's slowness and even threatened to call up a tank with a blade on the front to finish his job, but Morales sped up, finishing in record time to get them moving again.

They soon reached the sprawling business and industrial complexes Monterrey was known for, with massive vats of chemicals, fuel refineries, and factories stretching for miles around the outskirts. Morales pulled up to the first major junction and slowed to a stop at the obstructions ahead. All lanes had been cleared away to make room for Mexican anti-aircraft batteries and flack guns, all of them blasted to pieces across the road. A satellite dish sat crooked on the back of an armored vehicle, and several communications vehicles had been hit, too. There wasn't much for him to move, but the debris and unexploded ordinance lying around looked dangerous.

Captain Jones spoke through the comm line. "What's it like up there, Morales?"

"Our boys left a mess," Morales replied. "I've got anti-aircraft guns and flack weapons beat all to hell. There's unexploded ordinance all over the road. I can pick a path through, though."

"That's what I wanted to hear, son. We need to have boots in the Mexican National Armory in thirty minutes."

"I'm on it." Morales's eyes scanned the war-torn concrete and blown up weapons systems. He hit the gas and knocked aside a mobile missile battery, grinding his diesel's torque to a growl. Whipping the truck in the other direction, he brushed aside an old Humvee, a Mexican flag painted on the side, then hit fat pieces of plastic and metal debris, and he winced as he ran over an unexploded shell – fortunately without incident.

They made it through without issue and sped toward the National Armory in the center of the city, an ominous oppression closing in around them. The farther they outdistanced the main group of mechanized units, the more nervous he got. They were just a small group, the spearhead of a larger ground invasion, and as such were dangerously exposed. Yet, the captain pushed them harder and faster, only stopping when the convoy encountered a flood of refugees heading south across the highway. The dusty crowd came in all types; men, women, children, and elderly, wearing everything from threadbare T-shirts, jeans, and shorts to suits, ties and fancy dresses. Many were barefoot or in sandals, and the aroma of a thousand unwashed bodies and barnyard animals reached them from thirty yards away. Many of the refugees pulled wagons with ATVs, mules, and sometimes people, and most carried all of their worldly possessions on their backs.

Hundreds of smudged faces turned warily toward the US troops, their eyes dripping with resentment and accusation, disappointment and confusion.

"Damn." Morales shook his head with a deep frustration he couldn't put his finger on.

"What is it now?" Captain Jones asked.

"I've got a caravan of refugees heading south."

"You know what to do."

He lifted his hands off the wheel and gestured at the people. "I can't run them over, Captain."

A sigh came over the radio. "I didn't say run them over. Just push ahead. They'll get out of the way."

"Yes sir."

Morales edged his MRAP toward the refugee line, but the refugees showed no signs of breaking. He gave them a wave, but they only stared at him.

"Smith, shoo them out of the way."

"Got it." The man raised his voice and shouted at the refugees in English as he waved his hands wildly for them to scoot aside. "Get out of the way! Get out of the way or we'll run you over! Get!" He ducked back into the cab. "How do you say it in Spanish?"

"Oh, man. Let me think." Morales pinched his eyebrows as he thought about it, trying to remember what his grandmother always said when clearing the kids out of the kitchen after catching them in the cookie jar. "It's *muévete*. Move on, I think. That might be too formal, I don't--"

"Muévete, muévete!" Smith shouted, waving his hands at the crowd like he could shove them aside.

Morales kept edging his MRAP forward until a gap appeared as an ATV and mule moved to the center of the road, and a pair pushing two shopping carts full of goods stopped and held back the line. He gave them a peaceable wave and drove through the gap. It wasn't lost on him that he was being friendly to them while on their way to capture one of the few armories they had left to defend themselves.

"This is messed up," he whispered, making sure his mic was muted so no one else heard.

"We in the clear, Morales?" The captain's usual strained voice seemed even more stretched and thin.

Morales flipped his mic on. "Yes sir. We're clear."

"That's what I like to hear, son."

"Yes sir."

As they approached the center of the city and spotted the massive white dome of the National Guard armory, he slowed. From what Morales saw, and based on information in the briefing, it was a sprawling facility filled with a vast array of Mexico's heavy and light armor. There were stores of weapons and ammunition, and the surrounding base housed thousands of reserve personnel. According to the plan, the Mexican forces should have been drawn out and decimated in the field by air strikes the previous day, leaving the facility open to a ground-based incursion.

Morales saw great evidence of the success of the plan in the scorched buildings and melted hunks of metal that had once been assault vehicles strewn on the armory grounds. From their position on the road, he spotted cooked corpses still smoking from the attacks, graying flesh covered in military fatigues, the frayed edges of torn uniforms giving off trails of greasy smoke. Like at the junction, mobile missile launchers had been hit before they even had a chance to fire, and flack guns lay empty and unmanned.

"All right, soldiers," the captain called through the radio. "Let's move in and put some boots inside the building. Morales, take us in."

"Roger that, sir."

The massive facility was close to the road, so he exited and turned left at the end of the ramp. They flew beneath the highway bridge and drove fast along a tall fence with barbed wire stretched across the top, reaching the gate and finding it unmanned as well. Morales angled the MRAP into the chain link gate and plowed through the fencing, dragging it for a few yards before running it over. He cut across the bombed-out pavement, avoiding the bigger potholes but still bouncing along on debris and divots, the truck shaking and rumbling as he angled for the main training facility, a two-hundred thousand square foot building with bay doors on all sides and military trucks parked on its perimeter.

As they drew close, a small group of Mexican troops burst through the front doors with machine guns and rocket-propelled grenades. Two of the RPG handlers took a knee outside the door and a pair of rockets zipped off, arcing toward them across the concrete field.

Clenching his jaw, Morales jerked the wheel right, the first rocket ricocheting off their armor and exploding just behind him. The other flew overhead and detonated somewhere in the back of their convoy, and judging by the flurry of radio chatter, the Stryker had just survived a direct hit. Smith opened fire on the unit before they could reload, the high-powered rounds hitting three Mexican troops as they tried to duck for cover, blowing them back, and turning them into a fleshy, bloody puree across the pavement. The remaining half-dozen soldiers sprinted in the other direction as bullets chipped the concrete behind them.

Morales jaw, already clenched tight, gritted and turned, teeth grinding together, only half-believing the carnage that lay stretched out in front of him. He pulled past the front doors and brought the MRAP to a screeching halt, the massive frame leaning forward before settling back.

The captain's orders came through the channel. "All right, people! I want Morales, Smith, and Zellinger to guard our backs. The rest of you lugs to me. Let's go! Disperse!"

Morales and Smith stayed put along with Zellinger's Humvee while the troops all dispersed through the side door. The captain took a dozen troops with him to the armory and tried to force an entrance open and, when it wouldn't budge, they placed a charge, stepped back, and imploded it in a cloud of dust and a muffled *whump* of shaped explosives.

The group rushed inside, taking advantage of the confusion offered by the explosion, rifle fire cracking over the channel as the captain issued fast orders in the heat of battle. Morales cringed as he watched and listening, gripping the wheel tight, feeling alone with just the two armored vehicles standing against the unknown.

Morales felt his already churning guts turn to liquid at the sound of engines approaching, then six Humvees zipped around the armory's corner and sped toward them, their Browning M2 guns already firing. Hovering over them in support were three American-made UH-60 Blackhawks, all with the Mexican flag painted on the sides of their chassis.

"Captain Jones, sir," Morales tried to stay calm over the radio, but panic crept into his voice regardless. "We've got company out here!"

Chapter 18
Keith
Clarksville, Virginia

"That's another big win for you, Marge," Keith said, forcing a smile as she swept the mound of poker chips to her side. It was a friendly game between the three at the truck stop grocery store just outside of Clarksville, Virginia, twenty-eight miles west of Brodnax. In the half-sized cafeteria, a half dozen other drivers minded their own business where they hovered over steaming thermoses or bowls of soup, the atmosphere quiet as they kept to themselves.

The truck stop manager had been open to getting paid by the government to watch the place and keep the fuel supplies online and he had no problem with people hanging out and warming up – so long as they didn't ask for gas. Keith didn't have his Federal ID any longer, so he couldn't use his position to make the owner fuel them up, but they still had plenty of gas to get to Bristol – as soon as he could convince his companions to get off their fat butts and get moving.

They'd gotten through the town of Clarksville before the storm forced them to seek refuge at the truck stop, parking the semi beneath one of the awnings. It kept most of the snow off, and the other truckers parked there with their rigs still running provided a measure of comfort in the shared humanity, at least for Tex and Marge.

Keith, on the other hand, was a raging torrent on the inside as he looked out the window at the storm. He was angry at the snow, angry at his pair of patsies, angry over losing his ID and weapon, and especially angry that he was *still*, after so much work, trying to track down Tom McKnight.

"You look like someone just peed in your Wheaties," Tex said, remarking on Keith's glum expression. "What's wrong?"

"He's worried he's not going to catch his man," Marge responded for him.

Keith nodded in agreement, stifling the urge to reach across the table and throttle the woman. "It's just that my boss *really* wants me to find them and bring them in. I could actually get in trouble for not doing it."

"What kind of trouble?" Tex asked.

"Loss of privileges or demotion. They might even court-martial me."

"Do you think they'd punish us, too?" Marge looked worried.

Keith shrugged. "I've given them your names, so who knows."

"We'd love to get back on the road," Tex exchanged a worried glance with Marge, then glanced outside, "but the storm is way too bad."

"Your rig could probably handle it," he said. "You're a kick-ass driver."

Tex chuckled. "I appreciate the compliment, young man. But this storm might even be too big for old Tex."

"That's too bad." Keith didn't try to hide his disappointment. He sat back in his chair, looking around at the other truckers, contemplating his options. He didn't have a weapon to *make* Tex and Marge drive him, and he certainly couldn't drive the truck in his condition, even if he had the experience and expertise.

"I guess the snow might let up soon." Marge frowned and looked through the big front window to the billowing snow outside.

Keith shook his head as he followed the woman's gaze out the window. It was time to pull out all the stops with the pair, and hope to high heaven they didn't get a clue before he was done using them.

"The President said looting and lawlessness wouldn't be tolerated, so it'll be a sad day if they get away."

Marge gaped. "The *President* President? He knows about this?"

Keith lifted his eyebrows, acting surprised. "I thought I told you. He's the one who authorized the operation."

Marge and Tex exchanged a look caught somewhere between awe and worry, their similar facial expressions no doubt a result of being together almost thirty-five years.

"So, the actual President of the United States, President John Zimmerman, is counting on us to get this done?" Marge asked.

"Yep. You two are officially part of the mission. You can put a stop to this criminal and do a solid for the old Red, White, and Blue."

Marge leaned forward, still not convinced. "Can you tell me what he did? I mean, what could have been so bad that the actual *President* is looking for him?"

Keith had to think quick. It was hard picturing Tom as a criminal, and Sam as his captive, but he used his imagination, clearing his throat as if it hurt to speak the crimes out loud.

"He killed a family in cold blood, a military family. Husband was a high-ranking officer involved in helping coordinate the evacuations. Knifed them to death at a truck stop near Norfolk. Stole their vehicle and tried to get to Florida before we almost caught him. And he's still got their little girl with him. Now, I'm afraid we'll lose them the storms, and he won't pay for the damage he did to this country."

"Well, that's terrible!" Marge exclaimed, her face growing ashen, mouth in an O-shape. Tex's jaw locked and worked back and forth in anger as he stared holes in the table while Keith looked outside with a wistful expression, allowing a pained grimace to tug the corners of his lips.

"Yep. It's a damn shame."

The couple shared another look before Tex stood. "Marge, you want to come and help me?"

"What are we doing?"

"We're going to ditch the trailer and put on the tire chains. Then we're going to find that wicked man, rescue the little girl, and make sure he rots in jail for what he did to that family."

"Thanks a lot," Keith said, standing up, his expression of relief and surprise showing on his face actually genuine, shocked that they'd believed such a load of crap. "Do you need my help?"

"Not with your fingers and toes the way they are," Tex shook his head. "You stay here and keep warm. We'll be right back."

The truckers left the building and walked around where they'd parked the rig and, after twenty minutes, Keith bundled up and followed them outside. The wind hit him like a scythe, cutting through the coat they'd given him and chilling his skin, making the parts that had suffered frostbite feel like they were on fire again. He shivered but leaned forward, circling to where Tex and Marge were just finishing putting the chains on the last tire.

Gusts of snow blew deep beneath the awning, building up drifts against the tires. They'd parked the trailer off to the side and were walking around, checking the last of the chains. The husband-wife duo worked great as a team, and his hopes rose that things might get back on track without having to use even more elaborate means to convince them. One problem was solved, but they still had the storm to contend with, something Keith had absolutely no control over. And, with the evacuations well on their way to concluding, there'd be no snowplows on the road to clear the way.

Marge looked up and waved, and he returned the gesture. "We ready to roll?"

"Hop on in," she shouted back with a grin.

Keith tried to jog over, but his body was still too sore to do anything fast. He still had major bumps and bruises and swelling in one ankle, which was another reason he needed Tex to keep driving. He doubted he could make it even if he found a working vehicle, but resolved to pay more attention to how the man worked the rig, just in case things didn't work out as expected.

Climbing into the cab's warmth, he took his position on the sleeper bed. Tex and Marge assumed their usual seats, and the big rig pulled out of the lot and into a good six inches of fresh, puffy snow. Keith half expected the truck to stall and spin its tires, yet it plowed right on through like a big boat, the chains gave them the extra traction they needed to perform wonderfully on the icy parts.

Still, the going was tough as they got back on Highway 58 and fought their way west. The edges of the highway were barely noticeable, marked only by the indention of a ditch or a cluster of trees. Tex shifted and struggled with the rig to work through some tough spots. They got stuck in sudden drifts twice, breaking free thanks to the man's expert driving. It wasn't long before Keith thought himself foolish for pressing them to challenge the storm. After all, they'd been trucking for years and would know the highways and weather conditions better than anyone. Maybe he should have listened to them and stayed put for a while. He certainly couldn't collect Tom McKnight if he froze to death on the side of the road. But Tex proved him wrong by plowing ahead like a champion, working the wheel back and forth, shifting expertly to get the most out of the growling diesel engine.

The darkness of night bore down on them, and with no moonlight to illuminate their way, they relied on the truck's bright headlights glaring off the snow. The cyclonic cavorting of snow shrunk their visibility to a fraction of what it had been when they started, and Keith had no idea how the man could even keep the rig on the road much less keep them headed in a steady direction.

"You got an exact address, buddy?" Tex asked. "I figure you must have a good starting point."

"Just stay on Highway 58, and we'll be there soon."

In truth, Keith didn't have a specific address for the McKnight home. From what Tom had mentioned in passing, and his conversation with Banks, it sat on Highway 58, north of Bristol on Wyndale Road. The truckers would get them to the general location, then he'd rely on his gut instincts from there.

It took them thirty minutes to reach Buffalo Springs, just five miles from the truck stop, which was also just about the point when it really sunk in how difficult the journey was about to get. Getting stuck on the road and running out of gas wouldn't just be an inconvenience – it could mean the end of things, permanently.

He pushed the dour thoughts out of his head and continued to test his body's abilities. Fists flexed, sending painful stings through his hands and leaning, he shifted his weight, noting how his spine cracked and that there was an ache in his right knee. The LAV wreck had taken a lot out of him, robbing him of his honed muscles and reflexes.

"Do you want some medicine for that, Mister Squirmy Pants?" Marge quipped when she saw him moving around. "I've got some Aleve."

"Actually, that sounds great. Anything to lessen the inflammation and loosen me up a bit."

She rummaged through the glove compartment, found the bottle, and handed him two pills. Keith swallowed them and washed them down with a mouthful of water, trying to sit back and relax, though the bumpy ride made it nearly impossible. The massive seventeen-ton vehicle slipped and slid around on the road, hitting potholes and debris, jostling him relentlessly. Once, they rounded a bend going exceptionally fast and almost hit a snowbound car stuck in their own lane. Tex switched lanes in an instant, though, shifting into a higher gear and allowing the natural weight of the semi to navigate them safely around the bend without locking up the brakes.

"Good work, husband," Marge crooned softly, though both hands gripped her chair arms like claws.

They continued navigating the Virginia back roads in the snow-whipped winds like a ship on a stormy sea, plowing through tall drifts, shoving wakes of white powder off to either side. Gusts of screaming air rattled the rig on its frame and their chain-covered wheels shred through the frost packs and ice. The heating unit rattled reliably, thankfully, filling the cabin with warm, dry air that washed over them.

Over three hours, they passed ten small towns, all of which were dark and dead, the citizens evacuated. "Are those lights in the distance?" Keith asked, pointing ahead.

"By God, I think he's right." Marge leaned forward. "I'll bet that's Abingdon."

"Is that close to Bristol?"

"It's just a little to the northeast," Tex confirmed. "Is that close to where you need to be?"

"Yep," Keith said. "Stay on 58, and I'll tell you when to turn."

He leaned forward, studying their surroundings as best as he could given the storm, looking for homesteads showing any signs of life. Just a speck of light from a window or smoke from a chimney might be the clue he needed.

As they neared Abington, they spotted more vehicles on the road, cutting across in front of the big truck or pulling through parking lots, spinning tires and careening sideways as snow shot from beneath the rear fenders. They passed a gas station with the lights still on and people inside, and Keith briefly wondered if he should simply stop in and ask someone if they knew where the McKnights lived, but gave up on the idea for fear of even more delays.

"At least all the traffic has dissolved the snow and ice," Keith said, lifting himself up and looking down at the road. "It's all just slush." That allowed them to move a little faster, and Keith's anticipation kicked up a notch as he grew anxious to reach his quarry.

They left the outskirts of Abingdon and switched to Highway 11, Wyndale Road. The slush created by the traffic was beginning to turn to ice as the vehicular traffic faded away, and the twenty-five thousand pounds of rig shifted dangerously on the slick surface.

Keith sensed they were close, but finding the place in the pitch black was an exercise in frustration. He closed his eyes, recalling what few details Tom had told him about his homestead. There was the sloping front yard. Their livestock. The big red barn in the back. He opened his eyes again, looking for any combination of those as he watched both sides of the road.

Ignoring the sounds of country music suddenly emanating from the speakers thanks to Marge, he studied the dark and lifeless Virginia hills and forests, covered in a blanket of white. After a mile or two, the roads got worse again, the snow reaching above the front fender, and they found themselves plowing through it, sometimes slewing dangerously close to the edge. Tex swayed in his seat looking exhausted and approaching the end of his strength. If Keith couldn't find the McKnights soon, they'd likely have to abandon the search and hole up in Bristol.

A glint of light caught his eye off to the right. At first, he thought it was a trick from an interior dimmer or maybe a reflection off the window. But then it came again, a flash of dull yellow from the top window of a farmstead, like someone was opening and shutting a cover as they looked out.

"Slow down," he said, tapping on the back of Tex's seat.

"You see something?" Marge asked in a whisper.

"Maybe."

She followed his gaze and squinted. "I don't see anything."

The rig slowed as they approached a long driveway sloping up to a smart-looking home atop the hill. It had white siding and dark trim, its roof dripping with snow and icicles and, when he stared hard enough, he caught traces of light leaking from the window edges.

"Someone's in that house on the hill," he pointed past Marge. "They've boarded up the windows. And look there at the end of the driveway. They parked a truck there to block people from coming up the lane."

"It looks like something knocked it out of the way though," Tex said, eyes narrowing. "You think your man is holed up there?"

"I'd bet on it," Keith grinned, butterflies flitting in his belly, his adrenaline creeping up through the pain in his hands and feet. "Can you stop there?"

"You bet."

The rig plowed through the last twenty yards of snow and parked next to the beat-up pickup. Tex set his air brakes with a loud hiss, and Keith winced with the sound, hoping whoever was inside hadn't heard them. Not that it mattered, though. His gut was rarely wrong, and it told him that he had arrived. He'd finally found the McKnight home.

"I guess it's business time." Marge grabbed the door handle.

"Wait!" Keith held out his hand. "We shouldn't go in unarmed. This guy is extremely dangerous. You wouldn't happen to have a weapon on board, would you?"

"It just so happens, I do," Tex acknowledged. He nodded to a case strung above the sleeper cab. "There's an old shotgun inside it. I can cover you if you want."

Keith had already spied the case the first time he had awoken in the truck, but he wanted to get it willingly from them if at all possible. "If you don't mind, I'd like to carry it myself."

"I don't think that's a good idea," Marge said. "What with your fingers and all."

"I can still shoot just fine," Keith explained, "especially if it's a shotgun."

A frown formed on Tex's face as he half-turned in his seat, adjusting his hat. "Now, look, we did a lot to get you here. We did everything you wanted. But now you're asking to use my weapon, which is registered to me."

"Look, Tex." Keith replied, "I'm a trained soldier, and I can shoot my way out of just about any situation. Hunting people like this? It's what I do every single day. I guarantee you that you won't get in trouble for letting me use your gun." He glanced up the hill to the house for effect. "Trust me, as someone who's gotten in more shootouts than I care to remember, you don't want to be in a shootout with someone like this, especially if he's got support. You want someone who's been in situations like this taking the lead. I'm just thinking of your safety, yours and your wife's both."

Tex just stared at him, his jaw working steadily as he mulled Keith's words. The man's eyes finally shifted to Marge, and they shared a look he couldn't read.

"All right," the older man finally nodded. "You take the shotgun."

"I appreciate that."

"Well, we appreciate you taking point," Tex laughed nervously. "I've had to brandish a few times to run off kooks from messing with my truck, but I've never been in an honest to goodness shootout before."

"What's it like?" Marge asked as Keith removed the top layer of bandages from both hands, leaving just the thinly wrapped fingers.

"Not fun," he replied, distracted as he reached for the gun case, taking it down and placing it on his lap. "You have to go in mentally prepared to get shot and killed. It frees your mind, doing that. Makes you able to focus and react to the situation at hand."

The mention of being shot quieted the pair down, and Keith opened the lid, releasing fumes of gunmetal and oil, his nerves calming almost immediately at the familiar scent. He picked up the weapon and loaded it with shells from a small compartment in the case, then he stuffed a few spares in his coat pocket.

"I'm ready," he turned to them, raising the gun to show them he could hold it.

Tex seemed fidgety as he sat behind the wheel. "What's the plan?"

Keith had been thinking about how to approach the situation for a long time, and he didn't figure he could take Tom or his family by surprise, especially since he didn't know how many people were at the home. But, if he could confuse them, that might at least give him a slight advantage.

"You're going to blare the truck horn a few times. That'll make them think we're just regular folks, or maybe that we need help down here. I'll be up there, ready to take them down when they come out."

"How can we help you, though?"

Keith saw what they were getting at, and he quickly shook his head. "No, I can't ask you folks to come with me. Like I said, it's going to be a tricky situation, and I'd hate myself if either of you got hurt." Both of them frowned, and he silently cursed their stubbornness. "Look, if you get hurt up there, we'll be stuck. No one else can drive the rig. And I'd be devastated if something happened to your sweet wife."

Tex narrowed his eyes in thought. "I guess that does make sense. All right. Want me to hit the horn now?"

"If you could, please."

Tex tugged on a string above his head, and the unmistakable eighteen-wheeler air horns blared into the storm. He hit it five or six times, while Keith watched the window, then the light on the second floor blinked again, and the silhouette of a person appeared in the square frame. After it shut, Keith nodded vigorously at Marge.

"Okay, that's my cue!"

She popped the door and stood on the truck step as he leapt out into the brutal wind and snow. Head down, lifting his knees, he plowed into the waist-high drifts around the smashed pickup and trudged up the driveway. He'd done his best to prepare himself for a swift run through the snow, but he was still weak from the LAV wreck, his fingers and toes burning again as the cold bit into him.

Traversing straight up the driveway would have been a fool's errand in any other circumstance, but he was counting on the swirling storm to cover his approach. Hell, he could barely see the house himself in the blinding whiteness, so the chances of him being spotted were astronomically low. The wind churned the snow like a Christmas globe being shaken in a paint mixer and when he reached the top of the driveway, he crossed to the corner of the house and stepped onto the porch, walking slowly to keep from making any noise.

All the windows in front were boarded up, but he caught a sliver of light around the edge of one where someone was peering out. Steadying his breath, he stayed put, for if he moved, he could cast an errant shadow and give himself away. He wanted them think a friend was waiting for them down in the idling truck, or that some innocent soul needed help. They had to be curious - curious enough to lower their guard for the second Keith needed.

That was if Tom wasn't home, though. If he'd already managed to get back, he'd be armed and suspicious. And, if that turned out to be true, Keith decided he'd retreat to the truck and call for backup. Tom wouldn't be going anywhere in the storm.

Deadbolts on the front door snapped open, and Keith tensed his body to strike, waiting for the very last second to make his move so that the person at the window couldn't throw up a warning. A few seconds after the locks were unfastened, the door flew open, but no one stepped out right away.

Smart. They're waiting to see if someone will attack.

A boot appeared on the threshold. Keith imagined them peering into the swirling winds, looking both ways to make sure it was safe.

A shotgun barrel emerged next, pointed into the storm, shifting right and left, and Keith slowly drew a breath, calming his heartbeat, allowing his training to take over.

A second boot stepped onto the porch, and Keith pounced, sidestepping across the wooden decking in the blink of an eye, reaching for the rifle with one hand, the other still clutching his shotgun. A woman with strands of sandy blonde hair poking out from her cap stood at the threshold and, as he grabbed for the gun, she jerked it toward him, eyes wide as the barrel slapped right into his hand. At the same time he caught the weapon, the woman standing at the window cried out a warning, but it was far, far too late.

Moving with a fluidity that belied his injured state, Keith clutched her gun barrel and yanked what turned out to be a Benelli M2 away from her, but she held on tight, fighting against his attack despite her surprise. Still, the force of his tug threw her off balance, and she fell to her knees, grunting, shoulders straining to get the gun pointed at him and wrap her finger around the trigger.

He raised his own shotgun and brought the stock down on her head with a crack as the woman managed to squeeze the trigger, the shotgun going off with a heavy boom. Luckily for Keith, the buckshot missed, blasted out into the gusting snow, sending trails of snow and ice dropping from the porch awning. The smoking hot barrel seared his palm, though, and he screamed and struck her again with his shotgun stock, sending her tumbling off the porch and into the yard.

He tossed her gun away and stepped back, holding his shotgun on her, screaming over the sound of the storm. "I'm looking for Tom McKnight! Is this the McKnight home?! If you cooperate, you won't be hurt, just tell me what I want to know!"

He caught movement at the corner of the house and brought his shotgun up, a tall, broad-shouldered, portly man shuffling around with a rifle in this hand. "Run, Barbara!" the man shouted, firing his weapon as he came into view.

Keith lunged to his right and went to one knee in the snow, firing the shotgun from his hip, the impact of the buckshot knocking the man off balance and sending him staggering backwards. To the man's credit, he stayed on his feet, though and tried to aim his weapon at Keith despite his smoldering, red-stained chest.

Keith took two steps forward, jerked his shotgun to his shoulder, aimed at the man's head and fired again, most of the man's face evaporating in a spray of blood and bone. The gory debris flew into the whipping wind, absorbed by the whirling storm as his body slouched to the ground and fell backwards, landing with a stomach-churning wet thud on the porch.

"Darren, no! *No!*" A woman's blood-curdling wail cut through the storm, and Keith whipped around to see an older woman standing in the doorway with an American flag printed on a red sweatshirt. She hobbled onto the porch with a crutch under one arm, squeezing the trigger of her pistol repeatedly as she screamed incoherently at him. Something stung Keith's left arm at the same moment he fired, the blast taking the woman in the chest, sending her stumbling back into the house, the American flag smoking with hot pellets, her tortured screams silenced.

With two targets neutralized, Keith automatically pivoted to find his original target, seeing the woman called Barbara fumbling in the snow, blindly looking for her shotgun. He took two steps, slapped her hat off, and grabbed her by the hair, jerking her face up until it was just inches from his, spittle flying from his mouth as he yelled at her.

"Where are your children?!"

"Screw you!" she spat, eyes brimming with violence.

"If you tell me where they are, none of you will be hurt!"

"I know who you are," she hissed, swatting at his arm, though he'd locked onto her like a vice. "You won't get my kids, they'll blow your face off for what you've done!"

All of Keith's frustrations he'd been holding in bubbled up and he growled, reared back, and used the shotgun stock to smash her face with a sharp crack, blood bursting down her chin as she fell limp to the snow. He looked up to see the woman he'd shot no longer lying in the doorway and with an aggravated grunt, he jerked the shotgun's pump action to load another shell, jogged to the porch and leapt up, rushing inside, barrel sweeping the hallway. At the end of the hall, in the kitchen, the old woman was shoving a couple of kids out the open back door, blood dripping on the floor as she stumbled along, crutch still under one of her arms.

"Wait!" Keith shouted, stomping toward them. A dog barked in the background, but it sounded muffled like it was locked in another room, or the basement so he disregarded the noise, focused entirely on the obstacle in front of him.

The woman turned and faced him, her chest soaked with blood, cheeks smoking from the buckshot lodged in her skin. She held a pistol in her shaking hand, trying to raise it.

"Go ahead," he snarled. "*Try.*"

"You're an evil man!" she spat, fire burning in her eyes, her frame quivering with anger and pain. "You killed my Darren!"

"Go on!" Keith shouted again, daring her to shoot him. "Do it, then!"

She raised the weapon surprisingly fast, but he was ready, squeezing the shotgun trigger, the blast of buckshot hitting her in the gut at much closer range, spraying the wall with blood and dropping her on the spot. He crossed to her and knelt to make sure she was out of the picture when a noise came from across the room, a high-pitched, young voice screaming at him.

"You shithead!"

A pistol pushed through the open back door and fired, but Keith had caught a glimpse of movement at the last second and jerked back before the round could hit him. He dove forward and snatched the skinny wrist that held the gun, dragging a young girl in from the storm, her face a mask of rage, cheeks spattered with the old woman's blood, tears streaking the blood as she sobbed and screamed at him.

He snapped the weapon out of her hand and jerked her to the floor, then he lunged out the back door and snatched the boy just as he tried to sprint away, dragging the kid inside and throwing him on top of his sister. Both kids were crying by then, though the girl was scrambling for one of the pistols lying on the kitchen floor.

Little fighter, that one. Keith couldn't help but admire her tenacity, taking one step forward and bringing his heel down on the back of her hand, just enough for her to scream in pain but not enough to break any bones.

Keith tossed the near-empty shotgun aside and grabbed one of the pistols off the floor, checking to see if it was loaded and how many rounds he had remaining. With two children to wrangle, the smaller weapon made it easier for him to maneuver and, if necessary, fight.

"Try anything again and your mother gets a bullet in the gut!" He lifted each to their feet, wincing at the bloody nick in his left arm, shoving them toward the front door until they stood on the porch in the snow.

"Mom!" The girl jumped down and ran to Barbara, trying to roll the groaning woman over and the boy turned and punched Keith in the leg, yelling at him. "What did you do to our mom?"

"Shut up, you little shit!" He snatched the kid by the back of his jacket and threw him roughly into the snow, then he kicked the girl away from Barbara and grabbed the woman by her hair again, sweeping the pistol across her two children. "Look, this'll all go real easy if you just play nice, lady."

"You killed Darren and Marie!" the girl howled with her fists clenched at her sides, face streaked with tears.

"I don't know who the hell that is." He made a grandiose apologetic gesture. "And by that I mean I don't care about whoever you're talking about. I just want you people. The McKnights." The woman's pale face was the final confirmation he needed. "Now, where's your husband? Where is Tom Mc—"

"Keith! Holy fire and brimstone, man, what are you doing?"

He looked up to see Tex and Marge standing there in the snow after cutting a long trail up from the truck. The pair were glancing back and forth between the corpse in the yard and Keith, expressions troubled as they began adding things up in their heads.

"These are the fugitives I needed to catch." He gestured with his pistol at the three lying in the snow. "Well, a few of them."

Marge's eyes fell to the trio with a mixture of fear and betrayal. "That's... well that's just a woman and her two kids, Keith. That's not the killer you were talking about."

"They're *part* of it, you stupid hicks." Keith waved the gun around, still holding onto Barbara by her thick hair. "Don't you get it? If I get the family, I get *him*."

"By shooting them and beating them up?" The trucker shook her head in disappointment. "Using violence against kids? I thought you said you worked for the government. You're supposed to be the good guys, Keith."

"We are," he scoffed, laughing as if they just weren't seeing the obvious truth. "Believe me, it looks a lot worse than it really is. I have good reason for what I'm doing."

"We thought you were a better person, man." Tex's voice dripped with contempt, his eyes falling to Barbara where Keith swung her into a sitting position. "And there's never a good reason to hit a woman, or a kid." Tex raised a revolver and pointed it at Keith's chest. "Now, you'll want to stay right there while we sort this out."

"Oh for the love of..." Keith rolled his eyes and head, groaning with frustration. "I don't have time for this bullshit." He whipped his pistol up and put two into Tex, one in the neck and the other right between the eyes. With a cry, Marge lifted her own revolver and fired before he could pivot to her, clipping him in the same arm as the old lady. The noise that ejected from Keith's throat was half-howl, half-growl, and he shifted the pistol and shot five straight times, letting Barbara go as he took a step forward with every squeeze of the trigger, punching Marge backwards in a wild puppet-like walk. The woman gasped with each hit before plunging into a tall snowdrift with her arms thrown out like a snow angel.

The young girl screamed again, and Keith whipped around to see the little boy dragging Barbara's shotgun toward her. "Here, Mom," he yelled. "Shoot the bad man. Shoot him in the face!"

Barbara reached for the weapon, but Keith was there, grabbing the shotgun away and jamming the wearing-hot barrel of his pistol against her forehead.

"Barbara?" He gritted his teeth, head tilted slightly to the side as his voice tittered upward. "If you want to live - if you want your *kids* to live - you'll do exactly as I say. Got it?"

The woman's red-rimmed eyes glared up at him, blood running down her nose and over a pair of swelling lips that he might have considered pretty a few moments prior. Sheer, raw hatred burned in her eyes, a primal rage that almost caused him to take a step back, but his own crazed eyes narrowed, challenging her to do something stupid.

But Barbara wasn't stupid. He could tell that the instant he'd started tangling with her, and he admired her for it. That didn't mean he wouldn't blow her brains across the snow right in front of her kids, though, and she knew it. Tongue licking the blood off her lip, she nodded, sniffed, and spit red into the snow.

"All right," he sneered. "Let's go."

The gun barrel waved for her to rise, and she stood, staggering a little to the right before the girl rushed over and caught her. The boy joined his sister, slinging his arms around his mother's waist, staring at Keith as if he was a demon.

"Great. Now you guys need to follow me down to that rig there. We're going to go for a ride. I'm going to take you to a warm, safe place."

Barbara turned her eyes up to him, some of her senses returning in a fierce glare. "Where?"

"That's not for you to know right now." He waved the gun at her face. "But if you don't come nicely, it's not going to end well for your little ones. Got that, Mom?"

The heat drained from Barbara's eyes, and she nodded in understanding. "Come on, kids."

The snow tumbled from the sky in an endless wave of white as Barbara guided the children down the driveway to the waiting rig with Keith right behind them, his gun trained on their backs. Once there, he forced them into the sleeper cab where the woman turned and sat, shoving her children behind her.

Keith knelt in the passenger seat with his pistol pointed at the floor, breathing heavily. "Now that we've got a moment to rest, let me see if I can remember your names." He jutted his jaw at the boy, a warm smile melting away the rage. "I think you're Jack, and you must be Linda." They both gave hesitant nods behind their mother, who simply stared at Keith as though she could will him to die.

"We're off to a great start." Keith grinned, speaking congenially and casually, as if they were old friends. "Now, Jack." He motioned casually with the pistol, causing Barbara to tense up. "There are some zip ties in that drawer beneath the TV. Do you know what zip ties are?" The boy nodded. "Good, that's real good, Jack. Can you get those out?"

He did, and Keith directed him to zip tie Barbara's and Linda's hands behind their backs. Once secured, he took the ties from Jack and bound the boy's wrists as well. With a gust of relief, he set his gun in the driver's seat and zipped their feet up, pushed them onto the sleeper mattress, and started to shut the sleeper curtain.

"My husband is going to kill you for this." Barbara pushed the barely controlled, robotic tone between her tight lips.

"Oh yes, I know." Keith nodded wearily, exhaustion fighting with insanity as he drawled out the words. "He'll probably try. But we'll see if he's as successful the second time as he was the first."

He shut the sleeper curtain and fell into the passenger seat, the vents rattling as he hit the climate controls and cranked up the truck's heat. Outside the windows, snow was accumulating on the glass and hood, sliding down into a slushy puddle that pooled at the bottom. He engaged the windshield wipers, watching them sweep away the accumulated mess, entranced in the afterglow of the violence he'd just committed, allowing his adrenaline to drain off as the heat warmed him. Slowly but surely, his nerves calmed and his heartbeat slowed. He drew his hand down the side of his tired face and looked around at what had been Tex and Marge's whole world.

Now it was his.

Keith hadn't wanted to shoot the couple, of course. He just hadn't had a choice. It meant he had to drive the truck, something he wasn't totally comfortable with, especially not on the treacherous roads. But he'd faced worse challenges before, and he'd driven enough machinery in his life to figure it out. Yes, things were coming together, everything turning up Keith after so much failure, so much—

Whispering from the back reached his ears, soft breathless sounds in the darkness.

"Shut up!" Keith bellowed in sudden rage, pounding his fist on the center console so all the coins and pens inside rattled, needles of pain stabbing through his hand and wrist. The sleeper cabin fell dead silent except for soft sniffles from the girl. Cursing to himself, he opened the glove compartment, found the Aleve, and tapped two, no, three pain pills into his palm. Tossing them back, he washed them down with a big swig from one of the bottled waters sitting in the center console. On second thought, he tapped out two more and took those as well, hoping they might just be enough to take the edge off his stinging fingers and aching body.

After a few moments' peace and quiet, he removed his jacket and checked over his gunshot wounds. He'd been lucky. Damned lucky. One was barely a nick, but the other had cut a finger-sized slice of flesh from his arm. He pulled a first aid kit from under the seat, cleaned, and dressed the wounds with his good hand, the whole time listening for noise from the sleeper cab, *hoping* one of them would say one more *damned* thing so he'd have an excuse to bash them in the face and watch the bloody snot run down their—

No one piped up. No one so much as whispered.

He continued working, snorting at the idea of having a "good" hand. The "good" in his hand was all relative, because any intricate use of his fingers made him feel like he was dipping them in lava. It was a messy job, but he finished the dressing the small wounds in a matter of minutes, then sat back and waited, allowing the heat from the cabin vents to drive the last shiver of cold out of his system, then made the call.

"Military band, this is 3-ECHO-DANNY-APPLE-4-1. I need authorization on secure band 2-4-7-9-2. I need to reach Banks. Please acknowledge."

The operator recognized him as Arrowhead and asked for his security response, then he whispered the correct code and was patched through.

"Good morning, Arrowhead. This is Landry."

Keith paused. Landry was just a sergeant from one of the camps. One of Banks's trusted people, but still *not* Banks. "Patch me through to *her*," he snarled at Landry. "I want to speak directly with Banks."

"She's occupied at the moment. I'll pass along your message. I'm assuming you've secured the asset?"

"Next best thing," Keith sneered. "I got the necessary leverage to bring McKnight in. I'll have him in custody within a week, probably much less."

He felt Landry's frown through the phone. "Not ideal."

"No, but we have what we need to make him work, make him do whatever we want, and that's even better than what we expected."

"I'll let Banks know."

"*Thanks.*" Keith replied sarcastically, annoyed that Banks couldn't come to the phone herself. "Is that it?"

"Yes. Good luck, Arrowhead."

Keith waited for something more before realizing it wasn't going to come and he hung up the CB microphone and sighed deeply. Shutting off the truck, he put the keys in his pocket so Barbara wouldn't get any bright ideas.

"Stay here," he called back. "I'll be back in an hour or so. Don't do anything stupid, because I'm really not in the mood. Got it?"

Barbara's soft, muted agreement drifted up from the sleeper cabin, and Keith nodded in satisfaction. Carefully slipping on his jacket, he climbed down and trudged up to the house again, looking over the yard at the bloodbath. The three corpses were draining into the snow, blood pooling around them, bodies twisted up like demented Christmas decorations.

He sighed when he realized the amount of work he'd need to do to send the right message to Tom. Didn't matter, though. None of mattered. It would all be well worth it in the end.

Keith grabbed the one called Darren beneath his armpits and dragged him through the snow, hauling him up the stairs and dropping him there on the wooden planks. Huffing, panting, swaying a little, he stepped inside and hauled the old woman he assumed was his wife out to join him. He finished by dragging Tex and Marge onto the porch as well.

"The more the merrier," he huffed, wincing, grabbing his back and arching it as spasms ran through his muscles from the strenuous effort. The hardest part was over, and he could relax soon.

He placed his fist on his hip and tried to think creatively. He needed something that would really motivate Tom into action. While having his wife and kids in custody would likely be enough, he wanted the man so blind with rage and fear that he couldn't think straight. People blind with rage don't act rationally. And Tom, for all of his experience and smarts, was just like every other person – easy to exploit, if you found the right leverage.

Keith went inside the house and looked around, spotting a notepad and pen on the kitchen table. Ignoring the dog yammering and clawing to get out of the laundry room, he flipped through the notebook's first few pages and saw they were hand-drawn pictures of ideas for home defense. They had pit traps, trip wires, and other interesting contraptions.

"Cute," he said. "Too bad you never used them. *Major* fail." Keith cackled at his own joke for a few seconds, then he found a blank page and tore it free, taking a moment to think about what to say. Calculating the days in his mind, he quickly jotted the note and folded it, a smug sneer on his face.

The dog whined and pawed at the laundry room door, mixing in gruff barks and snarls. He thought about opening the door and killing the damn thing, but the four Aleves were doing their job, and his pain and violence were fading, replaced with gallows humor and pleasure over his job nearly being over.

"Have fun rotting in there, you stupid mutt."

The wind blew snow through the hallway, already accumulating inside the kitchen and foyer and Keith stepped out back and searched for something to put the note under, finding an aluminum feed pail that would do the trick nicely. Returning to the front porch, he cleared a space on the far corner, put the paper down, and covered it with the bucket, then he dragged the four bodies into place and positioned them accordingly. Stepping back, he surveyed his handiwork with a smile.

"That's a damned fine piece of art right there. Wish I had a camera. You could frame that."

After a moment of admiring the setup, he was left with just one thing to do.

Keith walked around to the backyard and found the fuel shed. The door was locked, so he shot the wood around the padlock, tore it off and stepped inside where the generator clacked away.

"Nice," he murmured, studying their efficient setup. He turned the generator off, then grabbed a can of gas from the shelf and carried it back to the house.

Pulling off the cap, he slowly and deliberately doused the siding around the rear of the home before spending the last half can soaking the living room carpet and furniture. He did his best to keep it off himself, but the smell was strong enough to sting his nose and eyes with a powerful burn. The dog pawed more feverishly at the laundry room door, its whines and barks more urgent, the long, trailing yowls almost humanlike in their tone.

"You're on your own, bucko!" Keith called out, cackling again, then he searched for something with which to start the blaze. A lighter next to a candle on the counter appeared after a brief search, and he walked to the living room, taking one final look around the house. It was cute, in a stupid, backwoodsy sort of way. The live wood mantle and small television. The mismatched carpet. The simple but homey decorations in the kitchen. He couldn't be certain it would burn down all the way given the storm raging outside, but it would be more than enough to make Tom realize he meant business.

Keith flipped the striker on the lighter and watched the flame flutter for a moment, then he tossed it on the carpet and danced away, giggling to himself as the conflagration whooshed to life in a roar of fire and heat. He skipped out the back door, slowly circling the place as it caught, the flames dancing in his eyes as they quickly climbed the rear of the home, burning all the way to the gutters, the dog barking frantically from the laundry room, barely audible above the fire's roar.

Keith watched it burn for five minutes before he dusted off his hands and walked back toward the truck, whistling cheerily to himself.

Chapter 19
Tom McKnight
Somewhere in Virginia

Tom woke to a gentle cry of wind. The ice still rained down, but not as bad as it had been the previous evening, the storm seeming to have reached its peak around midnight. The wind had shaken the sturdy barn until Sam huddled against him in fear where they'd hunkered in the loft, wondering if they shouldn't go try to make beds down on the hard concrete floor below, in case something were to happen to the roof.

Sam snuggled up next to him, curling an arm around his chest, reminding him of when she was a little girl and he'd introduced her to her first horror movie. She'd been too afraid to sleep, and he'd had to hold her to drive away the nightmares, sleeping next to her for several nights in a row until she'd recovered enough courage to sleep on her own.

Sighing, he pulled his arm out from beneath her neck and pushed the horse blanket off them, sitting up on the flattened hay. The fire they'd kept going through the night had warmed the barn nicely, though it was once again growing chilly, the flames needing constant tending to stay high in the drafty building.

Tom stood up, tucked Sam back in, and moved to sit on a hay bale, dusting off his dirty socks and putting them on with his boots over top, lacing them up for another day before walking to the ladder and climbing down to the ground floor. His body ached from the previous evening's and night's activities. Pounding on walls and furniture to make firewood had taken its toll on his shoulders, neck, and back, and running through snow, and having a horse bowl him over as a house collapsed didn't help, either. It was never fun getting older, and he didn't appreciate the constant reminders.

He winced as he walked tenderly to the fire pit. Reaching over, he grabbed a couple of table legs and placed them on top. With new fuel to burn, he sat and picked up his stick and stoked the fire, pushing the wood around in the orange coals to reignite the flames. His mind wandered as he worked. Mainly, it was still the guilt over having to put down the horse, Good Girl, that gnawed at him. It was just an animal – not even his own, or one he'd been depending on – but guilt ate away regardless. No matter how many books he read or people he listened to or plans he made for when things went south, it was always the little things that came back to roost. Practically speaking, he should have forgotten about the animal once it no longer served a purpose, not even bothering to waste a precious round putting it out of its misery. Reality demanded something different than practicality, though, even in the most dire of circumstances.

It's what keeps us human. Keeps us sane, willing to help others even to our own detriment. Without it...

He let the thought trail off, resting his hand on his belly to settle it, focusing back on his work. Once the fire had been rekindled, and the flames licked upward into the ductwork, he stood and walked to the barn doors. Unlatching them, he pushed hard at them, trying to get them open, but they were stuck tight. He shoved again, and the doors spread around six inches and a look through the crack showed the snow had risen at least two feet above what he'd cleared with the shovel. White covered everything outside, three or four feet high with trickles of it drifting down from the sky. The air snapped crisp and cold against his cheeks as his eyes crept over the ruins of the house and the lump of snow that was Good Girl.

With the storm finished, he could drum up enough wood for them to stay for a few more days, but staying was no longer necessary – nor was it necessarily wise. Tom nodded to himself, running scenarios through his head for a moment before he shut the door, cutting off the cold. He walked back to the fire and stoked it some more, throwing on a few more pieces to build up the flames, then he built a simple spit over the fire, hung a pot, and began heating water.

Once the water was boiling, he threw in two packs of Ramen noodles and let them cook, a shuffling from the loft followed by creaking wood an indication that Samantha was up, and he looked over his shoulder to see her climbing down.

"Hey," she said, walking over with her hands pulled into her coat sleeves and her eyes searching the fire. "Whatcha cooking? Smells good."

"Your new favorite." Tom made a flourishing gesture. "Beef Ramen Noodles."

"Oh, boy. Real breakfast of champions." Sam sat on her stool and rested her elbows on her knees. "How's it look out there?"

"Snow and more snow. The yard is completely covered. Three or four feet."

"Jeez."

"Yeah."

"What should we do? Stay here or move on?"

"Staying here isn't an option. The snow won't melt anytime soon, so it would be better to leave when we have the strength and supplies to get us somewhere, and while the storm's died down. Unfortunately, the streets will be covered, too."

Sam bit her lip. "And there won't be any plows coming to clear them."

"Right. So, driving isn't an option, even if we could find a vehicle that ran."

"We'll take the horses then?"

"That's what I was thinking." Tom nodded. "It's been a long time since I've ridden one, but I figured you'd give me some pointers. We'll get the horses fed and watered, saddle them up, and head out."

"After breakfast?"

"That's what I was thinking."

They cooked their meal and ate in silence, sipping the savory broth and slurping their noodles. They each had an energy bar and then split some of Keith's remaining chocolate before pulling down the saddles from the wall. Sam's knowledge was an invaluable reminder of what Tom had forgotten over the years. He used to ride, before they built the farm, but after that it had been all work and no play, driving the Gator to get around his property instead of on a majestic steed like he'd always dreamed.

It came back to him quickly, though, and they fed and saddled the horses in about an hour. After securing their backpacks to the saddles, they donned leather gloves from one of the supply cabinets, then they walked the animals outside to stand in the area Tom had cleared the day before.

Sam mounted the mottled white mare and Tom draped a horse blanket over her shoulders, letting it trail on her horse's flanks. Then he mounted the black and white gelding and peered up at clear blue skies filled with puffy clouds. The wind had died down, and a muted silence had fallen over the land, but the peacefulness was deceptively deadly. The temperature was well below single digits if not into negative territory, and they had to be careful not to leave their skin exposed too long to prevent frostbite.

Tom pulled his hat closer over his forehead and tightened the hood so only his eyes showed and, with a sidelong look at Sam, he questioned her. "Ready?"

"Yep. Let's do it."

They walked their animals around the collapsed house, Tom marveling at the spread of lumpy white debris scattered everywhere. He cursed himself for the hundredth time about Good Girl as they passed the slight hump in the snow, then he put it behind him for good.

Picking a path through the snow where the drifts only reached the horses' knees, he made it easier on the animals where possible. Their hooves kicked up the sludge and snow, accompanied by the animals' snorts and snickers, breaking the peacefulness of the scene, the animals seeming delighted to finally be out of the cramped, smelly confines of the barn.

As they crossed through the yard to the highway, no tire tracks marked the blanket of pristine whiteness as far as he could see, and he doubted they'd see any unless someone had a serious four-wheel-drive vehicle or a snowmobile. He guided the gelding along the right side of the road where the snow had sloughed off into a ditch, giving them a relatively easy path, and Tom glanced back to see Sam falling in behind him, riding with ease. Soon, they fell into an easy pace, and Tom swayed with his horse's movements, loosening up in the saddle, his body remembering old habits from years ago.

It was going to be a long, cold ride.

* * *

Hours later, the cold weather was beginning to take its toll. Tom, Sam, and their horses were already struggling as the air around them tried to overwhelm them and drag them under the disturbingly calm blanket of white that stretched in all directions. He estimated they'd gone over thirty miles on the snow-covered highways, making excellent time in spite of the rough conditions.

If Tom stared hard enough, the scene turned surreal. The unending, undisturbed whiteness lay between the evergreens and oaks, blanketing hills and valleys, covering homesteads to the tops of their windows. Green leaves occasionally poked out from the snow-covered branches, a reminder that they'd skipped fall and entered a dark and brutal winter.

Whenever he checked on Samantha, she swayed gently with her horse's movements, eyes-half lidded in sleep. "Almost there, Sam," he called back, and she perked up and nodded.

The sign for Abingdon came up, and Tom noticed tire tracks coming and going from the two-lane back roads they passed. The continued traffic had kept the snow from fully claiming the highway, making it easier for the horses to walk. Some parts of the well-traveled highway had turned to slush, though most was already refrozen. He'd also spotted a set of tractor-trailer tracks, slightly filled in with snow as if they'd driven in at the tail end of the storm. They passed the Abingdon Collision and Towing company with its doors shut and two big tow trucks sitting in the lot. One space in the lot was empty, its tracks joining the highway and heading north.

"Looks like some folks are out and about," Tom said. As he spoke the words, a small sedan sped across the road ahead of him, cutting through the snow like a speedboat in the water.

"Isn't that risky?" Sam asked as she pulled up beside him on the wider, clearer road.

"I can see where some small, front-wheel drives would do well in the snow. I had an old Hyundai Excel I could take anywhere."

Up ahead, signs for I-81 loomed, and Sam pointed at one that was half-covered in snow. "Should we take the expressway?" Sam asked. "That'll take us right to Bristol, right? I remember Mom going that way once."

"We'll stay on Highway 11." Tom nodded ahead. "It turns into Wyndale Road and will take us right to the house."

"Ohhh. Right."

They came to a junction with a pharmacy, animal hospital, and a Dunkin' Delights coffee shop. Most of the structures were lumps of white with snow drifts pressed against their sides, and some buildings were almost covered completely. Others had broken windows and bullet holes peppering the bricks, a reminder of Tom and Sam's first steps into what had become a new world.

"Let's pick it up a little. I think we can be home before nightfall if we push it, and I'd really rather not try to find somewhere *else* to hole up for the night."

"Awesome." Sam kicked her horse faster to keep up, as they made the switch to Highway 11 and passed directly under I-81. A pair of cars buzzed by on the bridge above them, but Tom couldn't see what they were or which direction they were going. A spattering of car engines drifted through the valley, and smoke lifted from the exhaust vents of several homesteads outside town, dead giveaways for the wood-burning ovens inside the homes.

"Do you think the military will come through here?" Sam asked, thick, foggy breaths gusting to the cadence of her words. "You know, keep sweeping the place to clean it up?"

"I don't know, but I hope the people staying behind are the friendly, capable type."

"Like Guy?"

"Exactly like Guy."

Tom rode nervously through Abingdon proper, keeping on the alert as they passed through windswept parking lots and stores, his hand resting on his pistol. He was tempted to try some side roads, but time was growing short and the horses were nearing the end of their strength.

As they left the small town, a pair of tire tracks persisted, and Samantha spoke up about them, a hint of curiosity in her voice. "Those are the same tracks we saw coming into town, right?"

"I can't be a hundred percent sure, but the treads look the same. And they're definitely wider tires than your average car. Seems they have chains on them, too."

The stores and strip malls disappeared, transitioning into the rounded Virginia hills once more and before long they joined Wyndale Road. *Their* road. The one that would take them right to the McKnight homestead, their own front door, warmth, and their family's loving embrace. Tom shivered, mostly from the chill, but also from a strange mixture of trepidation and joy.

"Almost there, Sam. Can you feel it?"

"Oh, yeah," his daughter said, barely able to contain her joy. "We're going to walk the horses up the driveway and take them around back. Everyone's going to come out to greet us, probably crying their eyes out."

"Even Jack?"

"Definitely, Jack. That little snot has a soft side. He's probably been driving Linda crazy the past few weeks. They'll *both* be happy to see me."

"And your mother will have something good in the oven, I bet."

"You know it." Sam was grinning, chin lifted, eyes glassy with brimming anticipation.

"If they harvested the crops, I'll bet it's mashed potatoes and roast." Tom's stomach rumbled with the thought of it.

"I hope that little jerk didn't eat all the pie," Sam shook her head. "You know they'll be hard to come by with all the stores closed."

"I'm sure they saved us a few pieces. They wouldn't have—"

"Hey, mister. Hey!"

Tom turned to see a man running out of the home they'd just passed. He wore a pair of long johns and boots, a pistol waving in his hand, his beard waggling in the wind as he high-stepped it through the snow.

"Come on," Tom growled, kicking his horse into a trot and Sam joined him, encouraging hers to keep up.

The man ran out into the street, screaming, "Stop! Hey, buddy! I said *stop*!" He fired his weapon into the air, and Tom and Sam kicked up their speed, jogging the animals around the next bend coming up.

"Can you believe that?" Tom's eyes were wide, mostly out of amusement instead of fear as he slowed the horse down and looked back.

"Yeah, that guy was like something out of a cartoon," Sam laughed.

Their elated spirits soon sobered, for the forest closed in around them, and the cold pressed deep. The horses breathed heavy, sides heaving, heads hung low, sweat accumulating on their necks, backs, and chests. Despite everyone's weariness, Tom recognized multiple landmarks that showed they were getting close. They rounded a forest-crowded bend that opened into a field, and a big farmstead sat off the road with a massive grain silo poking above the trees.

"That's the Tillman's property," Tom said, excitedly. "We're less than a mile from home!"

The snow was six to eight inches high across most of the road, and he forced the gelding to plow through it, kicking up gusts of white powder four feet high, then he cut to the center, following the eighteen-wheeler tracks that still stretched ahead of them. Tom's gut twisted a little as they ran beside a fence line, each post topped with a neat pile of snow. The tracks had been their companion for many miles, and he couldn't shake a strange flutter in his stomach every time he looked at them.

Clenching his jaw, Tom kicked the horse to a higher gear. The animal obeyed, flying along the truck tracks until they rounded the final bend for their home, and his mouth fell open as he gazed to the top of the rise where their house sat. Three plumes of smoke rose from the property, and he couldn't see the eaves over the treetops like he was used to.

"Oh, no!" Sam's voice cried in a panicked squeal. "Is it on fire? Is it burning? Dad?!"

"I... I don't know." Tom hunkered down over his horse's neck and rode hard, eyes watering with cold and worry as he kept glancing between the road and the house. Bile shot up from his twisting stomach as the tree line ended and he spotted the pile of black char at the top of a hill that had once held their homestead.

Tom's stomach churned at the sight, threatening to expel its contents, a mixture of rage and confusion consuming his thoughts. He slowed his horse at the end of the driveway where the eighteen-wheeler tracks had passed and turned up the snowy lane, maneuvered around their pickup truck, and raced to the top. At the end of the driveway, he shouted, "Whoa!" and leapt down before the animal even stopped.

His feet hit the slick snow, and he almost fell, but he stayed on his feet, staggering, stumbling toward the house, hands outstretched like he could somehow resurrect the remains. The entire first floor had caved in, leaving just a few wooden beams sticking up, and the heat coming off the place had melted the surrounding snow, creating a moat of mud that had yet to fully refreeze. There were still sections of the house that remained unburned, a function of the wind and snow no doubt, but the place – his home – was effectively gone. A waft of sooty smoke blew across his face and stung his lungs when he breathed it in, but he persisted, striding forward, barely able to believe his eyes.

"Dad! *Dad!*" Sam sobbed with hitching gasps. "Wait! Wait for me!"

Tom ignored her and sprinted through the front yard, stopping cold when he saw the bodies lying on the porch, a dark chill running up his spine and back down again. Four bodies lay on the steps, placed close together, splayed out unnaturally. Sam ran up and fell to her knees next to him, wrapping her arms around his side, grabbing at his hand. "Is that Mom? Is that..." Sam's face was a mask of agony.

Tom gripped her shoulder to keep her from going any farther, drawing the pistol from his waistband, his voice low, gravelly and quaking. "Wait here."

Breaking away from Sam, he approached the corpses on the porch with a lump so thick in his throat he could hardly breathe. The wooden slats were mostly intact, but the entire structure sagged on the right, their rockers and tables having been cast aside to make room for the bodies.

There was no doubt someone had positioned them specifically. They each lay on their sides, arms outstretched to his right, fingers pointing at something at the far end of the porch. Hair hung in burned patches from their heads, their clothes were singed, skin pink and roasted down several layers where the flames had peeled it away. A sickeningly sweet char wafted off them, and Tom had to look aside to keep from throwing up.

The memories came unbidden again, reminders of the past, of things he'd long wished he had forgotten. He let them wash over him, drawing strength from them, and after a moment, he looked again. He was no expert, and couldn't tell if the fire had killed them or something else. But someone had clearly stayed around long enough to arrange them in the way they had, so it was likely that the fire wasn't the culprit.

Two of them, Tom didn't know, except to say that neither of him were his wife. But the other two were Marie and Darren Everett, judging by the shape of their bodies and Marie's face. He knelt over them, still feeling as though he was in a dream state, closing his eyes and shaking his head with a mix of pain, relief and – most of all – anger.

"It's not them," he choked out, growling back toward Sam. "It's not Mom or Jack or Linda."

"Oh, thank God!" Sam cried, her eyes darting everywhere. "But where are they?! Where did they go?"

Tom lifted his eyes from the bodies, cupped his hands around his mouth, and shouted, "Barbara! Jack! Linda!"

There was no reply, and he looked back at the bodies, standing back, taking in the demented sight with fresh eyes. Whoever had killed four people and arranged them in some sort of a sick display wasn't just deranged. It was an act of pure, unequivocal evil, the sort he could hardly begin to imagine and couldn't even think of trying to understand.

"I'll go check the barns," Sam said behind him, trudging through the snow.

"Wait!" Tom whirled around, his voice booming. "It could be dangerous." When Sam started to go anyway, he snapped at her, his rage coming out in a snarl. "Stay right where you are, young lady! I'm serious!"

Sam stopped in her tracks, her face a mask of anguished protest along with mild shock over her father's tone. Tom turned back, tracing across the porch where the fingers of the bodies pointed to an overturned bucket with a light dusting of snow on top. He carefully walked across the charred floorboards, making sure he didn't fall through, and reached down with both hands to toss the bucket off the porch in one fluid motion, revealing a hand-held radio and a folded piece of paper.

He reached down and lifted both, tucking the radio in his jacket and unfolding the note, his eyes widening as he read it.

Hello, Tom.

If you're reading this, you'll know I've burned your house to the ground. Don't bother looking for Barbara, Jack, and Linda. I have them. Cute kids, by the way.

Banks has authorized me to use whatever means necessary to bring you around to the cause. No more playing nice. I hope you can see that we're serious.

So, if you want to see your family alive, you'll radio me within seven days of me placing this note on the porch. Otherwise, I'll kill them all.

We need your full and total cooperation here, Tom.

Talk to you soon.

Keith.

P.S. Don't make me wait. You know I'll do it.

Tom read through the note a second time before he squeezed it in his hand, crumpling the paper into a tight ball before throwing it to the ground.

"What does the note say?" Sam approached the porch, and Tom made no effort to stop her, his mind flying, whirling with a million emotions and thoughts, all overpowered with pure, unadulterated rage.

"Oh, Dad. That's Marie and Darren. Oh, no! No!!"

He turned to see Sam standing near the porch with her hand over her mouth and an agonized expression ripping her face to tears. She turned, staggering off the porch, vomiting into the muddy snow, hands on her knees as she retched. Tom stood, watching the bodies, mind broken, reeling, incapable of rational thought. When she had finished, Samantha turned her green eyes to him and her hand dropped, her expression changing to anger, her fist squeezing shut as she demanded answers.

"Who did this, Dad? Where's Mom and Jack and Linda?"

Tom pointed at the balled up note on the ground. "Your mother is okay. So are Linda and Jack. But it was Keith. Keith did it. He did all of this. *Keith* has our family."

"K…Keith?" She shook her head in bewilderment, as if saying the name for the first time in her life. "But… but how? I thought he was dead!?"

"I didn't check his body back at the crash site. He must have still been alive. Unconscious, but alive." Tom's voice was low, still growling. "He's been working for Banks the entire time, trying to get me to help them with some pointless project. That's why he aided our escape. But after we wrecked, he must have been picked up by someone driving a rig, based on those tire tracks we saw." Tom turned his attention to the two corpses he didn't know. "Probably those two."

Sam's expression was skittish, dancing between fear, anger, and uncertainty. She swiped the freezing tears from her eyes, hyperventilating as she spoke, unable to calm herself down.

"What are we going to do? How are we going to get them back? And where's *Smooch*? Smooch!" She yelled for the dog a few times then trailed off, staring at her father as he stood in the snow. He stood stock-still, barely breathing, eyes roaming between the house, corpses and balled-up note in the yard.

"Dad?!"

The memories were a tidal wave, crashing down upon him, each detail more vivid than the last. He'd tried to push them away when they moved to the homestead, bury them far down where they couldn't come back, but they had returned in full force, overtaking his mind, filling him up from the soles of his feet until they ran out the top of his head, flowing out into the snow and beyond, pointing him toward the only path left for him to follow.

"Dad?"

Samantha took her father's hand, gripping it tightly, and he shuddered, his whole body convulsing for a second before he turned to her, eyes dark, face set, tone grim. Tom shook his head, letting go of Samantha's hand and stepped off the porch.

"Come on. Grab your horse and follow me."

He walked to his gelding, ignoring Samantha's calls of frustration, and took the reins, leading it around the back past their charred Astro van sitting next to the garage. Part of the structure had fallen on the vehicle, leaving the window cracked and a big burn mark on the fender. Samantha caught up with him as they passed the metallic remains, and he angled past the generator house and approached their red barn, one of the first structures he and Barbara had built when they bought the property.

"Dad, stop!" Sam shrieked at him, "Smooch! Dad, it's Smooch!"

Tom whirled to see that Sam had let go of her horse's reigns and was flying through the snow toward an animal limping around the house. At first, he didn't recognize the creature with half of its fur singed, and covered in mud like it had been rolling in it. The wagging tail and doleful brown eyes that stared at Sam like a savior gave the animal away, though. It was Smooch. An injured, frightened Smooch, but Smooch all the same.

Tom let go of his horse and jogged after her, heart pounding as he caught up to his daughter. She was kneeling in front of the dog, ruffling her fur as the animal whined and danced in her arms. Falling to his knees beside them, he ran his hand through the matted fur, patting her, turning his face aside to avoid the rapidly licking tongue.

"Boy, she's glad to see us," a smile spread across his face at the sight of the first member of his lost family, a reunion he didn't expect coming much sooner than he had hoped.

"No kidding." Sam was giggling, tears pouring down her face. "What happened to her?"

"She doesn't look too bad," Tom remarked as he noticed she was favoring her right paw, a thick, dirty bandage taped to it. "Just some burned hair and an old wound, it looks like."

"She's shivering, Dad."

"Right, let's get her inside the barn. Come on, Smooch!" Tom scooped up the animal and took her to the barn while Sam guided the horses behind him. The door was locked, so Tom set the dog to the side and pulled out his pistol, putting two bullets through the latch so he could tear it off. He ripped the door open to the scents of hay, feed, and oil, welcome, invigorating aromas after breathing smoke and cold air for days.

He flipped on the light switch, but the barn remained dark, a reminder that the home he had spent years developing and crafting had been burned to the ground. Flashlight out, Tom illuminated the barn. Everything seemed in place. The Gator was inside, along with the stacks of feed, tools, and a smallish Bush Hog in the back.

Tom walked across the floor, following the trail set before him, grabbing the Bush Hog, yanking it aside with an angry grunt. He bent down and swiped away the hay and dirt to reveal a combination lock and handle and, with a steady hand, he thumbed in the code before throwing open the door so that it slammed against the floor with a thud. Flashlight in hand, he shined the beam down a thin set of stairs that descended into darkness. Trepidation held him back, though the memories bubbled up, guiding him, reminding him of the only choice left before him.

"What the…?" Sam came up with a confused expression. "When did this get there? I mean..." Her words trailed off in confusion.

Tom turned to his daughter. Standing tall, he seemed larger than he had since their trip began, and he spoke with a confidence and strength summoned from some hidden place. "There's a lot you don't know about me, kiddo. I've worked on government projects before, and… well. We can get into that later."

"What… what are you talking about, Dad?" Samantha knelt down, holding Smooch next to her, a bewildered expression on her face. "What *is* this place?"

"You were less than a year old when we started this project. Finished it up and built the new barn over it. After some things that happened on some projects I took on, your mother and I wanted a backup plan, on premises, in case something like that happened." Tom jerked his thumb back toward the house, growling, his expression turning dark. "Come on. Follow close."

Tom climbed down the steps with Sam right behind him. At the bottom, he stepped away from the stairs and shone his flashlight in a slow arc around the room. Boots hitting the floor, Sam turned and looked, jaw dropping as she followed the flashlight beam in bewilderment.

Tom spoke through clenched teeth. The anger had returned, but it was tempered, refined, directed. "Let's get loaded up. We've got six days to find Keith, kill the bastard, and save our family."

The path was clear.

All he had to do was walk it.

Book 4: SURVIVE

Chapter 1

Tom McKnight
US Marine Amphibious Base
Beirut, Lebanon
The Past

"It's hotter than you could ever imagine." Tom laughed into the phone, dragging his arm across his forehead, wiping the sweat away. The arm of his shirt came away soaked, the air in the prefab room like breathing a suffocating waft from an oven.

"Are you telling me they don't have fans or air conditioners there?" Barbara scoffed, the line crackling with static.

Tom held the bulky satellite radio away from his head and glanced in the corner where a single metal fan ground and rattled, doing more to circulate the sweltering heat than bring any type of relief. "Nothing that really helps. How's Sam?"

"She's doing great. She's excited about getting her first school assignments I set up on her computer. I'll tell you, this homeschooling thing will be interesting, but we're both looking forward to it."

Tom glanced out a tiny plastic window as helicopter rotors cut through the desert air and a voice bellowed over the loudspeaker for the SEAL unit to assemble.

"You don't have to do it, you know." Tom turned away from the window, closing his eyes, leaning in toward the phone box and lowering his voice. "We can send her to public school for now and homeschool her next semester when I'm there to help. I don't want you to feel pressured by this."

"No, it's fine," Barbara's voice was chipper, albeit with a hint of strain around the edges. "I'll get her started, and you can help after you get home. That's what we agreed on, so we should stick to the plan."

"And that's why I love you." Tom sighed as the rotors cut closer. "How's my little Linda?"

"She asks about you every day," Barbara's smile was like honey over the phone line. "Well, more like every second of the day. Daddy, Daddy, Daddy! That's all I hear."

Tom grinned, squeezing his eyes tight against the tears that threatened to well up. "I can't wait to get home and spend time with my girls."

"Us, too. When do you think the operation will be over?"

The swirling air currents shook the thin walls of the communication unit he was in and blasted through propped open doors. Tom's hair fluttered on his sweaty forehead, sticking to his skin.

"It shouldn't be longer than a week. We're entering the final phase in a little over forty-eight hours. This new Major's pushing everyone hard. She's tough, but seems fair."

The helicopter noise grew loud and almost drowned out the loudspeaker's bellows. "All trainees and service men assigned to Alpha Division, report to the liftoff pad. I repeat, Alpha Division, report to the pad."

"Honey, I've got to go," he shouted over the noise. "The team is waiting for me."

"Yes, I hear them. Okay, Tom. I'll talk to you soon. Please be safe. I love you."

"I will. I love you, too. And give my love to Sam and Linda. Bye."

Tom clicked a button to end the call and placed the bulky device in its cradle, gave the operator sitting at the desk a wave in thanks and picked up his backpack, heading out into the stifling wind.

The Marine camp was spread out in a combination of permanent and prefabricated buildings, the motor pool sitting off to the left next to a hangar and landing pad for the base's five helicopters. The barracks, mess tent, health center, and commissary lay straight ahead and the armory and training grounds claimed the dirt fields and hills off to his right. The Marines had been present for decades as part of the Multinational Force to protect western interests in the country and, in cooperation with the Navy, they also conducted SEAL training for forward operations.

A helicopter was just landing on the helipad and five SEALs were already waiting at the edge, doing last-minute checks on their bulky packs. Tom hefted his own pack to his shoulder, instantly weighed down by the heavy gear. He straightened as best he could under the weight and grabbed his white skis and poles where they leaned against the wall before jogging out toward the waiting men.

A short, wiry man with a stern expression broke off from the group and strode briskly to greet him, though he didn't offer his hand. While slim, he was powerfully built, with muscular shoulders and a sharp, a clean-shaven jawline. A pair of reflective wraparound sunglasses perched on his nose, and he was clothed in a light army green uniform. Arms held away from his sides, he nodded.

"McKnight."

"Lieutenant Commander Osaka," Tom replied tersely. "I'm ready for training."

"I see that. Come join the men."

As they strode over to the waiting group, Osaka shot him a sideways glance. "I can already tell by the shape of your pack that you took your first lessons seriously. Nicely done."

"I don't want to die because I packed something wrong." Tom shifted uncomfortably under the load.

"Excellent. Are you sore?"

"After two days of obstacle courses and prep exercises? Hell yeah, I am. You guys run a tough program here."

"You're getting an abbreviated version of what usually lasts weeks. It usually leaves most recruits in tears."

"I'm not a recruit."

The hint of a grin appeared at the edges of Osaka's eyes and he nodded again. "Fair enough."

They joined the SEALs at the edge of the helipad, each of them looking up at Tom as he approached. His stomach churned as he looked around at the group, trying not to appear nervous in the face of the withering gazes. Their shoulders bulged beneath their green T-shirts, biceps and forearms wound tight from years of training. One man wore burn scars on his left arm like tattoos while another had a pink, scythe-shaped mark that ran from his left temple to his chin, ending in a divot on his clean-shaven jaw. A few of them wore their sleeves rolled up, sunglasses propped on their foreheads, tendons bristling with tattoos and tension.

The men stood around their packs, jostling each other as they exchanged looks and raised eyebrows at Tom's expense. Compared to their experience and expertise, Tom was a nobody – a mere specialist, a civilian that they'd likely been ridiculing ever since they found out that he was going to be joining them. They were too professional to say it out loud – at least not yet – but when push came to shove, he'd have to pull his own weight, no matter what else was going on.

With nary a word spoken, they crouched and boarded the UH-1Y Venom and sat in their assigned seats, two rows facing each other in the front and back of the crew cabin. The aircraft lifted off and turned eastward, beating a path toward the Lebanese mountains, rising out of the dry desert and into white-capped snowy peaks that stretched jagged rows of ridges moving and stretching north to south. Turbulence shook the fuselage as the air changed from sweltering to mild, then to cold in a matter of thirty minutes and Osaka stood, grabbing a leather grip on the ceiling to help him balance during the rocky ride.

"All right, ladies. Swap to winter clothing. Let's go."

The SEALs removed their winter gear from their packs and stood on the wavering deck, balancing, switching legs as they stripped off their sweaty clothes and slipped on their winter base layers, then pulled on the tops, goggles, and white camouflage overcoats. Tom tried to remember the sequence he'd been taught, slipping into the assault uniform while crouching or on his knees. More than once, he glanced at the others for direction but mostly got changed on his own. The SEALs had done their dance a thousand times before, and a few watched Tom with amusement while offering a few chiding comments.

"Does McKnight have his shoes on the wrong feet?" one man asked with a raised eyebrow.

"Hard to tell," another replied. "The guy's got weird feet. I'm pretty sure he forgot his boot socks, though."

"Does he have his bobby socks on again?"

"Yeah, he thinks he's a cheerleader. Hey McKnight, you going to cheer for us while we train? Got your pompoms?"

"Yeah, yeah." Grinning slightly, nodding, Tom paced himself, making sure to get every layer of protective clothing right. Once finished, he stuffed his feet into his overboots, tied them up, and slid his hands inside his white mittens. His body heat instantly filled the material, leaving him with a warmth that was already starting to wither in the intense cold of the high altitude of the Lebanese mountains. Despite finishing last, as he zipped up his coat and hat and perched his goggles on his forehead he received an approving bump on his shoulder from one of the SEALs as Osaka turned to the group.

"Final checks, gentlemen." Their leader was dressed in full whites where he balanced near the back of the craft, shoving his fingers deep inside his gloves. "We're two minutes from our drop point. Keep it tight, and do not forget that this is a live fire exercise. Get me?"

A chorus of affirmations rang out and the SEALs settled back, feeling over their equipment and weapons, waiting in silence until the order came to drop. Tom had gotten mostly used to bumpy helicopter rides over his short time in training, though he felt his stomach rise and fall with the dipping aircrafts as he went over the steps he'd practiced in his head, imagining every grip and pivot he'd have to make. Without warning, Osaka stood and whipped open the side door, letting in a monstrous whirl of wind and snow that slammed through the helicopter, forcing Tom to plant his feet and struggle to stand. A repelling line was tossed out, and the first SEAL clamped to it and leapt out with seemingly dangerous abandon. Tom shifted forward without being told, slipping in behind the next one as gracefully as he could with skis and a ponderous bag attached to his back, waiting for him to go, then clamped himself to the rope, pivoted, and leapt without hesitation.

Stomach leaping into his throat, teeth clenched against the screaming wind, he flew toward the barren, white ground, using his hand brake to slow himself without coming to a complete stop or hitching too much. The SEALs below had already broken off, sprinting outward, working to secure the area. Tom landed a little too hard, the impact rattling his knees and pinching his spine all the way up to his hips and back. He shook off the pain and detached himself from the line, moving just as the next operator hit ground where he'd been standing.

Weapons raised, they performed an organized deployment to the edge of a tree line, moving in teams of two with Tom staying with Osaka like white on rice. Plunging into the woods, they smashed over the rough terrain, knee-high snow drifts, and brittle vegetation that crunched beneath his boots. The SEALs carried their rifles in the ready position, eyes up while Tom kept his gaze pinned forward, focused on keeping his feet, straying neither too close nor too far from his partner.

Osaka ignored the laminated playbook taped to the back of his arm, calling forth orders from memory, ordering the team to lay down a suppressive fire, and they fell behind the cover of logs and bushes to shoot at pre-set targets. With a heaving chest and burning legs, Tom was always a second behind them, removing his right-hand mitten to draw his pistol and fire at targets in the snow when Osaka prompted, sometimes actually hitting them. After each firing exercise, Osaka would call out, and they jumped to their feet and continued moving forward, marching, shooting and skiing through the untracked white all day, covering miles of Lebanese woods and mountains. They traversed valleys and climbed fast from them, spreading across ridges to fire down on make believe targets, and in a few hours, Tom's lungs ached, and his body felt ragged and worn.

When they stopped to camp, they assembled lightweight tents and ignited fires using sticks and tinder scavenged from their surroundings, then carved snow caves in the tall drifts and into mountain sides, building lean-tos and snow walls for shelter, concealment, and protection. While Tom was unpracticed, and his brain felt cold and numb, he paid attention and soaked up every piece of information he could, pushing his body beyond its limits to work as hard or harder than the sailors. For a full day and night they worked, barely stopping to rest for more than twenty or thirty minutes at a time, and on the second day they ate their midday meal as a unit before climbing aboard the helicopter for the trip back to base.

Soaring through the Lebanese mountains on the return trip from the sprawling heights, from deep snow drifts to flying sand that found its way into every crack and crevice. Landing in the hot, arid desert was a shock to his system, and after hopping out of the helicopter, Tom lugged his equipment to the edge of the tarmac and winced up at the sun like it was his enemy.

Their jeering subdued, the SEALs patted him on the shoulder as they strode by with their packs bouncing on their backs, heading to the barracks or commissary, chatting with one another as though it was just another day on the job for them. Tom, for his part, tried his best to act nonchalant, though his entire body ached, and he wanted nothing more than to flop down on the hot sand and fall asleep. Checking his pack, he sighed at the bits of cloth poking out of the top, stuffing them back in. He'd done his best to get his winter gear repacked on the return flight, but with only a few practice sessions, he'd likely be in for a long night of rearranging his gear. Picking up the heavy bag with a grunt, he started to follow the SEALs inside when Osaka planted his hand on his shoulder and he turned to see an uncharacteristic grin on the commander's face.

"Good job today, McKnight. If I didn't know any better, I'd think you'd been around a month or two."

"Thanks," Tom nodded tiredly, grimacing against the pain of his aching back and knees, spine still feeling compressed from the initial repel down.

"One more day of jump training, and an introduction to our HALO suits and you'll be ready for deployment." He grinned widely at Tom's flinching response to the reminder of what was yet to come. "Meet me in the briefing room in thirty."

The lieutenant commander gave his shoulder a squeeze and strode off and, with a sorry gasp, Tom turned and shuffled wearily back to his tent to stow his gear.

* * *

Forty-eight hours later, Tom was plummeting toward Earth with the wind screaming in his face. Goggles protected his eyes, but his cheeks were plastered back, undulating in the brutal airstream. Gut lurching, ground rushing toward him, he tensed his throat to hold down the water and crackers he'd had for breakfast. His stomach had been fine on the training drop but revolted with a vengeance as he plummeted over the Siberian wastes, the world a black void beneath him except for the faint glow of a fluorescent green tape marking the SEAL below and slightly off to the sight.

"McKnight, deploy your chute." Osaka spoke calmly in his earpiece, sounding like a manager giving an employee an instruction at the office water cooler. "I repeat, deploy your chute."

Tom's hand went straight to his ripcord handle, gripping it with his thick gloves, making sure he got his fingers fully hooked before he pulled. His parachute ejected in a whoosh of sound and his torso was pulled sharply from gravity's jealous grasp, his legs flying downward with a jolt, spine compressing inside his harness. An involuntary grunt came out as he tried to stay conscious with the blood rushing to his feet and he gasped for air, gripping the straps above his head, going back to his training to get his breathing under control.

"Good job, McKnight. Now keep your eyes on Reese and mark his location in your mind." Osaka's tone—professional, but tinged with compassion for his ward—focused him.

"Got him," Tom said, craning his neck to note the operator's direction as they swung in the freezing alpine winds, then began falling through pine branches, smacked, struck, and punched by them before landing hard at the edge of the woods, tumbling into the snow with his parachute canopy still hanging in the low tree boughs. On his hands and knees, his breath came raspy and raw, the cold burning his lungs like fire, discomfort aching through his body along with relief at being safely down and not splattered across the tundra.

"I'm down," he spoke as he stood upright, his voice looping back through his earpiece to confirm its transmission. To his right was the wide-open field he recognized from the mission briefings, the rocky features recognizable through his snow-dusted goggles. "I must have drifted to the left. I'm over by the edge of the woods. Cutting loose now and will walk to Reese."

"Stay where you are," Osaka said. "We're coming to you."

Tom didn't bother wasting energy in arguing, focusing instead on untangling his lines and cutting his canopy down as wind and snow gusted all around him, the dark Siberian sky stretching out above him. Already, the cold was seeping through his winter garb, but in short order the SEALs converged on him, briefly congratulating him with dry laughter on not dying before burying their lines and chutes deep in the snow, disguising the fact that they had ever landed in the area.

"The package dropped half a klick north." Osaka held up his arm, the low light of a small computer screen glinting off his goggles. "It's on our side of the lake. Move out, single file. Reese, you have point. Do it by the book, gentlemen."

* * *

An hour later the wind was picking up, whipping across the tundra, whistling between the Siberian pines and gray-barked peashrubs with their thin, waving branches. Tom sat on a snow-covered rock on the lake shore with his shoulders hunched over a blinking control unit with two horn-shaped joysticks jutting from the sides. His hands gripped the controls delicately, nerves finally settling after the harrowing jump. A small electric lantern spread a soft circle of light around him, just a few feet of real visibility in any direction except what was cast by the star-filled sky above.

Cross-legged, eyes narrowed in concentration, he allowed his surroundings to lull him into a sense of calm. The whispering winds and creaking branches surrounded him, embracing him, the frigid fingers of winter seeping through his cold weather gear. A thick cable that ran from his controller into a large hole cut in the ice and a soft hammering sound came from his right, and he glanced over to see a pair of soldiers dismantling a huge crate the package had come down in, burying the busted wood in the forest's snowy underbrush.

Osaka stood nearby, issuing orders to the rest of the team. "Reese, walk the northern shore. Irons, move south. The rest of you assume defensive positions in the tree line. I don't want any surprises."

Lake Baikal stretched in a gentle, massive crescent from south to north at his feet, the dark waters waiting, cold and bottomless beneath the icy surface. The deepest freshwater lake in the world, it reached depths of a mile or more, filled with hundreds of species of wildlife and plants – many unknown to science due to the extreme conditions and difficulties in accessing them. After a blink, he stared across to the other side where moonlight captured the mountain tops that extended along the western shore, their eerily-lit peaks haunting amid the stars peeking out beyond clouds. Turning his attention back to the controller, Tom guided the rover deeper, its spotlights paltry against the darkness below the water's surface.

"Status." Osaka intoned, peering over Tom's shoulder, his rifle gripped loosely as he stood guard.

"Doing good so far," he replied, banking the rover left to avoid a hitting a rocky rise on the lake floor. "We're over a mile down now. Getting close."

Tom focused on navigating the crusty rift bed, its stalk-like growths jutting upward while giant mats of bacteria and sponges covered the sloping lake floor. Fish and one-inch amphipods flitted in the darkness, briefly reflecting his spotlights in fractal flashes of light and he glanced to the picture-in-picture GPS navigator on the bottom right of his screen where their target's red light blinked in relation to the rover's blue hue.

"Now a hundred yards and closing."

The rover shook with turbulence from an unmapped hydrothermal vent and Tom made a quick adjustment, righting the scout vessel, pushing onward toward the target. His hands grew warm on the controls, chest dripping sweat beneath his layers that quickly grew cold from the relentless winds as he focused on navigating the rover and not crashing the three million-dollar piece of hardware.

"How likely is it the Russians will drop in on us?" he asked, mostly to break the silence as Osaka continued to hover.

He felt the lieutenant commander shrug more than he saw it. "Hard to tell. Our insertion was flawless, but they're not stupid. That's why I need you to hurry."

"Almost there," Tom's tongue poked out from between his lips as he concentrated, the minutes passing, fifteen, then twenty. Miles down, he pushed the rover over a rocky crust, spotlights spilling upon a dull, metal hull, rusted steep plating filling his view. He pulled the small craft to a stop and kicked the rover's six propellers into reverse, backed up, cranking his lights higher to get a better view of the monolith resting on the lakebed. While the depths were still mostly impenetrable, the unmistakable shape of an oddly configured submarine filled the screen, the vessel sitting awkwardly in a bed of rust-colored coral.

"Found it."

Osaka had already been leaning in but he moved even closer, one hand resting heavy on Tom's shoulder. The pressure caused Tom's grip to change, and the rover drifted to the left. He grunted his annoyance and adjusted the craft with deft movements, focusing the lights on their target again.

"Sorry," Osaka whispered and removed his hand. "Good work, McKnight. Access should be through the upper hatch."

"Right."

Tom guided the rover closer, sweeping across the vessel's upper decks, drawing upon his recollection of the dozens of briefings, grainy photographs and three-dimensional renderings he had been shown. Barnacles covered some of the steel hull, growing thicker along the bottom, and the rover drifted ever upward, Tom using the controller to angle the lights and cameras down. There were several hatches on top, and Tom paused over each one until Osaka told him to stop above one near the submarine's tower.

"That's the one. Open it."

When he was two yards from the hatch, he put the rover into hover mode and activated the arms, then took a flat black object from a basket beneath the vessel and placed it on the hatch and used one of the three claws to press the top. A burst of energy surged through the metal and disabled the magnetic locks holding the hatch shut, then he reached out with the claws and clutched the wheel, giving it a spin to the left. At first it wouldn't turn, and Tom had to increase the power to the propellers to gain more leverage. After wrestling with it, the wheel spun suddenly, causing the rover to fly sideways, off balance, in a wash of turbulence. Tom released the wheel so the arms wouldn't be damaged, and when the turbulence passed, he pushed back closer and finished turning the wheel. The hatch popped open, and he lifted it and let it fall back against the hull with a dull clang he couldn't hear.

"Good work. Proceed inside." Osaka whispered.

"Thanks. On it."

Tom let go of the joysticks, letting the rover drift while he flexed his cramped hands and took in a few deep breaths, loosening up his body for the next, most intense phase of the operation. When he was ready, he grabbed the joysticks again and pushed the rover forward, squeezing it inside without bumping the sides as he lowered it down into a cramped compartment, the rover's lights filling the space with ambient light. The ladder continued into the belly of the submarine, and two hatches led to the bow and stern. Rotating the rover, Tom got a good look at the instrument panels and emergency controls. A fire extinguisher still sat in its niche, the glass casing cracked and on the starboard side, near the bottom, a section of the hull had bowed inward as if split under tremendous force.

"Look at that damage," Tom whistled softly under his breath.

"Proceed towards the bow."

"Got it."

Tom turned the rover so that it faced the front of the ship and performed the same operation on the next hatch. After popping the lock, he gave it a gentle nudge with the left claw. When it wouldn't budge, he increased the thrusters and worked the joysticks to force it open, then slipped the rover into the next room, Osaka giving an approving grunt over his shoulder.

The rover entered slowly, pushing through debris suspended in the brackish water. A hat floated past, followed by clumps of softer materials like cushions and life jackets and he rotated the rover, letting the lights pick over the pipes and knobs running along the walls. The damage to the hull continued lengthwise, parts of a larger crack working its way downward into the lower levels of the ship. On the rover's left was a control chair and operation bay, a dead sailor sitting buckled in his seat, head bowed forward, arms drifting lifelessly in the solution. While his body would normally have been perfectly preserved so far down in the frigid waters, the damage to the hull had allowed extremophiles to invade, picking at the corpse, parts of the man's spine showing, his ears nibbled off and his eyes all but gone from their sockets.

"This is the control room annex," Tom whispered to Osaka. "We're getting closer."

Osaka took a step back and looked around at their surroundings, making a few motions with his hands, receiving a series of clicks on his radio in response. "We're still in the clear. Keep moving."

Tom navigated the rover into a room with more instrumentation, and they drifted past two manifold coverings, bumping another body. An arm floated by in the shadows to disappear behind them and Tom shivered a bit, shaking off the existential dread creeping up his spine as he pushed the rover forward. "This should be the bridge."

The door stood wide open and he gave the rover a little thrust, holding his breath as they drifted through. A large pipe jutted from the wall and bent toward the bow and Tom made a correction, angling into the middle of the room to avoid hitting it. A woman's face floated into the camera, the rover's blazing lights casting a dazzle across her blanched skin and hollowed-out eyes. A ripple of movement crawled across her half-eaten flesh as tiny worms were disturbed from their meal, crawling and writhing through the pockets carved into the flesh around her cheeks was stripped away, the gleaming cheek bone showing through. Tom jerked back but kept his hands on the controls, doing a quick rotation and using the rover's arms to shove the corpse toward the wall.

"Jeez. Sorry. Wasn't expecting to see half-eaten bodies based on the intel. I guess the hull breach was large enough to let them in."

As she drifted away, her uniform clung to her dwindling form, shoulders laden with bars and stripes that indicated a higher rank than the sailors.

"She was an officer," Osaka commented. "Not the captain, but she might have had the helm before they sank."

Tom allowed the rover to hang suspended in the thick, stagnant water as he maneuvered the lights across the cabin. Another two corpses floated against the bulkhead on their left, and four more sat buckled into chairs on the opposite side of the compartment. The room was packed with control panels, gauges, and a crescent-shaped wheel in front of one sailor and a few small, vibrantly-colored crabs moved about on one of the bodies before returning to feeding on their bounty.

"This is the bridge," Osaka confirmed, then touched his earpiece. "Bridge found. Prize incoming momentarily." Another series of clicks came in response from the team, signaling confirmations of his transmission.

Tom nudged the rover toward the first control panel, using the arms to hold a dead sailor aside while he searched the area for input slots. As he looked, particulates glowed in the stark light, shadows shifting all around them, his view through the remote feed clouding and becoming more difficult to deal with.

A voice piped over the earpieces in Tom and Osaka's ears. "Commander, I have lights along the north shore."

Osaka stepped up the shoreline and took the radio off his belt. "Copy that, Reeese. What about you, Irons?"

"Nothing here, sir," came the reply.

"What about the woods? Anything?"

"Nothing," another voice responded. "All clear here."

Osaka turned back to Tom. "Tell me you're close, McKnight."

Tom shook his head. "It's not in or around the control panel. Must be in one of the potential secondary rooms."

Urgent chatter barked over the radios, but Tom ignored it, backing the rover up and performing a deft half-turn in the confined space. Spotting a small hatch beside the command console, he pushed inside. A person would have had to squat to get inside, but the rover slid through the opening easily, revealing a compartment wide enough for three people to stand in. A stack of computer systems stood in a rack, Russian script scrawled across the front of each one. Tom immediately identified a hard drive array where the ship's data would be kept, and array of six drives, five of which were black, each one the size of a cigarette pack. Atop the five black drives sat a silver one, the same size as the others, but glistening in the bright lights from the rover.

Osaka stepped closer. "McKnight? We've got multiple contacts. It's about to get hot as hell."

"I've got the master disk in sight," Tom murmured. "I just need to pull it out."

He edged the rover forward, light glinting everywhere in the cramped space. Reaching out with the right-hand gripper, he clasped the drive with two claws, giving it a gentle tug, but the rubber tips slipped off, and the arm jerked back, empty, eliciting a quiet curse.

"McKnight?" Osaka was kneeling next to him, weapon to his shoulder, chatter coming in over the radios as the SEALs readied themselves for an engagement. "We're going to have to pull out if you can't get it."

Tom clenched his jaw and tried again, envisioning himself standing right in front of the drive array. He'd worked with them for years and had plucked out data drives a hundred times with his own two fingers, and knew the pressure required. The challenge was translating that knowledge into an automaton miles away underwater through a video link that was spotty at best.

Tom reached out again, clasping the drive's edges with the delicately thin rubber tips as far in on the body of the drive as he could. Instead of pulling with the arm, he reversed thrust on the submersible while keeping the control for the claw grips firmly depressed, applying constant, gentle pressure. The drive popped out two inches and Tom let go then immediately dove forward with the rover again, gaining a solid grasp on the exposed drive and reversed, pulling it free.

"Got it!" Tom hissed, relief flooding through him.

"Get it out of there, McKnight. Now."

Tom brought the drive in toward the rover's frame and placed it in a compartment in the submersible's underbelly, locking it tight. He then turned the rover around and worked his way back the length of cable he'd dragged inside, barreling through ports, knocking hatches aside that had drifted shut, only being delicate when it came to working with shifting the control cable when it bunched. While he worked, he heard Osaka issuing orders in a tight, clipped tone.

"We have inbound. I need an immediate exfil. Yes, directly at the site. No. No, we're unable to retreat. Yes. Confirmed." A handful of seconds passed before the commander addressed the team through their private channel. "Evac in fifteen. Get back here and form defensive positions. Prepare the sky hook." Then he addressed Tom specifically. "Hear that, McKnight? Evac in fifteen."

"Minutes?"

"Or less, if we're lucky."

"How do you expect me to…" Tom trailed off at Osaka's withering stare, focusing back on the work at hand.

Moving carefully but quickly, Tom brushed past the corpses and debris and exited the bridge, bumping against the walls with sharp jolts, stirring up sediment, worms and more of the tiny, multi-colored crabs. Two compartments later, he was back at the escape hatch, pointing the rover upward to shoot through the gap. He mistimed the maneuver and glanced off the edge, causing the rover to spin wildly as it exited the submarine. Holding his breath, Tom stabilized the vessel and rotated the camera down to make sure he still held the master drive. He sighed with relief when he saw it still in the compartment, secured, then leaned forward, engaging the main joysticks fully, driving the rover in an acrobatic flip, darting beneath the drifting cable, and shooting toward the surface.

"She's free and on the way up, Osaka."

"We're down to ten minutes," Osaka announced, tight-lipped. "Unless you can sprout wings, I suggest you hustle."

"If you want to pull on the cable to make this go faster, be my guest!" Tom snapped back, eliciting a low growl from Osaka, though the commander kept any reply to himself.

Using the picture-in-picture GPS, Tom kept the rover on target, driving it east at a steady ascent, balancing out currents caused by geothermal activity and keeping the engine in the sweet spot between going so hard it might burn out and hard enough to reach the surface in time. Particulates drifted by, whipping off the camera lens as the scout vessel surged through the murky depths. On the shore, the SEALs bustled quietly as they prepared a defense. Two men dragged six harnesses out on the ice before activating a self-inflating balloon that whooshed as it filled, lifting slowly off the ground, hauling a cable into the sky.

Tom glanced at the rover's gauges as he steered. "I'm fifty feet down and about two hundred yards out!"

In the rover's cameras, light glinted off the ice above him and a grin began to form, but his expression quickly dropped as something massive loomed in the shallows in front of him. An eight-foot-long sturgeon, glistening from tip to tail, turned, jerking with the rover's sudden appearance. With a grunt, Tom pulled back on the joysticks, whipping the submersible in a tight roll as it sped past, shooting over the fish, striking the ice in a glancing blow that sent it into back into a shallow dive. Tom moved with the change in momentum, years of experience working to bring the craft back around, the rover skimming beneath the hard ice, a mirroring shadow of itself reflected above as it churned through the water.

"Almost there," Tom's eked out the words through a clenched jaw.

The GPS screen showed the rover's blue light drawing nearer their green one. Slowing it down, he studied the screen, searching for the exit hole while Osaka stood nearby, rifle at the ready as he gazed north.

"We've got hostiles moving in the forest," the lieutenant commander said, "and evac is five minutes out."

Tom's normally steady hands twitched as he worked the joysticks, driving the rover in what seemed like circles as he scanned the screen, glancing up every few seconds to see if he could spot its running lights through the ice.

"What's wrong?" Osaka crouched next to him.

"I can't find the exit hole."

"Does the GPS match up?"

"Yeah. It should be right there." Tom's voice pitched sharply upward as he glanced out toward the lake. Part of him wanted to dive in and retrieve the rover by hand, but he held onto the joysticks. "But it's not. All I see is black ice."

"Take your time," Osaka spoke calmly. "Keep making passes."

"I've got two in the woods." Reese's voice came through the radio, his tone calm and cool. "Fifty yards. Permission to engage?"

"Granted."

The first shots cracked the night sky almost before Osaka replied, sending Tom's stomach tumbling, the sudden shock of sound knocking snow off nearby branches. Someone screamed in the distance as the gunfire quickly escalated and the Russians returned fire, bullets zipping by, smacking tree trunks and ricocheting off of rocks. Osaka began piling their equipment near the shore, nestled in the rocks and gravel. He tossed tents, packs, navigation devices, and extra radios together, then he jammed timed explosive charges beneath the gear. Snatching up his rifle again, he aimed out toward the woods and fired two shots, another scream echoing in response, joined by the sound of Slavic voices. Tom's stomach lurched with each shot and scream, trying to focus on the rover, but unable to concentrate in conditions that were utterly foreign to him.

"More coming in from the south."

"Sorted. I've got three at two-six-five."

"Two down. Irons, can you give me an assist?"

"Dispatched. Commander, it's getting rough out here – when's our evac arriving?"

Osaka squeezed off two more rounds, the sharp cracks drawing Tom's shoulders tight. "Three minutes, gentlemen." He turned to Tom, his relatively calm demeanor dropping. "Come on, McKnight! Get that rover up here now!"

A simple revelation struck Tom and, underwater, he doubled back with the rover until he came across a section of cable lying on the shallow floor. As gunfire cut the cold night air around him, he turned the submersible's nose down at the cable like a sniffing dog, following it ten yards until a perfectly circular round hole appeared above him.

"Found it!"

Thrusting the rover upward, he heard it shoot through the hole and land on the ice with a clank. He dropped the remote control and staggered across the icy surface, legs wobbling, stinging with numbness from sitting for so long. Osaka slipped past him with his rifle slung on his shoulder, reaching the rover first, bending to snatch out the master drive and stuff it in his coat.

"Assemble at the evac site!" Osaka called to the other team members, then he nodded at Tom. "Let's get this to shore so we can blow it up."

Tossing the rover controls in the pile with the other equipment, he staggered across the ice, slipping and sliding as he made his way out to join Osaka. They each grabbed a rover arm and dragged it toward shore, hauling it over the snowy rocks and dumping it atop the rest of the gear. As they were turning back to the ice, a half dozen rounds smacked the pile of equipment with heavy pops, sending up chunks of wood and plastic to sting Tom's cheeks. Something punched Osaka in the back and he stiffened and fell forward over the submersible.

Calling upon his training, Tom grabbed his pistol from his holster, crouched into a low shooter's stance and fired at the shadowy figures creeping toward them through the snow-laden trees, the Russians ducking for cover, buying him some time. Tom flipped Osaka over and leaned close to hear him groan, still alive. He dug out the hard drive from the commander's jacket and transferred it to his own pocket, then he grabbed the commander beneath his arms and pulled him backwards onto the ice, dragging him toward a circle of harnesses lying a fifty yards away. The flat part of his boots slipped on the slick surface, and he lowered his backside and dug in with his rough heels.

Osaka's head lolled on his shoulders, eyes rolling behind his goggles as he flitted in and out of consciousness, raising his rifle in his gloved hands, the weapon shaking as he fired back at the approaching Russians. Back bent and aching, Tom dragged him to the extraction point, grabbing a harness and shrugging it on, gazing upward as he buckled himself in, following the tether line stretching up to where it was attached to the white balloon and its flashing beacon.

"Irons and Plummer are down," Reese snapped through Osaka's radio to the staccato rhythm of bullets flying back and forth. "These bastards came in force!"

Osaka snatched his radio off his belt and barked into it, though the bite quickly faded from his tone. "Anyone still alive, get to the extraction point." His eyes lifted to the night sky where the sounds of propellers whirred loudly, growing in volume. "Our ride is coming. If you're not in a harness in thirty seconds, you'll be left behind."

Tom grabbed a second harness and held it open so Osaka could slide his arms in, but the commander wasn't concerned about getting away. His eyes stayed locked on the shore where the SEALs were still fighting, struggling and shouting as the main Russian force closed in around them.

"Leave me!" Osaka snapped, brushing Tom off. "Have to…" his head dipped again, then jerked back up. "Have to help them!"

The sound of the plane changed, as if it was altering its altitude, dipping lower. Tom ignored Osaka and forced his left arm into the harness, then tried to grab his other arm, but the commander elbowed him in the chest and shoved him away, lying half on his side, continuing to fire at the dark shoreline. With a growl, Tom circled and snatched the weapon from his grasp, tossing it onto the ice. He fell on Osaka, using his weight to pin the man, grabbing his wrist and forcing his arm into the harness. Still, the commander struggled against him, keeping him from locking the buckles.

"Stop fighting me!" Tom shouted. "They're already gone, Osaka! We have to go, now!" With a grunt, he shoved the larger man down, using his free hand to get the two buckles snapped.

Bullets skimmed across the ice as the Russians turned from their downed quarry and began to fire out at the lake, rounds skipping across the ice. The dull, steadily increasing roar grew painful as a massive plane swooped in from the east, its wings tilting and dipping mere meters over the tree line, blowing snow from branches like a massive, black bird in the night sky. The Russians lifted their weapons skyward and fired, bullets pinging off the fuselage with faint clankings.

Double checking Osaka's harness, Tom gripped his own harness and held onto the commander's arm, slamming his eyes shut, trying to relax his body like they'd told him to do. Above, the hook jutting out from the nose of the plane cut through the sky, aiming for a pinprick of flashing light that radiated out from the balloon, then snatched the tether and drew it taut, dragging the balloon and the harnesses with it.

A sudden force grabbed Tom, causing his entire body to go taut, launching them like rockets off the ice. Stomach somewhere in his feet, Tom could only cling on to Osaka as they both twisted in their harnesses, staring down as the muzzle flashes at the edge of the woods grew fainter by the second, then were overpowered by a massive flare of white and yellow from the charges detonating at the edge of the lake.

Chapter 2
Tom McKnight
Wyndale, Virginia

"You toggle the night vision scope using the switch here."

Tom leaned over Sam's shoulder with his arms wrapped around her, flicking the switch on the side of the scope which rested atop the AR-15. She nodded and mimicked his instructions, using her thumb to flip it on and off while peering into the lens.

"Got it," she replied, breath gusting in the cold.

Tom let her go and backed up. "Okay, now give it a few shots, get a feeling for it."

He gestured toward the paper target he'd nailed to a wooden post forty-five yards away. Sam raised the short-barrel, suppressed AR-15 to her shoulder, narrowing her left eye and looked down the sight with her right as the cold wind blew her long curls around. She took a breath and let it out, and somewhere in the middle of the release she squeezed the trigger, the rifle popping sharply in response, and a small hole appearing in the paper.

"Nice shot," Tom nodded. "Keep going."

Sam fired six more times, growing more confident with every trigger squeeze, and after hitting the paper five out of a total of seven shots, she lowered it, shrugging at her father.

"It's been a while," she murmured, ejecting the magazine and clearing the chamber before adjusting the rifle in her hands, gauging its weight and balance. "I like it. It's lighter, and I feel like I can control it better."

"It'll be great for close quarters," Tom added. "Let's hope it doesn't come to that, but just in case."

"Having something just in case is always good, right?" Sam smiled hesitantly at her father, looking more like her mother than Tom could ever remember.

"That's right."

"Why do you have this, anyway? It looks… I dunno, more military-ish than the guns we had in the house."

"I wish we could *get* to the ones in the house," Tom replied, side-stepping his daughter's question. "I doubt even the horses could move all that debris. Not in the time we have left, anyway."

Samantha watched him closely for a moment before dropping the subject, shrugging as they trotted back to an old folding card table next to the barn. Several weapons lay on its surface, different guns for Sam to try and for Tom to test the cold-weather resiliency of. Five below zero wasn't the worst he'd ever felt, though it was no laughing matter. The wind stung his cheeks and frosted up around his nostrils, sticking them together sometime when he inhaled. The snowdrifts were several feet deep across the yard, forcing them to dig paths all morning just so they could shoot. Whenever he labored too hard, his lungs grew painfully cold, forcing him to slow down and remember to keep his scarf up over his mouth. Tom looked up at the crystal-clear sky, devoid of clouds, the sun shooting golden rays through the deep blue, though it did nothing to warm the air.

"You did amazing for not firing a weapon in… what's it been, years?" he said, smiling.

"It's like riding a bike, right?"

"Uh, yeah." Tom chuckled, bracing himself against sudden gust of wind. "Let's go in for a bit. We've been out here all morning."

Sam nodded, and they gathered the guns and ammunition into a weapons bag and brought it inside. Shutting the door behind them, Tom placed the guns down and stood in the barn's relative warmth. A kerosene heater sat in the center, running on high to chase away the worst of the cold, though it still couldn't have been more than thirty degrees in the barn. The horses stood tied next to a food trough, blankets drooped over their backs, eating happily as they watched their riders rubbing their hands together before digging through the weapon bag.

"Looks like only one misfired." Sam held up an older model Beretta pistol whose slide was still locked back.

"Yep, that's one we'll leave behind," Tom agreed. "We can't have any misfires or issues due to the cold. C'mon, let's head down."

"Sounds good."

Tom picked up the gun bag and carried it to the cellar door, then grabbed one handle, lifting up a side, allowing Sam to slide past him and down the steps. He followed quickly and let the door fall shut behind him. They descended to the dirt floor, a wave of heat hitting them in the face as they went down. Underground, the average temperature was a more tolerable fifty-three, and the confined space mixed with a kerosene heater made for a nice shelter. Smooch whined from deeper in the room, and Tom turned to greet the German Shepherd as she limped across the cellar floor. Kneeling, he rubbed the fur around her head and Sam crouched down next to him, giggling as a long pink tongue greeted her.

"She looks so funny with her hair burned away," Sam wiped her wet cheek, grinning at the pup.

"It'll grow back, eventually," Tom rubbed gingerly at the short, blackened bits of fur. "I don't know how she made it out of there, but I'm glad she did."

After finding her limping from the wreckage of their torched home, Tom had inspected the old bandage and wounds, concluding that someone had gotten hold of her with a knife. He'd further assumed it was Barbara who'd sewn the Shepherd up, and after getting her warm, Tom had cleaned and redressed the wound while Sam brushed away the burned fur from her coat. The only problem once they were finished was what, exactly to do with her. Tom had a mission plan in mind that was as clear as day, but nothing about it included bringing a dog with them. Sighing, he pushed off the inevitable conversation about the topic and stood, ordering Smooch back to her bed, while he and Sam continued toward the back.

The underground shelter was comfortably laid out, if not more than slightly cramped. Rectangular in shape, storage shelves lined the walls while the cots and cooking appliances were in the rear. They had a kitchen table and a wood-burning stove that vented outside through a pipe that ran up the length of the back of the barn, and the shelter included a basic bathroom that consisted of a curtained alcove and deeply-dug hole over which a thick board and rubber-lined seat sat, which helped keep things sanitary and smells minimized.

The underground shelter was not perfect by any means, but it was better than a burned-out hunk of ruins and a drafty barn, and more than good enough to keep them alive. Tom walked to the small kitchen area and took off his coat, scarf, and hat, and placed them on the table, then plopped down in his chair, relaxing gently to ease the strain on his back. Sam joined him, stripping off her outer layers until she was down to a sweater and undershirts before she sat.

"Good thing you guys built this place." Sam put her elbows on the table and started rubbing her rosy-cold cheeks. "We'd be S-O-L."

"At the time, it was a big debate between your mother and I, but," he winked, "I eventually convinced her. It was a big expense, of both time and money, but it's one of those 'if you need it and don't have it' kind of things, I guess."

"No kidding. The wood-burning stove's a great touch."

"Coal bin, too. That was your mom's idea." Tom glanced into a recessed part of the room where the bin held enough black gold to get them through at least one winter, though the chances of it getting them through what they were enduring was less likely. *One thing at a time. One thing at a time.*

"I haven't started the stove yet, though, because I don't plan on being here much longer."

"I know," Sam nodded. "We're going to get Mom and Linda and Jack."

"That's right."

"When?"

Tom stared at the table for a long moment before replying. "We've got five days to get them back, but we'll do it in two."

"How?"

Tom placed his hand on a folded map resting off to the side, unfolding it and spread it out so Sam could see. Dropping his finger on an area southwest of them, near the Virginia-Tennessee border, Tom looked up. "In his note, Keith drew this map of where to come. I guess it's some kind of forward operating base where they're keeping them."

"That's a couple hundred miles away," Sam observed. "We've only got the horses. How can we get there in two days in this snow?"

"We ride the horses hard and pick up a truck or other large vehicle on the way there."

"It'll be tough on them." Sam glanced up to the barn.

"I know, but we'll be careful and make sure we don't drive them too hard. Plus, we don't have any other choice. If we can't get there early, before Keith expects us, then we won't be able to surprise him."

"When do we leave?"

"An hour."

Sam stared at her father, her eyes mirroring the same expression her mother would have made, showing that resigned toughness he'd always loved about her until, finally, she gave a hard nod in agreement. Layering up their clothes, they filled a set of makeshift saddlebags with extra-long johns and shirts, socks, survival kits, food, small propane tanks, and a burner. Sam found a thick knitted beanie with a ball on top and put it on, pulling it down over her ears while Tom grabbed a winter hunter's hat from an old box, letting the flaps cover the sides of his face. Once ready, they armed themselves with a pair of pistols each, two rifles and as much ammunition as they could handle. Hauling the gear upstairs, they saddled the horses, encouraging them with sweet whispers and plenty of pats on their necks while Tom tied their spare rifles to the saddlebags and gave his horse a gentle pat on the rump.

"What about Smooch?"

Tom winced, pausing at the conversation he'd been dreading having. "I… was going to leave her food bin open and leave some water pails for her."

"Why?"

"Well, she can't ride a horse, and she can't run in the snow. She'll just slow us down."

Sam narrowed her green eyes. "But if we don't come back, she'll die."

"If she comes with us, she could die, too."

"We can't leave her alone." Sam took a step back from her horse, her posture defensive. "Clearly she got hurt trying to defend Mom and Jack and Linda. She *deserves* to come along."

"So, you'd rather freeze out there, as long as we're together," Tom said, giving a half-hearted laugh.

"Something like that." Sam didn't smile, folding her arms, digging in deeper.

"It's not the time to be hard-headed, kiddo. You and I are going to saddle up, and we're leaving Smooch here."

Sam backed up and sat heavily on an overturned pail. "Then I'm not going."

"That's fine. You can stay with the dog. I'll go alone and come back for you when I'm done."

She gave him a sideways smirk. "Think you can ride a couple hundred miles without my help?"

Tom scoffed. "I can ride a horse, Sam."

"What about horse care? Do you know how to alleviate saddle sores? Can you identify symptoms of colic or laminitis?"

"You're not a vet, Sam."

"No, but I can tell when a horse is sick. I know when they might be about to keel over and drop you in the snow."

"Sam…"

"Besides, what if you can't get back? You'd really leave me here knowing that?"

Tom stopped his work and leaned against the horse, sighing in resignation. His bluff had been shoddy but he'd pushed forward with it anyway, underestimating his daughter's tenacity and stubbornness, a trait she had inherited from both sides of her family. With a groan he stood up, putting his hands on his hips, giving her an annoyed look as he conceded.

"Okay then, smarty pants. How do you suggest we transport her?"

"Easy. We make a sled. We can put her on it with her food and supplies. It doesn't have to be big or bulky, just something streamlined. The horses can easily handle it."

Tom scratched his chin. "Do we still have all our winter gear up in the loft?"

Sam cocked her head. "Maybe. But I haven't seen it in four or five years. Why?"

"Come on," Tom motioned toward the ladder leading up to the top of the barn and they climbed to the top. Bales of hay were stacked on one side, but the far corner contained what they'd called their long-term storage. It held items they hadn't used in years, including small pieces of furniture and plastic bins filled with miscellaneous odds and ends that they hadn't wanted to get rid of, but didn't want to keep around in the house any longer. Tom walked over and started picking through the nearly ten feet deep pile of odds and ends they hadn't seen in years.

"I wish we would have made rows to get through this stuff," he commented, recognizing things from he and Barbara's first apartment, before Sam was even born, tears forming in his eyes as memories of their early family flooded back. He wiped them away quickly, before Samantha could notice, and kept digging through the boxes and bins as she assisted.

"Well, here's our old skiing gear," she said, pushing aside a bureau to reveal three sets of skis leaning against the wall. "My old ones are too small for me but perfect to make a sled."

Tom snapped out of his brief reflection and took the skis, giving them a solid heft before nodding in agreement. "Yeah, this'll work. We can use a piece of plywood and bolt it down with carriage bolts."

"Awesome." Sam grinned. "Let's do it."

They found plywood easily enough, and an old tool chest had bolts and a hand drill which Tom used to connect the plywood to the skis, pushing the carriage bolts in from the bottom and locking them down tight. More than once Tom considered trying to find some of his electric tools in the remains of their home, but bore through the strain of the hand tool, and they were soon finished.

"What do you think?" Sam stood back from the sled as Tom gave a satisfied harrumph.

"Okay, you know what? I think this might actually work. Should be plenty of room for Smooch to lay on, plus we can carry some extra supplies. We'll need to be extra careful on hills and it'll slow us down some… but not much."

There was a long silence before Samantha sidled up to Tom, taking his hand in hers and leaning into his arm. "Thanks, Dad. Sorry for being so difficult."

"It's okay," Tom put his arm around her, squeezing her tight. "You were right – Smooch is a part of our family. I didn't mean to be so flippant about leaving her behind."

"I know." Samantha returned the hug as they stood, looking at the makeshift sled, before Tom patted her back and turned around, looking at the barn doors, snowflakes drifting through the cracks.

"I guess we're about ready to go. Just need to get the sled loaded and hooked up to one of the horses."

"What about the… bodies? The ones on the porch. Shouldn't we bury them? We don't know the other two, but the Everetts…"

"I don't think we have time," Tom replied. "The ground is frozen solid as a rock, and it would take us a day just to dig the graves. We'd get sweaty under our layers, then we'd have to change again after we were cooled down and dry. I want to bury the Everetts – and that other pair – as much as the next person – but our family takes precedence."

"Yeah… you're right." Sam sighed sadly.

"Plus, another storm could blow through at any time. If we get hit again, we'll never get out of here."

"It's cool, Dad. The Everetts were great people, but… well, I don't want to sound callous, but we're alive. And we need to keep staying alive. We can bury them after we get back, when it's warmer."

"Good idea."

They lined up the horses by the barn door and tied a rope to the saddle horn of Sam's mottled white mare, then used bungee cords to secure some dog food and extra supplies. Tom carried Smooch from the cellar under one arm and placed her on the sled on a thick layer of truck pads, the Shepherd whining at first, but Sam coaxed her down and covered her with several blankets. Once she realized they were going somewhere, and she didn't actually have to walk, she settled down and looked around expectantly like it was a ride in the back of the car.

With everything loaded up, they turned off the kerosene heaters, shut the cellar door, and hid it again, on the off-chance that someone might come by looking to scavenge. Sam mounted up while Tom opened the barn doors, leading his gelding out by the reins. Sam walked her horse out beside his, and they both watched to see how Smooch would react. As her horse moved through three feet of snow, the sled rose to ride on the hard layer, the dog wearing a look of confusion but soon realizing she was being pulled and her ears perked up and she panted almost happily.

"That's right, Smooch!" Sam called back with a laugh. "Just like when we used to go sledding when you were a pup." The Shepherd's chin lifted, and she gave a happy bark and looked around in excitement. "I think she's good, Dad," Sam said with a smile.

Tom grinned as he shut the barn doors and mounted his gelding, urging it through the snow with a slight kick of his heels, pushing ahead of Sam. Once lined up, they trudged down the driveway past the smoldering ruins of their home. Tom had avoided looking at it as much as possible since Smooch had come trotting out of the wreckage, every glance a painful reminder that he hadn't been there to defend his loved ones and their home. Fire burned in his stomach, his soul twisting, heart pounding so heavily that it hurt as a name reared its ugly head again.

Keith.

Burning their house down had been a brutish, cowardly act. Killing an elderly couple and two more strangers had been barbaric beyond measure. As long as Barbara, Linda and Jack could be retrieved, though, he could deal with the sorrow, anguish, loss and guilt. The only guilt he could not – would not – bear would be losing his loved ones.

With a glance back, he caught Sam swiping tears from her cold cheeks, his face twisting into a grimace of pain, heart breaking for her. The center of her comfort and safety had been their home, and it had been turned into charred ruins, her mother and siblings taken from her. They could rebuild and recover, but the pain would doubtless run deep for his children, their lives so traumatically interrupted by a force greater than anyone could have expected.

Lifting his chin, Tom took a deep, cold breath and pressed his teeth tight as he mounted his horse, giving a slight kick of his heels, forging a path ahead to – hopefully – a light at the end of a very, very dark tunnel.

Chapter 3
Barbara McKnight
Somewhere in Tennessee

The rig slugged its way through the snow and ice, slush and snow drifts plaguing it at every step, along with debris that they couldn't see that constantly knocked against the tires and chassis. Every time they hit something, Barbara flinched and the kids groaned, their uncomfortable positions amplifying even the smallest of bumps and jostles.

Barbara laid on her left side in the truck bed, just behind the passenger seat, her head angled against the back wall as she faced Jack and Linda on the far end. All of their hands and feet were securely tied in spite of Barbara's repeated attempts to free herself, and the curtain dividing the sleeper from the cab was drawn tight as Keith continued to drive, muttering and humming to himself. Both Linda and Jack's eyes were wide as the rig continually bumped and jostled around, occasionally slamming into things, sending everyone tumbling as Keith pushed onward with what seemed like almost negligent abandon – or perhaps he was just a terrible driver.

They slammed through a snow drift and the entire rig shook and shuddered, Barbara clamping her eyes shut as she awaited what felt like an inevitable slide into a ditch.

"Ow, Mommy," Jack sobbed and wiggled. "The ropes are cutting me!"

Barbara pressed her head against his, forcing the words into his ears, wishing desperately she could hold him in her arms. "I know, sweetie, just try not to struggle. They'll only cut you deeper. Lie still, okay?" He nodded and put on a brave face, Linda stoic next to him, her expression masking the pain that they all felt.

Keith had been overly aggressive with their bindings, the ropes so tight around Barbara's wrists that her fingers went numb if she laid in certain positions, and there was a constant tingling in her wrists and feet from a lack of circulation. She did her best to stay comfortable, but there was really no way to do it, especially with anxiety gnawing at her insides.

"Look, kids." Barbara whispered to them as quietly as possible, watching the curtain for any signs of Keith listening in. "We've been through a lot the past three weeks. A lot worse than this, right?" They both nodded. "We'll get out of this one just like we did everything else."

"How?" Jack whispered back, eyes wide.

"That's just how it is with us McKnights. We're tough." Her eyes flashed to her daughter. "Tell him, Linda."

Her younger daughter's face smoothed into something hard and mature. "That's right. It's been a hard month, but we've stuck together, and we'll get through this. Just like we always have."

Jack swallowed hard, shifting in his seat, wincing at the pain. "But our house is burned down. And what about Smooch? Is she okay?"

"I… I don't know, bud. I sure hope she's okay. As soon as we can get out of here, we'll go straight home. If Smooch got out, she'll be waiting for us. Until then, I need you to be strong for me – for us – okay?" She ground her jaw, speaking through clenched teeth, fighting to contain her rage at their captor. "I promise both of you that we're going to get out of this. Hear me?"

Jack sniffled quietly, nodding gently as Linda leaned her head against him. "We're good, mom. We've got your back."

"Good. Now, we just have to wait for an opportunity. Try to stay all smiles and be as helpful as possible if we interact with him. Make him think we're on his side."

Both children nodded and Barbara leaned back, trying to get comfortable as the eighteen-wheeler blasted down the highway. Whenever they hit a blockage or detour in the road, Keith revved the diesel engine too high, and it lurched every time he shifted gears, nearly stalling more than a few times.

"He's not a very good driver," she murmured to herself, looking around at the interior of the sleeper cab for anything that might give them an advantage.

A dilapidated, half-rusted metal bookshelf was filled with books and had bungee cords strapped around the front, keeping them contained so they couldn't slip out during turns and jostles. A basket of DVDs was nailed to the top of the shelf, and a small flatscreen TV was mounted to the wall as well. A minifridge sat next to the mattress, and a small pull-down desk rattled and thumped as the truck went along. Paisley curtains on the small side windows were threadbare, adding to the feeling that the sleeper was well-used, well-worn and not very well cared for by its previous owners.

Noise came from the front of the cab and Barbara gritted her teeth. *Showtime.* The divider curtain snapped open a few seconds later, and Keith looked into the sleeper cab, a suspicious gaze roaming over them.

"You folks okay back there?"

"How long are you going to keep us tied up?" Barbara tried to steady her voice, though anger rode just under the surface. "Our wrists are starting to bruise and bleed."

"Oh, I *am* sorry about that," he replied with a mockingly crestfallen look. "I know it hurts, but we'll be at our destination soon."

"Where's that?"

Keith shrugged as he glanced back at the road. "That's for me to know and you to find out."

"My daughter has to use the bathroom."

"We'll stop."

"When?"

"Soon."

Barbara's kept her tone light, giving the friendliest smile she could muster. "No problem. We'll try to hang on as long as we can. It's just, with all the bumps and stuff..." She let her words trail off. "I wouldn't want an accident."

"Got it." Keith intoned flatly, looking like he was barely able to stifle a roll of his eyes.

The rig bumped over something hard, nearly wrenching the truck from his grip and he straightened in his seat, jerking the wheel, getting them back under control before glancing back.

"Don't you want to know why I picked you up?"

"I already know. You're a government agent, looking for my husband. My guess is you're using us as bait to bring him in."

For the first time since Barbara had suffered the displeasure of meeting Keith, his self-assured visage all but dropped for a few seconds, his eyes growing wide and his jaw slacking before he regained control and responded sharply.

"How do you know that?"

"I was at one of the military camps in Bristol. I talked to a lieutenant there and she gave me the information."

Keith snorted. "Right. She just told you, huh? I find that challenging to believe."

Barbara tried to look innocent and gave him a half shrug. "With times being so tough and all, I guess she wanted to help me."

"What was her name?"

"Lieutenant Bratton, I think?" Briggs might have been in charge of the group that kidnapped her children, but Barbara wasn't about to sic Keith – or his bosses – on the woman.

Keith gave her a long, flat look in the rearview mirror, much like a sociopath studying a newly captured insect or small rodent trapped inside a jar. "Yeah, well. I'm sorry you're in this position. If your husband had just worked with us, it wouldn't have come to this."

"No, I understand," Barbara tried her best to sound genuine. "I'm sad that Tom did something wrong. I mean, he worked for the government a lot and he's always loved his job. I wouldn't even imagine him doing something bad."

"Well, he didn't love this one," Keith gave a dry, heartless laugh, "and it cost him dearly."

"So, you saw him?"

"Oh yes. I rode with him out of a camp in Virginia Beach."

Jack and Linda both began whispering between themselves, and Barbara shot them a quick look to silence them. Keith, thankfully, seemed to not notice their initial reaction, focused as he was on navigating a particularly deep snowdrift.

"You were in a vehicle? With my husband? What about my daughter?"

"Oh yes, we were all there. Both were fine the last time I saw them." Keith snapped the wheel left and shifted down, plowing through another snowbank. "But that was before the wreck."

Barbara's initial elation at hearing that Tom and Sam were alive faltered, and her heart skipped a beat. "The... wreck?"

Keith snickered. "Your husband and I got into a little scuffle, and he crashed the APC we were in. I woke up on the side of the hill a few hours later. Nasty case of frostbite, I might add. They were gone after I woke up."

"So, you don't know if they're okay?"

"I don't, but I assume they are. By the way, thanks for asking about *my* injuries. I mean, I got tossed pretty hard." He rolled his right shoulder. "I'm still aching all over. Not to mention the frostbite."

Barbara ground her teeth, her patience at putting up her charade waning. "You'll excuse me if I don't act particularly concerned for you, given what you're doing to us."

Keith glanced at her in the mirror, giving her a toothy, borderline deranged smile. "I'm sure Tom's fine. Both him and Samantha. They'll be home soon, if they're not already. They'll get my message and come looking for you."

"Message?"

Keith snickered at some joke only he understood. "Yeah. Your neighbors helped me write it."

Barbara vaguely remembered Darren Everett being shot in her front yard, but she'd taken multiple blows from her kidnapper, sent sprawling into the snow, dazed and confused, unable to focus on what had happened. A suspicion had been eating at her about the Everetts, though, and Keith's dark chuckle confirmed her darkest fears. She ignored them though, swallowing down her nervousness for the sake of Linda and Jack.

"What do you expect my husband to do when he finds your message?"

"He'll come looking for you, of course. He'll see that he won't get you back until he agrees to help us, and then he *will* agree. You'll be reunited with him once he does and you can all go on your way like one big happy family." Keith looked at her in the mirror again, eyes narrowed in another of his examining-a-bug-in-a-jar smiles. "Everyone will get what they want."

Not everyone, she thought. Not the Everetts, or the other poor people you killed.

"What if he and Sam—"

The rig skidded sideways with a sudden lurch, cutting her off, and Keith gripped the wheel in a stiff panic. He let out a string of curses before the truck slowed sharply, white powder shooting over the hood, dashing across the windshield in a gust of flakes as they slowed to a crawl. Keith jerked the rig back and forth, gunning the gas and spinning the wheels and the truck bumped something hard, slewing them to the right, throwing the trio in the back around against each other, Jack and Linda crying out. The rig finally skidded to a stop, though Keith continued gunning the engine for another few seconds before finally shifting to neutral and letting the truck sit idle. Cursing sharply, he repeatedly struck his palm against the steering wheel in frustration.

"Those are *no-no* words, mommy." Jack whispered at her and Barbara shook her head sharply, mouthing back to him to keep quiet.

After taking out his rage on the truck, Keith turned and looked back with a sour expression, panting slightly. "We're stuck. Obviously. It's going to take me a few minutes to get us out."

"Use the floor mats," Barbara told him. "Put them under the tires for traction."

"Thanks for the suggestion," Keith rolled his eyes. "But I'll try the winch first." A second later, the door whipped open, letting in a blast of cold and Keith slid out of the truck and slammed the door behind him, muttering something that involved the word "moron" as he went. The instant the door closed, words poured out of Jack and Linda as they peppered their mother with questions.

"Mom, what are we going to do?"

"How can we get these stupid ropes off?"

"What did he do with Mr. and Mrs. Everett??"

"Hush, kids," she shook her head, ignoring the babbling. "Let me think."

Barbara shifted to a sitting position, watching as the top of Keith's head appeared over the hood. Bending, he pulled on what she assumed was the hook and cable for a winch attached to the front of the rig. Pulling out the winch wouldn't take long, but it offered a unique opportunity to both keep an eye on him and try something that had been in the back of her mind for a while.

"What are you going to do?" Linda asked, eyes wide.

"I've got an idea. Watch Keith. Tell me if it looks like he's going to get back in the truck." With Linda keeping watch, Barbara swung around to her right side and brought her knees to her chest. Rolling her shoulders, she pushed her wrists below her boots, slipping them to the front. Hands up, she placed rope to the edge of the metal bookshelf where part of it was jagged from bits of it having rusted away. She began moving her wrists back and forth, the first fibers beginning to shred and sever. Soon, she'd cut through the entire strand of rope, and the rest of the tension evaporated as they fell off, and she smiled genuinely for the first time in what felt like ages.

"Give me your wrists, quickly!"

Linda held them out, still looking out the front, and Barbara went to work on them, plucking and pulling until she managed to get them loose and unwind the ropes, Linda's hands popping apart with a sudden sigh of surprise from the young girl.

"Now, work on your brother."

Linda reached around Jack and worked on his bindings while Barbara untied her ankles, then looked outside to see Keith dragging the steel cable out to a pair of trees some thirty yards distant. She squeezed her hands into fists as the blood flow returned to them, then glanced down at the scatter of cut rope on the floor, kicking it behind the driver's seat, staying as low as possible.

"Keep the loose ropes hidden behind the seats. When Keith gets back in, keep your feet hidden so he can't see them, okay?"

Jack and Linda both nodded.

"What are you going to do?" Linda asked, already working on her own ankles.

"Find a real weapon."

Barbara rose to a crouch and looked over the dashboard, watching as Keith walked the cable between a pair of thick trees, struggling to plant his feet in the thigh-high snow. She dove for the glove compartment, popping it open to see if there might be a pistol or knife inside, not terribly surprised to find it empty. She searched below the seats, feeling through food wrappers and garbage, and when she didn't find anything there, she scoured the cup holders, hands roaming over more wrappers, receipts and a pencil that was sticking out, point up.

She peered out to the tree to check on Keith's progress, but he'd vanished, and she felt her heart begin to race. She kept looking back and forth until the door flew open in a gust of freezing wind. Without thinking, Barbara grabbed the pencil from the center console and jerked backwards, landing on the bed with a gasp, shoving her hands behind her back, hiding her loose feet behind the passenger seat as she shot a warning look at the kids, and they mirrored their mother with stiff but quiet movements.

Keith rolled down the window and fed in a winch controller connected to a cable, then climbed into the cab and landed heavily in the driver's seat as freezing cold air chilled the cabin and snow gusted inside. He shut the door and sat still, fingertips over the vents as he shivered uncontrollably, panting harder than when he had left. After a few minutes of warming up, he glanced up at Barbara then flipped the power switch on the winch control in his lap.

"What are you going to do?" Barbara asked, trying to look like someone who was still bound hand and foot.

"I'm going to give it some gas as we're pulled forward," he growled, tone aggravated.

"That's a good plan."

"No kidding. Now shut up." The growl had dropped an octave, and Barbara took the hint, leaning back as she looked over at Linda and Jack, giving them a nearly imperceptible shake of her head. *Not yet.*

Up front, Keith pressed the clutch and put the truck into first gear as the steel cable drew taut and tugged at the rig. The sounds of groaning metal reverberated through the cabin as they inched forward. He gave it a little gas and the rig scooted forward, sliding sideways on the ice before straightening on the pavement. With the window down, the cabin filled with cold air, chilling Barbara's cheeks and turning them red.

By the time the temperature was starting to get uncomfortable for the children, the rig was grinding through deep drifts, the winch whirring and grinding in displeasure, but they eventually straightened out as they cleared the worst of the snow, the tires finding traction on the pavement. Keith gave a triumphant whoop and eased back on the winch, driving forward a few more inches to make sure they could still proceed under their own power. Jamming the emergency brake on, he left the truck idling while he got out to reel in the cable, Barbara sitting up to watch him walk to the trees and unhook the cable, teetering around, lifting his feet high and placing them into his original footprints. She leaned forward and looked out the passenger window, spotting strip mall parking lots, an office building, and other small-town structures.

"What do we do now?" Linda whispered, staying still in her faux-trapped position next to Jack.

Barbara shook her head and eased back as Keith returned with the hook, initiating the winch motor from the front of the rig, winding the cable slowly back into place.

"I want you to buckle up and wait for my signal," she spoke quietly to both of them. "When I tell you to, get out of the truck and run. Don't stop, don't look back. Just run. Think you can do that?"

Both Linda and Jack nodded, and Barbara held the pencil tightly with the sharp end pointed down like a knife, giving a few short jabs into the air, steeling herself for what was soon to come. With the hook and controller returned, Keith circled to the door, kicked his boots clean of snow, and climbed in. He rolled up the window and cranked the heat to high, sitting for a moment with his fingers over the vents again, shivering as the air slowly grew warm again. He spoke nothing and didn't bother looking back at his prisoners, and once thawed, he slammed his foot on the clutch and jammed the shifter in to first gear. The truck lurched forward too fast, spinning the back wheels before they finally gained purchase and he let out a mumbled curse. He continued to grumble for a quarter mile, occasionally shivering as the snow and sleet that had worked its way into the cracks and crevices of his clothing melted, dripping down his skin and irritating him all the more.

"If Tom had just done what we asked," he murmured, "we'd all be sitting in a nice warm military facility somewhere. Or on a beach. They promised me a beach. But oh no. No, instead, I'm out here slogging through the snow, dragging some idiot's family because he couldn't just do what he was damn well told."

"I didn't know you needed him that badly," Barbara ventured, raising her voice hesitantly.

Keith looked at her in the mirror, glowering, raising his voice. "He's got skills we can't find anywhere else."

Barbara was incredulous. "With all the people in the country to choose from, my husband is the only one who can do this certain job?"

"That's right." Keith shook his head, disgusted. "Believe me, I tried to get them to find someone else, but my bosses forced me down this path. They forced me to do all this." A bit of sing-song slipped into his voice as it raised and lowered menacingly. "It's all their fault… and his… I didn't want to do it…."

Nausea clutched at Barbara's gut as Keith sounded almost demented, his complaints falling back to low mutterings, arguments with himself, and she gripped the pencil tight in her hand as they slogged on, wheels spinning, engine grinding through ice and snow patches. Clearing her throat, she tried a different tack.

"Look… I know you're just trying to do your job, but taking us won't get Tom to do what you want. He's doesn't exactly go with the program."

"Yeah, we noticed."

"Let's say he does find your message and comes after you. It'll just be another fight you could lose."

"I *won't* lose!" Spittle flew from Keith's lips as he gripped the steering wheel with white knuckles. "Besides, that's the *entire* reason you're here. Insurance." He gave her one last look before turning back to the road, Barbara letting out a long-held breath.

"Look, we can still avoid all this," Barbra said, shifting in her seat, raising slightly. He was still too far away to strike, not without giving him enough time to respond and block her motion. "I know you're just trying to do your job. If you let us go, I'll make sure Tom doesn't pursue you. I'm sure I can even talk him into helping. Even after everything, we can still work something out."

Keith cackled inanely at the suggestion, wiping a tear from the corner of his eye before finally calming down. "Are you serious? Why the hell do you think I'd do that?" He scoffed, shaking his head. "We'll be at the base before nightfall and once I drop you off, you'll be Banks's problem. You can try your BS on *her* if you'd like."

Barbara didn't know who Banks was, nor did she care, as she was only half-listening to Keith's reply. Every time his eyes were pinned to the road she inched forward a bit more, still keeping her wrists and ankles concealed. She worked slowly and patiently, edging up on the sleeper cot until she was resting on her elbows and could see out the windows. The snowfall gusted listlessly, cyclones and dervishes whipping through the air, and another section of the small town came up on the right, shadows of buildings stretching into the gray haze. The two-lane highway had narrow shoulders and snow-filled ditches from someone's plowing attempts, leaving little room to maneuver, and Keith kept his attention on the road.

Barbara's stomach churned with anticipation and her hand was sweaty around the secreted pencil as she waited to make her move, her breathing shallow as she glanced outside and then back to Keith. With a quick breath, without so much as a glance at her children, she rose quietly from the truck bed, left arm gripping Keith's seatback for support as her right arm cocked back and she stabbed the pencil into Keith's shoulder at a downward angle, a scream of fury erupting unprompted, accompanying the sudden attack.

A gasp and cry of pain flew from Keith's lips as the lead tip punched deep into his flesh, the No. 2 wood burying itself a full two inches deep. He jerked forward, howling, ripping free of Barbara's hand, but she yanked out the wood and swung again, stabbing him crosswise across his chest, landing another blow on the back of the shoulder, digging in nearly as deep as the first one. A screech of angry pain rattled Barbara's ear as Keith let go of the wheel, backhanding her hard across the face, rattling her jaw, the truck slewing across the road.

"*Bitch*!" The expletive was barely comprehensible as Keith raged confusedly at her, still unsure as to what, exactly, was going on. "What the hell are you—?!"

Barbara lunged at him with both hands, gouging at his eyes with one hand and stabbing at his chest with the half-broken pencil, screaming at Jack and Linda to hold on at the same time. When he pulled his arms up to protect himself, she grabbed the wheel with her left hand and gave it a twist, giving Keith an opening he took full advantage of, shoving her head sharply into the dashboard, rattling her teeth and sending her off-balance. She held doggedly to the wheel, though, jerking it all the way around, causing the rig's front end to angle toward a ditch. Finally coming to grips with what was happening, Keith shoved hard at her, pulling his gun from his holster, trying to aim it at her, but Barbara let go of the wheel, shifting positions, stabbing repeatedly at his hand with the splintered remains of her weapon before he could fire.

An inhuman shriek came from Keith as he dropped the weapon and the truck slid sideways out of control, still running at forty, the brakes having never been applied during the several seconds the attack had been going on for. The ditch loomed faster than anyone could imagine and Barbara braced herself as they plunged into it, hitting the upward slope of the opposite bank, the rig's grill smashing into the dirt with a jolt that rattled her spine, flinging both herself and Keith forward.

The back of Barbara's head smacked the windshield, sending a spider's web of cracks along the inner layer of glass. Keith hit it face-first, though, his angry yell cut off like a snuffed candle, the world falling into an abrupt, eerie silence after the cacophony of sounds from the crash. Flakes of snow flicked against the rig's ticking hood and fell from nearby, disturbed trees, the smell of antifreeze and oil wafting into the cabin. A few seconds' worth of blackness cleared, accompanied by a surge of pain as Barbara sat still on the wide dashboard, eyes fluttering open, trying to regain her senses.

Blood ran down her temple, and her leg radiated with pain as she wiggled her extremities, and she looked down and saw she'd inadvertently jammed her broken pencil into her own leg during the crash, leaving a nasty, bleeding gash. Her ears were still ringing from the force of the impact and her head throbbed, but as she focused in more on her surroundings, she could hear Jack crying as Linda tried to hush and console him. Next to her, a groan drew her gaze to where Keith lay still, moaning and semi-conscious, but more out of it than she was, and sporting a face bleeding from multiple locations. With a wince and a muffled cry of pain, she pulled the pencil out of her leg and threw it down, then she leaned toward the back, blinking into the dome lighting.

"Come on, kids," she hissed. "Let's go."

Hands separated the curtain, and two heads peeked between the seats, with two pairs of wide, teary eyes staring back at her. Barbara motioned them to the front as she climbed off the dash and knelt in the passenger seat. Grabbing the door handle, she threw it open, snow gusting into her face, then she leaned back and allowed Linda to move past her.

"Are you okay?"

"Yeah, Mom."

"Are you sure?"

"I put pillows up in front of us. I'm sore, but we're okay, I promise."

"Good job, sweetie. Come on, hop down."

Linda's sneakers hit the slanted ground, and she slipped for a second before getting her balance, Barbara watching carefully for any signs of injury.

"Okay, buddy," she said to Jack. "You next."

He was already leaning toward her, holding out his arms and she hauled him across the seat, swinging him down to his sister. As she was helping him out, she noticed the matte black pistol lying on the floorboard and she bent and scooped it up, tucking it into her waistband before following the children out of the rig, heavily favoring her injured leg. Keith's slurred speech came louder from behind, spurring her on, and she turned and directed them up the cold, slick bank until they stood in a commercial parking lot covered in five inches of snow. Without looking back, she pointed to the first building she saw and ran for it, dragging the kids behind her. The wind gusted hard, knocking her around as she made a path for the kids through the white, teetering to the side, ice cold winds nipping her skin, cheeks tickled by spatters of sleet and blood still oozing from the deep wound in her leg. They came to the half-open front doors and stepped through into a restaurant, the tables and chairs all dusted with snow from the busted windows.

"Are we gonna hide in here?" Jack asked.

"No." Barbara panted heavily, hand pressed against her injury. "We're leaving through that broken window."

Barbara shoved them toward a booth on the opposite side, making Linda go first. She climbed onto the cushion, crept to the window, and jumped out the into the wind again, then Barbara fed Jack through to his sister and started to follow when she reached back and snatched a couple laminated menus off the table on a whim.

Landing outside, she shifted her shoulders, angling toward another building across the windblown lot. "That one."

They turned as one and pounded over the whitened pavement. Halfway there, she grabbed Linda by the shoulder, calling, "Jack, keep going. We'll meet you there."

"What, Mom?" Linda asked.

Barbara handed her a menu and squatted down, grimacing from the pain in her leg. She swept the menu back and forth, dragging snow in to cover their shallow footprints, and after a second of watching, Linda bent to do the same. Within a minute, they'd covered their tracks all the way to the next building where Jack stood shivering by a smashed-out glass doorway. Barbara pushed them through, shoving them between shelves, noticing it was a mini mart that had been looted at some point in the recent past, with wrappers and crushed foodstuffs scattered on the shelves and floor. She ignored the potential for supplies, focused purely on escape and survival as she angled them to the back, past the checkout counter, and into the employee break room where a door led outside.

"Are we stopping here?" Jack asked.

"No," Barbara said as she glanced at a line of wall hangars where three light jackets hung, likely left by employees that had left in a hurry. She snatched them off and tossed a pair to the kids, motioning for them to throw them on. Jack's was so big the sleeves hung well past his hands, and Barbara's was too small. Still, the sweatshirt material did wonders for staving off the chill, especially given that they hardly had any gear on when Keith had dragged them from their home.

"Okay, let's go."

"Why can't we stay here?" Jack started to whine, but Barbara pushed him ahead wordlessly.

They exited through the back door, where Barbara spotted a one-floor office building in the near distance. "That one next," she squeezed out in between long gasps, pointing at it. "Get inside, Jack. Now."

Jack ran for it while she and Linda covered their tracks with the menus, and by the time they reached it, Barbara's back ached and her leg felt like it was about to fall off. Looking down, she saw blood oozing from the gash in her leg, freezing in long streaks on her pants, though she wasn't dripping all over the place and leaving an obvious trail to be followed. They moved through the office building and two others in the same manner as before, covering their tracks between each.

After the maze of hallways and stretches of small-town courtyards, they came to a large house with blue shutters standing in an ice-covered snowfield. Barbara stopped to catch her breath, her nostrils frozen, eyes watering under the wind's brutal assault. She dreaded having to crouch the entire distance before them, sweeping the menu back and forth, but their survival depended on it.

Linda touched her lightly on the arm and stared up at her with concerned eyes. "You and Jack go ahead to the next one. I'll cover the tracks."

Barbara started to protest but then nodded briskly, glancing back toward the rig through the storm. Visibility failed at around fifty yards, so she couldn't see the highway or the truck anymore, though that didn't mean Keith hadn't recovered and wasn't somehow right behind them.

"We'll go ahead. If you see him, yell for me right away. And run."

"Sure, Mom. Now go!"

Barbara lifted Jack to her chest and trudged through the growing snow drifts toward the house. Going around the side, they passed beneath a wooden arbor and circled the garage to the front. Staggering past the front garden, she climbed a set of steps to the porch and placed her son down. The front door stood open an inch, and she pushed it in and looked into the foyer. It was an older style home with a living room on her left, sitting room on her right, and a staircase going up. The living room decorations were dated, with a faux leather couch and a TV on a stand in the corner, along with dropped clothes and personal items laying in the hall and trailing down the stairs.

She turned to Jack. "Kick your boots so we don't track any snow inside. If Keith comes and we have to hide, I don't want him to know we're here."

They both kicked their feet against the brick footer before she lifted Jack and set him inside. Turning, she watched Linda come around the side of the house, using her arms like a snow angel, sweeping the menus back and forth to fill in their boot prints. There were still spots that showed where they'd been walking, but the new snowfall would smooth it over in a matter of minutes.

"Come on, girl," she murmured. "You can do it."

Ten minutes later, Linda had backed all the way to the front stoop, leaving just a few slight marks behind her. She stood on the porch, panting, cheeks red, nose running with snot, eyes plaintive and apologetic at the same time. "Sorry, Mom. I tried."

"No, it's great." Barbara hugged her daughter. "You did great, honey. If we're lucky, it'll be covered up here before we know it. Now, let's get inside."

They finished dusting all traces of themselves from the stoop and shut the door behind them, turning to face Jack who was standing on the first step going upstairs with his oversized sleeves hanging to the floor.

"What now, Mom?" Jack asked. "Do we have to keep moving from here?"

"No, honey. This should be okay. Let's wait in the front room where we can keep an eye on things."

Barbara's leg screamed as she limped forward, pants sticky, the blood half frozen to her skin. "That hurts like a son of a gun…" She mumbled to herself, teeth grinding together against the pain.

She hobbled to the front window and peeked through the blinds at the front yard. The glass was frosted, and the snow swirled madly outside, blinding her with white, droplets of sleet crackling against the glass before whipping downward away from them. She slowly pulled a string to squeeze the blinds almost fully shut, gesturing at Jack.

"Come here, bud. I need your help."

He walked stiffly over, teeth chattering, arms pressed to his side. "Yeah, Mom?"

"Can you keep an eye out for Keith?"

"Yeah." Using a finger to part the blinds, he stared out between them.

Barbara ran her hand up his cold back and gave his shoulders a squeeze. "I'm serious. You have to look in all directions. If you see any dark shadows out there moving around, come get me right away."

"Okay." Jack's voice was small.

"In the meantime, I'm going to find something to get us warm."

Linda was already rooting through the kitchen and dining room drawers, and Barbara called out from the living room. "Anything good?"

Linda held up a flashlight, turned it toward her face and flipped it on, lighting her features like a ghost before she snapped it off. "It's not warm, but it'll help when it gets dark?"

"Good find," Barbara nodded. "Run upstairs and see if there's any blankets and pillows left."

Linda nodded and got to it as Barbara limped along the hallway to the kitchen, her leg stiffening badly. Her steaming breath hung in the air for several seconds before dissipating, the temperature inside not as cold as outside, but close. A quick check revealed no substantive food left in the pantry or cupboards, but Linda was back a moment later, carrying an armful of blankets and throw covers from the upstairs bedrooms.

"Good work, hon." Barbara hobbled into the living room as weariness pressed down on her, heading to her son and wrapping a blanket around his shoulders. "You doing okay? See anything?"

"Just lots of snow," he replied. "I'll tell you if I see Keith. He's a jerk."

"Thanks, buddy. Yes. Yes he is." She bent and kissed him on the head before turning around, swaying slightly.

Linda looked up from where she was spreading blankets out on the couch, eyes wide with worry. "I think you need to sit down, Mom."

"You're right." Barbara limped to the couch and collapsed on it, and Linda spread a blanket out over her reclined form, giving a firm, brave smile.

"I'll get some more."

While Linda went searching for things to cover them, Barbara rubbed her hands together and blew her breath down under the blanket. Her knuckles were sore from her fight with Keith and bleeding from the dry air, and her lungs ached from the cold and exertion. Being inside kept them out of the wind, but if they didn't make serious efforts to stay warm, hypothermia would get to them eventually, regardless of whether it was outside or inside.

Linda came back in a few moments with a comforter, two coats, and some pillows, making a pile around her mother and climbing beneath it. The effect of the added body heat was immediately palpable, and Barbara glanced over at her son as he kept his dutiful vigil.

"You okay over there?"

"I'm pretty cold." His voice was brave, but his teeth clacked together loudly as he spoke. "But I'm okay."

"Get over here, buddy," Barbara said, lifting the edge of the blanket. "Climb in with us."

"What if Keith comes?"

"We'll burn that bridge when we get to it."

"I'd give anything to burn a bridge right now," Linda snorted. "Or Keith."

"Oh, either one of those would make for a nice, toasty fire," Barbara laughed as Jack leapt onto the couch and slid in on her right side, fitting between her and the pillows, snuggling in close as he fed off his mother's warmth, sighing with contentment.

They rubbed their hands together and peeked over the top of the cover, three sets of eyes facing the window and the big black screen in the corner, Barbara's lingering on the front door as she felt heat slowly spread through her body. The house had been abandoned in haste and held little in the way of supplies to keep them long-term, but relief from the wind and cold was a major boon, enabling them to recuperate and recover until she could figure out what, exactly, to do next.

"I saw the cut on your leg." Linda interrupted her, nudging her with a sharp elbow. "We need to check it out."

"Go ahead," she nodded.

They ducked beneath the covers, unwilling to give up the precious bit of heat that had been generated by taking them off and Linda turned on the flashlight, shining it on the wound. "You've got a cut in your side, too."

"I do?" Barbara felt along the ribs on her left side, and her hand came away warm and wet. She tried to think where she'd gotten the injury. "Maybe it was when we were going through the windows. You know, the glass?"

"It could have been from the wreck, too. I think a tree branch came in through the windshield and might have stuck you."

"Maybe," Barbara replied tiredly, lifting her arm. "Can you check it out?"

Linda pulled her mother's jacket aside and placed her cool fingers against her skin. After a moment, she lifted her eyes, looking ghostly beneath the blankets. "Yeah, something cut all the way through your coat and got you."

"How long is it?"

"About five inches."

Barbara's eyes went wide. "Well, that explains why my side's been hurting. Though it pales in comparison to how my leg feels."

The pair leaned in again and inspected the cut on the top of her thigh. There was an inch-long rip in her jeans, and when Linda pulled the material apart, they saw bloody, puckered flesh beneath.

"I can't believe I did that to myself."

Linda frowned. "This cut is deeper than the other one. We need to get it cleaned out right away. I'll see if there are any medical supplies in the bathroom."

Barbara sighed tiredly as her daughter climbed from beneath the warmth of the covers. They couldn't have traveled more than a quarter mile from the truck, yet they were as exhausted as if they'd run a marathon. The deep snow had sucked the energy out of them, and all she could imagine was sleep. Barbara closed her eyes and let the tiredness take hold, trying to focus on something good, but her head swirled with dangers and darkness. She had no idea what to do next except stay away from Keith and guess where her husband and Sam might be.

"They took all the first aid supplies with them, just like the food." Linda walked back into the living room with a frustrated look.

"I have to get some bandages and antiseptic, or at least some alcohol," Linda continued. "You probably need stitches in your leg, but I don't know where to get the needle and thread for that. I guess some tight bandages will have to work."

"No." Barbara immediately saw where her daughter's train of thought was going. "You can't go out there, honey. It's way too cold. And Keith's out there looking for us."

"If I don't, you'll keep bleeding, those wounds will get infected and bad things will happen. No, we need supplies. Don't worry. I'll layer up with some clothes I found from the closets here, then I'll go out the back door and look for more houses or a pharmacy or something." Linda held up a hand. "I *promise* I'll be safe, mom."

Barbara stared at her daughter for a long, tense moment before nodding slowly. "I don't like it… but you're right." She shifted on the couch, pulling out a dark object from her waistband, handing it to Linda. "I should have used this on Keith as we were running away."

Linda scoffed. "Mom, you were hurt, he was coming to, and it was hectic as all get-out. We did good, all things considered."

"I know, but still. If I had, then we wouldn't be in this situation." She sighed. "I know you know how to use it. But try *not* to have to use it, okay?"

"Thanks, Mom." Linda accepted the pistol, double-checking that the safety was on before tucking it into her own waistband, giving her mother an assured smile. "I won't give him a chance to even see me."

"Be careful, honey."

"I will."

"I love you."

"Love you, too."

* * *

A sharp, chill wind blistered his cheeks as he fully regained consciousness, the ticking of the rig's engine mixing with the wind the only sounds he could hear, the truck cabin silent but for the sounds of winter and a dying engine. He slowly raised his head to see he was half-lying on the dashboard, his ankles on the edge of the steering wheel. His hand hurt, his legs stung and his shoulder had a deep ache not even the wind could numb. He lay at an odd angle, tipped forward with the truck grill buried in the ditch. The sights were all at once familiar and foreign as Keith's injured head reeled, trying to grasp what he was seeing and put it into context.

It all came back to him in a rush. Driving through the blizzard. Barbara stabbing him in the neck with something. *What the hell was that? A damn pencil? Where the hell did she find a pencil?* He remembered trying to shoot her, but she'd stabbed the gun out of his hand. *Along with everywhere else. Bitch.*

Groaning, he craned his neck, looking down past his feet into the silent cabin. The woman and her kids were gone. His guarantee that Tom McKnight would work for them had been dashed in the space of a minute and Banks would kill him if he didn't get them back. A growl escaped from his lips as he crawled laboriously back into the cab, moving slowly at first, testing to see what might have been injured in the wreck. He was sore all over – particularly on his head – and was likely sporting broken ribs, a concussion and multiple fractures, but nothing was keeping him from moving, albeit slowly.

While the storm had dissipated, snow covered everything inside, a thick dusting of it on the seats and floorboards. Standing on the tilted floor, he searched for his gun and when he couldn't find it, he stepped into the sleeper and opened a drawer beneath the bed, pulling out some of Tex's flannel shirts and an old beanie, and he quickly layered up before he dug deeper, hoping to find something an older trucker might hide away for a "just in case" situation.

Grinning, Keith pulled out an old shotgun, and upon inspection he saw it was loaded. Extra shells were rolling around in the drawer, and he stuffed those in his pockets, the discovery of the weapon slowly returning his senses to him. Keith crawled back through the cabin and exited the rig, staggering forward, trudging up the bank to stand in the parking lot before he surveyed his surroundings.

Clever girl. Keith crouched down, a low chuckle escaping his throat. There were faint footprints in the snow, barely visible even though they'd been made in a few inches of powdery white. Thanks to the snowfall – and was that someone covering their tracks? – they were almost hidden from view. Almost. Keith saw them, though, and he looked up, looking along their trail as they led across the parking lot to a restaurant ahead. Fresh snowflakes continued to fall, and the gusts picked up, the bare cuts on his face and back of his head aching in the chil. Another storm was brewing, and he had to get Barbara and her kids back before it hit. Gripping the shotgun tightly, Keith put his head down and plowed after them, rage and determination in his manic eyes.

Chapter 4
Specialist Lance Morales
Monterrey, Mexico

"Alright everyone, settle down. We've got a lot to go over in this briefing, and all of it is critical to the next phase of the annexation."

The crowd of soldiers inside the massive tent shifted on their wooden benches and began to quiet down. There were a thousand of them spread out in tight rows from the front to the back, most of them having taken part in operations across Northern Mexico. They stared up at the strategic commanders arrayed on the dais before them, most of them high mission brass, engaged leaders stationed close to the front lines while some were commanders and captains who'd seen recent battle.

The man speaking was of average build and height, about forty-five, with a silver buzzed haircut and sharp, dark features. He peered over his left shoulder and nodded to the assembled officers. One seat sat empty, and he waited for the last person to make their way from a side entrance and climb the stairs to join the others. Once settled, the man standing at the mic turned back to the crowd.

"Okay, folks. I'm Chief Staff Sergeant Tim Ranes, and I'm assigned to help coordinate our efforts here with the regional commanders. Frankly, I've got the best ground-level view of what's going on, and that's why I'm giving this presentation."

The lights dimmed, and a map projected itself on a giant screen behind him showing a view of central Mexico.

"As you know, the most recent phase was successful, and we've taken control of Mexican territory from Puerto Vallarta to Guadalajara, up to San Luis Potosi, and finally to Tampico on the Gulf Coast."

As he spoke, each city lit up, and a red line ran from the left side of the map to the right. The soldiers watched intently, some of them murmuring.

Ranes went on. "We're massing on the demarcation line, ready to move on Mexico City. You'll be part of that force. Time is critical, though. As you've no doubt noticed, the temperatures as far south as twenty-two-degrees latitude are rapidly dropping, and we need to move south as quickly as possible. That means you must be one-hundred percent ready for what's to come next."

Ranes's gaze slid across the group, searching for weakness or protest that might belie a less than strong constitution. Finding none, he continued.

"You'll be getting your individual assignments from your battalion commanders as soon as the briefing is over. Remember, our goal is to secure a new home for United States citizens. While this is tough to accept for the Mexican people, we're not here to harm them or cause any unnecessary damage. These people are suffering as well, and hopefully we can form a common bond.

"I know this is the height of hypocrisy to say this, but we'll do our utmost to ensure we help them once they come to accept this new reality. Once we *all* accept it. If you have any questions, feel free to see me or your commanders. Dismissed."

Morales and Smith stood and waited for the soldiers to file out before they fell in line and worked their way outside. Morales had been sweating in the tent with all the warm bodies, but the cold night quickly seeped into the gaps in his jacket and chilled his skin. He zipped up tight and pulled his jacket around him with a shiver, looking out through the camp and into the wide desert, surprised to see flakes of snow drifting down past the pole-strung lights.

"Do you believe this?" Smith said. "Snowing in the Mexican desert. The hell is this world coming to?"

The cocky gunner wasn't as mentally affected by all the fighting – or, at least, he didn't let it show - unlike the darkness Morales sometimes displayed.

"It was burning hot just a few days ago." Morales's watched more flakes as they fell. "Now it's below freezing."

"And they say it'll get colder. Like, Arctic temperatures."

"That's what I heard. It makes me wonder if any place will be far enough south." Morales turned to his friend and comrade. "Hey, you hungry?"

"Not really. I think I'm going to turn in for the night."

Morales sighed. "Yeah, you're right. We should get some rest before our convoy moves. I'll grab some breakfast before we head out."

They walked from the briefing tent and strolled along the outer sphere of tents and shelters. Morales watched as several groups of new soldiers marched across the training fields, being shouted at by their commanders, their spotless uniforms and clean, polished boots betraying the fact that they had yet to see action, and were likely fresh out of boot camp – if they'd even finished by the time they were forced to move south.

Smith spotted them, too, laughing and whistling at them as the pair passed by. "Looks like we've got some fresh meat coming on board!"

Several of the new recruits glanced their way with fearful expressions and Morales shook his head and smiled. "Knock it off, Smith. You'll make someone crap their pants before they get on the road."

"Just trying to prepare them." The gunner gave a toothy grin and waved at the recruits still staring at him as their sergeant began yelling at them to pay attention. "Things are going to get brutal soon."

They turned right and strolled up a winding dirt road to where their barracks perched on a hill, overlooking the rest of the camp. "It shouldn't be that bad," Morales countered. "We've already beaten the Mexican army to hell and back. I heard they don't have much left."

Smith gave him a pointed look. "Well, I heard a rumor they're massing to make a stand in Mexico City."

"How much can they mass? We left a trail of smoking armored vehicles behind. I overheard a couple of SIGINT guys talking about how we've already taken out three-quarters of their heavy equipment."

"Maybe. But maybe they don't need it."

The dirt road leading to the barracks got steeper, and Morales leaned into the climb. A camouflaged SUV blew past them, kicking up cold dust on its way down and an M939 heavy truck climbed up beside them and slowed. In the back were a handful of troops and equipment and a soldier leaned out. "You boys need a ride up top?"

"We're good," Morales waved, and the man nodded as the truck gave a lurch and kept going.

The battalion officers had been shuffling personnel in and out for days, expanding the camp in some places, shrinking it in others. It was a constantly evolving organism, always changing and taking on new forms to adapt to the unusual and constantly-evolving mission.

"What do you mean the Mexicans don't *need* their armored trucks?" Morales raised an inquisitive eye. "Anyone fighting a war needs heavy equipment. We outclass them in every way. It's not even close."

"Plenty of wars've been sustained with nothing but some rifles and sheer determination. I expect fewer stand-up fights and more guerrilla tactics. We saw some of that in Monterrey."

"That was rough," he admitted, "but I wouldn't expect this to turn into a Vietnam."

"I was thinking Afghanistan." Smith spread his hands wide. "We're on their turf, invading them, taking over their country. They're going to put up a hell of a fight, and that's going to put a major kink in our happy plans."

"I get it. It's not going to be easy. But we have three hundred million people moving into their backyard."

"They've got close to two hundred million. What's your point?"

"My point is..." Morales's words trailed off. "I guess I don't have a point. But I'm not worried about Mexican infantrymen hiding under my cot at night like the boogeyman."

"Maybe you should be." Smith elbowed him in the side and traipsed ahead. "Especially the closer we get to Mexico City. If you thought Monterrey was bad, you best be on full-alert driving through *those* streets. They're packed tight, ready for an ambush around every corner."

Morales shrugged off the soldier's goofing. "Give me a Stryker, and I can drive through anything." He gave his friend a sideways grin. "I think *you're* the one who's scared. Don't worry. I'll protect you. Keep you safe in your bed at night."

Smith snorted. "Just focus on your driving. I'll keep shooting straight and true."

He made gun motions with his hands while blowing rapid-fire gun noises between his lips. They shared a laugh, Morales's inside uncoiling a little with the levity as they circled up to the end of the sweeping dirt road and looked at the barracks laid out in front of them. A dozen large tents stood in the center, interspersed with smaller ones and prefab units for the higher-ups. Portable toilets were lined up in rows of six or eight, dispersed every fifty yards or so and a gargantuan mess hall and a rec center tent were nestled against a wide stretch of hills off to the left. Light vehicles drove by the dozens on roads lined with stones, reflectors, and a handful of speed limit and warning signs, ferrying troops, weapons and supplies to various destinations. Their battalion barracks was, in short, a small city, home for over two thousand troops and support personnel, a total of twelve Army companies to spearhead the assault on Mexico City.

Morales sighed and looked off to his right at the hollow sound of bouncing basketballs. It was still warm enough for soldiers to play a pickup game on the hastily erected courts and they were out with their shirts off, sweating and shouting jovially at each other as they played. Morales envied them, wishing he could join them to blow off steam after the intense first phase of the offensive. But, with just a few hours until they moved out again, he had to focus on rest.

He followed Smith around the courts to the northern edge of their camp, the rocky slope rolling down to the main base they'd just come from, lights stretching as far as the eye could see as the vast American force coiled around like a serpent preparing to strike. The gunner folded his arms and looked out over the sea of growling vehicles and drilling troops as evening came full force. "Now that's a sight that makes you proud, eh, brother?"

Morales pushed his hands into his pockets and nodded, smiling. "It never gets old."

A single-story surgical tent stood in the center as well as several first aid stations spread throughout the camp, each marked with a large red cross on top. A dozen more camps just like theirs were packed into the valley, army-green tents covering the landscape as far as the eye could see, divided in straight lines by gravel roads and lined with hastily-erected pole lights. Theaters and commissaries lined the roads to provide simple pleasures for the troops during their brief periods of downtime, with coffee shops and gaming centers where soldiers could indulge themselves over the military's private network.

Generals and high-ranking officers were stationed on the north side of the camp near the airfields where C-130s Hercules planes landed with massive amounts of supplies, heavy equipment, and soldiers. They took off as fast as they were unloaded, turning north to return for more. Helicopters buzzed around the edges of the camp where an attack and reconnaissance base had been set up a quarter mile to the east. From what he'd heard, it boasted two Full Spectrum Combat Aviation Brigades and an unknown number of pilots and troops, ready to be quickly tasked if need be. A land-based supply line wove north on Highway 85D as semi-trailer trucks and flatbeds hauled armored tanks, fuel, and supplies south before going right back to the States for more.

The streets below pulsed with movement and sound, almost enough to keep Morales awake the past few nights as a hundred thousand troops or more lived and breathed in the Monterrey Army Field, their numbers growing by the day.

Morales shook his head. "It's like we're picking up the entire country and moving it south."

Smith chuckled. "That's because we are."

"I wonder when it's going to be over? I mean, it's got to end sometime, right?"

"I wouldn't count on it being soon," Smith shook his head. "It's going to be a long, hard slog until we're even close to normal. I'm talking generations. And we can't do a damn thing to get settled down until we find someplace warm."

"How can you say that?" Morales lifted his chin toward the massive display below. "Look how organized this place is, man. It's proof we can do anything we put our minds to."

"That's the military, man," Smith scoffed, "and some civvy support. That's not tens of millions of desperate, hungry, cold people." He held out one hand and swept it across the entire base. "Our standing supplies will only last so long. So, look down there and imagine a hundred or a thousand times what you see, all starving and begging for a scrap of food. You think the commanders will give up what little supplies they have? I'm telling you, things are going to get ugly."

Morales shivered as he did, in fact, imagine what Smith was saying quite vividly. "It won't get that bad, man. They'll be setting up farms or something. The logistics boys will solve this mess."

"Yeah, well, I hope you're right, my friend. I hope it all comes up smelling like roses."

The guys playing basketball finally decided it was getting too cold, donning their shirts and coats, buttoning up tight, heading back to their barracks. Their mood was still convivial, but there was an air of worry as a cold wind blew across the courts, the soldiers starting to mutter and shiver as they hurried along. Smith gave a friendly smirk and patted Morales on the shoulder. "Anyway, don't let my piss poor attitude get to you. I just try to see things for what they are, you know?"

"You mean you're a pessimist."

Smith chuckled. "A *realist*. Come on, let's get some rest. We move out in a few hours."

Morales nodded and fell in beside his friend, cutting through the basketball courts and turning up the road leading to their tent. Soldiers and staffers bustled about the base with a sense of urgency, packing up supplies and preparing to move out. Part of him wanted to resent Smith for having such a confrontational attitude and he could be a jerk sometimes – not to mention incredibly cocky – but he was a straight shooter, and he told the truth, regardless of whether it was pleasant or ugly. With a resigned sigh, Morales found himself heeding his friend's warning. It was just the thing he needed to stay frosty and alert and if Mexico City ended up being as bad as he feared, Morales could stand to be a little more careful.

Chapter 5
Tom McKnight
Somewhere in Tennessee

The wind bit at them, icy fingers clutching their shoulders despite the warm sun hanging in the crystal blue sky, its warmth on deceptive display. They trudged stoically onward, focusing on the snow-covered road stretching ahead. They trudged along Highway 11E, heading south toward Asheville where Keith's forward operating base was located, the going tough on the old Virginia roads. Only some of the pavement had been cleared, but it was hard to tell as the wind had pushed the snow up into drifts, and in some places the snow brushed the horses' bellies as their heads hung doggedly, blinking against the wind-driven flakes of snow and ice.

The formerly green landscape had been completely altered. New ridges and valleys of soft white powder had formed on the shoulders, slopes, and fences. Untouched, the pristine white rolled in all directions. Forest trees jutted from massive drifts that reached as high as the low branches, sometimes feet over Tom's head. Time took on a different meaning when every ten yards felt like a mile, and distances that would've taken the horses an hour in normal conditions were taking four. He angled his gelding through the shallower drifts, trying to make better time and provide a smoother path for Samantha and her sled, while simultaneously going slowly enough to keep the horses from tripping on unseen obstacles or potholes. He could only travel so slowly given their situation, and at some point they would need to push it to reach Asheville in the two-day period Tom needed to enact his plan. It was already late afternoon, though, and they wouldn't be able to ride long at night on such treacherous terrain.

"Ease up, Dad," Sam called from behind him.

He'd just given his gelding a little kick to urge it forward, and the beast replied with a derisive snort, seeming to agree with her.

"Sorry." He shook his head. "I'm getting impatient. We should be making a lot better time than this."

"We can't kill the horses or have them fall and break their legs, or we'll really be stuck."

Tom nodded but kept his eyes on the snowy highway which was nothing more than a narrow groove curving between the trees and hills. While he tried to keep them in the center, he couldn't always be sure they weren't drifting toward one side or another, and he had to be on constant alert for changes in direction and elevation.

A half hour later, they passed by the white-coated remnants of a small Virginia town off to the side of the highway, an old gas station sign stuck up on his right, the building itself half buried on one side, covered by a snowy embrace that reached the front door. A mechanic's shop, feed store, and small grocer were clustered together like the ancient ruins of some long dead society, their peaceful appearance offset by bullet holes that peppered the exposed brick across all the structures and a part of the feed store that had caved in as if it had taken a hit from heavy ordinance. Just past the businesses, a Humvee hung off the edge of the presumed highway, its nose buried in a ditch and its tail end barely showing above the snow. Beyond it, homes lined the road with their front doors thrown open, new snow having long since covered any old footprints, not a single chimney blowing out smoke.

"The military was here, wasn't it?" Sam had trotted closer behind him and spoke quietly, in a reverent, hushed tone.

"They must have come through before the last storm. Maybe within the last twenty-four hours." His gaze roamed the abandoned homes, wondering if the owners had been moved to the forward base in Asheville as well.

"Think the soldiers will come back?"

"I don't think so." Tom shook his head doubtfully. "That last storm made it impossible for anything with wheels to move, but then again they've been pretty determined to get everyone out. Still, they'll have to give up evacuation efforts at some point." He gazed up at the sky as dark clouds loomed ominously from the south. "And it looks like another storm is on its way."

"I hope it isn't as bad as the last one."

"You and me both. Let's just put our heads down and keep grinding forward."

The rate of falling snowflakes increased by the minute, adding to the piles all around them as visibility quickly diminished, the air gusting sideways into their faces, sleet stinging their cheeks. Gray skies replaced the blue ones, clouds sweeping overhead, blotting out the sun as they ripped overhead like cattle driven across the plains. One burst of snow and ice howled and screamed for a full minute and a half before finally breaking off, and Tom recognized it as an exclamation point for what was about to drop on their heads. He glanced back at Sam where she huddled over the saddle horn, Smooch resting behind on her sled with her head under the covers, her snout poking out, eyes barely visible.

"Should we stop, Dad?" she shouted.

"Not yet," he called back. "I'm not convinced it's going to last very long. Strap in, though, it's about to get rough!"

They'd gone another two hundred yards when the storm proved Tom's naïve optimism wrong. A sudden howl tore viciously through the valley road, bending treetops and causing branches to snap, tossing the debris skyward and skimming across the white fields. Tom's gelding actually stopped dead in its tracks, refusing to go forward until he gave the horse a kick in the sides to get it moving again, the animal reluctantly acquiescing to his bidding.

Sam rode up beside him on the road, shouting to be heard over the wind. "I think we should stop!" Locks of her hair blew from her tightly bound hat, her hands cupped around her mouth. "The horses won't last long, and we probably won't either!"

Another banshee-like wail broke from the west and hit Tom full force, causing his gelding to lean into Sam's mare in a slight stagger, the trio assaulted by stinging bits of ice, snow and debris. Getting his horse steadied, he stared down the long road.

"I want to press on, but I think you're right!" He shook his head, his voice scattered by the assault. "I'm throwing in the towel for now!"

Looking to their right, he spotted a shallow depression in the field, beneath an overhang of trees where the wind wasn't blowing so hard and the drifts weren't so tall.

"Let's go in there and wait it out!" He pointed to where he wanted them to go, guiding his horse. The gelding must have sensed they were taking a break, because it leapt off the road and trotted up to the tree line without needing much in the way of encouragement. Tom stopped them at a decent spot where the wind was broken up by the trees and the snow was only up to his knees, and he and Samantha dismounted. They cleared away a snowy circle using shovels Tom had strapped to Smooch's sled, then blankets were draped over the horses' backs to keep them warm, and they tamped the snow around the area to build a thigh-high protective wall. Tom dragged Smooch's sled up and positioned it beneath the bulk of the larger animals, then he placed a blanket on the snow for he and Sam to sit on. They pulled a cover over their shoulders and huddled together in the shelter of the trees, snow and horses, watching the storm as it intensified, the sustained winds howling through their valley in a symphony of creaking wood and snapping limbs. An inch or two of snow poured down upon them before it began to let up nearly as quickly as it had started, clear skies moving in from the north. Within an hour of when it had begun, the storm had ended, and the sun shone down upon them unobstructed, as though it had never been hidden from sight in the first place.

"That was... weird," Sam said in a confused tone. "It doesn't seem normal."

"Must be erratic weather caused by the lack of warm air to the north." Tom stood, brushing snow out of the cracks and crevices of his clothing.

"Because the Northern Atlantic Current is broken, right?" Samantha stood too, shaking out their blankets and beginning to pack them up.

"That's right," Tom nodded. "It's just a part of the damage being done by the anomaly. I knew it would get cold, but I didn't imagine there would be storms like this. Not this fast, certainly."

"When will they settle down? Or will they ever?"

Tom winced into the clearing blue sky. "I wouldn't count on it being soon. If anything, they'll probably grow more severe as time goes by. They'll definitely make living up here difficult."

With the unspoken implication left hanging, the pair finished packing up the horses and got back on the road. The going wasn't much harder than before, the inch or so of new snow barely making a difference to the piles of it that had already accumulated. They continued following the highway until they reached a wider interstate junction heading east and west, it too covered in snow. Giant-sized drifts were piled up against a monumental accident, a twisted mess of cars and at least one semi-trailer truck forming a barrier of ice and metal. Tom removed a map from his coat and opened it, laying it across the horse's neck and Sam walked her horse up to join him, her cheeks rosy as she looked at the map with her father.

"What's the scoop?"

Tom raised his eyes and gazed ahead. "Well, this is a big mess. We can try to get around this wreck and stay on nineteen... or we can go east."

"Which one will get us to Asheville faster?"

"The first option, but look at it."

Though it was hard to tell what had happened beneath the blanket of white, it appeared that the trailer had jackknifed in the road and flipped on its side, taking out smaller vehicles going both ways. Icicles and sheets of sleet fused together with steel and glass, their jagged edges disguised from view, but no less lethal, especially to the horses.

Tom pointed at the map and gestured off to the side. "Let's take the exit and go left. There's another highway that joins nineteen at a second junction. It should allow us to bypass this mess here. If not, we'll have to go east and circle Elizabethton."

"But that's *way* out of our way," Sam sighed.

"Then let's hope the second junction does the trick. It's not far. Let's go."

They backtracked a bit and then walked their horses up the snowy exit ramp, taking a left at the end. Tracking a quarter mile east, they reached the second junction.

"Whoa!" Tom called, getting his gelding to pull up at the intersection as he looked north and south. The road was far less inundated with snow, and some parts showed bare pavement. There was still a large amount of white on the ground, but the path appeared to be easier than the other highway.

"Wow, I can actually see the asphalt down there in a couple places," Sam said.

"It's like someone took a plow to it after the first storm, but then the second one dumped more on top."

"I wonder if the highway looks like this all the way to Asheville?"

"Good question. I guess we can take it and find out. At least we'll be able to bypass the..." Tom trailed off at the sound of approaching engines from the north, where the incoming highway joined nineteen.

"Sounds like trucks." Sam cocked her head. "Coming closer."

"Yeah, let's hide. We have no idea who it is."

They turned their horses, hurrying over to a nearby parking lot where they dismounted behind an abandoned eighteen-wheeler. Leaving their horses tied up by the trailer hitch, they crept to the front end and peeked around the rig's grill just as a pair of massive dump trucks blew by, taking up both highway lanes, big knobby wheels pounding through the snow, plows grinding on the pavement as they shoved big mounds of snow toward the shoulders. Rock salt flew from spreaders beneath the hoppers at the back of the trucks as they drove in line with each other, looking like a single ship cutting through a blindingly white ocean on the two-lane highway.

"Wow." Tom whispered, nudging Sam. "Maybe we took the right road after all, eh?"

More diesel engines roared, and he looked back as a dozen Humvees flew by, pushing fifty or sixty, throwing salt and remnants of snow into the air. Two dozen APCs with mounted guns followed behind the Humvees and civilian vehicles poured in behind those, a mixture of cars, vans, and busses loaded for bear. Older military transport vehicles brought up the rear of the convoy, some uncovered with refugees sitting huddled in the backs, blankets flapping around their shivering shoulders. Supply trucks flew by next, loaded with crates and boxes tied down with straps, then eighteen-wheelers pulling tanks and helicopters on flatbeds. What had started off looking like a small military convoy rapidly turned into something much larger than either Tom or Sam could have imagined.

"There must be thousands of people." Samantha's whisper was full of awe. "Soldiers and regular people like us."

"They're really cooking, too. Going somewhere fast."

Something caught Tom's ear above the drone of diesel engines, and he looked to the sky to spot three Apache helicopters drifting toward them just a hundred and fifty feet above their heads, sleek and bristling with weaponry. More aircraft followed the Apaches, following the path of the convoy, flying just above the treetops.

"There's so many of them." Sam's mouth was half-open in amazement. "I've never seen helicopters like this up close."

"Those were Apache's," he pointed at the three that had passed by. "Attack helicopters. And here come a group of Boeing Chinook's. You can tell by the twin rotors."

"They're really big."

"They carry people and equipment, mostly." Tom had to raise his voice to nearly a shout as the massive craft swung lazily overhead. "Around fifty each."

"Wow."

"There're helicopters as far as I can see," he said, putting his hand to his forehead. "UH-1 Venoms, Cobras, and I think some civilian ones, too."

"Dad, be careful," Sam warned. "They can probably see you."

Tom had become enthralled with the sight of the aircraft and stepped away from the rig, and he quickly moved back to where Sam crouched. They watched as ten pickup trucks pulling trailers drove by next, the odd shapes in their truck beds partially covered in fluttering tarps and blankets. Beneath the ramshackle coverings were an Iwo Jima statue and another with a man riding a horse, both secured tightly with rope. Thin rectangular and square objects wrapped in brown paper and corners of antique furniture poked out beneath the blankets and tarps as well, hundreds of pieces in total, all being moved south.

"What do you make of it?" Sam asked.

"It looks like a total flush of DC. I mean, a complete evacuation of everyone and everything they could lift with a small crane. That means valuable stuff." He paused, hesitating to verbalize the inevitable conclusion. "They don't plan on coming back."

"They're going in the same direction we're heading," Sam pointed out.

"That's what I was thinking. We can definitely use the path they're clearing to make better time. It'll be way easier on us *and* the horses."

The flow of aircraft diminished, but the road convoy seemed endless, and soon Tom and Sam grew bored with watching and stepped behind the rig, sitting on the edge of Smooch's sled to rest while they waited. The shepherd had tried to get off the sled a few times during the trip but had been mostly mindful in spite of the rough, frigid conditions, and her fluffy tail flapped beneath her blankets as Tom and Sam gave her some attention.

"She feels so funny being bald in some spots." Sam laughed, her hands jammed under the covers, roaming over Smooch's stubble.

The dog rolled sideways and rested her head in Tom's lap, trying to paw playfully at him while her tongue lolled out. Her right forearm worked well, but she favored the left one, and it felt stiff as Tom worked it back and forth, trying to help work some movement back into the muscles.

"She's a gooood dog," Tom rubbed her jaws and neck, using the customary exaggerated tones as the dog bathed in the affection. "Aren't you, girl? Are you a good girl? Yes you are!"

"Dad?" Sam's voice was hesitant, barely audible over the sounds of the convoy. "Where did you learn all those names for the helicopters?"

He shrugged. "Just different missions and projects from my younger days, before you were born. I never told you guys all the stories, not even your mother."

Sam reached out and put her hand on his arm. "Do you want to talk about it? You always get quiet when we ask you about the old days, like you think we wouldn't understand. I'm a good listener, though. Mom even says so."

"You are a *great* listener." He chuckled lightly, then waved the subject off. "It's just stuff. Old stuff. Old jobs. A different life. Thanks, but it's just too boring, honestly."

"Okay." Sam stared at him, neither of them believing his response, but she backed off nevertheless. "No problem."

The convoy passed for another hour until it settled down to a trickle, Tom occasionally tilting his head when the engine noise grew silent, only to pick up again when a car or two flew by to catch the others. Eventually, after another half an hour, silence enveloped them again, the whistles of the wind and groans of overloaded tree branches replacing the noise and din of the convoy.

"Do you think it's safe now?" Sam asked.

"Let's feed the horses and Smooch. If we don't hear anything else by the time they're done eating, we'll move out."

"Okay."

They retrieved a bag of feed from their supplies and filled up a pair of heavy-duty feed bags, strapping them around the horses' heads to let them eat. Tom opened can of wet dog food for Smooch, dumped it in her bowl, and set it next to her. After getting some food for themselves, Tom and Sam sat, listening for passing cars. When they had finished eating and still none had driven by, they packed up their things and walked the horses back to the road to examine the conditions under which they'd be traveling. The road was, indeed, clear, and the pavement had been beaten down to a half-inch or so of slush, unable to fully freeze because of the salt layer, with a few thin layers of ice interspersed here and there.

"It's going to be rough on the sled," Tom remarked, "but much, much easier on us."

"Amen to that," Sam agreed.

Tom led, fast walking his well-fed gelding south along Highway 19, Sam right behind him, the sled grinding and creaking as it passed over the rough pavement. "We can make up for lost time if we ride deep into the night. What do you think?"

"I'm up for it."

"And the horses?"

"In these conditions? They'll be fine. We need to let them rest once in a while, but they have shoes, so they'll make it."

"Alright, let's get moving."

Tom settled into the saddle, his body moving naturally with the horse's gait. The animal seemed far more enthusiastic about walking without snow brushing his belly, and Tom patted the animal's neck, whispering to it as he and Sam settled into a light trot.

The briefest mention of his old missions to Sam had brought back a whirlwind of distant memories, some good and some… some, the word 'bad' was an extreme understatement for. His work with the military, while lucrative and rewarding, had also been a source for an intense amount of turmoil, both in his life and internally. He had survived, but at what cost?

Chapter 6

Tom McKnight
Beirut, Lebanon
The Past

"He's coming out of it," the balding doctor said with a blink. "He might be a little confused. Don't be surprised if he doesn't immediately remember your name."

Tom nodded and kept his eyes on the patient lying wounded on the bed. Bandages covered the man's cheeks and forehead, and his arm bore the traces of stitches under yet another bandage that covered where he'd been grazed by a bullet. He wore no shirt and had a blanket pulled up over his waist, and the bare skin that was visible was covered in bruises and small cuts.

"I'll give you a moment."

The doctor walked to the foot of the bed and conferred with a nurse about something on a chart. Osaka opened his eyes and blinked, taking a deep, groan-filled breath before looking at the doctor and nurse. His gaze roamed around the room before he finally turned his eyes on the man sitting next to his hospital bed.

"McKnight?" His voice was rough and dry, choking on the word as he forced it out.

"Yeah, Osaka. I'm here. You just got out of surgery. Doc says you might be a little foggy in the head." Tom leveled a hard stare at him and clenched his fist on the side of the bed. "I… I want you to know I'm sorry about what happened. I did my best. I swear I did my best."

"Did you… get… the drive?"

Tom nodded. "Yes. I gave it to the colonel five seconds after we got back to base."

"Good." A proud smile spread over his cracked and bloodied lips, then his jaw hardened. "Who else made it out? Reese? Irons?"

Tom gestured helplessly and shook his head, his hands falling limp at his sides. "I… no. No one else made it. Just us."

Something shifted in the commander's eyes, and he seemed to look right through Tom and north toward the Siberian mountains. His face drew taut, molars audibly grinding in a mix of anger and loss.

"It's my fault." Tom rushed his words, fist digging into the bed. "If I'd gotten the rover up faster, we could have called for the evac sooner. We could have called for it and got the hell out of there. It's my fault they—"

Osaka reached out to grab Tom's arm, his own arm trembling but his grip a steel vice in spite of his condition. "No. It's not your fault, McKnight." Osaka's voice grew stronger the longer he spoke. "Sometimes we're sent into unwinnable situations. You are *not* to blame. I just wish I could have traded my own life for one of theirs. They were all good men."

Tom allowed him to squeeze the top of his hand until it hurt, his face a twisted mask of pain and anger. After a moment, the doctor circled around to Tom's side and leaned in, glancing at Osaka's vital monitors beeping fast and hard.

"Mr. McKnight, the commander's blood pressure and heart rate are spiking. Could you please step out and give him a little time to relax? Perhaps you can come back later when he's calmed down."

"Of course." Tom nodded respectfully. "We'll talk later?"

Osaka nodded and settled back, his dark eyes drifting toward the ceiling, lost in a world of thought that Tom could only begin to imagine. Exiting the room, Tom walked slowly along the hallway to the elevators, then passed them, taking the stairs to the first floor, leaving the building to walk aimlessly through camp. He actively avoided the barracks and mess hall, imagining what everyone was saying about him. Tom had given his report to Colonel Banks, and she had barely said two words throughout, her icy stare all he needed to reinforce his self-flagellation.

Angling toward the edge of camp, he found a crumble of old Roman ruins that seemed like the perfect place to sit and reflect. There were scatters of them at the southern side of the base, buffering them against a nearby small town and Tom picked a spot where stones had spilled from an ancient building with tall columns and thick walls. He chose a rectangular-shaped cornerstone to sit upon and spun to face the dirt road that ran between the crumbled ruins. A group of children and young teenagers from town kicked a torn-up soccer ball around, shouting and laughing with glee as they scored points through imaginary goals, Tom watching and smiling wanly.

His thoughts eventually drifted back to the mission for the thousandth time, wondering how he could have gotten the rover to the surface faster. Perhaps if he'd followed the cable straight back from the submarine – though it had drifted in the lake's natural currents, and he wouldn't have had near enough time to follow it the whole way, especially with their enemies descending upon them.

No, he decided, he'd made the right choice to run it through open water. Once in the shallows, he should have looked for the cable right away – that had been his mistake. Or was it not thinking to look for the lights sooner? Perhaps he could have had Osaka go out to the hole and drop a flare, or shine a light? There were too many possibilities to consider and he could blame himself all day long, but at the end of the day, if he was honest with himself, he'd done his job to the best of his ability. Hell, he was one of the few people who could navigate the rover so expertly. Without him, they wouldn't have stood a fraction of a chance of retrieving that data.

Still, his gut churned for the loss of the SEALs. They'd all been good men, experts at their jobs, going into the fight without a care in the world for themselves. They'd known the risks of such dangerous work – it was their *job* after all – and he was certain not a single one regretted being on that frosty shore when the Russians attacked.

"Do you really believe that, Tom?" he muttered to himself.

On the surface, the answer was "yes." But who knew how he'd feel in a month or a year. After repeating the same arguments to himself nonstop since he'd been yanked from the surface of the lake, he still wasn't convinced of his own, honest answers.

Tom laid back on the warm rock, letting the sun beat down on his face and arms, dissolving the endless blackness in his mind. It evaporated the visions of the inside of the submarine, the thick soup of decomposed bodies and feasting sea life, the debris and leaking oil and fuel. He shuddered and let the warmth melt away the frigid Russian shores.

Tom thought of home. Sam and Linda and his discussions with Barbara about having a third child. And the *other* conversation where Tom was considering giving up the more dangerous side of his work. He was getting older and gallivanting around doing a young man's work wasn't something he could do forever. They'd have enough financial security with only a few more assignments, and he'd promised Barbara he'd talk to his boss about taking on safer jobs. When push came to shove, though, giving up what he was exceptionally, truly good at, was hard to imagine.

Tom stopped questioning himself, his tired body giving out on him as he slipped into a half-awake stupor, dozing in the sun's warmth with the solid stone beneath him. The kids' laughter was like pleasant white noise, soothing his senses even as they filled his heart with comfort. It seemed like he'd laid still for only a few moments before a young man's voice broke him out of his thoughts.

"Sir? Mr. McKnight?"

Tom's eyes popped open, and he sat up on the rock, head groggy and warm, a towheaded private standing in front of him with sweat stains around his armpits. Tom looked at his watch and saw an hour had passed. The kids playing soccer were gone, and his forehead burned despite the ample sunblock he'd applied to his skin.

He slowly nodded to the soldier. "That's what they call me. What is it?"

"Commander Osaka wants to speak with you. He's at the hospital, still."

"I know where he is," Tom snapped, then he shook his head in apology. "Sorry, just a little… yeah. Sorry."

"No problem, sir."

Tom rose from the stone slab and shook out his legs, then followed the private back to the hospital.

"What is it?" he asked as he kept pace with the man. "Has the commander's condition gotten worse?"

"They didn't tell me. A nurse told me to find you, so that's what I did."

"Thanks," Tom said, pushing past the private and leaving him behind as they climbed the hospital's front steps. Inside, he went up to Osaka's room and stood outside the door, giving it a gentle knock.

A nurse opened it for him and waved him in, the doctor still at the commander's bedside. Tom half-expected Osaka to be on the brink of death, though his monitors beeped steadily all around him, and the staff wore calm expressions and the commander himself was sitting up straighter in bed, looking dazed – no doubt from the pain medication – but otherwise fine. Relieved, Tom strode to the opposite side of the bed.

"He wanted to speak with you urgently," the doctor said. "I'd rather he rest, but he insisted."

"I'm not surprised," Tom chuckled, his eyes falling to Osaka's chiseled face. "He's got a bit of a stubborn streak, as I've learned."

"I'll give you some privacy. Just push the red button above his head if you need anything."

"I will. Thank you."

Tom turned back to Osaka, the commander's expression having grown tenser since Tom entered the room.

"What is it, Osaka? I came as fast as I could. What did you want to talk to me so urgently about?"

The commander swallowed dryly, his words once again hoarse, falling out in a whisper from his cracked lips. "Colonel Banks stopped by after you left."

Tom nodded, already jumping to conclusions about what was to come. The colonel hadn't reprimanded him during the debriefing, so Osaka was likely going to give him the bad news personally. Tom fully expected to be told to get packing, that he was off any future military missions and that the startup he worked for, Maniford Aquatics Engineering, would be put on standby until they re-qualified as a premier contractor.

"The intel you pulled out of the lake far exceeded expectations," Osaka whispered. "It will save many more lives than you know."

Tom blinked. "What?"

Osaka pressed on through the pain. "Banks told me they have a lead on another site they'll want your help on. The target date is four weeks out."

Tom's mouth fell open, speechless for a moment. "But… what about the men we lost? Isn't Banks concerned about that?"

"They were all good men," Osaka nodded tersely. "They were trained warriors, and they died serving their country." His chin leveled, eyes searching Tom's face. "She might not have told you this to your face, but you did well. I think so, and so does she. That's why she wants you on this next mission. You can think quickly, react quickly. You proved that at the extraction."

"I don't…" Tom tried to think of what to say, unable to process what he was hearing. "I don't get it. I failed you all."

"No you didn't." Osaka coughed, his entire body wincing from the pain. "Listen to me, though. This next mission... It's even more dangerous than the last. You should consider backing out. Don't take it. I don't want you risking your life again."

Tom's brow furrowed. "Are you going?"

"The bullet they removed was in a bad spot, causing the nerves to pinch in my spine. With it gone, I'm already able to move my lower extremities. The doctor said I'll be recovered enough by mission go-time." Nodding at his feet, Tom looked down to see him wiggle his toes.

"I have the experience and knowledge they need to pull it off," the commander continued. "The new team is shipping out in three days to start training and field exercises."

"I want in," the reply was without without hesitation.

"Tom, no. You were lucky last time. It almost cost you your life. And, as you no doubt know, losing soldiers can be a heavy burden on your soul."

"What happened at the lake was awful," Tom agreed, "but I'm going where you go. I'm going to see this through."

A regretful look crossed Osaka's face. "As much as I would love to have you, I can't recommend you come."

"You don't have a say in it." Tom pursed his lips. "When Banks offers me the job, I'm going to take it."

Osaka read Tom's face, and he gave a resigned nod and a slight smirk. "Fine. But don't say I didn't warn you."

Tom grinned. "I would never say that."

Osaka returned a hesitant smile. "Now go, so I can get some rest."

"I want to get in on the mandatory training with the new team," Tom pressed. "You mentioned they were shipping out soon."

"Yes, but you've already been through all the required training."

"I want more." Tom spoke with an urgent, almost desperate pride to do better than before. "I don't want to be a liability again."

"You're not a—"

"You don't need to lie to me, Osaka. I'm a dead weight compared to the rest of you. I want to be more than that. I *will* be more than that."

Osaka stared into Tom's eyes for a long moment, weighing the man like Anubis until, finally, he nodded. "I'll get you on the roster. Now go get some rest."

Chapter 7
Linda McKnight
Somewhere in Tennessee

Sleet crystals cracked beneath her sneakers as she left the house by the back door, waves of pristine white rolling away from her across an open field filled with micro-twisters of wintry flakes. Beyond the vast, untouched snow was a lightly forested area, the trees bowing and twisting in the shrieking wind, with the shadowy suggestions of houses up ahead through the mélange.

"That's as good a place to start as any."

Linda followed a shallow gully to the trees, covering her tracks until she was a few paces inside, where the wind was broken and lessened by the trunks. She hid the restaurant menu in the bushes and looked back toward the house to check for signs of Keith. When nothing human-shaped moved in the wall of whirling whiteness, Linda turned and bulled her way through the stiff stickers and low brush until she reached a road that curved away in both directions with an intersecting street right in front of her. Bundled up in thick long johns, two pairs of socks and two sweaters beneath a winter coat, Linda plodded down the middle of the road, peering through the two-inch gap between her hood and the scarf wrapped around her face.

With pink gloves on her hands, she gripped the pistol in her pocket while holding a flashlight up in the other hand, the potent beam cutting several feet ahead of her, illuminating both the swirling snow and the structures nearby. On either side, high drifts were piled up against houses, snow hanging in thick, flat sheets over the gutters. One home on the left was a rotting hulk, probably condemned even before the storms, so dilapidated that it leaned slightly to one side, its creaking and groaning audible above the wind. As she watched, a large section of snow and frost cracked free and slid from the roof, hitting the yard in an explosion of white powder. One house on the right was newer, although one corner had collapsed under a pile of winter white, and neither looked safe enough to enter.

Linda put her head down and plowed ahead, eyes focused on the shadowy buildings at the edge of the light. The wind punched her around, but the snow drifts held her upright as her legs dug deep into them to find purchase, keeping her wiry frame low to the ground for leverage, her head up and on a swivel. At the next intersection, a stop sign poked up out of the white, and she leaned against it and peered at a gas station on the next corner. The pump awnings were still visible, garage bay doors covered up to their windows. There were several more buildings scattered around, but they perched at the edge of her visibility, and she stayed focused on the mini mart attached to the gas station. Assuming it wasn't completely looted, they were likely to still have some food, and maybe even some basic medical supplies. Linda put her head down and walked across the street past the fuel pumps to the gas station door, her panting breath warm inside her scarf, moisture clinging to the material and freezing in tiny droplets of ice. At the window, she used her arm to swipe away snow and frost, putting her face and the flashlight against the glass, seeing displays and advertisements for food, drinks, automotive accessories and more, though it was impossible to tell if there was anything left in the place.

Movement reflected off the glass, something behind her, there and gone again in the blink of an eye. Gasping, Linda whirled, pulling out the pistol, holding it in a shaking hand as she stared across the street, squinting at a small, square building sitting in the middle of a lot. It looked like the office for a car rental place or cheap automobile dealer, judging by a few snowy lumps dotting the parking lot around it. Something shifted off to the left, a flicker in the snow, a shadow between the covered cars. Her gaze returned to the office building, heart leaping in her chest when she caught the rough shape of a head and shoulder poking around the building. Linda went cold inside, gulping, adjusting the grip on the pistol, preparing to fire, but when she blinked again, the shape was gone. She waited for a full minute, standing stock-still in the screaming wind, eyes watering as stared at the place she'd seen the shape, willing it to appear again. When no one showed themselves, she shook her head, murmuring.

"Must be the wind and snow playing tricks."

She turned around and shuffled to the gas station door, wiping her pink-gloved hand across it before giving it a tug, surprised to find it unlocked. The snow hindered it from opening too far, so she kicked it away and gave the door another hard tug, grinding it over the ice so it swung wide a foot. She squeezed through and left it stuck open behind her, stamping her feet on the floor to clear out the slippery chunks of snow and ice stuck between the grooves.

In the dark store, shelves were lined up in rough rows, crooked, knocked around and looted by those who had come before. Bags of chips and boxes of crackers lay on the floor, stomped up and squashed, interspersed with bottles of motor oil, empty beer cans and a dark red substance that looked suspiciously like frozen blood. Moving to the section that had basic medicine and medical supplies, she bent and shined her flashlight at the shelves, sweeping trash and detritus aside to look deep in the back. There were no first aid kits, gauze or antiseptics, and not even a trace of painkillers remained.

After double checking that nothing had been knocked under the shelves by the mad rush of looters, she circled the register counter and checked behind it, hoping to find the stereotypical first aid kit hidden out of sight, but came up dry. In the stock room were more shelves and a back door, and she pawed through the boxes of cleaning supplies, finding nothing that would help her mother. She was walking back through the store, intent on moving on, when she froze ten feet from the door, breath caught in her chest, heart pounding fast with fear.

The door was stuck open, like she'd left it, and snow whipped inside to dust the floor, but a shadow moved outside in the paltry gray light, and the faintest sound of boots crunching on the frozen snow slipped past the howl of the wind, chilling her far more than the temperature ever could. Linda slipped her hand in her pocket and gripped the pistol as she slowly retreated. The shadow grew deeper and more defined as it moved closer. What looked like a gloved hand came into view, reaching for the door, and she turned and fast-walked to the storeroom, moving to the rear where she stopped to listen, pistol raised, waiting for the approaching footsteps and someone to inevitably poke their head inside.

A good minute passed, and her gloved finger grew stiff resting against the trigger guard, her knees starting to ache from where she crouched on the floor, ready to put a round into the head of whoever entered the storeroom. There came no shuffling feet, though, and no one stepped through the door to threaten her. Linda finally released the breath she'd been holding, shaking her head and wondering if it the sights and sounds had been yet another trick of the weather. She started to go back to the front of the store but changed her mind, turning back to the rear door. It was an old metal slab, dented and chipped from years of abuse, a worn spot about shoulder level showing where employees had slammed it open with their palms over the years. Linda threw the deadbolt and gave it a hesitant push, but it wouldn't budge. Shoulder lowered against it, shoving it open three inches, it scratched across the pavement, snow beginning to fall into the room, followed by a chill burst of wind.

She glanced nervously over her shoulder, still seeing no one there, then, on a silent count of three, Linda threw her full weight against the door, banging it open so easily she practically fell in the snow. Windmilling her arms, she stayed upright, managing not to fall. She turned back to give the storeroom one final look when a tall shadow appeared out of the storm from off to the side near a dumpster, arm outstretched.

It was Keith. His face snarling, eyes glaring, nose red-tipped from the cold, he held a shotgun in one hand and lunged at her with the other, snatching at her forearm, growling and snarling at her. Linda cried out and jerked back, pulling free of his grasp and he stretched to hold her, tripping over something solid in the snow, falling to his knees in the soft fluff. He lurched for her again, hands like claws, but it was at an awkward angle, and she'd already sidestepped and was dashing for the back door. She plunged back inside the gas station, eyes wide with fear as she ran for the front door, throwing glances over her shoulder. She was back to the front in a flash, ignoring everything in favor of pure survival, squeezing through and rushing back the way she'd come, knees high and legs pumping through the drifts.

Keith screamed hoarsely after her, his voice faint on the wind. "I'm coming to get you! Your mother and brother, too! You can't run from me. You can't just cover your tracks and think you can get away! I'll still find you. Hear me?! *I'll find you!*"

Cold tears streaming down her face, Linda leapt from footprint to footprint that Keith had left in the snow, trying to get away while also keeping her path somewhat masked. She stumbled and tripped into a drift, her arms out to catch herself, cheeks hitting the snow and she sprung up and was off and running again in a flash. It was only after reaching the old houses from before that she realized she was leading Keith straight back to her mother and brother and she took a left down a side lane she hadn't previously noticed, weaving between the snowy rises, keeping low, glancing back repeatedly. While the deep piles of white slowed her down, they also worked to keep her hidden, but her footprints would inevitably give her away.

She staggered toward a home on the left-hand side of the road with a big oak tree squatting out front, branches laden with inches of white. Cutting a path through the yard, still looking back, she stumbled and knelt against the snow. She gasped for breaths, the air so cold it quickly became painful to take in air, the brutal chill reaching her skin through the gaps in the clothes, every nerve feeling it. Half a minute's respite was all she allowed herself before plunging between some bushes and lunging hard against the grasping branches, coming out the other side and smacking, face-first, into a chain-link fence. Ice crackled and broke off the frigid metal as she bounced back with a grunt.

With another fearful look back, Linda jammed the gun into her coat pocket and started to climb. The toes of her sneakers fit in the holes, but the metal was slick with snow and ice, causing her to slip several times. Finally, she threw her leg over the top and shifted her weight to the other side, dropping to land in the backyard. Teetering sideways, she caught her balance and plodded around to the rear, her eyes searching for an entry point. Trying all the windows and finding them locked, Linda pulled out her gun and smashed the glass with the pistol grip. It was an old pane that left several sharp shards poking out, and after knocking out a few of the larger pieces, Linda ducked inside, feeling the glass clawing at her skin and clothing, biting her lip to keep from crying out in pain. Finally, she ripped free and came to stand in a kitchen, leaning over on the counter, desperately drawing in gulps of air to quell the rising fire in her lungs.

After another moment of rest, her muscles and lungs still in severe pain from exertion and lack of oxygen, she forced herself up. *Think, Linda. Think! What would mom do?* There was no way to hide her tracks, but if she could grab a few things quickly, she could be gone from the house before Keith caught up with her, staying a step ahead of his mad, crazed pursuit.

Turning, she headed to find a bathroom, guessing one was in the hallway, and crept down the dark, shadowy corridor to find it. The floors were old hardwood, and every step she took creaked obnoxiously loud in the dead silence, her snow-covered boots slipping with each step. Linda found the first bathroom and knelt in front of the cabinet, pulling out her flashlight, throwing open the doors and shining the beam inside. It was crowded with shavers, dental floss, and shampoo bottles which she pawed through and knocked over before finally giving up. Back in the hall, looking both ways, she crept to the stairs and up to search a larger bathroom with the same result. Not a single bandage or bottle of rubbing alcohol could be found under the sinks or in the drawers. The people who had lived in the house either didn't keep medical supplies in the sink cabinets, or they'd taken it all with them during the evacuation.

She stood in the second-floor hallway with her hands on her hips, looking around, and a last-ditch thought sprung to mind. She crept to the hall closet and pulled open the old, creaky door, revealing clean towels, spare light bulbs, a bag of cough drops and a couple of dusty, empty backpacks. With a shake of her head, she grabbed one of the backpacks and crept back downstairs, gun raised as she descended to the first floor, making her way down the shadowy hall, stopping at the downstairs closet. Slipping her gun inside her pocket, she opened the door, murmuring a silent prayer before her eyes locked on the middle shelf where three plastic bottles marked "Isopropyl Alcohol" sat next to boxes of bandages, a thermometer, two tubes of antiseptic ointment, and several rolls of medical tape.

"Jackpot," she whispered, shrugging off her backpack, stuffing everything she could find into the deepest pockets before zipping them up so they wouldn't fall out when she trundled back through the snow.

With medical supplies secured, she began to relax, and started to head for the kitchen to see if there was any food or water available when the slightest alteration in the house's constant creaking and groaning caused her to stop and tick her head to the side. The bump – or was it a shuffle – was barely audible from the next room over, the noise a soft counterpoint to the wind's howling song. She froze, listening, hand holding tight to the pistol in her pocket, listening for the longest moment until she heard yet another.

Someone was in the house with her.

* * *

After leaving the rig, Keith had followed their footprints to the first building easily enough, though tracking them beyond grew much tougher than he imagined. They'd somehow covered their tracks leading from the restaurant toward town, helped by the fast-filling snow. Soon, there was no trace of them, and he walked aimlessly between the commercial buildings, scanning the nearly pristine white parking lots for signs of his quarry.

Sometimes he saw what looked like an unnatural disturbance in the frosty surface, though when he got there, he couldn't tell which way the tracks led. Sleet slapped his cheeks, and his nostrils and lips were minty cold as he breathed heavily. Eventually, he stopped going inside every building he saw and started using his gut feeling to tell him if anyone was inside. He spotted one house with blue shutters but bypassed it, not seeing any signs of disturbances in the snow, then passed by three more after it for the same reason.

Toes getting cold, cheeks stinging, he clutched his weapon angrily and stomped through the backyard of another home to where it met with a wooded area, and he fought his way through stickers and underbrush and stepped onto a road. From where he stood, it looked like the road curved off to either side, with a single street dead ahead of him like a valley cutting through the trees, but visibility was too bad to be certain. Farther up, Keith spotted movement through the crowded branches, at first assuming it was a deer, but his eyes adjusted to the swinging arms and knees and saw it was a person, low to the ground, likely one of the children. He couldn't see the face or hair, but there was no way that the youngest one would be out on his own, so it must have been the girl.

She was keeping low, plowing ahead with dogged determination, leaving obvious tracks behind her and the fire of pursuit warmed his belly. He quickly waded across the street and entered the roadside woods on her right where the snow piles thinned, and his long strides easily doubled hers. Soon he caught up to her and mirrored her movements from the cover of the trees.

He watched as she walked between two houses, looking left and right, pausing as if deciding to go inside before she moved on, Keith staying with her, circling the home on her right, walking through the backyard to stay out of sight. Soon, she came to an intersection with a gas station on the opposite corner. As she crossed to go inside, Keith took a chance and trudged across the street behind her, farther back, aiming for a small building squatting in the middle of a lot. It looked like a car lot where sleazy salesmen sold lemons at high interest rates to desperate suckers who needed a set of wheels.

Keeping an eye on her as she went, Keith kicked his way through the high snow to a car covered in a layer of white. Crossing behind it, using it as cover, he crept to other end and found the girl again. She stood at the front window, hands clearing off the frost before she put her face to the glass. While she was looking inside, Keith slogged another twenty yards to the dealership building, gun raised high to keep it out of the snow, feeling like he was wading through a high tide. He moved across the back of the structure to the far corner and edged his head and shoulders out to see the girl standing in a frightened position with her back to the glass, staring almost directly at him.

The wind was blowing snow up into cyclonic twisters everywhere, and under a sudden gust, he eased back into hiding and waited. It really didn't matter if she'd seen him or not. She'd eventually have to return to her mother, and all he had to do was stay close to her until the game played out. Still, he could end the chase and get warm again sooner once he actually caught her. Breath shallow, cold licking at his face, he edged carefully around the corner again, watching as she jerked the gas station door open and disappeared inside. Keith immediately took a circular route to the gas station, moving around the far edge of the car lot and crossing the street, concealed by the storm. He approached the gas station on its left side where the snowdrifts rose highest, covering much of the front glass.

Crouching low, he crept forward, edging past the repair bay toward the front door. While he moved quietly, he couldn't keep his boots from crunching and squeaking on the snow and icy pavement, wincing every time he made a sound. Shotgun cradled in his right arm, the butt resting against his hip, he reached for the door. A breathy gasp and faint shuffle of shoes froze him to the spot. Keith narrowed his eyes at the door as he waited for the girl to come out, but she didn't, and after ten seconds, Keith shook his head and slowly retreated, creeping around to the rear of the building, circling the massive piles of snow leaning against the brick. In the back was a dumpster and a back door and he shuffled past the dumpster and over to the door, placing his fingers on the handle. It suddenly pushed open an inch or two, causing him to jerk back in surprise, then smile in wicked delight as he realized what was happening.

He stood still, waiting for her to slam against the door again, ripping it open just as she hit it, causing her to stumble outside, nearly falling to the ground before catching herself. She stood, all bundled up with a pair of pink gloves on her hands, clutching his pistol in one hand, turning to look behind her. As quickly as he could in the snow, he reached out and snatched at her, grabbing her arm, but she reacted even faster, jerking out of his grasp, spinning on him, eyes wide and frightened. He lunged again, certain he could grab her, but he tripped over something beneath the snow and fell to his knees on the pavement and deep snow.

Linda darted around and back inside, gone in a flash and Keith struggled to his feet, but the pain in his knees kept him rooted. He leaned against the door frame, hurling a string of threats at her as she dashed away. Sucking air through his teeth, Keith waited for his knees to stop hurting. He could afford to give her a head start. It wasn't like she'd get very far. After settling his nerves for a minute, he got up and limped through the gas station, exiting out the front. The tracks were plainly visible where she'd gone back the way she'd come, stepping in her and his old footprints to go faster, but mis-stepping in half of them, making it obvious what she was doing.

"Smart," he murmured. "But not smart enough."

At first, the tracks led back toward the houses he had initially passed, then her tracks took an abrupt left turn and headed down a covered side lane.

"You don't want to lead me back to Mommy and Brother, do you?" he snarled. "Fine. I'll play along."

He followed Linda's footprints, anticipating catching up with her relatively quickly, but he soon realized she'd gotten a lot farther than he imagined, possibly outdistancing him by two hundred yards or more. Keith was starting to think he wouldn't catch up to her when he saw her prints angle off to an old house on the left. With a confident grin, he entered the yard and saw where she'd passed through some bushes and climbed a chain-link fence. He found the gate and shoved it open a foot so he could squeeze into the backyard, and - being especially quiet – he followed her tracks until he spotted the broken window on a slightly raised deck. He climbed three steps, putting his larger boots into Linda's much smaller prints, and peered through the jagged glass.

Seeing a few shards lying on the kitchen floor beyond, but nothing else, he slipped inside and stood, listening for movement. He heard nothing in the stillness, but a snow trail led straight ahead down a shadowy hallway to the foyer. Following, creeping along the hall, doing his best to keep his boots from creaking on the hardwood, he peeked into a bathroom, seeing sprinkles of white powder in front of the cabinets. *Medical supplies,* he thought. *She must be looking for medicine. For her? Her mother? Brother? Who cares. Someone's hurt. Good.*

By the time he reached the foyer, the snow trail had disappeared. To his right was a living room, and to his left was a shut door. Behind and to the left was a stairwell going up, the soft creak of movement coming down the circular stairs and he quickly backed into the living room, glancing around at the gaudy decorations. A large coffee table sat in the center, and a pair of flowery cloth couches faced each other across it. Hundreds of trinkets graced the end tables and shelves, forcing him to take extra care as he moved, lest he knock over a knick-knack and alert his prey. He listened as Linda came downstairs and snuck into the hall, then a closet door slowly swung open. Something unzipped, followed by soft shuffling sounds, then the zipping noise came again. *She found her supplies? Interesting.*

Keith was caught between circling to the kitchen to surprise her there and stepping back into the foyer. Deciding on the latter, he skulked forward in the near dark, hoping to catch her unawares. When the butt of his shotgun scraped against the back of the couch, he froze, the sounds from the hallway dying.

With a disappointed shake of his head, he called out, barely able to keep a smile off his face. "Hello, there. I just wanted to say how impressed I am at how you've handled yourself so far. Most kids your age would have been dead an hour ago. Not you, though. You're wise beyond your years."

He waited for a response, but none was forthcoming, so he continued. "That being said..." He raised his voice to a threatening level. "If you don't toss your weapon down and come out right now, I'm going to find your mother and brother and hurt them *very* badly. Worse than they're already hurting. I know they're back in one of the houses around here, and I won't stop until I find them, and then I promise you I will hurt them. So, drop the gun and get your ass out here right *now!*"

His voice had been rising until he hit the last word in a crescendo, and something crashed in the closed door by the foot of the stairs as he shouted. Keith rushed forward with his shotgun at the ready. There was no need to kill her; grabbing her and teaching her a lesson for making him chase her through the snow would do just fine.

He crossed the dark foyer and kicked open the door, staring at a what appeared to be an old dining room turned into a bedroom. A bit of light filtered inside, allowing him to see a perfectly made bed and an old writing desk beneath the window. A lamp lay smashed on the floor and clothes were strewn about, but there was no sign of the girl.

He sensed the movement behind him before he felt it, but his senses and reaction time were dulled from the cold and his injuries, and before he could turn, something stabbed into his shoulder in the same location Barbara had gotten him at in the rig. An angry cry burst from his lips as he stumbled forward into the bed, pain lancing down his side, right arm going weak, causing him to fumble with his shotgun.

"Bitch!" he growled, reaching up, jerking out whatever she'd stabbed him with, holding it up to see it was a bloody shard of glass with a bandage wrapped around it as a handle. Footsteps flew away behind him, and he spun and fired a wild shot with his left hand that peppered the hall wall with buckshot and stung his wrist and arm with the recoil.

"You little shit!" he screamed. "You're going to pay for that!"

Holding his shotgun at his hip, Keith charged out of the bedroom and clomped down the long, dark hallway toward the kitchen. He caught sight of the broken window and headed straight for it, expecting that she'd gone outside, and he'd have to give chase. Linda stepped into his field of vision by the kitchen sink with her pistol raised, brow furrowed, one eye squinting to near-closed. She didn't bother to say anything but squared her feet and fired, the first shot zipping past his ear like a summer bug, smacking the wall behind him and shocking him to a stop. The second jerked his left arm with a pinch of pain, and the barrel of his shotgun dropped before another bullet grazed his side through his thick coat.

"*Shit!*" Keith cried as he staggered backwards down the hallway, shoulders hunched, gaping in disbelief. A child? Doing such things to *him*? Impossible. Inconceivable.

He retreated to the far end of the hall, breathing heavy, teeth clenched as the new pain began to register in his body, rage boiling over. With a feral cry, he lunged forward, raising his shotgun and firing into the kitchen. The buckshot tore into the cabinets where the guttersnipe had been standing, chipping wood and shattering the window above the sink. But she was gone, the only evidence of her leaving a small piece of her ripped coat hanging from a glass shard in the entry window off to his left. She must have ducked into it when he retreated, and he initially started to follow, but hesitated. She could be standing on the porch waiting just like she'd done in the kitchen, ready to finish him off.

"I'm coming for you!" He screamed after her. "You're *mine*!"

He settled down long enough to do a quick check of his injuries. His right shoulder, where he'd been stabbed, he could neither reach nor see, though he certainly felt it, a giant ache as warm blood ran down his back. His left arm, meanwhile, was stinging and slightly numb where he'd taken a shot. Rolling his coat off his shoulders, he saw the round had penetrated the edge of his bicep and gone out the side, causing the wound to bleed, but not enough to cause him serious trouble. The last bullet had grazed his ribs on his left side. No big deal. An inch or two to the left and he would have had bigger problems. *Good thing she's not a good shot.*

Keith growled, grabbing a towel out of a nearby closet and wrapping it around his bicep, pulling it tight with his teeth before shrugging his coat back on and popping the shotgun breech open, ejecting the two spent shells. Hands shaking with rage and pain, he reloaded the weapon and snapped it shut. The fool who'd driven the rig at least had good taste in weapons, even if it was likely illegally acquired.

Eyeing the rear window warily, he turned to stagger through the front door where he stood on the porch, his hard glare piercing the storm as he stared at her footprints exiting from the side of the house, a white-hot rage growing in his belly and boiling his blood.

"I'm coming for you, McKnights! Oh, boy, am I coming for you!"

Chapter 8

Tom McKnight
Somewhere in Tennessee

The steady clip-clop of shoed horse hooves echoed across the barren roadway, quickly petering out as it reached the snowdrifts off to the sides, the drifts absorbing the sound, consuming it as easily as they had consumed the greenery far below. The wind had died down for the most part and there was a break in the snowfall, giving the pair of riders ample opportunity to examine their barren surroundings – for what little good it did. The once-familiar scenes of rolling hills, majestic forests and sweeping farmland were wiped away by the desolation of white, leaving them in a place as foreign as though they had been transported onto an entirely different planet. Silence had been the order of business since the start of following the convoy's trail, and it was only broken after hours of hard, grueling riding.

"I think this is a good time to stop." Tom peered up at the darkening sky. "It's getting way too cold to be out here and I'd rather not push them so hard when it's getting dark."

They'd ridden well past dusk, able to do so because of the clear highway. There'd been no snowdrifts to slog through, just potholes and occasional patches of ice, easy enough to navigate past.

Tom looked over his shoulder for confirmation from his daughter. "The next shelter we see, we'll pull off there. Sound good?"

"Got it," she nodded back.

They were both saddle sore, and the horses were tired from the wind beating on them on and off for hours on end, Tom feeling like a popsicle more than a human. Still, they'd covered a few dozen miles, tripling their previous day's efforts. After fifteen minutes more, he spotted a long, barn-like structure off the side of the highway.

He pointed. "That looks like a good spot. It's so big we can just hole up inside for the night."

"That's a Big Box!" Sam's voice rose with excitement.

Tom narrowed his eyes in the failing light, finally recognizing the big red sign he'd seen on dozens of commercials, the Big Box Home Improvement brand a massive chain of stores servicing Tennessee, Virginia, North Carolina, and Kentucky.

"They might have feed and other supplies in there," Tom agreed, tone rising with excitement. "Let's go!"

Tom flicked his gelding's reins and led them through the parking lot and to the front door. After dismounting, he walked over and tried to get the sliding doors to open. With a little prying and some help from Sam, they managed to spread them wide and guide the horses inside, then they closed the doors against the cold. The beasts shook their heads and snorted, sending flakes of ice flying in every direction, chuffing happily about being out of the wind. Tom patted his gelding on the neck and proceeded farther into the store, Sam following behind, Smooch watching them intently from her place on the sled.

"It doesn't look like anyone's touched the place," Sam said with a gesture, her voice low.

Tom nodded. "Everyone was probably forced out of the area before they could strip the shelves, or they didn't believe what was happening until too late. Lucky us."

"That's right," Sam grinned big. "Lucky us."

Tom pulled out a flashlight, flipped it on, and looked around. The open floor was enormous with big steel racks of supplies around the perimeter. The front few rows were dedicated to farming needs, seed, and tractor implements, the right side all tools and fixtures and the left holding plywood, drywall, and other building materials on racks or standing on their sides.

"Let's go to the back," Tom said. "If I remember correctly, that's where the feed should be."

They led the horses through the rows, the animals' big heads bobbing over the shelves as their steamy breath blew in the freezing air. Smooch's sled ground across the tile floor as they dragged her along, making sure she didn't get tangled on any corners. As they angled toward the animal and livestock related products at the rear of the store, Tom was ecstatic to see bags of feed packed on large pallets, most still wrapped in cellophane, the workers having been in mid-stocking when the order came through to evacuate.

"This is great," Tom grinned, giving Sam a light punch in the arm. "Here I was thinking we'd have to dig down to some grass for them or something."

They tied the horses to a steel rack that reached to the ceiling, unsaddled the animals, and left them near the back wall. They took their saddlebags and packs and placed them nearby then began wandering around, finding a camping display in the center of the store complete with foldout chairs, a metal fire pit with a spit, and cardboard cutouts of a family members standing around, ear-to-ear smiles on full display. They dropped their packs and looked around, using their flashlights to cut through the murky darkness of the store.

"It's everything we need right here."

"Yeah," Sam laughed at the cardboard people. "I wonder who the family is?"

"I don't know," Tom looked over them with a dry chuckle, "but they look *way* too happy. I feel like they're watching us."

"Yeah, pretty creepy."

He gently moved the cutouts to the edge of the camp and faced them away, then they returned to the horses, broke open a sack of feed, filled the horse's feed bags, and put them on. The animals munched happily, tails flicking against their flanks, muscles quivering and flinching.

"I'll get some starter logs and get a fire going. Can you stay here and brush them?"

"No problem."

Tom took a shopping cart and filled it with starter logs from a pile. Wheeling them back to the fire pit, he threw a couple on, adjusted the grate on the bottom and lit them. A few minutes later, the flames roared high, radiating a pleasant warmth. Tom held his hands out for a few seconds, reveling in the heat before getting back to work. He found a pair of metal buckets and took them outside and, after filling them with snow, he brought them in and placed them by the fire to melt water for the horses.

"What about exhaust for the flames?" Sam walked up with an extra horse brush in her hand.

Tom pointed up at the ceiling. "The roof's started to cave in a bit in a couple of sections from the weight of all the snow. The size of the place plus that should be enough we don't have to worry about it. We'll only be here for a short time anyway. And if it gets bad we'll just switch to some flameless heaters I saw on a nearby aisle."

"Okay. Want to help me with the horses when you're done? They're really cold and could use the extra attention."

"Yeah, be right there."

Tom pulled Smooch's sled close the fire and peeked beneath the blanket. The dog was lying in an almost complete circle, snuggled up in her own warmth. When he pushed the cover aside, her head popped up, sleepy eyes taking in her surroundings with a blink. After a moment, she got to her feet and shook herself, then sat and tried to lick at her bandage. When her tongue tasted the repellent they'd sprayed on it, she wagged her head and gave Tom a confused and agitated look.

"Sorry, girl," Tom chuckled, ruffling her jowls. "Can't have you licking at that. You'll just break the stitches and get it infected."

Once he had the dog situated near the fire, Tom stood back with his hands on his hips, proudly looking over their cozy campsite. "Not too shabby," he told himself.

Without the wind to blow things around, the air surrounding their fire was quickly warming, causing his body to kick off the remaining chill in a succession of shivers. He walked to the back of the store to find Sam brushing a pair of very happy equines and he removed their feed bags, grabbed a second brush, and went to work on his gelding. Using long, gentle strokes, he massaged the horse's muscular shoulders and flanks, the horses huddling together, making appreciative nickers and snorts. The gelding craned his neck around to nuzzle him, almost knocking him over, and he patted the beast firmly on his side.

"I know you're enjoying this. You deserve it. You did good today."

The horse shook his head with a snort.

"You always had a way with animals," Sam said from the other side.

"Not as much as you. They really love you, and Smooch does, too."

"Did you feed her yet?"

"Not yet."

"Want me to do it? I'm all done with Brownie."

"Brownie?"

"That's what I named my horse." She shrugged and patted the mare. "She's the color of a brownie, and I've been craving some of mom's desserts lately. So..."

Tom laughed. "Brownie, it is. Yeah, please go and feed Smooch. While you're at it, break open a couple cans of something for us to cook."

"You got it."

Tom finished working on his horse and went to check the metal buckets, finding they'd mostly melted. The sides were warm while the water inside was still pleasantly cool and he brought them to the horses and set the pails in front of them. Both animals sniffed at them and immediately started drinking and he left them alone, heading back to Sam where she was dumping the contents of several cans into their camping pot.

"They'll sleep hard tonight."

"I bet." Sam used a metal spoon to scrape around inside the cans, getting out every last bit.

"Chicken and dumplings?"

"Prepared by yours truly," Sam said with a flourish of her spoon.

"I'll bring the horses more water through the night," Tom said with a nod. "We want them fully rested and ready to finish the final leg."

"How far do you think we are from the forward base?"

"Probably about four hours out." Tom walked over to sit in the foldout chair opposite her. "Give or take."

Sam stirred the pot's contents and sat back. She picked up a bottled water from the floor and tossed it to her father. Tom caught it and unscrewed the top, tilting it up to drain it in one go, then Sam tossed him another.

"I guess we don't feel so thirsty in the cold, right?" she asked.

"Not as much as in the summer," Tom agreed. "But we still need to stay hydrated."

"At least there's plenty of water. Granted, it's frozen, but still...."

"Yeah," Tom chuckled darkly. "As long as there's a fire to melt it. Don't ever eat it straight from the ground. You do that in this kind of cold and you're just asking for hypothermia."

As the food cooked, the pair settled into the camping chairs, shucking off their shoes and socks, placing them around the fire to dry off while they leaned back and relaxed for the first time all day. Tom looked across the flames as Saman took off her hat, her brown curls falling over her shoulders. Her hair didn't have its usual sheen, as neither one of them had cleaned up properly in days, and both were covered in dirt, sweat and grunge from head to toe. Sam's green eyes were still sparkling, though, as stared at the fire, her thoughts in some distant place.

"You okay?" he asked her.

Her eyes lifted to him, and she gave him a pleasant smile. "I'm fine. Well, I'm not *fine*, but I'm trying to stay positive."

"I know what you mean. Just hang in there. Things are going to work out. We should appreciate we were able to find this shelter. It really is a blessing."

She nodded assuredly. "What's the plan?"

"Well, I figure we'll rest tonight and head out at first light. Once we get to the forward operating base, we'll find a spot to park the horses, then we'll set up an overwatch post for you. You'll have the rifle, of course."

She nodded wordlessly.

"From there, I'll try to infiltrate a weak spot in the camp, find your mother and brother, and break them out. It's a loose plan, but it's all I've got so far."

"Sounds good so far," Sam agreed. "But what about communication? Should we use our radios to stay in touch?"

"Not at all." Tom shook his head. "They'll be scanning all frequencies and would pick that up in a heartbeat. We want to maintain complete radio silence. I'll find your mother, Linda and Jack. You just cover me and…" Tom trailed off.

"Take out anyone who poses a threat." Samantha finished his sentence, still staring directly into the flames, her voice soft and somber.

"More or less, yeah." Tom shifted uneasily. "I gotta tell you, I feel uncomfortable asking my teenage daughter to kill people. Never thought we'd be in that kind of a situation."

Sam looked up, giving him a half smile. "It's okay, dad. I can handle it. I promise." A worried look passed over her face. "What if you can't find them or you get caught?"

Tom gazed into the fire. "Plan B is to do whatever's necessary. We'll just have to play it by ear."

Sam nodded and reached out to stir the contents of the pot, her expression still troubled, and Tom reached out, patting her hand.

"Are you sure you're okay?"

She hesitated, trying to find the right words. "I was just… wondering. If this is what a soldier feels like? Planning missions and stuff."

"A little." Tom chuckled. "But it usually involves a bunch of briefings and weeks of training."

"Which we don't have time for."

"Right. Not even close. I'm just hoping Keith isn't expecting us early. If we can catch him off guard, we'll have a chance. As soon as we have your mom and brother, we'll beeline it for home."

"Will it even be safe there?" Sam leaned forward and stirred the food again. It was boiling around the edges, the smells of chicken and dumpling soup filling the air and making Tom's stomach rumble. "I mean, if Keith knows we're back home, and he has our address…"

"Yeah, I know. Another bridge to burn once we get to it." Sam smiled at his malapropism, one of her parents' favorites. "If anything, there are hundreds of empty farmsteads around we can set up in."

"But we at least have to go back for our animals, right?" Sam pressed. "I know we put feed out for them, but they'll go through it by the time we get back." Her voice grew worried. "How can we just put them all in the back of a truck and move them to a new house?"

"I don't have that part worked out yet." Tom shook his head. "And I can't promise we can save all the animals, but I'm sure going to try. The important thing is that we get your mother, sister and brother back. Anything beyond that just doesn't matter."

Samantha took a deep breath, calming her nerves. "You're right, Dad. I'm sorry. One step at a time, right?"

"You got it, kiddo."

Tom grabbed a couple of metal bowls, leaned forward, and dished out their food. It vanished from their bowls nearly as quickly as he had spooned it in, and they sat back in their chairs, the savory chicken and soft dumplings filling them with warmth from the inside to match the fire's warmth from the outside.

After letting their food settle for a minute, Tom got up and used two more metal buckets to gather more snow which they melted by the fire and used to clean the dishes and utensils, as well as to quench their thirst. He placed a couple more buckets off to the side of the fire to use for easy refilling of their water bottles before setting out the next morning. Smooch got her dinner after the pair, a bit of leftover soup poured over her dry food to give it some warmth and added flavor, and Sam took her deeper into the store to do her business, the dog walking stiffly, but stronger than she had before thanks to the rest gotten by riding on her sled.

A few more minutes of chitchat were interspersed by deep yawns from the pair until they gave up trying to talk and laid out their sleeping bags, settling in to get some rest. As Tom breathed deeply, staring at the ceiling, his day-long back ache faded and his sore muscles finally got a reprieve as his entire body slowly, mercifully, began to relax. It took less than a minute for Tom's eyelids to droop and a moment later he was fast asleep.

* * *

Tom wasn't sure what woke him up first – the disquieting noise of the horses whinnying or Smooch's throaty growl. He sat up from where he'd been lying curled on his side and blinked, trying to figure out what was going on. Darkness still filtered in through the stores upper lights, and the only light they had was an electric lantern Sam had turned to low. Raising on his elbow, he saw her on the other side of the fire, completely passed out on her sleeping bag and oblivious to the noise of the horses and their shepherd. Smooch had been struggling to get up and finally rose to her feet, stepping off her sled as she glared toward the back of the store, still growling, her ears fully raised. Figuring the horses got their lines tangled on the racks or were fussing about something, Tom got up and went to the dog. He patted her good side and put her gently back on her sleigh bed, soothing her with a whisper.

"Stay there, girl. It's okay. I'll be right back." Smooch diligently obeyed, but kept her eyes pinned in the direction of the horses, hackles still raised.

Legs and back stiff from riding, Tom strolled to the rear of the store. They'd left a second small electric lantern on near the horses, and it was casting wild shadows across the big metal rack against the back wall. Tom froze as soft and urgent whispers reached him. He instantly ducked into the aisles and made his way between them, slowly drawing his pistol, verifying there was a round in the chamber before moving to end of an aisle and looking across the open space over the pallets of feed to where four people were wrestling with the horses' lines.

"We can double up and ride them," a woman whispered loudly where she stood off to the side. She was a bigger lady with one hand on her hip and the other holding a shotgun casually on her shoulder, acting like a supervisor.

"That's if we can get control of the damn things," said a man, struggling with Brownie.

A second pair of thieves, also a man and woman, were fighting with his gelding. The woman was trying to soothe his horse while the man jerked inexpertly on the rope, agitating the animal more than anything, none of them doing a very good job at keeping the animals calm.

"None of you even know how to ride," hissed the large woman with the shotgun. "I'm the only one who has any experience with that."

"Well, you're hardly helping," the man holding Brownie's reins spat back. "Maybe we'll just leave you here."

She made a derisive snort. "I doubt that. I got us this far, and I'll get us the rest of the way. Just take it easy with those ropes."

"Why don't you shut up and help me?" the woman whispering to Tom's gelding grumbled, finally giving up as she went to join the large woman in watching the men manage the horses.

After a minute, they finally got the lines untangled and led the animals to the store's rear entrance, their hooves clopping on the tiles.

"I'm riding in front," the man leading Brownie announced.

"Me, too," confirmed the other.

"How about *neither* of you are," the boss lady whispered, this time loud enough to put an exclamation point on it. "Women up front. Jerks in back."

"Aw, come on...."

Tom frowned, hefting his pistol as he slipped closer, glancing at it and back at the thieves. With the element of surprise, he could probably take them, but the odds were four against one, not a situation he'd normally want to go into, except for the fact that they'd be up a creek without the horses. Paying close attention to the woman with the shotgun, Tom began to stand up, preparing to step into the open and attack unannounced when Sam's voice rang loud and clear, echoing out inside the store.

"Leave the horses where they are and get out of here!" she screamed, "or I swear I'll blow your heads off!"

Breath caught in his chest, Tom rose and peered over the shelving, looking for his daughter, then back at the horse thieves. All four spun around, the large woman jerking her shotgun forward in search of the voice while the man holding Brownie's rope let go and drew a pistol from a holster under his jacket, aiming into the store with a scowl on his face.

Chapter 9
Keith
Somewhere in Tennessee

He scrambled after her footprints like a burning brand in the blizzard, the wind throwing him around as sleet peppered his cheeks, blowing sideways and even up into his face. His legs were wobbly and weak, his body drunk with pain and exhaustion, but he didn't stop for rest, shelter or anything. Rage was his fuel, driving him ahead like a missile without a guidance wire, armed, ready to explode at an instant's notice.

At one point, he staggered around in a circle, realizing he'd lost the girl's tracks for a moment, then he found them again, lurching forward through the blinding churn of white. Giving up was not an option. Giving up meant he'd never find her again, which meant not finding Barbara and the boy. He'd fail his mission, Banks would be furious and, worse of all, the McKnights would have gotten another one over on him, and that was an embarrassment he couldn't live with. He stumbled over what must have been a curb hidden beneath the snow, causing him to fall against a street sign. Pain lanced through his struck shoulder, his left hand almost completely numb trying to hold the shotgun. Backing off the sign, he switched the weapon to his right hand, the barrel cold in his fingers as he glared at the snow.

Her footprints angled off to the right, curving up through a copse of trees. Pushing off the sign, he followed the tracks, always trying to put his own boots into her footprints to move faster through the growing storm. As he trudged up the rise and passed between the trees, dry brush crowded in on both sides, swatting at his legs and hips. His boots struck objects beneath the snow, causing him to stumble, pain shooting through his feet. Keith had no idea where she was going, and he didn't have a layout of the town – he didn't even know the town's name. There were no more squarish shadows of buildings, just the vague outlines of trees at the edges of the driving storm. He was flying blind except for the footprints that filled his vision. The footprints he would follow until he had that little girl's throat in his hands, squeezing just hard enough to make her see stars, to force her to give him the information he needed.

Head down, eyes focused, he plunged on, smashing through a high drift to reach shallower snow. He made faster progress, growing more confident that the next bend or dip would reveal her hunkered down, given up, and nearly frozen to death. He toyed with the idea of forgiving her, as long as she admitted that he'd outlasted her and beaten her. Yet the tracks went on, seemingly forever, showing no signs of stopping or slowing down. Keith began to wonder just how far ahead of him she'd gotten. Fifty yards? A hundred? *Two* hundred? No. No forgiveness. None of that for her.

A tiny prickle of doubt wormed into his brain, but he quickly pushed it away. When he found her, which would be soon, he'd make her tell him where the other two were. He'd beat it out of her if he had to. Then he'd tie them all up again and spend a few hours getting warm before moving on to the forward operating base. He had no vehicle with which to get them there, but that was a problem for Future Keith. Present Keith had a job to do.

He saw a flitting shadow in the snow to his right, and he moved toward it until he caught a glimpse of someone running along the trail he was following. Switching direction, he lowered his head and gave chase, surging through a rising cloud of snowy mist with a cry of victory, lungs aching, burning from the cold. When he exited the cloud, he pulled up short, confused, leaning against a tree to catch his breath as he looked around. His vision swirled as the sleet stung him like a hive of angry bees, confusion smeared across his face.

She'd been right there in front of him, so close he could feel her scrawny neck in his hands, but she was gone, no trace of her to be found. Wincing into the screaming gales of wind, he kept his head down and plowed ahead, slower, body swaying as he fought to keep his balance. His skin was sweaty beneath his layers from his exertion, his entire body sweating and freezing and exhausted and confused. As the wind died for a moment, Keith stopped in his tracks, searching the perfectly pristine snow stretching around him like a heavenly blanket.

Her footprints were gone. The surrounding land was all white. Not a single foot of it was disturbed except for the lone set of tracks he'd made getting there. The wind gusted lightly like laughter teasing him and he jerked his head around, searching for the girl. Or, maybe it had just been the wind.

The tracks must have cut off or turned in a different direction a ways back, and he'd simply missed them. Standing in the middle of the blizzard, Keith spun in a circle, a heavy pit of dread growing in his stomach. He had no idea where he was or where he could find shelter, the kernel of desperation growing as he realized for the first time that he was freezing cold. So cold his bones felt like ice cubes, his blood as thick as molasses. The snow was starting to cover his own tracks already, so Keith swallowed and put aside his fear. He turned and placed one foot inside his last footprint, then another. Slowly, taking his time, he followed them back the way he'd come.

With the shotgun hugged tightly to his chest, he tucked his hands into his jacket sleeves to conserve warmth. He continued moving forward at a controlled pace, still seething, but his anger more controlled. Keith moved faster, head on a swivel to stay aware of his surroundings. The tree line ahead was distant and the failing dusk light wasn't making things any easier, but that was okay. He had his flashlight if it grew too dark and he'd always be able to find his tracks in the snow. That was important, the key to finding shelter or getting back to the relative safety of the rig if necessary.

He spotted something off to the right, ten yards distant, a disturbance in the snow, a mark on the pure undisturbed white that surrounded him. Keith hesitantly left his own tracks and tromped over the open ground to stand next to the spot. Looking down, he saw the disturbance was a set of footprints, hidden from view previously by a slight rise. That's how he'd missed them. He'd been moving too fast and rushed past them in the blinding snow, but they were the girl's exact size and shape. He slapped his hand to his cheek and chuckled, his voice weaker as he croaked out a whisper to himself.

"I've got you now. I'm back on the case."

He changed direction, surging over the shallow rise and down, gravity assisting his stagger through the snow, pulling him deeper into the cold landscape. He picked up the pace, pushing forward with gusto, growling and muttering about how he'd make her suffer for leading him on such a ridiculous chase. Definitely no forgiveness. Lots of throttling, but no forgiveness.

At the bottom of the hill, he leapt down onto an almost perfectly flat surface, flatter than anything before. Neck craning forward, he peered into a cloudy mist drifting off the snow, barely touched by the wind where the girl's footprints stretched into the haze. He had to be close. Even with the delay he had to be close to her, close to seizing her and wringing her neck until she squealed.

Grinning, Keith broke into a faster walk, almost jogging on the shallower snow. It was only a few inches deep, barely covering his boots, barely holding him back. It was only when something cracked beneath the snow, a muffled crunch of sound that rippled outward, that a sharp shiver ran up his spine. Every new footstep brought a new one, and the ground suddenly felt very soft and pliant. He froze, staring down, not wanting to move an inch until he figured out what was happening.

"No," he whispered. "No, she wouldn't have."

His confidence evaporated instantly, and his breath caught in his chest, his heated rage and need for vengeance secondary to the panic that came a fight for pure survival. Before he could do anything, there was a grunt from behind him, and he whirled in time to see a large shape arcing through the air to land at his feet with a heavy thud then vanish with a quiet *sploosh*, then the cracking grew louder, spiderwebs in the snow spreading beneath him, the ground suddenly thin and sagging, sagging and giving way, like rice paper valiantly trying to hold a wet stone but completely unable to do so.

* * *

Linda had never run so hard in her life. She pounded through the snow, using her knees to plow and churn and shove it aside. She'd just shot Keith two, maybe three times, and the adrenaline was still surging in her veins, lending strength to her limbs, dulling the pain of the bumps and bruises and intense physical activity. Hot gunpowder stung her nose, a welcome scent after the cold pine smells of the frozen forest and her hands still felt the concussion of the gun going off.

The bullets were death magic incarnate, inflicting pain, equalizing the playing field between herself and the much larger, *much* angrier man. As she ran through the side yard and out into the street, she realized that the weapon was her power and protection. She'd never let it go. A part of her felt terrible for shooting another human being, though an even deeper part was proud. The odds were evened, and she'd defended herself just like her mother had meant her to do, like she'd already done once before, and like she'd do a third, fourth and more times if she had to. If Keith wanted her so badly, he'd have to do better than that. Linda's life, and the lives of her mother and brother, wouldn't be taken so easily. She just needed to figure out what to do next.

Keith screamed behind her above the howling wind, wounded but alive. To him, she was weak and small, just a child, and he wouldn't stop until he had her. It was up to her to either be captured or resolve the confrontation in her own way, on her own terms. The finality of the thought calmed her nerves and she breathed deep and steady, setting a steadier, less manic pace as she ran back along the line of footprints toward the intersection. She found her original tracks leading to the gas station, but she plunged right past them, straight ahead, making new tracks, trying to give Keith no direction or ability to predict where she might be going. Leaving the street, she pounded over the sidewalk, angling through what must have once been a grassy field, but it was hard to tell since she didn't see any more buildings or landmarks to indicate where she was.

Vague recollections of winter survival tips flitted in the back of her mind, things from television shows or that her father might have mentioned. Things like 'don't exert yourself and avoid sweating,' and 'don't eat snow,' and 'dress in layers.' None of them addressed the potential of being pursued by a maniac through an abandoned town in the middle of a blizzard that was one symptom of a catastrophic, world-changing apocalyptic event. She focused back on herself and what she had to work with, shifting from the theoretical to the practical.

She was smaller and lighter than Keith, had a gun to even the odds, and she wasn't wounded. She was dressed better than him, too – he wasn't even wearing gloves, likely because he figured he'd have her wrapped up in short order. *For some kind of government agent, he sure does make miscalculations.*

Linda spotted a massive oak tree looming on a rise to her left, a beacon in the wasteland, and she quickly angled for it and plowed up the slope until she touched the tree with her palm. She kept moving past it, running over the looping, snow-covered terrain. There was no road outside the town, just sheer wilderness stretching out in all directions. Keith's shouting had stopped some time ago, so she put the gun back in her pocket and clenched her gloved fists to help keep her fingers warm. Linda was running to nowhere, just staying ahead of Keith, searching for something that would give her an advantage. She sidestepped down a rise and partially slid on an embankment to land in a quiet, flat area that stretched evenly in every direction.

Not thinking much of it, she walked thirty yards before ghostly cracking sounds whispered beneath her feet, muted by the layer of snow, giving away what lurked just beneath her feet. *Water.*

The ice on the lake or river wasn't thick enough to support even her weight without cracking, and she froze in place, feet planted wide to spread out her body weight as an idea sprung to life. She immediately backtracked carefully to the shore, following her own footprints, shaking her feet with each step to conceal which direction the prints were facing. Back on shore, she turned and backed up to her left along the bank, masking her footprints with wide sweeps of her hands, looking up every few seconds, expecting Keith to come flying over the rise toward her. But he never came, at least not right away.

She found a hiding spot not far from her tracks behind a cluster of lake reeds still poking out of the snow, then she dug furiously for the last piece of her plan. At first she didn't find anything, tossing several small rocks aside until her fingers scratched something larger. Scraping around the edges, she outlined a fifteen-inch log frozen to the ground. Anchoring her feet on either side of it, she grabbed a nub of a branch and jerked upward. It crackled but didn't come free.

The second time, she squatted and gave a hard yank, putting her back into it, tearing it away from the frozen grass and earth with a distinct ripping sound. She lifted the thing, just barely, carrying it back across the snow to reposition it. It was a bit heavier than she had hoped, and would be ungainly, but it would do. It had to.

Watching the rise to make sure Keith didn't surprise her, she squatted in the cluster of reeds, knees resting on the log. Silence lingered in the air as she waited, the only sound that of the wind and the only motion a few falling, flailing flakes blown to and fro. Her scarf had fallen down in her feverish run so she lifted it over her mouth and nose, breathing deep into it, the moisture left by her breaths cold, but the warm exhalations bringing back feeling to the tip of her nose. Long moments passed, but he still didn't show, and she started to wonder if she'd left enough of a path for him to follow, or if she had simply been too fast and he'd gotten lost, missing her tracks and stumbling off in some random direction. He could have also succumbed to his wounds, though she wouldn't know that for sure until she left her hiding place to check. Time passed, the cold seeping in through her layers to chill her skin, the wonderful heat she'd been producing when running beginning to dissipate as her sweaty skin cooled faster than was comfortable. Frostbite and hypothermia were real possibilities – in spite of her layers, none of her clothing was designed for long use in such frigid temperatures.

Mind lost in possibilities, she was about to leave cover when a shadow came over the rise and staggered down the hill, and she crouched lower. It was Keith, his movements sluggish and jerky, like he'd lost control of his legs. Still, his shoulders were hunched, his head bowed, eyes focused hard on her tracks as he passed within ten yards of her hiding place. His shotgun hung loosely in his right hand, swinging absently, in no position to shoot her and Linda briefly considered trying to shoot him as he paused for a few seconds. But then Keith stepped down onto the snow-covered ice and staggered out to the end of her tracks, stopping and staring at the wide whiteness all around him, head shifting back and forth as if in confusion until a faint crack echoed through the waters, barely audible to her, but unmistakable nonetheless.

Keith froze where he stood at the sound, motionless except for a slight swivel of his head as he looked around, slow realization no doubt seeping into him that he had just been lured into a trap. Linda gripped the log and lifted it to her chest, then her shoulder, getting her right hand under it, locking it in place. Stepping onto the ice, she ran forward as fast as she dared, feet kicking snow outward on the slick surface, the piece of wood balanced precariously at head level. Twenty yards away from him, then just ten, she started to stagger, tipping forward, launching the log with a mighty grunt before she fell with it in her hand, landing hard on her hands and knees.

The improvised weapon sailed in a high arc, landing with fierce impact on the snow-covered ice, and Keith turned at the last second, just in time to see the log hit near his feet. It plummeted through the snow with the sounds of cracking coming through the frost layer, revealing the full force of the truth he had no doubt been coming to grips with.

The log plunged through the ice with a sickening snap, the ice caving into a massive hole, taking hundreds of pounds of snow, and Keith, with it. The last thing Linda saw was his arms flying up, then he was gone without a sound, his face a mask of sheer terror and surprise. Standing doubled over, hands on her knees, she breathed heavily, gaping at the massive hole she'd made. Water bubbled by quickly, indicating a swift moving river beneath her and she felt a moment of triumph and jubilation before the cracks began to spread her way.

With no time to waste, she ran for shore and climbed the bank, following her footprints leading back to the intersection. Linda strode doggedly to her beacon, patting its bark with a dark and relieved chuckle as she went by, then plunged her numb feet into the tracks she and Keith had made until she found her original, lonely prints that would take her back toward her family. Taking a right, she stomped hard back the way she'd come, heart pounding with confidence and pride, certain the threat to her family had been neutralized.

Despite being cold and tired and exhausted beyond belief, she grinned fiercely. A monster had awakened inside of her. No, not a monster – Keith was a monster. It was an animal that had awakened. A beast who recognized the moment when it was time to fight or die, a creature bent on survival at all costs, especially when someone or something threatened the ones she loved.

Finally, the thin line of forest appeared, and she slipped through it back to the house with the blue shutters. She didn't bother hiding her tracks or masking her approach. Her enemy was gone. Dead. Sucked down beneath the ice into a freezing river no one could possibly survive, leaving her the victor in a deadly game of cat and mouse that she, the timid mouse, had won.

Chapter 10
Barbara McKnight
Somewhere in Tennessee

"You shot him *three* times?"

Barbara was incredulous as she held up her left arm so Linda could finish cleaning the cut on her ribs, squirting a little saline into it and dabbing alcohol around the edges before gently placing a large, square bandage over the wound.

"I shot *at* him three times, but I think I only *hit* him twice." Linda packed up the meager first aid supplies, got on her knees, and shuffled to the other side to check out the gash in her mother's leg.

Barbara put her arm down with a wince and shifted to make it easier on her daughter. She glanced at Jack, who sat at the edge of the couch, bundled up and watching them with wide eyes, taking in the story in the way that only a young child is capable of doing.

"What—nggh!" Barbara winced as Linda touched the wound. "What happened after that?"

Linda used a pair of scissors to cut Barbara's jeans, spreading the material to get a better look at the injury.

"This is really bad, Mom." She shook her head, seemingly unfazed by the amount of blood still seeping from the wound. "It needs stitches, but we don't have anything like that in here. Maybe I can find some needles and thread in the house."

"It'll have to be nylon thread," Barbara added, eyes never leaving Linda. "Until then, let's get it cleaned out and covered. I'll try to be easy on it when I walk. I promise. Now, tell me what happened next."

Linda's glanced at her brother, then back to her mother and Barbara nodded surreptitiously, then spoke to Jack, keeping her tone positive. "Honey, can you look through the bedrooms and find some needles and thread?"

Jack nodded and stood, keeping the blanket wrapped around him. "Nylon kind?"

"Yeah, it's like plastic thread. Super strong. We've used it for crafting before, remember?"

"I remember." He hopped off the couch and went in search of what they needed.

When he'd gotten out of earshot, Barbara looked at her daughter, eyebrows arching. "Okay, go ahead."

Linda launched into the last part of her story about leading Keith out onto the ice and sinking him into the river with the log. As the story came out, she worked on Barbara's wound, flushing out the deep cut, dabbing alcohol around the edges, and pushing it together while Barbara applied a bandage. To help secure the area, Linda placed a layer of gauze over the bandage and wrapped her leg with several strips of medical tape. It wasn't perfect, but it would keep her from bleeding until they found a medical facility or something to stitch it up with.

"You threw a big log at his feet, broke the ice, and sunk him in the river?"

"That's what happened." Linda nodded stoically, then her face darkened. "That was the right thing to do, right? I mean… he killed people and kidnapped us."

Barbara was equal parts impressed and horrified. Her fourteen-year-old daughter – looking far older than she had any right to – had gone out alone into a storm, found medical supplies, been hunted and nearly captured, shot her would-be captor and then killed him after a protracted chase. It was something Barbara could scarcely imagine herself doing, let alone her little girl.

She reached out and touched her daughter's head, tucking a loose strand of hair behind her ear. "Are you okay? Do you want to talk about it? I mean, you probably…"

"Killed him?" Linda sat back, giving a thoughtful tilt of her head. "Part of me feels sort of cold and dirty. Another part of me feels good, like I just did the world a favor."

"I know what you mean." Barbara thought briefly of the people she'd been forced to kill, those who'd invaded their property or tried to harm her family. "I had to do it, but it made me feel yucky."

"Yes," Linda nodded pointedly. "That's a good way of putting it. It feels a little gross. I'm not really upset with myself. I'm madder at Keith for making me do it. Does that make sense?"

"It totally makes sense," Barbara agreed, smoothing the bandage and tape over her wound. "That's spot on. You wouldn't have done it if Keith hadn't been after you in the first place, right?"

"Yep." Linda smiled warmly. "Thanks, Mom. You always make me feel better."

"I'm glad." Barbara raised an eyebrow. "Now, can I have the gun back?" Linda took the gun out of her pocket and promptly handed it over, grip first. "For your next assignment… I need you to get under these covers with me for some serious snuggling." Barbara laughed, raising her voice. "You too, Jack!"

"But I didn't find any thread!" he called from somewhere in the house.

"That's fine. Get your little butt in here and help keep us warm."

"Okay!"

Linda giggled as she crawled under the blanket and Jack came shuffling down the hallway, climbing beneath the covers on Barbara's left and snuggled against her.

"What now, Mom?" Linda asked, cozying up to her shoulder, freezing to the bone, shivering and cold.

"Let's all get some rest, and we'll move out in a little while. I'll keep watch for now."

"You don't have to do that. Keith isn't coming back."

"Well, if he does," Barbara squeezed the pistol grip in her lap, "I'll handle it."

"Okay." Linda settled against her with a sigh, and Barbara tried to give her all the warmth she could muster, rubbing her arms with her free hand.

After a while, her daughter's light snores came from the cover's folds and Barbara smiled contentedly, relaxing into the couch cushions, eyelids starting to droop before Jack wiggled next to her and she turned her attention to him.

"What about you, kiddo," she asked Jack. "How are you feeling after all this?"

She felt his shrug. "I dunno. I just want to see Dad and Sam. Where do you think they are?"

"I don't know, but we're going to find them soon." Barbara looked out the window as the blizzard raged, wondering how to keep that promise. She smiled down at him. "What's the first thing you're going to say when you see them?"

"I'm going to give them the biggest hugs of their life. Then I'm going to yell at them."

"Why yell at them?"

"For not coming home," he sighed. "And for making us so scared for them."

"I understand that." Barbara chuckled, leaned her head on him. "And, believe me, I want to know what's been going on with them, too. But remember, none of this is their fault. I'm sure they'd love to be here with us right now, snuggled and warm beneath these blankets."

"I guess so."

"And it's not our faults either." Her voice took on a drifting note. "It's just circumstances and how things turned out. All we can do is try to turn a bad situation into a positive one."

Barbara felt her eyelids getting heavier, and she wondered if she should even keep fighting sleep. Linda said Keith was dead – she'd seen him plunge into the frigid water, and they didn't have to worry about him anymore. Chin to her chest, snuggled beneath the blankets and wrapped in her children's warmth, she dozed.

* * *

Linda's stomach woke her up, growling and gurgling so loudly that it was the noise as much as the sensation that pushed her from a dreamless sleep back into the waking world. Pushing up and out from under the covers, she peered out the window to see that daylight was gone and night had settled fast upon them. Her mother was drowsing next to her, so she carefully pushed aside the covers and got up. The cold was unwelcome, but she couldn't ignore her cravings any longer – had been more than twenty-four hours since they'd last eaten, and they needed some food.

Her mother shifted beneath the blanket, her sleepy face peeking over the cover. "Hey, where are you going?"

"I'm starving." Linda shrugged. "I need to find us something to eat."

"Nope. You're not going out there again. I'll go instead." Barbara started to shift in her seat, but threw herself back suddenly, wincing in pain, grabbing at the wound on her leg. "Okay… maybe not."

"Relax, mom. I'll be fine. Besides, I know the general layout of the town."

"You sure there's nothing in the house?"

"Not unless they've got a secret basement somewhere." Linda shook her head, chuckling.

"Alright, well… I'm hungry, too, and you know Jack will be. What were you thinking?"

"The gas station was looted, but I think there were some boxes of snack food in the storeroom. Now that I know where it is, it'll only take me thirty minutes to go there and bring it back."

"And we don't have to worry about Keith anymore."

"Exactly." Linda nodded. "It should be an easy trip."

"That makes sense," Barbara agreed. She pulled the pistol from beneath the covers and held it out. "Take the gun, just in case you do run into trouble."

Linda took it and put it in her pocket, unable to deny a feeling of pride at having her mother's unquestioning trust with the weapon. "Okay, I'm heading out. See you soon."

"Stay safe out there."

Linda walked to the foyer and unlocked the door, stepped outside, and closed it quietly behind her. With the house quiet again, Barbara lifted the covers, turning to her son.

"You up, Jack?"

"Yeah." A yawn preceded his head poking from beneath the covers to see Barbara's raised eyebrow. "I mean, yes, ma'am."

"Why don't you go through the rooms and find anything that will burn? Wood, matches, sticks... anything."

"Are we going to make a fire?"

"We'll certainly try. Body heat alone isn't going to keep us comfortable for long."

Jack took off while Barbara eased herself off of the couch, the pain barely tolerable, hobbling over to check the bureau drawers for matches or a lighter. After a minute of searching, her son's eager footsteps came flying down the stairs and he whipped around the corner with a smile on his face. "Mom, they've got a fireplace upstairs in one of the bedrooms!" He spread his hands wide. "It has a *bunch* of wood next to it."

She'd seen the chimney from outside but hadn't found a fireplace on the first floor, figuring one of the previous owners had removed it.

"That's great news. And I just found these!" Barbara held up a pack of matches with a grin.

She checked some of the other drawers and found a stack of old magazines to use for kindling and, tucking a few under her arm, she followed Jack upstairs, taking each step carefully, wincing the whole way to the top. Walking the long hallway with one hand on the wall to keep herself upright, she stuck her head into each room until she found the master bedroom. True to his word, it had a fireplace in the back corner with a cord of wood stacked next to it. Hobbling over, she gave it a full inspection. It had a flue, so she reached in, grabbed the damper handle, and locked it in the open position, catching the faint whisper of wind through the ductwork. She ripped out some pages from the magazines and tossed them in, then put in a few logs, resting them on their sides to form a pyramid shape over the paper.

She lit a match and held it up inside the fireplace as high as she could reach until it grew too hot to hold on to, then lit the kindling and scooted away, feeding the flames every time they started to go down, waving her hand to add air, using the poker to push things around as needed. Soon, it got hot enough for the logs themselves to ignite, and the fire began to rage with licks of flame. Warmth billowed into the room and touched her cheeks with glorious orange light, the smokey scent of burning wood filling the air.

Jack grinned and held out his hands to the flames. "Oh, that feels good, Mom."

She closed her eyes with a smile. "Wait until your sister comes back. She'll love this."

His expression turned troubled. "Won't someone see smoke coming out of the chimney?"

"Very astute," Barbara pointed out. "I thought about that, but I'd rather risk being spotted as opposed to freezing to death. And that's why you and I are going to do some looking out, just in case."

Jack's expression perked up. "You mean like Linda helped you with before at home?"

"Sort of."

Barbara got slowly back to her feet and hobbled over to the window in the front of the bedroom. "I think we should do a rotation. You stay in here and keep an eye on these windows." She gestured to indicate the windows in both the front and back. "I'll take the other three bedrooms."

"You'll have to walk more. Won't that hurt you?"

"Don't worry about me, sweetie. I'll be fine. I want you to stay in here and get warmed up while you keep lookout," she replied. "Then we'll switch up and I'll get warm."

"Okay…" Jack frowned. "Linda probably won't like that you're moving your leg, though."

"She'll be fine," Barbara gave him a conspiratorial wink. "Just shout if you see anyone or anything moving out there, including Linda."

"No problem, Mom. You can count on me."

"I know I can." She ruffled his hair and gingerly walked into the hallway, taking a few steps and entering a bedroom facing the backyard.

It appeared to be a little girl's room with a ruffled pink bedspread and a desk with a purple laptop computer on it. The accordion style, slatted closet doors had been thrown open, and clothes lay strewn everywhere, likely due to Linda's searching for some of her extra layers. Barbara hobbled to the window and leaned against the wall, peering through the curtains at the weakening storm, the wind having dropped off to nearly nothing, leaving only a few scant snowflakes twirling in the air as they fell lazily downward.

* * *

The back storeroom had, indeed, been a treasure trove full of supplies, and Linda filled her pockets and her backpack with snack bars and drinks that had frozen in the cold. None of the drinks had spoiled since they were frozen – though she doubted energy drinks could spoil anyway – but the bad news was that they had to be thawed before anyone could consume them. She grinned when she found two packs of beef jerky, nearly hurting herself as she climbed up on a shelving unit to pull down boxes, tossing in several packages of salted cashews, peanuts, and other high-calorie foods.

The proverbial elephant in the literal room hung over her, and try as she might to not think about it, she couldn't help imagining Keith's shuffling footsteps behind her, and she caught herself tossing glances over her shoulders every few seconds. With a shake of her head, she tried to stay focused on the present and the positives of her situation. Her mother and brother were hungry, she had food to solve that problem, and getting it back to the house was the most important thing she could do.

She left the gas station and retraced her footprints. When she reached the point where her own tracks crossed, she took the restaurant menu from beneath her coat and started dragging it in the snow behind her, smoothing it out as she backed up. Covering her tracks was considerably harder as she was laden with all the food she carried, but she didn't want to give anyone a reason to follow her to the house, no matter how remote the possibility of pursuers might be.

Somewhere near the wooded backyard, she turned and saw smoke drifting up from the house's chimney over the tops of the trees. At that moment, the blizzard gave one final gust, seeming to give up its fight, the wind falling silent, leaving just a few snowflakes whirling in the air. Grinning, but patient, Linda clambered through the woods and crossed the backyard, covering her tracks the entire way. Holding open the back door, she kicked her boots against the old brick and stepped inside.

"I'm back!"

"We're upstairs," came her mother's faint voice called back. "We've got a fire going."

"No kidding!"

She locked the door behind her and traipsed up the stairwell. At the top, she peered down the hallway and saw her mother standing in the doorway to the master bedroom, smiling as she favored her right leg.

Jack flew from a side room and threw his arms around her. "It's *so* warm up here, sis."

"I know, I can feel it," she laughed, holding on to him. A gust of warm air touched her cheeks, and the smell of burning wood tweaked her nose. "Be careful, you're smashing the food!"

"Sorry!" Jack exclaimed. He let her go and took her hand, leading her down the hall, Barbara following behind.

Linda stared at the roaring fire, her face tingling from the heat radiating from the stone mantle. She tossed her backpack on the bed, unzipped her pockets, and emptied them next to the contents of the bag, bottled waters, chips, energy bars, and packs of jerky plopping on the comforter.

Jack dove for a bag of corn chips while Barbara tried to snatch them away. "Granola bar first, buddy."

"Aw come on, Mom," he complained. "It's the end of the world. None of this stuff is actually good for us."

"All the more reason to *try* to eat right. Bar first, chips second."

Jack sighed with disappointment but obeyed, opening a granola bar and chewing hungrily while Barbara reached out and scooped up a small brown can.

"Did you get me Mocca Burst?"

"Absolutely," Linda nodded. "But you'll have to wait until it thaws."

"Fair enough." Barbara picked up two cans, several frozen bottled waters, a bag of beef jerky, and an energy bar and carried them to the fireplace. "We set up some chairs."

"Awesome," Linda said, grabbing a few snacks of her own and taking them over.

Two puffy leather chairs piled with covers sat side-by-side, and a beanbag chair sat on the far right end. Jack flopped on the beanbag while Linda took the chair on the right as she unlaced her frost-covered boots and stripped her wet socks off, laying them out by the fire. She put her feet on a footstool and pulled a cover over her, starting to unwrap a snack but stopping for a moment as the raw heat washed over her. Leaning forward with a sigh of pleasure, she closed her eyes and absorbed it. Her toes were warming up and drying out fast, and she wiggled them luxuriously.

"Nice, huh?" Barbara placed some frozen coffees and waters near the fire and eased down in the middle seat next to her. A moment later, two pairs of bare feet rested on the footstool, getting warm. "I'll bet you were starting to feel like an ice cube going outside so much."

"Yeah, but this is super comfy." Linda's voice oozed between her lips as exhaustion washed over her. She finished opening the energy bar and took a bite, shaking it at the air. "It's okay, but not your cooking, Mom."

"It'll keep us alive for the time being," Barbara chuckled as she gnawed on a cold piece of jerky. "We're not out of the woods yet, but we're stable."

"What are we going to do next?" Linda asked.

"We need to get to that forward operating base Keith was talking about."

"Why?"

"That's probably where your father will be going, based on Keith's note he says he left."

"Why don't we go home and wait for him there?"

Barbara stared into the fire. "Well, home is pretty far away, and the FOB is close. According to Keith, it's just outside Asheville. I saw him looking at a map when he was driving. He had it circled."

"Oh."

"Plus… look, I don't trust Keith, but between what he said and what I saw on that computer when we were rescuing you kids, your dad really *is* being pursued by the military. And you know how your dad is. He'll make it home, see what happened, find the note and the first thing him and Samantha will do is try to come after us."

"It's what we would do." Linda spoke around a mouthful of jerky. "What'll we do once we get there?"

"We'll get there, and…" Barbara lost her train of thought and chuckled. "I guess we'll figure it out then. In the meantime, though, why don't you finish up your food and get into bed and get some rest. I'll keep watch."

"But your leg is—"

"Just fine. I can hobble around with the best of them." Barbara tried to keep her tone light-hearted, but Linda's suspicious gaze forced a further explanation. "Yes, it hurts. But I'm not hurting anything, and someone has to keep watch." Linda started to open her mouth to argue, but Barbara shook her head. "No arguing. Got it?"

"I… okay. If you're sure."

"I'm sure. The moment I need help, I'll tell you both, okay?"

Linda nodded, and she and Jack finished their meals before they both gave Barbara a kiss on the cheek, padding over to the big bed behind them. The old springs groaned as they climbed into it, giggling about some inane joke they were no doubt whispering about, giving Barbara the strangest feeling that she was once again at home. Hearing her daughter laugh relieved her more than she realized, especially given what Linda had been through. She had no idea what the potential long-term effects would be, but it was comforting to hear Linda and Jack both sounding like the same children they had been before the whole mess had begun.

Barbara watched the flames licking at the top of the fireplace, slowly dwindling as the fire consumed the fuel. Leaning forward, she grabbed another piece of wood and placed it on the others, then took the poker from its rack, using it to shift some of the embers around as a wave of heat rolled off into the room. Her body was warm, but it ached all over, the pain in her leg so bad she stood and paced to the other end of the room and back again just to get some motion to help reduce the stiffness. She paused next to the bed, listening to the snores coming from underneath the covers, Linda's question ringing loudly in her mind.

What are we going to do next?

While Barbara had only given a half-answer, it was because her choices were so limited. Their home was a no-go given the distance, and the FOB offered them a chance to stay warm and reunite with the rest of their family, even if it was in a cell. She limped back to the chair and sat down with a wince. Noticing one of the bottled waters had thawed a bit, she picked it up, unscrewed the top and took a drink, the water's coolness refreshing her dry throat.

There were risks with going to the FOB, of course. If Keith was an example of the sort of people who were after Tom, then the ones at the FOB could be a hundred times worse. The military had already taken her children once, separating them from her and using them as leverage. If they were willing to go that far, then who was to say that they wouldn't go a step – or ten – farther? In the end, no answer was easy, and she could only pray for the wisdom to make the right choice in the moment.

The one thing that remained clear in her mind was that she'd do whatever it took to keep Linda and Jack alive and to get to see her husband and oldest daughter again. She'd already been through hell and back and still stood to talk about it, and would make the trip a hundred times more if necessary. Mind roiling with questions, Barbara stared at the fire, looking for answers in the licking, crackling flames.

Chapter 11
Tom McKnight
Somewhere in Tennessee

As soon as the man's weapon went up, Tom's watching and waiting was done. He raised his pistol, aiming at the man threatening Sam and fired at a distance of twenty-five yards, his shot punching through the man's temple, exploding from the other side of his head in a chunky spray of bone and blood, the body falling lifeless to the floor like a sack of raw hamburger.

"Sam!" he hollered as he pivoted his hips to find another target. "Find cover! Now!"

The leader of the thieving bunch charged at him with a wild shout, swinging her shotgun around in Tom's direction, and he jerked back as a blast of buckshot shot shredded bottles of horse shampoo in the next aisle over. Keeping his back to the shelves, he stayed out of sight as the woman stomped toward him, screaming profanities at the top of her lungs. Tom held his pistol up, readying himself for when she came around, but Smooch's frantic snarl ripped the air as the dog charged out of nowhere, hitting her large mass like a freight train, the pair tumbling into a pallet of feed, spinning, and hitting the floor with the shotgun clattering away.

Tom crouched and came ahead, aiming at the woman, but Smooch already had her by the throat, jaws snapping her neck viciously back and forth, sending blood pumping across the floor. With her down, Tom spun to face the other two thieves, the remaining woman staring at Smooch in terror as the dog tore her friend apart. The shepherd's fangs gleamed in the garish light as blood and foam flew from her mouth and with half her hair missing and her wounded shoulder, the dog looked like something out of a nightmare. Before Tom could fire a single shot, the woman turned and ran headlong into the last man, shoving him toward the back door, the pair tripping over each other as they threw it open and fled into the cold.

Watching them go for a long minute, Tom eventually lowered his weapon and swung toward the sounds of Smooch's low growling. The dog stood over the dying woman, her paws splayed apart and her muzzle low, still on guard for any further threats. Tom stepped closer and looked down. The woman lay on her back with her head tilted oddly, ligatures and blood vessels shredded from the dog's vicious fangs. Smooch had punctured her trachea, judging by the sounds of her labored breathing and the bloody bubbles forming in the mess of her neck. The woman's eyes turned up to him with terror and a sense of finality, and Tom nudged Smooch to the side, giving her an all-clear wave of his hand, raised his pistol, and put a bullet between the woman's eyes, ending her suffering. The warehouse fell silent except for the horses' clattering hooves as they pranced off into the store, frightened by the snarling dog and repeated gunshots. The deed done, he looked up to see Sam standing in a nearby aisle, her jaw open and her eyes wide with horror.

Smooch tried to limp back toward Tom, holding her right paw up, favoring the wounded shoulder, her good leg shaking with exhaustion, and she finally made a pitiful noise and laid down at his feet. Tom holstered his weapon and knelt to assess her damage. She'd ripped her bandage off her wound, and it bled freely, caking her belly fur in red. It was too messy to really tell if she'd torn any stitches out, but she was still alive, which was more than he could ask for given the circumstances.

"Sam," Tom spoke softly, "Can you take Smooch back to the camp area and work on cleaning her up? She needs to be scrubbed down and have some bandages put on her wounds." When Sam only stared at him in wide-eyed fear, he leaned into the words, nearly shouting at her, his voice harder than she'd heard before in her life.

"Sam! Take Smooch! I need to see if those people are gone and clean up this mess."

"S-sure, Dad." She snapped out of her trance, her eyes still wide, watching Tom carefully as she came over, coaxing Smooch to stand, before gripping her under her chest and belly to carry her back to their small campsite.

After she'd walked the dog away, Tom grabbed the dead woman by the arms and dragged the body toward the rear door. The fleeing thieves had left it hanging open, letting in a cold breeze with gusts of snow. Tom kicked it open the rest of the way with his heel and looked around. Seeing no signs of the other two, he drew the dead woman out ten yards from the door and let her arms drop, then he went back inside for the man, pulling him to the same spot and placing him next to her, not bothering to cover them with anything. With the frequent snow and constant storms they'd be frozen through in a few hours, covered in snow to become yet another part of the hellish tundra landscape.

Stalking back in, he shut the rear door, but it fell open an inch and wouldn't close properly. Finding a rack full of rolled chain, he picked a pre-cut length and brought it back to wrap it around the door latch and then around a nearby rack before going off in search of the horses, stepping over the large piles of blood and gore along his path. He found the horses wandering in the back corner of the store, nickering nervously when he approached, tossing their heads and rolling their eyes.

"There, there," he cooed, forcing his still-hard voice to be slightly softer and gentler. "It's okay. Just a little scare. Nothing to be worried about."

A few pats on their necks, clicks of his tongue, and kind words comforted them and after a few minutes, they were calm enough to move. Taking their lead ropes, he guided them back to the feed section and tied them to the rack again before picking up the water buckets and fetching more snow out front, watching cautiously across the road, concerned that the other two thieves might still be loitering.

Satisfied they weren't there, he returned to the camp and placed the buckets by the fire where Sam had already fed another starter log in and moved Smooch back to her sled. Blood was smeared on the bedding and covers, but the wound looked much cleaner than when she'd been standing over the woman, looking more like a hellhound than a shepherd. Samantha had just peeled off the protective layer of a large bandage and was about to put it on the wound when Smooch's gaze lifted at Tom's approach, giving a soft whine and a wag of her tail. Tom watched as Sam placed the bandage over the injury and patted it gently so it stayed, neither of them speaking for a few minutes until Tom finally broke the silence with a cough.

"I, uh, see you've got some new first aid supplies." Tom gestured to several new bottles he didn't remember packing.

"Yeah." Sam didn't look up at her father, her voice barely above a whisper. "I found some really good stuff in the medicine section for dogs." After patting down the bandage, Sam turned and sat on the edge of the sled, eyes locked to Smooch as she ran her fingers through the dog's fur. "There's antiseptic, wound bonding powder, and these cool bandages that hold the skin together like stitches. I put those on first after I cleaned her up. She looked worse than she was, I think. Most of the blood wasn't…"

"Excellent." Tom interrupted as Samantha trailed off. "Good work." He coughed again, trying to smile through the tension that clung to the air. "The horses are all calmed down. As soon as the snow melts in these buckets, I'll take them some more water."

Sam nodded, still staring at Smooch, not saying anything. Tom walked to his chair and sat down, leaning close to the fire to warm up, his ears still ringing from the multiple gunshots. He took a deep breath, getting a nose full of the smoky warmth, then looked over at Sam.

"Are you okay?"

"I guess so." Sam stood and took her seat across from him, folding her arms across her chest, her green eyes staring at the fire, voice still whisper-quiet as it blended with the crackling flames.

"Do you… want to talk about what happened?"

There was a long silence, then another near-whisper. "You just shot those two people like it was nothing."

Tom nodded matter-of-factly. "I did shoot them. I killed them without hesitation and I'd do it again in a heartbeat. It wasn't *nothing*, though. You think I should have handled it differently?"

"No…." She shook her head. "I… I know *why* you did it, but the way you did it seems so… callous. You had this strange, empty look in your eyes, like it didn't bother you." She looked up at him, the fire dancing in her eyes. "It's like you just said. You had no hesitation."

Tom sat quietly for a moment, staring into the flames, rolling the words over in his mind before letting them out. "Do you remember the coffee shop, when I used Jerry as a battering ram, and you ran that gang off with your homemade flamethrower?"

She snorted, nearly smiling at the memory. "Yeah. I remember. That was crazy."

"I intentionally restrained myself that day. I hesitated, because I didn't want to hurt anyone too badly. I haven't stopped thinking about that since then."

Sam's face twisted in confusion. "You barely touched any of them. If anything, *I* was the one who hurt them."

"That's right. But I felt bad because I didn't do *more* to protect you and Jerry." Tom's voice lowered, slipping into a growl. "I should have taken them all out for even *trying* to mess with us."

Her eyes lifted to him with a fearful and confused expression. "Dad, you're really starting to freak me out. You're acting like some heartless soldier, but… you're not."

"No, I'm not. Not by a long shot." He shook his head, letting out a sigh that felt like it had been a decade or more in the making. "But it's time you knew a few things about me."

Chapter 12
Tom McKnight
Somewhere in Ukraine
The Past

Bullets smacked the hull of the rickety fishing vessel as the three circling motorboats fired relentlessly. Tom instinctively ducked every time a round pinged against the rusted metal hull or struck the winch that hung off the bow, his ears having become attuned to the zipping, ricocheting rounds as they bounced all around him.

The SEALs shot back from their hunkered positions on the deck, lifting to the rail to spit automatic gunfire across the churning sea before ducking back again. The sputtering motor kept them on a slow course forward, but they couldn't truly leave their position until Tom had the rover up and on board. He sat on the deck of the ship as it rocked back and forth, head craned forward, eyes fixated on the controller screen as he guided the remote vessel through the murky depths.

Lieutenant Commander Osaka fired his rifle over the rail and jerked his head around, checking on Tom. "Hurry it up, McKnight! We're running out of time."

"Hey, if you want to come drive this thing, be my guest!"

Osaka laughed and resumed firing at the circling boats as Tom focused on the rover, trying to ignore the stinging stench of gunpowder, salty gusts of wind, rifle chatter and the constant up and down motion of the small craft. A SEAL screamed and fell onto the deck, writhing and clutching his neck as blood slicked the wet wooden slats and Osaka called for some heavier ordinance, Tom glancing up in time to see another member of the team throw himself against the starboard rail with a long tube on his shoulder. He shouted something before depressing the trigger on the weapon, and in a whoosh of smoke, a rocket-propelled grenade zipped from the barrel, flying across the frigid waters to blast one of the pursuing boats.

An explosion of debris shot upward, and the enemy boat instantly slewed off course, a man on fire screaming and careening over the side only to meet a frozen end in the icy sea. Burning hotter, the boat angled away, out of control as the fighters on board wailed like dying animals, smoldering bits of wood and flesh raining down to sizzle on the water's surface. Tom noticed an instant reduction of incoming fire as the other boats backed off and, letting go of the joysticks, he shook out his hands to loosen them, giving his tired knuckles a brief rest. He bent back over the controller after a few seconds and grabbed the sticks with renewed intensity, focusing in on his part of the mission.

Far beneath the surface on the sandy sea floor, the rover circled a piece of equipment that had been ejected from a sunken, imploded submarine. Parts of the vessel were scattered over a quarter mile, and it had taken Tom almost two hours to find the section he was bathing in his spotlight. The hull sides were jagged around the edges where it had ripped free from the sub, but the main computer drive array was intact on the sea floor, though he had to work the rover close to the bottom and angle it slightly up to see it the actual drives.

Barnacles and sand covered the water-sealed computer equipment as the sea tried to bury the priceless information it held, but Tom wasn't about to let his prize slip away. Similar to how he carried out the last dive, he used the rover's rubber grippers to take hold of the master disk and reverse direction so it popped two inches from its slot before letting go, adjusting his grip and pulling it all the way free.

"Got it!" Tom shouted. He secured the disk inside a compartment, spun the rover toward the surface, and kicked the engines to full before glancing at his GPS picture-in-picture to see the boat had drifted a bit off course. "It'll come up a hundred yards off the starboard rail! ETA three minutes!"

"Copy that!" Osaka yelled back in confirmation.

The commander turned from the rail and motioned to the pilot of their craft, pointing off the starboard side. "Go a hundred yards that way! Once we have it, be ready to run!"

The man nodded through the bullet-riddled glass and spun the wheel to take them closer to the rising rover as the rifle fire picked up again, the enemy seeming to sense that they had collected what they needed, and they were going all-in to keep the SEALs from running off with it. Tom tuned out the noise, keeping his head down and eyes focused on the screen, his hands tight on the joysticks, forcing the vessel through undercurrents and turbulence, rising swiftly to the surface from a half mile below. Despite the arctic temperatures, he was sweating badly, his neck itching and his blood pounding with intensity.

Their boat bounced in the churning waters, bow lifting and falling on the waves as the enemy fell in behind them. After a hundred yards, their pilot cut the engine and let them drift. Tom saw the surface light on the rover's screen and the bottom of their hull in the far distance on the rover's left as another of their team took a hit and fell to the deck, clutching his chest before he gasped and fell silent. Tom fought to pull his eyes from the body, flashbacks of his previous mission flooding his mind, having to work overtime to push them away.

With tightened jaws, he put the rover on auto-pilot and placed the control module on a coil of rope. Snatching up a rifle from a dead SEAL, he joined Osaka at the rail as the remaining two enemy boats began circling again. Tom rested the weapon on the rusted metal and took aim at a skiff as it came around, looking down the gun sights to pick a black-garbed figure on the deck, focusing his aim as both ships bounced in the waves, trying to calculate trajectory and distance in the impossible swells.

He followed the man with his sights as he moved from the deck to the upper level, ascending a flight of metal stairs. Tom squeezed the trigger, trying to lead the target and his bullet struck the rail next to the man's hand, causing him to jerk. Tom fired several more shots, angling upward, chasing the man up the stairs, watching as he hit flesh and blood painted the faded white bulkhead. The man crumpled to the steps, lifeless.

"Nice shot, McKnight!" Osaka shouted as he rattled off a handful of shots himself. "Your extra training didn't go to waste after all!"

Tom nodded, trying to match Osaka's excitement, but his stomach bubbled with rising bile. He clenched his belly and hammered the sick feeling down. Another SEAL joined him on his right, and together they kept the attackers at bay, Tom choosing his targets randomly, sweeping his rifle barrel across the deck. He got a good angle at the man driving the boat and fired at the acrylic glass, adding a few more holes to it but missing the pilot altogether.

As the enemy boat dipped, he switched targets and took a shot at another man peering over the rail. His round hit home, drilling the soldier in the forehead, the impact splattering the deck in clumps of gore just as the boat leveled out and the rail rose to obscure his vision.

"Another one down!" Osaka's matter-of-fact attitude and cheerful tone chilled Tom's heart.

The SEALs fired an RPG on the other side of their boat, followed by curses that indicated it was a miss, though the vessel they were targeting backed off, circling farther out to avoid a potential follow-up shot. An alarm rang out on his controller, and Tom's looked to the water to see the rover had popped up and was bobbing next to them.

"It's here!" Tom yelled, disengaging the engines of the rover.

"Grab the hook!" Osaka shouted.

Tom dropped his weapon and picked a fifteen-foot pole off the bulkhead. Falling against the rail, swinging it over the side, he angled it toward the water, its hooked end scraped at a loop on the rover's frame as Osaka's men provided cover fire. After several tries, he finally caught the loop and drew the vessel closer toward the boat. The thing weighed two hundred pounds, and Tom could only get the front lifted up, banging it against the hull. Osaka shouldered his own weapon and moved to the controls of a large winch with a clawed end. He activated it with a high whine and lowered the claw toward the water. With Tom's quick guidance, Osaka grabbed a crossbar on the rover's chassis, reversing the controllers to lift the delicate machine as the boat's driver masterfully turned their vessel away from the enemy to give them some cover.

"Be careful of the master drive," Tom called, using the hook to keep the rover from banging against the hull. "Don't damage it!"

"Got it!" Osaka shouted back as he worked, fighting with the crane's controls, bringing the rover over the rail.

Together, they guided the machine to the deck and set it down gently. Tom dropped his hook and flew to his knees next to the rover to inspect the rover's undercarriage, pulling the storage receptacle open to reveal the disk lying inside. Plucking it out, he handed it over to Osaka.

"Good work." The commander smiled, then motioned for the boat's driver to take off.

They lurched forward, their bow shooting high, their enemy right behind them, firing as they gave chase. The remaining SEALs on board lined up along the stern rail, shooting back with a vengeance and bloodlust fueled by the loss of their comrades. Deceptively fast for its size and age thanks to some clandestine upgrades, the fishing boat quickly outpaced the smaller craft, and the sounds of gunfire dwindled to silence. Tom turned away from the rail, circling back to the front of the boat to kneel beside his controller. He disconnected it from the main line and quietly packed it away as the boat continued to the next waypoint for their extraction.

Once he'd secured his equipment, he sat on the rolling deck with his back against the bulkhead, adrenaline fading as he breathed the crisp salt air, swaying side to side with the ship's rocking motion, both gladness and a dark anxiety plucking at his heart. After the last mission, the sense of accomplishment and fulfillment of duty nearly outweighed losing most of the team. But something else had changed inside him, a sense of foreboding weighing heavier on him than he thought was possible. His eyes drifted to the two dead SEALs lying on the deck in front of him as the survivors respectfully prepped the corpses for travel.

The loss of the men, while tragic, hadn't affected him in the way the first mission's losses had. Perhaps his change in mindset had something to do with the images flashing through his brain. His own bullets painting a white bulkhead with blood, blowing bone and gristle across the deck. Gruesome, but in defense of his teammates, and necessary for the success of his mission.

Still, he couldn't help but think those men probably had families waiting for them at home, wives and children who would never see their fathers again. It could have easily gone in the other direction. He thought of Barbara and his own children and something stirred inside him, warring with the excitement and sense of duty he felt, casting a dark shadow over the entire event.

* * *

Eight hours later, Tom sat in a debriefing room on a Naval Vessel in the Mediterranean Sea as Lieutenant Colonel Rachel Banks sat across from him. She levelled him with a hard look.

"You alright, McKnight?"

Tom stirred from his deep thoughts and raised his eyes to the woman he'd gotten used to seeing, the one in charge of the missions he was on, tied somehow to multiple branches of US Special Forces, as well as other, more secretive organizations that he wasn't sure he wanted to know even existed.

"Sorry, ma'am," Tom said. "I was distracted. Can you repeat the question?"

Banks' cold, formal tone dropped momentarily, a trickle of sympathy showing through. "Look, McKnight. You killed two men today, two men that – despite your weapons training – you probably didn't expect to have to kill. More importantly, you weren't trained on how to handle the killing when it was over." She spread her hands on the table. "We have services that can help you with that, so why don't you let me sign you up for a program?"

"No. It's okay." Tom sat up straighter and squared his shoulders, his fingers tapping restlessly on the desk, his insides feeling strange and hollowed out. "I'm fine. What was the question again?"

Banks's look darkened again, looking down at her notes before turning back to Tom with a hardened expression. "My bosses want Osaka's unit to perform one last mission before they're split into new teams the Joint Chiefs are developing. And they want *you* to join them."

The dread and uncertainty Tom had been feeling doubled itself, his neck growing hot and his breathing growing faster and shallower. He looked down at his hands clasped on top of the table, trying to relax his white knuckles, feeling like an animal trapped in a cage.

He coughed into his hand, then replied. "I can't do another mission." Banks's already dark expression somehow darkened even more, and he continued. "It's not just up to me. After the last mission, my wife wants me back home, and I'm in agreement." He cleared his throat again. "In fact, I'd like to know how I can make arrangements to fly back to Virginia right away. That was part of the agreed-upon contract."

"Yes, I'm aware of the contract and what's inside." Banks added an edge to her tight tone. "But this new job comes with significantly more pay than the last one." She slid a piece of paper across to him, the number written on it higher than Tom could imagine. "Osaka is already onboard, too. The two of you make a formidable team. Your search and retrieval methods are unmatched."

Tom shook his head slowly, building up the courage to turn the woman down, but the Colonel pressed on before he had a chance to.

"Look, Tom." Banks smiled slightly, softening her tone, trying a new tack. "We have friends in the private sector who love to see this kind of experience on a resume. Complete a few more missions for us, and you'll never have to ask for work again. People will be begging to have you as a consultant on any number of key operations. And they're positions where you won't get shot at."

Tom closed his eyes and thought hard about it. His last two missions had been incredibly dangerous, so dangerous that he kept picturing his own brains splattered across the deck in some remote part of the world. He pictured a pair of SEALs prepping his corpse for transportation out of the operation zone to be delivered to Barbara, his children crying next to her.

Shaking the image from his head, he settled back again. On one hand he'd be a fool to accept. On the other hand, perhaps he shouldn't be so hasty in dismissing another op. The number written on the paper in his hand would set his family up for life. Not just for their lives, but for a few generations to come. If he could convince his kids to enter similar fields of work, they'd have jobs already lined up when they got out of college. The future prospects were tremendous. How could he think about his own state of mind when he had others to look out for? Over time, he could learn to live with anything he'd done. It would be worth it to see his family prosper.

The Colonel sensed his weakness, pressing in on him. "I'm telling you, McKnight, this is the chance of a lifetime. And if you're worried about the *extremely* unlikely event of not coming back, you can rest assured that your contract will pay out the full amount to your family."

"Extremely unlikely, huh?" Tom snorted.

"The team for this mission are the best of the best. You'll be very well taken care of."

Tom took a deep breath and shook his head. He could already hear Barbara's voice in his head, reasoning with him. She'd say his resume was already packed full of impressive accolades and experience and that in another five years, Maniford Aquatics would put them exactly where they wanted to be, financially speaking. From there, they could retire early to the farm and leave the high-pressure life behind, without the risk of him losing his head on another mission.

Still, the Colonel's words weren't lost on him. The chance of a lifetime. An unmatched resume. Security beyond measure. Not to mention the pride of having succeeded at another mission. Barbara would be pissed at him, but she'd understand in time. Hopefully.

He nodded to the Colonel. "Okay, I'll do it. One more."

"Wise choice. My bosses will be extremely happy to hear this." Colonel Banks stood, passing over a piece of paper which he signed as quickly as possible, trying to avoid the guilt that was already starting to weigh on him.

"Now, get your things," Banks said. "You're leaving in three hours."

The Colonel turned to go, but Tom sidestepped with her, a confused look twisting his face. "Wait a minute. Three hours? That's all the time I have to get ready? I was expecting there to be some weeks of training and preparation, like before."

The Colonel shook her head. "Sorry, Tom. But this one is extremely time sensitive. You'll be briefed en route."

Banks gave Tom a nod that told him she was done talking and left the room, leaving Tom to deal with a growing discomfort and a sinking feeling of having made a terrible mistake.

Chapter 13
Keith
Somewhere in Tennessee

His frozen fingers burst from the water's surface and clutched the cold hard ground like a claw. Ramming his other arm up through the ice, he slammed it down, leveraging his weight on his forearm. Gasping and grunting, he dragged his waterlogged body out of the rushing waters, crawling until he was lying fully on shore where he rested his cheek on the snow. The wind blew across his wet clothing, but he hardly felt it, barely felt anything at all. Something in the back of his numb brain told him that was a bad sign. A *very* bad sign.

Teeth clacking, body convulsing with shivers, Keith raised his head from the snow and saw he was on a riverbank. Looking down the shore, he watched the river bend around the woods, and he didn't see anything to show where he'd fallen in or how far the waters had carried him. His hands felt like ice blocks as he curled his fists and pushed himself to his knees, crawling sluggishly up the bank until he crested the edge of a snow-covered field. Getting one foot beneath him, he forced himself to stand, shivering against the gusting wind, shoulders slouched as he looked around. Behind him, the river passed under a bridge and the road leading from the bridge extended ahead of him with just some brush and trees separating them. Fifty yards distant, he spotted a hulking shadow bent forward in a ditch, one that was familiar to him through the fog in his mind.

With the faintest hint of a smile, Keith pushed through the snow-covered bushes and staggered down into the shallow gully. He tried to go slow and be careful, but alarm was growing in his brain. He was freezing, probably frostbitten beyond belief, and he wasn't feeling much in the way of pain, not even from his gunshot and stab wounds. His body was quickly approaching full-on hypothermia and was likely in shock. Warmth was paramount, and fast.

Climbing haltingly up the opposite bank, he finally reached the road. From there, it was another fight against the snowdrifts and whipping winds as he approached the hulking truck. Keith kept his eyes pinned on it, lifting his frozen feet and putting them down, one after the other. Yard after sluggish yard, he willed himself back to the truck. When he reached it, he saw the front end pitched downward, half buried in snow that rose to the rig's underbelly. It would be impossible to climb through the driver's side, so he circled the rear, noting the wheels and trailer hitch were covered in white, yet he could still reach the passenger door by scooting along the fuel tank until he came to the step.

Keith put his boot on the tank and hauled himself up, his soles slipping on the rounded, frozen metal. Face pressed against its cold surface, he worked his way along the truck's side, grabbing the exhaust pipe, swinging around until his toe touched the steps. He threw open the door and climbed inside, immediately falling into the driver's seat. Snow had piled up on the hood, some drifting in through the shattered front window. Back in the sleeper cabin, Keith stripped off all his wet clothes, his fingers barely cooperating, operating off of sheer force of will alone until he was bare, leaving his exposed skin pale and clammy.

Before he could get any colder, he bent and opened a drawer beneath the bed, revealing a stash of Tex's jeans, socks, underwear, and shirts. He layered up as much as he could, topping it off with a flannel shirt over several white T-shirts, then he pulled on a pair of beige work boots. Everything was too big, but that beat being too small, especially in his condition. Once he had every inch of his skin covered, he dug the key fob from his wet jeans and climbed into the driver's seat, holding the key up, hoping the water hadn't ruined it. If he could get the truck started, he could turn on the heaters and really get warm. Warmth was good. Necessary. Vital.

Reaching out, he inserted the key and turned it. The lights came on, but the engine growled once and died. "Damn," he mumbled, surprising himself with the far-off sound of his voice.

A second press of the button did nothing except cause him to shiver in the brutal cold. Flexing his hands in front of his face, he winced at the waxy, bluish tips of his fingers. They were numb and prickly, the first signs that his body was trying to conserve blood and heat for his vital organs. He glanced in the truck's side mirror and saw his nose had the same waxy look, tipped with white. Frostbite was setting in all over his body, from the tip of his nose right down to the tingling in his toes when he wiggled them.

Keith gave a frosty sigh, still shivering uncontrollably, realizing there'd be no more venturing outside and trudging through the snow until he warmed up, at least not unless he wanted to lose every finger and toe he had. As if that wasn't already a possibility, or a probability. The rage he'd been feeling toward the McKnights took a back seat to surviving the oncoming night. He had to live first. Life, then revenge.

He looked around for pieces of scrap paper on the floor, finding the vehicle documents and other paperwork in the glove compartment, hamburger wrappers beneath the seat. He piled it all on the sleeper bed and searched for a lighter, but Tex and Marge weren't smokers, and they didn't have anything that produced a flame. He caught sight of an auxiliary power outlet above the bed with a lighter adapter in it and pressed in the handle. Eight seconds later, it popped out and he pulled it from the socket and put the warm coils close to his face. It radiated heat across his cheeks, painful and burning, but necessary, and he drew strength from the pain, shifting it from aching hand to aching hand, trying to salvage what parts of him he could.

With a newfound sense of determination built on the smidgen of warmth, Keith shut the divider curtain between the sleeper cab and front seats and drew it tight, hoping to seal out the cold, then he sat on the bed with his back against the wall, dragging the covers over him. With the auxiliary outlet right by his shoulder, he reached back and pressed the handle in, holding it for a good thirty seconds before pulling it out. It was blazing hot, and he held it near his chest with his knees drawn up, rotating his left hand over it, feeling it bake across his fingertips, pain radiating through his hand and arm.

When the light cooled, he plugged it back in, coaxing another spark of warmth and light into the coils to warm his tingling fingers. After thirty minutes of pressing and pulling the plug, and passing it over his fingers, the tingling and numbness began to fade and he could make a strong fist. With the returning feeling came an intense ache beneath his fingernails, worse than the initial sharp pain but growing sharper by the moment, promising to be excruciating by the time he was done. Jaw clenched with determination, Keith switched and warmed up his right hand, staring at the lighter's simmering glow like a caveman held in thrall of his first small fire. He pulled the covers over his head to collect his breaths, then he took off his boots and socks but kept them under the covers in the warmth.

With his feet together, he ran the warm lighter above them, trying to bring them back to life. His right foot was the worst of the two, the bluish skin on his big toe completely consuming it. His left foot was almost perfectly fine, with no real damage other than a red discoloration that was fading beneath the cover's warmth, though as it grew warmer beneath the blankets, his gunshot wounds started aching, too. His left arm went numb twice, and he finally let it hang limp at his side as blood seeped into his clothes. His shoulder wasn't much better, the stab wounds deeper than he remembered and the muscles around his scapula and neck spasming uncomfortably. Still, he kept on inserting and removing the lighter over and over, working through the pain and agony, because that was all he could control. Warmth first. Recovery second. Then, the McKnights.

Over many hours of working with the lighter and shivering beneath the blankets, his core temperature finally rose, and more feeling returned to his extremities. With this new life came a sharp pain in every finger and toe joint, and his fingertips, in particular, were on fire. Any time he passed the warm lighter near them, it felt like he was plunging them into lava, yet he continued to work on thawing out, clenching his teeth against the delayed pain his body was registering.

It was sure to get worse before it got better, but at least he would survive the night, though at a great cost. He didn't know how long he'd spent in the frigid river, probably no more than a minute, but it had been a brutal minute, Keith punching at the ice in blind panic before busting through a thin patch. He'd still be floating in it, face-down, if not for that single bit of luck.

He sniffed and wiped snot from his nose with the back of his arm, wincing at the sharp rawness at the tip. Putting his palms to the sides of his head, he pressed his cold, fleshy earlobes against his warmer skin. They weren't frostbitten as far as he could tell, though they sang with the same cold pain as the rest of his body. Keith grabbed a pillow from next to him and pulled off the pillowcase, wrapping it around his head and tying it tight like a bandana. As he got warm, he thought about his mistakes over the last twenty-four hours. His first slip had been taking his eye off the McKnight woman for one second. Allowing himself to be distracted with the stuck truck and the winch had given her the opportunity she'd needed to break free. He should have known she'd be as wily and indignant as her husband.

Worse was the chase with the girl. He'd made several rookie mistakes that had culminated with him getting stabbed in the shoulder with the piece of glass and shot – twice, no less. It would never have happened if he'd just watched his back like he knew to do. He shook his head and crossed his arms over his chest, giving the lighter a rest as he shifted and grumbled on the mattress. A child. A child had tricked him onto the ice and plunged him into the river with a tossed log.

"That's *twice* you got the best of me. But it's the last time you make me look like a fool."

Keith steeled himself against the cold, taking courage that he'd get through the long night, finish his mission, and inflict revenge on those who'd played him.

* * *

After several sleepless hours filled with pain and misery, light chased away the darkness and brought a new day. Keith had started up with the lighter again before dark broke, going through the motions like a robot. Reach back. Press the knob. Hold for thirty seconds. Remove and pass the hot coils over his cold skin. He'd repeated it so many times he didn't need to even look.

His thoughts felt like rubber, bouncing around inside his head as sleep evaded him. There were vague recollections of what he planned on doing, though he couldn't bring himself to move from his spot beneath the covers. Hunger gnawed at his belly, but it was a lot easier to simply sit and cling to the little bit of warmth he had. He'd formed a tentative truce with the cold, and any slight change in the situation might send him on a downward spiral.

Something burning hot touched his left arm, ripping him from his stupor. He flinched, eyes flying open as he jerked the lighter off where he'd accidentally touched it to his wrist.

"Dammit!" He hissed, staring at the irritated skin, rubbing at it, happy to see there was no burn mark or blister. The lighter wasn't that hot, just enough to give him a harsh jolt. Keith pressed the adapter home, held it in, and pulled it out, flipping it around to see that the inner coils were hot, but the outer ones were not.

"Great," he murmured. "The battery is running down. Either that, or these coils are shot."

His fingertips radiated a fiery pain all through his right hand and wrist, and he realized he'd been gripping the adapter too hard. He put it back in its holder and slowly drug himself from his cocoon. Peeling back the divider curtain, he climbed into the driver's seat, looking for something to eat. In the center console, he found a half-eaten chocolate bar and a quarter bottle of cola and he ate and drank mechanically, occasionally glancing at his oddly colored fingers. His hands didn't even feel like his own anymore, just a pair of pain-filled appendages someone had stuck on the ends of his arms. He compartmentalized it, shoving the agony into a box and closing the lid tight, then pushed it to the edge of his consciousness and started to think of it as more of an inconvenience than anything. He'd lose a couple fingers, that was a given, but it was something he was coming to grips with. In the end, he'd be fine, so long as he learned from his mistakes.

He took the last bite of the candy bar, letting the piece warm in his mouth so it wasn't such an ice cube. As the sweet chocolate settled on his tongue, Keith turned his head and looked outside, eyes widening at what he'd just missed. A pair of horses were walking by behind him, already reaching the bridge and were passing over the river. While the riders were bundled in layers of clothes, he could tell they were two completely different sizes. The one on the left was an average man with broad shoulders and the other was a much slighter form, probably a girl or older teen. A sled dragged behind one horse, packed with supplies and a covered lump Keith swore he saw move. His eyes narrowed as he watched them, possibilities forming in his head.

It can't be. Can it?

Once Tom and Sam found his note, Keith had fully expected them to take roughly the same highways south to Asheville. Had they left at the same time, he might have even expected to run into them, but not out in some random backwater town. Still, he should be in Asheville already, not stuck out on the road, and the delay could have easily given Tom and Sam time to catch up. Keith hadn't checked the entire farm, though he knew they had animals on the property and it wasn't out of the question that they could have saddled up a pair of horses and set out at a brisk pace. In fact, the horses would have come in handy in the long run, making it much easier to navigate the rough, snowy terrain. The lump behind them confused him, until Keith remembered hearing a dog pawing at the laundry room door while he was burning the McKnight home down.

That mutt survived?

He shook his head, his breathing coming faster as he watched the figures ride out of sight. No, it most likely *was* the dog. And those two... They were Tom and Sam McKnight, delivered up to him on the silver platter of sheer chance, giving him an opportunity to redeem himself, to make up for his disastrous failures. His expression lit up, and a rush of adrenaline fired in his veins. Keith clicked the rig's start button and watched the dashboard lights come on, then he flipped the CB radio on and grabbed the mic. It was already set to the military band he needed, so he raised the mic to his mouth, hoping he was in range to get the operator.

"This is 3-ECHO-DANNY-APPLE-4-1. I need authorization on secure band 2-4-7-9-2. Please acknowledge."

Three seconds passed before the reply came through the CB speaker. "Acknowledged, Arrowhead. This is the military switchboard. Please provide the security response."

The number popped into Keith's head like the keys to the kingdom, and he rattled off the sequence with anxious delight bordering on mania.

There was a pause before she came back. "That is the correct code. How can I direct you?"

"I need to speak to Lieutenant Colonel Rachel Banks of the United States Navy."

"Please hold for Colonel Banks. It may take some time to reach her."

Keith growled on the line, the pain from holding the CB mic fueling him. "This is an emergency, so hurry up. I don't have a lot of battery life left."

"Understood, sir."

Keith waited patiently, his fingers and toes still throbbing at the edge of his mind. He glanced into the side mirror to see his nose had backed off its waxy whiteness and had returned to a semi-normal color. Keeping his nose was a big win, and he was feeling confident there'd be many more wins to come. Sure, he'd lose a few fingers and maybe even his big toe, but he wouldn't allow anything to get in his way. He waited a good three minutes before a voice spoke over the CB speaker.

"This is Banks. Where the hell are you, Arrowhead?"

"Good to hear your voice, too." Keith sneered.

There was an angry pause before Banks continued in a hard-clipped tone. "I repeat, where the *hell* are you?"

"I'm on Highway 19 stuck in a rig in North Carolina, but that's not the important part."

Banks virtually shouted through the CB speaker. "Arrowhead, what's the status of Tom McKnight and his family?"

Keith grinned, basking in the commander's rage. "All you need to know is that Tom McKnight and his daughter are inbound to the FOB in Asheville."

There was a pause, and the voice quieted on the other end. "How do you know this?"

"I guess you could say I put them on the right path."

"You actually saw them?"

"Yeah, I saw them not five minutes ago, but there's a lot more you need to know." Keith worked his jaw back and forth, readying his delivery. His plan depended on it. "Send me a pickup and I'll tell you everything when I get back to base."

"That's going to be a tough request, Arrowhead. I've got every chopper occupied with work, and the FOB will be moving soon."

"Well, that's too bad for you, Lieutenant Colonel." He spoke the title with dripping sarcasm. "You don't know how many he's brought with him or what direction he's coming from. I repeat, send a pick up, and together we'll bring him in without a fight."

"Like you've so masterfully done up to now?"

"He's heading your way, Banks. I'm just asking to help finish this peacefully without him destroying the base."

"What makes you think he can do that?"

"I've seen the briefings and I've seen him firsthand. You know as well as I do what he's capable of." Keith nodded and grinned, certain he was about to get his way. "You need me to finish this and bring him around. Everyone's survival depends upon it."

Another pause followed Keith's last word. "Okay, I'll send a chopper along nineteen until we spot your rig. We'll pick you up there."

The call abruptly ended, leaving him sitting alone once more. He rested back with a sigh, flexing his fists as pain radiated from his ice-cube fingers up through his wrists. His left arm was one big, aching throb, and his right shoulder still twitched from being repeatedly stabbed by the McKnight women. That wasn't counting all the other aches and pains that had taken a backseat to the really big ones. Sure, he was going to lose some digits, and probably the ability to perform mundane tasks like hold a cup or write, but as long as he could pull the trigger on a gun, he'd survive. Keith tucked his hands against his belly in anticipation of a warm room back at base with an actual heating unit inside. He was curious to hear what the doctor would say about his frostbite, and he wouldn't bat an eye when they ordered the amputations. It would bring an end to the nagging pain, and a new beginning for him.

Chapter 14
Barbara McKnight
Somewhere in Tennessee

Barbara's eyes snapped open and she sat up with a groan. She'd been dreaming of being in bed at home, so waking up in a chair with daylight filtering in was momentarily disorienting. Looking up at the vaulted ceiling, a spike of panic struck her in the brain and she remembered.

They were holed up in an old house in a town with no name, there was a madman on the loose, and he wanted to capture them and take them back to a base to be used as leverage against her husband. The madman had burned down their home and killed their friends and he could be in the house with—no, that wasn't right.

"I shouldn't have fallen asleep," she murmured, shifting, brain foggy, trying to straighten and remember what had happened the previous day and night.

Barbara rose from the chair but promptly sat again as pain pinched at her side and leg. It wasn't debilitating, but it hurt like nobody's business, and it brought to mind the injuries she'd sustained in the truck wreck, then their process of trudging through the snow to hole up in a random house where they'd built a fire. She shifted her eyes to the crackling fireplace, watching the smoldering coals as they radiated heat. Not only had they built a fire, but Linda had brought back food, and they'd had a meager meal of snacks. Craning her neck around the chair, she spotted her kids sleeping safely in the big master bed, safe from… Keith.

Relief flooded through her as it all came back. Linda had drowned him in a freezing cold river the previous day. He wouldn't be looking for them anymore, nor would he be in the house with them. They were safe. Barbara settled back with a relieved sigh and a smile, her panic subsiding for the moment, and one of the kids stirred beneath the covers, Linda poking her head out, her thick brown hair tousled and sticking out.

A smile stretched her lips. "Hi, Mom."

"Hi, baby. Did you sleep okay?"

Linda shrugged and swung her legs off the bed. "Not really. I had bad dreams. But at least it was warm and cozy. Jack is such a *heater*."

"Tell me about it," Barbara chuckled. "When he was smaller, he always wanted to sleep with me and your father. But he was so hot, he practically ran us out every night. We couldn't wait until he slept in his own bed."

Linda hopped off the bed and padded over in her bare feet to give her a hug.

"Help me stand, will you?"

"Sure."

Barbara threw her right arm around Linda's shoulders and rose from the chair. After a few experimental steps across the room, she turned and came back.

"How's it feel?" Linda asked.

"It hurts like a son of a gun, but I can deal with it."

"Let me check for signs of infection."

Barbara rested back so Linda could check, pulling apart the ripped jeans and the bandage to inspect the gash with her flashlight. "Doesn't look infected to me."

"Yeah, it's pretty clean. Thanks."

"No problem." Linda put the bandage back in place and gave her mother a faint pat on the leg before bending to inspect her socks which lay next to the fire, putting her palms on them. "Ah, warm and dry." She scooped them up with a smile, sat in the other chair, and pulled them on her feet. "What are we going to do now? Still want to try and meet Dad and Sam at the FOB?"

"Yes, I still think that's the best bet for us, unless something changes." Barbara bit her lip. "It's probably close enough for us to walk to. Of course, we'll pick up a car or truck on the way if we can. My bum leg's going to make for slow going."

Linda grabbed the fire poker, placing the end into the smoldering coals, shoving them around, inducing a fresh wave of heat before she reached for two pieces of wood and leaned them against each other in the fire so they stood upright. "What about the eighteen-wheeler?" she asked. "Think it's still running?"

Barbara shook her head. "Probably not. We hit the ditch pretty hard, and it would be a waste of time trying to get it started. But maybe this house has a car we can borrow."

"Hey, great idea!"

"Well, sorta." Barbara tilted her head side to side. "If they do have a car, it just means we have to drive through that crazy snow out there."

"Oh yeah… there's that."

Waving off Linda's offer of help, Barbara reached down and grabbed her own socks and boots and quietly put them on, then shoved herself to her feet. "Why don't you get some breakfast ready for your brother, and I'll go check for a vehicle?"

"You sure you can walk?"

"Don't have much of a choice, do I?" Barbara smiled. "But yes, I'm sure."

"Okay, sounds good."

Barbara flashed her sleeping son a fond smile as she hobbled past him and exited the master bedroom. Her arms and legs groaned with stiffness, knees creaking as she moved along the hall. For the first quarter of the walk, she held her hands out with her palms against the wall to keep her balance, though she quickly gained confidence as her legs stabilized, blood flow returning to her extremities after a long night of intermittent rest. She took the stairs down to the first floor, carefully going one at a time.

In the daylight, the house was different than it had seemed at night when she was exhausted and in severe pain, an average home but in good condition. The walls were straight, the roof intact, and the hardwood floors creaked a little, but still in good condition. In the living room, snow was piled up against the windows outside, the drifts standing three or four feet high. The place was quiet, the snow holding them in a soft embrace, muffling all sound from outside. Barbara stepped into the kitchen and looked around. The cabinets were a newer cherry color, and the stainless-steel appliances were spotless. Still, it was a small place, and they didn't have a breakfast nook or very much counter space to work with. Moving past the pantry, she found the door to the garage and pushed it open to see light filtering in through the frosted garage door windows, giving her just enough to walk by.

She stood and absorbed the quiet as her eyes adjusted. The faint smells of oil and dust came from somewhere off to the side, and racks and shelves filled with gas cans and tools rested against the back wall. A net was bolted to the ceiling that held basketballs and other toys and, in the center of the garage, two cars sat side by side. One was a beige sedan, the other a black Jeep with an open top, no doors, and giant, knobby tires. The Jeep looked like the kind of off-road vehicle she'd often seen on the road with mud slapped along its sides after the owners had taken it for a joyride on the trails and Barbara gasped, hardly believing her luck.

With a hobbling gait between the cars, she slipped into the Jeep's driver's seat, placing her hands on the wheel, the rough leather firm beneath her palms. "This will be *perfect*," she murmured to herself. "After a few modifications, of course."

A distant sound drew her attention away from checking out the Jeep, a thumping, chuffing sound growing from somewhere outside. Brow narrowed with curiosity, Barbara limped to the garage door and found the cord for the manual release. Giving it a tug, she popped it and raised it two inches, then she took the handle, slowly lifting it as snow swirled in and whipped across her boots. She bent, groaning as her leg twinged, and stepped outside, the wind skirting around her legs, sending cold tendrils up her pants and shirt. Arms folded across her chest, she raised her chin to the sky.

The distant noise she'd heard grew louder, the unmistakable thumping of helicopter blades, though she couldn't tell where it was coming from. She searched the stoic gray clouds for signs of the aircraft, craning her neck around, ducking and peering through breaks in the tree branches to catch sight of it, certain it was close. To see it, she'd have to leave the relative safety of the garage and, figuring it would only be a few minutes, Barbara picked up her feet and stepped into the taller drifts, boots plunging deep as she trudged down the driveway.

When she still couldn't see the helicopter, she circled through the yard and around the side of the house where there were no trees. She stood in the snow, looking up at the gray sky, the cold about to make her give up when the aircraft finally moved into her field of vision.

"There you are," she mumbled, taking another step forward, eyes narrowed.

It hovered above the tree line, less than a quarter mile away, rotors spinning in a blur. She wasn't an expert in aircraft, though she'd seen enough TV to know it wasn't a bubble-shaped commercial helicopter. Its squat profile, gray color, and wide side doors screamed military, and if it was military, it meant they could be rescued.

Barbara took her pistol from her waistband and pointed it at the sky, about to squeeze the trigger and fire off a shot to get their attention when a paranoid nagging in the back of her mind stopped her. *What's a military helicopter doing out here in the middle of nowhere?*

It could be on a reconnaissance mission or other task, but something about it bugged her, the way it turned and then suddenly dipped toward the ground making her think there was purpose in its landing. She looked across the backyard where their footprints had long since vanished, imagining the trail beyond through the trees to the distant buildings she'd run through with the kids, settling on a place beyond that where the chopper appeared to be landing. It had to be going for the eighteen-wheeler.

Maybe they'd randomly spotted the rig from the sky, knew it was Keith's, and were trying to recover something from it, but a sense of dread grew like a balloon in her stomach, and a horrible thought entered her mind. What if it was Keith himself they were recovering? If he'd somehow survived being dunked in the river, climbed out soaking wet, and made it back to the rig, he could have radioed for help and brought in support from the FOB. That would, in turn, mean that those on the helicopter would decidedly *not* be friendly.

"Just friggin' great." Barbara shook her head and lowered her pistol before hurriedly limping back inside, pulling the garage door down behind her and calling out to Linda as she climbed to the second floor.

Linda greeted her halfway down the hall with a wide-eyed expression, hair still tousled on her shoulders. "What is it, Mom?"

Barbara's eyes were wide as she put a hand on Linda's shoulder. "Are you *sure* Keith is dead?"

Linda nodded vigorously but switched to shaking her head. "I mean, I'm not positive. I didn't see him die. But I saw him go under! There was a big splash, and he was waving his arms around and then the water bubbled up over the surface. Then he was gone."

"How far were you offshore?"

"Probably thirty or forty yards. We were *way* out there. I had to run back to avoid the cracks from after he fell in."

Barbara bit her lip, thinking, listening as the helicopter suddenly grew louder. She went into the master bedroom and crossed to the back window, standing to the side and splitting the blinds with her fingers. The helicopter rose above the nearby trees and banked their way, a gun barrel hanging off the craft's nose, pointed directly at them as it swept in. A pit formed in her stomach as she imagined the guns sparking like fireworks followed by the terrible sounds of bullets slamming into the house, but they didn't, and the helicopter buzzed right over them, sending a shudder of relief up Barbara's spine as the windows rattled briefly from the sound of the craft's engine. Quietly closing the blinds, she turned back into the room where Linda had been watching from behind her, looking up at her mother with wide, frightened eyes.

"You don't think that was..." She trailed off.

Barbara shook her head and shrugged. "I don't know for sure, but I'm fairly sure that helicopter came to pick up Keith."

"But *how*?" Linda's voice rose to a strained pitch, and she curled her fists at her sides, very much looking like a little girl again. "I'm telling you, Mom, it was so cold out there. And we'd been running around for two hours. He didn't have gloves *or* a hat on. He had to be way colder than me. I just don't know how he could have survived being in the water!"

Barbara reached out and put her arms around her daughter, drawing her closer. "Hey, hey. It's okay, sweetie. I believe you, okay? And I don't know how anyone could have survived it either. Maybe he had some training to help him or just got plain lucky. Either way, I want to be a hundred percent sure if it was him or not."

Linda broke from her embrace and backed away. "How are you going to do that?"

"Get your brother up. We need to go check something."

After she woke Jack, they had a quick breakfast of beef jerky, water, and packs of mixed nuts, Barbara and Linda each drinking a small can of coffee before she had the kids pack the rest of the food into her daughter's backpack and coat pockets. They grabbed all the blankets they could carry down to the garage, and Linda's face lit up when she saw the Jeep.

"Cool!!" Jack shouted with glee, resting his hand on the vehicle's knobby wheels with a gleeful expression, the Jeep looking for all intents and purposes like a giant version of a toy he might have gotten for Christmas.

"Don't get too excited yet," she warned, "I haven't even started it. I have no idea if it runs."

They piled the blankets on the floor while Barbara went in search of the keys. It only took her a moment to find the Jeep key fob hanging from a rack in the kitchen, and she headed back to the garage and slipped into the driver's seat, said a silent prayer, and pressed the "Start" button on the Jeep's console. No lights came on, and the engine didn't so much as burp. Barbara's lips twisted, then she bent and pulled the hood release with a pop. At the front of the truck, she lifted the hood and set the prop arm to keep it open.

"What's wrong with it?" Linda asked, coming up and looking in from the side.

"Let's see..." Barbra's looked over the engine bay, searching for something easy that might explain the complete lack of response.

"Ah! Battery cable's disconnected."

She limped to the tool bench and chose a pair of five-sixteenth-inch wrenches and carried them to the Jeep, then placed the loose battery cable on the positive terminal and used the wrenches to tighten the bolt.

"Is it going to start now?" Linda asked.

"I sure hope so," Barbara sighed. "Push the button for me?"

Linda climbed into the driver's seat and hit the "Start" button again, the dashboard lights responding instantly, the engine smoothly rolling into an idle.

"Awesome!" Linda exclaimed.

"Not so awesome," Barbara countered as she came around to side and tapped on the dashboard.

"What do you mean?"

"We've just over a quarter tank of fuel left. We'll be lucky to drive for an hour before we have to stop."

Standing next to her door, Jack pointed back at one of the shelves. "What about these cans? Isn't that gas?"

Barbara cut off the engine and got out, following her son to the rear of the garage where he grinned up at her and patted one of four five-gallon Jerry cans lined up in a neat row. They were all red, though one was marked "kerosene" in bold black writing. She pulled each of them out to test their weight, pleased to find them all more than half full.

"They should work except for the one that says kerosene." She ruffled her son's hair affectionately. "Nice work, Jack."

Using two cans to top off the Jeep's tank, she left spare fuel in the last two, placing them in the back of the Jeep, then stood back to look at the open top, sides and back of the vehicle.

"We're going to have to cover it, right?" Linda asked. "That's what the blankets are for?"

"That's right. I'd like to cut down on some of the wind we're going to be dealing with, if at all possible." Barbara tapped her finger against her chin. "If we can find some duct tape, there's enough framework to secure the blankets tightly. It should help keep the worst of the cold out. So, let's look for tape."

The kids scrambled around, rifling through the toolboxes and drawers, racing each other as they often did.

Barbara found a roll of black tape hanging from a peg and held it up. "Score!"

"Me, too!" Jack quickly added, holding his prize of silver tape high.

"That's enough to get started," Barbara said.

They spread two thin sheets over the entire roof, taping one to the top edge of the front windshield and pulling it tight toward the back. The other they secured to the rear seat frame and stretched it to cover the truck bed, fixing it to the tailgate. A pair of comforters were laid over the sheet and taped to the front and back, respectively, then they fastened the blankets to the sides wherever it had a framework to attach to, leaving just a few inches open at the bottoms of the doors so that they could squeeze in and out. Pulling a plastic tarp down from a shelf, they stretched it over the blankets and taped it over the top as a final layer. When they were done, Barbara stood back and checked her handiwork. They'd taped everything tight, which should hold in some precious heat and help protect the kids from any stormy weather that might hit them.

"Okay. Now, you two head upstairs and grab all the extra clothes you can find, preferably stuff that fits you or larger. Be back here in ten minutes."

They ran up and brought down a half closet worth of garments, a collection of hats and gloves, jackets and even an adult men's Super Workman's jacket which Barbara immediately slipped her arms into.

"Alright," she jerked her chin at the Jeep. "Pile in and start bundling up."

While the kids got ready, she raised the garage door all the way and let in the icy wind, then pulled her coat tighter around her and lifted the sheet to get behind the wheel, taping the sheet's bottom edge around the door frame from the inside to keep out the worst of the cold. After starting the Jeep for a second time, she stared at the daunting snow covering the driveway all the way to the street. Barbara turned the heat on full blast, hoping most of it stayed inside their makeshift cab, then she moved the gear shift into the four-wheel-drive position and pulled out.

At first, she went slowly, hesitant to move forward at any significant speed as the Jeep's front end lifted and twisted over the drifts, moving to the end of the driveway. They exited the driveway into the cul-de-sac, passing four other homes before reaching the street, bouncing harshly over the harder ice blocks but plowing through the snowdrifts like they were nothing. The steering was tight and responsive, the tires clinging to the road with remarkable traction, not sliding nearly as badly as the APC she'd driven home from the Army camp.

Barbara slowly gained confidence, and by the time they reached the main road, she was comfortable doing double digits. She took a left and pressed the gas, shooting snow out from behind them as they shot forward, the kids sitting bundled and buckled up as heat filled their makeshift cabin. Snow and icy gusts flew in beneath the gaps in the sheets, but it stayed mostly warm thanks to the multiple layers, and the generous amounts of tape kept the blankets and plastic in place, though they flapped around quite a bit.

Barbara focused on where she remembered the rig to be, trying to triangulate the road layout in her mind. After a quarter mile, she came to what she thought must be the main highway because it was so wide. Off to her right was a bridge and back to her left she spotted the truck buried, nose first, in the ditch. She pulled onto the highway and made for the vehicle, more curious by the minute to see if Keith had actually returned. Foot on the brake, she slowed as she approached, eyes narrowed and looking for movement.

"Do you see him, Mom?" Linda's voice quivered with apprehension, her memories of Keith pursuing her coming into sharp focus.

"I don't see him, but there are a lot of footprints." Barbara stared at the disturbed snow around the truck. "And I see the huge dusting of snow where the helicopter set down."

"Well, maybe you don't have to get out then," she suggested. "We can just keep driving."

"One second." Barbara put the Jeep in park and climbed out, plunging into snow that rose past her knees, working her way around to the rig's passenger side.

The door was open, though she didn't hear anyone inside and, doing her best not to re-injure her leg, she climbed carefully on the fuel tank, stepped on the side rail, and came to the door. Falling into the cabin with her left knee on the passenger seat, she leaned forward, reading the story of what'd happened. On the sleeper bed was a human-shaped cluster of covers and pillows, and further inspection showed a discarded cigarette lighter lying near the foot of the bed, along with traces of blood smeared on the blankets and mattress.

"You're a smart cookie when you want to be," she commented under her breath. "Just a pity you had to be *this* smart."

Seeing nothing else of interest, Barbara backed out of the truck and stepped carefully back the way she'd come. She trudged to the Jeep and climbed inside to settle behind the wheel, dusting off her lap and checking to make sure her bandages were still on, her leg throbbing with a dull pain, but feeling remarkably good all things considered.

Linda leaned forward with her hands on the back of her seat. "Is it true, Mom? Is he alive?"

"I… I'm afraid so," Barbara replied, and told the kids what she'd seen in the rig.

"Jeez." Linda looked crestfallen. "I thought I'd gotten rid of him."

"Hey, you should be happy to be alive yourself." She reached back and rubbed her knit cap. "That guy is pretty tough."

"I guess so," Linda shrugged. "So, where to now?"

"Well, we need to keep going to the FOB."

"But won't Keith be there?"

"Maybe, but if he gave up looking for us, it must mean something's up with your father and sister."

"That means we need to get there yesterday, right?"

"Exactly. Now, buckle up, please."

Barbara put the Jeep in drive and pulled out, rumbling over the frozen ground as Linda sat back and buckled herself in next to her brother, the wind whipping against the blankets and tarps, making them flap against the frame of the vehicle.

"But what are we going to do when we get there?" Linda pressed. "I mean, what if they try to hurt Dad and Sam? How're we going to help them?"

"Don't worry," Barbara said with a glance back at the pair, smiling at them with a confidence that was half real, half bluster. "We just need to get inside, and we'll figure the rest out."

Chapter 15
Tom McKnight
Rybachiy Nuclear Submarine Base, Russia
The Past

The rickety cargo plane rattled and shook like a cold, wet puppy in the gusting, turbulent squalls. It flew low over a strange coastline, trundling southwest, the alarmingly sharp scent of burning oil wafting heavily through the cabin. The engines sputtered and spat in protest as they struggled to hold a steady course while outside, rain-slicked rock faces and stormy, wave-swept waters flew by far too close for comfort, a sobering reminder of what an engine failure could lead to.

Tom sat in the crew section in the fuselage, on the floor with the rest of the SEALs and their gear. Commander Osaka sat to his right, staring at nothing in particular, not once flinching whenever the plane hit a pocket of turbulent air, including when the engines gave a long shudder as they strained to maintain altitude against a ferocious gust.

"You guys really need to upgrade your transportation." Tom spoke in a near shout to be heard over the engine noise.

Osaka scoffed loudly. "Are you kidding? This is first class for a SEAL team."

"Feels worse than economy class," Tom replied with a smirk.

"Don't worry, we just need it to get us there and back, which is well within its capacity. And the more we look like an old cargo plane, the better."

"Old cargo plane," Tom shouted. "Got it. Still, it'll be a waste if the engines crap out over the North Pacific and everyone drowns."

"Don't worry, my friend," Osaka patted him hard on the shoulder, chuckling, "we'll be fine. Now, do you want to keep bellyaching or do you want to know the details of the mission?"

Tom nodded, swallowing a lump in his throat. "Yeah, let's find out what fresh hell I just got myself into. Go ahead."

Osaka brought up a tablet linked to the team's mini network. He tapped on the shiny surface and pulled up an overhead map of a curved piece of land with a red dot inching along the coastline. "That red dot is us, and we're flying along Russia's Eastern Seaboard."

Tom reached over, put his finger on the map's surface, and slid it up to show the land farther south of them. They were near the southwest portion of the curve, heading for a deep bay with a narrow inlet. A series of small towns connected by glowing white roads dotted the edges of the ten-mile-wide bay. Tom wasn't an expert in geography, but he'd seen enough mission maps of the general region to know where they were.

"That's Rybachiy, Russia." Tom's stomach squeezed itself, and he squirmed in his seat. "Isn't that a Russian base?"

"Nuclear submarine base, to be exact," Osaka replied smartly. "Our current assault target."

Tom shook his head incredulously. "You actually think we can make it past Russian radar and assault a Russian base in a piece of junk like this?"

"It's better than dropping in on a military plane."

"Oh, really?" Tom raised an eyebrow. "You sure about that?"

"The Russians have six radar installations in the area, but we're on a course that should give us the lowest possible profile along a known cargo route. Even if they do see us, they'll think we're on a routine flight and our engines are crap, or that we're trying to smuggle something in which case we just bribe them."

"And I assume our pilots speak Russian in case someone calls us from the local radio towers?"

"That's right."

"Well, I guess that explains why we haven't been shot out of the sky yet." Tom eased back in his seat. "Go on."

"The intel we got from the last two missions confirmed they're about to deploy an advanced vessel from the Rybachiy base." Osaka zoomed in on the area where the target base sat on a slip of land that curved inland from the bay's southern point and Tom saw a scattering of buildings dispersed through the jungle on top of a plateau. "We'll be assaulting the base before the sub gets a chance to launch."

Tom shook his head again, eyes narrowed as he tried to work things out. "But why am I here? I'd be no help on a strictly combat mission like this." He gazed at the heavily armed figures sitting around him. "Sure, I hit a couple targets last time, but I'm not even a grunt, much less a SEAL."

"Normally, you'd be right. But you're here because of *that*." Osaka nodded to a large black crate in the back of the cargo area by the bay door, strapped in with canvas netting. "It's something you've never driven before."

Tom stared at the sleek looking box, about five-feet long and three-feet deep, unmarked but for silver handles with rubber grips. "What's that?"

"It's a Mariner rover, and you'll be piloting it."

Tom snorted derisively. "What's new about that, Osaka? I drove Mariners on the last two missions."

The commander smiled widely. "This one is a Mariner II."

"Oh." Tom blinked several times. "You got a prototype Mariner II?"

"You got it."

"What's it got on board?

"The II is sleeker and faster. It's got multiple ultra-high-definition cameras and improved LED lighting and its wider array of pressure-balanced thrusters work together to provide flawless maneuvering and the manipulators are unmatched. Or so says the advertisement, anyway."

"Same controllers?"

"Yes, though I'm told the responsiveness is uncanny. They say it will stop on a dime."

"Okay, that sounds pretty impressive." Tom scratched his head.

"The manipulators are stronger and more sensitive, made from a new lightweight metal. It's got better sensors, and it'll update regarding sea temperature, pressure, and depth every second. It's wireless, too. Completely untethered."

"What's powering it?"

"Lithium-ion batteries, enough for up to five hours of continuous work," Osaka said, winking at him. "No more cables for you to worry about getting tangled up in."

Tom shook his head and reflexively squeezed his hands into fists, wanting to test the controllers. "I have to admit, it sounds fun to drive. But what if we lose contact with it? What if we can't bring it back up?"

"The transmission equipment is top-of-the-line. It communicates on a hard-coded, secure channel using a new type of underwater transmitter. It will give you limitless freedom." The commander tilted his head. "And if we do lose connection, it's programmed to find its way out and return to the surface on its own."

"Okay, you've won me over. What do you want me to do?"

"You'll be planting explosive charges on the new sub while some of us create a distraction inside the base. It'll be a quick, in-and-out strike before aerial reinforcements can be mustered from Aerodrome Mengon way north of us."

Tom nodded. "Why don't you guys plant the charges manually? You know, swim into the docking bay?"

"It's too risky. The area is pretty confined and there's no way we can get a team inside through the water without them being detected. There's also a chance the sub might try to make an emergency exit, or be parked elsewhere." Osaka gave him a confident grin. "That's why command operations opted for a land-based insertion and the rover. It's faster and more agile than any diver we can put in the water, especially with you driving it, and we'll be able to secure our flank against reinforcements to buy you time to do your magic."

Tom leaned back, looking up to the plane's sidewall where chains and securing levers rattled, mulling the details about the mission over in his head before looking back over to Osaka. "I'll need to concentrate this time. I can't have bullets flying over my head if I'm planting explosives."

"You'll be safe. Shouldn't have any direct contact with Russian soldiers."

Tom took a deep breath and nodded, believing Osaka meant what he said, though he knew from experience that things seldom went as planned. He thought about Barbara and the kids, and part of him wished he'd been more adamant in turning Banks down. He could've been on a flight home to Virginia, not stuck in a rickety rust bucket of a cargo plane. None of that mattered anymore, though. He was committed and there was no turning back. The best course of action was to focus on his job and ensure the mission went off without a hitch.

* * *

Several hours later, Tom grunted, staggered, and regained his footing on the edge of the muddy road as he and a SEAL hauled the rover crate, following the others. It was cold and dark as they carried their awkward burden along a dirt road, Tom's gloved right hand continuing to slip on the rubber handle grip, and he put his knee beneath it to keep it from falling. The SEAL shot him a derisive look over the top of the crate, and Tom adjusted his grip and nodded. The outskirts of the Rybachiy facility were close, though he didn't know just how far, so he focused on his breathing and keeping the valuable machine he carried from hitting the ground.

Part of the team pushed through the undergrowth on either side of the road, on the hunt for patrols while others crept along the curve ahead of them where they disappeared around a cluster of trees. The distant soft pops of suppressed rifle fire occasionally reached his ears followed by surprised grunts and cut-off screams as small assassinations played out in the forest's undergrowth. The SEALs were killing fast and hard, giving no quarter to the enemy and leaving no trace of their presence besides the bodies in their wake. His nerves danced beneath his skin, and it was a good thing he was helping to carry the rover, because it burned off much of his nervous energy.

Around the curve, he spotted a gate where several dark forms gathered. One was Osaka, and he quickly split the lock with bolt cutters while a pair of bodies were being dragged off into the bushes. Tom caught the faint scent of gunpowder drifting from the forest as the team slowly crept out of the brush and joined them at the gate. Osaka issued quiet commands before he pushed through and led them inside, following one of several discrete dirt paths cut through the jungle trees and bushes leading away from the fence and toward the buildings ahead.

Each of the paths divided clusters of gray-sided warehouses with aluminum-shaded lights hanging over the doors, and smaller sheds sat between them. A wide, flat building squatted in the center of it all, looking like a headquarters of sorts, and to the right of the plateau was an abrupt drop from a cliff face a thousand feet to the water below. Osaka signaled to the SEAL team, and the group fanned out on the paths, slipping between the buildings like shadows. Once they had dispersed, he moved closer to Tom and gestured for him to relinquish his hold on the crate. Tom traded spots with Osaka as more suppressed pops filled the air and the guards were neutralized, though the distant crash of waves in the bay and the vibrations below his feet disguised them, giving away the heavy machinery beneath them.

As they crept along the path with the crate, Osaka spoke softly. "Okay, the base is immediately below us. There's the underwater entrance, but we're going to use the headquarters to reach it."

Wiping sweat from his brow, Tom drew his pistol and followed close behind them. "What does the building have to do with us getting inside?"

Osaka angled them along the dirt path to the right. "There's a secret stairwell in the rear, so get ready to fight. We *think* the upper base is lightly guarded, but it's impossible to know the strength of the force underground."

"I thought this was a quick in and out type of deal, Osaka." Tom edged closer to the man.

"It's been quick so far and still will be. Just giving you a heads up in case things go pear-shaped. Get me?"

Tom nodded and kept his feet moving, keeping in a crouch as he moved behind them, eyes roving to pick out enemy targets in the shadows. They stopped twenty yards in front of the headquarters, and two SEALs slipped inside. Another series of subdued pops reached them before the commander jerked his chin toward the doors and Tom sprinted ahead and held the doors wide while they carried the crate inside, being careful not to bump it against the frame. They entered a typical office area with computer terminals and cubicles, overhead maps of the area hanging on a side wall next to a dry erase board with Russian words scrawled across it.

The SEALs moved between a pair of desks, and he caught a glimpse of two other men dragging more bodies toward the right-hand wall. He tore his eyes away from the bloody scene and focused on keeping close to the leader and their precious cargo. Osaka paused at the head of a long hallway with a series of doors on both sides. Head tilted, he listened.

"What's wrong?" Tom whispered.

The commander remained quiet for a handful of seconds before he turned to look at the others. "I expected the facility to have only a few guards on the surface, but this seems *way* too light."

"Light?! You guys have been killing nonstop since we got here!" Osaka ignored the remark, and Tom sighed, muttering to himself. "Okay. Too light. Great. Love hearing that."

The rest of the team filtered into the offices, and Osaka waited until they were assembled to continue. The SEALs alternated moving farther into the building, moving in groups, one pair holding doors open while others slipped ahead to check for guards. In the office at the end of the hall, they found themselves in front of a steel door embedded in a thick concrete wall. Osaka and his partner set the crate down, and the commander moved to the center of the room, flipping open a section of his tactical suit's chest piece to view his computer tablet. Tom stood by as the commander reviewed the data on his screen, his angular features lit up by the digital glow. His eyes flared upward, looking around, before he went back to the tablet, sweat dripping down his temples. The SEALs remained perfectly quiet, standing by the windows and doors, peeking outside for signs of trouble while they waited for their next orders. The tension in the room grew, thickening around Tom in a stifling grip, and after thirty seconds of laborious thought, Osaka finally gestured to a soldier.

"Go ahead, hack it."

The man strode to the steel door and used a tool to pop the face off the keypad, then removed an electronic device from a satchel on his belt and connected it to the keypad using a series of wires. The entire time, Osaka shot concerned glances toward the exit, only once giving Tom a look he couldn't read. A high-pitched beep went off, and the lock on the steel door popped. The man who'd busted in swung it wide, and several SEALs filed inside, rifles raised to their shoulders. Osaka and his partner lifted the crate and followed behind them, silent as ghosts, with Tom right on their heels. They stood at the top of a dimly lit stairwell that wound down around a core of concrete, the steps rubber-coated, stretched wide enough to hold several people and cargo, giving the team plenty of room to operate.

"Stenborn, stay up here and cover our descent," Osaka ordered, and one of the men nodded and stepped back into the office.

The rest proceeded downward with a handful out in front leading the way, staying close to the inner wall, moving like quiet specters. Tom watched from the center of the pack, body tense as he crept carefully to avoid making scuffling sounds in the darkness, avoiding any mistakes that might give them away. They stopped every few steps to wait for the soldiers on point to clear potential guards or alarms, Tom swallowing dry as hard-fought battles played out on the steps below him. There came grunts, tussling sounds, and stifled cries, making his stomach clench with nausea.

After each fight, they moved on. Tom glanced down as they passed bodies lying against the inner wall in pools of blood. Once, the soldier who'd hacked the keypad was called up to dismantle a laser alarm that was sending crisscross patterns of red lights across their path. As the man crept between the lasers to a control panel and began working on it, Tom glanced up the stairwell, worried the alarm might be the end of the line, though a moment later, a faint beep sounded, and the lights died.

Osaka turned and jerked his chin at Tom. "Take the crate."

Tom holstered his pistol and grabbed the handle, following behind the line once again with his partner, their burden between them. Sweat poured down his forehead as the endless stairs wound into the darkness, Tom not realizing how tired he was getting until he slipped on a step, boots scuffling on the rubber, falling forward but catching himself at the last second. The man in front of him spun and steadied him to ensure he didn't take them all down and he nodded to the soldier, breathing a sigh of relief, but the line didn't wait for Tom to catch his breath.

They pressed on, moving down several more flights as Tom's thighs burned, his arms trembling, back so taut it felt like it would snap, wondering if the downward descent would ever end. A small part of him considered asking someone to take the load, though he quickly pushed the thought aside – he'd carry his own weight, even if it killed him. Luckily, they reached the bottom step a few minutes after his momentary weakness, and they set the crate down while the specialist went to work hacking the security pad there. The door popped wide, and the SEALs filtered through to clear the way, leaving the door propped open.

A salty mist drifted into the stairwell as Tom caught a glimpse of a massive, brightly lit cavern, hundreds of feet tall and at least a thousand wide. He spied rough-hewn walls, natural stalactite formations, and tall archways, the Russians having expanded a naturally-formed cave to suit their needs. They'd built buildings directly into the walls, flowing with the rounded shapes of the chamber system and a dozen prefab structures sat scattered through the cavern, lit by bright halogen lamps, covering the underground in a depressing glow.

Tom rose on his toes and saw the floor on the far left was covered with steel tiles, a raised dock area marking the halfway point where water stretched into a lagoon off to his right. Tom wasn't surprised that they'd built their secret Naval base in such a location – the roof and walls would be impervious to penetrating radar, and it would be difficult to get inside. Beyond the dock, two sleek shapes sat at the water's edge, a pair of submarines sitting side-by-side, black and deadly beneath the stark lighting. One was massive while the other was half the first's size, periscopes, communication, and sonar antennae jutting up from both their towers while the driving planes all sat level. Tom took a deep breath of admiration and let it out slowly, appreciating the sheer display of man-made power radiating from the two vessels, a part of him yearning to climb inside them for fifteen minutes just to have a peak at their controls and propulsion systems.

"That's the target," Osaka said, peering at the smaller sub with *Tishina* written in matte letters on its side. "It means *Silence*."

"A stealth sub?"

"That's right." The commander nodded, then gestured for the team to follow him through the door.

Tom and his partner lifted the crate and carried it into the facility where the SEALs were gathering in the shadows behind a towering stack of supply crates. They had a good view of the cavern and its horseshoe-shaped dock where it pinched around the lagoon to form a cave entrance off to the right and to their left the subs sat ominously in the water. Tom and his partner put the crate down and looked toward the big vessels. Dozens of Russian soldiers marched across the steel tiles between the barracks and other prefab buildings as workers loaded the subs using two massive cranes and winches. Osaka crept back and forth, assessing the situation while conferring with a pair of officers.

Finally, he waved them in. "Okay, everyone gather close."

Two SEALs kept guard while Osaka explained the plan, his dark eyes shifting to the soldier who'd been helping Tom. "You two will take the crate off to the right, using the buildings for cover. When you reach the beach, insert the rover, find a safe place to drive, and plant the charges along the *Tishina's* hull."

Tom and the soldier nodded.

"I'll take the SEALs and create a distraction near the barracks." He gave Tom a hard stare. "That should give you enough time to do what you need to do. The rest of the team will disperse around the storage structures and protect the others, especially Tom. Are we good so far?" The team all nodded, including Tom. "After the charges are set, I'll give the word to retreat, and we'll gather at this location and extract upstairs." Osaka's eyes passed over them all again, lingering on Tom for a second before moving on. "Once on the surface, we'll meet at the cliff and BASE jump down to the water where our plane will be waiting. It'll ferry us away beneath the radar just like how we came in. Is that understood?"

The SEALs all nodded again, unflinching and unwavering in their dedication to the mission. Tom took a deep breath, wishing Osaka had held back the BASE jumping part. He wasn't particularly good with heights, and it was a surefire bet that he'd be thinking about that it the entire time he was trying to pilot the rover. Pushing down a smart remark, Tom nodded along with all the others.

Osaka grinned with steely determination. "Okay, men. Let's get this party started."

* * *

Tom and his partner waited at the supply stack as the sounds of the dock workers and marching soldiers threatened to crush his nerves. Boots stomped and foreign voices called out to one another, sometimes shouting or laughing. They were just people doing their jobs, but they were Russians, and they'd kill Tom as soon as look at him, especially if they knew he'd stolen some of their most valuable military secrets. He squirmed where he sat, wanting to crawl out of his skin as he eased forward, picking out the shadows of SEALs dispersing to the cave's far side, putting themselves between the enemy soldiers and himself, unable to tell which ones were part of Osaka's distraction team and which were the second layer of defense.

"I'm Leech."

Tom sat back against the crate and stared at his partner sitting next to him. A stocky, rugged character, the man looked at Tom with dark eyes beneath a head of tight curls as his mouth worked in big chewing movements, gnawing over the wad of gum in between his jaws.

"What?"

"Name's Leech."

"Ah. I'm Tom."

"Yeah, the submarine driver. Everyone knows who you are."

They shook hands, and Tom rested his head back and closed his eyes, fists resting on his knees, squeezing them, then he relaxed them again, repeating the motion to loosen up and siphon off more of his nervous energy.

"We usually train with new guys for a few weeks before a mission," Leech said. "You know, so everyone can get to know each other."

"Yeah, I wish we could have this time, too," Tom nodded. "I feel a little detached from the squad, if you get my drift."

"Well, don't worry. I'll help you place the rover into the water, then I'll cover your back the rest of the time. Don't think about anything else but sticking those firecrackers on that turtle over there."

Tom laughed, uncertainly. "You bet, Leech. And thanks."

"No problem."

An explosion rocked the far end of the chamber and the air pressure changed abruptly, causing Tom to flinch. He glanced around the crate to see part of the wall in the back of the chamber blossom out, carried by a wave of billowing flame. Pieces of stone rained on the steel grating, collapsing over what once had been a barracks entrance, at least three Russian soldiers stumbling from the gray dust haze engulfed in flames, screaming as they staggered and dropped to their knees. Rifle fire pinched the air and tore into a group of marching Russian soldiers, many of whom had just barely raised their weapons when they were cut down.

"That's our signal," Leach said, still chomping on his gum.

Together, he and Tom picked up the rover crate and broke cover, running off to the right to find a good spot to set up. They ran along the steel grating until they reached a set of three steps that led down to a lower dock, then they descended, boots clanging over the steel where they placed the rover ten yards from the water. They unclasped the lid and lifted it free, tossing it aside and the end pieces fell off on their own, revealing the high-tech machine resting on a lightweight base shaped to fit its form.

Spindly framed with a torpedo-like body, the rover mirrored the other Mariners he'd driven and his eyes roamed over the advanced systems Osaka had alluded to, admiring the slim, sleek, modern aesthetic. "She looks intact. Let's get her in the water."

With gunfire hammering distantly, they grabbed the chassis handles and lifted the rover from its frame, walking it to the edge of the dock and dropping it gently into the water. Tom flipped open a control panel to initiate the startup sequence, watching the screen as it cycled through its diagnostic phases and it beeped loudly to let Tom know it was done.

"Okay, that's it," he said, slamming the panel shut. "Now it's up to me."

Tom headed back to the crate and grabbed the controller from a box at the bottom and turned it on. Circling the crate, he plopped onto the dock and kept the rover's crate between him and any potential incoming fire while Leech squatted behind him with his finger to his earpiece.

"Commander Osaka, Mariner is in the water. I repeat, Mariner is in the water."

The commander replied with a scratchy voice, the sounds of flames and gunfire close in his ear. "Okay, Tom. It's up to you."

Tom nodded as he waited for the controller to fully boot up, glancing to his left to see the Russian subs squatting in the water three hundred yards away. Workers huddled behind loading machinery as two dozen Russian soldiers protected them and their submarines, unaware that Tom was about to hit them from below. The controller screen came to life and Tom kicked the rover into action, sputtering and spitting up bubbles until it was fully submerged, then it blasted forward, diving to a depth of thirty feet before he turned it toward the submarine stalls.

The gun battle raged on, but Tom pushed the sounds far out of his mind, focusing on the screen and letting his muscle memory do the work. On screen, the murky blackness rushed by, particles in the water bouncing off his cameras and whipping away in the wake he created. He came to what he thought was the Tishina's stall and brought the rover to a full stop, then he backed up, directing his spotlight along the massive metal stall door, spotting a four-yard-wide tunnel through which the rover shot through, barely knocking against a wall due to the tight space.

The rover emerged inside the stall and Tom guided his beam up at the Tishina's gleaming hull beneath the bright surface lights fluttering above. Glancing over at the ship and back to his screen, he had a moment of vertigo from being in two places at once, but a shake of his head cleared it and he refocused on his task. He flicked a joystick toggle with his thumb and used the rover's arms and claws to take the first charge from a basket beneath the frame. Pushing the vessel along the hull to the Tishina's bow, he avoided hitting the thick dock poles that could easily disable the Mariner if Tom wasn't careful.

The first hockey-puck shaped explosive was attached about ten feet up the sub's side, sticking to it with an ultra-strong magnet. Tom punched the top with a rover claw to activate it, a light on the disk blinking red, then he reached for another. Alarms were ringing out through the base, and people were shouting as more Russian soldiers converged on the dock area, spilling out of buildings all across the area. Dead Russians lay sprawled in front of the blown-up barracks and across the steel grating of the dock, muzzle flashes giving him a fireworks display as men screamed and shouted and died. Leech knelt next to him behind the crate, staying out of the fight until someone noticed them. Tom placed the second charge and glided the rover another fifteen feet along the hull as a massive clanging sound rang out through both his ROV controller's speakers and inside the cavern.

"That's the stall doors banging open," he mumbled as the high whirring of engines kicked on, the Tishina beginning a slow drift in reverse.

"What's it looking like, Tom?" Osaka shouted into his ear as he fired off a burst toward the closing Russians.

"Three more to go," Tom said, "but she's trying to escape."

"You've got two minutes before she clears the dock!"

"I only need one," Tom growled.

He followed the sub as it backed into the stall doors with a tremendous clatter, shoving them open as it simultaneously tried to submerge in the lagoon, the captain clearly prioritizing the secrecy of the craft over its safety. Tom wove around another dock pole and pressed back toward the hull, setting the third charge, expertly punching the top with a claw. He couldn't tell if the explosives were evenly placed, but it would have to do.

The sound of heavier machine gun fire entered the fray, a layer of deeper reports, a slow staccato beat in counterpoint to the faster bursts from the soldiers' rifles. A SEAL screamed through the earpiece but was quickly cut off and Tom looked up to see a pair of Russians had mounted two heavy-caliber machine guns on a stack of bricks and construction materials, every burst of rounds chewing at the SEALs' defenses.

"Come on, Tom," Osaka shouted over the line.

"Two more to go!" Tom's voice strained with tension, nerves firing into overdrive.

He placed the fourth charge but had to pull away before activating it, circling with his right-hand to send the rover in a tight spin around a dock pole and back toward the hull. The vessel was coming in too fast, but he couldn't stop it. His claw hit the fourth charge hard, activating the explosive but bending the arm downward at the same time, breaking it as warning lights blared on his screen. Tom cursed under his breath as he tried to lift the dead arm and it wouldn't so much as budge so he used the left arm instead. The Tishina was almost to the submerged passage leading out into open water, and Tom angled the rover so it drifted toward the U-boat's stern.

Something pinged off of the dock near his feet, and he looked up to see the Russians had finally noticed them sitting off by themselves. He jerked his boots back behind the crate to avoid having his toes blown off, a glance to his left showing a handful of soldiers standing on the dock and shooting in his direction. Leech returned fire, bravely putting his long-distance skill on display and an enemy soldier's head snapped backward, spitting blood from the back of his skull. Another took a round in the chest, clutching the wound in disbelief as he tumbled off the dock and splashed in the water.

Tom gulped and threw his shoulder against the crate, hoping it would protect him from the growing number of incoming rounds. Back to the screen, he saw the rover had almost floated past the Tishina and, reversing, he got the machine under control and angled in toward the hull one final time. He was just about to place the final charge when the dead soldier who'd fallen off the dock swirled directly in front of the rover as the body churned in the submarine's wake. A dark cloud of bloody water obscured Tom's vision, and the man's arms and legs brushed over the submersible, getting hung up on the chassis. He reversed thrust and rolled the machine beneath the corpse, trying to get out from under it as a pair of rounds smacked the remaining pieces of crate and, kicking pieces of fiberglass and foam into his face. A hand landed on his shoulder, and he looked up to see Leech standing over him.

"Time to go, buddy!"

"One second," Tom spun the rover again and again, rolling it like crazy as the corpse's weight dragged it down.

Leech grabbed him by the back of his shirt and pulled him backwards with a grunt and Tom resisted, shoulders hunched over the controller, continuing to work the joysticks and get back on track. He was about to tell Osaka to blow the damn thing with four charges when the rover rolled one final time and broke free of the obstruction. He swung the submersible in and slammed the explosive against the Tishina's hull as Leech half-dragged him across the dock with one hand while sending out suppressing fire with the other. The rover was pushed away by a current, but Tom drove it forward again, left-hand claw punching at the top to activate it, missing, diving back for a second attempt and hitting it as the submarine rolled over the little rover and sent it to the bottom of the lagoon. Tom turned, staggering toward the metal steps while Leech continued firing the entire time, spreading shots all around to keep their enemies pinned and Tom pressed his finger to his earpiece.

"They're placed, Osaka! I repeat, the charges are placed!"

"Copy that! Duck and cover!"

Gunfire raked the air above them and he ducked as he flew up the stairs, tripping, throwing his forearms out to break his fall. Raw pain shot through his arm and up into his shoulder, but he got his feet beneath him and scrambled up as bullets sparked on the steel tiles. He ducked and flinched and half-staggered toward the supply stack, waiting for the inevitable round to smack his head and put him down for good.

Behind him, the Tishina was still descending, its tower protruding from the water, when all five charges detonated at once. A spray of water, steam, and flame shot skyward, arcing out over the dock area like a storm, the concussion pitching Tom forward just when he'd gotten to his feet. He tumbled through the air, arms windmilling, stomach plummeting and the toe of one boot touched down before he face-planted on the steel tiles, hand slapping the ground with a painful whack, saving his nose from breaking.

Leech was there, lifting him to his knees, helping him crawl until he finally got his feet back under him, then they made a beeline for the supply stacks as SEALs from the distraction team fired and retreated in waves. His eyes shifted to the water where a cloud of smoke and mist hung near the top of the two-hundred-foot tall cavern. The Tishina was in the midst of a death roll, its propeller jutting out of the oil-slicked water, smoke billowing from the rip in its hull as fiery debris rained down. The larger sub wasn't faring much better, sitting slumped in its stall, the explosion having crippled it due to its proximity to the smaller sub. The sonar and communication antennae had been cut in half, hanging over and sparking with electric fury and it was starting to list in the water, no doubt having suffered from multiple hull breaches.

Tom and Leech fell in with the rest of the SEALs behind the supply stacks, two of them carrying a limping man between them, placing him against the crates. One kicked a spent magazine from his rifle, rammed a full one into the magazine well and poked the barrel around the corner, shooting back at an intensified barrage from the Russians, bullets zipping by them and hitting the rock wall in small dust puffs.

Osaka joined them, crouching down behind cover and tapping his earpiece. "Stenborn, you still up top?"

"I'm here, commander. It's getting hot up here, though."

"Not as hot as it is down here. Get ready. We're coming up."

"Roger that, sir."

"Alright," Osaka shouted to the eight SEALs remaining. "We're getting out of here. We'll form two teams, lay down a field of suppressing fire, and fall back to the stairs in waves. McKnight, you're with me!"

Tom nodded and drew his pistol as Osaka crept near him with his left hand on his arm. "First team, go!"

The first four SEALs leapt into the open, crouching as they laid down a layer of withering fire, the sounds rattling off like fireworks next to his ear. The second group, including the injured soldier, moved in behind them, spun, and raised their weapons.

"First team, fall back!" the commander shouted.

The initial line of soldiers retreated and let second team take over. At the same time, Osaka yanked Tom's arm, and they ran for the door. Tom turned to shoot back at the Russians, but the commander snatched his arm and dragged him away. "Not right now!"

They entered the stairwell, and Tom glanced back through the open door to see the Tishina drifting, upside down, nose pointed toward the bottom like a dead fish. Its rudder and diving planes slewed along the surface, trailing the last bit of smoke before it went under and the SEALs all piled inside the stairwell. Osaka slammed the door behind them, and the soldier who'd first hacked the keypad plugged his electronic device into it.

"Stenborn, we're coming up," Osaka spoke with an intense tone.

"Roger that," came the reply, followed by a burst of gunfire over the line. "I've got at least three hostiles up here trying to break into the stairwell. I'm pretty sure they've radioed for backup, too."

"No shit. We'll be up shortly to assist."

The commander nodded to the man on the door. "Got it?"

"It's jammed tight now, sir." The operative gave a sharp nod and shoved his equipment into his pouch, then he grabbed his rifle and moved upstairs with the second team.

As the SEALs ascended ahead of them, Osaka turned back to Tom with a grin, motioning toward the pistol Tom still had clutched in his hand. "I told you that you wouldn't have any direct contact with Russian soldiers."

Tom nodded. "Well, unless you consider bullets flying at me direct contact."

"You have to expect it." Osaka shoved him up the stairs. "Now let's get you out of here alive, eh?"

"Sounds good to me," Tom fired back. Taking two steps at a time, he climbed quickly and quietly with his eyes raised to the next landing. Because the stairs had an inner wall, they couldn't see farther up, so they took every corner with caution.

Stenborn's voice broke across the line, filled with fear. "Sir, I can't hold the office. I'm falling back inside the stairwell." The sounds of a door opening and slamming followed. "I'm going to bar it."

"Hang on, Stenborn!" Osaka said. Then he called up to the other soldiers. "Move it, men. Let's go!"

Tom ran as fast and hard as he could, but even the commander left him behind. Soon, he was running almost alone, barely catching sight of him as he rounded the next corner up. An explosion ripped through the stairwell above, and someone screamed under a barrage of rifle fire. Tom hesitated but redoubled his efforts to catch up.

"Stenborn's down," Osaka called over the comm channel. "Engage in waves of two. Go!"

The thought of being left alone with the Russians coming up behind them drove Tom to climb harder, thighs burning, soggy pants tripling in weight, wet boots pounding the rubber flooring. He only stopped when he finally caught up with Osaka, who crept behind the SEALs, glancing back with a nod as they continued their quiet ascent. Tom held his pistol in a sweaty grip, eyes thrown upward toward the inevitable conflict. It seemed like he had no sooner finished the thought when rifles went off again above him, casting muzzle flashes on the walls, lead ricocheting off the concrete and zipping by, though the fight was over as quickly as it began, and the stairwell fell silent once more.

"Three down," a SEAL said in a calm but breathless voice. "Moving up."

The downstairs door crashed inward, and Osaka glanced past Tom with a worried expression. "We've got company below us, men. We need to push it."

They moved faster up the next two flights, but Tom still couldn't see the lead soldiers. Someone shouted and fired a test burst, then a sudden eruption of sound and light filled the stairwell in a mess of chaos. He could only squint and avert his face, back pressed to the inner wall. A man screamed, and another gurgled, yet the SEALs ahead of Osaka continued moving upward. Tom ducked and hunkered behind the commander, sticking close to him, wincing against the deadly struggle above, yet unwilling to back down the steps.

They passed three bodies lying on the stairs, two Russian and one SEAL, dead from atrocious wounds to their chests and necks. In the darkness, Tom spotted a pair of pistols and a bloody knife on the stairs and he bent to pick up the blade, stuffing it into his belt. On the next landing, two dead SEALs and four Russians lay splayed in grotesque poses, the walls and stairs slick with blood. As they passed them, one Russian suddenly came to life, coughing up blood as he rolled over and lifted his pistol. A SEAL casually turned his rifle on the man and fired a burst from belly to neck, zipping the man up.

Tom felt himself go cold, disbelieving the violence playing out in such close proximity. He swallowed hard as they climbed into the meat grinder, spitting men out like ground chuck, the stairwell growing claustrophobic, the stench of death suffocating him. He thought of Barbara and her agitated pause on the phone when he'd told her he was embarking on one last mission, remembering her words as she'd pleaded for him to just come home. Yet he hadn't, and the regret nagged at the back of his brain.

You were right, Barbara. I should have just come home.

Before he finished the thought, they came to the next landing where another SEAL and two more Russians lay dead. Their teammate had apparently taken out both enemy combatants, still gripping the handle of the blade he'd driven into a Russian's heart.

"We're close to the top," Osaka said. "Leech, pair up and go."

With four soldiers and the commander left in front of him, Tom wasn't sure of his chances since they didn't know how many more troops they'd have to grind through to break free of the stairwell. The pair gave a hand signal and Leech leapt onto the next landing, circling to the far side, quickly followed by his partner. They disappeared from sight, but soon came flying back down, rounding the corner just as a grenade exploded behind them, sending shrapnel into the concrete wall to their left. The concussion knocked him down three steps, boots slipping, knees coming down hard on the rubber stairs. While none of them had been hit, Tom's head was dazed and his ears rang.

Two Russians leapt down, squeezing their triggers as they rounded the corner, a pair of bullets zipping past Tom's ears like bumblebees. Another struck one of the SEALs, who flew backward down the stairs and Leech tackled the first Russian while Osaka fired between his men and hit the other with a burst in the chest. More were coming, though, a handful charging around the landing with guns rattling. Two SEALs absorbed shots while Osaka and the remaining SEAL returned fire, a point-blank exchange that left a burst of red mist in the air. Tom had been leaning against the inside wall, but he raised his pistol and shot one enemy in the shoulder, spraying blood from the exit wound. Face twisted in pain and rage, the Russian leapt the five steps and slammed into him, taking them tumbling down the stairs.

Tom's gun flew away, but he rolled backward, kicking the Russian past him as they hit the landing below. They scrambled to their feet, Tom still standing above the other man on the bottom few steps. When he saw the Russian go for his pistol, he jerked out the blade he'd picked up and leapt, hitting the man before he could draw and fire, thrusting the knife into his gut with an animalistic growl. The Russian grunted in pain and anger as the blade bit deep, Tom driving him against the wall. He grabbed Tom's knife wrist and flailed with his fist, punching Tom hard across the jaw, momentarily dazing him. Even so, Tom jerked the blade back and thrust it again, higher, punching through his thick coat, twisting the blade as he screamed and spat like an animal. They stayed clenched in an embrace for a moment, the man's struggles weakening, eyes wider as darkness took over and consumed him. Tom's face was mere inches from the soldier as he died, close enough to smell the rank stench on his breath and hear his death rattle as he gave up the ghost.

As the soldier sunk, Tom tried to snatch his pistol from its holster, but the gun slipped out of his bloody hands to clatter to the floor. He drew the blade out in a gout of blood and stabbed the soldier one more time for good measure, then he grabbed the sidearm off the floor and spun to look up. Shadows flew back and forth on the landing above as the combatants tried to kill each other and Tom streaked up the steps, spotting two men grappling, hardly able to tell them apart in their combat greens. It was Osaka with a Russian on top of him, their arms locked in a pretzel configuration, a blade two inches from the commander's eye.

All of Tom's fears, hesitations, doubts and hesitations went out the window at the sight of Osaka inches from death, and he calmly took two steps forward, put the pistol to the side of the enemy soldier's head and squeezed the trigger, blowing red clumps across the wall. Swinging left, he glanced over the dead and dying, seeing a red mist hanging in the air and dotted the concrete walls. The floor was slick with it, and the stench of blood and feces filled his nose.

He spotted Leech above him, weaponless, standing on the second stair, glaring at an enemy soldier up on the landing. The Russian held a pistol in one hand as he clutched his blood-drenched side, face drawn into an agonized grimace. Noticing Tom, the enemy soldier lifted his weapon and fired at Leech at the same time Tom did, both men going down with groans of pain. Arms shaking, head filled with violence, Tom took two steps up, firing his weapon four times more, punching holes into the Russian until he stopped gasping.

Tom immediately descended to check on Leech who slouched against the wall, hand gripping his throat where the round had taken him. Tom tried to ease the man to the steps, but Leech's eyes flashed brightly for a moment before he took his final breath.

"Damn it!" Tom growled, laying him gently against the wall, anger spinning inside him, rage spiraling out of control. He closed his eyes as boots pounded on the stairs below them, then lifted his head to see Osaka with his hand out, the man's voice cutting through the dark veil in his mind.

"Come on, Tom! We've got to go. Grab a rifle. Come on!"

The urgency in the commander's voice got him moving and, like a robot, Tom picked up a carbine lying on the stairs, grabbed a spare magazine from Leech's pouch, and followed Osaka up. They took the next three landings with Tom anticipating it might be the last moments of his life, but fear had fled his mind, replaced with a steely resolve to either survive or take as many Russians down with him as he could. He and Osaka worked as a team, rotating and covering each other as they outran the boots that chased them to the top. Once there, on the final landing, they found Stenborn, riddled with bullet holes. They moved into the office area, meeting no resistance, and continued to the front door. Exchanging nods, they kicked it open and charged outside into the night, rifles ticking back and forth, prepared to fire, yet there were no more Russians around despite three military trucks sitting idle on the dirt track. Tom, Osaka, and the SEAL team had killed them all.

"Come on." The commander's voice was razor thin, and he turned to his left and jogged along the path to the edge of the jungle.

Tom put his head down and followed, nerves jangling on an electric wire, struggling to put what had happened into the back of his mind. Another team dead, another mission gone to hell, the only survivors himself and the commander of the unit, the two who every rational mind would assume would die first having been protected by fate's twisted sense of irony.

They trudged blindly through bushes and weeds, arms up and swimming, their way lit only by moonlight, feeling their way to what Tom presumed was the jump he'd have to make. For the first time, he noticed Osaka limping and favoring his right side, ambling with an awkward hitch, holding his arm close. After moving another fifty yards through the woods, Osaka stopped and looked around, panting, blood dripping freely on the leaves. Tom went to step past him, but the commander grabbed him by his jacket and jerked him back, then pointed down. Tom peered hard through the brush and realized the tangled undergrowth hid a steep drop over the side. One more step and he would have plunged off.

"Over here." Osaka jerked his chin off to the right.

Tom followed him to a clear spot on the cliff. The commander stood on the edge, slouching as he peered down. Tom joined him at the sheer drop, blood still pounding in his head knowing what they were about to do. He stared down into the dark bay, water stretching for ten miles across it, so wide it looked like an ocean, lights blinking dimly on their cargo plane where it floated just a hundred yards from shore.

Blood smeared on his cheeks, pain in his eyes, Osaka gave Tom a pointed look, his voice turning thin and reedy. "Okay. This works like your standard chute. Only this time, you'll jump, count to four, then pull the cord. Got it? You want to do it pretty quick, but not so fast you hang in the sky and make an easy target for the Russians." The commander shrugged. "If we're lucky, they won't even look down."

Tom nodded robotically, his emotions so distant he barely felt alive. Double checking the harnesses of the small parachute packs on their backs, they nodded to each other as the shouts of Russian soldiers rang out behind them, voices dripping with outrage for their fallen comrades.

"See you on the water," Osaka said with a pat on Tom's shoulder. Then he turned and leapt from the cliff, stretching himself out as gravity carried him down.

Tom watched him for a second before he stepped back from the edge, taking one deep breath, then another. Arms held out, he sprinted forward and lunged into the open air. He plummeted straight down into the darkness, gravity gripping the core of his body and yanking him toward the water, his stomach swirling up into this throat, making him dizzy and nauseous. In the heat of the moment he'd forgotten to count, so he guesstimated and pulled the cord at his shoulder, his chute opening with a whoosh, his feet flipping up in a wild jerk of motion. He swatted at the handles above his head before finally grabbing them and engaging the chute's steering mechanism, gasping, grunting, and staring down as he angled himself toward the plane.

The seconds ticked by as he hung in the air. Osaka hit the water off to his left with a splash, and Tom angled right so he didn't land on top of him. The water rose quickly to meet him at the end and he slammed into it with a blast of salty ocean spray to the face. Quickly releasing his lines, he drifted down a few feet underwater before kicking himself out and away from his chute. Surfacing, he shrugged off his harness, then he spat water and treaded in a circle, looking for the commander.

He spotted Osaka's shadow swimming toward the plane, and Tom put his head down and did the same. It wasn't until he reached the commander that he realized Osaka was moving sluggishly, leaving a trail of blood in the water behind him that was plain to see just from the pale moonlight alone. Still twenty-five yards from the plane, the engines coughed to life as the pilot waited for them to board. Tom flipped on his back and grabbed Osaka beneath his shoulders, dragging him backwards, feeling his motions grow weaker by the moment. Panic exploding in his brain, he found a reserve of energy he didn't know he had and hauled the commander to the plane's floats where the pilot was standing by the door.

"The commander's hurt," Tom yelled. "Help me get him up!"

Tom lifted Osaka onto the slippery float, and the pilot reached down and grabbed him. Holding the commander in place, but unable to lift him aboard, he called into the cockpit. The co-pilot emerged and assisted them, and between the three, they got him into the aircraft where he sprawled on the deck. Tom climbed up next, arms shaking, skin clammy cold and dripping as he fell to the floor by Osaka. He clambered to his knees, panting with exhaustion as he quickly found the wound that had slowed the commander down, a shot to the stomach just below the sternum.

Wincing at the sight of it, Tom shook his head and gestured to the pilots. "We need a first aid kit! Do you have one on board?"

The co-pilot nodded, grabbed a first aid kit from the cabinet on the bulkhead, and handed it to the pilot. The pilot, in turn, gave it to Tom, glancing back toward the front.

"We'll have Russians all over us in a minute. We need to get out of here. Are there any others?"

Tom took the kit from the man and shook his head. "We're all who made it. Fly."

The pair returned to the cockpit while Tom held Osaka's top half up, grabbing a backpack lying on the floor and dragging it closer. He situated him atop it and turned to the wound, a sick dread filling his gut as he opened the first aid kit next to him, eyes glued to the large bullet hole where blood pulsed out with every heartbeat.

"Stop the bleeding," Tom murmured to himself, going for a big roll of gauze. "Stop the bleeding first."

The engines kicked up, and the rocking plane bounced ahead over the choppy bay waters. Osaka groaned and shivered deeply, trying to cover his wound with his hand as his eyes found Tom.

"We made it out."

"Yes." Blood pumped between his fingers, and Tom pulled his hand away, placing a folded wad of gauze over the spot.

Osaka's eyes rolled around the fuselage. "It's freezing in here, man. So damn cold."

Tom held the gauze in place and reached for a camouflage Jacket a SEAL had discarded. He pulled it over the commander so it mostly covered him, realizing the gauze he'd used to stem the blood flow had already soaked through. He looked around for a shirt or rag or anything else that might be more absorbent as the plane suddenly lurched and lifted off, throwing Tom forward, though he managed to keep pressure on the wound while breaking his own fall with his other hand.

"Sorry, Osaka. It's going to be a bumpy ride home."

Lips thin and pale, Osaka groaned, barely able to squeeze the words out. "I… I'm not going to make it."

"Shut up. You'll be fine." Tom smiled at the man, doing his best to keep up a brave front, even though his heart was sinking. "I'll keep pressure on this until we get back to base. Someone with more experience than me can take over. You'll be fine."

"You're a… a shit medic," the commander coughed as he laughed, a line of bloody spittle flying from his mouth and landed on his chin. "It's a four-hour trip back. I'll be long gone by then."

Tom didn't answer, keeping pressure on the man's wound, focusing on doing his job even as his hands turned redder by the second.

"Tom. Look at me."

Tom reluctantly met Osaka's normally dark, stern visage, though the sternness was replaced by pain and a sense of finality. Tom fought to keep a brave front as the man who'd been his mentor, guide and protector for several months coughed again, more blood trickling from the side of his mouth, his skin growing paler by the minute.

"I'm sorry, Osaka." The apology slipped from Tom's lips as helplessness took hold, eyes brimming with tears. "I've let you down."

"Hachiro," he said. "Just call me Hachiro."

Tom nodded, keeping his hands on the wound. Grabbing a rag lying off to the side, and he stretched to grab it and swapped it with the gauze in a futile attempt to staunch the flow. "I'm so sorry, Hachiro."

The commander sputtered on his next words, more blood flicking across his lips. "N-nothing to apologize for. You should be…" He coughed and grimaced in a wave of pain before focusing back on Tom again. "Should be v-very proud. We accomplished great things for our country, and you've come… a long way." The flicker of a smile appeared. "She… said you wouldn't make it. But she was wrong."

"Who… who was wrong?"

Osaka flinched for a few seconds, grinding his teeth together as his entire body seizing up. "Banks. She… thought you…"

Tom felt a chill run down his spine. "She thought I wouldn't make it? She told me in the briefing something about how it'd be safe… obviously that was a lie."

"Told me… thought you'd bite it… called you… expendable." Osaka's words were a mere whisper, every syllable a struggle to eke out. "Sorry… didn't tell you… before. Thought you… knew risks. Thought she was… honest."

The words rushed out through clenched teeth. "Hachiro, you don't owe me any apologies. It's been an honor to fight by your side. Thank you for seeing me safely home."

Hachiro nodded, and a cold hand slipped from beneath the jacket and covered Tom's in a firm grip, his eyes holding him in a gentle stare. "Go home, Tom. It's… time… for you to go… home."

Lieutenant Commander Hachiro Osaka closed his eyes and swallowed hard, hand weakening where it lay over Tom's, his breaths coming fast and hard for a few seconds and then he was gone. Tom sat with his fingers still pressing the dirty shirt to the wound, unwilling to let go for several minutes, trying to process what was going on. By some miracle he'd survived another mission in which multiple men – *good* men – had died, partially to carry out their mission, and partially to protect him. The revelation that Banks had lied to him about his safety when trying to convince him to come, and had fully *expected* him to die left him feeling unsure of what to think or how to feel.

Turbulence jostled him around, the space in the fuselage seeming wide open and endless, empty without Osaka's instructions and the chiding jokes of the SEALs to keep him company. Finally, Tom let go of the wound and sat back as a sob burst from his lips. His hands clenched into fists and he slammed them to his chest as if he could take some of his own life and give it to the man. The dread he'd been feeling inside swelled and rose to the surface, morphing into a sick rage that had no outlet. Tom placed his hand on Osaka's forehead, seething with sorrow, anger and regret as the plane shuddered and shivered in the cold Russian winds.

* * *

Four hours later, the plane landed on a remote airstrip at a forward base in Alaska. Tom had long ago placed a few jackets over the commander's body to cover it, resting the man's hands across his chest. When the plane finally rumbled to a halt, Navy personnel threw the doors open and blinked at the lone, living figure inside. Blood up to his elbows and caked thick on his chest and lap, face smeared with dirt, sweat and tears, Tom climbed out slowly with a gesture of futile helplessness at Osaka's corpse.

The sailors watched as Tom walked away on shaky legs toward the barracks, Colonel Banks standing off to the side with several other Navy brass, looking over the empty plane and whispering among themselves. Her eyes grew wide when he saw the soldiers lift the jackets back to reveal Osaka's corpse.

She immediately jumped in front of Tom, putting herself between him and the barracks, her voice dripping with rage. "What the hell happened out there, McKnight? How did *Osaka* die?!"

Tom stared at her for a few seconds, their faces scant inches apart, and he chuckled at her humorlessly. "What do you mean? Were you expecting someone else to be in a body bag?"

There was a twitch at the side of Banks's mouth and she opened it briefly, looking like she was going to respond, then shut it again.

"You might wonder what happened to the rest of them, too. Or do you only care about Osaka?" Tom's voice dripped with sarcasm. "Their bodies will be in a stairwell at a nuclear submarine base. As if you even give a shit."

Tom stepped stepped to his right to go around, but Banks sidestepped with him, pressing an arm against Tom's chest. "What about the Tishina?"

Tom's eyes narrowed, and he brought up his left palm and slammed it against Banks's shoulder, shoving him aside.

"Yeah, we blew it up." Tom grunted as he strode by. "Now get out of my way. I'm going home."

Three MPs rushed to cut Tom off, glowering at him as Banks chased on his heels. "You are absolutely *not* going home yet. You're the only survivor and we need a full debrief."

Tom stopped in front of the MPs, half turning to the Navy officer, resisting the urge to throw a punch directly into her face, Osaka's words echoing over and over in his head.

Go home, Tom. It's time for you to go home.

Tom lowered his voice to a growl, barely audible above the noise of the airfield. "Osaka told me what you said, Banks."

"What? What are you—"

"Shut the hell up." Banks took a half step back, blinking in surprise as Tom continued. "Let's get one thing straight – I'll give a debriefing. But not to you. Never to you. When I finish here, I'm going to turn around and walk away, and I'd better never see you or hear your name *ever* again."

Still covered in blood and filth from the mission, Tom turned to the MPs and they took a step back, looking between him and Banks. He split between them and marched to the barracks, warring emotions twisting his heart. He was alive, yes, and would be able to see his family once again. Those he had worked with, fought with and very nearly died with, though, couldn't say the same. The lessons he'd learned while with the SEALs spun in circles in his brain, though he couldn't say if they were good or bad. They just were. And they'd come at a terrible, terrible cost.

Chapter 16

Tom McKnight
Near Asheville, North Carolina

The outside wind whipped up, blowing against the chained doors, rattling them back and forth. Snow filtered down through cracks in the roof and the horses gently chuffed as they laid next to each other, ears dancing back and forth at every bit of noise carried through the large, empty store.

Sam sat in rapt silence as Tom finished his story, eyes wide, tears running down her face, staring at her father like he was a different person. Tom tried to smile, but it faltered, and when she didn't immediately say anything, he leaned forward and stirred the contents of the pan, putting another scoop of food in his bowl.

"So… I realize that's a lot to take in at one time. Just remember: I'm still your father, and I always will be. And I love you very much."

Sam wiped her eyes, the firelight dancing across her tearstained face. "So you *were* a soldier, sort of."

"Careful you don't say that kind of thing to any spec-ops guys you meet, or call them 'soldiers' either," he chuckled. "They tend to be picky about what they're called."

His attempt at humor fell flat and she shook her head, blinking. "Did you tell Mom about any of this?"

Tom nodded. "She knows about a lot of it. She was initially pretty mad at me for accepting that final mission, especially after saying I'd come home." He chuckled darkly. "Things were tense for a few months. She was mad and confused and very cold to me. We were busy trying to raise you and Linda while building the farm and it took a long time to earn her trust again. The months passed, and she finally realized I wasn't going to go gallivanting off on any more military missions." His expression changed to a warm grin. "One day, I was putting up some fencing, and she walked all the way from the house just to hug me. We stood there for a good five or ten minutes, holding each other. That's when I knew things were going to be okay."

"But you'd changed."

"Yeah, a lot. After that, your mother had to deal with my nightmares." Tom leaned back, taking a steadying breath, the images of the fight in the stairwell burned into his mind. "Those lasted a few years. I still get them sometimes. She was a bit antsy at first with the new skills I'd learned while on those missions, too."

"Like how to kill people?"

"How to *protect* them, if I need to," Tom corrected her. He sat back, poking at his food with his spoon. "I want you to know that what happened back then made me think very hard. I tried to turn those dark lessons into something I could use to benefit us. To make sure we'd be ready to survive through anything." He paused looking off to the side, in the direction of the back of the store, where blood still stained the floor.

Sam nodded, choosing her words carefully and honestly. "I'm glad you were able to take something that affected you so badly and turn it into something good."

"I scared you earlier, though. I regret that a lot."

Sam nodded hesitantly. "Yes… some. But I understand now. And you're right."

"I am?"

"You had to do what you had to do, with those people. Without our horses, we could die here in the cold. They were desperate enough to try and steal, so what would stop them from hurting us to get what they wanted?

Tom nodded, letting out a sigh of relief. "Exactly. That makes me feel better to hear you say that."

"Well," Sam gave a genuine smile, "if Mom learned to deal with it, I guess I can, too."

While glad to receive an inkling of understanding from his daughter, something tore at him inside. He put the bowl aside and leaned forward, looking hard into the fire so he didn't have to see Sam.

She caught his darkening mood. "What's wrong?"

"Despite everything… I still wasn't able to do it. I wasn't able to protect your mother, Linda, and Jack. Now they're out there with a maniac who'll stop at nothing to get what he wants. To please his higher ups. One of whom is the person who had their thumb on my back in the past."

"Banks?"

"Yeah."

"That's something I'm wondering, actually."

"What's that?"

"Why did you work with Banks again, on the thing with the anomaly? I thought you told her years ago you'd never work with her, like, ever."

Tom leaned back in his seat, nodding slowly. "Yeah. I've been thinking about that myself. Since that mission all those years ago, the company – well, Ray specifically – started pursuing more government contracts. At some point, Banks was attached, and Ray asked me as a personal favor to oversee things." Tom shrugged. "I should have told him to pound sand, but I was naïve. I thought I had to do it, to help the company."

"What was it like, having to do that?"

"Honestly? It was fine. She was professional, and so was I. The past wasn't discussed, and the projects the company worked on made a lot of money and a lot of people very happy. That went on over the years and eventually… I just got over it." He exhaled slowly, his voice taking on a sharp edge. "I never expected that I'd get turned on like this. But I shouldn't be surprised."

"It's not over yet, Dad. Mom and Linda and Jack are still alive. All we have to do is go get them. And from what you told me, that Banks jerk and all her soldiers don't stand a chance against us."

Tom laughed. "Yeah, I can't disagree with that. Us McKnights are pretty tough."

"Darned right we are." Sam gave him a genuine smile before diving into her food with a little more enthusiasm than before.

"So, we're within a few hours of the FOB," he said, turning the focus to rescuing their family. "I was thinking, tonight you can take first watch. I'll take the second. We'll get some rest and then move on in the morning."

"Do you think the other two who tried to take the horses will come back?"

Tom shook his head. "No, I think after they saw what happened to their friends, the last thing they'll do is come back." Sam nodded grimly. "I can take the first watch, no problem."

They finished their meals and cleaned the dishes in the lukewarm water near the fire, the simple actions bringing a sense of normalcy as Sam washed and he dried. After they finished, Tom took two more pails to the horses and then they boiled some for themselves and used a pump filter to refill their water bottles. Tom placed his head down on a camping pillow, thinking he might not be able to sleep, but the unburdening of his past to his daughter had brought him an unexplainable sense of peace, and he was fast asleep moments later.

After an uneventful night, they saddled up the horses the next morning and loaded them with supplies. Taking an extra soft dog bed from a shelf, they opened the package and exchanged it for the Smooch's old one, the shepherd sniffing at it warily for a moment before shakily stepping back onto her sled and making a few circles before finally settling down.

Smooch's weakness was mostly a weak attempt to garner attention, based on the events of the previous night, and if either of them ran into danger, the animal would not hesitate to attack, and Tom considered them blessed to have brought her along, especially when he was the one who argued against it in the first place. Once they got her tucked in, they pulled open the front doors and walked the horses to the highway and, after consulting the map, Tom turned south, intent on following the road close to the FOB without being detected.

"Keep an eye out for Weaverville, Woodfin, or Grace signs. Once we hit Grace, we'll know we're right on top of the base. We'll park the horses and walk from there."

"Okay, Dad."

Tom rode ahead, as usual, the day clear and the skies blue overhead, with the sun occasionally going behind an infrequent cloud. The frigid cold had backed off thanks to the wind tapering down to nothing and they rode for a solid two hours without pause, the highway running parallel to I-26 most of the time, soon reaching the first sign buried in the snow, which Sam pointed out.

"There's Weaverville!"

"Excellent," Tom said. "We're getting *very* close. I'd say another two hours and we'll be there."

They rode past the town, a sparse layer of homes and businesses poking up out of the snow like chocolate chips in a field of marshmallow topping. A few birds chirped in the trees, but there were no signs of life otherwise, any other animals and humans long since having moved on.

"Do you think we should stop off here and see if they have anything we can use?" Sam asked. "I mean, the Big Box had a lot of good stuff, but not much we could actually eat."

Tom slowly shook his head. "We've got enough to get us to the FOB. We'll rescue your mother and siblings first, then worry about more supplies later."

They passed several stalled cars on the side of the road and an 18-wheeler stuck in a ditch before crossing a bridge to leave the little town behind. They rode another hour and a half, the horses having no difficulty on the cleared roads. Suburbs replaced the farmsteads, and the highway took an easterly course, breaking away from the expressway and transforming into Merrimon Avenue. He was the first to spot a town sign off to the right, which stood perfectly straight in the pale white drifts.

"Grace, one mile." He grinned and pointed.

Sam shot him an anxious smile in return. "Should we get off here?"

"Let's go another half mile, then we'll stop and take stock."

A tree-lined lane that skirted the north edge of a wide, white field, Merrimon Avenue's surface was perfectly flat, unmarked by forests or shrubs, and there were no signs of roads or automobiles anywhere nearby.

"That big flat spot must be a lake," Tom said, pointing out at the unnaturally flat section of snow, Sam squinting into the brightness to make it out.

"Oh, wow. I think you're right."

"After we get your mother and Jack and Linda," Tom quipped, "maybe we'll go ice skating."

"Sounds good," Sam laughed, nervousness still tinging her tone.

Tom gripped his horse's reigns tightly, battling an overwhelming mix of anxiety and anticipation. The highway curved to the south, still lined with trees spaced ten or fifteen feet apart. Between them, streets angled off to the left into what he thought must be subdivisions. The ones on the right gave way to parking lots and businesses with cars buried beneath the winter whiteness at intervals throughout. He pointed to a pet store and market sitting off the road where part of the lot and the space between the buildings had been plowed, leaving some room to walk the horses without having to wade into the snow. Tom led them into the lot and around the back, then they dismounted and tied the horses to a dumpster out of sight from the road.

"Okay, we go on foot from here." He started pulling their packs off the saddles.

"Will Smooch be okay making the trip in her condition?"

"I was thinking about that this morning. We should probably keep her out of harm's way for now, just until we can assess the situation. In a no-snow situation like last night she'd be okay, but with her injuries in the deep snow, I'm afraid for her safety. We can put her in one of these buildings and keep her covered, though. She should be okay."

They checked the market's rear door and found someone had already busted it open and they moved Smooch's sled inside and put her in a storeroom, Tom ruffling her fur as he spoke softly to her.

"We're going to leave you here, girl. But don't worry, we'll be back."

The dog gave a high-pitched whine as her humans hugged her and shut the door behind them, leaving an electric lantern on for light. From there, they checked their rifles and pistols and returned to the road. Tom strolled carefully along the right side, easily within reach of the tree cover, keeping his eyes up and focused ahead, watching for signs of the camp.

"According to Keith's note, it should be just off the road to the left."

The first sounds of vehicles and a rumble of wheels on salt-covered pavement reached them, sure signs of a military encampment and they crept slower until Tom spotted two Humvees parked in a gas station lot on the right side of the road. Beyond them, a chain-link fence blocked entry, stretching into the woods on both sides for as far as they could see. Tom backed up and stepped to the edge of the road, peering over the bank of snow that had been plowed aside.

"You see the Humvees?"

"Yeah."

"They're not looking in our direction." Tom gestured at the other side of the road. "Let's cross here. Quickly now."

He crossed first and hit the opposite snowbank, lifting his knees to slam a path through the piled-up white. Sam followed right behind him, leaping along in his footprints until they plunged into the tree line. Breaking out from the crisp undergrowth, they entered a thin forest of pines and sycamores where the snow wasn't as deep, only six inches or so, making it easy for them to slow jog as they wove their way south. When they reached the fence, Tom used a pair of wire cutters from the supplies he'd taken from Big Box and cut a slit up the middle. Once through, he turned and held it open for Sam, then they took off jogging again.

"What are we looking for?" Sam asked, panting as she did her best to keep up.

"That."

Tom stopped behind a wide oak tree that squatted close to the ground, its gnarled branches bending off to either side, giving him plenty of cover to study the FOB. Falling against the trunk, he squatted down and peered beneath a low bough.

The FOB was amidst a stretch of parking lots and existing structures, a military base grown out of the civilian structures already there, with prefabs and thick canvas tents mixed in. Comprised of a dozen or more buildings, the facility was less guarded than Tom would have thought, but then again, remote, thinly guarded outposts would likely grow more common as the majority of US forces relocated farther south into Mexico, the northern areas becoming too harsh for anyone to survive without extreme gear and immense logistical support.

Sam crept up next to him, placing her arm on his shoulder. "Where are they, do you think?"

Tom looked along the freshly plowed street running parallel to the woods to a line of homes across from them. A Jeep sat on both ends of the road, facing the woods and, pulling binoculars from his jacket, he checked the vehicles to see the soldiers inside were bundled against the cold, gazing out into the trees. Past the homes extended a cluster of small stores, a gas station, and an apartment complex beyond. The apartment building was three-stories tall, guarded by a group of soldiers out front who were facing each other in a circle as they talked, and it appeared as though razor wire had been strung up around the windows, though it was hard to tell with so much snow.

"If I were a betting man, I'd put my money on the prisoners being in those apartments." Tom craned his neck up and down to check for any patrols lingering in the immediate vicinity. "They'd be easier to guard in there, and it'd be harder to escape, especially if they kept them on the upper floor."

"How are you going to get inside, though?"

"Follow me."

He backed away from the woods and moved left along the tree line, deep enough so the soldiers in the Jeeps at that ends of the street couldn't see them. Once on the other side of the guard vehicle, Tom crept to the tree line and peered at the rear of the apartments, looking across the street into the yards, all the way down to the far guard vehicle. The backyards were full of sheds, swing sets and other obstacles covered with thick snow, perfect cover for infiltrating the base. The apartment had a fire escape that ran straight up the back, each hallway with a dedicated window to egress out of

"I'm going to cross the street here and make my way to the apartment. I'll climb the fire escape and enter through a rear window."

Sam nodded. "What do you want me to do?"

"If you see anyone coming up behind me trying to nab me..." he let his words trail off, looking to Sam.

"Shoot them." Sam hefted her rifle, the one she'd practiced with back at the barn in Virginia. "Got it."

"Do you think you can do that?"

Not surprisingly, she nodded right away. "Don't worry. If anyone tries to hurt you, they won't try twice."

"Good," Tom smiled. "If that happens, we'll have to move fast; the whole base will go on alert immediately if they hear any gunshots. Regardless, though, I'll bring your mother, Linda and Jack outside, and we'll make our way back to you. From there, we'll get back to the horses and Smooch and ride off into the sunset."

Just saying their names out loud put a grin on his face. Sam nodded, and he gave her a brief hug before leaving the cover of the trees. Keeping low, Tom moved down a short bank to a lump of a car that had been pushed off the road by plow trucks. Using his binoculars, he peered off to the right at the guards in their Jeeps to make sure they weren't watching, then he sprinted across the road, plunging up a driveway and into someone's backyard. He kept his rifle raised, pulse racing at a steady rate as he scampered from one obstacle to the next, eyes always alight on the building where his wife and children were undoubtedly waiting.

Tom put his head down and sprinted to a dip behind the apartments where the grass came to his hips. Standing on a sewage grate with a big bushel of gnarly bushes around him, he stared up at the fire escape. Seeing no guards, he tossed a glance back to where Sam waited with her rifle before he crept from cover, crossed the back yard, and wove between snow-covered playsets up to the metal stairs. He reached up and pulled the first section down with a soft clatter of steel, climbing the rickety steps while staying hunkered as low as possible. On the second landing, he peered into the hall but didn't spot any guards or prisoners, so he kept climbing. On the top floor, he leaned his rifle against the wall and glimpsed through the window down a long hallway. Again, there were no guards by the doors or at the end of the hall and, putting his fingers on the glass, he tried to slide it aside, but it wouldn't budge. Pulling out a knife, he began working it around the edges, but when that didn't work, he bumped them with his palm, hearing the ice break and give way. Tom wedged in his blade on the bottom, lifting until the window broke free and cracked an inch. Just as he was about to finish opening it and climb inside, a rifle, swung down from the roof and pointed at him as two soldiers burst from rooms in the hallway, each with a carbine aimed directly at his chest, one of them screaming at him.

"Freeze right there!"

* * *

Sam watched her father cross the street and make his way toward the apartments, fear squeezing her chest. It seemed like a long shot, thinking her mother, brother, and sister were inside the apartment, but she couldn't deny it was the most logical choice based on what was going on outside. Watching him move from one hiding spot to another, advancing quickly and strategically, she saw not her father, but a soldier, a man with a purpose, a light she'd never seen her father in before. After hearing about his past, though, it fell into place, and she doubted she'd ever see him the same way again.

Sam leaned over her rifle where it rested on a low branch, watching him move from the low patch of ground to the fire escape, pushing through the snow like a bull. He pulled down the first section of stairs and climbed them to the second story landing, peeking inside before continuing up. The whole time, Sam swung her rifle barrel back and forth across the grounds, peering down the sights, waiting for someone to pop around the corner and spot her father digging at the window. Raising the weapon to find him again, she saw him lean inside but gasped when a soldier popped up over the edge of the roof, his rifle pointed down, joined by a flash of movement inside the window.

"Oh no," Sam whispered, watching her father slowly raise his hands, cornered and unable to respond to the threat.

Sighting in on the soldier on the roof, she remembered her practice lessons at the farm from just two days prior. She took a deep breath and kept the barrel steady, resting her finger on the trigger, putting slight pressure on it, mentally preparing herself to take out a threat to her family when something cold and hard pressed up against her cheek.

"Young lady," the soft, firm voice spoke directly in her ear, "if you discharge that weapon, I will spray your brains out all over these woods."

* * *

When a shot from Sam never came, Tom's heart sank and he kept his hands raised instead of going for his rifle. The men grabbed his arms and yanked him through the window, and he landed hard on his knees as they forced his hands behind his back and used nylon cuffs to bind them. Tom grunted as the material bit into his wrists, and he twisted when they jerked him to his feet. As he was being dragged down the hall, Tom jerked his head left and right, yelling out, hoping one of the apartments held his wife and children. "Barbara! Linda! Jack! Are you here? Answer me!"

"Shut up!" The soldiers hauled him roughly to the stairwell and, unable to catch himself, Tom tripped and dragged his feet, half staggering to the first floor where they propped him up and shoved him outside. A Humvee turned into the apartment lot, flew over, and came to a skidding halt in one of the parking spots. The door flew open, and the soldiers forced him inside where Sam sat looking uninjured aside from her pride.

"Sorry, Dad." She winced as if he'd be mad at her. "I tried to take them out, but they caught me."

"Don't worry about it, sweetie." He leaned over and put his head against hers. "Are you okay?"

"Yeah, they didn't hurt me. Just threatened to shoot me, that's all."

"You sure you're okay?"

"Dad, I'm fine." She insisted. "But how did they catch me? And you? It was all of a sudden and…" She stopped talking as realization dawned upon her. "Were we…"

"Set up? It's sure looking like that, isn't it?"

"But how'd they know we were coming? We were so careful!"

Tom shrugged and glared into the rearview mirror where the driver was watching them. One of the soldiers who'd guided him outside came around and climbed into the passenger seat, slapping the driver's arm. "Let's go."

"Where are you taking us?" Tom growled. "Where's my family?"

"Shut up back there!" The driver barked, throwing the vehicle into motion.

It was a short drive, just three buildings over past a small strip to an open lot where they'd erected a prefab headquarters, the Humvee whipping into the lot, pulling across and halting in front where a two-foot-high metal catwalk circled the structure. Several soldiers slammed through the front door, jumped down, and converged on the Humvee where they jerked open the back doors and grabbed Tom and Sam from the vehicle. With a strong hold on their arms, they guided the McKnights toward the building and held them in front of the entrance.

"Hey, buddy! Glad to see you again!" Tom's heart sunk as Keith hobbled out of the entrance to the structure, standing on the metal grating with a wide grin on his face. "You, too, Sam. I really missed you guys!"

Keith's entire demeanor had changed from when Tom and Sam had last interacted with him. The same fake joviality was on full display, masking a deranged sort of menacing tone that hovered just underneath the surface. He looked much the same as he had before, but a bandage covered his nose, his reddened cheeks were topped with a greasy balm and his hands were wrapped in thick layers of gauze. When he moved, he carried his left shoulder lower slightly, and he walked with a noticeable hitch.

"You're supposed to bring your animals in when it gets cold," Tom smirked. "Looks like your owners left you out too long."

"Very funny," Keith sneered as the soldiers pulled Tom and Sam up the stairs and into the building where they entered a main room with three hallways branching out. "Speaking of owners, *she's* in a really bad mood."

"Where're Barbara and the kids?" Tom shot back, craning his neck to see Keith smirk in response.

The soldiers pulled Sam off to the right and Tom to the left, but he didn't realize it until she cried out, "No! Hey, get *off* me!"

"Hey, wait!" Tom twisted and jerked to get away, hot anger rising in his cheeks. "Where the *hell* are you taking my daughter?! *Hey!*"

The soldiers held him tight, twisting and shoving him forward, taking a right at the next junction. At the end of the hallway stood a white door with a reinforced frame around it and a security pad on a thick latched handle. The guards stopped, and Keith stepped around them, using his bandaged thumb to stretch out an ID badge hanging from a lanyard around his neck. The badge touched the pad and a green light blinked on, the door popping open. Keith turned the latch handle with his forearm and stepped through, Tom hauled in right behind him. They entered a medium-sized meeting room with a conference table in the rear and several massive digital screens on the walls. A whiteboard sat on a stand next to the conference table, and next to that was a smaller black screen, devoid of any images.

It was just another briefing room to Tom, one he'd seen way too many times on his missions with Osaka, though for the moment the room was empty, save for the computer workstations set up around the perimeter, with racks of servers and a series of large batteries in the rear of the room to power it all. Up front, by the screens, were a series of workstations that looked more advanced than the others. Deep, heavily cushioned seats faced computer terminals and joysticks that looked a lot like the ones he used to drive the rovers. Keith gestured to a chair at the table, and the soldiers slammed Tom into it, spinning him around to face the wooden surface, causing Tom to wince as the bindings cut deeper into his wrists.

"Wait here," Keith said, walking outside, leaving Tom to sit alone with the two guards watching him.

A few minutes turned into fifteen, then thirty before the door behind him opened and Colonel Rachel Banks strode around the table to sit on the opposite side of him by the whiteboard. Popping open her laptop, she hit a few keys and studied the results. A moment later, she lifted her chin and regarded Tom with a cool stare.

"Sorry we had to meet this way again, McKnight." Banks's lips were pensive, his expression dark. "If you'd only cooperated last time, we could have gotten everything resolved."

"Where is Samantha?" Tom spoke through clenched teeth.

"Oh, she'll be with your wife and other kids." Banks held her hands apart. "We have no real interest in them, only you."

"Is that why you sent a killer after them?"

"You've only yourself to blame here, McKnight."

Losing his cool, Tom tried to stand up, shouting at Banks as a guard forced him back down into his chair. "I want to see them! Right now!"

Banks shook her head. "Not until you're ready to cooperate. I could just throw you in a cell and walk away." Banks spread her hands again. "See, you don't have the luxury of time and I've got the leverage here, no matter how badly you dislike me."

Tom's jaw worked back and forth, trying to think of another alternative, though as much as he was loathe to admit it, there were none. "What do you want me to do so bad that you had to burn down my house, kill my neighbors and kidnap my family?"

Banks clicked a few keys on her keyboard and directed Tom's attention to the small black screen behind her. A map of the anomaly appeared, a crevice in the ocean floor with cracks spreading up into the continental shelf.

"This is the latest rendering from our folks on the science teams, including your old friend, Sue Anne Wilkes. The plan is pretty simple. Our geologists have marked places on the map where we're going to set massive charges."

Tom studied the spots on the map, looking from one white dot to the next, noting their placement along the ridges and valleys. "I have to give you credit for not putting them right on the edge, because that would bust the anomaly open even wider. But, still, even if we could get the charges there, there's no guarantee the entire thing won't get a hundred times worse."

"All you have to do is pilot the rovers to the spots. We'll do the rest."

Tom shook his head, giving the Colonel a truly bewildered look. "Wait… what? I can't drive multiple rovers simultaneously."

Banks nodded like she'd expected the question, jerking her chin toward the specialized workstations up front. "You'll maneuver the rovers to their designated spots, and we'll have technicians hold them in place, then we'll remotely detonate the charges and collapse the anomaly. It will take a few years before the North Atlantic current kicks up again, but that's better than another ice age, don't you think?"

Tom tried to hold on to his anger over his family being held captive, but the lunacy of what Banks was spewing was too much for him to ignore. "Are you serious? What kind of models have been run on this?"

"Adequate ones."

"Adequate??" Tom scoffed, looking at the guards to either side of him as though even they could see the foolishness of what Banks was proposing. "What kind of analysis is that? You need deep simulations, thousands of them, plus on-site samples and measurements. Has *any* of that been done?"

"We don't see how it could get any worse, McKnight." Banks ignored his protest. "Tens of thousands are dying every day from cold and starvation, and we're at war in Mexico. Did you know that?"

Tom nodded. "Yeah, I heard. Not an ideal situation for anyone, but this is mother nature talking, and there's nothing we can do to stop it." He leaned forward, trying to get Banks to understand. "All we can do is weather the storm and figure out a way to start fresh."

"We disagree. We think there's a way to stop this thing. And if you want to see your family again, you'll do what needs to be done." His eyes narrowed. "Just like you used to do."

Tom pulled against his nylon restraints, arms straining, tendons standing out in his neck, but he wasn't nearly strong enough to snap them. "Despite the mistake I made in ever agreeing to work with your sorry ass after what you pulled back then, you don't get to order me around, Banks. I'm not one of your lackeys."

Banks shuffled her papers, gathering them together. "This is happening tomorrow. Either you help us, or you and your whole family will be put out in the cold."

"You wouldn't." Tom shook his head. "No, no, I take that back. You would, wouldn't you? You always were a cold-hearted—" Tom's defiance was interrupted by the walls of the prefab structure rattling as a distance, massive explosion sounded somewhere off in the distance, the floor quivering in response as the monitors on the walls shook.

"What the hell…?" Tom looked around.

"And here we go." Banks nodded sharply. "Right on time."

Tom narrowed his eyes. "What are you talking about?"

Banks clicked a few keys on her laptop and gestured to a different monitor up front on the wall, the screen divided into six sections, each showing a portion of the encampment from a different security camera.

Several minutes passed, and Tom grew impatient in his chair, not understanding what he was supposed to be watching. "What, exactly, are we looking for?"

"Should be any moment now."

The same Humvee that had transported him and Sam to the headquarters came flying around the bend of the main road and into the lot, disappearing behind a strip mall lot before reappearing again, circling toward the camera and whipping into a spot in front of their building.

"There we are," Banks said, a thin smile on her face. "Captured."

The same soldiers as before converged on the vehicle and yanked open the rear doors, one man hauling a little boy from the back seat. The boy squirmed and wiggled, but the soldier held him tightly by the arm and neck, forcing him toward the stairs.

"Jack," Tom whispered, stomach plummeting, anger swelling in his chest at the soldier's rough treatment. He strained to rise, but his guards placed heavy hands on his shoulders, forcing him back down.

Linda climbed out next without being held, calm compared to her brother's wild struggling, her thick brown hair lying in a tumble on her shoulders, as she studied the building in front of her. He'd expected to see fear written on her face, not the calm collectedness on display, feeling pride rise inside at her behavior.

Keith got out of the other side and stood back as two soldiers converged to pull a third person out. They grabbed her from the back, hands bound behind her, eyes up and looking around in a mixture of trepidation and defiance. Barbara wore blue jeans and a torn flannel shirt with a coat thrown over top, her sand-colored hair drawn back in a loose ponytail, though several thick locks hung in her face. Like Linda, Barbara's gaze roamed across the headquarters before finding the camera, seeming to stare straight at Tom.

"Barbara," Tom whispered her name like she was a ghost.

Standing at the front of the Jeep, arms wide, looking at the camera, Keith gloated over his victory. Barbara glared at him, her jaw jutting out, green eyes going ice cold as words were exchanged, though Tom couldn't hear what they were saying. Judging by Barbara's posture and hateful looks, she liked Keith far less than he did as she snapped off a sentence and he jerked his thumb toward the door. Two soldiers immediately descended on her and grabbed her roughly by the arms. As the soldiers dragged her off, Keith looked up into the camera and smiled, waving at Tom, the whole scene clearly an orchestration between him and Banks.

He went over to Linda at the end, her wearing a defiant expression, though behind it was a well of hatred and mistrust. The two looked to be in a heated exchange, far more than the one between Keith and Barbara, Tom realizing that something must've happened between them, something beyond just Keith's kidnapping and hauling them across the state. As if to confirm Tom's suspicions, Keith shook his head angrily and grabbed Linda by the back of the neck, shoving her into the arms of two waiting guards who dragged her inside along with her brother.

Tom wiggled in his seat, jerking against his bonds, struggling against the soldiers holding him down. "I'm going to kill him." He turned his attention to Banks, who'd been watching Tom the entire time. Through tightly drawn lips, nostrils flaring, he hissed, "If that bastard hurts any of them, or so much as touches them again, I'll kill the both of you!"

"Well, good thing he hasn't hurt them," Banks replied, matter-of-factly. "Yet."

Chapter 17
Barbara McKnight
Near Asheville, North Carolina

Jack and Linda sat quietly in the back of the Jeep as they approached Asheville in the growing darkness. The air was still warm in the covered vehicle, only gusts of cool air and snow blowing in through the gaps, making Barbara's left leg a little cold and leaving the floorboard wet with slush from the accumulating snow. If things went as planned, things were about to get much, much hotter, though. Her plan had been constructed on the fly, and while it seemed solid enough to get them inside the base, she would have to execute it perfectly.

They drove slowly along Merrimon Avenue, the Jeep's big front tires crunching on the salt-covered pavement. Linda had joined her in the front seat the last few miles and when they passed a wide, snow-covered lake, she shot a glance at her daughter, who responded with a slow nod of her head. Keith's assumed survival had been a blow to Linda, though she seemed to be handling it with as much bravery as anyone could expect a child to muster. Barbara slowed as they pulled into Grace and angled into a parking lot partially cleared of snow, strip malls on both sides of the white packed pavement providing some camouflage from prying eyes.

Parking the vehicle so that the back was facing a corner, she turned off the headlamps and turned to face Linda and Jack. "Okay, guys. Wait here. I'm going to walk ahead a bit and see what there is to see. Keep an eye out front, and if you see or hear anyone, I want you to get out of the Jeep and hide behind one of those buildings. I'll be back to look for you."

"Okay, Mom," Jack said, Linda nodding next to him.

Leaving the Jeep running so the kids stayed warm, Barbara undid the tattered, wet cover on her side and got out, walking down the road a bit. The street had been cleared by plows, though an inch of drift still swirled across the pavement, none of the newer tire tracks giving her any information on who might have passed by recently. She kept to the right side, creeping forward, boots crunching on the snow as wind gusted her hair around her cheeks, and she shoved the loose strands up into the beanie she'd taken from the kids' stash of clothing.

Around the bend, a glow of light slowed her movements, and she peered around an abandoned vehicle to see a gas station with a pair of parked Humvees in the lot. They'd pulled up close to each other, windows down, four shadows inside leaning forward and back, keeping warm as they chatted. A hastily erected chain-link fence blocked the road behind them, sagging in places, and it wouldn't be hard to break through it if she did things properly. Chest tight, lips pursed, she scanned the area another minute before turning and jogging back to the Jeep where she climbed back behind the wheel and shut the cover.

"Did you find the FOB?" Linda asked.

"Yeah, I did." She breathed deep, building up her courage. "There's a fence around it, and a few guards, but I've got a plan to get past them."

She put the Jeep in drive and pulled onto the road, moving fifty yards closer and parking just before the bend where she'd spotted the soldiers. She turned into a coffee shop lot and hid her vehicle behind a ridge of snow piled along the highway and kept the engine idling, settling back with a sigh.

"What now?" Linda asked.

Barbara looked up through the front windshield as dusk settled over them. "We wait until it gets completely dark, then we make our move." She tried to give her daughter a reassuring smile, though Linda only stared back, clearly wanting more of an explanation. "I'm going to bring down the fence and create a big enough distraction to pull all of their attention away. You two will hide until I get you, then we'll all cross over together. Does that make sense?"

Linda nodded, though Jack leaned between the seats, looking back and forth between the two, eyes curious. "How do you know it's going to work, Mom?"

"Don't worry," Barbara assured them. "It will. We'll get inside the camp without anyone noticing. Then we'll look for your father and Sam."

"Won't they be after us?" Linda asked.

"Maybe, but I'm betting that they might think there are people outside the camp trying to attack it, and they won't be looking for a few people sneaking in. We can't just sit and let them hold your dad and Sam, so we need to try something. And I'm sure as heck not leaving you two by yourselves." Barbara smiled bravely, her stomach sinking at the thought of taking her children into yet *another* risky situation.

Linda stared at her mother for a moment before she settled back in her seat with a faint nod, biting her lip, eyes wide and trusting. "Okay, Mom. We're ready whenever you are."

"Yeah, we want to get Dad and Sam back," Jack said enthusiastically, placing a tiny hand on each of their shoulders.

"How big is the place?" Linda asked, brushing at some snowflakes that drifted in beneath the loose covers. "I mean, how do you even know where to look for him?"

Barbara shook her head woefully. "I don't really know, honey. I'm thinking once we get inside, you two can look for a vehicle and hide out in it. That way you two will be safe and we'll have a way to get out of there quickly once I find your dad."

"You want me to drive?" Linda grinned.

Barbara smiled, patting Linda on the shoulder. "Welllll... I wouldn't normally approve of it, but you've taken everything I've thrown at you and done perfectly fine. I think you can handle it."

"I can," she replied with a confident nod. Something had definitely changed in Linda, both good and bad, and Barbara couldn't change it back any more than she could turn back time. Barbara reached out and took her hand, sitting in silence with Jack holding her other hand as the sun went down, the small group listening to the Jeep idle as it pumped warmth into their makeshift cab. An hour later, Barbara opened her eyes wide from where she'd been resting them, checked her watch, and glanced at the sky. The sun was nearly gone, and they had plenty of darkness to execute her plan.

"Okay, kids. Let's do this," she said, sitting up and stirring her children.

"So what's the plan, Mom?" Linda asked, rubbing her eyes as she stirred from a light, dreamless sleep.

"I'm going to set up the Jeep so it will run into the gate."

"Mom, no!" Jack exclaimed. "I don't want you to get hurt."

She took the his chin in her hand. "Don't worry, kiddo. I'm not going to be in it. I'm going to rig it so it drives by itself."

Brow wrinkling, he nodded. "Oh, okay."

"Linda, you'll take your brother to the left side of the road and follow the Jeep as it goes toward the gate. Stay in the trees. As soon as I know it's going straight, I'll get out of it, come to you and we'll wait to find an opportunity to slip through the fence."

"That sounds easy enough," Linda agreed.

Barbara gave them each a hug. "Okay, go on. Remember to stay out of sight!"

The two left the Jeep from the passenger side and she watched as they jogged across the road, Linda holding Jack's hand. On the other side, they climbed the snowbank and disappeared into the tree line, safe and well out of harm's way. Barbara put the vehicle in reverse and backed slowly onto the highway uphill from the camp, keeping her headlamps off. With the Jeep facing the camp, she put it in park and got out to execute the rest of her plan. She found a rope she'd taken from the last house and tied it to the left part of the steering wheel, leaving it hanging out the window next to the side mirror. Taking out the fuel cans she opened them and splashed fuel all over the Jeep, saturating the cloth roof and doors they'd made, leaving a quarter inch in the truck bed and soaking the back seats.

Finally, she took out a pint whiskey bottle from her pocket, also confiscated from the last home's liquor cabinet, filled it half-full of gas, and stuffed a cloth into the opening, leaving the dry end hanging out like a wick. After she was finished she had one half-full Jerry can left which she placed in the truck bed and poked a small hole in the bottom using her knife, so that it slowly leaked out. She had no idea what the gasoline would do, aside from what she'd seen in the movies. While it probably wouldn't cause any kind of big explosion, she was certain it would make for a nice fiery distraction that would draw a lot of attention and give them a chance to get inside.

Lighter in her left pocket, whiskey bottle in the other, Barbara went over the sequence of events in her head three or four times. When she thought she was ready and not forgetting anything, she walked to driver's side door, opened it, half sat on the seat, placed her right foot on the brake and put the vehicle in neutral. Taking a deep breath of the cold night air, Barbara released the parking brake and got out, waiting for the Jeep to pick up speed on its own as she jogged along beside it, guiding it around the bend until it was relatively straight.

The Humvees were up ahead on the right, still sitting in the gas station parking lot and as the Jeep straightened, it coasted to a few miles an hour, and Barbara had to run hard to keep up. Panting and gasping, she used her left hand to wrap the rope around the side mirror, jerking it tight so the wheel wouldn't budge in either direction, then she let go of the Jeep and reached into her jacket pockets for the lighter and bottle.

Once in hand, she flicked the lighter and watched the flame dance in the wind as she ran, the Jeep already getting two or three arms lengths ahead of her and was gaining speed rapidly on the slightly angled road. A tight squeal escaped her lungs, legs pumping as she put the flame to the wick and waited for the cloth to catch. After a painfully long moment, a flame blossomed and crawled up the cloth and Barbara carefully cocked the bottle over her shoulder and lobbed it toward the back of the truck in a high arc before it smacked off the rear seat, bouncing inside.

Her boot snagged on a rut in the road, and she staggered forward, pitching to the concrete, hands thrown out, palms scraping on the concrete and the Jeep rolled toward the fence with a small flicker of orange in the rear. Not the fiery explosion she'd counted on, but at least her aim had been true - then a blossom of golden light suddenly danced along the back seat and caught on the overhanging covers. The flames roared to life, throwing a bright glow into the night sky as the vehicle gained speed from ten to fifteen.

Grinning wickedly, Barbara shoved herself to her feet and sprinted toward the left side of the road, throwing glances at the coasting Jeep as it rolled past the Humvees, the soldiers pointing and gawking at it. She clambered over the snow pile and up the opposite bank and by the time she reached the tree line, the Jeep was rolling fast toward the fence, angling slightly to the right. The top was completely on fire, pieces of the blankets and comforters sloughing off in flying cinders, the soldiers having left their Humvees to stand in the gas station lot, rifles and fingers pointed at the rolling fire but unable to actually do anything to stop it.

"Mom!" Linda hissed as she and Jack practically fell into their mother.

Barbara took Linda's hand and pulled her along the tree line, stomping through the snow, kicking over forest debris. "Hold on to your brother!"

They'd gotten a few more yards before the Jeep bowled over the fencing, knocking snow and ice everywhere, the front end lifting up before it rolled right over it, trailing sooty smoke behind it. The flimsy fence collapsed backwards, all the way across the street and up to the tree line. As Barbara led her children over the snowy forest floor, the soldiers jogged behind the blazing vehicle, keeping a distance as it finally careened off the road and got stuck in a snowbank.

She and the kids reached a portion of the fence that had collapsed, and she turned and gestured for them to cross. "Come on, guys. Walk over it. Be careful."

They stepped carefully on the slick, icy metal, Jack slipping a bit before Linda helped him over, their weight pressing the fencing down until they finally hopped off the other side and made into the woods. Grinning that her plan had actually worked, Barbara took both their hands and let them deeper into the woods just as the Jeep finally exploded in a bright orange ball of light. Barbara ducked, flinching and throwing her arms around the kids, taking them to the snow as a wave of heat rolled over them and debris zipped by, smacking the tree trunks with clinks and clanks.

"Whoa, Mom!" Jack shouted as she shooed him, pushing them deeper into the woods inside the fence line. "You really blew it up."

"Yeah, that was awesome," Linda said, panting and exasperated as she ran alongside her brother.

"I guess I did." Barbara wore a reluctant smile, hardly feeling the cold in her adrenaline-fueled rush. "Now let's go find your father and Sam."

They made their way along the tree line, feet crunching over the frozen sticks and brush with gusts of crisp, cold air. Eyes up, feet tromping through the snow, she glanced toward the road to see vehicles rushing by on their way to the distraction she'd made. Shouts rang out, and they ducked down as a half-dozen soldiers jogged by on the road, the soldiers dispersing into the forest behind them, three to a side to search the woods.

"I think we got in deep enough," she whispered to the kids, "but we have to be very careful from here on out. We have to stay low and keep quiet."

"Okay, Mom," Jack said, gasping on the cold air as he staggered in front of her, helped by his sister,

She kept the kids well inside the tree line, scouting for signs of a place to catch their breath and enact the next phase of their plan when she spotted a string of fast-food restaurants on the opposite side of the road. The lots were lit by hastily strung up lights, the parking spaces full of military and civilian vehicles, all of them cleared of snow like they'd recently been driven. Hunkered down behind a big tree trunk, she pulled the kids close and let them catch their breath, hugging them tight to keep them warm and calm.

Once most of the soldiers had passed, she edged around the tree and pointed across to the lot. "Okay, Linda. Look over there. See all those cars?"

Linda leaned around with her, bent over, hands on her knees as she breathed heavy from the hard run. "Yeah."

"It looks like they're collecting them so they can drive them south later, maybe. I'll bet they've left the keys inside each one of them, you think?"

Linda shrugged. "I have no clue."

"Well, this is a small facility. There aren't thousands of troops or anything. So, I'm thinking they'd leave the keys inside to make them easier to move. They wouldn't expect someone to break in and try to drive one off, but that's exactly what we're going to do."

"You want us to go find something to escape in?" Linda spelled out her mother's plan.

"That's exactly right." Barbara nodded toward some select vehicles. "Like that black Ford Explorer over there or a Jeep like the one we drove in. Sneak between the rows, open the doors quietly, and look for keys. Don't start anything yet. Just wait for me to come find you. Can you do that?"

Linda nodded. "We can do that. Want us to go now?"

Barbara looked up and down the road, spotting vehicles moving through the trees, but none of them appeared close and none were coming their way. "Yeah, go right now." She gave her kids each a hug, holding them in a lingering embrace before gently urging them toward the road.

A tear rolled down her cheek as she watched Linda lead Jack by the hand, helping him over a snow drift before guiding him across the ice-slick pavement. On the other side, they melted between the line of cars and disappeared in the shadows. Barbara checked the pistol at her hip, then slunk off into the woods. With no idea which way to go, she crept in a southerly direction, moving *toward* the sound of voices and where the vehicle noise was loudest. It had to be the center of the base, and that's where they'd have Tom and Sam.

She skirted the tree line and gazed at a series of strip malls two or three blocks off the road. A large encampment sat in the midst of the interlaced parking lots and a big prefab building squatted in the middle, highlighted by field lights and surrounded by a handful of guards. There were plenty of places for Barbara to hide in the shadowy strip mall storefronts and between abandoned vehicles. She set her eye on one with a cell phone store, a nail salon, and carry out pizza place, looking both ways and spotting an apartment building off to the left where several windows glowed with light, narrowing her eyes with suspicion. It made sense to use the apartment to house some captives, but from what she'd read, Tom was a high government priority. Barbara's shifted her focus back to the prefab building, certain Tom and Sam were inside where it was more heavily guarded.

"Now I just need to get there," she murmured to herself.

Stepping out from the tree line, she crept between a pair of abandoned cars half-covered in snow. From there, she crept to the rear bumpers, peered both ways and sprinted to a nearby store, pressing her shoulders against the front brick. Head on a swivel, she shimmied along the storefront, sometimes sliding across the wide glass windows but not taking the time to look inside. It was only when she reached the far corner and peeked around that she realized her mistake. One of the doors behind her opened, and someone stepped out of the darkness.

"Hello, Barbara."

She grabbed her pistol from its holster and spun to fire, but a hand reached out and snatched her wrist, bending it back. Crying out in pain, she collapsed to one knee, gun clattering to the ground.

"Gotcha." Keith leered at her from a chafed face that was half-twisted in pain, half smiling at her discomfort.

Barbara tried to take a swing at him with her left hand, but he grabbed her easily and held her arms far apart. Hands covered in gauze, his grip was still strong as he squeezed hard, bending her backwards, sending lightning shooting up her wrists.

"Agh!" she grimaced. "You're hurting me!"

"Good," he scowled. "Now ask me if I care."

A light military Jeep pulled up with a squeal of tires, and he dragged her to it with one hand, threw open the door, and shoved her inside where she landed across a surprised Linda and Jack. With a bitter cry, she turned and kicked, punched, and snarled but Keith got in behind her and grabbed her ponytail, shoving her head away, keeping her held so she couldn't hit him. She snarled and threw an elbow that missed badly, receiving a hard jerk of her hair for her troubles.

"Stop hurting my mom!" Jack cried, taking a swing at Keith, his blow glancing helplessly off the man's jaw and drawing a stuff laugh, then his voice turned deadly as he leaned over them, glaring at Jack.

"Hit me like that again, little man, and I'll spray your mother's brains across the parking lot and leave her body to freeze in the cold."

Jack gave a whimper and backed away.

"No, he won't." Linda shifted in her seat, putting herself between Keith and her brother, and wrapping her arms around her Jack and drawing him away. "He needs Mom. He needs all of us. He'll get in trouble if he really hurts us."

Barbara looked up at Linda and quit struggling, holding back for the sake of her children and Keith let go of her hair, grabbed her hands, and forced them behind her back. A soldier leaned between the seats and zipped her wrists tight with nylon cuffs.

"Smart girl," Keith admitted to Linda with a cocky grin. "But that protection only lasts as long as your daddy plays along. As soon as he stops, you're mine." He nodded to the soldiers in the front. "Alright. Let's go."

The driver pulled around the strip mall and headed for the prefab building. He parked in a front spot, and Keith got out as a handful of soldiers descended on them. They grabbed the kids out first, treating Jack roughly, holding him by the back of his neck.

"Hey, knock it off," Barbara growled at them, but two more soldiers appeared at her door and pulled her from the vehicle, leaving her to stand in defiant bewilderment.

She looked up at the prefab building, but she couldn't see much through the tiny glass window on the front door, then Barbara caught sight of a camera perched above the door and stared at it hard, eyes narrowed as if she could see who was on the other side.

"Alright. This is the moment you want to really be good boys and girls." Keith stood at the front of the Jeep. "It's not the time to think about escaping or trying any wild stunts. And, believe me, I know you're thinking about it."

Barbara shifted her gaze from the camera to Keith. "You'll pay for this. You know that, right?"

He shook his head, sighing like a parent having to discipline a child repeatedly for the same behavior. "And, of course, you never learn your lesson. Take her inside." He hiked his thumb over his shoulder, and a pair of soldiers gripped her arms tight and walked her up the metal steps.

The men forced Barbara inside, jerking her up the stairs and shoving her through the front door where they stood in a small entryway with hallways branching in three directions. The men brought Jack and Linda in next, and she panicked as it appeared they'd be going in different directions.

Broken at the thought, her voice cracked, pleading with the man she despised. "At least let me stay with my children. You can't separate us. *Please.*"

"Shut up."

He walked down the hallway and returned a moment later with two guards and a young woman held between them, struggling stiffly, defiant in spite of everything. Barbara blinked at her wild tumble of light brown curls, staring into the familiar green eyes as they ticked back and forth, wide with fright, then focused, narrowed in disbelief, and widened again, her body going slack.

"Sam!" Both Linda and Jack shouted almost at once, their voices squeals of delight.

"Oh, Samantha!" Barbara sobbed, heart breaking from an overwhelming feeling of relief at seeing her eldest daughter alive.

"Mom?!" Sam cried, her face twisting in agonized relief, shoulders straining against the men holding her. "Linda? Jack! Oh my... I can't believe it!"

Barbara leaned forward, straining to reach her daughter, but the guards held her arms tight, not giving an inch of leeway.

"Now, now! No touching!" Keith warned, raising his bandaged hand and waggling it where he stood between them.

Barbara stopped her struggle and shot a smoldering glare at Keith, then looked back at her daughter. "Samantha. Are you okay?"

"I'm fine, Mom. Really, I am."

"What about Tom? Where's your father?"

Sam started to reply when Keith intervened. "It just so happens he's here, though it won't be the happy reunion you expected juuuust yet." He gestured to the guards holding them. "Come on. Let's get this over with."

Under heavy guard, Keith led the McKnights down the hallway to the left, then he made a hard right. Halfway along the next hall, Keith held open a door, and the soldiers ushered them inside a room. Barbara staggered through first, pulled off her feet by the muscular guards as they guided her swiftly to the right, half dragging her to the far side of the room. They turned her around to face a man sitting with his hands tied behind his back and Barbara's mouth dropped, voice faltering as she stared at her husband for the first time in weeks.

"Tom?"

The man she loved looked nothing like she remembered. He was thin and unkempt with a thick beard, and his hair had grown out considerably, strands drooping over his dark eyes that held a hardness to them even as tears ran down his cheeks, emotions twisting across his features.

"Barbara…" His voice had a flat, hushed note to it, filled with a deep emotion he couldn't get out.

They brought Linda through next, and when she saw her father, the grown-up façade melting to reveal her still-childlike exuberance. "Daddy!" she cried as she pulled against the soldiers that held her. "Daddy! It's really you! I missed you so much!"

"Dad!" Jack exclaimed right behind her, so happy he actually laughed, though his face turned sour when the guards wouldn't let him go no matter how hard he squirmed and twisted.

"Hey, guys," Tom replied, smiling, looking back and forth across the lot of them. "I really missed you, too. Hey, my little man. How's it going? Linda, my girl…" His words trailed off as he pulled against his bonds and settled back, helpless, a strained smile on his lips and eyes filled with tears and rage.

For her part, Barbara could only grin at seeing him again. It wasn't exactly the reunion or daring escape that she had pictured, but after so long her family was in the same room again. Her *husband* was in the room with her again. Tom shook his head slowly as he mouthed *I'm sorry* at her, then dropped his head, a pair of tears falling to the front of his shirt.

"Tom!" she snapped. When he looked up, she tilted her head to the side, showing him all the love and affection she could muster with her eyes and her words. "I love you, Tom. We all do. We love you *so* much. It's going to be okay. I promise. Okay?"

Tom met her gaze, and he nodded faintly in reply.

"Very nice reunion, everyone. Very touching. But your Tom here has a decision to make now, don't you, McKnight?"

Barbara turned her head to see a stranger sitting on the other side of a large conference desk, a stiff-necked woman wearing military fatigues and a few badges on her shoulders and chest, blue eyes piercing, haunting almost, an island of decorum and no-nonsense attitude. For the first time, Barbara noticed TV monitors hanging on the walls around them depicting various military scenes. One had a map of Mexico with small red dots blinking all over it while another held an image of the anomaly from the news with cracks and crevices stretching out across the ocean floor and other screens ran data and video she couldn't begin to understand.

Tom had turned his attention away from his family and was focusing on the woman who'd spoken. "If… if I do what you want me to do, this absolutely insane plan of yours… after it fails, you'll let all of us go, right?"

Chapter 18
Tom McKnight
Asheville, North Carolina

"Do what we ask," Banks nodded, "and I'll open the door and let you go myself."

"Fine," Tom growled, emotions boiling in his chest, pushing it down so he could deal with Banks. "I'll do it, but I want to stay with my family tonight."

"No." The Colonel gave Tom an apologetic look that had very little apology in it. "We need to see results first. You'll start first thing in the morning. Dismissed."

Banks jerked her chin at Keith and made a circle with her finger in the air. The guards immediately whisked Barbara and the kids from the room, Jack and Linda both screaming the entire way, Jack's face a mask of angry tears, kicking and punching at the soldier holding him, getting in a few good hits to his gut. The soldier started to jerk the boy, but Tom glared at him in warning. Easing up, the man simply picked Jack up and carried him away with Linda following behind, head raised in defiance of the guard behind her. Sam went next, jaw set, eyes focused confidently on Tom before giving him a firm nod of confidence. He returned the gesture and looked back to Barbara, her beautiful green eyes blooming with hard determination.

"I don't know what's going on here, Tom. But we're going to be okay. All of us." she said pointedly. "I love you. *We* love you."

"I love you too." He held his chin up, but once she'd left the room, his eyes fell to the floor once again.

After they were gone, the soldiers lifted him from his chair and took him away. Once in the hall, his head swiveled, trying to see where they'd taken his family, but they were nowhere to be seen as they took Tom to a windowless room at the end, cut his bonds, and tossed him inside. He turned on them, fists balled, trying to judge whether or not he could take the pair on in a fight.

"Don't even think about it." One younger guard shook his head, almost pleading for Tom to settle down. "You touch any of us or try to break out of here, they're just going to hurt your family. Just… do what they want you to do, okay?"

Tom stood still for a moment before he slumped his shoulders, fists unclenching and arms falling slack to his side, chin dipping in a brief nod. The door slammed shut, leaving him alone. His cell didn't have a window, though a small blue ceiling light illuminated the space enough for him to see the cold walls and magnetically sealed door. Three bottled waters sat just inside next to a couple of protein bars and a pail for him to do his personal business in. He picked up one of the waters and popped the top, pacing the room for fifteen minutes before he fell into the only chair in the room and took a cool swig, waiting for morning to come.

* * *

"Let's go, McKnight. Time to go to work."

Tom lifted his head from his arms where he lay on the floor, squinting at the bright hall lights that filtered into the room as Keith stood above him, waving Tom up. They hadn't provided him with a pillow, blanket, or mat to sleep on, so when he pushed himself up, his lower neck pinched painfully. Grimacing, he shifted to lean against the wall and rub his right shoulder, trying to work out the kinks.

"Come on, buddy, let's go. Time to earn your freedom."

"You're not my buddy, asshole. And I'll need something to eat, and some coffee."

Keith scoffed. "You aren't in a position to give me orders."

"You want me to succeed in this idiotic mission of yours? I need to have my brain working. It's just coffee, man. Black. And I'll take oatmeal or whatever you have to eat. Unless you're making scrambled eggs and bacon."

Keith actually chuckled and nodded, an oddly bright smile on his face despite what Tom could clearly see were some serious injuries across his body. "I can do the coffee for sure. I'll see what I can do about some eggs."

Keith shut the door, but ten minutes later it opened again, and a soldier brought in a plate of freeze-dried scrambled eggs with two sausages, a piece of bread, and a large cup of black coffee. Tom ate, downed his coffee, and splashed water on his face from a small basin in the corner, then he knocked on the door to let them know he was ready. The soldiers opened it and stepped back to let him out while another held out a pair of nylon cuffs and waited for him to place his hands inside.

Tom shook his head and rubbed his still-sore wrists. "I can't wear those, guys. I need to have all my circulation flowing to drive the rover, and you already did a number to me earlier."

The two soldiers looked at each other before Keith stepped in behind them. "He doesn't have to wear them. Just move him along."

The soldiers stepped back and gestured for him to come out. Tom turned right out of the cell to follow Keith and one guard to the entryway while another soldier came behind him. The short walk away from the cell gave him time to think – his time in it had been claustrophobic and surreal, and he'd been unable to shake himself from thoughts of his family, particularly after seeing them for such a brief period of time before they'd been ripped away. Jack, Linda and Barbara had all clearly gone through hell, but Jack was still fighting tooth and nail, Linda had matured years in a short amount of time and Barbara… was still Barbara. Beautiful, wonderful, and strong. His longing to put his arms around his family was overpowering, and the only thing fueling his sense of calm in a situation where he wanted nothing more than to tear everything – and everyone – around him limb from limb.

They ushered him down the hallway to the control room door, entering the wide, rectangular room with its large conference table, computer workstations and banks of communication equipment. Racks of powerful computer servers hummed on the far-left side of the room and there was a massive wall of monitors and a row of driver's seats with their mounted joystick controls on tables. While the place had been empty the night before, several young men and women sat at the tables, kicked back and drinking coffee as they chatted softly as a group of civilian scientists looked up from a conference table and nodded at Tom. At a workstation in the rear, a woman with a bob of red hair leaned away from her computer terminal and gave Tom a hesitant, relieved smile.

"Sue Anne," Tom said with a nod. "Glad you made it off the ship."

"Me, too." She stifled her smile and sobered up with a glance around at the military personnel, lowering her voice to a whisper. "None of us are here by choice. Give 'em hell."

"McKnight." Colonel Banks stepped away from a group of people she'd been talking to in the back of the room. "Are you ready to start?"

Tom nodded, biting his tongue, forcing himself to be less acerbic to make the entire process smoother. "Yeah, I'm ready to go." He jerked his head toward the row of workstations sitting in front. "Are those the techs who'll be holding the rovers steady?"

"That's right." Banks stepped across the room to the center where a large chair sat apart from the others, looking like a leather captain's seat with high arms, smaller monitors mounted in front, and a robust set of joysticks perched on the desk's surface. "And this is your chair. Take a seat."

Tom strode over but paused before he sat down, turning to give the Colonel a hard stare. "I have zero reason to trust anything you say, but I have to ask anyway. This is the last mission, right?"

Banks held Tom's eyes before nodding. "In spite of your recalcitrance and the difficulties you've put me through, I am a woman of my word. You'll be reunited with your family as soon as the mission is complete. We'll release you, and you'll be given transport south. You have my word."

Tom shifted his jaw. "Alright. Let's just get this over with."

He sat heavily in the main controller's seat, looking up and down at the line of drivers who waited for him to get started. All of them young, they seemed fresh-faced and ready to go. If he knew Banks, they'd all been recruited from the Army's drone program and had been practicing with undersea rovers for the past week. Most nodded at him, respecting his position in the group without question and Tom returned the greeting, then gripped the joysticks to get a feel for them. It had been years since he'd driven a submersible on a job, but feeling came back in an instant as he checked the toggles with his thumbs, index fingers on the triggers as Banks hovered by Tom's right shoulder.

"A lot has changed since you last drove one of these, but we found an older set of controllers and engineered it to work with the new style of rovers."

Tom ignored Banks, focusing on the twelve-inch video screen nestled between his joysticks, angled up from the desk so he had a perfect view for driving, along with the two alternate screens that flared out from the main one, giving him an assortment of cameras to toggle through, including a rear view.

He gestured at a series of switches on his left, numbered one to ten. "What are those for?"

Banks leaned farther over his shoulder. "You've got ten drones to get into position. Flipping one of those switches will allow you to share control with the subsequent technician. You'll drive first. When you have the drone in position, simply nod at your tech, and they'll hold it steady. From there, you can switch to the next drone and drive it into position, handing it off to its subsequent tech. Rinse and repeat until all ten are in place."

Tom nodded, then addressed the techs. "There'll be cross currents you've never experienced before and forces that could tear your rovers to pieces. I need you to listen to me and do exactly what I tell you to do when I tell you. Understand?"

One young woman nodded enthusiastically. "We've been practicing around the fault zone for three weeks. We can handle it!"

Three weeks? They'd clearly been planning things out for longer than he had realized. Tom nodded at the woman, then Banks continued.

"All the rovers have been pre-positioned just outside the anomaly zone, resting on the bottom with no currents. You'll start with Rover One, driving it out into position first and move on down the line from there." She stepped back, gesturing to the controllers. "We're ready when you are."

Nodding, Tom settled into his seat, taking a deep breath before flipping the switch for Rover One. The screen between his joysticks automatically switched to the submersible's view of the ocean floor. While he would normally expect to see a bit of debris drifting by and some sea life in a calm environment, the rover showed anything but. Dirt swirled and pieces of rock and chunks of dirt spun past, evidence of the anomaly's raging flow just a short distance away.

Tom shook his head, let go of the joysticks, and crossed his arms. "I'm telling you, Banks, this is a bad idea. You're going to end up blowing that thing wide open and causing so much more damage than you know. You don't know how deep that rift is, or if it's tied to other aquifers and fault lines." Tom shook his head. "We'd be fools for trying it. We could be murdering the world."

Her patience rapidly running out, Banks slammed her fist into her hand, turning and gesturing to the men and women gathered at the table behind them. "You're a damn rover driver, McKnight! You don't know about geology, fault lines, or anything else. I've got a dozen scientists here who've been working on this for weeks, and they've given the unanimous go ahead for us to proceed. Do your damned job or suffer the consequences."

Tom craned his neck and looked at the scientists standing off to the side of the room, hoping to see a bunch of confident people who couldn't wait to show him reams of data to prove their estimates, but they all shifted uncomfortably or averted his eyes.

"They look scared to me," Tom scoffed at Banks. "Maybe you talked them into their theories with promises and false pretenses. Just like the old days."

Banks ground her teeth together, then whipped her head at Keith, who in turn jerked his thumb toward a different door off to Tom's left. One soldier opened it while another entered, shoving Barbara in front of him, yanking her wrists downward, bringing her to her knees with a cry. Keith stepped over with a pistol in his hand, pressing the cold steel barrel to the back of her head. Tom bristled, coming halfway out of his seat while the scientists gasped and squirmed uneasily in their seats.

Banks came to stand directly between Tom and Barbara, hands on hips, her anger no longer masked. "I'm not messing around with you anymore, McKnight. If you don't do what I say, we'll put a bullet through your wife's head. Then we'll go get Samantha and do the same to her. All the way down the line until we reach little Jack. How do you think he's going to feel seeing his mother and siblings lying dead on the floor, shot dead because you couldn't follow orders?"

Vision clouding over with a red haze at her words, Tom took an instinctual swing at Banks but she blocked it, smashing him in the nose, sending shockwaves through his head as he fell back into his seat. When he looked back up, she had her own sidearm out, aiming it at his chest, glaring down at him.

"Do. It. *Now.*"

Head ringing from the blow to his nose, Tom eased back in his seat, facing forward once more, gripping the joysticks on Rover One and kicking the machine to life. It rose off the sea floor, and pushing ahead slowly as he got used to the controls.

"Be it on your head, Banks." He mumbled. "Be it on your head."

"The coordinates we need you to drive to are on the picture-in-picture, as usual." Banks's voice was calm again, her sidearm back in its holster, Keith having backed off of Barbara as well.

Tom nodded again as he urged the vehicle forward, skimming over rises and weaving between tall rock formations, avoiding any tricky driving at first. The gray floor slid by beneath him as the rover cut smoothly through patches of dead kelp and sea grass, staying close to the bottom to avoid sudden currents and as much debris as possible. It wasn't long before he got his bearings, the familiarity of driving the drone like riding a bike. When a rock formation suddenly loomed ahead, Tom dove into a gap between the boulders, banking the machine to the right just in time to avoid smashing it to pieces. The scientists in the room gasped, and more than one rover tech nodded appreciatively though Tom ignored them, pressing the joysticks forward, moving the machine into rougher waters, imagining his body was part of it, feeling the resistance of the thrusters through force-feedback in the control sticks as cross currents from the anomaly tried to shove him around. Glancing at the GPS view, Tom homed in on the first location until he was sitting at the right spot, bringing the rover to a stop, fighting the entire way.

"First target achieved," Banks confirmed.

Tom looked at the first technician. "There's a major cross current coming from the right. Test it." Tom kept the joysticks steady while the young man grabbed his controllers. Together, they held the rover in place until the kid got a feel for the tidal forces.

"Got it?" Tom asked.

"Yeah," the young man nodded.

"Okay, I'm letting go." Tom released his joysticks and watched his screen.

The vehicle swerved slightly to the left as they switched control, though the tech quickly corrected, keeping it perfectly in place.

"Good," Tom gave him a nod. "Hold it right there."

He reached down and flipped the switch to take Rover Two, driving it to the designated spot in less than ten minutes. He handed it off to the young woman who'd spoken up about her training, and she took over for him easily, holding the submersible and its explosive payload in place.

The other rovers were harder to manage as the target points got closer to the widest part of the anomaly where the currents were the strongest. Still, he placed Rover Three, Four, and Five flawlessly, then grabbed Six and drove hard for the placement site. Moving it into place and starting the handoff to the tech.

"Alright, Six," Tom said to the young woman who was to take over. "There's an updraft, so keep the nose down. Go ahead."

She took her controllers in hand, looking unsteady, her joysticks shaking in her grip so much that Tom didn't let go right away.

"A little help here, sir?"

Tom glanced over at the Rover Three driver. "What's wrong?"

"I can't hold the position," the young man responded, shaking his head in frustration.

"He's right," Banks said, stepping closer, glaring at one of the larger GPS screens on the wall, their rovers' positions marked with green dots. "He's already thirty yards off the designated spot. We have a fault tolerance of twenty yards. That's all we can allow."

Tom quickly switched to Rover Three, instantly grabbing the submersible as a side current gave it a right hook across the front. Tom angled the vessel back left, dipping down as he increased the thrusters by ten percent. He slipped in, hugging the sea floor as he maneuvered the rover into position.

"I'm losing it here!" The young woman on Rover Six shouted at him, panic in her voice, sitting stiffly in her seat, holding the joysticks in a white-knuckled grip.

"I said keep the nose down! Come on!"

"I'm sorry!" Her voice quivered.

The four techs who didn't have a rover to control yet chimed in, calling out to give them control, and Tech Two came to Six's defense, arguing with the others to leave her alone. Banks joined the fray, stepped around Tom, her hands raised, tone angry.

"Calm down, people. Don't get too--"

"Shut up, Banks!" Tom bellowed, shouting over her. "Three – hold this! Keep the rudder at ten degrees to starboard and watch your thrusters."

He switched back to Six and took control again, increasing the thrusters and using a rock formation to take a different angle. Head down, eyes pinned forward, Tom willed the rover into position, wiggling it back and forth like a fish, gaining ground yard by yard.

"That's it." Banks's nodded, stepping back to her original position behind him. "Steady as you go."

"Did you not hear what I said?" Tom snapped at her, and to her credit she did, indeed, keep quiet.

The techs quieted down as Tom regained control over the situation and the rovers, the tech in charge of Six giving him a half grin and gripping the joysticks again, keeping the rover in position as he slowly let go.

"Great job, Six," Tom nodded. "You still got it, Three?"

"Yep!" the tech called back.

"Alright. I'm moving on to seven."

Tom picked up where he left off, taking care of the next two rovers in rapid succession, the currents surrounding their destination more predictable than the others.

"One to go, people." Banks spoke quietly from behind him, Tom continuing to ignore her interjection. He struggled against the currents with the last one, eventually finding a shallow valley to cut through, weaving the rover toward the final position, sliding the vessel into place. Once he had it stabilized, he nodded to Ten, who quickly took over and Tom let go of his controllers and held his hands up, looking down the line of techs. All were sweating as their eyes focused on their personal screens, each of them maneuvering their rovers with their own controls, keeping them level and steady in place.

Banks walked down the line, staring at the larger monitors and noting their placement on the GPS maps. Once she reached the end of the line, she turned and nodded to the coordinator in the back. "That's it. They're in position, and the fault tolerances are acceptable. Proceed with the detonation."

"Proceeding with the detonation," a coordinator from the back of the room called. There was ten second pause, then the rovers all vanished from the screens, their camera displays turning to static. Tom relaxed, hands dropping into his lap, glad it was finally over.

"Status?" Banks asked.

"All were detonated successfully, sir."

"Good. Can we get some data from the ships near the anomaly? Any indication that it worked?"

"Checking now, sir."

Tom stood and nodded to the techs. "Nice work, all of you."

"You were great, Mr. McKnight," one of them replied, with another slightly too excited for his own good.

"That was amazing! Now we know why they wanted you for the mission. Mad props to you, sir."

"Amazing?" Tom worked his jaw as he stared down Banks, who was conversing with the group of scientists. "Do you think it's amazing that they kidnapped my family and held a gun to my wife's head to coerce me into doing this? Because I don't think it's that amazing."

Off to the side, the soldier guarding Barbara hadn't let her go, and she was watching him with a proud expression, lips pressed firmly shut. The tech who had spoken to Tom withered at his words and turned back to join the others who were watching the big screens as they waited for confirmation that the detonations had worked. 3D images of the anomaly began to take shape as the ships on the surface bombarded the sea floor with sonar and an overhead video from a helicopter showed an aerial view of Naval vessels circling the area.

When the results came in, they didn't appear on the screen but were instead felt beneath Tom's feet. It started with a low rumble like a train passing close by then it grew into something larger, the ground quivering beneath the weak, prefab building, shifting the floor tiles, anyone not seated throwing their hands out to steady themselves. Tom grabbed his chair and put his knee into it, looking at Barbara as unease grew in his chest. The monitors on the wall flickered and buzzed with white noise and one rattled free and crashed to the floor, causing one of the techs to yelp in surprise. The shaking didn't fade but grew in intensity, and the scientists at the table grabbed on for dear life as others staggered and fell.

"Status!" Banks shouted, knees quivering like some vaudeville dancer as she tried to remain upright.

"On screen!"

An image came to life on one wall screen, and Tom threw his eyes up to watch a rover spiraling down toward the anomaly. The debris thrown up by the explosions was massive, clouds of silt and stone swirling everywhere, and Tom could tell the way the vessel swerved through the currents that something was seriously wrong. The rover found a clear spot between the billowing muck, spotlights aimed downward, a massive gap yawning up at them from below, its sides a swirling mass of stone and silt, the gash wider than it was before. Tom watched as the lights poked along the rim. Some sections had collapsed, leaving collapsed edges as Banks's scientists had hoped while other parts had split apart even more, throwing up spurts of rock as the anomaly ripped open like a fresh wound.

"Colonel, at least three ships are damaged from the debris field!" the coordinator called out, her hand held against her earpiece. "They're requesting permission to—"

The ground gave a massive heave, tossing people from their chairs and toppling anyone standing to the floor. Tom grabbed the chair and hung on while the room erupted in a frenzy, several scientists beginning to shout and argue. A pair of techs cowered, hugging each other as tiles dropped from the ceiling while the soldier guarding Barbara let her go and she immediately began crawling toward Tom across the unsteady floor.

Banks somehow got to her feet, hand resting on the shoulder of a kneeling scientist. "Everyone get on your knees and cover up. Stay right where you—"

"No!" Tom yelled. "The quakes are from the explosion." He shot Banks a dark look. "Just like I figured would happen. We need to get outside right now before this structure comes down on us! Form lines and crawl toward the door. Come on people. Crawl!"

He grabbed a rover tech from her chair and shoved her toward the door. She got the hint and took someone else's arm, pulling them along.

"That's it!" Tom yelled as he crawled toward his wife. "Grab a partner. Form an orderly line and get out of the building!"

He turned, and Barbara was right there, a determined grimace on her face. Tom reached for her, but Banks stepped between them, her face a panicked snarl. Wordlessly, Tom balled up his fist and punched the woman in the gut, shoving her away where she collapsed the floor, toppling over. He threw himself at Barbara, grabbing her shoulders and pulling her close, the feel of her body against his was strange and familiar all at once, but he didn't have time to think about it with the building falling apart around them.

"Turn and crawl," Tom shouted, grabbing her wrists and turning her, forcing her to go in the other direction.

They made it a short distance when Tom saw one of the soldiers lying on the floor, hanging on to one of the scientists. He reached out and snatched the man's knife out of its sheath, then he tapped Barbara to get her attention. She turned, and he held up the blade. Nodding her understanding, she lifted her wrists, and Tom carefully put the sharp edge against the bonds and jerked upward. Hands flying apart, she reeled and scrambled harder for the side door with Tom right behind her while others were clambering through doors and into the hallways despite Banks shouting for the guards to keep people in.

"There, Barb!"

She shifted direction and headed for the direct exit outside when a guard reeled to his feet and put his back against the door frame, blocking their way. Two scientists staggered by and slammed into the soldier, knocking his rifle aside as they blew through the door. Cold air shot inside as another terrible wave of shaking ripped through the facility. More of it was falling apart behind them, and people gave up any semblance of following Banks's orders and dove for the nearest exits, shoving, pushing, and punching their way through. With a lurch, Tom picked up Barbara and stumbled with her onto the steel grating, diving off to land hard on the snow-covered pavement.

The ground lurched to a halt, leaving Tom's teeth rattling in his head, bones shivering. Instinctively, he turned to his wife and planted a quick kiss on her lips, holding the side of her face and running his calloused fingers through her hair. "I can hardly believe you guys are here. Are you okay?"

"You could have asked that before you kissed me," she said with a sideways grin.

"Sorry, I just--"

Before he could get the rest of his words out, Barbara grabbed his face and kissed him back, then yelled, "We have to get the kids!"

He nodded, staggering to his feet, dragging her up with him. "I'm guessing they have them at the command center."

"That's what I was thinking," she agreed with a vigorous nod.

The pair sprinted through the parking lot as soldiers and civilians tried to make sense of what had happened, some wandering around aimlessly while others were helping those trapped in collapsing buildings. The destruction wasn't confined to the prefabs, as parts of the strip malls had fallen in or were still in the process of falling, brick, glass, sheetrock and rebar spread across the ground in thick layers, people screaming from inside. Glancing back, Tom saw half of the command center collapsing, soldiers diving in to rescue their friends.

"We got out just in time," he said as they sprinted away.

"Let's hope the kids are okay," Barbara's voice was strained with worry, and Tom picked up on it. "They kept us over in the holding center. This way."

Grabbing his hand, she pulled him through the parking lots, rounding a crumbling brick building and sprinting toward another prefab structure that leaned sideways with crooked walls. Officers and soldiers ran past them or jumped into military vehicles to zip away and Tom looked back, half expecting Keith to be there, but all he saw was chaos.

"I missed you," Tom said, as they ran forward, huffing and puffing. "I missed you guys so damn much."

Barbara grinned at him, the first genuine smile she felt like she'd cracked since the whole mess had started. "I missed you two. The kids have been a pain in my butt. About time you decided to come home and help out!"

Tom laughed, elbowing her arm as they reached the building, Tom following Barbara up a short set of stairs to the wide-open front door. A soldier stormed outside and ran right past them but didn't seem interested in apprehending them.

"Where to?"

"This way!"

Barbara stepped inside and took a right, then she hung a hard left down a hallway. They moved quickly, keeping their heads down, boots thudding on the flimsy flooring turned to mush by the quake.

"There," Barbara pointed.

Tom spotted a uniformed man standing in front of a steel door like the one he'd been held behind the previous night, and as they approached, he saw that the guard was the same young man who'd let him out earlier.

"Are my kids in there?" Tom asked, pointing at the door.

The soldier re-gripped his weapon, facing up to Tom with a hint of panic in his eyes. "They're inside, but they're not going anywhere."

"Let them go," Tom growled.

"Sorry, sir. I've not been given order to do that."

"Look, kid. I did my part, and now it's time for you guys to keep up your end of the deal. Or," Tom curled his fist, "we can do it a different way."

The soldier didn't back down. "Like I said, sir. I need a direct order from Colonel Banks to let the children go free. Without it, they'll have to stay put."

Tom clenched his fist, then relaxed it, softening his tone. "Look, son. You can either try to keep us from seeing our kids – the ones that Banks kidnapped at gunpoint – or you can go help some of your buddies who are out there injured and dying. I'd vote for the latter."

For a moment, it looked like the young man might resist, and Tom would have to go for his gun, but finally he nodded slowly, turned, and punched in a code on the security keypad next to the door. The steel slab popped open, and the soldier slid past them down the hall without another word. Tom put his fingertips into the door crack and pulled, but the earthquake had warped the framing and it wouldn't budge. He grunted and jerked and strained with all his might, but he couldn't free it, then Barbara dove to her knees, sticking her own fingers into the gap, putting her left foot against the wall and pulled, crying out when it barely budged.

"Mom, Dad! Is that you?" Samantha's voice was tinny and quiet behind the thick door.

"It's us!" he shouted back.

"Push, kids!" Barbara yelled into the gap. "Put some elbow grease into it."

"On three!" Tom added.

He counted down, placing his foot above Barbara's against the wall. He hit one and then shouted "Go!" throwing every ounce of strength he had into a massive heave. The door scraped along the floor, coming open about six inches.

"One more time!" he called, then he counted down again.

The second time, the McKnights shoved the door open another eight or ten inches, and Jack, Linda, and Sam all plunged through, landing on Barbara with happy cries. Tom leaned against the hallway wall watching his family lying in a pile on the floor, scarcely able to believe what he was witnessing.

Linda lifted her glassy eyes to him, then she stood and threw her arms wide, falling forward to wrap them around his waist, her cheek turned against his stomach. A happy squeal of delight burst from Jack's mouth, and he leapt up from where he'd been hugging Barbara, slamming into his father and clinging to his leg with a sob. Tom wrapped one arm over Linda's shoulders and ruffled his son's hair, then closed his eyes and leaned forward to put his cheek on his younger daughter's head. He blocked everything out for a handful of seconds, relishing the simple closeness of the people he loved most in the world. "Oh, I missed you guys so much."

"You too, Dad." Linda and Jack both squeezed him harder.

The tiles beneath their feet shifted again. At first, Tom couldn't tell if it was simply the flimsy structure or another quake, then he realized the rumbling was deeper than that.

Barbara touched his arm. "I think we need to get out of here, Tom. That's another earthquake."

"I think you're right." He turned his youngest two down the hallway, with Sam and Barbara close behind.

They passed military personnel coming and going, but they were concerned about the earthquake, not the McKnights and a moment later, Tom had his family outside and moving away from the holding center, kicking up fresh snow as they staggered through the gusting winds.

"Do you know how much worse the shaking will get?" Barbara asked, shouting over the soldiers hollering and revving truck engines as winches were cranked to clear debris in desperate attempts to save lives.

"I can't be sure at all," Tom replied, searching for something to escape in. "I just know we need to clear the area as soon as possible."

Chapter 19
Specialist Lance Morales
Mexico City, Mexico

"Keep driving, Morales," Captain Jones commanded over the comm line. "Don't stop until you see the whites of their eyes. And then keep going."

Morales nodded vaguely, holding his wheel straight, his foot pressed to the pedal as he drove on a long, two-lane highway, moving eastbound into Mexico City. As the spearhead of the incursion, their company was scouting, prodding for weak spots, and dropping off units deep behind enemy lines. The area had already been softened by air strikes, the buildings on the outskirts smoking and ruined by heavy fire.

"They're sending us into a meat grinder!" Smith called down from the turret as he lit up targets on both sides of the roadway with his gun.

"No kidding," Morales said, coughing and choking on dust filtering in through the vents.

Smith's gun rattled as they kept moving, and Morales glanced in his side mirror to make sure the other trucks were following. It was a convoy of twelve vehicles, a half-dozen Humvees, two Stryker APCs, and a handful of support units, including an M1129 mortar carrier. Behind them was a line of tanks, closing on the city center, but moving slowly through the tightly packed streets.

"Hold it right here," Smith called down.

"The captain said to keep driving!"

"I said *hold up*! I saw something."

"Alright, but the captain'll stomp our asses."

"Let me worry about the captain."

Morales pulled to a stop in the middle of the road, glancing into his rearview mirror at the soldiers in back, waiting for their moment to get out and do something. The truck went quiet as Smith did some spotting from his high seat, and Morales peered through his smudged window at the Spanish-style hovels lining the highway. The M1129 fired off a round to the side of the road ahead, causing a massive explosion in a nearby building, sending up billowing smoke as stucco and plaster flew everywhere. The gunners on the Humvees behind them tore into another structure farther down.

After a pause, Smith called down. "Okay, take the ramp here to the right."

"Why?"

"Because I don't trust what I'm seeing on the road ahead."

"Alright," Morales said, and he kicked the Humvee forward, taking the right fork.

It swung them around to another highway, still following an easterly course. The company had come to trust Smith's gut feelings, and not even the captain interfered with the lieutenant when he guided them to an alternate route. The road was clear ahead, and Morales punched the gas, taking them to a sharp and steady forty miles-per-hour, peering ahead through his dusty windshield as the highway guided them along a ridge cut into the side of a hill. They rose steadily until they crossed a bridge at the top, passing through rows of quaint shops of wildly painted concrete and brick. Off to the right, several high-rise hotels sat, at least three of them smoking from earlier air strikes. The restaurants were beautiful yet dusty looking with low awnings and scattered patio furniture, plastic flowers clinging to fancy posts, walls painted with Mexican and US flags, smoke pouring out of windows and doors.

Around the next bend, Morales slowed to a crawl. A cement barrier divided the lanes, though he could see over it at the surrounding hillsides. Mexico City was a blender of hills and valleys. Every square foot of space was laden with homes stacked on top of one another, fancy high rises plopped in the middle of blocks of squalor. The houses were similar to the ones he'd seen in Reyes and Monterrey, nothing uniform in size or shape nor placed in any particular order. Painted pink or baby blue or just plain beige, they perched on rises, clinging to the roads that wound through the city at odd angles and bends which explained the need for light armored vehicles, as tanks were going to have a tough time getting through the tightly packed streets and every block would be a potential trap.

"Alright, Morales," the captain spoke over the wire. "Quit sightseeing and keep it moving. We've got to be at the city center in another two hours."

"Yes, sir." He hit the gas and pushed them ahead, driving fast past abandoned vehicles on the debris-strewn roads.

Sections of the city were smoking, but those were from precision strikes to drive the military forces out. The brass wanted to avoid hurting infrastructure and civilians, though Morales didn't see how they could possibly distinguish between military personnel and civilians with indiscriminate bombing in such tight quarters. The caravan took small arms fire a quarter mile later on a section of highway squeezed tight by three-story buildings, snipers and machine guns firing down on them from the upper windows, and he winced as rounds pinged off the Humvee's reinforced sides and acrylic glass. Smith and the other vehicles returned a vicious barrage of gunfire and Morales tore past them as soldiers tossed grenades through the windows, explosions filling the air behind them. Three Apaches flew in overhead, too late to offer cover fire before they banked to the left, the convoy already moving forward to escape the onslaught.

It was an endless highway, winding between an endless mass of human construction and thirty minutes later, they still didn't seem any closer to the city center. A string of distant explosions went off on a parallel highway and Morales looked around as big fire clouds blossomed off to the right. He listened on the radio as the someone said a column had been halted by IEDs; another group had lost two trucks.

"There's the resistance I was talking about," Smith spoke offline, just to the soldiers in the Humvee.

Morales grew more nervous by the second, expecting to get hit at any time, and when the initial big rumbles came, he thought it was gunfire. The Humvee shook and rocked, but nothing hit them and it wasn't until a building up ahead fell to pieces and spilled into the road that he realized it wasn't an attack. In a split-second decision, Morales hit the gas pedal and whipped the wheel hard to the left, flying around falling debris and barely missed getting buried alive. A glance in his rearview showed the other trucks passing around the rubble, but ahead the road started to buckle and crack.

"Morales, halt!" the captain called on the comm.

He hit the brakes just as a big section of the pavement fell away and they skidded, front tires dropping over the edge as the Humvee came to a stop.

"Everyone out!" Morales shouted.

Doors flew open. Soldiers evacuated on wobbly legs, staggering and falling against each other or onto the pavement. Yet, the ground kept shaking, jerking, shifting side-to-side, and bouncing, making it nearly impossible to stand. When he turned to lean against the Humvee, the four ton vehicle finally slid off the edge as the concrete cracked and splintered under it, plummeting to the pavement below in a crash of metal. The surrounding buildings quaked and shivered, plaster and siding falling away like sandcastle walls that had dried in the sun, some of it spilling down the hillsides while much of it poured onto the cracking, crumbling road. Morales fell to his knees, crawling directionless, wincing as the pavement squirmed and kicked dust into his face.

"It's... an... earthquake!" he shouted, though the words came out shaky, teeth clacking in his head.

He turned and looked for the other members of his truck. One man cried out as he windmilled into a gap that had suddenly appeared, then the road shifted again and slammed together, swallowing the man, cutting off his screams and replacing them with a terrifying silence. Eyes sprung with fear, every bit of courage deserting him, Morales scrambled for higher ground. A piece of pavement sunk, a soldier slid by and he grabbed the woman by her rifle strap as she clung to the stock for her life. Dust filled the air in a choking cloud as they battled – no, tried to survive – an onslaught they couldn't begin to understand. With destruction all around him and no way to escape it, Morales closed his eyes and waited to die.

And then, just like that, it was over. The shaking stopped, silence hanging in the air as the rumbling rolled away like retreating thunder. The soldiers looked around at one another, some groaning in pain while others slowly stood, helping their comrades to their feet, trying to process what had happened. As the smoke cleared, Morales looked down to see he still held the rifle strap, but the weapon and the soldier on the other end were gone, the only thing remaining of her were bloodstains and gore smeared between the slabs of concrete. He threw the strap away, twisting and crawling away from the crevasse, glaring back in the general direction of the team. A half-dozen trucks still sat relatively upright and a few had plummeted into crevices or simply been rammed into each other by the forces at play. The surviving soldiers were out milling around in bewilderment, one sitting against one of the Humvee wheels, sobbing into his helmet while another vomited his guts up where the side of the road used to be. Without the constant whine of engines and gunfire, Morales could hear air raid sirens coming from some far-off place in the city's center.

The captain's clear voice finally hollered out. "Roll call everyone! Come on, get it together; we're still in a war zone here! Who are we missing?"

The company gathered in a central spot, eighty soldiers in all after losing ten to the quake's rage and a few more to serious injuries. Morales checked in and then strode back to the edge of the rubble, staring down at his Humvee where it rested on its grill fifteen feet below them. Stuck straight up and down, it leaked fuel and oil all over the street below, buildings tilting this way and that around it, strange creakings being carried on the dust-covered wind from nearby.

"You okay?"

He turned to see Smith standing with a cigarette in his shaking hand, sucking vigorously at it and letting the smoke trail from his mouth and nose. His partner had never looked more nerve-wracked, which was nearly as frightening as seeing a city collapsing around him.

"Hell, no." Morales shivered. "I watched Ready and Hergot get crushed in some rock. I..." His words trailed off as a lump formed in his throat.

Smith rested his hand on his shoulder and gave it a firm squeeze, the nervousness not affecting his sense of dry, dark humor in the least. "That's heavy. I didn't see any of that. I was too busy pissing myself and trying to keep from dying." The way the lieutenant said it with a smirk made him laugh and Smith held out his cigarette.

Morales shook his head. "What do you think we'll do now?"

"Probably wait for air pick up, if we're smart." The lieutenant gestured at their wrecked trucks. "It's not like we can drive anywhere."

Morales took it a step farther and gestured at the long stretch of ruined road ahead. "Yeah, there's nothing to drive *on*."

"Right," Smith agreed with him, tossing his cigarette down pointedly. "That's exactly right."

Captain Jones waved his finger in the air, giving a low whistle. "Okay, soldiers, I just got word from central command. Grab all the gear you can carry from the trucks. We're marching double time into the city. Mission's still on."

Smith turned to Morales with a look of incredulity. "Do you believe this bull? We're double-timing it to the city?"

"Yeah, I *do* believe it. And our stuff is sitting down there in the truck. Tell me how we're going to get it."

"I'm sure Captain Jones knows a way."

* * *

Fifteen minutes of the most creative rock-climbing Morales had never dreamed of having to do, the soldiers had grabbed their gear out of the oil-leaky Humvee and were ready to march.

"Better not light up," he reminded Smith as they pulled out their packs from the side doors and shouldered them. "Or you'll set us on fire."

"Don't worry, I won't." The lieutenant laughed. "Not that it'd make things much worse, eh?"

"Okay, Morales and Smith are back on point," Captain Jones called out. "Let's move it."

The pair sauntered to the front of the line, lifted their rifles to their hips and strolled along the devastated roadway. The pavement was torn to pieces, buckled and collapsed in some places, pushed upward in others. They had to watch where they walked, every step a potential pitfall as lumber and brick covered the edge of the road, some of it spilling out to the center, jagged edges clawing at their legs and boots, threatening to penetrate even the thickest rubber soles. The city rang with cries and wails as Mexican citizens picked through the rubble, searching for loved ones and an occasional police siren squalled, though those were eerily sparse in the dusty haze that lay over everything. Deep, ominous groans echoed from still-standing buildings as they walked past, the foundations of the structures disturbed by the earthquake trying to settle into new orientations.

Morales spotted groups of people trying to move heavy sections of rubble with their bare hands, hardly paying attention to the soldiers as they marched by. One group had formed a line of twelve and were passing rocks from one person to another as they tried to rescue those trapped in a building. Five soldiers from the company broke ranks and started to help, but Jones and the other officers chased after them and hollered at them to get back in line.

"We need to get to the city center!" The captain yelled at the top of his lungs. "We're not here on a humanitarian mission. We're here to spearhead the attack, and that means we don't stop until we reach the objective. Is that understood?"

"Yes, sir!" the troops called out, though Morales's eyes lingered on the struggling citizens, wishing he could help.

The fires started slowly at first, gathering fury as the minutes passed, a building here, a gas line there mixed with the occasional explosion. Soon, they spread, the houses packed so tightly that the flames jumped from one dwelling to the other with speed and force, assisted by the earthquake's disruption of any natural or manmade fire-prevention measures. The flames tore upward to consume buildings and the dry scrub between them, embracing the city in a hellish orange glow. Heavy soot filled the air, burning Morales's eyes and nose. Faint gusts blew, sometimes clearing the air, allowing them to breathe, and soon, everywhere he looked, flames had broken out across the city. Two distant high rises were colored in a golden hue, trails of black smoke drifting up to the sky to form a cloud of doom. The captain and his entourage moved toward the front of the line, not too far behind Morales and the men from his truck. Smith fell back, taking an opportunity to shoot the officer a question.

"Are you sure we should be moving into an earthquake zone, sir?" he asked. "Look at the fires. I mean, we could all die of smoke inhalation or something."

"Headquarters is well aware of the situation, Lieutenant Smith," the captain replied, "but they want us to continue. Now, fall back in line."

"Are you sure, sir? I can hardly breathe."

"If you're struggling to get air, son, don your mask."

"Yeah, I've got mine," Smith pointed out, "but not everyone else has theirs. We lost a lot of trucks and gear back there."

"I'm aware of that."

"But, sir—"

The captain leveled a hard stare at him. "Get back on point, lieutenant. It's the last time I'm going to tell you."

"Right, sir. Sorry."

Smith saluted and jogged back to Morales where he kept a wary eye on the street and buildings.

"Heartless bastard," the lieutenant murmured under his breath as he hefted his rifle.

"Well, on the plus side, I don't think we'll have to worry about that guerilla warfare you were talking about before." Morales looked around. "There's nothing left to fight over."

They continued, the destruction growing worse the deeper into the city they went. Pieces of high rises broke off and crashed to the ground right before their eyes, the sounds of straining girders and groaning infrastructure echoing across the dying city. The top portion of a distant skyscraper shifted and crumbled in slow motion, Morales pausing to watch with a look of horrified amazement on his face. On some blocks, the reek of burning flesh wafted by, causing him to gag every few minutes, and trying to think about something else to forget about the smell only made it worse.

A quarter mile later, a woman ran out of the mist toward them, wailing and crying with a bundle in her arms. Three soldiers turned and raised their rifles, causing the woman to stop and cower in terror and two of the company medics broke rank and rushed to her aid. When they finally got her calmed down enough to convince her to let them have a look, she held her arms out to reveal a charred lump wrapped in a fire-tattered blanket. Some of the soldiers looked away, vomiting into the broken street, others stared in disbelief and after a few moments of comfort for the mother, the column moved on.

After some time, Smith leaned in as they walked. "How are you holding up, champ?"

"This is what hell must be like," Morales replied. "Just… what the hell is going on here? What happened? And the smell… the smell is terrible. Every breath makes me want to throw up but I'm pretty sure there's not even any acid left in my stomach."

"Put on your mask. It'll help, a bit."

Morales had thought about it plenty of times, but he wouldn't wear one if others in the company couldn't, though he was close to admitting defeat. "I might share with someone later."

Smith scoffed as his head swiveled. "Shoot, you think this is bad, just give it a couple of days."

"What do you mean?"

"Hundreds of thousands of bodies piled up under all that rubble. The ones that don't burn will rot, my friend. And it's going to stink to high heaven."

Morales's stomach turned at the thought, but still, he led the group through the desolation in spite of the impossible dread settling over him. Step after step he peered into the gloom, eyes open to the broken road ahead, staying focused on the crunch of rock beneath his boots, brain on idle as he processed sights and smells like a robot, keeping his emotions under wraps. When he finally spotted movement, it was so big couldn't believe it. He narrowed his eyes, blinked, and stared harder through the haze until they solidified.

People. Dozens of them standing in the street, murmuring or coughing, gathered together like a single living creature. He turned and hissed at Smith as he lifted his rifle to his shoulder and Smith gestured to the captain before crouching down next to him with his own weapon up.

"You got something, man?"

Morales paused for a moment before stalking forward, seeing more people standing right on the highway. The few dozen turned to a hundred, then it grew to two hundred as a breeze whipped in and cleared the smoke away. Those two hundred turned into a thousand, and he stopped and gaped at the sea of survivors, stretching as far as the eye could see. There were old women and men, boys and girls, families holding each other with dead expressions on their faces, their clothing covered in ash, dust and blood, ignoring the arrival of the US soldiers.

Off to the right lay a soccer stadium, parts of it lying in ruin, though many thousands of people were gathered in the parking lot and surrounding streets. A pitifully small number of emergency vehicles sat at one end of the lot where a handful of tents had been erected and workers were passing out medical supplies and water from the backs of trailers. A few Mexican police cars were present, lights spinning, though none were in any position to do more than scowl and mutter at the passing soldiers.

Captain Jones stepped up, jaw hanging open as he took in the sight. "What in the name of God..."

Morales shook his head, the barrel of his rifle falling as he stared over a sea of human suffering. "Complete chaos, sir. We'll never make it through all these people. We'll need to find a way around--"

Smith elbowed him in the side, pointing deeper into the crowd. "Look."

Morales narrowed his eyes and spotted a group of soldiers pushing through the throng toward them, moving steadily and with a purpose.

"Mexican Army," he said. "And they're armed."

"Fire team up front!" Smith shouted.

Morales raised his weapon and stepped forward. Five others joined him, forming a firing line while the rest of the company fanned out, some of them leaving the street to take cover in the rubble. Sweaty hands on his rifle, Morales watched as the Mexican soldiers pushed steadily toward them. While all of them carried rifles, they were all shouldered, and the soldiers moved gently through the crowd. A short man with a black mustache and soot-covered face gripped an old woman's shoulders and gently moved her aside, then stepped into the street and stood there with his hands on his hips, dark eyes raking across the US servicemen. He wore a sidearm and several gold medals were displayed on his uniform, and five more officer types filed out behind him.

"Is this guy some kind of big wig?" Morales whispered under his breath.

"Is that who I think it is?" Captain Jones answered the question with his own, confirming the mustached figure must be someone important.

The man's eyes settled on Morales, and he walked toward him with bold strides, Morales stepping forward in challenge.

"Stop right there!" he called, his voice strangely calm as he pointed his weapon at the officer's chest. The man halted five yards away, his hard expression wracked with sorrow the likes of which Morales could only imagine.

"My name is Javier Allende." He spoke in heavily accented English. "I'm the General of the Mexican National Defense Army, second only to our President, Manuel Rodillo de Brizuela." He removed his pistol from his holster, drawing stiff warnings from the assembled US soldiers, but the man didn't fire the weapon, instead flipping it around to hold out to Morales. "I surrender all of Mexico's armed forces to the Americans. Please take me to your highest-ranking officer."

Morales lowered his rifle and slowly took the pistol from the man's hand, turning to give it to Captain Jones who stood with his jaw hanging open. In the background, sirens wailed, and fires raged as Mexico City burned.

Chapter 20
Tom McKnight
Asheville, North Carolina

"I can show you where the vehicle pool is!" Barbara grabbed Tom's hand and pulled him toward the main highway.

Tom followed, pushing Jack along in front of him while Linda joined her sister, the two running alongside them as the intermittent quakes continued to rattle the encampment. Tom glanced back as soldiers and civilians gathered around the wrecked buildings where a few trucks had been pulled up to them, using their winches to remove debris from the piles, attempting to rescue those trapped inside.

"Where is it?"

"Along the highway on the left-hand side."

Tom scooped up Jack, handed him to Barbara and took the lead, sprinting across the street and running along the shoulder with the girls right behind him. Cars and military vehicles zipped by, some of them hitting ruts and crevices in the road, their suspensions jolting with the impacts. By the time they reached the row of lots, people were driving away with pickups and Jeeps, Ford Explorers and at least one Land Rover.

Barbara's shoulders slumped over. "They're taking all the good trucks."

"The pavement's screwed up anyway," Tom murmured, staring at the wide cracks and potholes in the road. "These people aren't going to get very far unless they have some serious four-wheel-drive power." He shook his head and led Barbara and the kids onward past the motor pool. "We've still got the horses. Come on."

They were approaching the strip mall where they'd left their animals, when a high turbo whine and buzzing rotors reached his ears. Tom turned his head to see a helicopter lifting up over a tree line off the road.

"Wait here." He trudged through the snow to a fence nestled against the trees, clearing some of the high snow drift away and looking out on a baseball diamond with several aircraft spread across it. As he watched, three Ospreys and a pair of military helicopters were spinning up, rotors moving lazily as snow swirled in small but powerful cyclones. He turned and waved his family to the fence line. Once they'd arrived, huffing and puffing, he gestured to the field.

"Are you thinking about taking one of those?" Barbara asked incredulously.

"I'm thinking that's our best option."

"Can you fly it?"

Tom's gaze was piercing as he turned to her. "No. But we can make a pilot take us."

Barbara glanced back at the kids, responding with a nod. "Let's do it."

Tom started to climb the fence when Sam called to him. "Dad?"

He turned to see her watery eyes leveled at him, eyes flicking toward the stores. "We'… we're not going to just leave her here, are we? Not after all of this?"

"Leave who?" Barbara asked.

Tom stared at his daughter for a second before he shook his head, remembering the other family member he'd nearly forgotten. "Smooch."

"Smooch?!" Jack shouted, nearly falling out of his mother's arms. "She's alive?"

"Sure is, buddy." Tom smiled at Jack, then looked at Barbara. "Wait here. Won't take more than a few minutes. I'll let the horses loose, too."

"Thanks, Dad." Samantha smiled at him.

He waded back to the road and sprinted another hundred yards to where they'd tied up the horses behind the stores. Untying them from the dumpster, he removed their saddles and bridles and whacked them on their rumps, sending them on their way trotting south along the broken pavement. It would be rough going for them, but they could paw through the snow and ice to find some grass, and the farther south they ran, the warmer it would get. He returned to the strip mall's rear door as a distant helicopter lifted off, anxiety driving his limbs as he shoved into the storeroom where they'd put Smooch. The dog sat up with a happy whine and Tom bent and scooped her up as she licked at his face, covers and all, carrying her back to the fence line in a stagger through the deep snow.

"Smooch!" Jack shouted, his arms out, face lit up like someone had turned on a light bulb behind his eyes. "*Smooch*! We thought you were dead!"

Linda covered her mouth with her hand, crying quietly at the sight of their beloved pet as Tom handed the animal to Sam and climbed the fence. He hopped down on the other side, helped Jack over, then took the dog, then the rest of his family climbed over and stood looking at him.

Tom gave them a nod. "Are you ready?"

Barbara's eyes were still the same color they'd always been, but they shone with a rugged determination, a newfound sense of self that he'd never seen before. "Now that we're together again? Always."

"Good. I lead, you follow, understand?"

They all nodded and Tom turned back to the field where a pair of Ospreys and a single helicopter remained, though they looked on the verge of taking off. He angled for one of the Ospreys, coming up behind it where the pilot and crew workers couldn't see them. As the cold wind generated by the aircraft washed over them, Barbara shouted at him to be heard over the noise.

"Where are we going to go? We can't go back home, can we?"

"No chance of that; the house is gone, and all we'd have are the barn and supplies underneath." he called back. "I overheard them talking in the control room, though. They have settlements south of the border where it's warm. That's where the refugees are going. I think we just have to go there, then try to figure something out after that."

"What about the animals? What about the farm? The years of work?"

"I hate to leave it behind, but the weather is going to get much, much worse, I think, especially now that the fools did what I warned them not to. I don't think it will be possible to live north for a long time. We don't have any other choice but to flee."

The ground rumbled again, and Tom waited for the aftershock to pass before he moved again, taking Smooch from Sam and clutching her tight to his chest. A few flight personnel ran around the remaining aircraft, speaking on their radios or signaling to the pilots and a helicopter lifted off the field while a dozen soldiers boarded the other Osprey. There was enough chaos and confusion that no one seemed to notice the family running along through the snow, or at least no one who cared enough to do anything about it.

Barbara shook her head, eyes glassy with emotion. "So, we're going to be refugees?"

Tom stopped near their Osprey's side door, turning back to face his wife. "I'm sorry, hon. We don't have a choice."

Barbara stared at him a second longer before her lips pursed tight with resolve, tossing a glance into the Osprey's crew quarters. "Okay, how are we going to play this?"

He handed over Smooch. "I'm going to ask the pilot nicely. If they don't agree… just keep the kids back."

Barbara nodded, and Tom turned and entered the Osprey's side door. The crew quarters lay empty, buckles and gear rattling with the rumbling engines. With a gesture, he got everyone to climb aboard while searching for something to convince the pilot to lift off. He found what he was looking for on a rack of rifles on the wall, liberating a weapon and easing a magazine into the well. He charged it as quietly as he could and walked down the narrow fuselage toward the cockpit. The pilot sat in the chair on the left, flipping switches and running through pre-flight checks and Tom glanced out the window, seeing field personnel running around.

"I'll need you to go ahead and take off," Tom said, tapping the rifle against the man's helmet.

The pilot was a young man with light brown hair, and he jerked his head around, eyes flying wide at the sight of the weapon pointed at him.

"Sir?" he asked in a plaintive voice. "What are you doing?"

Tom adjusted his grip on the weapon for emphasis. "I said, I need you to lift off right now."

"Who are you?"

"It doesn't matter. Just finish your pre-flight and take off."

The pilot shook his head. "I can't do that, sir."

"Then you're going to force me to do something I don't want to do."

"Dad. What are you doing?"

Tom glanced back to see Sam and Linda standing behind him. Both their eyes were wide as they looked between the pilot and Tom's rifle.

"I'm securing transportation, girls. Go sit with your mother."

Tom turned to the pilot, raising his eyebrows in demand. "Do you have fuel?"

"A full tank," he sputtered. "But I can't leave until the team gets here. I'm supposed to fly another group south."

"Instead of flying *them*, you'll be flying *us*. I need to get my family out of here before the next earthquake hits." His point was emphasized by a low aftershock that ran through the aircraft. It rose in power, causing Tom to wobble before it broke off and faded. "I'm serious," he growled. "Let's go!"

The pilot blinked fearfully at Tom's weapon, and his voice faltered when he spoke. "I can't do that, sir. I've got orders."

Tom shook his head and raised his weapon, pointing the barrel at his leg.

"Dad!" Sam cried, still standing behind him.

Tom turned to tell her to go to the back when Barbara pushed forward and stepped into the cockpit, placing her hand on the barrel of Tom's gun and moving it away. She gave the pilot a hesitant smile. "What your name, son?" she asked him.

"Lieutenant James Reeves. My friends, uh, call me Jimmy."

"Jimmy," Barbara smiled. "Been flying long?"

"No, ma'am," he admitted with a shaky tone. "I'm fresh out of flight school. I was still training when everything went tits up." He blushed at the words, stammering an apology. "S-sorry, no offense."

Barbara's smile widened. "I understand. We were happily living on our farm when all this happened. Kind of turned everyone's lives upside down, right?"

"Yeah," Reeves nodded nervously, glancing up at Tom. "I guess so."

"Look, this situation isn't the best for anyone. It's total chaos out there. My husband, Tom here, was part of the mission to close that anomaly in the North Atlantic. He told the higher ups it wouldn't work and would only make matters worse." Barbara clicked her tongue, looking up at Tom.

"But they didn't listen," he continued off of her lead, keeping the rifle lowered, but ready. "They made me do it anyway and that's why we're experiencing these earthquakes."

"Oh, no," Jimmy said, eyes genuinely concerned.

Barbara patted Tom on the arm. "Oh, yes. And that's why we're getting out of here before the next tremor kills us. That includes you." Barbara softened her tone and let her hand rest on the pilot's shoulder, her face stoic and calm as she spoke the next words, holding a pistol she had taken from the rear of the craft and aiming it at his gut. "Now, you can either come with us, or I'll shoot you, throw your body into the snow fly this damned thing myself. What's it going to be?"

The pilot's eyes went wide at the sight of the pistol, looking up at Tom, then back at Barbara, her expression remaining neutral through his blind panic. Making his decision, he turned back to his controls. "Yes, ma'am. Lift off in five minutes. I'll secure the rear ramp."

"Thank you, Jimmy. I'll secure the side door." Tom nodded his thanks to Barbara before pushing past his daughters. "Everyone, pull down the seats and secure yourselves, and Smooch. Buckle up. It could be a rough ride."

As the Osprey's propellers spun up, the rear door started to raise with a high-pitched, mechanical sound. Tom slammed the side door shut and locked it, then looked out through the slowly closing back ramp to watch for anyone who might want to stop them. Barbara joined the girls, helping them get Jack and Smooch situated before buckling themselves in and just as the engine noise reached a crescendo, Tom saw a half-dozen people making their way toward the Osprey. Four were clearly medical staff by their style of dress and the fact that they carried two men between them on stretchers, one with a leg wrapped in bloody bandages. One of the medical team raised head and shouted something at one of the others with a hopeful expression as they angled toward the Osprey's ramp. Tom had the sudden urge to leave them behind, but he shook his head and sighed before shouting up to the pilot.

"Jimmy, open the ramp again. We're taking on some injured."

"Alright!"

The rear door descended once more, and the medical team entered the aircraft, the leader with a grateful expression. "Thought you were going to leave us behind!"

"Not a chance." Tom forced a smile, waiting for them to carry their wounded on board before he turned and called back, "Okay, Jimmy. Close it up and take off."

"Roger!"

As his team got the wounded secured, the head medic stared at Tom, then at Tom's rifle, then Barbara and the kids buckled into their seats behind him. His expression turned hard with a hint of confusion in his eyes.

"What's going on here?"

"My family and I have joined this flight." Tom spoke in a flat tone. "We're heading south and will eventually make it to a US military base where we'll disembark and continue on our way. Do you have a problem with that?"

The man took another look at Tom's rifle, shrugging in deference. "No problem at all. We've got wounded to care for; we'll stay back in the cargo area until we arrive on site."

"Good," Tom nodded. "Make yourselves comfortable."

Tom shifted positions by the side door so he could keep an eye on the medics and wounded soldiers. The Osprey's rotors spun into an even higher gear, the tilting wings fully engaged in the VTOL position, the noise and wind growing to an intense level as the aircraft shook and quivered before finally lifting off the ground in a rumble that shook him through his feet.

As the Osprey swiveled to bring the command center back in the view, Tom saw Keith and Banks jogging toward them across the field, both shouting at the Osprey, arms up and waving back and forth. Tom snorted at the sight, not taking his eyes off of them as the Osprey continued to lift off, rising higher until the pair were just specs on the ground. Once they were clear of ground obstructions, the pilot retracted the gear and swiveled the rotors forward, and the Osprey turned from a lumbering beast into a swift one, tearing through the air and leaving the FOB far behind.

Safely away, Tom lingered at the window for a few minutes more before ambling back to a seat on the end, arm out to help him keep his balance as the craft rumbled and shifted in flight. Sitting next to Barbara he took her hand in his, resting his rifle across his knees, feeling for the first time that things were possibly, maybe beginning to look up.

Chapter 21
Tom McKnight
Somewhere in North Carolina

The Osprey bumped and knocked in the turbulence, the gentle jostling calming Tom's nerves as he sat in the last seat before the cargo bay, keeping himself between the medics and his family. He'd seen nothing about their demeanor to give him reasons to distrust them, but after being up front with them about the situation, he wanted to act as a barrier of sorts, to ensure that they wouldn't bother his family or try to change the course of the flight. In a discussion with one of the medics he'd explained a few of the highlights of their situation, and promised that the soldiers would be taken straight to a military base as soon as Tom and his family were dropped off near the Texas-Mexican border, which seemed to make them happy enough.

Tom looked away and watched Barbara and the kids. Sam and Linda sat in the middle of the row of foldout seats, holding hands as they talked quietly while Smooch was curled in a seat next to Sam, bundled up in covers with her chin on her leg. Jack and Barbara sat across from them, him fast asleep and leaning against his mother, her arm wrapped over his shoulders as she stared at her oldest daughter talking with her youngest. After so long apart, seeing his family back together was surreal, and felt like a dream that could fall apart at any moment if Tom lost his concentration.

With a final look at the medics who sat talking quietly around their patients, Tom stood and made his way up to settle in next to Barbara on the opposite side of Jack, both of his daughters glancing up at him with smiles on their faces.

Tom eased himself into his seat and gave his wife a kiss on the head. "Hey, honey. How's it going up here?"

She shrugged, happy face turned up to his. "You're looking at it. Three safe kids, a grateful wife and a dog that can't be killed. Flying to an unknown destination has me a little worried, but otherwise, I'm good. How about you?"

"I'm feeling okay, all things considered. Jimmy tells me we've got enough fuel to come within a hundred miles of the Texas-Mexico border where he'll drop us off. I'm just happy to be getting away from the endless winter."

"You really think it will be endless?"

"I have no clue, but it'll be long, that's for sure. What we did back there with trying to collapse the anomaly..." Tom shook his head as his mind raced through the possibilities for catastrophe. "It could be absolutely irreversible. We could be in for an ice age that lasts a thousand years."

"A thousand years? Are you serious?"

"Wish I wasn't. The more fresh water that gets dumped into the ocean, the more the currents will be disrupted and the longer it'll take for thing to balance out and for them to recover… if they ever do."

"So we can never go back home?"

"I'm not sure. If we can, we will, I promise. I just don't know when it'll be." Tom quickly shook his head and waved off the thought. "Enough of the negative. Tell me what happened to you guys."

Barbara told him everything, starting with how they'd tried to keep the farmstead locked down and their problems with first intruders, taking special pleasure when relating the part about shooting the first group in their rear ends with the shotgun to drive them off the property.

Tom laughed. "So, the Benelli M2 worked out?"

"Loved that shotgun," Barbara said with a wistful shake of her head. "I think that's one of the things I'll miss most."

She continued with how they'd joined forces with the Everett's and ran off even more intruders, detailing the big fight with the thugs when one tried to take Jack hostage, including the part about her ripping the thug's neck out and how Smooch had earned her keep that day. Tom listened with rapt attention, alternating between feeling angry at the situation, the people involved and himself for not being present to help protect his loved ones.

"So, that's how Smooch got hurt," Tom mused, jerking his chin toward the dog, "protecting you guys."

"Yep, she almost died doing it." Barbara sighed. "Took two stab wounds to the body fighting them."

Tom shook his head with admiration. "She protected me, too, recently. I'm glad we brought her along."

Smooch lifted her head from Sam's lap and gave a soft whine at the sound of her name being spoken.

"Was there ever any doubt?"

Tom's voice fell. "When we were getting ready to come looking for you, I hadn't planned on bringing Smooch. All we had was two horses, but Sam insisted we bring her." He chuckled at the thought. "Sat down and refused to move unless Smooch came with us too, so we made a sled for her."

"What's this I hear about horses?" Barbara leaned her head against his shoulder. "Sounds like you two were busy. Why don't you tell me all about it?"

"Well, finish your side first."

She smiled and continued, but when she got to the part about Keith killing the Everetts, Tom ground his teeth together, and his chest swelled with anger and resentment.

"I swear..." He shook his head. "If I ever see that guy again, I'm going to take him apart."

"Well, your daughter almost beat you to it."

Tom's eyebrows wrinkled in confusion. "What do you mean?"

Barbara told him about how they'd gotten away from Keith in the small town and Linda's run-in with the agent. As his wife told the story, Tom stared at his younger daughter in awe. "Wait… she stabbed him, shot him and then actually tried to kill him by sinking him in the *river*?"

"That's right," Barbara confirmed with a dark chuckle. "She lured him out onto the ice, threw a frozen log at his feet, cracked the ice, and *whoosh*, flushed him right down."

"Little Linda's gotten fierce since I last saw her," Tom chuckled, trying to cover for his heart that was thumping in his as he imagined the fear she must have felt. "So is that why Keith was all…" Tom gestured to his face and hands, and Barbara nodded.

"Yep. Probably got frostbite. I'm shocked he survived at all, let alone as well as he did."

"So that's why they had words after they brought you to the holding center." Tom smiled as Linda glanced over at him. Truth be told, he was in awe of her. Proud, elated, and impressed all at once. "I don't know what to say. That was insanely brave of her, and smart."

"That's what I said." She shifted against him. "Does that mean she gets a car for her sixteenth birthday?"

Tom laughed. "Absolutely. If there are any more cars left."

Barbara grabbed his arm and snuggled it. "Okay. Your turn. Tell me what you and Samantha have been doing this whole time."

Tom started from the beginning at the conference, describing them arriving on the Navy ship and his theories on the anomaly and she gasped when he got to the part about the Naval ships being sunk by the debris shooting up from the sea floor.

"We were on our way to the store when that happened," Barbara nodded, "listening to a news reporter when her ship sank. I can't believe you survived that."

Tom described their trek through the hurricane, finding Jerry, and their run-ins with the people Jerry owed money to. Barbara was elated during the part where Sam torched the bad guys, though her expression turned sympathetic sound when he told her about Jerry's death. Tom grew tired as he finished, detailing their trek through the snowstorm until they came across the barn and horses.

"If we could have only found each other sooner," Barbara sighed against him. "But I'm glad we're here now."

"Better late than never," Tom agreed, reaching up and stroking her hair. "I couldn't be prouder of you guys. You fought hard."

"You, too."

Tom took a deep breath and let it out in a long sigh, looking toward the cargo area where the medics had stabilized the wounded and were resting on their packs in the hold. None of them seemed concerned with the McKnights, so Tom let himself relax. "I'll go talk to Jimmy and see how things are going. I want to make sure we stay on track."

"Good idea."

"Do you have a weapon?"

"Just this." Barbara held up a fist and laughed. "Pistol's back on the rack. Didn't feel like holding onto it for right now."

Tom laughed. "Do you want it back?"

She glanced down into the cargo section at the resting medics, then leaned back with a shake of her head. "I don't think so. We'll be okay."

"When I get back, I'll ask one of them to have a look at your leg."

"That sounds great," she nodded.

"Holler if you need anything."

"I will."

He started to draw away, but Barbara held his arm. "Tom?"

"Yeah?"

"I love you."

"I love you, too." He leaned down and kissed her lips, then her nose, then her forehead. Exaggerated kissing noises came from close by, and he looked over to see the girls making faces at them, puckering their lips and giggling like they were back at home together.

"Glad to see some things have stayed the same," Tom laughed as he stood. "You guys get some rest, okay?"

Barbara nodded and nestled in with Jack as Tom walked toward the cockpit, rocking back and forth as the aircraft gently swayed. When he got there, he leaned his rifle against the bulkhead and stood behind the co-pilot's seat.

"Hi, Jimmy. Everything going okay up here?"

The young man regarded Tom with a hesitant grin. "Everything's good here. I've got her on autopilot and she's holding steady."

"Good to hear."

Tom looked out the windows as they cut through a massive cloud bank, trying to quell his nauseous stomach for a moment before giving the young man a grin. "Mind if I sit? I promise I won't touch anything."

"I think that would be okay. Just be careful, please."

"Thanks."

Tom took his time squeezing into the co-pilot's seat, heedful not to knock his knees against anything. Once he was situated, he glanced at the dashboard controls before turning to Jimmy. "Sorry about the gun and all earlier. Things were getting desperate back there."

The pilot nodded, not taking his eyes off his controls. "You seem like good folks, all things considered. Not the usual kind of hijackers. I understand, I think."

"Have they been calling on the radio?"

Jimmy nodded. "They have."

"What have you told them?"

"That I'm being held against my will, and I have no choice but to keep flying."

"That's right," Tom smiled. "You have to believe me when I say it was nothing against you or your fellow soldiers."

"I know. You wouldn't have let the wounded men on board otherwise."

Tom nodded. "I've worked with the Navy before on a lot of projects as a consultant. I just hope you understand that Colonel Banks and her agents have made things insurmountably worse."

"That's what your wife was saying before she threatened to shoot me." Jimmy spoke with a flat tone, though a hint of mirth danced in his eyes.

Tom snorted lightly. "Yeah… I owe you an apology for that, too. Threatening a pilot and stealing an Osprey wasn't on the agenda when we woke up this morning."

"I'm sure it wasn't." Jimmy's brow furrowed. "Still, you've stolen a pretty expensive piece of machinery and took a US serviceman hostage. They're going to be looking for you."

"Believe me, they'll have more to worry about than us, soon." Tom turned to look out the side window, watching the clouds below them whipping past.

"That bad, huh?"

"You know about the anomaly?"

Jimmy nodded hesitantly. "Some bits and pieces. They said it's a freshwater aquifer spilling into the North Atlantic, doing something to the currents. That's why things are getting cold."

"That sums it up pretty well. They've been chasing me for a while. Did some pretty awful things to me and my family to force me to help them set off explosives around the edge of it to try and collapse it. I told them it wouldn't work but they didn't listen, and now…." Tom gave an exasperated sigh. "I mean if they'd left it alone, the aquifer might have run itself out in a few months. The world could have returned to normal, eventually."

"But now?"

"Now, we're talking a prolonged event, probably another ice age."

The pilot gulped, reminding him a little of Jerry with his youthful nervousness and general mannerisms. "What about the earthquakes? That can't have been a coincidence, right?"

"I don't think so. The explosions may have caused a release of energy from the Rampo Fault all down through the East Coast Fault."

"What kind of damage would that have caused?"

Tom shrugged. "It's almost impossible to tell without more information. If it influenced the New Madrid Fault, the destruction would be astronomical."

"That's in Tennessee, right?"

"Yes, and that would explain the shaking we felt back at camp." Tom sat silent looking out the window, contemplating the situation before turning to Jimmy. "Anyway, the point is, we had a good reason for wanting to get away from Banks. She kidnapped and held my family hostage and made me an unwilling partner in all this, among other, worse things."

"I get it, sir."

Tom smiled at his honest sincerity. "You can call me Tom." He held his hand out, and the pilot shook it. "I like you, Jimmy. As long as you set us down close the border like you said you would, we won't have any problems. But, if you do something that puts my family in danger..."

"You'll probably do something I won't like."

Tom nodded, looking back at the cargo area. "I'm not interested in doing anything of the sort, but…."

"Yeah, I get it. You're just protecting your wife and kids. They seem nice." He smiled nervously. "Your wife is intense, though. I'd hate to see anything bad happen to them. I'll drop you off, no problem. This whole mess wasn't exactly covered in basic… to be honest, I wouldn't be surprised if they'll even know what happened by the time we land."

"Good," Tom nodded. "Sounds like we're on the same page. You'll have enough fuel to make it to the nearest base after you drop us off, right?"

"Should have."

"I'll leave you to it, then. Just shout if you need anything."

"Will do. Thanks, Tom."

Tom gave the young man a final smile and got up, taking his rifle and heading toward the back of the aircraft where everyone was quiet. Barbara and the kids were asleep, the girls with their heads together and Smooch's muzzle still in Sam's lap. Jack lay against his mother with one leg thrown over her leg and Tom sat heavily in the seat next to his wife, putting his right arm around her, letting her settle against him with a contented sigh.

He tried to relax and found, to his surprise, his shoulders lowering, and his mind feeling lighter despite how they'd left things in Asheville. They were still far, far from being out of danger, but with his family back together, anything was possible to achieve. Tom rested his head back and stared at the Osprey's steel-framed roof, closing his eyes and allowing himself to doze.

* * *

"How far do we have left to go?" Jack asked.

"Not long, buddy," Tom replied a few hours later as he stretched his hands over his head, working out the kinks in his muscles, soreness still lingering as it likely would for quite a while.

"It's a good question though." Barbara leaned forward in her seat. "There's not much light left. We must be getting close."

Tom motioned up at the crew cabin. "I looked at the instruments when I was up there, and we were cruising at two-hundred and fifty miles per hour. It was roughly a thousand miles to the border, so..." Tom was still barely coherent after his short nap, and the simple math came slow to him. "Should've taken us about four hours."

Barbara held up her wrist to indicate she wasn't wearing a watch.

"I don't have mine anymore either," Tom admitted. "I wonder where we're at?"

A sputtering resonated through the fuselage, causing the craft to shudder before returning to normal. "*That*," Barbara pointed out, then she shot him a worried glance. "Does not sound good. Do you think it's a malfunction?"

Tom shook his head. "No clue. I'll go check with Jimmy."

He stood and ambled toward the front of the aircraft, finding the pilot with his hands flying all over the dials and levers, flipping switches and making adjustments to the control rudder to keep the craft from dipping right. The sound came again, and the Osprey shuddered once more. Everything that wasn't welded to the fuselage rattled like tools in a tool chest and Tom blinked, suddenly wide awake as adrenaline pumped into his blood stream.

"What's going on up here?" Tom asked, his voice rising higher than he'd meant. "Everything okay?" The pilot kept working with his instruments, not answering right away. "Jimmy? Talk to me, buddy."

"Um, I've been losing thrust going on thirty minutes. I can't find the issue but it's something with the engines."

"Can I help?"

"Unless you can read my instruments and help me troubleshoot, no."

"I don't have any experience with hardware like this. I'm an underwater guy." Tom shook his head. "Can you put us down now?"

"Already on it. I've been dropping in altitude for the past five minutes, trying to find a place to land. We're coming in at less than a thousand feet right now."

Tom raised up and looked out the window to see a vast expanse of desert stretching beneath them, the Osprey's wings swaying back and forth as the right engine occasionally hiccupped and spewed out belches of smoke. "Can you tell where we are?"

"About a hundred miles from the Texas-Mexican border." The pilot hit a few more switches before turning back to Tom. "I need to focus on this... this is a two-man job normally, and these birds are tricky."

Tom nodded and moved back to his seat near the middle of the plane. The shuddering came more frequently, like they were on an old wooden roller coaster barreling around a curve with the rattling, head shaking vibration that left him with a headache every time. Barbara, the children and a pair of the medics looked at him anxiously.

"Engine trouble," Tom told them honestly. "He's not sure what the cause is, but we're landing right away. I'd suggest getting buckled up."

The medics nodded and rushed toward the rear, hands thrown up against the fuselage to help them walk. Barbara helped make sure Jack was buckled in while Sam took care of Linda, and Tom spun and gently forced Smooch into a lying position, putting a seatbelt over her and snapping her in, then he gestured to Sam. "Keep a hand on her, would you?"

"Sure, Dad." She nodded and rested her palm on the dog's side.

"Thanks." He turned to Linda. "Are you okay?"

"I think so." He could tell she was trying to keep her voice calm, though fear leaked out with the words. "Are we going to crash?"

"I don't think so. Just... hold on tight to your sister." Then he raised his voice. "Everyone keep your heads down and cover up."

He received a spattering of replies as another deep shudder ran through the aircraft and he sat heavily, snapped his seatbelt in place, and threw his arm around Barbara. She had one arm across Jack and the other hand on Tom's knee, head back, looking up at the ceiling, silently praying as the descent continued to grow rougher.

Having seen Ospreys land before, Tom was well aware that it was a less-than-graceful act as the aircraft essentially transformed from a fast-moving plane into a ponderous helicopter, the maneuverability of which was less than ideal. As it slowed, the rotors on the sides of both wings would begin to rotate upward, transitioning the forward thrust to upward thrust, both slowing their descent and giving them the capability of landing on a dime.

Unfortunately, though, as the propellers rotated up, Tom felt stress straining through the fuselage, the shuddering moving through the very frame itself, gripping the plane and straining the metal with a loud screech. The left engine joined the right in sputtering and revving, turbines straining and out of sync as they descended in fits and spurts, the pilot doing his best to keep them level and on course for whatever landing site he had picked out. The shaking rolled over them again, reaching a thunderous crescendo and not backing off. Aluminum rattled, and the frame groaned, the metal twisting into positions it hadn't been forged for, stretching to its limits and beyond, testing the extremities that it had been engineered for.

Tom's head was shaking from the inside out, and Barbara's fingers had bent into claws, gripping his leg like talons. All he could do was hang on to her and whisper assurances as he kicked his feet helplessly. Something snapped with an ear-shattering metallic ring, and they dipped hard to the right, Tom, Barbara, and Jack rising higher while the girls slid lower, their faces thrown up in wide-eyed terror as they screamed.

The Osprey started to level out, yet they slipped backward, the tail sinking low as they plummeted toward the ground, the engines out of power and the aircraft out of lift. Tom reached for Barbara's hand and grasped it tight, looking at her and his children as they plummeted downward, unwilling to accept that he was about to lose them so soon after finding them, but powerless as the aircraft slipped backward and slewed to the right, whipping them in a circle. Barbara's hair flew into his face and he locked his other hand to the arm of his chair, yelling at everyone to hold on, then something exploded, something else shrieked against the fuselage and they hit hard, the concussion whipping Tom's head forward, massive forces fracturing the craft and tearing it apart. Wind screamed in, tearing at his hair and face, bringing with it the thick stench of fuel and oil, Then his head snapped back again and the world turned off like a light switch.

* * *

"Honey, wake up. Honey?"

Someone whispered to him in the darkness, a child's voice cried in the distance and another moaned in pain as a warm breeze blew across his face. None of it was enough to bring him out of the unconsciousness that had so violently dragged him down. In truth, it was the stench of burning oil and high-octane airplane fuel that got his eyes open. It stung his nasal passages, making his eyes water.

"W… what's going on?" he moaned, looking around in the near darkness as small fires flickered everywhere.

"Honey, wake up. The girls - I can't get to them. My seatbelt's stuck."

Tom burst to life, kicking out his arms and legs as if someone had doused his face with cold water. At first, he was dazed, his body rattled, unsure if anything even worked, but as he moved his limbs, he realized he was mostly fine. Banged up and confused, but fine. On the other side of the craft Smooch was straining against her seatbelt, squirming and whining under Sam's limp hand, both her and Linda leaning forward in their seats, long hair hanging over their faces. A piece of flaming debris was caught in Linda's thick locks and Tom grabbed at his seatbelt, pawing at it uselessly before he finally settled down and made his fingertips work. He pressed the button, unsnapped the buckle, and lunged from his seat to grab the piece of burning fuselage from Linda's hair, tossing it aside. Ignoring his blistered fingers, he patted her smoldering hair and lifted her chin.

"Linda, honey. Are you okay?"

Her eyes came open, and she stared at Tom like he was a stranger.

"Linda, it's Dad." He gave her face a gentle slap. "Are you in there, honey? Can you hear me?"

She blinked and nodded, so Tom quickly turned his attention to Sam.

"Sam, are you okay? Can you hear me?"

"Yeah, Dad." She used her forearm to lift her hair up and push it back on her head. "I'm fine, I think."

Tom ran his hands up and down the girls, checking their arms and legs, half expecting some nightmarish injury and almost crying in joy when he didn't find one. "They're okay," he looked back to Barbara. "The girls are okay!"

"Oh, thank goodness," she said. "Jack is fine, too. Right, Jack?"

He was still crying, but he stopped long enough to nod his head exaggeratedly. Tom quickly grabbed Barbara's seatbelt, twisting, pulling, and punching the button until it broke free while Sam hit her seatbelt release and turned to help her sister. As Barbara and the kids worked to finish getting untangled and free Smooch, Tom spun in a circle to further assess the situation.

They stood at an awkward angle, the floor tilted backwards, the entire tail of the Osprey missing, shrubs and dry grasses burning on the desert floor in the dusk light. He started to head out in the direction of the missing tail section, then stopped and shambled to the front of the aircraft to check on the pilot. Unlike the cargo section, the cockpit hadn't fared nearly as well. Part of the roof had been smashed in, leaving wires and piping hanging across his path and fires lit the darkness, tiny sparks bursting from the melting electronics.

He moved aside a swath of cables and stepped into the cockpit to find the window shattered and the dashboard smoking and charred. Jimmy lay across the console, his head turned to the right, blood trickling from the corner of his mouth, eyes open, but staring at nothing. Tom placed his hand on the young man's shoulder and gave it a little shake.

"Hey, Jimmy?" Tom's voice was low and respectful, and he received no response.

With a bow of his head, Tom returned carefully to the back of the plane, the scent of burning fuel getting stronger, spurring him to think and move faster In front of him, the kids stood awkwardly in the tilted aisle with Barbara while Smooch sat up in her seat with her big rear paws sticking out.

"We need to get out of here before the rest of the plane catches fire." Tom bent and lifted the dog, nodding toward the back. "Go out that way."

"What about Jimmy?" Barbara asked as she held Jack's and Linda's hands, helping them keep their balance as they shuffled down to the rear of the aircraft.

Tom just shook his head and focused on his footing. Sam stepped onto the desert floor first, ducking beneath some twisted metal and past a burning bush, then Linda followed, then Jack and Barbara. Tom picked his way carefully behind them until he stood outside the wreck. The dusk light cast murky shadows all around, but Tom could see part of the left wing lying a hundred yards away as flames from the burning engines licked at the sky. Puddles of airplane fuel stood on the hard desert floor and the right wing was still attached – barely – and it caught fire in a gentle whoosh of heat.

Tom put his head down and moved. "Get as far away from the fire as you can." He huffed and puffed, explaining as he jogged. "That's not like regular gas. That stuff... once it gets on you, you can't get it off. And it burns super hot!"

He angled away from the burning wreckage, clutching Smooch tight to his chest, weaving around desert shrubs and stones, putting fifty yards between his family and anything on fire. Once he felt they'd reached a safe spot, he got down on one knee and gently placed Smooch on the ground before standing back up, gasping for air while he absently rubbing the dog's ears, watching things burn in the distance. The outline of the Osprey's remains was a dark shadow in the light of the fires, and in a moment later there was a muffled explosion from the newly ignited engine, throwing sparks and cinders into the sky – and the outline was gone.

The wind gusted cool across the desert, chilly enough to see his breath, but much better than the blizzard-like temperatures in North Carolina. Sam poked him on the shoulder and pointed off toward their right where a lump of dark wreckage sat. "Dad. Is that the tail? Could any of the soldiers still be alive?"

Tom squinted to see, and nodded slowly. "Possibly, yes. Stay here. I'll go check."

He worked his way back toward the tail section, no flashlight available to pierce the night sky, forced to work off of moonlight alone. As he drew closer, he could make out that the split in the Osprey's body had occurred right where the medics and their patients had been sitting. The rear fins rested on the desert floor, the open end positioned at a slightly upward angle. Stepping on part of the metal frame, he peered deeper inside, struggling to make anything out in the pitch black.

"Hello! Anyone still in here?"

A groan answered him, and Tom quickly bent and felt his way toward the back. He found a man on a stretcher, strapped to the side of the wall but angled with his head pointed toward the floor, surviving only thanks to whoever had secured him. Another stretcher lay nearby, but the person who'd been lying on it had fallen off and lay crumpled in the wreckage. Moving some of the cargo chains and truck pads, he knelt next to her unconscious, twisted form. Fingers on her neck, he found a thready pulse and started to move her but realized he couldn't do it alone. Staggering back to the edge of the opening, he cupped his hands over his mouth. "Barbara!" he called, "I need help!"

A few moments later, his wife appeared. "Are you okay? What's wrong?"

"I've got two injured here," he explained. "First, help me with this lady."

Barbara climbed up and followed him inside where they pulled the loose stretcher near the woman. Tom took her legs, wincing as he repositioned the twisted part. The break had occurred between her hip and knee, and it looked terrible, but they rolled her over and put her on the stretcher, gently shifting the leg to what he thought was a comfortable position.

"That's a bad break." Tom shook his head. "Real bad."

They strapped her in and carried her carefully outside, walking her out to the kids before going back for the man. The tangle of straps holding him in was impossible to sort out, so Tom found a medical kit and used a pair of scissors to cut him free. He was much heavier than the woman, and they were forced to pause at the tail opening, resting a minute to catch their breath before they lowered him down. With Tom at his head and Barbara at his feet, they gave each other a nod and lifted him out of the wreckage, carrying him to where the kids waited.

"Is that all of them?" Sam asked, kneeling by the woman but unable to help her.

Tom nodded as he stood, hands on his hips, catching his breath. "That's all the people I saw. The rest must have been thrown from the wreckage."

"It's going to get colder out here." Barbara rubbed Jack's arms. "We need to find some shelter."

"I'll go back and look for some supplies." Tom glanced back at the wreckage. "I saw some truck pads which could help keep us warm, too."

Tom jogged to the tail section and picked through the wreckage, folding two truck pads and setting them on the edge. Under an overturned seat he found a backpack with some clothes and a flashlight inside and after shouldering the pack, he flicked on the light, relieved to finally be able to see. With nothing else of use he could find, he threw the pads over his shoulder and stepped away from the tail section when shuffling footsteps approached on his left.

He reeled, swiveling the light and cocking his fist as a man and woman in military fatigues limped up, blood on their faces, arms thrown over each other's shoulders in support. Tom lowered his arm, recognizing them as two of the medics from the plane.

"Holy cow, you guys survived?! Are you two okay?" Tom asked, shocked to see more survivors.

"We're alive," the man replied with a disheartened stare. "We got thrown out of the ship when the tail broke. I'm surprised we didn't break our necks. What about our people. Did they make it?"

"We found two wounded and got them situated away from the wreck. We didn't find anyone else, but we haven't had a chance to search yet."

The medic nodded. "We're going to have a quick look around. We'll join you after that."

"Alright," Tom pointed to where Barbara and the kids waited. "We'll be over there. It's going to start getting cold soon, so we'll need to move south and try to find shelter."

"We'll make it quick," he assured him.

Tom took his meager haul back to his family, carrying it through the gusting desert winds, the wide-open space seeming massive compared to his long trek through Virginia and Tennessee with the constant canopies of trees. Barbara was standing on a boulder out away from the kids and Tom put the supplies he'd found down and walked over to her, the adrenaline starting to wear off and the aches and pains from being tossed around in the wreck coming clearly into focus. With a grunt he hopped up on the rock where Barbara stood on her toes, squinting into the distance.

"See anything good?" he asked.

"Not really," she replied. "I did just catch the sun going down, so I can tell you which way is south, generally speaking." She pointed off to her right.

"Well, that's a start." Tom gave a thankful nod. "I found two of the medics. They seem fine, miraculously enough."

Barbara held out her hand, and Tom helped her climb down. "Where are they?"

"Having a look around for their buddies. I'd help, but I've spent enough time away from all of you."

They rejoined their children and Smooch and waited in the growing chill, huddled together, arms wrapped around each other with one big truck pad thrown over the kids. By the time the medics joined them, darkness had completely fallen, and Tom could see his breath puffing out in the flashlight beam.

"All we found was a first aid kit," he said, looking glum, "but no sign of our partners. They could have been tossed a mile away."

"I'm very sorry to hear that." Tom frowned. "We're thinking of moving on south to find some shelter. Are you two okay with that?"

The man glanced that way before giving a terse nod. "That sounds good. My name is Lieutenant Brad Stevens. This is Private Saanvi Patel."

"Good to meet you both." Tom introduced the medics to Barbara and the kids before facing the direction they wanted to go, staring out into the wide darkness ahead of them.

"Do you mind helping us carry a stretcher?" Stevens asked, looking at the pair of wounded on the ground.

"Not at all," Tom said, looking at Barbara, who nodded in agreement.

"Much obliged."

"All right, everyone," Tom looked back at the children. "Stay close, kids. Sam, you're in charge of herding everyone. Let's get moving."

The adults each grabbed an end of a stretcher and started walking south with the kids and Smooch ambling behind them, carrying the supplies.

* * *

After two hours of marching across the desert, Tom's feet and back ached, his throat raw from the cold air, yet he kept his head up and continued trudging forward. Stomach grumbling, he realized how long it'd been since he had eaten, which reminded him of how long since he had a drink, too. If the rest of his family was fed around when he was back at the FOB, then they'd be feeling the same way – the kids more than anyone. He glanced back to see Jack and Linda walking together, sharing a truck pad for warmth while Sam followed behind, a pad on her own back as she kept an eye on both Smooch and her younger siblings. They were cold and had complained on and off, but the physical activities were keeping them warm for the moment, and Barbara's constant encouragement kept them moving.

Barbara and Private Patel carried the woman with the broken leg while Tom and Lieutenant Stevens took the larger man. During their last rest, the medics had checked out the wounded soldiers using the first aid kits they'd found, which was also the point Tom discovered both soldiers had sustained most of their injuries in the Asheville quake. They had internal bleeding aside from the broken leg, cuts, and bruises and there wasn't much the medics could do for them but keep them comfortable and pumped full of pain meds, of which they had precious little left. Real doctors, x-rays and surgery were desperately needed to fully assess and repair the damage – and soon.

They marched carefully through the desert scrub, Tom and Barbara both in front of their respective stretchers with Sam having eventually taken point, walking ahead of the group with Smooch, searching for a friendly town or encampment.

Tom's breathing became ragged, his lungs cold, back aching and he glanced over at Barbara to see she wasn't faring much better. Her leg bled openly, the deep cut having saturated the new bandage the medics had applied when they'd last stopped, though she remained stoic, walking with a limp without complaint. He was about to call for a break, when Sam gave a happy shout and jumped up and down ahead of them. Encouraged, the group double-timed it to her where she was pointing off to their right. "It's a town!" she shouted.

Tom stood taller, examining the horizon, though he didn't see any signs of life. "I don't see any lights or anything."

"Not lights," Sam said. "Shapes. You can see dark shapes there. See? It's a town."

Tom squinted and let his eyes move slower. After a moment of searching, he spotted a series of buildings up on a rise, spilling down into what must've been a valley. "I see them now. Very nice catch, Sam." He craned his neck to look back at Lieutenant Stevens. "What do you think?"

The medic shook his head, cold sweat glistening across his brow. "I say we give it a shot. I don't know about the rest of you, but I'm beat."

All in agreement, they made good time to the town, reaching the first structures in about fifteen minutes. They were ranch homes, and as Sam shined the flashlight around, Tom saw they were poorly constructed with metal roofs and ragged fencing dividing the properties. The group took a two-lane road into the center of town, which consisted of two gas stations, a market, a frightening-looking roadside motel, and some restaurants and taverns.

"This place is definitely abandoned," Sam looked around. "I wonder if they have any food or water? I'm dying of thirst."

"We all are." Tom's eyes moved across the buildings, trying to find a good spot to set up camp. "How about that hotel? It doesn't look very welcoming, but it's off the road. We can put the wounded in the rooms and get them out of the worst of the cold. One of us can look after them while the rest of us scout for supplies, then we can build a fire and get warm."

"Sounds great to me," Stevens said with a shiver.

They walked the stretchers to one of the hotel rooms. The door was locked, so Tom kicked it in, and they found two queen-sized beds inside. They offloaded their patients, leaving Stevens to care for them and Smooch to get some much-needed rest while everyone else went in search of supplies.

Standing outside, Tom looked around. "Sam and Saanvi. Why don't you two ladies check out the gas stations? Linda and Barbara, you can search the other buildings. Jack and I will collect some loose wood and try to get a fire started. We're looking for food, water, flashlights, matches, lighters, extra clothing – anything helpful. Be *super* careful, all of you. The place looks abandoned, but we can't be a hundred percent sure."

"Wish we could have found a rifle or something in the wreck," Saanvi said. "I'd feel a lot less nervous right about now."

"You and me both, sister," Barbara smiled at her. "Just stay alert, and shout if you see *anything* wrong."

While the women moved off into the darkness, Tom put his arm around Jack's shoulders and guided him off to find some wood. It didn't take long for them to find broken-down parts of the fence with loose pieces, which they dragged back to the hotel to drop near the door. Tom then broke into two more hotel rooms and took the chairs out of them while Jack scoured the drawers for paper they might use for kindling. Tom stomped the chairs to pieces, and soon they had a sizeable stack of wood. By that time, Sam and Saanvi he'd returned with a half case of bottled waters and a long-tipped lighter from one of the gas stations.

"Oh that is a *solid* find. Nice work!" Tom grabbed the lighter with a grin. Making a triangle out of the chair's wooden legs, he piled some wadded paper beneath it and set it alight. After messing with it a few minutes, he got the dry wood to catch and moments later a warm fire blazed just outside the room. Barbara and Linda returned a moment after the fire was started, carrying with them some canned goods, a half-gallon jug of distilled water, and a box of oatmeal packages.

"The whole place is picked clean," Barbara said, putting their findings in a small stack off to the side with the rest. "We had to dig to the bottoms of pantries for this stuff."

Tom nodded his thanks. "Do the water faucets work?"

"There's a trickle," she replied. Then she pointed up to the rise where a small water tower sat. "They must have drained that thing on their way out."

"Damn. I'll bet they were forcefully evacuated like everyone else." Tom frowned. "Okay. We each get a bottled water to start, but no more. We've got a lot of mouths, and precious few resources."

Barbara handed the waters around, and they all drank happily for the few seconds they lasted. Tom finished his in three gulps and instantly wanted more, though the refreshment rejuvenated him and he dragged out more chairs for people to sit in. Finally, after an hour of putting it together, the camp was set just outside the hotel door. Tom sat next to Barbara, the kids spread around in various places, plopping on loose fencing or in chairs. They kept Smooch's blankets close to the fire, though after her short rest the shepherd couldn't be kept still, wandering between her family members for as much attention as she could get. Sometimes she sniffed at Stevens or Saanvi but mostly kept out of their way, wagging her tail as she watched them work.

For their part, the medics didn't slow or complain at all, and once they'd seen to the wounded soldiers, Saanvi looked at the cut on Barbara's leg, peeling back the temporary bandage and cleaning the injury expertly before pressing down around the edges using a penlight from the kit to check it over thoroughly.

"It's not infected," the medic said. "But, like I promised you before, I'm going to stitch this up."

"Is now the time?" Barbara asked, biting her lip.

"It is." Saanvi smiled. "No anesthetic, I'm afraid, but it'll be over relatively quickly."

"Okay."

Saanvi stitched Barbara up while Stevens looked over the children, finding cuts and bruises Tom hadn't seen before, and he cleaned and patched them up in short order.

"Thanks for all this," Tom said.

"Not at all. It's our job." Stevens finished up by putting a piece of medical tape on Jack's nose, which he giggle at as he pulled it off, then raced to stick it to Smooch's fur.

"What about you?" Saanvi asked, finished with Barbara and coming over, snapping on a fresh pair of latex gloves. "Any rough spots?"

"Actually, I'm fine," he replied, though the medic shook her head and leaned in closer, guiding the flashlight like a weapon.

"I see at least three second degree abrasions and two possible avulsions around your temple," she said with a click of her tongue. "One may need a couple of stitches, or I can just bandage it."

"I guess I've taken a few knocks lately," Tom looked over at Barbara with a wink. "Go ahead. Bandages, please, though. No stitches for me."

"Coward." Barbara grinned, running a hand gently over her freshly bandaged leg.

Kneeling next to him, Saanvi moved around his chair, cleaning and disinfecting his wounds, placing bandages and antiseptic where needed. None of the wounds required stitches, but Saanvi stopped and gasped when she got to the back of his head.

"Oh, this is a big lump." She gave the area a gentle press with her fingers, causing Tom to wince slightly. "What's that from?"

"That could have been my fight with Keith or in the APC crash. Or it could have come from when a house fell on me and my horse, too."

She laughed. "Or the Osprey crash too, eh?"

"Ha! That too, I guess, yeah."

"It looks bad, but the lump's on the outside. Best I can hope for at this point is that there's no internal bleeding or pressure building up. Do you want something for the pain and swelling?"

"Actually, that sounds pretty good. Something light, please."

"You got it." Saanvi ripped open a package and placed two pills in Tom's hand.

He popped them in his mouth swallowed them dry as the medic continued checking him for wounds. A half hour passed, and the campfire was roaring, chasing away the cool of the night, the blazing flames holding everyone's attention, and soon they were all staring into the licking tendrils. Despite the comforting moment, Tom didn't feel like sleeping at all. In fact, he was wide awake, the pain medication pushing his aches and pains to the background for the time being.

"Why don't you two sit down?" Tom gestured at the medics. "You've been working your butts off."

Stevens finished by checking over Smooch for a few moments before finally collapsing on a stool, glancing back inside at the wounded soldiers.

"You're worried about them?" Tom noted.

The medic nodded. "There's only so much we can do with internal bleeding. They need a real doctor and a real hospital facility."

"I'm sorry. I can't help but feel partially responsible."

"You didn't make the Osprey go down." Stevens spoke pensively. "And with everyone moving south, there's not a doctor within a few hundred miles anyway. Going with you was the best chance they had."

"And you didn't cause the earthquakes," Barbara reminded him with a hand on his arm, "Banks did that."

Tom gave his wife a warm smile. "Thanks, honey."

"So, the rumors were true then," Saanvi said from where she sat on a piece of fencing, knees pressed together, sun-kissed skin looking dark in the firelight. "They couldn't leave well enough alone? They screwed things up worse?"

"That's right," Tom admitted. "And they made me help them. A lot of people will have to pay for their mistakes."

"Idiots," Stevens spat.

"The sad thing is, Banks is still alive. I saw her and Keith when we were lifting off. They were trying to catch a lift with us."

"Good thing for him he didn't," Linda scoffed, "I don't think he'd have a very good time meeting *all* of us at once, even with that Colonel lady on his side."

"So, that leads me to the next question," Barbara mused. "What do we do now?"

"We're going south." Tom spoke confidently, as though he had every detail planned out to a T. "Any place where the weather is warmer, and we can find a place to settle down for a while."

"No earthquakes, please," Jack interjected.

"Amen to that," Barbara agreed, leaning into her husband and squeezing his arm.

* * *

The next morning, Tom woke up with Barbara by his side, the sunlight shining through the sheer curtains to brighten the room. They'd spread out across several rooms for the night with Tom taking first watch, and when he'd finally crawled into bed, he was surprised that the linens at least *looked* clean, in spite of the outside appearance of the motel. Thankfully, no one had bothered them, as without weapons, the plan was to simply raise an alarm if anyone heard or saw anything threatening.

His shift had passed uneventfully, then they let Linda and Sam take over, both girls eager to stay up and do something productive. It had given Tom and Barbara some much-needed time together, keeping warm as they talked long into the night about recent events, then the medics filled in after the girls, giving Jack and Smooch a much-needed full night's sleep. With the morning's arrival, Tom rose and walked outside with Smooch to find the medics outside, stoking a new fire and eating a small portion of the food they had available, both wearing glum expressions as they picked at their food.

"What's wrong?" Tom asked, coming up.

"They didn't make it." Patel glanced toward the closed door with the injured soldiers. "Both of them passed overnight."

"Oh jeez… I'm so sorry to hear that," Tom said, stomach twisting with nausea. "What should we do?"

"We need to find the nearest base." Saanvi stood, pulled a map out of her pocket, and waved it around. "I picked this up at one of those gas stations this morning. Seems like we're somewhere north of San Antonio. The FOBs are all along the border now, so we'll head in that direction."

"So, we're going the same way as you folks," Stevens added.

"Travel partners, then?" Tom raised his eyes hopefully. "At least until we reach the next base?"

The medics exchanged a look of relief and nodded, Saanvi speaking for them both. "We were hoping you would say that."

"All right," Tom sighed with a little hope returning. "Let's look for a ride."

Chapter 22
President John Zimmerman
New White House, Cuba

President John Zimmerman sits at the head of a large table, staring at the report. After the devastating failure to collapse the undersea anomaly, the subsequent earthquakes that followed wreaked havoc across the United States and most of Mexico. The room is quiet as he reads the report, his advisors all sitting in silence, watching him as he finally places the report down and stares at it. When he finally speaks, his voice is rough with emotion and weariness.

"Do we have an idea of the death toll in Mexico City?"

Secretary of State Rita Cortez clears her throat and replies. "We don't have anything accurate yet, though projections are saying hundreds of thousands to upwards of three million."

"Mother of..." The President's words trail off as he stares at the report, scarcely able to imagine the sort of destruction that could lead to so much loss of life. "Those deaths are on our heads. On *mine*. But we have to keep our heads up and stay strong. Let's make sure we're doing everything we can to reach common ground with our new allies."

Cortez continues. "We've got our generals talking, sir. They're coordinating massive relief efforts with members and our armored divisions who were already entering the city when the earthquake struck."

"With the annexation no longer in question," General Davidson says, "we can change our mission goal to be completely humanitarian. We'll bring the full might of our armed forces to bear."

"Our goal is unity now," the President nods enthusiastically. "No more fighting. Make it clear to all the generals and officers. I've spoken to the Mexican leadership, and they're in agreement." He tapped his fingers on the table, casting his eyes around. "Now, what else do we need to make this happen? What about short-term supplies as well as augmenting the American-Mexican infrastructure?"

"The long-term plan for the infrastructure is simple," Davidson says, referencing a paper in front of him. "We've seized seventy-five percent of the Mexican power grids and will have those running full power within the month. Many will be getting upgrades as we improve them and make upgrades that have been sorely lacking. In some cases, we'll build completely new grids. Later, we'll start laying fiber optic cables, creating a one-nation network to have some semblance of connectivity again. That's still a few months off, but that's the plan."

The President nods. "We need to get messages out in front of the people – how's that happening?"

"We'll push as hard as we can, sir," Davidson shuffles some papers in front of him. "Until then, we're relying on good old-fashioned AM/FM broadcasts, both in English and Spanish, to communicate official news."

"Good enough. Has news leaked about the attempt to seal the breach?"

Davidson shakes his head. "No, thankfully. We've kept things well-contained and will continue to do so as much as possible."

"Let's keep it that way for the near future." The President looks to Rita and his assistant, Maxine. "I don't care how much Pierre begs to know."

"The Canadian Prime Minister has called six times, sir," Maxine reminds him. "I'm not sure how much longer we can ignore him."

"We'll ignore him as long as we need to," Zimmerman snaps as he rises. "The official word I want communicated is that we're busy helping the Mexican people recover from the earthquake that rocked their capital. We are *not* and *never have been*, enemies. Our general objectives of relocating the American populace south hasn't changed. I want nothing leaked about the explosions around the anomaly." Everyone nods in confirmation and he continues, turning his attention back to Davidson.

"What can we do about this newfound catastrophe in the short term?"

The general pokes his finger on the table. "Short term, I'd say the first task is to get mass amounts of food and other emergency supplies transported south."

"And how do we do that?"

"We scavenge from the frozen, abandoned portions of the country. There are still livestock, crops, machinery, warehouses and armories that can be tapped. Not to mention all of the stockpiles that are locked away."

"That would require reassigning some of our armed forces for this effort, correct?"

"That's right, sir. Now that we don't have a war to fight, we can afford them. We've got ample resources all over the south. We just need your authorization to move them."

"That makes sense to me," John says with a nod. "Let's set aside two divisions for the effort."

General Davidson shakes his head. "I agree we need to send a lot, but that might be too many. We still don't know what the Mexicans have up their sleeves."

"I'll talk with President de Brizuela. I'll let him know we're breaking off many of our troops for this effort, and that it will be to both our people's benefit not to fight. I'll make sure he has every soldier stand down across the board."

The general levels his gray eyes at the President. "And if he breaks the truce?"

"He won't, Mark, trust me on this one." John waves his hand at those assembled as he makes his final point. "Make our top priority salvaging everything we can from the continental United States. I want vehicles, entire warehouses of goods, ships, building materials, weapons, food stocks... Anything that isn't nailed down. Got it?"

A series of murmured agreements ripple around the table and he trudges on, sounding like a battle-weary warrior.

"We've made some mistakes, people. Hell, *I've* made most of them. But we have to learn from them and keep punching." He gives the room a grave nod. "Everything we do here today in the coming days will lay the path for our children's children. They can prosper and make our country greater than it's ever been. Or they can show up on some future documentary about the failed empire of the United States." He sits back down and gives the room another once over. "You can all go except for Rita, Maxine, and Mark."

The silence fills with discussion as everyone files outside, emboldened by the President's words. He watches them carefully as they file out of the room, then turns in his chair, looking out through a window that has been hastily refitted with three-inch bulletproof glass, the view distorted and wobbly.

"We've moved offices how many times since this started?" the President asks no one in particular.

"Four times, sir," Maxine reminds him.

"Four times," he scoffs. "Our people must be going nuts."

"Not as nuts as the Cubans," Cortez replies.

"What's the latest there?" Zimmerman stifles a yawn, pinching the bridge of his nose, trying to wipe away some of his weariness.

"Most of the Cuban government are on board with us relocating here and consolidating, given what we're giving them in return, but there are a few who are sowing a counter rebellion."

"But they're not very effective," Davidson counters. "They're mostly amateur fighters, idealistic kids who will surrender when we punch them in the nose. The Cuban authorities are doing a pretty good job clamping down on them, but we have teams working with them, too."

"When did we become conquering dictators?"

"Sir?" Davidson glances at the other two at the table with him.

"I mean, I know when," he continues, speaking largely to himself, "but I guess the better question is why. Why'd we let ourselves turn into this?"

"Survival, Mr. President." Cortez replies, looking at Davidson with a shrug.

"Survival." Zimmerman snorts. "That's just what we tell ourselves so that we don't feel quite as bad about invading sovereign nations and using them for our own purposes. At the end of the day, evil is evil and good is good. I wonder what side history will judge us as being on, hm?"

"Sir, are… are you wanting to pause our current operations?"

The President takes a long, slow breath then lets it out in a rush, turning back to the table, rubbing his hands together. "What? No. Ignore my ramblings. Just the thoughts of someone who doesn't like any of the choices we've got and wishes there was another way out."

"A no-win scenario, sir." Maxine adds.

"That's what it feels like."

"It's not a no-win scenario for the American people, sir." Davidson's tone is perplexed, struggling to understand what Zimmerman is going through.

"We're not the only people on the planet, Mark."

"Sir, I—"

"No, no. Like I said, ignore me. Too little sleep, too much to think about." Shaking off his introspection, Zimmerman continues their previous conversation. "Good work, everyone. Keep it up, and keep me informed. Mark, I want you to personally oversee getting those divisions moved up from Mexico City, understood?"

"Yes, sir." The general stands and marches off with his orders, notepad tucked under his arm.

Chapter 23
Specialist Lance Morales
Mexico City, Mexico

Heavy machinery dug metal prongs into piles of rubble, lifting and carrying them to massive, Caterpillar 797 dump trucks. Scavenger teams of combined Mexican-American forces dove in after the big equipment, shutting off any remaining power or gas lines and removing corpses. Occasionally, very rarely, they found someone alive, and choruses of cheers went up as the person was pulled out and passed along to awaiting medics for treatment and transportation out of the hot zone. Fire teams moved between the blocks in an effort to stem flames that still raged through the city, tapping into working water supplies wherever possible, trying their best to get the choking columns of smoke under control.

"Gather around, everyone," Captain Jones shouted at the top of his lungs. "We've got new orders from up top."

"What the hell is it this time?" Smith murmured as he put down the rock he'd been carrying and nudged Morales in the arm.

Shirtless, covered in sweat, soot, and grime, swimming in the stench of dead bodies, Morales straightened and put his hands on his hips. He winced as the strain in his back muscles complained for a few seconds before fading. Removing his air filtration mask, he staggered after Smith, following him to where their company was gathering around as shouts rang down the line and through the blocks where the soldiers had been working.

"New assignment?" Morales suggested as the eighty or so soldiers gathered in a tired group.

"Hard to say," Smith shrugged and popped out a Mexican blend cigarette he'd bummed off one of the other soldiers. He lit it up and looked around, squinting at Captain Jones as he addressed them.

The scruffy, red-haired man jumped up on a pile of rubble and waved his hands in the air. "Like I said, people, we've got new orders from the top. Gather your things, because we're moving out."

"Where to, Captain?" Smith called out.

"Need to know, soldier – and right now, you don't need to know squat," Jones shouted back. "Just grab your things, kiss your new best friends goodbye, and meet at the soccer field in an hour."

The company disbanded, each of them moving off to the area where they kept their gear, some grumbling, most looking happy to be done with the grunt work.

"This stinks." Smith finished his cigarette and threw it down.

"What are you so discouraged about?" Morales scoffed. "I can't think of a worse place to be than here. It's like hell. So, I don't know about you, but I'm happy we're getting out."

Smith scowled as they walked up the road about two hundred yards to a pair of Humvees. The troops stored their meager supplies in or around them, on constant guard from the local kids who sometimes absconded with their stuff. Morales and Smith pulled on their grungy, unwashed shirts and shouldered their packs, walking slowly toward the soccer field a little farther up the highway.

"It's just that I'm the kind of guy who likes to get into a groove," Smith said, finally explaining himself. "Over the past two days, I've made a lot of friends. Now, I have to leave them."

"You like to make friends so you can start trading," Morales chuckled. "Then you start a racket."

"Big deal," Smith shrugged. "I collect certain things, trade them for other things. I make everyone happy. What do you do?"

"I do my *job*, that's what." Morales laughed and slapped his friend on the back.

The soccer field where the Mexican Army had surrendered two days ago had become a designated landing pad for the combined Mexican-American forces, using it to ferry heavy supplies in and out. A section off to the side was being cleared of debris and reinforced for larger aircraft to come in as well, so that they could start bringing in bulk amounts of goods. The pair found a side road and made their way down to the airfield command center where military personnel and trucks trundling past them in both directions. Smith spoke to one of the marshals, who pointed them to the runway where a massive C-130J Super Hercules stood waiting, its ramp down and being loaded with supplies and manpower.

"I've never ridden in one of these before," he admitted.

"Seriously?"

"Yeah, I drove here, remember?"

Smith gazed up at the plane as they walked beneath the wide wings, each with two huge propellers and a set of jet thrusters used to get the behemoth off the ground on extremely short runways. "They must be sending us someplace far away if they got us tickets on one of these puppies."

"You think so?"

"Yeah, the range on these are something like two thousand miles."

"Wow," Morales gaped, staring upward as the sun glinted off the aircraft's steel gray sides. "I wonder where we're headed?"

* * *

After getting on board, another lieutenant on board confirmed they were indeed traveling a long distance away, flying north back toward the US-Mexico border where they would board trucks on a mission into the central United States. At first, Morales and Smith wondered if it might have something to do with a Canadian incursion, but the commanders couldn't confirm it. At the front of the C-130, the officers broke out crates of cold-weather gear, and everyone was issued heavy overjackets, pants and socks, their old boots traded out for a newer, insulated kind. They received thick hats and hoods and pairs of work gloves made of a matte black material and rubber grippers on the palms.

A few minutes after passing out the gear, the C-130's engines revved up, and the soldiers on board were told to take their seats. A few minutes of final checks and a bit of taxiing later and the aircraft turned onto the end of the runway. The engines fired up to the maximum and the thrusters engaged, throwing everyone at an angle backwards as the plane shot down the runway, pulling up into a steep angle before reaching the end, soaring into the sky faster than Morales would have imagined was possible. Once they had achieved altitude, the thrusters were shut down and the plane leveled off, making a long, banking turn and beginning its journey northward.

Morales unbuckled his seatbelt as the all-clear sign was given and finished bundling himself up in his new gear, looking at Smith and holding out his arms, feeling like a stuffed turkey. "I'm not sure I can fight in this."

"Maybe we're not fighting." The lieutenant stared up at a high portal on the fuselage that allowed in some of the fading daylight. "Maybe we'll be doing different work. Maybe this will be a different hell than the one we just left."

"Why do you say that?"

"These gloves?" Smith held them out and whacked them against his palm. "I've seen these before. They're rated for working in extreme weather. I'm talking well below freezing."

Morales looked up at the same window Smith had been staring at, watching as the clouds whipped past outside and the aircraft hit some turbulence, knocking him to the side before he caught himself on a crate. He sat hard next to Smith as he was pulling on his boots and buckled back in, waiting, the propellers loud in their ears, the temperature dropping considerably inside thanks to their ascent. Over the next fifteen minutes, the aircraft's shuddering and rumbling grew steadily worse, and Morales's nausea rose to match it. Still, it wasn't bad enough for him to look for the bathroom – yet.

A voice came over the loudspeaker, calm and attentive. "Attention, everyone, we'll be entering some heavy turbulence momentarily. The weather conditions have worsened, and we're about to fly through some clashing weather fronts. Don't worry, though. Just strap yourselves in and leave it to us. We'll get you boys and girls there safe and sound."

It wasn't long after that the wind picked up in long gusts, causing a faint prick of worry in the back of Morales's skull. As the turbulence increased, the plane dropped in altitude and he experienced a sideways slipping movement in the plane, measured by his turning stomach. Morales wasn't afraid of a few bumps, but the fact that the wind could toss around a giant C-130 sent a helpless feeling crawling up his spine. He and Smith did as the captain ordered, double-checking their buckles and making sure they were strapped in for the long ride. Things seemed to calm down for the next thirty minutes before they hit another storm pocket that shook them so hard it caused Morales to cry out and cling to the arms of his seat, certain they were going to crash. When he looked sideways at Smith, the lieutenant was cracking up at him.

"Shut up," Morales snapped. "It just freaked me out, is all."

Smith continued to chuckle and shake his head, but the plane dropped steeply into a pocket of smooth air that made Smith shut up and cling to the arms of his chair until the plane finally stabilized. It might have been funny any other time, yet Morales could only purse his lips tight and wait as the storms had their way with the craft. He squeezed his hands into fists and wished they would land soon.

* * *

An hour later, Morales was regretting those sentiments as the pilot's voice came over the speaker system, more nervous-sounding than he had been previously, though it sounded like he was making an effort to be strong. "Alright, we're coming in for a landing. Hold on to your butts and try to remain in your seats."

The plane shook so hard it felt like they were driving over a gravel highway, but instead of gravel, they were stones the size of Morales's head. The bumps were like punches, jolting him to the bones and his teeth rattled, his shoulders tense up through to his neck. Where there had been joking and razzing between the troops before, the entire cargo bay sat silent in the near darkness only a few running lights remaining on to illuminate the faces of the other eighty soldiers as they stared helplessly across the bay at one another.

The propeller noise suddenly dropped as the plane started its descent and the sensible part of Morales told him it was a natural part of the flight. After all, they had to slow down at some point in order to reach the ground. The irrational, animal part of him screamed internally in sheer panic, though, and he didn't want the engines to stop, because that meant they would somehow freeze in the air and plummet to the ground. He wanted them to keep plowing through the storms, endlessly staying aloft in spite of the quaking. Clinging to his seat, sweat broke out across his brow despite the near freezing air inside the cargo hold. It didn't matter what Morales wanted, for the C-130 dove into a blender of crosscurrents.

The wind punched them left and right as the plane slewed toward the ground. He expected the pilot to come over the loudspeaker at any moment, letting the troops know things were going to be fine and that they were just minutes from landing, but when he didn't speak again, Morales's worry grew. A glance over at Smith showed the false bravado gone as his friend squeezed his eyes shut, gripping the arms of his chair with white knuckles. The engines slowed even more, like they were trying to coast through the turbulent air and the nose suddenly bucked upward, and they seemed to hang in the air for the blink of an eye. Morales thought the end had come when the rear tires slammed down hard on the pavement, causing his head to jerk forward as the impact shook his bones. Metal scraped in the back of the plane, and they skidded sideways before finding purchase. The front tires tried to descend, though it seemed like the pilot was fighting colossal forces to get it planted.

Morales could only shake his head. "Come on," he growled. "Put the damn thing down!"

Finally, the front tires hit pavement with the familiar sound of screeching rubber on asphalt and a deep grumble shook through the entire frame of the aircraft. But at least they were down, and in one piece as opposed to many, with no fires or real damage to speak of. He sighed deeply and looked sideways at Smith, who'd settled back in his seat as the C-130 slowed and came to a near rolling stop before taxiing to another spot on the tarmac.

"Thanks for flying," the pilot finally spoke, his voice sounding weary but happy to be down. "Good luck on your missions."

"Okay, people, listen up." Captain Jones called from somewhere toward the back. "Grab your gear and prepare to disembark. Once outside, load into the transports and hunker down for a little sight-seeing trip, got it?"

The soldiers did as they were told, hefting their packs, rifles, and sidearms. As soon as the plane came to a full stop, the rear ramp descended, letting in a screaming wind that blew through them like a scythe, snow swirling in roaring gusts, finding every crack and crevice in their cold-weather gear.

"Let's go!"

Heads down, shoulders forward, the troops filed out, Smith and Morales somewhere in the middle of the pack. As soon as his boots hit the tarmac, a gust of wind threw hard little flakes of sleet into his face. He held his arm up to protect himself from the fierce gale, squinting ahead so he didn't run in to anyone.

"Where the hell are we?" When his words were lost to the wind, he raised his voice and repeated the same question.

"Somewhere near the US-Mexico border," Smith screamed back as they branched off and strolled toward an older-style military transport. The truck had big, knobby tires and a flapping canvas top stretched over five ribs.

"The border?" Morales squinted. "Weren't we just here a few days ago?"

"Yeah." Smith climbed aboard the transport and found a spot in the back, sitting with his pack in his lap.

Morales removed his own backpack and sat next to his friend, wrapping his arms around his things. "I don't remember it being this cold."

"But it was getting colder."

"Yeah," Morales murmured for himself more than anyone else. "But not *this* cold."

They waited for ten minutes as the trucks sat idle, the convoy getting set up to roll out. A pair of massive Letourneau dump trucks pulled by with huge snowplows on front, their tires alone standing twice as tall as a man. Three eighteen-wheelers hauling fuel tanks followed those, while three Humvees stopped close by. More trucks could be heard, their big diesel engines trying to rival the C-130 turboprops, the sounds nearly blocking out the roar of the storm. The captain made his rounds, moving from truck to truck, standing near the back where he shouted orders at the troops. When he reached theirs, he leaned in and rested his hands on the tailgate.

"Our objective is to drive into the interior of the country. Specifically, to a depot in Santa Fe, New Mexico where we'll be making a grocery run. We'll stop for periodic breaks to refuel from our mobile gas stations, but otherwise we expect to drive straight through. No camping or marshmallows, got it?"

"Are we going to be fighting, sir?" Smith shouted.

Jones grinned through the sleet. "Not likely, soldier, unless you count this damn blizzard as the enemy, in which case there will be *plenty* of fighting."

Smith cursed silently under his breath as the captain got the convoy moving. The enormous plows pulled out first, followed by a Humvee, then the fuel trucks. The troop transports came next, four personnel carriers packed with their entire company of soldiers. Morales watched as several semis filed in behind them filled with bags of rock salt and sand and two flatbeds came behind them carrying a regular-sized bulldozer and excavator. Three more Humvees fell in after them and a dozen cargo vans and assorted four-wheel-drive vehicles brought up the rear.

"Wow, this is some operation," he murmured as the massive train took a highway heading north.

"It's going to be a long, hard drive," Smith grumbled, sounding aggravated. "Cold, too."

"Oh come on," Morales elbowed his friend good-naturedly. "Better freezing on home turf than frying in the Mexican desert, eh?"

* * *

Three hours after the convoy left the border, it ground to a halt. While they waited, the men and women huddled together in the back of the troop carrier, pressed tightly together, trying to draw warmth from each other. The snow poured down on them like nothing Morales had ever seen, whipping into the back of the truck, spinning in a cyclone, slapping and teasing them, finding its way into the gaps in their winter gear no matter how tightly they bundled their hoods and coats.

Snow and ice were piled high on both sides of the roadway, a dozen feet high in some places, made worse by the snowplows shoving it off to the side. The pair of plows had been their saving grace, breaking through the big drifts and clearing them in billowing waves of white. As an added measure, they sprinkled rock salt from spreaders to give the vehicles coming behind them a better grip on the road. Still, something had stopped the convoy.

"How far north are we?" Morales shouted over the stinging wind.

"We're close to Albuquerque, I think!" Smith yelled back. "I thought I saw a sign for Highway 25 a few miles back."

"Oh, you've got to be kidding me," he mumbled. "A blizzard in Albuquerque? I mean, I know they got some snow, but all this?"

The captain poked his head around the back of the truck and hammered his palms on the tailgate. "Need some muscle up front," he yelled. "Everybody out. Let's go."

They jumped down two soldiers at a time, leaving the thin layer of protective canvas. The twenty of them made their way along the right side of the road beside the idling trucks, oil smoke and the smell of fuel permeating the air. It wasn't just snow the plows had been tossing aside, but vehicles, too, rounded white blisters of cars and trucks jutted from the drifts. Morales walked up to one, half buried with just the rear end sticking out, and put his hands against the glass to peer inside.

A pair of shadowy forms sat stiffly in the back seat under a pile of covers. They were huddled close, their heads bowed together, hats pulled tightly down and his heart leapt in his chest and he started to call for the captain when he caught the bluish tint of their skin. They sat frozen stiff with no signs of breathing, chests flat, no gusts of warm air drifting from their mouths. He shifted to the side to investigate the front seat but didn't see a driver or passenger, though a set of keys dangled from the ignition. He figured they must have found their way to the vehicle during a long cold night, turned it on, and sat in the heat until the fuel ran out. With a disgusted snort, he rejoined the company as they marched toward the front of the line.

They'd stopped in the middle of a small town, and Morales glanced out at the shadows of houses dotting the roadsides. Visibility was only about a hundred yards, and the temperatures must've been quite a few degrees below zero. There was no sign of civilization as far as he could tell. No golden lights blinked from windows. No chimneys gave off trails of smoke he might have expected in a wintry landscape scene. At the front, he found Smith.

"Why'd we stop?"

Smith gestured up the road ahead where the plows had scraped the snow for about fifty yards. Between them lay a string of potholes like he'd never seen before, strung together into a massive line, eight or ten inches deep in some spots. Nothing that would cause trouble for the larger vehicles, but the smaller ones would quickly get bogged down and stuck in the snow sitting in the holes.

"What are they going to do about this, I wonder?" Morales said.

"Fill them with sand or rock salt?" Smith shrugged.

Soldiers from another team brought up dozens of sandbags, stacking them up. Captain Jones ordered a few soldiers to build campfires on the sides of the road where they hung buckets of snow. While it melted, they busted open the sandbags and began scooping a few inches into the long pothole crevice.

Shrugging, Smith and Morales joined in, dumping in buckets of warm water over the sand. They worked for an hour and a half that way, filling the holes with sand and water until they were completely full. Once done, Jones ordered the soldiers to march back to their trucks where they were given rations and allowed a bit of rest. After eating, Morales waded into the snow to take care of his personal business against the side of the house, a cold and unpleasant experience with ice-cold snow whipping down his pants.

When he returned to the truck, he sat next to Smith and drank from his canteen. "What the hell are we doing?" Morales asked.

"Waiting for the water to freeze so we can drive over it."

"Think that's actually going to work?" He scoffed. "It takes longer than that for water to freeze."

"About three or four hours at zero degrees Fahrenheit." Smith patted him on the shoulder. "And I hate to tell you, friend, but it's a bit colder than that out here right now. No, give it ninety minutes, and that water will be frozen solid. Then we can drive right over the whole thing. And guess what? It'll still be frozen afterwards, so we won't have to do this on the return trip."

"What's the sand for?"

"Structural support and some grip for when we drive over it and wear down the layers of ice, most likely. Those Corps guys know their stuff."

"Okay, I guess that could work."

Smith tapped his index finger against his temple and returned to eating his MRE. True enough, a short time later, the convoy got back underway, driving over the small lake of ice with no issues. Morales was impressed that it worked, even if it might only be a temporary fix. As they pulled away, the winds kicked up in tremendous swirls that cut their visibility almost to zero, sometimes halting the convoy for several minutes, or even an hour, at a time. The storms always ended as quickly as they started, allowing them to make some progress before the next one hit. As they drew closer to Albuquerque, the destruction became worse. More abandoned cars had been shoved off the streets with frozen, shadowy forms still inside, Morales watching in horror as they drove past a cluster of about two dozen people lying frozen in the piles of snow moved by the plows. Hats and toboggans and arms with mittens on them jutted up from the white, jumbled together by the work of the plows.

Smith shook his head as they drove by, voice low and respectful. "They must have gotten frozen trying to march south, poor bastards."

Morales could only nod as they passed more groups of frozen people, hundreds, possibly thousands of dead refugees along the road, with who-knew-how-many lying under the undisturbed snow in the ditches and beyond. Some bodies were visible up in the yards and porches where the snow was shallower, and homes had been partially dismantled and burned to create enough warmth to survive another day. The cold was strong, though, and relentless, and together with hunger and thirst it had won out in every single case.

"This is pretty unbelievable, man," Morales groaned, his throat burning with rising bile.

The nightmare faced by evacuees was nigh-on unimaginable. A mass exodus, thousands of families grabbing what they could carry and moving south as fast as they could go, the first wave in vehicles, and the second on foot as the snow became too deep for passenger vehicles to traverse. They would have been confident at first, certain they could outrun the creeping cold, but as the hours passed, many mothers and fathers would've come to realize they didn't have the skills to start a simple fire without a lighter much less survive in such a brutal climate. Only the absolute strongest could have made it.

Morales tore his eyes away from the endless highway of the dead before he threw up as Smith shook his head sadly next to him. "Yeah, despite all the warnings and evacuations, a lot of folks didn't make it out in time. I guess the military couldn't force a lot of them out at the end because they ran out of time."

"Half of them probably didn't even believe it could get this cold." Morales shook his head. "And I wouldn't have either. The anomaly was a thousand miles away. Who would care about the freshwater surge into the North Atlantic all the way out here?"

"It's the butterfly effect, man. One thing happens on one side of the world that leads to changes no one would have expected a thousand miles away."

"Hardly a butterfly though."

"Yeah. Definitely bigger than a butterfly. An elephant effect, maybe, or a blue whale."

Morales smiled, then his face dropped as something occurred to him. "You know what?" He shot his friend a dark look. "If anything happens to us out here, like, like losing our supplies or getting trapped in the snow, we'll be S-O-L."

"Just like these people." Smith shook his head. "We should never forget the war on the eastern front."

"Huh?"

"When Germany invaded Russia during World War II."

"What about it?"

"Well, the Germans tried to fight in the Russian winter. It was so damn cold a lot of their equipment failed and soldiers froze or starved right out in the field. The Russians ran right over them after that."

"That's just what I needed to hear." Morales shook his head and swallowed. "Another omen of death from Lieutenant Smith."

"I'm not trying to scare you. It's just a little friendly advice not to underestimate good ol' Mother Nature. We better keep the engines warm, or we won't have anything to drive home." Morales held his head down, absorbing what Smith had said, his gaze flicking outside to the passing dead despite how much he tried to avoid it.

The convoy plowed their way through downtown Albuquerque amidst a surreal scene of frozen wasteland, the truck headlamps revealing more endless, lifeless marchers. Buildings and bridges looked as if they'd been cast in a mold of soft white plaster, the city a tomb frozen in time, destined to never see another spring or summer. Signs of attempted survival poked through the fields of white; remnants of fires, makeshift shelters and scavengers frozen while trying to find food and water abounded.

"You were right, man." Morales stared out the back of the truck.

"Right about what?"

"This is just a different *kind* of hell than Mexico City." He paused with a stiff shake of his head. "Think we can talk the captain into reassigning us back to Mexico?"

Chapter 24
Tom McKnight
Laredo, Texas

"How much longer?" Jack asked, complaining from the back of the raggedy van they were riding in.

"We've only got about thirty miles to go," Tom replied, glancing out the window at the drifts dusting of snow blowing through South Texas at an alarming rate. "Just about another forty-five minutes."

"Well, at least he doesn't have to pee," Barbara added with a grin.

"I do, though." The boy looked glum. "Sorry."

"I could use a break, too," Saanvi added from the second row of seats. "We don't know what Laredo will be like once we get there. Might not have a chance to take care of business, if you know what I mean."

"I do," Tom nodded, eyes already searching for an exit. "I'll stop the next chance I get."

The opportunity came soon enough, and Tom pulled the 1988 Chevy Ram off at the next rest stop. It leaked oil like a sieve and had bald tires, but the old van with *Grace Baptist Church* stenciled down the side ran, if barely. At the end of the exit ramp, he pumped the brakes six times before coming to a complete stop in a parking spot in front of the restrooms and vending centers. Once parked, he held his hands up off the wheel, letting out a sigh of relief that they hadn't crashed.

"Alright, 10 minutes, people, then let's get back on the road."

Stevens opened the side door and the medics got out, followed by the kids and Smooch, who jumped gingerly down. They wandered up toward the restrooms, and Tom walked halfway there, keeping an eye on them as they went inside while Barbara turned to face him.

"Luckily for us we found those keys inside the van."

Tom cocked an eyebrow at her. "They probably figured no one would be stupid enough to steal it. It's practically a death trap."

"Well, it's gotten us about fifty miles, wouldn't you say?"

"About that." Tom nodded and shivered. He'd kept their speed slow and reasonable as the roads had turned icy with a dusting of snow, thankful that it hadn't yet turned into the tundra that was Virginia.

"It's getting colder," Barbara said, hooking her arm inside his. "Think it will get as bad as home?"

"It's really hard to tell." Tom raised his eyes. "We're pretty far south. This would normally be a bad winter for South Texans, but I think it'll get worse."

Barbara looked around, too. "Hopefully, Stevens and Patel can help us once we reach the base."

They'd been listening to the radio for the past two hours on an AM channel used exclusively for emergency broadcasts, the message playing on repeat until Tom had finally turned it off. Much like the signs they'd read up north, US citizens were under a mandatory evacuation order and all refugees were instructed to make their way to the Laredo-Nuevo border for processing as well as encouraged to bring no more than a handbag apiece and some form of identification.

"I wonder how many made it down from the north?" Barbara asked absently.

"It's hard to say. All the towns we passed were deserted, so those people probably made it." Tom drew a deep breath. "But we don't know about the people in the cities. If they took the warnings seriously, they might have escaped. If they delayed, even a little... well, you mentioned how bad the traffic was outside the house after the evacuation orders were announced."

"Very bad," she nodded. "People were desperate then. Imagine what they would have been like later." She spotted Jack coming out of the restroom and gave him a smile. "You washed your hands, right?"

"Yeah, but there's barely any water."

"Well, at least you tried," Barbara said.

Tom grinned despite himself. Even though they were miles away from home, with nothing but the clothes on their backs, he appreciated every moment with his wife and kids. The phrase, *at least we have each other*, had come to mind more than once, and for good reason. The loss of what was closest to him had reinvigorated his love for them all, and he had silently resolved to never lose sight of them again – no matter the cost.

They stretched their legs a few minutes more before climbing back into the van and once inside, they had a little to eat from their meager supplies, not bothering to ration it like they had at first. According to the radio broadcast, they'd be given aid at the border and while he didn't like depending on the military or the government in general, they'd take any and everything they could get. As long as the border guards let them through into a warmer climate, he liked his family's chances. They'd just need some short-term supplies and a bit of land to get started, then they could find some seeds, a body of water with a healthy population of fish and a way to build a long-term shelter. They had the skills to prosper wherever they ended up, so long as they could survive till they got there.

After everyone got back inside, he started the van with a clank and whine of the fan belt, then pulled out of the parking spot and got back on I-35 south. They kept the radio off and the windows up, both to keep out the cold and because they'd been smelling burning oil for the last few miles, though the engine light still hadn't come on. They passed a sign for Laredo in twenty-two miles, and he muttered at the clanking van.

"Come on. Just a little more to go. You can do it...."

Tom stopped worrying once he spotted the first few homes and an industrial park outside Laredo. There were military personnel interspersed along the highway, and Humvees were lined up every few miles. At the I-69 junction, a soldier waved for Tom to take I-69 west where they skirted the city and pulled into a line of about a hundred cars moving across the border. He lifted in his seat and peered out as far as he could, noting a dozen or more uniforms lingering near a narrow gate stretched across the road. Green fencing had been erected, branching off miles in either direction along the Rio Grande River and the soldiers were pointing off to their left.

"It looks like they're asking people to park off to the side," Tom said.

"They're forcing people to get out of their cars," Barbara added, peering out the passenger window.

"They'll want them to walk across the border," Stevens answered Tom's concern. "You know, to get a proper headcount, check for injuries or diseases, and search the vehicles for contraband."

Tom nodded absently, though it was strange to see the vehicles ahead of him where the owners were arguing briefly with soldiers as their cars were practically impounded.

He scoffed. "Well, they can have this piece of junk."

A soldier directed him to pull off to the side, and Tom did so, guiding the old bus in behind a line of cars and trucks. Families were exiting their vehicles, milling around until the military personnel grabbed their attention and turned them toward the narrow gates hundreds of feet away. They all looked road worn, carrying supplies in their trunks and on luggage racks, though the soldiers didn't allow them to get anything down, simply urging them toward the gates. When the parents tried to grab the possessions off the roof, they were pushed harder, forced to give them up amidst shouts and threats of violence.

"Well, it's a good thing we packed light, eh?" Tom quipped, getting a snicker out of Barbara next to him in the front seat.

Everyone got out, and the kids brought Smooch around the side, the dog's ears up and alert, her tail wagging slowly back and forth as she took in the scene. Tom turned to Stevens with an arced eyebrow, the medic nodded for them to continue and they strode toward the gate as a group.

Tom tried to see what was beyond the fencing, though all he could make out were people passing through the security checkpoint after answering a few questions from Army staffers. More than a dozen MPs stood behind the staffers in their small area, their weapons shouldered, watching the crowd keenly for any disturbances.

"Hold it right there!" A staff sergeant rushed up and stopped them, looking past Tom to Barbara. "Ma'am, you can't bring the dog inside without a leash."

"It's okay, guys," Patel responded, stepping between them. "They're with us. I'm Private Saanvi Patel. Army, Twenty-Ninth Infantry Division. We just flew in from North—"

"Look, private. I've got my orders." The staff sergeant turned and gestured at a sign hanging near the gates. "No animals beyond this point without a leash."

Tom glowered at them, then he looked back at the ratty van where a soldier was just climbing in to drive it away. He was already thinking of how he could make a leash out of tearing up some of the vinyl seats when Saanvi beat him to it.

"One second." The private grabbed her belt and whipped it off, tying it loosely around the dog's neck and putting the end in Barbara's hand before gesturing at her improvised leash "How about now? C'mon, sir. We've just come a long way."

The man looked over the ragged group with a tired, beleaguered gaze before he shrugged and gestured toward the gates. "Go ahead."

"Thanks," Saanvi said, gesturing for the McKnights to keep going.

"Thanks," Tom told her as the staff sergeant went off in search of someone else to berate, looking back and forth between the medics. "Seriously, thanks to both of you. You've done so much for me and the kids."

Stevens nodded, looking uncomfortable with the praise, though Saanvi flashed them a smile. "We're all in this together, right?"

"Most definitely," Tom agreed.

He turned and made sure everyone was with them as they approached the gates and stood in line behind other families. After ten minutes, Stevens sighed and stepped out, gesturing for them to follow him. He cut them through several lines until they reached a few Army staffers standing off to the side.

"Hey, guys. I'm Lieutenant Stevens from the Twenty-Ninth Infantry Division out of West Virginia," he announced. "These folks helped us get here from North Carolina. Think we can get them checked in quickly?"

The staffers stood straighter and nodded at him, their eyes regarding Saanvi and the McKnights, suddenly eager to help. "Of course," one woman said. She pulled a tablet from where it was tucked under her arm and took Steven's and Saanvi's information before turning to Tom.

"Your name, please, sir. And the city and state you're from."

"Tom McKnight, Wyndale, West Virginia. This is my family." He gave all their names and started to walk through.

"One second, sir," she said. "I'll need your thumb print as well."

"Thumb print?"

"It's for your security. We need a way to identify US citizens until we can issue a new form of identification, like an ID."

Tom winced, but he wasn't in a position to argue. He placed his thumb on the computer tablet where the officer indicated, waited for it to beep green, then walked through a side entrance to the other side of the gate. Stevens came through next, passing Tom with a nod before going to speak with some of the MPs on guard. Just then, Jack came through and ran up, throwing his arms around his father's waist.

"Dad, we made it!" he sang. "We're going to Mexico!" His face scrunched up in thought. "It's kind of like a vacation, right?"

"Not quite." Tom ruffled his hair, happy to answer a million questions just to feed off the kid's energy.

Sam and Linda came next, skipping through and looking a little more like girls than the rugged young women they'd become. Saanvi came next, shaking hands with a few soldiers as she passed. They finally let Barbara through with Smooch, and she quickly heel-toed it to them with a curious, but careful, expression, glancing at Tom, gazing past him at the vast country they were about to enter.

"I'm ready to make this work, Tom." Her voice was wistful, and she locked her arm into his. "I'm ready to start over and—"

"Mr. McKnight?"

Tom turned to face a rugged-looking MP who's face held a straight-edged jaw and deep-set eyes.

"Yes, sir," he replied. "I'm Tom McKnight. We just got here."

"I'll need you to come with me, sir. You and your whole family."

Tom watched the other families walking by, heading toward busses or secondary check points. "I don't understand. What's...." He looked past the MP to find Stevens behind the group, talking to someone in uniform while pointing at the McKnights. "What the hell? Stevens?!"

"Please, just follow the guards to the next checkpoint." The MP gestured for Tom to walk ahead.

"Take him now." Stevens hissed from behind the MP. "He stole an Osprey. Do you think polite language is going to work?"

Tom glared at the medic while Saanvi stared at her partner with an accusatory look. "What are you doing, Brad? Are you turning the McKnight's in?"

"I'm doing what needs to be done." Stevens raised his voice. "This man held a pilot hostage and forced an unauthorized takeoff."

"Come on, man," Tom growled at the medic. "You can't be serious. You know we didn't have a choice. I explained it to you."

"So, you *did* hijack a military aircraft?" The MP narrowed his eyes, studying Tom and looking for a lie.

Returning the stare, he dared the MP to doubt him. "I took this man and his soldiers in when earthquakes were tearing up the base in Asheville."

"And the injured soldiers we had died," Stevens reminded them.

"That would have happened anyway," Tom shot back. "The Osprey had a mechanical fault that forced a crash-landing!"

"It's true," Saanvi said, intervening on the McKnight's behalf. She shoved Stevens to the side and rounded on the tough MP. "If anything, Mr. McKnight saved our asses by getting us out of there after the crash."

"But he left Lieutenant Colonel Banks behind," Stevens interjected, giving Saanvi a shove in return "He told us so himself. He left a ranking officer in danger as he hijacked our aircraft."

"Okay, come on." The MP rested his palm on his pistol, seeming convinced by Stevens's story. "Just follow us, Mr. McKnight. No one has to get hurt."

Two soldiers circled to stand behind Tom, while another handful moved to corral Barbara and the kids. His wife gave him a hopeless, wondering expression which Tom didn't have an answer for. The two guards edged him away from the gates, and the rest followed, Jack suddenly lunging forward between the two guards to get to his father, but a soldier cut the boy off and shoved him roughly away.

"Was that necessary?" Tom spat, calming only when Barbara rushed up and took Jack's hand.

"Keep the kid quiet." The MP glanced down at Smooch. "And the dog stays,"

Another soldier tried to take the makeshift leash from Barbara, sending Jack completely over the edge. He took a swing at the guard, clocking him across the cheek, doing no damage but angering the man just the same, and he shoved Jack away hard and snatched the leash again. Smooch lunged at the man's face with a vicious snarl, her fangs snapping just an inch from the man's nose and he jerked his sidearm free and aimed it at the animal. Tom felt the old familiar violence rise within him, both unsure and afraid of where it might lead him, balling his hand into a fist and preparing to swing.

"I've got her!" Saanvi rushed in from the side, quickly taking Smooch's leash from Barbara and putting herself between the gun and dog. Holding her hand up, she glanced up and then over at Tom. "Don't worry. I'll see she's taken care of. She'll be fine."

Tom gave her a thankful nod and allowed himself to be pushed along. Despite the de-escalation of the situation, the MP had seen Tom's balled-up fist and he nodded to the two guards, who grabbed him, jerked his hands behind his back, and zip-cuffed him before he could fight them.

"Seriously? Is this really necessary?" Barbara complained, her voice rising in anger.

"I'm afraid it is, ma'am," the MP replied smoothly. "At least until I can get someone to clear things up." The big soldier stepped back and looked across the group to make sure things were buttoned up, then he jerked his head toward the second checkpoint. "Okay, let's go."

Families who had gotten through the first checkpoint quickly stepped aside when they spotted the soldiers with the McKnights as their prisoners.

"Where are you taking us?" Tom spat words at the MP, struggling against his bonds.

"I'm passing you off to a lieutenant colonel. He's a real nice guy, but I doubt he'll take kindly to you leaving people back in Asheville. Chances are, he'll put you in our holding facility till we can get this ironed out."

Tom's jaw dropped. "A holding facility? A *prison*? Are you serious?"

The MP gave him an absent glance. "Just until we can get your story straightened out, sir. Please stop resisting."

"I'm *not* resisting," Tom growled, shoulders shifting, craning his neck to see the group of guards shoving and pushing the kids along. Unable to control himself, he shouldered the man on his right aside and kicked the other one in the back before trying another angle.

"I need to see someone in charge of the science division. I'm a contractor for the Navy. They're not going to be too happy—"

"I told you to stop resisting, sir!" The big MP stepped in front of Tom and cracked him across the cheek with the butt of his weapon, causing him to collapse to his knees. The kids screamed, and a curse rang from Barbara's lips. The MP stood in front of him, boots shoulder width apart, waiting for Tom to recover his senses.

"Sorry to have to do that, sir, but you left me no choice."

Warm blood ran down Tom's cheek, and he licked salty fluid off his lip.

"Now, are you finished resisting?"

Tom nodded feebly, forcing himself to stand, glowering at the MP. They passed through the next gate without waiting in line, refugees staring at them with wide, frightened eyes. The soldiers shoved him hard through the second checkpoint and past more guards, jerking him sideways, angling him toward a long, wide RV unit with antennae and satellite dishes springing from the top. A broad-shouldered man descended a short set of stairs and stood with his feet apart, watching them approach.

"What's the problem, corporal?"

"This guy's the problem." The rough MP grabbed Tom by the back of the neck. "What do you want me to do with him?"

Chapter 25
Keith
Asheville, North Carolina

The UH-1 Venom lifted off from the Asheville FOB in a heavy gale of wind, causing Keith's stomach to lurch, though the higher they got, the better view he had. The earthquake's destruction had left the place in ruin, schools, restaurants, and apartments no more than piles of rubble. Three soldiers had died, a hundred were injured, their operating buildings were smashed to pieces and the entire FOB was generally in tatters.

The aftershocks hadn't stopped for an hour or more, one going off every few minutes as if trying to finish off what was left of the place. Between quakes, Banks had tried to pull together the science team to analyze what had gone wrong with the anomaly, but the Navy had begun recalling their ships almost immediately, so they had no eyes and ears above the site. Even if they did, their computer equipment was in shambles so the scientists couldn't crunch any data, so they had nothing to go on and no additional ways to study the anomaly.

The order had finally come for Banks to fly south, but it had taken hours for another chopper to arrive. Tom had stolen their intended ride, and that burned her to the core. Once the Venom landed, they boarded it quickly with a handful of soldiers and a medic to keep tabs on Keith's frostbitten digits. He clenched his hands on the arms of the chair, wincing as the pain cut right through the medication he'd taken. The sting only intensified his hatred for the McKnights – Tom had made fools of them once again and gotten away. It was embarrassing to Keith, Banks, and the military, though the lieutenant colonel was taking it worse than him, and Keith listened closely as she spoke to his higher ups on a satellite phone.

"Are you sure we can't break off an F-22 to pursue them?" Banks pressed the big phone against her cheek. "The man we're talking about here is *extremely* dangerous. He single-handedly screwed up the mission to shut down the anomaly, and he'll get away if we don't stop them." He paused. "Well, I don't want them to shoot down an Osprey, but a simple threat might force them to land." He paused again. "No, I know it's a valuable aircraft. Yes, I understand the priorities have changed, and all available aircraft have been directed elsewhere. Yes, I know... But I need you to... Dammit!"

Banks slammed the phone in its cradle, glaring at Keith with steely eyes as the injured operative eased back in his seat, clutching the arms of his chair as the chopper turned hard to the south.

"Let me guess. You're not getting any help from your contacts at the Air Force?"

"*No.*" Banks's face was twisted with rage. "I hate to say it, but now that the mission to collapse the anomaly failed, they don't care about McKnight anymore."

"Well, I do."

"I do, too," Banks agreed with a snarl. "His unwillingness to help us early on caused this. If he'd just been on board earlier, we would have time to rehearse the operation and possibly find a better placement for the explosives. We could have had time for a second attempt."

"To be fair..." Keith gave a mockingly casual tick of his head. "And keep in mind, I'm just playing devil's advocate here. He did exactly what you told him to do. He drove the rovers right where you wanted them. I'm not sure having him on site any earlier would have helped. We certainly can't blame him for wanting to get back to his family."

"Yes, but he's arrogant and irritatingly recalcitrant. He ran from us when he should have helped, he wasted our time and stole a valuable military asset. He deserves every damn thing he has coming to him."

"So, you're saying we'd be justified in going after him despite not having a lot of... 'official' support?"

Banks gave him a covert look. "I suppose, in a roundabout way, that's exactly what I'm saying."

"Let's trump up some charges and have him arrested," Keith offered. "We could file the paperwork and take a contingent of marines after him. It's not like we have a lot of red tape to cut through, right?"

"Not particularly. Not anymore. Not with everyone focused on Mexico and Cuba and everything else except for stopping this whole mess."

"There you have it. You put in the request, and I'll assemble the team."

"Someone could question it." Banks growled. "I mean, everyone *is* distracted at the moment, but some see it as a way to enforce more security measures that weren't there before. They're increasing the level of approval for borrowing equipment and troops. They're even requiring mandatory thumbprints for citizens at the borders under the guise of safety and security. It'll be easier to keep tabs on everyone that way."

"Using the crisis to add layers of control." Keith nodded. "I get it. Can we use it to find the McKnights?"

"Possibly. But we don't even know if they're going to the border. That family is crazy enough to try to eke out a living in the cold wasteland." Banks shook her head. "We can go after him, but we may eventually have to accept that we'll never see the McKnights again."

"We should at least try." Keith could barely hide the resentment in his voice. "We owe it to everyone to see him brought to justice."

Banks stared off into the distance as she tapped on er knee, wearing an expression caught somewhere between anger and indecision. Finally, she turned and fixed Keith with a stone-cold look. "I want McKnight as badly as you."

"Is it that obvious?"

The lieutenant colonel nodded. "What did you have in mind?"

"I could call in some special favors, but it would cost you a lot."

"I don't have access to the assets I used to," Banks reminded him. "They're directing most equipment and resources south."

"No, but you have all the access codes to the US bases they left abandoned, right? You can get us inside, and I'll bet there's a lot of equipment and intel there, ripe for the picking."

A faint smile touched Banks's lips. "Sneaky as ever, aren't you? Fine. The codes are yours, *if* you can get me McKnight."

Keith grinned wide, feeling better already. As a plan began to form in his mind, his thoughts drifted to the McKnights and what he planned to do to them once he caught them. It wasn't just Tom who aggravated Keith. It was smug Barbara, annoying Samantha, their whining little son Jeffrey or Jason or whoever the hell he was, and Linda. Yes, sweet Linda. She'd gotten away with the worst slight of all; almost killing him. Multiple times. But she wasn't as smart as she thought she was. None of them were. And Keith was determined to prove it.

He picked up the satellite handset and flipped it over, flashing Banks a smile. "I'll make the call."

Book 5: COLLAPSE

Chapter 1
Medic Saanvi Patel
Nuevo Laredo, Mexico

A chill wind whistled through the loose-boarded buildings of the criminal containment center southwest of Nuevo Laredo. Tumbleweeds blew against the chain-link and razor wire fence encircling the holding area, a dilapidated block of houses and businesses stretching in a rectangle the length of a football field. Plywood shutters battened tight slammed in their wooden frames, thudding to the wind's pulse while haggard trees that had once provided shade were trimmed back to allow more precious sunlight to gift its fragile warmth.

In the backyards, the dirt had turned cold and hard from the bitter temperatures slicing their way in from the north, the sparse grass brown and withered and rough. Burn barrels filled the yards, refugees huddled around them, hands raised, faces pressed close to warm chilled extremities. Furniture arms and legs stuck up from the crackling flames as they burned whatever they could scavenge to stave off the freezing winds. In the southern section of the camp on the street's north side sat a boarded-up restaurant and an old-style pharmacy topped with a sign out of the 1950s. Its face bore the image of a smiling woman with curly black hair, the word *Farmacia* stretched across the top in faded red lettering.

The camp's inhabitants were refugees from the north, singled out as troublemakers by the Army officers in Laredo. Prisoners strolled briskly between the ramshackle buildings, an urgency in their step as they threw furtive glances through the chain-link at the guards on the other side. Many still wore the lightweight clothing they had brought from the States, inadequate to handle the brutal chill moving in.

Whispers twisted through tight alleyways where refugees protected dwindling supplies, bartering and organizing out of sight as rumors of a break-out gained traction. Reluctant guards milled around the fence line, rifles slung on shoulders, black beanies pulled over brows, hands tucked deep into pockets as they huddled inside thick Army coats, their cheeks glowing red in the punishingly stiff wind. Gusts of warm breath blew from covered lips before fading to nothing as they walked with brisk movements to generate heat, attention focused on the supply tents and mess hall where a smell wafted out that could have been cooking meat, beans, or something else the company officers had scrounged up.

The command center and barracks were located outside the fence on the west side, made of a warehouse and prefab buildings dropped off by helicopters weeks earlier. Soldiers had assembled them so fast that almost nothing worked - the lights were spotty, the vents loose and leaky, and the laboring HVACs clacked away, barely holding the temperature inside above 50.

Captain Jennifer Godwin stood in her office wearing a heavy Army coat, staring north at the more modern buildings of San Miguel Village, ones that might have offered more comfortable living conditions, though her commanders had been adamant about keeping the criminal elements away from the adjacent neighborhoods. Poor planning combined with a frantic shuffle of resources and insufficient logistical support had led those who had preceded her to throw together the camp in what was-in her opinion-the worst possible way.

The phone in her breast pocket buzzed, and she pulled it out, placing it against her ear.

"Godwin."

The voice on the other end was her staff sergeant. "Captain, we've got word on the transports for the remaining prisoners."

"Go ahead."

"They won't be coming in on time. In fact… they won't be coming in at all."

The captain's shoulders slumped, though she managed to refrain from clicking her tongue. "What do you mean they won't be coming in at all? You requested those transports days ago."

"Yes, ma'am."

"So, what's the problem?"

"They've been re-routed to carry supplies into southern Mexico to support relocation operations there."

"Who ordered it?"

"A general placed an emergency request, which allowed him to assume control of the vehicles. It's part of the new resupply directives straight from Washington. High-ranking commanders take precedence--"

"I know what the directives say." Godwin stepped to the desk and pressed her fingers against the aluminum surface, hand in the shape of a claw. "It's still unacceptable, Sergeant. We've got our own relocation efforts happening. These prisoners need to be moved pronto."

"I know, ma'am."

Throat tight, fingers pressing harder on the desk, words coming out clipped, frustration slipping through. "So, what the hell am I supposed to--"

Knuckles rapped on the office door, drawing her eyes. "Who is it?"

The door popped open, and a red-haired private poked his head inside. "Sorry to interrupt, ma'am, but something's come up."

"What do you need, Swanson?"

The private entered and shut the door quietly behind him, addressing the captain in a low voice. "It's the dozen Canadian refugees we picked up the other day. They're still in limbo in the processing warehouse, and they're causing a distraction for the troops. This morning we caught one of our soldiers sneaking them supplies from our own stores."

Godwin sighed wearily. "They shouldn't even be here. If we can't find a record of them, kick them out of processing and release them. Have the offender detained if he hasn't been already – I'll deal with them later."

The private took a step closer. "Let them go, ma'am? Like out into the desert?"

"That's the gist."

A strained grimace broke across the soldier's face. "But, technically, we can't let them go, according to the new border agreements."

Godwin placed a hand over the phone and lowered her voice to match the Private's. "I don't care what the new agreements say. They change all the damn time, and I'm sick of it. We don't have the supplies to care for refugees that aren't ours, so out they go. Do it now."

"Yes, ma'am." The private looked as though he was about to turn away, then spoke again. "But if the higher-ups find out--"

Godwin's knuckles hit the desk with a sharp crack, the reserved strike stopping just short of damaging her hand. "Do what I tell you and let me deal with the repercussions. That's an order – dismissed."

"Yes, ma'am."

The private turned on his heel and exited the office in a hurry, leaving the door hanging open. Another shadow shifted in the hallway, coming hesitantly forward as the captain lifted the phone back to her ear.

"Are you still there, Sergeant?"

"Yes, ma'am."

"As I was saying before, keep working on those transports. I want replacements inbound as soon as possible. I don't care where you get them. The prisoners need to be gone within the week. Is that understood?"

"Yes, ma'am. I'm on it."

Godwin ended the call and slipped the phone into her pocket, eyes darting toward the hallway as the shadow moved in, knuckles rapping gently on the door.

"What is it?" she snapped, then her expression deflated, shoulders sagging with relief when she saw who it was. "Oh, thank heavens. Please come in and shut the door behind you. Lock the damned thing, too. Weld it shut if you can."

Private Saanvi Patel stepped into the room in a soft shuffle of boots and a light chuckle, pivoting to push the door home with a click before spinning to greet her superior. "Good to see you again, Captain Godwin."

"At ease, soldier." The woman slid her backside onto her desk and shook her head with a defeated sigh. "It's good to see you, too, Patel. Been a while. Where have you been?"

"I was on a special project back in Virginia when Asheville got hit with some aftershocks. We hitched a ride on an Osprey that crashed a few miles north of here. Hoofed it the rest of the way in with some refugees."

The captain nodded. "I heard something about that. Miracle you survived the crash. What are you here for?"

"The commander put me in charge of prisoner health, and your camp was on my schedule today, so I'm here to report what I found."

"Right, yes. He said we'd be getting a visit from a medic. That's great. Best thing I've heard all day."

"Why's that?"

"I'm happy to see a friendly face and not someone who needs something from me."

Patel's dark eyes shifted, taking in the captain's drawn features, cheeks gaunt with weight loss, the corners of her mouth pulled into a perpetual frown. "If you don't mind me saying, you look a little stressed." An apologetic scoff quickly followed. "What I mean to say is, I'm surprised to find you here. When we last talked, you mentioned you might be heading south to take part in the fighting."

The captain spun off the desk and circled to sit in a chair. Ripping open the drawer, she produced a bottle of amber whiskey and two glasses and slammed them on the desk, nodding to the seat on the opposite side.

"Drink?"

The medic took three steps and sat with an emphatic grin. "*Yes.*"

Godwin poured the drinks and slid one glass over to the private. They raised their glasses in toast, then sipped. Patel relaxed back with a soft smack of her lips, the whiskey burn adding color to an otherwise cold and dreary day. After a pause and a swirl of her drink, the captain finally got around to answering the question.

"I *had* intended to go south and fight, but they reassigned me here when the truce-surrender, whatever-came."

"That explains it. Not having fun here?"

"You'd think this would be a pleasant spot to lie low for a few months, but we're one of many under-supplied refugee camps sprouting up, and there'll be a lot more. All I do is field a million questions from clueless guards about every little thing. Trust me, I'm not getting the best the military has to offer."

"Sorry to hear it."

The captain blustered. "Well, except for you. I've been asking for a competent medic, and it looks like they finally sent one."

"I appreciate that."

"And how are things in the camp?" The captain's voice sounded strained, even after relaxing with a drink. "I mean, how are the refugees?"

Shoulders stiffening, back straightening, the private started with a nod. "Ah, yes. Of the 247 refugees here, you have a low rate of infectious disease. I found three cases of the flu, and those folks have been quarantined, but there's no signs of anything that would spell trouble for you."

"That's good news."

"On the non-disease side of things, there is a man in the northern part of the camp who needs his leg reset if he ever wants to walk again."

"When can you do it?"

Patel had another sip of whiskey and gave a head shake. "No can do, Captain, not with my level of experience. I'll call a specialist to have a look. It would be helpful if I had your signature on the order."

"You've got it." Godwin's expression turned dark. "For what my word's worth. It feels like command tossed me into a dark hole to rot. They keep undermining my authority at every turn. We might not get that doctor for months. What else do you have for me?"

"I'm a little concerned about the cold, captain. Quite a few refugees were underdressed, and I assume they entered camp that way. Don't you have anything to give them?"

Godwin felt her chest squeeze as a weight pressed on her shoulders. "I wish I could, but there's barely enough winter gear for the soldiers and guards here. If I haven't mentioned it already, we're low on supplies."

"You might have said something to that effect," Patel replied with dry smile, the words respectful as she danced around the real reason for her visit. "What about transporting them somewhere else? Surely, they've got warmer camps farther south to place them."

The captain drained the rest of her drink and set the glass down hard with a wince. "I sure as hell would've if I could. I've scheduled three separate transports to come get them, but they never make it."

"Why not?"

"They keep re-directing them for other operations, leaving me S-O-L."

"I understand," Patel nodded before she polished off the rest of her whiskey and rested the glass in her lap. "It's just that I'm hearing the temperatures are falling faster and farther here than they originally thought. It could be well below zero within the month, and from what I can see, the detainees are burning everything they have to keep warm. Chairs, tables, beds, pieces of plywood from the walls."

"It's a sad situation,"

"What about letting them go? At least they'd have a chance to settle in a better climate. I hear there are plenty of fertile valleys left in Central Mexico. I just don't think it's right to leave them--"

"Between you and me, I agree with you, but it doesn't matter what we *think*." The captain's tone held frustration and a touch of resentment. "We can't simply release them, because many are criminals. They even moved a few here from a minimum-security New Mexico jail. And while it might seem cruel to keep them in the cold like this, it's our job to guard them no matter what our personal feelings. Don't worry, the transports will make it here before the weather gets too cold, and I'll see the *refugees* are relocated to a safer place."

"Are you sure?"

"You'll just have to trust me."

Patel nodded affirmatively but stiffly, her agreement hiding her fear. Placing the glass on the table, she stood to go. "I'll return in three days to check on things. In the meantime, I'll put in that order in for a specialist right away. You'll have the paperwork within the day."

"It was good to see you, Patel. Stop back in and see me." Godwin rose with her, posture slightly more relaxed than before. "We'll have another drink."

"I look forward to it."

"And if you need anything, come ask. I'll do my best to make it happen."

"Thanks, Captain."

With that, Patel turned and left the office, shutting the door quietly behind her. Her feet carried her through the prefab command center, relief and uncertainty causing her stomach to twist with a slight case of nausea. It was good seeing Jenny again, though alarm bells of concern rang in her head for the detainees – refugees, whatever the spin was – in camp. The cold was coming fast, and when it arrived, there'd be nothing anyone could do but freeze.

She stepped out into a heated tent that was draped over the captain's prefab housing where six guards sat inside the enclosed space with a large kerosene heater blasting warm waves of air. Light, scruffy beards lined their jaws and Patel frowned. Any good commander would snatch them to attention and make them dry shave in front of everyone for the lack of hygiene, though then again they also wouldn't be drinking on duty, either. *The small things go first,* she thought, *and signal the coming downfall of the larger ones.*

Instead of guarding the captain's building, two soldiers played cards at a table while the other four huddled around a computer tablet. One of the card players removed a flask from his jacket and poured whiskey into a cup of tea, stashing the liquor away before taking a surreptitious sip. The lights strung across the ceiling flickered and the electric heating unit in the back corner hitched and puttered on, ozone and oil smells hanging heavy in the air.

With a shake of her head, Patel stepped through the tent flap into the blustery afternoon. The wind bit her cheeks, freezing her nostrils shut, causing her nose to wrinkle as she clutched her coat tighter around her shoulders. Brisk steps carried her into the south lot where a dozen older model Humvees sat parked side-by-side along with a pair of M1161 Growlers. The vehicles had mismatched parts, fenders different shades of green and beige, dents in them, balding tires half flat.

The two guards at the entrance gave her a cursory glance and then returned to hovering over a burn barrel, hands out, fingertips cut from their gloves. Far from standing carefully at guard, watching for signs of trouble, their eyes focused downward, breaths coming out in tired puffs as they tried to stay warm above all else.

Behind them stood a massive pile of wood beams and broken furniture, old skids, boxes, and crates. Raising her gaze to the next block, she spotted a handful of soldiers busting through walls with sledgehammers, piling the salvaged wood off to the side. Without proper heating and shelter, they'd resorted to taking apart the town to stay warm, matching the detainees in desperation.

She pivoted left, looking over a low row of shrubs, across the dirt lane to the holding block and its chain-link razor wire fencing. Three guards leaned against the fence, talking, laughing with shivering lips. Her eyes came to rest on five figures standing around a crimson burn barrel, one man staring back in her direction. Tall and wide-shouldered, he wore a heavy brown coat with the hood pulled over his face. Patel glanced around to make sure no one was watching, then she shrugged and shook her head, hoping her disappointment showed in the gestures. The man tapped on his wrist, and she replied with a nearly imperceptible nod. With a slight turn, she strode over to a soldier holding a leash as he huddled in his coat, staring north up the road.

"I've got her now," she said as she came up, reaching for the lead. "Thanks."

The soldier gave up the leash without question or comment, then returned to his placid, shivering watch. The German Shepherd on the other end of the lead whined and licked her chops happily as Patel led her away, the pair angling around the south side of the holding block. The animal's fur was fast growing back over her wounds, the fire-burned sections looking less gnarly, making her seem less like a hell hound and more like a family pet. The dog walked with a slight limp, sad eyes glancing worriedly across the street where the man stood by the burn barrel, watching them go in stiff silence.

Chapter 2
President John Zimmerman
Air Force One, Southeastern United States

Crisp air circulates through the cabin as the fuselage of Air Force One shudders and dips in the rough currents. President John Zimmerman barely acknowledges it, his face caught in a look of disbelief. He stares at the dark oaken surface of his desk as it reflects the comfortable but bright overhead lights. A smaller version of the one in his office, it boasts a full communication suite with three pop-up screens, enabling him to watch multiple situations at a time.

The cabin is long and wide, the top half stark white, cut sharply in two by a line of dark trim with blue paint reaching the floor, its roundish walls giving it a high-tech, bubble-like appearance. His shoes rest on a soft navy carpet that covers the decking, shifting and groaning as the plane absorbs the wind's abuse.

His most trusted staff members are assembled in three chairs facing him: Secretary of State Rita Cortez, General Mark Davidson, Chief Scientist Rick Manglor and the President's assistant, Maxine. The other staffers sit in the forward compartment, tapping away at their laptops as they relay information back and forth with the various U.S. agencies.

Another brush of turbulence gives the cabin a rough shake, jostling them from side-to-side as if the plane is slipping on an oily piece of plastic. Rita shifts uncomfortably, clutching her stomach with pain on her face.

"So, that's it, then?" Zimmerman askes, expression dour. "There's no way we can stop the anomaly? It's done?"

Rick clears his throat and raises his finger. Hair standing up straight, shirt loose and coffee stained, blue eyes wild with lack of sleep, the man has reached the height of dishevelment. "Actually, Mr. President, we may have sped up the freshwater surge."

"You'd mentioned that as a potential risk," he nodded, "and I agreed we'd take the chance, anyway. Can you tell me how much the freshwater influx has accelerated?"

Rick shrugs, mouth moving but no words come out. When he finally speaks, it's after a nervous sigh. "That's difficult to say, Mr. President, though the North Atlantic Drift must be completely disrupted or at least sluggish beyond immediate repair. We'll know more as we gather additional readings. I think it's safe to say the cold will advance faster than we predicted. Already, they're reporting minus 10 degrees in spots on the Texas-Mexican border, and those temperatures will trend downward over the next few days."

"How low can we expect to go?"

"Arctic levels. Something like an average of minus 21, give or take."

General Davidson shakes his head, his face red with growing anger. "How could your people could have screwed this up so badly? I heard the bombs were useless except to split the crevice open like a damned wound!"

"They were the best figures we had to work with," the scientist argues, jaw tightening, "based on the current modeling we had."

"Yes, and to get that modeling we had to lose a nuclear sub and over 22 research vessels, warships, and equipment we could have used elsewhere."

"I didn't authorize the plan," Rick snarls, lack of sleep putting an edge on his demeanor. "I just put the data together to the best of my ability. And I don't have to answer to you--"

"Stop it." The President's voice growls, cool yet stern enough to grab the men's attention as he looks across at them. "I gave the go-ahead for the operation and I take full responsibility for what happened. I won't tolerate any in-fighting - we gave it a shot, and it didn't work. Blame me for it, and let's move on. Rita, Mark, tell me about Cuba."

The general recovers his composure, lifting a notepad from his lap, scanning the words. "The operation was successful, sir. Our forces overran the island in record time after communicating to the Cuban officials that it was a no-win scenario for them. They had one chance to surrender before we annihilated them with extreme prejudice."

"Our pro-American influences in Havana encouraged the Cuban general to submit at 0900, with only a few shots fired. We're setting up strategic defenses as we speak. That includes the takeover of every naval and air force base in the country, putting boots down. We've got thirty thousand troops on the ground and more incoming. The area outside the capital is secured, and most of our required infrastructure is installed at the OSH. That's the Offshore White House."

"What's it look like in the water?"

"Three carrier strike groups and 23 submarines guard the coastline."

"Very good, Mark. That's the kind of progress I want to see. Any word on civilian casualties?"

"Less than a thousand, sir, and most of those were from two missile malfunctions that hit a town near Cabañas during the first phase of the maneuvering."

"Finally, something working out in our favor." John sighs, the tension in his voice lifting ever so slightly. "Looks like we've got a place to call home for the next couple months."

"Yes, sir."

"What about the nuclear missile silos back on the mainland? Are we in any danger of losing them?"

"Of our four thousand missiles, we moved fifteen hundred to our secure military site in Mexico. For the other silos and launch solutions, we have teams on site to guard and monitor the equipment. They're mostly underground, with enough supplies and power to last five years, though I can't say it's too pleasant of a life."

"Make sure we stay on top of getting those troops relief as soon as things settle and figure out how to support them for the long term in all aspects."

"Yes, sir."

The pilot alters course and guides Air Force One in a more southerly direction, guarded by a pair of F-22s flying just out of sight in the clouds. As the officials settle in for the long trip, the President monitors their position on his in-flight tracker, their path taking them past Tampa, the plane easing over the Gulf of Mexico toward Havana.

John glances out the large port windows as winds and rain beat down on them, followed by several close lightning strikes. An hour and a half later, the Cuban coastline comes within sight, and the pilot calls for landing instructions.

They make a pass over Havana and turn toward the runway as uniformed United States soldiers ready the city for its new occupants. Swarming the streets in Humvees and camouflaged SUVs, they herd citizens from areas around the capital buildings to camps on the edge of town. Military checkpoints pop up on every block, soldiers occupying boarded up homes and apartments, using whatever means necessary to subdue the understandable anger and resistance on the part of the civilian population.

The thriving city, usually blaring with music and food and life, has completely shut down. Steel doors slam to the pavement, closing tourist establishments as vendors fold their carts and hide them. Revelers pause and scatter in the wake of the United States military machine, massive and ominous and efficient as it assumes control of the Cuban capital.

Air Force One's wheels touched down with a heavy impact, causing the president's desk to shudder as Rita Cortez groans with relief as the flaps lift, bringing the jet to a screeching halt at the end of the runway. As they taxi to a secure part of the tarmac, the president stands and paces behind his desk. The passengers have gone quiet except for General Davidson, who has been on the phone during the landing.

The burly man hangs up and places the phone in his lap with a nod to his commander in chief. "We're good to go, Mr. President. The checkpoints are all setup, and we've got complete control of the airport and surrounding buildings."

"Fidel Castro must be rolling over in his grave." Rita's brow arches in sour amusement.

"Good," General Davidson quipped back. "Hook up a couple of power leads and let him spin."

The President glances around with a hesitant grin as the staffers up front turn in their seats, some standing to stretch, awaiting his word with uncertain, fearful expressions.

"Look, this will be hard." He comes to stand behind his chair. "We're in a foreign country that we've just occupied and taken control of. Our families are 2,000 miles away. But things will get better. We'll seal the capital and bring our loved ones along soon after. Once we're settled in, we'll bring our resources to bear, and the Cubans will view us as friends, and they'll join us on our trek south to freedom. Together, we'll transform the Southern Hemisphere into something amazing, you'll see." The words sound strange as they come from Zimmerman's mouth, speaking of things that would have been unimaginable at any other time in history.

"Thank you, Mr. President," someone said from the back. Others echo the sentiment, and Maxine gives him a warm smile and a confident nod.

Coming around to sit on the edge of his chair, he turns to his chief scientist with a hopeful expression. "Rick, how long can we stay here before the temperatures force us to move?"

The man cleared his throat, voice raspy, eyes plagued with weariness. "We're estimating a couple months at most, sir. It's plenty of time to push through to the ultimate objective."

"I agree with him on this one," Mark adds. "Our advance teams are making significant headway in both prepping for the Navy's arrival and working to block others interested in the area."

"Good work. That's excellent news." John taps his fingers on his desk, looking between the pair. "I never doubted either of you for one second. Let's keep pushing."

In the ensuing pause, Rita slides a folder across the shiny surface toward him. "This might be a good time to review these documents."

Thin and seemingly harmless, the folder lays on the desk like a brick, unmarked and oppressive, the President regarding it as though it's poisonous to the touch. With a heavy hand he pushes it back.

"I'll... review it later. For now, I just want to get settled in."

"As you wish, sir." The Secretary of State takes the folder back and rests it in her lap.

The cabin pressure changes, and the door comes open with a whoosh, drawing Zimmerman's eyes toward the anterior fuselage as speakers above them crackle with static before a deep, professional voice fills the space.

"Attention passengers, this is your captain. Be advised we're ready for the President and his staff to disembark. Please do so at your leisure."

Nodding, Zimmerman stands and sweeps his hand toward the front of the plane. "Okay, folks. You heard the man. Go on and find your rides. I'll stay here for another minute or two."

The staff rises in a bustle of noise and motion, grabbing their briefcases and laptops before filing forward. As each leaves, the cabin grows quieter, dropping the president into a thoughtful silence that fit his mood. Rita and Rick exit, leaving just General Davidson and his personal staffer, Maxine, on the plane. The assistant stares at him, waiting for an order while the general toys with his phone.

"You can go, too, Mark. No need to hang around."

"Negative, sir. Protocol dictates that I stay with you at all times until the security level falls."

"Oh, yes. Well, I could use a drink." Zimmerman stands from his desk and strides to a serving table with glasses on top and a mini fridge beneath it. "Anyone else? Never mind. We'll all have a drink, and that's an order."

"You won't get an argument from me, sir," Davidson says as the pair follow him over.

The president pours two fingers of whiskey in each glass, adding ice cubes to Maxine's, then he presses a button and watches as a cover in the fuselage slides aside to offer a view of the bustling airport and city beyond.

Turning, he hands a glass to each, then lifted his in a toast. "Here's to new beginnings."

"Hear hear," Mark says, while Maxine only nods, eyes remaining locked on him.

Glasses clink and are tossed back, the president draining most of his, enjoying the delicate burn as the sweet liquor coats his throat and makes flames in his belly. Maxine sips hers while the general takes it a step farther and downed his with a single swallow, then holds up the glass in his large hand for another pour.

"We drink like this at every new beginning, we won't be able to function."

Chuckling, Zimmerman obliges him, and the three turn to capture what they can of the city through the vista window.

"We're involved in quite an operation here." With one arm folded across his chest, the president holds his liquor in front of his face, swirling the contents thoughtfully as the general agrees with a dignified grunt.

"No other administration has ever even imagined attempting something like this," Maxine says, her tone tracking the president's train of thought.

"Yes, but what's the cost, Max? We're annexing entire countries, forcing innocent people out of their homes, sometimes at gunpoint from what I hear."

The general grunts again and Zimmerman's eyes drift over the beautifully constructed historic blocks of Havana. "People from a different century erected those buildings. Will their ancestors, the citizens of this city, today, really see us as friends? Or will we still be enemies, and I'm just blowing smoke up my own backside?" With a light scoff, he shakes his head. "Likely, the latter."

"I'd say you're right on that point," Mark adds, already halfway through his second drink.

"So, does that make us the good guys or bad guys?"

"Probably a little of both."

"And that's how we justify what we're doing."

Maxine's eyes move back and forth between the two. "You're both good men. The best I've ever worked for. While none of this is ideal, it has to happen, and that's the bottom line. To be honest..." The words trail off as she draws her drink toward her stomach, retreating a half step.

"What is it, Max?"

"No," the woman curls in on herself. "It's not my place."

Zimmerman shakes his head, his mood lighter from the whiskey and open to ideas. "Please, speak your mind. You've never held back before."

The staffer glances up at General Davidson, who only shrugs. "Might as well."

"What I'm trying to say is that while your talks have been upbeat, I can't help but think things will get worse before they get better. The people of Havana won't welcome us with open arms. I expect there to be rebellion and fighting, and it'll happen no matter where we go."

Zimmerman's expression turns sour but amused. "So, I *have* been blowing smoke up my own backside."

The general winces with a knowing nod. "We've considered all that, and I'm right there with you, Maxine. People won't roll over just because we ask them to. I guess we were hoping things would go smoother than expected."

Zimmerman nods, part of him wanting to disagree with them, another part saying they are than right – they're spot on. "So, we're the bad guys, after all?"

"Not the bad guys." Maxine shrugs and downs the rest of her drink in one gulp. "Just the *strongest* guys."

Chapter 3
Specialist Lance Morales
Santa Fe, New Mexico

The transport bucked and bounced along the icy road, trundling over swaths of densely packed snow that had slipped beneath the earth movers' massive, modified snowplows. After Albuquerque, they'd hopped on I-25 where the LeTourneau L-2350s, spread across all four lanes, their thirty-foot-wide plows cutting through the frozen drifts with jaw-rattling grinding sounds that caused Morales to cover his ears with his arms at every opportunity.

The turbocharged aftercooler diesel engines churned in a single collective growl as they sent sheets of snow and ice flying off to the sides in twin arcs of blinding whiteness twenty feet high. They caught tangles of trees and debris and crushed them together, wood bending, shrieking as it washed over the guardrail. The plows slammed aside cars and SUVs, moving big rigs with the sounds of cold, crunching metal and the smooth sliding of rubber wheels across ice. The trucks spun and smacked the guardrails and medians, trailers falling to pieces as their contents scattered in the road, no obstacle too large to withstand the sheer force delivered by the powerful machines.

From the back of the transport, Morales stared at the passing landscape, a nightmare of winter white that carpeted every inch of ground, suffocating trees, bending them, snapping them in two. Icicles the size of cave stalactites hung from the larger boughs, their shiny points forming a crystal wall above the tree line. One cracked away and plunged into the waiting snow like a dagger, piercing the white all the way to the frozen ground beneath it.

His gaze followed crests of ice-covered hills, the frosted, crusted edges sharp and glistening in the grayish midday sun as gusts of sleet blew through the air behind them in dervishes of whistling wind and stinging flakes of ice. Smith gave him a light punch in the arm and gestured upward. Lifting his eyes, the soldier looked up to spot a V-shaped flock of geese, their honks masked by the plows' incessant grinding.

A heady wind gusted through, briefly disrupting the formation and several animals fell out of place, drifting back and forth on the air current before falling dangerously low to the point Morales didn't think they'd catch up. One did a slow spiral downward and disappeared out of sight behind the tree line and a second animal nosedived and plummeted, wings barely flapping in the frozen sky.

"Jeez," Morales said with a heavy head shake.

"They migrated south too late!" Smith shouted. "They can't make the flight. Probably exhausted."

"Dying as they fly. Nature is completely screwed. At least here."

"I can't argue with that." The lieutenant's constant grin faltered, the corners of his mouth dragging downward.

"You think we'll ever see another summer?"

Smith's gaze dropped to the road where the convoy followed, spread out across a pair of lanes as it curved around the last bend out of sight. More vehicles had caught up to them after Albuquerque - Humvees and APCs for defense, bearing massive snowplows themselves in case they needed to split off or one of the LeTourneaus crapped out. Huge army supply trucks and troop transports trundled behind those along with tractor trailers carrying heavy bulldozers and backhoes. The convoy was moving at a leisurely 20 to 30 mph, though to Morales it sounded like they were going much faster as miles of I-25 slid beneath the heavy machinery, the vehicles sticking together on the cleared road.

Captain Jones, sitting in the front seat with the driver, shoved open the hatch door and shouted back with a clipped tone. "We're getting out at the next exit, folks. Be prepared to work." Then he slammed the door shut again with a clack.

One LeTourneau fell behind the other, switching from a side-by-side position to in-line. The entire convoy began a slow shift off the exit ramp as the resounding vibrations of the plows lowered in pitch, grinding over a different type of pavement. They merged into a single long line on the narrower ramp, taking a right toward an unknown town, following the LeTourneaus like ducklings behind their mother. Massive snowdrifts all but covered the one-story buildings, gas stations and stores identifiable only by parts of signs jutting up from the layer of white. A steak house sign stood tall on the right side of the road, the bull's head mascot just visible, a dusting of powder caught in the glass etching to give it a highlight. Side roads were impossible to navigate, blanketed in six or eight feet of snow topped in a hoary, crusty frost they could have walked on.

"There's no way we could handle these roads without the GPS and those big plows." Smith gave a low whistle.

"Yeah, this is insane," Morales agreed, voice filled with awe, finding it hard to believe anyone could have survived the deep chill lying over the land. His eyes shifted, moving up a snowbank the plows had added to, where he could barely see the tops of trees that were twenty feet high. "I wouldn't be able to tell where the streets are without the tree lines, and even those are almost buried or they just blend in so damn well amidst all this white."

A quarter mile along the two-lane highway brought the LeTourneau's grinding to a sudden halt, the grating, ear-bending sounds stopping, leaving a deafening silence hanging in the air for a moment before the murmuring began. Truck doors opened and slammed shut and a moment later, Captain Jones came around the rear and leaned over the tailgate, the lower half of his face covered in a wide, green scarf.

"All right, men. Everyone out. Let's go!"

"Where are we, cap?" Smith called as the soldiers filed out and climbed down onto the plowed pavement.

A swirl of icy snow whipped into Morales's eyes, the gust invading his bare skin through the small gaps in his clothing. With a shiver, he thrust his hands deeper into his pockets and walked away from the truck, turning to stare past the gargantuan plows that dwarfed everything around them. An extensive field of white stretched off the left side of the road, lumps of buildings bulging like soft pillow mounds, the connecting driveway buried in an intimidating crust of hoarfrost.

"It's a FEMA storage facility southwest of Santa Fe," the captain responded with a grin, "one of the big three in the United States. We're standing next to six large warehouses atop a nest of underground bunkers. How's that strike you?"

Smith came up to stand by Morales, gesturing at the field of white before scratching his head. "That's great, cap, but how do you expect us to reach it? I don't think we brought any sled dogs with us."

Jones gave his lieutenant a hard slap on the shoulder. "That's what you're for, soldier. We're going to dig our way to it, then uncover the buildings and secure the supplies. I'm told great treasures lie below ground. Let's break out the maps and start cutting smaller paths between the buildings. Lieutenant and the specialist, you're with me."

"Yes sir, cap," Smith said, throwing a glance and an elbow at Morales. "You heard the cap, we're bringing this warehouse back to life."

The team leads, specialists, and drivers gathered at the front of the truck, hovering over the warm hood and idling engine, a facility map spread out before them. Morales stared at the layout and glanced back often to marry their current position to what was on paper in his mind. Serious for once, Smith put his finger on the warm map, tracing a path from the road up to a pair of smaller squares that represented buildings. "Let's send one heavy up the main street with an excavator behind it, clearing the lot while carving out some of the side lanes. Once we have an idea of what's there, we can bring in the APCs to do the bulk of the work with teams of shovels and picks to finish the details."

"Spot-on, Smith." The captain raised his voice and spun his finger in the air. "Let's make it happen."

The second of the massive LeTourneaus backed up ponderously while another team unloaded the excavator from its place on a trailer bed before trying to get it started. Being twelve degrees below zero without the windchill didn't help matters, forcing the crew to warm the engine with heaters before it finally started, the throaty diesel sputtering and complaining the entire time.

Morales, rated to drive the excavator, climbed into the cab and followed the LeTourneau up the main road as it cleared a path to the buildings. He worked the joysticks gingerly at first as the hydraulics warmed up, using his bucket to catch piles of snow the bigger truck left behind, carving around the edges to widen the path between the lines of grass. Once the main plow reached the parking lot between the first two buildings, Morales uncovered the beginnings of a pair of side roads that encircled the grounds.

The excavator's tiny heater clattered away inside his cabin, giving a hot edge to the oil and hydraulic reek coming off the machine. After a while, a fine sweat coated his brow, and he tossed back his hood and cracked one of the windows to allow in some cold air for ventilation.

While the LeTourneau pressed deeper and APCs with smaller plows drove in behind them, two hundred bundled troops with shovels and picks in hand took up the rear, watching the machines work while they stayed huddled in groups, chatting amongst themselves. The APCs took up where Morales left off, shoveling the side roads to provide access points for machines and men around the warehouses. Following the first earth mover into the lot, he chipped away at one warehouse with his bucket, eyes narrowed at the front of the building, looking for the door. The steel teeth crunched through hoarfrost and snow, dumping massive amounts off to the side. Someone beeped, and he turned to see a dump truck had edged in behind him along with a second excavator.

Joining forces, the two diggers focused on one area, moving tons of snow and ice, dropping it into the truck bed with heavy crunches and white powder billowing everywhere. They filled the first dump truck, and it pulled off only to have another replace it. Morales reached as high as he could with the bucket, knocking off dangerous overhangs that might break off and hurt the soldiers working below. With the parking lot nearly cleared, the second LeTourneau drove up and made quick work of what snow remained before joining its brother at the next lot over. As the APCs and other heavy gear pressed by, cargo trucks idled in parking spots, waiting to be filled with supplies from inside.

Soon, the excavators reached the walking path and the stiff, frozen bushes along the building's front. Morales used his bucket to tap at the top edge of the wall, causing a section to break away and reveal the dirty beige cement beneath it. Once the dangerous spots up high were removed, a hundred soldiers swarmed the building with axes and shovels, chipping away like a group of coordinated dwarves working deep in the mines of Moria. Wheelbarrows were filled with snow, carted across the road, and dumped and within an hour, the soldiers reached the wall and were working their way toward the door.

"It *must* be here somewhere," Morales murmured, backing his machine up, parking it with the engine idling.

He climbed from the cab and grabbed a shovel from a tired soldier, stabbing and hacking at the stubborn snow along with the rest. The sharp edge of his tool banged a support pole for an awning, and he worked feverishly to dig beneath the narrower space. Stepping back, skin icy with frozen sweat, Morales let a few men finish the job, watching as they cut a swath to the front door where their tools tapped against the glass.

Captain Jones jogged up with a half dozen soldiers, Smith included in the bunch. The lieutenant handed Morales a flashlight, and he leaned his shovel against the wall and joined them. A security specialist went to work on the keypad adjacent to the door frame, opening the cover to reveal a faint green glow of numbers.

"The place still has enough electric for the security doors and some lights," Morales said to his friend. "They must have seriously strong batteries."

"And probably almost dead in this cold," Smith added.

Three seconds later, the door's deadbolts popped, and Captain Jones traded places with the specialist, pulling the door handle to release a gust of stale, warm air from the building that brushed across Morales's cheeks.

The soldiers filed in, flashlight beams cutting to the end of a dark hallway where a thick, steel door awaited them. Emergency lights radiated a dim glow, illuminating wooden doors and another cross hall. With an eager grin, Jones led them toward the metal door, pushing past the offices and janitor's closets, the soldiers following in a scuffle of boots, their hard rubber soles squeaking on the wet tiles. Morales kept close, shining his light into the cross hallway that ran the length of the building in both directions. They went straight for the metal door, though, hacked the security panel, and popped those locks as well. Jones, shaking with excitement, threw it open and strode inside, the soldiers filing in fast behind him, their shuffling boots suddenly echoing as if standing in a cavernous chamber. Flashlight beams pierced the gloom, pointing in all directions to chase away the shadows.

Morales stepped in last, having to push between Smith and the captain with an aggravated sound, trying to get a good view. He lifted his own flashlight beam, shining it across the open warehouse, stopping in his tracks as he stood, gaping with the rest of them.

Chapter 4
Tom McKnight
Nuevo Laredo, Mexico

"Shouldn't she be here by now?" Barbara whispered the question as they stood on a street corner on the holding facility's north side.

"Yes, but let's be patient. She'll be here any minute."

Shadows surrounded the niche between a crumbling concrete wall and a stubby pine tree, already showing signs of encroaching cold, its leaves brown and wilted where they hung from sagging branches. The sun still offered no relief from the chill, hidden behind the late day clouds, the air turning bitter and biting with sharp, unforgiving teeth. Tom watched refugees as they hustled between buildings, passing the pair with furtive looks, meeting their stares with equally hard ones, causing them to turn away and hurry past.

Barbara glanced over her shoulder. "I'm just worried about the kids. They shouldn't be left alone, not with these strangers around. And I'm not referring to the guards, though they're bad enough as it is."

"Sam's in charge, honey," Tom replied, looking toward the end of the street where three refugees whispered over a burn barrel filled with branches and twigs gathered from tree trimmings. A woman moved off, hustling into the thick clusters of ramshackle buildings and Tom tried to push aside the thought of trouble, shifting uncomfortably. "She's been through a lot the past few weeks. She can hold her own and then some. She'll keep them safe, trust me."

Barbara settled back, leaning against the tree with a pensive, glassy-eyed expression. "Oh, I know the kids are more than capable of taking care of themselves, especially Sam and Linda. I'm just worried about the long-term effects this will have on them."

Tom snorted. "Well, considering our youngest two kids lived through a firefight, saw their neighbors killed, and had to perform first aid on their mother.... Oh, don't forget they were kidnapped, too—"

"Twice!" Barbara scoffed.

"Oh yes, kidnapped twice, that's right. And Linda shot a man and tried to kill another by drowning *and* shooting him." Tom chuckled dryly. "Yes, I'd say you're right. There might be a *few* underlying issues we'll need to address down the road."

Barbara smiled at Tom's trademark sarcasm, then her expression fell. "And Sam lived through a stint at sea on a lifeboat, had to try to burn people alive to survive, watched her friend die before her eyes.... Oh, Tom, our children have experienced an entire lifetime in just a few short months, more than we ever did."

"Okay, fine. I guess they'll all be equally messed up." Tom put on a smile, though his eyes brimmed over with tears and he swiped at them with the back of his sleeve. "I'm just sorry about everything that happened to you and Linda and Jack. If I could have figured out Keith's game sooner, none of this would have happened. I'd have put the bastard six feet under and spared everyone the horrors he's inflicted."

"You can't blame yourself, honey," she replied, her tone soft. "You couldn't have predicted any of this. We'll just have to help our babies the best way we know how." Barbara came off the tree and threw an arm over his shoulder, chest and thighs pressing against him. A warmth flowed between them, her physical presence like a bombshell. With shut eyes, he gently bumped his head into hers to return the affection.

"I wouldn't worry about the kids too much." The voice broke from the other side of the fence, a shadow against the chain link. "They bounce back pretty well, especially when they have great parents."

Tom looked up to see a woman's slight form standing in military fatigues, a black beanie on her head, heavy Army coat smothering her waifish shape. In her hand, she gripped Smooch's leash, the dog prancing on impatient front paws, tail sweeping leaves and loose gravel across the pavement as the shepherd's dark, baleful eyes stared up at the pair, a soft whine repeating in her chest. Unable to stifle a brief grin, Tom glanced both ways before jamming his hands into his pockets and casually approaching the fence with Barbara at his side.

"Smooch!" Barbara said, keeping her voice quiet as she knelt and put her fingers through the chain link to accept excited licks from the animal.

Tom gave a terse nod. "Good to see you, Saanvi."

"You too, Tom. How are you guys holding up?"

"Same as before. Food's low, and it's getting colder by the hour. Not to mention the unsavory types we're locked in here with."

"Tell me about it," Patel replied hesitantly.

Tom gave her a stony stare. "What is it?"

The medic shifted from one foot to the other. "I got a meeting with Godwin, and she mentioned there are inmates from a minimum-security correctional institute in there with you."

Tom's jaw tightened. "What else did she say? Is there any way she can move us?"

"The camp is a total shitshow." Patel shrugged apologetically. "Forgive my French. Godwin is an outstanding commander, but she's losing control of things." Patel inhaled and let out a heavy breath, glancing left and right, lowering her voice even though there was no one around. "The guards are just... not good. Morale is dangerously low across the board. And her own commanders are undermining her authority at every turn. There won't be a transport to take you south anytime soon."

"So, we're going to sit here and freeze?" Barbara asked from her knees, fingers rubbing Smoooch's ears.

Hand already gripping the fence, Tom squeezed as a trapped feeling rose inside him. "Did you ask her about letting everyone go?" "I mean, if she can't take care of us, then we have to be set free."

"That's what I told her, but she still wouldn't bite. Seems she's going to hold on to you until the last possible minute."

Raising on his toes, the weight of his glare pressed on the medic. "But what if that's too late?"

"It won't be," she replied, unaffected by the pressure. "She'll get the transports here, and they'll take you south to plead your case at another camp."

"That's an entirely different concern," Tom said, wondering how far their enemies were away from the holding facility. "I expect Keith and Banks to show up at any moment. If they do, and we're not gone..." The thought dangled as anger swelled in his chest, imagining their smarmy grins as they approached from the other side of the fence, the *free* side.

Patel frowned knowingly. "I haven't forgotten what you told me about those two and why you had to escape them."

Barbara stood and straightened "Can you help us escape?"

"That was going to be my next question," Tom said.

The medic leaned slightly away from the fence. "You know I can't do that. I've got a duty--"

"If you can't break us out of here, we'll be condemned to a death sentence," Tom argued with a glance back. "Not just us, but our kids, too."

"I don't appreciate the pressure tactics," Patel replied flatly, soft expression turning as hard as a statue. "I'm doing the best I can, given the circumstances. And you *did* hijack a military aircraft. That's hard to look past, even given your situation."

"C'mon, Saanvi... it's not our fault the plane crashed when it did. And it wouldn't have mattered if we were on it or not. I'm sorry... I don't mean to put pressure on you. You've really come through for us, and we appreciate it."

The medic's cheeks slackened into a rounded shape once more, eyes softening in rich brown color. "I know it's not your fault, but you're asking me to undermine my commander and friend. Not only is it wrong, but they could throw me in the brig for it... or worse."

Barbara moved closer to Tom as the wind picked up. "They wouldn't shoot you for something like that, would they?"

"Absolutely, they would," the medic said. "I haven't heard of that happening myself, but things are constantly changing. It's getting scary."

"They would definitely shoot someone," Tom agreed. "Particularly if that person's blatantly going against orders. Plus... us civilians are under martial law. Laws don't exist anymore, not like they used to."

Patel stepped back to the fence, eyes imploring. "Look, I'm on your side, but I've got my family to worry about, too. They're only protected because of my service. If I betray that by helping you escape..." The thought remained unfinished, along with a sense of inner turmoil.

"No, we can't ask you to do anything that would threaten your family." Barbara strained to keep an understanding tone. "But things are getting desperate in here. Every day we stay is another day of danger."

"I'll think of something." The medic's fingers reached out to rest on Barbara's where she clung to the chain link.

"There's something else, Saanvi." Tom glanced back to make sure no refugees stood within earshot. "Another reason why you have to hurry."

Face pressed closer to the fence, she nodded. "I'm listening."

"There's talk of dissent in the camp."

"What? Like, refugees planning to break out?"

"That's right."

"How many?"

"So far, less than a dozen, but the numbers are growing with the worsening conditions. They've got a couple of rifles, so the rumor goes, and they're preparing to fight. They could be part of the criminal element you were referring to."

"When will they make their move?"

"No clue, but you can expect violence sooner than later, and that timeframe will be shortened as the problems with food and weather compound. You mentioned the guards weren't so good."

"Morale is down, and they're not expecting a fight, for sure. They're disobeying orders, a few have even abandoned their posts, gone AWOL."

"Then do what you have to do, for your sake, too." Barbara pleaded. "But don't forget us. Please."

"Right, I won't." The medic's head shook, breath coming fast. Then, with a single deep sigh, she settled down and shifted to Tom. "I *really* appreciate the information. I'll run it up the chain and work hard to get you guys out of here."

"Thank you, Saanvi." Tom nodded, forcing a smile. "Anything you can do would be helpful."

With a faint nod, she looked around. "I'd better go."

"Right," Barbara said, falling to her knees in front of Smooch. "And we'll see *you* later, girl."

The dog whined and pawed at the chain link, then tried to press her muzzle through. Tom reached down with a genuine grin and stuck his finger in a gap to accept licks and nuzzles from the loyal animal.

"And we appreciate you taking care of our girl," he added. "If not for you, she'd be out wandering the desert alone, or dead."

"That part isn't a problem at all," Patel chuckled. "I've always loved animals, and she's a wonderful dog. I suspect it's because she has great owners."

"And receives plenty of love," Barbara smiled. "Thanks again, Saanvi. We owe you so much."

"No worries. Talk to you soon."

With that, the medic turned away, making a kissing noise to get Smooch to follow. At first, the dog was reluctant but allowed herself to be led away. Tom watched their only hope of escaping the holding facility without getting shot walk off.

Barbara clutched the fencing. "Think she'll help us?"

"No clue," he said with a shrug. "It's a lot of pressure to put on a young woman. If she goes to her superiors, they could stop the rebellion, though it might make us targets of the other refugees if they suspect we snitched."

"So, we need to watch our backs."

"Big time."

Hands interlocked, the pair retreated into the depths of the camp, avoiding people, working south through the back alleys and yards. They climbed over rubble from a missile strike and at the far end of the block they circled to the front of the crumbling pharmacy where the kids stood around a burn barrel, rubbing their hands close to the fire.

"There they are," Linda cried in relief.

"Yay!" Jack crooned, skipping over to embrace his mother.

Tom gave them both a hug, then headed to Sam. "How'd the watch go?"

The young woman broke from the barrel to stand nearby, arms folded, a serious expression on her face. "Fine, mostly. A few people came by wanting to share the fire, but I got them to go away. No sign of the *group*."

"Okay, good. I don't want us associating with them, especially now."

"I know, Dad. You told us, like, a billion times."

"Really? A whole billion? That's a lot. It might take me several days or weeks to say anything a billion times."

Sam rolled her eyes. "You know what I mean."

Tom quickly sobered, brushing off an amused chuckle as he ushered her toward the pharmacy door. "Okay, let's get inside. It's going to be dark soon, and we don't want to be out here in the cold."

Jack was the first one in, opening the boarded-up glass doors and moving into the sales floor. Tom had left the bell on the door as an alarm, and it jingled as they entered. The dated decor was from the 1950s with old posters for pharmaceuticals like Listerine, Pyrotone, and Placida, Tom estimating they were original prints, probably worth a fortune to the right collectors before the chill. Pictures hung further down on the wall, showing the first owner, Dr. Miguel Ortiz (1958) and the subsequent members of the family he'd passed the store on to; his son, his daughter, and a cousin who was the last proprietor, judging by the date scribbled on the photo.

Despite the store's vintage feel, it appeared to have been well kept with modern products. The rows of shelves were mostly looted of food, though they'd left behind toiletries, cleaners, brushes, and cosmetics. The pharmacy was stripped of valuable drugs except for a couple bottles of amoxicillin that had rolled beneath the counter. There were mild pain relievers, blood thinners, and others with names impossible to pronounce, none of which were of much interest given their situation.

After picking out the place to keep themselves safe from the cold and the other refugees, the McKnights had made modifications to the establishment, boarding up the big pane glass front window and using a pair of empty shelving units as a makeshift barricade for the door.

"A little help with this." Tom nodded to a row of shelving and took a position on one side. Barbara stood opposite him, and together they lifted the entire thing and slammed it firmly against the door. A screech of metal on tile caught his attention, and he spun to see the girls shoving the second set of shelves toward them. The parents jumped out of the way as the kids blew by, bashing the two pieces together with a bang before Sam straightened and dusted her hands off with grin.

"Nice work, ladies."

Tom gave a quick check to make sure they hadn't left any easy entry points and the family retired to the rear of the store, through the pharmacy door, and to an open living space that had been their home the past three evenings. Beds assembled from threadbare covers and army pillows sat on the floor back in the corner next to an old wood-burning stove, the highlight of the establishment and one of the main attractions for choosing the place. A single faucet above a utility tub spouted tap water of dubious quality, usable only after boiling, though better than going thirsty. Aside from their two primary amenities, the McKnights had made use of what pots and pans they found, making meals from meager military supplies plus other bits and bobs they'd scrounged from an adjacent storage room including three expired cans of beans and a tin of dry tea leaves well past the best use date. Still, they were flavorful enough to make hot drinks, and after adding a bit of sugar, perfect for taking the edge off the cold winter nights.

Tom nodded to the stove. "Sam, why don't you get the fire going?"

"I can do that," she said, moving to squat before the door and grabbing the poker from a nearby rack while Tom collapsed on a stool, elbows resting on a makeshift table with a door as its primary surface and two end tables as legs.

"Well, let's get you settled in for the night," Barbara told the youngest two kids. "What do you say?"

"Will you read to me?" Jack asked.

"I'd love to."

The two youngest McKnights pulled off their shoes but stayed fully clothed as they swept back the covers and climbed into the cold beds. Curled up, snuggling side-by-side, the children made exaggerated shivering noises as Barbara turned to a stack of books nearby. A few dozen rat-eared paperbacks had been left behind in the pharmacy, all of them in Spanish, though that hadn't stopped the ritual where his wife sat and read the lines with a questionable accent, the kids growing sleepy to the sound of her voice.

The gentle clatter of Sam's poker rustled in the background and she threw a few pieces of wood into the mix, shoving it around until flames leapt up before shutting the door with a soft clank. Waves of warmth began to pour from the stove as it started to heat up, filling the room, sending a shiver across Tom's shoulders. Barbara's voice read the delicate Spanish words and Tom's eyelids drooped, heart and mind floating in a dozy, exhaustion-induced state. His arms and legs hung loose, relaxed despite him being hungry and sore and worried about the approaching enemies. The nearness of his family was all he needed to see him through it all, the comforting sounds of them going about semi-normal activities, alive, safe and as content as their situation allowed.

Ten minutes later, Barbara's voice faded, and the kids' soft snores filled the room. That alone was its own kind of warmth, and Tom let out a sigh as his wife finished and came to sit across from him. Placing the book on the table, her index finger slipped from between the pages, allowing the heavy cover to fall shut with a gentle thump. The corners of her mouth were tight, though she was still beautiful, green eyes drawing him like a moth to a flame. Unable to resist, he reached out and tucked a lock of sandy dark hair behind her ear, fingers brushing her cheek as his hand withdrew. The gesture drew a shy smile from Barbara, shrinking her age by decades in an instant.

"So, how are you holding up?" he asked.

"I'm doing surprisingly well. I'm worried about things, and sad we lost the farm, but being together is just…." Head shaking, mouth moving without sound, she struggled with the words, then a glance at the kids gave her the resolution she needed. "Having us together is heavenly. Absolutely amazing. As much as I missed you two, I didn't realize *how* much I'd missed you."

He chuckled, hand slipping across the table to cover hers. "I was just thinking the exact same thing. It's crazy how much strength I draw from you."

Barbara bent and kissed the top of his hand, cheek brushing his skin before she straightened. "What do you think about what Saanvi said? Can she help us?"

"She *wants* to help, but I'm not sure she'll come through. There's a lot working against her. She has her own family to worry about, and the penalties if she's caught are pretty high."

"Well, I think we should wait for her. She'll come back with something."

"I can't say I agree with that. I vote we break out."

"You mean, join up with the rebellion?"

"No, that's not what I meant. I--"

Finished with the fire, Sam sat heavily on a rickety crate beside her mother, resting a shoulder against the older woman as the wood creaked beneath her weight. Barbara raised an eyebrow at Tom, eyes shifting to her daughter.

"What do you think?"

A perplexed expression crossed Samantha's face, brow wrinkling in confusion. "You're asking *me*?"

Tom shrugged. "Why not? You're in the thick of this with us, and you're not a little girl anymore. What's on your mind?"

Red rushed to Sam's cheeks, shoulders straightening as she formed a response. "I like Saanvi a lot. She patched us up and takes good care of Smooch. She wouldn't have done any of that if she didn't care. We should wait for her help."

"I'm not saying she doesn't care," he agreed, "or that she wouldn't help us if the opportunity presented itself. I'm just not sure it *will* ever happen. Regardless, we need a plan to break out, just *us*, just in case we need a backup. The weather's getting colder every day. Blowing open the anomaly will fully stall the North Atlantic Drift – assuming that hasn't already happened – putting us on the cusp of an ice age." Tom sagged forward, running a hand through his greasy hair as the weight of his words fell fresh upon his shoulders. "Remember what we talked about in the tunnel, Sam? I don't think it's a possibility anymore. I think it's happening. Right now. We're looking at the end of the Holocene Epoch and the emergence of a new one."

Sam leaned in closer to her mother as Tom continued. "Warmth's hard to come by and food's running low. There might come a day we have to fight the other refugees for it, and that's when things will get *really* ugly."

"You're not wrong, I'll give you that much," Barbara gave Sam a squeeze.

"You make it sound pretty bad, Dad."

"Sorry. I don't want to scare you, but we're we'll past platitudes and assurances." He looked at Barbara. "I need you – both of you – to see what we're facing here. Waiting could mean dying."

"Okay, how about this? Let's give Patel two more days to figure something out. If she doesn't come through by then, we'll blow this popsicle stand."

Sam's head bobbed in agreement, though her heavy exhale quivered with uncertainty, green eyes shifting to her mother as if to gain strength.

"It's a deal," Tom said, reaching out to clasp both their hands. "And two days will give us the time we need to build a foolproof plan. Sounds perfect to me."

Chapter 5
Specialist Lance Morales
Santa Fe, New Mexico

Sounds echoed deep inside the cavernous warehouse, the sound of footsteps and whispered conversations bouncing off the racks of shelves and concrete walls. Breaths came in frosted spurts as flashlights streaked upward and across the literal tons of frozen supplies, all sealed in boxes or on skids wrapped in plastic. The two massive columns of racks, thirty or forty rows of them, ran in both directions, reaching six stories high to the warehouse roof with more than enough space for forklifts to maneuver.

Smith whistled low. "Jackpot, boys."

"This way." Captain Jones strode ahead to the main aisle, which stretched from east to west, the full length of the facility, taking a right, moving toward a faint white light at the far end. Morales looked up at the frozen racks of products branded as *Rice, Legumes, Freeze-dried eggs, Freeze-dried fruit, batteries, Cold Weather Rations,* and more. Frost covered some packages, making their labels unreadable and barrels of water were stacked to the ceiling, almost all burst open, leaving ten foot icicles as thick as Morales's leg dangling from the shelving units.

Seventy-five yards away, they reached a wide space with a dozen forklifts plugged in, their charging lights as lifeless as the building. Two pickup trucks sat parked against the wall in front of a pair of garage doors twenty-five feet high and the far wall held a smattering of windows, stretching at intervals and illuminated by thin slivers of emergency lighting. Signs for cleaning supply closets, lockers, and break rooms hung on the doors, thin layers of snow and ice covering them all.

Jones angled for the first door on the left as two soldiers anticipated his move and jogged ahead, rifles up as they came to stand on either side of the door, ready to cover the captain. Morales figured none of them expected an ambush given the situation in the warehouse, but caution and training prevailed regardless of the circumstance.

The lieutenant eyed the door, then nodded and one man grabbed the handle and jerked it open while two filed inside, their mounted lights sending beams into the room, cutting through the pitch darkness as they swept the corners.

"It's clear, Cap," one shouted, voice shaky and low. "But you won't believe it, sir."

The captain shot a look over his shoulder at Smith, and the lieutenant shrugged and waited for their leader to go ahead. Jones stepped in, head swiveling, eyes darting around and Morales followed the others into the room, shouldering his way to the left for a better view. Six beams lit the open space, showing cabinets, a refrigerator, a coffee maker, and a sink, water having frozen in the broken spigot, a long icicle reaching down to the drain.

Ignoring the paraphernalia in the room, their lights converged on the center where five forms huddled on the floor. Covered in thick, all-winter coats, gloves on hands, hoods pulled tight over their faces, they sat in perfect frozen stillness in the dark. A shudder streaked from Morales's knees to the nape of his neck at the sight, and he glanced over at Smith who stood stock-still, jaw open.

"This place is a tomb." Smith whispered the words as he stared at the corpses.

Jones stepped closer, reaching for one hood to pull it back, the material cracking like rice paper, taking off a frozen, crackling swath of hair with it. With a disgusted grunt, he turned and addressed the others in the room.

"Smith, take Brozowski and LaPlante and get the bay doors open. Look for survivors while you're at it." The three nodded and left the room with the captain shouting after them. "And see if you can salvage some forklifts from the warehouse area. Warm them up, charge them, and try to put them to use. It'll make this a helluva lot easier."

Morales returned to staring at the dead, strolling around the group, the sounds of the outer doors cranking up comforting him as he stared at the frozen faces, blue cheeks and fleshy noses, eyes open and shiny as glass. Packs of ration bins sat in boxes behind them, snack wrappers and empty containers piled in the corner of the room. A couple of the figures were leaning against each other, others against the wall or desks, their forms slouched over as though they had died in their sleep.

"Look at this, Cap. There's food all around them, so they didn't starve." Morales pointed to a circle of bricks with paper and wood scraps crumpled and charred in the middle. "It looks like they had a fire going, but not for long. Yeah, they must have froze, or died from carbon monoxide poisoning or smoke inhalation maybe, yeah?"

"Or dehydration." The captain kicked a frozen water bottle across the room to smack against a cabinet.

Barely breathing, Morales stepped between two of the dead, leaning over, reaching inside one of the coats to pull out an ID card. "And look. Government IDs. They were probably working in the building or somewhere in the area when the heavy snows trapped them." Blood running cold, he frowned. "They must have huddled in here once the power went out."

"Yeah, that's what it looks like." Jones looked across the stiff figures then spun and pointed at the remaining soldiers in the room. "Get some burn barrels going near the entrance. I want people near a fire every fifteen minutes, and I want men assigned to keep them fed with whatever they can scavenge. You hear me? No exceptions. I won't tolerate any complaints about frostbitten toes or fingers. It'll be so damn toasty around here you'll have sunburns before the end of the day." Chuckles echoed down the line. "Now, get out there and spread the word. Make it happen!"

"Yes, sir!"

Morales followed the others from the break room, glancing back once at the huddled forms, shivering at their dreaded fate. Out on the floor, Smith and the officers had raised the bay doors and were chipping away at the wall of snow and ice piled on the other side. A soldier came in lugging a thirty-gallon tote and slammed it on the concrete, tossing the top to the side. The soldiers flocked to it, hands digging inside for the military grade heat packs, ripping them open, stuffing them into coats and gloves, taping them around legs beneath cold-weather pants. Morales covered his vital spots and jammed two packs into both sides of each boot. Activated by his movements, warmth blossomed in his clothing as he joined Smith at the ice wall.

Taking a pick from the lieutenant, he and thirty other soldiers broke apart the ice as plows and trucks chipped away on the other side. Burn barrels sprung up throughout the warehouse casting a bright orange glow wherever he looked, and at first the fires and heat packs seemed like overkill, but with the bay doors thrown wide open, and the wind penetrating gaps in the snow wall, Morales saw how paltry their defenses truly were against the elements.

Cheeks stinging, fingers growing numb despite the warmth of his gloves, he kept swinging, careful not to get too sweaty. Steel picks and shovels whacked against the ice, and soon the entire floor was filled with loose chunks of it. Wood burned, men shouted, and the powerful diesel machines on the other side dug closer. After an hour, Smith let his pick head drop with a clang, panting as he gestured toward the center of the warehouse. "Come on. Let's take a break."

Not wanting to argue, Morales followed the lieutenant to a burn barrel, resting his pick against the warm metal before ripping off his gloves. Frigid hands up to the fire, he tucked his chin into his coat and focused on getting warm while Smith chatted with a pair of soldiers nearby at another barrel.

"They found more bodies in two of the locker rooms." Smith removed his own gloves and laid them over his arms, head shaking dismally. "All frozen, just like the ones in the break room."

"They had power to the security systems and lights, but not to the HVAC units?"

"Nope. Without heat, it was only a matter of time till they froze."

Soldiers brought more bins filled with thousands of heat packs and dropped them onto the warehouse floor and Morales and his friend hurried over to exchange their expired packs for new ones. All warmed up again, the pair returned to the wall, attacking it with their tools, cheering with the rest of the men when a bulldozer's teeth broke through, collapsing the massive barrier in an avalanche of crystalline rubble. More bulldozers and wheelbarrows came to haul the chunks away until troops from the other side stepped through to greet their friends with high-fives and nods. Many made a beeline for the burn barrels, stripping off frozen gloves, rubbing hands vigorously in front of the flames as others brought armfuls of office furniture and broken-up pallets, stuffing the barrels full to keep the flames high.

As a path cleared to the outside, the eighteen wheelers backed in, doors thrown open wide to receive supplies and the soldiers stepped aside, gathering around the burn barrels as the machines took up the brunt of the work. Forklifts buzzed to life as six out of the dozen they'd found inside still worked, and drivers steered them into the rows and extracted goods from the tops of the tall racks. Another two forklifts entered from the Army's supply and joined the other six in grabbing pallet upon pallet, trundling up ramps and careening into the trailers, shaking them on their springs, dropping loads at the far end with a bang before backing out to get more.

A chorus of mechanical whines echoed through the warehouse space as oil and fresh electric ozone permeated the air and even with the wide-open bay doors, the stench of diesel fuel filled the air. An occasional crash or clatter of metal resonated as the operators sometimes brushed each other in the crowded lanes, and there were shouts from grunts and officers alike that echoed through the facility as goods were sorted through, selected and loaded up.

When a truck was filled to bursting, it pulled away and got back in line, ready to head out with the convoy. Empty trailers backed in to replace each one, the forklifts swarming around them like ants. Food and medical supplies were the priority of the day - pallets full of vaccines, antibiotics, and anything the cold wouldn't destroy were hauled away to the trucks first.

Captain Jones left the break room and strode across the warehouse floor, eyes on a swivel as he overlooked the operation, sometimes pointing at something to be done, other times shouting into a 2-way radio on his belt. Slowly but surely the racks emptied, and the trucks bulged with supplies, the number of full trucks starting to look more substantial.

The captain spoke into his handheld radio and then listened to the reply, nodding as he absorbed the information. When he was finished, he shouted to those assembled around the fires. "Okay, men, this warehouse is about dry, so let's clear a path to the next one. Smith and Morales, you're on point again."

Charged by their first success, Morales stepped outside between the eighteen wheelers and gathered the drivers to him where they stood beside one of the gargantuan LeTourneaus, one man holding the facility map out for him to find the best way through.

"Right here." Finger tracing a path from their current location and up a service road, he showed them where to go. "Take one LeTourneau along here and into the next warehouse's rear lot. I'll take the excavator and Smith's men and clear the entrance just like before. A two-pronged attack on both sides. Let's go!"

After receiving positive nods from the drivers, Morales stomped into the warehouse, calling soldiers to him as he exited the front of the building and climbed into his excavator. Engine already running, he buckled himself in and flicked the joysticks, jerking the machine to life. Trailing fifty men with picks and shovels, he drove up the pre-plowed path to the next building over.

The teeth of his bucket cracked the ice and snow as he dug toward the entrance. Dump trucks pulled in behind him, and he filled one with tons of frozen debris in just a few minutes. Burn barrels sprung to life, faint orange glows dotting the parking lot, soldiers operating in shifts to cut the path while staying warm. Morales worked himself into a trance, hands shifting with a smooth fluidity only someone who appreciated the machine's power could attain and an hour passed in what seemed like a few seconds as they clawed their way toward another treasure trove. Just as he reached the front walkway, a soldier stepped into his vision and waved for him to stop. He reluctantly stilled the excavator as Smith jogged up, the lieutenant climbing the steps to his cabin, shouting in through the half-open window.

"Hey, we need to shut things down!" He made a cutting motion across his neck with his hand.

"What are you talking about? We just got started!" Morales shouted back, motioning toward the mounds of snow he planned on eviscerating.

"New orders! Jones got word of a spin-up storm heading our way."

"What the hell's a spin-up storm?"

"Sub-arctic freeze, high winds, real bad news. They're ordering us to seek shelter *immediately*. Cap is pulling everyone inside the first warehouse bay, even the rigs."

"All right, man. I'll wrap things up."

Smith glanced at his wrist. "You've got ten minutes to get your butt inside, then we're closing the door. You don't want to be out here when that happens."

Morales nodded. "I read you loud and clear."

The lieutenant jumped off and ran at the soldiers, waving his arms emphatically, pointing toward the first warehouse as he repeated his instructions. The excavator and dump trucks turned and shifted backwards, waiting for everyone to move out of the way. Leaving burn barrels and wheelbarrows behind, the troops sprinted across the icy parking lot to the original building's entrance. Despite a mere distance of one hundred and fifty yards, the going was slow, men laden in heavy winter gear while the machines trundled along after them.

Through the window crack, a snippet of wind cut across Morales's forehead, bringing with it a sting that caused him to stiffen in his seat. While they'd been working in Arctic temperatures for several hours, his skin long having gone clammy and cold, the recent wind was something different. It bit against his skin, sucking the warmth from the cabin, leaving his breath gusting against the windshield. The winds kicked up, brushing the top of his machine, shaking it, rattling metal on metal, drops of ice assaulting the glass, some flying inside, stinging his cheeks until he rolled the window up fully.

As the soldiers entered the first warehouse, Morales continued on, driving the excavator toward the side road the big plows had cut to the rear of the building, but the entire convoy was trying to escape the storm, and traffic was packed tight. He pulled in behind an eighteen-wheeler and waited, the seconds passing slowly, and he sat there glancing nervously at the sky, watching as multi-colored, black and gray and white clouds converged on them from at least three sides. Fighting the urge to abandon the vehicle and make a run for it, Morales remained where he was, leg jiggling up and down nervously until the line finally moved, trucks inching toward the back doors, crawling to safety.

Ice chips sprayed his windows as if trying to break through and shred his flesh and the excavator's framework groaned as a powerful gust of wind shoved against it. In another thirty seconds, the bay doors came into view and he pressed forward, jaw clenched as the brutal winds marched across the rear lot, sending dervishes of snow and ice flying everywhere. Without a watch, Morales didn't know how much time had passed, or how much remained, fingers tapping on the joysticks as his stomach twisted into knots.

"Has to only be two or three minutes before the storm hits us," he mumbled, looking through the windows of the excavator at the rapidly-darkening sky. "Four, at most. I'm a dead man. I won't make it."

The traffic broke as the soldiers got the hang of guiding the trucks through the bay doors. One by one they slipped inside, entering smoothly to disappear from sight. Soon it was Morales's turn, and he maneuvered the excavator into the first bay along the first row of empty racks. Breathing a sigh of relief, he followed the retreating soldier who waved him in and then shifted to point him down the main aisle. As he was making the turn, a forklift flew in from out of nowhere, and he jerked the machine to the right, bumping the rack and shoving it toward the next one, the soldier nodding vigorously and spinning his finger in the air.

Morales narrowed his eyes in confusion. "Again?" he shouted, circling with his own finger. Then he rolled down his window a crack, shouting. "You want me to push them out of the way?"

"Yeah! They're empty! Just shove the bastards aside, or we'll never fit everyone in!"

Backing the excavator up, glancing back to make sure he didn't kill anyone, he angled the machine right, placed the bucket against the rack and nudged it across the concrete floor as it squealed in protest. He bumped the ends of the first two rows together, the groaning racks slamming tight, yet he kept pushing until both curved inward toward row three, then he backed up, shifting to his right again, kicking the excavator forward to zipper the middle section. Above the squealing and clanking metal, shouts went up and forklifts whined, soldiers shoving burn barrels and loose pallets aside to make room for the remaining trucks. A bulldozer flew in behind him and tried to squeeze in beside the next column of racks, its fender clipping the edge of the row, causing it to tip dangerously. The soldier who'd been guiding him screamed for the driver to stop, but the panicked man whipped the wheel and kept his foot on the gas. The first rack shifted and bowed, the thin support rails flimsy without thousands of pounds weighing it down. Somewhere in the middle, the lock-fit pieces snapped apart and collapsed the entire framework against the next three consecutive racks, causing them to fall inward like dominoes.

Soldiers scattered as empty wooden pallets toppled from the higher rows to shatter into splinters. A forklift shot from where it had been tucked in, barely avoiding being crushed as a clatter of metal hit the concrete in a spray of chips and cracks. After six rows, the destructive momentum slammed against a rack bolted to the ceiling and floor, abruptly halting the collapse before it took out half the warehouse. Hands shaking, Morales continued compressing the first column as the last of the trucks filed in behind him. A heavy flurry of wind, snow, and ice chips chased them inside, the brutal winds kicking up like a storm at sea.

Men's hoods blew back from their heads, ears glowing red from the instant frostbite. Still, they bravely guided the trucks in, trying to organize the parking in the freezing chaos. The last of the Humvees and utility vehicles buzzed inside, angling sideways to fit in whatever small space remained. Soldiers grabbed the bay door chains and jerked them hand-over-fist, dropping the massive steel doors as the spin-up storm slammed the warehouse full-force.

Gusts of freezing wind whipped through the ever-shrinking opening, sweeping men off their feet, shoving them together where they toppled in heaps. As soon as the door's rubber lips touched ground, the segmented metal bowed inward, groaning and bulging as wind whistled between every gap it could find.

Morales leapt from the excavator's cabin, boots hitting the floor with a thud. He immediately ran to a man who'd been blasted over by the gale and hauled him backwards until his back struck something hard. Feet sliding from beneath him, half bowed over, his eyes widened as the entire warehouse groaned under the cyclonic pressures. The ceiling made a fluttering, popping sound as if a thousand small stones were hitting it, the big steel I-beams creaking, struggling to hold the superstructure together.

Soldiers turned slowly in the new darkness, flashlights flitting across the walls like fireflies as they stared up at the deadly sounds, gripping each other's arms, half squatting, cowering beneath the immense display of pressure and turbulence. A single, brutal gust struck the warehouse hard, every atom shuddering and quivering as it threatened to fly apart and crash on their heads. The wind faded in a teasing way, rising and falling as it died down. It backed off, petering out, then grew into a steady current that pressed a continuous yet manageable bulge into the bay doors.

Body relaxing, Morales exhaled the breath he'd been holding and he climbed to his feet, gripping the arms of the man he'd been helping and lifted him up, the pair leaning on each other for support. Taking a flashlight from his coat, he shined it into the man's frightened face, jaw-dropping when he saw the edges of his ears and earlobes blackened from the cold winds that had struck them.

"Come on, man, let's get you a medic."

Shaken, he led the frostbitten man through the milling soldiers, striding across the massive bay filled with Army vehicles, arm raised as he called repeatedly for help. Finally, a medic with the Red Cross on his hood took the man off his hands just as Lieutenant Smith approached with his flashlight beam shining in his eyes.

Hand up, Morales scoffed in aggravation. "Knock that off, will ya?"

"Oh, sorry." Smith lowered the light and fixed him with a shaken gaze. "You holding up okay after all that?"

"Yeah, I think so." The constant rattling set his nerves jangling despite the protective mountain of snow around them, protecting the warehouse as much as it was pressing against it. "I just hope the place holds up."

"It probably will."

Morales gestured at the wall with the doors, leading Smith away from the chaotic bustle of men and machines. "Why do you say that?"

"I'm thinking this isn't the first storm that blew through." The lieutenant's gaze shifted along with his flashlight, lungs drawing a deep but uncertain breath. "And it didn't fall on *them*."

Morales turned and followed the beam into the gloomy break room where the lonely workers were still huddled together in a circle around their cold fire, frozen water bottles and discarded food wrappers scattered everywhere, their forms passive and immobile. Stomach sinking with raw dread, he looked to his friend, sharing a look of impending doom.

Chapter 6
Keith
Houston, Texas

The stubby-looking Bristol Freighter with its fat nose and high cockpit taxied toward them, swinging its wide body around as the massive twin propellers buzzed, vibrating the air with sheer power as the Hercules 734 air-cooled piston engines prattled and thundered, the smell of oil and fuel permeating the air. The fuselage was coated in camouflage that was worn from age, and spare fuel tanks mounted under the wings. Beneath the high cockpit was painted the languid form of a leggy pin up model wearing a flowered dress, legs gently crossed and staring across the runway with wide blue eyes. Dark locks flowed over her silky pale shoulders, her pouting red lips poised in a kiss and above her was scrawled *Lucky Lady* in perfect comic-style lettering.

"How do you know these people?" Banks repeated herself, the corners of her mouth drawn into an uncertain frown. They were standing outside a hangar at the end of the runway, a black SUV behind them with a pair of burly MPs keeping guard.

"We worked together on a few unofficial missions in countries nobody's ever heard of." Keith shrugged nonchalantly. "They're rough. *Very* rough, but they can get the job done."

"How can they do what we can't?"

With a scratch of his head, Keith stepped from the hangar's protection, pulling his coat tighter around his shoulders, shivering as he gestured for Banks to follow. "They've got resources, experience and – most importantly – they can do things we might find 'questionable.'"

"Doesn't sound like a smart gamble to me." Banks followed a little behind him, watching the circling plane as it taxied around. "I'm already wishing we hadn't gone down this road."

Keith scoffed. "What other choice did we have? What other road could we have taken? It's not like we have the access we used to. Hell, you can barely get anyone to get you a coffee anymore."

A growl came from deep within Banks' chest. "I get it. But I still don't like it."

"I understand." He folded his arms across his chest. "But have no fear, this group is the best I've ever worked with. As long as we deliver on our end, we won't have any problems."

The freighter pulled within thirty yards of Keith and Banks and drew to a stop, the props spinning down as the back door behind the wing flipped open. A set of stairs uncurled and hit the ground with a clack on the hard, cold concrete and four figures began to descend the steps. The first was a short, stocky man in rough travel clothes of brown and green, his entire form filled with a cocky confidence, his gaze searching around, taking in everything with a keen, practiced eye. A tall, lithe woman came out next, a bright blonde ponytail bouncing against her leather-clad back. The outfit hugged her slim form, complimenting long legs and slender hips, and her neck bore tattoos of digital code tracing up the side while exotic, flowery scent drifted off of her, detectable even in the strong winds.

The next was a slight-framed man dressed like the first, only he wore his light brown hair slicked fashionably back with an expensive pair of sunglasses perched on his nose. A massive shadow filled the exit as the final figure emerged, pausing at the top of the stairs. His thick, sloped brow turned slowly, the gray eyes beneath it scanning his surroundings, settling on Keith and Banks, sending uncomfortable shivers down both of their spines. His shoulders stretched a tattered wool sweater tight, suspenders taut against his body, tree trunk legs covered in combat fatigues which were tucked into thick boots.

"What the hell is *that* thing?" Banks whispered as she shifted, taking an involuntary step back. "He's not even wearing a coat."

"That *thing* is a Dmitri." Keith whispered back to her, then smiled as the group drew closer, hand reaching to shake hands with the first man who had emerged from the plane.

"Hello, Serge. It's been too long."

Serge's gaze raked over the pair as he accepted the handshake, searching for weaknesses and making judgments and assessments in seconds.

"It's good to see you again." The man spoke perfect English, though his European accent was thick with mysterious inflections, hiding his exact origins.

Keith nodded to the others as they approached. "Lena and Mikael," he said, giving them a genuine smile in spite of his twisting insides. The woman gave a terse nod, and the man with the slick blonde hair grinned wider. Looking beyond them to the massive pair of stomping boots, Keith's smile faltered a hair as he called out.

"And how could I forget you, Dmitri, my big Russian friend?" The giant grunted as he came up but didn't smile or otherwise show an iota of emotion, standing behind his comrades with his massive arms crossed over his chest.

"Long time, no see, Keith." The woman's accent was also thick, words bubbling from the back of her throat with a slavic edge, the unique tattoo on her neck twisted elegantly as she stood next to the leader with her feet shoulder width apart.

"Too long," he agreed, gesturing at the lieutenant colonel. "Everyone, this is my boss, Colonel Banks. We need your help."

"Why else would you have called?" Serge asked. "No one ever calls us to do shots or have beer."

"That's true," Keith laughed as the tension hung on a proverbial tightrope.

"Who is this Banks?" One of Lena's fine eyebrows arched above her tinted sunglasses. "What do you do?"

"That's not important," the Colonel replied stiffly. "All you need to know is that I'm good for the payment we promised you."

Keith cringed internally as the tall woman stepped forward, lifting her glasses to reveal a pair of sea-green eyes that bored into Banks, the women eying each other carefully.

"It matters to me," Lena replied, tone accusative. "While you don't wear their uniform, I smell US military all over you." Her nose wrinkled, lip curling as she made sniffing noises in Banks's direction.

"Is that supposed to be an insult?"

"It is not a compliment, for sure."

"What she is asking," Serge said, "is are you active military?"

"What if I am?" Banks heaved a disappointed sigh. "Keith, I thought you said these people were tough."

The lithe woman sauntered up to the lieutenant colonel, mirroring her stance, fists on her hips and sunglasses perched on her forehead. "We are not afraid. But we don't work with scum." The giant behind her grunted his agreement, and the other two men spread out a bit, watching Banks and Keith closely.

Banks spread her arms and shrugged. "If you want to get paid, you'll work with me. If not, you can get back on your plane and head back to wherever it is you came from."

Keith edged toward the pair, hands up in a conciliatory gesture, trying desperately to defuse the situation. "Guys, this is a black ops mission. Strictly off the books. What does it matter if we're Army, Navy, or attorneys for the IRS? Especially under the current circumstances. We have what you need, so let's get on with it, eh?"

"Lena, it's okay." Serge reached out and took her by the elbow, gently guiding her back to the group before turning to stare down Keith. "A friend of Keith's is a friend of ours. We've been on so many missions together, I think we can trust him. Can't we?"

"I trust no one." The first words from the gargantuan Dmitri dropped like a bomb on the gathering, his tone as deep as a bottomless pit, accent so thick it was hard to imagine that he could speak much more than a handful of words in English or any other language.

"You know me, my friend." Serge patted Dmitri's arm, a calm expression on his face. "I also do not trust people so easily, but let's at least let them give us the details."

Keith looked at the Colonel, giving the woman a hesitant nod, feeling his blood pressure dropping as the four mercenaries relaxed their stances.

"Okay, then." Banks clapped her hands together one time and continued. "I need a family brought in. It has to be done cleanly, quietly and with no casualties – especially any US troops."

"Who are these people?" Serge asked.

"Their names are Tom and Barbara McKnight, and they have three children. They're currently somewhere south of the frozen zone, though not sure where. I do have a solid lead for you to start with, though."

"What are they, special forces, or agents of the US government?" The swarthy Mikael spoke, his youthful voice lilting upward like a musical note. "Do they have something you require?"

"The man is a scientist." Banks replied. "An engineer, to be exact. The woman is his wife."

Mikael scoffed and the group – minus the giant – shared amused glances amongst themselves. "So, no challenge for us? Just a routine civilian pickup? Keith, why the hell do you need us for such a simple job?"

Banks's tone lowered ominously, tinged with a hint of aggravation. "They've proven… tough to bring in."

"Oh, really? Who did you send after them?" Lena scoffed. "How can *children* provide any challenge?"

"They got past *me*, okay?" Keith replied, annoyance bubbling in his chest as he relived his experiences with the McKnight's in a flash of remembrance. "Their kids are no joke, either. They're all resourceful and slipped through my fingers a few times."

"Not hard to do given your condition," Serge snorted at Keith's bandaged hands.

Lena looked him up and down. "Are they good at fighting?"

"No."

"Can they shoot?"

"They're not marksmen."

"How did they evade you?" She chuckled. "Please, tell us, so we can be prepared to lose like you."

Bandaged fists clenching at his sides, wincing from the pain, he fought to grant them an even-keeled reply. "My hands were tied much of the time, and they got lucky."

The mercenaries' eyes stuck to him, dancing with amusement, holding back snickering laughter and even the giant's mouth was pulled tight in a thin, quivering grin. Just when Keith thought they'd give him more grief, the woman retreated behind Serge and folded her arms across her chest.

"To be clear," Banks continued, "I need them brought in alive, though if the goods are damaged it's no skin off my nose."

"At least we get to have a little fun," Mikael stated flatly.

"Let's talk payment." Serge gestured. "Do you have what we discussed?"

Banks stepped forward, drawing an envelope from her pocket, handing it to the leader who took the package and passed it to Lena. She opened the unsealed top and removed a slip of paper with codes and an old-style set of keys. Holding those in one hand, she retrieved a handheld computer from the inside of her coat and thumbed in the codes. The group stood in uncomfortable silence as she looked back-and-forth between the page and the results on her screen until she finally nodded, folded everything up, and placed the bundle in her jacket.

"The information appears accurate. These are the coordinates to a bunker we have previously known about, and the access codes and keys appear to be legitimate."

Banks nodded smugly. "As promised, that'll lead you to King's ransom of weapons, ammunition, and medical supplies. And that's just the upfront payment. You'll have access to nine more bunkers once you bring in McKnight and his family."

"Am I to understand that this is probably one of those 'sensitive' missions too dirty for even our American friends?" Serge smiled, his dark eyes shifting between the two. "One that cannot be tied back to them?"

"That's right," Banks nodded. "It must be done with the utmost secrecy and discretion."

"Sounds good to me." Lena shrugged and shifted her stance.

"Easy peasy, as you Americans say," Mikael added with a laugh, Dmitri grunting his agreement from the back.

Serge stepped forward and offered out his hand, but Banks hesitated. "There is… one more thing."

The merc leader dropped his hand, his smile following suit. "What is it?"

A gust of icy wind blew between them, snatching at Banks's words. "You'll need to take Keith with you."

"Excuse me, what was that?" Serge leaned in, feigning confusion.

"You heard me. Keith goes with you."

Keith's face blanched and his blood turned cold. The group of east European mercenaries were used to working solo, and they weren't particularly fond of him – or anyone, really – despite Keith's earlier business dealings with them.

"We do not need middle management looking over our shoulders," Serge said with a snide sneer in Keith's direction. "No deal."

"Then you won't be getting the supplies." Banks shrugged casually. "Though from what I hear, things aren't exactly going well in your part of the world. Sure would be a shame to miss out on so much you could sell off to the highest bidder."

Lena stepped forward and gave Keith a rough shove on the shoulder, snarling at him. "Is this your doing, you snake?"

The agent absorbed the blow, stifling a reflex to return a swing, hands thrown up in exasperation. "No way! I had nothing to do with this! I didn't even know, I swear!"

"Then why?" Serge shifted his eyes to Banks, folding his thick forearms across his chest. "Why would you require him to go with us? I thought you didn't want our work to be traced back to you?"

"We have the codes. Let's raid the bunker." Lena's thin lips curled with resentment. "One bunker for our trouble, time and wasted fuel. That should cover it."

"I'll change the codes," Banks smiled coldly, "and ensure you never see the outside of a cell – or a grave – again. In spite of rumors to the contrary, our military machine is fully functional. I'm sure a few teams would love an excuse to get away from dealing with logistics so they can hunt you down. Assuming you were to escape, of course." Keith had to forcibly keep his mouth closed, taking a full step back as he stared at Banks in shock as she opined in a matter-of-fact, almost bored tone of voice.

The dismal sky darkened as clouds moved in, bringing frigid temperatures that hadn't come so far south in decades, or perhaps even centuries. The wind kicked up to flutter hair, sting cheeks, and turn the air sharp – but it still wasn't as cold as the look in Serge's eyes. With a dark chuckle, the merc leader shook his head, forearms flexing with bulging tendons and muscles. The pistol appeared in a flash, taken from beneath his coat, barrel pointing between Banks's eyes. Serge clenched the grip with malevolence, voice rough and angry.

"You threaten us with violence when we came to do you a favor, to take a job you did not want? I should blow your brains across the runway and be done with you." Lena and Mikael chuckled while Dmitri watched them with a stoic expression. "You insult us with your arrogance," Serge growled, putting an exclamation point on his sentiment.

"It is *very* arrogant." The woman nodded to Serge, nudging him with her elbow.

Nonplussed by the appearance of the weapon, Banks merely glanced over her shoulder at a low hill where a pair of Humvees rolled into position, a squat missile launcher mounted on top of one, and a heavy machine gun on the other.

"Go ahead and shoot me." The woman retained her bored tone of voice. "You won't even make it back to your plane if you do, though. And if by some miracle you survive, you'll be hunted down like dogs." Banks shifted her cold blue eyes to the cocky Mikael. "Would that be enough of a challenge for you?"

The blond-haired merc glanced at the Humvees, then gave a hesitant nod. "That would do it."

Serge held his gun steady for a long moment, eyes fixed on Banks, weighing her up, his finger flexing faintly on the trigger, a hair's breadth of movement before he finally slipped it out, resting it on the trigger guard, lowering the weapon as a smile spread across his face.

"You have balls," Serge holstered his pistol. "I admire that in a woman. Yes, we need the supplies." The man waved the pistol in Keith's direction. "And having him along will be no problem. We've worked together before, though not so closely. We will get to know each other better. Who knows, maybe this will be the start of a long relationship."

Banks nodded smartly, still unphased by the entire encounter, treating it like any other normal part of a negotiation. "Excellent. Glad to be working with you fine folks. Please wait out here while Keith gets his things."

The stormy weather deepened as the pair strode back to the airplane hangar, leaving the four mercenaries to close ranks behind them, whispering amongst themselves. When the group was finally out of earshot, Keith hissed at Banks.

"Are you insane?! What the hell was *that* about?"

"I need a man on the inside. You've worked with them before. You're my man on the inside."

"I can't return to the field right now. Just look at my hands." He held them up, fingertips still wrapped from the frostbite he'd suffered. "Losing a few fingers and toes, and almost my nose, should win me a little recovery time, don't you think? I said I'd get you the help you needed, not volunteer!"

"You done?" Banks snapped as they approached the camouflage Humvee where an MP stood near the door. "Because you screwed this up. Royally. You had McKnight in your hands multiple times and utterly failed to hold onto him."

"I—"

"Shut the hell up." It was Banks's turn to hiss at Keith, her eyes blazing with barely constrained fury. "I've taken so much flak because of *your* failures and I'm done with this nonsense. You're going with them. End of story."

Keith lifted his bandaged hands again, a whine creeping into his voice. "I'm not ready to go back out there yet,"

"You'll be fine. I'd send someone else, but we don't have the resources we used to. *I* don't have access to resources that *I* used to have access to, thanks in no small part to your screwups."

"I know, sir, but--"

"There're no buts about it." Banks gestured to the MP who reached into the Humvee's back seat and retrieved a backpack. "I packed you some things. Everything you should need, including a weapon."

At a loss for words, Keith accepted the heavy pack, shrugging it on his aching back, the pain from his gunshot wound and missing fingers lancing through his body.

"You'll also find a sat-phone inside. You can use it to keep me updated on the progress, like last time, though hopefully this time the updates are more encouraging."

"Last time I had to report to you, someone died." Keith's expression turned sour, the weight of the backpack hung from his shoulder like a lead sack.

Banks fixed him with a confused, somewhat disgusted look. "Are you seriously trying to tell me you're feeling remorse over that idiot kid who died?"

"Of course not. Just that distractions happen. I can't always check in on your timetable."

"Keep it as regular as a geriatric who chugs Metamucil every morning."

"But—"

"Or spend the foreseeable future as a guest at a black site. I can arrange that pretty easily if you'd like."

Keith sighed. "No... I'll take care of it."

"You just make sure the job gets done. When this is over, we'll start fresh." Banks patted Keith's back just a little too hard. "And you'll get everything that was promised."

"Right." The agent nodded, swallowing against the dryness in his throat as he adjusted the pack on his back, trying to work out exactly how he'd gotten himself into yet pursuit of the same people he'd already sacrificed so much to try and bring in. He turned from Banks and looked out at the waiting plane where the mercenaries waited for him, four swarthy characters standing in front of the classic airplane with the beautiful lady stenciled on the side. Lena shifted on her long legs, placed her fingers against her lips, and blew him a kiss.

Chapter 7
Tom McKnight
Nuevo Laredo, Mexico

Awaking to a biting cold, Tom McKnight blinked away his blurry vision, breath scattering above him in a cloud of moisture that obscured the grungy ceiling above. The constant, ever-present moving of Jack fidgeting in his half-sleep was next to him, the small heels and legs pressing into his side and ribcage while snores from other sleepers assured him that, yes, everyone was still safe and sound. Clenching the blanket to his chin, he resisted getting up and leaving the cocoon of warmth it had taken them hours to create, but it was his turn to take watch.

With a sigh, Tom flipped off the cover and tucked it under Jack to keep the heat from seeping out. He shifted on the makeshift mattress, swinging his legs off the side and grabbing for his boots. Feet sliding into them, he winced at the coldness. The pharmacy was an icebox, smelling of dust, cold wood, and traces of the MREs they'd eaten the previous night. Palms against their cot, he started to rise when his son stirred next to him, shifting beneath the covers, pale face peeking over the top of the sheets.

"Hey, Dad?"

"Yeah?" Tom settled back, wrapped his arms around his knees, and pulled them into his chest. "What is it, Jack?"

"What's a holo… cen?"

Tom chuckled at Jack's mispronunciation of the word. "Well, it's *Holocene,* and that's what scientists call the current geological epoch." He struggled against the fog of morning still lying low over his mind. "Basically, epochs are how they divide time into sections."

"Why do they need to divide it up? Why can't it all be one name?"

Tom scratched his chin. "You know how when you and your sister fold clothes, you put different clothes into different drawers?"

"Yeah…"

"Same kind of thing. There are too many clothes to lump them all together. If you wanted to find a pair of socks you'd have to dig through shirts and pants and everything else. If we didn't have ways of talking about different time periods, it'd be hard to do that, and to tell similar time periods from each other. It's categorization, buddy. Like with animals, plants, stuff like that, too."

Jack looked down at his socks as Tom was talking, tugging at them before he looked back at his father. "So… are we in the top drawer?"

Tom laughed again, nodding. "Yeah, I guess the top drawer could represent the most recent years."

"So, we're the socks and underwear?"

"That would be true. I mean, nothing comes after socks and underwear, right?"

"Right." Jack held his grin for a few seconds before it flatlined. "Is our epoch going to end, Dad?"

"It's not as easy as that, but it sure feels like we're heading into a colder time period. Things are changing very fast. Dramatically fast."

"Will we be like the cavemen and wear furs from woolly mammoths?"

Tom grew serious and leaned in close to Jack's ear, whispering conspiratorially. "I don't think so, but I wouldn't rule anything out."

Jack's eyes grew wide, and Tom laughed, wrapping his arms around his son and squeezing him tight. "That was a joke. There are no woolly mammoths. Now go back to sleep so I can relieve your mom from her shift. I'll send her straight to bed, and it'll be your job to keep her warm, okay?"

"No problem, Dad."

With a groan, Tom stood and pressed his hand against the small of his back, rolling his head around, feeling his neck joints pop as he wandered over to their makeshift table to retrieve a couple of folded blankets. Laying them on his shoulders, Tom shuffled toward the front of the pharmacy, creeping across the creaking floorboards as the wind whistled through cracks in the walls. The dried up, half-inch plywood the previous owners had nailed over holes barely kept the elements at bay, and their attempts to mitigate the cold's incursion had been fruitless for the most part.

Head swiveling, teeth on the verge of chattering, he paused behind the counter where they'd placed a set of makeshift weapons before crossing to the front window, his body heat warming the blankets as he lifted the curtain aside and peered into the road. With no light coming from inside the pharmacy, he remained hidden in the shadows, able to peer outside without anyone seeing in.

As he looked around for Barbara, he spotted a group standing out near the fencing, bundled up and talking amongst themselves, dark shapes emphatically gesturing toward the pharmacy. They shuffled closer, moving onto the sidewalk, their harsh whispers audible through the thin glass pane. With furtive glances, they entered the courtyard, heads swiveling as they approached the front door, Tom's blood turning to ice in his veins. He hefted the pipe he'd taken off the counter and patted his pocket, checking for the presence of a makeshift shiv he'd pieced together from jagged metal wrapped in cloth at one end.

From what he could tell, they weren't carrying weapons of any sort, hands pushed into pockets, heads lowered in reluctant postures and Tom eased back in the chair, hiding the weapons beneath the blankets. The group stopped in the yard, milling around with uncertainty as one middle-aged man in a thick jacket with a faded American flag patch on the sleeve looked over the front of the store. After a long moment he stepped forward and pressed his hands to the glass, scraggly beard dangling from his chin as he peered inside.

"Tom McKnight! I know you're in there. Why don't you come on out so we can have a talk?"

Kicked back in his seat, Tom cupped one hand around his mouth and called through the porous wood in a voice that was softer than a shout. "No thanks, Marty. We can talk just fine like this."

The man on the other side of the glass paused, consulting with the group before returning to the window. "Look, Tom, you know we're getting ready to make our move."

"I figured." He drew a long breath, trying to calm his nerves. "What's that got to do with me and my family?"

"Well, a lot of us are wondering if you'll stand with us or against us?"

"Do we need to take sides?"

"I think you know the answer to that."

Tom shook his head. "So do you, Marty. My family and I are on nobody's side. We're just trying to survive, that's all. Your plans don't concern us, so you can go away now."

"That's where you're wrong. What happens in camp affects us all. Our fates are connected, and we need to be on the same page if we're going to get through this. We need to protect our rights and overthrow these tyrannical government camps." The man's finger tapped on the glass, rattling it in its weak frame. "You know as well as I do it ain't right."

"It's not right," Tom fought to keep his voice calm. "And I don't blame you for being mad, but what you're talking about is dangerous as hell."

"Dangerous? Dangerous?! It's dangerous staying in here, Tom; you know that!"

"True, Marty. But I've got three kids, and I have to consider their safety before anything and anyone else. We wish you all the luck in the world, but the McKnights can't contribute to the cause. We won't stand in your way, but we can't be a part of it. Just be careful, whatever you do. And have a pleasant night, okay?"

Tom held his breath, waiting for shouts, breaking glass and the rattling of the front door as some big oaf threw his shoulder into it, busting through, threatening his loved ones, forcing him to use his weapons to a bloody, violent end. Instead, after several long, tense seconds, the group wandered off, hushed voices muted through the wood and glass. Tom leaned forward and eased back the curtain, watching their shadows follow them into the street where they conferred for a moment before breaking up into smaller groups of ones and twos. Tom released the breath he'd been holding high in his chest, shoulders sagging, the pipe in his hand resting in his lap.

If it had come to blows, he wouldn't have lasted long. The military wasn't treating them well, none of their grievances given an ear and there were too many of them, all upset, cold, and hungry. If a fight was what they had wanted, he'd give them everything he had and then some, but his odds weren't great. A slim shape appeared from the shadows, interrupting his thoughts, circling in front of him in a surprise move and Tom jerked to the side and half-cocked his arm back to strike. When he saw it was Barbara, he relaxed and even cracked a smile.

"Geez, you're getting good at that," he said, voice shaking as he tried to play it off. "I wondered where you were."

A smug but apologetic grin spread on her face. "Sorry, babe. I didn't mean to scare you. I guess I have a lot of practice at creeping around, especially after avoiding Marty and his goons the past few days."

"Yeah, it seems like they're focused on making us join them."

Barbara came to stand next to him, wrapping her arm around his shoulders. "I'm not sure why they even care. We're only two people."

"They consider Sam and Linda potential fighters, too. Jack as a distraction mechanism."

Barbara's expression soured. "They won't be using our children to fight their little war."

"Absolutely not. That's not how Marty's little gang sees it, though. If we're not with them, we must be against them."

"What happens when they come back?"

"I'm not sure." Arm wrapped around her waist, he squeezed her hips against him, resting his head against her side. "We might be able to convince them to leave us alone... or we might have to defend ourselves. Either way, doesn't matter. We need to get out of here."

A wordless silence hung between them for a moment, and Tom couldn't help but hold her a moment longer, feeding off her warmth.

"We'll get through this," she said, hugging him. "We always do."

"I know we will." Patting her waist one last time, he broke his embrace and straightened in his chair. "Go on and get some sleep. We'll discuss our escape plan tomorrow."

"Good night, honey." Barbara leaned close and kissed him on the forehead, then turned and disappeared into the pharmacy's shadowy recesses.

* * *

The next morning, a swath of warm sunlight spilled into the room from the clipped back curtains, taking the edge off the chilly air. Still, it was cold. Bone-numbingly freezing. While having no thermometer, Tom estimated the temperature must be dipping into the negative teens and likely lower. At their small table in the pharmacy's rear, the McKnights prepared a breakfast courtesy of the MREs provided by the camp supply officers, Sam sitting next to him heating a piece of pepperoni pizza in a hot pouch and at the opposite side of the table Linda helped Jack get his chili mac started. They were beyond tired of the flavor and texture of the meals, but no one was complaining too much, all happy to have something warm in their stomachs given how bad their situation was.

After Linda poured boiling water from a pan into Jack's hot pouch, she placed the macaroni bag inside and sealed it. The smells of pizza sauce and chili powder hung in the air, underpinned with the smoky flavor of the burning stove. Tom put a gingerbread cookie in his mouth and bit the crisp edge, following the sweet bite with a sip of black coffee that sobered him with its bitter taste. Barbara scraped Alfredo noodles from a pouch onto a chipped plate, digging in with a grimace, taking liberal sips of warm powdered milk from a glass.

"Sooo..." His wife drew out the word as she stirred the noodles in the pouch. "Any ideas?"

"We can try to find some metal cutters," Tom suggested. "We could snip open a section of the fence and slip through in the middle of the night."

"We'd have to trade something to pick up a pair, and that would tip off Marty and his goons." Barbara shook her head, talking around her food. "They'd immediately question our intentions."

"No, you're right," he agreed. "Any signs that we're trying to leave will definitely aggravate them." Tongue brushing against his fingertips, he licked off the cookie crumbs and relaxed, resting his coffee in his lap. "We have to make it look like we're staying put in camp and not show we have a separate plan of our own." He paused for a moment. "We could try to climb the fence."

"Like we did back in the Army camp?" Sam held her pizza folded in one hand, a glass of powdered chocolate milk in the other. "Find some barrels or crates, stack them up, then climb over when the time's right."

"But this fencing has strings of razor wire across the top," her mother replied.

"We got around that by placing blankets on top of the sharp parts," Tom said. "It didn't matter, though. Keith came up with metal cutters and snipped the fencing. But, like you said, that won't work here."

Finishing up her Alfredo, Barbara broke open her chocolate chip cookie pack. "Okay, then. Let's think of something else. Come on, people, get those McKnight brains going. We've been here four days now. Surely there's a way out we're not thinking of."

"The guard situation hasn't changed," Tom pointed out. "They're pretty distracted, trying to stay warm, not really worried about us. And that makes me wonder just how much Saanvi told her superiors, or how much they really care or have control over the situation here. I half expected them to double the troops ten minutes after she walked away."

"Yeah, me too." Barbara looked over at Jack, rolling her eyes at a stack of noodles on his fork that he was balancing precipitously. "Jack, quit playing with your food."

Leaning back in his chair, Tom ran his hands through his hair, interlocking his fingers behind his head. "Aside from getting past the fence, we've got the added problem of finding transportation. The chances of us stealing a vehicle are pretty slim, and we won't survive long, or get very far, without one."

Barbara sighed. "We'll burn that bridge when we get there."

"More like a frozen lake than a bridge," Linda quipped. "It's getting cold."

Chewing her food, Samantha made an uncertain sound, caught somewhere between a grunt and an "um."

"What is it, Sam?" her mother asked. "Did you have something to add?"

She nodded, swallowing her bite and clearing her throat. "When we were out walking the other day, trading up for some supplies, I noticed a weak spot in the fencing."

Tom leaned forward. "Where?"

"You know that burned-out house that caught fire from those people trying to burn tires too close? The one up on the north end of the block?"

"Yeah, I know the one you're talking about."

"When we went by, I saw the fence. It's all black and brittle from the heat of the fire. You can barely see it because it's hidden behind the corner, but I bet we could break through there."

Tom lowered his coffee cup to the table, looking over at Barbara. "I know the exact spot she's talking about. It's around the side where the house presses close to the fence. There's a foot of space to squeeze through, and I'd guess the building is 30 feet long. The yard was littered with junk and burned up trees. Plenty of places to hide supplies until we can break out."

"And I only saw one soldier guarding it," Samantha continued. "That's one guy for the entire section. If we could distract or incapacitate him, we could slip by the defenses and get out."

A slow grin worked its way onto Tom's face, and his eyes locked with his wife. "That might just work. We'll have to scout a bit, but I can't think of a better spot."

"Good." Barbara nodded confidently, leaning across the table and patting her daughter's grease covered hand. "I figured one of us would get it."

"Outstanding work, sis," Linda added with a smile.

"Thanks, guys." Sam's cheeks blushed red.

"Regardless, we'll need to gather more supplies." Tom switched to focusing on the strategic details. "We need makeshift weapons, extra MREs, and more blankets and clothes. Even if Saanvi comes through for us, we'll still have to have them."

"I can help with the weapons." Linda's dark eyes shifted between her parents. "I saw some of that… what's it called? Rebar? It's sticking up from a pile of rubble nearby, and there were smaller pieces broken off, lying everywhere."

"Good, just remember it needs to be inconspicuous," Tom reminded her. "We can't be walking around with baseball bats on our shoulders. Let's focus on things we can conceal in our coats or in our pant legs."

"What about the stuff we came in with?" Barbara asked. "Don't we have supplies in our old packs?"

"We picked up a few things from that last town, but nothing especially good. And the chances are slim that we can get them. Who knows, though, maybe Saanvi can find out where they're keeping them."

Linda stiffened in her chair, dark eyes lifting with excitement. "So when do we get started? Can I come help scout?"

Tom and Barbara shared a look before he replied. "Your mother and I will do that *and* pick up more supplies. You kids will stay here under lock and key."

"Oh, you've got to be kidding me." Linda frowned, pounding her fist on the table with the fork sticking up like a starving child demanding more food. "You can't do everything yourselves."

"We can, and we will," her mother said firmly, standing with Tom.

"We've been locked in here for days." Samantha piled on with her sister. "You guys always say we have to do things as a team. So, let us help."

"Under normal circumstances, you'd be right," he agreed, "but this is a different situation. There are dangerous people in the camp, and they're getting pretty desperate. It's bad enough your mother and I have to deal with them, and we can't be distracted worrying about you guys."

Barbara rested her hand on Jack's temple and brushed his hair from his eyes with her thumb. "You kids are so precious to us, and we understand you've been cooped up in here for days. You're probably going crazy. But this isn't the time to take chances. It's for the best that you stay hidden inside behind the barricade."

With the kids' reluctant agreement, Tom and Barbara bundled up against the weather, layering on extra sweaters and donning their heavy coats and hoods. Tom chose a small satchel with a strap and packed in the bottles of medicine and painkillers they'd found beneath the shelves and in the corners of the store. Included with those items were a pocketknife, steak knife, and a couple paring blades someone had smuggled into camp. After buckling it up, he slung it on his shoulder and met Barbara at the front door. Steeling their resolve, the Tom and Barbara moved the shelving and slipped out into the small grassy courtyard where the wind gusted in angry bursts. Tom held up his finger and listened as Linda and Sam slid the shelves back into place with a slam and once the barrier was reset, the pair nodded to each other and walked left, skirting the south part of the block.

Shoulders brushing, their gaits casual but stiff, they acted like it was just another day in the camp. The usual suspects gathered around burn barrels on every corner and in a few yards as furtive shadows moved in the alleys between houses executing secret exchanges; food for knives, blankets for coal, and whatever could be smuggled in from or past the guards. The McKnights nodded to a few regulars they passed, ones who they trusted marginally, Tom repeatedly glancing toward the center of the camp.

"I don't see Marty or his merry band around," Barbara spoke under her breath, whispering so that just Tom could hear her.

"They've consolidated everything in the center of camp." Tom kicked a rock and watched it bounce into the street and glance off the chain-link fence. "Keeps things away from the guards' prying eyes. I bet they're gathering supplies and weapons for when they break out."

"Well, let's hope we don't run into any of them."

"And try to ignore everyone staring at us in the meantime. Or is it just me?"

Barbara chuckled humorlessly. "No, it's not just you. People are definitely scoping us out."

Smoke drifted by above them, dark tendrils painting over the gray skies, sunlight poking through the taffy-stretched clouds to grace them with a sprig of warmth now and again. The stones from fallen homes had been re-stacked to form new structures, roofs topped with canvas tarps, smoke drifting up from old stove pipes. Garbage blew across the street, plastic bags caught on car tires or lodged in tree branches and large quantities of discarded MRE packages covering the street and sidewalks.

They stopped near a burn barrel on the southeast corner of the block, a half-dozen people crowded around the flames all glancing at them before pressing shoulders together to keep the McKnights from squeezing in. A blue van from the 70s rested off to the side on four flat tires, frame rusted clean through. The side door faced the encampment, thrown wide open, the grayish interior carpet dotted with mold and faded from decades of wear. A man sat in the side door, winter garb hanging off his thin form, his gaze fixated on Tom and his wife, his eyes narrowed and cold. Behind him were cardboard boxes tucked under the seats or covered in old blankets and clothing and a guard stood at each end of the vehicle, hands deep in their pockets, heads up and on the lookout. The pair glanced the McKnight's way and Tom stepped off the curb, striding up to the seller, calling back to Barbara to stay on the sidewalk as he went.

Serious eyes regarded him from a dark-complected face, skin dry and ashy from the intense cold, voice hoarse and cautious. "Tom."

"Hello, Scott. Got any cans for me today? I've got aspirin to trade."

"Aspirin, huh? A full bottle will get you four cans."

"Four? That's robbery. A bottle of two hundred tablets is worth at least fifteen cans of food."

The seller's stony face never changed. "Considering I'm not supposed to be trading with you at all, five cans is a great deal."

"How about 10 cans?"

"Five."

"Geez, man. Are you crazy?"

Scott's expression never wavered, though one corner of his mouth lifted with a slight grin, knowing Tom was bent over a barrel. "Five is a decent trade, risk aside."

With an exasperated sigh, Tom turned away but caught Barbara's steady gaze and the slight shake of her head, then turned back. "I'll give you the bottle for seven cans. And I want a mixed batch. Two corn, one stewed tomatoes, one beans, and two peas. That's as low as I can go, man."

The seller remained still, fiddling with something in his coat pockets, eyes flitting past his customer to peer deeper into the camp, the blue-tinted lips twisting, jaw set as he reached a decision.

"Alright. Seven cans. Never say I did nothin' for you, Tom."

They made the exchange, Tom digging out the full, unopened bottle of aspirin and handing it over for the vegetables. Trade complete, satchel heavier, he returned to his wife, growling under his breath as they walked away from the area.

"He gave us half of what it was worth."

"I have a feeling we'll get a lot more of that in the future."

"I don't understand it. We've been cordial to everyone in camp. I thought we had a pretty good reputation."

A trio of women passed them in the street, striding fast in a heel-to-toe fashion just inside the fence line, each of them bundled up, hooded heads turning in the McKnight's direction. Forcing a smile, Tom gave them a friendly wave.

"Morning, ladies. Hope your day's going well." None of the women replied, continuing their walk-in stoic silence, boots devouring the yards in a scrunch of hard soles on the pavement.

"Aren't they a fun bunch," Barbara frowned.

"I'm pretty sure they're spies for Marty."

"Are you serious?"

"Oh, yeah. Pretending to exercise while scouting for guard movements."

"Clever," she admitted. "And here I thought they were just three rude bitches."

Tom chuckled at his wife's raw assessment, then motioned at a group of people circling a burn barrel on the corner of the block near the fence where one refugee stood near the chain link, speaking to a guard.

"Hey, folks." He waved and received a few tentative nods in reply, then nudged Barbara. "Well, not everyone hates us."

At the east gate, they found a line of refugees reaching all the way to the north end of the block. A supply truck had backed up to the fence and a FEMA worker tossing down blankets to a pair of soldiers who in turn handed them out to the waiting refugees. The wary, well-armed guards were dressed for the weather while those receiving the aid wore thick, ratty jackets and jeans with rips, showing dirty long underwear beneath them. Hands were held out, shaking and cold, skin dry and cracked, bodies shivering to stay warm.

"Let's get some things here." They strode to the end of the line and took a spot, moving forward quickly as the refugees got what they needed and returned to their meager domiciles, eager to get out of the weather. Soon, it was the McKnight's turn and Tom stepped off to the side with their contraband, keeping a close eye out for trouble while Barbara collected the blankets with a nod.

Once done, they walked along the north side, coming across yet another burn barrel with two women and a man standing close around it, huddled in thick coats and gloves. The smell of some kind of meat – Tom didn't know or want to find out what it was – drifted through the air, mixing with burning wood and plastic, stinging his nose. Approaching slowly, he raised a hand in a halting wave. A tall, burly woman wearing a thick green jacket with braids of blonde hair hanging from her hood nodded to the pair while her two friends remained silent.

"Hello, Sandy. Things going okay?"

The big lady shifted away from the barrel, offering a brief nod to each. "Tom, Barbara. Still cold as hell, but who's keeping score?"

"Not us." He winced at the sky, glancing toward the fence line where a pair of guards walked by on the other side. "You got anything up for trade?"

"I might, but it's frowned upon to deal with you McKnights."

"That's what I hear. Is that an edict from some great refugee camp council?"

Sandy chuckled. "To be honest, it's all Marty. He put the word out that trading with you folks wasn't the best of ideas."

Tom nodded. "Not surprising. What about you? Do you do everything Marty tells you to?"

Turning from the burn barrel, the burly lady crossed to a woodpile, picked up a 2-foot-long two-by-four, and tossed it into the fire. Flames and cinders twirled up, and a waft of dark smoke blew right into them, causing Tom to turn his head and cough.

"I'm not one to take orders from folks like Marty. The man's just a busybody, and I hate busybodies."

"Sounds like you're willing to do business at least," he sighed, holding her gaze. "We've got medicine and a few other things to exchange for food."

"I can trade with you," Sandy nodded, keeping her voice low, "but I have to keep up airs around here. Can't have anyone in Marty's group thinking I'm going behind his back. You know, when we bust out of here, I'd like to be confident someone won't stick a knife in my back. At the same time, I can't let him kill my business."

"Riding the fence. I understand. What did you have in mind?"

"I'm going to tell you to get the hell out of here and don't come back. You go around the side to the alley marked with an orange ribbon. My sister will meet you in back. She'll have what you need, provided you have something for us."

Tom and Barbara nodded, and Sandy took a deep breath and pointed off to the left, opening her considerable mouth and unleashing a torrent on them. "I told you to get the hell out of here, McKnights! We don't do business with you! Go on, leave!"

Tom and Barbara backed up in a hurry, and not just because they were playing at it; Sandy had a tremendous, booming voice that carried halfway across the block. Boots crunching on debris, they hoofed it around the north end and, sure enough, he spotted a ribbon tied to a construction stick next to a pair of cracked beige houses. The pair angled toward it, peering into an alley cluttered with rubbish and fluttering snow, junk piled up in the corners. Wind whistled through in gusts and gnarly tree branches crowded in from yards, decrepit fingers reaching in to grab at them.

"Ready?" Tom asked.

"Yeah," she replied

Right hand gripping one shiv, he stepped in first, boots lifting over the rubble and garbage, his breathing calm but shallow.

"What are we looking for?"

"No idea."

A low hiss from the left drew Tom's attention to where Sandy's sister waited for them on a patio. A tilted awning covered the space, the sides crowded with old fencing and a stack of tires.

"Ellie?" he called.

"Yeah."

Tom and Barbara stepped through a gap in a crumbled brick wall and approached the patio where the woman straddled a clear plastic bin, stout form hovering protectively over the trade product. Through the side of the bin he could see it was filled with beige colored MRE bags, probably two or three dozen judging by the size of the container.

Tom pointed at the bin. "I see you've got some MREs there."

"That's right," she replied, her tone a few shades less harsh than her sister's. "This is all Sandy's letting me trade to you."

"How much do you want for the whole thing?" Barbara asked, shifting from one foot to the other.

"What'dya got?"

"We've got aspirin."

"What else?"

Tom started to reply that the aspirin was worth its weight in gold, but he backed off, ceding to Barbara and her ability to get what she wanted.

"We've also got these fresh blankets here." She indicated the folded material beneath her arm the soldiers had given them a few minutes ago.

Ellie pressed. "What else?"

Barbara's mouth fell open, and she shot Tom an exaggerated glance of disbelief, though at the same time he caught a hint of craftiness in her eyes and an almost imperceptible grin.

"We've got a good pocketknife, a flashlight, a box of bandages, some gauze, and a bottle of rubbing alcohol."

Despite her stoic countenance, Ellie couldn't stifle the look of surprise that flashed across her face, but she quickly wiped her expression clean. "I guess that'll do. Put it all down on the table."

Tom's insides squirmed as Barbara placed the blankets on an old patio table, the surface warped from the frigid temperature. Next came the pocketknife and flashlight, then the gauze and bandages. Just as she was about to give up the alcohol, she held it back, turning toward the larger woman with a slight stamp of her boot.

"What's wrong?"

"I think this would be a better deal if you had a second bin of MREs by your feet."

Ellie scoffed and shook her head. "We made a deal, lady. You already put payment down."

"Yeah, that stuff is for the one bin. But the alcohol and aspirin… well, that's going to take another bin."

Back stiff, the woman snorted. "You're crazy. We had a trade for one bin, and now you want to change it? The deal's off."

Ellie bent to grab the MREs and leave as Barbara spoke. "Suit yourself, but do you think your sister will be happy knowing she lost out on aspirin and alcohol, which no one else in camp has? Believe me, we checked." Tom's wife nodded, expression turning surer by the second. "Yeaaah, she'd be pretty pissed off if she missed out because you wouldn't play fair."

As the words came out, Tom didn't think they'd sway her, but Ellie stopped with the bin in her hands. After a moment, she raised up, facing Barbara again, her confident look having completely evaporated.

"And don't say Marty and his group have plenty of medical supplies, because they don't," Barbara continued. "We traded them two bottles already, as well as bandages." She held up the bottle and shook it. "This is the last one in camp." With a heavy scoff, she turned to Tom. "Come on, honey, let's go. We'll trade it with someone else."

Satchel open, he played along, shaking his head while she placed their possessions back. "I think Scott would give us a couple cases of canned corn for this," he agreed, both of them starting to walk away from Ellie, who was still standing with the MREs in hand, watching them go with an unsure expression.

Though he kept up a brave front on the outside, Tom was cursing because those MREs were gold. They had a long shelf life and were chock-full of calories, far more than ten cans of vegetables combined, and they were the McKnights' only chance of surviving outside camp.

They'd just reached the collapsed wall and were about to step into the alley when Ellie's voice rang out. "Wait! Come on back. I think we can make a deal."

Barbara grinned and winked at her husband before they turned around. Five minutes later, the pair walked away with two full bins plus whatever else they could fit in the satchel, even picking up a few extra pepperoni pizza MREs for Sam.

"Let's take the back way to the pharmacy," he suggested. "I don't want Marty or any of his people seeing us lugging these bins around."

"Good idea," Barbara said, carrying hers against her hip.

"I know a way that won't take us past their hideout. Follow me."

With a full satchel and heavy bin of food, Tom picked his way toward the block's west edge, stepping quietly through backyards of refugee houses. The state of the homes was abysmal, many half-collapsed or riddled with holes covered by plywood, the once beautiful dwellings with Spanish-style phrasings having become worse than a ghetto. Face lowered, arms growing tired, he avoided making eye contact with anyone, looking away from the faces staring back through the windows. Once they reached the west side of the block, he stepped onto the sidewalk and hustled south.

"That was some brilliant bargaining," Tom said, huffing as he lifted his tote over a group of metal garbage cans scattered on the pavement. "Sounded like you enjoyed sticking it to her."

"I wasn't going to walk away without securing this food. Plus, screw them for joining in Marty's little vendetta against us."

Soon they reached the end of the block and slipped into a path between the bushes where they entered the pharmacy's side courtyard and set the bins on a frost-covered picnic table, hidden from view by the trees. Lids removed, they looked over the meager haul, transferring the MREs from the satchel to the bins, shuffling the meals into order.

"It's not much," he said, "but it'll keep us alive until we settle in somewhere else." They repacked them and hauled them around to the front, eager to get the food inside.

"How can we transport them if we don't have a vehicle?" Barbara asked.

"I have some ideas about that—"

As he rounded the corner, Tom jerked to a halt, almost dropping his bin, shocked to see Marty and a couple of his men nosing around the door. The leader snapped straight, eyes wide with surprise beneath his hood and, jaw set, Tom dropped the bin on the pavement and stepped over it, spreading his legs, shoving his hand into his coat pocket to grip the shiv he'd hidden there.

"What do you want?" Tom's eyes bore into the intruders as he placed himself between them and his wife.

Marty glanced at the bins, raising his bushy gray eyebrows curiously. "Hello, Tom. Me and the boys wanted to have a little chat with you and the missus."

Chapter 8
Specialist Lance Morales
Santa Fe, New Mexico

Smoke curled up from the steel containers burning wooden skids, paper, and fuel, filling the air with a charred stench that stung noses and irritated eyes, yet the heat the fires generated was barely enough to keep away the creeping chill that permeated the warehouse. Dark greasy fog rolled upwards to gather in the rafters, covering the ceiling in an ominous cloud of noxious fumes that flattened across the roof to the far side and down the walls, coating everything in soot.

Having rationed their heat packs, the soldiers huddled around the fires in a love-hate relationship with the flames. On one hand, they needed the warmth and on the other the roiling smoke was a promise of a painful, choking death. The warm moisture of their breaths gusted in hundreds of puffs as they tried to draw close without burning their lungs, some keeping their faces buried in their jackets or crooks of their arms to little avail. The building shuddered around them from repeated hits of wind and sleet, the constant creaking like an old ship on the open sea.

Morales rubbed his hands together, leaning in and a little back, looking for a sweet spot where the fumes weren't so terrible. Smith sat next to him, grumbling and complaining as he hugged himself, rubbing his shoulders, gasping softly, hesitant to breathe too much of the toxic fumes. "Well, at least we see what killed the people in the break room," he said. "And we'll be right behind them."

"You don't know that," Morales replied, countering the lieutenant's skepticism with his own blind optimism. "It could have just as easily been the cold."

"I feel it in my bones." The lieutenant doubled down. "Just like back in Reynosa and Monterrey before we got jumped." The man shook his head, cheeks touched with soot, eyebrows dusted with frost. "I got the feeling in my gut, and a few minutes later, *boom*! They hit us."

The men and women of the unit all looked the same, hiding their stony hands, shoulders hunching in claustrophobic fear. With a hill of snow sitting on their heads and no place to go, arguments were growing more frequent, and morale was dropping quickly. Malaise hung over the warehouse and whispers of hopelessness and despair grew by the minute.

"Those were lucky guesses."

"I've never been lucky in my life," Smith said in counter. "I've never so much as won a door prize at a bingo. Nope, I'm all skill and intuition. No luck here."

"And I notice you never complain in front of the other soldiers, just me."

"Take it as a compliment." The lieutenant gave him a mock sneer. "I only complain to the people I like."

"Yeah, right."

A soldier stepped to their steel container and tossed a table leg into the flames, cinders shooting upward in a flare of heat and light, causing an uneven blaze of smoke to pour over them. Smith, choking and waving his hand in front of his face, jerked to his feet, fists stuck out to the sides. "Easy with fire, you idiot," he snapped, scolding the man. "Don't just throw stuff into it."

The soldier opened his mouth to retort but backed off, palms up in surrender, ceding the argument before it turned into something worse.

"That's what I thought," the lieutenant mumbled, glaring at the man's back as he moved to another bonfire and sat.

"Man, you're in a foul mood."

Smith shrugged exaggeratedly, returning to his place next to Morales, hands up to the fire. "I get this way whenever I realize I'm in a slow spiral toward certain death. Also, I haven't had a cigarette in a few hours. I just don't feel like smoking for some strange reason."

"Could it be that we're dying of CO_2 poisoning?"

"That might have something to do with it."

"You should take it as a sign to quit." Morales gave the suggestion with a straight face, a smirk lingering beneath his flat expression.

"Not funny, man. Not funny at all."

A pause filled the air, broken only by the crackling wood and the soldiers' whispered voices. A trembling icy fear gripped his body, and he hugged himself as he stared into the dancing flames, mind drifting to more pleasant things. "I was just thinking of being back home poolside on a hot summer day. Mom's iced tea and all my friends hanging out and soaking up rays."

Smith smirked in a good-natured way as the flames captured his eyes, too. "I was just thinking of Heather Morrison. Had two dates with her before I shipped off to basic. Smoking-hot redhead. That girl could have melted every inch of snow off the building."

An accidental chuckle escaped Morales, and he inhaled a waft of smoke coming off the fire. Fist over his mouth, he choked and coughed. When he was done, he lifted his hand away to see the mucus was a sickly yellow color.

Captain Jones stepped over, gesturing to them. "Smith, Morales. I need you over here."

The pair got to their feet and followed him to where a group stood around a Humvee, surrounded by heaters to keep the equipment from freezing over. Morales reached up and rubbed his nose, an unpleasant crackle of ice and frost rippling across his nostrils as he broke them apart from where they'd frosted shut. He couldn't shake the image of an endless tundra outside the warehouse, an eternity of frostbite and frozen corpses, anything that vaguely resembled summer long devoured by the winter chill. Shaking off the dreadful thought, he focused on what the captain was saying.

With hunched shoulders, Jones gazed across the sea of vehicles. "Look guys, we need to keep these trucks warm. Even with the chemical treatments in the fuel, it's 40 below and getting colder."

Morales nodded with dawning realization. "The diesel fuel will turn to gel."

"That's right."

"We can *not* allow that to happen. And we've got to make sure the fuel trucks stay thawed out, too." The captain leveled his gaze at the assembled lot. "I'm telling you, boys, if we lose the fuel, we're done."

He and Smith branched out along with the other officers, shouting for the soldiers to relocate the burn barrels and metal containers closer to the vehicle fuel tanks. They were too hot to touch, so the men and women were forced to get creative in how they moved them, wrapping chains around them and using pieces of wood or steel racks to drag and shove them into position. Once the burn barrels were repositioned, they grabbed generators and portable heaters and angled them to blow warm air below the chassis, hoping to warm up the underside of the vehicles enough to keep them from freezing over..

"Be careful!" Smith shouted. "Don't let any of the heating elements touch the tanks. And leave the gas caps on. Diesel's not dynamite but I don't think anyone here wants to find out what happens if a cinder flies into a fuel tank."

Smith and Morales teamed up to move their steel container closer to his excavator's fuel tank, using one of the fallen rack bars to shove it into position. Standing close, he placed his bare hands on the engine cover, grinning at the warming metal.

A soldier was assigned to each vehicle to monitor the flames and, crisis averted, the officers gathered back at the captain's Humvee in somewhat better spirits to find Jones sitting with a radio specialist in the front seat, still trying to reach central command.

"It's no use." The man spoke with a growl, head tilted back in frustration. "The storms totally knocked out our signal. We won't be able to call base until it passes."

"How long do you think that'll be?" one soldier asked.

"Impossible to tell," Jones replied. "Our meteorologists just discovered these spin-up anomalies, and they're still studying the behaviors. Could be two hours, or two days."

The soldiers groaned and Morales turned away, hands stuffed into his pockets, looking up the walls to where a faint line of frost touched the smoky ceiling. The oppressive claustrophobia pressed in again as he could swear he could feel the mountain of snow squeezing the warehouse frame, about to crush it like an eggshell and expose the soft insides. A shudder of fear rippled through his chest in gasps and he forced himself to calm down and get his breathing back under control.

A hand landed hard on his shoulder and Smith's voice cut through the panic. "This is tons of fun, right?"

"Yeah." Morales breathed deep, forcing a smile. "What's next on the itinerary? Forklift races? Snowball fights?"

"It's good to know you haven't lost your sense of humor, Morales."

"Are you kidding? How could I *not* be chipper in your delightful presence?"

While they were pulling each other's legs, the back-and-forth continued to ease his panic, driving away the roof's groaning tension. The pair returned to the Humvee, Morales hit with an idea. "Hey, Cap. I just remembered something. What about the LeTourneaus? They're still outside; will they be okay?"

Captain Jones stepped out of the truck, hands on hips as he looked toward the windy bay doors. "Those tanks are insulated with a foot or more of weatherproof material. They should be fine for now, provided the storm doesn't last much longer." He gazed toward the center of the parking area where the tankers sat. "And if we do lose that fuel, we'll just change it out. That's why it's crucial we keep it warm in here."

Morales coughed into his hand, eyes flitting back to the ceiling where the vapor and frost gathered. The continual lung-rattling coughs from the soldiers echoed in the open space, and their bloodshot eyes were another sign of smoke inhalation.

"We need to get this air clean, Cap," Morales said. "I mean, the warehouse is huge, but we're putting out a lot more smoke than we thought we would at the start."

Jones nodded. "Yes, we need to think of a way to vent the area."

"Can we cut some small holes in the roof?" He pointed upward. "The smoke would go right out then."

"Nah. There'd still be several feet of snow and ice to cut through. We'd need guys with chainsaws hanging around up there for a long time to do it."

"What about the shutters and vents? If we could clear those and get the HVAC unit running…" He left the sentence hang as he traced the ductwork barely visible through the thick cloud of smoke roiling above them like a storm.

"Yeah, we'd still get a little ice and snow inside, but most venting systems are built to keep out the elements." Smith flashed a look at the captain before raising his eyes to the roof. "Getting the ventilation going is probably our best bet."

Hands on hips, Jones lifted his gaze. "I agree."

Soon, the dozen officers were staring upward, pointing and discussing where they'd clear the blockage and wondering where the control units might be. The smoke was growing dangerously dense, an oily looking mixture of gases, reminding Morales of the thick black exhaust from an eighteen wheeler's tail pipe.

"Oh, hell, Cap," one soldier said, voice shaking. "It's looking bad up there, man. If we don't freeze to death, we sure as hell're going to suffocate."

Jones raised his shoulders, chest out. "Don't panic, Brozowksi. Just start scouring the place for the control panel to the ventilation units. It's probably in the machine room, off one of these side rooms."

"Even if we find it, we don't have any power," the soldier pressed.

"Maybe Santa Claus will save us," Smith shot back, drawing strained laughter from the troops.

"We can wire up a diesel engine like a generator," Morales suggested. "Splice in some power."

The captain gestured at him. "You hear that? We can use a truck to splice in some power and get the ventilation moving." The red-headed captain scratched his head. "Does anyone have the building schematics?"

"C'mon, man," Smith grabbed Morales's elbow. "Let's try the other end. The machine room must be around there somewhere."

Nodding faintly, he followed the lieutenant, weaving through the tightly packed trucks and soldiers where burn barrels raged to keep away the chill. The troops fed off the fire like fearful vampires, glancing around with bloodshot eyes.

"You really think we can make this happen?"

"It's a long shot." Smith nodded. "Even if we get the HVAC unit turned on, it'll take us a few hours to clear the vents. Hopefully, the storm will let up by—"

Something clattered in the superstructure, cutting Smith off, the metal girders above them groaning as some massive unseen weight shifted. A shudder gripped the building, resonating through Morales's boots, reminding him of a truck with bad brakes coming to a shaky stop. Trails of powdered snow drifted downward like dust and Morales threw his hands out, every instinct in his blood and bones telling him to run, though there was nowhere that was safe. Smith grabbed his arm, gripping hard, pulling him closer as something cracked like a tree branch snapping. Soldiers shouted, crouching, cowering beneath trucks, wide eyes staring up in terror as the building threatened to buckle and crush them all.

Chapter 9
Keith
Somewhere Near San Antonio, Texas

The long stretch of highway wove with gentle curves from east to west across the flat Texas desert, ravaged by the brutal throes of the new winter. Afternoon sun glinted off the crystalline snowdrifts and windswept trees leaned over, bent beneath the withering storms that had blown through. Dense stratus clouds moved swiftly overhead, conflated colors of black and gray forming angry faces that glared across the weather-beaten land. Cacti jutted upward, their thorny tough hides withered in the shrinking frost, scattered among the towns lying off the highway that slept under the snow-covered plains. White-topped roofs bulged, housing the corpses of souls who hadn't escaped, leaving them forever entombed in their frosty graves.

A pair of Stryker APCs blasted along the interstate, snowplows shedding white powder in sweeping wakes off to the sides of the road. The M1132 engineer squad variants were fully encompassing units with eight chain-covered wheels each, their own private network and communications suites, and a full array of external cameras used by drivers with virtual headsets. Each bore an M2 .50 caliber machine gun mounted on top, and though the barrels were locked down they could be brought to life remotely from within the cabin at a moment's notice.

Supported by all-wheel-drive suspensions and powerful Caterpillar C7 diesel engines, the pair of vehicles crushed through the snow at a slow but steady clip, pulling heated and covered trailers, bearing cans of chemically treated fuel to protect it from the brutal chill. Separate from the fuel in the trailers were an abundance of weapons and food crucial to staying alive and well-armed in the rugged landscape for an extended period of time.

The trucks trundled down the highway, slicing through banks of snow, muscling them aside with ease as the big chain-covered tires dug deep for traction, kicking out icy debris in all directions. Keith was in an uncomfortably familiar seat in front of the radio, watching Serge drive using the tactical HUD. The merc wasn't the smoothest driver, but he kept the vehicle stable as they traversed the icy Texas roads and highways.

Mikael lounged in the back, lying between the seats, feet perched upon a stack of duffel bags, head resting on his own pack, arms thrown to the side and enjoying the ride. Lena and Dmitri occupied the second APC that traveled behind them, loaded down with supplies including an array of rifles, rocket-propelled grenades, packs of explosives, electronic equipment, quick rations, and several trunks of cold weather gear.

In addition to everything else, Banks had provided a large container of high quality MREs and high-protein, high-calorie energy bars to keep them going through the next few days. Keith figured the vehicles and supplies were an olive branch, offered by the lieutenant colonel to mitigate being forced to take Keith with them.

"These are very good," Mikael said, waving an energy bar, wrapper half-peeled down and several bites taken out of it. "Maybe Banks isn't so bad, after all."

"I will disagree with that." The merc leader was more relaxed after getting on the road and shifted his attention to Keith. "What is up with her, anyway? Shouldn't someone at her level be able to find one asshole and his family? And don't tell me she's not well-connected. I am very familiar with high-ranking officers across various military structures, and she acts just like one."

"Yes, like her shit does not stink," added Mikael. "I hate officers like that. They are the first to throw you to the wolves while they cover their backsides."

Keith smiled despite himself. It'd been longer than he cared to recall since he'd been alone with the mercenary group, and had forgotten that in spite of their rough exterior, they were more pleasant to be around than Banks or most of her military support staff. Perhaps he was more like them than he cared to admit.

"You're right," he nodded. "She's been in the service a long time, involved with many high-level, extremely dangerous ops."

Mikael laughed. "But I bet she was never actually *on* a mission. She strikes me as the kind of woman who runs *away* from danger."

Keith smiled at the exact depiction. "Another correct statement. The bottom line is that Banks screwed up a recent job, and now she's stuck in a less than pleasant situation."

"She is in the doghouse, as you say." Serge grinned.

"Worse. She's locked in the doghouse and they threw away the key."

The mercenaries broke into chuckles and laughter, shaking their heads and snorting.

"So, she is over a barrel and desperate for us to bring this man and his family in?"

Finger raised, Keith pointed at Serge in a bull's-eye gesture. "Bingo." A small part of him felt guilty for giving up such detailed information about Banks to the mercs, though it was satisfying to hear them laughing at her expense, and to deflect away from his part in the repeated failures to capture and hold Tom and his family. Mikael had been spot on about Colonel Banks's willingness to throw anyone to the wolves. He recalled their conversation after the first APC wreck near Richmond where, despite him being injured and frostbitten, Banks had kept Keith on the job without so much as a by-your-leave.

"She's by the book and formal as hell," Keith said, finding himself almost apologizing for her behavior in spite of himself, "but, in case you didn't notice, there's a lot happening. A lot of moving parts. We've all had to make sacrifices."

"Right." Mikael's feet dangled over the duffel bags, giving Keith a look he couldn't quite process, though it thankfully only lasted a second before the merc got on to another subject. "Speaking of finding our target—Lena, have you made any progress? Can you point us in the right direction?"

Lena's voice filled the cabin through its twin speakers. "Hello, gentlemen. I've infiltrated the U.S. Military's communication systems and am actively searching for traces of our targets."

"That was quick." Keith raised an eyebrow.

"My presence is tiny. Just two little rabbit ears, listening to the data storm. I accessed the remaining functional data centers in the country as well as allied nations not hit by the destruction yet. I'm sending some data to your screen now."

Keith turned to his console and watched lines of text. "I see Banks's mission logs from Asheville, noting the McKnights were there. A short time later, they boarded the Osprey and took off, leaving us hanging." He shook his head. "We already knew that, though. Don't you have something more useful we can use?"

"I can get information from the Osprey's flight recorder."

"But that went down with the crash."

"That is true. However, today's recorders upload data in real-time. While we cannot access the physical device, we have a log of events up to three minutes before the aircraft crashed."

Keith's screen switched to a GPS map with a blinking waypoint. "What am I looking at?"

"That is the craft's last known location."

"That's near San Antonio, Texas," he said, leaning in to study the map, interest piqued. "Hell, that's just a hundred miles from here."

"The vehicle crashed three minutes after that, heading in a southwesterly direction. We can pinpoint their location to within 15 miles of the last transmission."

Using his fingers on the touchscreen, Keith zoomed out on the map to show cities along the Texas-Mexican border. "If they were flying to Mexico, that would put the accident right around here." He drew a circle on the screen, showing the location. "Does this look accurate?"

Lena paused as the network synced between the two vehicles. "Mm. Expand the circle by another two or three miles."

Keith made the correction and sat back, looking from the last known waypoint to the estimated crash site. "How's that?"

"Much better."

"So, after they hit the ground, they would have probably assessed their injuries and kept moving southwest to one of the military checkpoints on the border."

"Are you certain they are alive?" Lena's voice crackled as the wind whipped up a gust of snow, clouding the transmission. "Based on this information – which I am surprised your Banks did not have access to – I would assume they died on impact."

"Banks has fallen out of some favor," Keith replied idly, "and I guarantee you that Tom McKnight wouldn't die in a crash. He's too slimy for that."

"I have doubts," Lena replied, "but either way, our job is complete once he is in custody – dead *or* alive."

"We will assume they survived," Serge interjected. "This black box data does not have information on how hard the crash was, or if it was anything other than a soft emergency landing anyway. Which checkpoint would they have struck out for?" Serge asked.

"There are at least three major ones." Keith pointed at the map. "Laredo, Reynosa, and Matamoros, and another dozen smaller camps along the border wall. We can't be certain which they traveled to or if they even made it. Neither myself nor Banks have access to refugee lists anymore."

"I may be able to hack the camp records."

"That would be useful." Keith absently stared at the screen, imagining which of the McKnights had survived and where they might have gone after the Osprey went down. "We'll start with the last known location of the Osprey and go from there."

Serge snapped the wheel hard to the right, leaning, sending the APC blasting down an exit ramp to hit a connector road to the next highway. With a switch to his forward camera view, Keith watched them swerve through a foot of snow, the interstate outlined by trees sprouting up on either side with occasional glimpses of a guardrail poking above the snowfall.

"At least we're not moving farther north," he murmured. "The snowstorms have been brutal up there, so we need to be careful."

"No problem." Serge shifted the APC's gear and ground on, giving Keith a sly smile. "This is nothing we can't handle. Settle in for the ride."

* * *

After connecting to a highway that ran south in the long stretch of endless tundra, Keith spotted rounded white roofs of houses in the distance. A sign for the city stood bent sideways, twisted from the wind, making it impossible to name the place, not that such things mattered much anymore. The town lay in a perfect line southwest from the Osprey's crash site, and his raw gut instinct told him the McKnights must've headed in the direction of the town despite no evidence to back up his belief.

"Let's swing off the next chance we get," he said to the merc leader. "I've got a feeling about this place."

Serge nodded faintly and pressed the Stryker forward, watching the road through his virtual headset. The external front camera mirrored his head movements so he could see in any direction, magnify his vision and toggle to a rear camera view and look behind them if needed.

"Beyond the houses is a cluster of buildings that could be businesses," Serge said. "I think we should check those first. Your McKnights may have been scavenging for food or medical supplies."

"I agree," Keith replied. "Especially since we didn't find any evidence of them at the crash site."

Their arrival at the wrecked Osprey and subsequent search of the grounds had been an exhausting exercise. The plane's broken-apart fuselage had been empty, the broken rear of the craft stained with blood but no bodies to be found. They'd picked over the area, digging through the snow, spending two hours searching for evidence of the McKnight's direction or if they'd left anyone behind. After an exhaustive search they were convinced the entire family had survived and they got back in their APCs and rejoined the highway.

The lead APC rolled to the end of the exit ramp, slowed in a grind of chained tires against ice, and took a hard right to enter a dismal little town nestled between a pair of hills. Restaurant signs jutted up from the snow-crusted ground, bent by wind, glass broken and filled with white powder, long crystalline icicles pointing downward. Two gas stations bracketed two restaurants, a grocery store, a short strip mall, and a Dollar Saver. A separate roadside motel rested off to the left with only one floor with outside doors and an office at the end, an epitome of a solitary desert landmark if not for the snow scattered all about.

Keith unbuckled himself and stood with his hands pressed against the ceiling of the APC. "Okay, let's check it out. Just leave the engines running. We won't be long."

They parked the APCs on the middle line, lowered the rear doors with a high motor wine, and exited. Lena and Dmitri met them on the right side of the road, dressed in full winter gear: heavy boots, insulated pants and coats, and all-weather hoods and gloves. While each wore sidearm at their hip, they left the rifles inside the vehicles. Somehow, Dmitri stretched even the largest size apparel so that it made him look exceptionally muscular, though Lena's thin form practically swam in hers. Keith breathed in the cool, crisp air, the below zero temperatures already causing his nostrils to stick, eyes squinting, dry and cold. Seeing the mercs with their tinted snow goggles on, he remembered to pull his own over his eyes to cut off the brutally frigid wind.

"It is a long shot," Lena said, head swiveling as she scanned the town. "Based on satellite images and maps, there are at least 16 towns of this size within a hundred miles."

"Yeah, but this one is in the absolute center of our search area," he countered.

"We will split into two teams." Serge pointed to the far west gas station. "Keith and I will start at that end, while the rest of you take the other and move toward us. Move quickly. If there is no sign of them having been here, we will move on to the next most likely location."

All in agreement, they headed in their assigned directions, Keith putting his head down and trudging through the heavy snow to reach the distant building. On the way, he flexed his hands, fingertips still stinging from frostbite despite the strong pain medication in his bloodstream. Flashbacks of his frigid search for Linda McKnight badgered his mind, skin shivering at the thought of wallowing in the freezing river waters. With a low grunt, he shoved the thoughts aside, replacing them with images of him strangling her – followed by her mother. Since arriving at the base with the family, he'd felt himself feeling more rational, but out on the road surrounded by hardened killers it wasn't difficult to imagine slipping back into the insanity he'd felt overcoming him as he had chased after Linda, trying desperately to bring her down.

Bolstered by the warm gear and the pistol at his hip, a surge of optimism coursed through his veins and boots picking up their pace, he soon outpaced Serge to the gas station. The pair circled the building, noting several abandoned cars in the lot, one still sitting at the pump. Using their hands to sweep the snow from the windows, they peered inside to reveal two people sitting in the front seat, a man and a woman, both frozen stiff, skin turned blue and hard.

"This is… concerning," Serge said, face pressed to the glass.

"Yeah, how do people in a car freeze solid so fast?"

"I do not know, but that's what has me worried."

Keith straightened, looking toward the empty wasteland, then off to the north where dark clouds brooded on the horizon. "Back at the base I heard rumors of things they're calling spin-up storms. Nasty pieces of work. They're on you fast and they basically flash freeze everything in a matter of hours. Maybe it was one of them."

Serge's eyes narrowed as he looked off at the storm clouds, then spoke loudly. "The second we see a shift in wind or weather, we immediately return to the APCs. Lena, Dmitri, Mikael. Do you copy?"

The two-way communication devices on their right breast pockets sparked to life with the female merc's thick accent. "We read you loud and clear," she said in a clipped, professional tone. "If the weather changes, we return to the APCs."

The pair resumed their search of the gas station mini mart. The front window was broken out, snow scattered across the shelves and deep into the store and Keith stumbled upon a dead cashier lying frozen behind the counter, huddled in a blanket with days-old frost clinging to his broom-style mustache.

"This one must've survived the first few minutes of the spin-up storm." He stared at the stiffened form. "Poor bastard."

Serge only shook his head and walked across the floor between the stripped shelving, looking over the remaining snacks left behind by the looters when he uttered a sudden gasp. Keith looked up to see him pluck a peanut butter cup candy bar from its box and raise it, a grin stretching his lips wide.

"I cannot believe my luck." The merc leader's tone dripped with rare genuine delight. "My favorite candy bar found in the first store. We cannot get these where I am from."

Keith scoffed, pointing to the stiff wrapper in the merc's hand. "Yeah, too bad it's frozen solid. You can't even eat it."

Serge gave the frozen treat an optimistic look, lips twisting upward in thought. "I will let it thaw and see what happens."

With a shrug, Keith completed his search of the gas station and stepped back outside once more. When his partner caught up with him, the two men turned and walked east through a sit-down restaurant. Inside were more dead bodies, circled in the center with the cold remnants of a fire between them. They'd burned almost all the furniture yet had still frozen into blocks of ice, one mother holding a child in her lap, the smaller hands within hers as she tried to hold them out toward the heat.

Outside, Keith glanced warily to the north, even more untrusting of the bold, roiling cauldron of black clouds in the distance. Over the next hour they checked out the strip mall with its cell phone store and tavern and in the bar, bottles of whiskey and vodka sat frozen, the full ones having exploded into chunks of ice, amber liquid spilling to the floor in crystal shatters.

"This is also too bad." Serge held up a half-full bottle of Kentucky bourbon and gave it a stiff shake. "One does not usually see frozen liquor. Perhaps I will thaw this out too."

"Picking up souvenirs. Do you do this on every mission?"

"Not on every one. But this mission is, as you Americans say, a cakewalk." The merc leader chuckled. "I feel like a tourist."

With a grimace Keith left the tavern with Serge following him, weighed down with his finds. The group met back at the motel in what would have been the parking lot and faced the building, looking over the structure. Many of the doors and windows were broken, though some remained shut and undisturbed. Snow reached a quarter way up the wall, almost covering the doorknobs and slabs of hoarfrost hung over the eaves.

Serge glanced over. "Same groups. Pick an end and work toward the middle."

Keith and his teammate started at the motel's office where the ice crunched beneath their boots but never cracked enough to sink over two or three inches deep. There were signs of footprints partially covered in a new layer of frost, though he couldn't vouch for their freshness and he assumed anyone still in the area was dead, including the McKnights if they'd been around when the presumed spin-up storm struck.

They peeked inside the office window, but the door remained closed, the glass intact with no signs of occupancy, then they came next the hotel rooms. Starting at room number one, they used military shovels to dig around the doors, kicking them in and checking for people. The first five were empty, though the next held the corpse of a man curled up in a bathtub full of ice, arm hanging over the side and blood dripping from a cut wrist in a crimson icicle that pooled on the floor. With twin looks of disgust, the pair exited the room and continued their dismal search. Only when Dmitri's deep voice boomed over the line did Keith grow excited.

"Serge. I found something in twenty-two. Come look, please."

They stopped their digging and hustled across the hard packed snow to room twenty-two and, ducking through the open door, Keith gaped at what he saw. On the pair of twin beds were the frozen bodies of two United States soldiers, both wearing the familiar fatigues, hands resting comfortably over their stomachs, fingers interlocked in a state of peace. Mikael and Lena were inspecting them, the woman glancing up as Keith and Serge entered.

"There are older dressings on the floor," she said. "And if you lift up their shirts, you will see bandages across their belies." She lifted one man's stiff, frozen camo coat to reveal a crisp, bloodstained patch. "They might have sustained these wounds in the Osprey crash. Or, perhaps they were already hurt. Either way, it's a good chance these are your people?"

Keith slid between the beds, glancing from one soldier to the other. Crew cuts were brushed back as stiff as porcupine quills, faces covered with folded white washcloths and he reached in and tapped the collarbone of the corpse on his right. "Someone removed their dog tags after adjusting the bodies in a resting position."

"Yes, that is right," Lena nodded. "It appears they tried to administer aid to them, but they died and were left here."

"And didn't have the time to bury them." Keith bit his dry lower lip as he mulled over the scene.

Dmitri poked his head and shoulders into the door frame, drawing everyone's attention. "I have another to show. Outside."

Something in the man's voice made Keith's feet move, and he was the first out, stepping up from the dug-out entryway to stand atop the snowpack. Serge, Lena, and Mikael climbed out with him, turning to stare as Dmitri remained standing in the recession.

"I was digging and found this." He gestured at his feet.

Keith stepped around the group to get a better view, looking at a bundle of sticks and candy wrappers mixed with the ice chips and detritus the giant had dug up.

Bending and squinting, he picked through the rubbish. "Was this part of a campsite?"

Dmitri shrugged. "This is what I think. Perhaps we can dig. Find more."

Keith swung his military shovel off his back and pointed it. "Good work, man. Let's get digging."

The team spread out, tools in hand, and began chipping away at the tough, brittle snowpack. Putting his back into it, wincing as he gripped the shovel with his remaining frostbitten fingers aching in his gloves, Keith tossed aside a couple hundred pounds of snow. While the mercs worked hard, Dmitri was the real powerhouse, his massive arms swinging the steel shovel with sharp cracks, sweeping broken chunks of ice aside, barely breathing heavily as the others panted and labored with stinging lungs.

Soon, they had a 12 foot circle of snow cut out around the entryway, the excavation revealing a pair of logs and two chairs from inside a motel room. More digging showed the remnants of a fire, stones placed in a circle around it, half burned paper wrappers lingering in the frozen coals. Stepping back, one hand on his hip while leaning on his shovel, Keith surveyed the scene, piecing together the picture in his mind.

"So, they crashed the Osprey a few dozen miles away and walked in a southwesterly direction to reach this little town. They brought their wounded to the hotel where they could use the beds." Looking up, he used his shovel to make a sweeping motion from the northeast to the motel and across the thirty rooms. "They searched the town, grabbed some snacks and supplies, and hunkered down here."

"This is where they decided what camp to go to." Serge stood next to him and inspected the scene with the same critical eye. "But they left behind no clues."

Keith raised his hand. "No, I think-"

Something scraped the hard ice from somewhere to his left, just a snip of sound in the breeze that caught his trained ears. Head snapping up, he pinned someone peeking around the office corner wearing a hood, drawstrings pulled tight so the face hole was only a few inches in diameter. Reflexes kicking in, Keith dropped his shovel and took off in a dead sprint. Almost instantly pain lanced through his feet and up his legs as his frostbitten toes screamed in agony from his heel to his head. He pulled up short, falling into a staggering, limping gait as Lena and Mikael flew by him, boots churning up snow and ice chips. The person standing on the corner twisted and bolted out of sight, soon followed by the mercs. Cursing and hobbling, arms pumping, Keith reached the corner in time to see the chase was already over.

Lena had caught the individual and pinned them face first on the hard-packed ground. Knee pressed to their spine, arm bent behind them, the merc applied pressure and the captive cried out in pain, a woman's cry, nose and lips pressed into the snow, spitting and fighting. Lena only twisted the captive's wrist harder, drawing a louder, pained cry and Keith circled to get a better look, snapping at the merc.

"Ease up a little, would you?"

Lena relaxed her grip and loosened the drawstrings with her free hand, ripping back the hood, revealing the face of a dark-haired woman with light gray eyes in her mid 30s. Gaze shifting to Keith as he knelt in front of her, the captive curled her lip in a snarl, though Lena grabbed her by the hair and jerked her head backward, drawing an anguished yelp that took the edge off her anger. The other mercs circled to stand behind Keith, and when she saw them, her expression melted from scowling to fearful, doubly so upon seeing Dmitri's intimidating physique and stony glare.

"What's your name?" Keith asked, drawing the woman's attention back to him and her mouth clamped shut, looking toward the tundra as if searching for an escape.

"You won't get away." He gestured at Lena. "She'll break your arm if you struggle too hard. Luckily, for you, she listens to me."

"I do not listen to him," the merc spoke flatly, jerking the captive's hair for good measure.

"So," Keith spread his arms, "Let's have your name before she does something I can't control."

With fear-filled eyes, the woman croaked a word, sounding like she hadn't spoken in weeks. Finally, after swallowing hard, she managed something they could understand.

"M... Mary," she said. "My name is Mary."

"Good, Mary. Now, do you live around here?"

She nodded again.

"Were you here before the storms hit?" He gestured, shifting on his pained feet, trying to keep his expression flat in spite of the agony. "I mean, before all this snow?"

"I live just through the woods there on Hayes Road. I only came this far out to scavenge for food." She frowned. "But there's not much left."

"I got one of the last peanut butter cups," Serge held the candy aloft, grinning between it and the woman.

Keith shot Serge a flabbergasted look, shook his head and continued his interrogation. "You would have seen if someone was at the motel recently, yeah? Maybe a family? A group of people, with a fire out front?"

When the woman didn't answer right away, Lena dug her knee harder into Mary's spine, drawing a tight whimper from her throat, a compressed sound with no breath to drive it.

"Y... yes," she gasped. "There were some people here a few days ago. Camped out in front of the hotel. I didn't watch them for too long, because I was scared."

Excited at the information, Keith leaned forward, cupping her cheek with his palm. "It was a family, right? Was there a pilot with them? Anyone wearing military fatigues?"

She shook her head, greasy hair falling into her eyes, lips shivering. "Not a pilot. Doctors I think. They were looking over some kids, checking for injuries."

"Doctors?" Keith's brow furrowed in confusion, then he had it. "Oh, medics. You're saying there were medics with them?"

"Yes," the woman whispered hoarsely. "I told you everything I know. Please, let me go now. I've got to get back... I've got to get back to my boy."

"Where did they go?"

The captive's chin jerked toward the road. "South along the highway."

Looking the way she pointed, his blood pumped excitedly. "Okay, good. Yeah, we'll let you go." He nodded to Lena.

The merc gave the woman's head a shove, pressing her knee once for good measure before standing and backing away. The captive slowly climbed to her feet, head lowered, gaze darting from one person to the next. Feet sliding to the side, she retreated, looking for a gap to escape when Dmitri puffed up, jaw tightening in a clinch of steel. He lunged forward with a grunt, lips drawn into a fierce grimace and the woman yelped and danced back, twisting, half stumbling in the opposite direction before getting her feet beneath her. She ran in a dead-panic, boots pounding across the icy scree as the giant rumbled with laughter deep inside his chest, sounding like a slow roll of thunder.

"Very cute," Keith said as the woman vanished out of sight, then he turned to Serge. "So, the McKnights were here, and we know their general travel direction."

The merc leader nodded thoughtfully. "I agree. They are alive, and seemingly intact. We just need to locate where they went next."

Lena folded her arms across her chest and raised her chin. "Give me an hour. I will find them."

Chapter 10
President John Zimmerman
Havana, Cuba

President Zimmerman steps from the armored limousine into the warm Cuban air, looking slowly left and right, noting hundreds of military personnel lingering on the terraces, rifle barrels sweeping the grounds for signs of trouble. At the top, a long, imposing structure stands erect with a domed roof not unlike the United States Capitol building. Over one hundred years old, perched in the middle of the city, it dwarfs everything in the surrounding area, proud and stoic against a sky streaked with unusually dark clouds. Twelve granite columns stretch across the front of the edifice, gleaming grayish white, the paint along the top chipped and peeled away. The gardens surrounding the building are of European design, comprising wide sections of lawn dotted with royal palm trees and other exotic shrubs. It is *El Capitolio*. The Cuban Capital Building.

He begins his long walk up the fifty-six steps to the front door, heavily armed Secret Service members in military camouflage trailing behind, each heavily armed, only a few feet from their ward as they join the military forces in focusing on protecting the president. Civilian staffers in suits and overalls carry boxes and push carts of goods, swarming around and through the Secret Service detachment, delivering items from trucks and vans parked in the street.

As the president's shoes scuff on the pitted concrete, he raises his eyes and takes in the sky. The dark streaks of clouds stretch in from the north, the fingers of gloom reaching farther south by the hour. The obvious change in the jet stream is evidenced by the muted stillness and occasional bursts of unseasonable winds cutting sharply across the terraced stairs. While he's never before been to Cuba, the chill breeze ruffling his hair feels off, a far cry from the expected tropical heat and soft breezes he's been expecting.

They usher him up the stairs, flanked by the twenty-one-foot tall, greenish-gray statues of *El Trabajo* and *La Virtud Tutelary*, then lead him through the front door into the main rotunda. In the hall, directly beneath the domed cupola, Zimmerman comes face-to face with *La Estatua de la Republica*, the Stature of the Republic. The forty-nine ton, forty-nine foot tall bronze statue dominates the room as it stands tall on an eight foot pedestal, the striking figure of a woman gripping the top of a long spear as she stares at some distant danger.

He stops and admires her beauty for several minutes while his staff wait patiently and nervously behind him. After some time, he turns away and follows an inlaid marble floor framed with gilded lamps on the walls, the group's hard-soled shoes echoing in the cavernous passage. Next comes two semicircular chambers with seats reserved for the Cuban Parliament and Chamber of Deputies, empty now that they've dislodged the government. A set of side stairs brings them to a long hallway of normal size for staff and administrators.

Members of the president's relocation team are busy removing pictures of Cuban leaders from the walls, tossing gold-leaf frames with images of Fidel Castro into boxes and pulling statues from tables. In their place, they raise portraits of former U.S. presidents, NASA milestones, and scenic depictions of United States geography. Still, there is something different about the architecture that can't be fixed with simple changes to the décor. The stiffness of the carpets and rugs and the claustrophobic walls gives the President a sick, sinking feeling in his stomach.

At the end of the hall, his new office awaits. The Cuban Presidential Suite is a long room with tall, white walls, bathed in golden light from elegant wall sconces. Crimson curtains frame the windows, though his staff have removed the rest of the Cuban furniture and décor, both for aesthetic and security reasons. Inside, the Resolute desk stands stoic and heavy, its oaken sides and spread-winged eagle on the front filling him with a pride that lifts his heart. Workers continue to swap out pictures and shift more familiar furniture into place, setting his usual whiskey decanters and glasses on a table, doing their best to make it feel like home.

Circling the thick wooden desk, Zimmerman slips into his chair, gives it a spin and peers out through the windows. While there should be a view of the gardens behind the capital, construction workers stand in his way as they exchange the existing hardware out with six-inch panes of glass, both to stop attacks on the President and to help ward off the inevitable cold.

As he looks on, the staff bring in more chairs—three for Rita, Mark, and Rick—and two sofas are placed against the walls behind them. Maxine approaches with her tablet, halting on the other side of his desk.

"Sir, the Joint Chiefs of Staff are here as well as the new governor."

The window workers are wrapping up and they step away, giving him a view of the gardens and administration buildings beyond it.

Spinning back around, he faces his lead staffer.

"Bring them in."

"First, can you sign a few things?"

Laying her tablet in front of him, she points to direct his stylus to sign a dozen electronic documents. When Maxine is done with him, several more staffers move in to replace her with more things to sign. After forty-five minutes of signing and marking e-paperwork, his hand grows sweaty on the digital pen. Finally, blessedly, they disappear and Rita, Mark, and Rick enter, taking the three seats directly in front of him. Others come in, milling around, some sitting on sofas and talking quietly.

A sense of dread grips the President's chest and he lifts his arms and shakes them to release the tension, expanding his lungs and forcing himself to breathe and relax. The room quiets as people pull out their tablets and phones, receiving the latest updates from Central Command and Zimmerman clears his throat to kill the remaining noise before nodding to General Davidson to get started.

Mark's normally stiff shirt is wrinkled, sleeves rolled up, salt-and-pepper hair unkempt as he returns the nod and turns to glance over those assembled. "Hello, everyone. I think we should all take a deep breath and appreciate what's been accomplished. The Cuban annexation was successful, and we've moved into our new home away from home. Most importantly, we did it with as few casualties as possible, and with the cooperation of the Cuban government – along with the requisite assurances and promises."

"Bribes, you mean." Zimmerman murmurs, barely loud enough to be heard by anyone except the three closest to him.

"It's been a long, tough journey," Rita adds, standing to address everyone, ignoring the President's remark. "We moved the Cuban staff to the centralized headquarters just east of here and have assured them they'll resume their duties as soon as we leave."

Dark thoughts circling in his head, fingers tapping lightly on his desk, Zimmerman releases an impatient sigh. "Look, let's cut through the bullshit. We've invaded a sovereign nation and forced the citizens out of their homes, disrupted their economy and halted their way of life. While the casualties on entry were low, we're still condemning these people to an unknown fate. There won't be a return to normalcy for the Cuban staff. It will never be the same again for any of them. Things are *not* going back to normal."

Both hands resting on the surface of his desk, the president scans the entire room, hardened gaze rimmed with sadness and despair. "When the temperature changes arrive, this place will turn into one giant tomb." A dismal pause settles over them, and he let it sit until people shift in their chairs and glance around at each other uncomfortably. "So, let's get on with it. Tell me who we're invading next."

The advisor remained quiet until Rita speaks up, his Secretary of State clicking swiftly through items on her tablet.

"I'll start with the status of the casualties in our own country," she says, glancing up. "We base these numbers on a count of citizens we've moved to Mexico, what we know of current and future temperature changes, and what is being reported by the scavenging teams who are still deep in the country." She takes a deep breath as she scans the figures one last time before speaking. "As it stands, we've evacuated close to fifty million Americans from the continental mainland. That includes those who self-evacuated and were counted at camps and crossings. The rest are dead or will be if they don't get out soon. Anyone above the fortieth parallel died long ago, and anyone above the thirty-fifth is likely already dead as well." Gasps echo through the room. "Anyone above the thirtieth will be dead in the next week, based on temperature predictions." Her voice shrinks with each statistic. "But the numbers are what were estimated *before* our attempts to close the anomaly. It's bound to become reality sooner than later."

The silence that follows is deafening as the president taps his fingers harder on the desk surface, General Davidson stiffening in his seat. "Mexico, thankfully, is on its last legs, and we've quashed all major resistance."

"I thought they'd surrendered unconditionally." Zimmerman eyes him idly.

"A few groups of rebels gave us problems in the capital, against their government's orders, but they've been dealt with."

"So, we should expect no more trouble from them?" A part of Zimmerman's soul hinges on the general's reply, and he quits his tapping and presses his sweating palms against the desk.

"That's correct, sir. The Mexican resistance is over."

"But a lot of our people are dead," Rita continued, killing Zimmerman's initial exhale of relief. "In fact, well over half the country. Most of Canada is gone, too, and even Pierre has stopped calling. While we haven't been able to confirm it, we think the Canadian government fled across the Atlantic and set up offices in France."

Rick Manglor speaks up for the first time, hair tangled, eyes beyond weary with fat black circles beneath them. His beard has grown out in patches of scruff that he hasn't shaved in weeks. "And that won't do them any good. The weather's turning there as well, though not as severely as here. We've already seen reports of hundreds of thousands, probably millions, dead across northern Africa, Europe, and Asia."

"It's the only thing keeping our enemies and allies from attacking us," the general adds. "Good thing, because they're blaming us for what happened."

"Can you blame them after that shitshow we produced?" John mumbles, guilt spiking his heart for the thousandth time so far in the day. His fingers start their relentless tapping once more. "One more reason to be on guard."

The room grows silent again, the seconds lingering into long moments of discomfort until his quiet whisper breaks through the pall, voice hoarse and husky, betraying his failing confidence.

"Is that it?"

Rita clears her throat and continues. "I'm… afraid it gets worse, sir. Initial projections estimated that this cold snap would descend well below the thirtieth parallel." She shoots a nervous look at the chief scientist. "Now we think it will sink as low as the twentieth."

"That's the top third of Africa, and all of Mexico. And it could last for decades," Rick stammers. "That's why I'm suggesting Hawaii is a no-go."

"Plus, the logistics of transporting our citizens across the ocean would be near impossible," Rita adds. "We need a place that's accessible by land to escort our people. And it needs enough resources to meet our substantial energy requirements."

"We'll need heat no matter how far south we go." Rick shakes his head. "This could get worse than our wildest imaginations."

"Is our location certain to meet our requirements?" Zimmerman steeples his fingers.

"Yes, sir." The general answers. "More oil than we can shake a stick at, and in the last five years they've been overhauling their infrastructure and urban housing. Even with their own government getting in the way, they've put together a fairly stable backbone, perfect for what we need.

"And we're way ahead of the game," the general adds. "Our initial recon teams report their military is in complete disarray, and they'll be easy to move on."

"I'm assuming we've already got ships heading there?"

Mark nods, jaw set with firm resolution. "Three attack subs and several destroyers in the area. Stealth recon has been in the air for the past forty-eight hours, monitoring their movements. We've got them locked down hard."

A folder that had been sitting in front of Rita the entire time slides toward him. It is the same one she'd passed to him the day before, the one he's been reluctant to open. The Secretary of State's hand lifts, her eyes focused on John as if daring him to push it away.

Nervous fingers reach for the folder and he draws it closer, opens it, and pages through, scanning the military projections on casualties and the potential risks and rewards of an attack. He notes points of geographical importance and flicks through the main battle strategy for winning the conflict quickly and decisively. He wants it to be easy, but it has to come from the general's lips.

"We've been running our troops ragged for the last ten days, and I'm seeing reports of equipment failures and low resources. We'd be facing fresh, motivated soldiers who must see what we're going to do next. Are you sure we can do this?"

The general's gaze remains flat. "We have to, Mr. President. If we don't…."

John's eyes drop to the folder. All their hopes are placed in its hastily constructed pages and plans. It is the last of many he'd seen over the past couple months, all of which have yielded mixed results. He draws a long, deep breath, releasing it in a huff. "Okay. Do it. My God have mercy on us for it."

The president shuts the flap and slides the folder back to Rita, its black front marked with red letters.

VE ANX.

Chapter 11
Tom McKnight
Nuevo Laredo, Mexico

Marty's cold gray eyes stared them up and down, his fists clenched loosely at his sides as his two henchmen stood a little ways back from him, both large, big-bellied men with broad shoulders and beards, looking like angry, puffed up bears in their thick coats.

"What do you want?" Tom asked, hand gripping the shiv in his pocket.

"I heard a curious thing."

"Oh yeah? What's that?"

"Rumor has it you two have been going around and doing some trading. Now, that tells me either you're hard up for supplies or you're thinking about ditching this place early, without a single consideration for what I'm working toward."

"I don't answer to you. I answer to my family's own needs, and how I can keep us alive in this camp."

Marty's voice rose in an annoyed growl, his chin lifting, fists squeezing harder. "Are you trying to get out of here or not?"

"We were short on supplies, like you said." Tom gave a breathy sigh. "I was just securing more food and blankets." Stepping aside, he removed his hand from his pocket and gestured at the bins of MREs. "Look, we've got five people to take care of, probably the biggest family in camp. This is maybe two week's worth of food for us."

"Yeah, yeah, spare me the sob story." Marty pointed at the bins in an accusatory gesture. "That's way more than a couple weeks if you stretch them out."

"You don't know what you're talking about." Barbara stepped up on Tom's left, toe tapping the ground, green eyes burrowing into man. "Ever raised three children before, Marty? Growing, hungry kids?"

"I've raised two. Got them all grown up and out of the house years ago. So, yeah, I've got some experience with that."

When she responded, her voice shook with anger, words pressing through clenched teeth. "You don't know what it's like doing it so far from home in a refugee camp, wondering if you've got enough for the next meal. *That's* why we made the trades. *That's* why we went out today. You keep saying we have to escape the government, but the biggest threat to my kids and husband is *you*."

Marty's posture relaxed, some of the tension and accusation draining from his body, though his jaw still worked back and forth. "You shouldn't use your kids as a shield. You're hiding behind them, doing things your own way. Alone. If you would've got on board from the beginning, we wouldn't have to settle things like this."

"Let's get one thing straight." Tom pointed at the ground, using a finger to emphasize each word. "We've nothing to settle with you."

"You're the only family who hasn't joined in, or at least donated supplies to the cause."

Shifting his right foot back, hand squeezing the shiv handle, Tom cycled through his options if things became physical. "My wife just told you we have nothing to donate."

Marty glanced over his shoulder at one of his comrades. "Grab a bin."

The man came forward, ambling toward the McKnights and Tom crouched and turned sideways, ready to lead with his left foot. "I'm warning you, big boy," he told the enforcer. "Take another step, you'll be eating your teeth for dinner."

In an instant, Tom had transformed from his stand-offish self to someone with nothing left to lose. His voice dripped with violence and ill intent, his eyes a pair of twin fires that stopped the enforcer in his tracks, causing him to back up a step and give his boss a questioning look.

"Marty, take your boys and leave before one of them gets hurt," Barbara spat.

The laugh that came out was laced with nervousness as Marty tried to calculate Tom's change in demeanor. "If you don't give up a bin, feeding your kids will be the last thing you'll need to worry about."

Before the words finished exiting the man's mouth, Tom lunged forward, shiv in hand, reaching for Marty's wrist. Marty saw it coming and yanked his own blade from his pocket, taking a swipe but Tom blocked it with his forearm, then gripped Marty's coat near the wrist, spun him, and pinned his arm behind him. The man yelped in pain, the knife clattering to the pavement as Tom slipped his shiv to Marty's throat. Arching his back, he bent the rebel leader backwards into a defenseless position, the point of his weapon pressed firmly against Marty's skin.

Tightening his grip, Tom growled into Marty's ear. "What did you say about my kids?" He'd spent the last several days tired and weary from sleeping on the floor, being chased across the country, only to end up in a strange land with few friends. Having his enemy in an armlock sent a surge of energy coursing through his body and with a sharp jerk, he pressed the shiv into the man's neck, drawing a cowardly whimper and a trickle of blood.

"Tom, be careful." Barbara spoke softly, looking over toward the fence. "There could be guards on patrol. If they see you with that…"

Marty swallowed hard, barely getting the words out as he tried to reason with Tom. "Hey, buddy. Listen to your wife. How you gonna help your kids if--"

"Shut. Your. Mouth." Tom raised his wrist another few inches, drawing a stifled yowl as something popped in Marty's shoulder.

"We need to wrap this up," Barbara whispered. "People are starting to watch us."

Looking around, Tom spotted folks at the burn barrel in the southeast corner of the camp gazing in their direction, staring with open mouths at the altercation in the pharmacy courtyard. And while the street was relatively clear, his wife was right, there'd likely be guards along at any minute.

In the moment, Tom wanted nothing more than to flick his wrist and slice the blade through Marty's neck, ending the McKnight's threat in the blink of an eye. His patience had officially run out, he was exhausted and no longer in the mood for playing games or tiptoeing around people who intended to do him harm. Looking at Barbara, he gave her a pleading look, begging for her blessing to take Marty out of the equation, but received nothing except a hesitant shake of her head. *Not worth it. Not right now.*

Mind snapping back into focus, Tom glared at the bodyguards. "You two get out of here. Get going. Go!" The pair backed away hesitantly, eyes on their boss.

"Go on." Marty's voice was timid as he tried to speak without causing the blade to penetrate further into his skin. "No sensing risking my neck for a bin of MREs."

The men kept backing up until they reached the edge of the courtyard then they turn and ambled off, hands jammed into the pockets, feet moving swiftly. One glanced back before they turned and disappeared up the street. With the guards out of the way, and the immediate threat to his family gone, Tom jerked the shiv away, pushed Marty forward, and kicked him in the back to send him stumbling. Marty caught himself, stood slowly, and pivoted. Rolling his shoulder, he fixed the McKnights with a genuine glare of hatred as a thin line of blood trailed down his neck and dribbled on his coat.

Tom waved the shiv. "No more warnings. You come around my family again and you'll never see the outside of this camp."

"And let *me* say one last thing, *Tom*." Lip curled upward in a sneer, mustache twisting, the man issued a final demand. "You've got one more chance to join us, or pay the price. Don't make me decide for you."

Tom held the shiv at chest level, pointing the tip at the rebel leader, staring him down as Marty slowly backed away, retreating into the gray afternoon light before slipping into a side alley. As he vanished, Barbara's shoulder's sagged and she leaned against Tom's shoulder.

Tom held her, letting out a slow breath, willing his heart rate to slow. "That was *way* too close."

"No kidding."

"Are you okay?"

"Yeah, I'm fine. But what the hell was that?" Barbara stepped to the side, looking him up and down. "I've never seen you do anything like that before."

Tom chuckled as he tucked the weapon away and stacked the bins, lifting them with a grunt. "I'll tell you about it inside. Right now we need to get this food out of sight."

Barbara knocked gently on the door and shelves slid across the floor on the other side before the girls opened up the entrance. "You guys okay?" Sam asked, voice shaking slightly.

"We're fine." Tom strained, holding the supplies. "Help me get the food inside."

His daughters made room for him to carry the satchel and bins to the table at the back of the pharmacy. Jack was ecstatic to see they'd picked up several more packs of chili mac, but Sam was unfazed by Tom holding up a few pizza ones, jumping back to the subject of immediate concern.

"We saw the whole thing." Sam looked between her parents, hand resting on one bin. "We were standing by the window."

"Marty wanted to have a… discussion with us." Barbara started, when Samantha interrupted, shooting her father a look in the process.

"Looked kinda one way to me. Nice work, dad."

"You should have stabbed him." Linda spoke the words offhandedly as she sorted through the bags of MREs.

Tom couldn't help but snort at Linda's reaction, even as he took her arm and turned her around, drawing her next to her sister. "Probably true, but there's a time for everything, and now's the time for us to lay low and not draw attention. Besides, we can't be hurting people whenever want to, just because we can."

"Dad. Come on." Linda shook her head at him as she pawed through the MREs. "You're talking to us like it's a few months ago. I *shot* Keith, dad. Shot him, stabbed him and dumped him in a frozen river. Sam said she watched Jerry…" Linda trailed off as Sam's shoulders slumped.

"Sweetie," Barbara interjected, "Just because you've heard it before doesn't mean it doesn't bear repeating. Killing someone should be a last resort. Your father was able to defuse the situation out there without resorting to it."

"Next time might be a different story." Sam replied.

"You're not wrong," Tom said, "But we'll burn that bridge when we come to it."

Linda pressed on. "I just want to know when you'll teach us that move. I could have used that against Keith when he grabbed us at the last place."

"I'll have to talk to your mother about that." Shoulder tensing beneath his wife's gaze, he gave them an uneasy grimace.

After a meal of MREs and canned vegetables, Barbara got the kids busy with sweeping and cleaning their small living quarters. With little to do to pass the time, she'd insisted that they at least keep things tidy, both to keep them occupied and to expend a bit of energy in a safe environment. Once they were set up, Barbara motioned to Tom, leading him across the pharmacy floor to where a few old booths rested against a wall from the place's early days as a soda shop. Wind gusted across the pharmacy roof as they sat down, wood creaking and whistling like a ghostly birdsong and a draft wafted beneath the table, causing a cold shiver to run up his spine.

Barbara looked over at the three children for a long moment, then back at Tom. "So, when were you going to tell me you're a ninja?"

Tom scoffed, spreading his hands. "That was hardly a ninja move, hon."

"Maybe not, but it sure took me by surprise. And I'm smart enough to know what a professional move looks like. Executing a maneuver like that requires a lot of skill and practice."

Tom turned over his hands and made circles on the table's surface. "You remember those old missions I did for the government, back when we were first getting the farm going?"

Recognition dawned in her eyes. "Ahh. I should've known you'd had some combat training. That was years ago, though. How'd you remember to do it so well that you could do *that* to Marty?"

Tom grinned awkwardly, taking his wife's words as a compliment. "It's like riding a bike. You get rusty, but you never really forget what you learned. And, c'mon, Marty's not exactly some super-soldier."

Barbara fixed him with a skeptical look, though her crooked grin told him he'd postponed the full truth for another day. "True. Marty's not in fighting shape. He *is* ornery as hell, though, and you wounded his pride like I doubt it's ever been wounded before."

"You got that right."

Backside edging across the seat, she snuggled up next to him, sharing her warmth and settling his restless nerves. She slipped his arm under his and interlocked their fingers. "So, what are we going to do about him? I can't see a guy like that allowing the transgression to pass. Embarrassing him is one thing, but you embarrassed him in front of his men and others in camp. I mean, he's bound to want to get revenge."

"I've been thinking about that." Tom squeezed her fingers and tugged her closer, resting her arm against his chest. "If we're to avoid any unnecessary violence and attention, I think we might have to move our timeline for getting out of here up. Which reminds me." He glanced up at an old battery-powered digital clock sitting on the bar which they'd traded a handful of aspirins for two days prior, and which came in handy for keeping their pre-arranged meetings with Saanvi. "It's getting dark, and we're supposed to meet Saanvi in 10 minutes."

Barbara straightened and unraveled her arm. "Oh, no. You're right. We should get moving if we want to catch her."

As they slid out of the seat, Tom gave her hand an affectionate squeeze before letting go. "And we may need her more than ever if we're going to make an early break."

Covered in their warm weather gear, they put Sam in charge of the store, giving her an extra word of warning about Marty before they stepped back out. Standing next to the lifeless burn barrel, they locked arms and waited until the coast was clear. A crisp chill seeped through their thin layers of material, caressing their skin with icy fingers. Chills ran up the backs of Tom's arms, wind gusting hard from the west, forcing the pair to lean together to keep from being shoved around.

The usual suspects stood around the orange glow of nearby burn barrels, identifying themselves with coat patches sown on out of sheer boredom. Tom remembered his first day in camp when the jackets had been fresh and clean, recently handed out by the military supply team, and it hadn't taken long for them to grow soiled and worn due to their living conditions.

"Okay, I don't see Marty or his guards anywhere. Let's go."

They stepped into the street, glancing right 30 yards where Saanvi usually waited and the medic was there, walking away from the fence, leading Smooch by a leash. With a click of his tongue, he grabbed Barbara's hand and pulled her along, snapping his fingers quickly. The German Shepherd's head swiveled in their direction, eyes brightening, ears perking up. With a high, excited whine, the dog tugged Saanvi back toward the fence. The woman turned, caught sight of the McKnights, and rushed back with a wide smile.

"I didn't think you were coming," she said breathlessly, locking her fingers into the fencing.

"We didn't think we were coming either." With a look in both directions, Tom checked for eavesdroppers but saw no one within earshot. "We ran into a little trouble with the group we were telling you about earlier."

Barbara knelt and placed her palm against the chain-links, accepting licks and nuzzles from Smooch, cooing and making kissing noises to the dog's happy whining and swishing tail. The dog wore a makeshift sweater, holes cut out of the woolen material for her legs to fit through, along with booties that were tied around her feet.

"Can you tell me what's going on with them?" Saanvi fixed him with a hopeful expression. "Who's running the show?"

With a deep breath, Tom rotated his head in both directions, still afraid of getting caught and having to deal with more than just a few thugs. "It's a guy named Marty. He's leading the whole thing, basically forcing everyone to take a side. You're either with him or against him."

Barbara looked up. "Much as we'd like to just remain neutral to protect ourselves, we're the latter. Against him, I mean."

"That's good to hear." Saanvi nodded, looking from Tom to Barbara and then back again. "Whatever you do, don't get caught helping them. Central Command is taking cases of rebellion seriously, and they're punishing people hard."

"No problem there. But he's making it difficult to trade with others in camp."

Saanvi stiffened, shoulders straightening as she gripped the fence harder. "Are you getting the food you need for the kids? Because if you can't, I'll put an end to this right now."

"No, it's okay." Tom shook his head. "We've got plenty of MREs to last us a few weeks."

Barbara glanced up. "Thankfully, some people in camp aren't doing everything Marty says. We were able to get those MREs and keep them despite his bullying. Barely."

"But don't do anything just yet," Tom added quickly. "We want to make our escape first. If they lock this place down before we break out, things will get harder. The revolt... it'll happen within the next 24 hours or so, based on what we've been hearing."

"Got it. I appreciate the information." The medic tapped her fingers on the chain-link. "But where does that leave you guys? If I put my captain on alert in, say, 12 hours, that doesn't give you much of the window to get out ahead of time." The medic leaned closer. "What's the plan?"

"We spotted a weak spot in the fencing on the north block we can use to slip through. It sits by a burned down house that will give us enough cover to hide. Once the coast is clear, we'll break through the fence and get away. The problem is they have one guard on that side of the camp, always on duty."

"There are supposed to be two or three." Saanvi shook her head.

Tom scoffed softly. "They're underperforming then."

"That's not surprising. There's a lot of that going around. But after this revolt, I can guarantee a major lockdown."

"Exactly why we need to get out before that happens."

Saanvi breathed deep, thinking. After a moment, she tapped the cold metal. "Make sure you're at the fence when the revolt starts. I'll clear the guard, but you have to get past the gang."

Tom glanced at his wife and shifted a nod to the medic. "We'll get past Marty and his goons and be waiting."

Saanvi offered a confident smile, tinged at the edges with a hint of nervousness. "Okay, then. I'll take Smooch back."

Kneeling next to the fence, Tom put his fingers through and let the dog lick them. "Hang tight, girl. We're coming for you soon."

The McKnights stood, watching their beloved pet, and the one person who could bust them from the camp, stroll south and disappear between the Army green troop tents.

"Well, I guess we're committed now," Tom said. "We just need to make sure were ready."

The pair turned and headed back to the pharmacy with the night covering them in shadows. Back in the courtyard, they knocked on the front door and listened as the shelves slid away. The entrance opened, spilling out a faint light, and they stepped into what he hoped wasn't their last peaceful evening together.

Chapter 12
Specialist Lance Morales
Santa Fe, New Mexico

The shrieking, tearing infrastructure pierced Morales's ears, driving like a wedge down his spine, freezing his blood cold. Soldiers shouted and hollered, crouching low to the ground, hiding from the collapse. Smith grabbed his arm, pulling him in one direction, but Morales fought back, jerking the other way, backing toward the bay doors.

"Come on, man," the lieutenant yelled. "Get into the break room!"

"No!" He shook his head, pointing upward to the rear of the warehouse where light snowfall drifted through the dark, rolling fumes. "The roof is collapsing in back, but not up front. Call the men this way! Get the trucks and equipment pushed forward as shelter! We need to move them!"

Smith stared at him, blinked, then shifted his attention to the back corner of the warehouse. With a tilt of his head to home in on the sound, the lieutenant gave a slow nod.

"I think you're right," he said in a hoarse whisper. "We have to tell the captain." Twisting away, Smith searched for Jones through the crush of dark forms scattering in the glowing orange flames.

"There he is!" He pointed to the tall, red-headed man standing next to his Humvee with the long antennas, gripping an officer's shoulder in each hand, face a mask of grim helplessness.

Morales waded through the crowd, bumped hard by the shoving, shouting soldiers. He grabbed a woman by her coat and threw her past him, then kept going, not worrying if Smith was behind him. His fellow soldiers jostled and knocked him around like a pinball as he surged forward, slamming him against an armored car before he fought his way free.

"Captain!" he shouted, voice raspy from the fumes he'd been breathing, the sound not loud enough to cut through the shrieking warehouse. "Captain! Hey, cap!"

The last note found a silent spot in the noise, drawing Jones's attention as the specialist waved and pointed toward the back of the warehouse. "Get them to the front! Move the trucks! It's coming... ooof!"

Someone slammed into him, cutting off his sentence.

The captain's gaze shifted between the collapsing ceiling and Morales, understanding dawning in his eyes. Grabbing his nearby officers, he jerked them around, pointing toward the roof. Orders flew from his mouth as he pointed to the trucks and then towards the bowing bay doors. The troops caught on, spreading the word, panic turning to purpose and purpose to action. Two men climbed into the nearest Humvees, started them up, and drove them thirty yards to the bay doors. Three more trucks pulled in behind those, Captain Jones standing in the middle of it all, directing traffic with his waving hands.

Morales reeled to find Smith doing the same thing, spinning troops and pointing them toward vehicles. He made a beeline for his excavator, climbing into the cabin and powering the big machine to life. Carefully he put it in gear, spun it on its tracks, and edged it to the front, parking it tight behind the other trucks. With a gasp, he killed the engine and jumped down, dancing back to avoid getting hit by an Army Growler that flew up behind the excavator.

Morales climbed onto the Growler's hood, traipsing over the roof and down the backside, leaping to the next one. From vehicle to vehicle, he staggered and slipped, losing his balance and nearly falling a handful of times. Eyes on the collapsing ceiling, he watched as thick pieces of steel and insulation fell under the weight of tons of ice and snow. An enormous slab of ice broke away, shaped like a dagger, slamming through a Humvee's roof, pinning it to the floor in a massive crash of metal and breaking glass.

Even as the blizzard poured in bearing destruction, the toxic cloud flowed up and outside in a vortex of air currents, clearing the air of the fumes that had been choking them. With the gaps in their shelter came a blistering stiff wind that whipped through the warehouse, knocking soldiers to their knees and sending hats flying off. Morales slammed his hands to his cheeks as his skin felt like it was being flash-frozen and flames from a burn barrel sent a whirl of glowing cinders into the racks and rafters, catching some of the remaining supplies on fire. The flames flared up and expanded, growing into a proper blaze and Morales leapt from the truck, reaching into the rear seat and grabbed an extinguisher. He spun on his toes, looking for his friend and screaming at the top of his lungs as he wove his way toward the flaming racks.

"Hey, Smith! Smith!"

"What?" the lieutenant shouted back from where he stood halfway across the warehouse.

Morales pointed at the racks as flames engulfed old wooden skids, paper materials, and cardboard and Smith grabbed several soldiers, shouting for more extinguishers, pointing at the growing inferno. In the sea of creeping vehicles and chaotic stampede, Morales climbed on a hood, leaping across to another, dancing on the balls of his feet. His boots landed heavily, denting the hoods, slipping and sliding on trickling ice shards.

Finally he reached the main aisle, jumped down, and circled around the first rack, which was already partially collapsed from when the bulldozer had crashed into it earlier. Flames were dancing up to the second level and climbing and Morales pulled the pin on the fire extinguisher, aimed the nozzle, and squeezed the handle. A gust of powdery white squelching agent blasted the base of the skids, mingling with the falling snow and blistering winds. While his efforts partially snuffed the fire, the wind drove the flames higher, stretching them together like fiery tongues.

Morales's cheeks burned as hot and cold wafts of air alternately buffeted him. Squeezed into the thin space between the racks, he crept closer to the base of the fire, cinders flashed towards his face, forcing him to jerk away. The metal racking reacted to the intense, clashing temperatures, bending and grinding against pressures it wasn't built for. A moment later, six columns of fire-squelching agent shot through from the other side. Soldiers stood on vehicles and directed their nozzles at the flames, countering the fire's fierceness.

Morales was caught in a dangerous position, the wind and gusting extinguishers sending the soot and cinders back in his direction, loose material raining down on his head. A big section of smoldering wood separated and plunged toward him and he spun on his heel and dove to the floor, landing hard, catching his chin on the concrete as he kicked and crawled for the main aisle.

Timber and metal crashed around him in a storm of cold flames, the smell of his own burning hair stuffed up his nose. He winced and grunted and gasped, fearful of sucking in flying embers. Eyes closed, he wriggled ahead blindly until his hand landed on a boot, then looked upward to see that it was Smith, and the lieutenant snatched him by his coat and jerked him to his feet. He began a frantic, abusive swatting of Morales's head and neck, knocking him around and beating the flames until they petered out.

Morales threw back his own hood, grabbing the lieutenant's shoulders. "It's coming down! It's coming down!"

As the racks collapsed against one another, the top level dropping in a clatter of smoke and ruins, they sprinted away, clambering onto a truck. They leapt toward safety, skipping from one hood to the other like boulders in a creek. Fire nearly out, the soldiers gave up and scrambled to escape the collapse. Morales slipped and fell, landing on a windshield. Rolling over, he stared at the back of the warehouse where almost all the toxic fumes had escaped. All that remained was the constant avalanche of ice and snow, covering everything in a smoking white mist.

The roof split open like a ruptured ship, hull breached, pieces of fiberglass, metal sheeting, and drywall swinging in massive chunks, plunging, crashing. Captain Jones, in the thick of it, grabbed at soldiers, lifting any that had fallen into the gaps and shoving them toward the bay doors and away from the collapsing section. Morales scrambled to his feet, slipping on the wet hood and nearly falling again. He threw in with the captain, helping the troops retreat under the catastrophic barrage of elements. The wind whipped in blinding flashes of ice and sleet but, to his surprise, it had lost its sting.

The rumbling faded, tapering into nothing. He helped another man up from the crowded floor and stood with his shoulders hunched, gasping on cold fresh air, hating the ache but relishing its pureness after withstanding so much of the smokey fumes. The wind gave one more gust before it died off, leaving a swath of gray light illuminating the warehouse floor. The soldiers stared at the quiet snowfall drifting through the stark grayness, casting their faces upward, taking deep breaths of the crisp air, leaning over and coughing the gunk out of their lungs, spitting it onto the floor. Eyes clearing, the breeze sweeping out the toxicity, Morales turned to Smith with an exuberant smile as the lieutenant clapped him on the shoulder.

"In the future, we should try to avoid warehouses."

A deep belly laugh burst from Morales's chest, forcing him to cough and choke for a good 30 seconds. When it was over, they spotted Jones once again gathering the officers to him. As the pair made their way over, stepping from truck to truck, he placed his hand against his chin and brought it back with a spot of blood.

"Well, that could have been a hell of a lot worse," he said, wiping his fingers on his coat.

"You got that right." Smith chuckled again as they stood on the APC, staring at the captain as he issued more orders.

"Okay, people. It seems the spin-up storm has died down. Don't ask me how or why, but I'm not complaining."

Several of the men and women standing around echoed the captain's sentiments with nods and murmured comments.

"So, what I need from you people is a full damage assessment. I need to know how many trucks we have left and which ones are buried. As we move vehicles outside to clear the warehouse, we can use the excavators to dig out trapped ones as long as it's safe to do so.

"In the meantime, we've still got several trailers left to fill with supplies, and a replacement convoy on the way. So, let's pick up where we left off and keep things moving." The captain turned his bright blue eyes on the gathering crowd, where they stood half-charred and exhausted. "I want us to split up. On one team, I want the big plows and spare troops to get back to clearing the other warehouse. Morales and Smith, you're with me. I've got a special assignment for you. Okay, troops, let's get some fires going again. The fresh air is nice, but we have to remember to stay warm."

Morales gave his partner a confused look, but the lieutenant only shrugged and jumped from the APC to the Humvee's hood. They stood around and waited as the captain invited Brozowsi and LaPlante to joint them. Jones issued a few more orders, watching as the bay doors rolled up, allowing in a brutal wind that caused the soldiers to clench up again, then Smith turned to his assembled four.

"Get inside the truck," he said, dropping between a pair of vehicles and climbing behind his Humvee's wheel.

Smith entered on the passenger side next to the captain while Brozowski, LaPlante, and Morales took the back. Once they were settled, Jones waited until a few trucks pulled out before he started the Humvee and drove out into the rear lot where he parked the truck and produced a logistical map of the warehouses. He spread it across the dashboard, leaning sideways so everyone in the backseat could see.

"What are we looking for, Captain?" Smith asked. "Are we going for another warehouse?"

The captain grinned and tapped his finger at a spot on the map directly behind the bay doors in a wide field. "Nope. We're searching for this puppy right here. It's a bunker they wanted us to find while we were here. They lost contact with the entire facility when the electric and internet died. We don't know what or who's down there, but command wants it found, so that's what we're going to do."

Morales glanced between the top edge of the map and the thin sliver of light that showed the ice and snow covering the field ahead. "You mean out there? Captain, that's a whole lot of super deep snow, probably 6 to 8 feet of it at minimum going for a quarter mile or more."

"Big deal," Jones said with a narrow-eyed glance back at the specialist. "Need I remind you that we just uncovered this humongous warehouse? What's so tough about finding a little bunker entrance?"

Morales scoffed, laughing as he shook his head. "I don't mean to sound negative, sir, but at least the warehouses had a shape. Digging around out there… It's going to be like finding a needle in a haystack."

Brozowski and LaPlante both nodded in agreement where they sat next to him, but Captain Jones shrugged, his bright red eyebrows ticking upward. "Don't look at it like you're searching for a needle in a haystack. Look at it like you're digging for ancient, buried treasure. Like the tomb of an Egyptian king and queen." The way he said it made them snicker, and Smith interjected.

"We'll be digging up a tomb, but there won't be any Egyptian kings and queens inside."

Jones dropped a heavy paw on the lieutenant's shoulder. "Come on, you know this is going to be fun."

"Yeah, a hell of a lot of fun. Woo-fricken-hoo."

* * *

Morales worked the excavator controls in a well-choreographed dance between his two hands, shifting back and forth, pushing and pulling as he scooped up buckets of snow, spun the entire cabin around, and dropped the load into the dump truck's bed. He'd already dug a good 30 yards into the open field, cutting a six foot deep, twenty-five foot wide trench all the way through to a patch of frozen grass, the faithful Caterpillar engine grinding onward, unfazed by the unseasonable cold, willing to do Morales's bidding until it would eventually draw to a clinking, clanking halt, and die. The machine's tracks churned the grass and snow, turning it into mud as he shifted back and forth vigorously while Brozowski, LaPlante, and Smith worked a small crew of soldiers with shovels and picks who chiseled side paths like moles digging for a fat meal with the help of the smaller excavator, one with a sixteen-inch-wide bucket.

While the map showed the entrance should be about forty yards straight out, they had no landmarks to reference because of heavy snow burying everything. Still, the team worked on as night approached, the light from dozens of nearby burn barrels illuminating the sky with a warm orange glow. The farther he dug his trench through the field, the more he felt alone. The only lights were from the internal cabin and instrument displays and the two spotlights on the outside, pointed at the endless white tundra where the excavator's arm cast a long, ominous shadow.

Behind him, Morales sometimes spotted the headlamps of other trucks driving up to the second warehouse, digging it out beneath the chilling night sky. The fact that a majority of the troops were working on one goal while Jones's group was off on a side mission made him feel even more alone.

He grabbed the radio mic from his dashboard and pressed it to his mouth. "Hey, Captain Jones? I'm running out of fuel. Can you hook me up?"

The captain came back with an immediate response. "I'll have someone run a hose out to you right away. How are you feeling?"

"Like I'm pissing into the wind, but otherwise okay."

"You think this was a dumb idea?"

"No, sir. But I remember what the map showed us, and I've been thinking we're probably digging in the wrong area."

"How so?"

"If you look at how the first two warehouses are positioned, they're farther apart than the map indicated. And I'm sure it's not an exact match of the compound layout."

"All right. Go on."

"Well, I've dug an enormous circle out here, about 30 yards in diameter." Morales sighed. "I'd like to stop digging here and angle more towards the south. I think the bunker is farther than we think."

A pause lingered several seconds before the captain came back. "I'll tell you what. You've been out there digging all afternoon, and you know the area. I never doubted you back in Reynosa and Monterey, and I won't do that now. If you think it's a little farther south, go for it."

"Thank you, sir."

A pair of soldiers appeared around a curve in the trench, carrying a long fuel hose between them. They each waved, and he returned the gesture, content to sit in the warm cabin while they plugged the hose in and filled the tank. When they were done, Morales gave them a wave and kicked the excavator into motion, left with the trailing scent of diesel fuel being carried off into the night sky.

With a fresh wave of motivation, he drove the machine to bite into the snow like a hungry child eating an endless supply of frosty white ice cream. It took out big chunks and dropped them off to the side, leaving the smaller icy debris for the bulldozer crew to clear. The mechanical whirl of the hydraulics and engine became hypnotic, and over the next hour Morales maneuvered the machine deftly to its own song. Deeper and deeper he cut, falling into a tired trance, going by instinct alone, settling the machine into a slight indention in the grassy field. It was only when his bucket's teeth cracked on a concrete walkway that he grew excited.

Grabbing the radio mic, he pressed the talk button. "Cap? This is Morales. I just hit a walkway, sir. I think I'm close."

"Good work, son. I'll send Smith and the others right away."

Following the new direction, he dug excitedly, loosely and tiredly, the excavator responding like he was leaning on a drunken friend after a long night at the bar. He cut a swath on either side of the concrete as it wound its way to the south before stopping as Smith and his group meandered up and dug behind him, widening the path for more tools and implements to be brought in.

Morales focused on a flat piece of hard-packed ice and snow, bucket crunching as the caterpillar strained to cut through, keeping his motions more rigid and refined in order to avoid hurting any of the nearby men. Gusts of wind seeped into the cabin, frigid air slipping between gaps in the frame, turning his feet and legs numb with cold. Still, his chin remained down, eyes staring at the field of snow that had become his domain. His shoulders ached where they slumped over the controls, instrument panel a blur as he approached the end of his mission.

Soon, he'd dug to the ground and hit something that didn't sound like a piece of walkway stone. He lifted the bucket and lowered it again, the teeth knocking against a heavy, hollow structure. Smith appeared outside his window, tired eyes alight with excitement.

"Did you hear what I heard?" The lieutenant shouted.

"Yep. I definitely heard something. I think this is it. Call Jones up while I clear the entrance."

Just speaking the words sent a chill down his spine. Digging for the bunker hadn't felt like the most productive work before, but it suddenly became the *only* important work. The excavator attacked the snow with a vengeance, bucket falling, cracking through ice, curling, and lifting away mounds of frosted debris until finally Smith waved his hand for him to stop.

Morales raised the excavator's arm and tucked the bucket under. Leaving it idle where it stood, he hopped out, boots touching steady ground for the first time in hours. He staggered a little in the cold, leaning on Brozowski as he made his way to Smith. To his left, he saw the results of his ravenous carving: raised from the flat area was a concrete dais with two massive doors set into it.

Brozowski, LaPlante and their crew started clearing the ice and hard-packed debris off the top until they reached the security panels which they flipped up, hovering over them, using specialized electronic gear to break into it and enter the necessary codes. While they worked, Morales slapped the lieutenant probably a little too hard on the shoulder, a wide grin on his face.

"I just found us some ancient Egyptian treasure," he laughed. "What do you think about that?"

Smith had bundled himself up again, his blue eyes peering out at Morales through a pair of clear coated goggles. "I think you're delirious. You need to get some rest, man, you've been out here for hours without a break."

"And miss the find of my lifetime?" Morales forced a grin, though Smith's words rung true. His knees were buckling, his shoulders ached from hunching over the controls and his eyes burned with exhaustion.

Captain Jones jogged up just as Brozowski and LaPlante got the security code bypassed and the group conferred for a few seconds before one of them hit a button on the side panel, causing the ground to rumble. All eyes jerked toward the cement door on the right as it rose on a big hydraulic arm and they retreated, surprised that something actually worked. Once raised, the soldiers approached and stood around the yawning entryway, peering down a wide staircase that spiraled downward into the darkness with only the dim glow of emergency lights to see by.

Jones stepped to the edge and gestured. "Well, Morales. You found it. You can go first."

Smith tried to get in his way. "I don't think that's a good idea, Captain. He's-"

"I'm fine." Morales pushed past Smith and took the initial steps down, careful not to slip as his soles crunched on chunks of ice toppling inside. Grabbing a flashlight from his coat, he flipped it on and angled the beam downward, stepping carefully and quietly, the heavy footfalls of the others following him, their boots echoing in the oddly shaped chamber.

The stairwell's core was a thick slab of concrete with no doors or markings for the first fifty or so feet until, finally, a notation on the inside wall read *First Level – Administration*. A short time later, they reached a flat landing with a massive steel door facing them which Brozowski and LaPlante got to work on, cracking open the security panel and working their magic with their specialized instruments. Morales stepped back to stand next to Jones and Smith, the shadows of a half-dozen other soldiers on the stairwell behind them.

"They must still have generators or emergency power." Smith stared at the door with a nervous expression.

"The frost hasn't reached this far down. Yet." Morales noted as he breathed out, unused to *not* seeing his breath.

The security panel beeped and the massive slab clicked and popped with an echo that streaked to the top of the chamber. Another pair of soldiers joined Brozowski and LaPlante, all four gripping the thick handle, eight hands heaving it with a chorus of grunts.

The steel slab slid open, silent on its well-oiled hinges, a gust of warm air blowing across their cheeks, carrying with it the faint but certain smells of cooked foods, ozone, and habitation. Everyone leaned in as the door swung wide, peering into a dimly lit hallway with metal grating that stretched twenty or thirty yards into the darkness.

Ears straining, Morales's eyes shot wide as voices called to them. "Hello? Who's there? Are you military? Boy, are we glad to see you guys!"

Chapter 13

Tom McKnight
Nuevo Laredo, Mexico

The sound of a blaring alarm startled Tom awake from a restless sleep, the noise loud and blaring, shrill all the way down his spine. He sat bolt straight, looking around the room, trying to remember who and where he was. Daylight penetrated through the cracks in the walls, casting dots and squiggles of gold across the floor and next to him Jack and Linda cried out, throwing the covers off, squinting, blinking sleepily in surprise.

The revolt.

Swinging his legs off the sleeping pallet, Tom slipped on his boots and laced them up fast as Barbara flew in from the front of the store where she'd been on watch, movements hurried and stiff though her expression remained calm.

"I think it's happening," she said with a firm nod. "Alarms are going off across the camp."

"It's definitely happening." Tom stood and crossed to his winter gear hanging over a chair by the table. "Get the kids ready to go. I'm going out to have a look."

Barbara shot straight for Jack who, like his sisters, was already half dressed, wearing several layers of light jackets and long underwear. The MREs and supplies were bundled into four homemade backpacks, strung together with straps of leather and string, preparations made the night before. Outside a rifle cracked in the distance, someone yelled and shouts echoed as a rip of gunfire sent chills dancing along Tom's spine, and he threw on his coat, gloves, and hat, and zipped himself up tight.

"Come to the front when you're ready." He told the children, looking to Sam at the end. "Make it fast."

Without waiting for a response, he strode out to the pharmacy floor and retrieved his shiv and pipe off the counter. Hefting the weapons high, he shoved the shelving aside with his shoulder and unwrapped the cable holding the door shut. The door cracked open, muted sunlight spilling into the room, the blaring alarms washing over him in full force, seeming to come primarily from the outside of the encampment. A mist hung over everything, its thickest point five to ten feet above the pavement, clinging to the buildings and foliage and obscuring the view – the perfect conditions for an attempted uprising.

Boots pounded the concrete and a half dozen shadows sprinted through the haze in front of him on the refugee side, running hard for the eastern gate. Adjusting his grip on the pipe, Tom threw the door wider and stepped outside as gunfire popped off again, a sporadic rattle of small arms fire cutting through the brisk morning air, a slight waft of gun smoke arriving on a chilled breeze.

Someone screamed again and a chorus of people shouted back, though he couldn't hear what they were saying. His shoulders clenched tight, eyes narrowed as he homed in on the conflict's direction. "It's coming from the eastern gate, for sure," he said, glancing back to see if Barbara and the kids were ready. "I'm glad we're not heading there."

"You won't be heading anywhere."

He spun left on the balls of his feet, raising the pipe as one of Marty's hulking, bear-sized guards stepped from the alley. The big man appeared puffed up, wearing an extra large vest, arms thick with layers of winter weather clothing, the ear flaps of his hat pulled down and strapped under his chin. At his side, he held a long wooden ball bat with barbed wire wrapped around the end.

"Stay back," Tom warned, hefting his weapon.

"You're a little outmatched," the man said with a grunt, turning sideways, cocking the bat.

"I'd put my money on me."

The man feigned a swing, forcing Tom to shuffle backwards before returning the gesture, taking a swing cut at the man's head. The quick move startled his opponent, causing him to jerk back or have his jaw broken and, pressing his position, Tom swung the pipe two consecutive times, swatting the giant's left shoulder and arm, drawing pained grunts from his shaking jowls.

Tom was about to take another swing when a shuffle of feet behind him made him spin and duck away, his pipe thrown up in defense. A crowbar swept in and connected with a clang, knocking him backwards and off balance and with a gasp, Tom faced his new opponent. It was the other brute who'd been with Marty the day before, both men he'd run off by his threatening their leader's life with a shiv. The new threat wore a red coat to his partner's brown, arms thick with layers of long underwear and coats. The pair slid in beside each other to pin Tom's back against the wall, looming large, limiting his options to move. They were massive brutes - but they weren't fast.

The second man took another swing, but Tom danced to his left, away from the door and his vulnerable family. He slipped by them and spun to draw them into the wider courtyard, crouching, feigning an attack but quickly withdrawing. They rounded on him, crowbar and baseball bat weaving warily in the air, threatening to take his head off.

"Why don't you stay still, little buddy?" The first thug spoke through thick facial hair, mustache thick on his upper lip. "It'll be easier on you."

"That's okay." Tom leapt from his crouch with a swing, taking aim at the raised bat, his lead pipe whacking against wood then swiping at thin air as the slower man finally got out of the way. The other stepped in and drove Tom off before he could land something solid and with a curse of frustration, Tom took two paces back, unable to find an advantage against both at the same time, no matter how slow they were.

The pair shared a look, fat heads nodding like they'd planned ahead, spreading out to flank him again. Tree trunk legs carried them around to either side, trapping him, weapons sweeping in to attack him simultaneously with deadly arcs. He ducked beneath the crowbar first, lunging forward, but the heavy bat landed, smacking him across the small of his back. Grunting in pain, Tom swept his pipe in a backward motion, hitting the thug in the chest with a thud and receiving a surprised exhalation for his efforts as the man grabbed for the pipe, but Tom spun and jerked it away.

The crowbar clipped his elbow as he cleared the trap, numbing it with a flaring pain through his shoulder and neck. With his back toward the pharmacy once more, he feigned another attack, but the pair came at him together, wood and metal launching at his head in a flurry of motion. Retreating, flailing with the pipe, Tom stepped to his right, away from the pharmacy's front door as the blows rained down. Pain erupted all over his body as the men pummeled and clipped him with the ends of their weapons, his jacket tearing on the barbed wire, left forearm flying out to keep the man off him. He fought back, going toe-to-toe for a moment, grunting and growling like an animal as he connected, rewarded with a yelp of anger and shock at his vicious swing.

Dangerously exposed, Tom jerked away, throwing himself backward to barely avoid a vicious swipe, the ball bat's prickly barb catching his chin and slicing the skin in a sharp snap of pain. The men continued to close in, drawing nearer when a furious burst of motion took them by surprise. Barbara flew from the pharmacy's front door and charged at them, clutching a thick piece of wood high, screaming as she brought it down on the second man's head with a crunchy, meaty thwack. His shoulders jerked upward, hat ducking as he staggered beneath the blow. She swung again, but the man had already turned and raised his forearm to block it, but the heavy wood connected with a thud regardless, dust and splinters flying everywhere, the man's face tightening into a grimace as an anguished scream escaped from his lips.

Distracted by Barbara's attack, the man had no chance to defend himself against Tom's follow-up as he whipped his pipe into the man's face with a sick, bone crunching sound. The left eye socket smashed inward, collapsing like a crushed eggshell and the man's chin snapped to the side as his legs buckled, dropping him straight to the ground.

With a feral cry through clenched teeth, Tom turned to find the other man already bearing down on him, spittle flying from his lips, eyes wide with the realization that the odds had drastically changed. The brute snatched Tom's pipe arm with his left hand, holding it away while cocking the ball bat to bring it down. Tom flew against the man, pressing close, grabbing his opponent's weapon arm to lock them in a stalemate, heads butting, faces spitting at each other in rage as they jostled just a few inches apart.

Surrendering to his rage he tensed his neck and shoulders, whipping his head forward several times, smashing his forehead into the man's chubby, bearded face with grunts and growls. Tendons straining, a final scream flew from his mouth as he spasmed one last time, brow crunching the man's soft nose cartilage, driving it into his nasal cavity. Blood burst from the man's face like a popped water balloon, warm liquid splashing everywhere, yet they still struggled, each grasping and pulling for an advantage.

As they fought, Barbara circled behind the man, swinging for his head with her piece of wood, connecting with the back of his skull with an unearthly crunch, tipping the scales that had already been weighed down by Tom's efforts. The gigantic body staggered forward, eyes drifting shut as he stumbled and fell against Tom, sending them both to the ground in a heap. Tom lay beneath the unconscious man, three hundred plus pounds of weight crushing him, and with a twist of his hips and shoulders he freed himself and looked up to see Barbara staring down at them, panting heavily, her face dripping with sweat.

As she saw Tom emerge from beneath the man's body she dropped her weapon, the piece of bloodied wood hitting the ground with a clatter. Tom looked at the man closest to him, then the other one nearby, seeing no movement from either of them. The nearest one was still breathing, albeit very shallowly, and he couldn't tell about the one with the crushed eye socket and temple – not that he cared about the man's condition.

Raising his hand, Barbara slapped her palm into his and she backed up, half squatting to get leverage, pulling him to his feet. They fell into each other's arms for a brief embrace, then turned back to the door, all business, ignoring the fight in favor of sticking to their plan. Barbara leaned in and called to the children while Tom picked up his pipe and looked around for more signs of trouble.

"Let's go, kids," she said, her words a hiss as she still breathed heavy. "Bring the packs with you, your father's and mine, too."

The kids filed through the entrance, Sam and Linda holding their parents' extra packs. Jack ambled out with his own little makeshift pack on his shoulders, wide eyes glancing curiously from the two downed men to his father, gaping at Tom's bloodied chin and the hulking bodies that his parents had taken on and triumphed over.

Swells of shouts filled the air, answered by more rifle fire, the gun play more balanced than before. To the south, soldiers sprinted through a thick layer of mist toward the east gate, rifles cradled in their arms, not even noticing the McKnights.

"Let's go west around the block, like we talked about."

Tom grabbed Jack's hand and pushed him forward as the girls jostled each other, far less shocked at the bodies than Jack was, quickly getting their bearings as they fell in behind Tom and Barbara. Tom guided the group to the block's southern end where they crossed through yards of dilapidated homes filled with shivering trees, the street plagued with abandoned vehicles. With long strides, he stayed on their left, pipe held out and keeping himself between his family and the fence. Bullets flew in from the east side of camp, blowing through the cracked buildings, the soldiers' errant shots taking off pieces of stucco and wood in sharp dust puffs, zipping rounds hitting tree trunks, shredding branches, and sending dry dead leaves floating to the ground.

"Stay down!" he hissed, but it was an impossible command. Between the bursts of gunfire on their right and the threat of the soldiers on the left, the family was vulnerable. Boots crunching on the dry debris, they crept from car to car, from shattered wall to tree, staying hidden and low as the sounds of chaos made a symphony around them. Tom's body ached with the blows he'd received in the fight, back screaming with the pinprick sting of the barbed wire as the adrenaline drained from his system.

He drew his family to a halt at the end of the north block, staring across the road at the burned-out house with the twisted, charred fence. Off to his right, refugees squatted behind a burn barrel and shot around it with rifles they'd managed to get ahold of, no doubt thanks to Marty's machinations. A return round punched through the metal and hit one of the refugees in the chest and cinders flew up from the still burning coals as the man fell backward, the feathers of his coat flying up.

Tom grabbed Jack by the strap of his pack and rushed him across the street, angling left to circle the front of the burned-out building. He dragged the boy past stacks of melted tires and charred wood and garbage, slipping around the corner and squeezing in between the house and the fence. The girls joined them, Barbara forcing the kids to squat low against the chain-link as the mist drifted by, thick, gray and full of shadows.

"It's right there, dad." Sam pointed to a spot on the left where the fire had weakened the barrier. With a nod, he reached out, grabbed the fencing, and gave it a rough shake. Several of the links broke right away, so he gripped either side and yanked it apart like a strong man at a circus, peeling back the edges. Barbara took the other part, each pulling in opposite directions and after straining and groaning, they finally split it wide enough to pass through. Crouched, Tom watched and listened, heart thudding in his chest. With side glances, he caught shadows scurrying in the mist, though he couldn't tell which side they were on or if they were armed.

"Is there a guard?" Barbara asked. "I don't see one."

"I think Saanvi did it. She got rid of the guard."

"Should we go?" Her hand clutched his shoulder, squeezing through his thick layers.

With a deep breath, he searched the surroundings. Errant bullets still zipped and ricocheted off things, but none seemed directed at them. "I think so. I think we can make our move."

He slipped one leg through the gap as if testing the waters, then followed with tense shoulders. Creeping onto the sidewalk, he peered into the impenetrable mist. "There should be some ruins across the street where we can hide." He nodded in the general direction of where he remembered the buildings being, though they were impossible to see in the fog.

With a sidestep, he turned and waved them through. "Okay, let's go."

Sam came first with Jack, the fencing rattling as they crossed to freedom, then Linda and Barbara followed, all with a hunched, frightened postures like animals being released into the wild.

"Where to now?" his wife asked.

"I'm thinking straight ahead." He nodded due north. "We work our way quickly but carefully-"

Hands suddenly clutched his jacket, gripping and spinning him. Tom rolled with the turn, elbow cocked and ready to respond to whoever had grabbed him, but he lowered his arm and grinned when he saw it was Saanvi, the medic's eyes wide but relieved, a tense grin on her lips.

"You made it! I didn't know if you'd make it!"

"It's good to see you." Tom smiled. "We knew you'd come through for us."

"Smooch!" The kids called out in sync, falling around the animal and embracing her as the dog's tail wagged madly, soft whiny barks bursting from her throat as she licked and nuzzled them. The reunion was cut short as a sudden barrage of errant fire buzzed overhead, a pair of rounds hitting the chain-link fence farther east causing them all to duck and cover.

"They're fighting at the eastern gate," the medic said, looking back in the direction of the gunfire. "I sent the guard to help."

"Thank you so much for doing this," Barbara gripped Saanvi's hand tight.

"Yes, we can't thank you enough," Tom agreed. "Which way should we go?"

Saanvi nodded in the direction they were already heading. "I hid some supplies north of here. It's a deserted area with plenty of places to hide. They'll never look for you with this fighting happening." She handed him a piece of paper. "Here are the directions."

"Come with us," he urged, clutching her jacket as rest of the McKnights moved ahead.

"I'd love to go, but I can't." The medic shook her head and pulled back, dark eyes shifting toward the east where the fighting was heaviest. "I owe it to the captain and my fellow soldiers to help them. You're good people, but I can't abandon them in their time of need."

"But after the revolt, assuming it's successful, there'll be nothing here for you," Tom argued. "The camp will be in disarray, maybe even overrun. You could be killed by these assholes."

Still five feet from Tom, Saanvi hesitated, uncertainty mirrored in her eyes, her mouth moving wordlessly as she searched for an excuse. More gunfire erupted, closer than before, and Saanvi cried out in pain as a single shot tore from the mist and punched her in the chest. The round penetrated flesh, bursting from her back in a blast of blood and cloth. Her body convulsed, arms and shoulders thrown forward, a startled gasp ripping from her throat. Hands flying to her chest, she staggered backwards and fell as Tom lunged forward, arms reaching, catching her just before her head hit the pavement.

Holding her shaking form, he stared into her terrified, pain-filled eyes, blood trickling from the corner of her lip, a red spot blossoming on the front of her coat. At first she gazed at the sky, then shifted to meet his face, trying to say something, but it came out as nothing more than a gurgle of blood and spittle on her chin.

Frozen in shock, Tom clutched the woman close, holding her head with one hand. "Saanvi! Tell me what to do, Saanvi. What do I do to help you?!" Right arm supporting her head, he laid her back as far as he dared, trying to keep any more blood from entering her lungs.

The woman shivered and swallowed hard, her eyes blinking rapidly before a sudden calm relaxed her cheeks. She raised a hand to Tom's face, fingers cupping his cheek, blood warm and wet against his skin as her mouth again tried to form words, her breathing growing more intermittent and hoarse as her body convulsed.

"Saanvi," he whispered desperately as he tried to think of a way to help her.

Glancing back with a helpless expression, he saw Barbara's head shaking in disbelief, eyes wide and glassy. Off to the east, the gunfire escalated, more rounds coming toward them, and as he turned back to the wounded medic to start moving her into cover, her hand slipped from his cheek and fell limp at her side as the light faded from her eyes, her whole body sagging to the ground. In a panic, Tom laid her flat, fingers digging inside her hood to feel for a pulse, his heart pounding in his throat, head swirling with dizziness and confusion.

"No, Saanvi! No!" The last twitches of her heartbeat weakened to nothing beneath his fingertips and guilt and sorrow clenched his chest tight as he clutched the lifeless body of his family's savior.

"Tom, we have to go!" Pain flowed freely in Barbara's voice as she called to him. "They're getting closer!"

Nodding absently, he gently released Saanvi's body and turned to follow his family, but stopped at the sound of boots approaching through the mist, Marty and a half dozen of his cronies stepping from the gloom, rifle barrels leveled at the McKnights. The rebel leader's jacket was covered in blood, splatters of it across his cheeks and chin and the man grinned with wide satisfaction. He began to say something to the McKnights when a sound cut him off and he turned, looking into the mist as the sound of a deep, throaty engine grew in volume, roaring toward them, bearing down something emerging from hell itself.

Chapter 14

Commander Tilly

Somewhere in the Amazon jungle

Moisture ran down a grizzled jaw, clinging to the five o-clock shadow on the man's chin before dripping on the forest floor. Ignoring the distraction, ice-cold eyes stayed focused on their target, peering into the dense jungle through a night vision headset. The rainforest was ablaze with the sounds of life, even in the middle of the night, a cacophony acting as both cover for any human-made sounds and a potential alarm if they were disturbed by said human's movements.

The dark shapes of Commander Tilly's SEAL unit crouched in the thick foliage, silent as ghosts, their warm weather camouflage making them invisible as they waited for orders. Tilly spoke into a microphone that curled from his ear to his lips in a sliver of black, his voice barely audible amid the deafening din that assaulted them from all directions. "Echo One to base. We'll have eyes on target in five. Expect an uplink within twenty."

"That's affirmative," came the reply. "We're on standby. Good luck, Echo One. Now going to radio silence."

With a flick of his finger on his earpiece, Tilly switched to localized communications, the secure channel enabling him to speak to his unit as if he were standing right next to them, the jungle's noise filtered and removed.

"Move on me."

The commander emerged from the cover of broad-leafed plants, stepping through the mass of thick foliage that clung to his sweat-stained clothing. Branches swayed above his head as eleven ghosts rose and followed him in a tight V-formation in the darkness. The ground sloped downward to the left, the sweep of deadfall beneath their boots slippery and dank. They ducked under fallen trees and slid over rotting logs and massive stones on their backsides, swinging over to continue their hastened march.

Night insects continued their chatter, enormous ones as long as his hand buzzing by, fat shapes with stingers and stripes, appearing and vanishing in an instant across the night vision. Creatures twittered and chirped, strange hollow knocks and wild animal cries echoing through the jungle mountains. The dense scents of loam and tree rot filled his nose and clung to his wet skin and a thick flock of bats cut the air above their heads, and Tilly glanced up to see a moon eyed monkey staring back at them.

After another minute of marching, the dense canopy released them into a bright clearing, the pale green of his night vision revealing rolling mountains and peaks covered in a fine gray mist and an endless sea of foliage. Using a hand signal, he ordered the men to halt, and the SEALs shrunk into the forest floor like they were made of mist themselves. Flipping up his night vision headgear, he lifted a pair of binoculars to his eyes, his skin moist beneath the camouflage paint coloring his pale features.

Through the advanced night vision lenses, he spied two communication towers jutting up from the trees a hundred yards away, perched on the hillside, half covered with jungle vines and deadfall. Stuck between them, barely visible in the clinging growth, hung a flag and he tilted up his binoculars to see the yellow, blue, and red colors waving in the moonlight.

Lowering the frames over his eyes, he jogged to the right, sticking to the edge of the forest. "I've got contact just up ahead. Prepare to engage. Branson and McClure, you're on flanks. Alpha has the middle."

The clipped affirmatives sounded in his ear, and Tilly sunk into the foliage once more, giving the flankers thirty seconds to get into position. On his mark, they crept up a shallow slope and dropped, crawling to reach the top of a rise. The towers had fallen out of sight to the left, but he spotted the stone-gray barracks and guard buildings nestled into the side of the hill. As he lay on his stomach staring at the formation, sweat dripped down the sides of his face, his stomach tensing as it always did immediately preceding the first firefight of a mission.

"I've got two marks on the second roof and a pair of box bunkers between the buildings. Branson, pin those gunners while we clear the boxes."

Without waiting for confirmation, Tilly raised his hand and signaled, two SEALs standing to creep past him through the knee-high jungle brush. Tilly then rose to a firing position with members of Alpha team spreading out to either side and after a five-second count, he squeezed off several rounds at the sandbags, the quick soft pops of his suppressed weapon grabbing the enemy soldiers' attention.

The SEAL team's fire rained like a hammer from both directions as the soldiers popped up to see where the incoming fire was coming from, slicing sandbags and flesh, silencing the machine guns before they got started. From the corner of his eye, Tilly spotted Branson and his men swing in from ropes, dropping to the second building's roof, their carbon blades plunging in with quick stabs to neutralize the gunners before they fired a single shot.

Tilly sprinted through the jungle, slipping between saplings, sliding on the wet mossy soil toward the barracks as McClure's team hit the building on the left, having already circled around to their assigned area. Under the brush cover, they waited for the door to fly open, troops rushing outside to join the fight only to run into a controlled spray of the SEALs' rifle fire. Enemy soldiers spun and dove, falling to the ground in shrieks of confusion and pain and McClure sprinted up and soft-tossed a grenade inside the barracks, diving to the side and throwing his shoulders against the wall. A muted boom blasted light and heat from the building's seams, hurling fragments back through the door.

The jungle fell silent but for the drifting leaves and drip of water from the upper canopy. With a satisfied nod, Tilly wiped his arm across his brow to swipe away the never-ending sweat as he strode between the buildings, looking around at the carnage his team had swiftly wrought.

"Secure. Form up and converge on the command post."

The black shapes fell into formation behind him once more, slipping through the dense jungle, boots crunching on plush ferns and wide-leafed shrubs, stamping the soggy debris as they circled the top part of the next rise. Tilly spotted a massive tree laying across the forest floor, at least fifty feet long, partially hanging from tangled vines, crushing mounds of foliage as it sat like a dark lump in the pale green of his night vision. The shouts of foreign soldiers reached his ears, and he motioned his men forward to fall into position behind the thick trunk, rifle barrels resting across the rotted wood.

"Branson, McClure. This is your party. We'll draw them in and pin them in place for you."

The SEALs waited for the contingent of enemy fighters to approach through the brush and over the hill and soon Tilly spotted a group moving toward them in the flitting jungle shadows.

"Hold," he whispered as more shapes appeared, the movements growing thicker and faster as they approached in a run, eager to reach the barracks after hearing the distant gunfire of the attack. The commander used their distraction to his advantage, watching them rush headlong through the dense foliage, not noticing the SEALs concealed behind the massive, rotted log until it was too late.

"Now," Tilly spoke calmly as he sighted down the barrel at a target and ripped off a burst of rounds, the rest of Alpha team joining him, unleashing a barrage of hell on the Venezuelan troops. Enemy soldiers fell like puppets with their strings cut at the same time, crying out, arms waving, rifles rattling to the jungle floor.

A few remembered their training and dove for cover, turning to fire on Tilly's position and the SEALs ducked behind the dead tree, bullets plunging into the soft, porous wood, blowing apart clusters of mushrooms and pulp into the air, creating a layer of dust above their heads. "Anytime now, gentlemen," Tilly intoned, stifling a sneeze.

Branson and McClure swept in from the sides, the soldiers catching the remaining enemy troops unawares in a deadly crossfire and a moment later the forest fell silent, the cries of insects and nocturnal animals temporarily abated by the rifle fire and stinking smoke. Tilly let out the sneeze he'd been holding onto and wiped his nose and stood, rested his backside on the massacred tree trunk, swinging his legs to the other side.

The team reformed and marched in a V shape formation over the dead bodies and across the sloping jungle. The bugs and birds and beasts had come back into their full volume, voicing their aggravation over the invasion and interruption of their domain. Sweat poured down Tilly's cheeks and ran beneath his clothing, making his skin itch. The salt runoff dripped into his eyes, stinging and burning, making him want to take a towel to his face. Tilly ignored the agitations and focused on reaching the command post.

They found the domed-shaped building fifty yards farther through the dense jungle. Like a sphere cut in half, the dome butted against the sheer cliff that stretched a hundred feet above them, its drab gray concrete walls glowing dark green in his night vision, crawling with thick layers of creepers.

A pair of Venezuelan guards took potshots from their sandbag positions beside the building, but Branson's fleet-footed team made quick work of them, utilizing advanced flanking techniques which the enemy never saw coming. Threat eliminated, he strode to the command post door, moving to the left side as SEALs spread around the building.

The commander removed a package of explosives and slapped it on the metal just above the security pad, then stuck an ignition device in the soft clay and slid several feet along the concrete wall.

"We need the leader alive," he ordered. "The rest are KOS."

With the touch of a button, the explosives ignited, snapping the door outward, tearing it off its hinges to land in the dirt. The SEALs filed in, moving tightly together to the left and right. Gunfire rattled the air, striking the concrete wall on the other side for several seconds until they fell quiet and one by one the team members shouted out "all clear" reports.

Taking off his goggles, a waft of cool, dry breeze wicked away the moisture from Tilly's cheeks as vents circulated fresh currents through a room full of workstations and monitors. A series of larger screens were mounted on the wall across the room and the humming fans and smell of electronics ran counterpoint to the natural jungle just outside the door.

Four Venezuelan corpses lay around, two on the floor, and another pair collapsed over the desktops, their blood still dripping into their keyboards. In the back of the room was a fifth man, still alive, being held by his men – the commander of the local squad that they had just obliterated. Dressed in a beige officer's shirt, the man's clean-shaven face was a mask of barely restrained hostility and rage.

With a glance at the Venezuelan commander, Tilly strode to the workstation where two laptops rested on a wide black desk with steel legs, gesturing for the SEALs to bring the man over. He lifted the laptop lids, watching the data flow roll down the screens as he moved the mouse, prompting a sign in warning that requested verification via a biometric reader.

Straightening, he turned to the Venezuelan, speaking in fluent, accented Spanish. "What's your name?"

"I am Commander Jose Rivera of the Venezuelan Defense Force. What do you American dogs want with me and my country? Why did you kill my men?"

Tilly nodded to a biometric pad sitting between the laptops. "All I need is your hand, Rivera." He stepped aside to give the man room. "Just unlock it for me, then step away."

The Venezuelan commander only stared at the SEAL leader with contempt, his eyes widening slightly as Tilly unsheathed a black-bladed knife from a sheath on his leg.

"Your hand will be going onto the reader. Whether or not it's attached to your arm when that happens is up to you."

With a slow nod and hard swallow, Rivera strode to the hand-shaped pad and placed his palm and fingers on it, the device tracing a red ring around the outline. A moment later the lights turned green, and the warning signs on the laptop screen disappeared. While two SEALs pulled the commander aside, another stepped in with a pair of cables that ran outside to their primary transmitter. He plugged the ends into the laptop's USB slots and began typing on the keyboards, talking as he worked.

"Okay, I've just removed all the security required to access the mainframe. Now, all I need to do is merge the data and compress it for sending." His fingers danced over one keyboard, then switched to the other as he kicked off a series of data flows, the lines scrolling upward so fast Tilly couldn't read them.

"You killed all of my men?" Rivera's tone was accusatory, his dark eyes resting on the SEAL commander like he was the devil.

"Yes." Tilly nodded.

"Thirty. Seven. Men."

"And I'd do it again," Tilly responded in an emotionless voice.

"At least tell me how many casualties we caused you. It would hearten me to know my brothers stood up to you."

"I'm not interested in debating you, Rivera. Leave me alone or end up like your men. Your choice."

The Venezuelan's face contorted with rage, spittle flying from his lips as he spat the next words. "You American dogs will not get away with this. There are treaties against this type of unprovoked--"

Tilly whipped his sidearm from its holster and fired a bullet between the man's eyes, dropping him on the spot.

"Get him out of here and wait for us outside." Tilly motioned at the SEALs in the room, who dragged Rivera's body out, leaving Tilly and his tech alone in the room. The commander switched his communication device to a wider band and strolled toward the door, watching as one of his men knelt next to a five-foot tall mobile antenna, the web-like dish standing open in a rough circular shape of 10 inches in diameter.

"Status report."

The tech flashed him a thumbs up sign. "Transmitting data now."

Tilly glanced up, most of the sky blocked by the thick canopy stretching above them. "Base, this is Echo One, we've started the link. Can you confirm on your end?"

"That's affirmative. We are receiving the data stream from your location."

Commander Tilly stepped outside, scanning the surroundings where his soldiers kept watch, feeling satisfied with their overall performance on the mission. Somewhere around the halfway point of the data upload, the radio chirped in his ear.

"Echo One, this is base. Be advised, we are no longer receiving your transmission. Can you check things on your end?"

The commander crossed to the antenna array, squatting next to the operator. "They're saying the transmission failed. Is everything still good?"

The soldier bent and looked at a small panel on the side of the unit. Even the commander could tell the lights were green, and the data flow indicator blinked green. "Everything looks great. We've got solid link to the satellite."

Fists clenched and tapping against his thigh, Tilly strode back to the control post entrance to check things inside, but he stopped before crossing the threshold, keeping perfectly still as the distinct *chuff-chuff-chuff* of helicopters grew to dominate over the sounds of the jungle. Rotors cut through the air, growing louder, drawing him back outside to look toward the sky and the rest of his team joined him, gripping their weapons as they stared upward.

"Are we being picked up at this location, sir?" Branson spoke what they were all thinking, the small, tough soldier standing near the transmitter on the uneven ground. "Wait… no, those are definitely not ours."

"They're Eurocopters," Tilly confirmed. "Cougars, if my ears are correct."

Running lights slid into view above them, spotlights shining through cracks in the trees, beams bouncing off their sweat-glistening faces. The jungle canopy reflected the light as a gusting wind spun leaves and forest debris everywhere and Tilly made out the Venezuelan flag emblazoned on the choppers' undersides. Ropes descended from the Cougars' crew quarters, dark shapes sliding into the surrounding forest and Tilly pointed upward, giving the order.

"Fire on those aircraft!"

The SEALS began ripping off bursts, peppering the choppers' bellies and return gunfire erupted from the forest as the enemy soldiers touched down and took attack positions, firing at them from the dense foliage.

The lights around the transmission equipment and base made for an easy target and several rounds smacked into the delicate equipment, shooting up sparks and sending the SEALs scattering.

"Hold position and find cover!" Tilly shouted, stepping back into the control post as he flipped over to the wider band.

"Echo One to base!" He lifted his voice over the wind and sounds of ricocheting bullets. "We've got a problem here. I have three enemy helicopters above us, dropping troops on our heads. Our transmission gear is compromised. Please advise." As Tilly spoke, he gave hand signals to his soldiers, rounding them up into a defensive formation around the domed structure.

The call came back. "Echo One, we show more tangoes inbound. Advise you to rendezvous at the drop site."

"Understood." He switched to the local secure band. "Saddle up! We're getting out of here! Prepare to break through and return to the rendezvous point."

Rifle gripped tightly, he left the control room and fell into a crouch outside, counting eleven shadows, his men hunkered behind trees and ducking below the thick foliage.

"Move out, on me!"

In a chorus of condensed rifle fire, the SEALs shot east toward the flashing muzzles in the forest. With no time to take measured steps, Tilly charged ahead, head and shoulders down, plowing back the way they'd come. He spotted a muzzle flash to his left, rounds zipping through the foliage at him and the commander responded by firing on the fly, slightly off balance on the mossy, uneven forest floor. His aim true, his target screamed from the darkness, barrel blazing upward as he plunged backward, dead.

The SEALs fell in behind him, shadows encasing them as they ran headlong into the dense night, their tight formation breaking through the line of Venezuelans as they charged at full speed toward the barracks. Those in the rear turned and covered the retreat, moving back in groups to support each other and ensure they couldn't be overwhelmed.

"How the hell did they find us?" Branson asked, his words breathless.

"I don't know," Tilly responded, slowing to a crawl as he sighted two more Venezuelans ahead. He fired, peppering a tree, the rest of the team engaging the same target, their collective rounds biting through wood and flesh to end the threat. They were off and running again in a flash, approaching the original barracks they'd attacked when one of the team members screamed from somewhere close, the groans that followed adding insult to their already FUBAR'd mission.

"Who was that?" Tilly asked, searching the night for more targets.

"Reggie," someone responded. "Hit in the leg, but we've got him."

The SEALs moved slower through the dense foliage and deadfall, forced to carry the wounded soldier and Tilly bumped into logs and sharp stumps, hips and thighs taking a beating as he forged a path toward the rendezvous point. A pursuing Venezuelan helicopter found them as they neared the barracks, pinning them with their spotlights and Tilly guided them through thick patches of forest, hoping to hide beneath the canopy. In the clearing just before the barracks, the Venezuelan helicopter circled around, firing on them and another SEAL screamed, twisting to the jungle floor.

"I want guns on that chopper now!" Tilly shouted, turning his weapon up at the aircraft, sweeping the barrel back and forth, spitting rounds into the sky in a desperate attempt to scare them off. The soldier manning the machine gun flew back, shoulders clenching in pain before he fell from the crew quarters to hang from his tether and the Cougar peeled away. The reprieve was short lived, however, as more Venezuelan ground troops appeared, pouring in behind a hailstorm of bullets.

"Take cover at the barracks!"

Knees high, they sprinted the last thirty yards to the pair of buildings, wrapping around the corners and diving behind sandbags to escape the blistering gunfire. Tilly slipped inside the barracks' blown open door, protected by the thick concrete walls. Poking his head out, he spotted a handful of enemy troops break from the foliage and charge. They came in a staggered, run-and-fire formation, dropping, crawling, and popping up, covering each other expertly as they picked their way toward the SEALs. Their accuracy was uncanny, rounds striking the walls near Tilly's head, spraying brick chips into his face, almost blinding him if not for his goggles.

"Shit, these guys are good!" Branson squealed, firing from around the corner of the first barrack.

The SEALs spat back a withering volley, chewing up foliage and stopping the rush in its tracks, giving better than they received, and after a ferocious few moments the last enemy soldier threw up his arms and died at the edge of the barracks grounds.

Tilly's night vision goggles caught more movement past the clearing, reinforcements entering the fray, and he slipped inside the building, breathing slow and steady as he exchanged a spent magazine for a new one.

"These paratroopers are some tough bastards," someone said. "Definitely not like the first group we encountered."

Tilly lifted the bottoms of his goggles, spilling the accumulated sweat into his lap. "Get loaded and ready to move out."

"They're not Venezuelan," Branson interrupted. "Well, not all of them."

"What?"

"I said, these guys are not all Venezuelan."

Tilly stuck his head and shoulders out to see that Branson had crawled to the edge of the barracks grounds, inspecting the soldier who'd fallen at the edge.

"What's up with him?"

"The insignia on this guy's coat isn't Venezuelan, and he's got light hair and blue eyes. He's not from this continent, that's for damned sure."

"What the hell is he then?"

Branson held up the man's arm, showing a red, blue and white striped flag on it. "Russian."

"Shit."

"You said it."

Tilly clicked his earpiece, connecting to the wider band. "Echo One to base. Be advised. We have engaged with Russian soldiers."

Dispatch came back with a confused reply. "Repeat that, Echo One. Did you say *Russian* soldiers?"

"That's correct. The paratroopers they dropped on us were a mix of Venezuelan and Russian."

"Message received. Continue with your egress."

Branson swung into the barracks with a shocked and worried look. "We need to punch our tickets out of here. I spotted multiple incoming reinforcements. And we still have the choppers to contend with."

Nodding, Tilly gave the order. "Form a defensive posture and retreat to the drop point. Don't stop until you're there. I've got your backs. Beat feet! Fly! Let's go!"

Branson exited the building and fled east with the SEALs as they broke cover and entered the forest, dark shapes pounding across the uneven terrain, ducking beneath bullet-ridden trees and chewed up foliage. Tilly came behind them, backing up as he swept his barrel at the oncoming muzzle flashes, spitting one empty magazine out, tossing it to the ground, and jamming home another. Charging the weapon, he reversed his direction of fire, making it seem like there were more guns covering their retreat, trying only to distract and suppress, not actually hit any targets.

He had no trail to follow, only the pale images in his night-vision goggles showing him where his men had gone. Glancing back, he stayed near his team as bullets flew by, surprised every time one didn't smack him in the face and put an end to him. Eventually, the enemy soldiers realized he was only a single man, and they charged through the tangle at him, the surrounding foliage exploding in a whirling wind of hot dust and shredded vegetation.

Head lowered, Tilly turned and sprinted, leaping deep brush, falling and slipping sideways on the slope. His hip smacked a rock and he stifled a grunt of pain as he scrambled to his feet, keeping the barrel of his weapon out of the dirt. Back on track, he pulled out his GPS as he ran, focusing on the waypoint just two hundred yards to the northeast. Eyes lifted to the sky, he thought he caught the flashing running lights of the Chinook and two U.S. support choppers but the incoming fire distracted him, chasing him through the woods, forcing him to dive into a gully. Rolling to his feet, he picked his way along the muddy earth as it curled up near their drop point.

Exhausted, lungs heaving, he willed himself to keep moving as he crawled out of the ditch, slipping in the mud. Something hissed near his head, and his hand dipped into a slimy pool of muck. With a sneer of revulsion, he sprinted toward what remained of his men. By the time he reached the drop point clearing, the helicopters were just sweeping in. The big Chinook dropped its ladders and hooks to pick up the wounded SEALs while a pair of UH-1Y Venoms cruised over the jungle to engage the Venezuelan aircraft and provide cover for the Chinook.

He spotted seven SEALs either on the ground or being lifted by the pulley retrieval system, Branson strapping Reggie onto a stretcher when Tilly jogged up and they both stepped back as the wounded man flew upward. The air erupted in bright flashes of light, explosions and rattling machine gun fire ripping through the night as the choppers clashed and their lift ropes began to shudder and sway. Tilly started to grab one, but a hail of bullets from the enemy ground troops caused both men to drop and the pair exchanged a nod, raised up, and fired back at the onrushing enemy, blowing through their remaining ammunition.
* * *

A thousand miles away, in the Cuban Presidential Office, space heaters rattle as President John Zimmerman leans over his desk, tuned in to the SEAL team's egress through a conference line. Hands wringing, he listens to the explosions and gunfire as a Venom is chewed to bits by enemy fire, the screams of the crew turning his stomach, then sighs with relief as Commander Tilly and the last SEALs are lifted to safety, the Chinook taking heavy fire as it bends away from the drop site to stagger home with the remaining Venom.

The harrowing escape from the jaws of death is bad enough, but the revelation of Russian troops fills him with a deep, unsettling dread. "There's only one reason the Russians would be involved," he murmurs, looking to General Davidson where he sits on the opposite side of the desk, lips pinched tight in surprise and anger.

"According to reports, the Russians aren't experiencing the kinds of temperature changes we are." The general shifts in his seat, rubbing his stubbly chin in doubt. "They'd only be in Venezuela if they were trying to keep us out."

The two shared a dark look, both having the same thoughts.

"Should we proceed, Mr. President?"

The President's eyes drop to his desk, the last vestiges of hope slipping, falling away like sand through his fingers. When he finally lifts his chin, his expression burns with a determination to fight to the bitter end, regardless of the outcome.

Despite the cold in the room, beads of sweat break out on his brow. He nods as implications circle through his mind, then he swallows hard, the decision made. "We don't have any other choice."

"I concur." Davidson's expression mirrors the president's.

"Okay, then." John's fingers squeezed into a fist. "Pull everyone together. We'll proceed."

Chapter 15
Keith
Somewhere in Texas

The 18 ton Strykers plunged through the snowstorm southwest of San Antonio, sleet gusting off the armored sides as their lowered plows shoved snow from their path. Sixteen knobby wheels ground up icy white flakes as grey clouds chased them ever southward, a pair of hunters in search of prey, armored dogs with their noses down to the ground. The mercenary drivers used camera magnification to scan the distance, searching for blockages of snow and piled vehicles which could put them off course, and twice they'd gone thirty miles down long stretches of highway, only to be turned back and forced to find an alternate route.

The APC's heaters were running at full blast, but Keith sat huddled in the radio chair with his coat bundled tight around him, the older trucks having taken some tough knocks so far on their mission. Deep within the diesel engine's growl was a faint clacking sound, which he associated with suspension damage, and the air that pumped from the vents was only lukewarm.

Serge abruptly spun the wheel to the right, hitting the gas and putting the Stryker into a heavy slide, the armored front-end smacking something hard and metal, the jolt running through the crew quarters before the vehicle settled steadily once more.

"Hey, buddy, why don't you take it easy there?" Keith relaxed his arms from where he'd thrown them out to keep himself from falling out of his seat.

Serge shrugged. "Sorry. Obstacle in the road."

"You couldn't have just slowed down and gone around it?" Keith shook his head, feet planted firmly on the floor to keep his balance against Serge's wild driving.

"In this weather, you slow down, you get stuck. Then, you sit in here until the fuel runs out. Then you die." He turned toward Keith, raising an eyebrow. "You want me to slow down more?"

The agent shrunk into his jacket, saying nothing as Serge snorted and turned back to his driving. A glance back showed Mikael fast asleep atop a bed of backpacks, clutching two cold-weather blankets to his chin like a child on a wintry night, seemingly unbothered by the driving, and Keith felt his regret at joining the mission growing ever stronger.

"Can you read me up there?" Lena's voice crackled from the speakers.

Turning toward the radio console, Keith answered. "We read you loud and clear. Do you have something for us?"

"Another town up ahead we should check. I'm sending you the waypoint now."

"Received," Serge grunted back.

"What's so special about this one?" Keith studied his screen, eyes on the waypoint she'd sent.

"It's about as special is the last one."

"Which means not very." They'd passed three towns on their way to the Texas-Mexico border, each filled with ice and death and the echoes of the old civilization, and none of them with the McKnights.

"This one will be different, I can feel it." Lena's accented voice dripped with mock enthusiasm. "I caught satellite images of our prey traveling this way three days ago, though I could not tell if they entered the town or bypassed it."

Keith nodded, filling his lungs with a deep, hopeful breath. "It's definitely worth checking out."

After two miles they exited the highway onto one of a hundred side roads stretching across the flat state of Texas, all of them snowbound and wind blasted. At the end of the exit ramp, he spotted a sign sticking up from the frost-covered snow that read *Parseville*. Less than a handful of stoplights divided the main roads, signs bent, cables and power lines hanging loose, buried beneath three feet of white.

Serge found an ice-crusted lot to park on and they left the Strykers running as they exited through the rear door. The wind was a demon, whipping their coats against their legs, its bitterness exploiting every gap in their clothing. Like before, they split up, each team starting at one end of the town and working toward the center, leaning against the gusts, pulled their hats tighter and squinting behind their goggles.

Keith's frostbitten toes and fingers ached terribly, causing his teeth to clench in pain as he shuffled through town. Searching for impossible clues, anger fueling his body, he trudged from building to building, disturbing restaurant kitchens, sheds, offices and homes wherever he saw a hint of footprints that might show the McKnights had been there.

The refugees that hadn't evacuated south had raided the remaining pantries, but the food hadn't saved them. Keith and the mercs found groups of frozen corpses holed up inside employee break rooms and kitchens, signs of old fires and beds made of piled sleeping bags. They strode past a tall sign with a horseshoe and *Texas Steakhouse* emblazoned on it and Serge put his shoulder to the door, breaking it open with a crunch of wood. A gathering of thirty stiff frozen people sat bundled up in booths, furniture and partitions dismantled and tossed into a blackened heap in the center of the room. Two bodies lay near the edge, huddled together, candy wrappers and food scraps scattered around their heads, the scent of cold, rotting meat flitting in the air despite the cold, a bleak and nauseating aroma.

"Isn't Texas supposed to be hot?" Serge asked with a wrinkled expression. "I thought it was a desert."

Keith shrugged. "Desert or tundra. Two sides of the same coin." He stared at the frozen dead, piecing together the reasons they'd stayed put. "They must've balked at the evacuation orders, figured they could stick out the storm and take the spoils when things warmed up."

"They were fools," Mikael added.

"Yes."

They left the restaurant, no more informed than before, and met Dimitri and Lena at the APCs. Staring north, Keith pulled his goggles away from his frosted cheeks with a crisp snap and settled them on again. A chill wind blasted them, forcing them to go silent until the gust passed. With a shudder, he blinked into the cold radiating off the winter-rated lenses. In the short time they'd been out, the freezing winds had seeped through his coat, soaking into his muscles and bones. "It's getting even colder. We need to get back inside."

"Much colder than I am used to," Lena said in agreement, trying to stare into the wind but turning her face away.

"Yes, much colder." Mikael added. "And we are no closer to finding our quarry."

"If they're anywhere in these parts, they're either lost or dead. No way could they have gone north if they're still alive – Tom McKnight is too smart to do something like that."

"Then we go south from here on?" Serge asked.

Keith nodded once and they climbed aboard their vehicles and sealed them, leaving on their coats, gloves and hats, desperate to retain any scraps of heat possible. Taking off again, the APCs worked south in a straight pattern, crossing the flat, ice-covered highway, chased by the indomitable cold through the wintry night. The Stryker's tires crunched over ice, passing stubby bumps of cars with layers of hard-packed snow that had grown over them in cocoon shapes, their plows blasting through dense drifts, the frames shuddering with the blows.

Each new town was the same, every stop more agonizing than the last and even the silent giant of a merc dragged his feet when it was time to leave the warmth of the trucks and explore. The enthusiasm shown at the airstrip had worn off in the face of the elements and on more than one occasion Keith had to remind them to do their jobs. By the time they finished searching the city of Encinal, their eyelids hung with sheer exhaustion and refueling the Strykers was a stiff, unenthusiastic exercise that took them a full hour to perform.

Coming in from the snow, stomping his boots up the ramp, Keith realized they were likely done with their search of the surrounding towns. He flopped into the radio seat and eased back, counting the seconds for the mechanical door to shut and cut off the wind. When the clamps finally locked, he let out a heavy sigh and pulled his goggles up to rest them on his forehead. Serge turned in his chair, leaving his headset hanging on its hook as he fixed Keith with a stern look below his frosted eyebrows.

"This is getting tough."

Keith nodded, leaning forward to place his elbows on his knees. "We're not searching any more towns around here, but I don't know what to tell Banks."

As if on cue, a light on the radio console flashed, and he glanced up at the merc before turning toward it. Placing a headset over his ears, he pulled the microphone in front of his lips and answered the call.

"Keith here."

"Any luck?" Banks's voice cracked with static as the wind outside picked up. "Tell me you've picked them up."

"Actually, I don't have very good news." Before Banks could jump down his throat, Keith plowed ahead with his explanation. "Every city within a hundred miles of San Antonio is frozen solid. We've been out searching based on a few clues Lena got from the satellite imaging but if the McKnights hung around, they're dead and buried now."

"You really believe that?" Banks's words were a whispered threat. "They survived the Osprey crash, climbed right out of *that* mess somehow. And you think they'd let themselves freeze in one of those shithole towns?"

"I didn't say that. I'm just saying that if the storms caught them, they're dead."

Banks snorted in derision. "I thought you said these *people* of yours were good. I thought you said they'd have no problem locating our little issue and resolving it."

Keith's glanced around the cabin. Mikael had fallen back onto the packs once more, pressed against a vent, absorbing feeble heat straight from the unit. Serge continued to stare at him, unable to hear what Banks was saying, though he imagined the merc could guess.

"It's too cold." Keith released a sigh. "If we stay out here any longer, we're dead. There's no way the McKnights could be in this area. We need to move south and search there."

Fingers flicked across a keyboard from Banks's end before she came back with a response. "Go to the border camps before they finish their own evacuations." The Colonel paused, clicking a few more keys. "Yes, I think that's the best strategy. If it's as cold as you say it's getting, the McKnight's would have been forced to continue south."

"Any ideas where to start?" Keith placed the microphone on mute and released a heavy sigh, nodding to Serge with a measure of relief.

"I'm sending you a list of holding facilities. The first one on the list is fairly large, located just south of Laredo. Let me know when you receive it."

Eyes fixed to a screen, he watched as a message popped up, indicating a data packet was on its way. The download moved slowly, possibly due to the storm, but eventually downloaded to the Stryker's onboard computer. When the names of the towns came up, he scanned the top ones.

"First one is Laredo, like you said."

"That's the closest and most likely choice." Banks gave an exasperated huff. "Get down there, put boots on the ground, find the McKnights and deal with them. I don't think I need to express what happens to both of us if you fail and this eventually comes to light."

"No." Keith pressed the words between tight lips, voice hoarse from breathing hours of Arctic air. "If they're in the Laredo area, we'll find them. And if they're not, we'll keep looking."

"You don't have an infinite number of chances here." Banks paused, lowering her voice, a note of desperation creeping in. "There are too many questions being asked by those with too much time on their hands. There will be a reckoning soon, and you don't want to be on the losing side when it happens."

"Understood. Let me hop off here, and we'll get going."

"You do that."

Keith cut the connection and sat still, staring at his hands as the truck's heating unit strained and rattled against the unbearable chill. Looking to Serge, he tapped his one good finger on the console and pointed. "We're getting our wish to go south."

"Thank heavens for that." Lena's accent was even thicker in her exhaustion, the hollow-sounding speakers not making it any easier to understand her. "I also received the list of checkpoints Banks recommended. Laredo is eighty miles away."

"I have the waypoint." Serge reached for his headset and slipped it over his eyes. "If the roads hold up, I will have us there in less than two hours."

"Let's not waste any more time." Keith settled back in his seat, grabbing cover from the floor and throwing it over his shoulders, clutching it tight to his chin like Mikael.

"Buckle up," the merc mumbled from where he lay on the backpacks. "It's going to be a long, cold ride."

* * *

They reached Laredo from I-35, closing in on the first checkpoint at Killam Industrial Park, leaving the snow behind them, the roads finally clear of the massive drifts of the stuff. The icy winds still challenged the Stryker's heating system, though not like before, and for the first time Keith could feel himself warming up on the inside.

As they approached, Keith looked through the external cameras, spotting a pair of soldiers in a guard booth. Cars were left abandoned on both sides of the entry lane, doors hanging open, tires flat, belongings scattered on the ground, but there were no people in sight; no one was stampeding south toward warmer climates. They'd either made it through already or remained behind, frozen effigies of a dead civilization.

"I'm surprised they only have a single guard booth." Keith half-whispered his concern as he realized how far the evacuations were coming along.

"It is a ghost town like the others," Serge agreed, slowing as they drew near the small building.

The radio console popped to life, a soldier's voice hitting the line with firm authority. "Attention Stryker units. This is Guard Outpost Laredo One. Can you transmit your identity in key codes, please?"

Keith nodded to Serge as he brought the vehicle to a complete halt, with Dmitri drawing the second APC in behind him. Leaning in, the agent hit the talk button and spoke into the microphone. "Transmitting codes now." He clicked a switch on the console to send the data.

"Will they work?" the merc asked.

"Banks gave us everything we need," Keith affirmed. "At least I hope."

A moment later, the guard came back. "What's your destination, Stryker 298? Why are you here?"

"We're heading to the south barracks. Got a weapons delivery run to make. It's a last bit from the, uh, Asheville Armory. Orders are to deliver it to the captain there."

"Affirmative, Stryker 298. You're free to pass." There was a pause, and the soldier on the other end came through with a slight chuckle. "Any chance you can you take us with you?"

"Negative on that, guard post," Keith laughed. "I'm sure they'll pick you up soon and relocate you boys to a nice sandy beach."

"Roger that, Stryker unit. Good luck with your drop."

Serge edged the APC past the guards and into the warehouse district beyond. The massive lots were empty, abandoned tents flapping in the wind, some uprooted and drifting in the air, two broken down Humvees sitting parked side-by-side near a long, squat building. A pair of generator units rested on trailers nearby and MRE packaging and empty plastic water bottles rolled across the pavement.

"They're already abandoning this post," the merc said. "Not looking good for you Americans."

"They know what's coming," Keith murmured. "Cold, cold, and more cold."

The trucks wove slowly to the south, slipping between abandoned cars and at least two more broken down military vehicles. Turning a camera to the sky, Keith watched helicopters lifting off with cargo containers hanging from ropes, then looked to the GPS screen, using his fingers to zoom in on a map of Laredo. Using the street maps, he navigated for Serge, guiding them closer to the nearest border crossing.

At one point, a pair of soldiers stood in front of an unidentifiable smoldering heap blocking the road, forcing them to swing west along the Rio Grande. They rejoined the highway as it swung them back southwest to a bridge that spanned the waterway where they stopped at a checkpoint station halfway across that was fitted with automated wooden arms that blocked their path. Keith retransmitted his security codes to the guards, and they waved the APC through, though before he gave Serge the go ahead to continue, he fired off a quick question to the guards.

"Hey, guys. Can you give me the location of the internment camp?"

"Uh, which one is that, Stryker unit?"

"I'm not actually sure. We're supposed to meet a captain…" He referred to the list of camps Banks had fed them. "A Captain Godwin. You know him?"

"He's a she," the guard replied. "And yeah, Captain Godwin is in charge of the internment camp south of Nuevo Laredo. You can find her down there."

"Great, thanks; that's exactly where we're supposed to be heading." The wooden arms lifted, and the APCs pulled off down the expressway where they cruised for a mile to the exit for Nuevo Laredo. "Go left here," Keith directed, and the vehicles took a long, curved exit ramp and headed south toward an approaching city. Smoke drifted up from a sea of block structures on the horizon, gathering in the sky below the gray clouds and the wide road narrowed into a two-lane main drag that ran through the center of town.

"Just stay straight," Keith said, clenching the edge of the console. "Let's see if this takes us there."

They cruised past dilapidated houses until the lifeless streets exploded with action, flooded with cars and people. People of all walks of life were busy packing possessions into car trunks or backseats, blank stares on their faces as they were forced to move yet again, their race and creed making no difference in the face of the onslaught from the north.

Soldiers stood on corners, directing a line of traffic onto the main highway heading south. They ignored the APCs, their massive presence and military stature giving them the run of the road. Using the map, Keith guided them down thin alleyways where the Stryker's armor brushed tree branches and brick, plowing abandoned vehicles aside, avoiding jams where they could, taking side roads and shortcuts as they worked their way south. The haggard, zoned-out citizens watched them pass with the blank expressions of herded cattle and soldiers shouted through bullhorns as they broke up vicious fights driven by resentment and confusion.

"They are all at each other's throats," Lena commented through the radio link.

"Wouldn't you be?" Serge responded.

"The camp must be around here somewhere." Keith's eyes flitted over the screen impatiently as he pointed a side camera at the sea of pale brick houses. With a frustrated slap on the console, he growled, "Stop here. Let me out."

Pulling his hat tighter, bundling up like he had so many times in the past two days, Keith waited for the rear door to lower before climbing out and circling to the front of the APC, making a beeline for the first soldier he saw. Back in the truck, Mikael rose from the pack he'd been laying on and took Keith's radio chair, watching the agent as he waved Serge forward.

"You think he will find the camp?" Mikael asked, Serge replying with a silent shrug as the pair worked the external cameras with a tiny joystick, having a look around at the decaying situation. In a side alley, a pair of families fought over the last spot on a military truck, fathers pushed and shoved each other, children squalled and mothers tried to make sense of the confusion, arms thrown protectively over their kids as they awaited an uncertain fate.

"This…" Mikael frowned. "This is worse than I expected to see. Even in the slums and the poverty there is some semblance of order. Here there is nothing but chaos tied up with string, bursting at the seams to escape. I do not like it."

"Completely FUBAR, as the Americans say," Serge agreed as he watched Keith stride up to the soldier, waving to get his attention. "Let's see what Mr. Wonderful can find out."

Mikael scoffed, snorting a laugh. "I used to think he was good. But sometimes I think he's still in basic training."

"I know what you mean," Lena said, overhearing the conversation. "Do you remember Tripoli?"

"I remember it well." Serge nodded. "Agent Keith was a much better man then. Arranged the drop-off and pickup points with ease. Very professional. Now, he seems filled with dangerous emotion. Like his mind is not all there."

"Perhaps he is getting old," Mikael agreed, "or the McKnights took some fight out of him. He did not even want to go on this mission to begin with. Imagine that, being afraid of a family, of children." Mikael spat derisively.

"Perhaps his edge is gone after losing a few fingers and toes," Lena suggested. "It happens. I worked with a man who had his left hand amputated. Afterward, he was never the same. Retired to a small village in Minsk and became a baker."

Mikael snickered. "But I thought Keith was supposed to be some big hero."

"Look, it seems our hero found some information." Serge gestured ahead.

They turned their attention back to Keith where he was backing away from the soldier, waving for the trucks to follow him around the corner.

With a shrug, the merc guided the Stryker after him as the agent walked three blocks to where another soldier barked orders at civilians. At first, the soldier rounded on him, screaming into his face to get back in his car, which drew chuckles from the mercs. Then the trooper saw the two massive APCs backing Keith up, and he instantly became more helpful. After listening to his questions, the soldier raised his mitten and made chopping motions off to the west. Keith nodded at him then sprinted to the truck, waving for Serge to let him in. With a sigh, the merc punched the button, and the door began its slow descent, boots pounded up the ramp with a gust of icy wind and Keith stepped over the packs to exchange positions with Mikael.

With a sweep of his hand, Keith unbuckled his hat and pulled it back, blue eyes alight with excitement. "They say the camp is just two blocks to the West. Turns out that particular soldier worked on the prisoner list, and he remembers a family with the name of McKnight being checked in around four days ago." Keith smiled wickedly, settling back into his seat, rubbing his hands in front of the heater vent. "I think we found them!"

"Yes, yes, that is wonderful. I just hope he is not mistaken."

"Come on, man! Go!" Keith said, hitting the dashboard with both hands, ignoring the pain shooting up his arms, a wide grin broadening on his face.

The APCs kicked forward, leaving what remained of the traffic behind and entering a part of town cut off from the rest. Whipping the Stryker down a dirt road in a squeal of knobby tires, Serge circled blocks of dilapidated homes toward a cluster of green army tents off to the left and the APCs trundled through the trash-ridden streets, crossing a set of train tracks into an area that appeared to be even poorer than the neighborhoods they'd passed earlier.

A thick mist hung in the air and abandoned buildings stretched around them like ruins, looking like they'd been unoccupied for years. Boards covered the windows, frames leaned at odd angles and walls lay collapsed, the wood riddled with dry rot and holes.

"Yes. This is it. We must be getting close." While Keith had been riding waves of confidence and doubt, a sudden sense of hope made his pained fingers tick, wishing more than anything that Tom McKnight would appear before him so he could smash the man's face in. Revenge and redemption were just within his grasp.

Serge drove them closer to the cluster of green, tops barely visible through the fog as he brought the Stryker to a squealing halt in front of the nearest tent, tracking a sudden rush of soldiers that flew past. One man stopped and gestured at the APC crew.

"What's he want?" the merc asked.

"No clue."

With Mikael peering over his shoulder, Keith maneuvered the camera around, watching as soldiers sprinted through the morning haze toward a block of trashed houses encircled by abnormally new-looking chain link fencing and razor wire. Beyond the fence, an old pharmacy sat in the block's center, a pair of men lying in the weed-ridden courtyard. Muffled reports came from outside, and Keith looked over at Serge.

"Is that gunfire? Hit the external audio."

As soon as Serge pressed the button, the obscured sounds grew distinct, revealing themselves to indeed be gunfire accompanied by shouting. People chanted and hollered in a cacophony of noise, followed by more single rifle shots, the back and forth gun play familiar to him.

"It's a revolt." He frowned. "Prisoners must be trying to escape."

"The American soldiers have lost control of the camp?" Mikael asked, grinning, a hand resting on his sidearm as he looked over at Mikael with a raised eyebrow. "Maybe this will be fun after all."

Keith listened for another several seconds as chaos reigned around them and more soldiers ran past, gesturing for the APCs to enter the fight. Serge's head moved back and forth, eyes unreadable behind his headset. "What do you want me to do? Should we help them and then recover the McKnight's?"

"No. Turn around. Let's drive around the camp and look for them." Keith slapped his hand on the console. "If I know Tom McKnight, they're probably leading the damned escape themselves. Come on. Go!"

Serge pulled the APC in a tight circle, causing soldiers to dive out of his way. Dmitri followed him, and soon the pair of APCs trundled around the outskirts of the camp, skirting the fencing, looking off to their left as soldiers fired into a broken down part of the gates on the eastern side. A dozen or more camp occupants shot back from positions on the opposite side of the fence, hundreds more huddled around them, armed with pipes, knives, bats and scraps of wood. Others slipped through cuts in the chain link, escaping past the thin Army line, a few receiving fire from the guards as they ran.

Via the camera, Keith scanned across the firing refugees, looking for signs of the McKnights. "They'll be two adults and three kids, one of them small."

Squinting, he stared into the rising mist, vision obscured by the drifting haze and distracted by the occasional stray rounds that plinked harmlessly off the Stryker's armor. When he couldn't identify them right away, he made another circling gesture. "Take us around the bend ahead."

Serge whipped the Stryker to the left, squealing around the corner. In a break in the fog, Keith gaped at a scene playing out forty yards ahead. A small group stood in the middle of the road, backing away from another, larger group – not soldiers, though – armed with rifles and handguns. The smaller group was bundled up tight, faces barely visible in their hoods, but Keith made out five forms, and a swirling in his gut confirmed what he already suspected.

"Hit them!"

"Hit who?" The merc driver let his foot off the gas and the APC lurched.

"The people with the guns!" Keith turned and gripped Serge's shoulder. "Aim for the riflemen, but don't harm the family! It's the McKnights!"

"Just… run them over?" Serge's expression wasn't one of hesitation, but of confusion, wondering if he had heard the instruction correctly.

He slammed his fist on the console, screaming the words through a clenched jaw. "Yes! Hit them! Run them over!" Serge shrugged. "Okay."

The mercenary leader pounded the gas pedal and the Stryker flew forward with a jerk, its engine revving, bringing them to thirty, then forty miles an hour. Eighteen tons of metal roared toward the larger of the two groups as they gesticulated at the smaller group, hearing the massive vehicle coming and turning their useless weapons on it far too late. Two shots pinged off the armor before the truck's plow slammed into the rebels, bouncing them like pin balls to skid across the concrete, rolling and pitching, arms and legs flailing as their guns flew loose, crushing as many beneath the wheels as it knocked away. One man farther out than the others tried to dive out of the way, but Serge banked into him with a sickening crunch of bone. Another stood with his eyes wide, a deer in headlights as the Stryker's plow cut him in half.

"Stop!" Keith yelled and Serge brought the APC to a screeching halt. Keith toggled to the rear camera, seeing that they'd pulverized most of the group. Two people were crawling away, one with a hip and leg twisted impossibly out of the socket while others lay unconscious on the pavement. A handful were creeping toward the APCs with their rifles already firing, obviously in pain but still able to put up a fight.

"Come on, man! Get that back door down!" With a frustrated grunt, Keith spun out of his seat, pulling his right glove off and snatching his pistol from its holster. Knocking Mikael aside, he clambered to the rear and stumbled onto the ramp as it fell far too slowly for his liking.

Squatting, edging toward the growing sliver of light, he ducked as bullets ricocheted off the armor. His boots carried him to the pavement where he landed with a pained grunt, the ache from his mangled toes screaming up his ankles to his hips, but he didn't care. Nothing mattered except getting the family. Nothing at all.

He raised his pistol and fired it at an approaching survivor, putting a bullet into the man's throat, sending him gurgling, spinning to the asphalt as Mikael and Serge flew out after him, their own rifles popping off, scattering the forces like roaches. Wide eyes whipping left and right, Keith searched for the McKnights, but they'd slipped away again.

"Serge, Mikael! With me! Do *not* kill any of the family!"

The pair broke off their attack on the civilians and fell in behind Keith, seeming reluctant to give up the fire fight but professional enough to stick to their assignment. Errant gunfire flew toward them and something exploded off to Keith's left, but he kept his head down and focused, angling for the dense cluster of shattered homes to their right. He caught the flash of a jacket swinging into an alleyway forty yards along a deserted street and headed in that direction. Picking up the pace, wincing from the pain in his feet, he sprinted to the spot and plunged into the alleyway only to find it blocked with old furniture piled atop a rusted out washing machine.

With a cry of rage, he slammed his hands into the pile of debris, knocking it off and diving over the washer's smooth surface, swinging his legs around to land on the balls of his feet. He stepped out of the alley to face a string of broken homes, doorways and windows open and yawning. Shoulders rotating, direction uncertain, he listened for a clue to where the McKnights might have gone when glass crunched off to his right, followed by a dog's muffled yelp.

"How the hell is that mutt still breathing?" Keith growled to himself, hobble-running across the street toward an open door. Ducking his head and shoulders inside, he listened for more sounds and was rewarded with crunching debris. Heel-to-toe, he walked carefully through the room, sliding right into a hallway that divided the house.

Eyes narrowed, he peered into an entryway that was far too dark. Far too quiet. Memories of the small town and the bitch of a child came back to him, his vision starting to cloud over with red, the wounds flaring up in pain and he forced the anger down, determined to keep a clear head. Not this time. Not like last time.

As he walked ahead, a thick piece of wood swung at his chin and Keith jerked back in reflex. The board missed his face but slapped his raised gun hand, sending the weapon clattering off the door frame to land in the hall. Fingers on fire with pain, mouth twisted in an agonized grimace, he watched as a boot heel flew from the darkness and landed squarely in the middle of his chest, knocking him into the wall. Before he could recover, the wood whacked the archway in an overhanded swing, bringing a pile of rubble down in a crash to block the entrance and Serge and Mikael arrived and stepped over him, rifles pointed at the debris.

"I will go back outside and trap them." Mikael turned and took off the way he'd come, leaving Serge and Keith to break through the blockage.

They pulled off the loose boards and tossed them down the hallway, pushing the rest of the plywood and drywall over. Keith grabbed his gun off the floor, shoved Serge aside, and threw his feet over the pile, sliding to the other side, risking impalement on debris to land on his heels with a jolt. Growling, eyes watering in pain, he rushed out the back door in a blind-red rage, all rationalization gone again, focused again on the hunt.

An old concrete wall surrounded the yard with several holes in it. Instincts on fire, he staggered straight ahead, dodging a rusted swing set, plunging through the gap to come out in the street. He stood there panting, fingers and toes wailing their displeasure, chest heated with fury when Serge jogged up behind him, barely winded, shooting Keith a dark glance, Mikael close on his heels, speaking first.

"They did not come around this way. Did you see them?"

"No." Keith gave a breathless, frustrated sigh, chest still smarting from the kick, pride wounded more than his body. Serge reached out and dusted off the front of Keith's coat, causing him to jerk backward, swatting at the mercenary.

"What the hell was that for?!"

Serge smirked. "You have a boot print on your chest. Come, let us go back to the Strykers. We can pursue them from behind our armored protection. It is getting too dangerous out here."

Jaw churning, chewing on his anger, Keith spun on his heel and strode stiffly back to the APCs.

Chapter 16
President John Zimmerman
Havana, Cuba

Zimmerman paces across the presidential office in his new thermal boots, the footwear replacing his hard-soled dress shoes, a necessity in the ever-increasing chill. Gloved hands slapping together, he hunkers down in a heavy coat, the space heaters in the room rattling with clacking fans and the smell of burning dust. The extra heat is necessary in the hundred-year-old building with its high ceilings and poor ventilation.

Cold clings to the stone, creeping through to turn the air frigid and unforgiving, the extra insulation and retrofitting to the building doing little to stop the never-ending advance of the cold. The President comes to the window and looks down at the Marines interspersed throughout the courtyards and gardens, all of them wearing thick winter gear and standing near burn barrels, trying to stay warm while performing their duties.

"That sounds like a solid plan," he says to General Davidson, where he sits across from the President.

The big man has more meat on his bones than the rest of them, but he's bundled up just the same, as are Rick, Rita, and Maxine, all of whom also have a space heater near their feet. The general turns and shifts in his seat so he can see the President as he paces back and forth across the room. "Key to all this will be securing the oil refineries in the Orinoco Belt, on the Northern coastline."

The President nods. "We have the transports and supplies for that, right?"

"Despite the fact that every supply chain we've ever had is screwed up to the max, we're somehow getting it done. We're pulling all ships out of the North Atlantic and bringing home the South China Sea patrols and even those in the Baltic and Indian Oceans." The general shakes his shoulders in a sort of half shrug, as if he's reached a rope's end. "We're consolidating our assets, and that should give us enough firepower to protect the oil platforms and keep the Russians out."

"What about the refining plants inland?"

"We'll cover those with ground forces, inserted via sea and air. Once everything is secure, we'll immediately begin working on processing it into fuel and upgrading any facilities that need it. It won't be perfect for a hell of a long time, but it will give us enough to fight and stay warm."

The president paces to the other side of the room where he rubs his hands together as he stares at a picture of George Washington crossing the Delaware in the freezing cold, an ironic smirk tugging the corner of his mouth upward.

"The idea is to hit them hard, and go all-in," he said, turning back to his advisors. "We need the Russians to understand we won't be deterred, and we're staying in South America for the long haul. It's *ours*."

"That's been communicated to all who need to know it, sir."

"Once the Venezuelan and Russian troops know we mean business, they'll destroy every platform and refinery they can. Those must be secured right away."

The general nods, his heavy jowls shaking, his face having grown thinner over the past few days, covered with an excessive growth of stubble. "Scorched-earth policy, sir. That's what I would do if I were them. But that won't happen. We've got teams training round the clock, and they'll be prepped and ready to go. It will be the biggest air drop and naval maneuver since World War II."

Hands clamped together, the President nods and returns to his desk, circling to his seat and easing down. A female staffer comes in armed with a pair of pitchers and looks at the small group. "Tea or coffee?"

"I'll take some tea," Zimmerman says with a nod. After it's been poured, he gives the woman his thanks and sips from his cup, relishing the bitter, sobering taste. The others take a black coffee each, Rita with her hands wrapped around the mug to suck up the heat.

"The secondary mission will not only be to secure key infrastructure, including housing, power plants, and city centers, but to ensure those aren't destroyed. We can't have a repeat of Mexico. We need shelter for our people when we bring them over."

Davidson nods. "We learned a lot from Mexico, sir. We're going to hit the military complexes hard and keep the fighting away from the populated regions as much as possible. We've also upgraded our plan to cut off their key infrastructure and supply lines and get them to surrender within 24 hours. We won't fight in the cities unless the Venezuelans and Russians force us to."

"This will be huge for us," the President says. "Once those two objectives are reached, the last thing we'll need is to transport our citizens in. Rita?"

The Secretary of State draws her hands away from her mug and folds them in her lap. "While the General prepares for the invasion, I'll be working with administrators on the ground in Mexico to get our people ready. Part one will be to move half our entire civilian population to the border of Guatemala, where we've established over a thousand major camps. They'll be leaving by bus and troop transports from Chiapas, south into neighboring countries, all the way to Panama. We'll be using the rail systems whenever we can, obviously, but it's going to be messy. We'll get it done, though."

"What about protection? The people down there won't be happy with us using their roads and highways."

"For those going across land, we're working with General Davidson and his commanders to secure helicopters and jets for cover on the trips down. Each convoy will be fitted with plenty of firepower to defend themselves."

"It won't be easy, Mr. President," Mark interjects, "but we'll be able to hold our own against anything they can throw at us. We're already sending warnings to all the countries we pass through, threatening severe retaliation should any of those convoys be attacked."

"Good. Rita, what about the rest of the refugees? How are we getting them there?"

"We've secured major ports along the Gulf of Mexico and have already begun the transport of half the remaining population to those cities…." Eyes shifting upward, she stops and lets out a soft sigh, followed by a subtle gasp.

"Are you okay, Rita?" The president asked, leaning across his desk.

In an uncharacteristic moment of caring, the general puts his arm around her and pulls her close, squeezing her shoulders in a comforting but brief embrace. "It's fine," Mark whispers. "We're all very tired, but within two weeks we'll be working toward a new future."

She gives a nod, looking up and smiling. "Thank you." She laughs and looks to the President. "I haven't worked this hard since going for my doctorate degree, and I was 20 years younger with twice the energy. I can barely keep my eyes open."

"You're doing an outstanding job," Zimmerman adds, feeling his own frustration and weariness rise. "All of us are about to collapse. Just a little while more and we'll be through the worst of this."

Putting forth a confident smile, burying her exhaustion, Rita continues. "Like I was saying—as with the land convoys, we'll have the ports protected with yet more personnel provided by General Davidson. Cargo ships and a small fleet of cruise vessels 'donated' by every cruise ship company in the United States will begin transport of our citizens once the Venezuelan landing sites are secure."

"It's not like anyone's going to be taking vacation anytime soon," the General laughs, "so it didn't take much convincing for them to hand their ships over."

"It will take multiple trips, upwards of months' worth, but we think we can get the majority moved pretty quick. Protecting them at sea will be an endeavor, though General Davidson has promised destroyer escorts every leg of the way."

"Good." Zimmerman turns to his scientist. "How about it, Rick? Can people survive until the boats pick them up?"

The disheveled scientist nods as if he's been expecting the question, shifting forward in his seat. Since the last attempt to collapse the anomaly, his job responsibilities have diminished, yet he's still called upon for temperature predictions and general atmospheric and weather advice.

"It's going to get pretty cold pretty fast, Mr. President," he says. "Like we spoke about before, the twentieth parallel will be hit by deep freezes of near Arctic temperatures. We're already seeing major drops in the cities we just now settled in. It may remain slightly warmer on the coast, given the relatively temperate waters there, but it's not something we should count on."

"You think we need to get our citizens off the Mexican coast in an expedited time frame?"

"Unfortunately, yes. The chilling waters in the Mid-Atlantic will create sheets of ice forming as far south as Florida which will cause potential hazards for ships leaving from the southern tip of the state. Add to that the rapidly advancing cold and… well…."

Zimmerman nods. "If we don't get them out of those Gulf cities, they could be stuck there?"

"Exactly, sir. I discussed this with Rita, and we both agree. There may not be enough time to beat the ice."

"It's not that we don't *want* to do it," she replies with a single nod of apology. "We just can't guarantee they'll make it before the routes get congested or the people freeze to death."

"No, it's something we should consider." After a light tap of his fingers on his desk, the President points back and forth between the two. "Can you put together a plan to get half the citizens in the coastal cities down to the convoy camps on the Guatemalan border?"

Rita nods. "We can do it, but we'll need to use the spare fuel reserves."

"Then that's what we'll do." Zimmerman looks at the General. "But if we burn through the spare fuel, we'll need a fresh supply quick or the whole shebang will be dead in the water. That's why it's critical for us to get those oil refineries locked up."

"Consider them ours, Mr. President." The man looks exhausted, the bags under his eyes dark with sleeplessness.

"Get a few hours rest first, Mark," the President scoffs, but his expression is sober. "That's an order."

"Yes, sir."

"Rita? Rick? Do it. Pretend like you have all the fuel and resources in the world to get those people relocated. We'll figure it out on the other end. I'm not leaving any of our people to die."

"We'll do it, Mr. President." Rita nods assuredly.

"Good. The invasion will start in one week. We need this to work like clockwork. Now, on to other-"

A rattle of gunfire rips through the courtyards below and Rita and Maxine both cry out and dive to the floor as Rick sinks lower in his seat. Zimmerman instinctively leaps from his desk, sliding toward the window to have a look outside when General Davidson grabs him, spinning him away from the window as Secret Service agents burst into the room, securing the exits.

Another spattering of shots crack the air, rounds pinging off the concrete on the other side of the wall as the US troops respond, the automatic rifle fire causing Zimmerman's insides to clench tight. Shouts and the muted sound of a grenade blast go off near the edge of their encampment, not a massive explosion but enough to send trails of dust drifting from the old wooden ceiling.

The response from the US troops is brutal, an impressive chorus of firepower as bursts are rattled off, a siren wailing like a banshee as the Iron Dome silos are activated.

Boots sprint along the hall, and the office door bursts open. A half dozen more Secret Service agents fly in, more heavily armed and armored than the first who came in, carbines lifted and heading straight for the windows, plastering themselves on either side of the newly installed bulletproof panes.

The head of security leans forward and peeks outside to have a look at the grounds. The thick glass is struck with three quick shots, the impact of the high caliber rounds punching an inch into the bulletproof material and caroming off, leaving burnt divots in the composite material, causing the man to jerk back behind cover.

"What's happening?" Zimmerman directs his question at his head of security.

"There's been a slight breach of the defenses by a guerrilla group, but it's currently being contained. I'd say you're at no risk," he gestures at the window, "but they've obviously penetrated far enough inside to get a line of sight on us. Just sit tight, sir."

The President lets himself relax against the wall. With nothing else to do but sit and wait until the fighting stops, he listens to the gunfire exchange outside, topped off by sharp explosions, each causing him to wince. After the last few concussions, the shooting all but dies out. A few more rounds pop off, the sounds of shouts and revving engines, then the noise finally trails off to a halt.

"We good?" the President asks.

Mark and the security lead both nod at nearly the same time, listening to a feed through their earpieces.

"Yes, sir," the general says, backing up from Zimmerman to allow the President to move around again. "The threat has been neutralized."

"Thanks, guys." Zimmerman slouches against the wall and takes a deep breath while Rick helps Rita and Maxine off the floor while the security forces file out of the room except for two, the black-garbed agents staying around to watch through the windows.

"There'll no doubt be more," Mark says, patting the President on the shoulder before shuffling to his seat. "We should expect it at this point."

With a stiff stride, John steps to his desk and eases into his chair, huffing with uncertain relief, spreading his hands across the surface, bracing against it like an anchor. "I suppose it's the price we must pay for what we're doing."

"It's the price we'll pay for keeping our citizens – and our country – alive," Rita's tone takes a noticeably dark turn. "And woe be to anyone who doesn't think we're ready to pay that price."

Chapter 17
Tom McKnight
Nuevo Laredo, Mexico

Jack's hand gripped tightly in his, Tom led his family from the rough Nuevo Laredo neighborhood into a better part of town. Spread out around them were blocks of upgraded Spanish revival and adobe style homes with multi-level patios and rustic wooden trellises. The fog had lifted, revealing deserted streets and abandoned cars, dirt roads giving way to pavement and gravel with boxy courtyards surrounded by brick, stucco, or latticework walls on either side.

Explosions and the staccato rips of small arms fire filled the air, drawing closer as the fighting spread. Bullets flew out of nowhere, nicking the walls and zipping by like angry insects as screams penetrated the haze, the two sides battling in the gloom. A US military bullhorn roared for the rebels to give up their weapons, though they never did, and if anything the order only caused the battle to grow louder, more frenzied, threatening to spread outward through the town.

After the shock of seeing Keith, knocking the man down and barely escaping, Tom had guided Barbara and the kids to where he hoped their supplies waited.

"Saanvi said they'd be just north of here." He lifted the paper directions in one hand and grabbed Jack up with the other, carrying him so they could move faster. "It says to find the missionary home on Miguel Hidalgo Street."

"What kind of a missionary home?"

Tom swung Jack to his left side so he could see better. "I don't know, but it should be on this street."

"*Missionary* home? Like, a church? Or a house?"

"Or that," Tom said, pointing to a large, odd-shaped structure in the middle of a block of smaller ones. The light gray stucco with blue trim stood out above everything else, and a crucifix was displayed on the topmost peak. "That's got to be it."

The family angled across the street as the sounds of fighting grew nearer. Underpinning the gun fire were the roars of APC diesel engines prowling the neighborhood behind them. Barbara jogged ahead and opened a dark wooden gate nestled into a white outer wall. Beyond it was a small inner courtyard and a thick oaken front door on the building itself.

Tom strode up and grabbed the plastic yellow ribbon Saanvi had tied around the porch post, ripping it off and holding it up for Barbara to see, then he twisted the doorknob, shoving hard with his forearm to open the door wide and shined his flashlight into a wide foyer hall. When he hollered inside, no one answered, so he gestured for his family to enter behind him, still carrying Jack in his arm. Barbara ushered the girls in along a short, tiled passage to the back of the house where an open living room greeted them as Smooch trotted in behind them, looking around curiously. Tom placed Jack down, giving him a pat in Sam's direction, pointing across the room.

"Girls, can you take your brother over there while your mother and I search for the supplies?"

Standing straight, hands on his hips, he looked over the ornate fixtures in the chamber. Metal sconces and biblical images hung from the walls, along with at least a dozen crucifixes and Tom blinked at the peaceful reverence, his breathing slowing as his nerves calmed.

"That was Keith back there," Barbara said as the pair stood in the center of the room.

"Yes, it was." His voice dripped with contempt. "And it looks like he brought some friends with him."

"We can't let him get us. We can't let him get to the children."

"I know." He nodded, looking around as he searched for the gear Saanvi had promised. "Let's spread out, honey. Search for backpacks and other supplies. She must have stacked them around here somewhere. They shouldn't be hard to miss."

The kids stood by a modest couch pushed against the wall, facing a small tube television sitting on a stand. Almost every archway in the home was rounded, the end tables laden with ornate metal lamps and old fashioned lanterns.

"No flashlights, okay kids?"

They all nodded, but Linda spoke up. "Can we help look?"

"No," Tom replied. "I don't want any of you near the windows, especially not the front ones facing the fighting. Stray bullets are flying everywhere." He was already leaning into the kitchen, though he saw nothing on the floor, and when he threw open the pantry, it was bare. "As soon as we find the gear, we're leaving."

Barbara strode across the living room to a suite of back bedrooms while Tom glanced into a closet, then returned to the foyer to check upstairs. Wide tiled stairs with an ornate wrought-iron banister circled up to the next landing and as he ascended, he studied a series of black-framed pictures running up the wall to the top. They were mostly of a middle-aged man wearing a priest's collar, posing with people in remote locations across the world. At the landing, Tom caught the faint scent of cooked meat and laundry detergent, something the man might have been in the middle of doing when the evacuation orders came. He turned right down the hallway, peering into a bathroom, then into a spare bedroom with a perfectly made bed, cross hanging above it, Bible lying on a desk in the corner.

The window faced the front of the house and the encroaching gunfire, so Tom carefully approached, keeping the wall between himself and the fighting. Leaning forward, he glanced outside, overlooking the street and its tiny yards and crowded parking before turning back to the room, mumbling, "Come on, Saanvi, where did you put the stuff?"

He backed into the hallway and searched the master bedroom and an adobe-colored prayer room overflowing with potted plants and a skylight that illuminated a massive crucifix perched atop an ornate staff. Stomach doing anxious flips, Tom walked back to the landing and shouted down.

"Barbara, have you found anything yet?"

"No!" she called out. "Not yet."

"Maybe it's the wrong house."

Linda yelled from below, but her voice wasn't coming from the living room. "Dad! Mom! I think I found it. It's out here!"

Confused, Tom started down the stairs, then turned back into the hall, taking two strides to reach the master bedroom, walking past the meticulously made bed to the window. Head against the glass, he peered into a two-car driveway where his daughter stood behind a Humvee. At first glance, the vehicle didn't look like much, certainly not new with spots of rust and old tires, an early model likely out of service until recent events had brought it back.

Hands held out excitedly, he called. "Awesome! Stay there."

Stomach flipping with growing exhilaration, he flew down the stairs to the bottom floor, swung around the banister, and shot out through the double doors at the rear of the house. Jack and Sam had joined their mother and Linda at the vehicle, peering inside, hands pressed against the glass. Tom checked, too, staring at the things piled in the cargo section.

"I count six backpacks in there," he whispered breathlessly. "And a couple of rifles and pistols. Good job, Saanvi."

"Six backpacks." Barbara stepped back with a frown. "She wanted to come with us."

"I know," he said with a sinking stomach, remembering the medic's last haunting look, then he slid along the side of the vehicle, popped the door, and slipped behind the wheel. "I'd say this is it, wouldn't you?"

"Definitely," his wife replied. "Kids get inside with Smooch, now!"

With a rush of feet, the McKnights got in, Barbara in the passenger seat, the children filing into the back, the German Shepherd laying across the floorboards.

"Wow, this is so cool," Jack said, looking around with wide eyes. "It's a real army truck."

Tom pushed the start button and the old diesel engine shuddered, sputtered, then rumbled to life rattling and thundering from beneath the hood, its noise heightened by spotty exhaust pipes running up both sides of the front windshield.

As he adjusted the rearview mirror, Tom glanced back, throwing out a command. "Kids, get down, right now. You too, Barbara. There'll be bullets flying everywhere, and I don't want you to get hit. This thing's got some built-in armor, so try to use it, okay?"

She agreed with a nod, turning in her seat and sinking, motioning for the kids to duck. Tom searched the courtyard shared with the house next door, seeing two older model vehicles sitting with flat tires. While Tom could see the street directly in front of him, his view to the sides was cut off by the privacy walls penning them in. Above the encroaching explosions and small arms fire came the growling of APC engines, the diesel growls closing in on them from what sounded like two directions.

Tom shook his head, gritted his teeth, and put the vehicle in drive. Testing the brakes, he edged to the end of the courtyard and peered to his right, seeing an empty street, but on the left one of Keith's APCs rumbled slowly toward them, bearing down. Its front profile was a thin cut of metal, menacing and sharp, the mounted gun on top swinging around and pointing directly at them.

Tom slammed the gas pedal, shooting into the lane as a hail of rounds tore into the wall where they'd just been. Brick shards flew against the Humvee's roof and rear glass as the rubber shrieked on the pavement. Tom whipped them hard to the right, clipping a compact car and sending it spinning away, then he straightened the Humvee in a squeal of tires, punching forward to the next block and swinging into the first left turn he saw. Throwing his weight behind the wheel, he slid the vehicle hard, tossing Barbara and the kids against their doors, clearing the corner as more rounds streaked across the road behind them, tearing into a nearby house. Windows shattered, stucco exploding everywhere as tree branches were blown to pieces, dropping to the ground in shredded green and brown slivers.

The children screamed and Smooch whined as Barbara shouted, trying to keep her balance. "Are they crazy?! I thought they wanted to bring you in alive?"

Tom didn't answer. Shoulders low, he pressed himself against the wheel, glaring at the streets ahead, the neighborhood carved up into mostly straight lines with some back alleys and hidden driveways. Before he could make a decision, a second APC unit spun around the far corner, its eight wheels spinning at full speed, the bulky armor leaning and falling onto its suspension with a bounce.

Barbara flew into him as he whipped the wheel hard to the right, kids screaming in unison as the oncoming vehicle unleashed a brief volley of bullets at their tires. Tom had already cut across the next corner, splitting a pair of thick trees, the trunks absorbing machine gun rounds. The chaotic swerving pushed him toward a brick wall and Tom adjusted again, jerking the wheel hard left, throwing the McKnights back the other way. The Humvee clipped the wall with its right fender in an explosion of bricks, sending shards and dust flying out ahead of them.

Dragging grass, parts of the wall, and stripped tree branches behind it, the Humvee screeched across the road, engine growling as he pushed the pedal to the floor. A glance in his rearview mirror showed the two APCs swing in behind him, machine guns sweeping the ground, chewing up pavement, nipping at his tires.

"They're trying to take out the wheels!" Tom's voice was a horse, throaty hiss. "They definitely want us alive."

"Well, you could have fooled me." Barbara's tone rose to a fevered pitch, reaching back, hand thrown over Jack's knee. "Are you kids okay?"

The three nodded vigorously, eyes wide, clutching each other, slumped and terrified with Smooch at their feet. Tom searched for a way out, swerving back and forth, dragging the wheel in long, hard turns, taking one street after the other, pushing the old Humvee to its limits. The suspension shuddered, windows rattling in their frames and sometimes, when he hit the accelerator, the engine coughed before finally catching.

The rounds finally stopped firing, though, giving him a minute's respite, a moment to breathe and think. The next time he checked his rearview, only one APC hung behind him. "They're trying to flank me," he said, lips pressed into a thin line, skin itchy with sweat even in the intense cold.

Head lifting, eyes scanning back and forth like a hawk, Tom searched for a way out for a long moment before finally finding it. The Humvee angled toward a gravel road that led up to a neighborhood filled with blocks of construction and abandoned projects. Huge mounds of soil lay everywhere, piles of wood and debris, stone and insulation, dumpsters full of garbage from the old, torn down buildings. They climbed the steep rise to a grid of dirt streets, the lanes just wide enough for two large vehicles to pass.

"Slow down, honey," Barbara said, looking back. "You're kicking up a dirt trail."

"Crap." Tom eased up on the gas, cutting the dust trail drastically.

"This is perfect terrain for the Humvee," he mumbled, "but it's a little tight for them. I can turn faster than they can."

His wife only nodded as she peered through the windows, the big truck cruising past tarps flapping in the chill breeze, piles of construction materials, excavators and bulldozers sitting idle amongst the half-framed homes. The hulking vehicle eased over the rocky, dirt-frozen ground, the suspension shaking gently on its struts, the squeaky frame loose with missing bolts and parts. Tom rolled the window down, ear to the outside, listening as the APC engines growled up the gravel road after them, the sound bouncing off the surrounding hillsides, making it impossible to pinpoint their location. He leaned forward and back, trying to see through the gaps in the construction, directing them up a rise to a nest of houses scattered there.

"Maybe we can spot them from up here," he said. Reaching the top, he swung left onto a dirt lane, cruising, raising in his seat and craning his neck to look below. The road took him right, deeper into the neighborhood, on another nameless street, the Humvee's wheels shifting on potholes filled with crumbled blacktop, and he slowed more, the diesel engine thrumming softly beneath his feet.

"Hey, guys. Help me. You see anything?"

From the corner of his eye, he saw the family raising and looking everywhere through the windows, Barbara shaking her head and Sam's curly locks shifting around her shoulders.

"Wait, what was that?" Linda asked from her middle position in the back seat where she had completely turned and was staring out the Humvee's rear window.

"What?" Tom glanced back and forth between the road ahead and the rearview mirror.

"Oh, shoot. I guess it's nothing. I thought something moved around the last corner."

"You mean up on this level with us?"

"Yeah, but it was nothing." Her voice quivered, shivery and uncertain.

"Don't say that. It could have been them. Keep looking." The APC engines had gone quiet and he took another soft turn, pointing the Humvee toward the center of the neighborhood. Their rattling, shaking vehicle went two more blocks before he finally drew it to a stop in the middle of the street. They sat idling as he wondered if he should pull into a garage or if he should get out and try to find a vantage point to search for their pursuers.

As he was deciding, a wide section of tarp wavered and fluttered off to the left. Doubled up on itself, the opaque material was stretched over a passage that cut between two homes, yet it couldn't hide the massive dark shape behind it. There came a punch of sound, and the plastic exploded outward, the sheeting flying up as an APC shot from beneath it, kicking up frozen dirt and gravel as it banked toward their Humvee.

The roaring engine sent the kids screaming, a spike of adrenaline straight into Tom's veins. He double-pumped the gas pedal to keep the vehicle from sputtering and catching, then he punched it hard, the Humvee rocketing forward, the family thrown backward in their seats.

The APC slid out of the passage, skewing sideways, barely clipping the back of their Humvee as they sped forward. A quick spray of rounds chewed up the ground behind them, and Tom took the first hard left to get out of the way, but the turn put them right into the lap of the second APC. Its massive form sat in the road, thick armor looming over the Humvee like a bully and for a fleeting moment he thought about shooting the gap to get around it, but the APC angled across the road, driver sensing what he was thinking and blocking his escape.

A slam of his foot on the brakes brought the truck to a skidding stop. Thrown forward against the wheel, Tom jerked them into reverse and hit the gas, tires spinning, icy mud spraying the fenders, clattering like rain on a tin roof. The Humvee backed into the intersection as the first APC reached it. Wheels churning, he wormed around the charging vehicle, slipping by, and the APC missed them and rammed into the nearby construction materials, slamming into a pile of bricks and beams, riding up it until its huge front tires were left spinning helplessly, unable to get traction.

Tom didn't wait to see more. He spun the wheel, throwing their rear end into a stack of shingles, sending the packages flying before reversing direction, foot pounding on the gas, the Humvee shooting up the street with the second APC roaring in on his back bumper. The diesel engines growled in challenge to each other, Tom pressing the pedal down to the floor, stretching his speed to forty then fifty, the Humvee's suspension shuddering over the dirt road as he pulled away, every dangerous turn putting their lives in jeopardy.

The children clutched each other in the back seat, forearms pressed against the armored insides, feet resting on Smooch. Tom drove for several blocks, leading the APC on, keeping to the right side of the dirt track, inching forward, teasing the bigger vehicle to keep up. As he hoped, the APC pounded after them, eight tires carrying 12 tons of steel smoothly across the road, the pointed nose of pushing against the Humvee, bending the back frame, spider webbing the glass as easily as a foot crunching a tin can.

Tom hit the brake and spun the wheel, cutting a sharp right, the Humvee's wide base taking the turn, tires digging furrows into the dirt. The APC broke past, unable to follow the shorter arc, its trajectory carrying it into a corner lot where it smashed through a home, barreling into the 2 x 4 framing. Stucco sheathing split and exploded like eggshells, insulation and wiring materials dragging behind. The tires slid on swaths of slick siding and plywood, its front end jumping the stoop, plunging into a basement with a rough growl of metal on concrete, wheels left spinning in thin air. The rest of the home collapsed on the armored car in an avalanche of debris, the wide flat roof dropping in a rain of shingles and brick.

With a metal-bending squeal, Tom barely kept the Humvee on the road. It slid across the street and to the edge of the concrete courtyards and patios, slicing through stacks of building materials and tarps, clipping pallets of siding, slamming into garbage barrels. The tires vibrated on their axles as the vehicle bounced over the sharp, uneven terrain, Tom fighting to get them straightened back out. Not waiting to see if the APCs were back on his tail, he slowed, taking turns at speed, getting more and more lost.

"Tom, there's the exit road!" Barbara shouted, pointing to the road they'd come in on.

He gunned the Humvee, racing onto the gravel lane and down to the lower part of the neighborhood. The truck growled and clawed its way through the streets, searching for an exit. Barbara leaned to the side, spun in her seat, both hands on the headrest as she stared back through the cracked glass. "I think we lost them, honey. I think we got away!"

"Nice driving, Dad," Sam said as she deflated with a slack expression of relief.

No one had gotten hurt, miraculously, and something was grinding in the truck's frame, the engine still coughing and sputtering, but as he pulled out of the Nuevo Laredo neighborhood, Tom considered them lucky. *Very* lucky.

"Stay strapped in, kids," he growled, eyes flitting from the road to the rearview, half-expecting to see the impervious, dogged APCs on their tail. "We've got a long way to go, and we can't let up."

* * *

"Pull over here!" Keith screamed, fists slamming on the console, the pain an afterthought, more of a friend to him than a discomfort. "This is where they crashed."

The APC came to a grinding halt, back door dropping to the ground and he rushed outside, glaring at Dimitri's Stryker as it shifted back and forth to free itself from its stuck position. Spinning on his heels, he turned and ran to a dirt pile and climbed to the top, staring into the neighborhoods below, following the Humvee as it shot west along the cold Nuevo Laredo streets. Serge and Mikael flew up behind him, clambering up the dirt hill to stand next to him.

"There he goes, dammit!" Keith spat, pounding his fist into his palm, setting his fingertips on fire.

"Is he heading to the highway?" the merc leader asked.

The agent leaned forward, eyes narrowed as the vehicle took a turn north and then swung west once more. He lifted his gaze, glimpsing the highway in the distance, a long stretch that wound far to the south.

"Yeah, I think that's where they went." He nodded slowly. "That's where I would go if I were him."

After the Humvee disappeared from sight he turned and slid down the dirt hill, stalking to the APCs just as Dmitri freed his vehicle and backed onto the road.

"All right, people! Let's move it out!"

They clambered inside, shut the door, and pulled off to give chase once more. Keith settled back in the comm chair, frustration simmering like a rash beneath his skin. Tom McKnight had been within his grasp – quite literally – then somehow escaped, found a vehicle – where the hell had that come from anyway? – and managed to evade *two* armed vehicles hunting him down.

No matter. As persistent as the McKnights were, Keith was more so. He'd continue hunting them, chasing them down wherever they went to roost, and eventually he'd catch them. He'd catch them and rain hell upon their heads.

Chapter 18
Specialist Lance Morales
Santa Fe, New Mexico

"Hello? Who's there? Are you military? Boy, are we glad to see you guys."

Morales and Smith exchanged an uncertain look, Smith stepping around the captain, calling out. "This is the United States Army. Who are we speaking to?"

Shuffling footsteps greeted them from the dark hallway, and several figures came into view. Morales didn't draw his weapon, not with the four other Army rifles pointed down the hall, but he shifted to Captain Jones's right side and stared into the darkness.

The first two people stepped into the light, a man and a woman, each wearing loose-fitting military-esque fatigues with a special unit emblem on the arms that he didn't recognize. The woman was short with inky black hair hanging to her shoulders, her cold blue eyes picking over them beneath stark eyebrows. The man next to her was a swarthy type, his loose dark locks falling into his face, a growth of beard lining his firm jaw. A handful of others came behind them, clothes disheveled, shoulders slumped, not the postures of strictly-trained and disciplined members of the military. Morales read their haggard, uncertain eyes bearing the weight of being trapped under tons of snow and felt an immense pity for their situation.

The man stepped forward into the emergency lights. "I'm Chet Peterson, part of the special unit here at the FEMA facility." He gestured to the woman and those assembled behind him. "This is Shae Roberts and the rest of my team. Who am I talking to?"

The captain met him briskly, offering his hand. "I'm Captain Jones, United States Army, Special Scavenging Unit. We formed less than a week ago and were sent north from Mexico to transport supplies from this facility down south. How long have you folks been down here?"

"Since the big freeze started," Shae replied, raising a dark eyebrow. "We barely made it inside before the really icy stuff hit." Her eyes flashed past them and up the stairs. "What happened to the others?"

"You mean everyone up in the warehouses?" Jones asked.

"Yeah."

"All dead. It looks like they tried to hold out up there, but the spin-up storms were a little too much for them." The captain's gaze shifted back and forth between the bunker leaders. "Can you tell us why they stayed up there and didn't come down here with you folks?"

A mixture of emotions Morales couldn't read flashed across Chet's face. "I told them not to stay up there, but they insisted on sticking it out and waiting for rescue to show up. I guess they weren't counting on the spin-up storms to hit as hard as they did." He stepped forward to emphasize his point. "I saw the writing on the wall, so I got my people out of the warehouses and into this bunker as quickly as possible. We must be the only ones left alive on the grounds, right?"

"At the moment, yes," Jones replied. "But we haven't checked all the warehouses yet." The captain stood back and looked them over. "How many of you are there?"

"About a dozen. The rest of the group is downstairs where we set up some sleeping quarters." Shae gazed across at the array of soldiers who had lowered their weapons, eyes flashing from face to face. The corner of her mouth ticked up in a bone-weary smile. "You guys wouldn't be offering rides south, would you? We wouldn't mind a one-way ticket out of this frozen wasteland."

"We're just here to ferry the supplies and that's all." Jones kept his hands on his hips. "And we don't have room for stragglers, I'm sorry to say. Nobody told us there might be survivors, but I'll call it in and see what we can do." He turned to a staff sergeant. "Radio in, let them know what's going on and ask for guidance."

"I'll send a message to headquarters." The soldier replied then pivoted and moved toward the back of the landing, taking a radio off his belt and ascending the stairs as he spoke into it.

The captain nodded to the bunker team. "You folks up for some loading?"

Chet and Shae exchanged a glance, the man speaking up. "We're not full military, just a special hybrid unit. I'd like to keep my group separate from your units. You people look like you just came off the front lines. I don't think-"

"Don't worry," Jones interrupted. "We don't bite. Well, maybe Smith does." A humorous chuckle came from the soldiers, though the bunker team only shared uneasy looks.

The captain continued. "If anything, you can show us where the warehouse supplies are and get us a full inventory. We'd like to see what we're moving. Would make our lives a hell of a lot easier."

Chet shrugged and nodded. "Yes, sir. We can at least do that much. And if helping out will buy us a ride home, we'll do it."

Jones stepped to the side and gestured. "Morales. Smith. Take a small team and go with these two. Locate the supplies and manifests and determine a load-out order. And we need to know where the cargo elevators are so we can dig the doors clear."

"Yes, sir," Morales said, stepping with Smith over to the pair as the staff sergeant came running down the stairs with an update. "Headquarters responded. We can't carve out a transport unit for passengers back with our convoy, but the third transport wave will have some APCs with room to spare for survivors. That one should arrive in a few days."

"Thanks, Staff Sergeant." The captain turned to Chet and Shae. "How's that sound?"

"Perfect." The man grinned. "You've got our full cooperation, sir."

"All right. I'll let you get to work. In the meantime, I'll be overseeing operations in the warehouses."

Jones took his staff sergeant upstairs, leaving Morales, Smith, Brozowski, LePlante, and eight soldiers with the bunker crew. Lieutenant Smith jumped ahead with Chet, while Morales fell behind with Shae, followed by the mix of soldiers and crew. Together, the group moved deeper into the dark depths of the sub-floors, boring into the ground, circling a central core of concrete, the walls marked with bold letters. Boots tromped on the stairs, echoes banging in the enclosed space, the sterile smell of moist, warm concrete lingering in the air.

"Sub-floor 1 is dedicated to storage pods," Chet said, loud enough for everyone to hear. "Sensitive electronics are on Sub-floor 5. In between are larger warehouses, at least 10 on each level."

"How big are these spaces?" Morales asked as they moved past Sub-floor 2.

Shae scoffed. "The ones we found are huge."

"You don't know the square footage?"

"No," she said with an apologetic glance. "Well, the exact specs are in the system. I might be able to get them for you."

"Great. Thanks."

They stopped on the third landing labeled *Warehouse 3L,* where Chet paused at the door.

Smith turned to two of the soldiers. "Brozowski and LePlante. Why don't you take Meyers, Jennings, Johnson, Isaacs, and Richardson down to the next level? Check out the radio gear and see if there's anything we can salvage." Lieutenant Smith pointed to three soldiers to stay with them. "Stevens, Griggs, and Rupert. You're with us."

Brozowski and LePlante nodded and gestured for their team to follow.

Chet motioned at his four other bunker crew members. "Take them downstairs, boys. Shae and I will see after the lieutenant and his people." The bunker leader turned and pulled open the heavy metal door, stepping into another long hallway that stretched at least 500 feet, lit by pale circular bulbs nestled into the ceiling. "This way, folks."

As they walked, Morales's eyes roamed over the concrete walls, tracing over each warehouse door as they passed.

"The entire place is connected by a slick intercom system," Chet explained. "You can call to any room using the internal speakers. You just have to know how to work the buttons, but it's pretty easy."

"There's a hell of a lot of rooms down here." Morales glanced over several square security pads next to a few of the doors, their keys glowing green. Chet and Shae didn't stop at any of them. "What about the ones with the security pads?"

"We haven't been able to get into them." The leader threw his reply over his shoulder. "No one on our team has the codes, and those who had them either never arrived at the bunker or were in the warehouses when the snows hit. And, according to your Captain Jones, they're all dead."

"So, there were people down here originally?" Morales asked.

"Yep," Shae responded. "There was a staff here when we showed up, but some left as soon as the snow started falling. I guess they didn't want to be buried alive."

Morales flashed Smith a look, raising an eyebrow as they trudged along, their boots thudding on the tiles all the way to the end of the hall.

Chet paused and turned, spreading his hands at Shea. "Do you remember where food storage was? I get confused between those rooms and refrigeration units every time." He shrugged and glanced at the lieutenant. "This place is like a damn maze sometimes, more cells, cubicles, and compartments than you can count. But it's all organized. You'll see."

"Left up here." Shea gestured at a branching hall, a flash of annoyance in her eyes. "Sorry, I would've brought my inventory tablet if I'd known we were going to get to work right away. You guys didn't even text ahead. We didn't know you were coming."

"No problem." The lieutenant waved her off with a crooked smile, hiding his true aggravation that Morales might not have noticed if they hadn't become best friends over the last couple months. "Let's just get through what we can," Smith continued. "I just need an idea of what we're looking at so I can report back to the captain."

"No problem," Chet agreed. "Let's go."

Smith dropped back by Morales and let the other three solders walk up front as they strode through a series of intersections. The group took two left turns and another right, confusing his sense of direction. When the others weren't watching, the lieutenant leaned in to Morales, mumbling out of the corner of his mouth.

"Do you have a bad feeling about this?"

"Yeah. They don't seem to have anything together," Morales replied. "No codes to any of the secure rooms."

"And no clue about their inventory."

"And their story seems a little sketchy."

"Keep your eyes peeled, okay? Look for a chance to break away if you can. Have a look around yourself."

Morales nodded secretively as Chet brought them to a flat gray door marked Food Stores, 6-3L. "Oh, here we are." The bunker leader opened the door, stepped aside and gestured for them to enter.

Inside, he gaped at the massive room filled with endless buckets of freeze-dried fruits, vegetables, eggs, and other dry rations. It wasn't as big as the initial warehouse they'd broken into, but just three or four rooms like 6-3L would easily surpass it.

Shae stepped out between the rows, pointing toward the rear. "It looks like there's a centralized cargo lift in the back corner that connects with several surrounding warehouses."

Morales spotted the massive steel door and nodded. "Those will be extremely convenient once we start bringing up supplies. Do they work?"

"To be honest, we don't know," Shae replied. "We haven't had to use them because we haven't moved any product, but I'm sure you boys can figure it out."

"You've got some lights out up there." Smith pointed up to the rafters, steel beams crisscrossing in blue paint, at least two big white lamps with aluminum hoods blinking sporadically.

"Yeah, we've had little time for repairs," Chet said. "We were more worried about securing the facility, making sure we were prepared to stay here for the long haul."

"Your radios are down, right?" Smith asked.

Chet's eyes flashed to Shae as an uncertain smile tweaked the corners of his mouth. "They work, but we haven't been able to reach anyone in weeks. I guess the spin-up storm took out our radio tower or something. You want to see some of the other storage areas?"

"I want to see everything you have access to. We'll have Brozowski and LePlante dig at those security keypads later."

The small group left Food Stores 6-3L and walked the entire warehouse sub-floor, poking their heads into at least six other large storage facilities packed to the brim with supplies of every kind. One offshoot section of the hallway was completely blacked out with even the emergency lights dark and dead.

"What's going on down there?" Smith asked. "You've got a total blackout."

"It was like that when we arrived." Chet cleared his throat. "We suspect a possible wiring problem, or blown fuses. I have someone looking into it, but they've had no luck yet."

"There's got to be a load of goods down there." The lieutenant squinted. "We should prioritize working on getting this section of the warehouse up right away."

"Yes, sir."

Morales peered through the darkness, eyes narrowed, lingering behind the group as they walked on. He spied a smidgen of light glinting off several metal doors along the dimmest part of the hall and suspicion pricked at the back of his mind, but the party was moving on, forcing him to catch up with them or be left behind.

The next room was filled with batteries, racks of deep cycle rechargeable batteries pressed against the left-hand wall, and tens of thousands of smaller appliance batteries sitting in wooden cases on the shelves. There were chargers, spools of cabling and connectors, and solar panels by the thousands. Morales's jaw dropped as they strode across the echoing space. Two dozen massive Xtreme worksite generators were neatly parked in the center of the chamber, resting on their own trailers, ready to be lifted upstairs and driven off by Humvees. He also counted 50 High Max mobile generators rated for 36,000 continuous watts each lined up in 10 rows of five along with smaller civilian generators, too, enough to easily power a small city.

"Well, this is exactly what we need," Smith said with a grin. "Do we have the diesel to run it?"

"The, uh, fuel tanks are upstairs installed near the cargo door," Chet replied in sheepish tone. "I think the pumps are above ground. Just make sure you guys are careful not to hit them."

Morales nodded, wishing he'd known that earlier when he was up digging around in the snow in an exhausted half-daze. "We'll take that into consideration."

"You know how much fuel you've got?" Smith asked.

Again, the two leaders shrugged at each other. "We're not actually sure," Chet replied. "We've been poring through the inventory system, but it's not as easy to navigate as we thought."

The lieutenant rounded on the man, hands on his hips, neck craned forward with a hard expression as he threw off any semblance of understanding. "You guys work here, but you don't have any of the security pad codes. You don't know how much of anything you have, or where it is. You can't even get into the computer inventory. Wait, I thought you said you could before. Am I getting mixed messages here?"

Chet held his ground, giving Smith a faint nod. "Look, the actual warehouse managers, the ones who would have all those access codes, weren't around when we got here. Or they bolted when the storms hit."

"One manager promised to come back," Shea explained, eyes darting between the three men. "But he never did, and we couldn't go get him after the snow started piling up. Back in the control room, we tried to hack into the databases and get full access to the inventory, but we could only read the non-restricted lists. The rest were off-limits."

"And there are no tunnels connecting this building and the outside warehouses?"

"That's right," she nodded. "At least as far as we know."

Smith scowled at the pair with a degree of menace. "I know we just got here and everything, but you people don't have your shit together at all. I can understand about the security codes and inventory, but you've got entire sections of the facility without lighting. That should have been fixed right away. It's almost like you don't know what the hell you're doing."

Chet's body froze, shoulders stiff as he swiped a lock of hair out of his eyes. He shot a stone-cold glance at Shea, and Morales squinted at them, wondering what the answer would be.

"Like I said before, Lieutenant Smith, we're not soldiers," he said. "We work here as part of the civilian unit, part-time, too. We were never given full access or had enough training to run the entire place. Our jobs consisted of packing and stacking things. None of us are electricians, but we've been working on it. We got 6-4L lit up, didn't we, Shea?"

"Hell yeah, we did," she responded. For the first time, the woman's shoulders sagged, the raw weariness in her eyes showing as she mumbled her words. "And, man, we're tired. It's just 12 of us, and most haven't slept for days."

"It's true." Chet agreed. "Not to mention being stuck down here. It's damn claustrophobic. Believe me, guys. It hasn't been a picnic for us."

"All right, fine," Smith said with a dismissive wave. "We're sorry you had to go through all that, but we really need to get a handle on what's here and get it moved south as soon as possible." He looked around the room. "I'm thinking we're going to have to hack into those secure warehouse rooms and do an entire inventory ourselves, from scratch." The other three soldiers with them groaned in response, and a tight ball of dread formed in Morales's stomach.

The lieutenant shrugged and exhaled sharply. "Unless Brozowski can hack into the inventory system, too. It'd be nice to check any security camera footage, see if we can figure out what happened here before you guys showed up. Anyway, let's keep going."

Morales caught another strange look between Chet and Shae before they stepped ahead to lead the group on. As the team left the battery room, he lingered behind, pretending to kneel and tie his shoe. He watched as the three soldiers walked beside Shea, asking her questions, Smith fully engaging with Chet as they moved to another section of the warehouse.

Legs slowing, boots quiet on the tile floors, Morales allowed himself to drift farther and farther back. Hands behind him, he strolled nonchalantly, pretending to study the doors and the wall markings, arrows pointing backward to various other sub-floors. The group rounded the next corner, and the specialist stopped cold. He waited a moment, then backed down the hall, finally turning and marching forward with quick steps.

He traced back the way they'd come, twisting door latches and peeking inside the storage rooms they hadn't checked. Stopping at the first security pad he saw, he tried out the codes he'd heard Brozowski and LePlante whispering to each other earlier. He punched the numbers into the keypad but had no luck and the second try didn't work either.

Morales glanced over his shoulder before rushing ahead to the beat of his quickening heart. Reaching the darkened intersection, he tried to penetrate the gloom, but all he could see was a spot of light at the far end of the hall; the rest was pitch black. With one more glance back, he strode forward through the darkness, emergency lights above his head as dead as night, not a single monochrome blinker or exit sign anywhere. None of the security pads were working, their normally green glow gone. In passing he grabbed random latches and turned them, but every door remained locked.

Feet shuffling, boots clacking on the tiles, he approached the faint hint of light he'd seen earlier. Time was running out, and he was certain Shae and Chet would notice he was missing at any moment. At the end of the hall, one emergency bulb illuminated three doors. Two sat on the right, neither with the security keypad on them while another stood on the left, its security pad lit with soft green keys. Two steps took him to the keypad, shoulders hunched forward, finger raised and frozen over the buttons when his nose twitched.

A stench wafted up from around the edges of the door, sweet and familiar, subtle at first, mingled with the heavy perfume of pine-scented cleaner. It was the smell of death, the intense reek climbing up his nasal passage and tickling the back of his throat. With a hard swallow, Morales punched in the first security combination he remembered. Each button made a quiet beeping sound, soft against his fingertip but when he hit *Enter* the pad turned red and left him locked out. He tried the second code, punching in the numbers and blinking in surprise when the keypad beeped with an upward-lilting click. The door popped open a quarter of an inch and, stomach rising through his throat, guts squirming, he opened it and stepped in.

The stench hit him first, a sucker punch to the chin, head jerking to the right as he threw up his elbow to protect himself and try to keep from expelling the contents of his stomach all over the floor. It was a large storage room with shelves lining the rear wall, mostly cleaning supplies, rags, and brooms hanging from racks. Boxes full of plastic bags and even a tile polishing machine sat at the back between the last two rows and the space was dimly lit by a pair of dull yellow bulbs beneath aluminum hoods.

The dim wattage cast a weak glow across a dozen corpses lying in a haphazard line in the middle of the floor. They were completely naked, left in awkward positions, rigor mortis capturing their tortured forms in stiff poses. Their chaffed skin was stretched and bloated in the early stages of decomposition, covered in blood and grime, the yellowish light gleaming off the tiny dots of moisture.

Gaze falling to the floor, Morales saw that someone had doused the tiles with pine-scented cleaner and bleach, rags soaked and pressed across the bottom of the door. Sickened, Morales hesitantly approached the bodies. The victims had been beaten, skulls crushed, bones broken, jaws knocked sideways, hanging loose from their faces. Without warning, the rations he'd eaten earlier in the day exploded from his stomach and he spun, reeling as the food and water and coffee spewed from his mouth and splashed across the bleach-slick floor.

Stumbling around it, careful not to get his boots messy, he moved to the wall, leaning forward as he waited for his guts to settle. Belly empty, he turned back to the bodies with a colder eye, approaching with a focused squint. While they were mostly without clothing, he spotted a woman at the far right end wearing the tatters of a military uniform. She had on army green socks pulled up to her shins, a tight-fitting sports top covering her chest and dog tags on a thin chain around her bruised neck.

Morales crept to the other end, studying the faces of the people lying still. They were clearly military with buzzed hair cuts and chiseled features, the women with their hair pulled back into tight buns, wearing minimal makeup. It was a military work crew if he ever saw one.

Chet and Shae being in charge made no sense. They didn't know anything about the facility or how much inventory they had, and had failed to fix simple things such as lighting, not to mention every answer they gave was vague and conflicting. They'd seemed more than a little surprised to see the soldiers at all, in spite of their original assertion. Morales stared at the puddles of cleaner, cracking his knuckles as the pieces came together in his mind, then he launched forward, gripping the door handle and throwing it open, stumbling, staggering into the hallway, almost slipping from his wet boots.

He bolted back the way he'd come, slowing as he reached the corner where he'd left Smith and the work crew, peeking around to make sure no one was around to see the direction he'd just come from. Coast clear, Morales began a fast walk along the hall, covering several hundred feet quickly, turning to where they'd disappeared.

It was a hallway like the others, doors on both sides, lighting running along the center of the ceiling. About midway down, he heard voices babbling from a room on his right. The door stood propped open, and he approached cautiously, stomach churning, pressing his palm against the surface with his hand lingering near his side-arm before he stepped inside.

Inside was a boiler room with pipes of various sizes and diameters running across the ceiling and far wall. Valves and pressure gauges sat at even intervals and touchscreen computer monitors placed in the center with schematics of the plumbing and steam systems highlighted in white on the screens.

Smith stood in the middle of the room near Shae and Chet with the soldiers standing off to the side while three members of Chet's team lingered behind the warehouse leader, shirts off, grease on their skin, at least two holding massive wrenches.

"There he is!" Chet said, regarding Morales with a grin. "We were about to come looking for you."

Eyes falling so he didn't give himself away, he nodded and made a show of zipping up his coat, coming to stand on Smith's other side. "I had to take a leak. I've been in an excavator all day, and I hadn't made yellow snow for a few hours." The group chuckled, yet the hot, moist air remained thick with tension, or maybe it was all in Morales's mind.

He nodded at the service workers and the pipes. "What do we have here?"

"It's part of the boiler system," Smith said, explaining what he must've just been told. "They've got heated water that flows around the entire place, and steam systems that run the conveyors and cargo elevators, and provide some of the power."

"These are the guys I was telling you about, the ones making repairs." Chet turned sideways, gesturing at the three men who were covered in sweat and stains, one with a thick beard growth uncharacteristic of a military employee. While they'd certainly been working, Morales doubted they were experienced workers, and he couldn't keep his eyes from flitting over the big wrenches in their hands.

Before they caught him staring, he glanced away, elbowing Smith in the side. "Hey, man I need to talk to you for a second."

Looking annoyed, the lieutenant squinted. "Can it wait until the tour is done?"

"I just had an idea about where the main cargo bay is, based on what I've seen of the layout so far. I think I can dig it up, but I wanted to see if you agree with me on the location first." He shot Chet and Shae a grin. "Boring military crap."

As he and Smith stepped to the back of the room to the gentle hissing of pipes, the other three soldiers strode up to chat with the bunker team, arms crossed as they engaged them in friendly conversation. Morales turned to face the group, putting his back to the corner, the lieutenant facing him.

"What's up?" Smith asked.

"Don't react to what I'm about to say in any way, okay?" The specialist's tone was flat.

"Yeah, okay."

"No, I need you to promise me not to react."

Smith grimaced, annoyed by the lack of direction in the conversation. "I think you know me by now, Morales. Just spit the damned thing out."

"All right." With wild gestures of his hands, Morales pointed upstairs and along the hall in a show of conversing about cargo elevators and loading strategies. "I wasn't in the restroom just now."

"I figured that. Go on."

"I searched that dark hallway. There's a room at the end where the lights work." He winced uncomfortably. "That's where the, um, real bunker crew is."

The lieutenant shifted from one leg to the other, jaw tightening as he fixed Morales with his customary stony look. "What do you mean by that? Are they having lunch down there or something?"

"No, sir. They're dead, but not dead like the ones we found in the warehouse. Not frozen. Beaten. Bludgeoned. To a pulp."

The gears behind Smith's eyes rolled out of control, anger, confusion, and resentment clashing on his face, but he quickly wiped the look away, forming a neutral expression despite that the information was undoubtedly burning his brain to pieces. "That would explain why these guys don't know jack shit," he whispered.

"Exactly." He glanced up to see Chet looking over. The man's face remained relaxed, but his eyes held an odd hint of wariness Morales had previously mistaken as exhaustion. "Whoever these people are, they took control of the bunker somehow, killed the original crew, and have been living off the supplies ever since."

"The place never felt good to me," Smith said with a head shake, lips pursing as he realized their predicament. "I don't care what the situation is, these jerks are too frikkin' clueless to pass as actual military."

"What do we do?"

"We need to get our people regrouped as soon as we can, if they haven't already been attacked."

After receiving a nod from Morales, Smith turned and gave a single clap. "All right, folks. Tour is over. We're going to reconvene and arrange to get this stuff moved out."

Before the warehouse crew leader could respond, Morales grabbed the door and held it for the other three soldiers, gesturing for them to go outside. Smith followed them, with Chet and Shae behind him, but the workers with the wrenches didn't come out. As he walked by, the lieutenant whispered from the corner of his mouth. "Keep an eye on our rear, would you?"

Morales nodded, smiled, and clapped one of the soldiers on the back.

"So we'll go find Brozowski and LePlante," Smith said as he caught up with the rest of the group, masking his suspicions behind the guise of urgency. "Then we'll start the inventory and get load outs arranged."

"They should be down on Sub-level 4," Shea mentioned, studying the lieutenant carefully as she guided them. "It'll just take a minute to get there."

Conversations were low as they moved through the halls, Smith hurrying them along, cautiously trying to avoid appearing like he was concerned. Morales lingered behind, glancing back, looking for the shirtless workers. There was no sign of them by the time they reached the stairwell, though that didn't mean they weren't there, trailing the group, waiting to make their move.

The others passed through the doorway, but he waited a moment and only after hearing no footsteps and seeing no shadows moving in the hall behind them, he entered the stairwell and quickly caught up with the group, tromping along the metal stairs to the next landing. Chet beat Smith to the door, holding it for everyone in a game of musical politeness. The hallway beyond was exactly like the one upstairs, long and starkly lit, the tiles hard beneath his boots.

"So what do you do for the military?" Chet was suddenly at Morales's side, shoulders relaxed with a smile on his face. "You're not a big, stupid grunt like some of these other guys."

Stevens, Griggs, and Rupert laughed good naturedly, having formed a loose friendship with the bunker crew, though as far as Morales was concerned, that was a good thing. It would keep the impersonators off guard when the soldiers made their move, but they would have to regroup first.

"I'm a driver, actually," he replied. "I'm rated to drive almost any military vehicle, including most forklifts and bulldozers. Stuff like that."

"What about helicopters and jets?"

"Unfortunately, no. I can't fly," Morales chuckled. "I'm a grunt, probably lower on the totem pole than these guys."

"That's right," Griggs said, rifle bouncing against his back. "You'll always be a chauffeur, Morales." Chuckling, Morales started to reply when they came to a stop, having reached an open door at the corner of the hallway, entering to see three big refrigeration units purring inside. Four of Chet's people stood with two soldiers from Brozowski's group, Meyers and Jennings, but neither Brozowski nor LePlante were anywhere to be seen.

"Looks like you guys found our seed stores," Chet said, stepping past them to one door and throwing it open. "When I first discovered these, I hoped they were full of beer. Boy, was I wrong."

His comment got another round of chuckles from everyone, though Morales continued to notice the exchange of glances between Shea and the other bunker crew as they adjusted their positioning, moving to stand closer to the soldiers.

Smith took a radio from his belt. "I'm not sure if this will work, but I'm going to try calling Brozowski and LePlante." As soon as he clicked the button, all he received was a scratch of feedback and static noise. "Attention, those in Smith's team. If you get this, move to Sub-floor 4, to the refrigeration units at the end of the first hallway."

"Yeah, radios don't work in here so well." Shae shook her head, striding to an intercom on the wall near the door. Her finger raised to one of the buttons. "Want me to call down to them?"

"Nah, we got this." Smith shook his head and gestured at Jennings. "Hey, Jennings. Why don't you run down and grab Brozowski and LePlante from the communication floor? We've got some stuff for them to check out. Hurry it up. Bring everyone up."

The soldier nodded, spun, and exited the room, and Morales's spirits rose despite the thrumming tension in his body though his expression fell just as quickly when Meyers strolled inside the refrigerated room and started perusing the shelves. The big, toe-headed kid looked out at them with a wide, Nebraska-sized grin.

"Boy, my dad would love it in here. He used to have a shed full of seeds, and we planted new ones each year in the garden. By the end of the summer, I knew every type of seed there was."

Morales glanced at Smith, eyes widening, and the lieutenant waved the soldier back. "Yeah, yeah, Meyers, we've heard the stories before. Come on out of thre."

"Seriously, guys," Meyers went on, scoffing in amusement and mock disbelief. "You need to check this out. This is the most awesome display of seeds I've ever seen. There're tons of corn, potatoes, beans, even honey producing flowers. Wow, this is real Noah's Ark stuff. Come here, Morales!"

"No thanks," Morales called back, separating himself from the group, walking over to a bulletin board near the door where someone had made a sheet of climate settings for the seeds. Big digital consoles showing the refrigerators' temperature and humidity hung on the walls, and he pretended to study them as Shea meandered over and put herself between Morales and the others, both groups shifting positions casually. "He's right, you know. It's an amazing display. You should check it out."

"I was never really into farm stuff. I'm a junk food fanatic myself." He glanced back at the refrigerator, grimacing even more as Rupert walked in behind Meyers. Outside the coolers, it was Smith, Morales, Stevens, and Griggs versus Chet, Shae, and three of their people. All it would take was one of the bunker crew to slam the door shut to even the odds, and that wasn't even considering the maintenance workers who could walk in at any minute.

Morales glanced at the lieutenant, waiting for him to pull out his sidearm and arrest the group, but if he jumped too soon, it might put Brozowski and LePlante in danger. Still, the decision had to be made, and it had to be made quickly.

"Hey," Smith called to his men, trying to sound casual despite the note of tension in his voice. "I'm serious, get out here where I can see you. Can't have you in there screwing off--"

The other woman in Chet's crew threw her shoulder against the refrigerator door, slamming it shut on the soldiers inside while the two other crew members grabbed Stevens and Griggs, going for their weapons. Shea lunged for Morales's holster, but he spun in time to crack her across the jaw with a left hook, the woman crashing to one knee as a flurry of motion exploded in the room. Pistol whipping out, Morales tried to shoot her, but she struck his hand with her forearm, knocking the gun free. They dropped down, grappling for the weapon on the floor as it slid and bounced against the wall. Morales lifted his hand and slammed it down, finally pinning the gun to the tiles, fingers clutching the pistol but she collapsed on his arm, clinging to him like a banshee.

Smith grappled with Chet, the lieutenant grabbing the thinner man by the shirt, sweeping his legs from under him and slamming him to the floor. Unfortunately, the rifle they'd jerked away from Briggs swung around and pointed at Smith's temple, freezing him in place. Stevens's rifle had been taken, too, the barrel jabbing into Morales's ribs as the man holding it glared down at him darkly.

"Drop the weapon or the lieutenant gets his head blown off!" the one on Smith yelled.

Morales froze with his hand on the grip, looking back at the crews' faces, their expressions having turned from helpful to furious in a handful of seconds. Releasing the weapon, he held his hands out and Shea snatched the gun and leapt up, firing it once into the ceiling before leveling it at him.

"Get off the floor, asshole. Move it!"

Morales stood slowly, palms raised, eyes on the woman with his pistol, and without warning she cocked her fist and struck him across the jaw, leaving his chin stinging from the blow. "You should know better than to hit a lady," she snarled, backing to the center of the room, gun pointed at his chest. "Against the wall. All of you."

Hands raised, Morales did as he was told, working his jaw back and forth. Stevens and Griggs put their backs to the bulletin board with him as Chet stood and grabbed Lieutenant Smith by his jacket, throwing him in Morales's direction. The soldier caught himself before he slipped and fell, raising slowly, chin lifted in defiance as he stared holes in the impostors.

"You keep that attitude up, buddy," Chet said, grabbing one of the rifles, "and I'll wipe that look right off your face with this."

The soldiers trapped inside the refrigeration unit were pounding on the door and Chet walked over and pounded back. "Hey, you boys want to keep it down in there? If you annoy us enough, we might have to kill one of your buddies."

The pounding on the door fell silent, and the intercom exploded with the huffing, panting voice. "This is Larry down on five. I'm looking for Chet. Chet, are you there? Everything good?"

The bunker leader stepped to the other side of the door, pressing the intercom button. "This is Chet. Yeah. All's well. I'm on Sub-level 4 in the seed storage room. What's going on?"

"We heard the gunshot, and the Army boys panicked. We've got a pair pinned behind some equipment. They won't come out. What do you want me to do?"

Chet backed away from the speaker, gesturing at Smith with the end of the rifle. "Tell them to surrender, or we'll do to you what we did to the other shits that ran this place."

Chapter 19
Tom McKnight
Nuevo Laredo, Mexico

The Humvee flew over what was just barely a highway through a desert that had become gentle curves of flat, white-dusted tundra in every direction. Tom's feet were cold as he kept the accelerator pedal pressed steadily to the floor, weaving back and forth over icy spots and slamming through the rare drifts that were a foot and a half high. The snowfall accumulation wasn't as bad as what they'd seen near San Antonio, but things were getting worse by the hour.

"This place must've gotten hit with a storm right before we came through," he said to Barbara. "Look at the wind."

Even as he spoke, a gust of chill air skimmed the ground in front of them, blowing a soft patch of snow into their windshield. The road vanished in a dusting of white before the windshield wipers swiped it clean and Tom bent the vehicle around a stiff curve, the highway banking right to cut between a pair of hills covered in scrub and snow. The Humvee's knobby tires slid sideways, the rear end shifting dangerously, slinging itself toward the middle of the road, and had someone been coming the other way, they would've crashed into them.

"Forget about the snow, Tom. Please slow down. There's been no sign of Keith or those APCs since we left Nuevo Laredo."

"Right," he said, easing the speed down to thirty, leaning back and trying to relax. The winter driving kept him on edge, and every few moments he learned a new lesson on how to keep the two and a half ton vehicle on the road. "Sorry. Better?"

"Yeah, thanks."

Despite the heater kicked up to full blast, the cabin was still chilly. Cold air filtered in through rust spots in the floorboards and cracks around the doors, his toes as frozen as ice cubes on the pedals. The kids huddled in back with Smooch, covered in blankets, a pile of children and dog, shivering as they munched on snacks from their backpacks. The cracked rear windshield whistled and leaked, and not even the piece of duct tape Samantha had placed on the surface helped much.

"Boy, these things weren't meant for comfort, were they?" she said with a grunt as the bouncy suspension jostled her around. "I'll tell you, Tom, I'm about to abandon you and join the kids in the back."

"I wouldn't blame you at all. I can barely feel my feet or my rear end, and my hands aren't doing any better." Still bundled from head to toe, his body was warm except for his extremities, the thick gloves covering his fingers no match for the frigid chill that surrounded them.

They hit a slight incline and Tom pressed forward, not wanting to get stuck. Tires spinning, kicking out snow in arcing wakes he turned the wheel to the right, hugging the inside lane. The Humvee gave off a soft clatter of noise, every part rattling on the frame but still it held together, and they came over the rise and down the other side in one piece.

"Oh, Tom. Look!" Barbara pointed out the front window, off her side where an exit ramp branched off the main highway. Beyond that, nestled into the snow-covered trees, were three buildings that comprised a rest stop area. He saw a gas station with a mini-mart and two garage bays off to the side, what looked like a Mexican eatery, and another adobe style building that could have been a hotel. The signs were in Spanish with English letters written smaller beneath them.

"We're definitely not in the United States anymore," Tom said, tracing over the words.

"Let's stop and get our bearings," Barbara suggested, turning to face him in the seat. "We don't know where we are or where we're going. This highway could be leading us anywhere."

"As long as it's not north, I don't care." He slowed as they approached, creeping, keeping the tires moving fast enough to avoid getting stuck in the mounds of snow. "You're right. We should at least stop and see if there's something we can scavenge. We'll need all the diesel, food, and water we can find. I'm just a little worried because of what people back in camp were saying about the annexation."

Barbara nodded, looking on at the establishments with keen interest. "Yeah, I don't think the people around here would appreciate a family of Americans busting in on them right now. For all we know, they might consider us sworn enemies. Especially driving this sort of vehicle."

With a deep breath and a sigh, Tom turned the wheel toward the exit and trundled down the ramp. At the bottom, he didn't bother stopping, but spun in a short arc, drove straight for another 200 feet, then angled left into the gas station parking lot. The big Humvee swung in beside the diesel fuel pump and came to a skidding halt and Tom sat with his hands on the wheel, fingers wiggling, head on a swivel as he looked for movement. Peering toward the mini mart's wide glass, he found the insides dark and impregnable, the front section of the store lit by the dismal gray winter light, fading to darkness at the rear.

"I don't see anyone, so I'll take Smooch inside and clear the place. Be right back."

Tom popped his door and got out, shouldered one of the rifles Saanvi had left in their supplies and opened the back door for the dog to jump down. The German Shepherd walked in a quick circle, limping slightly but looking much healthier than she had when he and Samantha had first found her. Smooch's fur was growing back on her wounded shoulder, and the singed hair from the house fire was filling in, too. Saanvi had fed the animal well, her chest and belly round and thick, and after another month of healing she'd be as good as new.

Tom slammed both doors shut, leaving the truck running, treading through the snow to the mini mart with Smooch on his heels. He paused at the front door, putting his hands to the glass and peering inside. The new perspective wasn't much better, his gaze only able to penetrate a few yards into the back of the store.

"Okay, girl. Let's check it out." With a flick of his wrist, he grabbed the door handle and pulled the unlocked door open, stepped in with the dog, pushing the door shut behind him to lock out the wind. The air was chilly, frosty, his misty breath blossoming into the darkness, hanging for a long moment thanks to the absence of a breeze. Flashlight shining toward the rear, he moved straight down the middle, looking through the remaining snacks still sitting on the skewed shelves.

There was hardly anything left, just a few of the less popular candy bars, energy snacks, and chip bags. A cooler sat in back and when he opened the door, the foul smell of sour milk poured out from several broken plastic bottles, white liquid sprayed and frozen on the glass. The dog whined, and Tom reached down and rubbed her head.

"I know, girl. It's pretty gross in there."

Still, he took three frozen bottles of water out, their caps having exploded, setting the blocks of ice on the bright red pressboard counter next to the old cash register. If anything, they could thaw them out and drink them later and use the plastic containers to help collect and melt down snow after that. Circling to check the cash register, he saw the door was open, the money having been cleaned out. "No dinero," Tom mumbled as he slammed the drawer shut, only to have it pop open again, some mechanism on the inside frozen or broken by those who had plundered the place.

The bathrooms were dirty, borderline disgusting, with the faint scent of cold sewage wafting in the air. The mirrors were smeared with muck, sink stained with iron deposits and the pipes had long since burst. Whatever piping materials they'd used likely couldn't resist such freezing weather – after all, since when did anyone so far south expect such frigid temperatures?

Exiting the restrooms, Tom stepped along the hallway to the end, pushing through the door into the garage area. The petrol scents of axle grease and motor oil permeated the space, and his flashlight revealed one bay taken up by an old Ford F150, while the other was empty. He did a slow circle of the place, stepping over hydraulic jacks and tires, walking past cabinets, tool chests, and work benches littered with tools. Soiled rags were draped around and piled on a bench near the back and a wood stove with two flat plates on top sat along the right wall, its rusted pipe angling upward to disappear into the ceiling. On the left side of the second bay, a fuel tank shared the wall with a row of metal shelves stacked with cans of oil, paint, and grease.

"Well, it looks safe to me. Time to put the kids to work."

Smooch gave another soft whine, faithfully sticking to Tom's heels as he returned to the store. From the inside, he knocked on the door glass and waved to get Barbara's attention. His wife raised in the seat, nodding at his motioning and the truck doors popped open, the children rolling out of the backseat, bundled up, kicking snow all the way to the front door. Holding the door open, he ushered them in and took his wife's hand as she followed behind.

"It's safe in here. Doesn't seem to be a lot of food, but there's a fuel tank in the garage and some spare oil cans that might come in handy later."

Barbara nodded. "This is good. There could be some things in here we can use later on. Kids, why don't you go around and start collecting whatever you can find, okay? Anything edible, even if you don't think you'll like it, gather up. We can't afford to be picky."

"I put some bricks of water on the counter," Tom pointed over toward the register. "Just set everything beside those."

Sam snickered, repeating his words with a sarcastic mumble while nudging Jack, who giggled in response. "He said 'bricks of water.'"

The children got busy walking through the store, noisily and busily checking under the rows of crooked shelving, stooping to reach to the back where they discovered the looters had left a veritable treasure trove behind. Barbara strode over to one shelf filled with paper towels and napkins and grabbed some packages, placing them on the counter with the rest of their goods.

"For when we don't want to use cacti to wipe," she said with a playful wink and grin.

"At the very least, we can use it for kindling." He narrowed his eyes at his wife. "You're in a good mood."

"I guess I am," she replied, traipsing by and giving him a kiss on the cheek.

Hands stuffed into his pockets, he followed her along the aisles as she picked through what remained of the store. Stopping at the medicine section, she snatched up aspirin packets, lip balm, and lotion. "These'll come in handy for our noses and hands."

"I guess you're right. Those are things I wouldn't have thought about, but it makes sense. The air is getting drier by the day."

"Exactly."

"So, why the good mood?" Tom gave her a friendly smirk. "You're really that happy we finally got our vacation to Mexico?"

Linda heard him from the other side of the store and laughed, while Barbara shot him a crooked smile, batting her eyes. "You always take me to the fanciest places."

Jack rounded the corner, holding up canned dog food as the German Shepherd followed him, sniffing and licking at it. Around the sides, one of the cans had broken, and the meaty frozen morsels had popped out. "You think we can thaw this out so Smooch can eat it?"

Reaching down, Tom took the split can from the boy and held it up. "I guess it's possible. I don't imagine it would be bad for her. How many other cans are there?"

Jack spread his mittens wide. "I'd say a bunch. Like, 12."

"All right, put them in a plastic bag, and we'll take them with us."

"Outstanding!" He spun and flew back to the dog food section to collect more, Smooch following him with a click of claws on the tile. Once Tom and Barbara had taken everything worth taking from the medicine aisle, they dropped it off at the counter, their tiny stockpile growing by leaps and bounds.

"It's amazing what we can do when we work together." Barbara's bright spirit suddenly switched off like a light, her expression shifting and uncertain.

Tom took her by the shoulders and fixed her jade green eyes with a questioning look. "Hey, honey. What's wrong?"

"Nothing at all." She circled her arms around his chest, squeezing him through his thick coat and layers of long underwear and shirts. "I'm just happy we're together. Even when we were in Asheville, it didn't feel like home."

"I know exactly what you mean." Tom embraced her back, letting his chin rest on the top of her head. "Even in the camp, it was hard to be ourselves, but I guess we're adjusting to the new reality. I didn't realize how much stronger I am when I'm with you guys."

Barbara melted into his arms, falling against him completely, sighing into his coat. Lifting her, he swung her around and set her on the floor again as Linda came up with a can of beef barley soup in each hand. She took one look at her parents and rolled her eyes before she placed the cans on the counter.

Laughing, Tom let go of Barbara and chased after his daughter. "You think you'll get away without a hug?!"

Linda squealed as she rushed to the end of the aisle with her father chasing on her heels. They rounded the bend, and she ran into Sam, giving Tom the moment he needed to snatch her up, lift her from the ground and swing her with her feet flying out.

"Jeez, dad! What are you doing? Let me go!" Yet, even as she struggled, she laughed and kicked without trying too hard to escape. Releasing Linda, he feigned a lunge at his eldest daughter, who jumped back, finger in the air, pointing and warning. "Hey, hey! What's gotten into you guys?!"

"I guess it's that we're finally free and not surrounded by a bunch of armed guards or people trying to kill us," he said, grabbing at her hands and chuckling as she ran away. Tom sobered up, standing straight, fists on his hips as he watched his family gathering supplies in the store. "I missed goofing around with you guys."

"I want a hug, too!" Jack flew into his father's arms, laughing, clinging to his bag of dog food as the cans clattered inside. Tom lifted him up, heart swelling with elation for the first time since they'd showed up at the Nuevo Laredo camp. The tension unwound from his shoulders, the gut-turning nervousness fraying and giving way. With Jack placed back on his feet, he found his wife and wrapped his arms around her again, lowering his voice as the kids returned to searching. "I'm not kidding about feeling free. It's like a huge weight has been lifted off my shoulders."

Barbara nodded, grinning, glancing outside at the idling truck. "Too bad we can't just stay here and get warm. Have some family time away from that damn camp, Marty, Keith… all of it."

Tom followed her gaze outside, staring at the Humvee, not particularly thrilled about getting back in the driver's seat. They'd seen no signs of pursuit since the town, and he was relatively certain the pace he'd set had allowed them to outdistance the APCs. A sporadic dusting of snowfall suddenly picked up, a wash of flakes whipping back and forth in what remained of the daylight and he felt a sense of peace wash over him.

"Hey, you know what? Why don't we stay here? I think we're far enough ahead, and it looks like a storm is coming in, anyway. We don't want to get caught in it."

The pair walked to the window and looked outside, Barbara putting her gloved hands to the glass. "What about our tire tracks? Won't they see those?"

Tom shook his head. "I think our tracks will be almost invisible within the hour, and I know the perfect spot to park the Humvee."

"On top of the weapons she got us, Saanvi packed a small cooking stove in with the supplies," Barbara said. "We could use that to get warm."

"I can one up you on that. There's a wood-burning stove in the garage."

Barbara's jaw dropped in awe. "Are you serious? An actual wood-burning stove?"

With a shrug and nod, he replied, "Yeah, it's back there. There're some pans and skillets lying around, too."

"And we have a few cans of food we can cook up," Barbara's smile grew.

"Sounds like a plan." Tom moved toward the garage door at the end of the hall. "I'll bring the Humvee in while you guys carry those supplies to the back. Line them up on the workbench and we'll get this party started."

Tom crossed through the garage and found the manual release for the second bay door. He popped it open, dragged it up by the handle, wheels squeaking and protesting as it grudgingly rose. With the wind and sleet whipping across his face and flying into the gaps of his clothing, he jogged through the ever-thickening snow and got behind the Humvee's wheel. A moment later, he was pulling it inside, easing the truck to the back, leaving plenty of room for them to gather around the stove.

Tom climbed out and stood at the bay door, staring out, dancing motes of white powder drifting in front of his eyes, growing stronger even as the daylight faded to night. The cool scent of winter mixed with the petroleum smells of the garage, his nostrils flaring as he watched their old tire tracks filling bit by bit, masking their route.

He reached up and grabbed the bay door handle, pulling it down on its squeaky wheels until it struck the floor with a soft impact. Locking it, he called over to Linda, and together they covered the garage windows with old rags and duct tape. Saanvi had packed a pair of electric lanterns in with their supplies, and Barbara turned them both on and placed one on the work bench near the stove.

"Hey, Sam, do you think you can get us a fire going?"

"We need some kindling and wood." Samantha strode to the stove, hands on her hips, bending lower, opening the door and peering at the coals the last person had left. She reached down and grabbed a stick from the floor, using it to prod around in the belly while Tom pointed to a stack of logs on the shelf behind the stove, grabbing a couple of large pieces and carrying it over while his wife brought a napkin pack.

"Can you use this as kindling?" She asked.

"That might work," Sam replied. "But ideally, we'd use some smaller sticks. I think there's some down here on the floor."

"Well, you've proven you can make a fire just about anywhere." Barbara placed the napkins on the floor and took a step back, watching her daughter build the fire with an expert hand.

"I learned how to do it when Dad and I were on the road."

"I guess I didn't realize how independent you were," she said with a glance over at Tom. "You're quite the survivalist now."

Tom strode over and put his arm around his wife's shoulders. "We've all had to learn some new skills, right?"

Linda gave an affirmative nod while Jack brought his bag of dog food cans over to the fire and set it down.

"Hey, kids. Let's find some chairs and pull them up to the stove. I'm sure Sam will have things pretty warm here in a minute."

Tom pulled up a rolling tool chest while the children went back into the mini mart and grabbed two foldout chairs from the storeroom. Barbara dug up a pair of truck pads in a cabinet, and together they placed them in a semicircle around the stove. The heat from the Humvee's cooling engine had taken the edge off the chill in the small space, and Sam was working diligently on the fire.

Sticks went in with a small cluster of kindling, then she placed a match carefully inside, leaning forward on her knees to blow the resulting cinders into a spark of flame. Two more larger pieces of wood were thrown in, orange tendrils of fire catching and licking upward and at the first crackle of smoke, she dropped in a bigger log, adjusted its position, and stepped back to see her handiwork.

The McKnights relaxed in their seats, Tom on the truck pad with Barbara on his left. As he squatted and lowered himself to the floor, every joint creaked and groaned with discomfort. Shoulders stiff, feet gnawed through with cold, he placed his hands behind him and leaned back, putting his boots closer to the growing fire. Sam settled back onto the toolbox, ready to jump in and stoke the flames when it was needed and Smooch rested at the end of the truck pad, turning in a circle and lying at Tom's right hand while Jack and Linda sat in the foldout chairs.

After several minutes, the small flame was a roaring fire, blossomed in a halo of warmth, smoking wood masking the mechanic shop smells. Feet stretched out toward the open stove, Tom's boots soon grew warm, and he had to pull his legs back to keep them from growing uncomfortable.

"Awesome fire, Sam. Good job."

"Thanks, Dad. I learned from the best."

"What else can you do?" Barbara asked, sliding her hand over to hold Tom's.

"Not much," she sighed. "I can cook soup, but that's about it."

She rose off the toolbox and picked up the sack of frozen items they'd brought in, lining up waters, cans of food, and other iced goods around the stove.

"It'll probably take a few hours for these to thaw," she said, stepping back to her seat. "But Smooch will be glad when she can eat some real dog food. We weren't able to give her much on the road."

"But I bet Saanvi fed her well." Tom stroked the Shepard's fur. "She looks way better now. Her weight seems to have picked up."

"I'm just happy we still have her. I'm still shocked she survived the house fire," Barbara added with a fond glance at the animal. "That girl has been through quite a lot."

"The best friend ever!" Jack gleamed, leaning in and giving Smooch a big embrace before he settled back in his seat.

They relaxed for a short time, allowing the warmth to radiate outward while Barbara and Linda went through their supplies of snacks, thumping cans of soup into two pans, placing them on the steel plates as the stove grew hot to the touch. Soon, the salty-rich smells of beef and chicken broth filled the air, a welcome relief after so many of the same MREs in a row.

"Not the greatest meal, but the best we can do under the circumstances," Barbara said, her eyes picking lovingly across her family.

"Fit for a king, I'd say," he replied. "Better than we've had in a long time."

"Too bad Jerry couldn't be here." Sam's glum tone cut through the quiet, and Tom absently rubbed Smooch's head as he thought back on the young man they'd traveled so far with. "He was a pretty good guy, and I know he would've been a big help if he were still here today."

"I would've loved to have met him," Barbara nodded. "We owe him an enormous thanks for helping you guys."

"The kid had his problems." Tom tilted his head, eyes filled with a sense of loss. "But he had a good heart, and he kept us going when things got tough. It burns me up that he lost his life because of Keith. It was so stupid and random, and I get sick just thinking about it."

"I miss the Everetts," Linda added. "They were so fun."

"Darren was my buddy." Jack was suddenly crestfallen, his previously happy face sinking with the memory of the loss of his friend. "He liked to show me shark teeth and other stuff they found."

Tom laughed, glassy eyed. "Remember when he brought over that metal detector? The guy was finding all kinds of stuff. Old bullets, coins, he even found some lead shot in his field from when they'd used his property as a training ground for infantry during the Civil War."

"Darren loved all that sort of stuff." Barbara sighed deeply. "What a tragic, pointless loss."

"And Marie cooked some awesome dinners." Linda's smile widened as she stared at the fire, seeming to see visions of the past playing out in the flames, then her face slackened as a single tear streaked down her cheek.

A silence hung over the group as they got comfortable, the old stove driving the numbness from Tom's feet and fingers, replacing pure survival with memories of their lives and the lives of others.

"Here's to all the people we've lost." Barbara raised a water bottle, and everyone else lifted their drinks with him.

"To Marie, Darren, and Jerry," Tom said in a lofty tone. "Good friends who we'll miss dearly."

They clicked their bottles and cans together, drank, then fell once more into a somber silence. Tom's eyes went distant, the flames hypnotizing as they danced and wavered. "And let's not forget our good friend, Saanvi. If it wasn't for her, we'd still be back in camp, dealing with Marty."

"Or Keith and his new friends," his wife added, her own jade green eyes falling prey to the fire's movements.

Silence filled the space as Barbara and Linda got everyone a bowl of soup and spoons from the dishes they'd found lying around. The quiet lingered as they ate, the broth and vegetables and big chunks of meat hitting their stomachs with a satisfying warmth. Finishing his meal, Tom placed his bowl aside and slid to his elbow. Laying lengthwise on the truck pads, his wife stretched out in front of him, her sandy hair brushing his nose and cheeks. Arm resting over her waist, hand relaxed, his fingers rested on her stomach as the fire warmed the floor.

Linda fished out a piece of jerky from a side bag, smiling as she chewed. "What's that grin for?" Tom asked.

"I was thinking this is just like home, except we don't have the big screen TV and a movie playing."

"And the popcorn," Barbara interjected.

"Oh, boy, do I miss popcorn." Samantha leaned forward with her stick and shifted the wood inside the stove's belly, kicking up cinders and producing even more heat. She circled to the stove's rear, found the sliding vent, and opened it one notch, allowing more air to circulate through, making the fire even hotter. "I'd give anything to be back on the couch with a cover over me and my favorite movie with you guys." As she retreated to her seat, her light green eyes gazed lovingly over her family, trademark curls falling over her coat in ringlets. "But I guess this is better than nothing, right?"

"Way better than nothing," Linda agreed with a nod as she popped another piece of jerky into her mouth and unzipped her coat, the stove rapidly turning the small building into the warmest place the family had experienced in quite a while.

"I miss the farm, too," Linda jeered. "The week you guys were at the conference, we harvested all the crops and Mom taught me how to can the food. She said I was better than you, Sam."

Samantha let a scoff slip free, lips crooked, smirking. "I seriously doubt that, you twerp. I was the best at canning in the family."

"I don't know." Barbara raised her eyebrows doubtfully. "Linda was pretty good. We'd finished with all the produce and were about to make some freeze-dried potato flakes when things started heading south."

"Next place we go that has canning equipment, it's on," Sam growled at her sister who pointed back, accepting the challenge, nodding as she chewed.

"You're on. It's going to be a good old canning competition between me and you, girl."

"But where will we do that?" Jack said, slapping his thighs as he kicked his feet. "We don't even have a home or a place to go. What are we going to do?"

"I can't tell you where that'll be." Tom stared at the white-hot coals in the oven. "But I do know one thing. We need to get to where it's warm and safe from the cold. South. Far to the south."

"Is that where the rest of the Americans are?" Jack asked. "South? Did the Army people take them there?"

"Hard to say," Tom shrugged. "We probably have millions of citizens there who were evacuated by our government and whatever's left of the Mexican authorities. I'm not sure we can call ourselves a country anymore except in spirit. We're all just human beings, trying to survive and stay warm."

The quiet of the mechanic shop blanketed them in a pleasant cover, the crackling stove with its blazing heat giving the McKnight's a semblance of peace, though said peace was overshadowed by the constant threats lurking just out of sight.

Voice lifting, Tom spoke to the children. "Your mother and I will take first watch tonight, kids. Linda and Jack, grab the sleeping bags out of the Humvee and stretch them out in front of the fire, then get ready for bed. Just like at the camp, you'll stay dressed, ready to move at a moment's notice. You can take off your boots and jackets, but keep your cold-weather clothing on. Okay?"

Jack and Linda nodded and hopped up from their chairs, hurrying off to get the gear while Tom enjoyed another few minutes of warmth with his arm wrapped around his wife's waist. His eyes shifted back to the fire, wondering what the next day would bring.

Chapter 20
Navy Admiral Ben Spencer
Venezuela, South America

The sky was bright blue, the sun shining through cloudless skies, reflecting off the ocean waves in shimmering streaks of light. The water stretched flat and calm in every direction, no signs of storms or foul weather in sight. Schools of fish banked away from the massive fleet as it neared, eight sleek ships plowing through the water at full speed, leaving towering wakes behind them and marine turbulence trailing in aqua blue streaks. To everyone aboard Carrier Strike Group Eight, it was a beautiful day.

At the center of the fleet was a heavy aircraft carrier, the USS Harry S. Truman, a Nimitz-class warship powered by two nuclear reactors, ultra advanced sensors, a suite of electronic warfare decoys, and enough armaments to take out entire nations. The vessel was supported thirty-five hundred sailors, pilots, and assorted crew and atop the main tower, a dozen radar arrays and sensory dishes spun, searching for enemy ships and aircraft in the area.

The vessels surrounding the Truman were formidable in their own rights. One Ticonderoga-class cruiser, four Arleigh Burke-class destroyers, and two Oliver Hazard Perry-class anti-submarine frigates comprised the bulk of the task force while three Los Angeles-class attack subs lurked beneath the waters, running silent.

With the bridge windows open, the command crew enjoyed a warm breeze blowing through, carrying the heavy scent of the salt sea. Coming from the growing cold of the Cuban base, Navy Admiral Ben Spencer took a deep breath of the tropical air, his gaze stony as he studied the distant ocean. The carrier group was cutting through the Caribbean Sea toward Barcelona after deploying from a port in Puerto Rico to spearhead the invasion of Venezuela.

The Admiral was on hand to assist with Operation Heat Strike, the Navy's jab at the Venezuelan coast. Once they arrived, they'd give air support for the landing parties and act as a distraction to confuse the Venezuelan Army. The crew bustled around the bridge, tactical displays and control columns in the back of the room manned by experienced sailors. Shoes shuffled and voices quietly called out changes to engine speed and direction, keeping them on course per the captain's orders.

Captain Rogers sat in his chair to the admiral's right, monitoring a tactical display of controls, radar screens, and maps. The man leaned slightly forward, pulling down a mic that hung above them, placing it in front of his lips. "Air control, launch the Hawkeye. I want to know what's on that Venezuelan coastline."

"Yes, sir," came the controller through the tiny speaker on the console.

The captain raised a pair of binoculars to his eyes and peered ahead toward the Venezuelan coast where Barcelona lay in wait. Spencer raised his own lenses and studied the distance with a furrowed brow like he was reading a book. Past the lead battle cruiser and destroyer was a solid line separating the sky from the sea, the two differing shades topped off by a bank of white clouds. The shore was still out of range, though soon they'd see it, reaching the point of no return when the Admiral would give the final go ahead for the operation to begin, putting the fate and hope of an entire nation entirely in his hands.

"What do you think, Captain?" He lowered his binoculars and looked aside.

Captain Rogers was a middle-aged man of fifty-two. Dressed in casual Navy trousers and a windbreaker, he struck a relaxed but stoic pose in his seat, sunglasses perched on a wide, hawkish nose, shoulders hunched forward.

"It looks good so far, but I expect some resistance from the Venezuelans. They won't leave their coast unprotected." The man spoke in a commanding voice, keeping his tone low enough so only the admiral could hear.

From the deck, the twin turboprop Hawkeye took off in a burst of burring propellers. It lifted into the air and banked left, rising in altitude with its massively round dish perched on top. The array held transponders, radar, and a Mini-DAMA SATCOM system. As it rose higher, it began feeding data into the Naval Tactical Data System, filling their screens with information. Spencer and Rogers both glanced down at their tactical displays as the first sweeps were made. Almost immediately, six large blips appeared just beyond their battleships' gun range.

The captain leaned forward, expression never wavering. "Tactical, give me a reading on those marks I'm seeing. What am I looking at?"

"We see them, sir," came a voice through the overhead speaker. "One second, and I'll get an identification on them."

A brief pause lingered over the bridge as tactical determined what types of ships were waiting for them.

The admiral looked over at the Rogers. "Whoever they are, it looks like they're guarding the coast closely. Look at that formation. You think it's Venezuelan?"

"No clue," the captain replied. "If it is, they'd be foolish to challenge us in open water. But let's see what tactical comes back with."

The question was answered a moment later. "Sir, we're seeing six Russian vessels out there. There's a Kuznetsov-class carrier, one Parchim-class anti-sub destroyer, two Grisha-class corvettes, and a Gepard-class frigate."

"Russians," the Admiral snorted derisively. "Trying to beat us to the punch."

"That's a big part of their forces," the captain replied. "That confirms the intel. They're definitely working with the Venezuelans."

The admiral squinted and raised his binoculars, still unable to get a visual on the Russian ships. "The Kuznetsov is one of their only three carriers. They're serious."

"If we attack them, do you think they'll launch nukes?"

"At what?" Spencer scoffed. "The whole northern United States is frozen, and most of Russia, too. There's nothing left to bomb – nothing that doesn't have resources that they're already trying to secure. No, we'll win this war conventionally, but we have to strike first and hard. I just wish we had a little more backup."

"We only had the one East Coast strike group available for this fight," the captain confirmed. "We couldn't commit any West Coast ships."

"It'll take weeks for them to arrive." The decision loomed, the moment of no return hovering like a dark cloud. The Admiral squeezed the binoculars in his hands, gripping them so tightly the frame creaked. "We can't wait for them to get here."

"Is that a go to begin Heat Strike?"

A deep bite of doubt froze his mind. The conflict in front of them could ignite World War III. It wasn't a decision to take lightly. "No. Let me talk to the President one last time."

The Admiral stepped away from his position at the glass and strode to a small steel case lying open on a utility table, guarded by two Marines who stood like statues on the wavering deck. Inside the case was a communications array with a direct feed to the president and Spencer picked up the receiver and put it to his ear, not needing to dial any numbers. After two brief rings, John Zimmerman's voice greeted him on the other end.

"Hello, Admiral. How goes it?"

"Things are going well, sir. We're approaching the Venezuelan coast on calm seas."

"Have you given the authorization to move ahead with Operation Heat Strike?"

"Not yet. That's what I was calling you about. We've confirmed that the Russians are here, and in force. Pings on radar."

"That's what satellite imagery showed us. What's your take on the situation?"

Spencer looked out through the front window of the ship's bridge out into the open waters, imagining what was waiting for them just a short distance ahead.

"I say we punch through. We've got them outclassed and outnumbered, and they won't be expecting us to move in force. We can knock the hell out of them. Then we'll start the landings. Once we get those refineries stabilized, we'll be in business."

A pause came over the line as the President weighed his options and the admiral's advice. Spencer took a handkerchief and dabbed at his brow. He'd been a Navy man his entire life, from the time he was eighteen until his seventy-second year on the earth. While scoring high marks in battle tactics and simulated maneuvers, his true love was for process and procedure, the uniform and what it represented. He'd enjoyed many years being at the top of his game astride the mighty United States Navy, all culminating in what would be the biggest fight of their lives.

"I authorize Operation Heat Strike." The President spoke with a flat finality. "Give 'em hell, Admiral. May God bless you and those sailors."

Spencer hung up the phone, spinning on his heel and marching back to the captain. He held the man's eyes, giving him a terse nod. "We have the go. Engage Operation Heat Strike."

A flurry of motion began as the Captain relayed the confirmation of their orders. Jets lined up on the deck, preparing to lift off and crews swarmed them in orange or yellow jackets, moving like a well-choreographed unit. They guided an F-18 to its starting point with the catapult officer watching from a control pod on the deck, connecting the nose to the slingshot hook with a clank of steel. Steam shot up in thick gouts as internal cylinders below filled with pressure and the pilot engaged the jet's engines as they released the catapult, hurling the jet along the deck. Its nose flew up, ejecting cyclonic winds behind it as it lifted into the sky. The voice of the flight deck operator boomed from loudspeakers, echoing across the water between the ships as more F-18s and F-35s were lined up and launched in twenty-second intervals. Their turbo engines shrieked as they swarmed upward, quickly forming strike groups.

"Captain, this is tactical. We have two squadrons up and two more coming online."

"Has the enemy scrambled any aircraft?" Rogers asked, leaning forward in his seat, neck craned as he scanned for ships on the horizon.

"None that we can see, sir. Should we have our squadrons wait for the others?"

"No. Their primary objective is to neutralize their air support before it can take off."

"Roger that, Captain."

Spencer looked upward as distant formations banked in a wide arc toward the Venezuelan coast, rising even higher into the clear blue sky. The admiral and captain dropped their eyes on the horizon, sometimes glancing at the tactical screen, watching the warships as the fighter squadrons approached. Hand resting on the touchscreen, the admiral could zoom in on the triangular shapes to pick out individual fighters, familiarizing himself with the units.

"I've got visual on the Russian warships," someone said on the other side of the bridge. Both the captain and admiral lifted binoculars to their eyes, watching the distant specs of the Russian destroyers waiting for them.

"Have they seen us yet?" Spencer asked. "It doesn't seem like they're moving... Wait, there they go, getting into defensive positions surrounding their carrier. They're probably scrambling planes."

As if to confirm his suspicion, the tactical display showed smaller triangles appearing on the screen around the Russian fleet, indicating the formation of the enemy squadrons.

The captain peered through his lenses, lifting them away from his eyes to glance at his screen, his voice riding high with anticipation as the fighters started their bombing runs. "I wonder if they even have satellite capabilities to speak of anymore. Seems we caught them with their pants down," he murmured, lips tight around the words. "Come on, guys. Nail that deck."

In the distance, Spencer spotted thin lines of counter fire, anti-gun ordinance exploding in the air, flak flying from the destroyers' guns. Explosions lit up the Russian carrier's deck, one massive strike blasting across the base of the tower. A launching jet was caught up in the concussion, spinning toward the deck's edge. The aircraft tilted, wing catching the pavement, flipping it right off the side of the deck and into the sea.

"Yes!" Spencer spat quietly.

"This is tactical. We can confirm two direct hits on the enemy carrier. We've lost one fighter."

The Captain confirmed it by glancing at his screen, noting a squadron was down one jet. As the US ships drew closer to the fight, ships became visible to the naked eye, smoke and fire trailing up from the carrier as the Corvettes and frigates circled it in a protective formation.

"We've got another jet down, sir," came tactical. "The Russians got half a squadron in the air, and more are coming up. Also, we're picking up the signatures of two Akula-class attack subs advancing on our position."

"Engage them with our own subs," the captain commanded. "And get the frigates into position to take them out."

"Understood."

Within minutes, US planes angled downward and fired missiles at the ships before sweeping upward, harassed by antiaircraft guns and the growing number of Russian jets on their tails. A US fighter banked toward them, wings tipping back and forth, tail dropping as it shot into the sky to avoid an air-to-air missile that missed and plunged harmlessly into the sea. The Russian destroyers fired furious barrages into the air, at the risk of hitting their own jets, doing everything they could do to stop the brutal US air assault.

Soon the sky was filled with streaks of tracer fire, bright red even in the daylight, the black shapes of planes swinging, dancing, diving in and out of formation, one explosion after another. A jet fell from the air, spiraling, wobbling, exploding on the ocean surface, though the admiral couldn't tell if it was a US or Russian fighter. Glancing down at the tactical display, he saw it was one of their own, cringing at the loss. But the Russian squadrons were quickly being taken apart, the deck of the carrier beginning to smoke and catch fire.

Still, the Russians continued to launch planes only to be hit by F-18s in strafing runs. The 50 caliber rounds tore through their wings, buckling them, sending them spinning downward to crash in a spray of salt water and smoke. The ones that made it a few thousand feet into the sky faced the clawed talons of the US reinforcement wing.

As the US destroyers closed on the enemy ships, a massive explosion ripped the ocean surface a quarter mile behind them, directly in front of the Truman. A geyser of spray shot as high as the deck, jolting the admiral from the hypnotic scene of the air fight.

"They're coming for us now," the captain said grimly as he shifted in his seat, ordering the deck officer to turn the carrier out of harm's way. The bridge crew exploded into action, calling and reaffirming the navigational adjustments.

The massive engines grumbled in the ship's guts. Vibrations shook the decking and ran through the admiral's boots as the ship began a slow rotation.

"Get those frigates on the subs!" he barked. "We need--"

An enormous explosion rocked the hull, shaking the floor, throwing everyone to their knees. Sailors grasped railings, clinging to their kiosks as they fought to stay upright amidst thick binders of manuals and tactical information spilling from overhead bins. Thrown against his console, the admiral stared off to his left where the deck dipped 10 feet, bowing in the water, a massive geyser of billowing orange soot and ocean spray flying up. The bridge crew scrambled, repeating the captain's continuous orders to get the ship turned away to safety.

In a tight grouping, the anti-sub frigates circled an area a mile ahead of the carrier. Depth charges were lobbed off the sides to splash in the water, a dozen, then two dozen, sinking fast, detonating when they reached their programmed depth and sending blisters of air bubbling up to explode in sprays of white foam.

"Captain, this is tactical control. Our subs are engaging an Akula that slipped through undetected."

"No kidding? How the hell did they get within a mile of us?"

"They shouldn't have, sir. It looks like a suicide run--"

Another explosion ripped the carrier's hull, shaking the admiral from foot to jaw, sending a shock of dread through his belly. His old stubborn will flooded to the surface, and he glared down into the ocean as if he could locate the enemy sub with his bare eyes.

"Get that submarine, Captain," he growled.

"Damage report?" Rogers was half turned in his seat, staring at the smoke coming off the side of his ship.

"There's minimal damage to the hull, Captain. That last one just glanced off us, and we're sealing off the affected sections."

"Good. Now, as the Admiral suggested, someone take out that damned sub!"

"We've got a feed from two of our boats. They're on it, and we're launching torpedoes as well."

Billows of steam hissed from the frigates' decks as racks of torpedoes launched. Like arrows, they flew free from their tubes in a hiss of pneumatic ejection, plunging into the sea, motors spinning up and carrying them toward the charging enemy submarine.

"Sir, our destroyers have their battleships within reach."

"Engage them," Admiral Spencer growled, clutching the console. "Throw everything we've got at them!"

The captain nodded and passed the orders to the fleet. Out on the ocean, in the thick of the fight, the US ships launched their long range surface-to-surface missiles. Streaking through the sky, they blotted out the sun as they raced toward their targets, the impacts blowing the Russian boats sideways, throwing sailors to the deck, many on fire, spinning and dancing as they leapt over the side into the sea. Massive holes erupted in their sides, sooty black smoke racing upward. The engine compartments caught fire and burned away the oil and fuel as ammunition detonated freely, blossoming flowers of raging flames, blowing sailors to pieces, chunks of them splattering across the ocean surface, chum for the sharks to eat.

The Russian carrier was already listing heavily to port, men and women leaping off the sides in life jackets, lowering the wounded to lifeboats. Fifty planes still sat on the deck or down in the hangers, never launched. The high whine of a US rail gun threw hyper-velocity projectiles at the Russian Corvettes, the rounds chewing the fast ships to pieces, puncturing deep into their hulls with a sickening rip of steel, destroying their critical infrastructure before they could respond.

Spencer narrowed his eyes as the missiles flew toward them in streaks of gray. The US anti-missile arrays launched projectiles into the sky, intercepting the incoming rockets, filling the air with pops, bursts, and ear-shattering explosions as debris rained into the sea. A handful of Russian missiles broke through, slamming into the US ships, spreading fire and death deep into their hulls. None of them reached the carrier and the next barrage of US rockets put the Russian vessels to sleep, all of them dead in the water. Over a mile out, where the anti-sub torpedoes had prowled, the water exploded in black foam, the sea swirling and pitching as a swath of oil spread like blood across the surface.

"This is tactical," the cabin speaker piped. "We got the Akula, and the other Russian subs are retreating. The leader of their battle group would like to discuss terms of surrender."

"I want a full damage report ASAP." Rogers stood with his thighs pressed to the console, binoculars pinned on the scene playing out before them.

Out on the water, orange lifeboats blossomed on the ocean surface as the Russians tried to save their sailors. "Let's send rescue parties," Spencer said, eyes shifting to the captain. "No sense in those men dying out there for doing their duty."

"We'll see it gets done." Rogers gave a confident nod.

The admiral watched as the sky cleared of debris, the smoke drifting in thick clouds. F-18s and F-35s landed on the wobbling ship as the repair crews below tried to get a handle on the damaged sections. Rescue helicopters launched from the deck, Seahawks and Hueys lifting into the air, bending toward the destroyed Russian vessels.

Within 30 minutes, shaken and dazed Russian sailors began arriving on the carrier deck in torn, oil-stained, and bloody uniforms. Marines sectioned them into holding areas, laying the injured on the deck for the Truman's medical team to triage. Under Captain Roger's guidance, the fleet cruised through the obliterated Russian ships. Admiral Spencer stared down into the waters, the frigates and destroyers listing, horrific tears in their hulls, slabs of steel peeled back and smoking, the bowels of the lower decks exposed.

A debris field of flotation devices, garbage, oars, pieces of shattered wood, oil and fuel was scattered across the ocean's surface, corpses floating in the nightmarish stew. As for the big carrier, all that remained was a rear section of the ship, broken off from the main hull, still drifting in an inferno of burning petrol, occasional pockets of ammunition blowing off like fireworks. As the bridge returned to normal, the admiral and captain directed the carrier unit into a defensive position on the Barcelona coast, just out of range of any land-based guns.

When things had calmed, Spencer strode to his phone and gave the resident a call.

"Speak to me, Ben. What's happening?"

The admiral let out a long sigh, the pent-up tension he'd been feeling starting to loosen. "We punched through and forced a surrender from the Russians but sustained a few battle scars. We're now in a defensive position around Barcelona, awaiting instructions."

"That's fantastic news, Admiral. Well done to everyone there."

"No problem, sir. Just doing our jobs."

"Hold tight while we contact the Venezuelan government and try to enter negotiations. If we can do this without more loss of life, we will. Standby for further instructions."

The President hung up, and the Admiral placed his own handset in its receiver before returning to Captain Rogers's side. The man had retaken his stoic pose in his seat, sunglasses pushed back into place as he adroitly juggled repositioning the ship with assessing damage reports filtering in from the other vessels.

His dark lenses turned toward the Admiral. "What did he say?"

"The President expresses his thanks to both of us, and he wants us to sit tight while they negotiate with the Venezuelans."

The Captain nodded, and both men raised their binoculars to get a look at the Venezuelan shore where a bustle of tanks and earth moving equipment showed that the South American soldiers were digging in deep.

Chapter 21
Tom McKnight
Somewhere in Mexico

A hand rested on Tom's foot, patting it above the thick layer of blankets on top of him. Curled on his side, fists jammed into his chin, he breathed into the covers. While it was chilly so far away from the fire, he'd longed to lie on something softer than blankets and a hard floor, plus he'd wanted to be in a suitable position to jump behind the wheel if they needed to leave quickly. The Humvee's back seat had seemed like the perfect spot, the old crusty seats better than nothing.

"Tom, wake up. Tom?"

Keith.

With a jerk, Tom's eyes went wide to find Barbara standing in the open door, hands resting on his legs. "What's going on?" he whispered harshly. "Is it Keith? Did you see someone?"

She shook her head and leveled her green eyes on him, her hair out of its ponytail and hanging loose from her hood. "No, I didn't see anything all night. The snow is still falling, but it's tapering off. It's about eight, give or take. I thought you'd want to get up."

"Yeah, thanks."

With the swallow and a nod as his racing heart began to slow, Tom lifted the covers free, precious warmth escaping as he sat up and scooted to the edge of the seat. Legs thrown out, Barbara between his knees, he kissed his wife on the chin and reached for his boots from the floorboard.

She slipped her rifle off her shoulder and leaned it against the Humvee. "I'll get the children up and see what we can drum up for breakfast. Why don't you go keep watch while we do that?"

"Sounds good." Tom bundled himself up in his thick coat and hat, laced his shoes tight, climbed out of the back of the Humvee, and grabbed the rifle. "Morning, kids!" he called, waving as Linda and Jack ran up and gave him a brief hug in passing.

Sam was still lying beneath a pile of covers in front of the stove, resisting her mother's attempts to wake her up. Barbara was kneeling at her side, shaking the girl's shoulder, but she only pulled the blankets tighter to her chin, grumbling something about only wanting a few more minutes. With a smile, Tom stepped across the garage and through the door, entering the mini mart. He walked to the window where his wife had positioned a rolling chair near the glass, nestled behind a shelf where it was easy to watch the road and parking lot for any signs of the APCs.

The snow was still falling, but softer, less of a storm and more like something he would've wanted to see on Christmas Eve. Big fat flakes drifted down and had covered their tracks completely so that the entire parking lot was one even surface of white. The gas station awning had dipped lower, the middle section bowing from the weight of accumulated snow. Beyond the end of the lot, out in the flat desert, small groups of trees were clustered with bent branches, bushes sprouting through the bone frost that had settled over the land.

It didn't take much to imagine the frozen ground beneath it, the dirt freezing, wildlife and insects destroyed by the abrupt change in seasons. Off to the right, across another flat piece of land miles long, mountains and hills rose, their once green and brown sides turned to frosty slopes, a gray mist rolling overhead, drifting over the landscape.

A man stared back at him in the glass, a reflection of himself that made him wince. His face was gaunt, cheeks pulled thinner beneath his firm brown eyes, the growth of hair lining his jaw thick and long, the start of a woodsman's beard which would suit him well given the new reality they faced. He put his hands against the glass, taking in the beautiful scene as his brain came awake and his body threw off the sluggishness of sleep. The rest had done him some good, the sharp snow vivid in his sight, the zombie-like exhaustion that had plagued him the previous day all but gone. Soon the smells of food drifted through the hallway and his stomach rumbled, complaining with hunger.

The door at the end of the hallway opened and Barbara poked her head through. "Hey honey. Why don't you come in and grab some food? We combined all the leftover soup." She shrugged. "I guess it's more of a stew."

"One of us should probably stay out here to keep watch," Tom said, shifting his gaze back to the wintry scene stretching out before him.

Her crooked smile warmed him, loving eyes regarding him with an adoration he'd sorely missed in his weeks on the road. "Honey, it won't make a big difference if you spend 15 minutes having breakfast with the kids. It could be the last one we have for a long time."

"Yeah, that's what I'm afraid of," he replied in a flat, somber tone. "I want it to last."

"I do, too. But if you don't hurry, Jack's going to eat it all." She laughed. "That boy's appetite has been growing by the day. Come on, honey. Just a few minutes. Sam's already made you a bowl."

"Okay."

Tom left the glass, striding along the hall to greet his wife with a kiss and a brief hug. They strolled hand-in-hand around the beat-up Ford back to the stove where the girls had found some more bowls and dishes with antiquated floral designs tucked into a cardboard box. They'd used water and some dish soap to clean them and had poured three or four large spoonfuls of mixed soup into Tom's. Barbara grabbed it off the bench it'd been sitting on and handed it to her husband, followed by an old, dented spoon.

"Thanks, honey."

He took his breakfast over to the truck pads and sat cross-legged, watching Jack kick his legs as he happily dug into his share. Linda sat curled in her foldout chair, feet beneath her, knees to her chest as she ate and his eldest daughter sat on her rolling toolbox, feet dangling over the side, the blaze roaring from the stove's belly displaying the fruits of her morning labor.

"You're the fire girl now," Tom told her with a nod before he stuffed a spoonful of the hearty beef stew into his mouth.

"I guess it's kind of my thing," she responded with a shrug. "I'm not sure why, but I love doing it. I got up three times overnight on my own without anyone telling me, and I kept it going."

"You're taking responsibility for something, and that's a good thing," Tom nodded. "Thanks, Sam."

"No problem, Dad. I like helping." Samantha smiled, taking a last bite of her stew and placing her bowl next to her, dusting her hands off, resting them in her lap. "So, where do you think Keith and his buddies went?"

"I have no clue, but I'm not complaining," Tom said as he dug through his last few bites. "I'm just happy they didn't show up overnight. They either fell way behind or they took a different route."

"Which leaves us with the problem of what to do next," Linda added from her curled position.

Dishes rattled as Barbara got her own bowl of stew and sat by Tom. "I could've gone for some coffee before we decided anything. But, I'm not sure we'll ever have any. At least nothing fresh."

"I'd kill for a cup of coffee right now," Linda agreed with a sigh, looking to her mother. "What do you think, Mom? I mean, about what to do now? Dad already said we'll be moving south, somewhere warm, but where?"

His wife gave him a sideways glance, passing the buck to him without a word being spoken and, nodding, he offered a simple answer. "We'll go as far south as we can. I'm talking all the way to South America."

Sam scoffed. "Dad, South America is a long, long walk, unless you think that Humvee will take us there."

"No offense, but that thing is a piece of junk." Linda chimed in.

"That piece of junk saved our lives yesterday." Tom gave her a disapproving look. "And it might save our butts again. We should be thankful we have it."

"I *am*, but it won't get us to South America. I'm a kid, and even I know that."

Tom shrugged. "Not necessarily. These things are tougher than you'd think. But even if you're right, we'll just take it as far as we can and then we'll find another form of transportation."

"Do you really think we'll have to go that far?" Sam asked. "Isn't there someplace closer, past the winter storms, or maybe a military camp that's not as bad as the last one?"

"No more camps." He shook his head firmly. "Absolutely not."

"I just want to go home," Jack chimed in, still kicking his feet as he looked between his parents. "Can't we go home and put everything back together?"

Barbara smiled at him, reaching out to take his hand in hers. "Remember what we talked about before? About what home is about?"

"Home is…." Jack thought for a moment. "About the people, right?"

"The people, not the place." Linda nodded.

"Exactly," Barbara replied. "And look around this room. We're home right now. We have each other, for the first time in… I don't want to think how long. We're finally home. Here. In this old mechanic's bay in a strange country just trying to survive." Barbara glanced at Tom, eyes glassy with emotion as she continued. "Our old place isn't what it used to be. I don't think we can ever go back. We'll have to find a new place, like your dad said. It might be all the way in South America, far away." Her eyes lingered on each of her children in turn. "The important thing is that as long as we stick together, as long as we love each other, we can call anyplace home."

"I agree with Mom," Linda said, mirroring her brother's expression of hope. "She's right. We have to stick together. If we do that, everything will be fine. Think of all the stuff we went through, but we're here now."

Tom surreptitiously wiped a tear from the corner of his eye as he drank from a bottle of water, prouder of his family in that moment than he could recall. They were drifters, nomads searching for a home amidst the chaos of a new world, fighting the universe every day just for a place to lay their heads, to find a moment of peace, to share a meal on a cold winter night. But they were together. They were already home.

Samantha pushed her curls back from her face. "But what about all our animals?" she asked. "I never even said goodbye to them. I thought we'd be going back home. I mean, to the house. Are you saying we'll never see the farm again?"

"I know it really sucks, guys," Tom replied. "I had hoped we'd be able to sometime. But we have to keep moving south… Or die. We don't have a choice. Truth is, everything a hundred miles north of the border's frozen solid. Nothing can survive up there without extreme levels of gear and preparation. Not even our stockpiles could have gotten us through it. There's only one way forward, and we're going to have to do it together. You feel me?"

Sam slowly nodded, turning her head to look at her parents through tears in her eyes. "Of course, we're going to give it a hundred percent. We have to at least try."

"How about you, Jack?" Barbara held the boy's hand up and swung it affectionately. "Can you be brave, too, like your sister?"

"Yeah," the boy said, his voice husky, staring at Sam and his mother.

Linda stood from her chair, finishing her last bite of stew, and brought the old plate back to the stove. She placed the dirty dish in the box and tossed the spoon in behind it. "What do you guys say we get going? We've got a long way to go."

Tom and Barbara exchanged a look, nodding and smiling at each other, his heart lifting at his children's bravery. "Yep, okay. Let's get up and get moving, guys. Pack up the sleeping bags and clean the pots and pans and dishes. We'll take some of those with us in case we need them on the road. Put these chairs back, though, and make sure we douse the fire out before we leave. If Keith and his friends come by, we want it to look like no one was here, especially not us."

The family got moving, cleaning up after themselves, packing away the gear and stowing it in the Humvee's rear. Tom checked the fuel tank in the garage and realized the rusted lettering read "Diesel" and he ran a hose from the tank to their truck and siphoned it from one to the other, completely filling up the Humvee. Saanvi had left them two Jerry cans of fuel, so he topped those off and filled a couple more gas cans he found lying around the garage, sticking them in with their supplies. Within thirty minutes they'd packed everything up and were ready to go. Tom started the Humvee and stood by the manual bay door release, enjoying one last feel of the warm air inside the repair shop.

"Ugh. I dread doing this."

Closing his eyes, he popped the latch and threw the door up on its creaking, scraping wheels. An icy wind burst in, brushing across his cheeks, slipping into the cracks of his clothing, that dreadful winter freeze sending chills over his skin. Back behind the Humvee's wheel, he started it, the engine coughing to life, spitting once, then finally idling. The kids climbed in with Smooch, settling in with a blanket pulled over their legs. Tom backed out of the garage, lurching into 8 inches of hard-packed snow. The tires spun as they circled backward and pointed the nose of the truck toward the exit. Barbara, still outside, reached up and grabbed a rope hanging from the bay door, dragging it down to slam it shut, then she turned and jogged to the Humvee, jumping in on the passenger side and buckling herself in.

Brushing snow off her jacket, she shivered and flipped on the heater asa Tom threw it into drive, gently gassing it, guiding the vehicle through the parking lot and up to the highway. The tires spun as they slipped onto the road in a long sweep, rear end sliding to the left before jolting straight again. The knobby wheels kicked out sprays of snow as the old military truck plowed on, white flakes whisking against the windshield, glancing and spinning off the glass, the wipers sweeping off the rest.

With his seat pushed all the way forward and lifted to its highest setting, Tom stared at the road, enraptured in focused concentration. The wind followed them from the north, gusting at their backs, whistling through the cracks, the bigger blasts rattling the windows in their frames. With the heater turned to high and the fan clacking noisily, Tom sighed with gratitude for what it gave them, the bleeding warmth from the vents enough to keep the worst of the frost and shivers away.

As the highway wound south, Barbara pointed out gas stations and buildings off to the sides of the road. What once might have been adobe type structures with flat roofs had turned into squarish igloos, their chimneys long gone silent, owners evacuated to warmer climes. There were signs for motels, markets, taverns, and restaurants and if the places had been lonely before, they'd grown even more so with the storms. The occasional neighborhood they passed had a few desolate streets, all dark and foreboding and abandoned. Vehicles had become white bumps in the roads, snow-capped, a deep hoarfrost setting in across the landscape.

"Everything is gone," Tom said. "Frozen. Dead. And we're well into Mexico. I wouldn't have imagined the cold would drift this far south, but the North Atlantic Current must be almost negligible. All that warmth is trapped below the equator… but how far?"

"Mother Nature sure is pissed off," Barbara agreed, staring at the winter wonderland with a fearful resolve. "Did you ever think in a million years it would actually get this cold?"

"Not even when we were back traveling with Jerry. I figured in the worst-case scenario, the frigid weather would stop around the US-Mexico border, but it's clearly gone beyond that."

"Did Banks's little project she forced you into have something to do with that?"

Tom snorted. "Undoubtedly. I told them it was a bad idea."

Silence soaked into the Humvee's cabin as they drove another hour, then two, the storm shifting between levels of voracity. Sometimes it was a harsh slicing of sleet and hail, other times a soft flurry of fat snowflakes. Barbara reached across and let her hand linger on Tom's leg, patting it before withdrawing to her own lap where she pressed her arms together and shivered. Tom looked at his rearview mirror, glancing up like he'd done a hundred times over the past two hours, fixing his gaze to the road behind them, blinking, watching. *Was that… no… can't be.*

Shifting the wheel right and left, searching for traction, he glanced at the road and then the rearview again, peering back into the vast grayness. There came a flutter, a glimpse of definite brightness in the drifting haze before it vanished in the shadows, then the blink of light returned, staying. They were headlight beams for certain, a pair of yellow eyes in the gray and white.

"What is it, Tom?" Barbara asked, catching his worried glances. Turning around in her seat, she draped her arms across the back and stared through the cracked rear windshield. "Oh, I see what you mean. Is that them? Is that Keith?"

"I don't think so," he replied. "I see one set of headlamps, but I can't tell if it's an APC or not. Wait…" His stomach felt like it sank through the floor. "It *is* them. There're two pairs now."

Barbara muttered something under her breath, loud enough to stir the kids in the back. The girls turned groggily, climbing their seats to look outside as Tom started pushing the Humvee harder, driving them through the snow at upwards of forty-five when the distant echoes of machine gun reports cut the winter air. Puffs of snow and ice blossomed behind their rear tires, rounds ricocheting off the pavement and zipping by. Cringing, he pushed their speed even higher, engine grinding hard, slewing the vehicle around a long bend in the road, briefly losing the APCs in his rearview mirror. He brought the truck straight again as it flew over a ridge and down the other side.

"It's definitely them," he said, releasing his held breath in a whisper. "Or someone else out here has a real dislike for American military Humvees."

"Can we outrun them?" Barbara asked.

"We've got a pretty big lead on them still," Tom replied, "but they've got the firepower to shoot out our tires. These run flats won't mean jack if they punch a couple rounds into them; they'll tear up the axle and that'll be all she wrote."

As soon as the APCs reappeared, more rounds ripped through the air, streaking across the ground behind them. One clipped the rear left side to blast out the taillight in a flash of sparks and shattered polymer. The girls screamed, Jack flying awake with a gasp, Barbara leaning into the back seat to put her arms around them.

"Get down, kids!" Tom growled. "Take your seatbelts off and get down as low as you can."

Sam and Linda dragged Jack to the floorboards with Smooch, huddled behind what he hoped was enough of the Humvee's protective armor.

"You, too," he told Barbara as his hands gripped the wheel, slithering the truck back and forth in a tight pattern to keep the APCs' aim off. "Stay as low as you can."

Barbara slunk in her seat, still peering around the headrest to watch their pursuers. The enemy headlamps were closer than before, maybe three hundred yards away, the hulking shadows gaining by the second. They were real, their mounted guns visible as they spat flashes of light, grinding through the snow with immutable power.

"I don't think we can outrun them," Tom said. "The Humvee is faster, but they're plowing through that snow and ice like it's nothing."

"What are we going to do?"

"We have to get off the road." Stomach queasy with nausea, fear riding up his spine, he began looking for an exit off the highway.

"Will it work?" Barbara asked frantically. "If they can catch us out here in the straightaway, what makes you think we can escape on some side street?"

"I don't know!" Tom slammed his palms on the wheel. "I just know that if we stay on this highway, we're screwed. If we take the exit, we can hide somewhere…"

An exit ramp came up almost faster than he could turn off, with no sign to show it was even there, but the small commercial buildings and tall town signs caught his attention and he whipped the Humvee's wheel to the right, cutting back toward the ramp. They fell off the road into the V-shaped gully, smashing through a line of dust covered shrubs to throw tufts of snow into the air. The truck's suspension tilted, unsteady for a frightening moment, Tom thinking they might wind up in a ditch before the knobby tires snagged the shoulder of the pavement and pulled them back left again, slamming straight, driving to the end of the ramp.

Tom brought the truck to a sliding finish, turning the wheel right yet again. The Humvee veered onto a thin roadway, straightened, and shot toward a stretch of low-rise buildings. They ground past a corner gas station and supermarket, the parking lot covered in a foot and a half of snow, the accumulation engulfing cars that sat half on the road and half on the sidewalk.

The Humvee tore into a small neighborhood of one-story, flat roofed homes, many with tin walls or sections plugged with plywood and swaths of stucco siding. Gnarled trees stuck up from the ground between the houses, their once exotic looking leaves having turned brown and weathered, branches weighed down with clinging snow. Along the walkways, thick tufts of grass and shrubs had wilted dead beneath the frosted layers of white.

A glance in his rearview showed the APCs just reaching the exit ramp so Tom took the first immediate left, sliding into a side street that led deeper into the endless maze of squat, narrow roads. He wove a convoluted path between the dense blocks, circling with three hard left turns before taking a right through more snow swept squalor.

While he couldn't see them, the soft yellow glow of the APC headlamps filtered up from the ground over the buildings like a pair of halos in slow pursuit. Tom's cold toes worked the Humvee's accelerator and brake pedals, moving it through city blocks, taking hectic turns, wheels spinning beneath his hands. In the distance, he spotted a cluster of taller buildings, enormous warehouses and looming complexes, windows gaping and dark, icicles clinging to brick walls like crystalline cocoons. Tom imagined all the nooks and crannies that could hide them and he angled the truck in their general direction.

"Now I know how a rabbit feels trying to lose a fox," he mumbled to himself, focusing on the mechanics of driving over his emotions, drawing strength from the repetitive motions. While not an expert driver, Tom had gotten used to the old Humvee's little quirks. He'd learned that the steering had a certain amount of play, and it was slightly harder to turn right than left. His shoulders and arms anticipated the motions, forearms tightening, hands gripping the well-worn wheel.

The big diesel engine ground faithfully beneath his demands, coughing and sputtering as he rounded a bend and hit a straightaway. The tires pounded over a twenty-foot-long bridge that spanned a shallow gully, rattling the wooden planks and causing the entire span to shudder. With cringing shoulders, he half expected the thing to collapse under the Humvee's weight. But it held, and in less than five seconds, the truck trundled to the other side, plunging into another densely packed neighborhood.

"I'm not sure they can drive those APCs over that," he said as he glanced into the rearview to see the APCs headlamps turn toward them. "At the very least, they'll have to take it slow."

"I hope so," Barbara replied, whispering as she peeked up to watch out the back window.

Pushing along a narrow lane, he swerved back and forth to get around spurs of accumulated snowdrifts. The vehicle exploded through a drift, sliding left into another hard, snow-blinding turn. Tom straightened the wheel with big sweeps of his arms, wrestling the Humvee as they fell into a cluster of taller buildings, five to thirteen stories high. They passed a gray-stone structure with frosted glass windows, a hotel, and a hospital. Spotting a service alley between the latter two, he angled into the parking lot and pushed the vehicle through the gap, hoping it would be too narrow for the APCs to follow. Coming out the other side, he shot along the entrance lane and into a cluster of streets that divided the warehouses into messy square blocks.

"Where are we?" Barbara asked, shifting in her seat and throwing her eyes frantically in every direction.

"No clue," Tom wiped a bead of sweat from his brow. "I'm just hoping following us will be just as confusing for them."

A massive courtyard came up on his left, snow-covered stairs rising ten feet on all four sides. On each corner were hollowed out pavilions, concrete structures that might be for a market or town gathering, the pastel pink and orange colors showing in bright patches through the frost. At the head of the courtyard stood a massive church, its old gray stone matching the glum sky, the steeple looming high above them. Tom didn't slow a bit. He ran the vehicle right up the set of stairs, tossing the McKnights around in their seats with surprised cries as the big tires climbed the stone with ease. The Humvee streaked across to the courtyard's other side and down the opposite stairs then circled back and climbed into the courtyard from a third direction, crossing his own tracks before flying past the church to plummet into the street.

They hit with a lurching impact, tires digging deep furrows in the snow as he swung them south again. Brain in overdrive, Tom guided them between the taller buildings, sometimes stopping in the middle of a lane, slamming the vehicle into reverse, and backtracking in the other direction. If the APCs followed them, they'd run into a blank field of white, the Humvee's tire tracks disappearing as if they'd been sky lifted out of the city.

A few minutes later, satisfied his misdirection was complete, Tom slipped the Humvee through a side alley and along a short hill between some ritzy looking haciendas. On the other side, they entered another commercial area with corner stores and what might have been a pharmacy. The buildings flashed by, their bold-lettered signs unreadable in Spanish.

"I need a place to hide us." The buildings all started to look the same, squeezed together in gray and green facings, many as tall as ten stories high.

"We need to find one with a gate," Barbara said, eyes tracing back and forth across the road. "Or a garage. Like that one there."

Tom immediately saw what she was looking at. It was a pale brick building with a rust-colored garage door wide enough for the Humvee to fit. It appeared frosted shut, ice and snow crusting the edges. Pulling the truck to a sharp, skidding stop, Tom and Barbara got out and circled to the door.

He grabbed the latch, but it was frozen stiff. "Okay, we need to loosen this thing up."

Right boot flashing out, he began kicking along the bottom, fists pounding the sides to knock off the loose ice and snow. Together, they came back to the latch, and he twisted it several times, finally getting it to turn with a rusty groan.

"Grab the handle," he said, "and I'll lift from the bottom."

Barbara did as he asked while Tom slid his hand under the rubber seal. On the count of three, they heaved, and the door ground upward a few inches.

"Again." He slipped his fingers all the way under to get a better grip.

After another count they jerked the door up a few feet, ice and snow falling on their heads. Getting beneath it, each on a knee, they both put their shoulders under it and stood. Together they drove the groaning, protesting door upward, tall enough for the truck to fit. The inside was almost empty, just a few shelves pressed up against the walls, buckets and maintenance materials stacked in the corners.

Tom jogged back to the vehicle, climbed behind the wheel, and took a wide turn into the courtyard, sliding the Humvee into the garage, the armored sides fitting easily. He killed the engine, hopped out, and went to help Barbara get the door shut. They stood together, peering out into the frosted landscape as he looked at their tire track back the way they'd come, all the way to the end of the street.

"As soon as they get past the bridge and figure out where I misdirected them, it'll lead them right here. It's just a matter of time."

"What about the snow?" Barbara asked. "Think it'll cover our tracks?"

Tom lifted his eyes to the oppressive gray sky where the snowfall was picking up, flakes dancing in a flurry to the ground. While some were landing in the tracks, the cover offered by the surrounding buildings meant that there were less to fall directly in the tracks, unlike the relatively open area at the last place they had stopped.

"I don't know. Maybe..." he replied, pulling Barbara close in an embrace. "All we can do is hope, though. Come on, let's get inside, out of sight."

Chapter 22
Simon Sharp
Santa Fe, New Mexico

Private First-Class Simon Sharp jogged along the snowy path to the bunker stairs. The passage walls weaving through the snow towered over him like a maze in an Arctic fantasy world. Morales had outdone himself to uncover the underground bunker, the mysterious discovery the subject of intense discussion for the soldiers back in the warehouses. Everyone seemed to have a different idea of what was inside, some guessing it held military secrets available only to Jones and higher-ups while other speculated that vast quantities of supplies were buried there, ready to be transported south. Sharp was eager to see it for himself, which was why he'd volunteered to check in on the bunker crews.

The path to the door in the ground was marked with orange ribbons nailed into the snowy walls, impossible to miss in the stark whiteness. Boots crunching through the snow, he rounded a bend that brought him before the massive, circular opening, edges frosted with ice, a set of stairs leading into the bowels of the hill. Seeing no one on guard at the top, he clutched his rifle to his side and descended, boot heels stomping the steps in quickstep fashion, looking for Smith or Morales.

When he came to the first landing, he opened the hall door and peered in. The passage stretched on forever, pale light illuminating countless doors. Hearing no voices, seeing no one, he let the door fall shut and went down to the second level. He stepped into the hallway and jogged to the end, looking both ways along the intersection. There was nothing but a maze of passages and doors in both directions, and no sign of the lieutenant or specialist. With a frustrated huff, he reeled on his boot heels and ran back to the stairwell door.

"All right, guys," he mumbled, "where'd everyone go?"

As he proceeded to the third landing, he noticed the air turning warmer, remembering something about how caves always kept their relative temperature. They were never too cold or too warm. Still, he imagined the frozen temperatures would eventually work their way down at least some distance through the Earth's crust, just like it had seeped into his clothing and muscles to chill his bones.

When he reached the third landing, he whipped open the door in agitation, about to call out, then stopped as he spotted three soldiers standing near his end of the passage, rifles in hand, arms tensed as they tilted their heads, listening to someone speaking over the intercom. Grinning, he charged along the hallway, striding up to the team, slowing to listen to the strained voice coming from the speaker.

"... Specialist Morales here. All Army units come to Sub-level 4 to the refrigeration unit at the end of the hall. We're being held there. We need everyone to surrender right now, or they'll execute Lieutenant Smith."

The speaker made a crackling sound before cutting off.

"Did you guys hear that?" one soldier said to the others, his face a mix of anger and uncertainty.

"Yeah, that was Morales," a soldier named Isaacs replied. "Did I just hear him say they want us to surrender?"

"Surrender to who?" asked the third man, a big soldier he recognized as Richardson. "Surrender to the bunker crew? Screw that. We don't surrender. Why would Morales tell us we need to surrender?"

"Morales said if we don't, Smith gets executed."

"So, what the hell? What do we do?"

"Hey, guys," Sharp said as he came up, his tone curious and uncertain. "What's going on?"

The three soldiers spun at the same time, harrowing expressions written on their faces. The first one who spoke, a man named Johnson, swung his rifle around to point it at Sharp's chest before recognizing who it was and lowering his weapon. "Hey, man. Get out of here. Go tell Captain Jones what's going on."

Private Sharp squinted, once again looking at each in turn. "I don't understand. What are you talking about? Tell the captain what?"

"Didn't you hear Morales?" Johnson jerked his thumb toward the speaker in the wall. "The bunker crew aren't what they seem."

"You mean the people we found here?"

"Yeah, man. We thought they were from FEMA or a special unit or something, but they've got Smith, Morales, and the rest of the team trapped on Sub-level 4. That's why you have to go tell Jones."

The private absorbed the information, his mind reeling with the true reality of the situation, eyes widening as the danger dawned in them. He stepped up, unslung his rifle, and held it in a tight grip across his chest. "We can take them, guys. We're armed and they're not."

Johnson shook his head, lip curling in a snarl. "Dude, they've got a gun to Lieutenant Smith's skull and have captured at least three or four of our other soldiers. Maybe everyone who went down there. You don't think they've taken our boys' weapons?"

"Why don't you guys come out with me? We'll tell Captain Jones together. Then we can attack the situation as a team."

"We don't have time for that. They know how many of us came in initially, and they're asking for us by name."

As if on cue, the speaker cracked to life once more, and Morales's voice piped over the line, again sounding unnaturally strained, like someone was holding a knife to his throat or a gun to his temple. "Come on, Johnson, Isaacs, and Richardson. They know you guys are here, and if you're not part of the headcount in five minutes, they're going to blow Lieutenant Smith's head off."

The speaker cut off again and Johnson dropped a heavy hand on Sharp's shoulder, causing the skinny private to slouch. "See what I mean? We don't have a choice. We can't let our men die. Buzz off, Sharp. Go tell Jones what the situation is, but make sure he knows these people aren't messing around. You got that? We'll go surrender to help buy some time. You bring Jones and take these bastards out, got it?"

The private nodded vigorously, eyes darting across his buddies, a nervous sweat sprouting on his brow despite the chilly air. "Don't worry, guys. I'll get some help. We'll get you out of here, okay?"

The soldiers bobbed their heads and waved the private back through the door where he slipped away. Then Johnson, Isaacs, and Richardson turned to see three men come striding around the corner and along the hall, shirtless with thick pipe wrenches in their hands.

One of them, a giant with a grey goatee hanging from his jaw, pointed at Johnson, who stood in front of the door as it fell softly shut behind the fleeing private. "I'm assuming you heard the announcement?"

"Yeah, we heard it," Johnson nodded, voice filled with contempt.

"Then let's get this over with. Give us your weapons, or Smith gets a round to the head. It's about time we got upgrades."

The two insurgents behind him chuckled, their wide shoulders flexing with the heavy wrenches in their hands. Johnson glanced at Isaacs and Richardson before he unslung his rifle and placed it on the ground.

* * *

Back upstairs, Morales took his finger off the intercom button and turned to Chet. "They'll be here, don't worry."

"They better be here within five minutes." Chet pointed the barrel of his weapon at the other three soldiers standing on Morales's left. "Or we'll end Lieutenant Smith. Your buddies will be next, then you."

Morales glanced at Shae, where she held his pistol on him from a few yards away. Several other members of Chet's crew had come to the room, bringing Brozowski and LaPlante with them. Their weapons were stripped and in the wrong hands and Rupert and Meyers were still locked inside the refrigeration unit.

Standing on Morales's left, Lieutenant Smith stood with his fists clasped at his side, shoulders tense, veins pulsing in his temples. "Who the hell are you people, anyway?" he asked. "You're not some civilian group who stumbled on the bunker randomly. Everything about this seems a bit too planned to me."

"Glad to see you're not a dumb grunt," Chet replied. "You're right, we're not civvies. We're with The United Front, New Mexico branch."

Smith shook his head and made a disgusted sound. "Son of a… you're a bunch of damn agitators, insurgents, filthy rioters and troublemakers. Terrorists. Weren't you people the ones who shot that woman and her child in St. Louis?"

Chet's jaw locked in anger, shifted back and forth, his friendly blue eyes taking on a harsh and hostile gaze. "We didn't cause any of that. That was police brutality. The bastards always handle things with a heavy hand."

Smith continued. "And you're behind a bunch of other stuff, too. Last I heard, the FBI was investigating you for a string of pipe bombings."

Morales noted the militia group leader tensing, shoulders growing tight as the rifle slowly raised to Smith's belly.

"I don't think it matters much anymore," he interjected with a halting gesture. "What I am curious about though, is how you people discovered this place."

Eyes lingering on Smith for another angry second, Chet shifted his attention to Morales, causing his coiled guts to turn cold. Still, he didn't cringe or shy away, keeping the focus on him. Jones would eventually figure out what was going on, but until then, he had to keep the situation calm or risk having his people shot and killed.

"We saw what was happening in the North Atlantic." The leader said. "We got the reports and our sources said things were a hell of a lot worse than the government assholes were saying on the news.

"We tried to organize and take over, but the police and military were gone so fast there was nobody left to fight. Many of our people got caught up in the fascist forced evacuations, and we couldn't track them all south. We've known about this place for a long time, and we had all the entry codes." The man glanced at Shae. "We brought everyone we could find, but we didn't realize they'd already changed the security codes on most of the warehouse doors."

"I thought you guys could hack all that stuff?" Morales asked.

Chet scoffed. "All the people here are muscle, but not a single one of them is a tech-head. Our techs are probably frozen dead by now or gone south. Idiots didn't hurry up and join us when they had the chance."

Morales shared a quick glance with Brozowski before continuing. "So, you guys were planning on waiting out the apocalypse down here?"

"At least until you showed up. I guess things have changed."

"And what do you expect to accomplish now?" Morales asked, homing in on the big question. "What do you want out of us? You want us to get out of here and leave you alone? Seal up the bunker? We can do that." A lie, painfully obvious to most, but the ego of The United Front was well known, and if Chet was anything like his more notorious comrades, he'd be too self-absorbed to realize Morales was simply fishing for information.

"Something like that," Chet said. "But it won't do us any good if we can't get into the locked rooms."

Morales raised his hand, looking between Smith and Chet. "We can help you. I'll figure out how to get you access to the locked areas, but you have to let us leave. You can't kill us. And if we seal you guys back in here, you can't kill the other convoy drivers that come along."

"Don't you get it?" Shae said, her voice cracking. "We're not interested in killing. Just leave us the hell alone!"

"That's why you've got our guns on us, right?" Smith snarled. "You just want to be left alone?"

Ignoring Smith's swipe, Chet continued speaking to Morales, treating the specialist as though he was in charge of the situation, a position Morales was more than happy to take on if it meant Smith was less at risk. "And if we let you go, you'll just run to Captain Jones and tell him who we are. He'll launch an assault, no doubt." The leader swept his rifle across the lot of them. "Or, who's to say you won't bomb us from 10,000 feet?"

The door came open, and the three pipe workers they'd seen earlier guided in Johnson, Isaacs, and Richardson. They'd taken the soldiers' weapons, and the militia leader pointed for the new soldiers to join their comrades against the wall. Morales gave the newcomers a nod, realizing all of the soldiers who'd remained in the bunker were gathered in the room. Chet could execute them and no one would be the wiser for who knew how long. Long enough for them to mount up a defense against Jones and the rest, bottlenecking any attack and rendering it next to useless.

With an icy feeling radiating from his belly, Morales faced the insurgent leader again. "It doesn't have to go like that. You could let us leave in exchange for access to the supplies in this bunker. I could tell the captain the cargo lifts aren't working, and we need to get some specialists up here to fix them. But after a few hours, we'll claim they're irreparable. Something about needing a special tool we don't have on hand. The captain will cut his losses and pull us out. By then, we'll have moved on to another camp, and you'll have the place to yourselves." It was a bald-faced lie, all of it, but Morales had few cards left to play.

"It's not like it matters anyway," Brozowski hissed. "You can't live down here forever, especially after the big freeze hits--"

Morales gave Brozowski a sharp glance, but Shae immediately stepped over and put her weapon to the man's forehead. "What was that, grunt? What was that about a big freeze?"

"N-nothing," Brozowski stammered, both eyes crossed as he stared at the pistol barrel. "It's just, you know, getting super cold out there. We don't want to stay around too much longer."

Eyes narrowed, the woman adjusted her grip on the weapon, pressing the steel cylinder harder between his eyes. "You better come clean, buddy, or your friends will be wearing your brains on their jackets."

"What Brozowski is saying," Morales interjected, "is that we're well below the freeze point here in New Mexico. Above us are Arctic temperatures, with spin-up storms hitting every few hours or so, freezing everything, and killing anything. What we're hearing is that this cold won't end. It'll be around for a long time."

Shae's ice-blue eyes narrowed beneath her thick eyebrows, gun shifting from the stammering soldier to settle against Morales's temple. "So, what you're saying is that if we stay here, if we seal ourselves inside this bunker, we'd be stuck forever?"

Morales looked to Smith, who stared at him with an even expression, giving him a slight nod of approval to continue. Negotiating with a domestic terrorist outfit wasn't exactly operating by the book, but given their situation he'd start handing out free lap dances if it meant getting his people free, then Jones could come up with a plan to burn out The United Front. Unfortunately, Brozowski's ill-timed admission about the upcoming freeze had ruined his plans.

Looking back to Shae, he nodded in the affirmative. "We're not a hundred percent sure, but there's a good chance that if you stay here, you'll be here for the rest of your lives. Sealed in."

"Like a tomb," Chet snarled, bringing his gun up to Smith's head. "And you assholes would've left us down here."

"Hey, wait a minute! You wanted us to leave!" Morales took a step toward the two men when Shae grabbed his arm, digging the rounded end of her weapon into his temple even harder. "Take one more step and see what happens." The woman's voice was a tense grumble pressed through clenched teeth. Morales froze and kept his hands raised. Eyes closed, he recalled the corpses in the room from earlier with their bashed-in skulls and twisted limbs.

"Like I said," he quickly added. "We don't know for sure--"

"Shut up and get back in line." Shae sidestepped to face him, dropping the gun from his temple and jamming it into his chest, forcing him to retreat to Smith. She spun to the militia leader, expression anguished. "We have to change our plans. We can't stay here."

Chet was already nodding, eyes falling to the floor before lifting to the soldiers. "Yeah. There's no way in hell we're sticking around."

The pipe worker with the gray goatee spoke up. "I say we grab some of the convoy trucks, fill them with supplies, and bus our asses the hell out of here."

"We head south then?" Shae asked, shooting him a glance. "It's got to be warmer there, right?"

"Yeah, that's what I figure," the man said. "Get to warmer weather as soon as possible, outrun these spin-up storms. What do you think, Chet?"

"You can't do that either," Smith interrupted with a growl. "You'll end up getting caught, or the Captain will come after you. People will lose their lives. Your best option is to give yourselves up."

Chet grinned widely, looking over the soldiers with a mischievous gleam. "We've been taking risks for years. Things aren't any different now. We'll take our chances with a few of your trucks and all the supplies we can carry. At the first signs of screwing us over, we'll mow you down. Now, strip those uniforms off, boys. We're going to need them."

* * *

Morales groaned and slapped his freezing hands together as he, Smith, and the rest of the soldiers moved bins of supplies from the elevator platform to a trailer. The militia had connected it to a Humvee that was idling nearby and were prepared to pull out and drive away from the convoy. Two hours had passed since the militia group had taken control of the secret bunker, and the Army crew was fast at work, loading three trucks and a Humvee full of supplies.

Standing nearby were five United Front members in stolen uniforms, covered head to toe in military cold-weather gear. The rest of the soldiers were in the bowels of the bunker, piling stacks of stores near the cargo lifts. The mid-morning sun was trying to push through the endless gray clouds, their edges marked with black burns. Every time the icy winds kicked up, Morales's eyes lifted upward, expecting the next spin-up storm to roar down on their heads.

"You just had to go and tell them about the weather, didn't you?" Smith chastised Brozowski. "If it wasn't for you, we'd have these jerks sealed up and could be sitting around thinking of a hundred different ways to end them. Now, here we are doing their dirty work."

"Sorry, Lieutenant." The soldier's expression was sheepish as he hefted a large plastic bin with military stenciling on the side, slipping on the circular platform as he staggered over to the trailer to place it with the rest.

"Don't be so hard on him," Morales said, shifting supplies around. "I don't think he realized who we were dealing with until it was too late."

"Once a dumb grunt, always a dumb grunt," the lieutenant snapped in a surly tone.

"Need I remind you? You're a grunt, too."

"Yeah, but I'm one of the smart ones." Smith snatched a bin off the top of the pile and carried it over to the trailer. "And I could use a damn cigarette."

Morales rolled his eyes, following the lieutenant, slamming his bin next to Smith's.

The snow was still falling fast enough to create a layer of white on the crates of supplies. A militia member was always standing nearby with a rifle, dusting the tops off and monitoring the soldiers. Within a few minutes, they'd cleared the cargo platform and stood waiting to be sent back downstairs for more. A United Front guard stepped on with them and punched a button on a control panel. A high-pitched beep went off, then the platform grumbled and lurched, Morales's knees buckling as they sunk straight into the sub-floors, passing all the way to the fourth level where more supplies awaited them.

"I think they're going to get away with this," Morales mumbled low to Smith. "I was a little skeptical at first, but we've got one truck already loaded, and Jones and the rest of our boys are still in the second warehouse."

"Yeah, I was doubtful, but the bastards are efficient." The lieutenant looked back at the militia woman standing behind them, covered head to toe in military gear. "They look just like us, dammit. Even if Jones sends guys over here for a status update, they'll never know they're talking to the wrong people. Hell, it might even get some of our men shot."

Johnson stepped around and stood between Morales and Smith, nudging them both with his elbows. Under the grinding sound of the hydraulics and sliding plate, he turned slightly, glancing at the guard. "Hang in there, guys," he murmured. "There's help on the way."

The specialist refrained from reacting, but the lieutenant shot Johnson a narrow-eyed glare. "What the hell are you talking about, soldier?"

"Just before they captured us, Private Sharp came into the bunker looking for us. We sent him off with instructions to let Captain Jones know what was happening. I think he got away without them seeing him."

Smith stiffened where he stood, his arms held out from his body like he was ready to fight. The lieutenant stared straight ahead, head turning toward the militia member standing behind them with one of their rifles. "Is that so?"

"That had to have been over two hours ago," Morales whispered from the corner of his mouth, his own heart pounding with renewed hope. "Hopefully he got to the Captain."

"Jones'll eat these jerks' heads for lunch." Smith's grin widened manically. "We just need to be ready when the time comes."

"Hey, you three!" the woman snapped. "Shut the hell up. No talking on the platform!"

The big steel dais reached Sub-floor Four, coming to a jarring stop, the men standing on it wobbling for a moment before stepping off. Chet and Shae were waiting for them, dressed in thick military fatigues, the size mismatches easily hidden by the heaviness of the clothing.

"All right, Army boys," Chet said, pointing to another skid of supplies. "Let's get the rest of this loaded up. Hup, hup! Let's go!"

Chapter 23

Private First Class Simon Sharp
Santa Fe, New Mexico

Private Sharp leaned against the door he'd just come through, turning, reentering the key code on the other side and hitting "Enter" to lock it. After leaving Richardson, Johnson, and Isaacs, he'd trotted up the stairs, intending to head outside and over to the warehouse. But he'd turned back at the sound of two enemies standing guard on the landing above him, their harsh whispers and snickers about having captured the GIs sent waves of dread through him, weakening his knees.

Going downstairs was off limits, so he spun and slipped into the Sub-floor 2 passage, shutting the door quietly behind him, sprinting to the next hall, taking a right, and running even farther, fatigue causing his boots to hammer on the tiles. Unsure whether the enemy had heard him, he crossed to the first secure room he saw and punched in the code with his fingers.

He'd gotten two sets of codes from his time working with Brozowski and LaPlante in the original warehouse when he'd been on technician duty which was one reason Captain Jones had sent him to find Morales and Smith. The private wasn't a brutish worker, and he couldn't run any of the trucks or loading machines so they'd assigned him messenger boy duty, ferrying orders around to the various lieutenants and specialists when the radios got spotty. The captain hadn't asked him to come straight back, with the work on the second warehouse moving fast and furious and no one else was aware of the betrayal happening at the bunker.

Lungs strained, heart hammering, a deep sense of isolation settled on his shoulders. Inside the room, he slid onto his backside, letting his fists rest on his knees, squeezing his sweaty palms, head lowered as he realized he was cut off from his team. During his time with the military, he'd relied heavily on the members of his unit to get through the rigors of basic training and the nightmare of Mexico. All the blood, sweat, and tears, the callouses and bruises, the brief but brutal fights in Reynosa, Monterrey, and Mexico City.

The men being held by whoever had taken over the bunker were his friends and fellow soldiers, the guys who relied on him to come through. He relied on them, too. Without them, he had no one to command him or shout an order into his face, no squad leader or lieutenant to give him flack for screwing up, no one to pat him on the back and lift him up and be there at his side. It had always been tough, but the private thrived on the comradery and teamwork. There'd been few things he'd ever done alone, but cut off from his team he had to think of a way to either reach the captain or, barring that, pull off some kind of miracle on his own.

The underground bunker was massive, several floors of warehouses, hundreds of rooms, side halls, and equipment areas, all buried beneath tons of earth in a quiet claustrophobia. Sharp squeezed his hands one last time, took a deep breath, and tried to remember his training. He needed to make a list of things, mental or written, minor tasks that, when accumulated, would lead him to a bigger goal.

Calm down. Focus.

Sharp took a deep breath and thought. Johnson had told him to go back and find the captain, because people had taken Smith and the others hostage and were about to execute them. The bunker crew, the people they'd found underground, had not been waiting for rescue at all. They were dangerous, and they'd captured his friends and posted guards at the top of the shaft to make sure no one got in or out. So, there were two options. Sharp could try to get past the guards and return to the warehouse to alert Captain Jones, or he could break the guys out himself.

The bit of critical thinking calmed his nerves and he took another deep breath, stood, and dusted his pants off, then he scanned the room, bringing an instant smile to his face. He was standing in a mess hall. Not exactly a military version, but close enough. Basic tables were placed around the area, each with four plastic chairs. The buffet line cut across the middle of the room, clean glass partitions and empty cases telling him it hadn't been used in quite a while.

Glorious memories of basic training and of the staging camp before the Mexico invasion flooded back. Sharp had always seen the mess hall as a haven of quiet relaxation, where he could grab a meal and joke around with his buddies. It was probably his favorite place to be besides his rack, and it filled him with a sense of comfort, steadying his queasy stomach.

With a quick glance backward at the door, he strode between the tables toward the banquet line, angling to the left where he squeezed through to the kitchen area. Two prep tables sat in the middle of the red-tiled room, one with a knife block and chopping board on it. Shelves stood pressed against the walls, stocked with big cans of tomato paste, pickles, soups, and boxes of candy bars.

Starving, after a ten-hour stint of loading trucks with almost no break, Sharp made a beeline for the shelves. He grabbed two of the candy bars, ripped open the packaging, and double-fisted them like he was chugging beers back in college. As he stuffed his mouth with the sugary sweets, he strode around the room, thinking about what he was going to do. A small part of him realized he'd have to fight the bunker crew to bust his friends out, regardless of whether he tried to get past the guards or free them himself. It wouldn't be a simple task. He'd only been average on the gun range, and he wasn't great in hand-to-hand combat so there'd be no running around the place, shooting it up like a cowboy or snapping opponents' necks like Chuck Norris.

The answer flashed in his mind. Knife work. That was something he was efficient at, a skill he'd practiced a lot. Being of smaller stature, he'd worked extensively with blades of every size and shape, often defeating larger men in basic training. "But this is reality," he mumbled to himself around mouthfuls. "Can you use any of those moves in real life, buddy?"

He stopped at the knife block and set his half-finished candy bars down, then removed his jacket. He slid two thick-bladed knives from the block, each six inches with sharp points, testing the edges with his thumb before taking a few experimental swipes. Satisfied, he tucked them under his belt near his hips, handles jutting up for quick access. Candy bars back in hand, Smart resumed his chocolate binge, walking around and exploring more.

He found an empty sack with a strap on it and placed it on a table. With no idea how long he'd be inside, or how long his mission would last, he'd need supplies. There might be times where he had to hide for several hours, or a day, so having food and water handy would be helpful. Even if Captain Jones found out about the hostage situation, he might not be able to do anything about it right away. He'd need someone on the inside, working behind the scenes to cut off the head of the snake.

"So that's what it's going to be, Sharp?" He grumbled, speaking to himself in third person, voice full of toughness. "You going to break your buddies out?"

In the pack, he placed the rest of the box of candy bars, a box of pilot bread crackers, a can of peanut butter, and a can of jelly. He tossed in a butter knife, fork, and a 12 pack of bottled water from the storage closet in the back. With the supplies on his shoulder, and a modest array of weapons in his belt, Private Sharp crept from the mess hall, peering along the passage before stepping out.

Taking a right, he moved deeper into the facility, watching the walls for a map of the place or to gain some sense of where things were. The air simmered with a quiet tension, the only sounds his breath and his boot heels gently falling on the tiles. Keeping to the left side of the wall, he crept through darker sections where the lights were dim or missing. With one six-inch cutting blade lifted from his belt, he switched to the opposite side of the passage, holding the weapon in his front hand.

Turning a myriad of corners, he slipped along multiple passages with his shoulders to the wall, knife glinting in the emergency lighting. Still, he struggled to make sense of the surrounding maze. With a quiet sigh, he stopped for a moment, squatting and closing his eyes as he thought back on the whirlwind of training he'd gone through over the past three months.

He'd done basic training in Fort Knox, Kentucky, before returning home to Covington while awaiting his deployment orders. As the days passed, he'd wondered if they'd ever call him. Then everything had happened with the anomaly, the news reports about the North Atlantic current dragging to a standstill, cutting off the warm waters from the south and bringing with it frigid temperatures. What followed had been an apocalypse no one ever expected. His deployment orders came swiftly, and he returned to a military that had changed drastically in a few weeks. With new recruits flooding in by the thousands, they'd pushed his unit out to a massive warehousing complex with three underground bunkers similar to the one he was standing in. During that time, he'd completed several inventory runs for their trainer, the layout of the place sticking somewhere inside his head.

"I remember the orders from Lieutenant Anderson," he whispered to himself, the memory floating forward from the back of his mind. "I was supposed to go to the armory and get .50 caliber MK211 ammunition and deliver it to the range for gunnery practice that afternoon. But what floor was the armory on?"

Sharp shook his clenched fist, face wincing as he thought back to that day, tried to recall what he'd eaten for breakfast. It had likely been oatmeal and toast with a cup of coffee. Then he mentally traced his footsteps outside to meet up with his squad out on the range. There'd come the orders from the Lieutenant, and his aggravation that he'd been the one having to run for the ammo. It was only because he was a newbie, the youngest in the unit, and they'd punished him by making him fetch anything and everything.

"I came down the steps, just like I did today. At the second landing, I took a right and walked to the end of the hall. Then…" The directions solidified themselves in his mind as butterflies danced in his stomach.

A smile widened on his face. Not only did he think he knew where the armory was, he also remembered some hidden stairwells and other interesting facets of the building. If the layout was the same in the bunker as it was back where he'd been before, he could move around undetected and no one would be the wiser.

Sharp turned back the way he'd come, slipping to the other side of the hall, shoulders brushing against the wall as he held his blade in a forward position, ready to strike like a snake.

"I'm coming for you, brothers. Hang in there. I'm coming."

Chapter 24
Keith
Somewhere in Mexico

"Here! Stop right here!"

Keith leaned forward over the radio console, staring at the external camera screen from his spot in the Stryker's communication chair, maneuvering the joystick to peer through the city streets. When Serge didn't immediately pull in where he wanted, he slammed both fists on the console and cursed under his breath. "What are you doing, man? Pull up those stairs and into the courtyard. Follow the tracks!"

The merc leader shot the agent a dark glance and then whipped the wheel to the right, sending the APC rocketing up a set of short, snow-covered stone steps at 35 mph. The front end crashed onto a flat courtyard about 40 yards square. The merc slammed on the brakes, catching the tires in the snow and ice, sliding them to a fast and shuddering stop in the middle of a large marketplace.

Three other sides of the plaza had similar stairs, even at the north end where a massive grey cathedral stood slightly off to the right. The thick, grey walls and steeple were covered with sleet, decorative statues, and figurines all along the top portion. The four market corners were concrete pavilions with stone tables and wooden benches where traders might have once sold their wares.

"Lower the back door! Lower it, now!"

Keith leapt from his seat and shoved past Mikael as the rear door crept open. With a single thick coat on and a thin pair of gloves covering his fragile fingers, he jumped before the door completely opened, landing in the snow, circling to the front and staring at the crisscrossing Humvee tracks snaking off in every direction.

For the last thirty minutes they'd been trying to follow Tom McKnight's blighted path, his backtracking and weaving throwing the mercs into a state of confusion. Standing in the center of the marketplace, Keith glared at three sets of tracks going in opposite directions, all Humvee tires, none of them any fresher than the others. Hands on his hips, he stomped around in the snow, moving from one set of tire marks to the other, following them where they plunged down the stairs and out into the neighborhood streets. Glaring up at the big church steeple, he wondered if some supernatural force was trying to tell them something.

"Perhaps we can park the Strykers at separate ends of town and wait them out."

Keith turned to see Serge lingering behind him, rifle cradled gently in his arms, Mikael standing a few yards away.

Lena and Dmitri exited the back of their idling APC and came to join them. Rifles in their arms, barrels pointed at the ground, they stared with bitter eyes at the even colder surroundings. Breath drifted from their mouths to be consumed by the hungry cold.

"No. We will *not* do that." Keith snarled. "Let's split up, actively pursue them, and whoever finds them first will call in."

Serge shook his head, a crooked grin beneath his hood. "You're being too impatient, my friend. This family, this Tom McKnight, is reckless and smart. That is a dangerous combination."

The agent whirled on the merc, fist clenched at his hip. "They're just civvies. You said so yourself. What, are you afraid of them now?"

Serge raised his finger and shook it at Keith. "None of us are afraid, but we understand when we are facing an enemy with great instincts and ability. That is not an insult to anyone." A shrug lifted his shoulders. "It only makes it more of a challenge for us, one where we must take our time and do things correctly."

"Serge is right." Lena jerked her chin at the man, locks of her blonde hair hanging from her hood. "You are underestimating them like you did before, as evidenced by your injuries. Your missing fingers and toes."

The mercenaries snicked, even Dmitri showing a big, dumb grin as Mikael kicked at the icy ground with the toe of his boot. Keith glared at them in turn, gaze lingering on Serge before shifting to Lena. "You people think this is funny? You think a *family* will win this? They may have beaten me before, but they won't win. There're on the run, and they're scared. I won't let Tom McKnight's little slalom course beat me, and you should feel the same way."

"Oh, we do," Serge said. "We'd just rather do this more methodically than you." He shrugged again. "We prefer methods that work to ones that lose fingers and toes."

"Luckily, we're not on your dime," Keith snarled, gesturing for them to follow him to the APCs. When they didn't immediately come, he stopped and turned back, finger raised and pointed at them. "Were splitting up. Serge, Mikael, and I will move north. Lena and Dmitri, you go east. We'll search by grids. I want to check every track until we find them. Is that understood?"

"We're splitting up, but we're not going to actively hunt them." Lena jerked her thumb behind them. "Serge, Mikael, and Keith will head to the overpass just north of us. Dmitri and I will go back the way we came. Once in position, we will lie in wait."

The merc leader agreed with a calm, careful nod. "And we will be ready when they come out."

"You're ignoring a direct order." Keith stepped up to Lena and put his face two inches from hers, knowing he was pushing his luck with her but not caring. "Do that, and you won't get the rest of your payment."

Lena shrugged, her jade green eyes watching him carefully. "You are not in charge of this mission. We were hired by Banks, and you were only to come along and observe." Her gaze shifted to Serge. "The final decision on how to carry out the plan is up to us."

Keith spun to face Serge, squinting in accusation, the man only staring at him with his cold, impenetrable eyes. "Bastards," he growled, stomping up the APC's ramp, shoving his way to the front, and falling into the radio chair.

Serge climbed into the APC and slipped back behind the wheel with Mikael dropping into a seat, watching Keith with amusement. After the door was up, the merc leader put the vehicle into drive and pulled it off the market square, trundling down the steps and into the street with a clatter of equipment inside the crew quarters.

The APCs split up, Serge's vehicle cruising north along the narrow roads, making their way to the massive overpass Lena had mentioned. The merc leader found the entrance ramp and climbed the vehicle up the wide arcing overpass to the very top, putting them a hundred and fifty feet in the air with a perfect view of the city's center.

He parked the Stryker and left it running, using the external cameras to look around, fingers toggling the magnification as he peered across the city. Keith merely sat in his seat, arms crossed, jaw clenched in anger as he stared at the radio controls, thinking through what had just happened.

"We are in position," Lena said over the speaker, and the merc leader replied that they were, too.

Mikael relaxed back in a crew seat. "Now, all we have to do is watch and wait."

Keith tapped his heel on the floor of the truck. "You know, if McKnight slips out on a side road, he'll be gone for good."

"He will not slip out on a side road," Serge assured him in his thick accent. "Do not worry. This will be like the rabbit hunting I used to do on my uncle's farm. If we dig around for them and make too much noise, they will only dig deeper so we can never find them. If we wait patiently, we will be in a suitable position to smash their heads when they come out. It's simple."

"And just how long is this supposed to take?"

The merc shrugged. "As long as it takes."

"Listen to Serge," Lena said over the comms system, and Keith caught the slight hint of amusement in her voice. "He knows what he's talking about, and he has been hunting people many years."

"And I haven't?"

"Apparently not someone like Tom McKnight," the woman responded, her amused tone cutting through the line to stab him in the chest. The agent bowed his head, jaw working back and forth, throat clenching tighter and tighter until a low growl rolled from his gut.

Slamming a fist on the console, he leaned forward and tapped the necessary buttons to make a call to Banks. Fingers throbbing, every press of a key like a spark of lightning up his wrist, but he didn't care. The mercs were out of control and needed to be brought back in line.

"Are you calling your boss?" Serge asked, his tone incredulous, then he raised his voice to the speaker system, his tone flat. "Lena, he is calling his boss."

The sultry woman returned. "What? Keith, why would you do that? What can Banks do for you now?"

"She can pull the plug on the weapons caches," the agent nodded, fingers lancing with pain as he tapped the console, waiting for the connection. "She can have those shut down, and you'll get nothing."

Serge shifted and lifted his visor, the slight grin on his face turning harder. "Your plan was not good. What we presented is better. We can just wait them out here, no problem. No risk to us, except it might be a little boring. Bringing Banks into this is unnecessary."

Keith stewed in his chair until the connection finally died, a roar of snow and wind eliminating the possibility of contacting anyone.

"Damn it!" he shouted, the tendons in his neck bulging with anger, face turning hot. Pressing his fingers into the console, driving pain to his hands like a nail, he shifted his furious glare to the merc leader. "Let me tell you the first mistake about your plan. As we wait for them, it'll grow too cold for any of us to survive. Remember what it felt like in Texas? The Strykers could barely keep us warm then. Once it hits down here, we'll be done for. Do you really want to wait for that to happen?" The agent shook his head vigorously. "No, we need to move now before it's too late."

"You are one man, my friend." Serge smiled at him. "How are you going to force us to do what you want?"

Dmitri's deep voice chuckled over the speakers in harmony with the svelte woman's higher tone. Serge still grinned, his humor sending a spike of rage through Keith's chest. Snatching his headset off, he slammed it on the console, giving the merc a brief glare before he settled back in his seat in frustration.

"We will monitor things, including the weather, from the warmth of the Strykers," Serge pressed on with his mocking amusement. "You can sit on top of the truck if you want, or rest, or have a snack. Just do not touch my candy."

The agent stared at the merc for a handful of seconds. With a disgusted sound, he jerked out of the seat, rummaging for his equipment and weapons. He shrugged on his cold weather coat and his extra pair of gloves, then he gathered a small pack of supplies. Pistol holstered at his side, he snatched a rifle from its place on the wall.

"Where are you going?" Serge asked. "Did we hurt your feelings?"

"What is he doing?" Lena spoke over the speakers.

"I'm going out there to do this myself," he responded, stuffing a couple of spare magazines into his waistband and pulling his goggles over his eyes.

Serge chuckled and tossed him a radio, Keith catching it with a wince. "We will keep a look out," he said. "If you see Tom McKnight, flush him toward us, and we shall take him out."

"Finally, you're making sense," the agent snapped.

"You don't have to do this." Lena's voice held a somber, half-apology before bursting into a giggle. "But if you want to lose more of your extremities, please, go ahead."

"To hell with you people! Lower the door." Keith picked up his things, shoved past Mikael, and jumped out.

"Keith!" Lena called in a mock sing-song voice. "Come back, and let's talk!"

"He's already gone." Serge stepped to the door, watching the man tromp angrily through the dense snow. "He is going to do what he wants with or without us."

"Do you think he'll flush these McKnights out?" Lena asked.

Serge's head bobbed, lips pursed. "He probably will, yes. Right into our hands. It would be a shame, though, if he died in the process. Wouldn't it?" The mercenaries' chuckles resounded in the frozen winter air.

* * *

Anger fueled Keith's body like an internal nuclear reactor, and he fed on the wrathful energy like a vampire, grimacing into the ice-cold wind as it blew snowflakes against his goggles. As he left the mercs behind, all he could think of was *good riddance*. They did nothing but mock him anyway, none of them with an appreciation for his resilience and strength in the face of adversity. It was poetic, being alone again, hunting the McKnight clan through the freezing cold over hours and days, chasing his prey wolfishly across the tundra. Never bending. Never wavering.

Pain filled every ounce of his body, muscle and bone, his frostbitten fingers and toes laughing at the powerful painkillers he'd taken an hour ago. He kept his hands tight to his sides, fists squeezed closed, conserving his warmth and strength. Mind fraying against the coming storm, body bound by fragile threads of sinew and cartilage, Keith took solace in his own intense desire for revenge. The purity of the thought was all that remained, turning the sour bitterness in his stomach to raw fire, the malice in his blood, warmth.

The agent was still alive, still trudging on, held together by willpower alone.

Chapter 25
Tom McKnight
Somewhere in Mexico

Tom stood at the window, fingers dividing the second-floor blinders, looking back and forth along the street, taking in the wintry afternoon scene. It had been an hour since they'd parked inside the garage, and he'd seen no sign of the APCs, or Keith. While the skies remained gray and angry, the snowfall had let up some, a soft pattering against the windows of the old industrial building.

After parking the Humvee, they'd found a storeroom leading off the garage, filled with canned grease and machine parts he couldn't identify. Beyond that, they'd climbed one floor of rickety stairs to reach an open warehouse space, just to get off the street and get a better view of their surroundings. Lips pressed together, he allowed the blinds to fall back and turned to face his wife and family.

Barbara stood in the middle of a wide factory floor, boots spread shoulder-width apart on the stripped hardwood. The ceilings stretched tall with round columns placed every twenty feet. Old milling machines and parts converters lay around like iron hulks, tons of weight squatting on the bowed flooring, cobwebs hanging from the spindles and wheels, metal filings everywhere, the whole place smelling like dust and cold grease. The three children sat in chairs, lined up perfectly, eldest to youngest, left to right, Smooch sitting dutifully at Jack's side. They remained bundled in their coats, hats, gloves, misty breaths puffing into the air.

The kids stared at their parents with expectant eyes, still nervous after the rattling ride into the city. Sam sat quietly, eyes raised to her mother, hands folded into her lap, back stiff, shoulders square and ready to run at any second. Linda held Jack's hand, only slightly more relaxed, but only because she was trying to keep her brother amused. Barbara stepped closer to Tom, her head swimming inside her hood, lips cracked and dry from the intense cold, her goggles frosted around the edges.

"It's been an hour, honey," she said, shifting her rifle on her shoulder. "We've seen no sign of them. Can we leave?"

Tom entertained the notion of getting back in the Humvee and driving off, but something nagged at the back of his mind, something that told him it would be a dangerous move.

"This is Keith were talking about here," he huffed. "I can't believe he'd give up so easily. He has to know we're still hiding somewhere in town."

"Your false tracks probably threw them off. Maybe they're lost and gave up or moved on."

Shaking his head, Tom crossed to one of the gigantic machines, running his hand along a curved part as he passed. At the back window, he parted another blind and looked across the street to the lines of dark buildings behind him. The lifeless panes of dingy glass stared back at him, chilling him to the bone. But it was their drooping, sagging roofs and the undisturbed snow resting between them that left an uneasy feeling in his gut.

He turned and strolled back to his wife. "The snow is slowly starting to cover our tracks, but the storm is tapering off."

"Yeah, the one time we want it to storm hard, and it won't." Barbara shook her head dismissively. "Damned if you do, damned if you don't."

Tom took a sharp intake of breath and then cleared his throat. "Something tells me if we go out there, we'll be falling into a trap. It might serve us better if we go up to the next floor and have a look around. I think this goes up four or five stories, so I'll take Smooch with me."

"That doesn't make sense, Dad." Sam stood in her big coat with her hands pressed to her side. "You need a human up there, not a dog. Let me come with you and I'll watch from the other windows. I'll be your second set of eyes."

"That's not a good idea, honey." Tom placed his palms on her shoulders. "We need to think about your safety, and you being up there with me-"

"That's BS and you know it. We've done this whole big journey with me doing dangerous stuff all the time. Being a lookout is nothing in comparison. You need me up there to look around with you. Mom can stay here and keep an eye on Linda, Jack, and Smooch."

Tom looked back and forth between his wife and daughter, eyebrows raised in question, eyes directed toward Barbara. "What do you think, honey?"

Barbara shrugged. "Your call."

"I'll stay ducked down," Sam said in an imploring voice. "They won't even notice me. I'll just look around the edges and report what I see." The girl was already walking toward the access door to the stairwell, and she stopped and looked back. "Are you coming?"

Tom gave an exasperated sigh and shook his head. "I guess I am. You guys keep Smooch down here in case Keith or any of his friends show up." Finger raised, he met their eyes so they understood. "Just be ready to leave at the drop of a hat, okay? If either me or your mother say to get to the truck, you go ASAP." The kids nodded.

"Be careful," Barbara added. "Both of you."

Tom went first, stepping past Sam through the old metal door, its hinges shrieking up the shaft. The stairwell was wide, a typical U-shaped pattern, with no windows letting in a single speck of light. The hardwood creaked as they stepped over to a wooden banister with pale aqua paint flaking off. Adjusting his rifle on his shoulder, Tom retrieved his flashlight from his coat and shined it up to the next landing. With an assured glance back at Sam, he started up with tentative steps.

Fingers sliding up the handrail, he kicked aside piles of paper and garbage, sweeping the debris out of Sam's way. The first landing was empty but for the trash and a single door with a simple frame. Tom walked over and pulled the knob, opening the door a bit, peeking into a similar room as the one downstairs. The space was filled with old machinery and parts, gray light spilling through the smudged glass. It painted a dismal picture of what might have once been a robust factory with workers and machine sounds, smoke and motion and life, though it had become nothing but a skeleton of the past.

Sam's stifled shriek sent Tom spinning on his heels, flashlight aiming at his daughter on the landing, rifle sliding from his shoulder to a firing position. Legs stiff, eyes wide behind her goggles, she pointed to the floor where her boot had uncovered a frozen rat.

"Jeez, Sam," he said, clutching his chest. "You almost gave me a heart attack."

Sam let out a long exhale, stepping over the animal. "Sorry, Dad. Startled the crap out of me."

He shook his head. "That's okay. But come on. And no more scares."

They moved up to the next landing, finding their way blocked by a desk and office furniture, trash piled on top along with dog-eared cardboard, water stained with mold. The place smelled like old dust and lost time, the smells of abandonment, the building left behind.

"Careful up here." Tom shifted boxes aside and lifted an upturned chair from the desk, setting it on the landing. "The last thing we need right now is to get hurt."

"I know. I've got this."

Tom leaned forward, fists together on the table surface to test its weight, then he climbed up, crawled across on his knees, and put one boot on the other side, holding his hand against the wall to balance. Adjusting his rifle on his shoulder, he moved up a couple of steps and gestured for Sam to come over. She crossed easily enough, stepping down to where he'd been standing, nodding that she was ready to continue. They passed the next two landings and came face to face with a pile of piping and wooden framing spilled onto the steps. One hand out, he stooped and raised a little, craning his neck, peering up and looking for a way through.

He handed her his rifle. "Stand back for a sec." Sam accepted the weapon and backed to the lower landing, waiting for Tom to clear the steel, aluminum, and junk, dragging it out with a screech of metal and stacking it along the wall.

Tunnel opened, he took his rifle back from his daughter and pushed it ahead of him, crawling through the prickling debris and drooping drywall. His coat caught on a nail, snagging him for a moment, and he turned back and freed himself before moving on. Once past the jagged rubble, he ascended a few steps and turned. "Come on through but watch out for the nails."

Sam nodded and climbed carefully, kneeling, crawling on one hand while using the other to hold off the sagging debris. "Ugh, this stuff is gross," she said, standing, dusting her gloves and coat off.

"Are you okay?"

"Yeah, I'm fine. Not a fan of this place, that's all."

With a faint nod, Tom turned and shined his light up to the final landing on an aqua-tinted door. Tucking his flashlight away, he cradled his rifle in his right arm, opened the door, and stepped in two paces.

It was an open warehouse room like the others. Wooden slats stretched the length of the floor, three windows on both sides with large frames cut into four panes. There were more of the same abandoned machines they'd seen on the lower floors, stinking of oil and grease and the faint scent of something dead. Sam started to walk ahead, but Tom reached out and held her back.

"Wait a second. Let me check things out first. No sense in showing ourselves to anyone who might be watching."

Raising his rifle to a firing position, pointing it out the first window on his left, he peered through the scope, his view limited because of the narrow angle. They were elevated slightly higher than most of the other buildings, but not high enough to see above the entire city, or into the streets unless he walked up to the glass.

The scope swept across the flat rooftops with red-tinted shingles, some covered in gravel and blacktop, overhanging slabs of snow and icicles in a thick layer of whiteness. He swung the rifle around to the right and pointed the scope out the nearest window, catching sight of roads between buildings. One wound up into a hillside where the snow had yet to cover. There were a few scraps of land visible, distant patches of brown, at the edge of the scope's range.

He leaned forward, inching the rifle barrel farther north, squinting into the glass and watching the crosshairs move across the desolate landscape, the city devoid of life and enemies.

"Okay, you can come in," he told her as he kept looking.

The girl started to push past him, to walk to the other windows, when Tom threw his arm across her chest and shoved her backwards out of the room, stopping only when they reached the stairs.

"Dad! What are you doing?" Sam grabbed at his coat, catching his jacket before she took a tumble.

"Sorry, Sam!" He pulled her back into the doorway. "I thought I saw something. Just wait here, and I'll be right back."

Creeping up, angling to the right, he switched the rifle to a left-handed grip, easing it ahead and peering through the scope with his left eye. Shifting forward, a bead of sweat trickling down his neck, he zeroed in on what he thought he'd spotted previously. Toward the north, a tall overpass towered over the city, higher than most of the buildings in the surrounding area, with an unobstructed view of their spot in particular.

The crosshairs brought the hulking form into view, the dark shape of a Stryker crouching beyond the concrete barrier, its massive gun pointed downward, two men sitting on top, back-to-back. One held a pair of binoculars in his hands while the other faced their building, scanning the area with a rifle scope, idly sweeping it back and forth. Because of wearing heavy winter gear, he couldn't tell if either of the figures were Keith, but they were definitely lying in wait. As he looked on, the man with the rifle swung it in his direction, the barrel moving rapidly to line up with the window. Tom jerked back into the doorway once more, tripping over Sam where she lurked behind him.

"Is someone up there?"

"One of the APCs. Two people, too."

"Did they see you, Dad?"

Sliding around to the landing, he sunk into a sitting position and shook his head. "I don't think so. No, I'm sure they didn't. But I have no clue why they're there. The other APC must be close by, or roaming the streets."

"I guess that kills any plans to leave, huh?" Sam knelt on the floor in front of him, eyes dancing across his face.

"Yeah, we're definitely not going to pull out any time soon. We've got enough supplies to last a couple of weeks, but the cold is what will kill us."

"Could we wait for another big storm to hit? I mean, maybe we could find a map somewhere and take a side road out under cover. They'd never see us leave."

With a grunt, Tom pushed to his feet, gesturing for Sam to stay where she was while he slunk back inside the room. He edged closer to the window, staying back out of the direct line of sight from the APC, and raised his weapon once more. A gentle wind whipped snow against the glass as he leaned forward slowly, painfully, giving up as little of his body as he could until he had the APC back in view.

The overpass was a quarter mile away, and the two men sitting on top had turned to face south, though they weren't looking directly at his building. The one with the rifle elbowed the other in the arm and pointed toward the streets. His partner edged forward on his knees, bringing his binoculars up to follow where the man was pointing. The second one saw something and then nudged the first man back. He made a circling motion with his hand and jerked it toward the streets once again.

Tom stared at them for a moment, wondering what they were gesturing at, until he realized. Someone must be down in the snow, searching the area for the McKnights, hunting them, flushing them out.

Chapter 26
The Mercenaries
Somewhere in Mexico

Serge and Mikael had exited the Stryker to watch things from the top of the APC, the extra couple feet of height giving them a better view of their surroundings. The merc leader's hands and toes were chilly, but the air-activated hand warmers they'd broken out, stuffed into their clothing after Keith had left, kept them warm enough. The pair were sitting back-to-back, Mikael with his binoculars and Serge with the rifle and scope, gazing back in the other direction toward Lena's APC where it sat on the street amidst the buildings. They wore their earpieces so they could keep in constant contact with each other, though there was little to discuss of importance. The town was destitute. Everything from the ricketiest home to the ritziest hacienda had been abandoned, citizens having left their possessions behind, abandoning their homes in desperation.

"This reminds me of my hometown," Serge said. "Or like one of those movies where all the people simply vanish."

"Yes, I have seen an American movie like that," Mikael replied with a raised eyebrow. "But it was a Russian original though."

The merc leader laughed. "Every tragedy is a Russian original. The terrible story of our lives." He glanced around at the Mexican town once more. "I cannot believe so many people left here so quickly."

"I wouldn't be here myself if it weren't for this mission," Mikael agreed, "and if you weren't my trusted companions. We stand to gain a lot of equipment and supplies if we pull this off. And after we're done making the sales, I expect to be in a nice warm boat off the coast of South America within a week."

"I'll be right there with you, my friend." Serge nodded. "First, we have to capture these McKnight's."

Mikael chortled, shoulders shaking. "Yes, we must save them from Keith."

The merc leader chuckled. Mikael always got him laughing no matter how grim the situation. And they'd all seen some grim situations in their time together.

"Do you see him yet?" Mikael asked.

"He's down there playing in the streets," Serge said. The merc scooted to the edge of the APC, boots dangling over the side, rifle pointed into the lonely city roads, past the church and marketplace where Keith had passed earlier. "Let me find him again."

Squinting through his scope, Serge poked and prodded into dark alcoves and deep stoops, housing complexes with gated yards, courtyards with vehicles crowding the streets, everything snow-packed and white except for the occasional glimpse of the agent's tracks. He caught movement off to the left, and he guided his rifle toward the southeast, moving past a lonely figure trudging through the snow.

"There he is," Serge said. "I have him lined up. Should I take the shot?"

Mikael snickered, spinning on his backside, and drawing himself up to sit next to the mercenary leader. Binoculars to his eyes, he began searching. "I don't see him. Where is he? Don't shoot him until I can watch."

Serge laughed, following the agent's path as he stumbled along a narrow street within the shadow of taller buildings. The man was small against the backdrop of frozen abandonment, staggering, slipping, arms windmilling as he clutched his rifle to his side. "Do you see that cluster of buildings southeast of our position?"

The other merc gave a light gasp. "Ah, I see him down there now. He's standing in the intersection. I think he is looking at us." The merc pointed and laughed. "He's in the middle of a warehouse area, perhaps the manufacturing center of the city. What in the world is he doing? He looks drunk."

"The man is frostbitten all over his body. I think even his brain," Serge replied as his scope followed Keith's staggering progress through the knee-high snow. "I have to admit, I admire him a little."

"Admiration for that idiot? Look at him. He can barely stand."

Lena's sultry voice came through their earpieces. "You boys get to have all the fun, watching that clown stagger around. I would like to request that we change positions. I want to see, too."

"No way, Lena." Serge made a derisive scoff through his frosted lips. "It is boring and cold out here, and Keith is far too entertaining. Ah, damn. He just crossed out of sight behind a building. Hopefully, he will come out the other side."

* * *

Every step he took was a fresh experience in pain, his boots pounding through a foot of snow, painful waves reverberating into his ankles, knees, and hips. It was like wading in quicksand made from dry ice, his frostbitten toes on fire, feet sore and twisted from having to walk unbalanced. Tottering and swerving, he clasped his rifle to his side to keep it from rattling, flashlight in his other hand, shining it into the darkest corners of the desolate city for a sign of his prey.

The never-ending shade of grey daylight left everything captive in a perpetual shadow as he moved through a residential district, cutting into back alleyways and side streets there. The Spanish-style homes began to look the same to him, the buildings like sentinels. Shoulders hunched beneath the gaze of black windows, he passed gardens snowed over and windswept, trees bending toward the road with branches like wretched claws. Looking side to side, he searched for any signs of life, any indication that he wasn't alone in the abandoned city.

But it had become a place of shadow, a land of ill omen, and Keith was on his own, more so than he'd ever been in his entire life. A light snow began to fall, the flakes drifting on sudden gusts of wind. He plowed ahead, driving through the snow with his knees, gazing up at a large cluster of warehouses that had been his original destination. As he approached, the old buildings loomed massive over him, thick brick structures that looked like they'd been built in the 1970s.

The dark doorways invited him inside, wanting to chew him up like toothless maws. Shattered windows gaped and screamed, though no sound came out. He thought he caught movement in the front door of one warehouse, and he froze, crouching lower, peering through his frosted goggles. In a flash, he unslung his rifle, grasped it in both hands, and charged up the stairs to fly across the threshold.

Flashlight pressed against the barrel, stock raised to his shoulder, he swept the weapon back and forth over a massive open warehouse space. Back in the shadows where his light beam barely reached, hulking machines squatted like sleeping giants, hydraulic arms poised as if frozen in time. Pipes and hoses and gauges covered their thick steel forms. Flywheels and gears stretched belts between them, sitting stagnant and unturned for weeks. Off to his left, snowflakes drifted through a hole in the ceiling, fluttering in his light to fall softly on the old hardwood floor. But there was no one there, certainly not the McKnight's.

"Damn," he sighed. "Now I'm seeing things." He gave a quick shake of his head, palm pounding his temple briefly. "No, it's just my nerves and this cold, and Serge's useless ass."

Keith backed out of the warehouse, stepped slowly down the stoop, and rejoined his footprints out in the street. With a last glance at the dark doorway, he resumed his search for the McKnights. The thick snowfall sucked up the sound of his boots as he crunched through the top layer of frost, busting it to pieces like candy brittle. He had no idea where the McKnights were, or if they were still in the city. He only knew he couldn't stand the company of the mercenaries any longer and needed to be out on his own, fighting, doing something despite his growing weakness. The cold and snow were sucking the life out of him, yet a fire still burned deep within, the part of him that wouldn't accept defeat or failure.

Reaching an intersection, he glanced left over his shoulder to see Serge and Mikael just specs where they sat on the APC at the top of the overpass. They looked down at him and pointed, probably laughing at him, following his progress with their scopes and binoculars. He resisted the urge to flip them off and instead staggered forward quickly, ducking behind another high-rise factory monstrosity, five stories high and inlaid with frosted windows like ancient gems.

Playful breaths of snow gusted against his face, causing him to glance aside and bow his head. Then he threw his eyes up, gazing up into the grey sky, shining his flashlight beam upward as flakes danced in the light. While the weather played, his body sang with pain. It was no longer the honed killing machine it had once been. He was well beyond top form and had extensive wounds. Doubt entered his mind, tickling his stomach before trickling through the rest of his limbs.

Still, he trudged on, arms swinging wide to keep his balance, boots lifting over the snow and pounding down again. He stopped in the middle of a four-way intersection that had once been a well-lit city street. The lamp posts were dead, the electric gone, devoid of life like everything else. He turned in a full-circle, staggering sideways, held up by the snow, stopping when something caught his eye on the south-running lane.

He stumbled ahead a few steps, bending, eyes focused on a brick alley and a set of tire tracks that crossed in front of him. They were thin and shallow, moving from right to left, not exactly the width of Humvee prints but wide enough to be distinguishable. Willing himself forward, Keith staggered the twenty yards to the tracks, lifting his goggles and glaring anxiously down, raking his gaze back and forth three or four times.

Were they the Humvee tracks? Yes… yes. It was the only answer. There was no one else around. Hand coming up, he wiped the frost from his nose and mouth and breathed hesitantly. With the spurt of determination, Keith put his goggles over his eyes and took the left passage between two buildings, certain he was closing in on his prey. Driving against the snow and a wall of pain he'd built for himself, he sucked gouts of ice-cold air, freezing his nose and lungs.

Farther up, the tracks angled right along a dark alleyway lined with steel doors and an emergency stairway zigzagging upward. A spattering of windows looked down at him, amused at his sudden vulnerability, waiting for him to keel over in the snow. Despite his pounding heart, frozen throat, and every limb crying for relief, his flesh and bones still served him. Swaying and tottering, Keith plodded into the next street, watching the Humvee tracks go half a block before turning right and disappearing beneath a big steel garage door.

The space was wide enough to hold a truck inside, plenty of room for his quarry to hide like a rabbit in a hole. Suddenly, he was alive again, the most living thing in the entire damn dead city. He was a wolf in the snow, a brother to winter, and he was there to take his prey and complete the cycle of life and death. He unslung his rifle, gave it a tap with his palm to knock off the loose frost and ice then he took several deep breaths and crept toward the door.

Chapter 27
Tom McKnight
Somewhere in Mexico

"Come on, Sam. We need to get back downstairs. Now!"

Tom flew down the steps in a blind panic, taking them two at a time, Sam's lighter footfalls following. He slid beneath the pile of pipes and wood, snagging himself again on the big nail, pricking through his coat to scrape his skin, crying out, part in pain and part as warning to his daughter. Then he was falling down the stairs, boots flailing, rifle rattling, his backside bouncing three steps before he regained his footing. He didn't wait for Sam to catch up, but kept moving. A couple of flights later, he came to the desk with all the debris sitting on top. He threw himself across it, boots first, kicking aside a box of papers to send them tumbling to the floor.

As soon as his feet landed, he heard the smash of the front door and a gunshot from below. Nostrils flaring, Tom grunted sharply, pushing forward, eyes wide with terror and realization, staggering and falling to the next landing. Tom spun and leaped in a blur, body flying, spanning the entire length of steps, boots slamming on the hardwood. From his crouched position, he launched himself toward the machine room door, shoulder low as he crashed through it, throwing it back against the wall with another resounding bang.

His jaw fell, knees weak as he caught sight of Barbara on the floor, clutching her chest, gasping, blood soaking her coat, flailing to grab her pistol she'd dropped in front of her. As Tom looked on in horror, she pointed, bloody hand shaking, finger quivering. He jerked his head around and saw Linda, Jack and Smooch wrestling with Keith. His daughter's lips were pulled back in a grimace as she clutched the man's rifle, elbows locked over it and clinging like a monkey to a branch while Jack hung on Keith's coat, screaming, right fist striking out repeatedly, as ineffectual as a gnat but just as irritating to the larger man. Smooth had latched onto Keith's leg, but the thick winter fabric rendered him impervious to her teeth.

Tom jerked his rifle to his shoulder, leaning in, aiming at his nemesis, but Linda and Jack were in the way and he growled, the noise punching from his throat with raw emotion. "Get out of the way, kids! Get out of the way!"

They either didn't hear him or were so enraged by what had happened to their mother that they only felt their own crying hearts. Shifting the barrel slightly left, then right, then up, Tom realized in a split second he couldn't take a shot without putting a round into the back of his daughter's or son's heads. With a hiss of frustration, he tossed his rifle to the ground, diving toward the struggling trio. He grabbed Linda by the shoulder and threw her off then took Keith's gun barrel in his left hand, cocking his right fist, delivering a punch to Keith's jaw that rocked him backwards.

The agent ripped the weapon out of Tom's hands, falling to the floor, pulling Jack along with him and sending Smooch flying across the floor to smash into a pile of scrap with a high-pitched yelp. Sitting there dazed, head shaking, Keith swung the weapon around and fired at Tom, but Tom had seen the move coming, and he dove to the side before the round could connect with anything but air and wood and metal above.

Tom tried to roll forward and get to Keith before the man could do any more damage, but the agent was on his backside, kicking away, retreating with his gun clutched in his lap. Back slamming against the wall, pushing himself up to stand. Keith had no place left to go, so the rifle came up, barrel pointed at Linda before shifting to Tom. He stepped forward with a rictus grin, finger on the trigger when Sam's cry cut through the din, resonating with unrestrained rage.

"No!"

Tom's looked in her direction where she stood, holding Barbara's dropped pistol. A grimace stretching her lips wide, Sam squeezed the trigger twice, firing two rounds into Keith's chest. The first pinged against his armor and he slammed into the wall, howling in pain. The second round hit the drywall with a sharp puff of dust and Keith spun away, rifle clutched to his chest, looking for the exit as Smooch got back to her feet with a bark, charging at him. Sam fired again, willing the round to kill him, but Keith only grunted and arched his back, hammering his way through the door, stumbling outside and into the snow, Smooch snapping at his heels as the door closed in her face.

A moment's hesitation struck her as she debated between chasing after the man and staying, but she made the decision quickly, shouldering the door aside as it tried to swing shut, ordering Smooch to stay put as she stepped out into the growing snowfall. The agent was hobbling along the street, glancing back as he clutched his bruised chest. Sam stopped at the top of the steps, slipping a little, raising the weapon and centering to shoot. A squeeze of the trigger sent another round flying, zipping to his left, barely missing him. Hearing the gunshot, Keith put his body into overdrive, plowing forward with his knees pumping, heading for cover.

As he hobbled and staggered, he grabbed the radio from his pocket, slamming the transmit button. "Serge! Lena! I found them. I found the family. Come on, get down here!" Only static greeted him in response.

Back on the stoop, Sam tried to aim, tried to fire one more round, but the man had become a shadow in the snowfall, the wind sweeping white dust through the streets to obscure her vision. It was no use. He was gone.

With a pained expression, dreading what waited for her in the warehouse, Sam screamed a curse into the wind and spun back inside. Her father had stripped off her mother's coat and cut her shirt open with a knife, leaving her bloody wet skin exposed to the freezing air as his fingers danced over her abdomen, looking for the wounds. Throwing herself to her knees, opposite Tom, Sam saw her mother was unconscious, and she grasped her hand and looked to her father.

"What can I do, Dad? Tell me what to do!"

Jack was screaming in the background, crying and reaching for his Barbara, but Linda held him back, trying to cover the boy's eyes and turn him away from the bloody sight while she stared on, weeping. Smooch sat near the pair of them, Linda squeezing her with a free hand as the dog whined, adding to the mix of noise and confusion.

"Find a place to make a fire," Tom said, fighting a wave of panic and memories of the past swirling unbidden as he swabbed away the blood from Barbara's stomach with her shirt. "There's got to be a stove or something around. Something that would have kept the workers warm on cold days."

"I'll look, but won't the smoke give us away?" Sam implored.

"I don't care!" Tom roared at her, his calm demeanor shattering. "If we're going to save your mother's, we need a heated place to work. Go! Now!"

Sam leapt to her feet, knees shaking as she stared at the unconscious figure, her mother's chin and cheek smeared with blood. Then Samantha turned on her heel and ran into the back of the warehouse, searching across the wide-open space until she spotted a door at the far end on the right. She jogged past the machines, paint flecked and rusted, saws and pressure fitters, racks of rollers that reached from one end of the warehouse to the other. At the door, she jerked the handle, pulling it back with rough resistance as it scraped across the old floor. Sticking her head and shoulders inside, she saw it was a break room of sorts with tables and vending machines. But as her father had suggested, they had a stove in back with a single small door and vent going up into the wall.

The girl immediately started gathering scraps of paper and wood framing that had fallen. It wasn't much, so she jogged back across the warehouse and out to the stairwell, where she and her father had run across all the junk to get to the top. She grabbed two pieces of wood and shoved them into a box of old documents, snatching it up by the handles and carrying it two flights of stairs to the bottom floor.

As she passed, she shot a look at Linda and Jack. "Grab some paper and wood, whatever you can find! Bring it to the back so we can make a fire for mom! Hurry, and keep Smooch with you!"

Linda nodded and gave her brother a tug, pointing his shoulders toward the stairwell door. A whisper in his ear was all it took, and the two ran upstairs to gather more scraps, Smooch trailing behind them. Back in the break room, Sam opened the stove, threw in some wadded pieces of paper and grabbed the stick matches out of her pocket. With shaking hands, she lit the match and set the kindling aflame, watching the wavering orange tendrils lick toward the top of the stove. She fed it a little more and then added a small piece of wood, then more scraps, then more wood. The fire caught, grew, and began putting out some serious heat. Sam turned to exit, almost running into her brother and sister as they were bringing in more boxes of paper and pieces of wood.

"Put it over there by the rest of the stuff," she said as she squeezed passed them and jogged to where Tom was still working on Barbara.

Standing over them, she couldn't tell how many times her mother had been hit or where. Feet shuffling, fists pressed to her sides, she was caught between running away and screaming. Instead, she strode over and knelt by her mom, keeping her voice firm. "Okay, I got a fire going in the back room. What can I do next?"

"Help me get her next to the fire." Tom rose and put his hands beneath Barbara's arms, his expression stoic, eyes hard to read behind his goggles. "Grab her legs. Come on, hon."

Nodding, her insides shaking, Samantha stood and moved to her mother's feet, grabbing her boots and lifting them off the floor. On a count of three, they raised Barbara up and waddled through the warehouse. It was almost impossible to hold her mother's feet with gloves on, but Sam hooked her fingers beneath her mother's ankles, using her arms to pin the boots against her waist. After setting her down once to readjust, they finally got her into the break room and placed her in front of the stove on the cold, hard floor. The air was already warming up, the area filled with the scents and sounds of crackling wood. Jack, Linda and Smooch stood off to the side, Jack and Smooch having calmed down as Jack embraced his furry companion while Linda stood by them stoically.

"Kids, go to the Humvee and get some blankets," Tom said, fighting to keep the panic out of his voice. "And grab a sleeping bag, too."

Tom moved back to his wife's side, staring down at the abdominal wound on her left side, a few inches below her ribs. From what he could tell, it was only one shot, one bullet that had entered one side and gone out the other. That was a good thing, but if the round had hit any internal organs on its way through, he wasn't sure what he could do. Blood was still leaking from his wife's body, pooling on the surrounding floor in a big red stain, barely contained by his shirt that he had removed and ripped into pieces, putting them on her wounds. Handing Samantha a few strips of cloth, he took deep breaths, still fighting against the past, refusing to base future expectations on past tragedies.

"Sam, get on your mother's left side and hold that rag beneath the exit wound. That's it. Press hard. We want to stop the bleeding." While she did that, Tom did his best to keep pressure on the entry wound. He nodded at his hands. "Now, put your other hand where mine is and apply force on the top and bottom. I'm going to rip up some more rags."

Letting Sam take over the pressure responsibilities, Tom stripped two more shirts off, leaving him with just a long John top as protection from the cold. The sound of cloth ripping filled the room as the chill seeped into his skin, the stove's heat barely keeping it at bay. Soon, he had a pile of rags lying in Barbara's lap, ready to go in case they needed them. Feet shuffled into the room and he looked up to see Linda and Jack with bundles of blankets in their arms. Linda dropped a sleeping bag by the stove and held up a box with a red cross on top. "I found this packed in there, too. It's a first aid kit, right?"

"Yes, it is. Please set it down beside me and open it up. I want to see what's inside."

Jack dropped blankets on the sleeping bag, backing away from the horrific scene of his mother's shallow breaths, bloody smears streaking across her fire-lit, glistening skin.

"Come on, kids," Tom growled. "Focus up. Stop staring at your mother and make a bed for her. We need something to lay her on."

Wordlessly, Linda and Jack spread the sleeping bag out next to the stove. On top of that, they placed a blanket, then Tom asked Linda to take over pressure duty while he and Sam stood at the woman's head and feet again. On a count of three, they lifted Barbara onto the pallet they'd made, folding a towel beneath her head as a pillow. Still keeping pressure on the wound, eyes watering in the warming air, the McKnight family huddled around Barbara's still form, stoking the fire, praying for the bleeding to stop.

* * *

Back on the overpass, sitting atop the APCs, Serge glanced at Mikael as he swept his rifle back and forth. "I haven't seen Keith in a few minutes now. I wonder where he went?"

"Maybe he froze to death," his partner replied, pulling his coat tighter around his shoulders. "The storm is picking up, and it's getting colder, I think."

"We can only hope." The merc leader searched for a few more minutes, guiding the rifle back and forth, peering through the scope at what streets he could see, moving back to the last location he'd seen the agent. "I don't know. Maybe we should go look for him."

"Careful, Serge. You sound like you care about the man."

"I am just as amused as you are with him, but it would be bad form to let him die out in the cold. Banks might not like that. We should at least give him the benefit of the doubt. Lena can..." Something caught his attention off to the east, a little left of their position. "What's that?"

"What's what?"

The merc leader pointed in the direction he was looking, a thin tendril of gray rising from a squat warehouse, drifting out of a pipe in the side. "It's smoke. Someone lit a fire in one of the buildings. Someone is alive."

Mikael shrugged. "Perhaps Keith got too cold and couldn't make it back to us. So, he made a fire."

"He may be trying to send smoke signals," Lena's voice piped through their headsets, and the mercs laughed, Serge especially so as he imagined the agent huddled in a tiny room somewhere waving a cloth over a fire. Before his grin could grow any wider, the merc leader sobered up.

"Keith has a radio. He would have called us to let us know what he was doing." He stood atop the APC and aimed the rifle back down toward the smoke, the snowfall swirling around, obscuring his vision.

"Unless the radio signal is poor." Mikael looked up. "The storm is picking up quite a lot."

"I think, more than likely, it's the McKnights who made the fire," he frowned. "Why they are doing it, I don't know." Serge watched for another moment before he sat and slid down the APC's front end on his backside, feet kicking as he dropped into the snow. Mikael followed him without question, boots thudding on the snowy pavement next to him.

"Lena, we're going on foot to check things out."

"Would you like us to assist?"

"Yes, please." Serge walked to the end of the overpass, taking an exit ramp down, following Keith's fading boot prints. But a violent gust kicked up, lifting white powder from the ground and throwing it into his face, and he had to turn to the side and wait for the chilly gust to pass. "On second thought, let's move in with our vehicles. We will approach under the cover of the storm and then attack as soon as it lifts."

"Command received," Lena replied. "Will meet you in ten minutes."

As Serge and Mikael marched back to the APC, he glanced toward the gentle smoke seeping upward from the chimney, wondering what had come over Tom McKnight.

Book 6: RECOVER

Chapter 1
Tom McKnight
Central Mexico

With just a pair of thin long johns covering his arms, Tom shivered, teeth clattering as he stared at the first aid kit and then at the terrible wound beneath Barbara's ribs on the left side. Sam's face strained as she held one bundle of bloodstained rags on her mother's abdomen over the entry wound. Everything was bloody - their clothes, the stain growing on the floor and the slow trickle of red running down her pale side. The first aid kit only held a few bundles of gauze and bandages, none of which would be any better at stopping the bleeding than what they were already using. The old rags were doing next to nothing, and Barbara's life was leaking out across the floor. Her face had gone pallid, her breathing shallow, pulse weak where his fingers rested on her wrist.

In the back of his mind, a thin thread held him together, and Tom had to breathe to keep himself calm, caught in a moment of indecision. Jack and Linda were ripping up rags, staring wide-eyed at their mother as tears streaked down their cheeks. Smooch whined, muzzle sweeping back and forth, forelegs dancing on the floor as she reluctantly obeyed Tom's orders to stay away. Sam's expression was horrified, her eyes darting between her shivering hands and her father's face.

"What do we do, Dad? Please. What can we do?"

Returning to the first aid kit, Tom picked it up with his bloody hands, inspecting it for something more useful. Turning it over, he saw a zipper separating two compartments. Fingers grabbing the tab, he unzipped it, placing it on the floor and flipping the top section forward. Inside were four tubes with plungers and four sealed bags of silver packaging. Each was marked *Injectable Hemostatic Sponges*. His mind slipped back in time to a first aid course he'd taken on a trek through the Rocky Mountains, where a ranger had provided similar first aid kits. While mostly used for penetrating wounds like gunshots and stabbings, the ranger had been obligated to run them through a brief set of instructions on the sponges, since they'd been part of the training.

Tom remembered the ranger filling the tubes with tiny, compressed sponges that looked like aspirin tablets, attaching the plunger, forcing the tip into the wound, and injecting the sponges inside. With shaking fingers, he flipped one package over and scanned the instructions, seeing they were the same as he remembered. Taking a smaller tube in hand, he pulled the plunger free, ripped open a sponge pack, and filled the tube with a tumble of the tablet-sized shapes. Then he put the plunger back in place and pressed the tablets toward the end.

He shifted on his knees, hovering over the entry wound in Barbara's side, watching Sam's trembling fingers try to stop the egregious amount of blood coursing out. "Okay, Sam. When I say so, I want you to take the rags off."

"What are you going to do?"

"No questions. On the count of three. One… Two…"

Sam pulled her hand away, swiping the rags to the side as blood pulsed from the tiny entry wound and gushed down Barbara's pale skin. Tom placed the end of the tube into the hole. Blinking, remembering what the ranger had said about getting the sponges in deep so they could force pressure against the damaged arteries and veins, he pressed it even farther, two or three inches inside. Gritting his teeth, knowing if Barbara was a conscious she'd be screaming, he jammed the tube until he felt resistance, almost all the way, and pushed the plunger with his thumb. As he injected the sponge tablets, he withdrew the device, filling the wound to the edge. When he drew it completely out, the tablets swelled, turning pink as they became engorged with blood and pressurized the wound's sides. Sitting back on his haunches, Tom stared and blinked, fully expecting the blood to keep pouring out after the sponges were saturated. But it didn't. The five pink ends stuck out from the entry hole, pressing firmly against the sides. No blood leaked out, leaving just Barbara's glistening, rouged skin reflecting torch light.

"Holy crap, Dad," Sam said in total awe, her jaw hanging open. "It worked. It really worked."

Sighing, shuddering with relief, wiping his bloodied long john sleeve across the cold sweat on his forehead, Tom nodded to Sam. "Yep, it's actually working. The bleeding stopped. Let's get her covered up."

Tom checked the entry wound again to see the bleeding was still under control, throwing a pair of blankets over her to keep her warm. "Come here, Jack and Linda. Bring Smooch." Tom gestured to his two youngest, directing one to get on each side. "Unzip your coats and climb under the covers with her. Easy though. Just snuggle up against her. You can hold her arms, but don't touch her belly or chest, okay?"

The pair nodded vigorously and hit the floor on their knees. Coats were unzipped as they slipped beneath the blankets with their dog and gripped her arms.

"That's it," Tom encouraged as he reached for the cover. He and Sam tucked it in around the sides and top. "Rub her arms and keep her warm. Sam, I want to see that fire blazing hot."

She nodded and backed away from the huddling group, staring at her own bloodied hands for a moment before turning to the old iron stove sitting just a few feet away. Grabbing a stick she'd been using as a poker, she shoved around some coals and tossed in a few pieces of debris her siblings had brought from the hallway. Within thirty seconds, the flames were blazing, the heat rolling off the hot metal to radiate around the family, sending shivers down Tom's arms, drawing a relieved sigh. Fishing beneath the covers over Jack, he felt Barbara's pulse one more time, noting it had strengthened. Gripping her wrist, squeezing his eyelids tight to force tears out, he stared across at Sam's questioning gaze and nodded. "She's... okay."

"What now?" She asked.

Settling back on his heels, hands resting on his thighs, Tom looked around to take stock of the situation. The last fifteen minutes had been a complete blur, the events flying through his head in what felt like the space of two seconds.

Sam stared at her mother and the small lumps her brother and sister made beneath the covers. "I think her face has a little more color. Do you see it?"

Tom glanced down and nodded. "Maybe a little. But she needs a doctor right away. That much blood loss, she probably needs a transfusion. I just don't know…" His teeth clenched, molars grinding as he remembered they were in the middle of nowhere with no idea where civilization was. Worst of all, there were people right outside their door that wanted them dead. "What happened to Keith? Where did he go?"

Sam backed up and shook her head. "I'm pretty sure I hit him twice in the chest, but it barely seemed to faze him." Her face twisted up in confusion. "Is something wrong with the bullets?"

"He has body armor on. I'm sure of it. What else?"

"When he was running away, I shot at him a couple more times in the shoulder, and once in the back." A quick shake of her head showed her frustration. "Same thing. He took it and just kept running, but I know I hit him because snow popped off his clothes. Like dust flying up or something. Know what I mean?"

Tom nodded, happy Keith had paid a price for his evil in some small way, though the agent would undoubtedly be back to finish the job, likely with his friends in tow. "Wait here," he said, standing, finding his coat, and slipping it on. Exiting the room, he crossed the machine area with its bulky metal monsters, rusted hulks lurking in the shadows, oil and grease wafting in the chilly air. Their strange mechanical arms hung poised over clamps, conveyors silent and still. In the front room, Tom spotted his rifle laying in a pool of blood. Scooping it up, he checked it to make sure it was charged and stepped to the front window, slipping to the side, and looking out.

The snow was falling slower than before, fat flakes floating across his vision in an icy wonderland that filled the streets. The drifts curved upward to the brick walls and the stoops, and an eerie stillness loomed. When he leaned forward and glanced to his left, he saw Keith's frantic boot prints leading to the corner of the warehouse across the street, but no blood was visible. Cursing silently, he turned and looked around for anything they might've left in the room. All that remained were the tatters of Barbara's shirt and coat where he'd cut it free and there were big, billowing red droplets on the hardwood and bullet holes in the wall where Sam had shot at Keith. After a deep breath, Tom released a long sigh, stomping down the anxiety building within him. He watched and waited, expecting Keith or one of his goons to come slogging down the avenue or from an alleyway, at which point he planned to smash out a window and mow them down where they stood. But when they didn't appear, he began to worry, doubt and uncertainty tickling his belly.

Part of him wanted to find a basement or upper-story room with just one entrance where they could dig in and defend themselves. But their opponents had armored vehicles, big guns that could shoot through brick like a welding torch through plastic. If they tried to stay put, it would be the end. No, they had to go on the offensive, or at least make the next move before their enemy made it for them. After another ten minutes of watching and waiting, Tom strode briskly to the back room and stood in the doorway, watching his family sitting huddled by the stove, shadows flickering across the walls from the open stove door.

"How's your mother?"

"The same," Sam said, where she crouched near Barbara's shoulders.

The covers rustled and shifted, and Linda's head poked out, neck craning to see. "She's getting warmer, though. I can tell. And she moved a little, too." She glanced beneath their blankets. "Smooch, stay still!"

"I felt it too," Jack agreed from the other side, his voice muffled.

"You have a plan?" Sam asked from her crouched position.

"Yeah. We're getting out of here. Sam, you and I are going to get your mom loaded into the rear of the Humvee. I'll stay back there and take care of her, but I'll need you to drive. Can you do that?"

Her glassy eyes stared back, unflinching. "I can drive. Yep."

"All right. Let's do this. Quickly and carefully." Gently tugging the blankets off Linda and Jack, he coaxed them out. "Hey, you two. Take Smooch to the Humvee and get the back door open. Find something for your mother to wear. Long underwear. A shirt. Another coat if you can find one. Then make a place for us to lay her down. Okay?"

The pair hopped to their feet, nodding, Jack staring at Barbara lying beneath the wrinkled blankets, blood on his coat sleeves from where he'd been snuggled next to her. Seeing her brother's distress, Linda grabbed his hand and called to Smooch, inclining her head to Tom, starting to lead her brother off.

"Wait," he said, holding out his hand to Sam. "Do you still have your pistol?" With a nod, she stood, pulled the gun from her waistband, and slapped it into his palm. He pivoted and gave the weapon to Linda. "You know how to use this, right?"

"Oh, yeah," Linda said. Releasing her brother's hand, she turned the pistol into her right palm, finger outside the trigger guard, and pulled back the slide to check that it was loaded. "No problem, Dad."

"Good," he nodded. "If Keith or his goons come through the door, you know what to do."

Linda tucked the gun into her waistband, grabbed Jack's hand, and led him out onto the machine floor with the dog trotting behind them, limping slightly. Turning back to his wife, worried about her shallow breathing but with no other choice, Tom circled and knelt opposite Sam. They wrapped the blankets around her and checked the warmth of her face, and her pulse, seeing she'd stabilized.

"I'll get her shoulders," he said, already shifting in that direction. "You get her feet. Just like before, except we're going to take her out to the Humvee and put her in back."

Sam was nodding, moving to Barbara's feet, pushing up her pants legs to get a good grip on the backsides of her calves where they narrowed into her boots. With his hands tucked beneath her armpits, the covers still draped over her, he gave his daughter a nod. After lifting her off the floor, Tom maneuvered around so he was walking backward, glancing at the wide red stain they'd left behind. He retreated through the door with Sam shuffling in perfect synchronization. Weaving between the big hulking machines, they moved to the stairwell door, passed into the hall, and entered the garage. Linda and Jack had thrown the Humvee's rear door wide open and had shifted supplies to the side, tossing some into the backseat to make room. They'd spread out a couple of thick blankets and placed a small pile of folded covers in the back corner.

"I was thinking we could rest her head on the left side," Linda said, climbing down and pointing to the folded covers.

"Thanks, kids." Tom looked over what they'd done and saw she was right. It would be cramped, but she'd fit in easily if they put her in diagonally.

When they got there, Tom lifted one heel to the edge and climbed in without using his hands, keeping Barbara from bumping against anything. Backed into the cramped space, he twisted his body and placed her down. Sam set her boots into the other corner, easing her onto the soft bed. The wind gusted against the garage door, rattling it on its frame, chilling his lungs. The faint scents of machine oil and dust drifted around them as they situated Barbara as best they could, bundling her in more blankets.

"We put some extra clothes on that side," Jack said, his words coming out in puffs of steam.

While Tom situated his wife, he turned to Sam. "Hey, run back inside and see if there's anything we left behind. Grab the first aid kit, too, okay?"

Sam nodded and ran off, and Tom continued tucking Barbara in, shifting things around in the back so nothing fell on her when they drove off. He motioned toward his two youngest, "Why don't you two jump in the back seat?"

Jack and Linda climbed in the back with Smooch, slamming their doors shut, Tom gritting his teeth at himself for not telling them to be quieter. Jack turned and threw his arms over the seat to stare at Barbara, his eyes wide above his rosy cheeks. Linda grabbed the boy's jacket and pulled him down just as Sam ran up with one of the extra blankets and the first aid kit.

"Here you go, Dad."

"Thanks." Tom accepted the things and placed them inside next to Barbara before he fished the keys out of his right front pocket and handed them over. "Okay. You're driving. You know what to do, right? It's an automatic transmission, but the steering's pretty crazy. Hang on with both hands. Oh, yeah, the gas pedal has a… thing to it. You'll see. Just push through it."

Nodding, Sam clutched the key in a tight fist as she turned and dashed around to the driver's side door, jerked it open, and threw herself behind the wheel. Tom circled to the other side, sliding between the wall and Humvee as he made his way to the garage door, intending to throw it up to let them out. Just as he bent to grab the handle, a pair of shadows flitted across the frosted glass outside, two big shapes moving from left to right, growing larger as they approached. Blood running cold, Tom left the door where it was and staggered backward, swiveling on his heels, dashing to the back of the Humvee. He climbed in with Barbara and pulled the door shut quietly behind him.

"Who is that?" Sam hissed, staring at the shadowy figures.

"Start it up and floor it," Tom said flatly.

"But the door…"

"Will crumple like tissue paper." His voice shifted to a growl, palm slapping the back of the seat. "Don't worry about it, Sam. Start it up and go!"

* * *

Serge huddled against the unrelenting cold, holding his rifle with both hands, elbows locked at his sides. He barreled through the snow, lifting his boots and dropping them in the same tracks Keith had left. But he took shortcuts through alleys and passages where Keith had been circling, cutting his time to reach the man in half. The snowflakes weren't gusting like before, and the thick dusting of white no longer obscured their vision. Tall buildings loomed over them, massive warehouses and housing complexes, some with gated yards with lumps of vehicles resting in their powdered tombs around them. It was easy to see how Keith had gotten so disoriented in the oddly angled streets amidst structures that looked mostly the same. But with the agent's partially covered tracks, and the smoke rising from the warehouse chimney, they had a general direction to go, and Serge kicked hard through the snow, closing in on their prey.

A glance over his shoulder showed that Mikael was right behind him, slogging in the tracks he'd left, the hood pulled tight around his face. They'd just entered an alleyway one lane away from the building when a mumbling shadow staggered around the corner and ran into him. Serge hit the man's shoulder with a palm strike, shoving him backward as he raised his rifle to fire.

"Ow, damn!" Keith grunted, slamming his right hand to his left shoulder with a wince, cheeks lifted in a grimace of pain. "What the hell!"

"You better be more careful," Serge said, lowering his rifle barrel, a slow grin spreading. "I almost turned you into Swiss cheese. We thought we would come save you from the scary McKnight children."

Mikael walked up and nodded at Keith's tattered coat over his body armor. "It looks like we're a little late. Someone has taken shots at him."

Serge tried to remember if he'd heard the gunshots, but the storm had been loud, the wind howling across the overpass and there was a good chance he wouldn't have heard them. "What happened?"

"The little bitch shot me three times." The agent grunted and groaned, staggering back into the snow. "They were right there in front of me. I had them." He squeezed his fist tight. "I brought Barbara down, and I think I wounded one of the kids. Maybe. I don't know. Their damned dog was chasing me."

Mikael snickered. "You so tough, beating up on women and children like a true warrior."

Ignoring the quip, turning to go back the way he'd come, Keith gestured at the merc's to follow. "Let's go. I know right where they are. We've got them."

Serge dropped his hand on Keith's shoulder, fingers gripping his coat tight and jerking him backward and around. "You go back to the APC. Get warm."

"Yes," Mikael said, edging closer. "Leave this up to the professionals. We will return with the McKnights, dead or alive, in just a few minutes."

Keith was already shaking his head vigorously, a sneer on his lips, beard growth frosted by the winter chill. "No way, man. I've been wanting this for a long time. We're all going in and getting them right now."

Serge shook his head. "No. You are freezing and wounded. Your body had frostbite all over. You need to get warm, or you will not have any hands or feet left to get your revenge. We will bring the McKnights to you. Trust me, my friend."

Keith's gaze shifted between the mercs, the insane heat behind his eyes fading, the pain still etched in his features. Reluctantly, he nodded, slowly at first, then more vigorously. "Yeah. I'll go back to the APC, get warmed up, and wait for you to bring the McKnight's to me." With an anxious step forward, he leaned over the deep snow, grabbing Serge's coat and pulling him close. "I want Tom alive, you got that?"

"We will see," he replied, and jerking his shoulder free, circling around with Mikael in tow.

Serge watched Keith stagger away and out of sight, turning the far corner into the next alley. With a frosty scoff, he murmured, "That man is a complete mess."

"A cold mess," Mikael replied, chuckling. "Let us go take care of business now." The merc gestured with his rifle barrel for Serge to lead on.

With a brief nod, he turned and put one foot after the other, lifting his boots high and slamming them into Keith's old footprints. While it was all fun and games with the agent, he couldn't help but have a niggling sensation in his gut. As crazy and impatient as he was, he was still a trained agent, and that he'd been driven off by one man and his family was alarming. Serge didn't doubt this team's ability to finish the job in short order, but it would be folly to take anything lightly.

Throwing a glance over his shoulder, he said, "Stay alert."

Picking up on his leader's intensity, Mikael gave a sharp nod in response.

They reached the corner of one building. Serge leaned forward and peeked around, watching as Keith's boot tracks wove thirty yards along a street to the left before angling into a courtyard and up a wide stone staircase to a doorway. The snow on the stoop was a mass of footprints, likely Keith trying to get away as he was being shot at. The McKnights had put up a formidable defense at the door, and it would be smart for the mercs to pick a different entrance. He took his radio off his belt and held it to his lips. "Lena, are you there?"

A second later, the speaker squawked, and the mercenary's voice reached him through the static. "We are here, Serge."

"Do you see the building with the smoking chimney?"

"Yes."

"We are in front of that building right now. Where are you?"

"Coming up behind it and a little to the east. Do you want us to come to you?"

"No. Find a back entrance, stairwell, or something. Let us know when you are in position, and we will flush them to you."

"You want us to keep any of them alive?"

Serge stared at the snow-covered stoop, the mess of boot prints Keith had left, thinking back over their hunt and how the McKnights had evaded capture for so long. Any other time, he would've toyed with them, but something about the family told him that would be foolish.

"No. Do not apprehend them. Shoot to kill. Let us know when you're in position."

"Very well."

Over the next few minutes, Serge watched the building, catching glimpses of someone moving inside, the faint traces of a flashlight beam in the darkness, enticing him to charge up the steps and take them out. But unlike Keith, he had plenty of patience and would wait for the right time. The cold gripped him, icy fingers reaching between the gaps in his clothing, tickling his neck and shoulders, his extremities growing chilled.

Lena came back to him a few minutes later. "We are in position," she said in a flat tone, seeming unaffected by the freezing air, having grown up in the Siberian wastes. "Waiting for you to flush them to us now."

"Good. We are going in."

With a glance back at Mikael, and nodding his head toward the building, Serge left the corner's cover and stepped into the street, following in Keith's footsteps as he stared at the warehouse door. He looked up at the building to the shadowy interior, wondering if the family might be trying to get higher to make a stand in a well-protected room. They could hold out there for some time, but with the merc's equipment back in the APC's, any barriers they erected wouldn't last long and, in the end, things would be far messier and take longer.

Breaking off from the boot prints, he angled toward the garage door, noting the frosted windows and old faded paint job, a foot of snow shoved up against it. If it was unlocked, they could enter that way, flanking the McKnights through one of the inner hallways. Shifting, he pointed his rifle at the door and gestured for Mikael to open it. The mercenary broke off and edged to the center to grab the handle, kicking away the loose snow to reveal a rusted handhold. He glanced at Serge, and the merc leader nodded back, pointing at it, twisting his hand to pantomime unlocking it.

Mikael stooped and reached, and as soon as his fingers touched the handle, a diesel engine sputtered to life behind the door, puttering and coughing at first, then growing into a deafening roar. The glass panes in the garage door rattled and shook and the mercs stepped back at the same time, rifles up and ready to fire when the person on the other side threw it open.

But the door never flew up. The engine roared louder, the diesel transmission kicked into gear and growled like a cornered mountain lion and tires barked on concrete a split second before a Humvee's grill slammed through the door, wood snapping and taking on the vehicle's rough shape before exploding outward. Glass shattered and sprayed everywhere and Serge winced, jerking back as shards glanced off his cheeks and neck. He dove to the side, landing in the snow and rolling away, not having seen if Mikael had made it or not. The Humvee ripped past them in a spray of snow and exhaust, the merc swinging the rifle up and firing from a seated position. Mikael had gotten out of the way and was tangled in some bushes on the other side, floundering, shifting to a kneeling position, jerking his weapon up out of the snow and fired into the Humvee's side as it made a sharp left turn and tore off down the street. The rounds punched into the armored sides with loud pinging noises, sparks flaring in the ghostly cold. Glass shattered and exploded inward, but the vehicle kept going, swerving back and forth as whoever was driving struggled with the slick snow and ice.

Slipping, Serge staggered to his feet and jogged from the courtyard, firing at the back of the shifting truck, watching his rounds ping harmlessly off the armor. Mikael joined him a second later, adding his own gunfire to the mix, but by then the Humvee had gone around a long bend and out of sight, speeding away with ease.

"Dammit!" Serge slammed his palm against his weapon, screaming to the heavens as Mikael crossed the street, Lena and Dmitri rushing from a side alley, spotting them, and jogging over.

"What happened?" Lena asked, breath coming in puffs of cloud, eyes saying she'd already figured it out as she stared at the Humvee's tracks through the snow.

Serge's response was barely a growl, his heart still pounding against his rib cage, senses on fire after narrowly avoiding getting run over. "Get back to the APCs. We are going after them!"

The other two mercs turned and sprinted away while Serge and Mikael dashed back the way they'd come, retracing their steps to their APC. It was only after trudging past a set of buildings twice did he realize that were going in circles. Standing in the middle of the street, he and the other merc glanced around in confusion at the footprints leading in several directions.

"Which way is it?" Mikael asked, eyes narrowed as he walked off to the side. He shined his flashlight beam all around, peering between buildings in search of the overpass.

Breath coming in frustrated gasps, heat rising in his face, Serge shook his head. "I don't know. If Keith made it back to the APC, maybe he can get on top and look for us"

A rumbling engine broke through the quiet cold of deep night and Serge and Mikael's flashlights whipped toward the end of the lane, penetrating thirty yards into the darkness. Their APC burst from a cloud of snow dust, barreling in their direction with the driver's viewing slit raised up, Keith's eyes gleaming at them from the vehicle's interior. Serge waved and stepped to the side, giving the burly truck enough room to pass on the clogged road. It trundled past them, jerking to a halt, steel frame squealing and shrieking. The tires kicked up white powder before the thing settled on all its wheels, the rear door clicking open and sliding downward. The mercs stood at the back, waited for the door to touch down, and leapt aboard, climbing into the warm interior.

From the driver's seat, Keith turned to them, a cold smile tugging at one corner of his mouth. "You boys looked lost. Need a ride?"

Chapter 2

PFC Simon Sharp
Santa Fe, New Mexico

In his favorite hiding spot on Sub-level One, Sharp slipped off his boots to reveal his sweaty socks and placed his footwear next to the door. Cracking it slightly open he listened for any sounds of guards, and when all remained quiet he stepped out into Sub-level One with his flashlight and knife handy, looking both ways, moving left along the corridor. He was heading away from the main stairwell, which was the only exit as far as he knew, though it was always guarded by militia, impossible to escape.

Creeping through the abandoned corridors, he made his way through Sub-level One in search of an auxiliary stairwell leading to the lower levels. There weren't many guards on that floor, just the occasional patrol or some militia passing through to reach another stairwell, like he was doing. The soldier kept his chin low, eyes ticking back and forth, listening for the sounds of boots or voices, or even the faintest hint of breathing. He'd already run into several militia members sleeping inside supply rooms or catching naps when they should have been patrolling. Once, he'd almost stepped on one man who'd been lying in the hallway, barely leaping him, landing with his heavy boots and dashing around the corner as the guy was waking up, shouting for whoever it was to quit screwing with him. But that's when Sharp had abandoned his boots and traveled by socks, tiptoeing quietly over the tiles, slipping past patrols with soft steps and held breath.

Several turns later, he came to one of the side stairwells, turned the latch, pressed the door open, and held his ear to the crack. A current of air whistled through the shaft, a change in air pressure causing the sound to expand and contract like it was breathing. To Sharp, it felt like he was stuck inside the guts of a beast with its maw clamped shut and no way to get past the teeth.

Shaking off the thought with a shudder, he stepped into the stairwell with its solid concrete core and started down, his goal to reach the third sub-level and prowl around a bit, seeing if anything had changed in the situation. The last time he'd checked, the militia were hunkering down until the trucks were loaded, hoping to escape before the next convoy arrived. With Captain Johnson having moved on to another set of buildings, the new arrivals would be their only problem, and any confrontation could get his buddies executed.

Gritting his teeth, determined to save them, he crept down the wide concrete stairs, his socks making no noise except when they caught on a rough spot, only his breathing and heartbeat accompanying the rhythm of his steps. On the third floor, he peeked through the square window into the corridor beyond. With a sudden gasp, he ducked and leapt back, rolling toward the stairwell and flying down with quick, quiet steps as two militia members slammed the door open and stepped out. As Sharp fled, he heard voices on the landing, a man and woman, laughing with breathless whispers, the soft noises of secretive affection.

He growled in annoyance, moving past the fourth floor and going all the way to Sub-level Five. Once there, he stepped into the corridor and peered up where it stretched for hundreds of feet, with many side corridors and hallways. Like Sub-level One, five didn't have warehouses and supplies, so it was the least used by the militia. They kept their patrols to a minimum, no guards posted unless they were trying to escape their duties. He moved more easily through the passages, not so much creeping as jogging and two turns brought him to a room with a big red light over the door. When he punched in the correct security code on the keypad, the magnetic locks popped open, and he pressed his head and shoulders inside. A wide control board took up most of the space, buttons and knobs and meters on it, three screens arrayed across the desk's surface, though only the center one was on. Above the console was a window into the next room, the lights there very dim, one wall full of monitors with live video feeds of hallways and warehousing units in the facility. A door to the right connected the two rooms.

"Must be the internal monitoring station," he murmured.

While he hadn't attempted to use the equipment, he'd kept it in the back of his mind whenever his plan to bust out his comrades took its ultimate form, though it still drifted half-finished in the tired space between his ears. Shutting the door, he moved once more through the hallways, slipping past a small armory he'd found days ago, accessible by using one of the override codes LePlante had announced on his radio before the militia shot him. It had come in handy getting inside many side rooms. Best part of all, Chet and his people didn't have the overrides, which limited their access to many of the facility's important areas.

From there, Sharp hustled past a barrack area, then made his way to another stairwell going up. Being on the far side of the facility, it would place him farthest from his fellow soldiers, but it was also seldom used by the militia. Following his standard procedure, he cracked the door, put his ear to it, and went up to Sub-level Three, stepping into the corridor with no issues. The worst part about using that stairwell was the smell, as it brought him out near the room where he'd found the dead bodies. That mess had been a complete puzzle to him, and he wasn't sure if Morales and Smith knew about them. As he slipped quietly through the darkened passages, the pungent reek of rotting flesh and pine-scented cleaner turned his guts, almost making him vomit. But he held it in, and in a few quick turns, he came to a well-lighted section where the danger of running into the militia group increased.

In a half crouch, he heard the distant voices of people walking along the main corridor, likely moving between the refrigeration unit where they were keeping their prisoners and the warehouse where the teams were working. He took a side way around, coming to the edge of the junction that carried sound well, one he knew he could use to spy on them. But as he was drawing closer, heavy boots clomped toward him from the left-hand passage, a pair of men bantering, not sounding like they were going to stop.

Sharp spun on his heel, dashing a couple doors down where he remembered there was a safe storage closet. He swept the door open and slipped inside to pitch darkness, turning, holding the doors so it fell gently shut. With a sigh, he sank to his butt and rested with his back against it, the supply closet crowded in around him as he sat with sweat drenching his hair, legs quivering with exhaustion after hours of creeping through the hallways and warehousing units. It had been a delicate game of cat and mouse, keeping out of sight, mapping out the halls and sub levels in his mind while avoiding detection.

Flashlight in his left hand, one of his six-inch cooking blades in his right, he was ready to defend himself should they get curious. His knife training ran through his mind, special moves and attack postures resurfacing as he feigned stabbing gestures. Sharp stopped his practicing and closed his eyes, listening. With his flashlight off, he was blind, the closet almost perfectly black except for a thin sliver of light leaking beneath the door. When they didn't walk by, he flipped on his flashlight and looked around. It was a standard supply closet with a mop and rolling bucket, a broom and dustpan, small metal shelves that held bleach, paper towels, and urinal cakes.

The room gave off a reek of pine cleaner and a generic strawberry fragrance and the combined smells turned his stomach, the air stuffy around his head. Standing straighter, he kicked his feet a little to get the circulation back. Standing, he shone his beam down at his wiggling toes inside their thick socks. A foul smell wafted up from them, his nose wrinkling and forcing him to remember the last time he'd had a shower. It'd been way too long.

"Okay, quit screwing around, Sharp," he told himself in a hesitant whisper. "Time to move."

In a half crouch, he turned the door latch and pulled it open, allowing in some of the hallway's blinking light. Stepping out of the room's shadow, he glanced to the right and left, choosing left where the militia's voices still reached him. With his blade still held in a forward position, Sharp crept along the hallway, facing the wall, relieved at the quiet sounds of his shuffling socks on the tiles. With the weight of the heavy boots gone, he allowed his feet to slide. Sections of the pale walls flickered in the failing lights as the emergency power quivered through the wiring. Following the sound of the voices and the boots, his eyes darted everywhere and at the next four-way intersection, he caught the faint hint of a conversation and he tilted his head in different directions to home in on the sound. At first, he thought it might be coming from the right passage, though as he neared, the echoes changed and convinced him it was back the other way. Creeping to the corner, edging closer, Sharp waited and listened.

"… happens when the next group shows up early?" one man with a high, nasally voice was saying amidst their shuffling boots. "Chet and Shae were wrong about these Army pukes showing up. They could be wrong again."

"Chet and Shae couldn't have expected all that," a second man replied. His tone was deeper, voice made of gravel. Just by the sound of him, Sharp estimated he was physically bigger than the first guy. "But it was a blessing in disguise."

"How do you figure?"

"They questioned the prisoners and got some answers, too. Now we know when the next convoy will swing in. And it won't be anytime soon. We've got time."

The pair shuffled again, and the private estimated they were probably fifteen yards down the passage. With a quick glance behind, Sharp checked to make sure no one was creeping up on him, a paranoid feeling that had followed him through the dark, echoing halls. Not seeing anyone, he turned back to the intersection just as a waft of cigarette smoke drifted by, a cloud of it going straight up his nose, filling his sinuses with a terrible, flaring itch. Eyes watering, nostrils wrinkling with the raging urge to sneeze, he retreated several steps and slammed his index finger and thumb on the bridge of his nose. Squeezing tight, he waited until the oncoming itching faded and finally disappeared altogether.

With a head shake, he moved back to the corner, waving his hand in front of his face to clear the smoke. While part of him said he should retreat to the supply closet and let himself sneeze it out, the two militia members' conversation were the closest he'd gotten to any real information in a full day. Ear ticked up, he continued listening.

"But what if they came sooner?" the nasally voice asked, the tension in his throat shooting his high-pitched tone even higher. "What if one of those guys got the message out and warned them? They'd come crashing through all that snow easy. And what if there's a lot of them, like those Army boys said? They could show up at any time, and we'd be screwed."

"We could be outnumbered a thousand to one and still hold them off for months and even years," the other replied. "We've got tons of supplies. Hostages, too. No one's going to try anything, Stu."

"But you know these Army guys. They've always got some kind of backdoor with a secret code to get in."

The deep voice chuckled. "This ain't a James Bond movie. There aren't any secret entrances. This bunker is way underground, dude. We've got the main stairwell covered, and the Army boys are loading our trucks. We'll be long gone before anyone else shows up. I wish you'd stop worrying. You're making me nervous, man."

"I know, but things are way too quiet. My skin is crawling. It's like I feel a snake sliding into my sleeping bag or something. Think about all the hallways and passages in this place. How many cargo doors do you think there are? Just the one we're using? I don't think so. And there must be ventilation shafts, too. If mice and rats can get in here, so can those Army pukes."

The bigger of the two didn't respond for a moment, except for the sound of him expelling a lungful of smoke, boot kicking at the floor. Stu went on, his tone even more piercing than before. "Yeah, man. They could come in here and get behind us, or flank us, and we'd never know it until they hit us. They might not care about the hostages, anyway. Not when all these supplies are at risk. There's enough food for tens of thousands of people in here. Probably hundreds of thousands."

The silence thickened, and Sharp began to agree with Stu, at least in principle. He was probably right that there were some passages they hadn't explored, some that might lead to the surface, giving Captain Jones and his troops a hundred different ways inside, although Jones wasn't even aware of the situation in the bunker.

"You're probably right," the big man said as boots shuffled fast toward the intersection. "We've got a few half-assed patrols, but that might not be good enough. Chet and Shae might want to interrogate the Army boys a little harder. They might have even more information. Back entrance maps. Codes. Things like that."

The private didn't hear the rest. He was busy scuttling down the hall, retreating, heading back to the supply closet as the boots shuffled toward the corner, almost on him. Once they saw him, they'd sound the alarm, either before or after they filled him full of holes. Smart's hand flipping the latch downward with a clack of internal mechanisms. Grabbing it, whipping it open softly, he slipped through and in one smooth motion, he turned and allowed the heavy steel door to fall shut behind him, catching it with his fingers so it didn't make any noise. With no lock on the door, he gripped the handle and held tight, ear to the surface as the voices and boots approached. As the pair rounded the corner, one stray glance up would've revealed the door slowly shutting, giving him away, screwing up his plans, but the boots kept walking, not breaking their rhythm. The men were still talking, their voices muffled, the cadence and volume indicating they hadn't noticed the door shutting or the latch clicking.

Once they'd passed, a sigh slipped from Sharp's lips and he turned and put his back against the wall, sliding downward until he was seated on the floor. Breathing steadily again, Smart pondered what the men had said, mulling over their paranoia about a back entrance, ductwork, and Army codes. The possibility that unknown forces might creep in to outflank them, and that they were going to warn Chet. Maybe a distraction to take their mind off the prisoners long enough for them to escape could work. Not wanting to fail, Smart sat quietly with his flashlight beam to keep him company, closing his eyes as he played out scenarios in his head.

Chapter 3
Keith
Central Mexico

The APC trundled over the rough, icy highway, moving south in pursuit of the McKnights. The old diesel engine growled, wheels churning through the snow, the vibration shivering up the seats and into the back of Keith's head. The rear lights were dim, casting a deep shadow over the APC's crew section. Fists clenched, he drew the thermal blanket around him, slouching lower as he listened and bided his time.

After picking up Serge and Mikael, they'd met Lena and Dmitri at the north side of the city. Keith had handed over the reins of the lead APC to the merc leader and taken his gear to the second vehicle. The two had looked disappointed to see him go, since he'd been the butt of their jokes for most of the journey and Lena was especially pleased for Keith to join them, sneering with amusement as he'd climbed in, tossed his pack into the seat next to him, and pretended to bundle up and disconnect himself from the rest of the group. Shortly after driving out of the city and joining the highway, Keith had enlisted a range of false snoring sounds, shifting back and forth in the chair before falling into a steady state of heavy breathing. He kept his head positioned to keep a slitted eye on the two up front through his entire charade, though, their faces lit by the APCs consoles.

Lena occupied the radio seat in her thick but stylish jacket, the material hugging her svelte form while Dmitri drove, his hulking shoulders hunched over the controls, his arms wide and bulging even beneath his heavy coat. For the past hour, Keith had watched Lena watch him, the merc glancing back randomly, keeping the radio chatter normal until she was sure he was dead asleep. Keith's instincts had been burning with warnings and alarm bells for some time and while his anger and impatience often caused him problems, he never ignored his gut feelings. After two hours of driving, they proved him right once again.

Lena leaned forward, pressed a button, and tuned a knob. Lips close to the microphone, she whispered in her sultry European voice. "Serge, are you there?"

"I am here, yes." His response was quick and quiet, the volume turned down, his tone low as if he'd expected the conversation and the secrecy it required.

"I am having… doubts about our mission."

"And why is that?"

Through his half-lidded eyes, Keith saw Lena glance toward the massive driver before turning back to the microphone. "This family, these McKnights, are especially slippery and dangerous. How many times have they escaped us despite our best attempts to apprehend them?"

"Yes. Not to mention the number of times we've almost died at their hands," Serge growled.

"They almost ran you over a few hours ago," Lena whispered with urgent agreement, her voice barely audible over the grumbling engines and sliding tires. "Under any other circumstances they would be nothing more than ants. But this cold, these conditions… our continued failures make me nervous. We have to ask ourselves if it is so worth it."

"Our leader would not approve of such a move."

Keith barely managed to suppress his grin, keeping his cheeks and jaws slack.

"We would outvote him, of course," Lena continued. "He could not keep us from turning around if that was our desire. And if he does not like it, we would leave him on the roadside to think about this decision in the cold."

After a pause in which Keith assumed he was talking to Mikael, Serge came back. "We are of a similar mindset, but there are other factors we need to consider. There are the bunkers and the weapons inside them. How do you propose we get codes for those?"

"That is easy," she replied, a sneer in her voice. "We explain what will happen to him if he does not give us the codes. We explain this compellingly."

"What are you suggesting?"

As if the answer was obvious, she gasped, "I am speaking of torture, of course. Is that not one of Mikael's better skills?"

Another pause filled the space, the grumbling APC's tires driving through the snow the only sounds for thirty seconds before Serge replied. "Again, Mikael and I agree with you. Do you have thoughts about how to do this?"

As they were speaking, Keith had been shifting his hand toward a panel above his head to the right, having positioned himself in that seat for just that purpose. In the shadows, Keith flipped a latch and popped a small panel in the wall filled with electronic circuitry and tiny flickering lights. Reaching inside, his index finger and thumb felt around for a fuse, one of three in a cluster that kept the radio transmission alive. Grabbing one, he snapped it out and quickly shut the compartment door, flipping the latch to a locked position once more, arm sliding back in place. The fuse went into his jacket pocket in exchange for a six-inch carbon blade while, up front, the radio connection between the APCs died, breaking off into complete silence as Lena looked back and forth in confusion. Her gloved fingers flitted over the control panel, flipping switches and turning knobs to reconnect, but nothing she did worked.

Frustration slipped out with a breathless sigh, and she squinted at Dmitri. "The radio has died. Did you do something?"

The massive mercenary shrugged, head shaking in the negative as the rough ride jostled him. "I have just been driving. I touched no buttons or knobs."

"Of course not," Lena said, slapping her fingers against the control panel's edge, blowing a frustrated breath between tight lips. "Do you know what I can check? You have experience with this model of truck, no?"

A massive paw raised, thumb hitching backward. "The remote array is in panel in back. Rear seat. My side. Check that. Perhaps a wire has come loose. Happens sometimes."

Hands thrown up in a gesture of frustration, Lena stood, balanced herself as they went over a pothole, and slapped the driver on his right shoulder. "Thank you, my friend. I will fix. Until then, try to keep up with Serge."

The thick neck bent forward in a nod, and Lena staggered and bumped her way to the Stryker's rear. Keith gripped the carbon blade's hilt and drew it slowly from his pocket, leaving it far enough inside to remain hidden. Through squinted eyes and deepening shadows, he watched Lena's slender form approach, swaying back and forth, both arms out as she fell gently against either side, sometimes using a ceiling handgrip to stay upright. Soon, her face came into view, her green eyes piercing as she stared at him through the gloom, lingering on his supposedly sleeping form for a moment before lifting to gaze across the various panels built into the vehicle's side.

She leaned forward as if to open the panel he'd taken the fuse from, the faint whiff of a fragrance touching his nose, some old perfume or shampoo she wore and Keith tensed, his bandaged fingers gripping the knife blade. Pain radiated up his wrist and arm, but he didn't care; his body thrummed with energy, veins pulsing with adrenaline, jaw squeezing slightly tighter, but not enough for the mercenary to notice as the thick coat he wore helped hide his intentions.

The thrill of what he was about to do coursed up through his back and shoulders, sending shivers across his arms. It seemed impossible that she didn't notice, her eyes brushing over him casually before she started opening the higher panels. As she searched them, her stomach was mere inches away, leaning over him, but he still didn't strike.

The mercenaries had been holding him back. Worse, they'd made fun of him, laughed at him, jeered and snickered beneath their breath. He'd caught the words they mumbled to each other to describe him; unprofessional, weak, and crazy. Not the man he used to be. No, they were right about the last part. He wasn't the stoic agent who'd carried out hundreds of dangerous missions, suffered through a thousand intolerable environments, finding victory in the harshest conditions and against impossible odds. No, he'd transcended all that. The near-death experience at the lake had changed him. Filled his blood with a fire he'd never felt before. How dare soldiers-for-hire mock him. How dare they take command of the mission and force him into some child's role. And how dare they threaten to stab him in the back and leave him by the side of the road just because they were tiring of their mission. Payment was demanded for such treachery. And the price was steep.

Finished with the upper compartments, Lena sighed, her breath washing across him as she bent to the panel he'd taken the fuse from. She flipped the latch, pulled open the door, and peered inside. Face right above his, she reached in and traced the components, looking for something wrong and a soft gasp escaped her as she realized the fuse was missing.

As she was about to straighten and call up to Dmitri, Keith's bare left hand snapped up, his frostbitten fingers grabbing her blonde ponytail, jerking her head back to expose her long neck in the paltry light. Her green eyes flashed wide, lips parting as she grunted in surprise, the sound cut off by Keith's carbon blade plunging into the pure white skin just below her jaw. The blade pierced her trachea, slicing through her vocal cords to leave her voiceless, unable to make a single sound. When the knife came out, warm blood gushed over his hand and face, splashing on his coat and hitting the floor in a spatter.

Years of training sprung to life, and Lena's body tightened and tried to twist away, a natural defensive reflex kicking in. Swinging her right arm up, she tried to dislodge the hand buried in her hair, but it was too little, too late as the knife plunged in again, thirsty for her blood. The razor-sharp steel sliced through her jugular vein, ripped free, and stabbed repeatedly with short, hammering blows. Her legs flew wide, boots almost kicking equipment to the side, her gurgling bubbling over him in splashes of red. Damage done, Keith wrapped both arms around her, his boots coming up to lock her legs, pulling her tight against him in a bloody embrace. As she gushed and gasped and punched weakly at the back of his head, he only smiled and held her tighter, his cracked lips brushed against her earlobe, whispering death and vengeance as she wiggled and squirmed and, at last, fell still.

For a long moment, Keith relaxed and held the corpse, the Stryker bouncing and shifting from side to side, the ride made only slightly smoother by following the lead vehicle's tracks. Moving her body to his right side, he focused on the giant driving the APC, the smile fading from his face. Angling his hips, he shoved Lena off him, dumping her on top of their backpacks with a soft rustling buried beneath the diesel engine's pounding. Grabbing a loose shirt from their things, he wiped off his hand and the knife hilt, cleaning off the blood that might cause him to lose his grip. He sat forward and slowly unzipped his heavy jacket, shrugging it off to lighten his limbs and give him more maneuverability, then, on his feet, he turned and stalked between the seats, arms held out and holding his balance like Lena had done a few minutes earlier, coming up behind the big Russian.

Body relaxed, he went along with the vehicle's sway, allowing his legs and hips to shift naturally instead of fighting the movements. Still, keeping his footing sent ripples of pain from his toes into the arches of his feet. But the ache only drove him harder, cutting through any fear and doubt, infusing him with adrenaline as he looked along the back of the man's neck and across his shoulders, looking for a vital spot beneath all the muscle. There were no two ways about it - Dmitri was an impressive man, wholly intimidating by his sheer size alone, but the danger ran far deeper. The man was a born killer, ruthless when he needed to be, sometimes just for the fun of it. Keith had to be quick and deadly, taking full advantage of his surprise if he wanted to survive the next few minutes.

The colossal head started to turn, chiseled jaw angling away from the window slit as wind blew around in gusts of freezing air, battling with the rattling heating system that barely spit out any warmth.

"How is it going back there?" His voice boomed through the Stryker's cabin. "Have you fixed it yet? Lena?"

For a split second, Keith froze, still a few feet from the man, a solid lunge away, though it might as well have been miles when dealing with a brute like Dmitri. With a sharp intake of breath, Keith dropped into a crouch, gathered his strength, and then launched himself forward. The big man came to life in a spasm of movement, one fist flying back to stop the assault, even as Keith's knife arm swept in above it, both hitting at the same time, the razor sharp carbon point cutting into the base of the merc's neck, slicing through muscle and sinew, the blade scraping against bone. But Dmitri's enormous fist caught Keith in the ribs on his right side, knocking his wind out, sending him flying backward. He tumbled into the seats where the arm of a chair punched the small of his back, causing him to writhe upward. The two men paused in a flash of shared pain and the Russian started to rise but collapsed, palm slapped to the wound in his neck, blood pulsing between his fingers, flowing freely.

Ignoring the cracked bones and the lancing agony up his side, Keith shifted forward and lunged to his feet, face twisted in desperate urgency. Staggering toward the mercenary, he led with his left hand to block, right hand cocked back and waiting for an opportune time to strike. The Stryker cut hard, throwing him off balance, causing him to pause long enough for Dmitri to swing. Keith caught the backhanded punch in the chest, coughing with eye-watering pain, though he still clung to his weapon. He dove forward with a cry, imbalanced but somehow wrapping his left arm around Dmitri's shoulders, clinging like a child to a tree trunk.

The next few moments came in a blur of motion, Keith grunting, screaming, stabbing wildly at the man's neck and face. Dmitri thrashed and growled, threatening to throw Keith off as blood soaked everything, slicing Keith's grip, the rich copper smell filling his nose as his cheek pressed against the merc's drenched crew cut, repeatedly jabbing at the thick shoulders. He tucked his face down to avoid the big grasping hands, both off the wheel and snatching at him, blocking his thrusts. A majority of Keith's strikes hit home, though, slicing and cutting Dmitri's neck to ribbons.

The giant head swung backward to crack Keith in the cheek, sending him to his knees, eyes swimming in stars. He fell against the seat as the Stryker fishtailed to the right, slid sideways twenty yards and ground to a spine-jarring halt. Falling back, Keith avoided another flailing swing by the titan, the thick knuckles missing his jaw by a hair's breadth as he hit the floor. Dmitri hauled himself from his seat, falling forward into the driver's console, bloody hands streaking across the buttons and knobs as he turned to face Keith. "You... son of a..." He tried to finish the sentence, but a spray of red ejected from his neck and hit the ceiling. With a surprised grunt, he grabbed the spot, swooning on wobbly knees.

Keith gaped at what he'd done, the mess everywhere, the ominous mountain moving above him with eyes so furious they crossed and bulged from their sockets. A boot flew forward and caught Keith in the back of the leg as he tried to turn aside, shoving him into the rear seats again. Realizing he no longer held his knife, he frantically searched on his hands and knees in the darkness to find it, then he realized he had his sidearm, too, tucked under layers of shirts. Twisting, back against the seats, he struggled to get it out, part of him wondering why he hadn't used it on the giant right away. But that voice was small and distant, because Keith knew it was the *blood* he'd wanted to see, to feel his blade cutting his enemies, carving them to pieces, to extract everything out of them that he possibly could.

By the time his palm rested on his pistol, a round exploded inside the cabin, zipping past him, sending a shocked ringing through his skull. Frozen in place, Keith saw Dmitri had pulled his own weapon, the massive forty-five caliber gun wavering as he struggled to focus on him in the tight quarters. It should have been an easy shot, but the giant suddenly groaned and collapsed to a knee, bending forward, dropping the pistol with a clatter. The big shoulders and head swayed back and forth, a deep groan rising from his chest, both hands slapping to his neck as he tried to stop the bleeding. He shoved his jacket and shirt against the gushing wounds, but the warm lifeblood found ways to spurt free. With a high-pitched, maniacal chuckle, Keith spun on his backside, stretched to grab the pistol off the floor, and kicked backward to the seats again.

As he raised the gun, Dmitri dropped to the side, pressed down by the angled roof to crumple at the base of the wall. The enormous chest rose and fell for another ten seconds, each breath coming raspier than the last. His kicking legs slowed, strength fading, until he stopped altogether, one final gasp expelling like the relieved sigh of a train as it reached the station.

Gasping for breath, the pain in his hands and feet excruciating, Keith wobbled to his knees, turned, and staggered to the Stryker's rear. He found the fuse in his coat pocket, opened the circuit panel, and shoved it home. As soon as the fuse was in place, Serge's voice shot into the cabin.

"...there, Lena? I repeat. Lena, are you there? Do you require aid? We can come back to you."

Stepping over backpacks and spilled equipment, Keith lurched to the communications chair, fell into the seat, and threw the headphones on, adjusting the microphone in front of his mouth. Finger poised above the console's talk button, he made a couple of experimental sounds, drawing low grunts from deep in his chest, stretching his throat to hit the lowest possible note. As an added measure, he grabbed a loose shirt that had fallen into the aisle and place it over the mic to further muffle his tone. Satisfied he was somewhere in Dmitri's vocal range, he pressed the button and replied in the same guttural, clipped way he'd heard the giant speak.

"Unnecessary. We are having trouble with radio. Lena is working on it now. Will catch up. Standby."

After letting up on the button, he waited for a reply, half expecting Serge and Mikael to come storming back, their guns blazing to take Keith out, but Serge came back fast, his tone low and serious but with no hint of suspicion. "Fine. We will keep going but slow down so you can catch up. Hurry. We are losing ground on our quarry."

"Roger that."

Keith's slack expression faded, and his head ducked between his shoulders, the back of his hand slamming over his mouth to stifle a giggling fit. Hearing himself, he chortled and shook harder as he clambered to the rear and gathered his knife and pistol from where they'd fallen on the bloody floor. Huge Dmitri was blocking his way and would make it difficult to maneuver inside the vehicle.

"Got to move the big guy first," he mumbled, squeezing his hands, sending aches throughout his bones and fingertips. Grabbing Dmitri's left arm, he heaved and swung the corpse onto its back with a heavy thud. Repositioning himself near the man's head, he reached beneath his armpits, fingers slick on his wet jacket, then he squatted, hoisted, and leaned backward with a groan, muscles straining to stretch the two-hundred-and-fifty-plus pounds.

"You thought I'd be easy, but I was far from it," he grunted as he struggled with the weight. "Poor little Keith, so weak and frostbitten. He probably couldn't hurt a fly." He spoke that last bit in a mimicry of Lena's voice, not coming close to it but still causing his abdomen to clench in laughter, almost dropping his burden. With one more heave, he straightened out the dead merc, leaving some leg room for him to get around if he needed to. Wiping amused tears from his eyes, he knelt, rolling Dmitri back onto his belly so he was face down at an angle. Standing over him, slipping toward the driver's seat, he kept murmuring, his voice barely above a whisper. "Now who's stuck in the corner? All those muscles couldn't stop my knife, could they? Silly man. Big and strong and couldn't even handle little ol' me."

Leaving off with a dry, quivering chuckle, he winced as a shudder of pain ran through him. Keith slipped back into the driver's seat, adjusted its height, and grabbed the steering wheel. During the fight, the Stryker had gotten stuck, its tires spinning in a snowdrift, engine whining high. As soon as he put it in reverse, the tires caught and the truck jolted backward, knocking him around fiercely as he let his body loll with the lurching movements. Sensing he was approaching the edge of the road, he slammed the brake, put the gearshift into drive, and pushed the accelerator to the floor. The big APC rocketed forward, shoving him against the seat, eliciting more pained delight as the tires slewed back and forth as he sought out Serge's tracks.

The Stryker pitched and fought him, spinning freely across the snow-laden highway, swerving and almost slipping off the shoulder more than once. Pain screamed through his hands as he worked the wheel, his right foot minus two toes pushing the brake and accelerator pedals alternately, the limb already chilled from where the warm ventilation didn't reach.

"Come on," he hissed through a wincing chuckle, rising out of the seat, peering through the thin view port at the windy road. Tongue out in concentration, his abdomen muscles squeezed around his ribs, grunting and laughing through the pain. Mumbles filled the cabin, a strained, high-pitched voice he didn't recognize. After a minute, he realized it was him talking. Maybe he really was losing it, going crazy, cuckoo-for-cocoa-puffs, but at least he was back on track, back on the McKnight's trail. The inner fire fed him, radiating from his core, coursing through his bloodstream to warm his limbs. A part of him thought the warmth was all in his head, and that he could still freeze to death if he wasn't careful, but that was a far-gone concern, buried beneath his sense of invincibility and inevitability. After a colossal struggle, the vehicle straightened and the tires fell into the grooves with a bump. Chuckling low, patting the steering wheel, he shook his head and mumbled incoherently, though a few tangible words sprung from his lips.

"You're mine, Tom McKnight... kill your girls... slow... cold... pain..." His fingers wrapped around the wheel and relaxed again as he repeated the mantra. The Stryker plowed on through the snow, the distant lights of Serge's APC coming into view, two red taillight dots in the gray morning, clouded by flurries and mist. Chin lowered, leaning forward, he pushed the Stryker faster. The words, *kill... slow... pain...* rang in his head like a lumbering footfall, the fire shooting up through his throat and burning inside his brain.

Chapter 4
Tom McKnight
Central Mexico

The Humvee shuddered as Sam plowed it through the snowdrifts, struggling to find a path forward. The battered front end and cracked glass made it hard to see, and she craned her neck around to find a big open patch where she could watch the road as the windshield wipers pitched back and forth at a slow pace, dusting each new trickle of snowflakes off to the side.

Wind whistled through the Humvee's cabin, the rear passenger window shot out by the mercenaries, the bullet having punched a hole clean through, passing by Jack and Linda, and leaving out the other side. The rest of the rounds, as far as Tom could tell, had struck the armor and bounced off or not penetrated deep enough to get into the passenger compartment, thankfully, because Barbara's head lay in the left front corner of the cargo area, closest to where the mercs had been firing.

Rising, Tom scanned outside to see nothing but pure white hills and endless desert, highway signs buried in chest high drifts, cavorting snow dervishes skipping across the road in front of them in halfhearted play. The Humvee shifted, sloughed sideways to the right, riding up a crystallized snowbank with a bang and shudder, the entire truck rocking stiffly like a boat smacking a dock. The motion threw Tom into the side, both hands flying out to brace himself, cursing low, his gusting breath evidence of the Humvee's heating struggles. Fingers pressed against the frozen glass, he held himself there until the vehicle settled.

With a determined head shake, Tom sat back on his knees, right foot straddling Barbara's hips to keep his balance and have the best possible angle to access her chest wounds. She was still out cold, though her bleeding had stopped. He searched his brain for the next step in saving her life as he rifled through the large amount of gear Saanvi had packed for them. He'd just found another pair of emergency medical kids-one of them as long as his leg had been tucked beneath the rear seat-when a groan reached his ears, but it wasn't Barbara. Rising again, he settled his hand on the back seat and peered ahead to see Sam shifting and rolling her right arm in pain.

"Hey, Sam, honey. What's going on up there? Are you hurt?"

She rolled her shoulder again, chin turning to the right a little, the pain on her face clear. "I'm not sure. My right arm stings, though. Up by my shoulder."

Tom began gathering gauze and bandages, face hot with worry. "One of their rounds must've hit you, Sam. Didn't you feel it before?"

"I don't remember. Really, Dad. It must not be that bad, because I just now noticed it stinging."

With the first aid supplies gathered to his chest, Tom started to climb over the back seat. "I'm coming to bandage it up. Keep driving."

"Dad, no. I'm fine. They just winged me. Take care of Mom."

Pausing between seats, thinking, he finally squatted over Barbara, handing the gauze and antiseptic to Linda. "Here. Take these up front and check on your sister's wound. Clean it out and patch it. Start with—"

"I know what to do, Dad," she said, accepting the first aid supplies from him and turning toward the front. Climbing forward over the seats, past Jack and Smooch, she staggered with the swaying truck, knelt, and spread her things on the passenger seat.

Balancing himself once more, Tom stooped and rifled through the various first aid kits Saanvi had packed for them, grabbing a red canvas one with a decent bulge in the middle. Unzipping it and opening it like a book, he placed it next to his left knee, staring at the contents. Needles of different gauges were tucked neatly into pockets on the left side, cannula pouches behind them while syringes, IV lines, gauze, catheters, prep pads, locks, tourniquets, and flushes filled the kit's right side. Folded away, forming the largest part of the bulge, was a long bag of clear fluid. His medical training with the Special Forces bubbled up in his mind, though his experience was next to nothing. All he knew was that he needed to get Barbara connected to the fluid.

Hands dancing hesitantly over the contents of the kit, his mood brightened when he found the laminated instructions in an inside pocket. Scanning over them quickly, merging them with what he'd learned in training, the initial step hitting him. "Okay. I need to prep my IV set."

Swallowing hard, he grabbed a six-inch, purple catheter line and connected a fat syringe filled with saline to one end. Pressing the plunger, he flushed the tube to make sure there was no air. With a shaky breath, he forced himself to relax as more memories rose from his past, the whispers of past failures teasing at the back of his mind. Leaving the two pieces attached, he placed them on Barbara's lap for later use then he returned to the IV kit, flitting over the pockets until he found a tourniquet, tape, occlusive dressing, and standard IV cannula, leaving that in its container to keep it clean. With the pieces arrayed in a neat row across her lap, he gently pulled back the cover, exposing her right arm, wincing at the smears of blood dried on her skin.

"Please, baby. Stay with me," he whispered, breathing softly as he grabbed the tourniquet from its pocket. "Just a few more minutes."

With the tourniquet wrapped four inches above her elbow, pulled tight and tied firmly, Tom's fingers traced along her arm to push at the skin in search of a vein. After a full minute of trying, but only getting her flat, pallid skin, he shook his head and backed off, sighing, stretching his neck from side-to-side, back muscles stiff from stooping so long. "Come on, Barbara," he said, blinking loose a pair of hot tears that streaked down his cheeks. "You've got to give me something."

Slumping with exhaustion, a haunting moment from his past filtered forward in his mind. It was back on the plane in Russia after destroying the two submarines. Tom and Osaka had been the only ones to escape, the commander getting shot as they leapt from a cliff to the waters below. He shivered recalling the frigid ocean waves lapping over him, sucking seawater as they swam to the waiting plane, hauling Osaka on board, holding him as blood leaked out across the cabin floor. A pained expression crossed his features, reliving those lonely moments, pressing his palm into the commander's chest to revive him, but failing. And while Tom could blame himself for not saving the man, his anger rested solely with Colonel Banks. Forcing the missions upon him, knowing she was pushing the team too hard, too fast, she'd been both directly and indirectly responsible for Osaka's death. Tom would be damned if she caused his wife's death, too.

With a gasp of determination, Tom leaned over Barbara, bending closer, ignoring the pain in his spine as he tapped on her arm harder, index finger searching for the slightest bulge across her bare skin. "I can't see a damned thing," he growled at the dimness, releasing an exasperated sob, his aching back crying out for release.

A light suddenly flashed on, and he looked up to see Jack's pale face hanging over the seat, flashlight in hand, shining it on Barbara's arm. While the boy's eyes were wide with terror, nostrils flaring with every shallow gasp, a hopeful smile tugged the corners of his mouth.

"Thanks." Tom nodded, almost laughing with relief, and went back to feeling on Barbara's skin just below her elbow, looking for one of two veins he could tap. The one running straight down the crook of her arm suddenly stuck up, and a morbid grin of victory spread across his lips. Keeping his eyes on it, reaching for an alcohol prep pad, he generously cleaned the area with big sweeps, leaving a pale white swath in the middle of all the red.

Not bothering to put on gloves, he grabbed the IV cannula, unpackaged it, and pulled Barbara's arm taut while looking for the best insertion point. He turned her arm back and forth, measuring the cannula against her skin, stomach twisting with nervousness. With a slow hiss of air, he stuck the cannula into the vein and withdrew his hand, blinking at the dangling needle from different angles to make sure he had it.

"I think that's it." He grabbed the flush line, his blurry eyes causing him to fumble it, almost dropping it on the floor before snatching it out of the air. With a sniffle, he quickly attached it to the cannula and released the tourniquet.

"Is Mom saved?" Jack asked, voice quivering with fear.

"Almost, buddy." Tom wiped his eyes to clear them, throat raspy and dry. "We'll hook her up with some juice, and that'll help. Now, keep quiet while I finish, okay?"

The Humvee banked around a long curve, shaking and shuddering as it rode snowdrifts like ocean waves, white powder brushing softly against the windows, the roaring diesel just a distant, thrumming sound in Tom's head. After flushing the line with saline, he applied an occlusive dressing to cover the stick point and anchor the needle. Something dripped on the Humvee's floor, and he wiped his arm across his forehead, the sleeve coming back soaked with sweat. Tom taped everything down, removed the flush syringe, and connected the IV line and fluid bag.

"Now I just have to put this somewhere high." Looking up, he searched for something on the Humvee's roof to attach it to, finding one of many hooks along the upper seam. Bag hanging above them, he leaned in again, fingers hovering over the clamp that kept the fluids from entering Barbara's bloodstream. With a glance at her still face, he whispered a silent prayer, released the clamp, and the fluid began to flow. Relaxing back, hands held out as if waiting for something to explode, Tom watched. When everything seemed fine, he nodded and held his hand out over his shoulder.

"Give me your flashlight." Taking it from Jack, he rechecked the IV lines, confirming the fluid was dripping into Barbara's bloodstream. With a heavy sigh that ended in a chesty sob, he smiled up at his son with relief etched across his features. Jack's eyebrows sprung upward, a hesitant smile on his face as his small fist pounded the back of the seat. "Seriously? Mom's okay?"

"She's got a long way to go." Tom's relieved expression grew grim as he tucked the blanket in around her arm and shoulder. "But we just gave her a really good fighting chance."

After a quick check of her pulse, he reached across her body and lifted back the cover, exposing the entry wound with its sponges packed tight. A slim trickle of red dripped from the wound's tattered edge, practically nothing compared to what it had been before. Fingers tracing around the hole, he nodded, pleased to discover the sponges had kept the bleeding to a bare minimum. Craning his neck, he looked at it from different directions, trying to imagine the angle the bullet might have taken, wondering if it had hit her lungs. But a check of her mouth showed no blood on her lips, and she wasn't coughing or struggling with breathing.

"What are you looking for?" Jack asked, half hanging over the back of the seat, staring with wide eyes at the strange, puffy wound in his mother's side, acting surprisingly calm in the face of such gore.

Glancing up, Tom replied. "I thought for a moment the bullet might have hit her lungs, but I don't see any evidence of that." Lifting her slightly, Tom reached underneath, fingers tracing up the small of her back to the middle, feeling along her spine and beneath her shoulder blade. "And it definitely didn't go all the way through, because there's no exit wound."

"Is that good or bad?" Jack asked, his warm breath coming out in puffs.

"It's good and bad," Tom leaned to the side, stretching his back. "It could've gone in and gotten stuck somewhere, and we at least need to try to get the bullet out before I can patch her up. Can you help me out?"

Swallowing hard, Jack nodded tentatively.

"Okay, then. Come on back."

Tom held Jack as he swung his short leg over the seat and climbed back, the rocking and swaying of the Humvee almost sending him tumbling on top of Barbara. Looking up at Sam, he gathered Jack in his hands and sat him on the opposite side, forcing him to his knees.

"Stay right there and try to keep your balance. If you fall on your mother, you might hurt her. I'm going to open these first aid kits and place some things next to you. When I ask you to give me something, I want you to do it, okay?"

Jack nodded with big moon eyes, looking around at the kits Tom had pulled out. Rooting through them, he found a suture kit, more gauze and bandages, and a small pile of alcohol swabs. He gathered them and lined them up on Jack's right, separated so they'd be easy to tell apart. After a search through the med kits, he picked out a package with curved forceps and handed them over for Jack to hold. Ripping the top off an alcohol prep packet, he gave the still wrapped part to his son, then squeezed his fingers into some latex gloves, pulling the rubber tight around his wrists. Grabbing the alcohol pad from its wrapper, he instructed Jack to open the forceps pack halfway and hand them to him and Jack peeled back the top portion of plastic and held them out.

"Good job," Tom said as he took the forceps and wiped off the end with the alcohol pad. Leaning over the wound, Tom held the forceps in his right hand while gently tugging on the sponges with his left. After pulling two out and placing them aside, blood barely trickled from the hole, not nearly as bad as before he'd packed it. Jaw clenched in concentration, he plucked out one sponge after the other, using the forceps to reach in and grab the ones that were deeper inside.

"Okay, buddy. I need you to shine the flashlight on her wound and use the gauze pads to wipe off any blood that comes out, okay? Can you do that for me?"

"Yeah." Jack spoke almost reverently as he angled the flashlight beam into the wound with his left hand while dabbing at the edges with his right. "Like that?"

"That's perfect. Keep doing that."

Tom prepared to go deeper, touching the end of the wound with the forceps, looking for anything shiny inside, peering through the blood bubbling up and the bits of tattered flesh and fat in his way. For a second, he thought he saw the white gleam of bone, figuring it was her bottom rib. Biting down on a sudden swell of nausea, he glanced up at Jack. "Are you okay? You want me to get Linda to help?"

"No, dad. I'm fine." His voice was soft and a little hoarse, eyes filled with a mixture of wonder and fear.

"Okay, then. I'm going to need to look around for this bullet. Look away if you need to, okay?"

Without waiting for a response, Tom pressed the forceps inside the wound, pushing aside a small flap of skin, reaching in about a quarter of an inch to grab out one of the deep-rooted sponges. The truck gave a sudden lurch to the left, the tail end swerving around before straightening in a smooth slide. Tom pitched forward, leaning to his right, forcing the forceps deeper than he'd intended them to go and a soft moan escaped Barbara's lips.

Bending in closer, Tom whispered urgently, "It's okay, honey. We're here. Me and Jack and the girls. We're out of danger now, and you'll be fine. Just hang in there for me. Stay strong."

When Barbara shifted her hips, a shudder shot through her abdomen, causing her chin to rise, a groan straining from her throat, the sound like an animal in agony, piercing him with worry. Her cheeks were pale except for two tiny rose spots at the tops, her lips thin and blue. Angered annoyance crawled up his chest as the Humvee continued to swerve and shake in a fishtailing motion.

"Sam, can you keep the truck straight, please? You're knocking us around back here like a bumper car!"

"Sorry, Dad!" she called. "Linda's still trying to patch me up. She hit my arm!"

"She keeps flinching!" Linda shot back. "Anyway, almost done."

"Just keep us steady!" he growled, causing Jack to cringe away with his abrasive tone.

"Sorry," he said, nodding to his son, taking the flashlight from him. "Hold your mother's hand, would you? Talk to her. Let her know you're here."

"I'm right here, Mom." Jack leaned closer, whispering firmly, the tone forced through his fear while he rubbed her arm with both hands and tried to get her warm.

Tom put the flashlight end in his mouth, bending forward to shine the light straight down, grabbing gauze pads with his left hand and moving in on the wound once more. Just before he placed the forceps tip back into the bloody hole, the diesel engine's growl slacked off, the tires churning slower, the weaving easing to a manageable sway.

Tom raised up, removing the flashlight from his mouth, shouting over the seats. "No, Sam. Keep your foot on the pedal. Don't slow down, no matter what. And drive straight!"

"I'm trying!" Sam yelled back, a quiver of anger in her voice. When Linda tried to apply a bandage through a rip in her jacket, Sam jerked away. "Just leave me alone. I don't want to wreck and hurt Mom…" The girl's words trailed off in a low sob, though the diesel engine's growl clawed its way higher, the wheels churning, grinding, cutting a swath through the snow and ice.

"It's okay, Mom," Jack whispered, leaning in to give Barbara a kiss on the temple before going back to vigorously rubbing her frigid arm. "They're not fighting. They still love each other. Don't worry…"

A quiet sense of peace settled on Tom, a warmth blossoming in his chest as unbidden tears flooded his eyes. Biting back a sob, he rolled his shoulders to loosen the muscles and bent lower again, stooping over his wife, bowing his spine, letting the tears drip freely down his face. He shook his head to clear his vision as he placed the forceps into the wound, pushing aside fleshy tissue in search of a shiny prize. As he looked, he picked out any remaining sponges, drawing them out slowly and watching carefully for any signs of excess bleeding. In turn, he dabbed around the wound's edges with gauze, tossing it into the back corner when it became saturated with red, grabbing another clean piece to dab some more.

He'd been pushing deep into the wound, reaching solid muscle and sinew, telling him the round hadn't gone much father. "So, where are you?" he whispered in a soft puff of breath, retracing his path, investigating an area of tissue he hadn't searched before. And just when he thought he wouldn't find it, the flashlight beam glinted off something in the wound's right wall, protected from sight by the overlapping flap of skin and muscle.

"There you are, you sucker," he said, looking at the gleaming white rib bone. "You must have glanced off her rib and lodged in the other side. But not for long."

Wrists and fingers cramping from gripping the tool, Tom angled the light up into the affected section, using the forceps to push skin and flesh around the squashed piece of metal inside her. As he tried to grab it, the lead squeezed out and fell into the fleshy pocket, where he easily picked it out and held it up.

Jack's pale, round face raised on the other side, his big brown eyes blinking at the thing Tom held in his forceps. "Is that it?"

"Yep. This caused all this blood and pain for mom." He tossed it into the corner with the rest of the bloodied gauze.

Turning to the wound, something in the back of his mind was confused at how she'd escaped death. A round from a high-powered rifle should have punched right through her ribs and torn her insides to shreds, but by some miracle it had bounced off her rib and lodged in a spot where it appeared to not have caused much damage, relatively speaking. Eyes narrowed, he reached to grab her jacket from where they'd thrown it in the cargo area's front corner, wadded up with all the other gear he'd been tearing through. With one hand, he shifted the material around until he held up the left breast area where she'd been hit, his finger poking the entry hole, fingers brushing against something hard in the coat's inner pocket. Flipping the coat upside down, he gave it a shake, blinking when a thick leather book fell out along with a flutter of papers that flopped on the cargo floor.

"That saved her life," Tom pointed at the floor, figuring Barbara must've stuck the book and papers in her coat pocket for extra warmth. When the bullet struck, the thickness absorbed most of the round's kinetic energy, robbing it of its killing force. The source of the saving grace didn't matter – the miracle was still a miracle.

An incoherent murmur passed between Barbara's lips and her head shifted from side to side, throat vibrating in a pained moan as her feet kicked, her body contorting like she was trying to escape a torture chair. Tossing the coat back into the corner, Tom ripped the latex gloves off and fished through several first aid kits for a section stuffed with pockets of pain medication. There were some lighter pills, packets of over-the-counter NSAIDs and aspirin, and the last pocket with slender morphine sticks and a laminated EMT instruction card. Snatching out the card, he reviewed the steps, reconciling them with what he'd learned in his brief bouts of military training.

"What are you doing now?" Jack asked, backing up, his feet slipping through the supplies scattered on the floor.

Tom glanced down at Barbara's trembling form. "Just giving her a little something for the pain."

Sweating in the cold, back aching, fingers beyond cramping, Tom followed the instructions. Checking her blood pressure with a digital cuff, he made sure her systolic reading was over one hundred, then he grabbed a pre-filled syringe and fixed it to the open catheter in her IV line. With the flashlight shining right on the dosage lines, he pressed the plunger to administer the lowest possible dose. Less than three seconds later, Barbara's body relaxed, her feet stopped kicking, and her head quit lolling back and forth. Her lungs filled with a deep breath, and she released it in a long sigh before falling into a steady, if elevated, rate of breathing.

He checked her blood pressure again to make sure it was stable, then prepared to patch the wound. Plucking fresh supplies from one med kit, he cleaned around the area one more time, stuffed the hole with gauze, and applied a firm bandage, sealing it with several pieces of medical tape. A quick check of her IV lines showed she was still receiving a slow drip of fluid, but the IV bag had shifted on its hook, barely hanging after being jostled by the rough ride. As he raised to secure it, something changed in the Humvee's suspension, a brief slow down before the vehicle roared forward again. Eyes lifting to the rearview mirror, he met Sam's terrified stare.

"Sam? What is it?"

The words shot from her mouth in trembling fear. "Dad! Behind us! It's one of the APCs. It's... gaining!"

Turning, Tom threw his hands against the Humvee's rear glass, bloodied fingers chilled at the touch. Framed between his palms were a pair of headlamps cutting through the snow, winding toward them through the Mexican hills, tires glued to the tracks made by Sam's driving, making it easy for the mercenaries to narrow their pursuit. The visibility wasn't great, less than a mile in any direction, Sam's vision having been keen to even notice it. The fear that Tom was half-expecting to well up inside of him was absent, though, and instead a defiant anger grew, curling up from his stomach to fill his chest with a low growl.

"No. No more. We end this now."

Chapter 5
LaFleur Family
Abbeville, Louisiana

South of Abbeville, Louisiana, off an old country road, sits a farmhouse buried in five feet of snow. The driveway is nothing but a white groove from the lane to the house, cutting between trees with branches weighed down by layers of ice and frost with no animals scuttling in the high boughs to knock it free. In the front yard rests a piece of machinery, its shape vaguely like that of a tractor with a harvesting device attached to the rear, though it is covered with too much white to tell exactly what it is. Ice-covered snowbanks grip the porch, coated with a crust of frost and icicles hang from the railing, glinting in the late day sun, though nary a drop of water falls from even at the midpoint of the day.

The sun warms nothing, not with the frequent storms that blow through, bringing more piles of snow and winter white, temperatures continuing to drop more with each passing hour. From the rooftop, a trickle of smoke drifts upward, lost to the swirling winds while plywood and plastic tarps patch the weak and leaking spots, and part of the rear wall is bolstered by two-by-fours nailed to the outside to keep everything from collapsing. Clutched in winter's gnarled grip, the home sits in complete silence but for the quietly crisping snow.

Inside, the LaFleur family shivers around an old stove, dirty faces staring into the struggling flames through the iron beast's mouth, the flumes open to allow maximum air flow and heat. They huddle, clutching blankets against their bellies, teeth chattering behind puffs of frosted breath. Any piece of skin that's exposed is chaffed from the dry air, cheeks glistening with petroleum jelly and the last of ointments originally purchased for some far different purpose than a defense against the cold.

Two children sit side-by-side in blanketed chairs, their bodies bundled in coats and heavy hats, the youngest in his own one-piece winter jumpsuit they'd gotten from a charity shop before the real storms hit. The mother bustles between them, ensuring they're wrapped tight and tucked-in around the edges. Her face is haggard and worried, hands dry and cracked, all the while throwing resentful glances at her husband.

The father stands from his chair and tosses in a piece of wood from the couch, one of their last, grabbing the poker, stoking the coals to beg one final bit of warmth. Their modest home is an open floor layout, almost a cabin, with the stove against the back wall in the center, resting on a slab of bricks, dividing the living room and kitchen in two. Hunting-themed paintings from the local flea market decorate the walls. Simple family photos hang there, too. Some faces belong to relatives who long ago passed away, though there are cousins in those pictures who should still be alive, but they haven't heard from them in weeks. There are many blank spots, too, where pictures *used* to be, all but the wooden frames have long since been thrown into the fire with the rest of the kindling.

Grumbling, having coaxed as much warmth from the coals as he could, the father ambles backwards and sits heavily in his chair with a grunt, murmuring, "Won't be long before we're out. I may try to go outside and cut some actual wood. It's cold, though."

The mother glances up at him with consternation as she adjusts their girl's hood. Despite the crackling flames, the room is far from warm, the children shivering in layers of blankets and coats.

Their six-year-old boy speaks. "Dad? I'm really worried about Petey. We haven't seen him in a few days. Can we go look for him later?"

Their family pet, an older black retriever who gave them long years of love and loyalty, is who the young boy speaks of. The father glances toward the back door, past the frost-covered swing set in the backyard to the twenty square foot slaughterhouse where he normally would process deer meat during hunting season. But all of the deer died off a week ago, and there's nothing left to shoot, not even squirrels and birds. They've all either frozen stiff or moved south, but still the slaughterhouse table has a fresh layer of iced blood, red icicles dripping from its edges.

The father's eyes flit to the pan of stew bubbling atop the stove. "Son, you know I love Petey, but it's probably not a good idea to go looking for him, but I promise I will when I go out for wood in a few hours."

The boy's sniffling penetrates his ears like a knife. "But… Dad, you said we could go look one more time."

"Well, he's not out there," the man growls, something feral crawling from his throat, quickly followed by a pang of guilt. He sits back with a shudder and a sigh, thinking of all the hard things he's had to do since the harsh winter set in. The situation with Petey, though, was one of the hardest.

"No need to talk to him like that," his wife says, striding over and fixing the boy's blanket around him before moving to the stove where she picks up the spoon and stirs the contents, though not without a bit of hesitation.

While the room smells good, the rich scent of cooking meat and broth filling his nose with a sense of home and love, he knows it won't last, and neither will the supplies in their pantry. All that's left are a few cans of corn, green beans, and peas, some soup, chips, and snacks that aren't worth much, nutritionally. A few gallons of milk sit by the door where they teeter on the edge of freezing, though their calories won't last long, either. He throws an apologetic glance toward his son and his wife, and there's a fleeting glimpse of the man he once was, always kind and willing to teach and help and love unconditionally. But the heavy weight of winter and its burdens has settled on him hard, exposing the flaws in his decisions, forcing resentment to grow in his gut like a gnarled tree, the branches threatening to tear him apart from the inside.

Glancing into the living room on his right, he frowns at the discarded food cans, plastic water bottles, and wrappers. Dozens of them lie scattered across the floor next to the lump of junk that used to be the couch. It lies beaten apart by his sledgehammer, the wooden pieces stacked to the side, the cloth material tossed next to those. Pieces of the end tables, TV stand, and his favorite recliner are long since gone, already part of the coals in the stove's hungry belly. Yet it still demands more, promising a smidgen of life for every table leg, bit of cloth, or picture it devours; some small fraction of life in exchange for their memories and keepsakes. Other parts of the house are gutted, drywall and plaster pulled aside to get at the two by fours and plywood beneath, the flooring in the kids' rooms yanked up to reveal the dirt under it. Soon, he'll saw up the joists, too.

They're like a cancer to the place, eating it from the inside out, chewing it up until the body and spirit die, and they die with it. The kids haven't laughed in weeks, ever since he threw in their toys and clothes to burn, and part of him wonders what they must be thinking with their blank stares and closely pressed lips, their shivering jaws and tears and constant complaints and worrying about a dog that isn't coming home. And while he could tell them it's just hard times and things are looking up, it would be a lie.

As if to emphasize his thoughts, his wife finishes fussing with their little girl and comes to stand behind him, hands clutched at her waist, wringing her fingers. There's no pat on the back or warm touch of reassurance, and he knows if he looks into her eyes, they'd be filled with accusation.

"We shouldn't have stayed." Her frown is pensive, eyebrows pinched and serious.

"I know," he says in a breathless whisper. "You never fail to remind me."

Her next words are a verbal sneer. "All of your conspiracy theories, thinking the government was going to take everything from us and leave us out to dry. That it was all some government plot, and they were just doing it to get more power…" Her quiet voice rises in pitch and volume, the words pushed through her chattering teeth and trembling chin. "All of that was bullshit. But you listened to those stupid people, and you let them influence you. You let them tell you what to do, and look where that got us!"

She gestures angrily at the pile of broken furniture ready to burn, continuing with a scorn-filled tone. "You wouldn't listen to the government's warnings. You wouldn't let us evacuate, not even when I had the kids in the car and was ready to go to my mother's in Florida where they have the boats. You know, the ones going to South America? The ones that could have saved us?" The next part comes as an anguished howl, her hands grabbing his shoulders to squeeze, the tendons standing out beneath her chafed skin. "You made us stay, Jimmy!" she shouts, squeezing harder, balling her hands into fists, raining quick, violent jabs on the back of his neck and head as she screams. "You forced us to hang on to this little plot of hell when we should've followed the evacuation orders! You killed us! You killed all of us! All of us! Damn you, Jimmy! Damn you to hell for what you've done!"

A sob punctuates her tirade, and his nose catches the faint hint of her shampoo, a scent he grew to appreciate over the years, reminding him of better times. Now it's just a smell like any other, carrying the hint of cherished memories he'll never regain.

The children stare at them in sheer terror, too frightened to even cry, holding each other as if they're the only ones left in all the miserable world, their parents complete strangers. As her fury and strength flee her, she stops hitting him, collapses forward, and leans on him, crying tears of anguish and heartache. She reaches out with her left arm to circle the children's shoulders, pulling them close in a last semblance of togetherness. Jimmy takes his punishment without complaint, slouching from the blows, the physical pain nothing compared to the strike through his heart, the certainty that he's failing them and the knowledge that that their demise rests squarely on his shoulders for what he's done.

As her anger wanes to sullen acceptance, he leans forward with the poker and opens the stove door wide, then he reaches for a few small pieces of flooring, part of the sofa cushion, and a few felt-covered stuffed animals. He tosses them in one by one, the remnants of their life going up in smoke through the chimney. All that remains is his son's sniffling, his wife's exhausted breathing, and his daughter's soft sigh as she lays her head against her mother's shoulder.

The wind whistles through unseen gaps in the walls, making a hollow, ghostly sound, and the cold presses in around them, its frosty fist squeezing them tight.

Chapter 6
PFC Simon Sharp
Santa Fe, New Mexico

After hours of slipping through the shadows, avoiding militia patrols and creeping in the bunker sub-levels, Sharp was almost ready to make his move. Boots and socks stored in a maintenance closet between the food storage warehouses, he'd stalked the dark hallways of Sub-levels two to five. Focused on tracking the enemy's movements, he was gathering as much information as he could, mapping the bunker's layout in his head as he went.

His comrades were being held on Sub-level Three in the refrigeration units and the only time they were moved was to go to the massive Warehouse 3L to load supplies up through the service elevator to the militia's waiting vehicles. Over the last day and a half, they only had six people on duty, but in the recent few hours, they'd awakened everyone to run patrols in the passages, guarding the prisoners in shifts while the rest roamed the back halls in ragged patrol groups, rushing along the passages, never checking the closets and tight spaces Sharp liked to hide in.

But something else was happening, too. Their movements were more urgent than ever, and Sharp wanted to find out the reason behind all of the hubbub which is why he was standing at a locker room entrance on Sub-level Two, steam leaking from beneath the closed door. The insurgents were cleaning the place out, getting last-minute showers, and scrambling with extra patrols, loading gear and preparing for something big. Glancing both ways, he pushed open the door and slid sideways inside, bare feet treading on the sweaty tiles, knives held up and ready to strike.

A pair of voices echoed in the bath area as a wall of steam hit him from the left, the warm mist smelling soapy and inviting after so much time spent smelling his own stink. He danced to his right on the balls of his feet, spinning away and ducking into the dressing room near a row of sinks, benches, and lockers. Bathroom stalls and urinals sat behind the lockers, and the faint scent of toilet water drifted through the air. Two pairs of boots were tucked beneath the benches, T-shirts tossed aside, sets of fresh long underwear and coveralls folded on the wooden seats off to the side. A few of the full-sized lockers stood open, one with a rifle hanging from the coat hook.

The showers suddenly shut off and the voices that had been laughing and talking got louder, wet feet flapping on the tiles as they came around the far side. Sharp started to enter the row with the toilet stalls, but he wanted to hear what they were saying, so he stuck close, tucking his knives into his belt, climbing over a wooden bench, lifting a locker's latch and sliding inside, squeezing into the cramped space. It was a tight fit as he turned sideways, angling himself diagonally as he pulled the door shut behind him. The men's voices popped into the room, followed by flat footsteps on the wet tiles as they were drying off, chit-chatting, and joking with each other. One locker flew open, smacking back on the others and their voices became clear enough for Sharp to understand.

"We need to get upstairs or Chet's going to kill us," one said.

"Chet can cry all he wants," replied the second guy, "but there's no way I was going to miss a hot shower before the Army pukes show up. Hard telling when we'll get the chance to take another one."

"I guess you're right. It'll probably be months before we can." The first man's scoff was muffled by a towel drying his face. "Maybe never."

"That's what I'm talking about," the second man laughed. "I just can't find the locker I put my gun in. Do you remember which one?"

"No. Try the other ones."

The sound of metal doors opening and slamming shut echoed loud, and Sharp felt the vibration in his shoulders along with the racket. A shadow appeared in the downward-angled vent, and he leaned back, eyes wide as his stomach rocketed into his throat. The private grabbed the inside of the locker door near the latch, fingers wedged into the curved edge, knuckles pressing against the back of the door. The latch lifted and the man on the other side jerked it, but Sharp had it finger-locked hard, teeth bared, sweat pouring down his face. The man tried again, then a third time for good measure before, finally, he gave up.

"This one's jammed." The shadow moved to Sharp's left, followed by another rattling of a handle and a door flying open. "Ah, here's my rifle."

The private released a quiet sigh and tuned into the conversation, still keeping his fingers locked in place, just in case. Hurried rustling reached him from the other side as clothes slid over moist skin, pants were slipped on, and feet were shoved into boots.

The first militia member continued the conversation. "So, do you believe what Chet said about the radio chatter picking up?"

The second guy scoffed. "Yeah. Why would he lie?"

"I'm not saying he'd lie. I just wonder if he heard right. He said the Army convoy was showing up a day early. Wasn't supposed to be here until tomorrow. Chet and Shae thought we had an extra 24-hours to beat it."

"Who cares?" the second guy responded in a cautious tone. "The Army jerkoffs will clean this place out when they get here, and I don't want to be around when that happens. We should be long gone by then, if we hurry."

"But what if we don't make it?" The first man's voice quivered slightly, fear carrying his words. "What if we get caught trying to leave?"

"That's what the hostages are for, dummy. They won't do a thing to us as long as we've got guns pointed at their heads."

"But what about *after* we're gone? Won't they chase us?"

A palm slapped the back of someone's head. "Why do you think Chet grabbed another truck? We're taking some of them with us. And when we get in the clear, we'll dump them."

"Well, you don't have to hit me," the first guy whined, and Sharp had to stifle a snicker at the man's crestfallen tone.

"Don't ask stupid questions, then. Come on. Put your boots on and let's get out of here."

"Where are we going?"

"We're moving all the prisoners to the warehouse. We need to get them loaded up in a couple of hours. Kiss this place goodbye, Stipe!"

The sound of a hand slapping a shoulder hard reverberated off the concrete walls.

"Ouch! I'm telling you, Murphy. You better cut that crap out."

As Murphy laughed, the group finished getting dressed and gathered their weapons from the lockers with a clatter and slipped from the locker room with the heavy sounds of boots echoing on the tiles. When Sharp thought they were gone, he lifted the latch mechanism from the inside, and stepped out, noticing old clothes and personal items they'd left strewn on the floor. The entrance door suddenly whipped open, and the quick clomp of boots caused him to jerk into reverse, pulling the locker closed behind him, wincing when the metal clacked together. A shadow went past his door and tossed a couple of things around before a voice whispered, "Ah, there you are."

"Let's go, Stipe!" Came the call from the hallway.

"Sorry," Stipe shouted back. "I left my pistol in here. Coming!"

The boots shuffled and scraped their way toward the exit, the door flew open and the man scooted out, leaving Sharp standing in the locker room, alone. Heart beating with quivering palpitations, he waited an extra few seconds before moving from his hiding place, swallowing hard as his gaze skipped to the door, half expecting it to pop open again.

"I don't have a lot of time," he murmured, slipping to the door and putting his ear to it. Opening it a crack, he peered out to the left to see the two militia members round the corner, taking the wide passage to the main stairwell to Sub-level Three, where the rest of his group were being held. While Sharp could follow them, there'd be guards on the staircase, so he turned right and jogged down a darkened passageway with flickering lights where the door at the end led to a rear stairwell which would get him upstairs without running into patrols.

Still, when he reached it, he peered through the square portal to make sure no one stood on the other side before stepping inside to a staircase bathed in dim red light. He went up, feet padding on the stairs' rubber grips, tight hand taking a knife from his belt, feeling his way up the rail in the darkness. At the top, he did another window check, peering ahead to the main hallway a hundred yards distant, leading to the refrigeration units and Warehouse 3L. The militia would be taking their prisoners from right to left through the intersection when they moved them for final load out.

The soft slip of his calloused toes over the tiles matched the low, electric hum of the emergency lights. Faint ozone and his own stale sweat wafted over him as he moved, his arms and legs pushing it ahead of him. Slipping to the left-hand side, he made a mental note of which doors were unlocked and safe to hide in. He'd tried all of them in the past day, catching cat naps in them in between monitoring the insurgents' movements.

Moving slowly and deliberately in heel-to-toe fashion, Sharp crept ahead slowly, listening as the sounds of a door shutting and hushed voices reached him from somewhere up the hall. At the first small intersection he came to he slipped to the side, keeping his left shoulder pressed to the corner, peering around at the main passage just fifty feet ahead. A straggle of boots pounded from the right side, and he tensed as he waited in the shadows for a chance to wave. While it wasn't the perfect way to communicate, it would give Morales and Smith a warning to his presence and the possibility of a plan.

"Here they come," he whispered to himself, then he gasped in irritation when only three militiamen jogged by on the way to the warehouse, no prisoners with them. "They must have changed their minds. I'll have to get closer."

Swallowing hard, he waited until they passed and edged forward, glancing at the various doors along the right side of the hallway, taking stock of his options. There were a few rooms he hadn't fully investigated, entering just enough to know where his escape routes were if he needed them, but he had an idea one of them might lead to a back entrance to the refrigeration unit where his comrades were being held.

Clutching his left hand into a fist to stop its shaking, he hurried across the hall, opened a door, and slipped into a dark room filled with storage bins, skids, and small shipping containers. Two light bulbs illuminated the space from the ceiling and there were benches and rows of packing material, cardboard, plastic wrap and a foam machine in the corner. He slipped across the room and through a set of soft rubber flaps into a wider chamber, twenty degrees cooler but just as dimly lit. Racks of cold-stored goods were stacked to the ceiling, a miniature version of the larger warehouses like 3-L. With a map of the place engrained in his head, he angled toward the refrigeration units, wincing as his soles met the chilly floor, entering a short hallway that stretched fifteen feet before taking a hard right.

The walls in the section were cool to the touch, gray concrete with pipes and hoses running along the upper corners. The sounds of humming equipment vibrated through the floor, and a fan kicked on from somewhere nearby. Reaching the end of the passage, he stopped short, shining his flashlight at a dead end. The pipes and hoses branched up into the ceiling, carrying coolant and water out and three vents were built into the wall around the bottom; one on his left, another on his right, and the last straight ahead. Scuffling noises and talking echoed through the thin metal ducts, and Sharp dropped to his knees with his ear to the left-hand vent. While it seemed like the logical choice, the voices and sounds were stronger from the grating ahead of him and, using his knife, he unscrewed the fasteners and lifted the cover off, setting it aside. Stooping low, he shined his flashlight along a dusty duct, small piles of lint wafting in the breeze gusting through.

With a deep breath, the private ducked into the vent and crawled on the flimsy aluminum floor, his shoulders tight in the passage, hips bumping the walls as he shifted. Flashlight on but pointed down, he followed the ductwork until it reached a hard left, then crept another twelve feet before cutting left again. The more twists he took, the louder the voices got, their tones commanding as they ordered the soldiers around. Despite the distraction of potential danger and ice-cold air washing through the ducts and sending shivers across his shoulders, Sharp dutifully marked the number of turns he'd taken to avoid getting lost.

It wasn't until he reached a series of vent covers where the voices were exceedingly loud and more of the overhead lights came through that he realized he was in the right place. Dousing his flashlight, he ducked and narrowed his eyes through the cracks, identifying the cooling fans attached to the back of three large refrigeration units, hoses and pipes running up the backsides as far as he could see. Automatic thermostats kicked the fans off and on, one rattling badly in its frame.

"I hope they don't have any of our guys in there," he whispered with a shiver.

He tested each vent cover with his fingers, pressing gently to find each of them secured tight except for the third one down. Flashlight between his knees, he stuck his fingers into the grating and shook it back and forth until the loose screws popped off with a soft clatter. Freezing in place, he expected a stampede of boots, militia rifles shoved into the vent firing at him and filling him with holes. When they didn't come, he let out a slow sigh of relief to match the fans spinning just outside.

With a dry mouth and cold lips, he placed the vent aside and crawled from the duct. The space between the wall and refrigerators was only five feet, though the tall units reached to the ceiling some twelve feet above him. A glance to the right showed him a dead end with a power grid and emergency shut off buttons built into the wall while to his left the passage circled to the front of the units where he suspected the rest of his group was being held.

Sharp reached into his pocket, pulled out a slip of paper, and eased to the back corner of the unit, peeking around where the light and voices were coming from. The private glanced around, frowning when he found himself staring at a militiaman's back. The man sat at the end of the passage, blocking his view into the greater room, leaning forward with a rifle lying on his lap. Sharp jerked backward when the man raised from his chair, readjusted it, and sat again, still turned away. With a soft shake of his head, Sharp looked beyond to see into the room. It was well lit from above, and several gun-wielding men and women milled around, at least one pacing, casting shadows across the floor. While he couldn't hear everything that was being said, neither could he spot his fellow soldiers.

Jumping at the sudden chance, he inched forward, stalking, sweat dripping along his sides and back as he moved in on the sitting militia member, knife drawn and ready. The man shifted, half turned, causing him to freeze with a lump in his chest and Sharp quickly backed off. Even if he dispatched the man, there were too many others in the room and they'd more than likely hear the attack and retaliate before he could complete his mission. As he withdrew, though, he caught a pair of voices, a man and a woman, speaking from somewhere beyond his vision.

"We need to move them right now," the woman said, her tone flat and insistent.

"We're not moving them until Stiles and Murphy give us the go-ahead, Shae," a man he recognized as Chet replied, his tone tired and weary, a verge-of-frustration sound that teetered on the thin line of an argument. "The last thing we want to do is get all the Army assholes in the same place and give them a chance to try something dumb together. You guys won't try something dumb, will you?"

The sound of someone being kicked reached his ears, and Sharp wondered who'd gotten the end of that boot, though he couldn't tell from the mumbled reply.

"Well, I don't want to be here when that new group shows up," Shae went on. "With Johnson taking care of the warehouses, the first place they'll go for is this bunker, so unless you want to fight fifty Army guys, I suggest we're not here when they show up. It'll be a bloodbath."

"We've got enough weapons to defend ourselves," Chet reminded her. "And we're locked down tight. We checked for back doors and didn't find anyone. We've still got plenty of time."

"Oh, yeah?" Shae protested. "What about the radio message we just intercepted? Sounds to me like they're only twenty miles out."

"Twenty miles in this weather might as well be a hundred. I give them five hours at the earliest until they come knocking. We'll be fine." The last part was spoken in a low growl.

"Not if they're coming the way Johnson's group did," Shae shot back.

The woman was more right than she knew, and chances were that Captain Johnson had directed the new convoy to take a route through the tracks they'd already made on the way to the warehouses. They'd used the big dozers to clear the road to the Mexican border and, barring any new, massive storms, a new deployment of soldiers could arrive in virtually no time flat. Shae was also right that it'd be a bloodbath if either of the forces at play came together before Sharp could free his comrades. No matter how he sliced it, he had to get them out of before that happened.

Having heard enough, Sharp backed around the corner until he was standing behind the refrigeration unit once again. Searching across the pipes and conduits and rubber tubing, he spotted a thin maintenance ladder connecting two blowing fans that ran to the top. With an uncertain sigh, the private grabbed on and started climbing. Feet and hands cold on the rungs, he reached the top in a few seconds, leaned forward and stretched longways to wedge himself between the unit and ceiling.

He crawled through a layer of dirt and dust bunnies that blew off his cheeks, nose twitching with a brief, tickling sensation before he gripped the bridge and clamped down on a potential sneeze. Once it passed, he breathed easier, edging over a pipe running along the center seam, shifting and sliding forward, knees and elbows carrying him to the front rim. Gazing down, he spotted three militiamen, not counting Chet and Shae, two of them looking bored, the other standing between the two leaders, expression unreadable. Sharp's brow raised when he next spotted Smith, Morales, Stevens, Griggs, and Rupert on the floor to the right, backs against the wall, hands bound behind them, though their feet remained loose.

Changing direction, he edged backward the other way, sucking his stomach in to squeeze atop a second pipe almost eight inches in diameter that pressed him tight against the ceiling. He winced as his knees and elbows made slight bumps on the refrigeration unit in the cramped space, the agitated conversation from below driving his urgency. There was no good way to do it, no simple solution to the ever-changing situation.

His right hand drifted across something stiff and slightly fuzzy and he slowly turned his head to see the dried, skeletal remains of a rat resting beneath his palm, its bristly fur rustling up between his fingers. Head jerking upward to bump the ceiling, jaws clamped on a yelp, the private froze in position, once again saying a silent prayer to keep him from detection. When Chet and Shae continued arguing, he lifted his hand from the corpse and brushed by it, circling to the front lip which would put him above the prisoners.

Edging closer, peering down, Sharp gave a slight wave to get their attentions, then he glanced at Chet and Shea and the guards. All of them were off to his left, not looking anywhere but at each other, still arguing in a moment of friction he hoped would give him the advantage he needed. Leaning forward, forehead poking over the unit's edge, he tried waving again, but Morales and Smith were watching the militia leaders, their expressions dark, whispering between themselves.

Backing away, cheek pressed to the layer of dust atop the refrigeration unit, Sharp tried to think how to go ahead. With a blink at his right hand and the folded paper in his palm, he wadded it in frustration, setting it aside, fingers rolling around in the dust as he jogged his brain. After a moment, he saw how the dust bunnies congealed into a puffball of dirt under his calloused pads. Grinning, he rolled the dust beneath his palm until he had a thimble-sized puff of it, weighed down by a denser coagulation on one side. Scooting to the edge, he held it out and let it drop, backing up and out of sight.

Head lifted, he kept his eyes on Morales as the dust ball drifted to the floor, wafting in the gently circulating air. At first, the soldier was too distracted by their captors to notice, but his gaze flicked to Chet and Shea and came back to the falling dust ball for a second glance. The private edged forward, hand up so that his fingers almost touched the ceiling, waving to get Morales's attention. The soldier's eyes narrowed before he lifted his chin, eyes growing wide at the sight of the soldier wedged between the refrigeration unit and roof. Brow furrowed, he glanced aside at the guards again and up to Sharp, nudging Smith with his elbow, jerking his chin upward after getting the lieutenant's attention.

A wicked grin flashed across Smith's face as the private nodded, touching the side of his nose twice before grabbing the wadded-up note and holding it up for the soldiers to see. He gestured like he wanted to throw it, and the lieutenant acknowledged it with a slight nod. The question was, how to get it there? Gauging the weight of the paper in his hand, Sharp frowned. It was light and probably wouldn't carry far on its own, not without something to weigh it down. Glancing to his left, his gaze settled on the dried-out rat's husk.

Reaching out with his left hand, face twisted in a disgusting grimace, he allowed his fingers to sift through the bristly fur and jagged bones, tracing up its spine to the curved part of its skull. Tearing it free with a soft rip, he shifted it to his right hand and wadded the paper around it, giving the projectile some weight. Smiling through his grimace, he raised up and got ready to throw, the wrapped skull held to his chest so he could toss it out more accurately rather than try to force it side armed.

By the time he was done with his macabre craft project, the captives had all seen him and most were purposefully looking away or glancing up, though Stevens got a hard elbow from Smith so he quit looking and stared at the floor. Peering down, then at the soldiers, Sharp drew a deep breath and released it in a measured exhalation, waiting for the perfect opportunity to make the toss. Chet and Shea were still arguing, the woman turning and pacing toward the prisoners right as he was about to make the throw. Tucking it to his chest again, Sharp ducked and held off as the soldiers cast their eyes to the tile floor.

"Just give Stiles and Murphy a few more minutes," Chet was saying, the words harsh and forced.

"Thirty minutes," Shea responded, facing him with her hands on her hips, palm resting on her pistol's grip. "Thirty minutes, and we get out of here with our new friends."

"Fair enough," Chet replied before turning to the man sitting in the chair. "Hey, Stu, go down and check on the load out. When you're done, run your butt right back here and no stopping off for a snack or a shower. Got that?"

The man named Stu, Sharp figuring it was the guy he'd heard in the hall the previous day, rose from his seat and stepped past his leader, nodding, edging out the door, his boots echoing through the hallway as he jogged away. The door fell shut with a soft bang. The private waited as Shae stood there another moment, shaking her head before striding to the other side of the room, where she wrapped her arm around Chet's shoulders with a reassuring grin.

While the two talked softly, Sharp raised up and tossed his note in a smooth motion, watching it arc through the air and down toward Morales. There was a moment when he was sure it would bounce off the wall or floor with a loud enough clatter to get the guards' attention, but without Stu present and with Sharp's angle from above, the chances of a successful delivery had increased significantly. The paper-wrapped skull struck Morales in the chest and dropped into his lap, and he drew his knees up to hide it. Of the soldiers lined up, Stevens's hands were some of the few bound in front, and he reached across Smith, snatched the note, and brought it back.

All their eyes shifted to Chet and Shea and the last guard in the room, Sharp breathing a sigh of relief when none of them suspected a thing. Stevens went back to the note, opened it, and grimaced with disgust when he saw what had weighed it down. Putting the skull aside, he unfolded the paper and read it.

Not sure if this will work. Be ready. Soon!

Stevens showed the note to Smith, and the lieutenant looked up at him, mouthing the words, "Be careful."

Elation coursed through his veins, muscles infused with a new sense of purpose, Sharp retreated from the refrigeration unit's roof, edged down the ladder, and ducked into the ductwork, moving the vent cover back in place. Creeping through the cramped passage, he emerged in the cold storage area. Forearm resting against the wall, he leaned forward and breathed in relief, swiping the itchy rivulets of sweat off his face. His friends had seen his message and they knew he was coming with something big, and Smith and Morales would be ready. They were the smartest soldiers in the outfit. All they needed was a small window of opportunity to overwhelm the guards and get the situation back under control.

Leaving the cool storage area, Sharp stepped into the hallway and made his way to the side stairs, glancing over his right shoulder to make sure none of the militiamen moving between the warehouse and refrigeration units caught sight of him. Once on the stairwell, he descended two floors to Sub-level Five where the passages were narrower, the lights running along the upper corner a vivid red color, marking the area as a special sub-floor housing all the tech controls that ran the place. None of the enemy had been to Sub-level Five for an entire day as most of their efforts had been on loading the stolen trucks upstairs, preparing for the getaway.

He stepped into a room with a security pad that accepted his general passcode, finding himself in a small armory with shelves full of ammunition, weapons, cleaning supplies, and bottles of defluxer and oil. From one shelf he grabbed a vest with an armored plate in the chest section, a pair of rifles, two pistols, and more than a dozen magazines to fit the guns. He shrugged into the plate carrier vest, zipped it up the side, and shifted beneath its weight so it settled evenly on his shoulders, then he stuffed the rest of the loose gear into a military duffel and slung it over his shoulder.

Panting lightly, he exited the room, stepped into the hall, and took an immediate left. Several doors down, Sharp entered another room with a red light blinking above it, turned, and locked the door behind him. Grabbing a steel bar he'd found in a storeroom, he wedged it beneath the door handle as added reinforcement. Dropping the duffel on the floor, he walked to a workstation with a wide panel of control buttons, switches, and knobs arrayed around them.

Sitting in a cushioned chair, Sharp gazed at the transceivers, frequency knobs, and gauges, trying to remember what he could about radios and internal systems. A small computer terminal to his right called for a code to enter the system, and he plugged his personal password in, not surprised when the login screen requested *try again*. Fingers flitting over the keys, he put in LePlante's passcode he'd been using to get into everything else, uncertain it would work on the radio, but the numbers proved true, and the console burst to life in a series of lights and static.

While much of it was confusing, a lot having to do with the external antenna arrays and a satellite dish atop the facility's radio tower, the private focused on a section of the console dedicated to the internal PA system. The bunker and its sub-levels were displayed in an easy-to-read layout, lights blinking on each room, enabling someone to select specific ones to message, but that wasn't what Sharp focused on. Flicking switches for each of the five sub-levels, he watched every light in the place go from blinking to solid, telling him he'd opened a channel to everything. All the sub-levels and warehouses, refrigeration rooms, closets, maintenance rooms—anything with a speaker in it—would receive his message.

With a wide, mischievous grin, Sharp relaxed in the chair, going over exactly what he wanted to say. When he had it straight in his head, he leaned forward and pulled a gooseneck microphone closer to his mouth. Adopting a gruff, militaristic tone, he keyed the mic on and began to speak.

Chapter 7
Tom McKnight
Central Mexico

"Stay here, son." Rising, Tom gripped Jack's shoulder and gave it a firm squeeze. "Stay with your mother and let us know if something changes." Tom started to climb over the back seat when the boy grabbed his shirt. Tom paused. "What is it?"

"What change, Dad? What would change?"

"Just… anything. How she looks, feels, if she says anything."

Tom crawled over the seats, past Smooch who was standing on the floorboards, trying to stay upright with the swaying truck, body tensing like she wanted to jump up front with him. "No. Stay there, girl," he said, holding his hand out in warning.

He landed between Linda and Sam, boots planted firmly on the floor. The girls were sitting apart, Linda turned and staring out the back window at the lumbering APC slowly gaining on them. Sam clung to the wheel, struggling with the loose play in the steering column, perched on the edge of the seat with her right foot extended to reach the pedals. As she drove, she cast furtive glances into the rearview mirror, face ashen with fear.

Tom snapped his fingers near her face, pointing to the road. "Keep your eyes that way, Sam."

With a vigorous nod, she pressed her shoulders tight, head craned forward and eyes pinned to the hardened snow and ice. The Humvee stayed centered, weaving around lumps of white that marked abandoned vehicles and wrecks. Edging between the girls, Tom's right hand rested on the dashboard, squinting against the brilliant glare stretching ahead of them.

Out in front was a constantly curving lane of white and the only way to navigate was to stay between the occasional road signs and telephone poles as the hills grew more devious and twisting. The balding tires of the old truck struggled to grip the treacherous pavement and while they hadn't reached a full mountain range, the slopes rose on either side, dead gray clouds sweeping in with a mist that rolled off the tops like tumbling cotton.

"I'm going to switch with you, Sam." Eyes watering from the intense brightness, Tom placed his hand against his forehead as if he could dim the world. "Just looking for a spot to do it."

"We better do it fast, because I can't outrun them." Sam's voice rode waves of hitching breaths, chest rising and falling in shallow gasps, steam puffing from her mouth like a tiny locomotive. "They're catching up quick, Dad. What are we going to do?"

"First off, take a deep breath and calm yourself." Tom grabbed a pair of tinted goggles tucked into the sun visor and pointed to a spot up ahead. "See that bend up there?"

"Yeah."

"See how it rides up and to the left?"

"Uh-huh."

"Drive like hell to the top, and we'll make the switch there. I don't want to get stuck on an upward slope. Got it?"

"Yep. On it."

With a slap on the back of the seat, Tom turned and stared through the rear window at the yellow-colored headlamps growing rounder in the glass, estimating that they were probably a quarter mile away, or less, and gaining fast. "Come on, Sam. Hit it!"

Teeth bared, his eldest daughter leaned in and slowly pressed the gas until the pedal was pinned to the floor. The Humvee's engine crawled upward from a growl to a terrifying caterwaul, the frame rattling over bumps as they rounded a bend and angled up a shallow slope to the left, bracketed by slanted telephone poles and busted power lines that curled on the snow like black snakes. What could've been a guardrail on their right created a low ridge with a steep drop on the other side and as they started into a dangerous slide, the road straightened and they shot to the top, carried by Sam's low snarl as she battled the wheel.

"Excellent, Sam." Tom patted the back of her seat with his palm. "You're doing great. Come on, just another fifty feet."

She nodded. "I got this."

"Go, Sam, go!" Linda encouraged her sister from the passenger seat.

A few seconds later, Sam hit the brake, sending three tons of steel sliding over the crest in a sweeping spray of white, slick tires carrying them forward until the nose pointed slightly downward again. Once they slammed to a stop, Sam slammed it into park and Tom pressed himself against Linda's seat and threw his thumb toward the rear. "Get back there with your brother and look after your mom. Use the digital cuff to check her blood pressure and don't let her slide around too much."

Sam was already nodding, rising from her seated position, ducking beneath him and scrambling to the back.

Tom fell into the driver's seat, jerked the Humvee into drive, and hit the gas, grinding down the opposite slope, adjusting to the coughing engine and playful steering. The truck lurched and slid, bouncing, wheel slipping under his sore hands. The road swept them downward and to the right, descending from the low foothills to enter a wide-ranging plain covered in white with jagged brown boulders and frozen cactus plants breaking up the stagnant landscape, gnarled clusters of oak and chestnut trees standing against the brutal storms that had passed by.

Raising his head, Tom called back. "What's your mother's blood pressure?"

Sam hollered back. "One second. I'm trying to find the cuff… wait! There it is!"

While Tom waited for her to take the reading, his gaze flicked to the rearview mirror, checking on their pursuers. While he'd lost time switching seats, he'd still gained distance on them because of his smooth, yet risky, driving. There were bends and turns no sane man would've attempted at forty-five miles per hour on such roads, but Tom needed to take chances and buy them some time.

"One-oh-seven over sixty-two!" Sam called. "Is that good?"

"It's okay," Tom replied, though it had been higher before. His head snapped to the side, nostrils flaring. Barbara was slipping and they had little time and even fewer options.

A plan started to form in his mind as he watched both sides of the road, searching for a rest stop or gas station on the long stretch of flat straightaway. Jaw chewing in thought, Tom peered into the rearview mirror. "Sam, how much fuel is left in the cans back there?"

She met his eyes in the mirror, mouth hanging open in confusion. "Why?"

"Just check, please."

A moment later, after looking through the windows where they'd hung their jerry cans, she came back. "We have a full one left on the passenger side."

"Good. That'll be enough."

"Enough for what? What are you thinking?"

Tom shifted in his seat, raising, his view alighting on a series of small, snow-covered buildings in the distance on the right side of the road. The structures were nestled against a low ridge of hills with clusters of trees surrounding them. With a deep breath he leaned forward, face pressed closer to the windshield, foot weighing on the gas pedal and pushing the old Humvee to its limits. The front end lifted, plowing through a foot and a half of snow, banging over drifts that shook the frame, the steering wheel shuddering in his hands.

"Dad?"

"See those hills off to the right?" He pointed. "We'll set up an ambush there if we can make it in time. I'm thinking we can set something up in the buildings in the cluster of trees there."

Sam nodded, glancing off to the right where he'd pointed. "Okay."

"What about some flares? Can you look for some of those, too?"

With a brief nod she ducked again, rooting through the packed cargo area while Tom put both hands back on the wheel to keep the swerving Humvee straight. Sitting next to him, Linda opened the glove compartment, but all she found was paperwork, an empty holster, and another flashlight. Reaching between her legs, she rummaged under the seat, tongue sticking out of the corner of her mouth as she felt around and, a few seconds later, she jerked up with a red package in her hand, a symbol of a person lighting a flare on the front.

Holding it up to her father with a triumphant grin, she blurted, "I think I found flares!"

"Great," Tom grunted, whipping the wheel to the left as they hit a spot of hard ice and slewed. "How many are inside?"

She unzipped the case and paused briefly, "Looks like three. Is that good enough?"

"Yeah, I think so. Now, we need some string. Like, some cordage so we can rig up the flares to light remotely."

"Like a fuse?" Sam asked.

"Exactly. If we're going to pull this off, I need to ignite them from a distance. See if you can find some in the back or under the seats."

Sam ducked behind the seat once more, rummaging around, tossing clothing and covers into the next row. Linda searched, too, and Tom went back to driving, sliding too much from his distracted attention. Checking his side mirrors, he caught sight of the APC charging after them in a frenzy of spinning tires, snow flying off its sides as it crested the hill where he'd switched seats with Sam. Despite being able to follow in Tom's tracks, the vehicle still had some problems staying in the grooves due to its size, as it rode up the snowbanks, rear end whipping back and forth, chasing them in fits of speed.

"Wait a minute, Dad. What's this?"

He glanced over at Linda and the case in her lap, eyes flitting over the flares lined up inside, her hand gesturing at a side pocket with a black controller. When she lifted it and turned it back and forth, he saw three buttons and a switch on it, a short antenna sticking out its top.

"I think these are remote flares," she said, whipping out an instruction card from a pocket.

"You might be right. Put the controller back," he rasped. "Don't touch any of the buttons."

"Okay," she said, placing the device back in its groove, eyes still scanning the steps on the card. "Yep, I was right. These are remote flares."

"Even better," he laughed, calling back. "Hey, Sam. Don't worry about the cordage. Looks like we've got remote flares."

Sam hung over the seat, grinning when she heard the news. "That's awesome, guys. But what are you—"

Barbara's low groan rose above the engine's noise, a painful and deep sound like she was clawing her insides out.

Tom's laughter died on his lips, looking between the road and the rearview. "Sam, check on your mother, please."

"What should I do?" Sam asked.

"Check the IV lines and make sure she's warm. Take her blood pressure, too. Same as before. If everything looks good there, inspect her dressing for leaks…" He started to say more but trailed off as he narrowly passed between two large, frost-covered lumps, parts of the vehicles' roofs showing through the snow. The Humvee's rear end clipped one vehicle as it went by, giving them a jolt and sending a burst of white powder into the air before he shot through and when he looked in the rearview again, Sam had disappeared.

"Okay, Linda. Hand me the flares." Linda handed him the case, and he tucked it into his coat. "Do you still have your gun?"

She patted the bulge at her waist with a slight gulp. "Yep."

"Okay. When I stop, you and Sam and Jack stay inside the Humvee, no matter what. If the situation goes south, and Keith, or anyone else, comes after you, you know what to do."

"Pull the trigger until it goes click. Got it."

Nodding, breath coming shallow as he amped himself up for what he had to do, Tom lifted his eyes to the rearview mirror, raising his voice. "You're in charge of your mother, Sam. Keep her—"

"Warm. And check her blood pressure. Got it."

"Yes. And read the instruction card on the morphine injections." Gripping the wheel, eyes narrowed, he tried to think. "I gave her a dose about fifteen minutes ago and those only last about twenty at the lowest dosage, so she's probably about ready for another. If the pain causes her to squirm around, she could pull out her IV, so you'll want to hit her with one before that happens. Use the port on her IV line. It's right in the instructions. Can you do that?"

"I think so." Sam looked at him questioningly. "What are you going to do with the flares and diesel?"

Despite an ache at the base of his neck, he produced a grin he was fairly certain looked insane as his mirthful eyes flicked to the rearview. "I'm going to make a bomb."

Sam's confusion deepened. "But, Dad… diesel's not like gas. You know it's not explosive like that."

Looking over his shoulder, grin widening in a slow stretch, he shot her a wink. "Sure it is. You just have to give it some encouragement."

Chapter 8
PFC Simon Sharp
Santa Fe, New Mexico

Private Sharp shouted into the microphone, raising his pistol and firing it into the wall for impact, his ears ringing from the shot. Turning his head away, he let off a high-pitched scream of pain, pretending the bullet had struck him in the gut. Then he growled a random order to an imaginary soldier. "Keep them pinned down, Reed! If they so much as leave that storage room, fill 'em full of holes!"

He twisted his torso in the other direction, releasing another scream, followed by a moan, then he returned to his gruff, commanding voice, speaking into the microphone at the insurgent leaders. "Attention to those in control of storage bunker Alpha–Tango-Niner. This is Colonel Simon Sharp of the United States Army. We've infiltrated your facility and have taken at least one of your patrols hostage on Sub-level Two. We know you're holding prisoners in Warehouse 3-L, as well as the refrigeration unit on the same sub-level. Stand down, and no more of your comrades have to die. Respond on channel four-oh-one-dot-two-one megahertz within sixty seconds if you wish to negotiate the terms of your surrender. I expect to hear from someone named Chet, as I've been informed he's the leader of your group. You have one minute."

Sharp flipped off the microphone and settled back, spine stiff as he took a deep breath, held it, and let it out in a long gust, trying to relax. He shifted his chair, stood and peered through a window into a video room where several monitors had flashed to life. He circled the control panel and entered the video room through a side door where there were eight in total, some split into four-way views, all displaying various sections of the facility's hallways and warehouses. Most of them were dark or had no activity, and it only took him a minute to flip through the cameras to switch to Warehouse 3-L and the refrigeration unit his friends were being held.

A grin widened his sweaty cheeks as his plan fell into place right before his eyes. The six members in Warehouse 3-L were scrambling to get the soldiers against the wall and all loading activities on the elevator had stopped. Two of the insurgents were arguing with each other, gesturing to the hall door and then at the elevator while one seemed to be suggesting they jump on the elevator, likely to climb to the surface and escape in whatever transportation they'd arranged. Shifting to his left, he used another screen to search for the patrol he'd seen just before entering the refrigeration unit and getting his message to Smith and Morales.

He found the patrol not on Sub-level Two but right above him on Sub-level Four. As he watched, the three stood in the middle of the hallway, rifles held at the ready, heads spinning as they peered toward each end of the passage, expecting to be attacked at any moment. Coming to some conclusion, the trio put their heads down and ran to the bottom of the screen and out of sight.

Shifting to the control board, it only took him a second to access the refrigeration unit's camera where the insurgent leaders stood by the door next to the intercom, Shae with her weapon on the soldiers, but Stu was nowhere to be seen. The private's nerves kicked up when Chet started to reach for the speaker button, but Shea batted his hand away, then she threw her arms out, pointing at him as if to say she'd told him so about the Army guys showing up early, eliciting a soft chuckle from Sharp's lips. Having a good general location of all the insurgents, minus the three who'd run out of camera view, he nodded at his apparent success. Still, he had to seal the deal. As soon as he turned back to the control board to locate the patrol, the radio in the other room popped to life, Chet's voice coming through. A quick glance at the security screen showed the leader was leaning in closer to the intercom, the green light on the key panel glowing.

"Colonel Sharp? Are you there?"

Sharp dropped what he was doing and rushed back to the radio room, falling into his chair, the wheels carrying him away from the console until he slammed his bare feet on the tiles. Kicking himself toward the microphone, he placed his hands calmly on the console's edge and pressed the talk button.

"This is Colonel Sharp. Who am I speaking to?"

"Yeah, this is Chet. I guess you already know I'm the leader of this little group."

"That's right," Sharp growled. "We heard from your patrol member still alive that it might be you. He said you people have been living down here, sucking off the government's teat for a while. Is that true?"

"Not how I'd put it," Chet responded, sounding defensive. "A group of us came across this place after the big storms hit. Knew someone who could get us inside. Yeah, we've been eating the food and staying warm. But that's what they were meant for, right? Can't blame us for that."

"But I *can* blame you for holding my men hostage!" Sharp growled, his acting being overwhelmed with genuine anger. "You're up to your neck in shit, Chet, but if you release your prisoners, we'll allow you to exit the facility and flee south."

There was a pause over the line, and when the private glanced through the window to the video room, he saw Chet and Shea conferring again before Chet leaned closer to the speaker and hit the talk button. "I hate to press my luck, but why would the US Army allow people who murdered federal workers to go free?"

Sharp gulped, pressing forward with as much gruff and falsified boldness as he could muster. "Look, Chet. We don't have time for this shit! My men and I have a much bigger mission at stake. We're to get these supplies south as soon as possible. While what you've done is reprehensible, there's no time to argue. You're holding some of our men, and we want them back. What happens to you after that doesn't matter to me, but if you don't comply immediately, we're going to shoot one of your men. I've got two left to choose from." Sharp felt himself getting backed into a corner that he was woefully inexperienced in, but continued nonetheless

"And if you still won't concede, we'll get to you anyway. I can assure you, Chet, it won't be a pleasant experience. It's not worth holding my people if I'm giving you a clear way out." Keeping his tone gruff and commanding, Sharp pressed the issue. "I repeat, accept the deal or more of your people die. Your choice."

"How the hell does the US military justify shooting prisoners?" Chet shot back, a hint of disbelief at the edges of his voice.

"Martial law, son. Have you not been keeping up with the news?" Sharp snarled as best as he could through the radio. "Millions have died, and we're trying to bring back supplies to feed the survivors. Anyone that stands in our way will be taken out. Understood?"

Glancing up at the screen, the private watched as the two militia members leaned together again, heads shaking, Shea gesticulating while Chet backed away. After thirty seconds, the pair still didn't seem convinced, and Sharp jutted his jaw, lifted from his chair, and injected a bellow into his tone as he slammed his hand on the talk button.

"Okay, Chet. It seems like you don't believe me, so another one of your people has to go down. Go ahead, soldier; in the leg, if you please." Holding the pistol away from him, he fired into the wall again, cheeks drawn into a wince, ears ringing with the crisp report.

Chet's voice burst over the speaker in reply. "Okay, Colonel Sharp. We get it! Just quit shooting my people!"

"Issue the order now, Chet." The private leaned forward, hovering over the microphone, lips pressed close. "March them up to the stairwell to the top of the landing and let them go. For my part, I know you've been loading trucks outside, and I've instructed my soldiers to leave those alone. Your people will get in them and drive away immediately. Is that clear?"

"Yeah. All clear," Chet spat. "Give us ten minutes and we'll have them upstairs for you. Is that *suitable*?" The man said the last part with a sarcastic sneer, and when Sharp looked up at the video screen, he saw him with both palms pressed against the wall, leaning over the intercom and shaking his head in derision while Shea stood off to the side, hands on her hips, face pinched tight with anger.

"That's fine," Sharp said. "You have ten minutes to comply or your last patrolman will be shot. And it won't be the leg this time. Colonel Sharp out."

Kicking back in his chair, the private slapped his hands over his face, drawing them downward as if he could wipe away the chest-squeezing tension that gripped him. Watching the screens, a slow grin worked onto his lips as the militia got Morales, Smith, and the others to their feet and the third guard in the room was sent off to round up the soldiers in Warehouse 3-L.

Watching Shea and Chet, Sharp studied the monitors. Shae had her palm against Chet's chest, backing him away from the prisoners while keeping her pistol trained on them. Frowning, squinting at the meddlesome woman, Sharp's hand hovered over the talk button as he thought about dishing out another warning, but he refrained, resting his fingers on the edge of the console. Any interference might kick things into gear, but it could also backfire on him. As he watched the two leaders, something moved on a screen off to his left. Looking over, he saw it was a patrolman from earlier pounding up the main stairwell from Sub-level Four to Sub-level Three.

"No," he said, standing up, teeth grinding. "You jerks just needed to stay away for ten stupid minutes! And, wait… where's your other two guys?"

The patrolman smashed through the door to Sub-level Three and sprinted up the main hall to the refrigeration unit, pounding on the door, jerking it open to find Shea and Chet backing up with their guns raised momentarily. Realizing who it was, the leaders bent to listen as the guy pointed and gestured at the hall and then up at the camera Sharp was watching them through. Chet glanced in the camera's direction before giving the man some orders and sending him off.

Stomach sinking with dread, Sharp leapt from his chair and circled into the video room, following the patrolman as he sprinted to the stairwell, flew down the steps, and out of sight. The private flicked some keys on the console to find the man as he reached the bottom of the landing with Sub-level Five written on the wall. The militiaman threw open the door and ran into the hallway, but when Sharp tried to pick up the hall camera, the screen remained blank with "disabled" flashing on it.

Fingers frantically dancing over the console, heart gripped in the frigid hand of panic, he sputtered, "No, no, no," as he tried to find the men who were on Sub-level Five with him.

"Colonel Sharp? Sharp, can you hear me?"

Looking to the screen on his right, he saw Shea standing next to the intercom with their finger on the talk button while Chet stood in front of the camera, looking up with a grin on his face.

"Colonel Sharp?" he asked. "Are you there, buddy? I'd like to renegotiate our deal."

Swallowing a massive lump in his throat, the private stood and rushed back to the radio room. Still watching Chet through the glass, he tentatively pressed the talk button. "What is it? I'm hearing from my men outside that you haven't brought the hostages up yet. You've got four minutes to make that happen before your world starts getting ugly."

Chet grinned even wider, folding his arms across his chest, shaking his head, laughing. "I don't think so, *Colonel* Sharp. I'll wait to meet you face-to-face so we can nail down the finer points of our... *negotiation*."

The private's eyes fell shut, lips drawing back from his teeth as he shook his head in dismay. He was just about to respond with an angry retort when the door to the radio room was assaulted with pounding fists, heavy thuds that caused him to jump, jolting him upright in his chair.

Chapter 9
Tom McKnight
Central Mexico

Straining against the blanket of white lying over the road that reflected the spots of sunlight back into his eyes, Tom spotted a groove in the highway that branched off to the right. He pulled onto the exit ramp, the Humvee slipping and sliding to the left shoulder and almost tipping into a ditch before edging back to the center. Hardly slowing at the bottom, he swung right and fishtailed onto the main road, slicing through a hundred yards of snow to the nearest gas station.

The armored vehicle angled left into the lot, circled to the other side, and cut between a pair of storage buildings on a back lane. Directly ahead were the clusters of trees he'd seen from the highway which he pulled behind, fully hiding the Humvee from view from the main road before finally hitting the brakes and bringing them to a skidding stop. Leaving the engine running, Tom exited the vehicle, slammed his door and circled to the other side where the fuel container hung. On his way, he spotted Samantha throwing her leg over the rear seat like she was coming with him and he whipped open the door and held his hand out to stop her.

"No, Sam. Stay here with your brother and sister and Smooch. Watch your mother like I asked."

"But, Dad, you need me out there." Her voice strained with protest, and she didn't back off.

Slamming both hands against the door frame, Tom leaned in, head shaking in a hard no. "Sorry, kiddo. This fight's not for you."

"Who's going to watch your back?"

Smooch whined in agreement from the middle seat, wagging her tail in agitation, baleful eyes staring at him in question.

He shook off the dog's accusatory look and shifted to Sam. "You *are* watching my back by being in here with your mother… She…" Tom tried to say more, but his voice cracked with emotion. With time running out, the mercenaries right behind him, he turned his tone to steel again. "Just do as I ask. If Keith or any of his people approached the truck, you know what to do. If that doesn't work…" Shaking his head, he gave them the only piece of advice he had left. "Just run."

"But, Dad. Wait!"

He slammed the door, cutting her off, sidestepping to the jerry can and grabbing it off its hooks. Before he turned away, he glanced through the side window into the back, gaze passing over Barbara's pale form. Her expression was peaceful, the lips he'd kissed a thousand times looking dry and cracked, cheeks sallow and thin. Still, she was as beautiful to him as the day they'd met, the deepening lines in the corners of her eyes and laugh marks around her mouth only making her look more lovely. All the memories he had of them building their lives together flashed through his mind in a split second and there was nothing he wanted more than for those moments to continue, to be with his best friend and wife forever, to hug his children and laugh with them, no matter where they ended up in the world.

Something hard inside him rose to the surface, dashing the exhaustion and maniacal stress. Strength surged through his limbs, forcing his teeth together, heat rising in his gut as he grabbed the jerry can's handle and turned away. With a shot of adrenaline tossed on top, Tom strode briskly from the cover of the trees, breaking into a jog along the main road connecting the gas station with the other buildings. Diesel fuel sloshed around in the can as he looked back and forth across the road, looking for a suitable spot to lay his trap. The surrounding snowfall muffled the distant sound of the APC's engine, but it was getting closer by the moment, the haunting squeals of the axles and armor creeping up toward him.

Picking a random spot in the middle of the road, he swept at the snow with his boot, making a foot-wide trench across the pavement. Uncapping the can, he poured diesel into the groove until everything turned into a yellowish slush. Leaping that, he dashed forward ten yards and made a smaller circle, kicking and sweeping the area clean in a dusting of white powder. Placing the fuel can in the center, he retrieved a flare from its package and dropped it inside with a plop. Capping it tight, he rested the can on its side and slipped to his hands and knees. Fingers and toes already numb from the unbearable cold, he scrambled around the circular patch, shoving armfuls of snow into the middle, covering the fuel can so it looked like a normal feature of the street before he stood and retreated, smoothing out his footprints until he reached the trench.

By then, the stench of diesel filled the air, stinging his nose and causing his eyes to water. Grabbing a pair of flares labeled '2' and '3' from his pocket, he dashed from one end of the trench to the other, placing a flare on each side, pointing the combustible ends toward the slushy diesel. Backing up, he fished the remote out of his coat and flicked the safety switch off. When he was far enough away, he held up the device and pressed buttons two and three simultaneously, flinching as they sprung to life in a hiss of sparks and flying cinders. The sudden intense heat vaporized the fuel, the high temperature produced igniting both ends at once. Lines of orange-yellow flame raced toward each other and met in the middle with a singular *whoosh*, not quite as dramatic as if it had been gasoline, but still providing a nice show.

The unmistakable sound of the slowing APC crept through the parking lot, the rattling diesel engine almost as sick as their own Humvee, something clinking in the suspension, a puttering illness deep within the engine block. Tom turned, facing the oncoming beast with its thick green armor plates and slanted front, the bug-like headlamps glaring through the swirling snow. The mounted remote control machine gun swiveled on its base and pointed downward at him with a motorized whine and the two sets of front tires swerved a little as it centered itself in the tracks he'd left, exhaust puffing from the rear pipes. Swallowing hard, Tom stood stock still as the APC crept toward him, the trigger for the remaining flare still in his hand.

Chapter 10
Sam McKnight
Central Mexico

Crouched in the back of the idling Humvee next to her mother, Sam stared out the foggy side window in the direction her father had gone. In the distance, she spotted the fire he'd presumably made, an orange glow pushing upward against the endless gray sky, snow flurries breaking her view as they drifted in the wind. She'd just given Barbara another dose of morphine, the lowest amount possible, as Tom had directed, a simple task all things considered.

Barbara was breathing steadily again, no longer in such intense pain, warm with Jack cuddled up beside her. Linda had turned the heat to high and slapped duct tape on the punctures in the glass, but the rattling ventilation couldn't keep up with the quiet cold that settled over them like death itself. They were forced to wait for whatever fate had in store for them, and Sam hated it more than she hated anything else. As the seconds ticked by, her jaw squeezed tighter, nostrils flaring with frustration as the slow buildup of worry for her father crawled through her intestines like a hungry raccoon, eager to get out, chittering at her to move soon or never get the chance again. And while she didn't want to leave Jack, Linda, or her mother, she couldn't let her dad take on Keith and his small army by himself.

She'd been through so much with him, from the Atlantic Ocean to the beaches of Kitty Hawk, all the way home, only to find their farm destroyed. And when they'd tried to reunite their family, Keith had gotten in the way again, pursuing them halfway across Mexico, intent on settling some kind of score that still made very little sense to her. She pounded her fist against her leg, growling as she swung her feet over the seat, landing hard with her boots on the floor.

"Where're you going, Sam?" Jack called out from the back, teeth chattering through the words.

"I'm going to go help Dad. He needs me. No one else can do it. You two have to stay with mom." She looked to her sister who knelt in the next row of seats, staring back with wide eyes. "You've got Smooch here to protect you and Linda's got a gun. She knows what to do if she needs to."

The covers ruffled in the rear, and Jack's head peeked over the seat, his voice plaintive, a pleading expression on his face. "You can't go, Sam. We just got you back!"

"Hush," Linda told him, her words flat, then she gave Sam an approving nod. "Go. Go help Dad."

* * *

Tom stood with his boots planted apart, hands up, twelve yards in front of the buried gas can, watching as the APC rumbled to a halt several yards behind it. The diesel engine idled, the machine gun still aimed downward and tracking him, several tons of armored bulk waited to pounce. A face flashed in the view port and disappeared as a high motorized whine reached his ears, and thirty seconds later two men sprung from the vehicle's rear, dispersing on either side of him, approaching cautiously.

Their rifle barrels were pointed at him even as they checked in all directions, looking across the clusters of trees behind him, the deep ridges of white surrounding them, the new winter forming its own frost-covered wonderland of hard ice and snow. The man on the left was tall and thin with a shock of blonde hair falling over his goggles, smooth strides carrying him forward to stand in the APC's shadow. The other approached on Tom's right, a shorter, stocky man with a chiseled jaw and shaded features, the eyes behind his goggles half-lidded and stony, giving the impression of being the leader of the group of Keith's new friends. The pair stopped ten yards in front of the waiting fuel canister as they eyed him suspiciously, hyper-aware of their surroundings, frost covering their beard stubble and upper lips.

"I'm unarmed, guys." Tom spoke with a raised voice, drawing their attention to him. "I'll come willingly."

The one on the right fixed him with a hard look, glancing off to the side before relaxing from his fight stance, lowering his rifle to his waist, the barrel still pointed at Tom's stomach. "Mr. McKnight. It is good to finally meet you face-to-face."

Tom pegged the accent as Eastern European right away, Russian if he had to guess. "And who are you two? It would be good to know the names of the people who've been trying to kill me and my family."

The two men shared an amused look, the one on the left chuckling before answering. "I am Mikael, and this is Serge."

"I am not surprised we caught up with you," Serge said, taking an extra step forward. "It was only a matter of time. You couldn't have escaped us forever and it would've been much easier if you would have given yourselves up miles ago."

Tom shrugged. "That wouldn't have been very much fun. And giving up isn't something my family is used to doing."

"Speaking of your family…" Serge lifted his chin and gazed past Tom where the road wound away from them. "Where is the rest of the clan? We would like to collect you together into a nice package."

Bending his head toward one of the side roads leading away from where he'd parked the Humvee, Tom replied, "I sent my family well ahead. Colonel Banks only wants *me*. And here I am. Come on. Take me in." Tom put his hands together and held them out, ready to be cuffed.

It took a colossal strength of will for Tom to avoid glancing at the slight rise of snow in the road that covered the fuel can. At the same time, he didn't want to appear as if he was trying too hard not to look. A nervous pinch began twisting his guts like a candy wrapper, a defeated smile playing across his lips as the heat of the burning diesel warmed the back of his neck, willing the pair of mercenaries to step just a couple of feet closer.

He only allowed himself an occasional glance over their shoulders, looking for the second APC, expecting it to come trundling up at any moment. If Mikael and Serge were the only ones he had to deal with, though, he might just have a shot at turning the tables before the other one arrived.

"It's pretty cold out here," Tom added. "Why don't we get this over with so we can get warm, eh, boys?"

The one named Serge jerked his head toward Tom. "Mikael, please secure him. Then we will make call to Lena and see what she wants to do." Turning back to Tom, he snarled, "Honestly, I did not expect this to be so easy, but we were tiring of the chase, anyway."

Chuckling dryly, Tom did his best to act like a prisoner getting along with his new captors. "You guys are real tough customers. I tried to lose you a dozen times, and you kept on my tail..." He glanced at Mikael who'd started forward, eyes on Tom, his rifle cradled in his right arm. The weapon stayed tucked against his side as he reached into his coat pocket for what Tom assumed was something to bind him with. The mercenary was getting very close to the fuel can, might trip over it in a couple more steps and Tom eased to his left, trying to get the man to alter his direction and move around it. Mikael was fumbling with the handcuffs, though, drawing them out with a soft clack, the curved ends tangling on the tips of his gloves.

The mercenary glanced down and kept walking forward until his left foot kicked through the snow and struck the can with a deep thud. He craned his neck to see past the cuffs, making jerking motions with his foot to give the can light kicks and his furrowed brows deepened as he swept the toe of his boot across the top of the can experimentally, clearing the soft layer of white away to expose the bright green beneath.

With high-strung reflexes, the merc leapt back with a shout. "Serge! Gas can!"

The mercs' rifle barrels jerked to their shoulders as they retreated three paces, both staring at the ground, finally noticing the disturbances Tom had made in the snow. Serge's gaze darted to Tom's hands, squinting as he tried to figure out what he was holding while Tom cursed inwardly that his reflexes had been too slow, and he hadn't jumped away and activated the bomb. The long, cold days of frustration and weariness had killed his reaction time, but still his thumb hovered over the button, clashing emotions contorting his face.

"Whatever you are holding," Serge shouted. "Throw it down! Do it now!"

Mikael squinted, working his way to Tom's left as if trying to see what he was holding. "What is that? It looks like an antenna or something..."

"Drop it now!" Serge yelled again. "That is your last chance! In exactly one second, I will blow your brains all over the snow!"

Caught between a sudden bout of indecision, Tom's breath stuck in his chest. Part of him wanted to hit the button anyway, though it would surely kill him standing so close to the can. Either way, he'd be dead, but if he ignited it, at least he'd take out two of the mercenaries, giving Barbara and the girls a chance to get away.

Thumb settling on the button, he started to press it when three quick rifle shots stiffened the air with sharp retorts, one round zipping by, the second hitting Mikael with a horrific smack, jerking the mercenary stiff. The bullet punched through his neck and out the other side in a burst of blood, dropping him to the snow, writhing, screaming as he clutched his neck with both hands, his own weapon forgotten. A third round smacked the ground at Serge's feet, kicking up powder and ice and the leader lunged toward Tom, ducking low with his weapon held to his chest.

Another pair of shots followed the first ones, originating from a building on his right, traces of gun smoke and a flash of muzzle fire in the corner of his eye, but Tom was already spinning away, backpedaling to his right, stumbling across the line of burning fuel, plunging through the flames. As he staggered into a face-first tumble, he stabbed the last button with his thumb, praying he was far enough away from the blast zone.

Flare three, resting at the bottom of the fuel can, received the signal from the remote and the flare's primer lit its magnesium core, instantly blossoming into a two-thousand-degree inferno, well above the eighty-two-degree flash point of liquid diesel fuel. Constrained by the walls of the metal fuel canister, the heat source ignited the combustible vapor, the combination of liquid fuel, vapor and flare making a near-perfect improved explosive device.

The explosion flashed behind Tom in a crack of heat and light, casting his shadow a hundred feet ahead for a millisecond before the shock wave shoved him through the air, arms windmilling, face slamming into the hard ice, scraping his nose across it in a sharp pinch of pain. Dazed but rolling over, he glanced back to catch the end of the fireball as it curled upward and died in a drift of dark smoke above their heads. The APC's front end smoked with pieces of melted plastic, one headlamp blown out and dangling off. Mikael's prone form had stopped kicking and screaming, his coat smoldering and smoking, the hood's furry edges aflame. A thick drift of charred flesh and hair slathered in the stench of burning diesel wafted over Tom, causing him to turn his face away and start crawling.

More shots went off from behind him, closer though, not the original shooter – whoever they were. Snow and ice flicked into his face as the rounds peppered the ground at his feet then he was up, scrambling, running for cover, glancing back to see Serge stumbling away, firing at him even as his coat still burned in a wafting of gray-black smoke. Head low, legs pumping with every bit of strength he had, Tom sprinted for the tree line, fixated on a thin stand of pines connected with a twisted thatch of snow-covered brush.

Glancing back as he ran, he saw the mercenary flinch away as the mysterious attacker shot again, providing cover for Tom, driving Serge toward the APC. By the time Serge turned to fire, Tom dove into the thicket, battling his way through the brittle stickers and switches that tugged at his coat, snow and ice flying everywhere as he kicked and punched, slipping over a shallow ridge of snow that hid him from the mercenary's direct line of sight. Flipping onto his stomach, Tom scrambled to one of the standing pines and pressed his palm against the tree trunk, using it to leverage himself upward. Easing around, he spotted Serge ducking and hiding from the first shooter, who was still taking potshots at him and the APC, bullets hitting the snow and pinging off the armor with bright sparks.

Turning, sliding downward with his back to the tree, he drew a pistol from his waistband, pulling and releasing the rack to charge it, checking his left pocket for the two spare magazines he'd stuck inside. Removing his gloves, stuffing them into his coat pockets, Tom raised the weapon and locked his palm to the grip, finger resting outside the trigger. Whoever his savior was, he owed them his thanks.

But first, he had a man to kill.

Chapter 11
Keith
Central Mexico

Sitting in the driver's chair with the video visor on, Keith surveyed what was happening through the Stryker's external cameras, zooming in on the action, a grin on his face. The temperature inside the vehicle was near freezing, despite the heating unit's best efforts, but he hardly felt the cold, the pain in his joints having become part of his newly transcended self, thrumming inside him with a heady warmth.

"That looks like Tom McKnight out there, standing just past a group of buildings. He's got a fire going. All appearances would indicate he's giving up." With a shake of his head, he dug into a chili mac MRE bag with a fork, stabbing a noodle and piece of flavored ground beef, slamming it into his mouth, talking around the food. "But we all know that's not the case, don't we? The question is, will Serge figure out what Tom McKnight's going to do before it's too late?"

He tilted his head to the right, listening, and after a pause, he shrugged. "No, I don't care how good Serge and Mikael are. McKnight's a real clever SOB. I mean, look where we are." He gestured to everything around them. "We're in the middle of nowhere in Mexico, freezing our asses off, chasing this guy down. I've got to say, while I want McKnight dead as much as the next person, I didn't volunteer to be hands on for this mission. That was all Banks' doing."

Pausing, he listened again, then responded. "Hey, don't complain to me. I gave you plenty of chances to be on my side, but you shat on my parade every time. And then, in the epitome of treachery, you went behind my back and worked against me to take command of the mission. That was the worst slight of all." He flipped up his visor and turned to Lena, who sat in the communication chair, strapped in tight, head resting back to expose her slashed neck and a gore-covered coat.

Keith arced an eyebrow. "I don't care about you being cold and wanting to go home. You picked the wrong horse to bet on, honey. And you paid for it."

Swaying side-to-side, he took another couple bites of the chili mac before gesturing to the woman, a pleased grin on his face. "Thank you! I'm glad you agree. You know, you're a much better conversationalist than people give you credit for. You really know how to listen." A fit of giggles gripped his stomach, and he slammed the back of his hand against his mouth to stifle them.

Flipping down his visor, he continued with his play-by-play. "Okay, back to the action. Looks like Serge and Mikael pulling up in the APC. They're cautious, as would I be. They're coming to a stop. Oops, I think they parked a little too close. I would've stayed fifty yards back, creating some space between myself and a potential trap."

As he spoke, he waved the fork around. "Hmmm. They're both getting out. Probably not the smartest decision. It would've been better for one of them to stay inside… Now they're trying to apprehend McKnight. Good luck with that." The last sentence was a slur as Keith took another couple of stabs at his food, shoveling the bites into his mouth with enthusiasm, a sense of satisfaction growing warm in his stomach.

"What's this? It looks like Mikael figured something out." Keith squinted. "It looks like a gas can of some sort. And they're trying to get something out of McKnight's hand. He mumbled, "Looks like they stumbled on the trap by sheer luck and... Oh, someone *else* is shooting at them. Ouch! That's got to hurt, Mikael. Right in the neck! Mikael's down! The merc is down! It's a full-on firefight and—"

Keith's eyes went wide as light blossomed in his camera view, washing out the entire image in white. When the picture faded to normal light, he shook his head with a dry laugh. "And that was one big explosion." Kicking a foot happily, he lifted his visor and winked at Lena. "Glad we didn't go down there, eh? We'd be crispy, too."

Eyes wide, chewing his food, engrossed in the events unfolding in the visor feed, he watched bullets pepper the snow. "Looks like someone's got Serge pinned down. It must be one of Tom's meddlesome daughters, Sam or Linda. Couldn't be the queen bitch herself. No, she'd be out of commission still. Whoever it is, they're keeping Serge busy and off Tom's back. Okay, Serge is trying to put the APC between himself and the shooter. Smart move, but... wait for it... annnd McKnight escapes into the woods!" He slapped his thighs with a barking scoff, then threw Lena a bemused glance. "Another failure for your 'expert team,' but I guess we're not keeping score anymore, are we?"

His expression turned sad, the corners of his mouth falling into a frown. "Our merry band is shrinking. I'm already feeling lonely. Hey, why don't you give Banks a call for me?" Head tilting, he gave a soft tut-tut. "You say your throat's a little rough? Can't speak right now? You're probably coming down with something. Don't worry, I'll call her."

Keith placed his chili Mac aside, turned up his visor, and shifted to the radio console, reaching across Lena to flip a couple knobs and dials, grabbing the headset and slipping it over his ears. After punching more buttons, he initiated the call and fell back into his chair to listen. The line hissed and crackled, sputters of sound as the APC's antenna tried to reach through the clouds and make a satellite connection. He hadn't had much luck trying to get hold of the colonel earlier, and the continued snaps and squelches in his headset all but guaranteed a failed link. He grinned when, after a full two minutes of listening to the static, a repeated buzzing ringtone reached his ears and, a moment later, Banks picked up.

"This is Banks. Go ahead Keith."

The agent's face lit with amusement. "Colonel Banks! So glad I finally got you! The connection has been terrible out here."

"Where the hell are you?"

"I don't know," Keith replied with a shrug. "The GPS has been a little spotty. Someplace in Mexico."

"Are you still in the APCs? Are the mercs still with you?"

"Affirmative to the first question. Sort of to the second." A giggle threatened to trickle from his mouth. Sliding to his knees next to Lena, he took her hand where it rested in her lap, holding the stiffening claw like they were two lovebirds sitting at the movie theater.

"What do you mean, *sort of?*"

"Dmitri and Lena had a bit of an accident, but Serge is still alive, and he's putting in a great effort. Real bang-up job from that guy."

"Go on."

"He's currently in a defensive position at his APC, taking fire from at least one angle. I'd say it's Linda taking potshots at him… maybe Samantha… but he'll have double trouble as soon as Tom gets back into the fray. But, hey, I took care of Barbara earlier. Everything's under control. Tom won't be an issue."

"What the *hell* are you talking about?" Banks hissed across the line, her voice mixing with the trickles of static. "You're not making any sense. And why aren't you out there with him? Is Mikael there? Put him on!" The last sentence came through in a hollow burst, scratchy in his eardrums.

"Oh, Mikael can't come to the phone right now." By then, Keith's voice was trembling with amusement, enjoying every second of the Colonel's confusion. "He took a round to the neck a few minutes ago. That was just before he caught on fire. By the way, he asked me to ask you if he could get hazard pay for that?"

"You've lost it, Keith." Her voice fell flat, tone filled with growing aggravation and disinterest, and he imagined the colonel shaking her head on the other side of the line. "You've lost control of the mission, the mercenaries, and the McKnights."

Eyes narrowing, he shifted positions. "On the contrary, Colonel." His voice turned dark, and he squeezed Lena's stiff hand until the welcoming pain from his fingers crept through his wrist and forearm, his shoulder cramping with the pressure he applied. "Things have never been clearer. I've done some soul-searching and found a new me beneath the soldier I used to be."

The pause from Banks lingered as Keith kept chewing his food.

She finally responded in a flat tone. "Explain yourself, agent. A *new* you?"

"That's right, Colonel. This entire mission has really changed me. I was down for a minute there, but I'm back on my feet now." In the camera visor, Keith watched as Serge continued to exchange gunfire with his hidden opponent.

"Does that mean you're bringing in McKnight or not?" The Colonel followed up, her voice dripping with misgivings. "No need to take him in alive at this point. I'd be happy with him dead. That man caused irreparable damage to my career, or what's left of my future. It's a miracle I could hold my position with the North American forces. And if you want to cash in on your stake, I'll need some proof that you've taken care of business. A picture of Tom McKnight's corpse. His head on a platter. Whatever you can show me, and I'll put in a word for you with the new government. You'll be as good as in."

Chuckling at the idea of having a career in a world that had fallen into madness, Keith shook his head and fed himself the last bit of chili mac, tossing the empty package over his shoulder, turning to Lena with a wink. "Yeah, right Banks. I'll send you a snapshot with me and McKnight. No problem. I'll get the job done."

Another pause followed, longer than the last. "Keith, are you… okay?" Banks sounded more curious than concerned, and he could only imagine what must be going through her head.

"Yeah, Colonel. We're just dandy over here. Give me another few hours, and I'll get you that picture of McKnight. Hell, it'll be a family photo. Because I'd hate to miss out on an illustrious career in our new government."

He reached up and clicked the disconnect button, reveling in not caring what his superiors thought of him. Sitting back, chuckling, he gave dead Lena a friendly jab in the shoulder.

"What's up with Banks? The colonel doesn't have our best interests at heart, does she?" Keith grinned and patted her again, so her bloody head wobbled on her parted neck "No, I agree. I won't kill the McKnights for her, or some career in a whacked-out new order style government." With a glance at his comrade, he gazed ahead through the APC, hands held out in front of him as if imagining a sweeping landscape. "I'm thinking you, me, and the open tundra. Let's head down to Mexico City, have a cocktail, then find a nice beach resort where it's not thirty below. How's that sound?"

When the woman only stared upward with wide, unblinking eyes, their surfaces already clouding over white from the cold, he nodded. "I'll take that as a yes."

Chapter 12
Specialist Lance Morales
Santa Fe, New Mexico

After Private Sharp left, Morales shared uneasy glances with Smith and Stevens, making sure the latter kept the note tucked in his pants along with the rat skull while Chet and Shae talked in harsh whispers, preoccupied with their indecision over what to do next.

Morales put his head down, murmuring from the side of his mouth to Smith. "You think he got hold of Johnson? Maybe the captain sent him in here with a plan."

"I doubt it's anything Johnson ordered," the lieutenant growled under his breath, casting a surly look at Chet and Shae where they stood by the intercom, waiting to hear from their people in the warehouse. "He would have already come in guns blazing."

After the pair of captors had sent Stu off to check the militia's progress, Morales had his ear tilted to the heated discussion happening between the leaders. As far as he could tell, Shae wanted to get out sooner while Chet was keen on loading every last bit of supplies they could fit in the stolen Humvees before they bugged out. He couldn't blame Chet; it was a harsh world outside the bunker, and he was smart for taking everything he could. Aside from what they'd overheard while loading equipment for the insurgents, Morales, Smith, Stevens, and the others were working blind. All they knew was that Captain Johnson's teams had moved on to the next buildings, though the second convoy unit could show up at any moment. But the militants had picked up the pace over the last few hours, calling an all-hands-on-deck gathering to get it together and bug out.

"I see your point," Morales whispered back in agreement.

"What do you know about Private Sharp? He a competent soldier?"

"No clue. Never worked with the guy. He was in Second Crew. Seemed enthusiastic enough."

Someone knocked on the door, popped it open, and stuck his head inside. "Almost there," Stu said, looking between Chet and Shae. "We've got four trucks loaded and are working on the final two. Just give us another hour and a half, and we'll be ready to go."

"Good," Chet acknowledged. "Don't fully load those last two, got it?"

"There'll be plenty of room for them." Stu lowered his voice on the end of the sentence, grinning at the soldiers before glancing away.

"Alright," Chet nodded. "Get back to the warehouse and finish up."

"And do it quick," Shae threw in, shifting from one leg to the other, the short, rugged woman resting her palm on her pistol as she paced.

After the runner left, the pair of leaders put their heads back together, continuing the harsh whispering between themselves, casting glances back at the soldiers every few seconds.

"Did you hear that?" Morales murmured from the corner of his mouth.

"Sounds like they plan on taking us with them." Smith spoke low, too. "Any idea why they'd do that?"

"They don't know when the next convoy is coming, or how many troops will be with them. If they're here when our guys arrive, they'll need us as bargaining chips."

Smith stared quietly ahead at the refrigeration unit, pretending to be playing along. Morales was about to say something else when the intercom burst to life with a loud crackle and squeal of feedback, like the person on the other end was eating the microphone. A shot rang out, causing Morales's shoulders to jerk, his head popping up, and then came a gruff voice over the line, sounding like every commanding officer he'd ever had.

"Keep them pinned down, Reed! If they so much as leave that storage room, fill 'em full of holes!"

Chet and Shae spun to the intercom, staring at it like it was covered in feces. Then, realizing she'd left the soldiers uncovered, she stepped back with her pistol pointed right at Smith.

A moment later, the gruff voice returned. "Attention to those in control of storage bunker Alpha–Tango-Niner. This is Colonel Simon Sharp of the United States Army. We've infiltrated your facility and have taken at least one of your patrols hostage on Sub-level Two. We know you're holding prisoners in Warehouse 3-L, as well as the refrigeration unit on the same sub-level. Stand down, and no more of your comrades have to die. Respond on channel four-oh-one-dot-two-one megahertz within sixty seconds to negotiate the terms of your surrender. I expect to hear from someone named Chet, as I've been informed he's the leader of your group. You have one minute."

Shae snapped her fear-filled eyes to Morales, raising her gun and jerking it back and forth at them. "Do you know this colonel?"

Smith shook his head. When her weapon turned toward Morales, he shrugged. "Never heard of the guy. He must be with the convoy. I guess they came early, like you said."

She spun on Chet with vitriol in her eyes, her pistol raised and shaking in her hand. "I told you they'd be here." Realizing she was speaking loudly in front of the soldiers, she turned the militia leader away, whispering in harsher tones.

Smith's expression hung between a smirk and relief. Leaning back, he shifted his knees and said, "That's it, then. We're going to get out of here one way or another."

"Yeah, but that wasn't a regular colonel," Morales told him, chest deflating with even more uncertainty than before, lips pressed thin.

"What the hell are you talking about? That's *definitely* a colonel, and it sounds like he's a real ball buster. The guys already offed one of theirs. Serves them right." Smith's expression fell, casting a concerned glance at the militia, voice rising in pitch. "I guess we should be worried about that, eh? They might take it out on us."

"Keep your voice down, Smith." His eyes stayed stuck on their captors, pausing before leaning in closer. "That's a valid concern, true. But that was *Private* Sharp, not Colonel Sharp."

Smith stared straight ahead at the refrigeration units, blinking at the brushed chrome doors as realization dawned in his eyes. "That was Private Sharp *pretending* to be a colonel… because he can't get out to reach Johnson?"

"Exactly," Morales said, his thoughts driving deeper. "He might be worried about us getting caught in the crossfire if it comes to blows. Like, if the real convoy shows up early. Bullets fly…"

"We die."

"Exactly."

Morales was about to say something more when Chet and Shae came to an agreement, Chet leaning closer to the intercom, pressing the talk button.

"Colonel Sharp? Are you there?" Chet asked.

After a pause, Sharp came back. "Yeah, this is Colonel Sharp. Who am I speaking to?"

Morales glanced over at Smith, listening to the back and forth between the nervous militiaman and the supposed colonel. "I have to admit, he's doing a pretty good job. If he doesn't get a medal for this, he should at least get an Oscar."

"Or even a star on the Hollywood Walk of Fame," Smith scoffed.

They continued listening as Sharp yelled through the intercom, his voice distorting the speaker. "Look, Chet. We don't have time for this shit! My men and I have a much bigger mission at stake. We're to get these supplies south as soon as possible. While what you've done is reprehensible, there's no time to argue. You're holding some of our men, and we want them back. What happens to you after that doesn't matter to me, but if you don't comply immediately, we're going to shoot one of your men. I've got two left to choose from. And if you still won't concede, we'll get to you anyway. I can assure you, Chet, it won't be a pleasant experience. It's not worth holding my people if I'm giving you a clear way out." Keeping his tone gruff and commanding, Sharp kept on. "I repeat, accept the deal or more of your people die. Your choice."

"Nice," Smith whispered with an impressive nod. "That little private might just get us out of this yet."

And when Sharp fake-shot another insurgent patrolman to get Chet to believe him, using a gun to demonstrate how serious he was, Smith nudged Morales, suppressing a grin.

"That's pretty creative," Morales admitted.

That ended the negotiation, and Chet agreed to the terms, requesting ten minutes to fulfill their part.

"That's fine," Sharp agreed. "You have ten minutes to comply, or your last patrolman will be shot. Colonel Sharp out."

Smith's knee whacked Morales's. "Now, we really need to watch these guys. We've no idea what they'll do. Sharp might have just made them desperate."

Griggs was on Stephenson's far left, unable to hear most of their conversation, but Stevens leaned in closer to Morales with worried eyes and a face glistening with sweat. "Yeah, she doesn't seem like the type to take prisoners. We're just baggage to her, but she won't let us go, either."

Eyes pinned forward, Morales glanced aside, hissing at the soldiers to stay back, keeping his tone below that of the refrigeration units. Stevens was right about Shae, though. The rough-edged woman was constantly throwing glimpses in their direction, a dark glint in her eye, her movements panicky as she waved her weapon around.

"He's right about Shae." The lieutenant's tone was grim. "Whatever happens, you take her. I'll take the other bastard."

"*I* wanted him," Morales growled back.

"I'm giving you the tough job." Smith coughed and tried his best to look downtrodden and beaten. "Because you're faster than me. That lady's got an itchy trigger finger, and she's getting the heebie-jeebies like I've never seen."

The two militia leaders continued to go back and forth, time ticking, the end of ten minutes coming up soon. Shae had turned in a complete circle, waving her gun at the soldiers, bending, hissing at Chet with complaints too low to hear as the man bumped her away, soothing her with soft tones, his rifle cradled casually in his arm, barrel pointed at the floor.

"My hands are bound in front of me," Stephenson said, his voice growing more nervous. "If it goes down, I'll get up and charge them while you guys use the wall to get up. Play it by ear after that?"

Smith tilted to Stephenson, catching the soft whispers barely audible over the refrigeration unit's fans. With a deep breath and a smooth exhale, Morales nodded and lifted his eyebrows to indicate he'd both heard and agreed with the plan. Five minutes ago, he'd been certain of their release, but the continued hesitancy from the militia made him doubt they'd actually comply.

"What the hell are they waiting for?" Smith whispered. "There can only be maybe a couple of minutes left. Think they'll call Sharp's bluff?"

With a shrug, Morales remained tense and focused, awaiting Sharp's reply on the intercom, or for Chet and Shae to tell them to get up and move out. What he didn't expect was a new insurgent to burst through the door, eyes wide, chest heaving as if he'd run a marathon.

Chet and Shae jolted backward, weapons swinging in his direction until the man backed off with his hands up. "Whoa! Wait a minute! It's me!"

"Jeez, Miley. That's a great way to get shot." Chet stared at the man for a moment before his expression shifted from anger to disbelief. "Wait… weren't you out on patrol? Didn't you guys get picked up by Colonel Sharp's group? Didn't they shoot two of you?"

"I'm not sure who Colonel Sharp is, but if he's that guy screaming over the intercom, we think we've got him pinned down in the radio room."

"What the hell are you talking about? We got infiltrated by the Army pukes."

"We haven't seen any Army guys." The man shrugged. "None of us have been taken hostage or shot. We think it's someone screwing around in the radio room."

Chet's expression of disbelief and realization would've been comical if it weren't for the dark look he threw at the soldiers, his gaze lingering on Morales. "You sure you don't know anyone named Sharp?"

Morales lifted his head, giving an innocent shrug and Chet scoffed and turned to where his patrolman was pointing up to a camera positioned beneath some coolant pipes. With a frightening grin, the man approached the lens while Shea pressed the intercom button.

"Colonel Sharp?" The insurgent leader's grin widened. "Are you there, buddy? I'd like to renegotiate our deal."

The colonel who wasn't a colonel came back after a squelch of feedback. "What is it? I'm hearing from my guys outside that you haven't brought my men up yet. You've got four minutes to make that happen before your world starts getting ugly."

Chet's grin spread wider, and he folded his arms across his chest with a laugh. "I don't think so, *Colonel* Sharp. I'll wait to meet you face-to-face so we can nail down the finer points of our… *negotiation.*"

Wincing sharply, breath caught in his throat, Morales's chest clenched around his ribs. He shot a glance at Smith, then Stephenson. "This is it, boys," he whispered, tensing his legs to push himself off the wall and charge the first person in his path, be it Shea, Chet, or Miley. He figured Stephenson would beat him there, and he might have to shift directions and go after someone else. Either way, he'd have to be superhuman *not* to take a couple of rounds before he got into the action.

As Shea turned to the soldiers with a dark grin on her face, Chet grabbed her and jerked his thumb toward the door. "Shea. Come with me. We're going to go pay a visit to Colonel Sharp." He shifted to the patrolman. "You stay here. If any of these guys move, blow them away. Got that?"

Miley stepped farther into the room, lifted his rifle, and kept it trained on the sitting soldiers. "Yeah, I got it. They're not going anywhere. The colonel is on Sub-level Five. Our guys are down there trying to get in. You can't miss them."

"Thanks," Chet said with a hard pat on his shoulder. Spinning towards Shea with a wide smile, he led her to the door. "Let's go meet this 'Colonel.'"

The militia leaders left the room with a chuckle, the door shutting with a heavy clank, leaving Morales and the soldiers alone with Miley. Their new captor was an average sized man with an uneven beard, the front part of his chin having grown out far ahead of the rest as if it had once been a goatee, black laced with gray. Morales counted the steps between himself and the guard, at least twelve feet, an impossibly long distance on a crawl.

"Hey, man, you got a cigarette?" Smith asked, lifting his chin. "Haven't had a smoke since you guys captured me. I guess it's getting to me."

Morales nodded in agreement. "He smokes like a freight train. And he's aggravating as hell when he doesn't get his—"

"Shut up," Miley growled, stepping closer, pointing his weapon at the two, the sights coming to rest on Morales.

"Fine," he conceded, dipping his head submissively. "Don't want any trouble."

"Good, because you're not going anywhere or doing anything or even saying any-damn-thing until Chet and Shea get back from rooting your guy out."

"Yeah, let's wait and see if they make it back." Smith shot Morales a knowing glance before turning to the guard. "Meanwhile, Captain Johnson swings in here with some special ops guys to take you out, sir. What are you, a former schoolteacher? How long will you last against a bunch of trained lunatics?"

"The door's locked," the guy said, ignoring the barb with a snarl. "No one's getting in here. I don't care how trained they are."

Smith's chiseled jaw and firm blonde crew cut remained angled toward the man, the lieutenant's stone-cold eyes staring hard until the guard glanced away. Smith chuckled deep in his gut, light at first, but growing louder by the moment, shoulders hitching as it grew into a chortling snicker.

"Can you switch me places, Morales?" he asked. "I don't want to be up front to this show when the guys burst in and blow this sucker all over the walls."

Morales blinked at the lieutenant before giving the floor a dismal stare, a defeated sigh slipping free. "It depends on which unit they send. If it's just the Rangers, they'll probably try to take him alive. But if it's the—"

"Talon Squad," Smith added with trembling shoulders. "If it's those badasses, it'll be ugly."

There was no Talon Squad, at least so far as Morales was aware of, but it sounded good, so he went with it. "No, I get your point." He scooted left on the tiles, away from the guard.

"Half the time those guys don't care who they shoot, as long as it's *someone.*"

"You guys are full of crap," Miley spat.

Morales shook his head vigorously. "I wish we were, and you've got a big decision to make here."

"What decision?" The man circled around, squaring up to Morales, jabbing the rifle at his chest. "What *damn* decision?"

Pulling on as much bravado as he could muster, Morales continued. "I mean, if you want to surrender now, we could put in a good word for you. Make sure you don't get a bullet in your head for following those losers."

The man laughed, a chesty guffaw, mocking the bound soldiers as he pushed his barrel at Morales's face, hitting him in the nose and cheek with the hard metal. The soldier's hands were tied behind his back, and all he could do was move his face aside. "Oh, yeah. I'll just surrender. Maybe I'll even let you guys tie me up, and we'll all sit together and tell jokes, right?"

"If that's what you want to do," Morales said, forcing his voice to go flat to avoid any semblance of fear. "You're putting your life into Chet and Shae's hands. Don't blame me when those guys come crashing in here."

"I'll be dead any—"

Lightning quick, Stevens, whose hands were still bound in front of him, jerked forward and grabbed the rifle barrel, shoving it to the side. The gun fired, punching a hole between Smith's and Morales's heads and Stevens yowled from gripping the suddenly hot metal, though he hung on, forcing the weapon upwards as Smith rolled away. Morales kicked out the heels of his boots, smashing Miley's kneecap with a crunch of bone and cartilage. As the man straightened and started to scream, Smith barreled into him headfirst, crew cut bowed low, forehead pummeling the man's face, knocking him off his weapon to go careening into the stainless-steel door.

En masse, the soldiers were pushing themselves up the wall to stand, Stevens still holding the gun as Morales, Smith, and Griggs rushed forward and kicked Miley in a rain of hard boots, anger and frustration pouring out of them, only stopping when the man curled into a ball, his pistol clattering across the tiles.

Morales shouldered Smith aside. "Let's cut ourselves loose, eh?"

With Miley groaning on the floor, they searched for something to cut themselves free, finding a pair of scissors in a desk off to the side. Thirty seconds later, the soldiers were out of their bonds and gave the rifle to Smith. The lieutenant stood over the wounded militiaman, jamming the barrel into the man's ribs to ensure he wasn't going to try to stand up.

"Easy," Morales said, coming over. "Just put him in the refrigeration unit like they did our guys."

Smith looked like he was about to take out some of his frustrations until, after a long moment, he lowered his rifle and growled at Morales. "Fine. Get him in there."

Morales recovered Miley's pistol before Griggs and Stevens shoved him inside the refrigeration unit, slamming the door on the bruised and bleeding man. Moving to the door, hand resting on the doorknob, Smith turned to them.

"Any idea where we can get some weapons?"

Standing by the intercom panel, his finger poised over the buttons, Morales hesitated. "There should be at least one on this level, probably on the opposite side with the barracks." He shook his head, backing away from the speaker. "I want to talk to Sharp through this, but if I press the wrong key—"

"They'll know we escaped," Smith finished. "Let's just find us some weapons and get armed up, then we'll rock their world."

Morales turned to Stevens and Griggs. "We'll lead, and you guys cover. Got it?"

The pair nodded, and Smith slowly pushed the door open a crack, peering outside, looking down the hall before whipping it open, gesturing for the other three to follow him into the hallway. Warehouse 3L was straight ahead, but Morales slapped Smith's right shoulder at the first intersection, and the soldiers angled away, moving stealthily along the hall. A handful of overhead lights blinked while others filled the corridors with stark illumination as they crept past dozens of warehouse doors, clean storage and administration offices, the hum of the ventilation system accompanying them. Near the next junction, Morales gestured to each side, and Griggs and Stevens split up, clearing rooms, peeking in while Smith watched their backs and Morales kept his eyes on the passage ahead.

Pistol held at chest level, the specialist edged to the next intersection, resting his shoulder against the corner, leaning forward and looking both ways. Off to his left were the darkened hallways where he'd found the murdered workers, and to his right were the maintenance rooms, where there could be more of Chet's people. The three soldiers came up, Stevens and Griggs shaking their heads.

"Nadda, guys," Stevens said with an exasperated sigh. "Just storage, some lockers, and a small rec room."

"Okay, this way."

Morales took the lead, breaking into a jog as they turned left and entered the darkened halls, most of the lights still out or blinking faintly, the stench of corpses tickling his nose with an off-kilter rot that made his stomach churn. At the end of each passage, emergency lights burned red like embers, the rooms between them as abandoned as a ghost town, air passing cool and putrid across his cheeks. Several turns later, after checking a dozen doors, they arrived at a room with a security keypad. Morales called out various codes they'd gotten from LaPlante as Stevens plugged them in, the lock finally popping on the third one. Griggs and Stevens slipped inside, with Smith and Morales coming in behind them, letting the door shut softly in its frame.

Turning, he grinned at the medium-sized room filled with racks of rifles and pistols along the walls. A single column of shelving ran through its center, filled with boxes of ammunition, utility belts, and ammo pouches, the smell of gunpowder and gun oil filling the air.

Smith dove in, resting his rifle against the wall and filtering between the shelf and racks, taking a pair of holsters and clipping them on his belt. He grabbed two Beretta M9s from their hooks, loaded them with magazines, charged them with stiff snaps of the slides, and held them up for Morales to see, giving a satisfied smile. "We're going to take these jerks to town."

"Downtown, baby," Stevens spat as he and Griggs filtered in deeper and snatched up weapons for themselves.

Morales checked the pistol he'd taken off the guard, a Ruger, and exchanged it for a pair of M9s, loading up several magazines and stuffing them into his front and back pockets. He grabbed an ammo pouch and wrapped it around his waist, then searched the rear wall for a rifle, of which he had two choices, either one of three Springfield AR-15s or a handful of M4 carbines to choose from. He stood before the carbines, pulling one off its hooks and checking it out. "They must have missed this room."

Smith sneered with disgust. "After they bludgeoned those poor workers and left them for dead, they shut the light off and never came back. Probably couldn't stand the stench of their own mess."

Smith's words burned in Morales's ears, a vision of the bodies he'd found flashing in his mind. Their stripped, half-naked forms, crushed skulls, and broken bones, the floor smeared with blood, turned his guts like a meat grinder and fed his thirst to bring a swift, violent retribution to the militia.

Jaw locked, he slammed the magazine into the carbine's magazine well, charged the weapon, and turned. "This is it, guys. We're taking them down right now. No more screwing around with these assholes. They're a bunch of damn amateurs, and what are we?"

"We're gonna kill every last damn one of them." Smith growled as he grabbed a carbine off the wall and pulled the charging handle, letting it snap with a heavy clack. As he checked the weapon, his shoulders were stiff with tension, every movement tight and professional, his square jaw setting itself like a rock. "We're wolves in wolves clothing."

"Fangs and claws!" Stevens called as he stuffed a pair of carbine magazines into his ammo pouch.

"Hunting as a pack, baby!" Griggs fired back.

Morales grinned, not as flamboyant as his brothers in arms, though their words sunk in nonetheless, confidence pumping through their bloodstream with the weight of the weapons in their hands. Loaded up and armed to the teeth, ammo packs bulging, they stepped into the hallway with aggressive postures, Smith on point, Stevens and Griggs coming next with Morales bringing up the rear, glancing back repeatedly as they made their way toward the refrigeration units and Warehouse 3L.

Morales called up. "Who do we go for first? Break everyone out of the warehouse, or go help Sharp?"

"Warehouse first," Smith said flatly. "Then Sharp. We need numbers first and foremost."

"Roger that."

Only when they reached the main hallway leading through the warehouse sections did they slow down and move with all weapons pointed to the end of the hall. Shuffling footsteps froze them in place, the sounds coming from the right-hand passage and Warehouse 3L. Smith gave a signal, and Griggs and Stevens dropped to a knee, staggering their formation just as Chet stepped into view with five of his people. The one named Stu and a few others Morales recognized were with him, rushing from the warehouse toward the refrigeration units.

A second flashed by where three militia members glanced their way, one reaching to grab Chet's shoulder, turning him, his eyes snapping wide at the sight of the armed men spread out in front of him. A small part of Morales wanted them to surrender, even as Smith shouted for them to lay down their guns. But another part of him gripped his weapon tight, his barrel sweeping across the enemy, knowing they wouldn't give up or show the soldiers any quarter. Beads of sweat coated his temple as his finger rested on the trigger, one man dead to rights in his sights. Chet shouted something, and rifles swung upward as the militia dove left and right, splitting up, but Morales tracked his man with a flick of his barrel, already squeezing the trigger, a quick sputter of rounds punching his man from upper chest to hip. He staggered at the shots, blood spitting backward into the next passage and the others next to Morales were firing, too, sparks of light in the stark white hallways, another militiaman hitting the deck with a scream.

Rifles reached around the corner and fired back at them almost blindly, Morales crouching and ducking lower on instinct. On his left, Griggs cursed and threw himself against the wall, squeezing out the last of his rounds, chucking his spent magazine to the floor and slamming a new one home. Morales dropped to the tiles with a grunt as bullets zipped over him. Braced on his elbows, he leveraged his barrel up and shot at the heads and rifles as they peeked around to pick off the soldiers. Smith lunged to his right, grabbing Stevens, pushing him into a room, the pair returning to the opening and firing high and low along the hallway.

"Come on, Griggs!" Morales shouted, pivoting, dragging himself across the tiles on his elbows, thinking to join Smith and Stevens in the side room.

"Back the other way!" Chet yelled. "Let's gather everyone up. It's a ruse! The entire thing was a damned ruse!" The militia leader and his men on the left-hand side of the passage sprinted across, firing blindly as they went. The bullets mostly zipped harmlessly by, but Griggs cursed again, glaring as the fleeing figures disappeared, and started to give chase after them until Morales scrambled to his knees and shouted for him to wait.

"Smith, they're heading to the warehouse," Morales yelled. "Our guys are there!"

Nodding, Smith pulled Stevens out behind him, and Morales turned to check on Griggs. The soldier lifted his arm to show one grazed spot, his uniform sliced open above the elbow, blood trickling down his pale skin. On his left cheek, a bright streak of red ran from where a chip off the concrete wall had splintered off from the impact of a round.

"I'm okay," Griggs said, shoving past him toward the junction. "Let's go."

With Smith and Morales in the lead, the soldiers moved to the intersection, two of them dashing across, chased by gunshots, slamming themselves against the wall. Gasping, they swung their weapons around the corners and returned fire at the retreating militiamen. Morales took a couple of potshots down the passage, glancing back at the man he'd killed a minute prior, the body splayed in the hallway, eyes staring dead ahead.

Smith called out. "They've only got a few guys in the hall. The rest are retreating to the warehouse."

"What do we do?" Griggs asked.

"We're rushing them. On me…" The lieutenant re-gripped his weapon and checked his remaining rounds, but Morales grabbed him just as he was about to turn the corner and expose himself.

"One of us could find another passage around. Flank the bastards."

"There's no time for that," Smith snarled. "We've got to keep the pressure up. Keep them from worrying about killing our guys in the warehouse."

After a moment's pause, Morales gave him a slight nod. "All right. Let's go."

Led by Smith, the soldiers poured into the hallway, spraying the far end with focused fire where militiamen had ducked around side passages or were peeking from doorways. The enemy shot back, but their bullets flew wide, missing terribly as the soldiers' continuous firing punched at them, sending up cries of surprise and pain that filled the hallway as their foes broke cover and fled. One man sprinting away was simultaneously pummeled by Morales and someone else, his shoulders jerking forward as he tumbled head over heels and face-planted on the tiles with a wet, sickening smack of flesh and bone. The soldiers gained speed, stepping quickly, boots clopping on the floor, passing two dead men, their backs bloody and torn open from gunfire.

Smith pushed on past several warehouse doors, grabbing one handle, twisting the knob, and shoving it open, sweeping his rifle barrel inside before jerking out again. The sounds of more gunfire echoed through the passage, coming from 3L and Morales's head snapped toward the half-open doors thirty yards down. He and Smith exchanged a look, and the four sprinted the rest of the way, flanking the entrance, two on each side as more shots went off inside. Someone screamed and an image of his fellow soldiers being mercilessly mowed down by the militia flashed through Morales' mind.

Jaw locked tight as they burst into the massive warehouse chamber, Morales gazed at rows of racks and supplies stretching ahead, beyond which sat the packing area and elevators off in the left corner, the walls having several doors built in to them.

They'd walked into a battle scene, a soldier named Rupert standing behind a pile of goods on his left, rifle resting on it as he fired across the gigantic space. Automatically, Morales shifted positions, sweeping his gun back to the right, spitting two bursts of rounds at a group of militia retreating through a set of double doors. Their foes had formed a frail line of defense amongst the packaging crates and boxes, but when the new soldiers rushed in, they fled from sight and the warehouse doors settled shut as bullets punched holes through them in several spatters of focused fire. Smith turned and strode toward Rupert, the rest of their troops rising from where they'd been hidden behind the crates and stacks of goods. They were Meyers, Jennings, Johnson, Isaacs, and Richardson, none of them armed.

"Boy, is it ever great to see you guys," Jennings said, head shaking as he stood hesitantly, gaze flicking to the far side of the room.

The big kid from Nebraska, Meyers, nodded in agreement. "Yeah. We thought we were dead when we heard the gunshots out in the hall. That Shae chick was determined to take us out with them. She was about to shoot us… had us all pushed against the wall… but we rushed them, and Rupert grabbed a guard's rifle."

Morales glanced around to see a couple of the militia lying in pools of blood on the warehouse floor when Rupert staggered, dropped his gun, and began to slide to the floor against the crates, hand clasped over his shoulder with a pained grimace stretching his cheeks. Johnson and Isaacs rushed to him, easing him to the floor between the half-packaged goods while Morales circled to see the man was bleeding from the shoulder and neck, blood saturating his collar and staining the front of his coat, red over green.

Isaacs was on top of it, fingers gathering loose jacket material and pressing it on the wounds, speaking over his shoulder. "Find me some clean rags, medical kits, or something, quick! There should be an emergency station in this warehouse somewhere. Look along the walls."

All the soldiers rushed to do his bidding, but Smith grabbed Jennings by the arm and spun him around, speaking to all of them. "Jennings, help Isaacs take care of Rupert. Once he's stable, go get some weapons out of the armory on three and join us. Morales will give you directions and the keycode. Meyers, Johnson, and Richardson with us." Snatching out a pistol from its holster, he handed it over to Richardson with half his magazines. "Morales, give Myers something to shoot, and make sure Johnson has a weapon, too."

As they distributed the guns and rounds equally, Myers stared at the doors where the insurgents had disappeared, the giant charging his pistol with a clack of the slide. "Where're we headed, Lieutenant?"

Smith's eyes were a pair of hardened grey stones as he glared at his men. "We're heading down to Sub-level Five. We're going to save Sharp's ass."

Chapter 13
Tom McKnight
Central Mexico

Tom stalked the stretch of woods like a wolf, moving between the trees, hidden in the weeping boughs weighted with snow and ice, the white-dusted bushes giving him plenty of cover from the man crouched behind the APC. He crept south, where the line of foliage swept slightly westward in a move he hoped would give him a better angle on his enemy, ducking when the mercenary took a crack at him, a pair of rounds penetrating the broken branches, zipping through to ricochet off something behind him, reminding him that being hidden didn't mean he couldn't be hit.

His partner in arms, whoever it was – Samantha or Linda were the likely candidates, though he hadn't ruled out some third party living in one of the buildings – fired back at the APC, snow kicking up around the tires as the bullets tried to cut beneath the vehicle, the shooter wisely going under the armor to pick at Serge. Tom put his head low and sprinted the last few yards to the next thick tree where he crouched behind it, then peeked out. The angle on the APC was a little better, but if he wanted to flank the man, he'd have to step into the open and move west across the parking lot to one of three lumpy vehicles abandoned out there, or he could run all the way across to a small building on the opposite side.

Raising up, firing two shots that glanced off the APC's slanted front end, Tom called out with puffy breaths. "Hey, buddy! I don't have a beef with you. I just want Keith. Tell me where he is and you can get back in your truck and mosey on out of here. No hard feelings."

There was motion along the vehicle's front, and the mercenary's arms extended in Tom's direction, his rifle firing off two rounds, the bullets smacking the tree trunk and sending up chunks of wood just as Tom ducked. Another enthusiastic reply ripped from his mysterious partner's north position, a handful of rapid-fire shots pinging off the APC, one zipping by the truck's front end, causing Serge to jerk his weapon back.

"I would really like to do that, my friend," the merc shouted, "but I do not know where he is. The second APC is somewhere behind us, and my people had orders to finish Keith off."

Tom's eyebrows furrowed in confusion, staring at the tree he leaned against, his gloved hand resting on the rough bark. Edging around, he called out again. "You wanted Keith *killed*? Why?"

Serge gasped, followed by the sounds of him swapping magazines, then his voice echoed into the gray sky, the words muffled by the packs of snow surrounding them. "Keith has been pain in our ass since we started this mission. He is—how do you say in English?—a douche baggy. He failed to bring down even a little girl, and he is no longer of use to us. We are tired of chasing you, McKnight, and I only want to finish you before we collect our reward for this FUBAR mission." His frustrated sigh drifted through the windswept snow as it whipped gently around in the space between them. "We would never have taken the job if we had known you and your family would be so hard to kill." Serge chuckled ruefully. "We made fun of Keith at start, for being afraid of a family. You are crafty, McKnight. I give you that!"

"So, leave!" Tom shouted, narrowing his eyes at the shadows moving behind the APC, Serge still protected by the armor. Gaze shifting right into the frigid arctic wind, Tom searched for his mysterious benefactor. "Nobody's making you stay!"

"Unfortunately, we are all here now. You, me, and whoever your little friend is."

On cue, the rifle barrel poked from the corner of the building to the north, one gloved hand gripping the handguard, the end spitting another fat burst of rounds that picked harmlessly at the APC, a bullet flashing beneath it to bounce around and out the other side.

"Dammit!" Serge shouted. "Who's your little pet, McKnight? One of your girls, I suspect, since Keith said he'd taken care of the missus already. Is that true? Did he blow Barbara away like he claimed, or was that just another lie?"

"Barbara's fine," Tom growled, biting down on the volume of his voice, keeping it too low to hear. Despite the wellspring of anger bubbling up in his gut, he forced his temper down and looked toward the abandoned vehicles that were just lumps of white out in the street.

"That is bad fathering, to be honest, Tom McKnight. But that is how you do it in America, eh? You teach your children to be irresponsible. Where I am from, we are hard on our children. We teach them to respect their elders and to do what they're told. We teach them—"

More rounds flew in from the north position, and Tom used the distraction to abandon cover, slipping through the bushes to sprint into the street toward the shape of a sedan coated in ten inches of snow. Boots crunching on the ice layer, it was impossible to keep quiet. Still, Serge had been forced to the APC's rear where he returned fire at the person in the north, his gun's reports echoing across the stillness, causing Tom to flinch involuntarily with each shot.

Pulling up short, slipping and sliding to a halt, Tom crouched and crept along the car's side, boots crunching softer, under control, as he moved to what he assumed was the front fender. From his position, the flickering fires he'd started earlier wafted by, the greasy petroleum reek stinging his nose, forcing him to stifle a sneeze. He lifted his head to peer over the hood, gusts of wind whipping snow dust into his face, but he blinked it away with dry, sticky eyes.

While he still wasn't in a good position to pick off Serge, looked to the side, going wide when he finally spied his mysterious benefactor leaning from the corner wreckage of a partially collapsed building, the rubble providing the perfect sniper spot. Curls of brown hair stuck out from a furry hat and whipped around the figure's shoulders as she fired three more shots at the mercenary, and Tom smiled, relieved to have her help in spite of his initial insistence that she stay back.

Hand raised, waving, lifting over the car's hood, he struggled to get Sam's attention. She was crouched on one knee, ducked behind some tumbled brick and debris, the building's frame having shifted under the snow's heavy weight. Peering down her rifle sights, she shifted her shoulders, neck craning, sinking lower as she popped off another round beneath the armor, shooting at Serge's legs. Standing stiffer, Tom leaned over the hood, his glove sweeping across it to send a burst of snow dust into the air. It caught Sam's eye, and her head raised in his direction, eyes unreadable behind her goggles, but she saw him and waved, ducking and crouching as more shots flew her way.

With her focused on him, he pointed to himself and then off to the left, indicating he'd be circling to flank, then he made shooting motions and pointed to her, though he kept glancing Serge's way to keep tabs on the professional killer. Sam gave a nod that she understood just as Serge attacked her with another barrage, forcing her to duck as the surrounding building materials were ripped to pieces, brick and wood showering her hiding spot. Tom's heart leapt into his chest, fist clenched as his daughter cowered beneath the withering onslaught, but even as he watched, Samantha looked up and saw him, gesturing with her left hand, waving for him to go.

Tom crouched, hand on the car's hood, sweeping off snow as he edged to his left, one careful sidestep after another until there was nothing but open space between himself and the APC. Tom pivoted then sprinted toward the next vehicle over where it sat thirty yards away in a parking lot. Elbows flying, legs pumping, he pounded his way through the snow, keeping his eyes focused on the powdery white lump that could've been a pickup truck.

He made it halfway there before Serge started shooting at him. A round smacked the snow by his feet, vibrating through his boot heel and another zipped by in front of him, his chest tense with clipped breathing, expecting to feel the sharp pain of hot lead any second. He dove forward, staggering, feet flying out as he landed face first in the soft snow behind the pickup's tire. Rounds smacked the metal in a symphony of ricocheting sound, a couple punching through to the engine block and bouncing off the hard steel inside.

Raising to his knees in disbelief, he patted himself to check for injuries or blood, preparing for delayed pain, but he'd made it unscathed without as much as a scrape. Serge was still firing, but not at him and the distant rattle of a magazine's ejection and a new one slamming home reached him, then more shooting. Tom saw in an instant what the mercenary was doing. Knowing he was facing two enemies, one having just flanked him, Serge would try to knock one out quickly, preferably the weakest, so only a single foe remained – and Sam was the weakest.

Tom threw himself against the truck's hood, arms extended, his view of the mercenary clearer. Still, he was a good forty yards away, a tough shot along the side of the APC with just a handgun. He fired anyway, four quick shots to get the man's attention, then he ejected his magazine, replacing it with his remaining one. Serge turned and shot back at him before edging around the APC's rear end, his body poised to charge Samantha, but she returned fire, a fierce barrage that drove the merc back to Tom's side where he fired off three more rounds that struck the APC's armor, glancing harmlessly off the thick steel.

Serge's head whipped back and forth, the tension in his posture palpable as he prepared his assault. With a fast spin, he sidestepped away from the APC, firing three focused bursts, and Sam's scream of pain rocketed into the sky, locking Tom's lungs in a windless shout that never came. Before he knew what he was doing, Tom flew from behind the truck in a dead sprint toward the APC. Chin tucked low, spit flying from his mouth to freeze on his lips, he pumped his legs through the near knee-deep snow. The frosted air stung his gasping lungs, as he watched Serge standing stiffly, rifle barrel pointed at a downward angle as he picked apart Sam's hiding place. Raising his gun, Tom almost squeezed off his last few rounds, but even at twenty yards, he couldn't guarantee a hit so he continued to plow ahead.

Serge heard him coming and spun, his weapon snapping toward Tom's chest, but when he squeezed the trigger, the pin fell on an empty chamber. With expert efficiency, he ejected the empty magazine and popped in a new one, but Tom was faster, raising his pistol and firing three quick rounds that jerked the mercenary around, lead smacking off his body armor with puffs of dust and snow. Not stopping, he snatched Serge's rifle barrel, shoving it aside, the gun going off in a long burst of automatic fire, the explosive sound crushing his left ear.

He held on, jamming his pistol under Serge's chin as they spun in the snow, stumbling and staggering, tripping over each other before crashing in a heap with the mercenary landing on top.

"You won't be needing that," Serge spat as he caught Tom's wrist and bent it back with a sharp pain, the handgun flying into a snowbank.

Tom ripped his hand free, cocked it backward in a fist, and swung upward, missing completely. Serge jerked his rifle, but Tom clung to the barrel, teeth bared as he raised to snatch the man's goggles. Throwing his body weight back, he hauled the mercenary forward and off balance, their heads butting, snarling, faces just inches apart.

The men wrestled and fought in the slick, dry snow, grunting and gasping, Tom hanging onto the weapon, glove slipping down the barrel. With a bellow, Serge stripped the gun away with a final jerk, snatching it from Tom's hands, holding it high out of his reach. As Tom tried to rise, the mercenary shifted positions and slammed his knee on his right shoulder, pinning him to the ground. Swinging the rifle around with a snap, he jammed the barrel against Tom's forehead, a rictus grin stretching his lips back from his teeth, finger ready to squeeze. Tom's life flashed before his eyes, prepared for a spark of light that marked the end of everything as the sound of a distant report echoed across the wasteland.

Serge's head rocked sideways as the insides of his skull burst from his left temple in a muted explosion of flesh and bone, chunks of him showering the snow. Tom jerked his face to the side to avoid the worst of the splatter of gore, grabbing the man's slackening body and shoving it off to his right, rolling back the other way in a daze. Head on a swivel, he searched for Sam, though she wasn't standing in the road or near the APC, but he spotted movement in the building's rubble where he'd last seen her. Scrambling to his feet, kicking snow off, he got his legs beneath him and sprinted across the icy lane, picking over the debris as he ran up.

"Samantha? Sam! Sweetheart, where are you?"

A curly head of hair, a pair of shoulders, and then a teenage girl crawled out of the wreckage to stand there with a wide smile plastered above her chin. "Did you *see* that shot, dad? Did you see it?"

Tom grabbed her by her elbows, looking her over for any signs of a wound from Serge's shots, confused when he could find nothing. "Sam, you did amazing, but… are you okay? Were you hit anywhere?"

"Dad, of course not, I'm fine!"

Brow wrinkling, a disbelieving gasp punched from his lips. "But you screamed! Why did you scream?"

"Oh, that," she said with a high, delirious laugh. "I figured he'd focus on me more if he thought I was hurt." She shrugged. "That way, you could sneak up behind him. I put my acting face on. Then I took care of him for you."

Tom stared at her, blinked, and chuckled wildly as he snatched her up in another hug, holding her at arm's length again. "Way to go, kiddo. You saved me – saved us all."

"Team effort, dad. Your explosive trick worked like a charm on the other dude."

"Yeah, well, it's just a shame that it didn't take Serge out, too. That way you wouldn't have had to…" Tom glanced in the direction of Serge's mangled corpse.

"It's okay, dad. I promise I'm good."

After looking his daughter up and down and embracing her in a tight hug, Tom gave her a single nod before looking back at the APC and starting toward it, gesturing for Sam to follow. "C'mon. Let's grab Serge's weapons then check on everybody."

Striding over to the dead man, he motioned for Sam to stay back while he knelt and scooped up the rifle from the snow, unzipping the man's bloody coat and fishing through it for three more spare magazines.

"Any pistols?" Sam asked, and Tom glanced back to see she'd come up and was leaning over his shoulder.

"Yep." Tom lifted a handgun from its holster, spun it so he was holding it by the barrel, and handed it to Sam, followed by a pair of magazines. "Here you go."

She stuffed them in her coat and zipped herself back up. "Thanks."

Nodding, Tom gave Serge a final glance, the man's goggles twisted sideways on his face, bullet hole through his fur-lined hat, blood leaking down his bearded scruff-covered jaws, mingling with the frost. With a snort, Tom stood and walked past the smoking APC to where Mikael lay smoldering in the snow. Steam still rose off his body from the smoldering fires from the explosion, blood spread beneath him in a wide, slushy-red puddle. Tom shoved the man onto his back, turning his head with a frown as the fierce reek of burning flesh and hair rolled up from the melted snow. Grabbing the man's rifle, he held it up, the matte black finish covered in frozen blood like glaze on a cake and the lower received showing multiple cracks.

Expression twisted in a disgusted grimace, he threw the weapon aside, started to reach into the man's coat for another pistol, but drew back from the tattered material and flesh that had melded together in an ugly mess. "I think we'll skip this guy. That explosion did more damage than I thought it would."

He stood, sighed, looking across the still-idling APC.

"Can we take that?" Sam asked, striding over, avoiding the still smoking front end. "It'd have more room than the Humvee."

"I'll check it out," Tom nodded, handing her the rifle he took from Serge before moving around to the vehicle's rear end.

The bay door was open, lights glowing faintly from inside, a few overheads and console buttons adding their illumination. Ducking, boots settling on the steel plate, Tom crept in, looking over the backpacks and bins of supplies piled in the small cargo area and one of the six seats in the crew space.

"Anything good?" Sam was standing by the door, a rifle slung on each shoulder, one hand lifted to the roof as she peered in after him.

"Yeah, definitely some food in here."

Tom started rifling through the supplies, combining a dozen or more MREs into a half-empty bin, throwing in another first aid kit and a pair of blankets. He lifted the bin from its spot and slid it back to Sam, then he found some more guns and ammunition, making sure each family member had a weapon and enough spare ammo for a robust defense.

"So, we're not staying in the APC?" Sam asked, leaning in and looking around. "Couldn't this take us where we need to go?"

Tom was at the front, running his hand across the heater, noting there was very little warmth coming out. Looking over the consoles, he found the fuel gauge, picked up the external camera visor, and put it to his eyes, seeing the view was completely frosted over.

"Hmm. I don't know." Tom shook his head and clicked his tongue. "Looks like these guys were running low on fuel and using the cameras on this thing will be more of a pain than it's worth. It means we'd have to navigate with the viewport down, letting in the cold air. It'd probably be harsher in here than in the Humvee." Tom paused for a moment, cocking his head. "And there's something clanking in the engine that sounds worse than ours. No, I think we'll stick with old trusty. But, I *will* take whatever scraps of fuel they have left."

Tom motioned for Sam to grab the bin while he searched around the vehicle, finding a pair of half-filled fuel cans hanging on the side. With one in each hand and Sam lugging the supplies Tom had picked out, they trudged back toward their family.

Chapter 14
Tom McKnight
Central Mexico

Tom and Sam pushed through the snowdrifts back the way they'd come, fighting their way to the Humvee. By the time they got there, they were breathing hard, puffs of steam trailing out behind them before being absorbed by the frigid air. As they approached the truck where they'd hidden it in a row of trees, both Linda and Jack's faces appeared in the windows, smiling wide at them through the glass. Linda waved frantically, dimpled cheeks wrinkled from ear to ear and Tom couldn't help but return a grin, his anxiety finally starting to lessen after the intense battle. He turned and patted Sam on her good shoulder, ushering her toward the idling Humvee's rear door. After pulling it creaking open, Sam put the bin of MREs on the floorboard and crawled in with the others.

Jack leapt on her, laughing, slapping her back. "Sam! Dad! You're okay!"

Sam scooted in, cracking up, shoving off the boy with one hand while ruffling his hair with the other. Tom didn't get in but placed his hands on either side of the door frame, peering in, relishing the bit of warmth still kicking from the armored vehicle's heaters. Linda crawled into the last seat, leaning forward, fingers interlocked on the seat in front of her as she grinned at him. "We heard a ton of gunshots, and we weren't sure if you were okay."

"It was a pretty big fight," he confirmed with a weary nod.

"You got them?" Tom smiled faintly and Linda's expression blossomed with joy. "Keith, too?"

Tom was already shaking his head in anticipation of the question. "No, Keith wasn't there. But we got two of them, and one of them said the other APC got lost on the highway or something... it's a little fuzzy right now. So, maybe they broke down or something? How's your mother doing?"

"I think she's okay..." Linda glanced back, the corners of her eyes strained with worry. "Her blood pressure is stable... well, maybe just a little lower than before you left. She doesn't seem to be in serious pain, though."

Tom slammed the door and filled up the tank with what he'd taken from the APC, then he slipped back behind the wheel, adjusted the seat, and kicked the Humvee into motion. They used the single lane utility road where it circled to the surrounding buildings nestled in the snow, the Humvee's tires crunching ice, the chassis rocking gently on its springs as he found the gas station they'd passed earlier. A tall sign pointed at the sky, partially covered in a white snowdrift. Giving the armored vehicle a little gas, he pulled around to the front and parked sideways against the mini-mart's storefront, putting the vehicle into park.

"What are we going to do now, dad?" Sam asked.

"The three of you will hang inside here for a minute while I run in and try to find a map for us. I'll be right back out, okay?"

Receiving three vigorous nods in response, Tom placed his hand on the door handle, pausing as the heater's warmth blew over the dashboard to touch his face. While the heating unit had lost its full force some time ago, it felt a hundred times better than standing outside. With a short breath to steady his nerves, he popped the door and stepped out, once again blinking into the blinding winds, stinging ice striking his cheeks, tendrils of frosty air finding gaps in his clothing.

Slamming the door behind him, Tom hurried around to the store's front window and plastered his face against it to see inside. There were looted shelves, the far-right window shattered completely and he slipped over to it, raised his boot and stepped into the mini-mart, crunching on broken glass, frozen potato chip bags, and candy wrappers. A soft stillness blanketed the room, wind whistling softly through the half-empty shelves and open refrigerator doors, but the majority of the outside world was mercifully outside of earshot. With careful steps toward the front, he passed over a handful of dead bodies, one of them with a blossom of blood pooling around their head, thick and dusted with fresh snow.

The cash register had been cracked open, pesos scattered across the floor, completely useless except as kindling for fires. After a quick check for weapons behind the counter, Tom circled toward the front glass to a small automobile section with oil, funnels, and anti-freeze. He picked up a full oil jug and kept looking, snatching a few snacks and tucking them into his coat. Tom made a full round of the store, bypassing the frozen bottled waters to stop at the rack of road maps. He grabbed a regional one and then one of the entire country, opening them to make sure they were what he needed. Having gathered what he'd come in for, Tom took his things and stepped carefully outside, slipping slightly on the ice before righting himself, grinning at the kids who were watching him. Back at the truck, he got in and tossed them some bags of snacks.

Sam took her pack and held it up with a blank stare. "Great, frozen potato chips. Mom would think this is pretty nutritional." Then she broke down laughing, throwing her father a wink.

Tom laughed. "They might be frozen now, but you could probably put them next to the heaters and thaw them out."

The girls found the rear heating vents and placed the chips in front of them as Tom tossed the maps on the dashboard. Pivoting, he squeezed between the seats and climbed to the cargo section to squat next to Barbara where Sam joined him. He handed her the flashlight they'd been using before and lifted back Barbara's coverings as Sam shined the light over the wound. A quick glance showed the bandage was only slightly stained, and nothing was leaking from the edges.

"Okay, good." Tom moved his hands to her chest, fingers resting lightly on her neck, listening as she breathed steady and deep, though the ragged sounds from earlier remained. Her cheeks, while they'd gained some color, were still pale and mostly bloodless. "We need to keep your mother super warm now, okay, kids? She'll have to contend with the bullet wound and pneumonia or whatever else might come with the cold, plus losing a lot of blood. That goes for you guys, too. Let's use the hand and feet warmers, drag out the blankets, and find any gaps in the windows and seal them up with tape." He shifted his shoulders toward the front seats. "Can I count on you two for that?"

Both Linda and Jack nodded and Linda grabbed the roll of duct tape lying in the seat, held it up, and shook it. "Let's go, little bro. We're on air control."

Tom leveled his gaze at Samantha. "Are you okay staying with your mother while I drive?"

With a worried frown, Sam nodded. "I think I can do it. Linda, how long since mom's last pain injection?"

Samantha's younger sister made a thoughtful face, looking up at the truck's roof, jaw working back and forth. "I'd say she's about due. It's been fifteen or twenty minutes."

"I'll tell you what," Tom said. "Wait to see if she shows any signs of being in pain. If so, hit her with another small dose. If not, let her try to go without it. Got it?"

"Got it, Dad."

Leaving Barbara in Sam's capable hands, Tom crawled carefully over the two rows of seats to reach the front again, sitting in the driver's chair and checking the gas gauge to show they had about a quarter of a tank left. "I'm going to use the rest of the diesel. Be right back."

Leaving the warmth of the truck yet again, Tom snapped the door shut behind him to preserve the heat for the kids, then ambled toward the Humvee's rear to grab two quarter-filled cans of diesel resting in racks on the outside door. After topping off the tank, Tom put the empties back in their places and walked to the driver's side door. He paused there with the wind gusting harder, shoving him a little, gazing at the entrance ramp and expressway and across the roads and snow-covered buildings in search of the second APC.

When he didn't find it, Tom got back inside, shut the door, and rubbed his hands together to shake off the chill. When he was ready, he grabbed one of the larger maps of Mexico and unfolded it on the dashboard. His looked over the highways and towns for a moment and then glanced at the gas station window to pick up the address.

"Juan Aldama," he mumbled, locating the city on the map and tapping on the general area, noting an actual town just south of them. A slide of his gloved index finger down a highway to Mexico City brought a wince as he estimated what seemed like an impossible distance.

"Can you tell where we are, Dad?" Sam asked.

Tom looked at rearview mirror, watching Linda and Jack on either side of the truck as they put their faces up to the windows to detect any air leakages. Whenever they found one, they stripped off a piece of duct tape to cover the gaps.

"It looks like we're near Juan Aldama, and I think this is Highway 49."

"Where do we go from here?"

"South!" Jack sang as he slapped tape over a bullet hole they'd received during an earlier chase.

"That about sums it up," Tom chuckled. "I'd say we're trying to shoot for Mexico City, which is about four hundred miles from here."

"Geez, Dad," Sam sighed, throwing her arms across the back of the seat. "That's a super long way."

"Yeah, though if I'm reading this correctly, there are a lot of small towns between here and there. It's possible we'll find some people still living there, maybe even a doctor. We'll get past Juan Aldama first, just in case Keith's still after us. If we can put a snowstorm between us and him, all the better."

"Amen to that," Linda added with a slap on the Humvee's roof.

"But won't there be troops everywhere?" Sam protested. "I mean, with the annexation and all, there might still be a lot of soldiers in the cities. Could be even a few are kinda stuck like us. What if we run into them and get captured again?"

Tom put the Humvee in drive and pulled away from the gas station, taking the first turn slow until he found their old tracks and put his tires into the grooves. But when he swung south on the ramp to reenter the highway, he was on virgin snow once again, the wheels plunging through eight or ten inches of it, slipping and sliding as he punched the gas pedal and twisted the loose steering back and forth. The Humvee tore up an incline to rejoin the highway, bulling its way along at a solid forty, kicking ice and powder white off to the side, plowing through it like a boat in choppy waters. The chassis shivered, though the glass rattled a lot less thanks to Linda and Jack taping things down.

Once they were moving, he answered Sam's question. "I don't like it either, sweetie, but there's only one direction to go, and we don't have much of a choice. We have to be careful and take one thing at a time."

"Play it by ear, right, Dad?" Jack sang again, throwing one arm over the seat to pat Tom's shoulder.

"That's right, son. We'll play it by ear. And if we come across Keith and his...friends in their APC, we'll take them out just like we did the other ones."

Chapter 15
President John Zimmerman
Venezuelan Coast

John stands on the bridge of the USS Harry S. Truman, part of a second carrier strike group sitting off the Venezuelan coast, surrounded by a myriad of Navy support ships and battle cruisers, their dark profiles low and ominous in the water, a few still smoldering and smoking from the previous day's fight. A beautiful sun beats down on them, casting its brilliant light across the water, a calmness settling over the seas since early morning, the massive carrier perching on a blazing blue surface that stands still beneath them, barely rocking the ship. The pensive professionalism of the crew runs throughout the vessel, and Navy Admiral Spencer's presence on the bridge, after having already engaged and defeated the Russian forces, gives him an added layer of confidence.

Zimmerman strolls to the window rail, standing to Spencer's left, Captain Rogers on the admiral's right, all three lifting their binoculars to the activity taking place out on the ocean waters. Hundreds of landing vessels carve away from the cargo ships and carriers toward the Venezuelan shore, the surface coming to life in streaks of white foam as they race onward with their powerful engines burning hot winds behind them. Many are Beach Master landing craft mixed with sleek LCACs, vessels riding a cushion of air over the surface, racing toward shore with their massive twin propellers spitting sprays of salt water from beneath their sterns. Bows bounce over the rough waves as they plow toward the Venezuelan beach where the golden beaches bristle with steel obstructions and pits, ready for the invasion. Jungles stretch out past the gleaming sands, vivid green trees with long trunks and fronds that wave them in. Beyond those the thick, rolling forests and hills hide thousands upon thousands of Venezuelan troops and anti-tank batteries.

The first wave of LCACs are loaded with troops and tracked Caterpillars, barrier removal vehicles for clearing the sands of obstacles. The second wave haul light APCs and the third, tanks. Thousands of tons of armor head in to assault the coastline and drive any resistance back into the jungles and mountains where the real, desperate fighting will begin.

Zimmerman is certain they'll win it, though the cost will be paid heavily in blood. "Will they see what's coming and throw in the towel?"

"Hard to tell, sir," Spencer says from where his lenses search across the water, watching the tide of amphibious vehicles gathering strength, swaths of ships spreading out as far as they could see, shifting and straightening, heading for the sands. "Proud people will fight even when it makes little sense to do so. And the Venezuelans won't go down so easily."

"Perez is a sensible man," Zimmerman goes on, "and Rita knows how to negotiate. It's General Molina I worry about. That man has a fierce loyalty to his country, and it's boiling his blood that we're even here."

"He won't have much of a choice once those tracked units hit the beaches," Spencer says. "The only question will be whether they die on the beach or further inland."

"We'll have those beaches cleared in a couple of hours." General Mark Davidson comes to stand on the President's left where he watches the proceedings from another part of the ship, coordinating the ground forces.

The general joined them at the start of the beach assault, Davidson with a command desk off to the side where two colonels assist him, and a full communication suite tunes into his other officers arrayed across the various ships. "Trust me, sir. They won't stand a chance once we have boots down."

"Let's just hope we provide enough of a distraction so units can drop in and secure the oil processing facilities." The President shakes his head as numbers roll around in his brain - lists of fuel reserves, refineries, and the critical shipping lanes they need to keep the military beast fed with oil. It's their lifeblood for the foreseeable future, and if they can't control it, they might as well be in the Stone Age. Without those supplies, they are unable defend themselves at all, much less take another country by brute force.

They watch as the line of US vessels creep toward the Venezuelan coast, the President's shoulders tensing as he waits for the bombardment to fire from the forests. He expects streaks of land-to-ship missiles to soar in and punch at the incoming forces, but two squadrons of jets roar above them, white contrails in the sky, ready to scream down and unleash hellfire should the Venezuelans respond aggressively.

But no missiles come. Not a single shot is fired from the trees or low foothills, and nothing from the shore. As he turns his field glasses inland, he notices gaggles of Venezuelan troops lingering around the forest edge, though he can't tell if their postures are aggressive.

"Mr. President? Rita is on the line."

Zimmerman turns to see his head staffer, Maxine, holding up a heavy phone at the back of the bridge, nodding for him to take the call.

"I'll be right back, gentlemen," he says to his commanders, striding briskly along the center aisle to reach a hatch at the rear of the bridge. Stepping in, he slides into a chair, takes the radio from her, and leans back.

"Everything okay, Rita?"

"Yes, sir. We're all fine. President Perez and his staff are treating us well. Better than well, actually."

"I take it you have good news?"

"Great news, sir." Rita's voice reaches him from where she and her staff met with members of the Venezuelan government in Caracas after being ferried in overnight on a Venom. "The Venezuelans have accepted the deal unconditionally."

Zimmerman slumps with relief, a soft gasp escaping him before he recovers. "That's incredible news, Rita. Just in time, too. We were about forty-five minutes from taking the beach. Give me a second, will you?"

"Yes, sir."

Handing the phone back to the staffer, Zimmerman stands and leaps to the bridge where half the bridge crew is gathered in close, a few watching him from their battle stations. Admiral Spencer and Captain Rogers watch in anticipation of the forthcoming news, the ship's captain wearing a surly, skeptical look.

Zimmerman nods. "Rita got it done, folks. We're canceling Heat Strike. Move ahead with Operation Handshake immediately."

The tension in the room lifts like pressure from a clenched air brake, and sighs and gasps of relief fill the air. "Aye, sir," Spencer grins, flabby jowls trembling as the captain grabs his hand, shaking it with increasing enthusiasm. The admiral breaks off long enough to issue orders to the colonels and lieutenants, passing the word down the line. "Cease all aggressive positioning. The new mission objectives are to initiate Operation Handshake." Shouts of joy explode through the cabin, spreading around the ship, cheers ringing out as word reaches all decks.

"How long until they get there, Ben?" the President asks.

"Less than thirty minutes, sir," the admiral says. "Everyone's been briefed on what to do. They'll hit those beaches, but it will be with slung rifles, smiles, and extended hands."

"It won't go perfectly," Zimmerman frowns.

"No, but it's a hell of a better start than we'd have gotten had this gone the other way."

With a wave and a grin, he turns into the huddle room to grab the phone from the staffer. "Rita, I'm back."

"You're on speaker now, sir. I've got my entire staff in here with me."

He gestures for the man to shut the door, cutting off the outside noise before he falls into his seat, kicking back hard, one foot coming up to slam on the desk. "I want to personally thank all of you. Rita, Janice, and Craig. Everyone. Really well done, folks. I just issued the order to halt Operation Heat Shield and initiate Handshake. That means peace. It means a new start for the American people in a brand-new world. You should give yourselves a round of applause."

Cheers ring out from the other end of the line, and Zimmerman holds the phone away from his ear, grin widening, tears welling in his eyes.

"How'd you get it done, Rita?" he asks after the excitement died down. "I hear the general is a real ball buster."

Rita goes off speaker phone with a robust laugh that eases the tension in his stomach immediately. "Molina *is* a real ball buster, but he's also quite aware of our capabilities, even reduced as they are. He knows we could wipe his entire military out in a few short days."

"Did he bring up the fact that they could hold out in the mountains for weeks, months, and even years?"

"He didn't mention it. He knows all we need are the oil reserves and processing facilities. The Venezuelan citizenry could hole up in the mountains for the rest of eternity, living like cavemen, if that's what they chose. But Perez doesn't want their people bounced back to the Stone Age. He's keen on them being a part of this new age, welcoming United States citizens, technology, and resources. You should've seen the look on his face when I promised him every Venezuelan would be granted immediate US citizenship and all the benefits that come with it."

"Which isn't much these days," he sighs. "Passage on a ship, protection, maybe a ration or two. Endless American TV sitcoms playing over the government network." She laughs as he continues. "They've got more food than we do now," he goes on. "Probably more people, too."

"He realizes that, and he guarantees every American who makes it to a Venezuelan shore will be given food and shelter, and we'll have the full cooperation of their citizens. They've opened their doors wide to us, Mr. President. They know that they'll need us as much as we'll need them, and between you and me, I think they'd prefer to work with us over the Russians. Some of the stories I've heard are brutal."

Pure joy flows through his body, his heart beating lighter than it has in days. Shoulders sinking back against the chair, he releases an unapologetic sigh, long and pronounced, as he slaps the table. "We'll be landing on the beach in thirty minutes, Rita."

"With no shots fired, right, sir? It's vitally important we have no violence, despite how tense it will be."

"It won't be a perfect landing, but we'll keep it under control. We're here to make friends with the Venezuelans, not exacerbate old wounds. It might've been more appropriate to call this Operation Smile, because we're going to need all the goodwill we can get."

"I'll let you get back to it then, sir. Talk to you later."

"Yes, thanks, Rita. Your work has been invaluable here. You'll be getting a medal at the end of this."

"I'll take a little bungalow by the beach if it's all the same to you, sir," she laughs. "I might even consider retiring after this."

"No way," he grins back, heart stirring at the woman's ability to find the humor in any situation. "I'm going to need you to stay on staff for at least the next decade or more."

"We'll just have to see about that, Mr. President."

With agreeable chuckles, they sign off the call, leaving him resting back in his chair, hands stretched across his stomach, a cautious smile on his face.

* * *

Aerial drones circled above the beach as a hundred LCACs swept in from the ocean, bumping over the waves as they entered the shallows, kicking off huge gusts of winds that shot sand and water everywhere, the edges of the forest twisting and waving branches from the turbulence. Venezuelan soldiers stepped from cover with their rifles shouldered, arms up to shield themselves from the intense winds churning around them, golden grains whipping, stinging their faces as they squinted.

The heavy landing vehicles shoved onto shore, pushing sand, displacing mounds of it off to the sides in rolling brown waves. Massive diesel engines idled down the propeller RPMs to a bearable noise, settling into a low thrum that vibrated the ground like an earthquake. The heavy doors lowered, exposing tracked armored bulldozers, excavators, and trucks.

Two thousand Army soldiers and Marines stepped off, boots on the sand, striding up the beach with rifles slung, stern stares behind rows of sunglasses and helmets, stopping forty yards from the tree line where the Venezuelan forces waited. A pair of colonels gathered their lieutenants and captains in a small group, approaching the Venezuelans with hands raised, waving in a friendly fashion. From the tree line, a contingent broke free from the forest, angling in from the east to meet the Americans. Boots tracked through the sand, kicking it out as the wind from the LCACs died to a faint murmur and the two sides stopped ten yards apart. A pair of colonels recognized each other by the emblems on their uniforms, stepped forward, and extended their hands as approving murmurs ran along both sides of the line, arms relaxing off weapons, crossing over chests, or hanging loosely.

"Greetings, Colonel Prescott," the Venezuelan commander said in Spanish. "My men and I welcome you into our country with open arms, as brothers, with a common goal of achieving everlasting peace and survival of our two great nations."

The American commander gestured for his translator to step up. "Thank you, Commander Vasquez. On behalf of the President of the United States and all US Armed Forces, I want to say how much we appreciate your warm welcome." The translator rattled off the translation at a lower volume so the Venezuelan soldiers could understand. "May we join in a new era of peace and brotherhood."

The two sides stepped apart, though the officers remained facing each other, nodding, their smiles coming easier, stances more relaxed, hands clasped behind their backs. Many of the Venezuelan servicemen looked nervous as they threw glances at the massive array of armored vehicles still landing on the beach.

A young man came running up with a bucket full of sweating beer bottles that poked up from the ice. Walking the line, he handed out a beverage to everyone standing around before stepping through to the other side, turning and watching the proceedings with a grin.

"This is a local brew," Commander Vasquez said, raising the bottle high. "May this be the first of many we raise together as comrades in arms."

"Here, here!" Prescott tipped back the beer so the cool sudsy liquid flowed down his throat, leaving off with a smack of his lips as he cast his eyes along the beautiful bright grains of sand, reflecting the sunlight in a glorious sheen to brighten the day.

"Hear, hear!" The officers shouted, beers lifted in cheer, bottles tossed back, hesitant grins heralding the start of an uneasy but hopeful truce between them.

Chapter 16
Specialist Lance Morales
Santa Fe, New Mexico

With Morales and Smith on point, the soldiers followed the blood trail through the back hallways to a second stairwell separate from the main one. They slowed at the door, the specialist peering through the glass and jerking away, pausing, waiting to hear movement from the other side. Smith shouldered past him, grunting, grabbed the door and threw it open and the lieutenant peeked around the corner, slipped into the faint red light of the stairwell and threw himself against the inner concrete wall. Morales poked his head out, Smith gesturing at him and the other soldiers to follow. Morales, Stevenson, Griggs, Johnson, Richardson, and Myers all flowed in, watching the shadows for ambushes while Morales kept hunkered down, weapon pointed between the two, until Smith waved him through.

"Morales, hit that landing and secure it," he hissed. "I'll move past you and take the next one."

The specialist took a deep breath and flew down one step at a time, swinging his rifle around the corner, jerking back, then diving forward again to the next set of stairs. On the move, he descended with quick, efficient steps, his sweaty hands gripping his weapon. Landing on Sub-level Four without incident, he paused, then looked upward.

"All clear," he hissed.

The Lieutenant was already flying around the corner, barely making a sound as he shuffled quickly past him, the soldiers behind him breathless as they followed on his heels, half crouched with their rifle stocks pinned against their shoulders. Morales waited for Myers to pass before he joined the back of the line, looking nervously down through the darkness, anticipating what the militia force had planned for them in the stairwell's depths.

His assumption came true a moment later when a burst of rifle fire ripped off below, followed by Smith calling out for help. Someone shouted a commanding growl, return fire lighting up the dark stairs and casting fleeting shadows up the walls. A militiaman cursed and a door slammed shut hard, followed by objects striking the tiles on the other side, sliding against the metal surface. By the time Morales got there, the soldiers were gathered at the bottom of the stairs, Smith touching a nasty gash on his arm, glaring at the door. Slouched on the floor lay a wounded militiaman, near death, his body twisted, one leg caught beneath him as he continued to bleed. He took a final breath before falling still and Smith kicked him aside, grabbed the doorknob and tried to pull, but something was holding it on the other side. Foot against the wall, he jerked the door open an inch and jammed his rifle barrel in the gap to hold it open. Whipping out his flashlight, shining light into the gap, he laughed. "They're holding it with a rope." He ripped a long blade from its sheath, reaching through and giving a single slice.

The door fell open, bringing with it a bunch of trash and equipment the militia had piled up. Tables crashed inward, dumping equipment on them; mop buckets, bottles of pine-scented cleaner, bleach, and chairs had been piled against the door to make the passage treacherous for the soldiers to cross. Even as they started through, bullets whizzed past them, slamming the door, slicing the air with wispy sounds and smacking the wall behind them. Morales spun smoothly out of the way, as did the rest of the men, but Smith wasn't having it. As soon as the first wave of firing stopped, he and Myers plunged into the pile of trash, swinging their rifles, shooting controlled bursts down the dark corridor. Someone yelled, another cursed in a high shriek, leaving Smith chuckling dryly as he shouldered rubbish out of the way and stepped farther into the hallway, firing off bursts the entire time.

Morales glanced at the other men, shrugged, and spun into the hallway, spitting fire down the middle, taking carefully aimed shots at the shapes moving at the end of the hall. The militia were using open doors for cover where they could, but still the soldiers' rounds punched through, puncturing flesh on the other side, drawing screams and shouts. Morales stayed close to Smith as they plowed and kicked through the remaining junk and trash, pushing toward the open doors, firing sporadically as they drove the militia ahead of them. Grunting and growling, the pair swiveled apart, making deadly cuts with their weapons as the last of the enemy disappeared around the corner.

"Be careful, it's slick," Smith pointed ahead.

The floor was covered in blood, one militiaman crawling away on his left, head pressed against the wall. Remorselessly, Morales swung his rifle, flicked his carbine to single fire, and sent one round into the man's face. Turning forward again, he joined the rest of the men as they tailed the remaining militia. There was no more time for surrender, pleasantries or the giving of quarter; they were going to save Sharp and escape come hell or high water.

At the intersection, Smith angled to the left-hand corner, stopped, and listened, then he gave Morales the signal to move to the other side and wait. The specialist nodded, stepped back and sprinted across, half-turning and firing wildly as he ran, skidding to a halt when he got there. Returning to the corner, Morales peeked around and spotted fleeting glimpses of retreating shadows, but no one shot at them.

Smith was about to lead them down the left-hand corridor when the lights winked out in a click, the entire floor going dark. Red emergency lights snapped on, providing barely enough illumination for them to see almost to the end of each passage, though militia could still be lurking in the shadows. Smith side-glanced across at Morales, reaching into his pocket for a flashlight attachment, popping it beneath the barrel of his gun, flipping it on.

"We could leave them off, you know," he whispered to the lieutenant, absently affixing his own light to the end of his rifle.

Smith thought about it for a second before he shook his head. "We're going to need the lights. They'll see us coming, but they won't be able to stop us."

With that, the lieutenant took a sharp breath and spun around the corner, Morales gasped, shook his head, and dashed to catch up. The enemy fired more rounds in their direction, right through the center of the hall, causing the pair to split up and throw their shoulders against opposite walls. The rest of the soldiers came around, leading with a withering barrage of gunfire that lit up the far end of the hall in flashes of penetrating light, silencing the militia. They kept moving, Morales's training rising to the front of his brain, his reflexes firing on all cylinders, reflexes honed to a fine point. Head forward, crouching low, the specialist sought targets in the shifting darkness.

"You'd think they'd know when to quit," Smith hissed, the sweat on his brow glistening in the red emergency lights.

"They're fighting pretty desperately," Morales replied as he stepped over a dead militia man, eyes focused on the next passage. With no enemies in sight, he tossed a glance to his left. "Where you think they've gotten off to?"

"I've never seen the radio room, but they're still leaving us a nice trail of blood." The lieutenant pointed his rifle toward the floor, the bright light illuminating smears of red, thick drips of it, splatters angling around the corner to the left.

Using the same tactic as before, Morales moved across to the opposite part of the junction, though his jogging almost got him killed as a flurry of rounds, the most aggressive they'd seen yet, zipped past him, one or two nipping at the back of his fatigues as he skidded to a halt. Turning, he shot the rest of the group a wide-eyed glance, heart racing after the close encounter. Pressing his cheek to the corner and peered around, he saw – halfway down a long passage – that the militia had managed to muster up a barricade. There was a line of desks like a wall with filing cabinets and other obstacles placed behind it, a substantial barrier that might even stop their rounds from getting through. Beyond it, the radio room light blinked, showing several militia trying to break in.

Suddenly, Smith and Myers were flying across the hall to join him, chased by a hot wave of gunfire as Morales caught them and held them upright. The three huddled together in the near darkness as Morales shook his head and fixed Smith with a pressing expression. "What now? If we assault them in the hallway, no matter how we do it, we're going to get blasted to pieces. They're packed in like sardines."

As if agreeing with Morales, Chet called out from behind the barricade. "Hey Smith! I hope you're thinking about charging us. You'd be doing us a favor by dying fast."

"Or you could quit while you're behind," Smith shot back. "Leave the bunker and save your own skin!"

"Sorry, lieutenant. We can't do that. We're not giving up the bunker, and we're ready to fill you full of holes to prove it."

"He can't have a lot of people left, can he?" Smith groaned at Morales.

"They could've had more people scattered in different parts of the facility," he shrugged. "We'd never know it unless we ran into them."

Smith lifted his head and hollered. "We'll be along shortly, guys! Don't worry about it!"

"Quit talking to them," Morales nudged the lieutenant. "That's what they want. They're trying to figure out what our next step is."

"And we don't have much time," Myers said, motioning toward the passage as someone fired a pistol through the radio room door, trying to open it as Private Sharp shouted something obscene back at them. "Whatever we do, we need to do it fast, or we'll lose Sharp. And he saved our butts."

"Yeah." Smith leaned his head back and gently bumped it against the wall, willing some sort of idea to spring forth.

Morales glanced over his shoulder at where the other soldiers waited, something catching his eye as it moved in the hallway's shadows behind them. "What the… that's Jennings and Isaacs!"

The three turned to see the two soldiers from upstairs jogging along the passage, rifles slung on their shoulders, each carrying a duffel bag. Smith and Morales knelt near the corner, careful not to expose themselves to the militia, but close enough to speak to the men on the other side of the junction without being overheard if they kept their voices low.

The lieutenant grinned. "I didn't think you guys were going to make it," he hissed. "I take it Rupert's okay?"

Jennings dropped his duffel bag on the tiles, eyed the corner dubiously, and crept closer, the other men giving them room to squeeze in. "Can confirm. Rupert was fine. Just had some nicks and scratches, though the one in his neck was bleeding pretty bad. Anyway, he's patched up and hustling to get Captain Johnson."

"These bastards will be dead by then," Smith snarled, then pointed at the duffel bags lying in the passage. "What did you bring?"

Jenkins turned and pulled one duffel closer, flashing him a grin. "We went to that armory you told us about, got inside, and…" The soldier blew a low whistle. "You guys missed a lot."

"If you have something we can use to blow up a barrier seventy-five feet down that hallway, I'm in."

"I'm pretty sure we do, sir," Jennings whispered harshly, fishing around in the bag, pulling out several handheld grenades of different types, some pear-shaped, others cylinders with various markings and colors. The soldier held up a pair of the pear-shaped ones. "I'm assuming you want to use these? Blow the socks right off them. At the very least, you'll give them a hell of a shock."

Smith's eyes gleamed with a violent mirth as he stared at the two explosives, gaze shifting to the hallway as if imagining what it would sound like to throw them at the militia. He looked at the brightly colored ones, then shook his head with regret. "I'd love like hell to toss those bangers down there, but we could end up hurting Private Sharp, or at least put him in a disadvantageous situation. I think we're going to have to smoke and choke. Wait…" The lieutenant frowned, shaking off the idea just as soon as he'd said it. "Throwing smoke bombs won't do us any good if we don't have any respiratory protection."

Isaacs, a dark-haired soldier who looked more like a kid, grinned with a mischievous eagerness. Falling to his backside, he swept his duffel around and pulled the end open, then pulled out a pair of air filtration masks from its depths.

Smith met his grin with an even wider one. "Soldier, tell me you've got a half dozen or more of those."

"Yes, sir, I do. Like Jennings said, you boys missed a lot."

"Well, lob three over to us, and we'll get this party started."

The soldier nodded and began dragging the masks from his duffel, handing three to Isaacs, who was about to toss them over when Smith held up his palm. "Hold on. We want to make sure we do all this quickly and together. If they see us lobbing these masks across the hall, they'll know what's coming." He waited until the soldiers nodded that they understood.

Morales gave him a thumb's up before pressing up to the corner and peeking around at the barricade way down the hall, noting the thick piles slammed together with militia peering at them from the darkness, rifle barrels pointed their way.

"Issacs will toss us two masks," Smith went on. "As soon as we put them on, Morales will throw a pair of smoke grenades up the hall. Then Myers and I will take up positions along the wall and lay down some suppressing fire. Isaacs, Jennings, and Griggs, you follow right behind us, straight down the middle, spread out so we don't crowd the hallway. We'll be charging them hard, boys. No falling back and waiting, got it? I want to drive them off the barrier, then take it for ourselves."

The three men slated to take the middle slapped hands, gripped each other's arms, and passed around solemn nods.

"Johnson, Stevens, Richardson, and Morales will be our reserve units." His grim expression bore into them, fixating on each man with a hard look before glancing back toward the hall. "If I go down, Morales is the next ranking officer. He'll be in charge. Got that?"

A sliver of nausea crept through Morales's guts as the men nodded their understanding but he forced it down, focusing on the objective over the potential problems that might be in the way.

"Do you want the flak vest?" Isaacs asked, whispering the words across the space, pulling pieces of heavy gear from a duffel. "There were only three of them. One for you and Myers?"

"If I was standing over there right now, I'd kiss you." Smith grinned widely, then shook his head. "No. I want the first team to wear them. Isaacs, Jennings and Griggs."

The soldiers started arming up, the three assigned the flak jackets slipping them on, buckling them along the sides, standing, shifting beneath their heavier weight as they adjusted them on their shoulders. Morales grabbed all the grenades and placed them in a nest made from the duffel bags, making sure his smoke bombs were on the left and the explosive ordinance was on the right, as throwing the wrong one while his vision was impaired could get everyone killed. Once armed, Isaacs handed out the air filtration masks and they slipped them over their faces, adjusting them, the soft hiss of their breathing through the filters filling the quiet space. Another shot rang out as the militia kept pounding on the radio room door.

They're magnetic, Morales thought. You'd have a better chance shutting down the power.

"You guys ready?" Smith asked, standing with his shoulders forward, half crouched with anticipation, big Myers on the other side of him.

Isaacs held up two masks for them, standing side-by-side with Jennings and Griggs, all three nodding that they were ready to go. Their geared-up forms looked massive in the hallway, flak jackets bulky, faces covered with the air filtration masks. On Smith's signal, Isaacs tossed the other masks across the hall where the two soldiers caught them and quickly slipped them on their heads, taking rifles in hand, squatting as they prepared to engage. The lieutenant's gaze shifted to Morales, giving him a nod to go with the smoke bombs.

Tension tickling his stomach, he picked up a cylindrical canister in his right hand, twisted the tab, and pulled. On an internal count of three, he side-armed it around the corner, listening as it skittered along the tiles to slap off a table and bounce away. It had already started smoking by then, a massive cloud of purple trailing up the hallway, red emergency lights cutting through in fractals.

There were no shouts or surprised cries from the militia teams, sending a creeping feeling through him as he peeked around. The smoke was blossoming from the canister's top, shooting up to the ceiling, covering the lights before crawling down the walls. Morales turned back to his cache of smoke grenades, grabbed another one, activated it, and leaned farther into the hallway. With a much better angle, he flung it high through the air, hoping it skimmed across the ceiling to fly over the insurgents or even lodge in their barricade somewhere.

He turned back and nodded to Smith who charged ahead with Myers right behind him, the exchange of gunfire ripping off immediately. Morales leaned forward, following their progress as the pair spread to the walls and found anchor spots in front of the encroaching smoke. Isaacs, Jennings, and Griggs came next, plowing around the corner, rifles pointed straight ahead, their bodies in compact crouches as they moved on the militia. Weapons spat fire, brief flashes of light in the purple fog. At first, the five soldiers they'd sent made steady progress toward the fog, Isaacs jerking once when a round punched him in the chest, his flak jacket absorbing the blow.

Someone yelled from the militia side, and things scraped across the tile before a crash reached them. A surge of enemy fighters sprinted up the hall, mouths and nosed covered with shirts, towels tied around their faces, firing blindly ahead. Jennings jerked to the side, and Myers turned his face away from the wall as bullets punched the brick and the dark shapes were overtaken by the fog, still ten or fifteen feet from the soldiers.

"Full auto!" Smith shouted, and the soldiers' sporadic bursts morphed into wide sprays of ammunition, hurling spitfire at the rushers, forcing them to seek cover from the overwhelming suppressive fire.

Screams of pain and shrieks of agony cut Morales's eardrums, and he winced from where he observed the clashing sides. The cloud engulfed the five soldiers, smoke swirling around a bullet's path as it sped up the hall to smack Griggs square in the chest, though he shrugged off the shot and barely broke stride as he kept firing. Myers called out with a guttural grunt as the billowing clouds overtook him, followed by a screaming militiaman who slammed into him. Morales's elbows clenched to his sides, his first urge to charge up the hall to help them but Myers slung his man off, swept up his rifle, and pegged him to the floor with a brief burst, forcing Morales backward as a spray of blood flew all the way down the passage to land on the tiles in front of him.

The two sides met, rifles dropping, hand-to-hand combat taking the form of dark shapes dancing in the violet clouds. Bodies flipped in the air, landing hard on the tiles and Smith charged in to snatch a militiaman who was pummeling Isaacs. He grabbed him one-handed, slung him around, and slammed him against the wall. Stepping back, he fired point-blank into the man's chest, ripping holes through his body and coating the wall in red. The purple smoke engulfed everyone, blocking Morales's view, billowing toward him. Face turned aside, he watched his reserve team as they blinked wide-eyed behind their visors, ready for Smith's orders to charge.

The sound of running boots came next, then another flurry of rounds firing off, then Smith was shouting. "Morales! Get your people down here!"

Morales gripped his weapon and sprinted along the hall, taking the center, boots slapping on the tiles as he leapt over one dead form, then another, both of them militiamen. Shoulders tense, he made it the last fifty feet, spying the shadowy shape of the barrier stretched across the passage. The militia had shifted part of the middle out of the way to have a spot to charge through, and his comrades were kneeling or crouching behind it. He came in sliding on his knees right up to Isaacs as bullets smacked the surrounding barrier on the other side, rattling and clattering with noise and sharp, ear-splitting reports.

Isaac's shoulders were thrown against the barrier, his face gasping in pain as he gripped his arm. In the rolling, hissing smoke, Morales saw Jennings and Griggs to his right, Griggs on a knee and bending forward, left fist clenched at his side. Jennings leaned on the wall, clutching his hand to his chest, firing one-armed over the barricade at the retreating militiamen. They were back to single shots, conserving ammunition, covering themselves and holding their position.

In the blink of an eye, the soldiers ejected their magazines, grabbed fresh ones, and slammed them home, charging the weapons with sharp clacks, aiming them up the hallway, and firing again. Smith and Myers were shooting on his left, growling, grunting, swinging their rifle barrels back and forth, picking out gaps in the smoke and piled debris.

Morales leaned over Isaacs, waving his hand to clear the smoke, only to have it replaced by another velvet cloud that rolled past them, the canisters still hissing and spitting the colored smoke. "You okay, Isaacs?" Morales had to shout to be heard over the firing weapons, bullets pinging the backsides of what had become their own barrier as the militiamen fought back.

"Yeah! It's just a nick. Might want to check Myers. He took a couple good cracks."

Morales shifted toward the big Nebraskan, resting his hand on the thick arm, gasping when the man turned to him with red streaks running down his right temple to his cheek. A gash just outside his mask's rubber seal seemed manageable, but a considerable amount of blood was flowing from above his hairline and his visor had three nicks in it, the plastic striated in the upper corner. Morales tried to turn the big man around, but Myers shrugged him off.

"It's nothing that can't be taken care of later." The soldier barely winced as a handful of rounds landed on the barrier, sending shrapnel flying everywhere.

Nodding as he ducked away, Morales turned toward Smith. "Looks like we ran them off," he said. "What now?"

Morales pivoted back to the barrier, pressing his forehead against the slick metal surface. "I'll climb through and get the door open. You guys cover me"

"That's not the best idea," Smith stopped firing and gave his head a quick snap to the negative. "They've got some people down the hall there firing at us."

"What do you propose we do then?"

Backing away from the barrier, Smith assessed the blockage with a quick and critical eye, raising to look over the edge before ducking again. "There's not a ton of stuff on the other side. Just some rolling chairs, filing cabinets, mop buckets, and dead assholes. I say we put our shoulders into it and shove this whole thing about fifteen feet up the hall."

Morales blinked at Smith and then the barricade. "Geez, I don't know, lieutenant." Turning, falling onto his backside, he put his back against the barrier, setting his boots firmly on the floor, pushing it, seeing if it would budge without success. "Seems like we should lay down some cover fire, have someone climb over, and bring the private out. I'm already volunteering."

With a grimace and shake of his head, Smith raised his voice and twirled his hand in the air. "All right, boys. Let's put our shoulders into it and shove this crap down the hall so we can get Sharp out of there."

Myers gave the table in front of him an experimental punch, then grabbed the top and shook it. The men on the other side were nodding and grunting and Griggs said something about shoving it clear down the hall and up the militias' rear ends. With one eyebrow cocked at Morales, Smith placed his rifle on the floor, turned on his side and anchored his feet. Isaacs joined in, pressing his good shoulder against the barrier, fixing his boots on the tiles, the hard rubber soles catching.

"Ready, sir," Isaacs said.

"Yep. We're good here, sir," Jennings added from the other side where Johnson, Stevenson, Richardson, and Griggs joined him, testing the barrier's weight with their forearms and shoulders, twisting and shifting to get traction on the slick tile.

"All right!" Smith snapped, his voice rippling with authority. "Let's do it on a count of three."

On the count, the soldiers shoved, leveraging their strength and weight against the barrier as a single force, lifting the edge off the floor, moving the tables a quick six inches before letting them fall to the tiles again.

"Seriously, guys?" Smith growled the words, chin tucked low, eyes shivering in their sockets as sweat beads popped up on his cheeks. "You can do better! Let's get this moved and bust the private out! One more time. Let's do this!"

The soldiers shifted and changed their leverage points, Jennings turning on his hip, using one foot to get traction, pressing his head against the table with a grimace. Morales held his position, shoulders thrown low, boots planted flat on the floor, all within the bloodstains streaking the tiles. He took slow, steady breaths, glancing to his right, waiting for Smith's signal.

The countdown came again, and the men surged with grunts and groans, shoulders low against the barrier, hips and thighs straining to provide force, thrusting with everything they had. The tables lurched forward a good twelve inches, but they didn't stop and when the tables fell to the tiles, the soldiers kept shoving, feet kicking, legs extended and quivering with the effort.

The tables scraped and scratched across the floor as they thrust tables, trash and dead bodies up the hall like a snowplow. Morales dug in, back straining against the barrier, teeth bared as his left foot slipped in a puddle of blood. He quickly regained his traction when his heel dug into a groove between two upturned tiles, the edge enough to give his wet boot the bit of leverage he needed. His legs extended, body twisting straight as the soldiers shoved the barricade the last few feet to clear the door where Private Sharp had hunkered down.

"Yeah!" Morales shouted, laughing, unable to believe they moved what seemed like a couple of tons of junk along a rough hallway.

Myers was giddy, laughing and patting Smith on the back, and even Isaacs' face was trapped in a mixture of pain and joy as he slouched against the barrier, panting and exhausted. Their victory was short-lived, though, as the militia fired upon them, bullets rattling and clacking the weakened barricade, one slug punching through next to Morales's head, causing him to whip to the right and hit the floor hard. With a sneer, he swung around to his knees, threw his rifle to his shoulder, and began to fire back. With the team laying down cover fire, Stevenson crouch-walked to the door, pounding on it, shouting through the bullet holes the militia had made.

"Hey, Sharp! You in there, man? It's Stevenson and the guys."

Morales glanced over to see the private's eye peering through one hole, then his mouth pressed against it. "Hey, guys! I never thought I'd see you again. Get me out of here!"

Stevenson stepped back, checking out the keypad, looking for a way to break it open. "Can't you open it from the inside?"

"I've been punching in the passcode, but it's not working. Whatever they did to open it ended up breaking it. The electronics are totally screwed up."

"They're magnetically sealed," Morales said over his left shoulder. "Pull off the security panel and clip the power cables. That might do it."

He kept his attention forward as the smoke cleared, sucked up by the rattling ventilation, purple swirls spinning upward until he could see through to the end of the passage. Doors were thrown open, with shapes and movement behind them as enemy militia leaned out, fired toward the barricade, then disappeared again. The three soldiers did their best to pick them off, sending one hobbling away with a pained curse from the other side and a moment later, no one was shooting at them at all.

"We scared them away," Morales said, relaxing against the barrier, pulling his left hand off the rifle's handguard and flexing his fingers to get the blood flowing again.

"I think we ran them off for a bit," Smith agreed, "but that doesn't mean we're not going after them."

The security panel popped off the wall and Morales glanced over to see Stevenson pulling the damaged piece off, a tendril of smoke drifting up from the controller board. He shined his flashlight into a maze of wires, a dozen different colors staring back at him.

"I think it's these," Stevenson said, running his fingers along a pair of wires in the center of the bunch, one bright red, the other black. "I'm going to cut the black one."

Drawing a carbon blade from a sheath on his vest, he drew the tip gently against the black wire. A quick jerk, and it was snipped in two and, a second later, a pop came from around the frame and the door swung in an inch. Someone grabbed it from the other side and pulled it open a foot, revealing Private Sharp's grinning, sweaty, rosy-cheeked face staring back at them.

"Nice timing, guys. I was about to be roasted." He stepped out, hand up, expecting a high-five from Stevens, but Stevens grabbed Sharp by the front of his fatigues and jerked him into a crouch, forcing him to duck under the barricade's cover. "Ah, sorry. I was so happy to get out of there, I almost forgot there are still bad guys out there." Turning on his heel, Sharp motioned for the others to follow him. "Come on in. It's safe in here. And the cameras and radio system work."

Smith gestured for the team to go inside, saying, "Johnson, Richardson, and Stevenson, stay out here. The rest of you get the injured guys in there and check on their wounds. Myers got a real banger to the head. Do him first."

The troops shuffled in except the three left standing guard at the barricade, Morales relaxing his stance as soon as he got inside, his shoulders thrown back to shake loose the tense knot at the base of his neck. Placing his rifle on a nearby console, head bending to the left to stretch his neck, he looked over the room.

"Any first aid kits around here, Sharp?" Jennings asked, gesturing for Isaacs, Griggs, and Meyer to pull up three chairs.

"There's a first aid kit on the wall in the video room," Sharp said, pointing to a door leading to the back area.

Morales stood in front of a wide console, examining the intercom system with its array of switches and buttons, a layout of the rooms and various sections on the left, making it easy for someone to speak with anyone in the facility. Lifting his eyes, he peered through the glass partition at what appeared to be a video monitoring station with another console and three rows of screens lining the back wall.

As Jennings went for a first aid kit, Smith followed him, pointing through the video room window. "Is this where you were spying on them?"

"Yeah. That's how I tracked them." Sharp came behind the lieutenant for a few steps before turning and gesturing to the console. "But that's not all, guys—"

"So, this is where you are talking to them?" Morales motioned to the control board stretching out wide in front of him, broken into three sections with computer screens. The two side monitors were black, but the center one was on and glowing with data. Buttons and switches on the board flashed bright green or red, though some remained solid. Speakers were built into the console, as well as a microphone that curved upward.

Sharp stepped closer, nodding. "That's right. Once I got down here, I figured out the intercom system and hatched a plan to get you guys out of there." He gave a light scoff, a wistful grin tilting his lips. "Actually, I only wanted to distract them for a minute and give you fellows a chance to escape. In the nick of time, too."

"Great plan, Sharp. The distraction was all we needed to bust out of there. We appreciate it." Morales held out his hand, and Sharp grinned, color rushing to his cheeks as their palms slapped.

"And that's not even the best part," Sharp continued. "While they were figuring out what I was doing, and coming after me, I was messing around with the external communication array, trying to get an outside connection and—"

"Hey, Sharp. How do you see the other sections of the facility?" Smith was standing in the video room with the screens, scanning the warehouses and hallways the private had recently been spying on. The lieutenant leaned in, fiddling with knobs and dials, glancing up as he flipped through them, looking at various floors and storage areas and passages. "I'm just getting a lot of black screens over here."

Sharp took a deep breath and let out a frustrated sigh, hurrying to the doorway, pointing to something on the left panel. "See the sub-level floor switches there? They're labeled."

"These?"

"Yep. You can toggle through the floors with those, then use buttons here to tab between rooms. Some cameras are spotty, so you'll get black images every now and again. Okay, yeah. Switch it one more time. There you go."

Smith's grin glowed in the monitor light as he flipped through the screens, searching for the militia. "I'm going to find you bastards no matter where you try to hide."

"So, which ones did you use to get the intercom working?" Morales asked from the communication console. "I'm not touching anything. I don't want to turn something on by accident and let them hear our conversation."

Sharp rolled his eyes and strode back to the console, reaching across Morales before pivoting around him and pointing at the center screen, then gesturing to some other buttons. "These control the different sub-levels, and the rest are labeled accordingly. It'll show you what floor you're on, and I figured out it's even a touchscreen, so you can press the specific room you want. This switch here to turns everything on. That's what I did. But it's red right now, which means it's definitely off. As a matter of fact, all the rooms are off, so speak freely."

"Thanks for the tutorial." Morales crossed his arms, narrowing his eyes at the layout before glancing up through the glass partition. "Any luck in there, lieutenant?"

"Nada. I can't find them anywhere."

"We can always just follow the trail of blood again," Isaacs said, wincing as Jennings worked on cleaning the wound on his shoulder where the flak jacket didn't provide cover. Just finishing up, he turned to Griggs, bending to have a look at his chest where he'd been hit earlier.

"I'm fine," the soldier said, coughing into his fist then pounding it against his chest. "Just took a couple rounds to the old flak jacket. Knocked the wind out of me. See to Myers."

Jennings turned to Myers and loomed over his head, taking out some alcohol swabs and gently picking through his hair for the cut that had been bleeding down his face. The big Nebraskan leaned forward so the soldier had a better angle.

"We need to keep the pressure up," Smith said, slapping the desk in frustration, turning and coming back to the radio room. "We can't let them hunker down and set their defenses. They could ambush the next convoy."

"Sounds like a good plan to me." Morales shrugged, an encroaching nervousness crawling up his spine. He grabbed his rifle off the floor. "Okay, who's coming? So far, it's me, Smith, Stevenson, Jennings, Richardson, and Johnson."

"Jennings, Myers, Isaacs?" Smith asked with a raised eyebrow.

The three nodded, leaning out of their chairs, looking for their weapons.

"How about you, Sharp?" Morales grinned. "You in?"

"Of course, I'm in." With a frustrated gesture, he slipped between them, pushing them apart. "Wait, guys. I've got to tell you something."

Smith squared up to him. "All right, Sharp. Get it out, man."

"I was trying to," the private groaned, "but you wouldn't let me talk."

"We're letting you talk now." Morales flashed a grin at the lieutenant. "Go ahead."

"I've been trying to tell you guys the second convoy is topside, right now!"

Morales blinked. "What? Why didn't you say something?"

"If you guys would've shut up, I could've told you." Sharp growled, heat rising in his face. "After Chet's people figured out what I was doing and were coming for me, I panicked, hitting all the buttons on the panel's right side, trying to call out of the bunker for help. That's when I caught an incoming signal, something from outside. When I responded, they confirmed it was the new crew."

Morales grinned at Smith, excitement pulsing through his blood. "Our luck's changing fast and furiously."

"Can we talk to them?" the lieutenant asked.

"Yes." Sharp circled Morales, pointing at the radio layout on the console's right side. "It's basically just these control buttons here. I've got the channel tuned in, and they're waiting for our call."

The soldiers grinned stupidly at each other.

"I'm not sure what we should do with that information," Morales said, scratching his head. "Call them down here through another entrance? Put the squeeze on old Chet and Shae?"

"Nah," Smith said, lips pulled back from his teeth like he was holding in the greatest joke of all time. "I've got a better idea. Just put me through to the outside to clear it with the Captain, first."

* * *

The soldiers gathered around the radio console as Sharp sat in front of the microphone, leaning forward with a tense expression, face dripping with sweat. Morales bent lower, Smith on the man's other side, the pair sharing with a hopeful yet amused glance before turning their attention back to Sharp.

"Think this'll work?" Morales asked.

The question didn't phase Smith's hard-chiseled look. "Yeah, it'll work. Based on the blacked-out cameras we found, Chet and his people have to be holed-up in the rec room and barracks. That'll leave them cut off from the warehouses upstairs."

"A pretty vulnerable position, if you ask me," Morales added. Part of him squirmed for doing what they were about to do, though it was somewhat of a mercy compared to what the military up top would do, and it would be a measure of poetic justice to boot.

Smart glanced up at Smith, then Morales. "Okay, guys. I'm going to open the intercom system to the entire facility. Every warehouse and storage area will hear me."

"Do it," the lieutenant said.

The private ran his fingers down the script they'd written out, reaching up to the console and flicking a switch on the board before tapping a couple of spots on the screen in front of him. Morales watched as the lights turned solid green, showing every room lit up and ready to receive Sharp's last broadcast.

Swallowing a lump, the private took a deep breath, strained his neck and shoulders, the hinge of his jaw clenched tight as he assumed a harsh, no-nonsense attitude. The air burst from his lungs in a harsh tone, voice like thunder rumbling through the microphone. "To everyone remaining in the facility, this is Private Sharp of the Unites States Army. Sorry about that whole colonel thing before – it won't happen again."

Smith snickered softly, turning his bright eyes up at Morales who held his own stifled laughter.

"Since you so kindly retreated and allowed my team to rescue me, I'm here to explain how the rest of this operation is going to go! Since you've been so incalcitrant and murderous, we'll be pulling out of the facility and leaving the bunker to you – albeit with somewhat limited access to the facilities. Provided the heating units continue to run maintenance free, you'll have some time to assess your situation and un-bury yourselves."

* * *

Several passages from the radio room, Chet and Shea stood next to the intercom after having been roused by Sharp's thunderous introduction. They'd holed up deep in the barracks where they'd originally found the workers they'd killed, dragging them from their beds or work posts to bludgeon them and stick them in a side room on Sub-level Three. The soldiers' attack had been brutal, driving Chet and his remaining people back through the dark hallways like roaches running from stomping boots, but he'd gathered all his forces from around the facility, rallying them to the barracks rec hall, gathering even those with radios who'd been posted out of sight for days on Sub-level Four to add firepower to their last stand.

"They're… giving up the bunker to us?" Chet asked, turning to Shae.

She stared at the intercom with a haggard expression, blood still staining her cheeks from their hasty retreat. Hair hanging lank around her face, her voice haunted and slack, she grumbled, "I don't like the sound of this."

"What's not to like? They're leaving?"

"There're still a lot of supplies here." The doubt in her eyes forced a head shake. "Why would they just abandon all this?"

Chet turned and looked at the rest of his men and women standing from where they'd been sitting around the rec tables. As if in direct response to her, Sharp came across the intercom again. "You people aren't worth the fight, and we don't want to lose any more men trying to pry you out of your hole you've dug yourselves into. It's going to get pretty chilly up here over the next few months, so we plan on finding us a nice warm beach somewhere south. As per protocol, we'll be changing the security codes on all the warehouse doors and locking down the stairwells when we go. So, when I mention you have limited access, that means *extremely* limited access. Get comfortable where you are. I can't say it's been fun working with you, but I wish you folks good luck trying to get out. Oh, and Chet? Rot in hell."

Chet and Shea shared a glance, the woman's eyes going wide, genuine fear exploding across her features, sending shudders up his spine. The doors around the rec room clicked with a deadly sound, the magnetic locks sealing it tight as she leapt into action, grabbing a chair piled atop the desk and throwing it off with a clatter, turning, screaming at the remaining militia.

"Come on, you fools! They're locking us in here! Unless you want this rec room to become our coffin, we need to break out!"

* * *

"You didn't have to add that last bit." Morales grinned, then laughed as the rest of the men laughed and doubled over, slapping each other on the backs.

"That was classic," Myers said, chest hitching with chuckles as he threw his arm over Jennings's shoulders.

"They're in the rec room crapping their pants," Griggs snickered, standing, grabbing his gear from the floor.

"Yeah, that was pretty good, Sharp," Smith agreed with his chest out, hands on his hips.

"Thanks, guys." He stood from the console, grinning for a moment before he pushed past Smith to stand at the right-hand side of the console, sitting in front of the keyboard with the right-hand screen lit up. "Okay, guys, I've got everything set. Once I hit this button, we've got five minutes to get upstairs before the security codes on every door in this place switch to a new encrypted password. That'll keep Chet and his people locked out of the warehouses, armories, and stairwells. If they want to get any food, they'll have to bore through the floor to do it."

"As long as it's hard as hell for them to do it," Smith said, "it'll be worth it. And with the snowstorms coming down, they're bound to be locked in here for the rest of their considerably brief lives. No medical attention, nothing to do and no way out. Chances are they'll turn on each other before too long. Even if they could by some miracle make it outside, there won't be any vehicles left to take them anywhere. Captain Johnson and the convoy teams are aware of our plan, and they've confiscated the Humvees Chet and his people were loading. They found them tucked behind some of the tall snowdrifts near the road leading out."

Smith clapped his hands once and rubbed them together vigorously. "Everything's working out pretty damn well." He turned his attention to the others standing in the room, saying, "Okay, boys. I'll bet Chet and his people are thinking of how they can try to get at us right about now, so grab your stuff and get ready to roll."

The team picked up their duffels, armor, and weapons, and stood by the door, glancing back at Private Sharp where he hovered by the keyboard, holstering a pistol Richardson had given him. Once secured, the private looked up at Smith.

With a solemn nod, the lieutenant said, "Myself, Myers, Griggs, and Jennings in front. Johnson, Isaacs, Stephenson, Richardson, and Sharp in the center. Morales will bring up the rear."

Weapons clacked as the soldiers charged them and checked the rounds in their magazines, nodding at Smith's orders, shoulders shrugging as they prepared to move out.

"Okay, Sharp. Go ahead. Hit the button."

The private pressed the Enter key on the keyboard, and the screen lit up with red boxes, showing an alarm that the security systems had activated, a clock in the center counting down from five minutes. "Okay, guys," the soldier said with heightened elevation in his voice. "It's done. Let's go."

Morales stepped to the side to let the private pass, holding his weapon tightly in his hands, falling in line as they moved out, glancing left past the barricade before turning right to make their way back to the stairwell. Heads on swivels, staying grim and focused, rifles tensed to fire at anything that moved, the soldiers hit the stairs at a run, slamming the door shut as alarms blared out and a calm female voice intoned.

"Attention. Four minutes until lockdown."

As Morales flew up two steps at a time, he called up to Sharp, who was moving ahead of them. "Hey, Sharp. What's so funny?"

The private was panting and giggling to himself as he ambled up the stairs. "I didn't have to add the alarms or that annoying voice, either."

"An added feature?" Isaacs asked, voice dripping sarcasm.

"When I lock down a facility," he replied, "I try to scare the shit out of whoever's left inside."

Chortles and chuckles ran up the line as they raced against the clock to get outside before the entire bunker clamped shut. Boots stomped, lungs billowing with heavy exhales that reverberated through the stairwell. Not stopping at any of the sub-levels, the soldiers hit the upper shaft, alarm bells chasing them the entire way, the female voice echoing that there were two minutes left before the doors slammed shut. The warmth of the lower levels slowly dissipated into icy gusts, particles of frost blowing through the stairwell, concrete steps turning to rubber coated ones. They reached a point where it was easily below zero, steam puffing from their mouths, wind diving into loose gaps in their clothing, Morales pulling his shirt tighter around him to seal it out.

"I wish you would've brought our winter gear up with us," he murmured, though none of them had even mentioned it after being downstairs for so long.

Reaching the final landing, flying up the last flight of steps covered with frost, ice, and snow, they emerged into a freezing jet of wind that buffeted their fatigues and shoved Morales a few paces to his left. Soldiers with rifles were surrounding them, all clad in white outer coats, full winter gear, each emblazoned with an Army insignia. A soldier with captain's markings stepped from the group with a brief wave, goggles perched on his nose, fur hat pulled over his ears.

Smith walked up, smiling. "Captain Johnson! Good to see you, sir. Never thought I'd be so happy to see your mug."

"Lieutenant," the captain laughed, catching his hand. "We've almost got the entire east side of the warehousing campus loaded and are ready to head back south again." Stepping aside, he gestured to another man who walked up, dressed in standard military greens, eyes covered in goggles, tips of black hair sticking out from his hood. "This is Captain Lee from the second convoy. He and his men will be taking over for us. He would've been here to tackle loading up from the underground bunker, if we weren't about to seal it up. By the way, Smith, if I'd known you boys were in trouble down there, I would've sent help sooner. Good work handling the situation."

Smith waved him off. "We were in a tough spot, and once we got in touch with the surface things were under control. No sense in risking more lives just to pry a bunch of roaches out from inside a hole in the ground. The private did the trick, sir. He really turned a number on those bastards."

"There's plenty left in the other warehouses for us to grab," Lee said, turning to Smith and his shivering group. "Captain Johnson filled me in on what was going on down there, Lieutenant. A radical militia holing up in one of our facilities? I couldn't have written a movie script that well. Quite a predicament, and it's good you made it out with none of your men getting killed. Great work."

"Thank you, sir." With chattering teeth, Smith turned to Johnson. "Pardon my tone, sir. I've never been so glad to see snow before, but where in this frozen hell of a wasteland can we find something warm to get into?"

Morales nodded, shoulders shivering, teeth rattling in his head at the sub-zero temperatures. The snow he'd dug up around the top of the bunker with the excavator had turned as hard as stone, the massive five-foot drifts surrounding them like solid walls.

Johnson laughed, exaggerating a bow and gesture. "Right this way, Lieutenant Smith. You know who to talk to for gear assignment."

Behind them, the massive door to the underground bunker began closing, grinding on ice that had formed on the hinges since they'd first entered. The big hatch swung up and then over, slowing as it fell as the female voice chirped from below, cheery in her final pronouncement.

"Attention. FEMA Bunker One-A is now shutting down. You have zero seconds to evacuate the facility."

The massive slab of steel slammed over the hatch entrance with a final thump that sent a hollow ring up Morales's spine as heavy bolts locked with a clack, sealing the fate of those inside.

* * *

Twelve hours later, the edge of the rec room door popped open, crowbars and metal pipes squeezing out to bend the steel back wide enough for someone to slip through. One by one, they wedged themselves out, handing weapons through and guarding the hallway doused in sharp red emergency lighting. The alarms had stopped blaring, the final warning from the computer system letting them know they'd just been sealed inside.

"I don't think heating will be a major problem down here," Chet said, taking a rifle from a woman in the group. "But we need to get to those supply warehouses. Are there any on this level?"

Shae slipped through last, her face betraying her fear as she stood looking around, the surly confidence she'd once had sucked out of her. The woman who'd always been full of fire, the one always challenging him and keeping him on his toes, was cowed and... afraid. Chet motioned for a man and a woman to take point.

"You two up front, everyone to the main stairwell."

The two hustled ahead, peering into the gloom, footsteps frantic as they backtracked through the halls, pushing past the barrier they'd made earlier, the bodies of their comrades lying scattered in the wreckage or splayed on the floor, dead and already starting to smell.

Shae spat. "Can you believe they knocked us off that and took it for themselves?"

"We should have trained harder," he replied, uneasiness crawling up his spine.

"We shouldn't have charged them like that."

"What choice did we have?" Chet shrugged, instantly regretting the nonchalant gesture. "The smoke bombs were a good move on their part. We would have all died if someone hadn't sacrificed themselves to slow them down."

Shae shot him a surly look. "We should have done a lot of things differently."

"What's that supposed to mean?"

She remained quiet as she marched next to him, looking down as they followed those on point back to the main stairwell. Their boots echoed on the tiles, ventilation shafts blowing warm currents of air up the hall.

"Don't worry," he told her in a reassuring tone tinged with doubt. "We'll get to the supplies. Just like the rec room door, we'll wedge it open. We've got the tools to do that. Once we get everything open, we'll work on getting the place fixed up, then settle in for a long winter." Though he couldn't shake the sick dread filling his insides, spreading through his limbs, prickling at the base of his neck.

And as they reached the stairwell doors, the ones running point turned and glanced back with shaking heads. "It's not looking good, boss. We've got the same magnetic locks on these, but the bolts are way thicker, and there's four of them on each side, all around the inner seam. We'd need a jackhammer, a bomb, or welding torch to get out."

"Are you sure?" he asked, swallowing hard against his doubts.

The man who had spoken turned to the others. "Anyone have any tools that can cut through this?"

A couple more people stepped up, feeling around the seam, sticking knives between the door and frame, finally turning to shake their heads no. Chet shifted with his hands on his hips, a heaviness like warm, salty water settling in his gut. The fifth sub-level was mostly barracks and radio gear, the brains of the entire facility, but they couldn't eat copper cabling and wires. Aside from snacks and a few rations that might last them a week, all the real food and supplies were upstairs, above a ceiling of concrete and earth with thin shafts cutting up through it.

Turning, he looked over his people, their smudged and bloody faces, eyes surly after the drumming they'd taken from the Army boys. Words escaped him, no way to salvage a situation that was quickly getting worse. Already, his stomach grumbled with the first hints of hunger, and he sulked beneath Shae's heated glare. Some of his more aggressive people, ones who often sided with her, stepped forward, rifles cradled in their arms.

"Okay, people." His voice shook, knees weak, the weight of the bunker pressing down on his shoulders. Still, the leader inside him surged up and told him if he didn't get them up to where the food was, he'd be the first to die – maybe even Shae would attempt to do it herself. "Let's spread out and search the floor. We need some heavy-duty tools, or a way up through the ventilation shafts. If we don't, we'll die."

But the stairwells to the upper levels were bolted shut, the magnetic seams strong and impenetrable. He split his people into three groups, each dashing off to search every room for an air shaft that might lead up, yet they could only get into ten out of the thirty rooms on the sub-level. The rest were locked and the air shafts were only wide enough for a small dog to pass through them.

Gathering back in the main corridor, Chet took in the bad news. "Okay, let's look for emergency lifts or exits we might have missed—"

"It's no use," a woman said from the rear of the group, shouldering her way to the front, gaze plaintive and angry. "We've checked every possible exit and cargo elevator. All of them are sealed up tight."

Chet swallowed, heat rising to his chest. "Do we have anyone left on the upper floors? Maybe someone injured or stuck up there?"

"You radioed everyone to come down here," Shae said. "This is it. It's all we have. We can't even get to the machine rooms to make sure the water and heat remain on. If these units go out…"

She didn't need to finish her sentence for him to know how screwed they were. Standing amidst his simmering, beaten fighters, surrounded by grumbles and doubtful whispers, the heat of Shae's glare boring into him, Chet gripped his weapon and grimaced into the maw of the beast he'd created.

Chapter 17
Commander Justin Clem
Trujillo, Venezuela

Commander Clem led the troop of Marines along the ground-fixed power line that stretched deep through the jungle for miles and miles, forming a pipeline of energy, the foliage cleared away for monitoring and maintenance. They patrolled off in the brush where the cover was thick, marching parallel to the line, keeping it just in sight, avoiding the cameras and other electronic surveillance protecting it. Its source was the El Boqueron Geothermal Power Station in the middle of the most mountainous, forested land they'd ever traversed.

Captain Green came up, pressing through the rough foliage on the sloping hillside, rifle pointed downward, eyes scanning back and forth for any treacherous spots hidden beneath the grass. "You say you've got experience with this terrain before, sir?"

"That's right, captain. I trained extensively at Camp Gonsalves in northern Okinawa."

"Is this matching up to the training?"

"Not hardly," he replied, wiping sweat off his brow with a backhanded sweep. "It's… different here."

The forest was dense with thick green brush, interspersed with vivid wildflowers and boulders, with vines clinging like veins. Musky pollen assaulted his nose, softened by the scents of wet earth and tree bark while wild birds called incessantly with trilling sounds, fighting with insects for control of the audio landscape. There was the ever-present chemical smell of the repellent the Marines used to keep the bugs off them, fighting to keep away the mosquitoes carrying bacteria and viruses that could turn a man's guts to water. If not for the power line, and his infallible sense of direction, he could have easily gotten them lost in the sweeping slopes and deep spurs with their trickling creeks and rivers.

Clem continued leading as they picked their way through the dense foliage. The unit was fairly new, pieced together from a couple of different groups as the military shuffled and reshuffled resources to fit their ever-changing needs. It was their fifth mission as a unit, and though a lot of the newer men had joined after Mexico, Green had been with him from the start.

"You say you trained in Louisville?" Clem asked.

"That's right," he replied. "At the extension training facility. So many of us were signing up. Then it got too cold, and they moved us south to Ft. Worth. After that, they shipped us to the big camp in Monterrey. We were one of the first groups in Mexico. That's when I was assigned to you."

As they crossed a prominent ridge, with the pipeline even higher on the right, he guided them down the trail over moss-covered rocks, stepping over gullies trickling with water. At least one soldier tried to stifle a cry when a snake slithered through the branches above them, the rest of the team laughing but quickly sobering when he ordered them to quiet down with a single low whistle.

Down in the vale, fields lay spread out in almost perfect squares, though they were tilted and angled to fit the landscape, some sloping at ten or twenty degrees, wrapping around the forest's edge. A faint hint of smoke drifted up from a controlled fire near a ranch home with its old brick and wood construction. Closer to the bottom of the hill, a farmer plowed a slanted field with a pair of oxen, the beasts lowing and snorting as he guided them to pull the ancient equipment he was still using. On a still lower field, family members in rough-spun clothing harvested potatoes and other crops into burlap sacks, carrying them to another cart sitting between the fields.

A few months ago, Clem would've laughed at the thought of running a farm and hollering at a pair of cattle to cut rows in the dirt. "What a life," he spoke ruefully, sweat dripping off the end of his hawkish nose. "Everything that's happening out in the world, a new Ice Age and everything, and these people are hardly affected. Unless they had a radio, they wouldn't even know what's going on."

Green chuckled, his already sunbaked skin glistening with a sheen of sweat. "Ignorance is bliss, right? They see us walking up here and probably have no clue why we're here or what we're doing. Not to say they're dumb, but how would they know?"

Clem sighed in agreement. "They're the smartest people in the world right now."

"I'd miss my dentist back home, if I was out here living in the middle of nowhere."

Turning, he watched one of the new marines stride up behind Green, an ordinance specialist named Martin, the broad-shouldered man's pale, freckled skin shining bright red from sun exposure.

"What makes you think you're going to have dental care still?" Clem added a high note to his growl. "We're not in Kansas anymore, Toto."

Green chuckled as he pushed through the brush between them.

"It came out with the government announcement," Martin replied, calling up anxiously, pollen and brambles covering his legs like he'd bulled his way through a field of sticker bushes. "They say we're going to make Venezuela the fifty-first state. Can you believe that? We'll get a joint military force, a healthcare system, training people for the future and all that." He shrugged. "I guess they'll fix all the things they never could before. You know, get the new United States off on the right foot."

"I thought America was already on the right foot," Clem replied, not sharing the Marine's soft sentiments. "That's why they're adopting our rules, buddy. Believe me. They need us more than we need them." He tilted his head. "Still, I can see where having some national systems would help, especially now."

"We've got to work together more than ever," Green agreed.

"But just remember," Clem went on with dry sarcasm in his tone. "We're not here to save the world today, or secure checkups for you. Our goal is to lock down this geothermal facility while the suits assemble the statehood and make it official. So, don't be thinking about settling down with a nice Venezuelan lady yet. And don't fret over what might happen tomorrow. All that matters is this mission today. There're a lot of other units out there securing power stations, dams, and oil refineries just like us. Let's get this done."

"Right." Martin gripped his rifle tighter, moving sideways down the hill, looking serious again.

"So, what's the deal with the station?" the captain asked. "We were barely briefed."

"It's a geothermal power station that produces about two thousand megawatts for the surrounding area," Clem said with a breathless sigh as he repeated the boring parts of the briefing he'd received earlier in the morning. "It services areas including Valera, Escuque, La Mata, and several other small towns and villages. They just built it five years ago, so it's fairly new, but it's a critical piece of infrastructure in the Trujillo region, and not one we want to lose in any way, shape, or form."

"How do these geothermal power stations work?"

"I'm not an engineer, Green, but I know the gist of it. They drill down to a geothermal field, pump up the hot water, leech off the heat to make steam to turn the turbines, and send the water back underground to heat up again."

"That's pretty slick," the captain replied, impressed. "I'll bet it costs nothing to run."

"That's the point." Clem chuckled at the enthusiasm. "Geothermal energy is great if you can find the geothermal fields. But they're not everywhere."

Glancing up at the power line, he saw they'd strayed from it, and he angled the dozen Marines up the hill, thighs burning with the climb, breaths coming hard and heavy as they swatted bugs and gripped their carbines one-handed.

When they came within twenty yards of the power line, Clem pointed at a sign. "Look, just a couple more kilometers to the station. Keep your eyes open. Stay sharp," he snapped and murmurs of agreement echoed along the line. As they trudged the last distance to the station, Clem pushed them at a good clip, glancing at his watch to see they were thirty minutes ahead of time. The tropical forest was stifling, slick with wet spots and hornet hives he gave a wide berth to while blue covered the sky above them with just a hint of broad, puffy clouds.

"You think they could have air lifted us in," Martin complained.

"They wanted us to follow the power line in to check it out," Clem responded, answering the easy one. "Because that comes with the power station."

"Oh, yeah." Martin scratched his arm. "I guess it does."

"Are we expecting trouble, sir?" Green asked.

The commander shook his head. "Not specifically. Command was in touch with the facility as early as yesterday afternoon, and now they just want boots on the ground to ensure the place stays secure. At least until more permanent troops can be assigned." Clem pointed ahead. "And there it is, boys."

Big stacks emerged above the tree line, and as they worked their way forward, the plant revealed itself where it perched on the crook of a spur. Two ridge lines wove away from the facility, the one they walked leading straight up to a chain-link fence surrounding the place, topped with curls of nasty-looking razor wire. Just inside the fence, and to their right, was a separate fenced-in area holding transformers and maintenance sheds. In the back of the complex stood a single gigantic structure, venting towers billowing gray smoke from the roof while massive brown water tanks sat clustered in three groups of six. Off to the left, nestled into an even higher rising slope, was a camp and support buildings for the staff that worked on rotations to keep the isolated plant operational.

"Let's get closer to the power line," Clem gestured, "now that we've secured it. No need for stealth at this point."

With varying degrees of joy and sighs of relief, the Marines hoofed it up the last twenty yards to the cleared area and stood easy. The brush was cut down, the grass trimmed, and a concrete walkway led just beneath the big conduit with rust spots streaking down its sides. Commander Clem jumped on the path and moved toward the gate, the thrum of the place vibrating through his legs, the hum of electricity in the air.

"Think they've got a decent mess hall here?" Martin called to anyone who'd listen. "I'm starving like—"

"Shut up, Martin," Clem snapped, his voice tight as he squinted at the gate, slowing his stroll.

"What is it?" Green asked, speaking over his left shoulder.

"I figured there'd be some guards at the front gate, wouldn't you?"

"Yeah," he responded flatly.

"What's the deal, then?" When they came within thirty feet of it, he slowed, a feeling of dread growing in his stomach. "And why is the gate off its hinges?"

When he popped his rifle to his shoulder, the entire group followed suit, snapping from jocular to alert, instincts and training flipping on like a light switch. He looked across the open lot, taking in everything at once, glancing over the main building, which was a massive, fifty-thousand square foot edifice. No one was walking across the complex, entering or exiting the main building or were playing basketball on the court out by the recreation park.

"Steam's still venting," he said, staring up at the big circular towers. "So, the place is definitely operational."

Glancing up at the security cameras, not knowing if they were working or who was behind them, he reached out to grab the gate and pull it open, slipping inside with the other eleven Marines. He angled them toward the tall transformers, massive steel skeletons with wide arms bound in a spiderweb of cables that fed directly into a building that read "Transformador." From there, the main power line stretched off into the forest behind them to feed the nearby cities.

The humming was almost unbearable as they walked by the vibrating metal frames, moving quietly over concrete paths and flat stoops, creeping past buildings with signs that read "Alternador I" and "Alternador II" above the doors, sticking close to the walls, taking time to look around before progressing to the next one. The main building loomed in front of them, a massive white structure with water-stained brick, its roof tall and rounded with different sounds rumbling from inside, a high-pitched grinding like something turning fast, the drone wavering slightly in his ears.

"The turbines are in there," Clem called back, strengthening his voice to be heard over the white noise drowning him out. "Let's go!"

After a quick check around, he sprinted to the turbine hall with boots pounding behind him. Windows dotted the building's face, perfectly square and modern, and pipes ran up the sides in grooves. He threw his shoulder against the wall and crept along its front to the double doors, which stood ajar.

Leaning back, he pointed at the doors, and Green and Martin nodded their understanding. Clem slid to the opposite side while Green grasped the handle, and Martin and three other Marines stepped up with their rifles ready. The captain threw open the door, and Clem charged through first, gliding into a thirty-foot-long hallway, lights with aluminum covers hanging from the ceiling. Barrel shifting, his scanned the walls lined with cork boards and employee messages, safety procedures, warnings and sign-up sheets. Beyond the corridor lay a wide-open floor space filled with pipes and catwalks, control rooms and valves. Steam hissed at them, and the turbines screamed into their faces, and with quick sweeps of his barrel back and forth, he waved the others in, waiting for Green to step to his side.

"What you think?" the captain asked, eyes darting beneath his sweaty brow.

"Not sure what to think, except that there should be people walking around the place. It's the middle of the day, and there's not a damn soul in sight."

"It's definitely creepy," Green nodded. "What do we do? Split up?"

"I don't think so. Let's stick together and find the workers." He gestured ahead. "Take point. Start with the sections off to the left and work around the building's perimeter. I've got your back."

"On it."

The Marine stepped to the front, half crouched, rifle raised as he moved along the hall and shifted his barrel in wider sweeps as they entered the open turbine room. Clem's eyes grew wide as he glanced up a hundred and twenty-five feet to the roof, gaze drifting across the fifty thousand square-foot generator area. Huge steel catwalks ran along the walls with landings where control panels sat with tubes, ducts, conduits, and gauges surrounding them. Two hundred feet ahead, four massive turbines spun, oblong shapes made of thick metal, hugged by large steel pipes which curved around the structures. Each had their own wall of controls and valves, measuring six inches to a foot wide. Skylights filled the ceiling, letting in plenty of daylight, though it left the corners and control rooms in each corner cast in shadow. Hanging lights and bubble glass bulbs were built into the gauge boxes to illuminate the dark spaces. Everything was metal, with soft curves or sharp edges, miles of piping shaped to fit, clusters of it running above their heads in brackets, dripping, leaking steam.

"Over here." The captain still held his rifle barrel up, though he was looking at the floor, where a puddle of something glistened. Clem stepped to the side and approached, kneeling next to it, dipping his index finger, and lifting it to his face with a deepening scowl.

"Blood. We've got a situation."

"That's what I was thinking."

The commander wiped his finger off as he stood, nostrils flaring, finally muttering, "Off to the left, Green."

"Yes, sir."

The marine took an immediate left along a stretch of hallway formed from pipes and machinery. Side alleys and corridors wide enough for one person to fit branched off in every direction. Carefully searching the shadows, he listened for any sound different from the loud, obnoxious white noise groaning in his ears, unsure what to expect except that it would mean trouble in some form or fashion.

In each corner of the turbine room sat a separate control area with its own wall of gauges, valves, and switches, massive sections of piping running off and connecting to the turbines. He figured the holding tanks and boilers must be in a room below where the geothermally-heated water would be brought up from the ground into the boilers, mixed with chemicals or heated even further, then pumped to the turbines via the surrounding pipes.

As they stepped into the first control panel area, Clem motioned for the Marines to spread out and check every nook and cranny. They worked through the space with a stoic efficiency, their job made harder because there were no actual walls to use as a secure point of reference, just layers of pipes and venting and gauge panels everywhere.

"Hey, Commander. Over here."

Clem rushed to where Martin was kneeling next to a cluster of blood spots, running his finger through it, looking up. "It's fresh, sir. I'd say within the last hour or so."

"Damn," Clem murmured his acknowledgment and jerked his rifle at the corridor.

Green jumped back on point again, moving with even more careful precision, stopping, fist shooting up once for them to pause before he lowered it and continued forward.

Must be seeing ghosts, Clem thought.

But up the corridor, near the next control area, the captain suddenly threw his body to the left, hiding behind a vertical cluster of pipes, waving for the others to do the same. There came a soft shuffle of boots as the men slipped aside and melted into the scenery, leaving the passage wide open as if no one had ever been there.

Clem shuffled up, reaching the captain's shoulder, whispering. "What is it, Green?"

He stared forward for a long moment before shaking his head. "I'm not a hundred percent sure, but I think I saw some shadows moving up near the next turbine control area."

Clem edged forward, shifting around the man, peering ahead where the surrounding lights illuminated an enclosed room with the upper half partitioned in glass, a door in the center, slightly ajar with a dim bulb above it. Figures moved inside, though they were still a respectable distance away, their voices drowned out by the glass and turbine noise. Something in the shadows' movements seemed urgent, their arms working up and down, a figure stalking from one end of the room to the other, pointing at a massive control panel glowing with lights and blinking indicators.

"Go on," Clem ordered, signaling to the rest of the Marines that there was trouble ahead.

Moving from one curved section of pipes to the next, Green led them, edging closer, foot by foot, the figures growing more visible by the second. From behind a cluster of pipes that ran vertically and horizontally, Clem watched as men took form, turning into soldiers, the objects cradled in their arms becoming assault weapons, their uniforms a stout green color in two different shades and styles. A pair of what he presumed were officers growled from the control panel, gesticulating angrily, browbeating someone he couldn't see. The words were unintelligible, though he didn't think it was English or any typical South American language, either. On the other side of the glass, two soldiers flanked the cracked door, but instead of guarding the corridor, they'd half-turned and were watching the action by the panel.

Green pivoted to receive his next order, and Clem sent him forward to get a better look. Nodding, the captain bolted along a thick, foot-wide pipe before diving behind a waist-high metal power unit, pausing a moment and then peeking over, raising when the guards still didn't turn to look. His head shifted as he took in the scene, ducked, and eased back to their position by the clustered pipes.

"What do you make of it?" Clem asked.

He shook his head in confusion, then finally responded. "It looks like two groups of soldiers up there, with two different uniforms. Six in total. They've got eight power plant workers on their knees in front of the control panel. The guys yelling are officers, but they ain't from the same Army."

Half turning, Clem relayed his orders back to Martin in harsh whispers; they'd be approaching an in-flux situation, and would need to go forward with stealth in mind. Then he shifted to face Green. "All right, Marine. Move in and—"

A gunshot cracked the air, snapping sharp against the turbine's white noise. Jerking forward, Clem lifted on the balls of his feet to see inside the room, just in time to catch sight of one of the kneeling workers falling face-first into the control panel, blood coating the front, dripping from the levers and gauges. The man who'd shot him stood behind him with a pistol leveled where the man's head had been. He shifted to his right and raised his gun at the head of the next worker in line while the other officer hovered nearby, leaning in and screaming at the kneeling man.

A jolt of heat rose in Clem's chest, catching his brain on fire, hands tightening around his gun. "Go, Green!" he growled at the Marine's back, but the captain was already moving, forcing Clem to lunge after him, hissing, "Take the guard on the right!"

By then, the two guards flanking the door had turned fully and were watching the grisly proceedings with their backs to the Marines. Green shouldered the door open and stepped straight up to the first enemy soldier, his gun raising as he fired, the automatic weapon stitching the man up the side and blowing the top of his skull clean off, splattering the glass with dots of red and bone. Crouched low, Clem threw his shoulder against the swinging door, blasting it into the soldier on the other side who was just turning, the door hitting him with a thump and a shatter of glass as he fumbled for his rifle.

On one knee, at a distance of eight feet, Clem focused on a clean shot and put three single-fire rounds into the man's chest, the soldier staggering backward like he'd been shoved by a heavy hand. The commander walked forward, swinging his weapon right as the rest of his men poured inside, splitting off to either side of the door, rifles up and setting the room ablaze with spitting muzzles and sharp snaps of sound. Blood-curdling screams rang out in every conceivable pitch, gurgling voices falling to the floor. A few enemy soldiers raised their weapons and popped off a handful of shots, but were quickly mowed down by the Marines. The surprised officers whipped toward the bulk of the troops pushing through, not even noticing Clem back in the corner, hidden in a swath of shadow as he fired at will.

He took the first officer down with a single shot to the head, sending him slewing and gasping to the left, knocking aside the second officer's gun arm where it was pointed at a Marine, causing him to fire into the glass and punch a hole clean through. Someone else's bullet separated that officer's eyes with a neat, red dot and dropped him before he got another shot off.

Heavy silence settled over the room in a matter of seconds, the cloying scent of gun smoke burning through his nasal passages with every breath. Clem straightened and stepped past the trembling workers to the opposite door, looking into the next passageway. Not seeing any other soldiers, he motioned for a pair of Marines to stand guard while he moved to the downed officers, kneeling by the second one, flipping him over, noting the deep green color of his uniform, his Asian features, and the odd lettering stitched into the jacket.

"Chinese," Clem sighed, the implications growing to a fevered pitch in his mind.

"And this guy's definitely Russian," Green added, rifling through the other officer's bloodied uniform, its style different from his counterpart's, with its collar and Russian markings. "So, these guys are working together now?"

"It sure looks that way." The commander shook his head, stepping away, reaching for his radio. Before he walked out of the room, he turned to Green, gesturing at the workers who still cowered on their knees in the smoky haze, not even glancing up to see who'd saved them. "Get these guys up off their knees, and sit them somewhere that doesn't have blood."

"Yes, sir," Greene replied, standing, moving to the workers and taking one man's arm, lifting him up. "Okay, guys. Everything's okay now. Martin, tell them everything's okay." The big redheaded soldier came forward, semi-fluent Spanish slipping from his mouth, the workers turning with hesitant grins and hopeful expressions.

"Americans," a skinny man said, smiling wide, his construction helmet sitting skewed on his head.

Clem stepped out of the room, raising the radio to his lips as he stood with his hand on his hips, looking back the way they'd come. "Command, this is Marine Unit Two. We're out here at the El Boqueron Power Plant, and we've got a problem."

The radio crackled, static playing over the line before a man's tight, professional voice came back. "Go ahead Marine Two. What's the problem?"

"We just broke up a little party here. Seems some Russians wanted to blow away all the plant workers. And he had a Chinese buddy with him, too. That can't be good, right?"

After a pause, the man spoke again. "Understood, Commander. Were any of the other enemy combatants Chinese and Russian?"

"Affirmative. We only cleared a small portion of the plant, though. What you want us to do?"

An even longer pause followed, the dispatcher relaying the message to someone higher up in the chain. "Secure the rest of the facility. You are weapons free for all hostiles. It's crucial you guarantee the plant remains functional. Is that understood, Commander?"

"Yes, sir."

"Good. We're aware of the Chinese-Russian joint presence and will be sending backup ASAP."

"Great," Clem grimaced. "Orders received. Marine Two out."

Returning to the control room, he called the other Marines to him, relaying the news from central command as he waved his hand in front of his face in a vain attempt to clear out some of the gunsmoke.

"It's an awful big place, sir," Martin said. "There could be a lot more. Maybe even up at that camp."

"Count on it," he nodded. "Here's what we're going to do. Tracy and Pike head back to the front and guard the doors with an eye on that camp. You see anyone coming down the hill, radio me pronto."

"On it," Pike said, slapping Tracy on the shoulder, the pair dashing off with a purpose back through the passage they'd come through.

"Okay, the rest of you with me." Clem moved toward the second door. "Green back on point."

"What do you want me to do with these people?" Martin asked, gesturing at the huddled workers who were crouched in the corner looking at the Marines expectantly, except for a few who stared at their dead friend with tearful expressions.

"Tell them to stay here until we've cleared the place." Clem shook his head. "I know it's messy in here, but they'll have to deal with it."

Martin instructed the workers while Green jumped on point, leading them along the next passage of pipes and machinery. Stalking the halls once more, their boots shuffled fast. Clem ducked beneath a leaking valve and moved on, the turbines still spinning, the low vibrations shaking, beads of condensation breaking and streaking down pipes and gauges. Suddenly, something shifted in the plant's mechanized sound, its loud drone wavering as one turbine kicked to a higher gear, grinding on their ears, sending new vibrations through the superstructure.

"Someone's screwing with something," Green muttered, and Clem nodded in response.

"Any chance they shut the place down wrong and make it blow sky-high?"

"No clue. Let's make sure that doesn't happen."

Green picked up the pace, quick-timing it to the next control junction, but Clem caught motion out near the turbines, grabbing the captain and jerking him backward just as bullets flew between the piping gaps and impacted into the opposite side with metallic clanks.

"Cover!" Clem shouted, and the Marines threw themselves against the porous wall, ducking, poking their rifle barrels into the pipes to fire back. "Let's get some eyes on them, Green!"

The captain scurried ahead, glimpsing movement between the gaps, turning, pointing, then lifting two fingers up. Clem spotted someone approaching around the noisy turbine, a Chinese soldier sidling along, firing, trying to hit them through the crevices. Clem jammed his barrel between a valve's spokes and fired, missing, jerking his weapon free, shifting left, shooting over a conduit box. His rounds chased the soldier, finally cutting him down and sending him flailing and shrieking as he fell.

Bullets ricocheted between the piping, kicking up bright sparks, smoke, and gong-like sounds whenever shrapnel impacted upon a hollow section. Steam hissed angrily, whipping at their faces and one Marine grunted and spun to the side, rifle clattering away, and the rest of the unit swung their guns to the right where three enemy combatants were approaching in crouches, pressing the Marines with withering automatic fire. Clem's men held their ground, the staccato rips of return fire shredding the incomers, the enemy soldiers flailing and screaming as they pitched in different directions to the floor.

"Someone see to Almero!" The commander glanced at the fallen Marine as he went to Green's aid, the captain pinned down on the near corner of the next control section where the enemy had trapped him behind a triangular gauge panel sitting atop a pole with just a few thin pipes providing cover.

Sparks flew as the enemy soldiers kept him from showing even an inch of skin, the man drawing his arms and shoulders in, making himself as thin as possible. Clem approached while firing, sidestepping across the control area, feeling suddenly very alone and unprotected in the middle of the eighty square-foot space. But his aggressive attack sent the enemy ducking, giving him enough time to find protection within the seams of machinery. While his bold move had provided Green a chance to locate better cover, the two sides were at a standoff, taking random potshots with minimal effect.

Turning, Clem spotted his Marines hanging back, led by Martin, looking in his direction, waiting for an order. He pointed to the floor, then forward, then spun his finger in the air, indicating they should go around. Martin nodded, leading the Marines up the steel corridor, finding an opening into the generator room and crossing to the opposite side to get in behind the attackers. Clem and Green kept them occupied while Martin's men moved into position and a moment later pinpoint shots from up the passage rained in on the enemy, hitting them hard to send them crumpling to the floor with muted cries.

The commander waited until he saw Martin signaling the way was clear, then he turned and nodded to Green, the pair jogging up to join the other Marines in the passage. "Good work," he told Martin as he strode by. "One more control room to go, boys. Let's go secure it and see what those bastards did to the place."

Dashing ahead, Clem took point, running along the spitting pipes where scalding water leaked from their joints, at least one turbine spinning with a sickening, clattering sound, separating itself from the others' smoother rhythms. Gauges and warning lights began flashing red, and an alarm blared from somewhere above, its insistent din somehow louder than anything else, sending hot prickles of worry up his neck. Sweating, the Marine commander slowed to a jog, working his way to the next windowed control room, just like the one they'd found the officers and workers in. Not seeing anyone, Clem pushed through the door, popped on his rifle's flashlight, and cleared the corners, searching the shadows for any lurking enemy. The other Marines entered behind him, Martin carrying Almero, the wounded man holding his left hand to his side, wincing and gasping as he hobbled. The commander motioned for two men to guard the next passage which angled back toward the entrance while he turned to the flashing panel.

As wide as the wall itself, the panel consisted of flickering status symbols and fifty or more levers thrown in different on-off positions, gauges, and warning lights screaming next to them, glaring red. The already agitated pipes surrounding them sizzled even louder, the air turning hotter by several degrees, moisture beading his cheeks, dripping down his neck and back.

"You know what to make of this, sir?" Green came up, fingers digging beneath the rim of his helmet, scratching away.

"No idea," he replied, "but—"

The radio at his belt popped and crackled, a voice piping through. "Commander Clem? This is Pike and Tracy over at the front door. We've got a contingent of soldiers moving down from the worker camp. There's about thirty of them, and they don't look happy."

"Roger that," the commander growled. "We'll be right there. Hold your position at all costs. Martin?"

"Yes?" he answered, standing from where he'd just leaned the wounded Almero against the wall.

"Run back and grab some of those workers." His gaze returned worriedly to the blinking controls. "Bring them here and see if any of them can fix whatever the hell is happening. Then you and Almero hold this position. Got it?"

"On it!" Martin snapped, turning and lumbering back the way they'd come with heavy footfalls.

"Green? Take three guys out the back door. I saw the exit as we were coming down that last passage. Work your way around the east side of the building and pop in on our new friends. We'll go join Pike and Tracy by the door to anchor that spot. Got it?"

"Consider it done." The Marine said, grabbing three other men and following Martin back the way they'd come.

Clem took his remaining three and left the control room, finding an opening out to the generator floor, jogging past the sick, clattering turbine as its sound degraded into a pulsing whine that climbed upward in pitch, the vibrations itching the hairs inside his ears as they passed. The sheer noise radiating from the fifty-foot-long steel form made him wince as it threatened to shake his brain loose in his skull. Hot winds exploded from ventilation slits cut into the massive casing, almost blistering as it blew across the Marines' faces, then they were past it, sprinting around big, curved pipes that sprung from the ground and curled back downward for what seemed like no apparent reason.

In less than a minute, they found the short hallway they'd entered through previously. Tracy and Pike stood next to the wide-open doors, keeping low behind a metal cabinet they'd pulled up and turned on its back, bolstered by some steel shelving. The flimsy barricade was already hammered through with bullet holes, daylight sifting in. Sticking close to the wall, Clem's looked upward to a catwalk running beneath the first level of windows, and he gestured at the men he'd brought. "You two get up there, break out the glass, and give them something to think about."

The Marines nodded, angling through a doorway, searching for a way up while the commander kneeled behind the cabinet.

"What've we got here, Pike, Tracy?"

The Marines ducked as a barrage of gunfire hit around them, the rounds impacting the metal with heavy pings, pieces of it flying up even as they squeezed closer to the floor, wishing they could bury themselves beneath it. Clem held his face pressed to the concrete, helmet pulled low as bullets whipped just over his head, slamming the cabinet and vibrating it.

At the next pause, the three rose and returned fire, shooting across the wide-open lot where enemy soldiers had taken cover behind a ten-foot-long utility shed dead ahead and a small cluster of trees in a grassy area to their left.

Pike gasped and fell back from where he'd been shooting, clutching his chest, his green jacket blossoming in a pool of dark red, glancing down at himself before shifting to the commander. "Sorry…" His voice was breathless with pain, fingers already smeared red with blood. "One must've got me through the cabinet. I…"

"Heads up!" A Marine shouted from above them. Glass shattered and rained on their shoulders and once the downpour ended, Clem glanced up at the two men he'd put there who had already started taking shots at the enemy from the higher position, immediately cutting off the incoming fire.

Clem turned to Tracy, the soldier shooting as stoically as a robot, picking targets, teeth pressed tight and bared, not even wincing at the rounds that had been flying their way. "Get Pike out of here," he commanded. "Stop the bleeding, then get your ass back here."

Tracy wordlessly put his rifle on the floor, grabbed the Marine, and helped him away from the barrier, the two crawling toward an open doorway to disappear, leaving Clem to anchor their position. He looked upward again, seeing his men taking a withering barrage of fire, pieces of brick and parts of the window's framework shattering off and raining on his head through the catwalk. After swapping out his magazine for fresh one, he returned to shooting, focusing on the men behind the trees for a pair of shots, then shifting to the ones at the utility shed, his angle on them too poor to do much good. The rhythm of his weapon played counterpoint to the still blaring alarms, a couple speakers mounted in the yard pouring the warning notes out across the field of battle.

To his right, a handful of enemy soldiers sprinted across the open ground, Russians with their Chinese counterparts moving hard and fast toward the utility shed. Clem turned his shoulders toward them, leading the running men and popping off three quick rounds, two of them hitting their mark. One soldier pitched forward on his face, the other flailing to his knees before collapsing backward. Despite the brief delay the injuries might cause, the enemy was still about to charge his position. Ducking, he removed his remaining full magazines from his ammunition pouch and placed them on the floor beside him. He had three grenades with him as well, which he lined up next to his ammo.

A soldier up on the landing cried out, and he glanced up just in time to see the man pitch sideways, boots stomping across the steel grating, hands thrown to his face. His rifle clattered away as he fell backward, toppling from the catwalk, plunging fifteen feet to land with a sickening thud on the cabinet. Clem reached up with both hands, grabbed the wounded Marine, and jerked him with a grunt, dragging him to the floor before he could be pulverized by more incoming fire. He flipped the man over, wincing at his injured face, one eye gory with blood, something not right with the socket. He was breathing, though, gasping, his good eye staring up at the commander as he weakly grasped Clem's arm.

"Come on, Parker!" He pulled the man a few feet away from the barricade, clenching his jacket, shouting into his face. "Stay down, son. We'll have help for you in a minute!"

Clem crawled to his weapon, positioned it on the cabinet and watched in horror as twenty soldiers left the utility shed and sprinted toward him across the open ground en masse. Picking one out, he shot twice and missed, but his third shot hit home, putting the man down. Before he could line up another target, he was forced to duck again as the enemy returned fire in tandem, punching two dozen holes in the already weakened metal, a sting hitting his shoulder, something else glancing off the top of his helmet. Clem's pained grimace shifted to a suicidal leer as he gripped his rifle and prepared to die.

"We're in position!" came Green's blessed call over the radio, and the captain snatched it off his belt, put it to his lips, saying, "Perfect timing, Captain. I've got Chinese and Russians all over me! Give 'em hell!"

From off to his right, a withering barrage of rifle fire cut into the sides of the approaching men, sending four spinning, toppling to the ground with ear shattering shrieks and gurgling lungs as bullets punched through their chests. The commander rose, he and his last man pouring everything they had into the onrushing soldiers, the combined firepower mowing down half of them, sending the rest off in a hasty retreat, three more dropping before they reached the utility shed.

The heavy gunfire suddenly fell off, leaving thick drifts of gun smoke wafting across the yard, a stillness settling over them despite the still blaring sirens and turbine caterwaul. But just as soon as it died down, more guns rattled off from his right, sounding like someone firing on Green's position. Radio in hand, he spat into it. "Green, what's going on out there?"

"There're another twenty or thirty soldiers approaching from the camp. They got us pinned down over here behind a pair of sheds!"

"Can you get around them? Flank them?"

"I've got a wounded man, sir. I can try an offensive maneuver, but we're badly outnumbered. It'll be a miracle if we can keep from getting flanked ourselves."

At that moment, Tracy crawled back to him, picking up his rifle, setting it atop the cabinet, and opening up on the enemy soldiers at the cluster of trees.

"Roger that, Green," Clem said. "I've got some help here, so we'll hold them off on this end. Fall back inside the facility and guard the rear door. You understand me? Nobody gets past you!"

"Consider it done!"

"It's just us now, Tracy," the commander said, joining him in taking potshots at the Chinese and Russian soldiers.

"Fine by me, sir," the Marine added stoically, shooting off to his left, then shifting to the right as the group of enemy combatants Green had mentioned sprinted to the utility shed to add to the force there.

The pair picked off a few more enemy soldiers, switched magazines quickly, and peeked over the cabinet again. Clem imagined them lining up behind the shed, huddled in a tight group, whispering among themselves as they worked up their courage to charge the stubborn Marines. Half rolling onto his back, he looked up at the man still standing on the catwalk. The Marine remained steadfast, shoulder pressed to the chewed-up edge of brick, face dusty, blood streaking to his chin.

"Hey, Cox! They're about to hit us hard! I want a steady toss of grenades out there. You, then me, then Tracy, alternating fire in between until we've mowed all the bastards down. You got that?"

"Affirmative!" Cox shouted, and he reached inside his fatigue jacket and exposed a trio of grenades attached to hooks.

With a satisfied nod, Clem rested his rifle on the cabinet, shaking his hands loose before gripping the weapon again, sweeping it across the silent field, counting the seconds until the enemy came hard for them. Time floated in a drifting of smoke, his numbed ears picking up the turbine's slowing whine, its dangerous rattling starting to fade.

"Martin must have gotten those workers to shut down that sick machine. If we can just hold this position now..."

His words faded as enemy troops poured out from around the utility shed. The group at the cluster of trees sprinted in from the left, joining them. Rifle fire erupted from the right, hitting the barrier as the soldiers from the camp sidestepped into their view, laying down suppressing fire for their comrades who were running full bore at the last three Marines.

Shifting slightly to his right, Clem aimed into the raging, screaming faces of the charging soldiers, squeezing the trigger mechanically, moving from one to the next, dropping them, watching a handful of others being shot by Cox and Tracy from the corner of his eye.

Cox's grenade flew in, bounced off the concrete and exploded somewhere in the rear of the enemy group, the brief blast shaking the ground, small shrapnel fragments catching a trio of Chinese soldiers in the backs. The men staggered forward, though, still rushing in and with a quick twist, Clem grabbed a grenade, pulled the tab, and hurled it low so that it hit the pavement and skimmed across, bouncing off a running leg before it exploded in a muffled flash, sending one man spinning through the air, two others sinking to the ground with agonized screams. Tracy was winding up to throw his, but the enemy was upon them, a half-dozen Russian soldiers slowing and swinging up their rifles, unleashing a withering barrage of gunfire, causing the Marines to duck behind what was left of their flimsy barrier or be chewed to pieces. Tracy's grenade went off, but Clem remained low, ready to stand up and shoot at the first set of eyes to cross his field of vision.

The sudden chuffing of helicopter rotors came out of nowhere from over the thick treetops into the yard, followed by the staccato rip of at least two fifty-caliber machine guns pumping out a steady barrage of heavy rounds, lead punching the ground, slamming through flesh and bone as they sent up gurgling screams that gave him shivers of simultaneous dread and elation. Tracy rose next to him, mouth stretched wide in a bloodied grimace, helmet thrown off, shrapnel wounds bleeding on his face as his weapon rattled off. Clem gripped the cabinet's edge and drew himself up as well, watching as the Russian and Chinese soldiers who had been so certain of their victory fled in horror and were mowed down. A handful began shooting up at a pair of Huey Venoms descending on their heads in an angry buzz, the aircraft slipping slowly across the open field, gunners on each side picking careful targets, firing down, the heavy weaponry pulverizing the concrete and tearing the enemy troops to shreds.

The Russians in front of the barricade had turned and were staring upward when Tracy and Clem fired into them almost point blank, sweeping their weapons back and forth like they were scraping filth off a window. The Russians screamed, stiffened, crumpled, and spat blood, and Clem only stopped when they were all still.

At the tail end of the slaughter, Clem's radio piped up. "Attention, Marine Two, this is Captain Alexander. You still with us down there?"

He grabbed his radio where he'd dropped it on the floor next to his ammunition, shouting joyously back over the thumping of the rotors. "We're still here and kicking! Great timing, Captain!"

"No problem. You mind if we scatter these roaches?"

"Be my guest," Clem replied with a grim chuckle. "Give me the chance to get my men together, and we'll help."

"Negative on that, Marine Two. We've got three more Marine units dropping in on you in five. Command says take care of your wounded and guard the facility."

Clem was nodding, somewhat disappointed that they wouldn't get a chance to send the bastards back to hell, but grateful to catch a breather. "Roger that, Captain. Happy hunting."

As the helicopters peeled off to continue their hunt, Clem realized that the alarms had faded along with the damaged turbine, leaving him with his groaning Marines and a bad case of tinnitus. Tracy was slumped over the barrier, coughing blood into his hand and the Marine who'd taken a shot to the eye was still gasping, his good eye darting around with tears streaking from the corner, mouth forming wordless sounds.

Clem knelt beside him, resting his hand on the man's chest. "It's going to be okay, Marine. We'll get you out of here. The cavalry showed up after all. And they kicked ass." The man clasped his arm, nodding, swallowing hard, relaxing at his commander's words.

Chapter 18
Tom McKnight
San Felipe Santiago, Mexico

Tom slapped himself across his cheek. His bleary, dry eyes blinked painfully, sore from keeping them wide open and alert. The all-night drive had carried them through to morning, the snow-covered roads stuck in his vision, hallucinating movements as he glanced off to the sides at the dozens of small towns they passed. His neck and upper back ached from keeping the vehicle straight, and his lumbar region felt strained and stretched as he wiggled to get comfortable in the threadbare, cushion-less seat. Borrowing pillows and jackets from their supplies, he'd already tried a dozen different configurations, placing folded blankets behind his lower back, slipping coats beneath him for more padding on the thick cloth, taking deep breaths and rolling his shoulders to keep them loose. But the hours had rubbed him thin, every mile sucking a little more of the strength from his body and mind, forcing his head lower, his whole body drawn into a slouch by the unbearable chill leaking in by his feet.

With Jack sleeping in the seat behind him, Linda sitting up in a bundle of covers in the next, and Sam still in the back with Barbara, all he could do was snack on the food the girls had piled in the passenger seat, making sure he drank enough water, stepping out and stretching, emptying his stuffed bladder every three hours or so. There'd been no sign of the second APC, the roads behind him pitch black all night except for fleeting glimpses of far distant lights that always set off panic in his brain yet, whenever he blinked and looked again, the lights were gone.

He almost didn't notice when their bald tires weren't sliding back and forth across the road anymore and the gusts of snow-laden winds tapered off, no longer shoving the old Humvee around or blowing snowdrifts directly into Tom's view. The chill in the truck's cabin was approaching something less frigid than before, his misty breaths lingering only a second before fading.

"I think it's getting warmer," Tom commented over his shoulder, realizing the girls hadn't said anything in some time.

Linda shifted and rose from where she'd been lying back, her eyes popping open in the small circle she'd left herself to see out of. "Oh, sure. It's almost tropical in here, Dad." She replied with a sarcastic giggle.

Tom chuckled and turned back to the road. His immediate wish was for a few moments of rest before they continued on, but Sam's regular reports about Barbara were growing steadily worse. Her blood pressure was dropping a little at a time, and she'd stopped sipping water when they put it to her lips. Only his grinding teeth and blinking eyes kept him going, his tenuous grip on a last thread of hope.

"No, I mean it," Tom laughed tiredly. If he didn't laugh, he'd break down in tears. The woman he loved was dying just a few feet from him, and all he could do was drive. Keep driving. Stay on the road. Don't fall asleep.

"There's a lot less snow on the road, too. We're not getting hit with those minor storms like last night."

Linda blinked at him, turned in her seat, and pressed her face closer to the taped-up window, peering into the darkness. "You know what, Dad? I think you're right." There came a slight rustling as she freed her arm from the blankets and put her hand on the glass. "It's not freezing my fingers off anymore. It's still really cold, but definitely not as bad as before." She shifted forward. "Do you want me or Sam to drive? I know I'm not old enough yet, but I learn quick."

Tom hadn't been listening fully, as something had grabbed his attention up the road. "Are those lights I see up ahead? I think it's a small town."

Throwing off her covers, Linda came forward, resting her arms on the back of the seat, looking through the dark cabin at the distant, dim lights. Her eyes narrowed, blinked, and narrowed again. "Bingo, Dad. Spot on with that call. There are definitely lights up ahead."

Tom tugged the wheel left, the tires screeching slightly on actual concrete instead of ice, kicking up a dusting of snow as he passed two slouched figures walking on the right shoulder, shuffling along like elderly people, not bothered by the couple inches of light powder on the ground. Shoulders bundled, they turned toward the truck, smudges of faces watching as the McKnights flew by. After moving past, Tom pulled the vehicle back to the right-hand lane, glancing into his side mirrors, then at Linda.

"Those were real people, right?"

"They were definitely real."

"Good," Tom tried to shake the road shadows out of his head, glancing one more time at the very real people in the side mirror.

Linda threw her cover aside and swung her legs over the seat, partially landing on Jack and waking him up with a grunt of protest. She fell against the passenger side seat, one arm thrown over the top as she leaned in. "That's it. I'm driving. Or Sam. You look super tired, Dad. And without so much snow on the road, there's no need for you to be behind the wheel."

"Normally, you'd be right. But I think we're going to need to stop in this town and find a little help." He looked to the left and the right at the shabby buildings, old dirt roads winding off between them, a full dozen people out shuffling in the early morning dawn as it crept over the horizon. Still, the main cluster of lights was even farther ahead. "It's got to be a small town on the outskirts of Mexico City."

Linda hopped into the passenger seat and grabbed the map where it lay on the dashboard, unfolding it in a rustle of paper as she tried to find exactly where they were, alternating between glancing up and looking at the spiderwebs of highways and city dots.

"Can you make out any of the road signs? If so, match them with the map."

"The signs are hard to read," she replied, trying to catch sight of one that wasn't bent or covered in a thin layer of frost, swiveling to look at the buildings, stores and restaurants crowding the road.

"We can probably grab some more fuel in town, too." They'd scavenged several gallons of diesel overnight, siphoning them from abandoned trucks and vehicles, yet they were running low again, the indicator trembling over empty.

"I don't know, dad," she replied. "They're giving us some pretty nasty looks."

When Tom looked, he saw she was right. Residents shot them dark glances, pointed, and gestured in ways that were clear across all language barriers. Thinking twice before they got too close to town, he took a quick side road to the right that wound up a shallow hill, following the rumbling dirt track as it ran parallel to the highway. Less than a quarter mile up, he stopped and pulled over, hiding the Humvee in a gravel lane surrounded by trees.

"I'm going to get out and take a look," he said, grabbing a pair of binoculars from the center console. "Sam?"

Her curly hair popped into view, one arm raising to stretch, her cheeks drawn with worry. "I'm here."

"How's your mother?"

Sam glanced down and swallowed hard, then leaned over the seat. "She had a little water about thirty minutes ago, but that's it. And she hasn't moved much either." Sam's jaw tightened as she spoke, forcing down some of the worry that was bubbling to the surface.

"Okay, sweetheart," Tom replied, burying the spike of worry in his voice. "I'm going to get out and have a look at the town. Should be easy with the sun coming out. I'll just be a few minutes."

With a sigh he threw the door wide and stepped out, two other doors flying open as Jack and Linda joined him outside the truck.

"We're coming too, Dad!" Jack said, slamming his door shut, shrugging on his coat.

At first, Tom wanted to protest, but he couldn't think of a good reason to keep them from coming. With a shrug, he gave Jack a second glance, then spoke to Linda. "Get your brother bundled up, would you?"

"Yeah, Dad. I'm on it."

After looking both ways, Tom jogged across the road, pistol on his hip, binoculars in his gloved hands. The kids fell in behind him, reaching the opposite shoulder and running up a shallow embankment. They climbed higher into a copse of trees that clung to the side of the hill. Entering the woods, Tom pushed stiff boughs aside, holding them before they whipped backwards, pressing into a small clearing with a dusting of snow filtering through the brittle canopy.

"Look, there's a perfect spot." Tom pointed to a large stone lying flat between the cluster of brown and withered foliage, just enough room for the three of them. Groaning, he settled to his knees, pitched forward to his hands, and crawled to the edge to lie on his stomach. The slope rolled away below them, swooping a few hundred yards to the town, the lights still bright against the early morning haze. "Come on up, kids, but be careful. If you fall off, it's a good tumble down."

A moment later, Linda had crawled up on his right, Jack on his left, the kids stretching out and gaping at the view. From where they were, Tom spotted figures walking around town, even more than earlier.

Just like any other winter day in Mexico, he thought sullenly. Lifting the binoculars, he started on the left side of town where the lights were dimmest, sweeping slowly across it.

"What are you looking for?" Jack asked.

"Anything that resembles a hospital. An ambulance. A building with a big red cross on the side. Stuff like that."

"I'll help look, too."

Tom glanced to his right to see Linda also had a pair of binoculars pressed to her eyes. "Hey, where did you get those?"

"Saanvi left them in with the other gear. In one of the backpacks."

"Okay," Tom nodded. "You start on the right side of the town."

"I'm on it."

The two searched back and forth across the small town, the daylight chasing the shadows away, exposing dark recesses and revealing signs with Spanish writing. Cars started up and rolled along the streets, offering a sense of shocking normalcy to the scene that had been absent in Tom's life for longer than he cared to contemplate.

"This has to be a suburb of Mexico City for sure."

"Why do you say that?"

"I don't know." He shrugged. "It just doesn't seem like the other small towns we passed. They've got running cars, and people are out by the dozens. Those apartments there in the middle look nice. See the ones I mean?"

"You mean the ones with all the pretty colors?"

"Yeah, those. They've all got gates, too. I'm not saying it's Beverly Hills, but they must have a hospital around here somewhere."

Linda's voice held a somber tone as she glanced over. "And what if they don't? What if they don't have the hospital, or doctors, or anything else? Is Mom going to die?"

Tom shook his head once with a sharp snap. "No. Don't even think about it. They've got to have *something* around here. The question is, will they be friendly?"

"What you mean?" Jack asked.

"I mean, will they even let us in?"

The boy's face wrinkled in confusion. "Are we bad guys to them or something?"

"What would you think about someone invading *your* country? And here we are driving around a military Humvee, so there's bound to be some issues with that, too." Tom searched the area for adjoining roads, trying to get a layout of the place as he looked for emergency vehicles, police cars, or military trucks. It was still a tossup how anyone would act once they entered town.

"Is that a hospital, Dad? Over to the right, in between those tall white buildings. I see a sign on it that kinda looks like a red cross, but it's faded."

Tom angled his binoculars in that direction, picking through the various buildings, clusters of them squeezed so tightly together he couldn't see between them. "You'd think they could spread things out a little," he scoffed in frustration. When he craned his head, taking a different angle, he finally spotted part of the faded cross between the structures. "Hey, sweetheart, nice find! I think that's it. And it's on the other side of town, too, so if we can approach from the south, maybe we'll get in without too much trouble. Let's go!"

They squeezed back through the trees, crossed the road, and climbed into the Humvee. Linda and Jack took the seat directly behind him, Sam still in the back with her arms thrown over the seat.

Tom turned, addressing the group. "Linda spotted a hospital down in the southern part of town, on the outskirts. We need to get your mother there, but I'm a little worried about driving the Humvee in."

Sam gave a frustrated sigh. "You're right. I remember what it was like back in the prison town. The people that lived there didn't like us much, and it'll probably be the same thing here. Even worse if we come rolling in there with this thing in military camo…" The implication hung in the air. "I don't know, dad. Do you think this is a good idea?"

Tom leaned sideways against the seat, letting his head rest to the side, closing his eyes and taking a deep breath, giving himself a few seconds to relax. It was only when Linda reached out and touched him with a gentle shake that he came awake, realizing almost a full minute had passed.

"Are you okay?" she asked, the corners of her mouth turned downward with worry.

"Yeah. I'm fine, sweetie." He lifted a firm gaze to his oldest daughter. "I see what you're saying, Sam, but we can't carry your mother all the way down there into the back door. We're all exhausted, and I don't have a lot of gas left in the tank. Neither does the Humvee. We're going to have to give this a shot, okay? It's either this or nothing. I'm just letting you guys know, because it could get hairy down there."

Linda patted the pistol on her hip. "And we might have to use these?"

"Only as a last resort," Tom nodded. "And only if we run into people like Keith, or those mercenaries. Know what I mean? When this is all over we're going to have some hard talks about the things we've all had to do, but until then just…"

"Oh, we know," Sam replied for them both. "Trust me, the things we've done... they're all in the aid of survival, dad. I hate it. Hate all of this."

"Me too, kiddo." Tom smiled. "I'm just glad you've kept your humanity through all of this." He took a deep breath and rubbed his eyes until he saw stars, then shook his head several times. "Okay. Let's get this show on the road."

Tom put the Humvee in drive and pulled back onto pavement, moving south over the hill, sweeping down and dipping into the valley, swinging closer to the main highway they'd come in on. The town passed out of sight when they dropped too low, the trees and buildings obscuring it to some degree, but the location was locked in his mind and he angled the Humvee through the lower part of the foothills past farms, businesses, and even a corner bar with neon lights glowing in the windows. Finally, he caught a spattering of porch lights ahead through the woods, and he stuck to the straightaway until he turned onto the highway, coming up to a sign that read *Mexico-15*.

Edging closer to the wheel, a rising sense of confidence crushed his exhaustion, senses brightening with the hope they'd find Barbara the help she needed. Increasing their speed, he wove around a couple of bends, past a hotel with a long series of bungalows off to the left, hugged by tight clusters of trees. They swept past more small businesses, garages, a gas station, two food marts, and what looked like an old drive-in theater sitting far off the road. Lights glowed dim from store stoops while the wind blew scattered pieces of paper and garbage everywhere. Sniffing, wiping his nose from the cold, Tom pressed on to the edge of town, finding the hospital off to the left, easily visible from the road, a three-story structure with a grungy façade. Its parking lot was cracked and oil-stained, and a sign out front read *Centro de Salud El Jacal*. A handful of patients hobbled along the sidewalk, some standing near a side entrance where an ambulance was parked. People caught sight of the Humvee, and their expressions went dark, many turning and limping back inside, helped by caregivers. A pair of nurses pointed and bundled their coats around them, backing away in fear.

"I guess you were right, Dad," Linda whispered. "They really don't like the looks of us, do they?"

"No, they don't." Tom searched for a way into the hospital lot, the place cordoned off from the road by islands of cold-wilted trees and bushes.

A group of teens bundled up in coats stood across from the hospital, their breaths puffing out steadily, chins tucked low as they stared. Tom started to pull into the front lot when something smacked the top of the truck, smashing with a clatter of glass against the armor that made Linda yelp. Soda drained off the side as Tom took a quick left on a side lane, the dirt track rattling their suspension as he punched the gas pedal, speeding to the back. The rear parking lot was wide with multiple choices of doors into the building, and he searched for a place to hide between the vehicles, driving past several signs in Spanish he didn't understand.

"Sam, honey! You remember any of your Spanish from school?"

Sam leaned over the seat, lips twisted to the side, jerking when Tom pulled the wheel to the right to guide them across the back of the lot. "I remember a little, but I'll be pretty rusty."

"What do these say coming up?"

Face pressed to the window, Sam craned her neck to see between the smudge marks on the glass and the taped-up bullet holes. "There's one that says Visitor's Parking, and one for Emergency Only. This other one… I think it's for the doctors? You know, when the doctors have their own lot."

"Physician's Parking?"

"Yeah, that's it!"

Tom carefully turned the vehicle down the last row, looking toward the far end where a pair of vans sat parked almost side by side against a retaining wall. He pulled the Humvee into a tight, shallow curve to the right and then banked it into the spot facing the wall. Popping the truck in park, he shifted and pointed to Linda. "You're in charge. Same as before, when your sister and I were out fighting those people. Keep an eye on your mother and don't let anyone in unless we're with them. Got it?"

"Yeah, Dad," the girl said, voice somber as she switched positions with Sam, crouching next to her mother in the back.

"Are you ready to go, Sam?"

She was shrugging on her coat, nodding, pulling the hood up over her matted curls, giving Jack a quick hug before she edged closer to the door. "Okay, let's go."

Leaving the Humvee running with the heat on, Tom stepped into the cold, not bothering to put his hood up, the tips of his earlobes stinging, cheeks chafed from days in the terrible weather. Moving left, the pair bounded up a short set of stairs between the retaining wall and hospital, old pipes and ductwork running up the back of the place with water stains on the brick. They circled the corner, coming up on the side of the emergency entrance. The ambulance they'd seen driving up was parked off to their left in a spot, a pair of shady-looking EMTs standing outside the van, one smoking a cigarette, blowing a billowing waft of haze from beneath his hood.

"Can they help?" Sam asked, her feet shuffling fast to keep up.

"I don't think so," Tom replied, angling toward the emergency room doors, the glass squeaky clean as they came up and pushed inside, stepping into a small lobby.

Chairs were neatly placed along the walls, and a TV with a black screen hung in the far upper corner of the room. Families were camped out in the seats, bundled up in covers, pillows piled on the chair arms for them to rest on. An old man in a robe sat with one arm connected to an IV stand, the other wrapped around a crying girl as he nodded and whispered to her. Straight ahead, a pair of nurses helped a patient in front of the emergency room doors that opened into a hallway beyond. Two administrators worked behind desks just to the right of that, with a nurse's station wedged between them and the corridor.

Tom started to grab a nurse's attention when he stopped in his tracks, glancing at Sam, eyes blinking. "It's warm in here. Can you feel that?" It wasn't the coziest room he'd ever been in, but heat was cranking through the ducts, gusting through the lobby, grazing across his stinging cheeks and lips.

Sam held out her hands, marveling at them as if she'd just stepped into a magical wonderland. "Yeah, this is amazing. We've got to get Mom in here. The heat alone will help."

Nodding, he guided Sam to the side and walked over to the nurses, one having just helped an elderly man into the corridor beyond. The other stood by a wheelchair with a crying boy in it, his injured leg elevated, mother hovering nearby and fussing with him.

Reaching out, Tom touched one nurse's arm, and she turned, regarding him with deep brown eyes from a thin face. She was tall, and her thick black hair curled to her shoulders in a long sweep. Her name tag read Henrietta Guerrero.

"Excuse me, ma'am," he said, leaning in. "Henrietta, we need some help outside. Can you get someone to help us?"

Her dark eyes raked over Tom in a blink, widening when she saw his tousle of brown hair and fair skin, backing away, whispering, "Americana."

"Yes, we're Americans."

"Militar…" the woman gaped, one hand patting at the other nurse.

"We're Americans, but we're not here to hurt anyone. We're not soldiers."

While he attempted to keep his voice soft and sincere, his words were struck with tension. He closed his eyes and tried again, patting his jacket, expression plaintive. "Not enemies. See? I'm not wearing a uniform. We won't hurt you. This is my daughter, Sam. Samantha."

When he stood to the side, gesturing to his daughter dressed in her dirty jacket and hood, the nurse softened. With drawn lips, she pushed the boy's wheelchair through the double doors to the other attendant, then turned back to face them. The boy's mother followed the wheelchair, casting dirty looks at the Americans while the nurse was speaking in Spanish, too fast for him to understand.

"Did you catch that, Sam?"

Brushing back her hood, her green eyes searched the nurse's face before shifting to him. "I think she asked what we're doing here. Something about us being in the wrong building or camp."

With a hand on Sam's shoulder, he kept his tone calm. "Just keep asking them to help us."

Sam turned toward the woman, face up, eyes wide, eyebrows raised. "A-ayuda. Por favor!"

"Tell them your mother is injured."

Nodding, Sam kept on stuttering, forcing the words out. "M-mi madre es-esta herida."

The nurse's face stayed locked in confusion as she peered past Sam, eyes searching for someone.

"No," Sam said, waving to the woman, pointing outside and then back at herself. "Mi madre. Um... carro."

The woman's expression turned from confused to doubtful, retreating from Sam, glancing around as more patients and nurses noticed the discussion and the two dirty Americans who'd stepped into their peaceful lobby. A pair of older men wearing coveralls, their fronts stained with oil, rose from their seats, one man holding his bloody elbow, both with dark, agitated looks.

Taking Sam's upper arm, Tom turned her toward him. "Tell her she's your mother, and she's close to death. Please, Sam. Try."

"I'm trying, Dad." Tears welled in Sam's eyes as she took the nurse's hands, gently pulling her toward the door. "Mi madre... Ella está c-cerca de la m-muerte. Por Favor!"

Trusting Sam was getting the words right, Tom stayed back, searching the nurse's face as conflicted emotions crossed her features. Fear and uncertainty lingered in her eyes, caught between the smudge-faced girl and her far more dangerous looking father, neither of which spoke her language very well – or at all. The swinging doors pushed open, and a short, stocky, younger man pressed through. In his thirties with clean cut hair, a shaven face, and wide shoulders stretching his button-up shirt, he glanced from Henrietta to Sam to Tom, light hazel eyes missing nothing, his nametag reading Carlos Gonzalez.

"Henny…" he said, whispering urgently at the nurse.

The next part of his sentence went by too soft and fast for Tom to pick up. Even Sam squinted, stepping closer as he took the nurse's arm and turned her away from the McKnights. He said something else, but the nurse only shook her head, one hand raised to the doctor's chest, holding him in check while she tried to explain, gesturing to Sam and then Tom before pointing toward the door.

Carlos's body language shifted, suspicion and doubt showing, head shaking vigorously as he motioned at Tom. "Americanos... militar. No podemos tenerlos aquí!" Taking Henny's arm, the doctor started pulling her back through the swinging doors, looking toward the administrators behind the glass. Both were standing, staring at them, one with a red phone raised to her ear.

Voice tense, Tom turned to Sam. "What's he saying, Sam?"

"I think he's saying we're with the military camp," she replied, her face confused but attentive as she tried to catch the words. "Yeah, he said we're Americans and not wanted here."

Tom lifted his chin, patting his chest more vigorously, coming closer, his words came out in a pleading growl. "Yes, we're Americans. But were not military. No militar!"

Still, the two were almost through the door, Tom and Sam following them, the pair of rugged looking Hispanic men circling behind them, one of them closing in on Sam.

"Stop!" Tom snapped at the man with spittle flying from his dry lips. Then he turned back to the doctor. "Look, I know we seem crazy, and we are Americans, but my wife was wounded by the American military. Shot by my people! Please! They've been chasing us. Sam, tell them we're being chased by our own people."

Nodding, tears streaking her cheeks, Sam swatted at the guy behind her when he tried to take her arm, staying focused on the doctor. "N-nosotras estamos s-siendo per-per-perseguidas."

"Carlos, por favor!" Tom added on top of her pleading. Hands up, chills of frustration and anger racing up his spine, he wouldn't quit. "Save my wife, please. Don't leave my kids without a mother. Don't leave me..." His words faded, buried beneath the confusion. Slumped over, tears wet on his face, he looked down to the tiles, then back to Sam, grabbing her, pulling her behind him.

A moment later, a firm hand took Tom by the forearm. Head jerking up, he came face-to-face with the young doctor, gesturing toward the exit doors, his heartfelt expression and soft eyes calming the situation. "Muéstrame. Muéstrame."

Tom's beleaguered eyes turned to Sam. "Muéstrame. What does that mean?"

Sam was already reaching for the doctor's hand with both of hers, drawing him toward the doors, saying to her father, "He wants us to show him. He wants to see Mom."

"Yes! Si!" Tom exclaimed, stepping in behind them, nodding vigorously at Nurse Henny while firing dark looks at the two rugged men as they slowly backed off.

The group stepped through the hospital's emergency doors and turned left, striding to the building's rear, moving past the retaining wall with its wilted shrubbery, descending the small flight of stairs where Tom walked in front of them, motioning them toward the idling Humvee. Both physician and nurse saw the armored vehicle and drew back, eyes wide as their coats whipped in the freezing winds. But Sam held onto the doctor, gripping his one hand, tugging him toward the waiting truck.

"Ella está cerca de la muerte," she begged him, leaning backwards and using her leverage to get the man to take two steps. "Por Favor!

"Please. My kids are inside there. No militar! Kids. See!"

They made it far enough to see Linda and Jack's wide eyes staring back at them through the smudged glass, the boy waving faintly as the group approached, Smooch panting next to him, head tilted questioningly. Seeing the two children and animal in the vehicle, the doctor murmured something to the nurse, and the pair rushed forward in a flurry of motion, coattails whipping in the wind behind them.

Carlos tugged at the door handle, jerking it open, stepping back with a gasp. Linda was kneeling in the cargo area, her shoulders thrown against the seat, expression fearful. Barbara lay stretched diagonally across the floor, pale-faced and gaunt, her breathing more shallow and ragged than before, a bundle of coats and pads supporting her weight and more were heaped over her. Bloody rags were piled in one corner, first aid kits spread on the rubber matting by the door. Both doctor and nurse retreated, their shock wearing off, murmuring to each other, looking back at Tom in accusation.

"No. You don't understand." Tom circled them, standing next to Barbara, letting his left hand rest on her chest. Despite the tears streaming down his cheek, gut sinking with frustration and doubt, he kept his voice steady through sheer force of will. "We broke out of a military camp and were being chased by soldiers. They're the ones who did this. The *soldiers* shot her." He mimicked a rifle firing.

"No militar!" Sam added, one hand on the nurse, the other on the doctor, gently pushing them closer to the truck, her Spanish falling to English once more. "Please, you've got to help her, sir. Please!"

Tom rested his hands on the blankets covering Barbara's wounded side, lifting them back to show the part of her chest below her left ribs. "They shot her here, and I removed the bullet, but she's slipping fast. Her blood pressure…" With pumping motions of his fist, he tried to get them to understand, then shook his head again, spinning in frustration.

Carlos stared at the wound as he reached to clasp Sam's shoulder, gently pushing her away, turning back to Barbara and her shallow breathing, the steam rising off her bare skin, her beauty still showing beneath her rough, gaunt features. His traced the IV hanging tenuously by its hook, the line running to her arm and he leaned forward, reading the words on the side of the bag. As Tom stepped away, the doctor relented, gesturing to Henny, saying something in Spanish she didn't understand.

The nurse suddenly dove in, uncovering Barbara's right arm, her hand slipping to the woman's wrist, fingers checking her pulse as her left hand rested on her temple, thumb brushing across her cheek. She murmured something to Carlos, who slipped in on the other side, hands pressing around the wound, lifting one corner of the bandage, remarking again to Henny. With a tight, professional expression, he turned to Tom and nodded, gesturing for him to step in and help. Together, he and Carlos lifted Barbara from the vehicle, still draped in blankets, Tom with his fingers digging beneath her armpits, the doctor at her feet. She weighed next to nothing, her head pressed against his stomach as they carried her toward the steps.

Sam and the nurse ran ahead while Tom called back, "Linda! Jack! Lock up the truck and weapons. Then get in here with Smooch. Got that?"

"I'm on it, dad!" Linda was already rounding up the boy and dog.

As they carried Barbara up the stairs, Tom nodded to the doctor, who was walking backwards, hands grasping her ankles. "Thank you, Carlos. Please save her."

The doctor's expression remained dark as they circled the corner and scurried toward the emergency room doors being held open by Sam and Henny. The ambulance drivers stared at them as they carried her inside. A gurney flew up, and two more nurses and a curious physician rushed up. Carlos nodded at the rolling table, and Tom acknowledged it, lifting Barbara high and placing her gently down, resting her head on a thin pillow, grabbing her arms and putting them against her sides. He started to tuck in the blankets, but the nurses snapped them away and Carlos and the other doctor bent over the gunshot wound, stripping off the bandage as an orderly shouldered Tom aside and wheeled her through the swinging doors.

"It's going to be okay, honey," Tom whispered, stretching his arm, pushing her hair behind her ears as the crowd of hospital staff slowly squeezed him out.

When Tom tried to push through the swinging doors after them, an orderly stepped in to cut him off. The wide-bodied man held a flat expression, putting his hand on Tom's chest, giving him a stoic head shake.

"That's my wife," he said, eyes following the gurney as they wheeled it away. "I have to be with her."

"No señor." The orderly separated himself from the hospital group, holding Tom at the edge of the hall. "No puedes pasar de este punto."

Tossing a glance back, he asked, "What's he saying, Sam? What's he want me to do?"

"He's saying you can't go back there." The beleaguered girl shrugged helplessly. "It's only for staff. We have to stay out here in the waiting room."

"No. You don't understand," Tom snapped at the guy. "I promised her we'd never be separated again. I told her that when we found each other back in North Carolina. I promised…"

The man fortified his position, one leg anchored as he leveraged his weight while Tom pressed forward, shoving him back, the orderly using his thick arms to sweep Tom away, grabbing his shirt and thrusting him backwards. The move took him by surprise, but his old training kicked in, and he regained his balance, pivoted, and punched the man just below the ribs, knocking his breath loose, forcing him two steps into the swinging doors.

"Dad, stop!" Sam pleaded, her small hands wrapping around his right arm even as he cocked it to swing again.

"Cut it out, Dad!" Linda was suddenly on his left side, gripping his jacket, jerking to keep him off the orderly.

The stocky Hispanic man had taken Tom's punch and was coming at him with a low growl, anger rising in his glare, but right before the two could clash, Carlos and Henny pressed through the swinging doors, the nurse grabbing the orderly while the doctor continued toward Tom, stepping in front of him, holding his hands up in the air.

"Settle down, sir," he said in thickly accented English. "I cannot allow you to go past those doors. Rest assured, your wife will get the best possible care here."

Jaw falling open in shock, Tom's panic and anger drained, one hand resting on the doctor's arm as he was guided away. "Wait, what?"

"I'm telling you to let my people do their jobs if you want your wife to live. I've got the best surgeon in the hospital working on her. He'll go in and make sure there's no additional internal bleeding. We'll get the infection washed out and get her some blood, though our supply is limited."

"I… I can give," Tom said, eyes wide as he stared at the doctor. "I'm O-negative."

"That's great, sir. I'll send someone out to collect from you, but you must settle down first."

By then, Henny had convinced the orderly that they had the situation under control, and she joined them where they were guiding Tom into the waiting room. His spike of angry energy had completely vanished, leaving him feeling extra drained after days of exhaustive fighting and driving over the rough Mexican highways. Tom hit the seat with a heavy sigh, deflating with a shudder. Sam and Linda jumped into chairs on either side of him, Jack squeezing between his legs to fall on his chest, the boy's weight pinning him down.

Head shaking, voice quivering, hands trembling, he gave Carlos and Henny an apologetic look. "I'm sorry. I'm so sorry. I've been driving all night, and I can barely see straight."

"Exhaustion will do that to you," Carlos nodded kindly. "And that's even more reason for you to relax. You're in excellent hands."

"You speak perfect English, doctor. Why didn't you just say that to begin with? We could've cut through all the…" Tom gestured toward the orderly across the room. "All of my nonsense."

Carlos stood a couple feet back from Tom, arms folded across his chest. "As you know, the world is uncertain these days, and I couldn't be sure you weren't part of the military. They sometimes deceive us in order to get medical treatment, and some even steal from our facilities. Our doctors have been harassed and held hostage by Mexican gangs, too, so we have to be careful on all fronts."

"I'm sorry to hear that," he replied. "Like I was saying, we were running from the military. Or, at least, a very wrong-minded part of it." Tom's instinctively looked toward the doors as an image of Keith in his APC flashed through his mind.

"When I saw your children and your injured wife," Carlos continued, "I knew you were telling the truth. And we always help those who are truly in need."

"Thank you, Carlos. You too, Henny." When the woman nodded at the sound of her name, Tom shot the doctor a bemused grin. "Does she speak perfect English, too?"

"Not as well as Carlos," she answered for herself, smiling at him as she knelt in front of the children, giving Smooch a pat on the head. "But I am learning fast." She gestured at teary-eyed Jack to come over. "Hey, little boy. Do you want some snacks? Maybe a candy bar or some water?"

Jack hesitated, wiping at his sniffly nose, face turned up to Tom, waiting for his approval. When he nodded, the boy slid from his lap. "My name's Jack."

Henny laughed, her voice musical in the dismal lobby. "Well, since it is okay with your father, young Jack, I'll take you to the lunchroom. You girls want to come, too?"

Linda nodded and came out of her chair, giving Tom's leg a quick pat before standing at Henny's side.

"I'll stay here with dad and Smooch," Sam said. "But if they've got any bottled waters, I'd love one."

"I think we can accommodate you," Henny replied, touching Linda's shoulder. "We might even have a Coca-Cola or two."

"You guys have Cokes?" Jack stared up at the nurse with wide-eyed wonder, like she held the keys to a fantasy land or castle.

"Someone just contributed two cases to the hospital. They will not last a long time, but I think I can set a few aside for you children."

Jack chirped with glee, reaching out and taking the nurse's other hand, the woman leading both children to a side door that led into a different hallway. Leaning forward, Tom dropped his face into his hands, fingers rubbing his forehead and temples, dragging down his cheeks and through his beard, palms slapping on his thighs as he stared up. "Can you tell us where we are, doctor? We were trying to get to Mexico City, thinking things might be better there."

"You're not too far away. This is San Filipe Santiago, a suburb of the city. Not like a suburb in the United States, but more an outskirt."

"That's what I thought when we first drove up, and I was already skeptical we'd get a warm welcome. That's why we came around from the south—"

"Closer to the hospital, yes," he nodded. "That was a smart move, Mr.…?"

"McKnight. We're the McKnights. I'm Tom, and this is Sam. The other girl is my middle daughter, Linda. And Jack introduced himself already."

"And your wife's name?"

"Barbara."

"You say she was injured by the US military?"

"It's a long story, but yes. A special operations force they sent to track us down did it."

"Special forces, eh?" The doctor raised an eyebrow. "You must be a valuable target."

"No, not really. Someone put us on their shit list, and they really wanted to take us out because of a personal grudge. We were in a military camp up north when some of the refugees started a coup. We escaped in the confusion, but the specops stayed on our tail, chasing us through a bunch of cities I don't know the names of." Tom looked out through the doors as an EMT walked in. "What's going on here in Mexico City? Is there a big US presence here? It seems everyone's pulled out."

"That is true, mostly. Mexico City is under military control, and your government has settled millions there, though with the temperature getting colder, they may only be there for the short-term."

"Short-term? If they're going to be moved, I wonder where?"

"Somewhere in South America, to be sure. I've heard as far south as Venezuela." The doctor took a pointedly long breath, releasing it in a sigh. "Until then, it looks like Mexico City will be the main resettlement area, and other places along the coast, of course."

Tom stared at the daylight leaking in through the doors that cast a vivid swath of light across the floor. "So far to go," he said wistfully.

"You mentioned being in a camp. Do you remember where that was?"

"Nuevo Laredo was where the internment camp was. Mostly for…" Tom was about to say criminals, but he stopped himself short as he looked up at the doctor.

Carlos waved off any concern. "It's okay, my friend. No matter where you were, or who you are, you're here now. I've committed to taking care of you, no matter what. Speaking of which, why don't you start at the beginning. Where did you come from?"

Tom was certain the doctor wouldn't turn them in to any authorities, especially not American ones, and definitely not Keith, if the man ever showed up again. Staring at the floor, he thought about where to start. It made no sense to go back to when the anomaly was discovered or why they'd ended up in North Carolina. The important part was that they had, and he'd reunited with his family there, so that's where they started.

"We went through a lot of hell when the disaster first hit, but managed to get reunited right before we were in a camp in North Carolina. When an earthquake hit the town we were in, my family and I escaped by 'borrowing' a military aircraft."

The doctor chuckled. "I can appreciate a man who puts his family first."

"We were heading south to warmer climes, but the aircraft crashed somewhere near Fort Worth, we think. We barely made it out alive with a pair of army medics who helped us get as far as Laredo. There, we got into a little trouble thanks to that personal vendetta I mentioned, and that's when they stuck us in the camps. Like I mentioned, a bunch of people formed a rebellion, and we escaped in the chaos, grabbing that Humvee you saw out back and motoring all the way down here."

Carlos's expression remained a face of mild surprise through Tom's entire story, head shaking in disbelief when he talked about the crash in Ft. Worth, though he'd left out the crazier details of the story.

"It's always been cold." Tom reached back and scratched the base of his head where a tired itch was working. "Where we crash landed, everything was a frozen desert. Nothing but frozen, abandoned towns."

Carlos blinked. "The people?"

"Those who didn't get out in time were basically turned to blocks of ice. I saw a lot of them, frozen like statues, and I'm sure I didn't even see the worst of it."

The doctor's expression fell somber, resignation written across his face. "We haven't heard a lot about goings-on north of the border, but I guess when you put it that way I can't blame the Americans for coming south. It must've been pretty bad for them to want to come here."

"It was total annihilation up there." The weight of it rested heavily on his chest. "Believe me, Carlos, we wouldn't have come all this way if the cold hadn't been so bad. We had a farm, in Virginia, and it's gone now. We didn't have any other choice but to flee south. Our entire country is just… gone."

The doctor was nodding, and whatever mistrust he had initially had toward Tom and his family seemed to have completely vanished. "Then God has looked favorably upon you, Mr. McKnight. You should consider yourself very lucky to even be here."

The words were like a lock and key for Tom, twisting, snapping the deadbolts in his body open, allowing him to fall slack in the chair, after pushing himself to the limits and having done everything he could to keep Barbara and his children alive. Smooch circled and laid down at his feet, seeming to agree with his exhaustion and sudden relaxation.

"Do you think we'll be okay in one of the US camps?"

"Absolutely not." Carlos was emphatic. "If the military is looking for you, any of the camps around here would be a bad idea. They'd be sure to notice a family of new arrivals. The nearest ones are just south of us, so steer clear of them."

"Thank you, we'll do that. Speaking of… when will you know more about my wife's condition?"

"I'll keep you informed as soon as we have news," the doctor said. "In the meantime, why don't you get some rest. We don't have any cots or beds around, but feel free to spread out across the chairs. No one will bother you while you're here. You're safe."

"Thank you, Carlos." Tom clasped the man's hand. "I can't say it enough."

"Yeah, thanks, Carlos," Samantha chimed in with a smile.

With a nod, the doctor turned, the click of his hard-soled shoes marching across the tiles and disappearing into the emergency hall double doors, the pair swinging softly shut, leaving Tom and Sam together, his thoughts turning dark with an impending sense of doom. Before he could break down in tears again, he turned to Sam and nodded at the door Henny and the other two had gone through.

"Why don't you find your brother and sister, and I'll start setting us a section up in the corner where we can wait."

She nodded and got up, bouncing off to see after them, somehow still charged with energy. When she'd gone, he hauled himself to his feet and began rearranging the chair setup with Smooch sitting back on her haunches and watching with keen interest.

Chapter 19
President John Zimmerman
Caracas, Venezuela

Marine One's turbo engines wind down, the blades spinning lazily, swirling winds sweeping from the rotors and blossoming outward, buffeting the Marines and secret servicemen in their suits and ties on the roof of the Hotel Eurobuilding in Caracas. Their profiles stand strong against the distant Venezuelan hills, rolling green stretching off in every direction, rich brown mountains looming behind those.

Huey Venoms and Apache helicopters swarm the skies like insects set against the deep blue, the air filled with their ominous buzzing. A pair of F-35s race by overhead, cruising over the city. And, while they don't have troops on the ground, thousands of them wait on the beaches to receive the order to enter.

The President steps off Marine One, his shoe touching the rooftop landing pad. Two men from his security detail split up, one gesturing for him to follow them toward a set of sliding doors near one end of the roof, the hotel's golden insignia emblazoned upon them. Ducking, clinging to the briefcase tucked under his left arm, he follows the Secret Service personnel, glancing back to see the rest of his staff stepping off the chopper.

General Mark Davidson descends the stairs in full uniform, his stout appearance confident and reassuring. Admiral Ben Spencer follows him, his rotund belly pushing out against his white Naval jacket, jowls shivering in the gusting winds. Out next comes Colonel Prescott, a tall man in his standard green fatigues and sidearm, his long, grizzled face sporting sunglasses, and Tenika Brown with Rick Mangalore are soon to follow, the chief scientist's disheveled features only slightly less haggard than in the previous weeks. After their attempt to blow up the anomaly, Rick's expertise has taken a backseat to military priorities, though with the recent operations completed, they need him to address the upcoming climate changes brought by the freshwater surge. Bringing up the rear of the group is Zimmerman's lead staffer, Maxine, who remains steadfast and strong, keeping him on point and informed, well-rested, hydrated, and all the simple things he's apt to forget.

At the sliding doors, they meet a half dozen Venezuelan special forces, hands clasped behind their backs, General Frederico Molina at their head. Molina is a short, stocky man with a weathered face, pockmarked and scarred from a long-ago battle, his hard brown eyes welcoming the President, thick salt-and-pepper hair parted on the side.

"Hello, Mr. President. I am General Frederico Molina. Welcome to our beautiful country. I hope you will be proud to call it your new home." While the man's words say one thing, the tension in his tone and the unwavering stoicism in his expression tell the President the man is far from pleased.

Zimmerman accepts his extended hand, shaking it firmly, wincing inwardly at his extraordinarily firm grip, but he locks his jaw, speaking with confidence. "Thank you, General. I mean it when I say it's a privilege to be here in your country, and our appreciation for your heartfelt welcome will not go unrewarded."

Molina's gaze rakes over the President, as if adding the two lines of conversation to an ongoing case of evidence locked in his mind. "Please, sir. Follow me. President Perez is waiting for you just one floor below us in the Great Meeting Room, as planned."

"Very good, General. Lead on."

In a small atrium stands a set of elevator doors with a button for going down. The doors slide open, and he and a pair of his officers step inside, motioning for the President and the first few members of his entourage to join them. The elevator is deep and wide, easily large enough for at least half the group to step in, including five of the President's secret servicemen and two burly, sharp-eyed Marines with M4 carbines hanging from their shoulders. As they squeeze in, he takes a position next to Molina, chin held high in the awkward silence that follows, and it's a short, one-story drop before the elevator dings and the doors open wide.

The president and his team step into the hallway while Molina remains on the lift. "I'll go up and retrieve the rest of your people, if you don't mind staying here for just one moment, sir."

"Of course," Zimmerman replies.

The doors slip smoothly shut, and secret service personnel spread out along a corridor that stretch across the building in both directions, lined with a dozen doors. A thin carpet with elegant golden designs cover the floor, and the walls are layered with a deep red wallpaper, golden stripes running from baseboard to ceiling, fancy wall sconces hanging at regular intervals. Simple pictures adorn the walls, images of vases, scenes of rolling Venezuelan hills. There are tables every twenty or thirty feet, decorated with lamps, casting a warm glow throughout the hallway.

He turns to General Davidson. "Are you surprised we've been left alone here?"

The general glances at Prescott, then peers up and down the corridor. "I don't see how it makes a difference. We've got the outside covered, so any attempt on your life would end in terrible repercussions for them. There is really no reason for them to try anything."

He bows slightly in acknowledgment as his people spread out across the hallway. One secret serviceman stops near a door, hand poised over the handle, glancing at the President with a curious expression. Zimmerman shakes his head, and the man backs off with a nod, relaxing into a casual stance.

"We need to keep the sanctity of this meeting pure," he murmurs. "Getting this treaty signed and sealed is of the utmost importance. I don't want to insult the Venezuelans by showing mistrust. It's bad enough we brought these guys." He nods to the burly Marines who stand stock still, armed to the hilt and wearing flak vests, their eyes moving behind sunglasses.

"We insisted on it, sir," Davidson says. "While this meeting is about trust, we also have to be careful."

Not long after, the elevator doors open, and the rest of the group files out; Rita, Maxine, and Rick shuffle closer to him.

General Molina and his officers step around the presidential contingent and move across the hall to a deep alcove with a set of double doors built in. With a flourish, two men stride to the doors and open them while the general gestures for the President and his people to enter. The big Marines and two Secret Service members go first, their heads swiveling, glancing across the room as they spread out with confident, calm strides. Expression flat, the President comes behind them, loosely gripping the briefcase tucked beneath his arm, eyes drawn to the far end of the chamber to a long table where President Perez, his military officers, and officials stand beside their chairs. It's a grand meeting room, elegant, yet functional, with a small contingent of staff people standing off to the side next to carts of coffee, clear dispensers full of ice water and other refreshments.

He nods to the Venezuelan President and strides briskly to his seat, waiting as his security team spreads out to greet members of the Venezuelan special forces and guards arrayed throughout the room, dark suits and sunglasses meeting and shaking hands, quickly stepping back from each other, turning to the officials gathered at the table. President Zimmerman gestures for his people to sit. On his right is General Davidson, Admiral Spencer, and Colonel Prescott and to his left, Rita and Rick. The Presidents wait until everyone is seated, eyes locked, smiles cordial. Rita, having already met the Venezuelan contingent, grins broadly, reaches across the table to her counterpart, Nina Herrera, and shakes hands. Zimmerman is struck by how similar the two women look with their shoulder-length hair and sharp suits, both sharing a smile and nod before turning their faces up to Zimmerman and the Venezuelan President.

Rita's making inroads, he thinks, that's good.

They sit slowly, his eyes never leaving President Perez's, and after getting comfortable, he speaks, "Rey. It's good to see you again, my friend."

Reynaldo Perez sits with his thin shoulders stiff, spine straight in his white shirt and tie. A kind, round face with sharp eyes stares back at him, salt and pepper hair thick on his head and parted on the side. The man gives a curt, friendly nod and reaches across the table.

"Hello, John. It's good to see you, too," he says. "I wish it were under different circumstances." The man's accent is thick, though his English is perfect. "Let me first offer my condolences for what happened in the United States." They shake hands and relax back in their seats. "I heard the temperatures are unbearable there now, and you've lost tens of millions of souls. I couldn't imagine that hitting my country. May God bless you and your people."

"Thanks, Rey. It's pretty bad. We've got an Arctic freeze all the way to Mexico and beyond. I'm talking minus twenty degrees. It's taken a lot of lives." Being frank with another acting president for the first time causes his breath to lock in his chest, teeth clenching to hold down the sudden, hard-edged emotion, closing his eyes, waiting for the moment to pass before continuing. "We've heard rumors of some trying to live on the southern tip of Florida and Cuba. I suppose it's doable, but it's going to be a hard life for them."

"How far do you think the cold will reach?" Perez asks, his concern and surprise mirrored in his eyes as they shift down the line to Rick Manglor.

"As soon as we're done with our business here," Zimmerman says, drawing his attention back, "sealing the bond between our two peoples, we'll provide you and your experts all the data we collected over the past months and days. Full transparency."

Rey nods, gesturing toward his briefcase. "Yes, John. Let's finish with the official business and get on to saving lives. Perhaps we can talk more openly about the situation then."

He pops the locks on his case and pulls out a stack of papers. Maxine and her counterpart, Stephano Aguilar, a young man with a thin mustache and goatee, pick them up and take them to a separate desk. There, they triple check the documents against each other, flipping through the pages for ten minutes before standing and distributing a set to everyone at the table. They each have something to sign, from the two nations' civilian leaders to those in the military. Each are to be held accountable for the Great Annexation. Papers shuffle, and whispers flit through the room as Maxine and Stephano make their way around, answering questions, clarifying paragraphs and amendments. Rita leans across to Nina to discuss and shed light on recent updates to a specific section about housing and supplies for the incoming refugees. Pots of coffee and tea in hand, staffers walk around the room, filling cups, asking if anyone wants snacks or other refreshments, the workers' quiet as they serve the presidents and military leaders. Zimmerman glances up to see Rey making a show of going through the documents himself, a quiet intensity in his gaze, the rest hidden behind a stoic front.

"Thank you for this, Rey. You won't regret it."

Perez gives one of his curt nods, though he breaks free from his stoic expression and relaxes his jaw. "I hope you don't mind, but in anticipation of a successful signing, we've taken the liberty of starting Phase One."

"Here? Outside of Caracas?"

"That's right," Rey smiles. "We're clearing the forests for farms and living spaces south of the city in a massive swath of beautiful land. After today, we'll add your heavy equipment to the mix. Soon, we'll have enough room for the first million of our new brothers and sisters to join us."

The American President nods with relief, though his fingers still tap nervously on the desk. "I'd heard our teams were already working together on this, and I appreciate everyone's initiative."

"I sense your tension, but you can relax." Perez smiles. "I speak for everyone when I say you'll soon come to know the warmth of the Venezuelan people."

"The American people, as well." In his head, Zimmerman reviews the full run down he had with his experts earlier. Prior to the anomaly, Venezuela was stuck in a downward spiral, so he doesn't doubt Rey's sincerity at wanting American equipment, know how, and protection inside their borders, especially with the Russians and Chinese on the doorstep.

He lifts the corner of one document. "It will certainly be interesting."

Rey smiles warmly. "Yes, indeed."

After thirty minutes of back-and-forth, Rita stands with the stack of papers. "Okay, folks. Let me go over some of the chief points of the document to make sure we're all on the same page. According to this new US-Venezuelan Heartland Treaty, the following things will take place. An initial clearing of one million acres of land for American citizens including farms, living facilities, hospitals, and schools. More additions will be added right away as we ferry in people from Panama thanks to the secure convoy route through South America." Rita shifts to her other hip, tapping her pen against her chin. "For now, our shared military forces will become the Joint US-VE Command and will begin formal training immediately, with the primary goal of having a fully combined force within ten years."

The military folks at the table raise their eyes at each other, Davidson and Molina giving each other a long stare, breathing heavy sighs, finally offering up hesitant nods before Rita continues.

"This treaty will spawn several acts, including the Venezuelan Admissions Act, the US Constitutional Amendment Act, and the Joint Commerce and Trade Act, all aimed at bringing integral parts of Venezuelan law in line with current US law. The amendments to the US Constitution will be small and will address specific concerns as they pertain to geological locations and resources owned by the Venezuelan people. All land ownership, rights, and laws will remain the same for now, with the appended US Constitution and codes of law to take effect within six months. We only had to modify the wording in one section, which you should all have. Maxine and Stephano have initialed the documents to say they provided oversight to the linguistics changes." She smiles at the assembly. "Seems everyone is happy."

Pens are passed around, plain, black styluses with the express purpose of signing what could be the most life-changing document in the history of both peoples. From the edges of the table inward, signatures are scribbled, moving down the line, eventually reaching the generals. Molina and Davidson stare across at each other in a tense moment, their hard eyes locked, as if testing the other's honesty and resolve. In simultaneous understanding, the two generals nod to each other, lean over the documents, and flick their pens across the paper.

With a soft outtake of breath, Zimmerman raises his eyebrows briefly. "Well, Rey. This is it. Are you ready to sign, my friend?"

"Yes, I am. For the betterment of our two peoples. May we face the future as one nation."

Eyes glassy, chest squeezing, the American President leans forward and looks at the typed print. All their recent failures and victories flash through his mind, culminating in this one moment. The two men bow their heads, scribble their signatures with soft scratches across the paper, flip to the next page, sign again. They repeat it four more times throughout the document, setting the treaty in stone.

* * *

Three floors beneath the meeting room, President Zimmerman, Rita, and General Davidson share a view from the west side of Hotel Eurobuilding, watching the first US refugees flood in. The room's west and north walls are mostly glass, giving them an expansive perspective of bustling Caracas, its beautiful but crowded downtown area, the clusters of dirty white buildings bumping against the foothills and mountains. Vivid green jungle trees cover the high slopes, a mist clinging between the spurs, and on the lower sections, piles of houses and apartments fill every available space, colored with wild degrees of bright blue, orange, and lavender, perching on ridges or making trails down to the city outskirts.

With shallow breaths, the President watches the first wave of refugees come in, mostly heavy workers, construction crews, and military personnel, big rigs with tracked excavators and bulldozers on the flatbeds, a few Humvees and APCs entering behind them to offer protection against any elements of the populace that may be resisting the cooperation between the two peoples. After the twelve-mile journey from the beaches up north, the massive convoy turns south along the main highway through Caracas, which is shut down to regular traffic to make way for the flood of Americans.

The US landing forces have taken control of the coast, thousands of troops and heavy equipment disembarking, rolling west and east along the coastal roads, heading for the oil refineries where they'll add to the already edgy Venezuelan security forces that have been made nervous by rumors of Russian incursions on Brazil's eastern shores. The sea is filled with American ships as the full flotilla rolls in, all the East Coast carrier groups joining them, and soon the escorted military haulers will steam in, ships carrying hundreds of thousands of American citizens from the Gulf and Florida.

"Well, it's sure a beautiful place," Rita says, coming up with a glass of ice water in her hand, her heels kicked off so she's in her bare feet, relaxing as she stands to Zimmerman's right, one arm against the window frame, staring out to the north.

Caracas is bustling as gaggles of citizens, thousands of them, gather along the highway, watching the massive convoy of US citizens rolling into their city, many waving and dancing, music ringing out in a festive atmosphere. Food stalls stand off the boulevard on corners and in the lower streets, smoke tendrils drifting up to fill the sky.

"Are they actually happy to see us?" Standing with his top few buttons undone and his sleeves rolled up, the President can't quell the queasiness he felt since his arrival, though the cheering, vibrant crowds go a long way to remedying it.

"You would be too if you've been living under that regime as long as they have," Davidson replies. "While I respect General Molina, his troops have been brutal on the citizenry, cracking down on protests with vicious killings and beatings. It'll be tough at first, sir, but we'll rely on our strong training contingent to get them straightened out. We'll make soldiers out of their ragtag forces yet."

Zimmerman nods. "You're right about the protests, Mark. I've seen the reports."

"These people are more than glad to see us," Rita cuts in. "It's a dream come true for many of them. They've been living under such militaristic and bureaucratic oppression for so long—"

"Will they expect us to solve their problems for them?"

"Not all, but some."

"So, our people are being driven straight through the city and to the south?"

"It's the most favorable land right now," she continues. "Government owned but undeveloped so far. A perfect place for our folks to start."

Glancing back, he speaks to General Davidson, who sits at a table behind Rita, punching buttons on his tablet, occasionally looking out the window. "I'll take a tour as soon as possible. I want to be down there as much as I can, every step of the way. Our people are in the middle of a foreign land, facing unknowns around every corner, everything totally alien to them, and I won't let them do it alone."

Davidson nods. "Yes, sir."

"We'll all have to make changes." Rita watches the streets below. "But there're a lot worse places to restart our lives."

"The clash of cultures will be significant." Zimmerman shakes his head.

"I wouldn't worry too much about them influencing our people," Rita says with a reassuring glance. "Most Venezuelans love American culture, and there will be over one hundred and fifty million of us coming in compared to their thirty." She chuckles. "I think we'll have them a little outnumbered in that regard."

"That's true, I suppose." Turning away from the window, he walks over to sit by the general. "But they're partial to communist influences, especially that of Russia. You know, the guys we just ran off their coast?"

"Tell me about it, sir." The general punches another few buttons on his tablet, putting that aside to pick up a second one he carries with them, holding it in front of his face, reading lines of text. "We just received reconnaissance reports from Brazil's East Coast."

President Zimmerman leans forward, shoulders tensing, cheeks wincing at the potential news. "We know the Russians have landed on the coast, but we don't expect they'll be a problem when we get our other carrier groups around the southern part of the continent, right?"

"They still have a significant naval force," Davidson says, "but we wiped out a major part of their fleet. They won't try to challenge us on open water anytime soon."

"Any word on how they're doing?"

"We've been able to send as many overflight missions as we want, so we've got the best data on the Russians we've had in years." The stout man sits back in his chair, shifting slightly, crossing one leg. "They've got a foothold there now, with a good contingent of tanks and troops. And they're trying to do a similar thing as us, but they don't have any people on shore yet."

"They don't have the equipment and ships, for sure," Zimmerman agrees. "Where are they staging their people?"

"For starters, they're bussing them to the coastal naval bases near China. But they have to trek all the way across the Pacific, then around South America, a significantly longer journey than what we have. Volkov is just doing what we'd do, taking the path of least resistance."

"What does the CCP think about all this? Any news there?"

Rita scoffs. "China doesn't want their territory anymore. They've taken advantage of their extensive networks in Africa and are essentially doing the same thing we're doing here, and they've got the forces to do it easily. They're trucking in tens of thousands of troops and citizens across multiple nations, daring anyone to attack them. I spoke to Rick today, and he said most of the Northern Hemisphere is uninhabitable right now. Someone should send a note to Canada."

"It's smart of China to leverage investments they've made in Africa over the last thirty years," Zimmerman scratches his head. "What about the other nations?"

"England is trying to hold out, but it's brutal." Davidson jumps back in. "Though they have some fingers in West Africa. Same as a lot of European nations, including France. I imagine they'll form an alliance and try to make a stand against China."

"Sounds to me like we could have World War III on the African continent," the President muses, picturing those countries with hundreds or thousands of years of mistrust and war suddenly forced to come together on a single piece of land, although it was a big one.

"It won't be much of a war if they can't get to any oil reserves. Before long, most of those will be buried under ice, so whoever's got the equipment to dig it out of the ground will survive."

"Rita, as soon as we get settled here and work is underway, I want you to put your Secretary of State hat on and reach out to some of these nations, let's see if any of our allies need our help. Back to Canada. Any word?"

"Pierre hasn't been happy with us through the entire process," Rita says. "They've barely spoken a word to us throughout the entire tragedy."

Davidson shrugs. "They still have a military command."

"Have they made any headway south?"

"As far as we know, they've not made the effort. It's just as cold there as in the north. Last we heard, the Canadians were setting up hotspots across the major cities to bring in people from the cold. They've been living in frigid temperatures forever, so they might make it work."

"I just don't see how… And that's why we need Rick here to help us talk through—"

Three quick knocks hammer the door, and Rita turns and makes straight for it, popping it open a crack, whispering to the guard on the other side. She steps back to let Rick Manglor in, the man in jeans and a button-up shirt, the collar wrinkled, his brown hair tousled on his head, as uncombed as when they met earlier that day. Tucked under his arm is a tablet and notebook.

Slouching, giving a hesitant wave, he passes around tired nods. "Hello, Mr. President. General Davidson. Mrs. Cortez."

"Speak of the devil," Zimmerman says, standing, gesturing to the chair he'd just been sitting in. "Why don't you have a seat, Rick. We've already gone over some other updates, and we need to know about the anomaly. What's it doing, and what we can expect to see over the next weeks and months?"

"Thanks, sir." Holding up his tablet and papers, shaking them, he strides to the chair and sits heavily. "I've got that right here."

The President pivots, moves to a nearby table, and pours him a glass of cold water, bringing it over and placing it in front of him. "Here you go."

"Thanks." Rick sips, sighs, and flips through his tablet until he had what he was looking for. "First things first. We have a trio of ships in the area over the anomaly, monitoring, working between bouts of mass seafloor ejection."

"That's when that bastard breaks off a piece of the ocean crust and shoots it to the surface, right?" Davidson asks.

"Exactly. They've been able to detect when those start up and get out of the way before they get blasted out of the water."

"I wish we would've known that a few weeks ago when we were trying to shut the damn thing down," Zimmerman replies with a derisive scoff. "We lost a lot of people out there because of our ignorance."

"We're more informed now, sir. And ships are doing a great job of staying out of the way while monitoring the situation." Rick pushes his glasses up on his nose. "The bad news is that the anomaly is still spewing freshwater into the ocean. The good news is that the rate of flow has significantly changed. Meaning, it's slowing down, though it will continue to push water out for at least another six months if the flow rate change stays constant. Oceans will rise another three inches or more, and our advanced projections show this will keep on for the next fifty years at least."

The President straightens and moves to the window. "So, we've got a chance of going back someday?"

"That's a little harder to discern. Provided the anomaly stops pushing out water as we expect, the earth will need time to re-adjustment. The North Atlantic Drift, the Gulf Stream, and the Canary Current will have to restart. That could take hundreds of years, or a few, or anything in between. We'll know more as time goes on. But once it makes that correction, it'll take a while for things to thaw out and for life to return to the north. Some species will have survived, though others will have been devastated. It'll be at least a generation or two before we can even think about resettling in the Northern Hemisphere."

Zimmerman shifts his gaze to the window, his blue eyes drifting out across the breathtaking mountain expanse, the mist rising as the late day sun burns it away. "Thanks, Rick. That's what we needed to know. Let me ask you this. Do you think anyone can live up north? Is it survivable?"

"Well, sure, sir. The temperatures aren't much lower than they are in the Arctic, and folks have lived there for thousands of years."

"Not an easy life," Davidson adds.

"No, it's not, but it can be done. There're plenty of fuel sources besides oil. The endless expanses of forests will be vital for anyone to survive, though there won't be much to hunt except in the lower regions around the Mexican border. Plus, without a cycle of growth each year, those resources will eventually dwindle, depending on how quickly they're exhausted."

Folding his arms across his chest, the President turns and addresses his most trusted advisors. "I think we have to stop seeing things in terms of land, though I'm as guilty as anyone in thinking we'll go back soon. The truth is, we can't. Not for a long time. And even though we don't have our home anymore, we're still a great nation, and we *will* endure. That's going to be my legacy. *Our* legacy." He steps forward. "We have to see this as a chance to start over, and fix what we got wrong last time. Our Constitution will stay strong, and the Republic will stand."

"We've all got your back on that, sir." Rita steps closer, locking her arm with his, patting his shoulder, the freckles on her cheeks spreading with a reassuring smile.

"That's right, sir," Davidson stands, his stout form facing the President, gesturing out the window. "This is our new home base, and we'll do everything it takes to advance future generations. That starts on the ground floor. We can't expect it to be easy, but if we focus on taking it step-by-step, we'll get there. And don't worry." The big man's wink looks goofy above his stern jaw and hard eyes. "I'll keep an eye on the Russians for you."

A chuckle wells up from Zimmerman's belly, and he clasps the man's left arm in his. "You've done amazing work to get us through this, Mark. Both of you. And I know I can rely on you the rest of the way." His grin slides to Rick. "And you, my friend..."

The scientist gives a half grin. You're about to tell me I'm going to have more work than I can handle. That's fine, sir. Who needs sleep? I'll do that when I die."

The four laugh, though Rick looks seriously doubtful, the stress in his face overwhelming as a soft knock reaches them. Maxine pokes her head in, waving a small stack of papers. "I need you for a minute, sir. The Senate and Congress have all signed off on this in an emergency meeting this morning. And I just came back from the Venezuelans' office. President Perez has signed off on it, too. They're all waiting for you now."

The President breaks free from his friends. "Come in, Maxine. We're done here for a while."

The staffer enters wearing tennis shoes and a pant suit, her hair pinned back, bags heavy beneath her eyes. With a hesitant smile, she hands the documents over, and Zimmerman takes them to the table, leaning in, reading the first page. At the top, it reads *Venezuelan Admissions Act*. Flipping through the sheets, he skims past the addendums and corrections, realizing it must've come fresh from the command ship with the verbal agreements from Congress and the Senate, not even printed anew.

He glances up at Davidson and Rita before turning back to the document, holding out his hand for the pen Maxine gives him. "Thank you," he says as he stoops lower, putting his initials in handwritten spots to show he's read them. With a sigh, he signs and dates each page with a long sweep of his hand, and when finished, he holds up the documents so everyone can see. "That does it, folks. Venezuela has now become the fifty-first state of our union. Kind of anticlimactic, after all of that."

"It won't be enough," Davidson says, clasping his hands behind his back. "We'll need to consider annexing Colombia and northern parts of Brazil, as well as Guyana."

"When I call Rey to let him know the good news of his statehood, we'll start up those conversations." He hands the documents to Maxine. "Go ahead. Run these back please."

"Yes, sir."

She turns on her heel to deliver the formal paperwork back to Central Command.

Chapter 20
Specialist Lance Morales
Morelia, Mexico

"I tell you, Smith, it's good to have wheels down on real pavement again." Morales sat back, relaxing in the Humvee's driver's seat.

"Yeah, no kidding," the lieutenant scoffed. "Nothing but a winter wonderland from Santa Fe to Morelia. And your driving, man…" He lets out an exaggerated sigh and roll of his eyes. "Let's just say you needed the practice."

"Be glad I didn't let *you* drive back to Mexico at any point," Morales chuckled. "We never would have made it."

Smith only grinned and shook his head, kicking his boots up on the dashboard as they watched the road ahead, Captain Jones's convoy slipping closer to the next camp south of San Filipe Santiago, just a hop, skip, and a jump from Mexico City. They'd been re-routed multiple times because of highways affected by the earthquakes that had ravaged downtown and some outskirts, finally finding a road in from the west. The massive line of supply trucks, Humvees, snowplows, and support vehicles, trundled along, though the going was easier compared to trying to plow through four or more feet of snow up north, battling for every mile, begging their trucks not to die.

"Yeah, I hope we never get assigned back up there again," Smith said, resting his hands in his lap, as relaxed as Morales had ever seen him. "Although I have to admit, I'd love to know if Chet and his people got out of that bunker alive."

"It's been a week." Morales shrugged, as if that meant anything. "They've either starved or they got out and died in the cold."

After escaping the bunker and locking the militia inside, the soldiers had rejoined Captain Jones's unit and helped the second convoy load up supplies from the remaining buildings. Avoiding a couple of spin-up storms, they'd made their way south, fighting the constant cold, the persistent winds biting at their faces, freezing equipment, and creating problems for them at every turn. The convoys had made it into Mexico two days prior, driving south ever since, dropping off supplies and taking part in massive troop movements toward Mexico City.

"I'm torn which fate I'd prefer for them," the lieutenant sneered. "Those a-holes don't deserve to die fast in a winter storm, so I'll go with starving alone in the bunker, hopefully eating each other to stay alive."

Morales shuddered at the idea, knowing how close to the truth it could actually be. The pair fell into a silence, nothing but the grumbling of their Humvee filling the surrounding air, trucks in front of them and behind. He occasionally glanced out his window at the small towns dotting the landscape, snowed in, white bumps with signs jutting up the only markings that there was anything there at all. But the farther south they drove, the more lights they saw, little places still alive and kicking after the power had been restored to Mexico City thanks to the U.S. Army Corps of Engineers and a lot of muscle and grit. In some villages, people walked the streets as if it was any other day, going to markets and standing in the parking lots, trading food and goods. Smaller convoys filled with US citizens passed them, making their way south to one camp or another, perhaps even the one Morales and Smith were going to.

The radio on the dashboard sputtered to life, lights blinking on the front face. "Good afternoon, soldiers. This is Captain Jones. I wanted to be the first to give you spectacular news that we'll be heading to Venezuela after a brief stop in Mexico City. We've got a one-way ticket to the new country to join the operations there, so dig out your sunblock and put your snow boots away. Rumor has it that Venezuela will even be our fifty-first state. Jones out."

"You hear that?" Smith asked, staring at Morales with slack-jawed incredulity. "We're heading to Venezuela, my friend. End of the line for us."

"End of the line for everyone," he murmured back.

"Fine sand, fine sun, and fine *fun*!" The lieutenant kicked back with his hands behind his head, stretching his legs even farther. "And it'll be the fifty-first state? Did I hear that right?"

"You did. But for all we know, it's just as cold there as it is here."

Smith blew a raspberry. "No way, Morales. You gotta get that negativity out of your head, son."

"Oh, you're Mr. Positive now?"

"I am now that we're heading to Venezuela. We don't even need a passport! I'm all in! I've had all I can take of the cold, and I want some nice sunshine beating down on my shoulders, buddy."

Morales shook his head, watching another town pass by. "And as soon as we get down there, you'll be complaining about how hot it is and how you want an assignment farther north."

"Not this time." He gestured at the world around them. "I think I've learned to appreciate the simpler things in life."

"Like steady warmth?"

"Exactly. That's why I think going to Venezuela will be the best thing for us. Pristine beaches. Girls with surfboards. Shoot, we'll have it made down there."

With an assured nod, Morales laughed. "We definitely deserve a weekend off. Think they'll make us drive down?"

"Good question. Probably. No, *definitely*."

683

The next few hours passed slowly, the snow tapering off until it was just an inch on the ground, then a quarter of an inch, the wind abating, still crisp but not near as biting as it had been. Not as bad as Santa Fe, when Morales had gotten worried about frostbite on the trip back, though the tips of his fingers were still pink after a day of thawing out. They rolled past another two dozen Mexican towns, residents staring at them as they passed, not appreciating the danger of the encroaching cold. Part of him wondered if the Mexican citizens would come to Venezuela with everyone else, though they didn't appear to be in any hurry to leave.

The air grew thick with helicopters and jets, swooping low over the treetops as they landed outside visual range and soon the radio announced they were within five miles of camp, and they had come to their first checkpoint. Bundled MPs stood to the side as the massive train of supplies rolled through, Morales giving them a wave as they passed, the soldiers halfheartedly returned the gesture with frowns.

Smith shook his head. "What's up with those guys? You'd think they'd be in a better mood."

"You're on a high because you're still alive. It's a damned miracle we survived Santa Fe."

"I guess you're right."

They pulled into an enormous parking lot, bigger than any department store or stadium lot they'd ever seen. It sprawled between the low foothills and snowy forests, part pavement, gravel, and dirt track, with stadium lights atop tall poles casting a brilliant white glow over everything. Beyond the lot stretched a series of runways dotted with blue and white running lights reaching toward the south. At its head was a parking lot filled with more than a hundred planes, their rumbling engines vibrating in a din of noise like he'd never heard. The aircraft trundled out and joined a queue, idling as they waited to taxi. Four massive C-130s were lifting off, their propellers saturating the air with a rising vibration, their colossal forms swinging south as they gained altitude. Out in the middle of the lot, a grand exchange was happening. Two other convoys like theirs were pulling in from different highways. The trucks lined up to allow crews to transfer goods from the convoy vehicles to smaller vans and pickups that were being driven out to the tarmac to be loaded onto planes.

Morales's jaw dropped, voice falling to a hushed whisper. "There must be ten thousand people..."

"Try twenty thousand," Smith replied flatly, though his stare was wide and wondrous as the convoy pulled to a stop.

There was a five-minute pause before Captain Jones came over the radio. "All right, team. This is going to go smooth and easy. Follow your guides and go exactly where they tell you."

"Guides?" Morales asked.

Smith lowered his window, letting in a frigid blast of air, sticking out his head and shoulders, peering past the line of trucks to the front of the convoy. "Ah, I see what they mean."

A moment later, a woman in camo with a pair of orange batons stepped into view, both arms raised and waving the sticks off to the right. The trucks in front of them began breaking off and heading in that direction, and Morales followed suit, angling off toward the waiting hands of the cargo crews. He parked between another Humvee and a semitrailer truck, the workers jumping on those vehicles first.

With a shrug to Smith, Morales popped his door and got out, jogging around to the rear and opening the back door. The lieutenant joined him, and soon the two were offloading their own supplies which were comprised mostly of rice and beans, smaller parcels of seeds, and data processing equipment. Once they'd unloaded the cargo area, they slammed the doors, grabbed a pair of foldout ladders, and climbed to reach the goods strapped on top. Within fifteen minutes, Morales was sweating and winded, a welcome break after driving the Humvee for so long. The pair worked wordlessly and tirelessly to get the job done, putting all the goods into the backs of waiting vans and pickups.

A soldier receiving the supplies commented, "I see you guys have done this before."

"More than you know," Smith laughed, sliding a bin inside and slapping the van's side as they made their way back to their empty Humvee.

"This is incredible," Morales said, his dazed expression drifting across the intense bustle, listening as planes roared along the runways, the turbulence blowing back across the lot. "It almost seems like we're going to be fine with all this heading south. You could feed two small armies with all the stuff."

"And it's just a drop in the bucket compared to what we'll actually need."

Morales hopped up on the hood of their idling truck, sitting and watching the show as helicopters of every kind swooped in, noses lifting at the last second as they touched down on their landing pads. Even as their skids set down, others rose, massive Chinooks stuffed with people and supplies, guarded by Huey Venoms and Apaches flying in perfect formations as they turned into dots in the distance, blending with the purple-orange clouds of dusk. Troops jogged in precise form, shouting cadences, moving toward a wide grouping of military barracks to the east, the buildings' rounded tops looking more like real prefab units and not just tents. And beyond that, a sprawling, endless, far-reaching spread of refugee facilities sat, a combination of hastily erected temporary housing and awnings crammed full of bundled up civilians, burn barrels as far as his eyes could see, spotlights sweeping back and forth across the sky.

Smith hopped up beside him, the soldiers sitting as the heat from the idling engine warmed their backsides. "You're right, Morales. This is... I've never seen anything like it."

Chest swelling with emotion, a tear streaked down Morales's check, but he didn't wipe it off, content to sit there feeling very small in front of something much larger than him. "This is us surviving. This is humanity."

Smith started to respond when a heavy hand slapped the side of their Humvee, and he turned to see Captain Jones coming up between the trucks, stopping to pat him on the shoulder. Both soldiers saluted and shifted to face the captain.

"I was looking for you two," he said, swiping back his hood to reveal greasy hair stuffed beneath a black beanie. His reddish beard stuck out scraggly and unclipped, his blue eyes dancing as he gazed past them. "Magnificent, isn't it?"

"We were talking about that, sir," he replied. "It's amazing."

The captain's eyebrows raised when Smith had nothing to say. "Well, as beautiful as this scene is, I need you boys for something."

Straightening where he sat, the lieutenant nodded curtly. "What do you need, sir?"

"The bean counting eggheads in logistics are trying to pull in every bit of loose equipment we can find. As you can probably imagine, a lot of assets are finding their way into these surrounding towns. Someone reported a missing Humvee just a few miles up north in a little village, and we need a couple of men to get it back. You boys know any volunteers who'd like to do that?"

Smith hopped to the ground with the sharp nod. "You found your men right here, sir. You got directions?"

"It's off the main highway, just north of us. You can't miss it. The Humvee was last seen parked at a hospital in that area, and the ID matches with a vehicle that was marked as stolen in the database." Jones looked at a clipboard and sighed. "It's an older model, probably some piece of crap not even worth going after..."

"Orders are orders, sir," Morales said, hopping to the ground. "We'll be back in a snap."

The captain was already nodding, grinning as if he expected Morales's answer. "If you do get that thing back before midnight, I'll make sure you get some decent grub and a solid pair of cots to take a load off."

Smith circled to the passenger side door, hopping in and Morales nodded to the captain and jumped behind the wheel. Jones grabbed one of the parking lot guides and had them make way for the pair. Less than a minute later, they were heading to the far end of the tarmac where a dark highway awaited them, lightless and shadowy compared to the camp's magnificent brightness.

Smith scoffed. "Been back five minutes, and we've already got a new mission."

"Yeah," Morales replied with a head shake. "Military life, man. Never a dull moment."

Chapter 21
Keith
San Felipe Santiago, Mexico

Keith leaned back on the couch, still panting from his bloody work, hands and arms smeared with it, red caked into his soiled finger bandages. He wiped his arm across his forehead, glancing into the kitchen, then looking away toward the closed blinds, examining everywhere in the strange apartment with Spanish-inspired décor. There was a coffee table made of old wood with a striped vase on it, end tables held decorative lamps and the walls were adorned with one crucifix and a few images with religious messages. While he couldn't read the Spanish phrases, he recognized references to Mark, James, and Matthew inscribed at the bottom of each one.

During the struggle, a few of the blessed symbols had been knocked off, crashed to the floor along with a smattering of family pictures and knickknacks. Casting a bleary look at the smashed decorations, he reached for the bottle of Jimador tequila from its spot on the coffee table, unscrewed the cap, and took three long swigs that burned from lip to gut, fire pouring into his belly in a moment of heat and pain. He pulled the bottle away from his mouth with a smack, body cramped in a sudden coughing fit as flames radiated throughout his stomach and legs. It hit him so hard that he threw his head back against the couch cushion, gasping for breath.

The apartment was scorching hot compared to the freezing APC, the damn thing having turned into a giant block of ice since they'd left Texas days ago, the heating system all but shot, the diesel engine the only thing left to warm the steel walls. He was thankful to be out of it for the moment, the alcohol's glow sinking into his muscles and bones.

With a wet belch, he stood, slewing to the side before staggering toward the window, parting the blinds and peering through at the hospital across the street. The sign out front read Centro de Salud El Jacal, and he leered at it for a moment, imagining what the McKnights were doing inside before he allowed the blinds to snap shut.

Keith turned away from the window and shuffled across the bloodied floor to the kitchen where he dropped into a seat at the table, slamming his bottle of tequila down. With a glance at the five bodies piled by the sink, he glared hungrily over the meal the family had been about to eat and began spooning big helpings of rice, refried beans, and a pepper-steak stir fry onto his plate. Everything was still warm and tender as he shoveled spoonfuls of it into his mouth, a ravenous hunger rising from his guts, jaws chomping, head shaking as he swallowed bite after bite.

"Home cooked food," he nodded graciously. "Beats the hell out of MREs." He pointed his fork toward the former lady of the house, who lay staring at the ceiling with bloody holes for eyes. "Very delicious, Mamasita. You should be proud. Such an excellent cook. Your husband and kids were lucky to have you." He paused for a moment, then nodded. "Yes, well, that's too bad. I wouldn't have had to stab you through the eyes if you'd let me in like I asked." He stopped chewing for a moment, utensil paused in the air, an angry expression crossing his face. "Look, lady. I said you're a good cook, so you better stop talking to me that way unless you want to end up chopped to pieces and tossed into a garbage bin. That's right. I can deny you a Christian burial just like that." Snapping the fingers on his other hand he winced until the pain faded. Chewing again, he mumbled, "That's what I thought."

Snatching the tequila, he swallowed another few swigs, his throat and belly craving the burn, letting the food and alcohol warm him. In fifteen minutes, a quarter of the bottle had disappeared, as well as most of the meal, his head swimming, fingers and toes pleasantly numb from the pain that had nagged him the entire trip. A warm comfort settled over him and he nodded at the blessed reprieve, surer than ever that his path of retribution and redemption was righteous. The mercenaries were out of his way, and nothing remained between him and his quarry.

Stuffed to the gills, Keith dropped the fork on the plate with a clatter, sitting back and releasing a grotesque belch that rattled in his chest and throat for a good three seconds before tapering upward into a high note that made him chuckle. Slamming his boots on the floor, he shoved himself back, coming to his feet, the dead family lying in plain view. Their corpses were bloody and twisted, facing randomly in the pile, a family portrait gone horribly wrong. The children were the least mangled because they hadn't put up a fight, their three angelic faces staring from the mass of bodies, limbs caught beneath them. The mother and father had resisted enough to get themselves butchered by Keith's carbon blade, the same one he'd used on Lena, its efficient, razor-sharp edge slicing the man's flesh like warm butter, putting him down fast.

Mama had fought like a demon, bless her soul, and Keith respected her for that. She'd attacked him with swinging fists and wild kicks he could barely follow, almost knocking the knife from his hand once before he got her under control and shut her up before the neighbors could become curious. For her bravery, he left her facing upward in the pile, allowing her to stare toward the Heaven she'd prayed for her entire life.

Shuffling through the bloody streaks on the kitchen floor, making new ones with his dragging feet, Keith stepped onto the old, bloodstained carpet, turning left and entering a hallway. Arms held against the walls, he staggered to the bedroom and began rifling in the dresser for something to wear. Checking for clean underwear and socks, he tossed out a pair of each, adding extra socks for his tender feet before stooping to the lower drawers to find an outfit that would help him blend in better with the locals. A moment later, he stood grinning with a pair of blue worker's coveralls in his hand. They were used and ragged, thick and loose, easily able to hide his flak jacket while fitting layers of long underwear beneath them.

"Bingo," he said, dropping them on the neatly made bed with the rest, staggering wearily, half drunk, to the bathroom.

It had been some time since he'd consumed so much alcohol, and it was rushing to his head all at once. While it would hinder his judgement and coordination for a while, it was the perfect anesthetic for his pain. In the bathroom, he leaned over the bathtub, turned on the water, and ran his palm beneath it, waiting for it to warm. It poured hot from the spigot, steam rising from the cool shower floor in a billowing mist.

He removed his flak vest and tossed it on the toilet seat. Next came his outer coat, jacket, and several layers of long underwear, each one grungy from a couple weeks of wear, peeling off him like a second skin of sweat and grime, the reek drifting off the soiled garments with a terrible odor, the staleness stinging his nostrils. It signified his days on the road, moments of battle, the time he'd put in taking nothing but backtalk from the mercenaries only to end up being the lone survivor and to get the last laugh.

His boots and pants came next, the rugged stench drifting off his bottoms worse than his shirts, a deep animal smell that went beyond an oxen's musk. The scent assaulted his nose as he kicked the garments into the corner along with his underwear and socks. Steam had begun filling the room, drifting across his wind chafed skin with a stinging touch, his calloused cheeks chipping off dry flakes, still rosy-red from the abrasive cold. When he looked at himself in the mirror, he was a different man. His blondish crew cut had grown out and was caked with grease and dirt, looking three shades darker than normal, wisps of it falling across his forehead and temples. The beard lining his jaw was rough, blonder, spattered with the family's blood in vibrant red drops within the hairs. But it was his eyes that had changed the most. They were the eyes of a stranger. Colder, bluer than before, with their own permafrost coating, flames flickering deep inside them, beneath the ice.

Holding up his hands, he tugged at the first bandages on his right hand, wincing as the old bindings pulled away pieces of skin in a slimy browned mucous. The tips of his first three right-hand fingers were dead and rotting, and a piece of his index fingernail came off with the bandage. He tossed it in the sink with a grimace of disgust; the fingertips would need to come off soon. The good news was that the rest of his initial frostbitten parts seemed to be healing, the stinging pain evidence of nerves still alive.

Keith sat on the edge of the tub with warm steam crawling up his back, stooping, reaching for the bandages on his feet. What the doctors hadn't already removed in North Carolina seemed okay, traces of frostbite on the knubs of his right big toe and pinky toe, his left foot mostly fine, his skin clammy cold in the heated bathroom. Standing, turning naked toward the shower, he held his left forearm out to test the water's temperature.

Once it was warm enough to enter, he pulled the stopper and activated the shower, gingerly withdrawing to the rear of the tub, heels down and toes lifted. He slammed the door behind him, palms open beneath the water before he jerked them back again, wincing in pain as rods of fire lanced up his fingers, through his wrists, and into his forearms, setting his nerves alight. Stepping back, holding his hands to his chest, he closed his eyes and sputtered, head ducking low to catch some of the spray. Slowly, he lowered his toes, the pain intense but tolerable.

Edging forward, dousing his head, he turned and backed up so the warm shower ran over his frozen shoulders and back, dripping down his buttocks and legs, shivers coursing through his muscles, days of aches whittling away into nothing. His fingers passed through his hair, the warmth stinging his sore, frostbitten knuckles, though the alcohol kept it at bay, allowing him to back in a little more. With water running over his shoulders, he rubbed away the dirt on his ribs, the bruising sharp from where Sam had shot him, the flak vest saving his life but not sparing his breastbone from the impact of the rounds.

When he finally gave in and turned into the full spray, he almost shrieked. The shower beat against his bruised chest and frostbitten hands and his jaw clamped tight on the shock, eating the scream that rose from his lungs, wanting to lash out, but striking anything with his fists would only bring more agony. Nerves on fire, rotted flesh wafting to his nose, Keith grabbed a bar of soap. Ignoring the ache, he massaged it between his hands, lathering up, running it across his chest and down his arms, scrubbing his armpits. He washed every part of himself he could reach, focusing on the tequila's pleasant buzz, grinning as the pain faded. Pouring shampoo over his head, he used his palms and a couple of fingers to rub it in, getting soapy. Fruity smells filled his nostrils, and he turned his face into the spigot, letting the water blast his cheeks.

Within fifteen minutes, the heat waned, the spray getting colder by the second. Keith turned the knob off, flipped the shower curtain open, and grabbed a towel, dabbing himself off gently, more relaxed than when he'd stepped in, a mysterious headiness in his brain, his entire body radiating a glorious warmth. Beneath the bathroom cabinets, he found some gauze and bandages, antiseptic and alcohol.

Dried off, he took everything into the bedroom and stood in front of the bureau mirror, spreading out his supplies, wrapping his fingers and toes first, slathering them with antiseptic balm. Next came his scars and cuts, which he used smaller bandages on, leaving the rest alone. Then he dressed, pulling on all the underclothing, wearing his flak jacket over two pairs of long underwear, tugging the coveralls overtop and grabbing his old boots and tying them on tight.

With a last glance around, giving the dead family in the kitchen a 'tsk tsk' and a wag of his finger, he shouldered his pack and stepped from the apartment into the hallway. Striding briskly to the end, he popped outside to a gust of freezing wind at the top of a staircase landing. He hardly felt it, warm on the inside and out as he descended the stairs two floors to the bottom, ducking into an alley between the buildings, seeing the massive APC parked by a dumpster at the end. The next building over were some businesses, side doors built into the lengthy wall. A pair of curious workers strolled out to watch as he went by, his leering grin driving them back two steps, murmuring words he couldn't understand, nor did he care to.

At the rear of the APC, Keith punched in the code, shivers of cold on his neck and shoulders. The electric motor whined high as the back door lowered, hitching and sputtering, the mechanisms wearing out. Keith hopped inside, whistling softly and a moment later he emerged with a pair of pistols in his hands, lifting them so the workers could see, then tucking them into holsters inside his coveralls.

Seeing Keith's grotesque leer, the men turned and shoved each other back into the establishment in comical fashion, running and bumping shoulders, wedging themselves in the door frame before they finally pushed inside and the door slammed shut behind them.

Well-armed and stepping lightly on the balls of his feet, Keith strode along the alley toward the hospital, smiling and whistling through the pain. "Okay, McKnight," he whispered. "It's showtime."

Chapter 22

Tom McKnight

San Felipe Santiago, Mexico

In the lobby's corner, beneath the dead television, Tom and the children had set up a veritable fort comprising three sets of armless chairs crammed together, blankets from the Humvee thrown on to form a bed. Jackets and extra clothing Saanvi had supplied made perfect pillows, more sheets tossed on for them to lie under. Linda and Jack rested comfortably while Tom and Sam slept side-by-side in a pair of chairs nearby, sitting up, each with a pistol inside their coats. Smooch lay on a pad under Sam's feet, the animal's ears ticking back and forth as she watched the patients and staff come and go, her good behavior earning her a pass from being kicked out into the cold by the staff.

While Tom sat with his feet up, he wasn't sleeping much. The hospital had handled three emergencies since they'd arrived; a nasty fracture, a stabbing from the north side of town, and one man who'd been involved in a fistfight, found in a ditch outside a bar and brought in. As for the nurse, she checked on them frequently, bringing them snacks and water and generally keeping them company. The kids had been so tired not even the sugar and caffeine could keep them awake for long, and they'd passed out soon after settling in. Even Samantha, her thin form curled in the seat next to him, had somehow dozed off on the coats and blankets she'd piled on the chair's arm.

A helicopter's rotor blades chopped the air above them, moving from north to south toward the US military base. The aircraft was one of almost two dozen he'd heard since arriving, topped off by an occasional jet zipping by overhead. He'd asked Henny how often military convoys came through town or visited the hospital, and she'd replied "quite often," which explained the rough welcome they'd gotten from the town's residents.

Rising from his chair, Tom turned and motioned for Smooch to stay before striding around the administration desks to a second waiting room on the opposite side of the ER. Daylight spilled across the floor from a pair of wide windows set into the south and west walls. Stepping to the south one, he glanced up at the sky to see the helicopter disappear over a tree line in the distance, its shape and form that of a military attack helicopter, though it was too distant to see what kind. Turning, he smiled at an old woman who sat in a nearby chair—she was used to him getting up and coming over by then—and she smiled in return, holding up her coffee cup in a toast before sipping. When he swung back to the glass, he caught sight of another big plane sweeping in and landing at the airfield. While he couldn't see the camp from his position, it must be less than five miles away.

He'd done his best to be positive during the long hours of waiting even though he'd squirmed and worried, digging deep to grasp the last sliver of faith that remained inside him, using everything in him to keep from falling into despair. With a sigh, he turned and shuffled into the north lobby, hands shoved into his pockets, worry gnawing at his guts. When he got there, he saw Sam was up and talking to a pair of nurses at the station between the ER doors and administration desks. She offered him a brief wave, and he waved back, grinning tiredly as he circled to check on the other two kids and Smooch. As he started to sit, his knees creaked, spine cracking, legs and feet weary and sore, hands and arms bruised from the fight with Serge but at least they were warm and fed, and had a place to sleep.

For the next hour, Tom faded in and out of consciousness, sometimes glancing up to see Sam laughing with the ladies there, the nurses seemed to have taken a liking to her. But the next time he looked up, Carlos was stepping through the emergency doors, looking around the room until he found Tom. He walked straight over, the flat expression on his face turning Tom's insides to mud, a weak gasp escaping his throat as he bounced from his chair to hear the news.

"Hi, Carlos." From the corner of his eye, Tom caught Samantha and Henny coming over, an expectant look on the girl's face, eyes glassy with raw, exhausted emotion.

"Barbara is alive and stable," he stated, the corners of his mouth lifting in a slight smile.

Tom turned to Sam, barely able to get his arms extended before she leapt into them, long curls flying everywhere, her body vibrating with joy, words coming out of her mouth that sounded more like whimpers and cries than an actual language. It was all he could do to hold her with one arm, squeezing her tight as he shifted his attention back to the doctor, desperate for details.

"I got the bullet out and stabilized her," Tom said breathlessly, "but she just kept getting worse. What was the problem?"

Carlos was already nodding. "It was touch and go for a while. The internal damage was from a splintered rib, and that's what was causing the bleeding. But the surgeon did an excellent job, and he specifically said that you saved her life by removing the bullet. I saw her x-rays, and she's going to make a full recovery. Her blood pressure has stabilized and she's on the mend."

"That's the best news I could've ever gotten," Tom sobbed, striding forward to grab the doctor with his other arm, clinching him briefly before letting go.

Laughing, straightening his coat, Carlos backed away, glancing at Henny who was grinning from ear to ear while over by the improvised bed, Linda and Jack Rose, heads poking up.

Jack rubbed his eyes and blinked. "Gosh, guys. I was sleeping so good." Then he caught their smiles, and a hesitant one formed between his boyish cheeks. "Is it Mom? Is she okay?"

"Yes, she's fine. She's stable." Tom rested his hand on Sam's shoulder and guided her toward her siblings. "Fill them in, Sam, okay?"

"No problem."

Tom turned back to the doctor, relief etched on his face, an eyebrow raised in question. "How soon can we move her?"

"How did I know you were going to ask that question?" With a dark chuckle, Carlos shook his head, expression sobering. "The surgeon says she can't be moved for a while. She must stay here and rest for a few days minimum." Stepping forward, he laid a hand on Tom's shoulder. "I know you want leave, but she'll need constant monitoring to make sure we didn't miss anything. Moving her right now, in her condition, could be extremely dangerous. Do you understand what I'm saying?"

Tom was nodding, a mixture of relief and worry entwining his heart and mind as he looked past the doctor to the lobby's north side and beyond that to the airfield and military camp he knew sat in the distance. His gaze dropped to Carlos. "Can we at least stay with her? I'm sure you don't want us camping in your lobby, and we really don't have any other place to go except the Humvee."

"Of course, you can stay with her. I know we told you we didn't have any cots available, but the doctors offered some we keep as spares for on-call physicians so they can rest on long shifts. Everyone agreed you can borrow them while you're here."

"That's… amazing of you, Carlos." Tom fixed the man with a confused look. "But you don't have to do that. Your people need those. We can make do with the blankets and clothing we have on hand."

"No, I'm afraid we insist." Looking to Sam, he stepped closer, voice low. "Sam made friends with the nurses today."

"Yeah," Tom issued a scoff that was more a snort than anything, caught between laughing and crying. "She's a friendly girl."

"Well, she told the ladies what your family has been through to get here. You left out quite a bit. She mentioned how you were separated and had to find your way back home, losing a good friend in the process."

"Jerry," Tom nodded, a discomfort rising inside him because of the young man's death and because of Samantha's willingness to share information that might make the doctors and nurses more wary of them. "He was a good kid."

"She talks about how you survived the worst of the cold. Your time at the camp in Virginia, then North Carolina, where you found the Osprey." Carlos shifted, arms folded across his chest, looking at Tom in a different light. "It took a lot of resilience to reach that point and reunite as a family. Hats off to you, my friend. And you never mentioned in Nuevo Laredo that you lost another close ally. One of the medics who traveled with you from the crash site?"

"Saanvi," Tom said, another name, another person he would've gladly called a member of his own family. "She took care of the kids from the start. Always concerned about them. Then she kept Smooch for us while we were inside the, um, prison section. That's how we got the Humvee and all the gear we brought with us here." The impossibility of it drew a light scoff from him. "That truck barely made it, but we never would've had a chance without her helping us."

"She told us you had to shoot people." His eyes flicked to the girls. "Them, too."

Tears reformed along the rims of Tom's eyes, the weight of the guilt clawing at his soul, every squeeze of the trigger a gash in his subconscious, an irreparable thing he'd have to live with his entire life, even if it was for the greater good of his family. "Sam's coping with it pretty well, Linda, too." He glanced at his kids as they folded the blankets around the tent area and rearranged the chairs back into their normal positions. "I try to talk to them about it, because I know how things like that can weigh on a person's conscience. It certainly weighs on mine. It's been tough to find time so far, constantly being on the run like we have."

"It's hard enough being a father," Carlos nodded. "Even in the best of times. Doing it now seems… impossible. I've got two little girls of my own."

Tom smiled. "What are their names?"

"Elsa and Sophia. Ten and a half and thirteen. They are the lights of my life, and I protect them, though it means keeping them locked away, mostly. I don't know what…" The physician's eyes misted over, glassy and red, but he held his head high as he wiped the moisture away. "I don't know what I'd do if someone tried to take them from us or hurt them. I'd turn into a madman. A raging demon."

"Sometimes I feel that way, believe me," Tom nodded. "It hasn't been easy, and they've had to take on a lot of responsibility for their own protection. That's how I know we raised them right." Looking up, he blinked. "Never doubt yourself, Carlos. As long as you have your girls' best interest at heart, things will be okay in the end."

"That's what it comes down to, Mr. McKnight. That's why we want to do everything we can to help you along the way." The physician turned and gestured around at the staff. The two ladies at the administration desk were smiling back, and the big orderly he'd almost tousled with gave a faint nod from where he stood by the doors. Henny glanced over with a grin as she drove an empty cart to where the kids were packing things up, talking excitedly amongst themselves. Carlos continued. "It's been rare to see good people come through here lately, and your family is the real deal."

Standing, legs still aching, Tom shuffled forward and embraced the young doctor, gripping him fiercely before letting go. "I really don't know how to thank you for helping my family. We've seen the worst of humanity, and the best. You and your staff fall into the latter category, for sure. We can't thank you enough."

"Henny will get you situated upstairs," Carlos said with a flourishing gesture. "Now I've got some rounds to make, so I'll let you get on with it."

After a brief handshake, and a strong pat on his shoulder, the doctor turned and walked away, striding through the emergency room doors to disappear into the hallway. Tom pivoted, moving to help the nurse and his kids load up the last of the blankets onto the rolling cart. With a grin, he took the handles and spun it, whistling to Smooch to come as they followed Henny and the children into a side hall stark with illumination. Restrooms and meeting rooms sat off the corridor, even a security window where a pair of armed guards stood behind the glass partition. Two turns later, they found an elevator bank. Waiting until they'd all stepped on, Henny hit the button to go up.

On the top floor, the nurse got out and guided them along the hallway to room 307. They passed more nurses and doctors bustling through, food carts being wheeled around and cafeteria workers carrying trays in to waiting patients. She knocked gently on the door before turning the latch and going inside. The children skipped in behind her, Tom pushed the cart in, parking it at the foot of the bed as he looked for Barbara. The kids lined up on the other side while he shuffled to the near side, swallowing on a tightening throat, gaze tracing over his wife's sleeping form.

They'd connected her to a vital signs monitor, her heartbeat pumping a steady, comforting beat on the screen. An IV hung above the head of the bed, holding a unit of plasma and making all the difference in the world. Her cheeks were flushed with color, a faint pinkish hue, lips glistening with a smudge of moisturizing salve, an oxygen line running to her nose with the cannulation peace connected behind her ears. They'd cleaned her up a little as well but her hair was still greasy and dark where it was pressed back from her temples, though the dirt marks on her forehead were gone, her skin radiating freshness, hands resting on blankets pulled just above her waist.

"Oh, honey," Tom said, leaning against the bed. "I don't know what to say."

Linda and Sam stood looking at their mother's prone form solemnly, their hands clasped in front of them on the side of the bed. His eldest daughter's lips trembled, and a tear trickled down her cheek. Standing in the middle, Linda reached out to take Barbara's hand, wiggling her smaller fingers beneath it, touching her palm. When Tom tried to take a deep, steady breath to calm himself, the air came out in a shudder, emotion locking his chest, his mouth going as dry as a desert. His fingers crawled along the top sheet and took his wife's other hand, rubbing his thumb gently across her wrist.

Jack rested both forearms on the bed, shoving himself up, frowning with fear at his mother's face. "She doesn't look very alive."

The boy's matter-of-fact statement broke through Tom's weighty emotion, and he broke down into a laugh. "I know she doesn't look that great right now, but trust me when I say she's doing really well. See her cheeks? There's a lot more color there, and her blood pressure and pulse rate are way better than they were inside the Humvee. She's just sleeping right now, buddy."

Sam turned, glancing back at the monitor, face slack with relief as she nodded her agreement. "It's true. Mom's blood pressure was dropping off the charts, but it almost looks normal now. One twenty over sixty-eight isn't bad, right?"

"Actually, it's amazing," Henny said, coming to stand behind the children with her long arms stretched around all three. "It means that as far as we can tell, any internal injuries she had are fixed, and her internal bleeding has stopped. But..." The nurse's voice rang with a slight warning. "She's still not out of the woods yet. That's why Doctor Gonzalez wants her to stay a few days more for monitoring. And..." She dragged the word out, leaning in to hover over the kids with a smile. "That's why we're going to set up a camp here for you."

Jack's head whipped around at the folding cots resting against the far wall. "Is that what those little beds are for?"

"That's right. So, why don't we start setting things up." Turning them away with a solemn glance at Tom, she left him standing by Barbara's side.

"How long before we can speak with her?" He asked with a thankful nod.

"The anesthetic should wear off within the hour, and you can probably talk to her then. Though I'm not sure how coherent she'll be. Her body has undergone a lot of trauma, and she'll need lots of peace, quiet, and love to recover." Pointing to the cots, she guided the boy over. "Can you kids handle that?" Jack and Linda gave rousing replies, while Sam nodded and stared at her mother with pursed lips as she absently unfolded a cot.

The next forty-five minutes were spent setting up four cots side-by-side along the far wall, blankets and coats spread out evenly atop them, Jack bouncing on each one to test their strength and softness. The first notes of laughter sprang from his lips, and Linda got sucked into it, wrestling with the boy as he ran circles around them, never-ending energy radiating from his body like a nuclear reactor. Sam took things more seriously, organizing the beds properly, fetching pillows from the cabinets by the bathroom, making sure everything was doled out and they were ready for an extended stay. At some point, Henny had excused herself to go find them dinner, and Tom took over helping the kids. Jack had a million questions, which he tried to answer as honestly as he could.

"What if mom takes longer to heal and we have to stay here for more than a few days?"

"Then we'll stay here for more than a few days."

"What if mom gets sicker again?"

"We'll leave her care to the doctors and go by their advice, but I don't think she's going to get worse, son. She's looking great, if you ask me."

"What if the Humvee won't start when we try to leave?"

"That's probably the best question you've asked yet," Tom said with a chuckle as he fluffed up some pillows and tossed them down. "It's cold and getting colder. So, it's possible that piece of junk might not start and we'll have to look for a new means of transportation. We'll burn that bridge when we get there."

He reached low and patted Smooch's head as he stepped around to help Sam center blankets on the final cot. Between them, they finished tightening up their camp, and Tom was about to go back to the Humvee to check on their weapons, thinking he could hide them in the room when Henny returned with a food cart with four trays. Tom's grumbling stomach made him forget the weapons, and he sat on the cots with the kids, trays on their knees, digging into the simple Mexican fare of albondigas, rice, chongos, and hot, tomato-based soup.

Henny didn't stay to eat with them but excused herself to continue with her rounds, but not before the kids all circled her, hugging her, thanking her intensely for her help. Tom came last, holding out his hand in appreciation, but she pushed it aside with a smile and embraced him in a warm hug, both laughing before breaking off. After she'd gone, the children played and talked quietly as they settled onto their cots, their spirits uplifted by Barbara's presence and the eventuality that she would wake up at any moment to speak with them. Sam was the most anxious of them all, and try as he might, Tom couldn't distract her from her frequent glances over to the bed or occasional visits where she double-checked the vital signs monitor and held her mother's hand.

Still, not even the anticipation of Barbara coming awake could keep Sam's eyes open, and the past twenty-four hours of excitement drew her eyelids shut. Eventually, she ended up next to Linda and Jack on cots, their snores filling the room, a quiet peace settling over them. Tom had been sitting on his own cot by Jack, the boy's arm thrown across him as they chatted and joked. But with them all fast asleep, he gently lifted his arm and slipped from beneath its grasp, returning to Barbara's bedside, drawing up a chair to sit.

With quiet, steady breaths, he watched her face, following its lines and features, appreciating her elegant jaw and cute nose slightly upturned at the end. Memories of when they'd first met rushed back to him. Their times strolling along Virginia Beach, the only place they could afford in those days, riding the Ferris wheel, eating junk food on the boardwalk, though sometimes they hit the better wharf restaurants with fresh seafood and wine, every moment topped off with her smile. Barbara's thin but graceful lips formed that familiar expression of love and amusement she'd had whenever they stared into each other's eyes. Heart fluttering, he reached out and took her hand with both of his, loving its warmth and the steady pulse that raced along her wrist as he whispered to her.

"I know things have been hard on you, honey. I know we've barely had a moment to catch up since North Carolina, but I have to take this time to let you know how much I love you. A lot of old memories are keeping me going right now. Remember, before we had kids in that apartment at Virginia Beach? Those strolls along the boardwalk, eating hot dogs and ice cream. Having Sam was when the true test came, when our lives really changed. And all the years later, having Linda and Jack. So many incredible moments, they flash through my mind like a carousel. You're just…"

He swallowed and gripped her hand firmly, determined to tell her how he felt without tears getting in the way. "You're the best mother these kids could ever want. You've been there with them from the beginning, mentoring them, guiding them, and disciplining them when I couldn't be there. I'm sorry for the times I had to be away with the military, before and after Sam's birth, though I'm glad we made the most of what little time we had together. And one of the best days of my life was becoming a senior member of Maniford, knowing I'd be able to spend so much more time at home with you guys. The rest is history."

Tom was forced to back away, catch his breath, and swallow the swell of love that threatened to suffocate him with tears.

"I think we've rounded the corner," he said, chuckling. "That sounds crazy, given where we are now compared to where our home is, but it's true. And I know we've always talked about togetherness being more important than any farm or retirement accounts. That's never been truer than now. But…" He shook his head, looking upward with a disappointed note in his voice. "We worked so hard for that place. Long days and nights, a lot of weeks running together in blurs of time. When we put up that red barn out back, it about killed us. And you were pregnant with Sam, waddling around and putting hay down, working right up until the last minute of your pregnancy." Exasperated thoughts gripped him, and he turned his head to the side. "I hope the animals are okay. We left them facing a deadly winter, but there was nothing we could have done for them. I wonder if they wandered south at all, or just froze? If they were lucky, maybe someone from the government came by, loaded them into a cargo truck, and drove them south. I wouldn't complain about that. I guess we'll never know. And the house… those beautiful woods. I'm just so sorry it had to go, but it all comes down to what I was saying before."

He squeezed her hand, fingers tracing along the inside of her arm, looking over toward the children where they rested peacefully on their cots. "It comes down to the people in this room right here. Me, you, and the kids. And, of course, Smooch, the wonder dog who apparently can't die." He laughed softly, laughing alone, though he searched her face for any sign of life other than her shallow breathing and the constant beep of the vital signs monitor. His voice rose with deep strength. "It's just amazing we're still here, holding on despite everything. And we'll make it no matter what. No matter where this crazy road takes us, even if that's all the way to Venezuela, or the South Pole. We're in this together, and that's how we'll stay. And the running… That has to stop soon, and it will. But where that'll be, I have no clue."

He clung to the silence for a short time, one minute turning into ten, nothing but the sounds of the kids' snores, Barbara's shallow but steady breaths, his own heartbeat in his ears and always the regular beep of the monitor's chirp.

When a brisk, unrelenting knocking struck the door, his head jerked up from a daze. Smiling at Barbara, he said, "It's probably a doctor coming to check on you. Or maybe, Henny, who you'll love." Tom released her hand and stood with a soft smirk. "She's really good with the kids and has helped us adjust here today. I'll be right back."

With a sigh, Tom swung his tired feet forward, ragged jeans and heavy boots weighing him down as he shuffled to the door, grabbed the handle, and pulled it open.

Chapter 23
Keith
San Felipe Santiago, Mexico

Keith strolled across the street, stifling his eagerness to keep from bouncing on the balls of his pained feet. The town was a glum place, so appearing too excited about anything would make him stand out like a sore thumb.

People were out, carrying on with their regular business, visiting, shuffling toward the corner markets and dilapidated storefronts. A group of youths stood in front of a liquor store up the highway, hands stuffed into pockets and huddled close, the chill dampening their roguish spirits. Catching their sidelong glances, he pulled the coverall hood over his head as he reached the street. Not bothering to look both ways on the sparsely driven road, he crossed and strode past the hospital sign and over the grass partition to squeeze between some bushes with brittle, crispy-cold branches that scraped against his legs.

His body thrummed with a simmering fire as he went toward the hospital's drive-up entrance and front doors. Orderlies wheeled a pair of patients to a van off to the left and two nurses stood on one side of the front doors, waiting for someone, barely noticing him, no one concerned with the hooded man in the mechanic's overalls with Pedro emblazoned on his name tag. The sky had turned one of its thousand shades of gray, the clouds lying overhead like a splotch of old pancake batter, rolled out smooth in the middle, jagged around the edges in puffs of white highlights. The occasional ray of sunlight burst through to touch the ground, but its warmth was bare and paltry against the winter chill. As he was about to step inside, two guards walked out, their heavy coats covering the nightsticks and pistols on their belts, each with a radio mic attached to their coat breasts, their beanie-style hats marked with a circular security emblem.

Turning on his heel, Keith took an abrupt right, stepping out of the grass onto a cracked walkway that led him to a side lot and the emergency doors. From his head down posture, he glimpsed a couple of ambulance drivers with their truck pulled in nose-first to a spot, doors open as they hauled out a patient, the stretcher legs elongating automatically, wheels touching the ground with a clatter. The EMTs turned and pushed the gurney toward the emergency doors, breaking into a fast walk as they headed right at him. With a quick glance into the lobby, he hustled on by, staying out of the technician's way, not catching sight of Tom or his family.

Angling for the next corner, he circled to a sidewalk that ran along the rear of the building parallel to a retaining wall, glancing past the wilted shrubbery and grasses into the lot below. A spattering of cars filled the spots, over half with rust decorating the paint, fenders hanging off, at least a dozen at the far end likely left abandoned. He next searched the hospital's rear wall, its ventilation and pipes running along the exterior, windows staring out into the dead gray sky, at least three doors giving him optional entry points. The first two read Employees Only, while the last was a physician's entrance. He stopped, pivoted a hundred and eighty degrees, and marched back to the middle one, bracketed by bushes and a couple of lawn chairs, cigarette butts tossed into the frozen mulch.

Looking both ways, Keith edged up to the door, putting his ear to it, not hearing anyone on the other side. There was no window or sidelights, so he turned the latch and pushed quickly inside, spinning, shutting the door behind him, right hand wrapped around the hilt of the carbon blade in his pocket.

The sounds of running machinery greeted him, tumbling clothing and the squeaking and squealing of a rotating drum. The smells of detergent and fabric softener filled the air, faintly underpinned by the pine-scented cleaner. Turning, looked across a long room with shelves full of folded linens, sheets, pillowcases, and towels. Across from those were four big industrial-sized laundry machines, two washers and dryers and at the end, a cluster of wide-mouthed clothes baskets hung in stands.

As he finished his turn, he almost slammed into a short woman with her arms full of folded towels. Initially gasping, the woman backed up a pace and stopped with a hesitant smile on her face, words in Spanish coming from her mouth as she ducked forward to see beneath his hood. Keith had no experience with Spanish, didn't know a single phrase or even how to say please and thank you. All he knew was, "Si, señor." Anything else was gibberish to him. When he didn't immediately reply, she leaned in farther, caught sight of something she didn't like, and danced back a step, glancing over her shoulder where two corridors led away.

When she turned back to Keith, her smooth neck met his blade, the knife plunging in deep, penetrating her esophagus, slicing through connective tissue and tendons, jerking it out to leave her gurgling and staggering backward. Before she could fall too far, Keith's left hand grabbed her by the hair, keeping her up, slamming the knife into her eye, to the hilt. It sliced through the soft brain matter, scraping bone as he yanked it free and he put his hand beneath the stack of towels she was still holding and pushed them against her gushing throat.

As she choked and collapsed, he snatched the back of her shirt, jerking her upright, dragging her through the laundry room. Her feet kicked faintly, fists flailing at him weakly as he found an empty bin, lifted her thin frame off the ground, and slammed her backwards into it. With her legs sticking up, he thrust the blade a half-dozen more times into her before she finally stopped moving. Glancing aside, seeing no one, he shoved her feet all the way in and tossed a pile of towels on top of her. Grabbing a clean one for himself, he wiped off his bloody hands and threw it in after her, then he draped another rag over his arm, holding it against his chest, still clenching the carbon blade under it.

The floor was smeared with blood, shoe prints spreading it everywhere, streaks of it on the tiles, mixing with moisture from a dripping pipe. There was no time to clean anything else so he walked around it, past the vibrating machines to stand at the junction where one hallway went left, the other right. An array of doors lined both, and he figured one was just as good as the other, choosing the left on a whim.

As he passed through the dank corridor, he spotted a mop bucket and broom sitting in an alcove halfway down, miscellaneous tools on a shelf above them. He grabbed a wrench, carrying it in his left hand like he had a place to go and something to do. Whistling low beneath his hood, he strolled along until he reached a short branch to the right. After twenty feet, it opened into a kitchen area, with a few bustling cooks flitting by at the edge of his vision. The smells of baking bread drifted through the hall along with a faint wash of spices, sizzling peppers, and roasting meats. Not knowing where he was, he strode boldly up, shifting sideways to avoid a passing worker, turning left, walking across the kitchen's rear wall.

A stove door slammed shut and an empty rack rattled by. Someone stepped from an office with a checkered cook's shirt, and Keith held back with a polite nod, letting them pass, saluting them with his wrench before moving on. He cast sidelong glances at the staff, a few of them looking his way, but none too interested in a guy named Pedro who was going to fix something. Ahead of him stood a cart with a coffee urn, a pile of plates and cups, and a bowl of strawberries on it. With a quick twist to his left, he poked out with the carbon blade, stabbing at a strawberry and popping it in his mouth, chewing happily as the sweet juice dribbled down his throat.

Keith stayed to the outside, looking around in search of any doors or passages that might lead him to a nurse's station or anyplace that would tell them where Tom McKnight and his family were. A group of cooks were walking his way when he noticed a short, left-hand hall with a wide elevator at the end.

"Perfect," he mumbled as he banked left and strode toward it, stepping inside and bending to study the numbers on the control panel. There were three floors, not including the roof, and two basement levels, one marked Boiler Room.

As he was deciding which one to push, someone hollered out in Spanish, followed by the clattering, rattling wheels of a food cart. Before Keith could protest or press a button, the heavy cart rolled across the threshold, its wheels clanking over the trim, a big, boisterous guy shoving it in.

Keith stepped back, watching as the guy maneuvered the massive cart and its trash bin around inside the lift, finally getting it situated, saying, "Dos, por favor," to him.

"What?" Keith asked.

"Dos... Pedro," the guy repeated, leaning in and staring at his nametag. When Keith didn't immediately respond, his thick shoulders and a head of brown hair pushed past him to punch at the buttons.

"Oh, I see," he said with a slow nod.

The doors paused for a moment before rattling shut, but the elevator didn't rise. It sat parked as something wound up in the mechanics, vibrating the floor and shaking the walls. The man turned to him, speaking fast in Spanish, chuckling, pointing at the doors. Keith figured he was trying to tell him the elevator was a piece of crap, but he only nodded and stepped to the side, waiting for it to go up. But the worker kept laughing, tossing him a friendly elbow, firing off a joke that meant nothing to him. When the man boldly lifted the top lip of Keith's hood, the agent's cold eyes shifted upward, sending the kitchen worker jerking back in surprise, just like the lady in the laundry room.

Keith whipped the wrench up in a sweeping motion that clocked the worker across his temple with a crunch of bone, dropping him against the doors as the elevator lurched and began its ascent with a high grind of machinery and clattering of gears. A moment later, on a different floor, the doors rattled open, and Keith stood there alone, folding a bloodstained towel over his hand, the faux wood flooring slick with blood, the edges of the stainless-steel trash receptacle marked with bloodied fingerprints and splatters of red. He settled his hood back in place, unable to find the wrench, though it hardly mattered anymore.

Stepping out, he walked straight ahead into the main corridor of a hospital patient ward. A circular nurse's station sat in the center, two halls branching off to either side. Directly across from him was a short passage that housed another few rooms. The corridors were quiet but for a gentle murmuring of doctors and staff, one patient standing near the junction's corner, clinging to their IV stand and staring at the floor. The lights were on, but shadows lingered in the hall as daylight waned.

Putting on his best smile, Keith strode directly forward and up to the nurses' station, leaning against the waist high partition, beaming at the doe-eyed beauty behind the desk. He stood there with blood splattered on his coveralls, his blade and bloody towel resting on the partition, his cold blue eyes staring down, grin plastered to his face like he had just stolen it from death itself. The nurse clacked on her keyboard, eyes drifting across the screen, mouth moving wordlessly as she read what was in front of her. Her brown hair was bundled atop her head, held in place by a pair of decorative sticks, lips lightly rouged and just a touch of makeup on her face.

"Un momento, por favor," she muttered.

While he was looking directly at her, his head was filled with the layout of the place, noting the near comatose man standing at the corner and the shuffling feet and murmurs of the hospital staff as they performed their regular duties. He estimated there were five staff members on his left, another three off the other way, none of them formidable, not like the guards downstairs at the front door.

Perfectly still, he watched as the nurse finished clacking her keys, shifted to her left, and turned to face him with her hands clasped gently on the lower portion of the desk. She started to speak, but her lips stopped moving two or three words in, eyes staring up at his bloody coveralls, the red splatters across his cheeks, and the rictus grin beaming down at her.

"Hello." Keith smiled, speaking politely. "I'd like to know where Tom McKnight is."

When she replied in Spanish, head tilting, swallowing hard, he repeated himself, pronouncing every word carefully so she fully understood.

"Tom. McKnight. Or, any McKnight." He pointed at her computer, mimicking keyboard typing with his bloody left hand.

"Ah, sí, quieres saber en qué habitación están?"

"Yeah, whatever," he replied, jabbing his finger harder at her keyboard "Mick. Night. Look it up, lady."

Nodding faintly, her expression disturbed, she made a sweep of her keyboard, clicking through some screens, eyes flashing wide for a moment as she paused, casting a sharp glance in his direction. To her credit, she moved fast, lunging across the desk to a red button by her computer, but Keith was faster and moreover he'd expected the move. Flying forward, he grabbed her topknot and jerked her toward him, using the high partition as leverage where it was nestled snugly against his stomach. As he dragged her closer, screaming for help, his carbon blade struck again, its razor-sharp point drawing out blood in a spatter of red, followed by her face slamming into the lower desk. As she rose, the knife cut three quick swipes across her neck, then he shoved her over her chair, toppling them both to the floor with a clatter.

Spinning away from the desk, he glared at an oncoming doctor who'd heard the commotion and was rushing to the nurse's aid. With a growl, he swept his blade across the man's grasping hands, drawing a yowl, forcing him back. As the doctor fell, he took a knee to the chin on the way down, dropping him on the spot.

Keith waved the knife at him. "Trying to be a hero, are we?!" he yelled.

Before he could stoop to finish the job, a nurse stepped from a room right there, eyes flying wide when she saw the bloody doctor lying on the floor. She slipped as she tried to run, stumbling on her own feet, but he was on her in a flash, snatching her by the back of the neck and slamming her against the wall, turning her head to the side with his knife at her throat.

"McKnight! Tell me where McKnight is!"

"No sé! No sé!" she cried, face twisted in a terrified grimace, tears streaking to her chin.

"I'll take that as you don't know." The carbon blade swept in to take care of business, and the nurse's bloodied form slumped to the floor, one arm trailing down the wall as the other clutched her open throat, scream stifled, vocal cords cut like brittle parchment.

Reeling with an enraged howl, Keith stomped along the hallway, gaze flitting across the door numbers, chasing terrified workers back into the rooms, doors slamming everywhere as the hospital staff ran for their lives. Just when he thought he'd run out of options, a bewildered nurse stepped from a supply closet, looking to the left and then right, spotting Keith barreling down on her. Before she had a chance to flee, he grabbed her by the arm and slammed her into one of the nurse's carts, pens clattering to the floor, a pair of plastic bedpans crashing in a splatter of yellow urine. He jerked her aside and shoved her against the flowered wallpaper, blood-slick blade waving in front of her face. She sniveled and trembled, eyes darting around, widening when she saw the bloodshed farther down the hall, her voice rising in panicked whimpers when she spotted the dead nurse fifteen feet away.

"Look at me," he commanded, but when she remained fixated on the dead woman, he shook her harder, screaming, the tendons in his neck stiff with rage. "I said look at me!"

Head jerking straight, trembling, wet with a stream of tears, her terrified eyes fixed on his. With a leering, angry snarl, Keith pressed forward, his nose touching hers, each syllable squeezed through his teeth in a hiss as he spoke. "If you want to live, tell me where Tom McKnight is. Tom McKnight."

As he brought the knife near her neck, the woman's eyes flicked toward a door at the end of the hall. Keith glanced in the direction she was looking, pointing with the carbon blade. "Right there? That door right there?"

She nodded vigorously, trembling in his grasp, guilty eyes streaming tears as she looked away. Grinning, Keith threw the woman to the floor and crept over to the door, ear placed to it but not hearing anything on the other side. The nurse he'd been holding scrambled across the tile hallway, getting to her feet, sprinting away with pounding tennis shoes and gasping, sobbing breaths.

It didn't matter, because he'd found his prey, through trials and tribulations and torture and death and destruction and the loss of everything he'd held dear. None of that mattered – he'd achieve final, glorious retribution in just a few short seconds. Straightening himself, twisting his head in a circle to stretch his neck, Keith raised the blade, reached up with his left hand, and began to hammer the door with repeated, insistent knocks.

* * *

Tom pulled open the door and blinked, confused by the bustle coming from the hallway, the air filled with a new sense of urgency. "Hey," he nodded. "What's going on out there? I thought you had rounds to go on? Come on in." Tom moved aside to let Henny in.

"No, Mr. McKnight." She stepped just inside the door, head shaking vigorously, panic stitched across her face, eyes darting to the children. "We have to get the kids up. We have to go right now."

Hair raising on the back of his neck, he jerked her inside the room and leaned into the corridor where a pair of doctors and a guard were running toward the elevators. The officer carried a pistol in his hand, the doctors each bearing a blunt weapon. Pulling the door shut, he turned. "What's happening? Is it a military raid?"

"I don't know," she replied. "They found a dead worker in the laundry room and another in the service elevator. I think it was Carlita and José. They were stabbed to death..." She grabbed Tom's shirt, uncontrollable tears pouring from her eyes as her face twisted to remain in control. "Some nurses are dead, too. But one escaped and reported someone in the second-floor hallway killing people. He looks like he works here, but he doesn't! And he's searching for you! He's screaming for McKnight!" She motioned at the children again, pleading as she jerked his shirt. "You've got to go right now! I don't know who he is, but you must go!"

Looking at the door, Tom's shoulders slumped, lips tightening into a thin line, a deep breath filling his tired chest as, once again, their brief reprieve from running was at an end. He nodded.

"I know who it is."

Book 7: RESTORE

Chapter 1
Specialist Lance Morales
Central Mexico

The big Humvee trundled along the service road away from the massive parking lot and airfield, vast convoys of eighteen wheelers, Humvees, and every kind of supply truck in the military's arsenal passed them on the way in. Chinooks swooped in from the north, huge pallets of goods swaying beneath their bellies from chains as they approached the tarmac. Massive C-130s rumbled along the runway, noses lifting off the ground, pointing to the sky, turbo propellers hauling their bulging bodies upward as endless amounts of provisions moved south.

The sky was cloudless, filled with night except for a slight bit of pink off to the west, darkening clouds to the north like a distant fog carrying cold and snow with it. The vehicles passing them with supplies were dusted with it, white powder whipping off the hoods, crusted ice breaking off door frames and antennae, crashing onto the pavement in shards.

Morales turned right, leaving the main highway and joining a secondary road, heading north toward the small town Johnson wanted them to investigate. The traffic died to near nothing, the streets lightless except for a few lamp posts and homes with porch lights, modest fixtures glowing from the windows. Ranches sat off the road, surrounded by trees and fences, the occasional corner store lit up, cold and bored teenagers standing around with winter coats pulled tight, hoods covering their faces, tattered gloves on their hands. They stared at the Humvee as it passed, dark expressions hidden.

"You think they know what's going to hit them?" Morales asked, shivering. "The cold is coming. It's just a matter of time."

Smith scoured the shadows off the roadside with his eyes, shoulder pressed firmly against his door. He cradled his rifle, the hand guard resting on his knee, barrel pointed out the front window. "These folks have some tough times ahead unless CENTCOM plans to send transports to retrieve them." He shot him a sharp look. "Anyway, it's not our concern. Let's just grab this wayward Humvee and get back to the runway. I want to be on the next plane out of here."

Morales gave an affirmative grunt as he turned the wheel, taking a long curve, foot resting on the brake when they reached a rough spot in the road, a scar from the big earthquake that had hit when their unit was entering Mexico City. Many homes had structural damage, though lights still shined from inside despite the sunken windows and stoops. The only cars that passed them were a pair of beat-up sedans and a rusted out van with a missing headlight, the interiors dark and foreboding.

"Looks like we're getting close to town. You know where we have to go from here?" Morales motioned to indicate businesses springing up on the roadsides, a parking lot filled with broken-down cars, snow dust whipping between their tires, a closed garage out front. Stores and shops dotted the roadside, mixed in with clustered homes and a spattering of apartment buildings.

Smith referenced part of a folded map in his left hand, looking over the red lines marked on it, glancing up at the signs as they passed. "I think this is the right highway, but I'll radio in." He reached for the mic as Morales cruised at thirty-five, catching trickles of snow as it swept off the windshield and spun upward in a slow-spinning dervish.

"This is Search and Retrieval Unit Five calling Los Berros Supply Base," Smith said, his tone clipped. "Come in, Los Berros Supply Base."

"This is Los Berros Supply Base," a woman's voice chirped back. "Go ahead S & R Five. What do you have for me?"

"We're out here on Mexico 15 looking for that lost Humvee. There's a small town coming up. Can you point us in the right direction? Where is it?"

After a pause, the soldier came back. "The last known location of that vehicle was at the town hospital, Centro de Salud El Jacal. I probably butchered that pronunciation."

Smith chuckled. "I wouldn't know it if you did, base. Thanks for the info. We'll be bringing our lost puppy in shortly."

"Roger that, S&R Five. Good luck."

Smith hung up the mic, leaned back, and shrugged. "It's at the hospital."

"Yeah, I got that." Morales scanned their surroundings, the number of streetlamps growing, illuminating the cracked business establishments, brick fronts broken away, yellow sawhorses and tape stretched around them, a pair of small excavators nearby. "The whole place is nothing but hovels."

"I'd say the hospital is in slightly better shape than the rest of them," Smith replied flatly. "It's pretty important, especially here."

"You've got a point there. Oh, what about this?" Morales gestured to a large apartment complex on the right, then back at a pharmacy and gas station on the left. Off that same shoulder was a three-story building with a half-filled front lot where raggedy bushes framed a big sign that read "Salud El Jacal" along the bottom, matching with what Smith said. "Yep. This is it."

The Humvee slowed as they pulled in, gravel crunching under the tires. A yellow and red ambulance came into view, the drivers sitting inside, the glow of the interior lights painting shadows on their faces.

"Hey, cut through the lot and slip off to that alley on the left," Smith said, pointing behind them a little. "We'll check around back."

"Got it," he replied, whipping the wheel, circling the sign and cruising slowly through the lot.

A spattering of patients stood by the front door, a nurse nearby with her coat pulled tightly around her shoulders, a cigarette in her hand. Their narrowed gazes followed the Humvee as it moved past the first row of cars and turned between the hospital and a side building that might have been a school. They barely fit, the truck's armor scraping the brick on both sides, sparking where it touched.

Entering the back lot, their tires hit patches of slush, spraying off in waves. Morales's shoulders clenched, and the hairs at the base of his neck rose as a pair of hospital workers burst through one of the rear doors, staggering away from the building, throwing fearful glances back. A car jerked out of a parking space, causing him to slam on the brakes to avoid hitting it, Smith cursing the man as he tore off. Easing the Humvee forward again, he tried to read the various hospital signs, but there were several sections broken into visitors' and physicians' lots. The fancier vehicles, if he'd call them that, sat on a lower level than the others.

Smith scanned over the cars, row by row, turning in his seat and craning his neck suddenly, pointing deeper into the lower lot toward the hospital. "Hey, there's the Humvee! It's right there!"

Nodding, catching sight of it, Morales carefully angled into the next row over, wanting to sweep to the end and come at the stolen vehicle from the other direction. He straightened the big truck, its massive frame dwarfing the smaller cars parked there as he edged forward. A nurse flew through a different door and sprinted up some steps along the back of the building.

Eyes narrowed with doubt, Morales said, "I don't like the looks of this." More people poured from the hospital, running up the rows, getting into their cars or rushing past them into the cluster of apartments and houses beyond the lot. Rolling down his window, he tilted his head, picking up a loud ringing coming from inside the building. "Is that a fire alarm?"

"Sounds like it," Smith said, eyes pinned forward, getting a better angle on the stolen military vehicle. "Damn. Would you look at that?"

Morales shifted his attention to the Humvee, noting several bullet holes through the glass, massive dents in the armor, bits of ice and snow caught in the crevices. The chassis sat awkwardly on its suspension, the left side tilted at an odd angle, one tire low.

"Looks like it took some small arms fire," Smith continued, edging forward in his seat, gripping his rifle tighter. "Is that duct tape over the holes in the windows?"

"Looks like it," Morales responded, bringing the Humvee to a stop, ducking as the sound of gunfire ripped the air, joining the blaring fire alarm.

* * *

Bundled in his coat and hat, Tom made his way down the hallway, one hand on the stretcher where Barbara lay, rolling smoothly along with a bag of fluid hanging from the metal rod over her left shoulder. Carlos stood on the other side, Nurse Henny behind them with another friend of hers, ushering the kids and Smooch along, stooping to zip their coats and pull their hats down tight as they went. The doctor directed them to an elevator and hit the down button, the doors sliding open for everyone to step inside.

Catching a moan, he glanced at Barbara, her head rolling to the side, eyes blinking open but barely, no recognition there, just a dazed look from the pain medication. Sam stepped closer, staring up and listening as Carlos gave them instructions on her care.

"It is absolutely critical that you keep her warm. Try not to move her. Try not to stress her out at all."

Tom raised his eyebrows and glanced around, the fire alarm ringing throughout the hospital. "I'll try, Doc. But we're not off to a good start. Will she be okay riding in the back of the Humvee?"

"I cannot promise you anything, Tom. I can only tell you to keep her stabilized to give her the best chance of survival." He leaned forward, fingers resting gently on Barbara's arm. "This is a vital point in her care, and any sudden changes, the least little thing, could be dangerous to her. Do you understand that?"

Sam's eyes were filled with tears as Henny and her nurse friend handed the kids bottles of medication and another first aid kit which got tucked under Linda's right arm. The nurse held up a bottle and gave it a shake, instructing the girl in broken English on how many pills her mother needed each day as soon as she was conscious enough to take them. Jack's head bobbed, eyes wide, pretending to understand when it was clear he didn't. Linda wore a similar expression, though she nodded more confidently, repeating the directions back to Henny.

"Take two of these per day for pain, and one of the others for infection," she was saying, holding up two bottles and shaking each one in sequence.

"And make sure she finishes every pill," the second nurse replied. "If you skip any days, you may give the infection a second chance to take hold. Understand?"

Linda stuffed the bottles in her coat pocket as Henny brought out more medications to explain. The elevator doors slid open, and the fire alarm blared in their faces. Carlos directed them to the right, leading them down a long passage where hospital workers rushed by as they helped patients hobble outside. One male orderly stepped inside a room, throwing a dark glance into the hall before he slammed the door shut, the sound of chairs moving into place to bar the latch.

"Where are we going?" Tom asked.

"This is the fastest way to your Humvee," Carlos responded. "We will go through the cafeteria and out the laundry room. There is a walkway there where we can wheel Barbara into the parking lot."

"But where should we go from there?" Tom asked, holding the gurney's corner and pulling it faster down the hallway. "We can't go to any of the US bases around here, but is there a safer place in Mexico? A haven?"

Carlos was shaking his head, gripping the other side of the stretcher, and jogging to keep up. "I cannot say with any certainty that anywhere in Mexico is safe at all."

At the end of the hall, he pointed them to the right, guiding the gurney along a short hallway into an open cafeteria, tables and chairs filling the space, a half dozen nurses and orderlies nodding curtly at Carlos and Henny as they rushed by. Tom noted one man's hands were covered in blood, the front of his scrubs also stained with splotches of red, sending Tom's stomach into a fit of knots.

"What then?"

"The best piece of advice I can give you is to take your family as far south as possible, to Venezuela if you can."

"Venezuela?" Tom's face scrunched as they pushed the gurney between the buffet line, entering the kitchen proper with its prep tables, massive soup pots, industrial sized blenders, and carts full of bulk tomato paste, beans, and rice. "That's a damn long way from here."

"Yes, it is. But we've heard through official channels that US forces have taken Venezuela. Rumors are that it will become the fifty-first state and is safe for Americans to enter."

"All right then," Tom nodded. "Venezuela it is. But that Humvee won't make it all the way."

"Then you will need to find secondary transportation. Go to Panama and take the ferry the US government has set up into Venezuela. You will be provided with a home and a job—"

"No. We can't do that, Carlos. That'll put us right back in the military's crosshairs. Any alternatives?"

"There are none," Carlos said. "If you want to ensure Barbara's ongoing improvement and to keep your family safe, you'll do as I suggest."

As they reached the back of the kitchen, the doctor gestured for them to go left, and Tom pulled the gurney's front end around, heading to another short hallway that looked like it had been rebuilt several times, the floor turning to gray-painted concrete with drops and smears of blood everywhere. A pair of red boot prints marched in their direction and disappeared behind them, leading from a big puddle of blood in the middle of the floor. They wheeled the gurney through it and entered a large industrial laundry area where the bloodstains were worse, dark splotches and streaks reaching the far end of the room. A woman lay on the floor with her hands resting at her sides, unmoving, her hospital scrubs stained red. Sam gasped and threw her hand to her mouth while the nurses turned Linda and Jack away and Tom swallowed hard. "Is she...?"

"She is dead," Carlos acknowledged, his dark voice taking on a hard edge. "That is the first nurse the maniac killed. And that is why you must leave right now."

"We heard you talking," Nurse Henny came forward, sparing a glance at the dead woman as she wrapped one arm around Sam's shoulders, the other holding a dog-eared travel book. "And we think we might have a solution for you. A place for you to take your family."

The other nurse stepped up, guiding Jack and Linda. "Your children told us about your lives before the anomaly. They said you worked your land, and you had many animals and crops?" She shook her head, struggling with the English. "What is the term? *Prepper*? You are a prepper?"

"I prefer *homesteader*," Tom replied. "Yeah, we had goats and chickens. A fair number of other animals, too. We can farm the land and live off it if we need to."

"Then the Darien Gap would be the perfect place for you." She shot a doubtful glance at Carlos but gave the book to Tom.

The doctor made a cutting motion with his hand. "Absolutely not! It is a harsh and dangerous environment, not friendly to outsiders. Nature would kill these poor people within an hour of them setting foot in the place. I am sorry, Tom, but I cannot recommend you go there."

Tom glanced at the book, which had a picture of a lush, forested area in front. "The Darien Gap? Is it just a big stretch of woods or something?"

Henny leaned closer, reaching across to double-check Barbara's IV. "The Darien Gap is an old smugglers' corridor, an inhospitable jungle that connects North and South America through Panama and Colombia. It is beautiful, but dangerous and remote. As Carlos said, it is an extremely harsh environment that has its share of violent people."

"Oh, I saw a documentary on that one time." Sam was standing at the foot of the gurney. "There are a bunch of legends about the place. Hundreds go in there every year and never come out. It's *hazardous*, Dad. There's no way we can go there. We'd be crazy to try it."

"You can't believe everything you see on TV," Henny corrected her. "I know people who have gone there and have carved out a life."

"While I agree with the young miss," Carlos said, tilting his head to Sam, "Henny is right. Whatever Sam has seen on television is probably exaggerated, and many good people have created small communities in the wilderness, choosing to live away from civilization. I have heard that the colder temperatures have cleared out the criminals. Whether that is true or not..." he shrugged "... you would have to see for yourselves. But, again, I don't recommend it. Not with young children and your wife in such a condition. Your best bet would be to continue to Venezuela and connect with more Americans."

"Yeah, but you said the bad people might be gone. Maybe there's something left there for us."

"Think about it, Tom. If the criminals are leaving because of the cold, the animals will leave, too. Not only the dangerous ones, but the ones you could hunt for food, which would be crucial to your survival. It may be safer than it was, but—"

An anguished scream ripped through the hospital, and their heads whipped that way, eyes wide with fear as the nurses guided Jack and Linda closer to the door.

"That's from right down the hall," Carlos said. "You need to go, now!"

"Henny, are the directions to get there in the book?" Tom asked, shaking it.

"Yes. Everything you need to know is inside. Now, go! It's the gringo who is looking for you. He will come soon!"

Tom folded the paper and stuck it in his pocket. "Thank you," he said, briefly shaking Carlos's hand. The nurses zipped up Jack and Linda and all the medicine and first aid supplies they were carrying. They embraced the kids before ushering them toward the door. Carlos shoved it open, and chilly air gusted in, the brisk breeze rushing across Tom's cheeks and down his neck.

Tucking in a blanket over Barbara's shoulders, he said, "Come on, kids. Sam, help me wheel your mother out."

They pushed her onto the sidewalk, partially lifting the gurney so the front wheels clicked over the cracks, the fluid bag shaking on its stand. Heads lowered against the wind, they drove her along the path and into the lot, watching as nurses and hospital staff fled through other doors, staggering off, some holding bleeding wounds, rushing past vehicles to get away from the muted gunshots still sounding from inside the ward.

Tom angled them toward the Humvee, nodding at Sam. "We need to get the cargo area cleared out so we can fit your mother inside. When we get there, hop in back and toss stuff into the backseat, got it?"

"Yeah," Sam replied with a nod, squinting against a gust of freezing air.

Dervishes of wind spun between their legs, jackets fluttering, Sam's curly hair whipping around her head as a pair of nurses rushed through the upper lot, glancing back fearfully at the hospital as if expecting Keith to bust out at any moment. Tom pushed Barbara faster, the wheels clicking over gravel and cracks, shifting sideways, sliding on icy spots. They were a quarter way to the Humvee when Sam slammed her palm on the corner of the gurney, pointing off to the left and Tom's breath caught in his chest as a second Humvee cruised toward them, one row over, its height towering above the other vehicles in the lot, though the soldiers inside hadn't appeared to have caught sight of them yet.

"Just keep going, Sam," he hissed. "We can make it."

Heads down, they pushed the gurney faster, the frame rattling, Barbara's body quaking with the rough ride. They'd almost reached the truck when the door they'd come out of shoved open violently, slamming back with a bang. A handful of hospital personnel stumbled outside, one woman hitting her knees and crashing onto her stomach. An orderly stooped to help her up, shouting for her to move while two kitchen staff split off and sprinted toward the second Humvee while another pair ran for the upper lot. As Tom opened their Humvee's rear door, Keith thrust through after the nurses, catching the door as it was falling shut, crashing it against the brick. Dressed in coveralls, his expression was calm as he strode toward the downed worker. Pistol in his hand, he ejected a spent magazine and slammed in a full one, charging the weapon as he approached.

The orderly lunged at Keith, but he was already shooting, two shots to the man's chest, blowing him sideways so he staggered into the bushes. Shifting his body, arm still extended, he fired at the woman who was clambering to her feet, putting a bullet into the back of her skull, the round exploding through her nose, spraying the icy pavement with blood as she pitched to the ground. Sam cried out, but Tom grabbed her by the coat and shoved her into the Humvee, watching Keith as he caught sight of them across the lot, a slow grin spreading on his face, triumph in his eyes.

"Linda and Jack, get inside!" he growled, circling the gurney, pushing the kids between the Humvee and the vehicle next to them. His rifle suddenly appeared, Sam holding it out, and he grabbed it and spun toward Keith, who was just taking aim when the second Humvee swept in with a roar, tires squealing and angling at the agent. Keith reeled, arms thrown up as the truck sideswiped him, sending his gun clattering away, body spinning to the ground. The Humvee went another ten yards before screeching to a halt, the doors flying open, two US servicemen jumping out with their rifles pointed at him, shouting at him to stay still and not reach for his weapon. Tom slung his rifle onto his shoulder, putting his finger over his lips to urge the kids to be quiet, nodding for Sam to keep working. Reaching in to help her, he grabbed all the bloodied rags they piled in the corner, blankets and pillows, several first-aid kits, Sam taking them and passing them up to Linda and Jack, clearing the cargo area quickly. Tom stooped to see how he could collapse the gurney, unable to find the latches, clueless as to how it worked when Sam hopped out. "Henny showed me how. You get at the end and push the front surface wheels to the edge. I'll lift the folding legs up."

Nodding, he moved to Barbara's feet and pushed the gurney forward so the wheels on the front part of the table hit the edge. Sam bent and tried to fold the legs up, tugging and jerking them to get the thing to work. Tom glanced at the soldiers as one collected Keith's pistol while the other rolled him onto his stomach, kneeling next to him, pulling a pair of nylon cuffs from a pouch on his belt.

"Got it, Sam?" he asked, holding Barbara steady.

"Almost." Sam grunted and jerked some more until the entire frame shifted and folded upward, allowing Tom to take all the weight and roll it inside.

Sam climbed in, grabbing the edge and hauling it to the left while he moved Barbara's feet to the right, sliding her in sideways until she was firmly in. The entire time, he was glancing over, watching as they lifted Keith and put him in the back of the truck. Slowly shutting the rear door, Tom circled to the driver's side and got in, easing the door closed behind him, then he slipped the key into the ignition and turned it, the Humvee coughing and sputtering to life, kicking off fumes and a waft of burnt oil. The vehicle in front of them had already pulled out and was gone, so he put the truck in drive and let it coast into the other row where he turned left and headed for the exit.

"How's it look, Sam?" he asked, unable to see what was happening in any of his mirrors.

Moving back and forth, stooping and craning her neck to see, she murmured, "They haven't seen us yet. One of them is on the radio... Wait, the other guy's walking toward our spot. Dad, hurry!"

Giving it a little gas, he sent the Humvee lurching forward to the end of the lot where he turned right, edging toward a row of trees and a thin alley that cut between rows of houses and apartment buildings. The massive truck barely fit in the passage, hitting branches covered with snow, white dust trickling over their windshield, Tom kicking on the wipers to clear the glass.

"What just happened, dad?" Linda asked from the very back seat.

"I'm not sure, but we need to get as far away from here as possible."

"Were they looking for us?" Sam's voice was a whisper in the truck's quiet interior. "Those were soldiers."

"Yeah, I know. And I'm not sure." He glanced into the rearview mirror at Linda. "Hey, why don't you and Jack organize all that stuff? Tuck the first aid kits beneath the seats, fold all the blankets and make some room. Sam—"

"I'll keep an eye on Mom," she replied, a faint grin on her face as her hat came off, and she squeezed in next to the gurney.

"Good girl."

Heart filling his ears with a pounding thrum, Tom reached out to see if he could coax some warmth out of the rattling heater.

Chapter 2
Keith
Central Mexico

Morales pulled into the camp, taking a side entrance to bypass the convoys still rolling in from the north. The man in back was screaming and yelling, kicking their seats, once forcing them to stop and bind his feet, Smith cracking him across the face to get him to shut up, but the blessed silence had only lasted a moment as he exploded into a fit again, frothing at the mouth, spittle flying as he cursed them.

"Oh, you're going to pay for this! You shouldn't have stopped me! She'll hear about this! You'll pay!!" He was screaming, calling him and Smith every name in the book.

"I'm already paying for this," Smith mumbled, rubbing his temples.

Cringing, Morales turned to the Lieutenant, trying to ignore the man. "You think he is who he says he is?"

"Of course I am!" Keith growled, leaning forward but jerking to a stop when he reached the end of his tether which was locked to a bar beneath the back seat.

Smith's patience had fled him ten minutes ago, and he turned around, fist raised. "I don't care who you say you are, buddy. One more word out of you, and I swear I'll stuff a sock in your mouth, and I've been wearing the same pair for four days."

Morales glanced in the rearview, tossing the man a warning look. "You think he's kidding? You should've seen what he did to the last assholes we had to deal with."

The man's wild eyes shifted between the two before he settled back, still seething, shoulders and arms straining to break the cuffs around his wrists. They pulled through the lot, using the temporary lanes set up with orange cones and soldiers standing at the intersections directing traffic. The route circled to a series of makeshift buildings, big heating units pumping in warm air and electricity, lights glowing from every window.

"This the place?" Morales asked.

"Yeah. It's building INT-3. There it is, written by the door. That's where base command wants us to park."

They'd already called it in, explaining who they'd found and asking if base wanted them to pursue the Humvee that had mysteriously disappeared, surprised when they were ordered back right away. Swinging around three parked helicopters, he pulled into the lot and found a spot with plenty of space between them and the other vehicles, watching as a pair of MPs strolled toward them. Morales got out, slamming the door behind him, the man inside breaking out into more hysterics, face pressed against the side window, smearing the glass with foam and spit.

One of the MPs shot a salute to Smith before staring past him. "Geez. Who's that? He looks a little—"

"Disturbed?" the Lieutenant replied. "Yeah, he seems to have some anger issues. Bastard's tied up tight so he can't budge."

"What's he in for?" the other MP asked, adding his salute to the mix.

"Shooting up a local hospital."

"Geez," the first MP repeated. "Want some help with him?"

"Affirmative. Base needs us to bring him inside and get him situated. Says he's been working with a Colonel Rachel Banks. Ever heard of her?"

The second MP responded. "Nope, but I hope she's a psychologist, because this guy needs some help."

"All right, boys." Smith gave a dark chuckle. "Get him out of the truck and inside."

Morales approached from the driver's side, letting the bigger MP lead the way. Smith and the other MP circled around, the Lieutenant jerking open the door and shouting in, "I swear, if you spit on any of us, it'll be lights out for you."

Keith shifted, cold blue eyes glaring at Smith, saliva dribbling down his chin as he cursed under his breath. The MPs leaned in and unfastened him from the bar, pushing him out on Morales' side. One MP grabbed him while the other came around to secure him, and together they muscled him toward the building. The guy thrummed with tension, the tendons in his neck standing out, causing Morales to retreat a couple of paces while the MPs shoved him along.

As they walked toward the building, Smith caught up with him, saying, "We need to figure out if this Banks lady is real."

"Yeah, and what does she have to do with a guy who just shot several Mexican citizens in cold blood?"

* * *

Morales stood outside the hanger doors, his jacket pulled tight around him, a warm mug of coffee in his hand, listening to the bustle of mechanics as they wheeled helicopters into the repair bay in a constant rotation, the aircraft needing round-the-clock maintenance to keep them flying. Out in the massive parking lots, supplies continued to roll in, trucks and big rigs, troop transports and ammunition haulers, soldiers loading up the C-130s and Ospreys before they lifted off and banked south into the dark skies. There were at least twenty-five other hanger bays spread out along the airfield's outskirts and the drone of engines filled the air, motorized wind to blow the light snowfall and wispy white dustings around, still not enough to accumulate or create any dangerous ice fields yet. A handful of MPs and soldiers wandered the grounds, but if they weren't helping the mechanics haul equipment, they were on patrol duty, sometimes stopping in for breaks, grabbing meals from the commissaries.

"I could get used to this." Smith took a draw from his cigarette, washing it down with a swig of bitter black coffee.

"Until the Cap sends us off on another oddball mission," Morales said with a wry scowl. "Not that I'm complaining, but Cap always has something fun for us to do."

"I'd hate for it to get too boring around here," the Lieutenant snickered. Then he turned and looked back through a window in the supply area. "This Keith guy is pretty interesting."

"Is that what you'd call him?" Morales half swiveled to peer inside with Smith.

The man named Keith sat handcuffed and chained up, sitting on a stool in the middle of the room, surrounded by green bins of supplies with a pair of stark white lights glowing down. A medic was checking him out, shaking his head as he inspected Keith's right hand, the blackish fingertips on the first three fingers looking rough and rotted, the knuckle skin chaffed and dried out. Dozens of cuts, bruises, and scrapes marked his face, patches of blonde beard lined his chin, though it was the crazed gleam in his eyes that sent a shudder up Morales' spine. The medic said something to him, gesturing at his frostbitten hands, and Keith snapped with spit flying from his mouth as he jerked against his chains. The medic jumped backward as an MP strode over, towering above them, glowering at the agent like he wanted to pound him through the floor. Keith glared right back, rising on the stool, putting his nose close to the bulky MP's like he might break his bonds and tear the man's head off.

"I couldn't guarantee the MP would win that fight," Smith scoffed.

"Tell me about it," Morales nodded. "That dude has zero fear."

"Nice thinking to take the guy out with the Humvee. We would've had to kill him otherwise."

As the medic approached to check Keith's other hand, Morales turned back to the airfield, shuddering against the brisk winds blowing in from the north. The soldiers stood in a comfortable silence, looking across the bustling parking lots and tarmac, clusters of lights sweeping in with the arctic gales.

The next sip of Morales's coffee curled his lip, cold and bitter, and he tossed it on the ground with a splash. "Man, I'm going inside for a minute. You want anything?"

"Wait," Smith said, nodding to the sky.

Morales turned and followed his stare to a cluster of six helicopters rolling toward them in formation, four of them continuing south while a single Black Hawk broke off and banked in their direction, lights gleaming from its belly as it swept in for a landing. He pulled his jacket tighter in a defense against the chuffing rotors as wind tore across the tarmac.

As soon as the wheels touched ground, the side door flew open, and a slim woman in military fatigues hopped out. Turning on her boot heel, she gestured and snapped angrily at the Marines inside, pivoted, and strode away. A Marine slammed the door shut, the pilot shaking his head, pulling into the sky before she'd even left the pad, stomping toward them, blue eyes glaring above gaunt cheeks, hair tied back loosely as the wind whipped strands around her face.

"That's her," Smith snapped, tossing his cigarette and squishing it out with his boot toe, both soldiers jerking stiffly in salute. "Welcome, Colonel Banks. We—"

She stalked straight by without a pause, jaw working back and forth, a soft curse on her lips as she grabbed the door and threw it open with a bang. Striding into the hall, she slammed her forearm against the right-hand door and shoved through. The MP stepped up to meet her, but she shouldered past him, fist cocked, delivering a sharp swing at Keith's grinning face. Her knuckles cracked across his jaw, snapping his head, bending him off the stool. Straightening, he lifted his chin in defiance, lip cut and bleeding.

Arms thrown out to her sides, Banks took a massive breath, chest expanding upward beneath the uniform, and screamed, "You son of a bitch! You almost cost me everything! What the hell were you thinking shooting up a damn hospital?! We're trying to keep peace with these people. This is a delicate operation, and every general in Mexico wants to know why my agent's screwing up! It took every last favor I had to fly down and straighten this crap out!" Head agitating, she cocked her fist, threatening to open his bloody lip even more, then her hand relaxed and she pointed a bony finger into his face. "You better have some good news!"

Smith and Morales exchanged a confused look, meandering closer to the door but not daring to go in, the Lieutenant saying, "She's got a nice right hook."

"That's one mad officer," Morales murmured back with a nod.

"I *do* have some good news," Keith replied with a leer, glancing at the glowering MP and medic. "But it would be best if we discussed it in private."

Banks' furious glare rested on Keith another moment before she turned to the MP and jerked her chin toward the door. "Take him to a huddle room. I want to talk to him alone." Nodding, the soldier gestured to another, and the pair approached the agent and released him from the stool.

Smith turned to Morales, holding his arm as the MPs guided Keith along the passage to a door at the end. "Come on," he said, pulling him inside the hangar. "Follow me."

The pair stepped past the mechanics and racks of helicopter parts. Amidst the ratchet clatter and banging of tools, they watched through another glass partition where the MPs secured Keith to a table in the smaller room. The Lieutenant Colonel strode in and gestured for the soldiers to go, and they turned and left, shutting the door behind them.

* * *

Banks stood across the table from Keith, arms at her sides, fists clenched, feet spread in a stance of discontent. Her narrowed eyes glared as he scarfed down his ration, palming his fork in his right hand, unable to grasp it because of his rotting fingers, but her anger superseded any hatred or sympathy she might have felt for the man, more concerned with getting something out of him, salvaging a hopeless situation. Over the past several days, she'd noticed a shakeup in CENTCOM, a shuffling of ranks, and she wasn't close enough to the generals and other civilian higher ups to guarantee her small team's continued latitude in the new government.

Their failed mission to blow up the anomaly was a dark scar on her record, and the resulting turmoil coming from an agent under her control was drawing the eyes of those in charge. Someone at CENTCOM was questioning her requisition for the two APCs and gear, and the shooting at the hospital was the last straw. Keith was an animal, slavering over his meal, grunting and groaning like a starved dog with every mouthful, stopping to grab his cup of chocolate drink, slurping from it, leaving a mustache on his upper lip that dripped to his chin.

"So, you're saying you have something for me? Hard to believe." With a head shake, she gasped. "What the hell happened to you out there? What did the McKnights do to you?"

He stopped eating, hand squeezing around the metal fork, face low and staring at his food. A wave of tension passed through his shoulders like he might spring out of his chair and stab her in the throat, but she'd made sure the MPs had chained him to the table.

Something shifted in his body, and he relaxed, eyes raising in good humor, a smile taking up in the corner of his mouth. "What's wrong, Colonel? You seem upset."

Uncoiling, Banks slammed both fists on the table, causing his tray to rattle on the surface. "You're the reason I've lost everything, and I should've never come this way. I should've just kept going to Venezuela, where at least there's a chance to recover my reputation. There's nothing left for me here." With an exasperated sigh, she straightened, gave him one last stare, and turned to go.

"Wait a minute, Banks." When she didn't stop, his voice raised with an angry edge. "I said, wait!"

Standing at the threshold, she closed her eyes and spun back, lips pursed. "What is it?"

Holding up his right hand, he wiggled his rotting fingers, and she caught a faint malodorous reek that made her nose wrinkle in disgust. "I've lost everything, too. And keep in mind, I didn't even want to lead that mission, but you forced me to do it. And that's what I'll tell the inquisitors when they come for their pound of flesh."

"Is that a threat?" She paced forward, ear bent. "Because if it is, it's the last one you'll ever make."

Both hands raised in placation, he shook his head in apology. "No, not coming from me, but I'm obligated to respond truthfully in a military tribunal. It doesn't have to get that far. We can never return to what we had, but I can offer both of us some catharsis."

"Oh, yeah? And just how are you going to do that?"

"I know where McKnight is," he grinned. "I was right there when those soldiers sideswiped me, bastards."

With a barking laugh, Banks turned to face him, head shaking with derision. "I don't give two shits about Tom McKnight or his family. They can fly off into the sunset as far as I'm concerned. Attempting to seal off the anomaly failed, and my credit is shot because I burned so many resources trying to convince my diminishing circle of influence that he still might be useful. If I'm lucky, I'll be left sitting at a desk in a nice comfy office in Venezuela until someone with the time digs out more info on me and gets me court-martialed. But, make no mistake, that won't be you."

Keith gave a light snort, nodding at everything she said. "And that's why you want McKnight and his perfect little family just as badly as I do. You want to see them suffer. I know you do, despite denying it, so we've still got some business to attend to."

* * *

Morales and Smith stood deep in the mechanic's bay, hidden in the shadows, peering through the glass into the room as Banks and Keith argued back and forth, arguing, shouting, the Lieutenant Colonel walking a tightrope between disgust and rage. Fists clenched at her sides, she spun away from him, saying something with a head shake. Keith replied snidely, causing the seething officer to turn and grab a chair, throwing it against the opposite wall, crushing the big screen TV, sending spiderweb cracks shooting across the surface before it crashed to the floor.

"What in the hell's going on with those two?" Smith asked, reaching absently for the pack of Mexican cigarettes in his coat, then drew his hand away with a shake of his head, remembering how the hangar crew had already admonished him for smoking in the bay with all the fuel and oil.

"I don't know." Morales stared at the two, measuring the tension through the glass. "Whatever's going on between them… it's dangerous."

"No kidding. Did you see the look in that guy's eyes? He's more than a few cards short of a full deck."

When Keith barely flinched at the Colonel's outburst, she lunged forward, snatching the front of his jacket and jerking him half out of his seat, her face two inches from his, words spitting from her lips. The agent's expression stayed flat, eyes calm, arms resting on the table, though he'd picked up the fork and held it tight in his right hand. Morales grabbed Smith by the arm, gesturing toward the window.

"We need to break this up, or he's going to kill her," he said, rushing to the bay door. "Look, he's got a damn fork in his hand, and she's way too close."

The two men started moving to the bay doors, Smith calling for the MPs standing just outside, when Morales glanced once more into the room to see Banks let go of Keith's coat and straighten.

"Wait," he said, holding Smith. "They're calming down."

The Colonel and her agent exchanged a few more words before Banks turned and exited the room with brisk strides, pulling her coat tightly around her shoulders.

"Oh, hell," Smith said, grabbing him by the sleeve and rushing toward the bay doors, the pair beating her outside, but barely.

Morales shoved his hands into his coat pockets, whistling, trying to look like they hadn't just been spying on them. Banks caught sight of the soldiers and angled straight at them. When she didn't brush past them, Morales turned and proffered a stiff salute, Smith spinning and adding his.

Banks returned the gesture, eyes still burning with heat. "I'm going to need you two for a side mission."

The soldiers shared an uncomfortable look, Smith seeing the panic in Morales's eyes, turning and addressing the higher-ranking officer. "I'm sorry, Colonel, but you need to clear that with Captain Johnson. You're Navy, and we're Army, so—"

"Never mind that." Her seething glare was masked by a layer of professionalism. "This is a wartime situation, and my commanding officers have a standing order that cross-branch operations follow the same chain of authority. Since I outrank your captain, he'll mark you as resources for what I need. In the meantime, we'll get started. Come with me."

Spinning, Banks marched off without another word, heading toward the motor pool and the small guard station there as a soft gust of wind twirled snowflakes across the pavement. Morales didn't immediately follow but stood there with a raised eyebrow. "You okay with this?"

The Lieutenant shrugged. "I'm outranked. Not much I can do. Let's hope Captain Johnson steps in when he hears about this. Until then, we're on the hook."

With a shake of his head, Morales followed Smith as they moved to catch up with Banks. In the huddle room, Keith watched through the open door, looking toward the end of the hall past the MPs as they shuffled in to release his bonds, grinning wide as his two new recruits helped Banks prep for their journey.

Chapter 3

Tom McKnight

Osa Peninsula, Costa Rica

Beneath a rich green canopy of jungle, an unseasonably cool, dry wind blew. It was the middle of the day, gray clouds pushing in from the north and west, bird calls and animal cries sounding unsettled and anxious. The woods shuddered, the first signs of a mysterious change taking place, a shift in temperature Costa Rica hadn't experienced in hundreds of years. While silvery light broke through the canopy, the woodland floor lay in a dense canvass of lush foliage, hiding the creatures that stirred beneath it.

Along a deer trail crowded with fern-like shrubs, bushes, and dangling vines, Tom moved carefully and quietly, boots crunching on twigs and broken limbs. Pistol in hand, he scanned the dense brush off to either side, tracking the movements of small animals and even a monkey or two up high. The air thrummed with life despite Carlos's indications that the changing climate would drive the creatures away, though he suspected that reality loomed on the horizon. Already, several species of flowers appeared to be withering, their stalks bent low as they rotted from being just a few degrees out of their native temperature band.

"Dad, I think I see tracks moving off to the right," Linda said from behind him. "Is that our guy?"

Glancing back, he saw her following close, pistol in hand, sleeves rolled up, jeans cut off at the knees. Her hiking shoes were covered in dried dirt, and mud streaked her lean, girlish legs. Despite it being just a few degrees below seventy, sweat beaded on her forehead and cheeks, and her hair hung lank and greasy, pink clips keeping it out of her eyes.

"It could be," he replied, breathing softly and slowly. Shifting attention off to the right, he caught sight of breakage in the brush, and he crept closer to spy small hoof prints angling toward the top of a bush-covered ridge. Taking a deep breath of jungle air he gave Linda a nod, whispering, "Be ready to climb if he charges us, got it?" Tom motioned to several trees with low-hanging branches surrounding them, easily able to hold her weight. She nodded and glanced around before peering anxiously up the trail.

Weaving up through the brush, sweat trickling down the sides of his face, Tom pushed aside frond-covered boughs and itchy leaves, ignoring the fat bugs that buzzed by. Their skin was saturated with bug spray to ward off the worst of them, but the insects were industrial sized predators, and his arms and legs had more than a dozen bites. He hoped the chemical stench didn't reveal their presence to their prey, but the breeze was blowing into them and shouldn't carry their scent too far. A soft grunt and crunch in the underbrush ahead caught his attention, and he dropped to one knee, stooping low, trying to peer up through the dense brush. Movement up by the ridgeline drew his eye, the bulky brown shape two feet tall, its bristling hide shifting beneath bulging muscles as it rooted around for grubs and other morsels.

"There it is," he said in a whisper, eyes lingering on Linda until she nodded that she understood. "Remember to aim for its chest. Heart and lung, okay?"

He didn't wait for her to respond, focusing all his attention on the boar, tracking its progress as it moved off to the right. Mirroring it, Tom stepped off the trail and into the brush, barely able to see the boar's mud brown shape against the ground. It stopped for a moment, head and tusks punching at a rotted log, breaking apart the wood to reveal a prize clutch of grubs and insects, feasting on them as Tom raised his pistol and took aim. A trickle of sweat caused an itch between his eyes, and he swiped it away before refocusing. Staring along the gun's sites, he gently squeezed the trigger until the weapon bucked in his hand, the muzzle flash and hard pop against the natural jungle sounds.

The boar squealed and jumped, bunched shoulder muscles quivering and jerking as it whirled, caught sight of Tom, and charged. Leaping backward toward the trail, he screamed, "Linda, get in a tree!" before firing off a second hurried shot at the barreling beast that missed, landing wide off to the side. Its burly form cut a pathway through the underbrush, knocking down everything in its path, white tusks jutting upward, its head the top of a piston on its powerful neck, eager to gut and gore him. Linda stepped into view on his left, feet spread in a firing stance, weapon raised, taking aim.

"Linda, get out of here!" he screamed as he led the beast with his pistol, sweaty finger squeezing the trigger in a last-ditch shot.

* * *

Near an old dirt road at the north end of a small forest, Sam shifted the kettle of boiling water to a stone off to the side, giving it a chance to cool before they put it to use. Their smokeless fire blazed where they'd sunk it into the ground, masking them from any nearby prying eyes. Jack was tidying up the campsite like she'd told him to, a too-large T-shirt dangling from his shoulders, face and arms smudged with muck. He'd gotten over his morning's complaining about not being able to go with their father and Linda on the hunting trip as someone had to stay and help her tend to Barbara, who needed constant attention and care, especially considering the wild animals and criminal element Carlos had warned them about.

Smooch lay on a bed made from a patch of soft vegetation covered with a blanket, the dog recovering well and thriving in the warmer weather. Whenever Jack finished with his chores, they'd go romping off through the grass, playing like they used to. The dog walked with a slight limp, barely noticeable, her burned fur growing out thick and new. Sam glanced up at the sky, a canopy of gray mixed with blue, the bitter winter not having reached so far south yet, the heat a welcome blessing after weeks of navigating the frozen roads of Virginia and Mexico. With a blink, her gaze fell on the rifle resting on her sleeping bag nearby, her father reminding her to keep it handy as well as the pistol in its holster on her right hip.

"I feel like I'm finally thawing out," she commented, tossing a rag on a stack of dirty ones.

"But now it's so hot," Jack replied, his voice lilting downward.

A gunshot fired in the distance, echoing through the jungle, the flock of birds squawking in annoyance as they tore off into the sky. Two more shots went off, and Sam stood with her fists clenched at her sides, staring at the trailhead her father and Linda had taken. Jack rose, scratching his head and glancing over at Sam with wide eyes.

"Was that Dad and Linda?"

"Yeah."

"Are they okay? Should we run and help them?"

Sam forced her tense shoulders to relax. "Don't worry about it. They're just out hunting. They probably shot something."

"Like what?"

Sam shrugged. "I don't know. A nice fat dear. A steak sounds pretty good right about now. What do you say?"

Jack went back to work, moving a plastic bin, setting it down heavily and placing a stack of blankets on top. "You know what sounds good? A pizza. A nice big extra large pepperoni pizza with cheeeeeese." The way he said cheese, all dragged out with an exaggerated smile, made her chuckle.

Their makeshift camp had a small table set up nearby with several gallons of recently boiled water, a pot to wash and clean dishes, and two tents nestled beneath the tall canopy of trees stretching over them. Off to the right, she spied telephone poles running parallel to the road, old wires dangling from them, some construction project the government had never finished. She didn't know how far it continued, but parts of the road they had taken were rough to say the least, shifting between pavement, dirt, and gravel.

Grabbing a clean rag and moving to the "sink" area, Sam picked up a gallon of fresh water and wetted the cloth, stepping over to where Barbara lay on the makeshift pallet made of logs and a single piece of wood they'd found at an abandoned garage on their journey south. Kneeling by Barbara, she moved aside the first aid pack filled with her bottles of pills and dabbed at her mother's forehead, wiping the beads of sweat away from her cheekbones and jaw, her eyes still sunken but face generally looking more alive than Sam had seen in a while.

Barbara's eyelids fluttered open, a faint smile tugging at the corners of her mouth. "Thank you, sweetie. That feels really good."

"No problem, Mom. Are you thirsty?"

"Yeah." Her voice was still hoarse, and when she swallowed, it sounded dry and crackly.

Nodding, Sam returned to the kitchen and poured a plastic cup of water, bringing it back and putting it to her lips. "Why don't you take your pain pills while we're at it? It's a few minutes early but should be fine."

After another nod, Sam fished out the proper pill and fed it to Barbara, holding her head up with one hand, the cup in the other, trickling water between her lips. She swallowed much better the second time, smacking her lips, green eyes lighting up when she saw Jack come over and plop down next to Sam.

"Hi, Mom," he said with a slight wave.

"How's my big boy?"

"Pretty good. Just hot and sweaty."

"He's had a rough morning," Sam said apologetically. "Hey, buddy. Why don't you put a couple more sticks on the fire?"

Jack sighed and let his hands drop on his thighs, but he did as he was told, getting up and dragging his feet to a pile of wood they'd stacked off to the side and covered in a plastic tarp in case it rained.

"He's listening to you," Barbara said, impressed. "How did you manage that? I could barely get that boy to help me do anything sometimes."

"Don't sell yourself short. Also, Dad threatened him pretty good if he misbehaved."

"Ah. That would do it."

"Speaking of your father. Where are he and Linda?"

Sam glanced into the forest. "They're out hunting. Our supplies are getting a little low, but there's a stream nearby, so we've got plenty of water. We just have to boil it." She gestured to the sink area and the fire.

"I see. How long was I out?"

"What do you remember?"

Barbara's eyebrows wrinkled as she tried to think. "I remember being shot… then there was the hospital, your father talking to me…" Her head rolled to the side, teary eyes shifting to the forest. "Anyway, I recall being in the back of that damn shaky Humvee."

"Yeah," Sam laughed. "That thing is on its last legs. You've been a little out of it. You're probably pretty hungry."

Blinking, Barbara thought about it, then shook her head. "I don't feel very hungry, but that could be because of the pain medication, right?"

"Henny said it might affect you that way."

"Henny?" she asked, giving a slight shake of her head. "Who's that?"

With a deep breath, Sam launched into what had happened, starting with her mother getting shot at the abandoned warehouse, all the blood and the desperate attempt to save her life. Barbara's eyes turned glassy with emotion when Sam told her about how they tried to keep her warm by the little stove in the back room, and Tom's decision that they should break out and make a run for it once they saw people coming. Sam had driven the Humvee through the warehouse garage door, barely getting away from the mercenaries as they took shots at the armored truck, then came the long trek south until the group caught up with them, going into detail about the trap they'd laid.

"Explosions, huh?" Barbara said with a light chuckle. "Geez. I sure missed a lot?"

"Yeah. So, we got back on the road, hoping we were done with them. We found a hospital… I have no clue what town it was. I had to speak Spanish to them, but Carlos and Henny helped us, and they're the ones who got the doctors to operate on you."

"I think I remember just before going into the operation." Barbara stared at the sky in deep thought. "It was all pretty chaotic…"

"You were out of it, but they were so cool at the hospital. They let us all stay in one room together, but that didn't last long. Keith showed up." Sam continued the story, detailing how they'd gotten away because some soldiers had clipped the agent with their Humvee. Finally, she recounted the two-day drive to reach their camp.

Barbara's hand slipped over hers, giving it a squeeze. "Thanks, Sam, for looking after me. I know it must've been hard."

Shrugging, she brushed off the compliment. "It's nothing, Mom. We all pitched in and—"

"It's not *nothing*," Barbara said, for the first time in days fixing Sam with a hard look. "You're just a teenager, and you've done so much to protect our family. I'm so proud of you I could cry."

"Well, don't do that, because then *I'll* cry, and Jack will get upset." Laughing, Sam wiped at her eyes.

"Okay, but where are we? Looks like a forest of some sort."

"A jungle," she replied, gesturing around. "Before we left the hospital, Henny suggested we go way south, so we've been on the road for the past two days."

"And where is that, exactly?"

"Central America. Like, just inside of Costa Rica. We've been siphoning fuel all the way down, and we dodged a bunch of military patrols, too."

Barbara's eyes flew wide. "Wow. Costa Rica."

"Dad wants to find a place to resettle here. Well, farther south."

"Resettle? What about home?"

Sam picked up the rag and slapped it in her palm with a sigh. "Dad doesn't think the US will be habitable for decades, maybe longer. He said we could go back when things thaw out. Meanwhile, Henny mentioned a place between Central and South America that's remote, and a lot of people are settling in the area. You know, people trying to get away from civilization?"

Barbara blinked, her eyelids falling half shut before popping open again. "Yeah, I think I understand. And your father thinks this is a good idea?"

"Yep. We've been talking about it on the way down, going through all the possibilities."

With a faint nod, Barbara's eyelids fluttered. "Home doesn't matter anymore… the only home I need is my family."

Sam reached to touch her mother's face, stroking her cheek as the pain medication pushed her into a painless sleep. "I love you, Mom." Her endearment went unheard as Barbara drifted off into oblivion.

"Me, too," Jack said, standing there with dirty knees, wiping his forearm across his nose with a sniff.

"We know you do." Sam rose and gave him a quick hug, ruffling his hair. "You need a haircut. That's the first thing Mom's going to do when she gets better."

"I hope not."

"Yep." Sam grabbed a metal bowl off the sink. "She's going to put this on your head and snip around in a circle. That's right. You're getting a bowl haircut."

Jack gaped. "No way! I'll shave it bald if Mom does that."

Laughing, she ruffled his hair again. "Keep working on getting stuff organized. We want this place looking good when Linda and Dad get back."

Sam crossed to the fire, sitting, grabbing a metal rod and stirring the lagging flames back to life. She glanced at the woods before taking the warming kettle to the sink to fill another plastic jug full of water. Something crashed through the brush, and she dropped the kettle and scrambled for the rifle lying nearby, suddenly frantic since the sounds weren't coming from the trail her father and Linda had gone into.

"Get back, Jack," she said, holding the weapon up, barrel pointed in the general direction of the noise until a shout caused her aim to waver.

"Hey, Sam!" Tom called. "It's us!"

A moment later, Linda stepped from the woods twenty yards off to the left, grinning from ear-to-ear, Tom followed her out, laughing, carrying a massive, muscled form slung over his shoulder, arm thrown across its prickly, bloody coat. The thing was so big it bent him to the side, but that didn't keep him from smiling.

"You got something!" Sam called, lowering her weapon even more and trotting over. "What *is* it?"

"A big, fat boar!" Tom announced, voice straining as he strode toward camp. "We're having bacon for dinner!"

After two days of eating bland rations, Sam's mouth watered at the word. "Amazing, Dad! You guys are hunters!"

"Your sister's the real hunter. I just wounded it."

"Dad made it mad," Linda nodded knowingly. "I had to finish the job for him."

"You sure did!" Tom chuckled, then looked for a spot to put the thing. "Thankfully, your sister didn't run for a tree like she was supposed to because I was about to get gutted. She nailed it in the heart like I should have done."

"Maybe *you* should have climbed the tree, Dad," Linda snorted, and Tom laughed so hard he slipped sideways and almost dropped the boar.

"How much does that thing weigh?" Sam asked, gesturing to a spot of soft grass a ways from the fire.

"Probably about a hundred and twenty pounds," he replied, ambling over to the spot and dropping it with a thud. Swaying backwards, he dusted off his hands and glanced at his shoulder where his shirt and arm were soaked with blood.

"I'll get you a new shirt," Sam said.

"Don't worry about it right now. We still have to skin and clean this thing, but we'll have meat for weeks."

"Some water then?"

"That sounds great," he nodded.

Sam started to pour cups of water for them when Barbara cleared her throat and raised her fingers in a weak wave. "Tom… what did you get?"

Expression turning serious, he glanced at Sam and rushed right over, kneeling next to Barbara, taking her hand, whispering, "Hey, honey. How are you?"

"She woke up earlier," Sam added, coming over and giving Linda a cup of water. "But the pain medicine knocked her out again."

"How are you feeling?" Tom was asking, leaning close and kissing her forehead.

"Much better, thanks to Sam," she said, her voice little more than a croak but clearing with every word. "She told me everything that happened. You guys are so brave, bringing us so far."

"We didn't have a choice," Tom replied, squeezing her hand and putting it against his cheek. "It's getting cold up north, and there were military camps all over the place. Plus…"

"Keith," Linda said, her lip curling in disgust. "I swear, I hate that guy."

"All of us do." Tom glanced back. "But we shouldn't be seeing any more of him. Those soldiers took him away."

"I want to help skin and dress the animal," Barbara said, raising off her bed on a quivering elbow.

"No, Mom." Sam came up on the other side and eased her down. "Rest. We'll handle dinner."

"Linda and I will do it." Tom planted another kiss on her forehead.

"I want to help!" Sam said with a slight pang of jealousy.

"You can watch this time," he agreed, "but it's Linda's kill, and she needs to learn, anyway."

"What do we need to do it?" Linda asked, staring at the dead animal, a sudden look of disgust on her face. "It's going to be pretty bloody, isn't it?"

"Super bloody," Sam said, nodding and winking at Tom.

"Your sister's trying to scare you," Tom added, considering the boar and glancing over to where they'd parked the Humvee and covered it with brush. "We'll need a long tree branch and some rope to string him up."

"I'll get the rope!" Jack shouted, taking off running with Smooch sprinting and yapping right behind him.

As Tom and Linda walked off to find a suitable spot to work, Sam called, "I can help, too. I'll watch Mom from here. She'll be fine!"

"Okay," Tom relented with a chuckle. "I guess we won't be far."

She jogged after them with a grin, grabbing her mane of hair and wrapping it in a soft hair tie. At the jungle's edge, they spent the next few minutes finding a pair of thicker saplings four feet apart and a fallen branch that could span the distance. Taking axes from a satchel, the three stripped the big branch clean and hacked off the thinner end, tying it six feet off the ground across the two trees with the rope Jack brought.

"Okay, now we have to drag the boar over here and hang it," Tom said.

Tying the hog's feet, they hauled it through the brush to the cross branch, Jack and Smooch trailing behind them, the German Shepherd's ears perking up, nose nudging and sniffing at the dead animal. Once there, Tom tossed the rope over the branch and took the loose end, nodding for Sam and Linda to each grab a leg and lift while he pulled on the other side.

Squatting and grunting, gripping the boar's legs just above the hooves, Sam strained to get her half of the beast off the ground. Linda, teeth bared, arms straining, tried to help her sister, but they could only raise it a few inches, both of them struggling to keep the carcass up. Tom pulled his end of the rope, and the boar shot straight up, causing the girls to fall on their backsides, laughing as Smooch barked worriedly at them.

Tom anchored the rope to the bottom of a tree trunk, stepped up, and patted the boar on its side with a hard slap. "This will sustain us for a little while, so take a moment to give thanks for this animal giving up its life so that we can continue to live."

When she glanced at her sister, Linda looked back with a serious expression and reached out and took Sam's hand. After saying a short prayer of thanks for the bounty, Tom removed his knife and started skinning it. Two years ago, Tom and his friend had gone hunting, and Sam had tagged along, watching them kill and dress a deer. So, she knew how to do it, sort of. He quickly worked the blade through muscle, fat, and skin, separating it, peeling it back, showing Linda the fine details and letting her make some cuts until her fingertips were smeared with blood and gristle. Sam followed with her eyes, trying to remember the steps herself, only missing a few. Linda gently and awkwardly cut the bristly rough coat away to reveal the thick musculature beneath, like something out of an anatomy book, perfectly formed, the overlapping layers of red meat in tight bunches, shot through with fat, all held together by sinew and ligaments.

"Sam, why don't you keep a closer eye on your mom? The jungle is super dangerous, and we're getting blood everywhere. It'll definitely attract some predators."

Nodding, Sam stepped toward camp, glancing at Barbara still resting peacefully on the bed they'd made her. But she couldn't help looking back as Linda started disemboweling the animal, their father showing her all the right cuts, removing the boar's insides, intestines, heart, lungs and everything else.

"Don't pierce the intestines or stomach," she murmured.

With one hand on the carcass and one on Linda's back, he let her finish cutting and dragging the entrails out to plot on the ground, Smooch immediately running up to sniff at them. Tom shooed the dog off and they sorted through the pile for the heart and liver, finishing with heavy cuts to the body to separate the more select pieces of meat. Jack ran to get plastic bags, paper, or anything they could use to wrap the parts and when they were almost done, Linda turned away, breaths shallow, face ashen and a little green, smudges of blood on her cheeks and forehead.

"Congratulations," Sam said with a grin. "You didn't hurl."

"I thought I was going to a couple of times," Linda replied with a lurching stomach. "That's really tough work."

"You did awesome, hon."

"Thanks."

With the heavy scent of blood in the air, they carried the meat closer to the fire, storing some in a cooler they'd found at a gas station to keep the bugs off, cutting the rest into strips, grabbing a pan for the campfire, and laying the pieces inside. Tom skewered several thin slices with sticks and stuck the ends in the ground so they hung over the flames. It was bloody, hard work, but within forty-five minutes the smells of cooking food drifted thick in the air, Sam's stomach growling audibly.

"Hungry?" Tom asked, walking around camp and glancing up toward the truck.

"Sounds that way," Sam replied, letting her hand rest on her stomach.

"Oh, that smells amazing," Barbara said from her dreamy haze, and Sam filled another cup with water and took it over.

"Now we just have to protect it." Tom gazed into the forest. "I'm not sure what animals are left out there, but if we found one boar, there'll be a predator around. This entire place smells like blood. We probably should've butchered this a little farther away."

"How can we preserve the meat?" Linda asked as she stood at the sink, using water from their jug to wash her fingers.

"I thought I saw some stuff along the side of the road that might make for a good smoker. We'll walk up later and see what we can gather. In the meantime, let's make dinner and talk about our supplies."

Making a semicircle near Barbara, Linda, Jack, and Smooch sat on one side of the fire, with Sam and Tom on the other, their father leaning in and adjusting the skewers and strips in the pan, the meat sizzling, fat spitting everywhere. After a minute, he snagged a piece with a fork and blew on it until it was cool enough to eat. Then he bit off the end, chewing, grinning. Cutting them each a chunk, he passed them around for everyone to take a nibble. Sam fed Barbara, who took the piece with her fingers and popped it in her mouth, gnawing happily, eyes wide.

"This is incredible, you guys," she said, swallowing it and reaching for the last strip hanging from the fork. Handing it over, Sam returned for more, and they each had another snack before Tom grabbed a can of baked beans from a nearby backpack and poured it into a pan, placing it next to the skillet to cook.

By then, the spit they'd set up was packed with smoking, sizzling meat, the smells wafting through the camp. Tom handed out the skewers he'd started, Sam taking hers and sitting back, pulling thick chunks off the stick with her teeth, chewing the salty meat and swallowing with satisfied groans. Tom tossed Smooch a big hunk before prepping more skewers.

"So, Sam. What do our supplies look like?"

Crouched on a log, Sam gazed upward as she thought about it. The afternoon sun was almost directly overhead, though the jungle canopy stretched over them, protecting them from the worst of the heat, if not the humidity. "I checked all our bags and had Jack stack things while you guys were gone. Between everything out here and in the Humvee, we have a dozen MREs, a few cans of this and that, and enough medical supplies for Mom. We've got water, but not a lot. Carlos and Henny put tons of purification tablets into the bag they gave us, though, so we should be set with those."

"With the stream nearby, water won't be an issue," Tom said. "Between what you've been boiling, and the tablets, we should have plenty. I don't think we even have to consider it very much, which means we can all get cleaned up a little."

Sam sniffed. "A makeshift shower?"

"Maybe," Tom said, looking around. "It would do us all a bit of good to have at least a hot sponge bath."

"I'd settle for lukewarm," Barbara mumbled, shifting on her pallet.

"Hygiene will be a big deal out here with no doctors and hospitals to take care of us," Tom went on with a smile. "It's critical we try to keep our cuts clean and watch out for parasites, bug bites, and anything that could make us sick. I had a book on jungle survival, but that's back home in Virginia under six feet of snow and ice." His smile fell. "If it even survived the fire."

"What else do we need to worry about, Dad?"

Shaking off the memory of the house, he pressed on. "I say the next big concern will be the trip to Panama City and the military presence around it, based on all the radio chatter we heard coming down. Most of it was in Spanish, but I'll need you to brush up, and we'll have other languages to contend with. I'm betting English and Spanish will carry us most of the way given the situation and the US's agreement with Mexico, but who knows."

"No problem, Dad," Sam nodded, though that had been an unexpected frustration. While she'd done well in her high school Spanish classes, it was way different listening to strangers talking over radio static in clipped phrases.

With the beans boiling, Tom took bowls and spooned everyone an equal portion, putting more cooked meat on the edges. Sam delivered a plate to Barbara, holding her up while she ate. At first, she chewed hesitantly but then devoured everything, bean juice on her chin, lifting her plate for another piece of meat.

"You're getting stronger." Sam watched as her mother finished and raised up to hand her plate over.

Resting back with a sigh, Barbara said, "Oh, boy. That was... amazing. The best meal I've ever eaten." Her eyes fell to Tom. "Thank you, honey."

"No problem," Tom nodded, head hanging heavy, though Sam was glad to see him smiling again. "But I can't take all the credit. Linda slew the beast, and both of the girls helped put it on the fire for us." His eyes moved between the two of them. "There's a ton of hunting in all our futures if things work out like I think."

"I don't even care," Barbara said, watching them, hands resting contentedly across her stomach. "We're out of the danger, I'm with my family, and I'm happy." Eyelids drooping, she gave them a final smile and settled on her blankets, blinking at the gray-blue sky for a moment before going to sleep.

Silence fell over them, marked only by bird calls in the trees, the distant squawking of strange animals, bugs chirruping and buzzing, and the crackling fire still sizzling fat in the pan. They finished eating quietly, tossing Smooch the scraps.

Tom stood and brushed his hands on his pants. "All right. Let's go find stuff to make a smoker!"

Chapter 4
Sergeant Brody
Guayana City, Bolivar

The Black Hawk cruised low over grassy plains, weaving between flat-topped mountains and swaths of forests that reminded Sergeant Brody of the woods back home in Indiana with their grand maples and oaks packed together between rows of cornfields. Flying over Venezuelan farmlands, they passed open stretches of fields with neat lines of crops southwest of the massive sprawl of the city.

The helicopter made a gentle turn, crossing one road to fly parallel to another, keeping a respectful distance off the ground, always watchful for surface-to-air missiles that were becoming all too frequent in the area. A thirteen-man Marine squad crouched in the crew quarters, equipment checked and packed away, the three fire teams decked out in M4's, M249 Squad Automatic Weapons with night-vision scopes and IR aiming devices, and M203 grenade launchers. The aircraft swayed gently as it turned again, and Brody, the squad leader, looked over his Marines with a discerning eye. The team leaders, Smith, Mitchell, and Bash, were on the ball, quietly checking with their rifles, communicating via hand signals and nods, ensuring they were ready to go.

Coming out of his crouch, Brody peered out the window and watched the grassy plains pass beneath them, shades of brown and green with gentle sweeping hills to the north topped with shaggy trees. Hanging on as they made a deeper turn, the chopper swept over treetops and angled to the southeast, maintaining a steady altitude. Piled into a single Black Hawk, they were heading to the Caruachi Dam on the Caroni River to support the Venezuelan troops guarding the facility. With an output of twenty-one hundred megawatts, the gravity dam produced power for the lower valley and Guyana City, and CENTCOM was concerned after a local farmer reported seeing two boats full of Chinese and Russian soldiers moving up the river toward the dam several hours ago.

Of course, mission objectives were subject to change, and he wasn't surprised when his earpiece burst to life and the dispatcher's voice piped in. "CENTCOM to Sergeant Brody' squad. Come in, Brody. Do you read me?"

"I'm here, CENTCOM. What do you have for me?"

"Be advised, we have lost communication with the Venezuelan troops at the dam, so you won't be landing on the helipad as previously planned. It's recommended you drop in a couple miles to the west and survey the situation before moving in. Over."

"Roger that, CENTCOM. I'll take that advice."

Overhearing the conversation, the pilots descended in altitude, and Brody motioned to Corporal Smith, leader of Alpha team, to join him in looking at a map, the pair picking a wooded area to the west of the dam to land. After passing the new coordinates to the pilot, Brody sat back and fell into his normal routine of quiet, clearing his head of distracting thoughts, allowing them to fade into dust as he filtered out the noise and focused on his training.

"Sergeant Brody, we're making our descent," the pilot said in a clipped tone.

With a nod, he stood and readied the squad, grabbing the side door handle, swinging it wide as soon as they touched down, three teams leaping out and heading for the forest's edge. Brody jumped out last and followed them, a rattle of gear on his back, legs chugging, carrying him through the gale of rotor wash until he was surrounded by green woods and the chopper had lifted off and gone.

"Men, let's head up toward the dam, staying low until we reach a good recon point, at which time Alpha team will scout the area and let us know just how far the Russians and Chinese are along."

The layout of the dam passed through his mind; they'd be approaching from the southwest, moving parallel to a road that turned sharply east and rose to the dam's causeway where the power was generated by radial gates that controlled the water's flow. Past the gates was a powerhouse with a control tower on top, then another thousand feet of right-abutment rock fill with a concrete slab face, the entire wall one hundred and eighty feet tall.

"I want to know if they've really taken the facility," he said, "and what they plan on doing with it."

The team leaders relayed the orders and the Marines moved out, creeping through the lightly forested areas, sprinting over open ground, sweating, working to stay hidden in the oppressive heat. After a mile, Brody found a comfortable clearing to rest in and ordered Smith's Alpha team up ahead to run some reconnaissance. Standing at the edge of the woods, he stared north toward Guayana City, the evening dusk settling over the town, the lights glowing in the dimming sky. While they waited, Bash stepped over, the lanky Marine Specialist giving the Sergeant a nod.

"What is it, Bash?" Brody said, voice low.

"What if they've taken the dam and have a solid defensive perimeter?"

"Two boats of Russians and Chinese… that sounds like two dozen soldiers, wouldn't you say?"

"That sounds about right, sir."

"Then we'll take them apart bit by bit until there's nothing left of them."

The Specialist gave a grim nod and turned to wait along with the Bravo and Charlie members, an uneasy silence settling over them as Brody ran through a hundred different scenarios in his mind, anticipating what Alpha team would come back with. They didn't have to wait long before Smith and her men returned, lugging their gear, sweating and panting as they double timed it across an open field to sweep into the forest's cover.

"What's it looking like, Smith?" Brody asked as they turned to the map of the facility and surrounding grounds spread out in the dirt, corners held down by small stones.

The stocky Marine took off her helmet and swept her sweat-stained hair back, eyes scanning over the map, pointing at the elbow shaped road leading to the spillway, the powerhouse, and the rest of the concrete face. "They've got six guards at the entrance to the spillway, and it has a wide causeway on top with some blasted out Venezuelan armor, giving them a little protection. Nestled behind those is a scattering of troops all the way to the powerhouse."

"Is that armor functional?"

"Doesn't look like it, sir," she replied. "Smoke is rising from one, and the others have blown tires or apparent engine trouble. The mounted guns could still work… but that's not the worst of the situation."

"Do tell."

"They've got soldiers hanging off the side of the spillway and are planting charges on the concrete braces. It looks like they're drilling into them to get the explosives deeply embedded. They want to blow the entire power station."

Brody was already nodding. "That's what I figured, and we can't let that happen, Marines. We've got a million people in the city depending on that power, and if they flood out that valley, thousands will die. Let's mount up and get ready to roll."

As the fire teams readied themselves, Brody gathered the leaders around the map searching for potential attack points, looking for suggestions.

"I could take my guys across," Smith said. "Get on the other side of the river and attack from the east as a distraction."

"We don't have time for that. They'll have that spillway blown in two or three hours. No, we have to do it now." Brody tapped at a spot on the map. "See this little finger of land that goes out into the river? It's about eighty yards south of the spillway, with some brush cover and rocks. Smith, take Alpha team down to that snippet of land and start picking off those guys hanging over the side. On my mark, you'll get the party started, and Bravo and Charlie teams will sweep up the road from the west, secure the elbow, and charge the guards at the spillway. But even if we clear that pavement, they could still have control of the powerhouse…"

"Forgot to tell you, sir." Smith slapped her head. "It looks like some workers and Venezuelan troops are holed up in the powerhouse, so if they can hang on there…"

"That makes our job a little easier," Brody said with rising hope. "Okay, fellas. Let's go."

The squad moved out in a staggered formation with Brody moving from the rear to the middle, Alpha team branching off to the south once they were a quarter mile from the dam, the remaining two teams making a beeline for the road, heads down and chugging along in the growing darkness, the Sergeant hoping to start the attack when the dusk light would work to their advantage. The roadway came into view, the paved lane winding up from the valley about a hundred yards, rising to the level of the spillway before taking a sharp right to the entrance. At the top was a small parking lot, a gate, and a pair of concrete guard houses with wide windows in front. Otherwise, the open ground between the elbow and the gate offered very little cover, and the river came about even with the road, the waters gently lapping at the rocky shoreline, leaving no shelter there either.

Brody took the lead, pushing to the front of the line and guiding the Marines along the westernmost edge of the road where a thick line of trees clung to the muddy edges, the dark waters breaking along with the rustling trees. The wind was barely gusting, the sweat dripping down his face, heat building in his body as he geared up for action, though he was careful to keep his breathing steady, his muscles harboring a slight thrum of tension. The sound of rushing water grew to a roar as they crept closer to the spillway, using the brush to mask their presence, eyes thrown upward toward the road whenever the foliage thinned. And as they reached the slope below the elbow, he stopped and put his hand into Bash's chest, forcing him back into the cover of the thickets.

"What is it, Sarge?"

"Two guards standing at the edge of the road up there, but they didn't see me, so we're still good."

"Change of plans?"

"Not at all. We just have to go through them before we attack the gate."

Just then, his radio crackled with Smith's voice. "We're in position, sir. Great idea having us set up on this little sliver of land. We're about eighty yards from the spillway and have a good bead on the guys setting those charges."

"How far are they along?"

"They've still got an hour of work to do, and they're going to be real surprised when we hit them. Be advised, sir. They've got some automatic weapons up on the causeway, so your trip up won't be a friendly one."

"Understood. You have permission to open fire. We'll go on your mark."

"Roger that, sir. Give us five minutes."

Time ticked slowly as they waited for the first shots to go off, the nervous sensation at the bottom of his gut making his limbs liquid and weak, like he could collapse to the dirt and lay there, though it was just his body's natural reaction to the upcoming conflict, that fight-or-flight fear that consumed everyone in the moments just before combat. Facing it allowed him to fall back on his training, controlling his breathing while keeping his eyes on the two Russian soldiers standing above them with their rifles held loosely in their hands, controlling the high ground.

It was only when Alpha team began firing in the distance, the sounds barely audible over the roaring waters, did Brody' nervousness finally flee, and with that signal given he gripped Bash's shoulder, ducking past him to the front of the line, turning and signaling for how he wanted the dispersal to go. Once agreed to, he crept from the brush, scrambling up the hill, left hand on the dirt, eying the two Russian soldiers who'd spun toward the gunfire and were walking out of sight. Panting, the toes of his boots kicking rocks and dirt behind him, he breached the ridge, fell onto his stomach with his M4 pointed up the road. In burst mode, he fired on the two Russians, breaking the first one's back and sending him twisting with an anguished howl to the ground. The other had just turned, finger squeezing the AK's trigger when Brody' bullets made a stripe across his chest, shoving him backward, weapon flung wide and hitting the pavement as Bravo and Charlie teams rushed past him with Bash and Mitchell disbursing in a staggered formation on the road.

"Smith, we're engaging," Brody spat into his radio before climbing to his feet and running, finding an angle to fire on the guard houses flanking the gate.

Gunfire rattled the sky, M4s and the heavier M249s firing in bursts and in single shot mode respectively as they took advantage of their surprise. The Marine team leaders and riflemen charged ahead, laying down a suppressive fire, sending Russians dying and scattering behind whatever concrete cover they could find, their weapons turning toward the Marines and rattling off a response. Everyone in his squad remained miraculously untouched for the first thirty yards which he chalked up to the fading light and the excellent conditioning of his men, and by the time a Charlie rifleman was hit and fell screaming to the pavement, the enemy was in range of their rifle-mounted M203s.

Bash and Mitchell reached beneath their carbines and began firing fragmentation grenades, each exiting the barrels with deep thuds, the projectiles arcing toward the Russian positions to explode with sharp bursts of sound that were followed by screams and curses from the enemy. Flushed out, two Chinese soldiers sprinted from behind a concrete block toward the shoreline, and the remaining Bravo rifleman angled in their direction, shooting four bursts from a crouched position, cutting them to pieces before he himself was hit and fell with a shriek.

Brody rose from his firing position and sprinted straight ahead, coming within range of his own M203, squatting, reaching beneath to the mounted weapon and cycling five grenades at the concrete guard houses, putting one through each window, the explosions rattling the buildings, glass shattering in a flash of light and pained howls from inside as a Russian dove from a cloud of black smoke through the front where someone quickly tracked his motion, putting him permanently to rest. By then, Bravo's and Charlie's machine gunners were on their bellies with their M249s resting on their bipods, assistant riflemen feeding them quick ammunition for a barrage of heavy firepower focused on what remained of the Russian forces. Bullets chewed up concrete like it was paper, biting into flesh, breaking bones, more screams erupting from the dying men inside.

Out on the causeway, Brody spotted enemy reinforcements rushing up, and he took off in a dead sprint toward the guard houses, equipment pounding on his back, choking on smoke and the reek of the dying, shouting for Bash and Mitchell to get there. Brody raised his M4 and fired at a Russian crawling to the shoreline, spraying the rocks with blood as he fed the man a full burst, then switched to another soldier who was miraculously still alive and firing from the guardhouse, his defiance put to an end by one of the machine gunners. Reaching the concrete buildings at the same time as Bash and Mitchell, Brody ducked to evade a barrage of bullets from the enemy soldiers behind the armored trucks.

"Hold here!" he shouted, turned, and waved the others up before swapping out a fresh magazine. Leaning around the corner, he fired at shadows behind the parked armor and peppered the figures rushing to take up positions close to the gate. Dead Russians were sprawled everywhere, blood seeping across the pavement from mangled limbs and shredded faces, one man's leg hanging by a thread of muscle and sinew, the bone stripped clean by M203 shrapnel. Grabbing his radio, he barked into it. "Are you done down there, Smith?"

"Yes, sir!" came the reply.

"Then get your asses up here!" he shouted, ducking away as concrete spit from the corner of the building, and the first Russian fragmentation grenade bounced past them to explode farther down the road, the shrapnel eating into the dirt and pavement.

"It won't be long before they lock down our position," he shouted.

The rest of Bravo and Charlie teams reached the guard houses, but when he asked about wounded, one of the machine gunners only shook his head and looked for a better firing position, their assistants dropping duffel bags full of ammunition and preparing to feed them it as needed.

Gathering Bash and Mitchell to him, he shouted in their ears. "Alpha team swept those bastards off the spillway. We're good."

"Not good!" Bash shouted back. "I spotted some Chinese setting more charges along the causeway."

"We've got to clear it, then!" A quick glance around the corner showed the chain-link gate was mangled, shredded by explosives from the attack. A short brick retaining wall hugged a walkway that angled down toward the river, and the Russians and Chinese were using it as cover. And sure enough, along the causeway, dark-haired soldiers were setting up boxes of squares with wires running between them, each position covered by a single soldier with a rifle. "They're dug in pretty tight, and they're putting charges down."

"Can we hit them with the M203s?" Mitchell asked in his deep, booming voice as all three men loaded fresh grenades into their launchers.

"Not until we get a little closer, and position ourselves to the left, where we can fire against the rail."

"Can we call in the Black Hawk for support?"

"There's no time for that."

As if agreeing with him, another grenade blasted off behind them, pieces of shrapnel dry-spitting against the top of a concrete guard house, showering them with gray dust. The exchange of gunfire was even, and he figured they'd taken out seven enemy soldiers to their two losses, leaving them with more than a dozen to deal with; the odds were stacked against them by any estimation.

"If we charge in, they'll take half of us quick, sir," Mitchell said.

"Not all of us will be charging in, Marine," he stated. "And we can't let them blow this bridge. So, on my mark, myself and Mitchell will charge through that gap in the fencing while Bash fires a couple grenades onto that pathway. You're the best shot we have, Bash. Lob those high so they come down on top of their heads, got it?"

"Yes, sir."

"Take those out, and we'll have a chance to back them off." Shoulder to the wall, he glanced around the corner, watching as Russians moved mortars into position behind a pile of debris. Shouting for the machine gunners to provide cover, he nodded to Mitchell. "Mark!"

The two men charged around either side of the guardhouse, carbines raised and firing in a dead sprint toward the gap in the fencing, the jagged edges charred and rough looking. Brody fired at any Russian raising above the retaining wall before sweeping his weapon toward the armored trucks, launching a burst in that direction. At the same time, a buzzsaw of bullets chewed up the air, pinging off the concrete, making him flinch when a pair zipped past his right ear. Mitchell grunted as something hit him, yet the Marine kept running, beating him to the fencing, getting caught as he slipped through, leaving the sharp metal dripping blood.

The M249's ripped off strings of burring bullets, and Brody closed his eyes as he slipped through the fencing, going two steps before his boots ran into something and sent him tripping to the ground. Glancing back, he saw Mitchell writhing on the pavement, clutching his throat as he squirmed, blood spouting between his fingertips. Brody crawled fast toward the retaining wall with his carbine in hand, thirty yards to cross with bullets pecking at the surrounding concrete, spitting up dust and stone fragments. Still, he was determined to clear it alone if he needed to, and he was almost there when Bash's grenades fell, three heavy thuds exploding in perfect synchronization, spaced out evenly behind the wall, each punch drawing screams and grunts. Parts of bodies, blood, and debris shooting upward and landing near him before he buried his face in the crook of his arm.

When the explosions stopped, he glanced back to see Bash running toward him in a crouch, so he finished his crawl, reaching the retaining wall, grabbing the edge, and flipping over—the path was sunk another two feet deeper, making his total fall a good five feet—to land hard on his side, knocking the wind out of him with a pained grunt. The path was a mess, both walls covered in blood and gore, viscera slapped on the brick, dripping in slimy, lumpy trails. The reek of charred flesh caught in his nose even as he tried to suck air, leaving him gagging and coughing and looking for his carbine. A bloody figure staggered into view, a Chinese soldier, helmet blown sideways on his head, his right eye socket nothing but a ragged hole, dripping gore on his fatigues. The man's weapon swung up and popped off a round, which smacked the concrete near Brody's head. Rolling into a seated position, the Sergeant grabbed the soldier's belt and hauled him backward like a rower, forcing the soldier off balance, making him fall forward over Brody to sprawl on the pavement.

As the Sergeant twisted and tried to get up, the man's knees locked around his head in a vise-like wrestler's hold, and then something was stabbing at his helmet, metal striking at Kevlar until he realized the soldier had a knife. The blade sliced his hands as he fought off the angry stings, ducking, squeezing from between the man's legs, but it was a death grip, and he couldn't break free. They rolled until the Chinese soldier rose to a seated position, knife poised to strike, Brody staring into the gory hole where his eye had been, throwing up his bloody hands as a sacrifice to the blade. Bash's boots landed next to him, and a sharp snort of bullets blew the soldier back in a short shower of blood, ending the fight.

Crawling from beneath him, Brody stood on shaky legs, dusted himself off, and staggered in a circle in search of his carbine. Scooping it up, he threw himself against the opposite retaining wall, facing the remaining resistance gathered behind three armored vehicles, the first truck angled toward the rail. The thick tires were impossible to penetrate, the armor even less so. Dropping his backpack, Brody pulled out a pouch of M203 grenades, tossed it to Bash, and got another one for himself, and they talked about what to do between sending bursts of rounds at the enemy troops.

"Thanks for the assist, Bash."

"No problem, sir. Too bad about Mitchell."

"If we finish this fast, maybe we can get him some help."

"Yes, sir. How do you want to do this?"

"You lob 'em over the armor, I'll skip 'em below. On my mark... *mark*!"

Sliding to Bash's right, Brody kept his rifle level with the ground, firing his first grenade so that it skipped twice across the pavement and exploded before it reached the Chinese position. Popping another grenade in, he raised the barrel just a fraction and fired again, the second round skipping three times, flying beneath the first armored vehicle and slamming into the rail, blowing a hail of shrapnel backward into the Chinese soldiers, shredding a rifleman and tearing the face off the man bent over the square of explosives.

"Two down," he growled, loading another grenade, hyper focused on the next spot he wanted to shoot.

In the meantime, Bash was firing his grenades in a high arc, dropping them behind the armor, listening to the screams as Chinese and Russians tried to escape his expert marksmanship. The rest of Bravo and Charlie teams rushed through the gap in the fencing, the two automatic rifleman firing single shots from their shoulders, their assist-men opening up with their M4's, showering the armored vehicles with flying lead, sparks and gun smoke wafting by in thick clouds, clogging his sinuses with a sharp sting. Between the drifting fog of combat, Brody fired another M203 round between the first two armored vehicles, nailing the concrete rail, blowing shrapnel and pieces of rock back at the Chinese soldiers nestled there, the concussion blasting one man back ten feet, his entire front smoking, hair and clothing and boots on fire. The two remaining men in Mitchell's Charlie team saw their leader lying dead and charged the enemy position in a fury, hollering, mindless with rage and battle lust, their training momentarily forgotten.

As they sprinted by, too fast to stop, Brody glanced at Bash. "Let's go, Marine."

"Yes, sir."

Swapping out a fresh magazine, shrugging on his gear, Brody pulled himself over the retaining wall, landing in a stagger before getting his weight set right. Charging behind Charlie team with Bash coming up on his left, they crossed from the wider concrete yard riddled with dead enemy soldiers to the narrower causeway. The machine gunners swept between the first two armored vehicles, and a brief exchange of flashing gunfire erupted before everything fell deathly quiet. When he and Bash got there, another Marine lay dead along with a half dozen enemy soldiers, the remaining machine gunner standing over their corpses with a smoking gun, panting and shaking as the battle rage blazed in his eyes, though when he turned to his squad leader, he slowed his breathing and regained his composure.

"Orders, sir?"

"Private Adamu, right?"

"That's right, sir."

"Go see if there's anything you can do for Mitchell, and be careful, because Alpha team is coming up the road. When you see them, tell Smith to join us up here pronto."

"Yes, sir," the Marine replied, jogging back along the causeway into the drifting, blue-gray smoke.

"The rest of you with me," Brody said, grabbing Bash and the Bravo team, kicking a nearby Chinese soldier in the ribs to make sure he was dead before striding toward the rail where the explosives had been set.

The Marines walked a causeway littered with corpses, everyone dead from weapons fire or shrapnel from the grenade rounds, even the ones setting the explosives. They made a mess along the concrete rail, pieces of them lying in the road, smoking and smoldering from the onslaught, three of them writhing and groaning in pain. The Marines disarmed them, dragged them to an armored vehicle, and secured them there. Above them, the big powerhouse loomed, red brick all the way to the top where a handful of faces, men and women in hardhats, the dam workers, stared down at them through the glass with wide, blinking expressions. A set of steps ran along the outside of the building, stacked high with chairs and tables and pieces of furniture, obstacles to block the Russians and Chinese from getting in.

Brody waved up at them and gave them a thumbs up signal, surprised when one of them pointed at the causeway where the smoke was thick and clung to the pavement like a mist coming off a cold forest floor. With a narrowed gaze, the Sergeant strode through the drifting smog, carbine barrel sweeping left and right until the smoke blew away to reveal a Chinese man crawling toward the rail, blood smeared down the sides of his face, his leg dragging behind him, useless. One good eye rolled up to stare at Brody, going wide with fear when he realized it wasn't one of his own countrymen. In a burst of frantic movement, he rolled onto his belly and crawled urgently across the pavement, fingers scraping at the concrete, a bloody grimace on his face. When the Sergeant saw he was headed toward a black controller with two red buttons and an antenna on it, he aimed his M4 at the man and squeezed the trigger, the body jerking and rippling before falling limp, blood slowly spreading in a halo around him.

Brody looked up at the folks at the top of the tower, giving them a thumbs up sign before continuing along the causeway, looking for more enemy troops, but they'd killed them all, to a man, the bloody pavement riddled with corpses a testament to the fight for freedom they were embroiled in. He went to the rail, peering over into the rush of water billowing and foaming from the radial gates, the roar deafening as he grinned into the spray, allowing the mist to soak his face, bathing him in a refreshing coolness.

Taking his radio off his belt, he turned away from the rail. "CENTCOM, this is Sergeant Brody. We've secured the dam and eliminated the enemy presence. We took three prisoners, lost four. Please advise."

"Brody, this is CENTCOM. Roger that last message. Good work, Marine. Hang tight for more orders."

Radio tucked away, he walked back the way he'd come, meeting with Bash and Smith to help with the dead and wounded, putting the perished Marines in a respectful row near the rail where the cool mist rolled over them and left them covered in crystal clear beads of moisture.

Chapter 5
President Zimmerman
Caracas, Venezuela

Standing at the wide glass window, he stared at a vibrant green valley that stretched at their feet, a river flowing through the foothills and into a town along the Pan-American Highway. It swelled with an influx of refugees, the restaurants and hotels overcrowded, construction areas spread out in all directions, excavators and bulldozers tearing up the earth. Marine units and Army MPs ran patrols throughout the streets, guard stations dotted the forests and clearings, and a formation of Black Hawk and Apache helicopters flew in regular sequence as Venezuelan residents stared up with curiosity and more than a little worry.

"This is hardly secure or remote," the President said to General Davidson, who stood next to him to survey the scene.

"It's Perez's former presidential bunker and the best the Venezuelans could do on such short notice." Davidson brushed a shock of salt-and-pepper hair back and gestured behind him as he turned his square shoulders. "And, as you can see, we're getting there. The *new* US CENTCOM will be fully functional in the next couple of days, if not sooner. We wouldn't want to be standing here during a missile attack, but the lower levels can withstand heavy artillery."

"But not a nuke," Zimmerman replied.

"Not a nuke, sir."

They stood on a raised catwalk running along the bottom of a massive chamber carved out of the mountain, the central hall rough-hewn and gray with passages cutting deeper inside, covered by smooth drywall or brick. Behind them cascaded a short flight of stairs down to the main floor where high-ranking military officials floated around an oval table in the room's center. Smaller dividers hung off to the sides, three-foot tall partitions with computer desks, telephone systems, and other communications gear. Techs ran everywhere, connecting cables, running conduits through the floor, all supervised by the Secret Service and a strong Marine guard. Monitors stood side-by-side or in twos and threes at the heads of the tables, though only a few were actually lit up and working, bathing parts of the hall with flashes of light.

"I wish we could enjoy this view longer," Zimmerman said, "but we've got a ton to do." He briskly descended the stairs, the General behind him, nodding at scientist Rick Manglor, who approached with hurried steps. "Thanks for overseeing the network build," the President said. "How's it going?"

The disheveled man ran his hand through his hair, his expression tired but sharp. "As good as can be expected, sir, but still too slow."

"What's the problem?"

"We're merging our computer gear with the Venezuelan equipment, but their stuff is old. I'm talking 2000s Hewlett Packard servers running outdated HPUX operating systems. They haven't been upgraded for fifteen years. I'm surprised they even work."

"Damn." Zimmerman lowered his head and frowned. "Do we have to use theirs? Can't we just do a complete swap out?"

"We need every bit of power we can get, sir."

Davidson's next words came out through tight lips. "Perez made it sound like the stuff they left us was useable."

"It's usable to process backups," Rick replied, "but that's about it. We're plugging our hard drive arrays into them, so at least we have some space to store data, but they don't have the CPUs or memory to do any real crunching. About a quarter aren't even booting up."

"Thanks, Rick," Zimmerman said. "Do the best you can. Hey, can you join us for the briefing in five?"

"Yes, sir. Can I have a minute to tie a couple of things up?"

"See you in a few."

They strode across to a side table, separate from the regular bustle with higher dividers and better computer equipment, where Davidson's top officers waited, including Navy Admiral Ben Spencer, Venezuelan Commander, General Molina and his staff, and the lanky, ever-scowling Colonel Prescott. Rita Cortez had joined them with updates outside military purview, things like refugee statistics, settlements, and ratios of sick and wounded in the quickly rising hospitals.

"Okay, people," Zimmerman said to the gathered brass, gesturing at some workers nearby. "Grab something to drink. We've got Rick incoming in less than five."

Servers with security clearance staffed by Venezuelans and Americans moved in with carts of food and beverages, passing them around. His regular coffee mug and its presidential seal appeared before him, and he nodded his thanks, smiling encouragement at the young woman in the white staff coat who'd brought it.

"I was going to cut back," he said to the General, "but these Venezuelan beans..."

"Delicious," Davidson agreed.

Rick joined them a few minutes later with his tablet tucked beneath his arm, weaving around staff members and approaching to stand at his customary seat on the President's left. The man blinked at the glowering crowd of military people, nodding to a few, rocking on his feet with practiced confidence.

"You can go first, Rick," Zimmerman said, "so you can get back to the computer situation."

"Let's shed some more light on things, sir." He pointed to three monitors behind the President and then at a group of technicians who were stooped inside a section of raised flooring nearby. A tech dipped and made a network connection and the screens lit up, flaring to life with global tactical data, supply statistics and a map of the Americas marked with various weather indicators like wind and temperature. "We've got you all tied in, Mr. President. It'll take us some time to get the other groups up and running, but they'll still be sending data to your channels here."

"Excellent," Zimmerman said with a relieved sigh. "I'm glad we've got our real-time views tied in with the *new* United States CENTCOM, thanks to Colonel Molina and his staff." He motioned to the former General, who nodded back. The man had been integrated into the officer core at a lower rank, as determined by part of the exhaustive negotiations between the Americans and Venezuelans.

"Okay, go ahead, Rick," Zimmerman said. "Fill us in on the environmental changes we're facing."

"Yes sir." The Chief Scientist circled to the monitors, using a remote control to shift the map so Central and South America came into view, zooming in three steps for a closer look. "Everyone's wondering about climate, so I have some good news on that front. The average daytime temperature in Central America has dropped from around ninety-two degrees Fahrenheit to somewhere in the mid to high eighties. Still very much tolerable, and well-within the threshold to sustain the wildlife there. It's even better news in South America, where we've only seen an average overall drop of two degrees."

The officers around the table nodded, breathing in relief, some patting each other on the shoulders, many continuing to stare at the map, stepping closer with folded arms or hands on their hips. Confidence seemed high, though the men and women were constantly looking for weaknesses in the plans, ways to improve things, and factors no one else might have thought of. A single map feature could provide a breakthrough.

"Still..." Rick went on, pulling a wince. "The northern freeze could have more of an effect on the south as the weeks and months go by. See..." He pressed the remote, zooming out to include North America again, using his finger to point at the fast-speed overlay that showed weather systems merging and circulating across the continent. "The warm and cold air fronts are battling it out around the twenty-eighth parallel, and it's hard to tell who's winning right now."

"What does that mean, *battling*?"

"We're looking at completely new weather systems spinning up across the entire globe," Rick said, scratching his tousle of hair. "Patterns we can't begin to predict due to their rapid changes and ebbs and flows. We could see extended hurricane seasons up and down the South American coast while the storm patterns in the north may settle into long-term freezing periods. It could get brutally cold up there, making supply retrieval nearly impossible. Or... the stabilization we're seeing now might last for generations."

He hit a button on his remote, flipping the screen so wildlife migratory patterns replaced the weather ones. "We've got folks out in the field to monitor what's happening to the animals. And while the temperature shift hasn't killed anything in South America, we'll no doubt see a lot of locals migrating here."

"What about the cartel highways? Are the thugs and drug lords coming south too?"

General Davidson cleared his throat. "We've been working with Rick's team on this. It's hard to track the movements of the criminal elements, but there's signs they're shifting south."

"Go on."

"Fighting in the Darien Gap, Santiago, and San Jose continue. That tells us there may be a power vacuum happening in those places, though it's far too early to know for sure."

"That doesn't sound too terrible." The President rubbed his chin and nodded. "We can handle the shifting populations."

"So much of our livestock was wiped out." Rick made a slight choking sound in his throat. "But considering our needs are far less now... If we focus on conservation, we could create sustainable fishing and cattle for the remaining citizens."

General Davidson nodded. "In other words, we've lost a lot of food, but that's no problem since half our people are dead."

Rick cast his eyes to the floor. "In no uncertain terms, yes, sir."

"What about the crops we plan on growing here?" Zimmerman glanced up at the window where sunlight was pouring in, shedding light into the room, bringing the screens into more vivid focus. "What are the chances we can grow corn and wheat?"

"We lost a lot of arable land," Rick replied, "but the soil here is good. Very good. If we can avoid an actual winter, we should be able to plan with the local farmers to grow hardier crops."

"Just in case, I want your team working on some genetically modified samples for us to look at within six months."

"Yes, sir. We've already been experimenting with the possibilities there, like the hardier Ukrainian winter wheat and corn breeds. Over the last few years they had record-high yields, so we're hoping to duplicate those results."

"Thanks, Rick. Anything else?"

"Yes, sir. Our field agents, along with General Davidson's joint patrols, have discovered something interesting."

"What's that?"

Rick shot General Davidson a look. "We came across landing craft with Chinese and Russian markings. Dozens of them in jungle regions along Darien National Park, Necocli, and El Tutumo."

Zimmerman's jaw dropped. "Did we engage those forces?"

"No, sir," Davidson replied. "We snapped some images and are stepping up our patrols in the area. Here are the ships we found." The General gestured at the military operations screen, and Rick used the remote to put up pictures of boats with sleek, gray hulls towed up on rocky beaches, covered with jungle foliage, odd-looking swoops of Chinese lettering along with choppy Russian symbols stenciled on the sides.

"Those are older Russian Ondantra-class ships, correct?"

"Yes, sir," Davidson replied. "But we spotted one Russian Project 21820 craft, one of their advanced hydrofoil vessels."

"There could be hundreds of enemy troops landing on the Colombian and Panamanian coasts."

Davidson nodded, jaw set. "Yes, sir."

"We can't let them have those strategic spots." Beads of sweat formed around the President's collar as his head filled with more worries. "They're trying to chew at our edges."

"We'll have joint forces moving in with the second wave of field agents within five hours," Davidson remarked.

"We're going to find them and hit them hard." Zimmerman's shoulders stiffened, his hand forming into a fist. "They need to know, in no uncertain terms, that landing in our backyard will be met with extreme force."

"Yes, sir," the General said, turning to his commanders.

* * *

Low lights illuminated the CENTCOM control room, the techs having finished the last of their upgrades and moved off to other parts of the facility to harden it with wiring and computer gear. The civilian leaders had relocated to the inner chambers to leave the President, his officers, and staff in the primary control center with their communication systems. Operators flipped switches, murmuring as reports came in, data flashing across screens, notifications beeping in the quiet tension. The big scenic window had been barricaded against the outside world by thick plates of steel, the faint buzz of Black Hawk turbines a constant reminder of war.

The scent of ozone filled the sanctum, carried by the upgraded ventilation, rattling vents that pushed cool currents around, drying the moisture leaking down the cave walls and giving the air a cold, sterile taste. Colonels and captains stayed close to their operators, commanding forces arrayed throughout the Americas and in both oceans where they challenged hundreds of minor threats with counter attacks and defensive measures, outmaneuvering two world powers hellbent on their destruction. Marine guards walked the chamber in pairs, never far from the lurking Secret Service personnel who'd changed into full tactical gear, locking the place down like a high-tech tomb, the ceiling tall yet somehow close and compressing.

Zimmerman was sweating despite the coolness of the room, his undershirt damp, hair clinging to his forehead as he scanned the five displays, a claustrophobic feeling weighing down on his shoulders. Molina, Spencer, Davidson, and Prescott wore headsets and were in direct and constant contact with their forces on the ground arrayed across the face of South America.

"What do you have for me, General Davidson?"

"Sir, we've got drones monitoring a pair of drug cartel caravans heading south into Colombia, out of Darien National Park." The General directed his attention toward the far right-hand screen, where the sky view showed them a dense jungle, long lines of mules and locals transporting massive amounts of supplies on their backs in rucksacks and on wooden frames, looking like ants crawling across the ground to a new hive.

"The detail on these images is astounding," the President said, eyes narrowed at the dense line of people carrying their lives southeast toward the Colombian border. "What happens when they reach Colombia?"

"We've got assault teams waiting to intercept them there, and a squadron of drones prepared to provide air support if necessary. If they give up peacefully, we'll detain them. If they fight us, they'll be liquidated."

"Any signs of the Russians and Chinese in Colombia?"

"Sir, we've doubled our patrols in the last five hours and aren't seeing anything from the sky or on the ground, though they're likely moving in much smaller numbers than the drug cartels."

Zimmerman shifted his attention to the middle screen and then slid to the left one, where other military operations were taking place in Venezuela and in the various provinces where Russian and Chinese forces had been spotted. "Will it be enough? It almost seems too quiet out there, and I don't like it."

"We're taking a flow-to-the-battle mentality, saving our heavier hardware for a pair of activities happening in Trinidad as well as attacks on power stations along the border of Guyana, sir."

"We've got to be prepared for a major assault there, I understand." The President studied the camera views taken from the helmets of captains and colonels in charge of the jungle strike teams monitoring the cartel caravans. Experiencing a momentary sense of vertigo from the helter-skelter motions, he watched soldiers and Marines march through dense woods or ride in the backs of Humvees on vast tracts of dusty roads. The center display was the most confusing, with three smaller square camera views along the bottom, a kaleidoscope of movement and activity as troops repositioned.

General Davidson shifted to the side, fingers pressed to his ear, something coming through on his earpiece. Nodding, he conferred with Prescott and Molina before turning back to him. "Sir, one of the drug cartels is approaching our south positions, and we need your approval to strike."

"You have it, of course," the President said with a curt nod, shifting to the right-hand monitor, resting his fists on his hips as he focused on those angles. Twisting his neck, he popped the vertebrae, loosening his tense shoulders as a satisfying crunch rippled through his spine. "Is this the tactical team here?"

"No, it's this one, sir." Davidson used a remote control to flip to a soldier's view from atop an outcropping, staring down at a trail that wound out from the jungle canopy, his head swiveling as he watched and waited. The bold lettering at the bottom of the screen read *Commander Decker*. "And that's our new expeditionary force, I-Corps, 2nd and 5th Divisions, arrayed throughout the Darien Region, outfitted with as many jungle-trained troops as we could find."

"Very good, General. What's the ETA on that combat?"

"I'd say within the next forty-five—" The General twisted to the side, jaw dropping as someone else got his attention in his earpiece. "Wait, sir. I'm getting some reports of an attack on I–Corps 1st and 3rd Divisions as they were moving to intercept the second drug cartel group." Davidson pointed to the center screen and spun his finger in the air, and instantly that view switched to another soldier's helmet cam, the bold across the bottom reading *Commander Wilcox*.

The display's tinny speakers suddenly burst to life, the Commander calling orders in a strained voice beneath a dense barrage of machine gun rounds that tore up foliage and trees, wood chips and vibrant green pieces slicing off and whipping around like someone was taking an army of chainsaws to the jungle. The President winced as the soldier grabbed the man next to him and broke left through the spiraling confusion, the flash of his rifle barrel bright as they entered a clearing, charging from the tree line, stopping to fire at a group of fighters just fifty yards away.

"That's not the cartel," Zimmerman grunted. "They're wearing combat gear."

The two sides clashed in a brief exchange of zipping lead before Wilcox grabbed a man and pulled him back behind cover. Soldiers shrieked and wailed in agony, damage inflicted by piercing shrapnel and explosions, whizzing and snapping ricochets of sound popping through the speakers. Wilcox sprinted away, his swiveling head nearly impossible to follow in the confusion as they dove toward a thick cluster of trees. A spray of red hit a tree trunk ahead of him just before they ducked behind it. The view went dark for a second as the soldiers panted and groaned. The President held one hand up to the screen as if he could command them to fire back, or run, or do... *something*. If it was twenty years ago, and he was in a jet, he could swoop down and launch ordnance at the enemy to wipe them out in a single lethal blow.

A flurry of pops and cracks ping-ponged over the line, growling Hispanic and American accents hissing and cursing, pissed off soldiers shouting back at the fighters who'd just hit them, yet Wilcox's voice remained calm as he covered his mic and gave orders, peeking around the tree toward the clearing where four dead servicemen lay. A moment later, a half-dozen soldiers stepped to the edge of the woods, raised their rifles, and thumped heavy rounds from tubes attached beneath the barrels. The view shifted to the clearing as the grenades arced through the air to lace the jungle with fist-sized bombs. Explosions rocked the air, shrapnel ripping the opposite tree line to shreds, pieces of plants, soil clods, and body parts filling the air along with a chorus of screams.

After the barrage ended, the Commander reported. "Uh, CENTCOM, we're engaging what appears to be a medium-sized force of Russian and Chinese troops. We've got them locked down using M203 grenade fire but we could use some air support."

"Confirmed, these aren't cartel fighters." General Davidson scoffed and turned to Molina to confer. "It's the Russians and Chinese we've been looking for."

What followed was a measured retreat to a fallback zone by the joint US–Venezuelan forces as MQ-1 Predators swept in and unleashed laser-targeted Hellfire missiles at the Chinese and Russians, massive explosions rocking the camera in violent jiggles as pinpoint bombs turned the jungle into pulp, rattling the treetops in waves. After a quick thanks to CENTCOM, Wilcox gathered his troops and pressed onward through the forest in support of the other I–Corps units.

"Good work, UAV flight teams," Davidson barked before shifting to receive intel from the additional expeditionary forces. After nodding and murmuring to people on the other end, he turned back to Zimmerman, his voice loud enough for everyone to hear. "Sir, we're getting more reports of contact with enemy troops, and we still have that cartel convoy incoming."

"I trust you to do what's needed." The President paced slowly as he watched the screens. "Again, you have my sweeping approval for non-nuclear military action. Engage as necessary and let's take them down."

Zimmerman took a backseat as the operations continued, absorbing views of both I–Corps units while keeping tabs on a digital overhead map of South America, where several red dots blinked. Navy Admiral Spencer and Colonel Prescott got his attention and drew him to the map while Davidson and Molina monitored the cartel situation.

"Trinidad is looking like a definite point of contention," Spencer said. "We've got joint Russian–Chinese assets moving toward the island, and we just don't have the boats right now to intercept them, but—"

"I'm assuming we've got auto-counter measures initiated?"

"That's right, sir," Spencer replied. "F-35s incoming from our carrier strike groups west of the attack point."

"Where are the landing vessels coming from?"

"From what's left of the Russian fleet off Brazil's east coast, sir. And the Chinese, too. Seems they have solid footing there, with the Brazilian government's help. They're bringing the fight to us."

"And you think we need to change that?"

"Yes, sir. With carrier strike groups One, Three, and Five just coming around the tip of South America, I say we engage them immediately. We can wipe them out in less than twenty-four hours and limit their offensive capabilities there."

"It would effectively cripple them for good," Molina added with a puffed chest. "We'd have unfettered air and sea superiority."

Excitement tickled Zimmerman's gut, and he rubbed his sweaty palms against his smooth slacks. "Do they realize we're coming around the tip of South America?"

"Impossible to know for certain, sir." The heavy-set Navy Admiral shook his head, which caused his jowls to shake menacingly. "Unless they've got a satellite view of us, I don't see how they can. We've got drones and planes crawling all through the skies, and our first strike nearly wiped out the Russians surveillance and aerial capabilities all together. There is no doubt the Chinese have held something back in reserve, but I'd say we're about to give them a big surprise."

"Let's do everything we can to keep them out of Trinidad while assaulting their remaining carrier groups."

"You need to know something first, sir." Rita Cortez approached with brisk strides, nodding a greeting to the Navy Admiral and Colonel before addressing the President. "The Prime Minister of Spain has just arrived, and he's seeking a conference with you."

He exchanged a confused look with his officers. "I thought the Spain was moving into Africa?"

"They were, sir," Spencer said, guiding them away from the screens where the noise faded. "It's just another long line of things we need to address. Too many at once, I'm afraid. But, yes, two hours ago, AWACS picked up a fleet of ships on radar, and the Spanish Navy Admiral responded to our hails. They're parked fifty miles north of Trinidad. Military vessels and countless troop transports and supply boats filled with people."

"What's the fleet's condition?"

"Not great, but they're on our side, and they're looking for our approval to come ashore in Trinidad."

"Well, they can't do that with the Chinese and Russians invading."

"Exactly. We think the enemy's plan is to block the Spanish from landing, knock us off the continent, then pick off those waiting ships. Africa must be getting crowded."

"Let's welcome the Spanish," he said with a relieved sigh. "I've got a great relationship with Prime Minister De Leon, and I'm certain we can count on them as an ally. Rita, set up that meeting with him immediately and let them know our intentions is to clear the way for them to land. In fact, tell them I'll talk to De Leon within the hour."

"I'll give them the message, sir." Her expression turned dark. "There's another request."

"Go ahead."

"Five minutes ago, the Russians and Chinese asked for a meeting. They want to talk to you and General Davidson."

"We can definitely accommodate that. I'd love to give them a piece of my mind."

"But they don't want the Venezuelan leadership attending."

"Too bad." Turning to the men who were directing the combat, he caught Davidson's attention and gestured him over. "General Davidson? Colonel Molina?"

"Five minutes, sir?" Rita asked.

"That works for me. We'll be right over."

Rita spun away, slipping back into her Secretary of State duties easily, salvaging what remained of foreign diplomacy as the commanders came up.

"Can you two spare fifteen minutes?"

"The jungle fighting is getting pretty hairy," Davidson said, "but I've got eyes and ears on it. What's up?"

"The Russians and Chinese want to meet."

"What for?" Davidson's expression turned to steel. "I've got nothing to say to those bastards."

Molina glanced at the monitor array, nostrils flaring with contempt. "They want to parley while making incursions into my... into *our* country? What hubris!"

"They think they have us over a barrel," Zimmerman said.

"But they don't," Spencer replied. "Not with three full carrier groups coming around the southern tip of the continent."

"Either that, or they want to talk to us about nukes."

Molina gave a knowing nod. "I had assumed those would be out of play for the sake of not killing everything on the planet, but I suppose anything is on the table with those fiends."

"What do you think, sir?" Davidson asked with a hard gleam in his eye. "I'd love to give them a piece of my mind, especially after we nearly destroyed the entire Russian fleet without a blink.

"Let's feel them out and see what they want," he replied. "First, we take nukes off the table, then we give them a piece of our collective minds."

"They'd be stupid to even consider nuclear weapons." Molina's voice was gruff yet plagued with a note of fear. "Would they?"

"They'll use it to frighten us, certainly, but that's not going to happen. Come on. Let's go."

Zimmerman strode through the bustling CENTCOM chamber with his chest out, preparing himself to meet a man he'd only spoken to a handful of times during his entire presidency, nodding as staffers parted to let them through. Stomach twisting, he pulled out a small computer tablet from an inside pocket and gripped it in his sweaty hand. The Secretary of State guided them along the cavern's outer wall, its rough-hewn shape somehow comforting as they prepared to meet their adversaries. It was *La Rom de Guerra*, as Molina called it, the War Room, and the name fit perfectly.

Rita waited for them, holding open a door leading to a short passage with a honeycomb of chambers woven into the rock, heavy Marine guards standing by, lukewarm air circulating from vents. Much of the civilian leadership was gathering in the smaller rooms, congress people, senators, state representatives functioning in tandem to redraw the new lines of government. With no more states to oversee, they were dividing up Venezuela into sections already, their Venezuelan counterparts both amused, confused, and a little angry, but at least they were working together.

As the President strode to the end of the hall, a Marine briskly saluted them before grabbing the door handle and jerking it open. Inside was a short oaken conference table with the presidential seal in the center, a single large screen at the far side, mounted to the rock. The rest of the walls were made of drywall and thick insulation, rendering the room completely soundproof. Zimmerman stood at the head of the table, gesturing for Molina, Davidson, Rita, and Spencer to take seats on either side. Once they were situated, he nodded for Rita to go ahead and start the conference. She reached for a control panel beneath the screen, punched a couple of buttons, and activated a camera fixed atop the display.

She cleared her throat. "Hello, this is President Zimmerman, General Davidson, Navy Admiral Spencer, and Colonel Molina, formerly of the Venezuelan forces. I'm Secretary of State Rita Cortez. To whom are we speaking?"

The monitor came to life, at first a blink of blue, followed by two figures standing in an elegant room with rich paintings, Victorian style door moldings, and a single window covered by crimson drapes. A faint beep reached them over the line, and the two men in the camera frame turned. Both leaders were decked out in sharp military uniforms, the Chinese President standing several inches shorter than his Russian counterpart, a group of officers murmuring behind them, some Zimmerman recognized from past briefings over the years, while others were fresh faces.

Nodding to each man, he stood stiffly. "President Xiaodu. President Levashov." He didn't care that he was pronouncing their names poorly, hoping it aggravated them as a flash of anger flared up his spine.

"President Zimmerman," the Russian started, his icy blue eyes framed in a hawkish face, blond-gray hair parted neatly on the side and combed back perfectly, every indication giving the impression he was in good health and spirits, though worry lines etched the corners of his eyes, and dark bags coloring his skin beneath them, barely covered by a dusting of makeup.

"Mr. Zimmerman," Xiaodu announced, purposefully insulting him by not calling him by his given title, but he'd expected the extra vileness from his Chinese counterpart.

Jaw clenched, he ignored the slight. "I'm assuming your call is to concede that this fight is over, and you've lost. We demand the immediate withdraw of Chinese and Russian forces from Colombia and any part of Panama, including the Darien National Park."

"It is just like you Americans to throw your weight around," Levashov said with a smirk. "It is that kind of reckless bravado that enables us to keep making headway despite your best efforts. Thank you for being so bold and stupid." The last sentence dripped off his lips like poison.

"Let's not mince words, Levashov. We've soundly defeated you in the skies and on the water, and you're only still viable because we haven't had the time to completely wipe those hulks you call ships off the map. And believe me, we'll get to them soon. In case no one told you, it's all about air superiority." He turned to his admiral. "Where are they along the coast of Brazil, Mr. Spencer?"

Davidson shot him a warning glance, though Zimmerman gave him the faintest nod to show he knew what he was doing.

The Navy Admiral held up his own small tablet, scrolled through several reports that highlighted troop movements and other intel he'd gathered from AWACS. "Sir, I'm showing four battle cruisers tucked into the islands off the eastern coast near Vitoria, and mixed in with those are Chinese naval vessels, including three submarine groups. As a side note, there's a fourth joint Russian-Chinese sub fleet cruising toward our northern carrier positions, which we'll neutralize over the next hour. Most of their strength is arrayed between Brazilian bases in São Paulo and Rio de Janeiro. The Chinese South Sea Fleet is deployed there, along with the Liaoning and Shandong aircraft carriers."

"Just two carriers?"

"That's right, sir."

"It's a sizeable force," Zimmerman said with a mocking sigh. "What can we do against it?"

"Well, much of the equipment is outdated, sir," Spencer went on, eyes scanning his screen. "While they have a lot of materials and weapons, and two railgun boats, they're missing about half their fleet."

"Where's the North and East Sea Fleets, Xiaodu?" Zimmerman looked at the camera, one eyebrow cocked. He backed off the table and folded his arms across his chest. "Didn't have fuel to bring them?"

Xiaodu huffed and glared, but he wasn't half as imposing as his Russian counterpart. Still, Zimmerman had to be careful. The Chinese forces were nothing to scoff at, and briefings showed they had plenty of destroyers, frigates, and amphibious vessels, submarines, coastal defense units, and enough aircraft to make life difficult, though they didn't have a full accounting of them.

"You have no idea what you're talking about," Xiaodu replied. "Just because you can't see them doesn't mean they're not there."

"If they're anywhere close to South America, we'll find them. Now, what do you want?"

Levashov held back his counterpart with a soft look, then turned to the camera. "I'll be short and to the point, Mr. President. We want to understand your stance on nuclear weapons, and we're hoping you won't force us to use ours by using yours in the upcoming conflict."

Zimmerman shot General Davidson a glance, saying, "We've stood by all the nuclear treaties and agreements, though we've moved our arsenals to secure locations. We could launch at any time." While the US stockpile was in complete disarray, a quarter of their weapons still locked in frozen bunkers back in the states, the Russians and Chinese didn't need to know that.

"Us as well." The Russian President spoke slowly and carefully.

"And us." A slow grin spread on Xiaodu's face. "Perhaps they are on one of those missing fleets you are so curious about."

The line went silent, the men staring across the miles, his enemies somewhere out there, their shaky connection glitching and fluttering with static as satellite crews struggled to keep the signal strong. As the months and years rolled by, more systems would go offline, orbits degrading, equipment falling to pieces until they had the technology to attempt space travel again.

"Will you then agree to withdraw from the continent?" Zimmerman pressed.

"No!" The pair shouted at the same time, the Russian adding, "Besides, it is impossible. There is no place left to go."

"Africa," Zimmerman stated. "Weren't you settling there?"

Xiaodu stepped forward, words spitting from his lips, dark eyes simmering like hot coals. "Our mortal enemy, India, has allied with England and France. They forced our landing party off Madagascar. South America is our last hope."

In a moment of conciliation, for the sake of thousands of lives, Zimmerman nodded. "Then go to Argentina. Abide by a set of rules, and your people can settle there."

"And trust you filthy Americans to stay faithful to your agreements?" Xiaodu scoffed and spun away with a violent head shake, Levashov turning to catch his ally before he abandoned the conversation completely.

"You should talk," Zimmerman hissed, all the frustration he'd felt toward the Chinese bubbling up from his gut, twisting his face into a sneer. "Your infiltration into Taiwan was a direct betrayal of the Taipei Peace Accord, and we can never trust you after that."

Levashov spit. "What about Afghanistan and Israel? What about Cuba and Mexico? Have you left those citizens to rot?"

"And the Ukraine?" Zimmerman fired back, insides burning from the Russian invasion that had spanned decades. "How many people died in that conflict? Are you landing Ukrainians on Peruvian shores to show your grand mercy?"

The Russian leader rose toward the camera, his fist balled like he wanted to take a swing at it, though he backed off, his anger fading until he finally conceded with a nod. "As much as it burns me to admit it, you are right."

"None of us can be trusted," Zimmerman said. "Our pasts haunt us with every step. And while we should be talking peace--"

"Our only choice is war," Levashov sighed. "A fight to the bitter end."

"Then it's settled." Zimmerman blinked as he realized what he was agreeing to. "We fight to the end, though no nuclear weapons are to be used."

"Or chemical," Davidson added where he sat with his hands clenched on the table.

"Agreed," Levashov said. "No nuclear or chemical weapons to be used."

Xiaodu glanced at his counterpart skeptically before he gave a curt nod. "Agreed."

"We'll keep video copies of this meeting as a historical record," Zimmerman told them with a bitter smile, "holding us to our words. Not that there'd be anyone left if we did resort to nuclear weapons, but should the world end in fire, those remaining will know who started it."

The two men on the other line agreed, and Rita punched a button on the control panel, cutting them off. The room deflated with sighs and slumping shoulders, hands slapping on the table as the officers released the breaths they'd been holding for a long minute.

"I trust Levashov to keep his word," Molina said, his tone thick with distress. "But Xiaodu is ruthless. Do not expect mercy from him. We have had enough dealings with the Chinese over the years to know their promises are like leaves in the wind."

"Are you sure we should have gotten into specific logistics?" Davidson asked. "We basically just told them we know where they are."

"I just wanted to get a rise out of them," he replied. "Seems like it worked."

"And we got them to agree to no nuclear weapons," Rita said. "Good job on that, sir."

"That's an easy promise for them to make right now, but when we come to the end of this, and they've lost, we'll see if they still keep their promises. The temptation to use nukes as a last resort may be too hard for them to pass up, especially if they've got nothing left to lose. And I'm fairly certain the Chinese have their other naval groups around. It's just a matter of where. General, can you locate those fleets?"

While they'd been talking, Davidson had been distracted with his computer tablet, scrolling through a constant barrage of incoming reports, his expression ranging from slack and focused to red-faced and angry, big fingers pounding on the screen to fire back replies to his people in command. Finally, the General shook his head and lifted his eyes. "Sir, we've found the Chinese Northern Fleet."

"I'm getting a notification, too," Spencer said, also occupied with his tablet.

"Where?"

"Sailing toward Florida, on a collision course with some of our convoys heading this way."

A shudder coursed up his back at the thought of missiles and rail guns taking out their transports. "They're going to attack a civilian convoy?"

"It looks that way, sir."

"Do we have assets in the area?"

The Admiral shook his head. "We have a few destroyers and subs guarding those ships, but not enough to take on the entire Northern Fleet. Our best bet would be to get those convoys to move west around Cuba, and we send two carrier strike groups in pursuit of the Chinese, one trailing and one heading them off. If we can knock out that force, it will be a tremendous victory for us."

"Make it happen. Now, let's get back out there and do our duties. New America is counting on us." He turned to leave but paused when he saw Rita unmoving in her chair, palms resting on the table, tears wetting her cheeks. Nodding for the others to go, he sat across from her, trying to read her distraught expression. "What's wrong, Rita?"

With a sniff and a heavy sigh, she said, "It's never going to end, is it, sir? The fighting. The killing. Not even when we're facing annihilation can we pull back from the precipice."

He slumped and ran his hand through his hair. "For a second there, I almost pulled back and gave them an out. For the sake of our people and theirs. Think of all the Russians and Chinese citizens on those boats, looking for a place to land, hoping with all their hearts to find a new home. They're not responsible for what their governments do."

"Like ours aren't responsible for us?" Lifting her glassy eyes, she wiped her cheeks with her fingers. "Why didn't you pull back? Why didn't you give them an out?"

"Because I realized just how doomed we are, and that someone…" A dark chuckle slipped out. "*Someone* has to perish in all this. Even if we saved every human the cold didn't kill, there'd be mass starvation and death."

"We couldn't feed people fast enough, because it'll take years for farming to catch up to the millions of refugees."

"The world's been craving this war for decades, and this is the perfect excuse to have it."

"You really think they won't use nukes?"

With a hopeless stare, he shrugged. "I don't know, Rita. I honestly don't."

Chapter 6
Tom McKnight
Osa Peninsula, Costa Rico

The Humvee cruised along a quiet stretch of highway, the center line faded, the asphalt smooth and unmarked, not like the roads up north with their ragged potholes and cracks. The jungle crowded around them as the diesel engine coughed and sputtered and carried them forward after coming down from the humid heights, warm breezes blowing through the open windows and sunlight hitting the ground in long, dust-filled rays.

Tom leaned over the wheel, blinking blearily at a highway running north to south. "It's great being on smooth pavement again."

"Yeah, those back roads were tough on Mom," Sam said from the passenger side, glancing over her shoulder to where Barbara was buckled up in the seat between Linda and Jack. "This should be Highway 34." The book Henny had given them sat open in her lap, her fingers flipping through rat-eared pages of maps and area descriptions.

"And that will take us south, right?"

"Highway 34 goes through the rest of Costa Rica and into Panama, all the way to Panama City." Gesturing at the map, she glanced at the road with a hopeful expression. "If we can stay on this, we'll be home free."

"I can't imagine there won't be a detour or two," Tom grumbled, looking both ways, "but it's been pretty clear so far."

"And the ocean is, like, right there," she said, pointing out her window at a deep blue line on the horizon.

"Can we go to the beach?" Jack called, kicking his legs and leaning into the middle over Barbara's lap.

"That does sound pretty cool," Linda said, her eyes shifting from the jungle forest to the vast blue space off to the right. "It's been forever since we went on vacation."

"I don't know," Sam shrugged. "After paddling through a hurricane, I think I'm done with the ocean for a while."

"I'm sure it's beautiful," Tom added, "and sitting on a beach for a few hours sounds amazing, but we're not on vacation. We're all fueled up thanks to that farmer back at the last village, so we can keep on going for a good bit. We have to take advantage of it while the weather is warm."

"That farmer was so nice to fill our tanks," Barbara said with a tired smile, hand raising to stroke Jack's hair.

"Yeah, they loved the smoked meat we traded them," Sam nodded, picking a piece from a plastic pouch and popping it in her mouth.

"We had to give him almost half of it, though," Tom said with a head shake. "Man, that guy drove a hard bargain. Thankfully, we didn't have to give him any of our ammunition or medical supplies."

"Can we really afford to trade away any of that?" Linda held her pistol holstered in her lap, one that Saanvi had left them in their backpacks, a smallish Springfield Hellcat she'd found tucked in a side pocket, so small they'd missed it at first. While camping, she'd been combing through every last inch of their possessions when she came across it, claiming it and its two spare magazines.

"A taste of civilization sounds nice right about now," Barbara said happily, though her voice was underpinned with intense weariness.

Tom smiled into the rearview mirror. The trip had been hard on her, every bounce and bump along the Costa Rica dirt roads an experience in pain, but she'd whittled her medication in half, stating she'd rather know if something was wrong than float mindlessly through the day. While her voice drifted, dreamy and slightly slurred, it was gaining strength by the hour, her mental acuity sharpening with every sentence.

Tom nodded. "We'll see. There's bound to be bigger towns on this highway."

"Oh, yeah." Sam's finger trailed down the map. "There are a bunch of them."

They passed through a dense cluster of trees that stretched a hundred feet over their heads. Barks and long, chesty howls rose in a chorus throughout the forest, and Tom glanced off to his right to see shadowy shapes shifting and bolting from branch to branch, muscular arms swinging them around, clinging there, dark faces peering back at them through the foliage.

"It's the howler monkeys again," Linda said, chuckling, grinning up into the trees.

"They're so awesome." Jack gawked through his bullet-riddled window.

"Maybe we can get one for a pet," Linda twisted her lips to the side in thought.

"Bad idea," Tom disagreed. "Monkeys do not make great pets."

"Yeah, but we'll be living in the forest anyway," Linda mumbled. "Might as well have some monkeys."

A vehicle barreled in from the north with a creaking suspension and a slither of tires on pavement, an aluminum grill coming into the picture behind them, gaining fast. Hands clenching the wheel, Tom held his breath as a small white pickup shifted lanes and roared past them, the truck bed filled to the brim with crates of goods covered in fluttering tarps, a half-dozen people clinging to the ropes and bungees that held it all together, blinking at them as the wind whipped around their heads.

Ever since coming out of the heights, cars, trucks, and vans filled with people and every last possession they owned flew past them, a mixture of Mexicans and Americans heading south, fast. The air occasionally fluttered with chuffing helicopter rotors, big formations of them spotted through the overgrown canopy. The Humvee cabin grew quiet as they settled in, the lush forest giving way to farmland stretching on both sides, massive mountains rising off to the left with green spilled across them like an artist's painting. Tom caught sight of roads winding up through valleys between spurs, but the highway was the most crowded, vehicles pulled off the degrading shoulders as loads were adjusted, flat tires fixed, hoods lifted over smoking engines filling the air with burnt oil and antifreeze.

Even as the highway grew thick with traffic, so the forested hills became even more beautiful. Clusters of bright blue butterflies fluttered across the road, bird calls descending upon them from the tree heights, and always the howler monkeys sang to them for miles. Signs written in English and Spanish dotted the roadside with arrows pointing off to rest stops and forest preserves, former tourist spots filled with citizens and joint US–Mexican military forces with their sleeves rolled up as they ferried supplies south or helped stranded refugees.

Soon, vehicles crowded in behind them, and Tom sweated nervously, reaching up to tug at his white T-shirt collar, casting a wary eye all around. Even in the morning light, the headlights grew thicker, a sea of humanity flooding south to escape the mysterious winter nipping at their heels. Roads swelled with convoys, civilian vehicles interspersed with Humvees and military medical trucks, though no one gave the McKnights a second glance, everyone too caught up in their own distress or urgency to care about the family inside the old Humvee. Signs for Ciudad Cortes sprouted up pointing to tourist destinations, waterfalls, walking paths, and fishing spots. The road split at times, branching off toward small villages, Tom taking the least congested routes over gravel or dirt tracks, always ending up back on the main highway again.

Sam had shrunken in the passenger seat, one foot on the dashboard, gaze shifting from the road to her side mirror, left hand itching at her neck as a thin sheen of sweat glistened on her skin. She read from her book. "We're entering the Osa Peninsula."

"What's that?"

"It's a place where the South American jungle meets North American forests. It's like a regional crossroads, I guess. The book says it holds two-point-five percent of the world's biodiversity. Lots of tourists."

"So, it was already packed with people *before* the anomaly," Tom murmured, glancing in his rearview. "Sounds like a mess."

"Definitely a mess," Sam replied, eyeing the traffic another second before gazing out her mirror. Suddenly, she rose, back stiffening, neck craned forward in alarm. "Hey, Dad. Do you see—"

"Yep." Tom watched in his rearview at the massive beige vehicle far behind them, hardly noticeable in the crowd. "I see them."

"How long—"

"For at least the past hour, maybe longer. They're keeping pace with us, stopping whenever we do, turning when we do. It's like they're waiting for something."

"Are you sure it's him?"

"I'm pretty certain. It's a Humvee, like ours, just newer and looks like it's loaded down with gear. It's *got* to be him."

"That's what I thought," Sam replied, glowering at her mirror. "Think we can lose them?"

"I'll try… right here."

They were approaching a broken-down vehicle in the center of the road, with a pair of lanes branching to either side. Whipping the wheel to the left, he put the Humvee on the lane that wound up through a mass of colorful houses, dirt flying up from the tires, a cloud of dust rising behind them. The truck windows rattled as Tom punched the gas and passed several vehicles, jerking the wheel again to put them back in line on the highway, causing Jack to cry out in glee as he was whipped around. Sure enough, the Humvee mirrored their movements, taking the left-hand lane, surging through the traffic, and sliding in behind them to keep pace.

"Definitely them," Tom said. "Crap."

"And it looks like we're coming up on a checkpoint, too," Sam added, gesturing to a newer looking sign on the roadside, *Ciudad Cortes Checkpoint. US Citizens Only,* and then an arrow pointing to the newly paved lane running off to the right.

The road funneled them toward the center of town where the sea of humanity thickened into a veritable soup of engine exhaust and noise, people packed into small villages and neighborhoods, shouting, music blaring from a hundred different speakers, drums and horns battling it out in strained Spanish melodies. They passed three consecutive checkpoints where Tom saluted the soldiers from behind the wheel, expecting them to make him stop, though they were waved through and kept driving until they reached an empty stretch of road that joined them back with highway traffic.

"It looks super crowded up there, Dad," Sam said, voice rising with alarm when Tom punched the gas. "Are you sure we're—whoa!"

The Humvee rocketed forward before slowing suddenly, Tom whipping the vehicle left and flying across the tight-knit traffic, cutting off people to the sound of blasting horns. Facing oncoming cars for a second, he jerked the wheel again and tore up a gravel path that wound along the outskirts of a massive marketplace filled with brightly colored tents, wood-framed booths, and clusters of mostly smiling people. Half were clearly Mexican, but the rest wore denim and cotton T-shirts with college or branded logos, marking them as American, though they were dusty and threadbare, many of them with shell shocked expressions from travelling the Central American highways. US and Mexican soldiers strolled through the crowd or stood in pairs where hard-packed dirt lanes intersected. Barrel fires with spits kicked off the scents of roasting meats and vegetables. Red, green, and yellow fruits were piled high in carts, hands sweeping in to make quick trades, filling baskets and shirts and plastic bags.

Tom's stomach growled, but he didn't stop driving, working his way toward the other side, cutting through a wide grassy field full of dusted vehicles and crowds hawking their wares, gesturing wildly, laughing, and shouting. He drove the truck to the end of the packed lot and circled around on flattened grass, the Humvee barely able to fit, the suspension rocking as he glanced over his shoulder for any signs of pursuit. Finding some empty spaces at the end of a row, he pulled in and stopped with a lurch, putting the truck in park but leaving it running. "Wait here," he said, getting out of the vehicle and crawling onto the hot hood, crouching there and peering over the taller vans and pickups stacked with goods, scanning from left to right as the late morning sun cut across the grounds.

Not seeing the Humvee, he jumped down and climbed back in. "I don't see any signs of them anywhere. I think we're good here for a while. We'll wait another thirty minutes before we head out."

"Why don't we just stop for a couple of hours?" Barbara asked from the back, glancing toward the crowds, eyes glinting eagerly over the bustling activity.

"Yeah, Dad." Jack lifted his head from where it had been resting on Barbara's lap. "Let's get out and walk around. There's a bunch of kids out there."

Linda yawned and leaned in, one hand rubbing the side of her face, eyes tired as she tried to wake herself up. "Actually, that doesn't sound like a bad idea. We've been in this thing for how many hours?"

"At least four," Sam said. "But it's hard to tell with no watch or anything. I just know that when we left it was dark, and now it's what, afternoon?"

"It's getting close," Tom confirmed, his internal clock nearly spot on with such things ever since hourly time went mostly away. There was no 10 a.m. or 1:30 p.m., just morning, noon, and night, and various shades in between, the position of the sun always etched in his mind, its rays pushing through the forest canopy from the east, not quite above their heads. "It's not a good idea to get out right now. We should hang tight."

"Oh, come on, Dad," Linda replied, her tone plaintive. "We've all got to use the bathroom, and we're super hungry. Plus, where else are we going to see so much stuff and so many people in one place again?"

Leaning forward, Barbara reached out and clenched Tom's shoulder, giving it a gentle squeeze, surprising strength in her fingers. "If we're going to start over in South America, we'll need some kitchen supplies, right? Like utensils and real cookware and a ton of other stuff."

Tom ran his fingernails through his beard, itching the sweaty skin beneath it. "True, but I didn't think we'd do it here... today. I figured we'd wait until we got settled in a spot first."

"And we have no clue where that's going to be," Barbara countered. "We need to gather what we can on our way to our new home, wouldn't you say?"

"She's sounding pretty logical," Linda said, resting her hand on her mother's knee, giving her father a knowing nod. "I mean, it's Mom, right?"

Tom winced as he looked at them in the rearview mirror, noting Barbara's sideways grin and the mirthful gleam in her eyes. Shifting to Sam, he said, "What do you think?"

"Well, we have been riding for a while." She nodded toward a pair of soldiers walking between a row of cars. "There's a lot of guards here for protection, and they don't seem to be looking for us. Heck, they waved us right on through."

Tom stared at the soldiers, sighing softly as he yielded to the pressure. "I guess you're right about that. It definitely feels a lot safer than other places we've been. And I could stand to stretch my legs, too."

Linda and Jack squeezed forward with cheesy grins, and Barbara, the mastermind, smiled behind them and rubbed their backs in encouragement.

"Does that mean we're going?" Jack sang.

"I don't know," Tom said, sighing, pulling a mock look of concern. "What you guys are talking about is having fun, and I don't think we're ready for that yet, do you?"

All three kids screamed, "Yes!"

Laughing, patting his palms on the steering wheel, Tom finally conceded with a nod. "Okay. We can go, but only for about an hour and only if you promise that we stay together and watch each other's backs. Do you promise?"

Again, a simultaneous shout blasted through the truck, Barbara laughing and adding her own soft, "Yes!" to the mix. A minute later, they were getting out, holstering their pistols but leaving the rifles behind, wearing jeans and boots except for Linda and Jack, who had on tennis shoes. They pulled their dirty T-shirts over their guns and got ready to walk. At the back door, Tom reached in for Barbara, helping her scoot to the edge of the seat and step gently to the grass, holding both of her hands until she was steady.

Drawing away, she said, "Okay, honey. I can take it from here."

"I don't think so, babe," he replied, gently guiding her as she turned. "This field has a lot of ruts. One false step and you'll—"

"I've *got* it." Barbara pulled out of his hands, moving gingerly toward the back of the Humvee, palm resting on the upper part of the frame to keep herself steady. "I don't need any help."

Tom started to catch up with her, but he couldn't get around because of the vehicle they'd parked next to, a small pickup truck, brown, filled with crates of goods. A woman sat in the back on several wooden boxes, her dark, friendly eyes watching them with a bemused smile, seeming pleased at Barbara's bravado. The shin-high grasses made it impossible to see where they were going, and her boot plunged into a rut and twisted, her knee buckling as she teetered sideways. The woman in the pickup gasped as Tom and Sam converged on Barbara, four arms grabbing her before she fell and hurt herself, lifting her upright and leaning her back against the Humvee.

Clutching her chest, Barbara gave a breathless murmur. "Okay, maybe I need a little help."

Sam squeezed in next to her. "Put your arm over my shoulders. I'll carry you."

"Are you sure, honey?" Barbara swung her arm over and gripped her tight. "I'm probably too heavy for you."

"Oh, please." Sam rolled her eyes. "Just lean on me. I've got you."

"Hey, Jack, where are you?" Tom asked, looking around. "Why don't you get on your mother's other side and help, too?"

"Okay!" he sang, dashing out of nowhere to get on Barbara's right, hugging her tight with a big grin, calling cheerily, "You can lean on me, Mom!"

Hobbling away from the Humvee, they turned toward the massive wall of forest that encircled the field, gazing up at hundred-foot-tall trees, exotic foliage jutting out everywhere like a shaggy painting, wide leaves as big as his chest dripping from the recent rains. A beautiful blue and gold bird leaped from the middle branches and soared across the edge of the trees, much to Jack's delight. Tom stepped back, having another glance around, noting their parking spot was both inconspicuous and a quick shot to the highway should they need to escape.

"Yeah, I think this will do just fine." He gestured to the surrounding vehicles. "These trucks are stacked high with so much stuff, no one will notice us. But maybe…"

Stepping to the back of the Humvee, he opened the hatch and removed the backpack filled with ammunition and a good share of smoked boar meat they planned on trading, and set that aside, then he reached in for a ratty blue tarp they'd used to keep the rain off at the campsite. The plastic was split in spots, stripped away from where they'd folded and unfolded it multiple times.

"You want to cover the truck with this?" Linda asked, taking one end as Tom unraveled it.

"Yeah, but do it kinda messy." Tom shut the rear door and lifted his end, Linda following his lead.

He dragged the tarp over the back, opened the front door a few inches, tucked some of the tarp in, and slammed the door tight. "No one can take it now. Smooch can guard our things just for a little while. There's plenty of shade, and we'll be gone less than an hour. Put a bowl of water on the floorboard for her."

Tom came around to supervise Linda as she opened the back door and intercepted the eager dog, keeping her inside, rubbing her neck and fixing her a bowl of water. After some more love, she held up her hand, saying, "Pas auf!" *Guard!*

Smooch hopped from the floorboard onto the seat, pawing at the cushions and licking her chops and giving a playful yelp.

"No, Smooch. Pas auf!"

The dog gave a more confident bark and flick of her snout.

"Good girl!" Linda patted her head, locked the door, and slammed it shut.

Windows cracked, and with plenty of shade on the inside, they stepped away from the Humvee, Tom nodding appreciatively at the job they'd done. "If someone drives by, they're just going to assume it's another pile of junk, like most of these trucks."

"Well, it *is* a piece of junk," Linda replied. "But I kinda love it now. It's our little rolling house, isn't it?"

Tom laughed and patted her on the back. "I guess it *is* our rolling house, and it needs a new set of wheels. Think they'll have Humvee tires here? Or a new engine?"

Linda shrugged as they meandered over to the rest of the family. "You never know, right?"

"I won't count on it. Okay, you guys ready to go on a little adventure?"

"Yes!"

They guided Barbara down the row of parked vehicles, their boots and tennis shoes treading through the soft grass, the ground moist with rain and puddles, Sam acting as an anchor. Tom glanced back to see Smooch watching them from the window, partially covered by the tarp.

Linda looked, too. "You think anyone will try to get inside?"

"If they try to steal our truck, I wish them the best of luck." He gave her shoulders another quick squeeze. "They'll be pulling back a bloody stump or two."

"Smooch is such a good dog."

"She is. Tough as nails, too."

MIKE KRAUS

Loose leaves and seedlings fluttered down, carried on a warm breeze, a cluster of them clattering on car roofs and at their feet, where they were ground into the rich earth by their shoes. The crowd's murmurs grew louder, the aroma of hot food drifting their way, making Tom's mouth water with delicious possibilities. He could imagine how the kids must feel not having snacks like pizza and mac and cheese for weeks, yet they were always happy just to get what they were offered. Grinning, he couldn't wait to see what the bazaar had cooking.

Linda glanced up. "I heard you and Sam talking about someone following us. You think it's Keith?"

"It probably is," Tom conceded with a sigh. "If there's one thing I've learned in all this, it's that he'll never stop until he…" Tom pursed his lips, unwilling to guess out loud what was in Keith's head. "Yeah, it's him."

"Good," she said in a deadpan voice.

Tom chuckled. "Why do you say that?"

"Because that asshole needs to get what's coming to him," she spat.

Tom laughed harder and then caught himself, clamping his mouth shut. "You shouldn't talk like that, especially…" With a sad head shake, he sighed. "Oh, never mind. You're right. He does."

The bazaar blazed in the middle of the makeshift parking lot with brightly colored tents and shouting vendors, crowds spilling from the center into the rows of vehicles, cooking from the backs of their pickup trucks and vans, holding up bottled waters or steaming meat on skewers.

"This is a lively place," he murmured to himself, keeping his eyes on anyone who might look threatening, but he couldn't find a single person who did. Everyone milling around was caught up in their own world, doing everything they needed to do in order to survive. Something caught Barbara's eye, and she turned Sam and Jack toward a couple of Americans selling items from the back of their pickup, a woman with a bright orange Tennessee Volunteers T-shirt and what was likely her husband.

"Hey, there!" In her fifties, the woman wore her dyed blonde hair pulled back in a bun with a big black clip, the dark roots grown out four inches. "Are you guys from the States? Of course, you are. I can just tell you're not natives to these parts."

Nodding with a grin, Barbara hobbled in her direction, Jack and Sam dutifully holding her steady as they approached the covered truck bed, scanning the items the woman was selling, each one marked with yellow sticky notes with handwritten prices scrawled on them. There were lanterns, tent packages, blow-up mattresses, plasma lighters, pots, pans, and grills... and Tom would have bought all of it if he could have.

A short man with a round belly and scraggly beard stood next to the woman, returning Barbara's smile and gesturing her to come over excitedly. "Greetings, folks! I'm Greg and this is my wife, Cindy."

"Nice to meet you." Barbara glanced into the truck bed at the stacks of goods. "This is my husband Tom, and my kids Sam, Linda, and Jack. We're from Virginia."

Greg raised his fist. "Go Cavaliers!"

Tom smiled and gave a halfhearted fist-pump. "Go, Vols!"

That made Greg laugh harder, and he patted Sam's shoulder. "Hey, we've got all kinds of camping stuff you guys might need. Used to run a shop back in our hometown and brought the whole damn store with us, as you can see."

As Greg and Cindy selected items at the front to show them, Tom peered inside to see the prices were high, though each one had "or will trade" written beneath the costs, and he doubted they'd want anything the McKnights had. Shrugging off his backpack, he placed it at Sam's feet, nodding to her as he backed away to give himself some breathing room. Linda stepped aside with him, hands on her skinny hips, looking around at the milling crowds with an adult's wary eye.

Tom smiled when Barbara laughed at Cindy's enthusiasm, the woman running through explanations of her wares faster than they could blink. Barbara gestured at the big blue truck, commenting on their little store and inquiring how they'd made it so far. Cindy obliged in a more serious tone, rattling on about driving through Mexico, armed to the teeth as they protected their precious supplies, recalling how they'd traded their way to the border, even bribing a local official of a small Mexican town to let them cross into Guatemala. From there, they'd jumped in with a US military convoy, tailing them through El Salvador and Nicaragua. Tuning them out with a deep breath, Tom allowed a surge of inner peace to settle on his shoulders. With a quick step to Linda, he wrapped his arms around her and squeezed her tight. Gasping, laughing a little, she embraced him back, pressing her cheek against his rib cage, clutching him with a strong grip.

"What's that for?" Her voice was muffled at first until she gave him a final hug and backed away. "Do you like me or something?"

"I don't know what's gotten into me," Tom laughed, then his expression sobered. "I guess I'm sorry for everything you've lost, kiddo."

"What are you talking about, Dad? We can get a new house and more farm animals. It's like Mom said. It doesn't matter where we are, as long as we're together as a family."

"That's not what I meant, sweetheart. I'm talking about the important things that can't be replaced… things that were stolen far too early for reasons that make no sense." His voice faded as he failed to put it into words she'd understand.

Linda grew quiet, and together they watched Barbara, where she was laughing at something Cindy had said, her hand moving to clutch her chest as she broke into a light coughing fit. Sam and Jack held her steady as she wavered, their expressions worried, Cindy's smile fading. Then Barbara recovered, waving it off, chuckling and pointing at more items in the truck bed.

Linda stared at her mother a moment before her pale face turned up to Tom. "You don't mean things we can touch, do you, Dad?"

"No, sweetheart. We've kept each other alive, and that's the best we can ask for. I'm talking about the intangibles. For that loss… I'm so sorry."

Linda's mouth fell open to reply, but Jack spun away from the truck and sprinted over, holding up several slim boxes in his hands, the pictures on the sides showing eight-inch-long cylinders with thin tips.

Tom leaned in. "What do you have there, Son?"

"We traded some smoked pig and ammo for these filters," he replied, grinning from ear to ear. "Aren't they cool?"

Tom took one from him and had a closer look. "Oh, these are straw filters. Very nice."

"What do they do?" Linda asked.

"Supposedly, you can stick these into a pond, suck on the straw, and draw the dirty water through a filter where it will come out perfectly clean."

"Can you even do it with poo water?" Jack asked with a disgusted face.

Laughing, Tom shook his head and handed the filter back. "Well, maybe not *that* dirty of water, but in any old creek or river, they should work great."

Barbara was just finishing up with Cindy and Greg, waving goodbye and turning away, Sam at her elbow, the two laughing at a joke. Tom ducked in, grabbed the backpack, and closed the front flap, giving a nod at the couple before stepping off into a cool breeze that gusted between the rows of cars. His eyes settled on Barbara and Sam, a loose, cheery grin on his face, chest swelling with happiness to see them getting on so well again. Sam stood about Barbara's height, the pair looking like a couple of friends rather than mother and daughter, and Sam had more filters in her hand, while Barbara carried a tall paper bag tucked under her left arm.

"What's in the bag, honey?" Tom asked, and she held open the package so he could peer inside. "A couple of aluminum cooking pots?"

"These are the start of our new kitchen," she replied with a smile and a gleam in her eye, glancing between him and the package, measuring his response. "Pretty cool, right?"

"Yeah, these are awesome!" He rolled the top of the paper bag up tight. "But how did you talk them into it? What did you give them, an ammo magazine and some boar meat?"

"Well, Greg wasn't too happy about it," Barbara admitted, "but Cindy insisted we take the pans after everything we've been through." Expression turning thoughtful, Barbara glanced back. "I'm just thrilled there are still good people in the world, and I wouldn't be disappointed if we ran into them again. We started to exchange numbers and then realized we don't have cell phones anymore."

"They're definitely good people," he replied, watching in amusement as Jack traipsed over to a vendor at the edge of the bazaar who was selling tortilla-wrapped South American food, big piles of rice frying on a sheet of metal, pots and pans cooking chicken and peppers and a myriad of other toppings.

Hands on the side of the cart, Jack rose on his tiptoes, peering at the food, turning and waving them over. "Dad, can we get some of these?"

Linda followed her brother, eyes going wide at the sizzling food and delicious smoke that billowed off the griddles around their heads. "Oh, dad! These look amazing. I think Jack's right… we need to try these." Glancing back, her tone diminished. "I mean, if we can afford it."

Stomach growling, mouthwatering with the rich smells, Tom hefted his trading pack and wondered what it would cost to buy one for each of them. "Tell you what, guys. Let's just split a couple, okay? And since we've got stuff for our kitchen," he said, smiling at Barbara, "we'll eat up and get right back on the road. We need to start on the final leg of our journey. Sound good?"

"Yes!" they shouted at once, surging toward the food booth.

Chapter 7
Specialist Lance Morales
Osa Peninsula, Costa Rica

Morales kept the wide Humvee on the highway heading south, the vast canopy of trees fifty and a hundred feet tall casting a shade over the pavement, leaving brilliant rays of light piercing through the gaps, glinting across the windshield in golden fractals. Thick tree trunks wove together, a tangle of twisting roots grown deep into the soil, intertwining, strangling each other quietly within the misty lowlands.

Bird cries echoed in the air, carried into the truck cabin through his half-open window, flocks of them scattered by hunting howler monkeys that barked and groaned in long choruses, suddenly fading to nothing, only to rise again even louder than before. Behind the forest wall, mountains rose to the east in a vast swath of green, varying shades and shadows reaching as far as the eye could see. The stretch of road had a few cars but plenty of potholes, and parts of it were simple gravel or dirt tracks meeting rickety bridges that spanned rushing rivers and streams.

"At least it's warm," Morales murmured to the grumbling Lieutenant Smith. The Lieutenant sat in the passenger seat, leaning forward, elbows on his knees, sulking since Banks had ordered them to take the man only introduced to them as 'Keith' south as a VIP.

"Yeah, things are way better now," Smith smirked. "Nice and warm while we taxi this maniac around." While his words were soft, barely above a whisper, he glanced over his left shoulder with a curled lip.

"It's only until Banks joins us in a couple of days," Morales replied. "The Captain fought hard to keep us home—"

"But she outranked him, I know. Cap was so mad." Leaning closer, he whispered. "What's your over and under on how long this guy can stay quiet?"

Morales shrugged, clutching the wheel, smoothly swinging the Humvee down a long dip and back up to the crest of a shallow hill, then sweeping the other way again, grinning at the fun drive. Keith kneeled in the very last seat, balancing as he leaned into the cargo area, using his left hand more than his right to shift around the Pelican cases, checking over the equipment Banks had provided. They each had a Colt M4 carbine, a case full of Beretta M9 pistols, hundreds of rounds of ammunition, and a surprise piece of gear: three Javelin missile launchers.

Keith was favoring his right hand after having some quick surgery by the camp doctors to remove tiny pieces of his rotting fingertips, a procedure performed under mild sedation with the agent recovering with surprising ease. Morales shivered, recalling Keith walking out of the infirmary, sweating and wavering a little, his lips drawn tight in a pained grimace, hands wrapped, nodding at them that he was ready to go.

"He seems pretty into that gear," Morales whispered back. "As soon as he gets bored again, he'll start railing."

"Or after his pain medication wears off," Smith snickered, "whichever comes first."

"I give him thirty minutes before he calls one of us a name."

"Fifteen." Smith held out his hand to shake. "Bet me a pack of smokes?"

"I can hear you guys," Keith grumbled as he shifted something around and dropped it on the floor with a bump. "You assholes would be wise to shut up and drive like your lives depend on it."

"I win," Smith grinned. "You owe me a pack of smokes."

"But I don't smoke," Morales sighed, glancing at his rearview with a frown.

Along with the weapons and ammunition, they'd loaded up with a few cases of rations, older stock by the date on the MRE packages, plenty of empty duffel bags, three crates of water, purification tablets, and straw filters in case they took to the jungles and found themselves without an adequate water source. Morales reached back and rifled through an open container sitting on the rear floorboard and pulled out a couple of toasted corn nugget bags, tossing one to Smith.

"There you go," he said. "Debt paid."

"Hilarious," Smith shot back, but he grabbed the top of his bag with both hands, ripped it open, and dug inside.

Keith turned around, saying, "Hey, you're keeping up with them, right?"

Morales nodded and pointed. "Yeah, late model Humvee filled with bullet holes. Got it. They're a few cars ahead, but it's getting crowded. We blend in with the rest of the military presence, but they might have caught on that we're following them."

"I don't give two shits. Just don't let them out of your sights," Keith growled, going back to his sorting tasks, lifting one of the M9s from its case and popping a magazine into it, charging the weapon with a snap.

By Smith's estimation, they were coming up on a town called Ciudad Cortes, on the north side of the Osa Peninsula, a "rich jungle-forest region with some of the most biodiverse species on the planet," he'd read from a small paragraph at the bottom of the tourist map they'd gotten off a local vendor in Uvita. The roads were rough, pavement cracked and filled with untended potholes, which the Humvee's tires handled easily. Harder to traverse were the constant broken-down cars that made choke points as people tried to fix them on the road instead towing them off to the side. Sometimes the traffic narrowed to one lane, smoke and antifreeze reek wafting through the air, shouts, and honks adding to the chaos.

Morales tracked the old Humvee, not kidding in the slightest about it being a hunk of junk. The armor was dented in several places, bullet holes peppering every window on the vehicle, the spots covered with what looked like duct tape, cloth thrown up so he only saw the shadows of people inside, five or six of them with no way to know if they were men or women, soldiers or civilians. He assumed they were armed and dangerous fugitives who'd taken something from Lieutenant Colonel Banks. At least that's how Keith made it sound, and so he'd kept close with extreme caution, not tailgating, confident he could catch them at a moment's notice.

"Think we should call for backup?" Smith asked to anyone who would answer, though Morales only glanced over with a shrug.

"We can handle them," Keith said absently. "Just shut up and keep driving." Turning, he looked forward and pointed. "They're five cars ahead of you now. Stay on their tails."

"I'm on it," Morales said, swerving right into the dirt shoulder, heading straight for an abandoned vehicle, whipping the wheel left to jerk them back onto the highway with a roar of tires. When he found the old Humvee again, it was just four cars ahead, almost invisible behind a pair of pickups with the truck beds stacked high with crates of chickens, pigs, and people, the barnyard stench coming off it stinging his nose.

"Stay at least two lengths back, Morales. We're still too far away."

"With all due respect, *sir*," he replied, "I'm a specialist, top rated to drive just about any vehicle the Army has. So, why don't you lay off a little?"

"Because you don't know who you're dealing with here." Keith continued his weapons sorting, glancing doubtfully toward the front.

Morales shot Smith a dark stare, a wordless communication of aggravation, and when he shifted to look at the road again, the Humvee wasn't there. He searched for the truck up ahead around the cluster of vehicles, but when he didn't see them there, he punched the gas and roared forward, scanning a couple small neighborhoods filled with side streets and crowded avenues, people and automobiles packed in tight.

"What's going on?" Keith asked, turning and leaning over the middle seat as he peered ahead, a scowl forming on his face. "You lost them, didn't you? Dammit, Morales..."

"Just hang on a second." Looking left, Morales caught sight of the big beige vehicle shooting up a side lane, cutting through a local neighborhood, and disappearing over a shallow rise and deeper into a community of brightly painted houses. "Got him."

Morales hauled the wheel left, the big truck responding, flying across the road to a buzz of beeping horns, like a hornets' nest stirred up. Their fender bumped another pickup that had partially blocked the turn, nudging it aside, denting them. The men in the front seat cursed, but Smith shut them up with a glare as he tapped his rifle barrel on the window frame, then they were rocketing up the side street, sailing over the rise only to slow through a small marketplace in a cobbled square with shops skirting the edges. Morales laid on his horn as people walked in front of him as casually as they pleased. Only when they saw it was an American military vehicle that wasn't slowing down did they whirl and scatter with dark scowls and angry gestures.

Gripping the wheel with agitation, Morales shot them onto a right-hand lane, angling back toward the main highway, sweeping through a fifty-yard patch of forested jungle with animals howling at them, dispersing throughout the branches. Reaching the highway, he laid on his horn as they flew in front of a white van to rejoin the slower-moving traffic, passing a small dirt lot where US servicemen were loading supplies into civilian trucks. The Humvee wasn't there or anywhere on the road, leaving his face burning with embarrassment.

Keith raised his leg and climbed over the Humvee's middle seat, landing heavily. "You should have stayed right on them like I told you to. Now they're gone, and that's more wasted time, you idiot!"

"Hey!" Smith scowled back.

"I had him right there," Morales said, spreading his hands on the top of the wheel as he continued to search for the other truck. "Took my eyes off of him for one second, and he was gone."

"Better listen to me next time!" Keith pounded his fist on the back of the seat, lifting it with a wince of pain, sucking air through his teeth. "I'm telling you, the man we're following has taken down his fair share of soldiers and mercenaries. You might be a decent driver, but you're not as good as him. Now,watch the road and find them!"

"Hey, just calm down," Smith said, turning around with his palm up, then his eyes caught sight of English signs off to the right. "There's a side road to a military checkpoint. Why don't we pull over there and get our bearings?"

Keith stared at the long line of traffic ahead, more populated areas dotting the highway on both sides, entire neighborhoods nestled into the hills and jungle with busy roads and crowds of people. The gravel road through the checkpoint looked freshly built with two guard stations, and soldiers milling nearby. As he worked the gas and brake in the slow traffic, Morales shifted his gaze farther to the right, where another single-lane road wound off into a field with several prefab constructions and tents, guarded by thicker ranks of military units. In a side lot tucked in behind the forest, lines of American and Mexican refugees were being sorted and guided toward troop transports.

"There might be someone there who can help us," he suggested, nodding at the military buildings. "An officer or something."

"More bureaucracy," Keith snorted, watching the road till he finally nodded slowly. "Yeah, get off here. Maybe we can get some additional eyes on the situation."

Nodding, Morales guided the Humvee off the main highway, leaving the thick strands of traffic for a relatively clear two-lane gravel road. He shot them around a big troop transport with its nose angled into the grass on the right, soldiers hopping out and jogging along the roadside with their packs and weapons. At the first checkpoint, the guards took one glimpse at the Humvee and waved them through, but Morales shook his head and pulled to a stop, rolling his window down. The pair flashed their IDs, and a private stiffened and saluted the Lieutenant, glancing back at Keith, who didn't show any ID at all.

"All US military vehicles can go on through," the Private said, gesturing at their truck. "No need for identification."

"Who's in charge of this outfit?" Smith asked across the seat.

"That'd be Colonel Whittington. Why?"

"We need a little bit of help. Hoping to get some of you boys on the case."

The soldier was starting to reply when Keith leaned over Morales' left shoulder, speaking in an authoritative tone. "We need a few warm bodies to track some people down." He looked at the first guardhouse. "I'll take you and your partner there. Hop in."

"Excuse me?" The Private stared, glancing at Keith's bandaged hands and bruised and cut up face for the first time. "Just who the hell are you?"

"He's a special agent," Smith assured him. "And we really need that help. Can we borrow you two for a couple of hours? We can have you back by chow."

"The Colonel would rip us a new one if we just walked off guard duty."

"We still need the help," Keith pressed, "and we've got the authority to get it."

The Private waved them through and backed away from the window. "Sorry, sir, but you'll have to run it past the Colonel. I'd need a direct order from him to leave our posts."

"Fine!" Keith slapped the side of the seat and pointed at the military buildings. "Take us there. I want to talk to Colonel Whittington."

"Yes, sir," Morales said with a glance, and he gave the Private a final wave and drove through, keeping to the side as the gravel road widened. The left lane branched off toward the next checkpoint, the right curving to the military buildings, two clusters of them with a parking lot between them. In the lot, soldiers drilled in formation around stacks of supplies in rows of organized chaos, trucks and workers bustling everywhere, diesel exhaust drifting through their windows. Morales pulled off as an Army Growler shot up the road and whipped around them with careless abandon, leaving him to coast the rest of the way, being more careful as they eased into the busy lot.

"Morales, you're slow as tar," Keith scoffed. "Pull into the lot on the left. Yeah, the bigger building there. I'm guessing that's where the Colonel is."

"Yes, sir." Morales fought to keep the sarcasm from his voice as he turned the Humvee into the proper spot and shut it off, sitting there with a ticking engine, sweating under his Army shirt. Keith got out, slammed the door behind him and marched up to the guards standing on either side of the entrance, already making demands of the soldiers who were leaning forward and listening, looking confused.

"Something tells me this guy's going to get us killed," Smith said with a frown. "And what's with you calling him *sir*? You don't even know his official rank."

Morales shrugged. "Colonel Banks asked us to treat him like a VIP, and Captain Johnson went along with it. Orders are orders."

"That they are," Smith nodded.

By then, Keith had turned and was gesturing feverishly for them to get out and come up. With a sigh, Morales grabbed the door handle, popped it, and stepped into the Costa Rican heat. Distant bird cries and animal calls grew louder, the last vestiges of the icy north slipping away as sweat broke out on his chest. They strolled up to the soldiers, and one guard faced Lieutenant Colonel Smith, popping him a casual salute.

"Sir, this man won't show me his military ID, but he claims he needs to see Colonel Whittington. Is that true?"

Nodding, Smith returned the salute and folded his arms across his chest. "I'm afraid he's right, Private. We need to get in and see the Colonel as soon as possible, by order of Lieutenant Colonel Banks. You can check. She's on the active roster."

"I'll be right back." The soldier nodded and went inside, pushing a flimsy door across the prefab mat flooring.

He returned a moment later and ushered them into a long, hot, crowded hallway that cut through the center of the building. Doors flew open and slammed shut, staffers turning and sliding past one another, privates and MPs moving with a purpose, the stench of body odor and sweat filling his head. The passage led to a central lobby where several haggard high-ranking officers stood in groups next to whiteboards, issuing orders to clusters of lesser officers as they mapped out steps and directions. Lines of dirty refugees slipped by, led by two sergeants who saluted Smith awkwardly as they passed, pushing through the hub of noise and confusion. Keith grinned and returned the gesture exaggeratedly, looking around at the bustle as if it was the funniest thing he'd ever seen.

"Right this way," the Private said, taking them into a hallway, stopping in front of a plain door where he stopped, knocked, and pressed inside without waiting for a reply. Turning, holding the door open, he gestured for them to follow.

Keith shoved between Smith and Morales to stand in front of a short black desk, which was little more than a hastily constructed frame assembled from prefab kit, the thing so flimsy it shook beneath the man whose arms rested on it. Keith stood there with his feet spread apart, hands clasped behind him, cold eyes staring down at the Colonel. The Colonel was shuffling through papers on his desk, a gruff-looking man with a five o'clock shadow lining his jaw, glancing up once as he shifted to a laptop computer and clacked on the keys. Keith rocked from heel to toe, his hard gaze growing more bulging as Whittington continued working and ignoring him. Taking a deep breath, he stepped to the edge of the desk as if to start the conversation, when a soldier flew into the room, slipping between Morales and Smith, her dark, pinned-back hair losing strands, cheeks rosy as if she'd run a couple of laps around the facility.

"Sir." She pressed past Keith, circled the desk, and leaned in to hand him a paper.

The Colonel murmured back, taking the paper, signing it, sending the soldier hoofing out of the room before returning to his work. Morales held his stiff posture, glancing at Smith and watching the standoff at the desk.

Keith put his hands on the edge, leaning closer, a hint of impatience in his tone. "Excuse me, Colonel, but we've got important business to discuss. I'm currently searching for—"

"I've got that requisition for you, sir!" Another soldier popped into the room, peering over Morales's shoulder. "You want to sign these now or later?"

"Let's hold off until I hear from CENTCOM," Whittington said, barely looking up from his laptop, continuing to punch at the keys, one or two fingers at a time.

With a grunt, Keith slammed his palm on the edge of the rickety desk, rattling it, causing the Colonel's hands to freeze over the keyboard before his glare turned slowly upward.

"Sorry, sir." Keith backed up a step under his hot gaze. "It's an order from Lieutenant Colonel Banks from the Los Berros Supply Base."

"Never heard of him," Whittington replied with a dry grunt.

"He's a she, sir."

"Never heard of her." The Colonel corrected himself, hands coming apart slowly. "As you can see, I'm up to my ears in refugees, military integration with the Mexicans, and more fires than I can put out in a lifetime. So, unless it's an order from the President of the United States, or General Davidson, there's nothing I can do."

"Please, Colonel Whittington." Keith's jaw shifted. "Give me a minute. It's of national importance that you listen."

The man stared at him a moment and raised a hand to stop a staffer who'd come in with another question. "You've got thirty seconds."

"Thank you." Keith spoke in a fevered pitch. "There's a criminal in the area, sir, and he's a threat to civilians and military personnel alike." He raised his gnarled fist with its amputated fingers covered in stained gauze, and squeezed it tight. "This man and his family are running all kinds of illegal contraband south of Venezuela, and I don't think—"

"Can't be any worse than the drug cartels we're dealing with," the Colonel responded tersely. "They're not real happy with things being shaken up the way they are, and I've got a random shooting every couple of days around here. What do you need from me? Wait, *who* are you?"

"I'm a special operative out of DC," Keith sputtered, "when it was still DC. I gave your guard my ID and mission code, and he checked it out."

"What do you want me to do about this man and his, um, dangerous family?"

Morales and Smith exchanged a look, the Lieutenant mouthing, "*Family?*"

"I need to borrow a few of your men and women to help me search around town for them. I promise it won't take long, and I'll have them back to you in short order."

"I can't afford to give you any soldiers or staffers, American or Mexican, to hunt down a single family, and I question your assertion that they're a national security risk. Sorry, Special Agent, but there's nothing I can do for you."

"But sir—"

"Dismissed," Whittington spat, raising his pen and pointed it toward the door. "You can go now."

"Sir!"

"Get out of here!" the Colonel growled, rising from his chair and glaring at Smith. "Lieutenant, get this man out of my sight right now or I'll have all three of you thrown in the brig."

"Yes, sir!" Smith rushed forward, grabbing Keith by the arm, trying to draw the stubborn man away as he stood there rigidly, his face growing redder by the moment.

The agent jerked from his grip, spun, and stalked out of the office, grumbling under his breath, Morales and Smith following right on his heels. Then they were in the hall where sweating staffers and soldiers were rushing around, carrying boxes of papers, cases of bottled water, and ammunition. Mexican troops pulled civilians by the hand through the mix, a thousand smells colliding inside the compact passage, English with Hispanic notes flowing over them, bathing them in confusion and chaos. Keith jumped out ahead, losing Morales and Smith at the busy officers' junction, the two pausing and taking their time getting through the crowd.

"He said he was looking for a *family*," Morales said.

"The way he went on about it back at base, you'd figure we were after Darth Vader or something."

"Think there's kids involved?"

Smith shrugged, stepping between two sergeants, neither one of them bothering to salute him as they rushed by, hounded by someone shouting orders and a baby's wailing cries.

"And a follow-up question. Are they really the cold-blooded killers he makes them out to be?"

"No clue," Smith replied, squeezing sideways through the crowd. "Let's see what he wants to do next. I'm hoping he'll give up and turn back to base."

"Wishful thinking."

* * *

Keith's teeth ground together as he shoved his way through the crowd in search of the exit, his jaw just about the only thing on him *not* in excruciating pain most of the time. His fingertips and toes ached in the warm southern climate, chest still bruised from the shots he'd taken from Sam McKnight. Head spinning with anger, it pushed his insanity to the outside, providing a moment of clarity. Mood shifting between rage and calmness, his sense of duty and pride clashed with what would be the liberating feeling of simply pulling out his sidearm and shooting everyone he saw, starting with Colonel Whittington, until the guards finally gunned him down.

Only then would his pain truly end after a brief flash of glory, an exclamation point to the life he'd lived as an operative in the United States Armed Forces. One thing kept him from exploding, and that was the fevered dream of putting a gun to Linda McKnight's head and blowing her brains out right in front of her parents, followed by the other two children, and finally Barbara and Tom. Only then could he even think of the next step, whether it be ending his own life or fading into the Costa Rican jungles forever, the lush denseness calling him, enticing him into its wide green embrace to thrive amongst the wild beasts. Pushing through the front doors, he walked to the back of the Humvee, hands on his hips, head swiveling to scan across the bustling parking lot, watching vehicles come and go, lines of refugees marching off to the side lot, buses and cars honking, enough to drive someone insane. With a deep breath, he forced the rage back down inside. Cooperation, not destruction, would be required to accomplish his goals.

"What next, sir?" Morales asked, he and Smith coming outside to watch the chaos with him.

"Going to be tough to find those people in all this insanity," Smith added. "And we won't be getting any help from Colonel Whittington. Maybe we should call off the search and get back to base."

Wordlessly, Keith strode away from the truck and walked toward the side road that led to a refugee lot where soldiers and Army staff were rounding up people and ushering them onto buses. Clusters of dirty luggage and rucksacks were being sorted, kids wailing and crying as they clung to their parents, sergeants shouting orders with barking urgency. Biting his cracked bottom lip, he wondered how they could find a needle in a haystack, then he saw Mexican soldiers guarding a grassy clearing beneath a cluster of trees, picnic benches set up and covered with refugees, kids playing or crying, holding toys or suitcases as their eyes desperately scanned the throng for parents or siblings. The older ones wore grubby faces and had street smart looks, keeping pace with the crowds and noise, not bothered by the chaos. A crooked signpost read *Huérfanos. Buscando Padres – Orphans, Looking for Parents*. Morales and Smith had followed him through the lot, staying a little behind him as they waited for further instructions. The two were anxious to get home, dragging their feet, too ready to give up when the prize was *right there*.

"Hey, see those kids over there?"

"Yeah, what about them?" Smith replied.

"Go grab the older ones... tell them I'll pay them to perform a little mission for us."

Smith and Morales exchanged a look, then the Lieutenant asked, "How much?"

"Tell them it's a year's wages or something, and it's a big mission for the Americans, that we need them to help us find someone." With growing enthusiasm, he shot them a stony grin and walked off, the noise and bustle giving him a headache.

Strolling back to the Humvee, he leaned against the rear hatch, grabbed the handle, and flipped it up, digging into their supplies for a bottled water. Wiping sweat off his brow, he popped the top and chugged half in a few gulps, glancing toward the main road. Beyond that, a forest rose to touch the bright blue sky, trickles of gray mist seeping through the high boughs, distant showers raining across the lush landscape. The sight of all that green made it seem impossible that there were freezing storms heading their way, the slow descent of an ice age creeping ever nearer by the hour. Putting the water back, he closed the Humvee's hatch, leaning against it, rubbing his aching chest and shoulder as a sense of calm settled over him. Recent memories flooded into his brain, arms shuddering as he remembered the cold trek through Virginia and North Carolina, the frigid waters of the river hugging him after Linda McKnight had dropped the log through the ice.

"Hey, Keith." Morales said, striding up from the side lot. "We found some kids who want to help."

The soldiers had a dozen kids in tow, twelve or thirteen year olds, all of them lean and lanky with hungry eyes. "Oh, this is great," Keith nodded and rubbed his palms together. "Excellent work, guys. I couldn't have done better myself." Raising his chin, he said, "All right, boys and girls. Where heading into town for a little scouting mission. Hop in."

One of the bigger kids strolled forward, scowling at Keith beneath a pair of bushy eyebrows and tussle of dark brown hair, spitting words, his accent so thick he barely understood him, though he grinned at the kid's fearless attitude.

"Hey, Morales," Keith gestured. "You have any idea what he's saying?"

"I'm not *that* good with Spanish, but I don't think he trusts you. The gist is that he want to see payment before they set out."

Keith stared at the kid for a long moment, grinning grimly, trying to penetrate the boy's dark eyes, but a hard shell protected them, impossible to pierce. Like fingers prodding at a brick wall, the kid's emotions were locked up tight, well-guarded, his psyche probably as damaged as Keith's, and no one was going to bully him.

"All right," he said, turning and popping the Humvee's hatch, lifting it, shifting their supplies around to find a bulging duffel bag. Reaching inside, he pulled out a wad of cash and held it up. "There's a thousand dollars in here for each of you if you help me find a family. They're Americans… Gringos like me. It's a father and mother, with three kids, and they have a dog." Holding up his last stubby fingers, he patted his chest. "The mom is injured, shot here. You understand?"

When the boy shook his head, Morales intervened, stumbling through a description in Spanish until the kid finally nodded that he understood.

Keith turned and patted the Humvee. "And they're driving a truck like this, only theirs is beat up bad. Bullet holes and dents. Go ahead, tell him."

Morales did as he was directed, walking to the Humvee and patting it like Keith had, struggling to explain in Spanish, muddling the words, much to the children's amusement, though finally the leader nodded that he'd gotten it.

"Good," Keith said, his headache backing off as their odds of finding the McKnights had suddenly flipped around. "I'll need you to get started right now."

"Okay, Gringo," the kid said. "We go now."

Chapter 8
George Lee
Cargo Ship Ocean Trader, Colombia

The cargo vessel Ocean Trader cut smoothly through the gentle waves off the northern coast of Colombia, rocking back and forth in the gentle waves of the Caribbean Sea. The waters were black, the sky dark and filled with stars, moonlight streaking in from the northeast to leave a gold reflection across the ship's port side. One ship in the middle of a larger string of boats ferrying people from Cartagena to Venezuela, the Ocean Trader carried five hundred passengers on board along with their tattered luggage and belongings and food and water for the trip.

After their recent transfer to the vessel, George Lee and his son were in good spirits, laughing in the pre-dawn light as they navigated the confusing steel bowels of the ship to come up in the kitchen and his first cup of coffee in days. Ricky had a pastry as they left the busy cafeteria, seeking the freedom of the open sky. The crew, a mix of American and Venezuelan sailors, acted kindly to everyone on board despite looking haggard, and that went a long way with George, whose family had endured a lot since leaving Minnesota.

It had been a rush of packing, piling into their Subaru SUV and heading south to flee the cold, traveling along the back highways as the snow and frost gripped the land. Their engine had frozen solid one night, stranding them on an icy roadside surrounded by wrecked vehicles and entire families turned to ice in the winter storm. They'd been lucky enough to find a troop transport returning from a supply run and jumped on, then were dropped off in Nuevo Laredo where they'd lived with a Mexican family for a while. After that, it had been an arduous drive to Matamoros in the back of a farmer's truck before going north again to Port Mansfield where they were forced onto a smelly cargo ship with four thousand other people, cattle, and supplies to Cartagena, Colombia. George shook off those memories and guided his son through the port-side door to step on deck to the scents of the salt sea. The tough times were best left for revisiting later, years or decades later, when they could look back on everything that had happened and laugh, at least a little bit.

"Ahh!" he declared, taking a deep breath of fresh air. "This is what I'm talking about!"

Ricky ran to the rail and put his hands on the top, standing on his tiptoes to peer over the side at the foaming wake kicking off the hull. "Dad, check out all the boats."

George came up, resting his hand on the boy's shoulder, looking forward and behind at strings of lights from other boats trailing into the darkness, red and white, with the spattering of blinking blue ones that Ricky enjoyed. There were old Venezuelan naval ships, cargo vessels, and fishing crafts, carrying refugees to their destination in harbors near Caracas. "That's a lot of ships with a *lot* of people."

"Do you know any of the boat's names?"

"Nope. Just ours. The Ocean Trader."

"When do you think we'll get to Ven… Vene--"

"Venezuela," George laughed. "It's pronounced *Venezuela*. The man at the port said we should be there by tomorrow morning, so we've got a whole day to enjoy this great air and weather, and it beats being on that transport ship from before, right?"

"That one smelled bad," Ricky agreed, wrinkling his nose and holding his head high as the sea breezes ruffled his hair and T-shirt, an old baseball shirt he used to wear when he played little league back in Minnesota.

"That's because we were all packed into the cargo hold, and they wouldn't let us out because it was too cold. Remember all the icebergs in the water?"

"That was bad," he nodded. "I was so scared we were going to run into one and sink."

While some of the big chunks had been bad, George hadn't been too frightened of one piercing the hull. He was more worried about making sure his family had what they needed in the crowded hold, when food and fresh water had been scarce, families packed together on a cold metal floor, side-by-side on blankets or, if they were lucky, inch-thick foam mats. Dozens, if not hundreds, had died on the way down from dehydration, lack of hygiene, and restrictions on medicines. He had to explain to Ricky why an older woman in her seventies a couple of spots over from them had passed away from complications from diabetes because the ship doctors had been unable to find her insulin, and George suspected that would continue to be a problem for many people settling in Venezuela. But the Lees didn't have any lingering health problems—Sheila had once been a smoker but had given it up a few years ago—and he was hoping they'd have time to adjust and start making a living before any major issues cropped up.

"The good news is we made it, right?" he asked, smiling into the wind.

"Yeah. What happened to Grandma and Melissa and Cousin Jon?"

George frowned. "Like I said before, buddy, we don't know if they got out of the state. The phone lines were down, so I couldn't call them… but I tried. Once we get settled in Venezuela, the first thing I'll do is search for our family until everyone is reunited. They're supposed to populate the northern part of the country, so we might be closer than you think. It's just confusing right now, but don't worry, everything's going to work out fine."

Ricky gave a rare smile, gazing out toward the sea, watching as a sleek-looking ship slipped through the darkness, its profile sitting low in the water with the faint outline of a big gun perched on its bow, a massive United States flag fluttering from the pilothouse pole. "What's that boat, Dad?"

"That's one I know. That's the USS Firebolt."

"*Firebolt?* Cool!"

"That's right. It's what they call a cyclone-class patrol boat." He slowly pronounced the words. "And its only job is to guard us from the Chinese and Russians. They're guiding us home. Isn't that awesome?"

"Just one boat against all the bad guys?"

"It seems like tough odds," George replied, "but you'd be surprised at how much firepower that puppy has, and they're going to do everything they can to keep us safe."

"And they have sailors on the Firebolt?"

"Yep, about thirty guys and gals, I'm pretty sure."

"Wow. I'm so glad they're on our side."

George took a sip of his coffee, watching as the compact vessel motored out ahead of the convoy with its sleek shape bathed in moonlight. "Me too, son. Me too."

* * *

Lieutenant Commander James Stewart rested back in his captain's chair, the Firebolt's powerful diesel engine sending smooth vibrations through the superstructure as they lead the civilian convoy to ports north of Caracas along the Venezuelan coast. The waves were quiet, no storms on the horizon, just the golden glint of moonlight off the shimmering sea disturbed only by the wake they left behind.

"You'd think they could've given us a partner boat, sir," Deck Officer Tinaz said, watching the passing waters from the port window of the cramped pilot house.

"I know it's been a tough shift, but the Navy's stretched thin right now. No buddies."

"You got that right," Petty Officer Duane scoffed as she looked over the radar, scanning for blips and signs that the Chinese or Russians were around. It had been a quiet night, and he'd caught her yawning once or twice through her long shift.

"We'll rest as soon as we deliver these packages," Stewart said, glancing up at the ships in front of them, the slow line of boats motoring to friendly shores.

"Once we get these little civvies all tucked into their beds," Tinaz added, "I'm going to sleep for about a week."

"They're giving us *one* day off after this run," Stewart corrected him, "so you'll have to cram all that sleep into a short time. That's the life of a sailor at the end of the world."

"Aye, sir."

The fourth officer in the pilot house was Seaman Second Class Mintz at the con, standing watch over the throttle controls, telltale panel, and speed log, keeping the ship on course as per the commander's orders.

"Steady as she goes, Mintz."

"Aye, sir."

Before the anomaly, the USS Firebolt had been scheduled to be decommissioned after a quarter century of service in the Middle East, patrolling off Iranian shores and surviving fights with fighter boats out in the Black Sea where the rules of war were sketchy at best. After the anomaly, and the sudden freeze of the Northern Hemisphere, she'd been recalled, all her guns replaced, hull patched and repaired, and put on guard duty with thirteen other cyclones in the Navy's arsenal.

There was plenty of work to do protecting Venezuelan shores from Chinese Russian incursions, and the Firebolt was lightweight, swift, and armed to the hilt with a pair of MK-38 chain-driven autocannons, machine guns, grenade launchers, and two quadruple mounts for short range griffin missiles. Stewart's only concern was the length of the convoy they had to protect, the trailing boats easy pickings for any fast-moving assault ships, destroyers, or even submarines. But as he'd told Tinaz, the Navy was making do with what they had, and the sailors of the Firebolt would have to deal with the shortcomings and continue to be the best boat in South American waters.

"Anything on the radar, Duane?"

"Negative, sir."

The Commander nodded and turned his attention to the window, watching the distant horizon sharpen with the rising sun, the sky lightening, the faint watercolor clouds showing, streaked with gold and blue, and no enemy ships anywhere on the waters.

"What are our chances the Ruskies will leave us alone today?" Tinaz asked.

The Commander shrugged and reached for his sunglasses case, dropping it into his lap for later when the sun would reflect off the ocean waters. "It's been seven days of cat-and-mouse with them, and only one actual engagement." He glanced down at the deck where enemy rounds had struck the starboard side rail, finger-sized dents making patterns down the side. "Your guess is as good as mine. Just keep your eyes on the water. Stay sharp."

"Aye, sir."

* * *

A mile and a half from shore, the Chinese commander sat inside the cramped cabin of a Type-05 amphibious fighting vehicle, peering through a periscope as the floating tank bounced on the choppy waters, riding up wave crests, plunging down the other side, smacking hard, causing his stomach to lurch and the headache at the base of his neck to pulse.

Fans circulated fresh sea air through the compartment, but it couldn't vent all the heat, and beads of sweat trickled down his face to drip onto his light naval shirt. The three-man crew punched buttons and hunched over radar screens, watching pressure gauges and prepping weapon systems for a landing. Within the hour, they'd assault an oil refining facility before breaking back to the sea to be picked up in the open ocean later. That was if the F-35s or the United States Navy didn't find them first.

There were twenty-four Type-05s in the column, a row of floating armor, cannons, and machine guns, their chassis riding low in the water, almost impossible to see unless they were right on top of someone, the vessels performing far outside their intended scope of operation. Biting his teeth against the pain and nausea, the Commander barked for the driver to keep them together with the other assault vehicles and put his eyes back to the periscope lenses, spotting a long line of lights in the distance, ships of various shapes and sizes silhouetted against the Colombian mountains.

The navigator had seen them, too. "Do you see that, sir?"

The Commander nodded. "I count two dozen cargo ships in front of us, none of them fitting a U.S. Navy profile."

"Should we call off the assault?"

"Why would we do that?"

"Our formation will be disrupted if we try to pass between them. At the very least, we should pause our operation, lie low, and wait for them to go by."

"That will put us too far behind schedule," the Commander replied firmly, "and the General was quite clear that he wanted the objective destroyed before midmorning. Continue forward."

"But the civilian column. We cannot—"

"Sailor!" he barked. "Our orders are to destroy any ships that get in our way. Do you understand?"

The navigator lifted his face from the glow of the digital periscope screen, fear in his eyes but standing firm. "Are you sure, sir? Those boats could be packed with civilians."

"Yes," the Commander replied, turning away from the viewfinder to stare at the sailor. "But you *will* do your duty, or we will toss you into the sea and promote one of the Marines in the crew quarters to your position. Do you understand?"

The navigator glanced past the Commander where a contingent of special operations soldiers sat cramped in seats along the vehicle's sides, their faces pale as ghosts in the interior red lights. They blinked back at him with stony expressions as they waited to hear his response.

"Yes, sir!" The navigator resumed looking at the screen while the Commander got on the radio and tapped into the secure channel.

Guts turning with what he was about to say, he put the mic to his lips and spoke. "Tank crew 234. This is Commander Sun. We are approaching a column of civilian vessels, who may be blocking our path to shore. We will not delay our actions but continue forward, not breaking formation. This is a war, and if we do not realize our goals, the Americans and Venezuelans will leave us stranded at sea. They stand in the way of our survival… for our families, our culture, and our names. It is not something anyone takes joy in doing, but if any of these boats get in our path, we are authorized to fire upon them so we can pass. Do not stop. Fight with the understanding that to fail in our mission is to fail our people. We shall *not* fail our people."

He hung up the microphone and wiped the sweat off his brow, putting his eyes to the periscope lenses once more, wishing the civilian line would move faster. A few minutes later, the lead Type-05 tank fired, punching a hole in the side of a big cargo ship with rusted sides, and his jaw locked tight. There would be no mercy if the American Navy found them.

* * *

"Sir, I've got some marks on the SPS-73 navigational radar," Duane said, her face lit from the faint glow of the screens.

Tinaz left his spot at the window and walked over, looking over Duane's shoulder as Stewart rose in his chair. "Enemy ships?"

"The signal's in and out," Duane replied. "Whatever they are, they're not giving off much of a profile, but they're definitely there."

"We saw a similar signature about five days ago," Tinaz mentioned, "but Duane wasn't on radar that day."

"Wasn't that a group of Type-05 amphibious tanks we ran off?"

"One and the same."

The Commander let out a heavy sigh and shifted forward in his seat, glancing out the port window. "Damn things are nearly impossible to see riding in the water. What's their position?"

"Looks like they're toward the middle of our column, heading straight at the—"

"Attention, USS Firebolt, this is the captain of the Ocean Trader. We're not sure what hit us, but we just took several shots to our hull. We could use an assist back here."

The Commander turned on his radio. "Roger that, Ocean Trader. This is Commander Stewart of the Firebolt. Do you see anything out on the water? Is it a destroyer… maybe a sub?"

"Negative, sir. We've got a column of—"

Boom! An explosion cracked over the line, bringing a scowl to the Commander's face. "Ocean Trader, are you still with us?"

There was a pause before the Captain came back. "Roger that, Firebolt. We're here, but listing to port, and got some smoke coming off our sides. Working on a damage report now, but I may be giving it to you from the bottom of the ocean."

The entire time, Stewart had been signaling to his conn officer, spinning his hand in the air and punching his fist forward to say he wanted them turned around and heading back ASAP. Mintz worked the throttles, turning them in a tight arc, lurching starboard as the Firebolt's four Paxman diesel engines churned hard.

"On our way, Ocean Trader. Hang in there." He came out of his chair and pointed to Tinaz. "Get on the horn with CENTCOM and see if they've got any air support in the area. If so, get them over here."

"Aye, sir," the deck officer replied, activating the alarm for battle stations.

While they did that, the Captain switched to the onboard intercom system. "Attention, crew, this is Commander Stewart. We've got a column of Type-05 amphibious assault vessels, heading for shore. They've fired upon one of our civilian ships, and I expect we'll be seeing some casualties shortly. I want the griffon missiles armed and ready to fire. Gunners, remember that these tanks have a low profile in the water, so keep your aim flat and tight!"

By the time he cut off the radio, they were racing back to the middle of the column, the USS Firebolt skimming over the water as the sun's first rays broke the horizon and shot across the bow in glorious golden beams. The civilian ships at the head of the line had pushed their speeds to maximum, foam exploding from the aft sections as they sped to get away from the certain destruction behind them. Dark smoke rose from the Ocean Trader, the long cargo liner with its belly bulging with civilians listing hard to their port side. Rising from his seat, he walked to the pilothouse window and raised a pair of binoculars to his eyes. Tiny figures poured out of hatches and flooded the deck, climbing to the starboard rail as the vessel began to dip dangerously the other way. Lifeboats plunged toward the water filled with people, and Stewart winced as one came loose from its pulley, the front end falling, spilling everyone into the sea.

"How many are aboard that ship?" he asked Tinaz.

"That's one of our big ones, sir. Five hundred or more, I think."

The Commander cursed softly. "Tinez, put in a call for rescue while we deal with these tanks." Shifting his binoculars to the right, Stewart watched as the tank column spread out across the water, leaving foaming wakes behind them, dipping atop the ocean waves that washed over the tops, the mounted cannons swiveling, switching to a different target and firing with a heavy thud and cloud of smoke. "What's the status of the CIC? Are we ready to fire those griffons?"

Tinaz switched to another information screen, grabbed a radio headset, pulled it on, and muttered into the wraparound microphone. A second later, he glanced over. "We're in range of the griffons."

"I want those lead tanks taken out right now and get that autocannon firing up the line!"

"Aye, sir!"

"Con. Sweep us across their path."

"Yes, sir!"

From midship came heavy pops and blossoms of smoke as the missiles launched into the sky, four of them ripping through the air, swinging up high, acquiring their targets, and diving like hawks toward the ocean. They rammed the bobbing tanks, explosions tearing the waterline, metal and debris flying upward in dark plumes and a rain of armament. Stewart stood at the window, searching the water where a few tanks were already turning in their direction, slow and ponderous, though they didn't need to be fast in taking up a strong defensive position. The Firebolt's autocannon began popping off thunderous rounds at the low-riding tanks with bursts that sounded like ripping cloth, foam spraying off them, but he couldn't tell if they were penetrating the armor.

A half dozen big cannons lined up, answering in kind with bright flashes and rolling booms, smoke peeling off the water to rise high in the sky. The Firebolt shuddered as the heavy rounds slammed her hull, explosions ripping through the vessel, one cracking them right below the pilothouse, throwing Stewart back into his chair. Port side glass fractured as manuals, flashlights, and radios toppled from an overhead bin to crash on Mintz's head. The man brushed off the clutter and returned to the con, angling the ship slightly to starboard to cut across the enemy's noses, pushing their speed to maximum.

"Second wave of griffons…" The Commander eyed the tactical screen in front of Tinaz, watching as the CIC cycled through new targets. "Fire!"

* * *

Another explosion ripped through the Ocean Trader, sending a ripple of screams through the ship's passengers, the floor vibrating beneath George's feet. The shock of the burst threw his son forward, but George let go of the port side rail and grabbed him with both hands even as they dipped dangerously toward the water and then lifted higher with a swelling wave. Turning toward midship, he climbed up the slippery deck with Ricky in his arms, grabbing a steel pole sticking up from the decking, hanging on as people tumbled head over heels or slid across the wooden planks to bang against the rail.

Smoke burned his nose as the clouds of it billowed over the port side, drifting past the radio tower and bridge, and then the ship was tilting back to port again, dipping deeper, edging down. To free his other hand, George swung the boy on his back. "Hang on to my neck, son! Don't let go!" Ricky threw his arms around his father's neck, which allowed him to fall forward onto his hands and knees and shimmy toward the bulkhead where there was more to hold on to.

"Watch out, Dad!" Ricky shouted, squeezing so hard it almost cut off his breath, but George caught the warning and looked up.

A woman was sliding down the slick planks, screaming as the ship hung to port, her feet scrabbling on the wood as she tried to break her fall. George wrapped his arm over a steel pipe jutting from the deck and swung out to catch her wrist as she slipped by, dragging her to his body and anchoring them. Gravity tugged at her weight, and her sweat-covered arm began to slip through his grasp, but he hauled her closer with a heavy grunt, shouting into her face, "Hang on to this! Come on, lady!"

Momentarily dazed, she crawled over him to grab the pipe and hang on, kicking and scrambling to get leverage, almost knocking Ricky off his neck.

"Stop it, lady!" he shouted, stabilizing himself. "Hang on here and wait for someone to get you, but we're moving lower."

With a glance up, she screamed, "No! Help me get to my husband! Don't leave me!" More people tumbled by, one grabbing at her and almost ripping her from the pipe.

George shook his head. "I have to move lower! I have to find my wife! She was inside when we got hit."

They'd been standing at the railing with Ricky pointing to what looked like a floating tank off the side of the ship with its monstrous cannon pointed right at them. George's first reaction was incredulity that something like that could actually *float*, but its nose was elevated, its green camouflage color mixed with lighter shades of blue that blended with the waves. It was only when a heavy shell pounded the Ocean Trader's hull he realized how much trouble they were in. To his horror, there were several more bobbing tanks, spread out in rows of three, their big guns firing repeatedly with ear shattering booms that rocked the ship's frame and sent bodies scrambling away from the rail to reach safety, though there was no place to go. Thirty seconds later, they started dipping to port, and the initial surprise at being shot at turned into full-fledged terror, people screaming and running, falling to their hands and knees as the angle took on a sudden, precarious lurch, at the same time wailing for loved ones in the panic-stricken crowd.

Ricky screamed in his ear, gasping in breathless confusion. "Are we going to drown?"

"No!" George shouted, glancing over his right shoulder, getting a perfect view of the ocean just in time to see missiles scream down to hit the floating tanks, blasting their tops off in fracturing slivers of metal and foam, big splashes of dark water as the first two armored vessels plunged beneath the waves, leaving an oil slick burning on the surface. A moment later, they heard the staccato blast of machine gun fire, not the firecracker noise of someone shooting a nine-millimeter pistol, but something louder, somewhere between a cannon and a rifle. Bullet sprays traced a line straight to the next tank, punching the armor with loud *clangs*, bursts of metal shards, and more smoke. There must've been twenty or more of them, and they were all shifting to face the racing Firebolt as it flew into the fray.

Even the sight of the glorious gunboat brought no relief, because George's arms were straining tight, barely hanging on as the Ocean Trader was pulled deeper into the foaming waves. When the boat tipped on the starboard side, he got his legs under him, let go of the pipe, and loped toward the bulkhead, knocking into someone coming the other way, trying not to shove them down but unable to help himself. Cursing and grunting through clenched teeth, he kept moving, scrambling over a passenger rolling down the deck, somehow landing without sliding backward. He lunged and grabbed a light post jutting from the bulkhead, feet dangling as the ship dipped back in the other direction.

"Hang on, son!" he shouted over his shoulder.

"Mom! We have to get Mom!"

"I know!" he gasped and spat. "Just hang on! Don't let go!"

"I won't!"

A wave rose to meet them, waves crashing over the port rail and splashing on the deck, people screaming at an earsplitting volume, hollering as they plunged into the foamy water and disappeared beneath the surface in a spray of foam. Husbands and wives were lying across the rail almost flat, reaching into the salty sea and sweeping their arms back and forth in search of their lost loved ones. And then the Ocean Trader was rocking the other way, separating those still hanging on from those floating in the sea, screams of anguish rising yet unheard in the roaring, swelling battle taking place on the water.

* * *

The diesel engines drove the propeller to churn, bouncing the Firebolt over the waves in pulses and Stewart leaned against the arm of his captain's seat, peering at the Chinese Type-5s spreading out to attack. Mintz had the throttle hammered to ninety percent full steam and the autocannon continued to beat the enemy's armor, griffin missiles pounding down in sprays of sea foam. Another shot from the enemy fractured the top of the pilothouse, and the window on the right side exploded in fragments of glass, showering the rubber cabin floor.

Stewart came off his captain's chair and pointed at the nearest Chinese vessel, shouting at Mintz, "Ram the bastards! Run them over!"

"Yes, sir!"

With a quick shift of the twin throttles, the Firebolt gave a lurch, jumping a wave, slapping down and speeding directly at the waiting Type-5. The gun went off, firing point-blank into their faces, the round rocking the floor in a shock of vibration and partial collapse. More glass shattered, and someone screamed, and the ship's control panel lights blinked rapidly and died, but not before they rammed over the Chinese vessel, the thick steel hull slicing across the hapless water tank, ripping the big cannon clean off. The Firebolt heaved like it'd hit a speed bump, throwing everyone forward into consoles, sparks and fire bursting from the electronics throughout the raised deck. Stewart slipped and grabbed Tinaz as he crashed, the two men balanced each other until the ship finally settled, the diesels still running but with an odd clank from deep in her guts.

Mintz was muttering, holding his head as he climbed to his feet, trying the throttle, pounding his fist on them. "Looks like I lost control, sir."

"What's the damage?"

The sailor looked over his displays, shaking his head. "From what I can see, we've got one broken propeller and my controls are locked up thanks to the fire damage, but we're still moving."

"Take the auxiliary controls and get us sweeping back and forth across those enemy craft." He started to flip the switch to call downstairs, but the light for the intercom was out, too. "And see if you can reach the engine room while you're out there."

Nodding, Mintz was already heading for the door where a second set of controls sat behind the pilothouse, the same ones they used to guide the Firebolt in to dock for resupply. Falling forward against the ruined panels, Stewart peered through the shattered glass, wafts of oily smoke drifting into the cabin, forcing him to turn away until it finally cleared. "What do we have left, Tinaz?"

The deck officer was at the controls, watching the overview screen. "CIC is still targeting, so weapon systems are up and working."

The Firebolt was wandering, listing to the right even as she turned in that direction, dipping as it circled around the Type-5s. The bow was leaning dangerously, though the autocannon and the fifty caliber guns on the starboard side were still firing, trying to disable the rest of the Type-5s that were banking toward the cyclone-class ship.

"How many enemy targets do we have left?"

"Only fifteen, sir!" Tinaz growled back.

"Duane!"

"Yes, sir?" she called, clinging to the radar terminal, eyes glued to the screen as smoke blew across her face.

"Get out there and assist the gunners!"

"Yes, sir!" The sailor pivoted and followed Mintz out the door, not skipping a beat as the pair hit the stairwell going down. Everyone on the Firebolt did everything, from engineering to gunner work to cooking and electrical maintenance, and he counted on them to take up the slack when they needed a gap filled.

"It's just me and you," Stewart said, sweeping over to the right side of the pilothouse, where some radio lights were working. Punching buttons, yelling into a curved microphone, he finally reached the engine room. "I need a full report. What's the damage?"

"Diesels are ninety percent good, sir!" came the shouted reply. "We've got some serious fluid leaks, but nothing we can't repair. One of the starboard side propellers isn't doing so hot."

"I heard we might've sprained an ankle." Stewart's eyes flashed. "Keep that engine running, sailor. Any noncritical personnel, send them up top, got it?"

After receiving an affirmative from the engine room, the Commander turned back to the pilothouse window as the Firebolt suddenly lurched to port, the ship swinging hard to the right, guns blazing, taking another heavy shock from a cannon round across the bow, barely missing the autocannon but shredding parts of the control rigging and sending deck planks shooting skyward in an explosion of debris. The patrol boat made a big slow circle around the gathering Type-5s, and both officers saw their mistake right away.

"There clustering up," Stewart said. "Get those F-35 in here *now*!"

"Aye, sir!" Tinaz grabbed a secure two-way radio off the hook and started to call CENTCOM again when high caliber machine gun rounds ripped through the pilothouse, chewing up paper and glass and metal, sending both men ducking to the buckled floor as the Firebolt absorbed the ordinance. Someone screamed below, another shouted for fire extinguishers as a half dozen sailors tried to put out blazes before they could hit the ammunition caches.

"They say they're on their way!" Tinaz yelled. "ETA, four minutes."

"We might not have four minutes," he murmured back. "Tell CIC to empty out the missile stack and keep on CENTCOM about those birds. I'm heading downstairs to see what I can do!"

"Yes, sir!"

With his orders given, and the Firebolt's weapons still going off, Stewart lunged for the pilothouse door and flew down the steps toward the aft part of the ship, pausing and ducking as more missiles launched from their tubes in a hiss of fire and smoke, arcing high upward, turning and shooting at the ocean to strike with massive booms that sent water jetting skyward. A sailor staggered by him, swatting at the oily flames covering his right leg, heading for the port rail where it looked like he was going to leap over. The Commander shoved him to the deck as another sailor raced up with an extinguisher, spraying him with white powder, sending a cloud of it billowing upward into his face, momentarily blinding him. The smoke cleared, the fire squelched, and the soldiers were ducking and scrambling to get under the missile shielding as the enemy's fifty caliber guns responded like a sudden hornet's nest attack. Stewart dropped, hands thrown over his head, but once the barrage passed, he climbed to his feet and kept moving to the rear of the boat, grabbing more sailors and shoving them beneath the protective screens.

He slammed into bodies by accident, ducked, and spun, coming to the split section in the rear where a dead crewman sat slumped in the M2HB machine gun chair. Shoving the man aside, Stewart took his place, checked the ammunition feed, and swung the weapon to the left, spying a handful of Type-5s bobbing in the water. Picking a spot, he squeezed the trigger and pounded the surf well ahead of his first target, raising his aim until he hit with a *chink* of metal striking metal, holding his sights there and watching as metal shredded metal, smoke wafting up from the Type-5s turret.

The way they were listing hard to starboard, it wouldn't be long before they sunk, and off to his right the Ocean Trader was tipped up, the port side dipping deeply, people bobbing in the waves or on the deck, hanging on to whatever they could. A Type-5 round hit the Firebolt hard, breaking something in the bowels, the diesel engines vibrating and clanking under his feet. The white foam off the aft faded to a sputter, the propellers barely spinning, the ship slowing to a crawl. Leaving the gun seat, he made his way back to the pilothouse, grabbing soldiers from the port side and shoving them toward the rear of the boat where RHIB combat craft sat nestled in the aft section.

"Get everyone you can, and get the RHIBs launched!" he shouted, then he kept moving up the port side, ducking as machine gun rounds smacked the metal bulkhead in pings and sparks. Grabbing a pair of sailors working to un-jam one of the twenty-five millimeter guns, he pushed them to the back, too. "Go on! Abandon ship! Get out of here."

He found Mintz at the auxiliary controls, the lower part of the panel flung open as he tried to fix something messed up in the electronics, but the Commander sent him back with the others. Ten more feet along the rail, Duane was laying with her arms hanging over the side, a bloody hole in her chest, face turned and staring at nothing. With an angry grimace, he surged ahead, reaching the front of the ship, gaping at the damage the cannons had done to the armor skirting the pilothouse and autocannon. Holes the size of his fist had been punched through, leaving metal bent outward and smoking. Something detonated inside, and pieces of shrapnel flew from the gaps in a blast of heat and flame.

He jerked his head to the side as rounds of ammunition caught fire and exploded. The gray radar shielding at the base of the pilothouse blew with a sharp concussion, coming off its housing, swelling with hot vapor that rolled over the sides. A half dozen sailors rushed by him toward the aft, and he grabbed them by their arms, slapping shoulders as they passed. Remembering Tinaz, he turned back and climbed the stairs to the pilothouse door through the pouring haze, forcing his eyes shut, and gagging on the petrol stench. He ascended hand-over-hand on the twisted metal, boots slipping on the grating, finding the deck officer squatting outside the pilothouse door beneath the oily smoke, shoulder against the wall as he coughed and yelled into his radio.

"Tinaz! Tell me you've got those F-35's incoming, sailor?"

"Yes, sir!" The man grinned and pointed to the sky.

* * *

Clinging to an exterior light fixture bolted to the bulkhead, George held on to Ricky, every muscle in his body quivering with weakness as ocean spray covered them. Chin dripping saltwater, his eyes searched below for any signs of his wife, Sheila. There were lifeboats in the water and a pair of overloaded ferries were trying to pick people up despite the pitched battle happening a few hundred yards to the north.

It wasn't looking good for the Firebolt, the ship listing badly, its engines seemingly dead, and the tanks were taking pot shots at the military craft. Still, the part of him that wasn't in complete panic gave the patrol boat a blessed thanks because it was absorbing ordinance meant for the civilian vessels, and the Ocean Trader would've already sunk – or worse – if it weren't for the Firebolt's swift action.

"Dad! Where's mom?" Ricky called, still clinging to his neck but slipping, and if the boy let go, he'd plunge fifty feet to smack the port deck rail or water, both certain to have a deadly outcome.

"Hold on, son," he gasped, shoulders straining. "Don't let go. Your mother… she was somewhere below when we came outside…"

His numb right elbow was locked around the light fixture, tennis shoes barely touching the deck. Even with plenty of lifeboats, they couldn't get down from where they were unless they simply let go and plummeted to the railing. Maybe when the boat was leaning to starboard, he could slide down first and turn up to catch him when it was his turn.

"Mom!" Ricky shouted, his voice raspy from the saltwater. "Dad! It's Mom!"

"Where?" he asked, gaze cast along the bulkhead at the people bobbing in the water or squatting on the rail as waves washed over them. If Sheila was down there, her light hair would be darker, plastered to her cheeks as she swam or treaded water. "I don't see her, son! Where…?"

"Over there! Hanging onto that chain!"

While it seemed impossible that she would've made it up to the deck between them coming outside and the ship being attacked, she could have been right behind them. Things were confusing below, and with the maze of passages and twisting stairs, anyone could get lost or turned around, and she may have exited on the starboard side. Squirming his body, he shifted in the other direction, crying out when he saw Sheila clinging to a chain with ten refugees above her, kicking her in the face, people screaming as the boat flattened out a little and allowed them to rest on their knees.

Sheila's eyes locked on them, holding a faint glimmer of hope, the corner of her mouth twisted into a scared grin. It seemed she was about to cross to them when the boat began tilting back to port, the deck shifting past forty-five degrees, to fifty, to sixty and a little farther, everyone's feet lifting off the floor to dangle. More people slid by, someone trying to grab her as they flew by, plunging down, slamming the port side rail, back cracking in a sickening snap of bones before they drifted away in a daze.

George was shaking his head, "No, baby, don't come, don't—"

As the boat began pitching back the other way, Sheila let go of the chain, crawling on hands and knees, slipping downward as the deck fell to thirty-five degrees flat, still almost impossible to traverse across the slick planks with people falling all around her. And the ship was tilting back faster, sinking farther until the rail was submerged beneath the waves. Sheila screamed as she was dumped toward the ocean, but then she was diving, scrabbling, grabbing a bubble-shaped light casing jutting up from the deck. Its glow illuminated her chest and face as she clung to it, eyes wide and staring across the thirty yards where her husband and son watched helplessly.

With grim determination, George gripped his son's arm with his left hand, pulling the boy higher. "Climb over me and hang on to this light post. That's it. Yes, now lock your arm over it like I'm doing and grab your hand. Don't let go, okay?" He left Ricky with his skinny elbow locked over the bolted lamp, face wet with saltwater spray as he spit and sputtered.

"Hurry up! Get mom!"

The urgency in the boy's voice spurred him on, and he stared across the deck at his wife, seeing she was just about level with him, maybe thirty yards away. "I'm coming to get you. Don't let go, okay?"

She nodded, and when the boat swept back to starboard and flattened out, he let go and fell to the decking, scrambling, clawing his way in her direction. The wet metal kept him from getting a foothold, and when he put both hands down to brace himself, his right arm failed him, too numb to hold his weight. Clutching it to his side, he crab-walked out to her, reaching her in just a few seconds, but the ship was moving back the other way, gurgling and bubbling, sea waves crashing in and riding twenty feet up the deck, splashing them with foam.

"George!" she cried in joy.

Squatting next to her, he shouted. "Come on!"

There wasn't enough room for him to cling to the bubbled protrusion, so he took her arm and pulled her off it, hauling her toward the bulkhead. With a grunt, he crashed to the hard wood, pulling her with him, grabbing what he could, kicking until the angle finally spilled them in the direction he wanted to go. Bouncing to his knees, drawing her along, they dashed to the bulkhead, and he slapped his palm on the steel, fingers sliding along the slick metal, snagging a big bolt sticking out from the side. Instantly, he stretched and caught Sheila's wrist, and as the Ocean Trader tipped past seventy degrees, he clenched his teeth and held on. The tendons in his arms strained, the pain in his shoulder reaching a crescendo, but he wouldn't let go, wouldn't let her end up like the rest of them, thrashing and flailing in the waves until she was consumed. Mercifully, the ship rocked back the other way, and their feet touched down again, allowing him to crawl up to where Ricky was still hanging on, craning his neck to see what had happened to his parents. When they reached him, they fell on him with an embrace, clinging to the warm, dirty bulkhead, each with one arm around their boy.

Sheila rained kisses on them, squeezing them, shouting, "What do we do now?"

George craned his neck to see where the battle was still raging. Above the ocean swell and explosions came the slithery sounds of jet engines somewhere, drawing closer by the second. Preceding their arrival were four streaks of gray shooting in from the coastline, missiles on a downward angle toward the water tanks, blasts sending smoke sizzling off the top and shimmering upward in a spray.

"It won't be enough," George whispered, clinging hard to his family against the bulkhead, but then four more projectiles streaked in, pummeling the steel hulks floating in the water, silencing their cannons as a jet formation shot by in a blast of sound, four screaming aircraft tipping their wings, the engines covering them in a glorious shriek that brought a grin to his face.

The Firebolt sat stagnant out in the waters, its starboard rail tilting dangerously into the ocean, crewmen in life vests drifting in a fiery oil slick, trying frantically to swim away from the flames. Just when George thought there was no hope for any of them, a rubber raft shot from the Firebolt's aft, motoring out to pick up the bobbing sailors who were waving and calling for rescue. All around the Ocean Trader, lifeboats converged, and people tossed life vests out to those who didn't have them, reaching with poles to let them grab on, drawing them in, *saving* them.

"What do we do?" Sheila asked.

Spitting brine, licking it from his lips, George peered at the foaming sea thirty feet below, almost close enough to safely drop. "We'll wait for a few more minutes, and when the water comes up a bit, we'll let go."

Sheila was already shaking her head. "No, we can't let go! Ricky... he'll get hurt. He can't handle a fall like that!"

"We *have* to. When a big boat like this goes down... sometimes they can suck people and objects down along with them. We don't want to be right here when that happens, okay?"

Wincing against the ocean spray, wet hair clinging to her cheeks, she nodded vigorously. "Okay. We'll wait a little longer and then drop."

The battle on the water was done, and the surface was bloated with debris and dark patches that rode the waves, covered with orange flame. Unused life vests floated around the boat in a tangle of rigging, articles of clothing, hats, shoes and sandals, toys and paper clogging the foamy swells. All George wanted was for his wife and child to be safe again, to find a place to sit and rest his shaking arms, to hug them close and pray for the nightmare to be over. His shoulders ached, and his eyes stung with salty spray, and there was a moment when he thought the boat might actually leave them suspended there, still too high to let go. But on the next dip, the sea smacked against the deck and splashed their feet, and George looked across at Sheila.

"I'm going to go first, then Ricky, then you. I'll let you know when it's okay."

Sheila nodded, and they shared a long kiss before George grinned and let go.

Chapter 9
Tom McKnight
Costa Rica

"We need to get going, guys," Tom said with a belch, bending to pick up their paper plates and take them to a nearby trash can.

They'd just finished a meal, and he was trying to round them up to keep them from spreading farther through the bazaar, calling back Jack and Linda who were running between vendors selling colorful clothing and travel bags, cutting off the kids' adventures before they got carried away. Despite their groans and feet dragging, they did as they were told and came back to help him clean up.

He couldn't blame them for wanting to stay. The food was amazing – rice, beans, and sharply-flavored meat filling their bellies, delicious scents wafting through the air. Voices rang out cheerfully, full of positivity, laughing good-naturedly at the McKnight's attempts to order food or inquire about directions. Everyone had been most impressed with Sam, whose Spanish had come a little farther after being forced to speak it at the hospital and from constantly reading signs on the trip down.

Reluctantly, they gathered their goods and walked across the grassy lot toward the Humvee, taking off the tarp and refolding it. Sam popped the rear hatch and lifted it, dropping the things they'd purchased inside. Linda and Tom leaned in to rearrange their supplies so they fit better, and he blinked at the stretcher, part of him wanting to trade it since Barbara was up and walking, but if something happened to her – or any of the rest of them – it would be incredibly useful.

"Where are we going now, Dad?" Sam asked, hands on her hips, sticking her belly out in a stretch.

"Onward down the highway, I suppose. Ever southward."

"Actually, we're heading east at this point," she added with a grin.

"Right. You're the map person."

Nodding, her smile widened. "I'm your navigator."

"That you are, dear."

Linda and Jack let Smooch out, and she pranced from between the cars and did a turn in the row, the boy chasing her, laughing as they wrestled around.

"Okay, everyone. Let's—"

A rush of braying and cackling voices swarmed them, kids giggling and shrieking, feet running and the hallow tone of a ball being kicked. Tom whirled around and looked down the row, reaching out and grabbing Jack and Smooch, pulling them out of the way as a ragged soccer ball zipped past them with pieces of its leather cover hanging off, bouncing to the end where it rested at the edge of the forest. Linda turned to run after it when a group of children rushed by, two younger ones spotting the ball and racing for it while the others waited near the Humvee. More youngsters sprouted out of nowhere, flowing around the truck and brushing past them to stand out in the row, staring at the McKnights a moment before watching the race. A little girl fell on the ball, rolling and stealing it from beneath a boy's grasp, both howling as he chased her back in their direction. Barbara and the kids chuckled in amusement as the two charged through the gaggle of children, dodging hands to escape out the other side, the lot of them sprinting into the bazaar.

"I'd love to kick with them!" Jack said, turning to Tom. "Can we stay a while longer and play?"

Tom's heart broke, because Jack hadn't been able to play with anyone his own age in months. Reasonably normal on its own, with being home-schooled, but worse when their closest neighbors were miles away. The last few weeks had been nothing but traveling in the back of a frigid truck with just his older sisters and Smooch to keep him company, something that had worn on everyone – least not of all Jack.

"They're so adorable!" Barbara said, turning to him with raised eyebrows. "Come on, Tom. Can't we stay a little while longer? Let the kids play."

"I could pick up some Spanish from one of the girls," Linda added hopefully.

"No," Tom said, still watching the kids, an unsettling feeling growing in his gut as one of the older boys glanced back at them before melting into the crowd. "We need to get going."

"Yeah, let's go, guys," Sam said with a worried look, and she finished arranging things in the Humvee's cargo section and guided Barbara to the side door. "Come on, Mom."

Smile fading, Barbara nodded and allowed herself to be led around while Tom slammed the rear hatch and pushed Linda and Jack to the other side, the two of them kicking through the grass, Jack complaining about never being able to do anything or have any fun.

"Hush yourself and get in," Tom said, slipping past them and circling to the driver's side door, where he slid behind the wheel and started the truck in a cough of smoke and hot oil.

Smooch yipped excitedly and did circles in the back seat. "Easy, girl!" Barbara said, nudging the dog aside as they all piled in.

Jack got into the rear on the passenger side and threw his arms around Smooch, wrestling and fussing with her, getting the dog worked up again, and when Linda slipped in, she shoved them back toward Barbara, ruffling Smooch's fur and causing her to bark excitedly.

"Settle down, guys!" Sam slammed her door and rolled down her window, resting her arm on the edge.

"Yes, please," Tom added, also lowering his window to allow in a cool breeze that dried the sweat on his brow and neck. "Listen to your sister."

With the engine coughing and sputtering, Tom backed out of the spot, the suspension rocking as they moved over the uneven ground, reversing until the big truck was straight. Before he could put it in drive, the same soccer ball careened through the air, bounced off a car and then smacked the Humvee with a thump. The laughing children surged from the bazaar, twice as many as before, a flood of them sprinting toward them, flowing around the truck with tiny hands slapping the sides, dirt smudged faces peering through the windows, shouting in Spanish.

"What are they doing, Dad?" Linda asked in a strained voice as she pushed at a pair of hands that were reaching inside.

"Roll the windows up!" Tom barked, grabbing his window handle and pumping it in a circle. Sam did the same on her side, trying to block the hands that were grabbing at her shirt.

Barbara yelped in surprise as two kids snagged her hair, tugging it and calling out like little beggars, hanging on as the Humvee pulled away and left them straggling. Smooch stepped into Barbara's lap, snarling and snapping at the hands until they jerked back, allowing her to crank her window closed. Still, they slapped and beat at the truck's sides, faces pressed against the glass with a mixture of laughter and desperation, Tom hitting the gas and pulling to the edge of the lot, joining the dirt track that circled to the highway. Glancing in his rearview, he watched the children falling behind, shedding them like a second skin.

When he had to slow down on a rough patch of dirt, the kids caught up with them, surrounding them again, getting in front and forcing him to stop or else run them over. Cursing under his breath, Tom leaned on the horn, hitting it repeatedly, bleating at them as he edged forward in fits and stops. Instincts on fire, he glared back through the rows of cars toward the market, scowling as three men stepped from the crowd of vendors, dressed in military fatigues, bearing rifles and pushing through the throng of people.

Sam straightened, face pressed against her window as she peered over the crowd of children. "Dad! Do you see them?" She pointed, finger poking at the glass as she hissed. "It's the soldiers… And that's Keith!"

"Great," Linda growled from the back seat as she checked her weapon.

"Yeah, it's them," Tom said, edging the truck forward but too late, the crowd of kids thickening around them, three layers of them leaning on the hood, slapping their palms on it, laughing and jostling and shrieking. "These kids are completely blocking us… I knew it as soon as I saw them."

"What are we going to do?" Barbara asked, one hand on the door panel, the other palm resting against Tom's seat to hold herself steady as she gaped at the kids pressed in.

Putting the truck in reverse, he edged backward, but the crowd of children floated with them, some trying to crawl up the sides and get on the back, but he jerked them forward again and knocked them off. Tom pounded his palm against the window. "Hey, get off! Leave us alone! Come on! Yah! Yah!"

The rest of the family joined in, Sam slapping both hands against the glass, yelling and screaming, Linda tapping the butt of her weapon on the window, shouting at them, and the whole time Barbara waving them away, gasping softly, unable to catch her breath. The kids only leered and laughed louder, banging harder, their own voices rising with the McKnights' desperate pleas.

"Little jerks!" Sam hissed. "Get *off* us!"

Tom stopped hollering and slapping the glass, clenching both hands on the wheel, blinking at the innocent faces surrounding them, the ball of his foot poised over the gas pedal. Pawing at the Humvee, the kids were laughing like it was a game, but the truth was they were just children, brought into something far more dangerous than they could comprehend, and they didn't deserve what he was about to do. But the alternative was worse—Keith's past threats to shoot his kids in front of him flooded back in a wave—and it drove a spike through Tom's heart.

With a glance in his rearview, he caught Barbara's eye, and she read his thoughts like a book, eyebrows arcing in realization of what he was about to do. "Wait!" she cried desperately, reaching up and pounding her fist on the Humvee's roof, snapping a couple of latch seals, pointing and shouting for Linda to help with the other side. A moment later, she had her pistol in hand and was pressing upward through the opening, throwing back the hatch with a heavy clank against the roof, stretching as tall as she could. Trying not to step on Jack or Smooch, she kicked at the seat, finding purchase, pushing herself higher. Tom clenched the wheel, foot shifting back to the brake, eyes on the approaching soldiers as they closed in but still hadn't seen them. Barbara fumbled with something, knocking around while sweat trickled down Tom's temples. Gunshots cracked the air, jerking his shoulders taut, and he glanced left as bullets punched the ground, dirt popping up in chunks just inches from the kids' feet—*pop, pop, pop*—scattering the children like a flock of birds in a chorus of high-pitched squeals. The sea of little ones in front of them parted, and Tom hit the gas pedal, rocketing them forward over the rough dirt, squeezing between the last cars in the row and the dense jungle, bouncing them in their seats as they rumbled ahead. People in the lot ducked and dashed away at the sounds of gunfire, grabbing their children, pulling them into the grass, wedging them between cars and trucks to protect themselves.

Sam screamed. "Go, Dad! They see us!"

"I know, I know." he grumbled, searching for a road as he picked up speed, the suspension shaking them like beans in a box.

"It's Keith! He's aiming at us!"

"I know!" The words squeezed between his teeth as he came to a tight spot, clipping a pair of cars as he bulled his way past, knocking them aside in a crush of metal and a jolt to everyone in the Humvee.

"Dad, hurry—"

"I *know*!"

The heavy reports of a rifle ripped off, preceded by fat thwacks against their armor, punches that smacked them hard, rocking them on their suspension, adding to the grueling drive. Shoulders clenched tight, right foot pressed on the gas pedal, he shouted, "Everyone down! Get down now!"

The kids took cover and Barbara fell sideways with a pained grunt, throwing her arms around Smooch and Jack. Tom caught sight of light traffic up ahead, the main highway weaving away toward the south, smooth pavement calling to him like a golden stretch of hope. The last few yards were worse than anything before, the drier dirt churned up by tires from when it had been muddy, creating massive ruts that were almost impassable. A sudden dip and bump sent their pots and pans clattering in back, Tom's head smacking the roof, reminding him he'd failed to buckle up properly before pulling out.

Whipping the wheel, he pointed them down a shallow bank and lashed them back to the left, the Humvee's right front tire hopping onto the pavement, bumping them upward with another heavy jolt. Sam squealed as she was tossed in his direction, rolling, landing between the seats, one hand clinging to his arm.

"Almost there!" Tom growled, cutting off a small pickup that hit them in the rear bumper, knocking the Humvee forward, everyone's heads snapping back against their seats. The impact shoved them ahead, and Tom whipped them into the right-hand lane with a sharp squeal of tires and clatter of settling cookware, straightening them out as they shot along the road toward the next village.

"Are we safe?" Barbara asked, her breaths coming in short gasps as she glanced back.

"I think so. For now."

"Were those kids working for Keith?" Linda asked.

"Of course they were," Sam replied, "but I'm not sure how. Who'd work for that guy?"

"There's a lot of hardship happening right now, kids," Tom said. "If you offered someone supplies or money, they'd probably do just about anything to survive."

"I wouldn't do that," Linda snorted. "I'd never work for Keith. He's a jerk, and he deserves to die."

"Those kids probably don't understand what a bad man he is, honey," Tom reminded her. "They don't know what he's done, or what he's trying to do, so we can't blame them."

The truck cabin fell silent except for their labored breathing, hearts pounding as he drove along the winding highway, moving fast, weaving around slower vehicles as if the hounds of hell themselves were on his heels.

* * *

Keith was running with his rifle, stock raised to his shoulder as he popped off three more rounds at the fading Humvee until it disappeared around a bend. Cursing, he shook his hand, pained fingers aching from the weapon's recoil, his shortened reach having forced him to adjust his aim. Still, he'd hit them a few times, though not enough to make them stop. Boots rushed up, Morales and Smith panting, lowering their guns as they glanced between Keith and the fleeing vehicle.

"You could've helped me!" Keith shouted, gesturing at the road. "Thanks!"

Morales shook his head and scowled. "Man, there're people everywhere. You could've hit someone or killed one of those little kids."

With a huff, Keith gave the road another glare before pointing at them. "Well, don't just stand there, go get the truck. Bring it up." When they didn't go right away, he fixed them with a furious stare. "Move it, soldiers!"

The pair exchanged an uncertain look, which brought the blood boiling to his face, and he was about to raise his rifle and shoot them when they finally turned and jogged back toward the bazaar. With a satisfied nod, Keith walked to the road, limping on his pained feet, his body a canvas of agony, but he didn't feel terrible. In fact, he felt alive with pumping blood, adrenaline surging through his veins, the fading percussion of the AR-15 against his shoulder just the jolt he needed to get back into the swing of things.

"I've got you now, McKnight." A cheerful grin found its way onto his face. "You can't get away now. And next time, I won't miss."

* * *

Hands still shaking, Tom released a deep sigh, letting his shoulders sag, head dipping forward to bump against the wheel before lifting it again.

"Are you okay, dad?" Sam asked, followed by her gentle hand resting on his shoulder.

Nodding, Tom raised his head, eyes coming back to life as he peered ahead at the winding road that took them into a valley town with more dense traffic and branching neighborhoods, dilapidated houses with brightly colored roofs. "Yeah, I'm okay. Thanks." Glancing at his rearview, he caught Barbara's eyes as wind whipped through the open hatch and tossed her hair around, light strands snapping across her cheeks. "How about you, honey? Are you okay?"

"Yeah," she replied, gripping her ribs with a pained wince. "I got knocked around a little, but I'll be fine." And while that was probably true, a troubled glint flashed in her eyes before she looked away.

"First chance we get, check Mom's bandage," he said with a glance at Sam.

"Yeah, I will."

Outside, they were passing a string of new signs nailed to thin sticks, plain black letters on white written in Spanish and English. "Can you decipher any of these? I don't want to read them while I'm driving. Looks like directions to Panama or something."

"I'm on it." Sam pressed her face to the window, lowering it to peer even closer. "Yeah. It's just saying this is the road to Panama." Whispering the words, her mouth made shapes to form the Spanish, adding them together with the English ones. "Actually, there's a directive on some of these, too. An order by the US military for Americans to stay on this highway. It's about ninety-six kilometers to the Panama border... Let's see, that's sixty miles?"

"Sounds close enough. A half day's drive from here, barring any more problems."

"Hey, it even says there are residences waiting for US citizens!" Sam was studying the signs hard, head whipping as they drove by one.

"Does that mean a free house?" Jack asked, wrestling Smooch into a comfortable position on his lap, the dog struggling to settle down after all the excitement.

"Something like that," Tom replied.

"Does that mean we'll get our farm back? And we can get more rabbits, dogs, and chickens?"

"I doubt it'll be anything like we're used to, Son. Actually..." he sighed. "I'm not sure we'll be stopping there for long, but it's worth checking out."

"It's a straight shot." Sam shrugged.

"And we've got all the fuel we need," Tom agreed. "So, we shouldn't have to stop."

The faithful Humvee carried them ever southward, a silence falling over them as the tires buzzed on the pavement, the gentle flow of traffic less frenetic than before as they left the Osa Peninsula and its highway towns behind. And while the lush green jungle towered over them comfortingly, Tom continually checked his mirrors for signs of Keith bearing down on them, only relaxing after a half hour passed in the growing heat, their sweaty skin cooled by gusts and breezes blowing through. In back, Barbara had been fidgeting for the past few minutes, shifting, staring out the window before her gaze settled on Jack, who'd finally fallen asleep with his head on Smooch. Absently, her fingers stroked his hair, her troubled expression growing deeper by the moment.

"I'm not going to take back what I did," she finally spoke, glancing at each of them, head shaking as if denying some dark accusation.

"What do you mean, Mom?" Linda asked.

"Those kids..." she replied, as if that explained everything, but when no one seemed to understand, she sat straighter, forcing the words out. "I shot at *children*. That's something I never would've done before, but I'd do it again in a heartbeat if it kept you guys safe."

Linda reached across Smooch and Jack and gripped Barbara's arm. "But you didn't hit any of them. They're all okay."

"Yeah, but Sam and your father are right, and Keith used them to get to us... tried to use our *humanity* against us, but he made one mistake; this family comes first." Barbara ran her fingers through the dog's thick fur, Smooch rolling her head up and happily licking her hand. "You guys matter more to me than anything else in the world, and I don't care what our enemies try to throw at us, we'll never flinch, and we won't back down."

"You did the right thing, Mom." Sam shifted in her seat, fixing Barbara with an understanding look. "That was a hard decision to make, and you could have hit one of them... but you *didn't*. Somehow, you just scared them away."

"And what you did was better than what I was contemplating," Tom added somberly. "You and I are aligned in our thinking, hon. You saved lives out there today. They don't know it, but you did. It'd... I don't know how I'd live with myself if I had gone through with running them down to escape. If it had just been me, I'd have given up. But I'm not giving you guys up. Never."

Smiling with something like relief, Barbara turned her troubled gaze out the window. "But what if they hadn't been afraid of me shooting and missing on purpose? What if I'd had to..." Her words fell away like soft leaves cast aside in a gust of wind, and a thoughtful silence settled over them, Jack starting to snore and drool, the girls staring ahead as they considered their mother's words.

"The good thing is that we're away from there and safe," Tom said. "We'll always stay one step ahead of them. We've been doing it this whole time, and we'll keep on doing it no matter what."

Chapter 10
Tom McKnight
Panama

The Humvee cruised along the stretch of Highway 1, sweeping through the Panama countryside, surrounded by warm, embracing mountains, rolling foothills covered in tropical green, sunlight highlighting the ridges with touches of golden light. Flocks of birds soared from the treetops, diving into the lowlands, banking and switching direction on a dime as their darting shapes beat against the dark blue sky. Only the occasional belch of smoke from the diesel engine tainted the fresh air, the swell of hot grease tossed with a hint of sweet antifreeze, but Tom'd gotten used to it over the weeks.

It was quiet in the cabin, everyone sleeping, Jack and Linda's snored lightly as they leaned on each other with Smooch between them. Barbara's head rested back and was lolling, mouth pressed tight as she dreamed of something feverish and troubling, and Tom wished he was lying next to her, arms wrapped around her and whispering that everything was going to be okay. Their supplies rattled in back, his rifle hanging from a hook, the cooking gear they'd purchased clattering as the Humvee's suspension creaked and groaned with each bump and bend. The alignment wasn't quite right, and one front tire was wobbling badly, causing the steering wheel to vibrate in his palms. At best, they'd be hobbling into Panama City, but if they could make it across the canal, Tom thought they had a good chance of reaching the Darien Pass in a day or two. From there, who knew what they'd do, but there was uncertainty around every turn, and all he could do was grip the wheel and keep the Humvee on track, always watchful for Keith.

The sun burned the mist off the wet road, disturbed by the traffic growing thicker up ahead, the Humvee breaking through, parting the haze in wispy curls as red lights blinked in the distance. Foothills gave way to more lines of vehicles packed tighter, engine fumes swelling in the air. Residential areas sprouted up on both sides, homes stacked atop one another against the hillsides and the Humvee passed a shopping center on the right filled with civilian cars and military trucks. Coming up on Guadalupe, the roads split into two main highways and a dozen offshoots, bumper-to-bumper vehicles, groups of young men pushing abandoned cars onto the already crowded shoulders while would-be mechanics sweated beneath frames quivering on flimsy jacks. The entire place stunk of engine exhaust, oil, urine and worse. Shouts and arguments broke out in yards and fields, civilians and refugees fighting over bins of supplies and clothing, police lights and horns blaring to add to the morning din.

Sam stirred next to him, yawning, rubbing her eyes, blinking at the chaos. "Where are we?"

"We're coming up on Guadalupe, and the roads are splitting. There's a checkpoint up ahead, it looks like."

Sam rose in her seat, reading the signs spotting something, gesturing for him to get over. "Dad, Americans are to take the left-hand lane and stay on Highway 1 up here."

"Sorry." Tom flipped on his turn signal and nudged the big truck into the next lane, receiving a flurry of honks and gestures in response. "I must've missed the signs. I guess I'm a little tired."

"You've been driving all night. You should've woken me up like I asked."

"I wanted to let you sleep, but maybe you can take a shift once we get on the other side of Panama City."

"Okay."

Angling to the left, Tom came to the first military checkpoint, weapons-ready armored Humvees blocking the road along with concrete barriers with orange reflectors tacked to them. There were only two sections open, each wide enough for up a big truck to pass through. Handfuls of soldiers walked up to vehicles, peeked in at the drivers and passengers, and gave them little more than a glance before waving them on. Tom received the same treatment, no one blinking twice at their Humvee, an obvious piece of Army equipment with civilians inside. Tom sped up on the clear highway, taking the exit that kept him on Highway 1, hitting sixty and racing through the north section of town, the wind whipping through the cabin, everyone coming awake with yawns and groans.

Barbara leaned forward and peered around the seat. "Where are we, Tom? Anywhere near Panama City?"

"We just made it through a checkpoint on the outskirts of Guadalupe."

"How much longer do you think we have?"

"I don't know. The traffic is up and down. The city is a complete mess, but at least the checkpoints are keeping things from devolving into chaos."

Restaurants and cafes lined the four-lane highway, laundromats and phone stores, quaint places with old walls, cracked paint and signs that were faded or hung crooked. People crowded the sidewalks, groups of South and Central Americans watching them pass with curious expressions as they followed vehicles with license plates from New York, Texas, Kentucky, and even Minnesota. There were civilians in military trucks, too, old Growlers, stripped-down Humvees, camouflaged SUVs, and flatbeds, none in worse shape than what Tom was driving. A herd of people rushed across the street ahead of them, and he hit the brakes, jerking to a crawl as combined US-Mexican troops sprinted up, shouting, ushering the crowd to the opposite side, waving Tom and the other cars through. Rocketing forward in a belch of smoke, he pushed the speed to sixty, racing past businesses with their doors shut and locked, a handful of them with broken glass, plastic taped over them as guards walked the side streets.

At the next five-way intersection they reached a second checkpoint which sat at the base of two lanes circling upward toward a neighborhood in the heights, quaint Spanish-style houses with fences encircling terraced gardens. Past the roadblocks stood a police station with tiny cruisers and blue lights spinning, cops standing in the road wearing yellow vests and hats, milling near the crowds, keeping them from spilling onto the roads. At the checkpoint, a more strenuous check as one vehicle behind them was directed to pull off to the side for a search, while others, including the McKnight's Humvee, were allowed to pass. Waving to the soldiers, Tom shot through the checkpoint and continued into an increasingly crowded part of town, the sounds of music bouncing off the brick-and-mortar walls, echoing in the valley around them as streets packed with houses and people climbed the foothills.

Sam had been studying the signs along the way, and she pointed to one, saying, "Dad, this is the Pan-American Highway."

"I was wondering about that," he replied, shaking his head. "I didn't know if it was on Highway 1 or a different one. But I guess this is it."

"What's the Pan-American highway?" Linda asked from the back.

"It was supposed to be a highway connecting North America to the tip of South America," Tom replied, trying to recall everything he'd read about it.

Sam had her book open in her lap, thumbing through the pages. "They built the majority of it, I'm pretty sure. But I don't think it ever got finished, because a lot of environmental groups didn't want them tearing down the South American jungles. It looks like the highway continues on the other side of the Panama Canal, and ends on our side at… yep, The Darien National Forest."

"Just like Carlos said," Tom nodded. "The area is so wild they never finished the highway through it. That gives me hope that maybe we can stay safe there."

Tom started to say more, but they were merging into a suburban area of fields, neighborhoods, and signs. "Sam, can you tell me which direction to go?"

Samantha studied the signs, finger held up and poking at the writing as if she was reading down a page. "It's another highway junction. We're supposed to stay on Highway 4 and pull off at the next checkpoint." At first, she didn't seem sure, but her voice rose with confidence. "Yep, straight ahead. It'll be coming up soon."

The traffic was moving well, the roadsides framed by grassy lanes, suburban areas with vast neighborhoods stretching up into the north, a blanket of rusted tin roofs, clusters of residents out in the streets, watching the fleeing Americans go by. Around the next bend, a wide-open field lay off to the right, packed with vehicles of every conceivable make and model, American and Mexican plates, people surrounding them looking slumped and sweaty, soldiers jogging between the rows in massive numbers as they lugged equipment and personal possessions, pointing and ushering crowds in the congested space.

The highway ahead of them was blocked, barricades lined up side by side across the road with no visible way through, and behind those loomed military trucks with mounted machine guns and manned by soldiers who looked both relaxed and bored. Standing tall in the distance was a wide swath of forest, the empty expressway winding around it, but with no one allowed that far. Huge warehouse buildings and a shopping mall stood a hundred yards off the road, a big sign reading Arraiján Town Center up near the entrance.

"Dad, see that soldier? He's gesturing for you to get off the highway here."

Tom was already slowing, driving beneath an underpass, waving to the guard as he joined a gravel road branching to the right and cutting over a grassy field, the entrance to the dirt lot where more guards directed people to stop and park in a wide line. The Humvee hit the rough terrain and bounced them around, another soldier pointing for them to go even farther left. Blinking through the rising cloud of dust, Tom drove that way and stopped in front of a half-dozen guards coming up, wearing weary expressions.

"These are Marines," Tom murmured, noting the ranks on their fatigues as he put the truck in park. Rolling down his window, he started to say something when one man gestured for him to get out.

"Sir, please exit the vehicle!" The Marine wasn't shouting, though he bellowed in a loud monotone as if he'd been ordering people to do it all day, making rolling motions with his hand. "Please, sir. We need everyone out. The whole family. Come on."

Glancing over his shoulder at Barbara, Tom popped the door and stepped out, looking between the soldiers. "What's going on here, guys? We're Americans, coming down from Virginia, trying to get across the canal."

"No problem, sir," the Marine said as his fellows strolled toward the back of the Humvee. "No one's getting punished for having a military vehicle. CENTCOM understands the nature of the emergency, and they're happy you made it. Now, please get everyone out, so we can process the truck through."

Barbara and the kids popped their doors, slid out, and blinked at the surrounding Marines. Jack grabbed Smooch's collar as she leapt down and tried running in circles, her sniffing, yapping barks driving the Marines back before Linda stepped in and snapped her leash on, snatching it tight to get her quickly under control.

"Wait a minute!" Tom raised his hand to the Marine. "What do you mean, *process* the truck through? We've been driving this ever since we left the states. If you need me to explain how we got it, I can--"

"It doesn't matter, sir." He started to maneuver Tom out of the way.

"Hey, man!" Tom growled, starting to grab the Marine but pulling back. "This is the only transportation we have. You can't just take it."

"You're going to have to walk to the ferries from here, unless you can grab a bus carrying people in. There's ten of them, and they're constantly running, but I wouldn't wait on one if I were you. If you start walking now, you'll see the camp in an hour. Check in there, and someone will give you food, water, and a place to sleep while you wait to be taken to the other side."

"So, this is the last stop before the ferries?"

"Yes, sir. The camp and canal are just past that wooded area there. All the bridges are closed to thru-traffic."

Tom turned and gazed across the field to where crowds of people flowed through the lot to join Highway 1, a sea of humanity jam-packed with refugees, not a single vehicle on it but for a spattering of blue roofs he assumed were the busses. "That's a four-mile walk, Marine."

"Yes, sir. Sorry about the inconvenience, but we're processing all vehicles here and allowing folks to hoof-it the rest of the way. It's the only way they can get everyone settled quickly and efficiently."

"I get that, but—"

"Hey, Sergeant, we've got an issue here." That was from a Marine medic who stood by Barbara, where she was leaning against the Humvee, holding her ribs with one hand, hugging Jack to her as he came around with the rest of the kids and Smooch.

"What is it?"

"This lady doesn't look so good," he said, craning his neck. "She's pale, her breathing is off, and I'm pretty sure that's a heavy bandage beneath that shirt. We should check her out before she goes any farther."

"That won't be necessary, guys," Barbara said, trying to laugh it off, though her eyes were pained, and her medication was slurring her speech. "We can walk there just fine, really!"

"Is there a way to drive a little closer?" Tom asked, gesturing to Highway 4, which was wide open.

The Marine glanced backward. "Negative. CENTCOM wants to keep that clear for military maneuvering. All foot traffic is being directed along Highway 1 to the docks. Please, sir, grab what you can carry and make your way over to the infirmary. We've got a lot more folks to process today."

"I don't need an infirmary," Barbara insisted as another Marine joined the medic. "I can walk to the ferries—"

"But Mom!" Jack said plaintively. "We're not getting on the ferries, because we're not going to--"

"Hush, Jack." Barbara gave a pained smile, brushing his cheeks to quiet him down. "We'll get on the ferry if we have to."

The Marine Sergeant stared at Barbara before his eyes shifted to Tom. "You didn't come here to get on a ferry, sir?"

Tom stepped away from the truck, hands on his hips, glancing over at Barbara and Jack and the medic, waiting to help her. More Marines moved to the back of the Humvee in preparation to unload their equipment, and one opened the driver's door, holding his hand out for the keys.

"Answer the question, sir." the first Marine said, circling to stay in front of Tom, turning and tossing his keys over to his buddy. "You weren't getting on a ferry? What were you planning to do?"

Tom sighed resignedly. "Long story short, we're trying to get to a place on the border between Panama and Colombia. It's a spot called the Darien Gap. Not sure if you've heard of it, but people are settling there… It's supposed to be pretty remote, and that's what we want."

"The Darien Gap?" The Marine glanced at his buddies.

One who'd overheard them came over, shaking his head. "You really don't want to go there. Things are heating up in that area."

"Heating up?" Tom replied. "It doesn't matter. That's where we have to get to. Can't we drive through on the highway and keep going?"

The first Marine's lips pursed as he gestured to the rear of their vehicle. "Sorry, sir. It's either the ferries or nothing. Now, we've got work to do, so grab what you can carry, and Corporal Hodges will escort you to the infirmary." Tom started to argue more, but the Marine briskly stepped away and motioned him toward the back of the Humvee with a snap of his hand. "Please, sir."

With a sigh, Tom turned and directed the kids. "Okay, guys. Let's grab a single backpack each. Just take the important stuff."

Linda popped the hatch, Smooch's leash firmly wrapped around her hand, the Marines giving them some space to work. Pulled in tight, they sorted through the backpacks, stuffing food and clothing inside, making sure they had all the water they could carry, their straw filters, and things to start a fire.

"Stay close, kids," Tom murmured. "Don't let them see…"

"We're keeping our pistols," Linda whispered back, slipping hers from the front of her waistband where she'd been hiding it, sliding it into her backpack toward the bottom. "I've got Sam's and Mom's, too. They left them on the seats."

"Good job," Sam murmured as she nodded to an ammunition pouch hanging from a hook in the back, though not reaching for it right away. "How are we going to get that?"

"I'll distract them." Tom took his rifle where it hung from a nearby hook, casually slinging it on his shoulder and turning so the Marines saw it.

"Whoa, sir!" One man rushed forward and reached for the weapon. "You're not allowed to have this in camp."

Tom appeared baffled, then smiled and chuckled, letting the gun slip from his shoulder into the Marine's hands. "Of course. We don't want any trouble." And when he turned back to finish loading, he noticed Sam had taken the ammunition pouch down and hid it in one of the packs. Tom slung his heavier backpack on his left shoulder, Barbara's smaller one on his right. Linda and Sam fussed with the arrangement of theirs, taking clothes out, putting different ones in, rearranging and messing around as the Marines grumbled behind them. Tom rested his hands over theirs, quieting their movements, pulling the front flaps closed as he glanced at each of them.

"This is good, girls. Let's go before they decide *for* us what we can take or not."

"I know," Sam said with a mopey frown. "It's just… we've been in the Humvee for what seems like forever. It's been our home away from home."

With a troubled expression, Tom looked over the cargo space with its bloodstains and dirty clothes, parts of the disassembled smoker in back along with their recently purchased cookware, rat-eared books written in Spanish, and all the little odds and ends they'd picked up.

"They're just things," Barbara reminded them, putting her arms around Sam and Jack. "We can accumulate more possessions wherever we go. The important thing is, we have each other."

"And our home goes where we go," Linda finished for her with a single firm nod, sliding her backpack on and tossing her mane of hair to her other shoulder. "I'm ready."

"This way, folks," Corporal Hodges said, gesturing them into the narrow spaces between vehicles, ushering them away from the Humvee as the Marines descended on it, rooting through the back, starting it up with the familiar belch of black exhaust.

Tom understood what the girls were going through, though he'd been too distracted by the Marines for the sentimentality to hit him. As he glanced back, he squashed a pang of resentment that someone could sweep in and take what they owned so easily, and it was the perfect reason not to allow the government to ever control their lives again. Steely determination stiffened his resolve to find a place for them where they could be truly free.

"The infirmary's right over here," Hodges said, a few steps ahead of them, guiding them toward a tent sitting in the middle of the sea of cars, the green canvas with a red cross on the front.

"Help your mother, but not too much," Tom murmured to the girls, Linda moving to her left, Sam on the right, each holding her arm over the trickier parts of the field, letting her walk on her own where the going was easier. With Smooch on a tight leash, they passed rusted out vans and pickup trucks, small cars covered in dust, newer model Cadillacs and BMWs with barely a scratch on them, worth thousands of dollars in the old world. There was even an ambulance that looked beat up, its fenders smashed and half falling off, like it had been in a dozen wrecks before landing there.

As they approached the infirmary, Tom watched civilians, soldiers, and Marines come and go, some helping people hobble along or carrying them on stretchers. A man leaning on a pair of crutches turned sideways to let them pass, then slipped out with a small family trailing behind him.

"How long is this going to take?" Tom asked.

"Not long at all, sir," the Marine said. "We need to make sure you're not sick, and that your wife can complete the trip to the camp."

"What if they decide she can't?"

"She'll have to stay in the infirmary while the rest of you move on to the docks."

Tom shot a dark glance Barbara's way, throwing her a terse head shake, and she replied with a curt nod as they stepped in. The place thrummed with urgency, a simmering bustle of noise and motion as medics, doctors, and nurses with haggard but patient expressions attended the injured who rested on cots or wheelchairs. Shell-shocked people stared at nothing, faces miserable, coughing or nursing stained bandages wrapped around their shoulders or knees. The air had an iron tinge to it, the reek of blood, illness, and festering wounds, and he noticed there were two additional parts of the infirmary for long-term patients plus a closed-off space with a sign that read, *Surgeons and Critical Care Staff Only*. A shriek of pain ripped from behind the tent flap, and worried faces paused to stare before going back to regular business.

"Careful, sir," Hodges said, putting out his arm to keep the family from running into a pair of orderlies carrying bowls of soup and trays of mystery meat and mush.

"I'd rather have smoked boar," Sam murmured, her nose wrinkling.

The unexpected declaration made Tom chuckle. "Me too, dear. Let's get this over with and get to the docks. We'll figure the rest out from there."

The medic directed them to a hospital bed off to the side, Barbara leaning on the end with the family crowding in, the Marine pulling the privacy curtain all the way around, saying, "Wait here, and I'll have someone come over. Good luck."

Tom nodded and parted the curtain as soon as it shut, peeking out at the bustle of people, sensing nothing immediately threatening except for the uncertainty of what they'd have to do if Barbara couldn't make it. Shutting the plastic curtain, he turned back to her. "I know we told them you can walk to the camp, honey. But how do you really feel?"

"It hurts, but it's mostly just in the muscles, and a deep soreness if you know what I mean."

"The last time I changed the dressing, there wasn't a lot of blood." Sam leaned against the bed next to Barbara where she shifted her ponytail of curly locks over to her other shoulder. "It's healing pretty well."

"I guess we'll let the doctor determine that for sure, but we need to be careful here, guys. We want to move quickly, but we can't force your mother to make a trip she's not up for."

"The doctor can give their opinion, and we'll go from there," Barbara said.

With a swish of the curtain, a doctor stepped through, wearing standard green scrubs, dark hair cut to her shoulders, and exhausted blue eyes that looked them over with a glance

"What a nice family." Holding up a clipboard, she checked the scribbled-on sheet. "My notes say bed five has a chest wound." She arced an eyebrow at Barbara. "Are you my chest wound?"

"Guilty as charged," Barbara replied, raising her hand with a sheepish grin.

"Well, hop up and let me have a look. I'm Doctor Ramsey."

"Good to meet you." Barbara wiggled onto the thin mattress, threw her legs up without help, and laid back. With a pained grimace, she began pulling up her shirt to the bottom of her breast, revealing the thick bandage Sam had applied earlier. "Long story short, I got shot in the ribs."

"Ouch!" Ramsey whispered in a tense tone as she leaned over the wound, peeling gently at the edges of the bandages, wincing when she saw the stitches and puckered pink flesh, blood encrusted on the dressing and in the indention the bullet had made. "You weren't kidding."

"Nope."

The doctor prodded the wound studiously. "You probably won't tell me who shot you, but whoever stitched you up... this is excellent work."

"We got her patched up in a hospital north of here a few days ago," Tom said. "There were some doctors there, and they took great care of us."

"They sure did." Ramsey peeled off the dressing the rest of the way, tossing it in a garbage bin, grabbing a new one from a table nearby. With swabs and alcohol, she cleaned the wound, causing Barbara to wince and suck air through her teeth. Antiseptic went on next, followed by a bandage.

"What's your prognosis, Doc?" Barbara asked.

"We can clear you to walk to camp, provided you can take the pain."

"I've been dealing with it so far. What's another day?"

"Do you need anything for it?" Ramsey stood back with her hands on her hips. "I can give you some pain pills for that."

"We'll take what we can get," Tom replied before anyone could say no. "Thanks."

"No problem," Ramsey smiled. "Be right back."

The doctor swept out through the curtain and disappeared, and Tom stepped in and rested his hand on Barbara's arm as she pulled her dirty shirt back down, shifting to the side to keep the bandage from bunching up.

"Don't we already have pain stuff, Dad?" Jack asked.

Linda was nodding at the foot of the bed. "A bottle and a half of what Carlos and Henny gave us. Won't that be enough?"

"We have some left, but we should take everything we can when we can get it. We don't know if we'll have access to pain medications later. One of us could get hurt and might need them, whether it's a day, a week, or a month from now. Let's load up and prepare to walk."

Hoisting their backpacks to their shoulders, Tom took two like before, nodding appreciatively when Sam and Linda both helped Barbara off the bed and to her feet. Five minutes later, Ramsey returned with a small bottle of pills and extra dressings in a sealed bag.

"Here you go," she said, handing them to Tom. "Be careful out there."

"We're supposed to get on the highway, and that will take us to camp?" Tom asked, gladly accepting the supplies.

"That's right. Just follow the horde of people." The doctor grabbed one end of the curtain and swung it open in a clatter of clips over the metal rod.

"Thank you," Tom said, leading the family into the principal thoroughfare and toward the exit, bunched around Barbara to keep anyone from accidentally bumping her. Outside, Tom motioned them to the side, pushing through the ever-growing throng of civilians who threaded between the cars, climbing over them, the sounds of feet on metal hoods making a clatter. As he led them, he looked across the thousands of families just like theirs, somber husbands and wives, older couples, brothers and sisters and groups of kids. Rags hung from their thinning frames, old brand-name T-shirts and blouses, torn and stained from the journey. Dirty faces stared at the ground, shoulders laden with backpacks, one man pulling a boy and a girl in a rusty red wagon that reminded Tom of someone they'd walked with back in Virginia, though he couldn't remember her face against the thousands of others. The crowd thickened as they reached the highway, all four lanes packed with ambling refugees, staring east toward Panama City and what they hoped was salvation.

"Stay close, kids," he said, shepherding them along, glancing back to make sure Jack didn't get knocked around and lost.

The highway cut through a wide swath of forest, birches and oaks and more exotic vegetation that Tom didn't recognize. The overbearing stench of sweat and body odor clogged his nose with the reek of humanity, the kids' noses wrinkling. Jack was clinging to Barbara's arm, so Tom tried to keep the boy from crowding her, but she smiled and shook her head that she was fine with it. Like the Marine said, buses drove up the highway though every seat was taken, people hanging off the sides, an occasional fight breaking out when they wouldn't let an elderly or injured person on. Tom started to guide them that way, fully planning on fighting for seats if it meant saving Barbara some pain, but she took his arm and turned him toward the middle of the highway where there was more room to walk. Carrying on his guidance, his heart swelled at his wife's bravery, her defiance of the pain, battling every step of the way. Once, she needed to take a rest, and they pushed to the side, cutting through the crowd, finding a shady spot beneath the trees where Smooch had a few more feet of freedom. There, Tom wrapped Barbara in a gentle embrace, pressing his cheek against hers and whispering that he loved her, rewarded with her smile and a breathless, "I love you, too," that brushed lightly in his ear.

Once she caught her breath, Tom gestured for them to rejoin the crowd, making their way east, hearing murmurs of "Lacona" and "Panama City," Spanish accents and English voices filled with fear and uncertainty, and when Sam checked her map, she showed him Lacona was a small town near the boatyards on the canal. The throng quieted as they walked, weariness and fatigue settling on them like a pall. There were a few random acts of kindness as refugees helped each other along, too weak to argue or fight, eyes continually lifted to the end of the curvy road. The forest on both sides was lush, bursting with screeching birds, almost jungle-like compared to Guadalupe and the surrounding towns, which were full of congestion and chaos. Plodding on, Tom watched Barbara, the only evidence of her injury a slight lean as she kept walking, staring ahead with Jack held tight against her.

Sam rose on the balls of her feet, calling back, "Hey, guys. There's a sign for Lacona coming up, and I see some houses."

At the edge of the town, joint US-Central American soldiers stood on the corners of the major byways, gesturing to the flood of refugees, guiding them north onto a road called Bruja. Lacona faded off to the right with more glorious estates on the left, modern style houses and mansions, a row of fancy hotels and spas that sat way off in a wide green field. Military trucks blocked the lanes in, troops standing with rifles in hand, studying the crowd as it passed.

Sam read a gilded sign as they walked by. "Ropa al Mayor Panama. Tucan Country Club." Her face screwed up. "Seems kind of weird for the soldiers to be at the country club, wouldn't you say?"

"Sounds like it's a government official's house to me," Tom replied, glancing across several square acres of well-trimmed grounds, homes with fancy pools, a glorious mansion resting at the top of the hill. "The first thing any military does during a crisis is take over whatever civilian facilities they want. So, not surprising they'd secure a fancy place like this. There's probably some pretty important people there."

"Oh," Sam replied. "I see what you're saying. No matter what happens to the little people, the big guys will always have it good."

"Now you're catching on." Tom winked, trying to keep his voice from sounding sour, though it was hard, knowing the rich wouldn't suffer at all, not even as humankind collectively stared down the barrel of a gun. Placing his palm in the middle of her shoulders, he prodded her forward, not dwelling on what he couldn't control.

A half mile up the road, a line of soldiers swept their arms toward a gravel lane that cut through a patch of woods, and on the other side sprawled a massive camp of civilian refugees, a sea of tents, thousands of milling people stretching to the water's edge. The Panama Canal flowed dark under cargo ships that bobbed on the gentle waves. Ten or twelve ferries cut paths across the water, motoring toward a series of docks on the other side, and shipyards were filled with massive containers stacked beside two enormous warehouses, all protected by military trucks and patrols. Smaller Navy boats with guns mounted on the front cruised the freight lanes, a pair of them idling at intersections where the ferries passed.

"Wow! Look at all the boats!" Jack said, standing on his tiptoes and pointing.

"Yeah, pretty cool, huh?" Sam asked, mirroring his excitement.

"Are we going to get on one of those?"

Neither parent replied, and Tom guided them over to a pair of soldiers who stood at the edge of the camp, holding up signs in English and Spanish, shouting in both languages at once.

"Welcome to the Rodman Port Camp," spouted a man with a bullhorn, "where you'll wait to catch a ferry to Panama City, after which you may continue on to your new homes in Venezuela. Please note that all white tents are emergency services, blue are for food, and green are for lodging." He held up his other arm, which had a white band around it. "The white band indicates a camp advisor. If you get lost or need to add a name to the list, see them right away, and they'll be happy to help. You must sign up within a day of your arrival."

"Or what?" Tom murmured to himself, looking off to the left.

"Failure to do so will result in you not receiving an armband, which will lead to forfeiture of special privileges, housing, and financial help when you get to the other side. Please remain calm at all times, as your safety is our biggest priority."

"Well, that answers my question," Tom said, guiding the kids between the shouting administrators and angling them off to the left where a dirt track circled the entire encampment. To the north was a second camp, just as massive as the first, connected by thin gravel roads. Beyond those were the locks and port authorities who allowed big commercial vessels through the canal using a series of floodgates.

"I can find someone and get us signed in," Linda offered, dancing on the tips of her toes as she walked backward while keeping Smooch close, glancing around her to avoid running into people.

"That's not what we want to do," Tom replied. "The first thing Keith will do when he shows up is check that list, and if we're on it, he'll know we're here or that we passed through."

"He kind of knows that already, right?"

"Maybe, but I don't want to give him any additional clues." Tom nodded toward the north. "Let's just keep walking until your mother needs to rest." Glancing at Barbara, he said, "Are you okay, honey?"

"I can go a little farther."

"We'll go to the north part of camp and rest there, it looks less crowded."

"There's more room without all the cars and trucks," Sam added as she glanced up at the huge horns affixed to poles, blaring a constant list of names and numbers.

A woman bellowed, "Bracelet numbers twenty-one thousand to twenty-two thousand, report to Rodman Dock Three! I repeat, bracelet numbers twenty-one thousand to twenty-two thousand, report to Rodman Dock Three. You're allowed a single backpack each. Please do not attempt to bring more, as it will be confiscated in the shipyard."

A connector path took them to the north part of camp where entire families clustered at picnic tables, sitting on benches with their possessions stacked on top, staring into space, fingers toying with the white wristbands as they waited for their numbers to be called. Some milled around, others stood with backpacks hanging from their slouched shoulders, munching on fruit and snacks. Tom bulled through the crowd and closer to shore, focused on spots nearer to the canal, finally coming across a family who were evacuating a picnic table, hooting and hollering after their numbers were called.

"There, guys. Grab that one."

Linda and Jack sprinted ahead with Smooch bounding next to them, throwing their packs on the tabletop, Tom glaring at anyone else trying to move in. After putting their things down, he dug out a pair of binoculars and climbed on the table, peering north at the locks and closed floodgates, then across the canal to a wide campus with pristine red roofs and blocks of gray walls. Pivoting south, he studied Panama City itself, a vast cluster of highways and roads, rooftops with trails of smoke drifting upward in a light smog, though downtown didn't appear to be on fire. There was a shipyard with a dozen temporary docks bobbing in the water, held afloat with massive black bladders. Ferries pulled up, and people flowed off them like ants to where military trucks and packed buses drove them to camps on the other side.

"They're taking people south from there." Tom shook his head. "Boy, it looks like a mess."

Increasing the magnification on his binoculars, he passed over clusters of refugees by the thousands, a sea of stinking humanity everywhere he looked. Sweat dripping down his face, swallowing with a dry throat, he turned the binoculars north again, peering at the fancy campus on the other side of the canal.

"That's the City of Knowledge," Sam said, climbing up next to him with her travel book in her hand.

"What's that?"

"The City of Knowledge is like a business park, I think. Not sure what that means."

"We have them in America, too," Tom said. "It's just a place where local businesses have headquarters and warehouses and stuff. I'd imagine in a city like this, there are officials there, too."

"What are you thinking, hon?" Barbara sat with Jack next to her, while Linda sat on the table with her feet on the bench.

"With the automobile bridges closed to foot traffic and cars, we're going to need to cross someplace less conspicuous. I'm thinking about those locks over there."

"Locks?" Linda asked, expression curious as she stood and joined them. "I don't see any locks…"

Tom chuckled. "Locks are what the boats pass through to get through part of the canal. The locks are just wide enough for one ship at a time, and they use extendable floodgates to raise and lower the water level, allowing the ships to cross."

"Can regular people walk over those floodgates?"

"I don't know," he replied, "we'll find out." Stooping, he returned his binoculars to the pack and sat on the table like Linda with his feet resting on the bench. Giving Barbara's shoulder a light squeeze, he asked, "Think you can make it over the floodgates if I find someone to let us cross?"

"I think so," Barbara replied with a sigh. "I can't run a race, but a brisk walk won't kill me. Actually, I feel pretty good right now."

"That's what I was hoping. Okay, kids. Grab your stuff. I want to scout it out a little."

Linda and Sam passed around bottled waters, everyone drinking their fill before abandoning the table. Other families were already hovering, swooping in as soon as Tom stepped away, arguing and fighting over the prime real estate. Pointing at the locks, he ordered Sam and Linda to take the lead, and they pushed their way through the crowd, always glancing back to make sure Jack, Barbara, and Tom were following. They circled the outside, edging toward the canal, boat engines growing louder beneath the din of muttering people and crying kids. Groups of refugees sat on the grassy shore, staring across the waters, sharing a meager meal as they waited for their numbers to be called. The waterway smelled moist and muddy, thick with the stench of fish, a flat reek that made his stomach turn. A long wharf connected to the nearest canal lock, a sort of guide rail for a big cargo ship that was coming in, aided by tugboats with churning motors. The approaching vessel's deck was laden with orange and maroon shipping containers that towered over everything, colorful, rust-stained things marked with white letters, numbers, and country designations.

"Wow!" Jack exclaimed, looking up. "That boat is huge!"

Tom chuckled at the boy's delight but kept his eyes on the floodgates. As he watched, the first gate drew inward, opening with a smooth groan for the incoming ship. With his hand lightly on Barbara's shoulder, he called up, "A little faster, girls. I might have an idea."

The pair nodded and picked up their pace, Smooch trotting alongside Linda, stepping along the rocky shoreline and coming up near the Floodgate Control House One, surrounded by stark white sheds dotting the green lawn. Workers in coveralls went on break, standing in groups, smoking cigarettes, some exchanging words with refugees and civilians who'd claimed parts of the yard, blankets thrown down as temporary picnic spots. A paved path led from the smaller sheds to the main control building, a dirty, three-story structure that stretched a few hundred feet along the canal and boasted an entire wall of observation windows. Workers with coveralls moved between the pressure systems and mechanical boxes, making repairs or releasing valves in hisses of steam. Tom stared at the enormous ship edging toward the lock, barely keeping pace with them. Its rusted hull loomed over them with the scent of corroded steel, creaking and groaning under the weight of its load. Guide trains rode along the dock, workers catching ropes and chains cast off from the ship's deck and tying the beast down.

"Is that where you want to go, Dad?" Linda asked, voice filled with awe. "Those bridges there."

"Yeah. That's what I'm thinking."

"But how? We can't just walk across them, can we? What if they move or open while we're on them?"

"We might need a little help." Tom gestured toward a section of the yard behind the main control building, dropping his packs to claim the spot. "Put down a blanket here, girls. We'll have a bite to eat and let your mother rest."

They settled as Tom glanced at the armored vehicles parked on either side of the building with their gun barrels lowered, the soldiers relaxed in their turrets, enjoying the late day warmth. Workers came and went, exiting through rear doors, striding toward sheds, using key codes to get in and do whatever maintenance function they'd been assigned. No guards were escorting them, and the refugees left them alone to work, which gave Tom an idea. With their backpacks in the center of the blanket, they eased Barbara down to rest on the pile of soft canvas, and Sam and Linda dug out a package of smoked meat and random vending machine snacks they'd picked up along the way, bags of sour cream and onion chips popping open, candy bar wrappers crinkling, a dog bone for Smooch. Bottled waters were passed around, and someone ripped open a flavor pack for Jack they'd found in an abandoned store, tapping the sugar crystals into his top, shaking it, and watching the liquid turn red with cherry flavoring, much to the boy's delight. While they ate and drank, Tom put together a small sack of goods and tucked the loose end beneath his belt so it hung from his hip. With a bottled water in hand, he gave Barbara a quick kiss on the forehead and stood.

"I'll be right back," he said, glancing toward the control house. "Holler if you need me. I'll stay within earshot."

Barbara smiled up at him, the kids enjoying the picnic-like atmosphere as Jack and Smooch ran a few circles around them. Still, Tom's nervousness cranked through the roof as he strode toward the control house, glancing to the opposite shore, knowing that to get away, to truly be *free*, they'd need to reach it without registering with government forces. Their last hope was to completely vanish at Panama City, fading out of sight and out of mind forever, making the Darien pass and settling there, creating a new life for themselves that would be something close to what they'd had in Virginia.

Tom strolled casually across the yard, stopping to gaze upward every now and again, taking a swig of water as he got ever closer, the bag of goods jostling against his leg. Workers ambled by wearing dark coveralls, their faces smeared with grease and dirt like they spent a lot of time in mechanical rooms and maintenance shacks, but he wasn't sure any of them could help him. A quick right turn took him past several doors until he reached the building's back corner, and he walked across another grassy part to face the canal, watching the crews continued to align the cargo vessel, slipping it into the first lock. A dozen refugees stood against a fence that kept onlookers from getting too close. A father pointed to the massive ship and then at the floodgates that were sliding shut behind it, and the channel filled with water, the boat slowly rising to come level with the next lock. Minutes passed, and the vessel drifted forward into the second lock. Out near Panama City, a mile or more away, another bulky cargo ship was pulling into the canal, moving in behind the first one, though it would be awhile, and Tom had time to figure out how they'd get over the fence and dash across fifty yards of pavement, past hydraulic maintenance boxes and mechanisms, to the floodgate, all with Barbara's injured side to deal with.

Two men stepped around the front of the control house and into the sun, one dressed in blue slacks and a collared white work shirt, lighting a cigarette and passing it to his co-worker in orange coveralls. Tom took another swig of water and strolled in that direction, angling more toward the fence and the other refugees gawking at the locks. When he came within ten yards, he tuned into the workers' Spanish conversation, inwardly cursing himself for not bringing Sam along. But it was too late to go back, so he kept working up his nerve as he watched the cargo ship glide forward, listening to the lock's mechanics click and bang as the third lock opened to let the big boat in. Soon, it would be released to the other side and could travel up the canal to the Caribbean Sea. The ship's engines kicked on in a deep, gurgling burst, moving it ahead at a snail's pace, inch by inch, the distant sounds of workers calling to each other as they guided it through. One of the men sharing a cigarette said something and walked back to the control house, leaving the man with the white shirt to finish his smoke alone. After a glance over, Tom turned and meandered that way, looking casual and relaxed like he was enjoying a long ferry wait, though his yes narrowed briefly as he read the man's name tag.

"Mr. Horatio," Tom said with a nod. "Hola! How are you? Do you speak English?"

The man drew on his cigarette, one eye squinting as he inhaled, the tip swelling bright red as the tobacco burned. Head rotated away from Tom, he exhaled the smoke into the twirling breeze.

"Hello, sir. Yes, I speak English."

"I was hoping you would." Tom smiled and scratched his head. "My daughter… she knows a little Spanish, but I don't know any."

"It's okay," Horatio replied. "Normally, I take people on tours of the facility, but those have been canceled for the foreseeable future, so now we just work to keep the locks open so the flow of vessels constantly moves."

"It's incredible," Tom said, glancing at the approaching ship with more stacks of shipping containers, a contingent of military guards standing at the rail, and a pair of gunboats trailing behind it. "These locks are a feat of human ingenuity. How long have you worked here?"

"I've been at this lock system for three years, though I've spent time at all of them before that, all along the canal."

"What else do you do here, aside from giving tours?"

"I'm the on-duty controller." He gestured toward the approaching cargo ship. "When that boat gets closer, I will go inside, prepare the floodgates to open, and let them in. I manage the entire process."

Tom looked him up and down, judging his tired face and slumped shoulders, though he had smart, kind eyes. "Let me guess. Things were much easier before this flood of refugees showed up?"

"We always welcome visitors to the locks," he chuckled tiredly, "but it's very stressful now. We work long shifts, and there are rumors about Russian and Chinese forces in the area, causing trouble. Everyone is on edge, though we might appear relaxed."

"What do they pay you here?"

"I work for the government, so I'm happy just to receive rations for myself and my family. That's all we need right now."

Tom glanced out at the ship and then at the floodgates, still trying to remain casual despite the anxiety tearing at his insides. The gently lapping waters and the faint odor of rot and mud was soothing somehow, and he focused on that as he prodded the worker. "I guess things are going to get even tougher soon, huh?"

"Yes, my friend," Horatio said, nodding and laughing. "But the people of Panama City are always happy. We face whatever we must with a smile, and we care for our fellow humans. What about you? What'll you do once they ferry you across? Will you live in Venezuela like the rest?"

"We're not looking forward to it." Tom winced. "In fact, no. We're not going to Venezuela."

"What do you mean?" Horatio blew a long puff of smoke off to the side. "Will you stay here in the camp?"

"My family and I… we're hoping to get across." Tom nodded at the floodgates.

Horatio looked confused. "With the ferries, yes?"

"No, I mean right there." Tom gestured at the floodgates with more emphasis, blood pounding in his head, knowing that giving up his intentions could get them caught and held. "We're hoping to find someone to let us through, and we have some things to trade for anyone who helps us."

Horatio's cigarette paused near his lips. "Help *how*?"

Tom kicked at the ground. "Well, if we could jump that fence and use the floodgates. They seem safe enough to cross with the rails and all."

"It *is* safe to walk across," he confirmed after a pause. "But where'll you go, my friend? If you do not get on the ferries, you can't be counted. As the announcements say…" He raised his cigarette, gesturing at the voice droning over the speakers, calling the next set of numbers. "You'll lose your privileges. No land or job for you, and you'll miss out on the benefits you'd be entitled to as an American citizen."

"We don't want those privileges," Tom explained. "We're homesteaders, or, we were. We have a farm… Well, we *had* a farm. We raised chickens and rabbits, and grew crops in a greenhouse and in a field—"

"I know what homesteading is. My cousin talked about his farm a lot, and we got a lot of our tips from his family."

"You farm, too?"

"Simple gardening, mostly. My wife loves the activity, and I eat the fresh vegetables it yields."

Tom laughed. "Yes, it's the best food you can ever get. Anyway, that's why we want to cross right here." Looking straight at the man, he put it on the line. "Can you help us?"

"Where will you go?"

"The Darien National Forest. We hear it's beautiful."

"It *is* beautiful, but it is also extremely dangerous."

"We've been warned about the criminal elements, but no place is going to be truly safe. It all comes down to where you want to settle, and that's what you call home."

"I couldn't have said it better myself." Horatio took another draw on his cigarette, eyes darting to the side. "What do you have to trade?"

With a blink, Tom lifted the sack hanging from his belt, taking out a plastic bag full of smoked boar. "We killed the animal ourselves and processed the meat. I have four pounds here."

"I'll have a piece first."

Tom obliged, handing him a sliver of reddish meat, tough and fibrous looking. "Here you go."

Horatio popped it into his mouth, chewing slowly at first and then faster, nodding his approval. "Very good, my friend. You've smoked meat a lot?"

"I did it as a hobby when we started our farm, but this is the first time I've done it in a while. Glad you like it."

"What else do you have?" Horatio nodded at Tom's bag of things like he was Santa Claus with a sack of toys. "If I were to look away and let you cross, I could lose my job, so I would need something else as payment. I'm sure you understand."

"Yes, of course. Well, I've got this handy water straw filter." Tom pulled out a thin box they'd gotten from the Tennessee couple and handed it to him, not expecting to impress him at all. "This has never been used, and I'm sure it would be valuable if something happened to the water supply here."

Horatio stared at the straw with a gleam in his eye. "May I?"

Tom handed it over. "Yes, of course."

Opening it, he looked inside, pulling the filter out a couple of inches to check it. "The sewage system in our neighborhood has never been the best, and it's bound to degrade even worse now. Many of us worry about bacteria and disease."

"Well, there you go! This would come in handy. Do we have a deal?"

Horatio stared at the straw for a long moment, peering at the incoming ship as it crept toward the locks, then shifting his gaze to an armored vehicle sitting between the two camps, marked with the emblem of the Panamanian Defense Forces. For a second, Tom thought he might give the straw filter back or even shout for a guard, but he pushed the filter back inside, closed the box top, and stuck it in his pocket. Holding out his hand, he said, "Now the smoked meat."

"Of course." Tom gave him the whole bag.

Horatio stuffed the items inside his shirt and buttoned himself up. "That boat will pull up to the first lock within the hour. Bring your family to the fence, and when you hear the bell, climb over and run to the floodgate. The gates slide open on this side, so be quick. Once it opens, anyone trying to stop you will have to go to the next lock. That will give you a head start."

"If someone tries to cross on another floodgate, can you make sure those come open so they can't follow?"

"That will be much harder to hide."

"But that's what I need you to do."

With a pause and finally a head shake, Horatio started to hand back the straw filter.

"I've got a second straw filter," Tom added hastily, opening the sack and showing him another one along with a magazine of 9 mm rounds and snacks he'd thrown in.

Horatio's frown deepened, and he pulled back slightly.

"Come on, man," Tom said. "This is *two* straw filters. That's a lot of clean water for you and your wife. All you have to do is look the other way and keep anyone from following us. It shouldn't be too hard to do. If they question you, just tell them you screwed up or something and accidentally opened the other gates. Please. Can you try?"

"I've been doing this a long time, and they won't believe me."

"Tell them you're *sick*…" Tom replied in a rush. "You mentioned there were some questions about the water. It's dirty, right? Tell them you were sick and hit the wrong button or something."

"I've not been feeling so well lately," the man said with a terse nod, sweat beading on his brow. "That would probably work if I *must* make an excuse."

"There you go." Tom drew out the straw filter a little more. "Do we have a deal?"

After a long pause, Horatio nodded, and Tom handed it over to seal their bargain. "Thanks, man."

"Gather your family," he said as he stuffed the second straw filter in his other pocket. "Come here to the fence. After the bell goes off and you climb over, keep running. None of the workers are armed with weapons, so don't worry about being shot, but I won't be able to help you once you're on the other side of the lock. Someone might try to stop you there."

"I'll deal with that when the time comes."

"Okay, my friend," Horatio nodded, tossing his cigarette down and rubbing it out with the toe of his shoe. "I must get back to work now, but good luck. I will do everything I can to ensure you reach the other side."

"Thank you," Tom replied, shaking the man's hand before turning and rushing away.

At the picnic area, Sam saw him coming and stood from where she was playing with Smooch, the dog rolling around on her back, rubbing her healing stab wound against the rough grass to scratch it. Linda got up, too, the pair side-by-side, Sam's curly hair next to Linda's thicker mane.

"What is it, Dad?" Sam asked. "Is somebody onto us?"

"No, but I found a way to get us across, and we've got to get ready to go." Looking down at Barbara, he gave her a questioning look. "Can you climb a fence?"

"With a little help," she replied, raising into a seated position, holding her hands out for the girls to take.

Together, they put everything in the backpacks, tucking the spare clothing atop the food and water, heavier items on the bottom, softer ones placed between them. Once done, they folded the picnic blanket and stuffed it inside Tom's bigger backpack, and with a nervous sigh, Tom shouldered both his and Barbara's packs and waited for the others to get theirs on.

"What's the plan?" Barbara asked.

"Follow me." Tom locked arms with her, the kids crowding in around them, Jack's hand slipping into hers on the other side, while Sam and Linda went a little ahead with Smooch.

"Just walk over to the side of the control house," Tom directed them. "Yep, that's right. That way."

The McKnights reached the back corner, and Jack saw the other refugees gathered at the fence, the father and son still there along with a couple of families who were looking off to the right where the second cargo vessel was cruising closer. It was thirteen-hundred feet long and a hundred and ninety-seven feet wide, its profile flat on the canal, shipping containers stacked eight or nine high as it loomed over them, casting a massive shadow across the surface of the water. The military boats turned and sped off as the tugs took over, the train crews jogging out on the wharf to greet it.

"What are those little train cars doing?" Jack asked, pulling on Barbara's hand to get closer, finally releasing her to trot ahead.

"Workers on the big boats toss down ropes and chains to the workers below, and they connect them up to the trains to help guide the ships in."

"Oh, wow!" Jack exclaimed, skipping to a free spot along the fence, throwing himself against it. The families standing around smiled and gave the McKnights room as they came up.

"Thanks," Tom told them as Sam and Linda joined Jack at the fence, Barbara behind them with a hand on each girl's shoulder.

Barbara nodded at the black chain link. "Is this the fence we have to climb?"

Tom nodded. "Yes. When we do this, I'll climb first, followed by Jack. You girls hand me the backpacks and then help your mother over. I'll be on this side to catch her. How does that sound?"

"How do we know when to go, honey?" Barbara asked, smiling as her eyes darted across the locks and then slipped toward the massive ship approaching.

"It won't be long... probably within the next fifteen minutes. We'll know it's time to go when the bell rings for the first floodgate to open. That's when we make our move. The gate will open on this side and slide to the other end." Tom held his hand out and made a pushing motion away from him. "We need to get there before the bridge separates, got it?"

"I don't see any guards."

"The guy I talked to—the guy who's going to help us—said there're no guards, but everyone's on edge. Still, we should be able to get across without being followed. He'll open the other floodgates if they do."

"And we can trust him?"

"I don't know." Tom shrugged. "I guess we'll have to have a little faith in humanity."

Several nervous minutes passed, the big cargo ship slipping closer, its bow reaching the end of the long dock, the tugs nudging them in. Chains clanked, and the trains were connected up. A man in yellow coveralls cross-walked toward them, hands waving to someone in the control house who was communicating with the ship's captain.

Tom swallowed hard, gazing out toward the floodgate, gauging the sprint to get there, noting no other dockworkers around except for some guys way off at the end of the lock, busy with mechanisms and switches. "Get ready. It has to be soon... within the next few minutes. Kids take you packs off."

Smiling at the couple to his left, who kept glancing in their direction, Tom let his backpacks slide off his shoulders and prepared to toss them over ahead of them. Then it was a waiting game, the dark waters lapping at the shore, birds darting through the sky, the mysterious grinding and clicking noises under their feet as the lock started to open. Someone shouted, sending Tom's heart leaping into his throat until he realized it was just two workers waving at each other across the channel. Fist clenched atop the fence, backpack straps resting on his thumbs, Tom counted the seconds with deep breaths, calming himself against what they were about to do. The cargo ship had become a monolith in the water, its dark shape looming above them, and he leaned forward to ask the kids if they were ready, when a heavy bell rang out, its clanging resonating across the lock and causing Linda to jump. Several refugees made awe-filled sounds as they pointed to the floodgates, gaping as motors and gears clacked and vibrated in the ground. Tom tossed the backpacks over with heavy thuds, grabbed the rail, and swung his body across. As soon as his boots hit the ground, he seized the packs from Sam and Linda, dropping them next to his in a neat row, catching Jack as he climbed awkwardly, feet clambering, tongue jutting from the corner of his mouth. Tom snatched him off the rail and plopped him down.

"Hey, are we allowed to climb over?" asked a man who'd been standing on their left.

His wife put a hand on his shoulder, looking around him. "Yeah, I didn't think we were allowed to climb over."

"Well, I got special permission from the controller," Tom replied with a terse nod, reaching out for Barbara as she clutched the fence and pulled herself up, a girl on each side, holding the tops of her arms and supporting her back. She got one knee on the rail, but her left boot toe got stuck in the honeycombed mesh.

"Come on, honey," Tom encouraged her. "Just fall toward me and I'll catch you, then you can bring your other foot over and drop."

"I don't think you're allowed to do that," the man said, pressing in with narrowed eyes. "Hey, wait a second!"

Tom shot him a warning look. "Everything's fine. Mind your business."

With a stricken expression, the guy backed away as Tom caught Barbara and placed her down. Sam and Linda were already handing Smooch over, the dog wiggling as Sam held her up, Tom snatching her up and dropping her gently on her paws. The girls were climbing, but the man lunged and grabbed Sam's arm, jerking her down.

"You guys can't do that!" he cried. "It's dangerous—"

Tom flew forward, reached across the fence, and slugged the man in the shoulder, knocking him back two steps. He responded with a surprised cry, grimacing as he rubbed the sore spot, his wife gaping and sputtering in offense. Sam leaped up and threw her legs over in one smooth motion, landing with the rest of the family.

The man's face twisted with pain and fury, eyes watering with tears. "Hey, man! That frigging hurt!"

"I *mean*t it to hurt!" Tom growled.

Before the man could say another word, they were moving toward the floodgates, Jack and Smooch running out ahead as the boy struggled to get his backpack properly situated, Linda reaching and snagging him and helping him shrug it on as they ran. Barbara came next, with Tom and Sam guiding her quickly to the gate. When the ground beneath them rumbled, and the floodgate started to come open, Barbara stiff-armed them off and lurched forward in a jog. "I've got this! I can run!"

"Honey!"

"Go!" she shouted, the words squeezed between clenched teeth.

Jack and Smooch stepped onto the floodgate, murky waters on either side, the lock snapping, the gate breaking away six inches, then a foot. Sam and Linda both made the jump easily enough, Barbara hesitating a second before hurling herself forward, landing on one foot, collapsing into the girls, and Sam somehow turned and caught her before she fell on her face. Tom came down right after her, backpacks rattling on his shoulder, eyes looking toward the other side.

"Come on! Almost there!"

The family shuffled in a half run across the floodgate as it flowed open, dog claws clicking on the metal surface, tiny figures against the massive cargo boat that loomed above them. Its horn blasted the sky like a bellowing bull, the hairs inside Tom's ears quivering, Barbara groaning from the ominous sound. Glancing up, he saw a group of Panamanian soldiers standing at the bow rail, looking down, pointing, a couple of them laughing.

"Almost there!" Tom called out, motioning ahead where the gate met pavement, stopping when they reached the other side so Barbara could step off like it was an escalator.

Tom cast his eyes toward a second smaller control house where three workers stood, watching the McKnights but not making any effort to follow them. Tom ushered his family across a paved courtyard, pointing them to the second lock with thinner floodgates, all of them closed and no boats coming up. They reached the other gate and staggered across it, gasping, hands grasping the flimsier cable railings that bounced and wavered. It was thirty-five yards to the opposite side, their feet pounding past a round control house that resembled a castle tower with gray concrete walls dripping moisture and moss.

"Where to, hon?" Barbara asked, bent over with her hands on her knees. Everyone was breathing hard except Smooch, who was barking and trotting like she wanted to do it again.

Tom pointed to an elevated overpass that crossed a narrow channel of water. Not knowing where it went, he herded them in that direction anyway. "Let's get on that road and see what's on the other side."

"Hola!" someone called, and Tom turned to see the trio of workers strolling over, looking amused.

Stomach curling, he kept the family moving toward the bridge, Barbara walking with much more confidence, only occasionally reaching for someone to keep her upright. It was fifty yards to cross the overpass, and on the other side was a main road surrounded by parking lots and tall administrative buildings, clean with red roofs and beige clay walls. The City of Knowledge, free of refugees and civilians, the warm pavement baking under the sun. The buildings stretched along both sides of the road, forests and more lanes branching out from those, a helicopter flitting over the distant rooftops, heading toward Panama City. By then, they couldn't jog anymore, all of them exhausted, Linda holding her ribs, Smooch with her tongue out and licking her chops. Tom glanced in both directions, tensing at the sight of the military trucks flanking the corner buildings, two old Jeeps with Panamanian symbols marking their sides, four soldiers in each, heavy mounted machine guns perched in back. Their engines were off, and they appeared to be guarding the road leading into the locks, all eyes focused on the McKnights.

"Dad, do you see the soldiers?" Sam asked with a warning note.

"Yeah, I see them, hon." Tom spotted a wooded area dead ahead between the buildings, and he kept them moving in that direction.

"What do we do?"

"Keep walking," he mumbled. "Smile and nod, but don't stare."

They kept going, walking briskly, the girls nodding and smiling, Jack giving a slight wave as he gripped Smooch's leash. Tom held up one hand in a placating gesture, hoping they understood his family was just passing through and were not looking for trouble. A driver elbowed his buddy in the passenger seat and stood, leaning forward over his windshield, shouting something in Spanish, pointing to the east and south, shaking his head with emphasis.

Tom glanced over. "What's he saying, Sam?"

She was watching him, her lips moving with the Spanish words, finally raising her voice until she was speaking them out loud. "… no prote-ccion, no proteccion. *Protection*. He's saying they can't protect us if we keep going this way."

Tom nodded to both groups of guards, showing he understood but was still taking his family into the woods. Crossing the sidewalk, their feet carried them up the shaded yard, disappearing into the trees and the coolness. They found a soft dirt trail and moved deeper, the scents of crisp honeysuckle and pollen drifting beneath their noses, bird cries and animal calls filling the air, the sounds of freedom to Tom.

"We made it across," he said with a weak note of triumph, hands on his knees as he caught his breath. "Let's take a break. Grab something to drink if you need it."

"Where are we going now, Dad?" Jack asked, fixing a small bowl of water for Smooch and placing it on the path, soon followed by the dog's sloppy, lapping tongue.

"I'm not sure," he said, walking up the trail a little way, peering through the dense woods. "Sam, let me see the travel book."

Backpack hitting the ground, Sam pulled it out and opened it to the map of the Central American Provinces, handing it over to Tom as he came back down the trail. "It's about ninety miles from here to the Darien Province," she said, shaking her head helplessly. "Without the Humvee, it'll take forever."

"Okay, so Panama City is directly south of us, and we want to avoid that because of the military presence there. It would make it too easy for Keith to track us down, but the main highway picks up and carries through several towns to there, and I can see there are entrances off the interstate."

"Yeah, a bunch of trails and footbridges," Sam replied, gesturing toward Barbara. "But we can't walk all the way there. It would take us at least three days, and Mom…"

"There are some back roads that will take us most of the way there," he said, but it was still too far, seemingly out of reach. "We'll just need to find another means of transportation, something that can get us there fast. Or… we'll walk if we have to."

"More walking?" Jack asked, swiping his palm across his sweaty brow with a grimace. "Smooch'll never make it."

Linda stepped over to the dog and ruffled her fur as she sat, water dripping from her tongue. "Smooch is just fine, aren't you, girl?"

Smooch barked in reply, tail sweeping back and forth excitedly. Barbara stood straight, wincing, holding her side, lifting her shirt up to show her bandage was leaking blood down her stomach in twin red rivulets. Heart pounding, Tom rushed over, bending with concerned eyes. "Are you okay, honey?"

"I'm fine," she waved him off, gaze shifting to Sam. "Sweetheart, can you change this bandage real quick?" As Sam dug out the medical supplies, Barbara's eyes hardened. "As soon as she's done, we're leaving. It's just a few more hours to our new home. We can make it. We *have* to."

Chapter 11
Rifleman Teddy Barnes
Arauca, Colombia

The short Humvee column worked its way along a dirt track after being dropped off by a light maneuver support vessel on an Arauca River beach. It was a full Marine squad, three armored trucks armed to the hilt, midday sun glinting off their windshield as they readied for action in the nearby city of Arauca. A member of Alpha team, rifleman Private Teddy Barnes—six foot four and skinny as a rail—sat in back as the big knobby wheels bounced over the rough terrain, hitting the edge of the road and launching them high enough to crack his helmet on the roof.

"Geez, Tucker!" Greer shouted. "Can you drive any worse?"

"Shut up," growled the Private.

They rumbled onto the road, straightened out, and raced toward the smoke-filled sky where Arauca was burning from several days of intense street fighting. With Bravo and Charlie team right behind them, they sped toward the explosions and the faint sound of gunfire reaching them through their open windows, dusty wind blasting them in the face along with the flowery jungle green.

The assistant rifleman, Private Greer, sat to Barnes' left, chewing a big wad of gum. "Hey, Sarge, can you remind us what we're doing here?"

"You were debriefed, Marine," Sergeant Ackerson said from the passenger seat, shooting Greer a dark look, but everyone knew Greer only craved the chatter to distract him from the fact that they were driving into a live combat zone, so, he went on. "The Russian and Chinese forces are occupying the oil-rich Arauca region of Colombia, which borders our new home of Venezuela. To keep them from securing critical oil reserves key to their military machine, our illustrious generals have given us the auspicious task of taking the city from them. At the very least, we are to be extremely disruptive. Is that understood?"

"Right, sir." Greer seemed genuinely curious, though he was only pulling the Sergeant's leg. "But since we're shelling the hell out of them from El Amparo to the north, won't that put us in the direct line of friendly fire?"

Ackerson played along. "That is correct, Marine. However, the part of town we're going to isn't currently being shelled, and we'll be allowed to go in and get our boys. We've got one crashed Black Hawk and some stragglers to pick up, six to ten Rangers and Marines, your friends and allies. Is the mission clear to you, Marine?"

"Crystal clear, sir!"

Sweat trickling down his face, Barnes grinned, glad to have the banter, wiping the dust off his M4 carbine instead of looking up past the Sergeant to the deathtrap they were about to enter. He was chest-busting proud to be going to help his fellow Marines, but there was no escaping the swirling in his gut and the nagging headache pounding at the back of his head. All that combined with the lingering sense that he'd never see his family again. Soon after the news of the anomaly reached the world, Barnes had joined the Marines, passed basic training, then gone off on more missions than he could count, from patrolling the streets of Mexico City to helping American refugees in Costa Rica, and finally ending up in Venezuela staring at a list of names on a computer screen hoping to find his family. Mom and Dad, brother and sister, and a few aunts and uncles… all of them made it on a ferry and settled into temporary housing outside Caracas. The Sergeant had been kind enough to let him visit for two days before sending Greer to fetch him off the little tract of land his father was trying to farm. A day later, he was in a Humvee, rolling down the road with the same boys he'd been with since he started.

"You okay back there, Barnes?" Ackerson asked.

"Oorah, sir," he replied.

"It's just that you get quiet sometimes, son, and it's hard to read you."

"He's shy, sir," Greer snickered.

Barnes' gaze lifted to the encroaching scene, the Humvee slipping along the road, past small tracts of farmland and patches of jungle, always coming out to the same view of the smoke-filled sky and burning buildings, only closer each time.

"He's just nervous," Tucker said. "He doesn't have an empty head like Greer back there, which comes with the benefit of not being able to be afraid."

"Up yours," Greer laughed, ducking and checking his duffel full of ammunition as he had been chosen by the Sergeant to assist the automatic rifleman because he was stocky and could haul the extra ammo for miles without complaint.

Reaching the city outskirts, Tucker wove between burned out husks of vehicles with their insides still smoldering from direct missile hits or fifty caliber gunfire. Potholes and cracks caused the Humvee to swerve, though it was impossible to miss everything, and they bounced against something hard, and Barnes was rocked upward again, knocking his helmet against the roof.

"What's your feeling about IEDs, sir?" Tucker asked, where he leaned over the wheel. "Being our first real fight down here, can we expect the road to be booby-trapped? What should we look for?"

"The Russians and Chinese just got here a few days ago," Ackerson replied. "I doubt they would've had time to tee up too many surprises for us. We'll have enough to worry about with them shooting at us from the rubble."

"Oh, that makes me feel a lot better, sir," Greer said, chomping the wad in his mouth. "I guess we should--"

They'd just come to a cluster of buildings on the outskirts of town, bicycles and wood and other debris scattered through the street, when the lower floors lit up with flashes of orange from both directions as slugs ripped into the Humvees' armored sides, bouncing off the bullet resistant glass. Divots and hairline fractures stitched a violent pattern in front of his face, sending him wincing away. Tucker punched the gas pedal and the Humvee rocketed ahead, Bravo and Charlie teams keeping right behind them in a roar of diesel engines and smoke, racing along the country road chased by gunfire.

"That was close," Tucker scoffed.

"They were just saying hi," Greer snickered from the back, shifting some of his gear around and pulling the whole duffel into his lap.

Ackerson was slouched in the passenger seat, a map spread out in his lap, looking from it to the road ahead and up through gaps in the trees to spot the taller apartments and office buildings. "The chopper is five blocks down and two blocks to the right of the Mobile One gas station."

"What are the street names?" Tucker asked.

"Don't worry about it," Ackerson replied. "You can't pronounce them, anyway. Just turn when I say turn, okay?"

"Oorah, sir."

They were entering a residential area, farms and trailers spread out in rough lines, city residents fleeing in groups of twenty or fifty through the fields to the south, wearing sandals, jeans, raggedy T-shirts, carrying their remaining possessions with them. Barnes spotted a brown-skinned man slapping the backside of a mule, the beast dragging a wobbly cart over the rough, grassy field.

"Seems almost too easy, sir," Greer said.

"Yep," Ackerson replied. "Don't expect it on the way out, son."

The Humvee reached a three-way branch in the road and took a soft left, running parallel to the Arauca River. The road was filled with debris and dry brush, and every time they ran over something Barnes clenched up, thinking of all the stories of Humvees with their bottoms blown out by IEDs and Marines sprayed all over the insides. Once over the deadwood and junk, he relaxed until the next enemy attack, which came from a pair of Russians in a corner house, a brief spattering of rounds barely denting their armor, leaving him sucking air between his teeth.

"All right, Greer," Ackerson said. "Get up in the turret. Let's give them a how-do-you-do of our own."

"With extreme pleasure, sir."

Greer threw the roof hatch open with a wide grin and climbed up as the Sergeant called back to the other trucks to do the same, and soon the Humvees were spitting fifty caliber gunfire to both sides, chewing up brick walls, shattering house windows, leaving a trail of dust and ducking figures behind them.

"Nice shooting, Greer," Ackerson called as the tracers sliced up a row of brush and scraggly trees, the Humvee plowing through a cool bank of shade before bursting into the bright sunlight.

They zipped past an old park with rusted swing sets and monkey bars, a group of civilians sprinting toward the river throwing frightened glances back at the Marines as they sped by. A block later, the road was jammed with vehicles with flat tires, freshly cut trees and brush tossed on top and Russians and Chinese firing from the gaps right into their faces from about thirty yards away.

"Two more streets up," Ackerson called, pointing off to the left as they entered a debris-strewn battlefield, brick-and-mortar spilled into the street, windows shot out and seeping smoke, gaping holes in the walls, leaving dust tendrils to trickle the sidewalk.

"Where?" Tucker asked, face pressed forward as he clung to the wheel.

"Past this street… watch out!" The Sergeant was pointing the other way to avoid hitting a blasted hulk of a van with all its doors flung wide and black smoke rolling out. The Humvee swung around to miss the wreck, front right tires bumping over a pile of stones and sending Barnes' helmet cracking against the roof again, the tall Marine groaning and hunching over.

Once they'd straightened, the Sergeant continued in a calmer tone. "Okay… one more street…. Go left!"

Tucker was already whipping the wheel in the indicated direction, tires skidding across the dirt as they sent up a cloud of smoke to billow up the front of a three-story apartment, a barrage of enemy gunfire pouring down on their heads. Greer cursed as rounds peppered the Humvee roof with *plinks*, bouncing off the shielding on his machine gun as he ducked and sprayed bullets across the building's top floor.

"Two more blocks!" Ackerson called.

"I thought you said we'd be there by now, sir!" Tucker replied, tight-chested, hands clenching the steering wheel like there was no tomorrow.

"Just keep driving, Marine!"

Barnes held his carbine in his left hand, the door handle in his right, eyes sweeping upward below his helmet rim, staring into the soulless black windows at the flashes of movement and fluttering curtains. Swallowing hard, he remembered his training, though it was easier said than done with bullets raining on their heads as they flinched inwardly at each ping and ricochet, ready to duck every time they came to an intersection. At the Sergeant's direction, Tucker steered the Humvee into an alley between buildings, swung right onto a side street, and whipped left again, entering an empty parking garage covered in graffiti and garbage. The short column of armored vehicles moved up a ramp, turned into the lot, and pulled back down to the entrance.

"This is good right here," Ackerson said, raising his radio and talking to everyone at once. "Charlie team, you'll stay here with the trucks. You've got a roof over your head, so watch the entry and exits and terminate with extreme prejudice anyone wearing a Russian or Chinese uniform. Alpha and Bravo teams, with me."

On cue, Barnes stepped into the heat, which was still cooler than inside the Humvee, a breeze blowing up the ramp to dry his sweaty face. He strode to the end of the ramp and crouched, keeping his right shoulder pressed against a short concrete wall, looking both ways with narrowed eyes. A round shattered the stone, kicking up rock shards that sprayed off his helmet, and he immediately shifted in the direction it had come from and fired at a distant window where he thought he'd seen a flash of light.

"Easy on the ammo, Barnes," Ackerson said, creeping up with Tucker and Greer behind him with Bravo team pulling up the rear. "Okay, men. We'll cross to the southeast corner and then make our way to the next block. Our friends should be on the top floor of a grayish building with a bunch of murals drawn on the side. We can't miss it, they said."

Barnes nodded as he looked across the debris-strewn street, clutching at a mental image of his father standing in a field somewhere in Northern Venezuela, laughing with his mother as they tried to get something to grow. Pushing that thought aside, he focused on the bullet-ridden cars, bricks and cement spilled into the street, a flutter of paper and garbage skittering by. Ducking, he looked under the vehicles to spy any Russian or Chinese feet, and when Ackerson ordered him to go, he leaped from behind the wall and sprinted northeast to the next bit of cover, a delivery truck sitting on busted tires, a strip of bullet holes stitching it up the middle right through the windshield, making a perforated seam from front to back. Shoulders flat against the side fender, Barnes slid to the rear corner, peeked around, and gazed across to the nearest building and its chewed-up brick and mortar, assessing the threat and searching for a place to shoulder down.

"In twos!" he yelled over his shoulder. "Come on!"

When Bravo team reached the delivery truck, Barnes sidled to the rear and dashed in a continued northeasterly direction across the street with Greer on his heels, running to the corner where a bomb had blown a three-foot-deep hole in the dirt, knocking over a tree and flipping a bench in a scattering of metal framing. He and Greer hit the wall with their shoulders pressed against it, scooting to the edge, Barnes peering around to the east to find the next rally spot, figuring they could duck into one of the many holes in the wall if anyone shot at them. A few streets off to the north, a Russian APC rolled by, heading west, and he waited to see if they'd return. When they didn't, he turned back to wave the Sergeant and the rest of the men over.

Ackerson and Tucker jogged across the street, packs bouncing on their backs, Tucker with the big M249 rifle swinging with its bipod hanging off the end of the barrel. While they were running, Barnes was peering around the edge eastward into another garbage-strewn lane, covered in a cloud of smoke, the buildings close and crowded in on both sides, old brick apartments with their corners blasted off, thick debris clogging the roadway, glints of light flashing in the upper windows through the haze.

He turned to the Sergeant. "Sir, I can't see much of anything. The smoke is thick…"

"Can we use it as cover?"

"Probably. But if the smoke clears at any point, we'll be sitting ducks. I'll be flying by the seat of my pants."

Pressed to the wall, face glistening with sweat, the Sergeant calmly nodded. "We'll follow with staggered spacing. Get on it, Marine."

"Oorah, sir." Barnes slipped around the corner, sliding against the rough brick, moving east as he watched for breaks in the smoke, boots clipping fallen garbage and popping pieces of glass.

Swallowing spit, he kept moving and breathing, ignoring the sweat trickling down his face. Tucker and Greer were shadows to his left as smoke billowed up the walls, carrying dust and a burning reek that stung his sinuses. Parts of the sidewalk were just wooden planks, sometimes gravel or cracked and crumbled pavement, unable to bear the weight of the armored trucks that had been driving by.

Barnes caught movement in a window across the street to the north, and he turned and scooted backward through a doorway with a chewed-up frame, his head banging against the top, rifle barrel striking the brick as he plunged awkwardly inside. Machine-gun rounds smacked the walls and whizzed into the room as the other Marines filed in quickly behind him, cursing and ducking. Barnes was already shuffling east inside the building, finding a window about twenty feet down, throwing his gun across the sill, firing a burst through the haze to cover the incoming Marines. Then he was moving east again, navigating the old warehouse guts with its big metal tables, bins of textiles everywhere, and rolls of cloth. Rows of sewing machines were tipped over or skewed, all of it layered in dust and cotton lint.

Barnes met a wall and stepped through a second door into the same street, falling to his knees by a spill of brick with an entire window frame buried in it, curtains caught and drifting on the wind. A cloud of dust from all the shooting billowed from the west toward him, obscuring his view, nothing but shadows moving through the haze. Crouched there before the empty pane, he peered across the street to the other building, looking for the enemy soldiers who'd shot at them, alerted by boots crunching on glass. Finger on the trigger, he paused, uncertain if it was friend or foe, shifting as Greer and Tucker settled in beside him. With his M249 bipod resting on the bricks, the Marine pressed his shoulders over the sights, measuring the flitting shapes with narrowed eyes. He fired a long burst—*thip thip*—peppering the mist with heavy rounds, drawing screams and a gurgling groan from the darkness. Barnes hovered in anticipation, jaw grinding at the thought that Tucker had fired on his own men, followed by relief when a Russian soldier staggered from the mist and pitched face first in the dirt, squirming for a moment, squeezing his neck until he went still.

Return fire hit the brick pile in front of him, spitting dust and chips into his face and he fell forward, crawling over the rubble to the far-right end where he squinted and responded with his carbine, catching a shadow and swinging to fire at it, his rounds landing on a charging shape, punching the soldier back, the man's weapon raising, bullets spraying the building behind Barnes. The other Marines joined in, a barrage of gunfire to clear the lane, the amount of rounds cutting up the haze and leaving the road full of writhing bodies.

With the Marines firing from their defensive positions, Barnes peered east down a long block looking for the next piece of cover. Buildings showed through the drifting smoke and at the far end he spied a single grayish wall of brick, almost dark blue with part of a mural captured on the side. But at the end of his street stretched a double-walled barricade of old cars, furniture and trash from north to south, blocking the way to their target. Enemy shadows moved behind the barricade, firing up at the Rangers on the higher floors of the building. The enemy soldiers hadn't noticed Barnes and his comrades yet, though, giving him a few precious seconds to find a way through.

The machine gun fire slowed down, and Sergeant Ackerson knelt next to him, adjusting his helmet and staying low behind the tumble of brick. "What do you think?"

With a long arm, Barnes pointed east. "Enemy's right there, sir. End of the block. But I say we cross the street, climb through some windows, and make our way east *inside* the building. Maybe we can ambush them."

"The enemy just came from where you're indicating."

"That's right, sir. But they gave up their defensive positions to take us out, and lost. Right now, the enemy soldiers at the barricades don't know who won. Once they figure that out, we'll be pinned down. I say we get to them first."

The Sergeant hesitated for a few seconds before nodding at Barnes. "Lead on, Marine."

Barnes always trusted his gut feelings, sniffing out trouble long before anyone else, and Ackerson had noticed his skill back in the streets of Mexico when the Marine had consistently warned them about roadside ambushes, citizen terrorists, or dangerous places in the earthquake-torn city they should avoid. That's what had gotten him the position of point man, the team trusting the Marine's instincts almost without question. Bolting from cover, Barnes moved north across the street, staying as low as his gangly form would allow, creeping through the smoke, head on a swivel, looking for an opening inside the building.

A wide window presented itself, crooked and broken beneath the weight of a crumbling foundation, and he put his chest on it and swung his legs over, dropping a little too loudly on the wooden floor. Inside the warehouse was near pitch darkness, thick with dust and oil and gunpowder smoke drifting through holes in the walls big enough for a person to walk through. He kept his rifle trained on the gaps until his Marine buddies slipped in behind him. Once the room was secure, and all the openings covered, he turned around, quickly scanning the countertop, the old cash register, ice cream machines dented and broken, bombed out with their doors flipped down and paper cups littering the floor.

Crossing to the room's east wall, he put his ear against it and whispered. "Sarge, the enemy's right next door. My bet is that the barricade is right off the corner door of whatever store is next to us."

"Can we go through the wall?"

"Maybe."

Nodding, he swung his legs over the counter, carefully putting his boots down and creeping to the rear of the store with his rifle pointed ahead, cursing his awkward height, dirt and sweat mixing to form muddy streaks on his face. In the back storeroom he found a makeshift doorway that had likely been carved through the brick with sledgehammers, the smell of urine thick in the air and the soft sounds of Russian and Chinese accents using stilted English to speak with each other on the other side.

Tucker and Greer circled off to his left where racks of industrial-sized food cans lined the back wall. Ackerson came up and listened quietly to the shifting boots and clacking weapons on the other side. Before the Sergeant could issue an order, someone stepped through the opening, a stocky man with choppy black hair falling across his eyebrows, who didn't see the Marines at first. He was unarmed except for a pistol on his hip, belt loose, hands undoing his zipper as if he'd just come to do his business.

When he finally raised his eyes, there was a flash of recognition and then Tucker blasted him back through the opening with his M249, crimson dollops spurting from the exit wounds in the man's back as he tumbled into the next room. Ackerson stepped toward the hole and chased the dying soldier with a fragmentation grenade, sending a second one through before the first detonated, rocking the walls with explosions. After a third one popped off, he backed away as a thick cloud of dust and a blast of heat and the smell of scorched flesh poured out, everyone turning heads to cough as the building's framework groaned and complained, pieces of the ceiling falling, smacking off their helmets, plumbing exploding in bursts of water.

Giving it five seconds to clear, Barnes charged through with his carbine rattling in his hands, shooting at shadows that shrieked and shouted, wincing as rounds flew back in his direction. To hesitate, to succumb to a moment of fear, would be his undoing so he kept going, plowing through obstacles in the darkness, soft material and thick clouds of dust brushing against his face. When his shoulder plowed into a rack of clothes, he slipped and fell, bringing the whole thing down on his head, chin smacking the floor, jaws snapping as enemy rounds tore through the place where he'd been standing. Climbing from beneath a pile of clothing, he threw the rack aside as shouts and screams echoed out.

Barnes came up behind a counter that was chewed to bits and falling apart, and a doorway to the street let in a spill of light across a half-dozen men writhing in the rubble. The Marines kept spitting rounds, peppering the wounded Russians and Chinese until Ackerson shouted for them to cease fire, leaving one man alive, whimpering and groaning like a baby on the floor of the ruined clothing store. The air thickened with the scent of iron and death, filling Barnes' nostrils, forcing him to push aside the crumbling counter and step over the groaning Russian for some fresh air by the door in the southeast corner which opened to the barricade entrance. Barrel lowered, he peeked outside and saw the narrow barricade passage ran south to the opposite corner, empty but for a dead Russian shot on his way in. The grayish-blue building was directly across the street, itself smoking from several floors, big chunks of it fallen into the street. Scanning to his right, he picked over the shadows, checking the other corner before ducking back inside.

"Sarge, it's clear out here for now, and our target's just across the street. I don't see anyone over there, but I have a feeling—"

"That they're over there waiting for us to cross," Ackerson replied, striding to the corner of the room with his radio as Alpha and Bravo teams stepped all the way in, boots crunching in the rubble as they searched the dead. "Give me a second."

Greer was cursing, limping through the mess with his back stiff, raising his pistol, firing point-blank at the last dying Russian with a single hard *pop.*

"I said cease-fire, Greer!" Ackerson shouted.

"Sorry, sir!"

As they waited, Barnes guarded the door, breathing the semi-fresh air and staring out where the enemy troops had locked themselves down behind a row of junk, big metal cabinets and furniture, stuff dragged outside and piled high. Helicopters chuffed in the distance, machine guns rattling, explosions echoing, armored trucks revving, beeping, and roaring through the streets as other units clashed in desperate fury. The east-running lane was empty of barricades and barriers, but that was enemy territory, and he didn't doubt they were waiting for the Marines to come get their comrades.

Stomach finally settling, wiping the sour look off his face, Barnes turned inside to see the medic from Bravo working on Greer and two Marines with light wounds, the whites of their eyes glowing from their dusty faces, one man nervously punching at his leg. He was a haggard private, having joined the squad during their patrols in Costa Rica after his unit had taken losses in the brief but violent fighting in Mexico. When they locked eyes, Barnes caught his haunted look, and he spun back to the door and searched for enemy combatants in alcoves and dark places across the haze-filled street, thoughts of home tugging at the edges of his mind.

"All right, Marines," Ackerson coughed, stepping away from the corner. "I just spoke with the captain of that crashed bird, and it's buried in the roof of that building across the street. We've got eight service people up there, spread out on the fifth floor. There are Russians and Chinese in the building trying to get up the stairwells at them, which might explain why they were a little thin down here. Oh, and they know we're coming. CENTCOM wants us to get inside the building pronto, and the captain up there has promised a diversion to make our journey easier."

That got nods from the other guys, and Ackerson turned to Barnes. "Marine, you're up again."

With a grim nod, Barnes cleared his head and tried to think of something random, letting his eyes and ears absorb the surroundings out there. Moving away from the door, he stepped over to the east-facing window, glancing up to the fourth floor, seeing nothing suspicious, just more broken glass and black panes like empty eye sockets. A queasy feeling hit him as he scoured the lower windows, and he imagined leading his Marines straight across, hearing the eruption of gunfire and his buddies screaming as enemy soldiers mowed them down. With a discouraged scoff, he walked off, staring at the floor as Ackerson came up.

"What did you see?"

"Nothing… And that's what worries me."

"Give me something, Marine."

"Call up that distraction," Barnes said with a frown, then he moved back to the corner door, gesturing for the guys to get behind him.

"We're not going through the east-facing window?" Greer asked, limping up with his massive ammunition duffel weighing him down.

"We're taking the scenic route. South through the barricade, then east again. We'll enter the target from the side. Trust me. Stay low."

"I'm not getting any lower than this," Greer said, standing stiff, his dirty blonde hair sticking out from his crooked helmet.

"Then you're going to get shot."

"Everyone, stay low," Ackerson repeated, "and follow Barnes."

A moment later, the distraction started with Rangers shooting inside the building, and Ackerson slapped Barnes on the shoulder. "Go, Marine!"

Leaping out, he ducked and sprinted between the two walls of the barricade, moving south, stepping over bags of rations and water, backpacks and weapons the Russians and Chinese had left when they'd charged inside. At the opposite corner, he glanced back to see Alpha and Bravo teams following close, so he gripped his rifle tight and ran east to the next corner, head swiveling, looking for enemy soldiers. Now to the north, the gray-blue building and its mural of playing children loomed above them, and as Barnes left cover and sprinted toward it, two Russians shot at them from behind a car farther east.

The trailing members of Bravo team took the hits, one falling to his belly, squirming, rifle raised and firing back. A pair of riflemen went to their aid and shot at the Russians, driving them backward, killing them with barks of pain and twisted grimaces. Without waiting for the teams to catch up, Barnes reached the other side, where the mural of brown-skinned children playing towered over them. More enemy units poured into the street from the east, firing as he stopped behind two broken-down vans, followed by the rest of Alpha team, and the Bravo group bringing their wounded with them. Bullets slammed the metal and pinged off the ground in ricochets of dust, but they'd all made it alive.

With all of them gathered, Barnes dashed toward an open side door, leading with his rifle, stepping into the musty shadows of an old hallway. The tile floor was buckled, and cracks lined the walls, dust trickling down as a firefight raged above, punctuated by the blast of a fragmentation grenade. Stairs led upward into more darkness, and Barnes paused as the fire teams entered behind him. With boots rushing to greet them from down the hall, he split-second decided to climb the stairwell, two steps at a time, rising into uncertainty with sprinkles of light pouring through gaps in the drywall.

At the top of the first landing, a long swath of gray light stretched to greet him from a window on the far side, and shadows stepped from side rooms to tangle the light across the hardwood. Barnes unleashed on them, firing three quick bursts to clear the hall, dropping one man with a scream, the others leaping for cover before he could get them. Tucker was right behind him with the M249, the automatic weapon hammering whoever was left in the hallway, errant rounds striking the walls in a spray of drywall dust and lead, and then he was swinging around the banister and climbing to the next level, eyes up as they moved to the floor above. At the top, Barnes paused, wanting to wait on the rest of the team, who *weren't* coming. Bullets were still flying, Ackerson shouting, a man screaming repeatedly with such raw intensity it sent shivers up his spine. Weapon clenched in his sweaty hands, he peered down a similar hall as the one below, light spilling in from open doorways, swirls of soot, the occasional ricochets glancing up through the thin wood and tile, forcing him to duck back in a guarding position. Boots pounded up the stairs, and Tucker and Greer were there with Ackerson coming up behind them.

"Go ahead, Marine," the Sergeant ordered, then he cut off Barnes' question before he could ask it. "Bravo has two injured, so they're going to guard the stairwell leading down."

Barnes nodded and swung up the next set of stairs, taking it slow and steady, stepping over a dead Russian sprawled on the landing. On the third floor, he flinched at a shadow approaching, though he ducked back before they saw him, resting his right shoulder against the wall to give the men behind him some room. Three Chinese soldiers jogged into view, boots thudding on the old hardwood, glancing down at the last second as Tucker's machine gun chewed them up in a crimson cloud before they fell to the floor in a heap. While Barnes was beyond gagging, beyond the horrors of seeing dead and bleeding men, the red drips from the banister and over the top stair sent his stomach into full revolt, clenching up and spasming, forcing his mouth to lock tight to keep from vomiting.

"You okay, Barnes? You hit?" That was Greer, gripping his shoulder and squeezing.

"No. And no." Barnes rose and stepped into the bloody hallway, over the bodies and up the stairs with the others coming fast behind him. Enemy soldiers rushed from the hall doors, shooting at the Marines as they were rounding the corner, pinning Sergeant Ackerson in a blender of deadly projectiles, their heat billowing up the stairwell. Barnes turned and fired at a downward angle, clipping helmets, shoulders and faces, driving enemy soldiers back momentarily until Tucker swung his SAW around and unleashed a non-stop, withering spray of linked ammunition, clearing the hall in less than fifteen seconds, leaving a stinking cloud of smoke hanging in the air.

The three soldiers panted in the silence, waiting for another attack, though only a moan from Ackerson broke them from their frozen stares. Barnes flew down the steps, pushing past Tucker and Greer to kneel by the Sergeant's side. The man was covered in blood, shoulder to hip gunshot wounds and a couple in his legs, fatigues smoking, equipment shot to pieces. His left knee was twisted back behind him, looking like he'd come up the stairs and slipped backwards on the Chinese soldiers' blood as the rounds pummeled him. The Sergeant's eyes locked on to Barnes as if he could somehow cling to the young man's life force, gasping and sputtering, grasping the Marine's forearm.

"B... Barnes," he spat blood on his lips.

"I'm here, sir," he replied, throwing a dark glance at Greer. "Give me your first aid kit."

"Screw the first aid, kid. Look at me."

"Yes, sir." Barnes turned his eyes back to his Sergeant, blinking, feeling like a little boy stripped down and afraid, warm and cold clashing inside him to send shivers through his guts. "I'm here, sir."

The man's breathing grew shallower by the second, coming in gasps, eyelids fluttering as he spoke. "G... good... Marine... t-tell... my kid... get a... chaaaa..." The last word was unintelligible, slipping out like a sigh, the Sergeant taking his thoughts to his grave with him. His eyes shifted to the ceiling, staring upward, leaving a final murmur as he died.

The first aid kit appeared over his shoulder in Greer's shaking hand, and Barnes only shook his head and waved it off. "He's gone, guys. They killed Sarge."

Tucker's jaw clenched, and he put his eye to his gun sites, rage building in his chest until he screamed. "Commie bastards! Get your asses out here! You want to shoot at us… I'll give you something to shoot at!" The soldier's continued screams devolved into a series of curses to make a sailor blush before he began firing back and forth across the hallway in a steady stream of rounds, tearing up the walls and stirring up another cloud of smoke, sending Barnes' already raging headache into overdrive.

Standing from their fallen leader, he stepped over a dead Chinese soldier and slapped the Marine's shoulder. "Tucker! Stop!" The rifleman ceased firing, leaving them stewing in stunned silence, breathing dust trickles and scorched clothing, blood and grime.

"What are we going to do?" Tucker slumped.

"We keep it together and finish the mission," Barnes snapped, throat tense around the command. "Next highest rank picks up Sarge's gear. That's you, Greer." When the Marine didn't reply, he looked back to see the man staring at the Sergeant like he was a ghost. "Your next in line, Greer. You've been here the longest, and you're next up for a promotion. Grab his rifle and radio, and let's go. We've got another floor to get up."

Greer shook his head. "Nah. I don't want it. Tucker?"

"What's wrong, man?" Tucker replied, blinking like someone coming out of a daze. "You a coward or something."

Greer came off the stairs, jaw jutting. "I'm not a coward, but I don't want Sarge's job. I never could lead worth a crap, but I can follow better than anyone. Take it, Tucker. It's yours. I'm *giving it* to you."

Tucker swallowed and glanced back at the dead Sergeant, his lifeless eyes locked on the stairs like he could get up and lead them for one last charge. "Same here. I don't want it. Never was good at decision making. Barnes, it's all yours. You've been leading us the whole time, anyway."

"I'm just a private… I just started… I can't…" The hesitancy in his teammates' eyes, the way they stared at Ackerson with hopelessness, stirred him into action, and with a clenched jaw, he stooped and grabbed Ackerson's radio and ammunition pouches. Then he slung his own M4 and took the Sergeant's weapon with its M203 grenade launcher affixed beneath the barrel.

Putting the radio to his lips, he clued-in the team. "Attention Army Rangers, this is Private Teddy Barnes. Sergeant Ackerson has been killed, and I'm resuming Alpha leader responsibilities. Bravo is guarding the second-floor landing, and we're coming up the south-side stairwell. Prepare your wounded for exfil. Give us thirty seconds to clear the way."

"Roger that, Alpha leader," came the reply. "We're ready."

"Let's go," Barnes said with a rasp.

Leading Tucker and Greer to the next floor, he jumped a hole that had been made in the steps, the charred, jagged edges giving him a view of the stairs below, realizing he hadn't seen it before. Putting the mistake past him, he kept climbing, silent boots on old wood creeping up to the fourth floor, running into a barrage of gunfire from enemy units from behind a pile of furniture about halfway to the other side.

"Let it sing," he called to Tucker, rolling aside.

The rifleman came up, lying across the top four steps, dropping the M249 on its bipod and pointing it down the hall. With a two hundred round drum attached, he pumped bullets at the barricade, chewing up bed frames and desks and thick wooden bureaus, filling the passage full of stinging smoke, sending Russians and Chinese diving into side rooms as their cover disintegrated.

"That should do it," Barnes murmured, calling up the stairs. "Come on, Rangers!"

Staggered footballs pounded the steps, two Army riflemen dropping to their knees beside Tucker, though there was no one left to shoot at. The wounded were brought next, tired, bleeding forms with arms slung over shoulders, shrapnel-laced bodies dragging, groaning as they tripped down the stairs. Swinging around the banister, the Rangers moved past the Marines, who continued sending obligatory bursts at the enemy to keep them at bay. Barnes turned and led the way, descending to the third-floor landing, covering the retreating Rangers. With Bravo just below them, the mixed US units exited the apartment through a cloud of dust and smoky haze.

Barnes pushed them hard west across the street, limping and staggering along the side of the building with the children staring down at them, eyes gleeful in the war zone. Reaching the front corner, he ordered cover fire in all directions as the wounded were carried across to the Russian barricade, where they slipped into the corpse-ridden clothing store. Barnes gave them thirty seconds to rest, the thick stone walls keeping out the dangerous barrages as enemy units crept closer, surrounding them. Rounds gnawed at them through the broken window, ricocheting inside, forcing them to abandon the position. After retreating to the ice cream shop, they found another opening to the street and snuck west up the block, crossing to the sewing factory in a haggard line, ducking as gunfire peppered the brick and pavement, half-hearted attempts to stop the withdrawing Marines. When Tucker and Greer fell behind to exchange shots with the Chinese and Russians, Barnes went back for them, grabbing them out of the street, cycling grenades from his M203 east down the smoke-filled lane until the enemy abandoned their position.

Once everyone had entered the sewing factory, he used the holes in the walls to move to the end of the block, Barnes leading, sidestepping as he moved from window-to-window, ducking, flinching, and firing, driving the enemy back long enough for the rest of the troops to slip by behind him. Safely tucked in the last room on the block, he called in an artillery strike on the combat zone and sent everyone over to the delivery truck and parking lot where the Humvees waited. While covering them, he stared up at the lifeless windows, the gaping holes where dangerous enemies hid, a final thought for Sergeant Ackerson where he lay dead on the third floor of an old building in a Colombian town. Then he turned and ran after his men, elbows swinging less than before, his gait smooth as he rejoined the soldiers filing up the ramp to their waiting rides. The Marines got the wounded situated, cramped, bleeding, and sweating inside, hacking on smoke and dust... alive, except for one brave Sergeant. The diesel engines coughed to life, and several tons of rolling armor prepared to move.

With rockets zipping across the sky, pounding the enemy positions, the chipped brick and decimated streets, before getting in on the passenger side and slamming the door shut. Ackerson's map slipped off the dashboard into his lap, and he spread it, glancing over the Sergeant's scribbled notations, tracing the alleys and roads that would take them back to the beach. "All right, Greer. I need you in the turret. Tucker, let's go!"

Chapter 12
Specialist Lance Morales
Panama City, Panama

Horns blared in the hot sun of midday on the outskirts of Panama City as people shouted on the sidewalks, milling between the squeezed tight traffic, exhaust fumes choking the air. Keith in the backseat cursing and swearing as he stared at a squarish device in his hand. They'd been driving for countless hours, leaving the winter behind, ice roads and frost-covered trees giving way to warm winds and sun, passing through Guatemala with its clogged borders, every highway choked with stringent checkpoints. El Salvador had gone by quickly, with beautiful volcanic scenery to the north and ocean views from the byways. Keith wouldn't allow them to stop for a second, pushing them ever south, guided by the handheld device, using it to direct Morales on the old roads and motorways that cut into the wild landscape. They'd driven through Honduras and Nicaragua, crossing several checkpoints, Keith flashing his new ID to get them hurried through.

Finally they reached the lush forests and jungles of Costa Rica, the highway crowded with towering trees and flashes of wildlife like Morales had never seen at any zoo. There were monkeys and wide-winged birds of many shapes and colors along with a sloth hanging upside down from a vine that stretched overhead, perfectly still as it stared at them. On one stretch of highway, a herd of what looked like large cats with long snouts and ringed tails snuffled around, hunting for insects, scattering when the Humvee flew up. Keith had gotten angry, yelling at Morales for slowing down, giving him an earful when he replied that he wanted to avoid hitting the animals.

And as they approached what he hoped was their last stretch, Panama's capital city, Morales looked at Smith for help, but the Lieutenant just shook his head and turned to the window, watching the crowds. Traffic picked up, and he was able to pull ahead, shooting a gap to the right and hitting an open stretch of highway. They drove through Guadalupe and San Vernaldino, passing signs written in English and Spanish, though he wasn't using them, instead going by what Keith told him, the man snapping commands from the back seat as he checked the coordinates on his device.

"Where are we?" Keith asked. "Highway 1?"

"No. You didn't tell us to take that turn. We're still on Highway 4."

"You should have gotten on Highway 1," he uttered, gesturing at the signs they were passing. "That's for American military and refugees... we'd already be there by now if you'd paid attention."

"You didn't tell him to turn," Smith said with a scowl.

Keith pointed ahead and to the right where cars were moving in a loose line. "Go that way! Shoot the gap! We need to get around this traffic."

"That would put me on the sidewalk," Morales said. "There are people there."

Keith swung himself between the seats, snatching the wheel, jerking it out of Morales' hands to send the Humvee jumping to the next lane, clipping a vehicle behind them with a crash and a screech of tires. Someone cursed them, and the person whose vehicle they'd hit thrust their arm from the window, flipping them the bird while people on the sidewalk scattered with shrieks and dirty looks.

"All right, man!" Morales snapped, grabbing the wheel back and slamming on the brakes before he took out a group walking ahead, jerking the vehicle to a halt in a squeal of tires and shivering suspension. He laid on his horn and pushed the Humvee forward, popping onto the sidewalk and causing more of the crowd to part. For each of those shaking their fists or shouting at them, Lieutenant Smith raised his rifle to display the weapon through his window, his hard expression proving his willingness to use it.

"Yes, that's it!" Keith leaned between the seats with a leer.

Morales pushed forward in fits and starts, bleating his horn, working his way through the traffic snarl and rejoining the road before hitting the gas and rocketing them ahead. They moved quickly after that, Keith directing them to a junction that took them up to Highway 1 where the lanes opened up for them, although crowds of people still gathered in massive clusters on corners blocked off by local police and Panamanian forces.

"Keep following the highway here," Keith said, staring at his device. "Now... to the right. Turn right here, Morales!"

"I am!" The Humvee pulled off the highway and onto a gravel track, the suspension bouncing them in their seats, clouds of dust rising from the tires of the cars in front of them.

"Okay, keep going." Slapping his palm on the back of Smith's seat, he barked. "Go!"

"We can't go any farther," the Lieutenant said as they came to a full stop.

"What do you mean?" Keith's growled as he looked up, his eyes going wide as he stared over a massive impound lot, rows upon rows of vehicles of all kinds lined up for miles in all directions. Cars, vans, and semi-trailers reached to the distant treeline and filled every conceivable square acre of land. There were delivery trucks, busses, coupes, and SUVs, brand new and old, all of them covered with a layer of dust, the windows scrawled on by passing refugees.

Repent!

Terry loves Ricky (with a heart shape).

Wash me (with a smiley face).

"I mean, we can't go any farther," Morales said, nodding forward, speechless as the midday sun glinted off metal rooftops for miles. "Literally."

Off to the right of the parking lot was a herd of people moving along a highway heading east, sweeping past large green medical tents, groups of soldiers and Marines posted as guards or assisting injured refugees. A pickup truck pulled in next to them, a half dozen Americans hopping out of the back, the driver and another woman exiting to stand around with the same perplexed expression Keith wore.

"This can't be the end of the road," the agent said, throwing the rear door open and hopping out.

A dozen dusty soldiers and Marines were striding up, armed with just pistols, their sleeves rolled up, shirts sweat-stained around their necks and armpits. They moved toward the pickup, pointing and giving orders for the occupants to hand over the keys, to get out and take one suitcase of personal possessions. The Marines broke off and intercepted Keith as he walked up, gesticulating at the wide sea of vehicles and then at the Humvee. The Marines stood with their hands on their hips, listening intently but tiredly, exhausted faces trying to remain stoic amidst the crush of people as new vehicles pulled in.

"Think we should get out and help him?" Morales asked.

"Before he gets himself shot?" The Lieutenant shifted in his seat. "I'll take a wait-and-see approach on that."

"Come on," Morales said, rolling his eyes and popping his door. "Banks will have our heads if anything happens to him."

The pair got out and circled to the front of the vehicle as Keith was trying to slip past the Marines, two of them stepping in to bar his way while the Sergeant spoke to him.

"Sir, we can't let anyone into the lot, for security reasons," the leader said. "I'm sure you understand."

Keith edged to the left, sizing up the two burly Marines blocking him as if deciding whether he could take them in a fight. "We need to get inside for a minute and check one vehicle."

"Sorry, Sir. No can do."

Danger gleamed in Keith's eyes, and his chest swelled in a way Morales was used to seeing whenever the guy was about to explode, and he knew it was best to cut it off before that happened. He stepped in with a salute to the Marine Sergeant and a nod to his men, motioning to Smith as he walked up.

"I'm Specialist Lance Morales," he replied, "and this is Lieutenant Smith."

"What can I do for you?"

"Just hoping you fellas could let us in to track down a truck we followed here from Mexico."

"It's a direct order from Lieutenant Colonel Banks," Keith said, taking out his ID and flashing it.

"Your credentials don't work here, sir," the Marine Sergeant replied. "We're under orders not to let anyone in."

"I promise we won't tamper with anything or try to take anything off site," Morales added. "We just have to verify something. Please, sir."

The Sergeant's eyes shifted across them, his gaze lingering on Smith, who kept one hand resting on his slung rifle, looking disinterested. "I'm under express orders not to let anyone into the lot, and refugees are to be guided directly to the camps to await a ferry ride to the other side."

"Can you make an exception, sir?" Morales asked, his eyes pleading with the man in what he hoped was a shared sentiment. *I've got a pain-in-the-ass officer I'm dealing with, so can you help me out so I can get this guy off my case?* "We'd really appreciate it."

"What he said," Keith jerked his bandaged thumb at Morales.

Finally, the Sergeant stepped aside and motioned for the other two to do the same. "You've got an hour, but that's it. Go ahead."

Keith bolted straight through, but Morales paused, "Thanks, fellas. We'll be out of your hair shortly."

Smith and Morales followed Keith as he waded into the thick sprawl of vehicles, hopping on the hood of a red sedan and leaping to a brown Honda Civic. Morales shrugged at Smith and jumped up, boots buckling the metal and kicking up clouds of dust as they ran to catch up.

"Look how close these are parked," Morales said. "You can't even walk between them."

"Yeah, they pulled them bumper-to-bumper and side-by-side," the Lieutenant replied, "and then they climbed out through the windows."

Morales leaped onto a silver BMW, wincing as he stomped across the expensive car's hood. "Saving space, right?"

"Well, when you have what's left of the United States and Mexico population parking here... it's the last parking lot at the end of the world, man."

"It looks that way."

Skipping across the vehicles, they followed Keith as he navigated around larger trucks and vans, stopping, checking his handheld device before moving off in another direction. Oil and gas fumes filled the air as groups of soldiers carried hoses and five-gallon fuel containers, siphoning what was left out of the tanks, other teams going through the vehicles and throwing whatever the owners had left inside into bags.

"Getting closer," Keith announced, his sweaty hair clinging to his temples, wild blue eyes darting everywhere. "There!"

Morales followed his finger and spotted the beat-up beige Humvee they'd seen back at the bazaar, squeezed between a semi-trailer truck and a row of smaller cars. Keith had shot at the family inside, a couple of young girls, a father and mother, and a boy in the rear seat. Wiping his arm across his forehead, giving a heavy sigh, he gave a doubtful look at Smith and pounded over the last dozen vehicles to come up behind the Humvee. Keith climbed down and sat on the hood of a Ford Escape, peering into the Humvee's slanted rear end. Reaching between his legs, he popped the hatch and lifted it high, putting his boots in and sliding inside.

Morales stepped on the SUV's hood, bending down to see. "Looks stripped out to me."

"The soldiers took everything," Smith agreed, nodding at the open fuel port. "Even the gas."

Keith crawled to the front and back again, poking his head out and holding up a small black device the size of a quarter, a single red light flashing in the middle. "This is the tracker," he said breathlessly as he climbed up on the Escape with them, his eyes scanning the sea of vehicles spreading in every direction.

Morales jumped to the next truck over, hands on his hips. "And they're nowhere to be seen."

"Yeah, looks like we lost them, sir," Smith said, glancing toward the flood of humanity making their way east along the highway. "The chances of locating them now would be like finding a needle in a haystack."

"It would be a good idea to head back now," Morales suggested. "Or, if you've got other business here, Smith and I can check in with Captain Johnson and see if he has something for us to do."

"Oh, no," Keith said, stomping across the hood and leaping on the Escape's roof to stand there like a conqueror with his legs apart and gazing eastward. "We're not done yet."

"What do you mean?" Morales asked, his skin crawling with a nervous sweat. "It'll take us years to find them in all this. The family is *gone*. It's a dead end."

"No, it's not," Keith said, pulling out a long device from his pocket that looked like a satellite phone. The agent punched a few buttons on it and put it to his ear, face raised to the sky as if he could see the celestial body he was connecting to. After a moment, he turned away from them, murmuring to the operator on the other end. "That's right. De-activate receiver one."

When he held up the handheld device he'd been using to direct them, Morales leaned closer, watching as the red light blinked out. "What are you doing?"

"Yeah, you got it," Keith told the operator. "Now activate tracker two." There came another pause before he turned to them with a wicked grin, sticking the smaller tracking device in his pocket, then watched as a different light showed up on the handheld. "That's it," he said into his phone. "Tracker two is online."

"There's a second bug?" Smith asked with a confused glance at Morales. "How—"

Keith shook the handheld with a chuckle. "I gave those little brats we hired *two* trackers and told them to toss one in the Humvee and put the other one *on* someone. This works over ultra-long distances, but it can only track a single bug at a time. That's why I had to call in and have them make the switch." Hanging up his phone, he stuffed it in his pocket and punched a few buttons on the handheld. Morales and Smith watched as the black screen cleared and then returned with the new red light superimposed over a miniature map.

"Got them," Keith grinned. "They're across the canal and heading southeast at a good clip. We're back on track, boys! Let's get to the Humvee." He moved with a hop in his step.

"There's no way they're going to let us drive into that mess," Smith said. "And you're in no condition to jog through Panama City."

"We won't be walking. Trust me."

The trio stomped over car hoods, hopped down to the dirt, and jogged to the Humvee parked by the Marines with Keith hobbling on his heels more than actually running, his hips hitching awkwardly, body deteriorating before their eyes. As they came up, the Marine Sergeant broke away from his men and addressed them. "I take it you found what you were looking for?"

"No," Keith replied. "We need to drive into the city. What's the best route to take there?"

"You can't, sir. All vehicular traffic stops here. Anyone wanting into Panama City needs to walk, following the rest of the refugees."

"That's bullshit and you know it," Keith snapped, looking at Highway 4 where it cut away north past the barriers and through the forest. "The military is using that highway in case they need to move quickly, and it'll take me to…" He glanced at his handheld device. "To the Puente Centenario Bridge."

"Centennial Bridge," Morales murmured.

The Marine Sergeant looked at his men, who'd stepped closer and started to surround them. "Again, sir. That's primarily for the Panamanian forces, but we can use it in support of them should they request it." He glanced at their Humvee with its American markings on the sides and stickers on the windows. "They won't let you cross in that."

"We'll see about that," Keith replied, firing a look at Morales, heading toward their truck. "Come on. Let's go."

Smith pursued him. "Hey, man! *Keith!*"

"What?" He'd reached the back door and was about to open it when the Lieutenant caught up with him.

"Are you sure we should be doing this? You heard the Sergeant. We'll be dealing with Panamanians, and we won't have the pull we have here with these Marines. And let me ask you something else. Can you speak Spanish? Because you might need it to get across that bridge."

"Passable, and Morales can help me. Now get in, or I'll make sure Banks hits you with some big fat demerits. Imagine trying to start fresh in Venezuela with black marks on your record." With that, he flung the door open, slipped inside, and slammed it shut.

Mouth gaping, Smith turned to Morales, and for a moment he was certain the soldier wanted to simply walk away, but he only shrugged. "You heard the man. Let's drive a little more."

With a sick feeling in his gut, Morales groaned, got behind the wheel, and pulled the door shut, glancing up at the Marine Sergeant who stood with his arms folded over his chest, glaring as they ignored his advice. He gave the man a helpless shrug and started the truck, buckling himself in, backing out from where he'd nosed in between some other vehicles. Spinning the wheel, he got them on the gravel drive, clinging to the right-hand edge, tires going into the grass as two cars came past them, more American citizens packed in, windows down, sweaty faces staring back at them from inside.

Pulling onto the highway, he turned toward the barriers, the concrete structures topped with orange reflective plastic, green spray paint scrawled across the front, *Panamanian Military Personnel Only*. There were small gaps between them, enough for a person to pass through, so he had to drive to the left-hand side, sweep up into the grass, and go around the far barricade. The suspension bumped and knocked, tossing them in their seats, causing Keith to grunt in pain, which gave Morales a grin of satisfaction. The truck hit the highway with a lurch, all four tires barking on the pavement, and he punched the gas pedal and rocketed them forward, jerking the wheel exaggeratedly to get them straight.

"Easy, asshole," Keith snarled.

"Hey, you want to get there fast—"

Smith cut him off with a glare, and Morales remembered both men outranked him. With no vehicles on the road, Keith leaned between the seats, anxiously watching out the window. "Come on, Morales. Let's go! Pick it up!"

Punching it, he took them to fifty, blasting past the jam packed impound lot which gave way to more trees and a town off to the left with crowds of civilians walking to Panama City. Two miles farther on, he was forced to draw the truck to a halt as a thick line of refugees crossed the road, fences and barriers made of wooden planks funneling them into a single-entry point. Panamanian soldiers in beige uniforms kept the flow tight and compact as they crossed and Keith began to punch the roof of the Humvee in frustration.

Cursing under his breath, Keith nodded ahead, saying, "Push through that line. Blow your horn! Come on!"

Before the lunatic could reach between them and grab the wheel again, Morales pushed the truck forward, palm slamming the horn as he stopped just short of ramming through them. Refugees looked up with weary eyes staring from smudged faces, and they only moved when he edged closer, threatening to hit them with his bumper. A pair of Panamanian guards rushed toward them, waving and shouting, but the crowd had already parted, and Morales pressed through, reaching the other side and punching the gas pedal. The diesel engine growled, hauling them fast along the highway, leaving the refugees and soldiers behind.

"That's it, Morales!" Keith shouted. "Great job."

"You know they'll come after us, right?" Smith shot the agent a hard look. "We're not getting across the bridge without being stopped."

"It's not going to be a problem, Lieutenant. Banks' order is a joint-force order, which means the Panamanians *must* comply. I've got my ID and mission number with me if they need it."

Morales shook his head but kept driving, swinging through a swath of forest with towering trees and a pair of short bridges that crossed trickling streams, finally hitting a straightaway devoid of guards and people. The Humvee flew past a small town and over a rise where the Panama Canal came into view, spanned by the Centennial Bridge. The beautiful structure had a tower on each end, anchoring a single ridge of cables bolstering the roadways. Muddy waters flowed beneath it north of the main lock, and as they watched, a massive cargo vessel cruised under the span, its flatbed over a thousand feet long and two hundred feet wide, stacked high with shipping crates.

"There's the checkpoint!" Keith's voice rose as he stared ahead, his tone more excited by the moment. "Drive on through, Morales."

"Sir, I'm not driving *through* that," he fired back, nodding at the middle of the bridge, slowing his speed as they hit the span, tires buzzing on the lighter pavement. Armored trucks stretched across the roadway, big guns mounted in the beds, a sliver of space for a single vehicle to pass in the center. A handful of soldiers left the line of protection and strode toward them, spreading out with rifles cradled in their arms.

"Just go straight through," Keith ordered, still staring at his device. "Our target has stopped, and they're a few miles up the road. Drive ahead!"

"No, sir," Morales said, stomach turning, unwilling to weave dangerously between the advancing soldiers without hitting one. "Let's stop and show them your orders, then I'll drive through."

Nodding and waving to the troops, he brought the Humvee to a halt and put it in park, dropping his hands into his lap. The approaching soldiers wore ragged uniforms, some with their shirts untucked, messy hair and unshaven chins, carrying older-model rifles and ammunition pouches. A Panamanian Captain came closer, hand resting on the hilt of his weapon. "Turn the vehicle off and step out," he said.

"All right. I'll handle this." Keith popped the back door, climbing out on the left-hand side.

Morales and Smith followed suit, leaving their rifles in the Humvee, the guards directing them to the front of the truck, where they leaned on the warm hood and waited with their arms folded over their chests. The soldiers stood ten yards back, regarding them with tired, wary expressions, though their guns remained pointed at the ground.

Keith argued with the Captain. "Look, I've got orders from Colonel Banks of the US Navy to get across the canal and pursue some dangerous people who just crossed."

"I do not know this person," the Captain said in thickly accented English, his mustache trim and flat, lips barely moving as he spoke. "You must turn the truck around and go back now."

"The United States Government doesn't want these criminals making it to Venezuela. They've kidnapped a family, and they're extremely dangerous. The order is straight from Lieutenant Colonel Banks herself, and she's backed up by the United States-Venezuelan Joint Chiefs. That's the top of the line, buddy, and if you don't want to hear from my superiors, you'd better let me through."

The Captain spread his hands in a helpless gesture. "I'm sorry, but I have my orders, too, and no American soldiers may cross at this point. If you want to cross the canal, you must do it on a ferry."

Keith laughed in the man's face, shaking his head. "I'm not getting on a damn ferry. Go check your joint orders and tell me I'm not allowed to cross. I can make some calls, too, and I'm sure I can get help from our Marines." He nodded back the way they'd come, up Highway 4 where the rest of the US forces were deployed. "You want to deal with them?"

The Captain fixed him with a frosty stare, cold despite the sweat beading on his brow, the rivulets running together and trickling down his face. With a gesture, he called a soldier forward, who pulled a notepad out of his pocket, leaning in to get Keith's ID number off his badge, pen scribbling across the paper.

"Follow us," the Captain said, striding briskly away, motioning for his men to come with him.

"Wait here." Keith chased after the Captain.

Feeling uneasy, Morales took a deep breath and sighed, leaning back against the Humvee's hood, glancing over at the massive cargo ship passing beneath them in the lazy day's warmth. Smith shared his pensive expression, looking at the surrounding soldiers with the uncertainty of a trapped animal.

* * *

Eyes narrowed at the Panamanian Captain's back, Keith followed the two men between two large, armored vehicles, turning left toward a big radio truck with a pair of long, flimsy antennas hanging off the rear, a small dish planted on top. While his fingers and toes radiated pain with every step, Keith was so close to the McKnight's he could see their faces right in front of him, and he imagined their surprised expressions when he walked up to put a pistol to little Linda's head. The moment was at his fingertips, but the Panamanian scrubs were keeping him from his prey because of some stupid order from their degenerate government. And while he didn't want to wait, exhibiting patience for a few more minutes might save him time and effort later. At the very least, it would keep them from being shot at while running McKnight to ground, and as soon as the Captain checked out his order, they'd be right back on track.

Reaching the truck's side door, the man put one foot on the step and turned, saying, "Wait here. We will go inside and verify your order with our commanders."

Keith gave a faint nod, resting his hands on his hips, wincing as the heat-soaked in. The bridge was wide open, with no real protection from the sky, and the massive cargo ship slipped beneath them, its sudden horn blast piercing his ears, squeezing the headache that had settled at the base of his neck hours ago. Taking a deep breath, he let it out slowly, eyeing the soldiers milling around, bored to death with their guard duties. Rifles shouldered, they paced or chatted in small groups, one man removing a pack of cigarettes and passing them to the others, while another pair moved to the bridge rail to watch the ship cruise beneath them,

Shuffling invoices came from the radio truck, and Keith turned, smiling. "As you can see, Captain, my orders are perfectly…" His smile faded when he saw the Captain's expression, grim and dark, head shaking ominously as he motioned at one of the smoking soldiers, who tossed his cigarette and trotted over.

"I don't understand." Keith took a hesitant step back. "What's going on here?"

"I'm sorry, agent, but your authorization from Colonel Banks is invalid."

"That can't be right," he gaped, gut stirring in agitation. "I just received the order a few days ago. Maybe it's taken a while to get approved down here, or there's something messed up in the communication log."

"That's what I thought, and I made a phone call to United States CENTCOM to get to the bottom of it. Turns out your Banks has been marked as AWOL, and so have you. We have orders to hold you until otherwise notified."

Keith scoffed. "Give me a second, and I'll call CENTCOM myself and figure out what the screwup is. I've got some other numbers I can provide off my order papers, but those are back in the Humvee." With an annoyed look, he held up a bandaged finger. "Just one moment, okay? I'll make that call and bring my ID, then you can try again. I'd really hate for you guys to get in trouble for holding an American officer by accident. CENTCOM is unforgiving when it comes to things like that, especially these days. What do you say?"

The Captain glanced at his soldiers, then turned to Keith. "Go make your call. Hurry." The last word came out gruff and condescending, his expression annoyed.

"I'll be right back," Keith said, moving backward with one hand up in placation. "Give me just a second... Thanks!" He turned and almost ran into a soldier standing behind him, but with a murmured apology, Keith circled the man and dashed between the armored vehicles, heading back to their Humvee, Morales and Smith coming off the Humvee's hood when they saw him approach.

"What's going on?" Morales asked. "We okay to pass through?"

"Yeah," Keith said, hobbling toward the driver's side door. "But I'm driving now."

* * *

They'd been betting on the chances the Panamanians would let them through, Morales hoping they'd be denied so they could call off the chase, but when he spotted Keith walking back, fidgety and with a crazed gleam in his eye, he knew it wasn't meant to be.

"What's going on?" Morales hopped off the truck. "We okay to pass through?"

"Yeah," Keith replied shifting direction, heading toward the driver's side door. "But I'm driving now."

"What?" Morales shot Smith a warning look and circled behind Keith. When he got there, the agent whipped open the door, smacking Morales in the knees and forcing him back with an angry grunt.

"Hey, man! What are you doing?"

"Shut up and get in," Keith said, slipping behind the wheel and starting the vehicle. Staring at Smith through the windshield, he called, "Grab this handheld and guide me while I drive." Then he shifted his eyes to Morales. "And *you*... get in back."

A small part of Morales told him to stay put and turn himself in to the Panamanians, because something wasn't right with Keith, but his duty superseded everything, and he finally frowned and popped the rear door, hopping inside. The Lieutenant followed suit, coming around to the passenger side and getting in with Keith's tracker in his lap. The second he shut the door, the gas pedal was punched to the floor, and they shot forward in a squel of rubber. Two Panamanian soldiers jumped aside, diving to the pavement with their weapons flying in the air.

"Hey, man!" Morales shouted. "Be careful! You're going to—"

The Captain and another soldier stepped around an armored truck, stricken with surprise as the Humvee bore down on them, smashing the soldier straight on and clipping the Captain in the side, spinning him away with a shout. The one they'd hit square tumbled over the hood, skull smacking the windshield in a burst of blood, the man's body rolling off the back to hit the pavement with a crunch. Gunfire chased them to the other side of the bridge, bullets ricocheting off the armor with *pings*, two rounds punching through the rear glass, Morales rocking sideways in his seat as Keith laughed and swerved.

At the end of the bridge, they joined the main highway sweeping southeast around toward Panama City. Using the rear seat as protection, Morales peeked over the top, looking back as the soldiers faded from view. With a grimace, he turned and slammed his palm against Keith's seat, rattling the crazed driver with his face locked in a sneer, hands gripping the wheel as they veered.

"Hey!" Morales shouted. "Pull the truck over now, man! Pull it over now or I'll—"

"Shut up! Just shut the hell up!" Keith screamed, spit flying from his lips, half-turning in his seat as he ratcheted their speed up to sixty-five, the vehicle swerving in punctuation with every word. "We've all got our orders, and there's no one who can stop us from capturing this dangerous criminal... Not even the idiots who can't follow commands and who try to interfere with US business. Believe me, the Captain's going to pay as soon as I talk to Banks!"

"Unless he's dead," Smith murmured as he tried to keep himself steady.

"You shut up, too," Keith said, taking one hand off the wheel to jam a finger in Smith's face, causing the truck to swerve harder, tires yelping on the pavement.

"Okay, man... *okay*." Morales held up one hand, feet spread on the floorboard to anchor himself. "Just chill out, dude. You're going to kill us."

After one more swerve, Keith let off the gas, shaking his head like he was coming out of a trance, and the low-geared Humvee ground slower, back under control. "Okay..." he nodded. "Okay, yeah." Wiggling his remaining fingers on the wheel, he relaxed with a deep breath, easing the truck to a solid forty-five miles per hour. "I'm cool. Don't worry guys... I'm right as rain. I won't wreck."

Smith held up the tracker, saying, "You want me to track them on this?"

"Yeah. The red dot is our target, and you'll see the distance and direction parameters hovering above it. Just guide me to them using the map overlay. How many miles are they ahead of us?"

The Lieutenant rotated the tracker, eyes narrowed and fixed over the red dot as he got used to the interface and screen. "I'm showing less than fifteen miles."

"And their heading?"

"Definitely east and south... um... it looks like they're on a smaller highway that runs parallel to this main one. Okay, wait... stay left. That should put us back on the Pan-American Highway, and we can catch them easily after that."

Morales had been looking over Smith's shoulder, watching the device where the red dot was blinking. "We can even get ahead of them," he suggested.

"Good thinking." Keith pointed to his temple. "We can cut them off and set up an ambush. *Yes*. But even if we can't... we're right on them!"

Morales nodded, eyes narrowed at the red dot, which was moving fast and keeping well ahead of them. While he hoped their mission was coming to an end, his insides grew hot and heavy with dread, the madman behind the wheel frightening as he grinned at the road, teeth bared, hands firmly on the steering wheel, the one small saving grace that he wasn't weaving anymore. The Humvee moved swiftly over the empty highway, only a few Panamanian armored vehicles pulled to the side of the road to potentially stand in their way, though none of them seemed aware of the incident at the bridge as they didn't give chase. The truck flew by regular traffic, Keith laughing and grinning at the drivers as they passed.

Smith said, "Looks like they're keeping ahead of us. They must've found a vehicle of some sort."

Keith tapped the steering wheel with his palms. "That's fine. We can catch up with them as soon as we reach the Panama City outskirts."

"Yeah, just follow this highway, and it'll take us all the way around the city and then east through a bunch of small towns."

"Perfect. Settle in, boys. Get some rest. Once we get there, there's going to be hell to pay. No mercy for this guy, got it?"

"So, this guy we're after," Morales said, "he's a pretty bad dude?"

"He and his accomplice are horrible people." Keith nodded. "That poor family they kidnapped... they're really paying the price. Did I tell you there were two young girls with them?"

"Yeah," Morales said with a shallow breath. "You mentioned that earlier. I'm clear there. It's just..." His words trailed off, duty and uncertainty clashing inside him, Smith watching him from the corner of his eye.

"You have a problem with the mission, Morales?"

"No problem with the mission in and of itself."

"Then what is it, Specialist? Are you getting weak? Because if you are, this world's going to be a big wake-up call for you."

Stomach writhing with resentment, Morales' words came out slowly and carefully. "We've seen combat, more than enough to last a lifetime. I'm not weak."

"Then what is it, soldier?"

Bile welled up in Morales' throat, but he swallowed the burning fluid and shook his head, relaxing back in his seat. "Let's just get this mission over with."

Keith returned to driving as Panama City slid by them on the right, Morales watching the city and its rising smoke, a thick haze that hung over everything. The occasional cluster of helicopters lifted off the airfield and headed east, zooming overhead and disappearing over the jungle, and as they moved toward the outskirts, it became clear that the Panamanians wouldn't be hunting them down for what happened at the bridge.

Pulling his phone from his pocket, Keith punched a button and put it to his ear, pausing before a smile alit on his face. "Yeah, it's me. Yes, Morales and Smith are still with me. That's right... McKnight's about to run out of road. We'll have them within a few hours. If you want to meet us, we'll rendezvous where our waypoints merge. I'll send you the feed from my tracker. Yes. See you shortly."

Chapter 13
Tom McKnight
Darien Gap, Panama

A beat-up Ford truck rolled along the Pan-American Highway, the rough road bumping and knocking them around in the pickup bed as they rumbled through the wild, ragged jungle, crossing stone and wooden bridges over murky waters, trees and vines tangled with verdant foliage. They'd left behind all other symbols of civilization long ago, and the last man-made structure had been a lone church with whitewashed slats for siding, chipped and battered by years of rainstorms, the steeple on top with a golden crucifix standing as tall as Linda. The pickup stopped in a squeal of old, poorly-maintained brakes at a small town at the end of the Pan-American Highway, nestled against the sharp curve of Chucunaque River, a green sign marking the place as *Bienvenidos a la Comunidad de Yaviza.*

"Yaviza," Sam said, standing up in the truck bed and grinning at a narrow road stretching into the jungle. Birds flocked from one side of the verdant tangle to the other, sweeping through the higher boughs in a burst of squawking noise.

Tom stood with a groan, put his hands on his hips, and bent backward, then he swung his leg over the tailgate and hopped down. "Okay, kids. Let's go."

Sam and Linda climbed out, tennis shoes hitting the ground, while Tom picked up Smooch and Jack, one at a time, and placed them on the cracked pavement. Jack watched closely as a group of kids wearing bright clothing sprinted past them and hit the trail in bare feet, laughing and shrieking in joy. Before he could run off, Tom had him take Smooch's collar while he turned to help Barbara down, bracing her as she got over the tailgate and dropped to the ground, holding her until she stopped swaying.

"Okay?" he asked.

"Yeah," she said with a breathless sigh.

Tom grabbed Jack's backpack from the truck bed, hung it from his son's left shoulder, and reached in for his and Barbara's packs. Securing those, he made sure the girls had theirs before walking alongside the pickup, placing his hand on the driver's side roof and leaning in with a smile. Inside sat a man with a ruddy appearance, sweaty-dark hair clinging to his forehead and smelling like tobacco smoke.

"Thank you, Javier," he said. "We appreciate the ride."

"Yes... is fine," the driver replied in broken English, giving the family a wave and a big smile. "Take care."

"We will," Tom said, leaning into the dusty, oil-smelling truck cab. "Wow. It's so beautiful out here."

Cheeks smudged with dirt, Javier shook his head, fixing Tom with a grim look. "This is last of nice places. All out there..." he waved his hand in the jungle's general direction. "Very hard. Very... danger. The Gap is no good for Yankee."

With a deep laugh, Tom patted the top of the truck with a dull thump. "Point well taken, Javier. We'll be careful, and maybe see you back here in Yaviza sometime, eh?"

The man's dark scowl faded into a friendly smile as he looked back at Tom. "Maybe, Tom. Good luck, you and your family."

"'To you, too, Javier."

Tom backed away from the truck, and the farmer put it in drive and made a sharp roundabout, giving the horn a toot before rumbling out of sight around a bend in a puff of tailpipe smoke. "Let's go," Tom said, stepping onto the road with a sigh, using one arm to push aside long branches with leaves as wide as his face. As they walked, the sounds of a crowd reached them through the forest din, adults shouting and clapping, children laughing and playing, causing Jack to try to sneak past him with Smooch.

Tom held out his arm and stopped him. "Hold up a second, son. I don't want you getting too far ahead." He looked at each girl in turn. "That goes for you two as well. Everyone stay together, okay?"

"Right, Dad," Linda replied, and Sam gave him a thumbs up.

Turning back to the road, Tom moved ahead, locking arms with Barbara, who was walking easier after recovering from lying in the truck bed for so many hours. The family passed more signs written in English, confirming they were approaching Yaviza, the end of the Pan-American Highway, and the start of Darien National Park. The road led them through a short patch of jungle, Barbara giving a soft gasp as the village spread before them. Locked in the river's elbow, a row of brightly colored shops with deep wooden awnings and old rusted placards stretched ahead of them, beer signs and a few pieces of neon lighting casting pink and blue hues across the dirt lane. At the very end, flanked by more jungle, was a steel bridge spanning the Chucunaque River.

"That's where we're going to go," Tom said, pointing.

"Right now?" Jack asked in a frightened voice.

"Not now," Tom laughed, "but in the next day or two."

A gentle bustle of locals and Americans glanced up as they stepped into a wide-open park around sixty yards square, filled with tufts of scraggly grass and dozens of abandoned vehicles. Off to the right stood a line of dirty scooters chained to a rail, and an old, rusted swing set sat in the center. The nearest building was a two-story tavern with chipped concrete walls on the first floor and faded brown wooden slats on the second. Past that, a cluster of old structures butted against a swath of forest with mist clinging to the treetops and bird calls filling the air. The same group of kids they saw earlier exploded through the street again, ducking into a narrow alley, bringing a smile to Jack's face. The little town sat on a finger of land, surrounded by water on all three sides, grassy slopes reaching to the Chucunaque River, the shores crowded with long motorboats, their drivers congregating there, talking, trading, and sharing meals. Floating in the muck were deadfall drifts that would have clogged parts of the wide waterway if not for the efforts of two small crews dragging the clusters of loose vegetation and brush to the shores.
*****

Stepping into the town proper, Tom turned and checked that the kids were still with them. Linda was helping Jack with Smooch, keeping them herded close even as they wandered past the small shops and restaurants, the scents of exotic cooking drifting past them along with the faint whiff of stale beer and earth as people dumped old water into trenches that ran between the buildings. They passed a small shop boasting wilderness supplies Tom marked as a place to visit before journeying farther south, and in the window were several styles of machetes, locally made, and bundles of rope and canvas bags, compasses, and flashlights.

"We'll check that place out before we go," Tom mentioned. "Hopefully, we have enough supplies left to barter. We had to leave so much back in the Humvee, it makes me sick."

"Don't worry about it, hon. We definitely need to stock up before…." Barbara clutched his arm harder as she wavered, her breaths coming short between words. "Before we venture into the forest. But we've got a little time. Let's just try to chill out."

They passed the largest building yet, with a wide awning and people standing on the second-tier landing, leaning on the rails, holding beers and relaxing. A sign reading *The End Line Hotel and Eatery* hung sideways above the door, and the aroma of cooking fish and vegetables wafted out of a first-floor kitchen in a gust of steam. The floor was sturdy wooden planking covered in dust and grease spatters, and a haggard American couple stepped outside, slouching under the weight of their backpacks, bellies bulging, the man pointing to the steel bridge at the end of the lane as they turned in that direction.

"Whoa!" Sam exclaimed, stopping and tugging on Tom's shirt from behind. "That smells amazing!"

"Yes, it does," agreed Barbara with a smile, leaning harder against him and clutching his arm with both hands, though her grip wasn't as tight as it had been on the trail, and her legs were wobbling.

"Are you okay, honey? You seem a little shaky."

"I'm getting tired," she replied, her smile faltering.

"Well…" Tom looked through the hotel's flimsy screen door where more Americans sat, a young Hispanic woman whipping between them with trays of food and drinks held high while a boy cleaned up a large section in the back corner, wiping off the tables with a soapy rag. "Why don't we go in here and eat?"

Barbara looked inside, smiling wanly. "Babe, we don't have any money."

"That's true, but we can try to barter for food."

"Do we have anything left someone would want?"

"Maybe," Tom said, venturing over and pausing to glance back at Sam. "I'm going to need you here, sweetheart. Can you help me translate?"

"Of course!" Sam grinned and took the door handle, pulling it open and marching right in. "I'm on it, Dad!"

As Linda, Jack, and Smooch followed her, Barbara and Tom shared a look, her eyebrows raising in amusement while his grin widened. Snatching the door handle as it was swinging shut, he bowed his head for her to enter as another mouth-watering blast of steam wafted over them from an inner kitchen. The brisk flavors of spice and something peppery tweaked his nose with a pleasant burn, enticing his stomach to life more than any restaurant he could remember.

"After you, my dear," he said, hand resting in the middle of her back as he guided her inside.

Sam was already working with the waitress, pointing to the corner table, speaking to her in Spanish. The young Hispanic woman caught sight of Smooch and shook her head. "I'm sorry, sir, but you cannot have that dog in here."

Tom grabbed her collar. "I get it… can we—"

Turning sharply, the young woman snapped her fingers in the air, calling for the boy who was bussing tables. "Jose, can you please take…" She looked at Tom with a question in her eyes.

"Her name is Smooch."

"Smooch." The way she said it, her lips puckered in a round O-shape. "Take her out back to play with Rodrigo." Glancing at Tom, she explained. "That is my little brother's puppy. They will be fine together."

"Okay," Tom replied with a smile and a nod.

Jose stopped when he was doing, put his plastic dish bin down, and motioned for Linda to bring the dog with her and follow him through a wide doorway to a back room. Tom leaned in to watch them, peering into another meager dining area and an opening to the backyard with a big metal fan facing outward and pulling air from the hot kitchen to the outside. Out in the dirt yard, old toys were strewn around, and a medium-sized mutt sat on its haunches, watching them and wagging its stubby tail where it was tethered to a tree. The two took Smooch out, introduced her to the smaller dog, and tied her leash to a pole sticking up from the concrete.

The young waitress gestured to the table in the corner, and Tom smiled his thanks and motioned for Barbara to sit first with himself on the end, Sam and Jack opposite her, leaving the end for Linda when she returned. Letting his backpack slide off his shoulder, he swung into a chair, looking around at two other American couples seated nearby, throwing them casual glances but not staring. With a curt nod toward them, Tom turned to say something to the waitress, but Sam was already leaning in and explaining to her in halting Spanish, rubbing her fingers in a money gesture, then pointing at their backpacks. The young woman wore a doubtful expression as she listened, finally holding up a palm to stop Sam, turning, dashing in a flourish of her skirt past a short check-in desk with a single bell and an old gray-haired lady sipping tea.

"What was that all about?" Tom asked.

"I told her we didn't have money," Sam replied, "but we had things to trade."

"Why did she take off like that?"

"No idea. She's--"

The young woman returned with an older version of herself, both women with copper-toned skin and ink black hair tied back in long ponytails, except the girl had a pair of thin braids that hung past her cheeks. Their light skirts brushed against their legs, white blouses glowing in the dimness. The two stopped near the table, the younger woman gesturing to the family, at Sam, and finally at their haggard backpacks.

"This is my Aunt Alia," the girl said. "She runs the place. If you want to barter for a meal, you must speak with her."

The older woman turned to Tom, her English good with a crisp Spanish accent. "Sophia says you have no Panamanian money, but we will accept United States dollars as well."

"We're completely broke," Tom shrugged, "But we've got some supplies here. What do you need?"

"As you can see, we do not need much." Alia gestured around. "What is happening in the world has only brought more visitors to the end of the road, more business. Otherwise, life is the same here."

"Surely we have something you'd need for a hot meal and a little time to rest… for my wife." He gestured to Barbara. "She's hurt and recovering from a gunshot wound."

The woman shook her head as if she didn't understand, turning to Sophia to explain, the girl firing off some quick Spanish words and getting a nod from her aunt, whose eyes shifted to Barbara with concern.

"You are hurt. You have come… a long way."

"That's the short of it," Tom replied with a sigh, "the *real* short of it."

The woman shrugged. "This is our home, and we have what we need." Then she mumbled something else in Spanish, looking at Sophia to explain.

After a moment of chatter, the young woman nodded and gestured toward their backpacks. "My aunt is saying that she does not believe you have much to offer, and we simply cannot give food away for free. We struggle to get by every day."

"No, I get it," Tom nodded, and he almost stood to gather his things to go, but a glance at Barbara, her slumped shoulders and tired face, forced him to try harder. Pulling his backpack closer, he removed what had worked with the guard at the canal. "I have some straw filters left. Do you need these?"

Alia accepted the box, studying it, lips twisted to the side before she returned it. "No, I do not think so. Good water… we have this."

With a sigh, Tom placed the box back inside his pack, moving past the smoked meat they had left, considering his pistol and a couple of magazines before he got a better idea. Switching to Sam's backpack, he flipped the top open and dug out their two remaining MREs, glancing at Barbara with relief, glad they'd not finished them off, instead relying on what they'd caught or scavenged on the way through Mexico and Central America.

Holding up the bags, Tom said, "these are American Army MREs… They've got a shelf life of twenty-five years. If you ever ran out of food here, these would come in handy. They're nutritious…" He showed the back to Sophia and tapped the list of nutrients. "Tell her these are packed with calories, a full day's meal for an adult. We'd love to trade these long-lasting rations for hot food *today*, if you can find it in your hearts."

As Alia stared at the packages, Sophia explained what Tom told her, the woman pursing her lips and taking the MREs, pausing to study them before looking across the table at Barbara and the kids. Finally she nodded at the offer. "Ci. *Yes*. I will accept these. You stay. Eat, please." She walked off, and Sophia stepped in with a smile.

"Would you like some water, chicha, or a beer?"

"Water for me… what is *chicha*?" Barbara asked, leaning against Tom with a sigh.

"It is a sweet drink, refreshing and fizzy."

"That sounds awesome, Mom," Sam grinned.

"As long as it doesn't have alcohol in it?" Barbara raised an eyebrow in question.

"We serve non-fermented chicha," Sofia nodded.

Tom's mouth watered. "Make it two."

"I'll be right back," Sophia replied, sweeping away in a flourish.

Tom settled back, closing his eyes as Barbara leaned against him, watching the kids as they smiled and looked around, Linda and Jack's attention drawn toward the other Americans in the dining room.

"This is a pretty cool little place," Tom said, allowing his shoulders to rest back, lungs deflating in a final, comfortable sigh.

They enjoyed a couple of minutes of quiet before Sophia brought the drinks, the kids sipping their chicha, faces lighting up at the taste of it. Tom left their food order to Sophia, since he couldn't pronounce most of the names on the menu, much less argue about what was inside them. There was *guacho*, a soupy rice dish bursting with vegetables, *carimanola*, which were handmade yucca balls stuffed with ground meat and cheese, and *ropa vieja*, a plate of shredded beef simmered with tomatoes, garlic, cumin, and oregano. And when she brought it out ten minutes later, the steaming dishes made everyone's faces light up like there was pure gold on the trays, accompanied by bowls of seasoned white rice and plantains. The kids dug in with forks and spoons, not minding at all that it was far different fare than what they'd gotten at home months ago. They quieted, shoveling food in their mouths, Sophia standing by for a moment, watching with a grin, but once they were settled in and eating, she went away, telling Tom to holler for her if they needed her.

"This is so good," Barbara said, dumping rice on her shredded beef, mixing it up, leaning her face over the steaming plate.

Tom was digging in, too, grateful for the larger portion, washing down the spicy meal with the beer. "I can't believe we reached our destination," he said, eyes wet as he spoke around a mouthful of food. "But I'm not sure it's going to get any easier after this."

Barbara finished a bite and leaned back. "When I was speaking to the traders at the bazaar, the lady overheard some locals talking about the Darien Gap people. She'd heard they were a mix of folks from the United States and Mexico who didn't trust any government, and that the cartels were moving out of the area, leaving room for others to move in."

"Back at the hospital, Carlos mentioned the colder temperatures would drive the thugs out," Tom said, "but I don't think it will be so cut and dried."

"Still, a lot of travelers were stocking up at the bazaar for that reason. They sold hundreds of filter straws to them."

"Those would definitely come in handy down here, unless you know how to get a regular, clean supply like Sophia and her aunt."

"She told me there were fertile farmlands amongst the swamps and jungles, near enough to like-minded people without calling it civilization." Barbara shrugged and had another bite. "Sounds perfect for us."

"Carlos mentioned that, too. So, we can agree a lot of people are saying the same things, but whether they're true or not is up for debate. The first task will be to find good land to live on. It might take a while, but we can get some help from the locals or team up with other Americans at the beginning." Tom stared at those eating in the dining room and strolling outside, decent looking folks with hopeful eyes like theirs, and he wondered if they would become friends down the road. "We can trade for some tools to build with, either get them from local people or from the equipment shop we saw coming in."

Barbara started to reply but clutched her chest, a pained expression crossing her features as she coughed and held her side. Tom placed his fork on his plate and reached for her cup of water, but she wasn't choking on what she'd eaten, whatever it was had come from deep within her chest.

"Are you okay, honey?" he asked with a concerned look. "Here's your water."

"I'm fine," she waved him off, sipping, swallowing hard. "Seriously... As I was trying to say, before we build something, we should check out some of the former cartel establishments. The woman at the bazaar said there were small areas where they'd abandoned houses, structures, even farmland – nothing we'd see on the map. If we asked the locals—"

"I don't know, honey. That might be a little too dangerous. What if some thugs stayed behind? They could still be in any of those buildings."

"That's what I told her, but she had it on good authority from someone who had a connection to the place--a satellite radio or something--that the cartels are really leaving."

"It's a possibility, but we won't know until we have a look around, and this is rough terrain." Tom kept his voice low. "I almost feel like I need to scout ahead while you guys stay here, but I can't imagine being apart from you for even a second. And we don't have much left to barter with..."

Barbara shifted, edging away from him, keeping her voice soft. "What's this all about, Tom? Where is this coming from?"

"I guess... I didn't realize how tough it was going to be here," he said, throwing a glance at the door. "The US military is so much farther south now, and they'll be breathing down our necks, eventually. Let's say we find a building that a cartel was using and move in. What then? If the temperatures drop anymore, it'll be hard to grow what we want. We'll have to figure out which crops will work, and it'll be months or years before we have anything we can eat. I don't know what we'll do until then..."

"But at least the warmer average temperatures will allow us to grow year-round." Gripping his shoulder, she pressed on. "That'll give us plenty of time to experiment with the crops. And between the supplies we have left, foraging and our ability to trade with some of the more established people, we'll figure out a way to make it work. We *will*, Tom."

"We barely made it here, honey. The kids are resilient, but how much more can they take? We may need to ask ourselves if we really want to put them through any more."

Barbara's brows creased, forcing her eyes into narrow slits. "What do you suggest we do?"

"We could hitch a ride back to Panama City, hop on a ferry, and head for Venezuela. That will guarantee us work, and the kids will have security." Tom let the doubts flow, everything he'd been feeling on the drive through Central America, the wide, desolate jungle, the abandoned cars and dead refugees on the roadside. Yaviza was the last town in the world before they gave themselves over to the wilderness. "And with your injury, how much farther can we actually go? What if the wound gets infected again?"

"Infected?" Barbara glanced at the kids, who were only half paying attention, eating their food, talking, and looking outside. When her eyes returned to Tom, her voice was a harsh whisper. "I can't believe what I'm hearing. We've come all this way…" Catching her own rising tone, she pressed the words through tight lips. "I did *not* risk my life and the lives of my children just to give up now."

"I'm not saying we should quit." Tom's words were agonized. "It's… a possible change of plans. I thought we could give the kids more by coming here, but it seems impossible now."

Her grip on his shoulder loosening, Barbara swung around to fully face him, her dark green eyes turning hard. "We *must* do this, Tom. For us and for the kids, and to ensure they have a future free from dependence on a government, the weather, or anything else. We won't be living in an apartment building in the middle of some strange country at the mercy of everyone. We *can't* be."

Tom sat back, staring at the table, eyes burning with weariness. "So, you really think we can do this…"

"It won't be easy," she said, her tone softening, her hand sliding around his shoulders in a hug. "But we'll be self-reliant, away from everyone and all the trouble that's been chasing us. It'll be the life we very nearly had in Virginia, only we'll be doing it here instead."

Glancing up, Tom caught the girls and Jack staring at them, blinking back tears. Finished with her food, Linda grabbed her brother's attention and pointed out the window. "Hey, check it out! There're shops across the street. Maybe we can go look out those when we're done eating."

"That would be cool!" A grin sprouted on his face as more kids walked by with their families, talking and laughing in the busy streets.

Eyes back on Barbara, Tom watched her pull up her shirt to partially reveal the bandages packed over her ribs. "If I… if *we*, made it through the last month, we can make it anywhere."

"You're right," Tom agreed, head bobbing under Sam's and Barbara's stares, his mind already working on what they'd need to do starting the very first day. "I was wrong for even suggesting it. We'll find a place to rest tonight and cross into the wilderness tomorrow. Then we'll set up a small base camp and reach out to make some local friends. From there, I'll run scouting missions with the girls, searching for a safe place to call home."

"That's the man I love," Barbara said, resting her head on his shoulder and giving him another hug.

A knowing smile broke out on Sam's face, and she winked at them over her glass of water. As their meals settled, they watched people stroll the dirt lane out front, locals with Americans thrown in, wearing backpacks, carrying satchels, and eating as they walked. A man had a rifle slung on his shoulder, though no one appeared alarmed about the weapon being out in the open. Sophia returned and filled their glasses once more, telling them to stay as long as they wanted, but Tom's backside was hurting from the hard wooden chair.

"I think we should go, guys," he said, getting up, glancing across the kids. "Let's free this table up for someone else who needs food and rest. Grab your packs and let's explore the town before it gets dark."

Jack and Linda got Smooch from the back while Tom walked toward the front door, raising his hand to stop Sophia as she was going by. "Thank you so much for your help. And thank your aunt for us, too."

"I will," she said with a friendly smile. "Please come back any time."

"We will," Barbara added with a wave. "Definitely."

"I hope so." With that, the girl swept into the kitchen and disappeared in a faint haze of smoke.

The kids' shuffling feet followed them to the door, but Tom paused, heart stopping as he heard a distant sound. Arm held out, he kept Barbara inside, head bent to catch it again, a faint chuffing noise, rotors cutting the jungle air and getting louder by the moment.

"Wait right here," he growled, stepping through the open door and into the dirt lane, head tilted, scanning the sky for the source.

People were gazing upward, hands lifted to shield their eyes from the sun as the whooping beat at the air, growing louder and closer. Back past the open park, a Black Hawk swept over the treetops, its nose rotating as it skimmed over Yaviza, flooding the jungle with powerful winds, paper, leaves, and twigs gusting through the lane, sending people scattering with surprised cries, shouts of anger at being buzzed so close. Others ran from the scouring winds as the helicopter settled into a hovering position over the park, floating downward, blowing Tom's longish hair in flutters around his forehead and eyes. With a silent curse, he turned and rushed back inside, the expression on his face flat. Jack stood in the middle of the dining room, holding Smooch's leash, fearful and shocked, though Sam and Linda didn't seem surprised, both girls' lips pursed as they looked at him for what to do.

"Great." Linda rolled her eyes, cheeks turning rosy with anger and fear. "It's Keith, isn't it?"

"I wish that guy would leave us alone," Sam said in agreement.

"Everyone, grab the spare ammunition and leave your packs here." He let his backpacks slip off his shoulders, catching the straps and plopping them on the floor.

Sophia rushed out of the kitchen, leaning to the side with her aunt behind her, both women peering toward the door and then at Tom with questions in their eyes. "Who's out there?" Sophia demanded. "Are they soldiers?"

"You could call them that," he grunted, kneeling, digging three magazines from his pack and stuffing them into his front pockets. "Hide. They just want us."

Sophia's eyes went wide when Sam and Linda took ammunition from their packs and thrust them in their pockets, each checking their guns to make sure they were loaded. Barbara, already armed with her pistol, turned to the door and looked outside, the wind from the slowing helicopter rotors blowing her hair around her shoulders, the turbine drone blaring in their ears.

"Tom, I think a military truck just showed up," Barbara said, squinting toward the dirt lane they'd come in on. "Yep, it's a Humvee."

Blood turning to ice, Tom fumbled a magazine and dropped it on the floor, pausing to take a breath and calm down before he grabbed the magazine and shoved it in his left-rear pocket, gesturing at their things as he spoke to Sophia and Alia. "Could you ladies look after our stuff? We'd appreciate it."

Sophia bent to grab the girls' backpacks and slid them into the kitchen, while her aunt snagged the other three and hauled them away. Tom pivoted and scanned over his family, Barbara and Sam looking at him with apprehension, Linda staring at the doorway with hatred in her eyes, both hands balled into fists at her sides. Jack studied his face, bottom lip quivering, a single tear staining his cheek. Tom forced a confident smile, his stomach doing a backflip as he ruffled his son's hair and bent to rub Smooch between her ears.

A loudspeaker clicked, a faint static buzz crackling in the air, Keith's wicked chuckle blasting at them above the wind. "Good evening, kids. This is your local neighborhood bounty hunter, looking for Tom McKnight and his accomplices." His laugh tittered, high-pitched and frail, having fallen far from the edge of insanity. "You thought you could get away from me back in Panama City, but I was right behind you the whole way. And this is the end of the line, man! Your day of judgement has come!"

Shaking off anxious waves of nausea in his gut, Tom's shifted toward the door. "All right. We finish this right now."

Chapter 14
President Zimmerman
Caracas, Venezuela

In the mountain fortress, with its metal shielding closed tight, the massive stone chamber shrouded in darkness but for a handful of lights up in the rafters, and the glow of the computers, the President and his senior officers were gathered. Each monitored various battle situations, following protocols for operations scattered across the content, spreading into Colombia and Brazil, the Russians and Chinese like fire ants in the jungle, crawling all over them in a desperate attempt to secure the key resources required for throwing the American military off the continent.

Sea and air superiority had been established, though the enemy's foothold off the coast of Brazil remained strong, and they were working their way inward, still landing troops and civilians, a million people pouring into South America, delivered by cargo vessels and transport ships the President was reluctant to attack. It wasn't the Chinese and Russian citizens they despised, but the continual aggressive moves by government forces in a battle that had no end.

"Sir, do you want some more coffee?" Maxine Stafford asked, his assistant already there with his cup.

The President took his eyes off the screen where they'd been viewing an operation in Arauca where a contingent of Marines had just rescued a downed helicopter crew from behind the lines. "Yes, thank you, Maxine."

"Two creams," she said, placing the mug next to him, her eyes flitting to the screens. "Are you okay, sir? Is everything going well?"

Standing, he moved from the table, guiding her away from images and the carnage they sometimes showed, real-time streams of soldiers fighting and dying, occasionally interrupted by Rita Cortez who was back to her Secretary of State duties, working with the other nations on the continent to secure relations and resources, combining climate experts to better understand the odds for survival. It was a conversation Zimmerman wanted to be a part of, but his immediate priority was protecting his people and their new constitutional republic as it took root.

"It's going as well as it can," he replied, moving her around a temporary wall section they'd erected in the great chamber. "We're fighting to keep this new framework we've created from burning to the ground."

"Yes, sir. I'm sorry for bugging you."

"It's okay," he laughed. "How about you, Maxine? Are you guys making progress over here?"

"Almost everyone's happy to be working side-by-side with elected officials." Looking around at the bustling tables and desks, where agencies were spread out, some of them with branch names hanging above them as they streamlined the paperwork and logistics of settling an entire country. "We're getting to know the Venezuelans, and it's nice to walk across the room and talk to someone from another agency. Yes, it's working out well."

"Good. At first, I didn't like this enormous chamber at all. I thought it was too open and would distract the officers, but it's nice to have direct access to people by just walking over and talking to them. It sure beats the long-distance videoconferences from the old days."

"Yes," she laughed. "If you need anything, don't hesitate to ask. Assistants to the Joint Chiefs of Staff have a table right over there, and I've joined them."

"Very good, Maxine. Thank you."

His chest rose with pride, watching her return to her team where they were merging skills, building a synergy that promised to be the anchor for a better future for their people; provided he could defend them from the communists. With a sigh, he turned back to CENTCOM and joined Davidson, Spencer, and the rest of the team, staring at the middle screen of South America. Red dots and swooping arrows depicted current operations and troop movements, and the spot that drew his eye was the two-hundred-mile stretch of ocean between São Paulo and Rio de Janeiro where the largest remaining Russian and Chinese ships floated. Farther out, a contingent of US carrier groups stood ready to attack them at his order.

Spencer wore his admiral's uniform buttoned down like everyone else, voice strained as he turned and gestured for Zimmerman to join them. "We've got new intelligence, sir."

"Go ahead," he replied.

"I'd like to draw your attention to the center screen."

"Okay. What am I looking at?"

General Davidson stepped around to his other shoulder. "We still have quite a few of our satellites working, and with air superiority, we've been flying successful recon missions, tracking their ships, using radiation-based detection to determine where they're moving the nuclear warheads. I'm talking thousands of flights, sir, with every available plane we have in our arsenal. Long story short, we don't think the Russians or Chinese got many nuclear weapons out of their respective countries before the big freeze. With Russian infrastructure already struggling *before* the anomaly, we're confident a majority of their nuclear missiles are still sitting in Siberia somewhere."

"That's great news," John replied with a nod, "but where does that leave us?"

"We believe the Russians have moved all remaining nuclear warheads, roughly seven hundred of them, to their last carrier off the coast of Rio de Janeiro, protected by planes, anti-aircraft artillery, and submarines. I mean, they've really got a tough defensive shell there."

"Could we take them before they launched a missile?"

"That's just it, sir," Davidson replied. "We're not sure they even have that capability anymore."

"It would only take one to destroy Caracas," John murmured. "Though they promised not to use them."

"If you believe those bastards," Molina said

Davidson nodded in agreement with the Venezuelan commander before continuing. "We think this could be an unprecedented opportunity to remove their nuclear capabilities altogether without confronting them in another large ocean battle."

"Go on."

Davidson took the laptop from him and handed him a printed packet with *Operation Golden Cobra* written on it. "Since getting our network back online, we've had our cybersecurity teams working overtime to bust the Russian ZETA Operating System, which controls all their ballistic missiles and firing solutions. Previously, with their forces spread out across the world, and redundancies in place, we could never breach their security."

"But now we can?"

"We think so, sir, and Admiral Spencer assembled another mission packet for such an operation, which you're holding right there in your hands." Stepping into the light, the General nodded at the hard gray cover. "With your permission, we think we can cut off the head of this snake and end this war with one quick strike."

John carried the packet around the table, flipping pages, skimming through the mission summary before digging into the details. The gathered commanders stepped aside, watching, waiting for the President's word. Coming full circle, he nodded at the center monitor, the admiral clicking a remote to put the last satellite images of the remaining Russian carrier on screen. The grainy picture showed the damage it had sustained in skirmishes with US Navy forces, plus all the destroyers surrounding it in a defensive formation.

"We're not even sure this ship is fully operational, since they just finished building it before the anomaly. But they're making modifications now…" Spencer came around to face him. "Sir, we may never have another chance to catch them with their pants down. If we give them time to regroup…"

Scanning the estimated success percentages, and the likely outcome for the operatives, he ran his fingers through his hair, gazing at the ship. "Are you sure our SEALS can pull this off?"

"Certain of it, sir." Spencer gave a curt nod and stiffened resolutely. "Our special forces have been training non-stop for a potential sea assault, and they're ready, sir."

"And they know what it might mean, for us and *them*?"

"Yes, sir. We have volunteers for this mission. These are the best of the best of the best. Highly dedicated resources, and they understand the consequences should they fail… and even if they succeed. One of them had a father in the Russian Navy who defected to the US when she was a girl. The government was not kind to their relatives after that, sending pictures of them from prison camps, tortured and maimed."

"That's… terrible."

"Needless to say, she's got a chip on her shoulder, and her patriotism is unmatched."

Crossing his arms over his chest, John stared at the Russian carrier and finally gave his approval.

* * *

Seaman Anne Sidorovich clung to the sea scooter as it hauled her through the dark waters fifteen feet below the surface, her legs kicking slowly, eyes turned to the RNAV-2 screen as bubbles slipped across its surface. Shadows sliced the surrounding waters alongside her, seven other SEALS embraced by pitch blackness, a vague sense of direction, and the rebreather in her ears with gentle suction, stale rubber taste in her mouth, bubbles floating around her head and up. On the nav display, the Russian carrier gave off a faint blue glow, massive against the green dots that marked the rest of the SEAL squad.

She barely registered the chill as more than a slight discomfort, nothing like the recent two weeks of training she'd undergone to fight with the team, picked for her combat and espionage skills and her proficiency in Russian. The last name helped, too: Sidorovich, stemming from her Ukranian roots. Another scooter pulled up closer, giving off a faint squall of bubbles in its torpedo-like shadow, the upper half cut off, and Lieutenant Templeton lying on top with his hands on the controls. His muscular shape slipped through the waters with languid ease, face mask turning toward her, his green eyes staring across seven feet of black ocean.

She nodded, and he angled his scooter to the left, careful not to disturb the water too much or be heard by Russian monitoring systems. The ultra-quiet vehicles were powerful and sleek, carrying their weight plus gear in waterproof duffels tied to the sides. With a glance at her screen, she saw they were fifty meters from the carrier, closing slowly but steadily, and when she peered into the distance, a dark shape grew against the coal-colored waters, the sharp angle of a ship's hull, stretching hundreds of feet away. Templeton and two other SEALS kicked on their low-light beams, and Anne gasped in shock at the massive propellers and rudder looming in front of her, as big as a building.

The earpiece in her helmet clicked on, and a soft voice whispered through the respirator's clacking. "SEAL team. This is Lieutenant Templeton. Prepare for ascent."

Even though they had a secure connection, any sound beneath the water—the softest talking, bump, or knock—could alert the Russians to their presence, so Anne breathed steadily and let the scooter hover in place. Tethering her duffel to her wrist, she snatched a secondary backpack that held her mission uniform and prepared to surface.

After everyone had their gear, Templeton's flashlight blinked twice. "All right. Let's go."

Anne took one deep breath and removed her rebreather, hooking it where her duffel had been, then she turned the scooter off and swam to the ship's hull with a magnetic tether, pressing it lightly to the rusting side and activating it with a soft click. Lungs screaming for air, she moved along the hull, feeling her way with slick gloves against the rough side, making sure her bag didn't bump the steel. As soon as she broke the surface, a wave shoved her forward, but she caught herself against the ship's hull with a gasp, sputtering salt water, going with the flow of the current as she gently rocked. Other heads bobbed around her, Templeton swimming close, then kicking off the side, producing a long tube about as thick as her arm. Treading water, aiming the tube at a lower deck jutting from the ship, the Lieutenant squeezed a trigger, and it gave a muffled pop and puff of smoke. A pair of metal prongs shot upward, spreading out as the magnetic ends hit the bottom of the platform less than a foot from the edge. When Templeton pulled the end taut, an aluminum ladder six inches wide unfolded and snapped open.

With a grin that glowed in the dark, the leader clung to the last rungs, gesturing for the first SEAL to climb. It was arduous going, with the flimsy ladder swinging back and forth, twisting and spinning. There wasn't much to grab onto, and no way to balance, but the SEAL reached the top and clambered over the precarious lip, feet kicking, legs wiggling until he vanished out of sight. A moment later, he appeared and gave a hand signal, and the rest of the SEALS started up, one after the other, coiling and turning with Templeton hanging on at the bottom, leaning backward with all his might to keep it as taut as he could. And when he nodded at Anne, she wordlessly grabbed on, taking several deep breaths before climbing into the darkness. It didn't take long for her shoulders to ache and scream, but she put one boot after the other and scaled the thin rungs, gritting her way up.

A glance back, and the bright lights of Rio de Janeiro shined in the distance, the harbor full of patrol boats, the distant sounds of music drifting from the city, though she kept her laser-focus on the ladder and reaching the top. Every step, every pain, was her sacrifice to her team, pulling her weight, dedicating herself to the success of the mission above all else. At the top, two helping hands grabbed her arms and lifted her up, another snatching her shoulder and sweeping her onto the deck, where she scrabbled and crawled to her knees. Turning, she looked at the incredible view, a couple of hundred feet above the sea's surface, the city blazing behind it.

"Over here, Sidorovich," someone called, and she moved to the corner of the platform where a cluster of pipes was built into the decking. The other SEALS were already there, half geared up, pulling rifles out of their waterproof duffels and checking the loads.

Panting and dripping water, she staggered over, the men nodding to her, bringing her into the fold where she dropped her packs and stripped off her wetsuit. For a moment she stood in her undergarments on the cold, wet steel, the ship lilting on the calm sea as others rolled up the aluminum ladder and checked their gear, a pair moving to the deck door to guard it. A SEAL named Kerry helped her sort her dry garments, handing her one piece at a time, rubbing her shoulders and cheeks to warm her chilled skin as she zipped up her Russian blue coveralls. Anne shook out her long blonde hair, gathered it, and pulled it through the backstrap of a ship's cap, letting the tips brush the middle of her back.

"Thank you," she murmured to Kerry and slipped her feet into a pair of Russian-made deck boots and added a splash of red lipstick so they didn't look so chilled and blue from the trip in.

By the time she'd finished, Templeton had changed into his own coveralls, grinning as she checked her Makarov pistol and slipped it inside her coverall pocket. One by one, the SEALS disappeared upward, climbing up to the next deck, leaving her and the Lieutenant standing alone.

"Are you ready for this?" he asked.

Stepping over by the door, clutching her hands behind her back, Anne shrugged to loosen her tense shoulders from the climb, tossing him a curt nod. "I am ready," she said in a Russian accent.

"Good," he replied, mimicking her accent. "You sound very naturally Russian, so you will do most of the talking."

Slipping into full Russian, she nodded. "So, we wait until we get the word, make our way to the CIC, and—"

"You're going to do all the talking. Remember that."

"I *will*," she agreed, "but I just want to make sure—"

"And we'll break into the CIC, complete the mission, and be sipping vodka in the mess hall before we exfil."

"Are you going to interrupt me while I'm speaking *Russian* to the *Russian* soldiers so we can complete this mission on this *Russian* vessel?"

The SEAL shook his head and laughed. "No more interruptions. All business from here on out, but I will still have that glass of vodka on this boat before we leave."

Anne allowed herself a smile, pacing a little but stopping to dispel the nervousness, getting into the mind of a Russian sailor on duty, dealing with the stress of the job. *I'm tired. The Americans are closing in. Their jets are flying overhead every day.*

"Are you okay?"

"Yeah," she said, shaking her shoulders and rolling her neck. "I'm getting into the role." Then she went over it again, speaking it out loud. "I'm a Russian sailor. I just want to do my job. These damn Americans are breathing down our necks, and an attack could come at any moment…"

Templeton raised his eyebrows. "Pretty grim, but I get your point." The Lieutenant paced with her, bantering back and forth as they got into their roles; five minutes, ten, then a half-hour passed standing in the chilly breeze, waiting for the diversion to start. Buzzers in their pockets went off, and they shared a long look, Anne took a deep breath and prepared to enter the ship.

Templeton was reaching for the door handle when the latch turned and flipped open. The SEALS leaped back, going for their pistols as two Russian sailors stepped through wearing sloppy coveralls, dragging out a rolling garbage bin, overflowing with refuse and a swarm of flies. The man on the front end jerked back, startled to see Anne and Templeton out on the deck, but she quickly improvised, looking embarrassed, gesturing at the Lieutenant and then at Rio de Janeiro.

"Please do not tell our commander," she sputtered, eyes falling to the floor. "We could not find any other place to go, so we came here."

The garbage men shared a bemused glance, and the one in the back snickered at Templeton. "You could have found a more romantic place, my friend. You should be better to your woman."

"It was such a good view," the Lieutenant explained, awkwardly.

"Do not worry," the first man said, pulling the garbage through, spilling paper off the sides. "We will not turn you in."

"Thank you," Anne replied, nodding, stepping into the passage, throwing a glance back to see the men lift the bin and dump everything into the sea.

Templeton pulled the door shut and they walked along a corridor that smelled like rotted vegetables and grease, lit by a sparse bubble lighting built into walls that dripped with moisture, the air thick and warm. Anne swatted at more buzzing insects as they reached the end and entered an enclosed stairwell, floors marked in Russian, fire extinguishers and emergency equipment hutches everywhere, though much of the gear was missing. She recalled the ship's schematics in her head, their position in relationship to the CIC, and the path they'd go to get there. Up one floor, they traversed a myriad of passages and halls leading to the front, stepping aside to let sailors rush past, a few with second glances at Anne as they passed.

"I should have died my hair," she murmured to Templeton as they passed a short brunette woman double-timing it to another part of the ship.

"You're fine."

"Until some long-timer realizes I'm not a crewman."

"The Russians are confused and changing personnel all the time…" Both saluted an officer as he moved past them to the upper decks, hardly noticing them, and Templeton's voice lowered. "Much like we are. So don't worry."

The pair stuck to the inner railing as boots pounded on the steel grating, sailors flying down the stairs, shoving past them with disinterested looks. When two Russian soldiers approached she tensed up, ready to grab her pistol should they stop to question them, relaxing when they moved on by.

"Looks like our boys are working hard," Templeton murmured, saying a silent prayer for the other SEALS who'd made their way to the engine room to create a disturbance. "The Russians are awake, at least."

"Let's make it count," Anne replied.

They continued going up, stopping only once on a stairwell to let some Russian Marines pass, men with AK-74s in their hands, their eyes tired, expressions haggard. The SEALS weren't challenged the entire way up, though soldiers and sailors rushed past them, carrying out their duties, one man even whispering an apology as he bumped Anne. At the top was a circular chamber with four passages branching off, each guarded by a pair of stout Russians who wore aggravated looks.

One stepped toward them with a scowl, hand on his slung rifle. "This is a secure area. You must have special access to even be here. Who are you?"

"Yes, comrade," Anne sputtered, feeding on her natural anxiety, glancing at the floor before snapping off a formal salute. "We came over from the Ushakov and are supposed to report to the CIC. We have orders…" She gestured to Templeton, who fished past his pistol to pull out the set of papers and hand them over. The Marine snatched the Russian-marked documents from him, unfolded them, and scanned them carefully, mouth moving as he read.

Another Marine stepped from the passage to their right. "You were on the Ushakov?"

"That is correct," Anne nodded, her shoulders and back stiff. "It was… terrible."

He looked her up and down, skeptical. "If you were on that destroyer, you would have had injuries. No one escaped those bastard Americans and their bombs."

"We were in the ship's CIC when they struck…" Eyes watering, she shook her head as she pretended to remember being on the destroyer during the attack. "The bombs came straight down, crushing all the systems, and we couldn't fire back." Shrugging, she glanced at Templeton, who was watching the exchange nervously with a light sheen of sweat on his forehead, body on a hair trigger as she continued. "Men like you protected us, got us all off the ship and to safety. It is because of men like you we survived and escaped injury." Eyes flashing to the passage, she said, "Now our orders bring us here to fight on against the American pigs."

The man with the papers folded them and handed them back to the Lieutenant before shifting to Anne. "You are very brave to have gone through that. The Ushakov is now at the bottom of the ocean, and you could've easily been there with it. It is good to have you here on this ship. Please go ahead." He looked at the second man. "Their papers check out."

"Thank you, comrade." Anna looked for the right entrance to the CIC, her Russian and English mixing for a moment before she identified the proper section, which was straight ahead. "We will go to our posts now."

Gesturing for Templeton to follow, she pushed between the Marines and stepped briskly down the passage, boots snapping on the steel grating, tossing a swift glance back at the other SEAL. His firm green eyes and calm smile settling her nerves before his attention shifted to the door at the end of the hall, guarded by a single Russian Marine. Placards in bold writing stated only authorized personnel were allowed, and a security ID reader was built into the heavy steel hatch with its double-enforced bolts. Minor details leaped out at her, like the dirty walls with chipped lettering and glass cabinets with old emergency equipment inside, looking untested in years, nothing she would've seen on a US Navy carrier in the worst of times.

They were halfway down the hall when the alarms rang out, a flat *wah-wah-wah* that echoed off the steel guts of the ship, causing her to wince inwardly as the sound stabbed her ears. The SEAL's distraction had started a few seconds too soon, though they'd planned for such an event, and the pair kept walking, a relaxed expression on Anne's face despite her pulse rate rocketing to an insane speed. Nervous tension gripped her shoulders, threatening to rush her into action, and it took every bit of control to hold back, staying calm, spine stiff as the Marines behind them shouted.

"Sidorovich, wait!" the first one yelled. "Comrade Sidorovich, stop! I will fire if you do not *stop!*"

"Keep going," Templeton mumbled from the corner of a smile, nodding at the guard as he stepped away from the door toward them, peering past them at the troops running after them down the hall. Producing the paper orders, the Lieutenant started to hand them over, but grabbed the guard's wrist when he got close enough. Drawing a surprised grunt, the SEAL twisted behind him, bent his arm back, and wrapped his forearm around the soldier's neck, pulling his body taut. Anne was already lunging for his rifle, jerking it out of his hand, wincing and ducking as rounds flew at them, pinging off the metal, dangerous shrapnel tearing through the air.

Throwing the weapon down, Anne dug into her coveralls for the key card that would grant them entrance, the Russian soldiers screaming and shooting, the guard Templeton held between them taking bullets to his chest and face, painting the heavy walls in crimson splatters. In a flash, she had her badge out and swiped it across the flat surface, the red lights around the pad blinking red for a moment before clicking to green, tumblers clacking, gears spinning, the steel slab popping open an inch. Anne grasped the handles and tried to wrench it wide, but it was immense, nearly twelve-inches thick and moving like molasses.

When there was enough room, she slipped inside, turning and waiting for the Lieutenant, who dragged the dying Russian guard in with him, rounds hitting the metal, boots pounding the floor. Anne took the inner handle with both hands and threw her weight backward, grunting, shoulders straining against its impossible size. A piece of a bullet hit the wall and ricocheted past her face, forcing her to turn away. The Russian Marines were there, gripping grabbing and pulling from the other side, the barrel of a rifle trying to twist in and shoot her, but the door slammed home and snapped tight, the magnetic locks keeping it sealed while the larger tumblers rolled into place with a *clank*.

Without hesitation, Anne pivoted and crouched as slugs hammered the inside of the door where she'd been standing, the dark CIC filled with popping rounds, flashes, and the shouts of Russian officers. A roughly sixty square foot room, the CIC held rows of computer servers with a circular center of computer terminals and screens that glowed soft blue and white. Glancing up, she watched as Templeton, bleeding from a few places, swung the dying, twitching guard high to absorb more shots before he dropped the body and ducked into a row of computer servers stretching to the end of the room. Drawing her pistol from her coveralls, Anne crept in the other direction, swift and quiet behind the humming equipment, bullets slamming the thin aluminum cabinets as she scouted what they were up against.

It was a square area with a low ceiling covered in ductwork and cabling, vents blowing a cool breeze through the room, the air thick with ozone and warm metal. Tossing her ponytail off her shoulder, Anne put her back to a cabinet and waited, listening, breathing quietly as she took it in. The initial surprise had worn off, and voices were arguing, a man whispering orders, receiving hissed replies. On the other side of the thick steel door, fists hammered with faint blows, and she figured they had a few minutes before someone arrived with enough clearance to get in.

"Where did they go?"

"Behind the cabinet, you idiot! Go... shoot to kill!"

A woman's voice shook. "I'm a systems analyst. I can't-"

A gun went off in the room - Templeton's weapon - followed by a gurgling sound and a body hitting the floor. Anne swept away from her position, glancing between the computer equipment to see the Russian CIC specialists in the center of the room, hunkered behind several bolted-down desks and flat screen monitors that offered them a modicum of protection.

"I said shoot them," the officer commanded.

"No!"

"Damn you!" the man snarled, and a struggle ensued, some grunting, others punching and shoving.

"Enough!" Anne shouted. "Put down your weapons, and we won't hurt you. We only want access to the computer systems to stop this war!"

"You're surrounded," Templeton barked from the opposite side of the room, though his voice sounded pained and angry. "Give up, and we'll let you live."

"You Americans pigs do not take prisoners!" The Russian officer growled in defiance. "Maybe *you* should give up!"

"Whatever your leaders are telling you," Anne called, "you cannot win this. Give us access to the computer terminals, and we can stop this without violence!"

"Go to hell!"

Anne turned in the other direction, peering through the low light given off by the warm servers, blue and green and yellow flashes, showing active processors and network connections. As her eyes adjusted, she spotted Templeton on the far side of the room, staring back at her from the depths of the equipment rows, expression filled with pain. Pistol held high in one hand, he was covering a wound she couldn't see with his other. A Russian guard was creeping around to shoot him, so with two smooth steps she swung into the open, fired a pair of shots at the soldier's head and retreated behind the cabinet before the man hit the floor.

The Russians cried out in whimpers and sniveling coughs, the officer shouting, "Stop shooting! We're giving up! We will surrender. Just one minute…"

Peeking around the corner, she had a look at Templeton, but he'd slipped lower, eyes closed, head thrown back, either dead or unconscious against the wall. Cursing softly, she shifted in the opposite direction, crouch-walking to another cabinet, having a glance at what the Russians were up to. With pursed lips, she kept moving, edging between the rows, watching as the officer raised up over the computer monitors to find her in the darkness.

"I said we're giving up! Okay?" Pistol held high, he waved it to get her attention. "We are surrendering now. Please, take my weapon."

By then, she'd come to the other side of the computers, sweat pouring down her temples, eyes darting through the gaps between the desks, noting every shadow in the ghostly lighting as the Russians tried to trick her. Approaching a corner section where someone was fiddling with something on the floor, she rose and pointed her weapon at a female sailor, no older than twenty-five, buried to her elbows in the sub-flooring where she'd removed a square tile and was about to cut some cables. Her sweaty-pale face turned up with a gasp, blinking in a mixture of apology and fear, the clippers poised to cut what Anne suspected was power to the terminals. When the tech didn't drop the wire cutters fast enough, Anne popped off two shots, and the woman collapsed into the hole. Swinging her pistol up, she fired at the officer who was spinning to shoot back, but her rounds arrived first, perfectly placed in his chest and neck, crumpling him over the desk to spill on the floor. The remaining Russian techs screamed and cowered, hands thrown up, weapons tossed down.

"Everyone, stand and move to the door!" she shouted, pistol shifting between them, all six looking terrified. "I said *move*! Do it now or I will simply rid myself of you!"

They slunk from behind the desks and walked towards the big metal slab where two women stood shaking, one man with his hands and forehead resting against the steel as the Marines beat on the other side. One of the female techs turned and glanced at her shoulder. "You are shot."

"Shut up and put your palms on the door," she replied, blinking at the pain radiating through her side and neck, muscles twitching, making her want to scream. "If I see any of you move…"

Letting the sentence linger unfinished she came around and slipped between the computer desks, taking a USB drive from her pocket and stepping to a terminal that faced her prisoners. Fingers dancing over the keys, she pulled up a login screen and used an account by a captured Russian sailor to access the ZETA Operating System. With a few more taps, she initiated a file on the USB drive, kick-starting the viral sequence that would destroy what remained of their computing capabilities.

Picking up her pistol, she took two steps back, brain swimming with dizziness. Going to the end of the server rack row to see if Templeton was okay, finding the Lieutenant slouched forward with no pulse. She hugged his head to her chest, closed her eyes and sent a thought to him beyond the grave, letting him know they'd finished the mission, won the fight, and, God willing, brought peace and an end to the conflict.

Something exploded out in the hall, and the room shook, cables falling from the ceiling as the techs backed up with startled cries. Anne stepped away from the Lieutenant, moving to the computer terminals, wincing as her shoulder started to go numb. Sitting in front of a blinking screen, she held her pistol in her lap, remembering her mother's stories about her father's work for the Russian Navy, his supreme sacrifice for the Sidorovich family by leaving his homeland and risking everything to give his wife and daughter a future. Anne's brothers and sisters were settled in Venezuela, none of them aware of what she'd done that day, though she hoped her actions guaranteed their survival and their children's survival, and on and on for every new Sidorovich that ever came into the world. In some small way, she wished all Russians might think of her fondly for what she'd accomplished to put an end to the fighting, just one tiny sacrifice on the backs of many selfless gifts by many other people.

More booms detonated outside in the hall, rattling the thick metal slab on its hinges, dust and water trickling from above, giving the impression the room would collapse before the door ever fell in. "My friends," she said to the Russian techs, who were all standing back away from the violent explosions, shooting her fearful glances as if caught between two immovable objects. "Please, yes. Step aside. When it comes down, it will not be pleasant. I hope-"

A final explosion ripped through the room, and the hinges sprung with pieces of shrapnel flying everywhere. A female tech grabbed her throat and collapsed as the others scattered from beneath the tumbling door, AK-74s flashing like fireflies in a cloud of dust.

* * *

It was well past midnight in the new CENTCOM headquarters, and an expectant silence filled the chamber, the mountain sealed up tight in the event Spencer's operatives failed in their mission and the Russians and Chinese struck back. Every unit in the joint US-Venezuela armed forces was on full alert, tired Marines, sailors, soldiers, and support personnel, uncertain of why they were on emergency standby other than something big was in the air. The President and his officers sat in chairs in a semicircle around the three monitors, the table behind them littered with half-filled coffee cups and MRE wrappers, empty plastic bottles and fruit peels. The long day of planning had gone without basic support staff to keep the details of the mission under tight wraps, leaving Maxine and her fellow staffers to quietly clean up, throwing away garbage in paper bags, refilling coffee urns, occasionally glancing up to listen for the results of Operation Golden Cobra to come in.

While there was activity happening across three continents, all eyes were on the center screen where the Russian carrier was being observed by a high-flying drone, the officers looking for any indication the enemy had caught on to the infiltration. Something like a scrambling of boats, planes, and helicopters would have been a sure sign, though waters near Rio de Janeiro remained calm, the ships cruising on their normal patrols, the carrier sitting quietly with just her running lights on.

"We could take those jets out right now," Colonel Molina said, the former Venezuelan General not convinced the mission would be the golden bullet the Americans expected.

"Give them some time to work," Spencer replied, the heavy chested man leaning forward, fingers interlocked in front of him. "They just need time to do their jobs..."

The contingent of officers were glued to the center screen, occasionally giving other operations attention but mostly focused on the one they hoped brought an end to the fighting. General Davidson sometimes stepped off to the side to take a phone call from his lieutenants about patrols and troop placements. Colonel Prescott often snuck off to pace alongside the CENTCOM meeting desk or to check some news regarding actions in Central America before rejoining the other commanders.

Molina was persistent. "They were dropped off, correct?"

"That's correct," Davidson said, annoyance in his tone. "A submarine placed them a few miles outside the harbor, and they motored in on submersibles. If they failed before then, we'd know."

"But if they were deep inside the ship, they could not send a message."

"Until they break into the system and secure the Russian codes, we won't know anything."

"And if we do not hear before dawn?"

"The mission will have failed," Zimmerman snapped, glancing to his right where Rick Manglor waited patiently with his computer in his lap, eager to take control of the ZETA operating system.

The chief scientist shook his head and made a helpless gesture at the blank screen, the cursor blinking as it attempted repeated reconnections. With a nod, John got up, stepped closer to the Russian carrier, noting it was already around 3:30 a.m., and the SEALS would've been dropped off three and a half hours ago, which meant they'd had plenty of time to complete the mission. A headache tapping at his temples as he cycled through the long list of contingency plans based on whether their enemies would say nothing or if they'd feel threatened enough to take things to the next level. The US commanders had considered a third choice, that the Russians would capture the SEALS and use them as propaganda to strengthen the solidarity of their soldiers and citizens, but with millions of them spread all over the world, from the Chinese coast to the Brazilian waters and everywhere in between, they figured the propaganda wouldn't help the Russians like it might have during normal times.

"I'm going to take a walk," Zimmerman announced, striding out to the open floor, stepping past Colonel Prescott and moving in a circle toward the far side of the rock chamber. There, a smaller section of work pods was set up labeled *Logistics* and *Comm Systems*, occupied by twenty dispatchers with fingers dancing on their keyboards, talking quietly into headsets, keeping the government and military conversations secure and timely. The agents were trained on several wireless and physical communication systems throughout Venezuela, and their mastery of the equipment was impressive. A young lieutenant sitting alone glanced up at him, did a double take, pushed away from her desk and stood, saluting him with a sharp snap to attention.

"At ease, Lieutenant..." he replied, leaning down to see her nametag.

"Jennings, sir." Her shoulders sagged, and there were dark circles under her eyes.

The President was about to tell her to carry on, but he wasn't ready to return to CENTCOM yet. With nothing he could do about events happening hundreds of miles away, he could think of nothing better to do than talk to the Lieutenant.

"How are you tonight, Jennings?"

Jennings started to sit down, as if expecting him to go, but she remained standing when she realized he wanted to talk. "Okay, sir. Just waiting to hear about the mission."

"Are you assigned to Cobra?"

"Yes, sir. Myself and two other communication specialists have extended responsibilities to handle all calls regarding Operation Golden Cobra ourselves, so we've been on point all night with this one. The team is taking a quick break, since it's a waiting game now."

"So, you heard the SEALS when they were being transported to the carrier?"

"I was listening in just before they disembarked from the SDV and took to their scooters."

"Oh, very good." John nodded, then grimaced. "I'd heard one of the operatives... well... she has a Russian background, and their government didn't treat her family too well after her father brought them to the United States."

The Lieutenant glanced up at the chamber's tall ceiling, the corner of her mouth ticking nervously. "I don't know all the SEALs' backgrounds, Mr. President, but you're probably referring to Chief Petty Officer Anne Sidorovich, since you said *she*, and she was the only woman on the team."

"Yes, I'd say you're right. What can you tell me about her?"

Blinking, she gave a guarded smile. "I'm not sure what you mean, sir."

"I mean, how was she before the mission? Did she seem…"

"Confident?"

"Yes. Was she confident and in good spirits?"

"Professional, sir. She seemed very professional." Jennings shrugged. "Anne was excited about the mission and left a…" Glancing away, she continued. "She left a letter for her family in the event of her passing. But mostly, the SEALS were busy with equipment checks and going over mission variables and things like that."

John paused, trying to imagine moving through the ocean in an ultra-quiet submarine, total darkness surrounding them in what could be the last hours of their lives. "Thank you for that. It took a lot of bravery for them to volunteer for the mission, and we can all learn something from them."

"Yes, sir," Jennings nodded.

They stood in an awkward silence before he gestured to her chair. "Well, carry on, Lieutenant. We're still waiting to hear, but hopefully—"

"Mr. President!" Davidson called from across the room, waving him over. "Mr. President! News!"

With a nod to the Lieutenant he launched into a brisk walk, covering the distance in just a few seconds, circling the big desk where the officers had gathered around Rick. Admiral Spencer and Colonel Prescott, Molina, Maxine, and many others… and Rita Cortez was jogging in from the far side of the room, flashing John a hopeful smile as excited murmurings began to swell.

"What is it, General?" Zimmerman asked as Davidson met him before he got there.

"We received a two-pulse signal from the Russian ship. One for us here, and one for the Russian forces, calling for their surrender. They're the ones we planted on the USB drive."

"So, they did it? The SEALS were successful?"

"They did, sir, but Rick hasn't officially connected yet… his team doesn't have control of the Zeta OS."

John patted the General on his shoulder and stepped through the excited crowd of officers and staffers joining them. Rita was waving over those who'd been on the outskirts and had played a role in the operation, acquiring resources or logistics, adding to what appeared to be a military success. Clapping, clasping their hands together with hope, they stood shoulder-to-shoulder and waited for the official news.

Circling around, Zimmerman pushed through the crowd to stand before Rick, the chief scientist still tapping keys on his laptop, his unkempt hair sticking straight up, so busy over the past few days he'd forgotten to even comb it. Sweat trickled in rivulets down his cheeks, a sheen of it glistening on his brow and dampening his shirt. Scanning the screen, his eyes widened with excitement at some success, then frowned at something else, typing in a long string of commands only to cycle through the same expressions.

Zimmerman placed his hands on his hips, locking his jaw against any false emotion that they'd succeeded, that they'd *won*. Looking over Rick's shoulder to where the logistics teams and communications specialists were gathered, he spotted Lieutenant Jennings and her fellow teammates standing around with their headsets on, arms folded, fidgeting or whispering to each other.

Finally, the scientist pounded a key and leaned forward, eyes big and bulging as he traced the lines of code flowing down the screen. "That's it," he spoke breathlessly. "That's… I'm in. I got into the Russian system. I…" Mumbling something, he continued typing.

"Talk to me, Rick!" That was Admiral Spencer from where he'd squeezed into the crowd, shoving two people aside, his jowls shaking with intensity, a fist clenched at his side. "Did they succeed or not?"

"Yes, sir. They succeeded!" Rick replied. "Templeton and Sidorovich got into the Russian carrier's CIC and inserted the USB drive. I'm connected… just checking the logs now…" He shook his head and grinned, wiping sweat from his brow and drying his hand on his pants. "They're trying to get control back, but it's too late." Eyes flashing up with nerdy glee, he nodded at the Admiral and then at John. "Mr. President, it appears our plan worked, and the Russians have lost control over their primary weapons system. They'll still have some basic functionality, but anything running the Zeta OS is shot. What do you want me to do?"

Zimmerman gestured impatiently. "You've got a post-mission protocol. I want an inventory of their nuclear warheads and how many we control. Once you get that, shut down everything they have… every missile battery and autocannon. Cripple their ability to launch anything that ties into the Zeta OS."

"Yes, sir. We'll work on it right now." As Rick bowed over his laptop and sent messages to the systems team, John stepped away from the crowd and motioned to Rita.

"Yes, sir?" The woman was exasperated, her wistful expression somewhere between disbelief and joy. "What do you need, sir?"

"Get me the Russian and Chinese presidents on the line. We need to have a talk about their unconditional surrender."

A roar of elation went up in the room, hats flying, people cheering and clapping in every department, members of the new Congress and Senate, logistics and dispatch, all smiling, patting, and shaking each other hard, though he couldn't blame them. The sense of relief was palpable, and many stood alone, arms folded and sobbing, eyes swelling with tears as they realized what'd happened.

President John Zimmerman turned to the screens and released a satisfied sigh, staring at the big Russian ship, silently thanking Chief Petty Officer Anne Sidorovich and the SEAL team for their ultimate sacrifice, and then he rolled his shoulders, loosening up for his meeting with his Russian and Chinese counterparts.

Chapter 15
Keith
Darien Gap, Panama

"We're four or five miles away," Smith said, his voice excited from where he sat in the passenger seat watching the tracker.

Keith couldn't keep the clownish grin off his face, cheeks hurting from his gleeful fantasies of driving up on Tom McKnight and seeing the man's surprised expression when he realized they'd been hunted to the end of the road and wouldn't get away. His fingers fidgeted on the steering wheel, pained palms sometimes beating out a happy little rhythm on it, an old tune he couldn't remember the name of that kept ringing in his head.

It was warm in the Humvee's cabin, but with the windows down tropical air rushed inside, drying his sweat as it whipped dust around. The dashboard radio sometimes crackled with voices, US military units communicating with each other or up to CENTCOM, but he kept the volume low, not interested in what they were saying no longer caring about troop movements and orders. All the cold and disappointment was behind him, and parts of his rotted fingers and toes, too, and he chuckled out loud, thinking about little pieces of himself trickling all the way back to North Carolina like breadcrumbs.

The Humvee rumbled along the rough highway, the asphalt showing signs of neglect, cracks and potholes rattling the suspension every time they hit one, drawing smart remarks from Morales in back. The truck passed over bridges and spots where the road turned to dirt tracks, threaded with deep tire grooves. There were too many abandoned cars to count, luggage and backpacks left on the roadside, flat tires and windows shot through with bullet holes. Sometimes there were bodies, too, lined up in threes or fours, some with bandaged limbs, others with their faces or bodies covered in sheets, all arranged in a way that showed someone was giving respect to the dead, and at one spot, a pair of farmers had pulled over and were digging graves twenty yards off the shoulder.

"Waste of time," Keith scoffed and given their effort a head shake. "Idiots."

"They're not idiots," Morales snapped back. "They deserve a medal for doing something no one else would do."

Keith shot a dirty glance into his rearview and scoffed. The soldier had been sulking in the back seat since the bridge in Panama City, and he was getting on Keith's nerves, but nothing could ruin his mood, not even Morales' moping and scowling. The important thing was that the man would shut up and do his duty, or he'd get a bullet in the head for his defiance.

"They're two miles out," Smith said, "and they haven't moved for an hour and a half. They must be resting or something."

"Not for long," Keith laughed.

A distant turbine cut above the wind, fluttering rotors beating a staccato rhythm against the blue sky, and he grinned upward at it, catching sight of Banks' Black Hawk soaring overhead and getting out in front of them as it started its descent.

"There she is," Keith said, waving vigorously up at her. "Hey, Banks! Save some for us!" Turning to the soldiers, he smirked. "Check your weapons and get ready to take out these terrorists. This is going to be huge for your careers, trust me."

"Terrorists?" Morales asked. "I thought you said they were fugitive criminals who'd kidnapped a family."

"Same damn thing, soldier." A glower replaced Keith's grin. "Are you going to keep correcting me? Do I have to add to my final report that you were a problem?"

"No," the Specialist scowled. "I'm good."

"You better be, because we need to be on the same page if we're going to bring this guy and his accomplices down. They've already taken out some pretty tough hombres, so get your head on straight and be ready to fight, or I'll have to hire those farmers back on the road to dig a grave for you, got it?"

"Yeah. Got it. Crystal clear."

"Good." Keith nodded, satisfied when Morales picked up his rifle and started checking it and his equipment.

"One mile." Smith looked up the road. "Dead ahead." A moment later, he added, "A quarter mile, now. We're almost there."

The pavement turned rough, gravel spitting from beneath their wheels, the road thinning until there were no more shoulders and the edges were crumbling off. Ahead it narrowed even more, changing into a dirt trail that led through a thick swath of jungle too slim for the truck to pass. The treetops were swaying, rotor wind driving leaves and debris up the path to rattle against the windshield. Brakes slammed, tires squealed, and the Humvee came to a jarring halt before it plowed into the trees. With the wind dying down, the radio burst louder, a CENTCOM dispatch coming over the line in clipped tones.

"To all units in the Osa Peninsula of Costa Rica and those in Central to South Panama. Be advised of two missing soldiers in your area who are AWOL and considered armed and extremely dangerous. They've stolen equipment and are wanted by the US and Panamanian forces. Their names are Colonel Rachel Bank—" Keith reached up and snapped off the radio.

"That could have been important," Morales grumbled as he charged his weapon. "Turn it back on."

"It was nothing." Keith picked the radio mic off its holder and flipped the switch to activate the Humvee's rooftop horn, grin wide and unwavering. "Keep your mind on the mission."

Putting the mic to his lips, he hit the transmit button, and the loudspeaker on the roof burst to life. After a faint scratch of static, he laughed, his voice blaring through the forest above the chopper's fading engine noise.

"Good evening, kids!" he shouted, smirking, jerking the microphone in front of his lips. "This is your local neighborhood bounty hunter, looking for Tom McKnight and his accomplices." He laughed like a madman, throat swelling with tittering tightness. "You thought you could lose me in Panama City, but I was right behind you the whole way. And this is the end of the line, man! Your day of judgement has come."

* * *

Morales sat frozen in the back seat, ears still ringing from the name he'd just barely heard mentioned over the radio. Colonel Rachel Banks was someone of interest by both the US and Panamanian forces, and when Smith looked at him, he fixed the Lieutenant with a long stare, head shaking slightly, eyes shifting to Keith with obvious doubt, listening as he cackled over the Humvee's external speaker, mocking Tom McKnight and his accomplices.

Still, when Keith ordered them out of the truck, Morales did as he was told, stepping outside and shrugging off his heavier fatigue coat to leave only his sweat-stained, olive-green T-shirt. He reached in to grab his rifle, slammed the door, and met Smith at the front of the Humvee. Ahead of them, the highway turned into a dirt track that disappeared into the forest swath, the blowing debris dying down along with the engine noise. Dogs barked above the crowd's murmur, and the pungent reek of pollen and weeds stirred up by the helicopter tingled his sinuses.

"Is that town on the other side of the woods?"

The Lieutenant nodded. "Yeah, that's Yaviza."

Morales stepped away from the truck, gesturing for Smith to walk with him, saying, "Did you hear what CENTCOM said on the radio?"

"Not really," Smith admitted. "I was getting my gear together. Did you catch something?"

"Yeah, man. US and Panamanian Armed Forces are looking for—"

"You guys ready?" Keith walked by, still grinning, a hop in his step as he jerked his head toward the town. "Let's go meet Banks."

Morales and Smith fell in behind the agent, strolling along the dirt path, muddy earth beneath their boots, jungle bugs clicking and chirruping, birds and other animals squawking with exotic sounds. They walked for a hundred yards and emerged from the jungle, stopping at the head of a grassy park with kids' toys strewn around, several half-deflated soccer balls, a baseball bat, and an old-style merry-go-round, rusted and bent to the side on its shaft. Off to the right, the big Black Hawk sulked on the ground, its rotor blades slowing to a near stop. Behind the windshield sat a single pilot, wearing a headset and sunglasses perched above the same gaunt cheeks he remembered from the Los Berros camp in Mexico. Colonel Banks nodded to Keith, removed her headset, and kicked the door open to step out in full military fatigues with an olive-green flak jacket covering her chest. She reached behind the seat, pulled out a pistol, and holstered it, then she grabbed an M4 carbine from a storage bin, holding it by its hand guard as she fished out a handful of magazines, storing them in a pouch at her hip. Cradling the weapon in her right arm, Banks turned and strode to them with brisk steps.

"Gentlemen," she said when she got there. "Good to see you made it."

Keith didn't salute the Colonel, though Smith and Morales both gave one, Banks returning the gesture with a curt nod. Morales walked off to the side while the others talked, getting a glimpse of the village. The dirt lane ran right between a row of shops, a few eateries, and a hotel. Towering over the buildings was more jungle, providing a cool layer of shade over the town, and the shores on either side were filled with boats. It smelled muddy and fishy to him, though the delicious aromas of exotic foods drifted through the air, and he put his hand to his belly to keep it from growling.

A few dozen locals stared back at them, the dirt-smudged faces of people eyeing the soldiers and their helicopter with haunted and suspicious eyes, many backing away, turning their children into side alleys or taking them indoors. More than a few looked on in defiance, though they didn't appear armed except a few wearing machetes strapped to their backs, the blades stained green from regular use.

"Glad you made it, Banks," Keith was saying. "Are you ready to finish this?"

"More than ready to tie up this loose end," she agreed in a terse reply, and Morales caught her out of the corner of his eye as she shifted nervously, anxiously, gripping her weapon too tightly.

"You didn't bring an escort with you, Colonel Banks?" Smith asked the question Morales had been wondering, the Lieutenant's gaze moving between Banks and the Black Hawk.

"CENTCOM couldn't spare any more soldiers," she shrugged. "And I've got everyone I need right here, wouldn't you agree?"

"Yes ma'am," Smith said, straightening. "We're glad you have faith in us."

"After it's all said and done, I'll see that you boys are taken care of."

"Just glad to do our duties," Smith said, "right, Morales?"

"What are we dealing with here?" Morales asked. "A couple of gunmen?"

"Three or four with guns," Keith replied with a nod.

"All of them trained fighters?"

"Only one of them is truly dangerous, but they've got a dog, and they're…" Some thought turned the agent's head, and he stared into the village with a haunted look.

Smith exchanged an uncomfortable look with Morales but pressed the agent. "So, they've got some weapons, but only one can fight?"

"Yeah, but they can be a little tricky, is all." Snapping out of his thoughts, Keith turned a simmering glare on Smith. "Don't give them any quarter. Shoot first, ask questions later, no matter what. Got it? Now, let's fan out and start looking for them."

Smith nodded. "Yeah, okay."

"I'm going to need a little more clarification," Morales stepped into the circle, standing between Keith and Smith. "Who, exactly, are we looking for? There are people all over the place here, and the last thing I want is to point my weapon at someone who doesn't deserve it."

Banks stepped in. "You're right, soldier. It's a mother, father, and three kids. Caucasian, so they're going to stand out amongst the locals. And, like Keith said, they've got a German Shepherd."

"Wait, did you say *kids*?" Morales glared at Keith, who'd taken a step back, staring at Banks, gripping his rifle tight enough for the barrel to rise an inch or two. "We're hunting kids? You said—"

"Just get the job done, men," Banks said. "Kill the adults. Bring the kids to me, and I'll sort out the rest."

"But if you don't take down the adults, you're dead." Keith's eyes traced across them. "I hope that's clear. They're heavily armed, and they'll be looking to blow your heads off. Don't be weak!"

"The adults we can handle," Morales said as a rebellious spike streaked up his spine. He shook his head and pointed at the dirt. "But the kids…"

"We won't be killing kids, right, Keith?" Banks reiterated, fixing the agent with a clear look.

"I'll do my damnedest to make sure they don't get hurt," Keith nodded, "but as soon as one of them points their weapon at me, all bets are off, and you'd be smart to adopt that same philosophy."

* * *

"What do we do, honey?" Barbara asked, eyes flashing to the entrance, voice filled with tight determination. "Should we hide?"

Tom leaned past her, glancing toward the lane's end where the helicopter had idled down, watching as Banks strode away from the aircraft to where Keith and a pair of soldiers stood. One soldier was six three, skinny with light hair and a commanding stance, likely an officer. The other was shorter, broader, and of Hispanic descent. The two soldiers were having a heated discussion with the officers, the Hispanic man pointing at the ground, making a demand Tom couldn't hear. It wasn't the troops he was worried about, or even Banks. It was Keith, the man a scarecrow of his former self, scrawny, fidgeting with tension, gripping his gun as he glanced their way.

Tom backed inside to avoid being seen and turned to his family. "We won't hide, because they'll expect that. No, we're going to go out and meet them. Jack can keep Smooch here and hole up in the kitchen. Sam and I will cover the lane out front and try to isolate them and pick them off one at a time. Barbara and Linda, you two head out the back door and get behind them. Watch out for crossfire. We'll take out as many of them as we can and then fall back to the bridge if things go south. Got it?"

They nodded to each other, the girls sharing a frightened look before Linda threw herself at her sister, slamming her arms around her in a tight hug. "Shoot straight sis."

"You, too, Linda," Sam said, wiping away a tear as they separated.

Jack sniffled and whimpered, and the girls descended on him, embracing the boy, rubbing his head. "I want to go with you guys."

"You have to stay here and keep Smooch safe," Linda said with an assured nod. "And be ready to help us retreat if necessary."

"Yeah, we're depending on you," Sam added, swallowing a lump in her throat, her voice quivering on the edge of tears. "You've got to be our little soldier. Think you can do that?"

"I think so," he said, his eyes hardening even as moisture filled the bottom rims and streamed down his cheeks in twin rivers, holding Smooch's leash like it was a lifeline. "I don't know."

In the meantime, Tom turned to Barbara, taking in her striking green eyes, brushing a lock of sandy brown hair back from her face to push it behind her ear, bending to give her a quick kiss on the forehead. "Sorry it came to this, honey," he said, bumping his forehead against hers. "I don't want the kids to be involved in this…"

She touched his face, quivering fingers drifting lightly across his skin, voice trembling in the soft half-light. "They've grown up and become stronger, and they're in this together. We *all* are. No matter what happens, Tom McKnight, I'll always love you. Now, let's take care of these evil people once and for all so we can get on with living our lives."

Tom kissed her hand and squeezed it lovingly before pivoting to Sam, motioning her to stand by his side as he peeked outside. The two soldiers were just breaking off from the officers, their plans made. Gesturing for her to follow, stepping into the milling crowd, he crossed the street and entered an alleyway between buildings. With a glance back, he saw Barbara and Linda go out the hotel's rear door, Smooch's tail disappearing into the kitchen, and then the soldiers were there at the end of the lane, the Hispanic one slipping around the building while the officer entered the first shop on their side.

"This is a United States military operation!" His voice reverberated through the walls. "We're looking for an American family, two parents, three kids, and a dog. Have you seen them? Anyone seen a family…" The soldier repeated the request, voice raised above the crowd, townspeople slipping away as he continued making his demands.

"Where's the other one, Dad?" Sam whispered beside him.

"He went around to the back. Let's get him!"

Tom stepped deeper into the alley, moving over trash and garbage cans, slipping past a rotting storage shed squeezed between the buildings, leaving barely enough room to get by. The rich earthy scents were thicker there, the ground nothing but dirt and weeds and scrubby grass. When they reached the end of the alley, Tom edged past the corner, holding his breath, half expecting the soldier to be right there. When he wasn't, he gave a breathless sigh, eyes skittering in every direction. Out back of was just more brush, a couple of cracked concrete patios with lawn furniture, sheds, and crates of bananas stacked high enough to block his view. Two sheds stood side-by-side out in the back yard amidst tangles of trees and drooping vines as the river slipped by.

He kept his eyes on the stacked crates, expecting the soldier to step out from behind them at any second. When he didn't, Tom pursed his lips and shook his head, turning back to Sam. "Lost him—wait, there he is. Down by the river." Tom edged away from the building, gesturing for Sam to stay there, slipping to the stack of boxes, peering through the trees where the ground sloped to the brown, flowing waters. The soldier was moving amongst the boats and boat people littering the shore, looking into the shallow hulls, asking questions in halting Spanish even as several of the boaters dragged their longboats into the water, started the engines, and buzzed away.

The soldier suddenly turned and walked up the slope, eyes down as he climbed over the rough terrain, and Tom crept over to a thick tree near the two sheds, spotting the perfect place for an ambush. Glancing at Sam, he held up a single finger, and the girl nodded and raised her pistol, ready to back him up. Edging around the tree, Tom caught sight of the soldier stepping over a fallen log, jogging up the last twenty yards to come nearly level with them, still looking around but not seeing him. Before the soldier could look up, he leveled his gun and fired three quick rounds, the bullets popping off in the woods, scattering a flock of birds in a burst of angry squawks.

The soldier was fast, his rifle whipping up, barrel spitting fire just before he slid out of sight. Tom had already jerked backward as the three consecutive bursts of rounds peppered the tree, sending wood chips and bark flying, spraying the forest floor in a rain of debris. The thick trunk quivered against Tom's back under the onslaught of bullets. He kept his eyes pressed tight, wincing, grimacing in anticipation of a deadly bite of lead through his flesh. But when it didn't come, he shifted in the other direction, stealing a look around, catching the soldier still sliding up the hill to his left, moving in behind a tree, closer to the concrete patios and even more protection. Cursing, knowing the other soldier had likely heard the shots and was coming, he gestured for Sam to come to him. She nodded, breaking from cover, taking three steps before freezing to the spot, her brown curls falling over her shoulders as she stared at something Tom couldn't see. Shifting to the other side of the tree trunk, he saw that the soldier had come around fast and was in a crouch, rifle pointed at Sam's chest. A single squeeze of the trigger, and she'd be gone.

"No!" Tom shouted, whipping his gun up and firing, tracking the soldier as he hit the ground and rolled to Tom's right, ending up behind a tangle of deadfall. Not stopping to see if he'd hit the soldier, Tom grabbed Sam and pulled her away, using the sheds for cover as they dashed through the backyards.

Pistol in one hand, Sam's hand in the other, he dragged her through the crunch of forest debris, over concrete and dirt paths, sweeping around stacks of junk and plastic garbage bins, boots staggering, tripping, kicking rubbish and beat-up furniture out of the way. They dashed straight up to a partition made of latticework and vines, flying around it, stumbling into a group of old people sitting around a table. Tom pointed at the back door and hissed for them to get inside, and then he and Sam were off again, ducking beneath a clothesline, breaking into a dead sprint for the end of the row of buildings. The soldier pursued them, boots hammering on the ground, but at least he wasn't shooting, and Tom's eyes darted through the woods, looking for a hiding spot.

Breathing heavy, running hard, they reached the very end of the shops and houses, and Tom pushed Sam around the corner and followed her, slamming his back flat against the wall. Keeping his breathing calm and quiet, he turned back and peered around the corner, expecting to see the soldier again, though there was only the fleeting glimpse of old people going inside and the slam of a door as they shut themselves in.

"What now?" Sam asked, panting next to him.

"To the bridge," he whispered. "Like we planned."

"But Mom and Linda—"

"To the bridge," he growled, pushing Sam east toward the river and the steel bridge where it spanned the churning waters, stretching to the Darien wilds, lurking like a vast green monster. He led them through the woods where the foliage was thick, pushing past tangles of saplings and bushes, throwing glances back at the buildings, finally able to see down the lane where the crowds were cowering in doorways or in front of the shops, looking around in confusion.

"Sorry, I screwed that up," he said in a breathless whisper, brushing a branch out of his face. "I can't believe I missed him."

"Well, maybe we lost him, or they called him off or something."

"Maybe…"

They trudged up toward the bridge where steel cabling anchored it in place. Only five feet wide, the concrete bridge had steel rails and blue mesh fencing along the bottom half, the entire construction looking new and out of place against the backdrop of overgrown woods and ramshackle shops and houses. Crouched near the walkway leading up to it, partially hidden, they stared back along the lane, not seeing Keith, Banks, or the other soldier. Gripping Sam's arm, he pulled her aside to let a pair of locals in threadbare clothes slip past them and sprint to the other side, and another dozen people were rushing up, fearful expressions on their faces as they hurried across.

"If I'd waited a couple more seconds, I would have had him." With a grimace, he started to push Sam across to the other side. "You go. I'll see about your mother and Linda."

"I'm not going without you," she said, pushing his arm away. "We can set up a defensive spot here and –"

Movement came from his left, and Tom spun that way, but the officer's boot arrived a second faster than he could react, connecting with his gun hand and knocking it up with a sharp snap, his pistol flying straight up. As he tracked it with his eyes, the butt of a rifle swept around and cracked him across the face, sending him staggering backwards to land on his backside. The few locals still standing around scattered, bare feet pounding the dirt. Sam turned to shoot, but the Hispanic soldier stepped out of the woods on the other side, grabbing the top of her weapon, shoving it down, making her shoot dirt. She screamed and reeled on the soldier, trying to swing the gun around to blow him away, but his foot swept in from the left, and her feet flew out from beneath her, sending her airborne and landing on her tailbone with a yelp, her pistol ripped from her hand.

Face stinging, eyes watering with tears, Tom spotted his weapon lying in the deadfall a few feet away, and he rolled and crawled toward it, but the light-haired soldier was back, boot slamming down between his shoulder blades, the hard rifle barrel butting against his skull.

"Freeze, buddy," the man said. "You crawl another inch, and I'll paint the woods with your blood. Don't make me do it."

Squinting moisture from his eyes, Tom stopped crawling and caught Sam's look, the girl's expression furious, teeth bared, raising one eyebrow in question, but the men had their weapons pointed at their heads, dead to rights.

With a curt head shake, he said, "Don't do it, Sam. It's over."

* * *

"Check outside." Barbara swallowed hard and raised the weapon. "I'll keep an eye on the front door."

Linda poked her head out of the back door and looked both ways. The woods behind the hotel were moist and rank, the river scent drifting up through the trees along with a swarm of gnats, fat bugs flying in like bomber planes through the insect clouds. There were pieces of old lawn furniture scattered around, quaint latticework and trellises amidst the impoverishment. Hushed voices whispered in the shadows, doors slamming as locals disappeared inside.

One soldier was shouting something across the street, sounding to Linda like he was going building-to-building in search of the Americans with the German Shepherd, and she scanned back in the other direction, passing over the puppy Smooch had been playing with. The little dog was tugging on the end of his leash, Rodrigo, the mottled brown and white mutt, barking his head off at the helicopter that was parked about fifty yards away. But as soon as he saw Linda, he scrambled at her, jerking his rope tight with a happy *yip* and a *woof!*

"Shhh," Linda said, putting her finger to her lips, shaking her head when the puppy only barked harder. *Yap-yap-yap!* Turning inside, she motioned to Barbara. "Come on, Mom. We've got to get out of here or he'll give us away."

Barbara followed her outside, and the two crept east toward the bridge, skirting the excited puppy as it yipped and barked and bounced on the end of its leash, but they made it to the edge of the woods, sliding between a stand of saplings and short bushes with spiky leaves that reminded her of the ferns like the kind her mother kept around the house, only gigantic. Once they were hidden, the puppy stopped barking, ears perked up and shifting in every direction like radar dishes scouting for sounds. The shade was cool, quiet and dark, with a mist drifting up through the palm trees and thick brush, hiding the river from view.

Hunkered down, eyes on the backs of the dirty buildings, Linda leaned in, her voice barely above a whisper. "What do we do now, Mom?"

"Your father said to flank them," Barbara replied, shifting to a larger tree, peeking around the left side. "But if we walk out there now, little Rodrigo is going to go nuts."

"Yeah," Linda said. "Maybe we should—"

Three pistol shots popped off on the other side of the street, followed by heavy bursts of machine gun fire, and Linda's stomach lurched, the food she'd just eaten threatening to come up. "That's Dad and Sam!" she hissed. "They need our help!" Jumping up, she rushed through the brush, but her mother lunged and grabbed her arm, jerking her back into the tangled cover with a grunt.

Linda turned, eyes on fire, trying to rip free, but Barbara put her finger to her lips, shaking her head, gripping her fiercely. The finger moved from Linda's lips to point back toward the buildings where Rodrigo was going nuts again, barking his head off at something. One of Barbara's eyebrows raised to make sure Linda understood, a message she'd given countless times during her childhood. It meant heads up. Pay attention. *Beware.*

Swallowing hard, Linda nodded, and Barbara released her, Linda rising slowly to spread the ferns apart. Rodrigo was barking at the end of his leash at a man working his way toward them behind the buildings, moving in careful spurts, peering into windows and leaning inside open doors, testing doorknobs and locks, a rifle in his hand. The sight of Keith made her ill all over again. Scarecrow-ish and lean, the man wore bandages on the tips of his right fingers, spots on his cheeks and nose still raw from the frostbite she'd given him back in North Carolina.

Rodrigo saw Keith and trotted as far as his leash would allow, barking and yapping and seeking the man's attention. Keith grinned at the puppy, rose from his crouch, and strode over, stopping just short of being licked in the face as the dog spun and jumped and stretched his leash taut, dancing on his rear paws. A hollow fear touched Linda's belly, a lilt of unease at the sight of Keith's slow smile, the sensation expanding when the man suddenly stepped back and pointed his rifle at the puppy's yapping face. Roderigo barked louder, snapping playfully at the long metal barrel.

Linda came out of her crouch with blazing eyes, raising her pistol and getting ready to shoot. A hand fell heavily on her shoulder again, Barbara gripping her tight, head shaking, whispering, "No, Linda. You'll give us a way. It's too long a shot."

Linda shifted with a snap of her shoulder, the heel of her boot pressing harder into the turf, crushing a twig beneath it. She dropped, but not before Keith whipped his attention in their direction. At Barbara's warning look, Linda stayed in a crouch as Keith's footfalls crunched carefully, deliberately, on the debris-strewn ground, his light chuckles chilling her bones as he crossed the couple of dozen yards to them.

Barbara made quick hand signals. You go through the brush that way, and I'll go the other way. We'll hit him at the same time…

Linda nodded vigorously that she understood, and she squared up to the tree, holding her pistol ready to fire. Barbara mirrored her position, one hand raised and counting a silent three.

One… Two…

A branch crackled behind them, the distinct sound of a heavy football cracking through brittle leaves. Barbara whirled as a rifle stock struck her in the chest, reversed direction, then returned with the crack across her jaw, knocking her sideways into the brush.

A croak burst from Barbara's throat. "Run, Linda!"

Linda threw a glance at the woman who'd just struck Barbara, legs spread, forearms bulging with tendons as she turned the rifle on her. Linda spun away, firing once blindly, missing badly, bursting from the bushes and sprinting across the grass toward the hotel. She made it three steps before a shock punched her in the side, needles of pain lancing her ribs, followed by an electric jolt that stiffened her spine, muscles spasming up her back as a cry gurgled from her throat. She pitched face-first to the ground and flopped there, clutching her side, trying to get control of her body. But her arms and legs were completely useless, every muscle with a mind of its own. She shivered, bucked, and moaned, foam forming on her lips, a sound like simmering fire in her ears. And then it stopped, her body falling into a tired slump on the ground, exhausted as she gasped for breath, muscles twitching. A boot kicked her in the side, pitching her onto her back with a pained cry, adding to the aches already streaking through her muscles, pins and needles in every nerve. Keith stood over her, grinning down, snorting and laughing as he shook his head. "I've been waiting a long time to do that, little Linda," he said, kicking her in the ribs for good measure, spit flying from her lips as she curled up in pain. Glaring up at him, she tried to swing her leg around to kick, but her limbs were useless and dead. The lady who'd hit Barbara dragged her out of the brush by her hair, kicking her in the back to send her crashing to her knees next to Linda.

With a sob, Barbara threw herself on Linda, grabbing her hands and pulling her into her lap, supporting her back while gripping her chin. "What happened to you, Linda? Linda!"

When Linda tried to speak, a moan came out.

Barbara's head whipped around, snarling at Keith. "What did you do to my baby? You son of a—"

The rifle stock flew in again, cracking Barbara at the base of her neck, slumping her forward in a heap with a pained gasp.

* * *

Holding Smooch's collar, Jack stood by the back door, one hand clamped over the dog's muzzle as he peered outside, watching Linda be taken by surprise and his mother get struck in the head with the rifle. He tried to do what his father had asked, had tried to stay hidden with Smooch so he wouldn't get in the way and cause any problems, because the last thing he wanted to do was make his dad angry. But a deep gnawing feeling was devouring him on the inside, unbidden emotion bursting from his chest, a scream crawling from his throat.

Just when he was about to let Smooch go, to rush out and run at Keith with his fists swinging, voices out front caught his attention, his father's among them, growling in defiance. Pulling back into the shadows, Jack tugged the whining dog away from the door, shushing her, trying to keep her claws from scrabbling on the old wooden floors. Finally obeying him, the German Shepherd turned and allowed herself to be led to the front where Jack peeked outside, watching as Tom and Sam moved ahead of the two soldiers, rifles trained on their backs, shoved and pushed by the armed men.

"You don't have to do this," Tom was saying, half turning, shoved again by the shorter, darker soldier.

"Shut up and keep moving," the man said, his mean tone of voice lancing Jack's heart with fear and confusion, his eyes shifting to the back door, uncertain of what to do.

Smooch pawed at the floorboards, whining and growling deep in her chest, but they were too far for the soldiers to hear. Face scrunched up in fear and anger, Jack fell to one knee and wrapped his arm around the dog's neck, whispering in her ear. "Everyone's in trouble, Smooch!" he sobbed. "What should we do?"

* * *

Tom staggered and nearly fell, shoved from behind by Morales, the soldier's name learned when he'd spoken with Lieutenant Smith. While the two were under Banks' command, the soldiers hadn't shot them, not even when Morales could have easily put a bullet between Sam's eyes, and that gave Tom a glimmer of hope, a sliver of light in the darkness.

"You don't have to do this," he said, hands on his head, half turning to meet Morales' eyes. "We haven't done anything wrong!"

"Shut up and keep moving," Smith replied, his hard expression shifting from Sam to Tom.

"What they're doing is outside of military jurisdiction," Tom continued, eyes darting to the shops and eateries along the lane, everyone having cleared out, just a pair of faces disappearing as some blinds flew shut. "Keith's a maniac. If you spent any time with him, you'd know he's crazy."

"Shut up," Smith snapped. "Next time I have to say it, you're going to feel it."

Tom snapped his mouth shut, glancing at Sam. Her cheeks were wet with tears, lips trembling as she held her hands on her head, fingers interlocked, dead leaves caught in her hair. They reached the end of the lane and angled toward the helicopter, when Tom glanced over and saw banks and Keith shoving Linda and Barbara in the same manner, laughing uproariously when Linda stumbled against her mother, Barbara catching her before she fell.

Tom started forward. "You son of a—"

Smith stepped around to his left, blocking him. "Look, buddy," the Lieutenant said, peering down his rifle sights, stopping Tom in his tracks. "The only way this is going to go well for you as if you shut up and do as you're told."

"You don't know what you're doing." Tom balled his fists at his side. "If you help these two, you're helping known criminals."

"Funny," Smith said. "They're saying the same thing about you. Now put your hands back on top of your head and *move!*"

"Over here by the helicopter!" Keith shouted, gesturing toward the Black Hawk with his rifle.

Tom edged toward Keith, but Smith pulled his weapon back and shoved him straight again, the soldier backing up and jerking his weapon back to his shoulder. "I'm telling you, man. Knock it off."

As the groups converged on the Black Hawk, Tom caught Barbara's gaze. Cords stood out on her neck as she fought against her own instincts, a hand resting on her chest while the other arm wrapped around Linda's shoulders. At first, Tom thought Linda had been shot by the way she stooped, clutching her left side and crying, white spittle caked on her lips.

Jaw clenched in fury, Tom raised his fist like he wanted to hit someone. "What happened? What did they do to her?"

"They shocked her, Tom."

"Gave her a little taste of my taser," Keith said, proudly holding up the device, flicking a button to let the spent cartridge fall to the ground. "I wanted something special for little Linda after what she did to me." He cradled his rifle in his right arm as he stepped closer. "I might hit her with it again just for kicks."

"You keep your hands off of her, you *bastard*!" Tom growled, pushing his chest against Smith's rifle barrel, turning when he heard Sam's cry. Morales had shoved her to her knees on the rocky soil. A moment later, the soldiers grabbed Tom by the arms, one rifle stock cracking him on his lower back, buckling him, forcing him to his knees next to Sam. The cold, hard barrel returned, bumping against the base of his neck.

"Colonel Banks, do you have any zip ties in the Black Hawk?" Smith asked. "Let us know where they are, and we'll get them bound up for transport."

"There won't be any transport," Banks said as she grabbed Barbara by the back of the neck and forced her to her knees with a cry, Linda falling out of her grip and pitching forward into the grass. "We're going to take care of this here and now."

"I'm glad you didn't shoot them," Keith said to Smith and Morales. Then he turned to Tom, the man's footsteps behind him in the grass. "It will be so much more satisfying to do this like I told you I would, starting with little Linda." There was a pause as he looked around. "Hey, where's the kid?"

"We didn't have time to look," Morales said. "These two were hard enough to handle."

"I told you they would be," Keith smirked. "But don't worry. We'll find him later."

"Leave them alone," Tom croaked, his mind reeling with pain and confusion, still dizzy after the rifle strike to the back of his head.

"Sorry, Tom," Banks said, stepping closer, switching places with Keith. "This has been a long time coming, and it's going to be a pleasure to see you die. You caused me a lot of problems."

"*You* caused yourself those problems," Tom glared up at her. "I told you we couldn't stop what was happening, but you kept going, kept pushing… you made everything worse."

"I followed *orders*." Banks circled to face him, the barrel of her rifle swinging dangerously close to his face. "Something you couldn't bring yourself to do. If you'd helped us sooner, we could have—"

"I *told* you it wouldn't work, but you wouldn't listen," he snapped, spittle flying on his lips. "You were trying to please your bosses and stroke your own damned ego, just like the last time. Is that why you kept after me? Is that why you rushed things? You know, what we did… we unleased those earthquakes, and people *died* you bitch. I should have never worked with you again. Not after the last time, you evil, lying—"

"Shut up."

"It was *your fault*!" Tom screamed through clenched teeth, barely able to keep his hands on his head where they shook with rage.

Banks' lip curled as she stared down at him, eyes narrowed, one cheek twitching, and she turned to Keith. "I'm tired of listening to this. Go ahead. Do it. Execute them *all*."

Keith got in behind Linda, leveling his rifle at the girl's prone form where she was slumped on her side in the grass. "Hey, little Linda. Get your ass up. I want you to take this on your knees, not lying on your face."

Tom clenched his hands over his head, gathering himself to rise and grab at Banks' rifle barrel. He'd likely be shot by Smith first, but he couldn't bear to see Linda killed. No, he'd die before she did. He'd grab Banks' rifle, wrench it out of her hands, and kill them all, no matter how many times they shot him, no matter how many bullets he had to take. Before he died, he'd give his family a chance to survive.

The barrel poised against the back of his neck suddenly pulled away.

"Wait, what?" Smith asked. "What the hell are we doing here?"

"Yeah, we can't just execute an entire family," Morales' voice was filled with doubt. "We need to call this in to CENTCOM. We can use the chopper's radio–"

"Negative, soldier," Banks said. "Get those weapons turned around and step back."

There was a pause, Tom holding his breath as the tension thickened around him, the faint traces of hope still alive. Turning his head slowly to the left, sweat dripping from his nose and chin, he watched Banks and Keith out of the corner of his eye, all their weapons pointed at the ground for the moment as they dealt with the new wrinkle in their plan.

"Sorry, sir. We can't do that," Smith said, the Lieutenant's rifle shifting up to cover Banks. "Morales, go to the radio and call CENTCOM now. Killing kids does *not* sound like an authorized operation."

"Roger that, sir," Morales responded with a relieved tone.

Tom's eyes met Barbara's, their deep green color alive with hope, wheels turning in her head just like they were in his. Tom kept looking slowly between their captors, sizing them up, searching desperately for an opening.

"You guys win," Banks said, backing off, stepping away from Tom with her rifle pointed off to the side. "Call it in, and you'll see we're justified in this."

"It's a waste of time," Keith shrugged, but he also stepped back, shoulders relaxing, weapon shifting away from Linda. "But, yeah, call it in like Banks said."

Morales circled around to the Black Hawk's cockpit, lowering his weapon as he looked inside. Faster than Tom could have imagined it was possible given the man's wounded state, Keith's rifle snapped up, a quick burst firing toward Morales, then shifting to Smith and shooting again. Morales spun and hit the ground while Smith cried out, a spatter of hot blood spraying Tom's neck before the Lieutenant collapsed on his back, but he wasn't dead and tried to get his weapon up in response. Banks rushed forward, her boot flying past Tom's head to kick the soldier, knocking him into the grass where he howled and writhed and clutched his arm to his side.

Spinning on his knees, hands out, Tom looked for an opportunity to charge, but Keith's eyes were on him, his snarling lips curled on one side, swaggering with his rifle wavering above Linda's whimpering form, the barrel still smoking. Planting one foot, Tom turned back to Banks, ready to dive at her, but a flash of motion stopped him, a shape running low to the ground, ears pinned back, tail flying behind it, teeth bared as it sprinted at Keith while Jack was shrieking from behind.

"Fass, Smooch! *Fass*!!"

Keith spun, his mouth falling open, head jerking away as the furry missile hit him, sending the rifle flying away, driving him to the ground as jaws clamping on his throat with a snap, the dog's powerful neck twisting back and forth like his windpipe was a chew toy. Screams ripped from his chest as he punched and swung futilely, voice climbing upward into gurgling shrieks, but Smooch held on with ease, sinking her fangs deeper into his soft flesh.

With bulging, furious eyes, Banks swung her rifle at the dog, but Tom was already on his way, shoulder lowered, hammering her in the gut with a hard tackle, slamming her into the Black Hawk's fuselage, punching the air from her lungs. The rifle flew away as they hit the ground with a grunt, Tom swinging a fist, cracking her across the side of the face and eliciting a pained howl. He tried to grab her arms or wrists, anything to hold her down, but she was fast and squirming, twisting beneath him, protecting her right side where her pistol was holstered, elbowing him with her left arm.

When she flipped onto her stomach, Tom wrapped his left arm around her neck but she tucked her chin and bit, teeth penetrating flesh, sending pain bolting through his forearm as he screamed. The pistol came free from its holster and she tried to roll right and shoot him under her left armpit, but Tom had expected the move and swiveled as the shot flew into the sky, then he reached around her waist and grabbed her wrist, pulling, keeping the weapon pinned beneath her. She kicked backward, twisted, tearing a piece of flesh from his forearm, head snapping back, cracking his nose in a spiderweb of shock that ignited every nerve in his face.

"Son of a bitch!" Tom cried, raising up and jerking his arm free before bringing his forearm down on the back of her head, pummeling her with his elbow, driving her face into the moist earth, leaving bloody streaks in her hair. Shoving his left arm on her shoulders, he leaned in with all his weight, wrenching her gun arm from beneath her, twisting it backward, her shoulder cracking as he jerked it at an awkward angle. Tom pulled once, twice, then a third time until she howled and dropped the pistol into the dirt. They both scrambled for it, but he pinned it down, gripped it, and swung it up to slam the barrel against her skull.

Three quick shots split her head in two, hot blood spraying his face as bits of hair and bone flew off in chunks. Ears ringing, Tom shoved himself up, climbing, staggering to his feet, swinging the pistol up to end Keith, but Smooch had dragged him across grass, painting the long blades red. The German Shepherd's jaws were locked on his throat, no longer twisting and trying to rip it out, but strangling, her eyes up and looking at Tom, sides heaving while Keith's arms pummeled at her weakly, his screams dying in a gurgle of pain and agony. Tom didn't call her off, instead watching quietly as Keith's last breath rasped from his throat, blood-spattered face staring blankly at the sky.

* * *

Standing next to the Black Hawk, rifle in his hands, Tom stood guard with Sam. She'd collected Bank's gun and patrolled near the chopper's tail, watching for any new soldiers who might roll up, her jaw set, gaze hard as she scanned the slopes leading to the river and the woods beyond.

"I'm telling you, it's just us." Smith winced where he sat on the edge of the chopper's crew cabin as Barbara tended to his wounded left shoulder, a pair of nasty bullet wounds that had taken off a huge chunk of skin and muscle out and rendered his arm nearly useless.

"Yeah, we got roped into this whole thing," Morales added. "We're so sorry about all this. I wish we could take it all back…" His voice faded, eyes glassy with emotion as he glanced at Linda who stood to the side with Smooch and Jack, the kids cleaning up using water from a bucket Sophia had brought to them.

"We'll keep the guns anyway," Tom said sharply, then he caught Barbara's look and shook his head, sighing wearily. "It's fine. You're not the first ones Keith swindled into helping him. A lot of people died because of those two. Friends and strangers alike." Tom's looked off in the grass where he'd dragged Banks and Keith, leaving their bloodied corpses to the insects and scavengers, unwilling to give them a proper burial.

"You need to get this seen to right away," Barbara said, finishing wrapping the man's upper arm before shifting to Morales where he slumped shirtless, white bandages on his tanned side, three deep grazes that had taken a good-sized piece of flesh off him. "Yours will probably be fine, too, but you should find a field hospital as soon as possible to keep the chances of infection down."

"Yes, thank you," Morales said, and his dark eyes lifted to Tom. "Thank you so much for your help. Again, we're both so sorry."

"I said it's fine," Tom nodded, stepping closer to the soldier. "I saw you had my daughter pinned in your sights, and you could've shot her dead, but you didn't. That's when I knew you weren't on board with what they'd intended to do. At least not fully."

"I'd never shoot a child," Morales agreed with a haunted look, wiping his hand down his face, shaking his head as he glanced over ashamedly at Sam before he averted his gaze.

Barbara finished packing up the first aid kit and stuffed it into their duffel bag, which was filled with more supplies and magazines taken from the Black Hawk. "I'm ready to go."

Tom faced the soldiers. "Now, the big question is, will you try to bring us in? Are you going to pursue us?"

The soldiers shared a look, an unheard communication between them, and Tom sensed they'd been together for a while, maybe even from the start of the Mexican annexation, their camaraderie reminding him of the past and what Banks had taken from him. He didn't make a show of pointing his weapon at them, didn't want to end the conversation on a threat, trying to give them the benefit of the doubt in spite of the circumstances.

The pair finally nodded, and Smith shifted to better face Tom, wincing as his shoulder moved. "Oh, geez, that hurts." After the pain faded, he met Tom's gaze dead on, voice filled with honesty and regret. "As far as we're concerned, Mr. McKnight, the actions taken by the deceased were unlawful, ultimately resulting in their deaths. The unfortunate victims of Lieutenant Colonel Banks and her special agent vanished before the situation was completely resolved, and no further information on them is available at this time."

"Thanks," Tom said with a nod, his stance loosening. "You can't imagine how much it means to us."

"After everything you've told us," Morales said with a heavy headshake, "it sounds like you folks have been through hell. All we can do is wish you good luck. So… good luck."

"Yeah, seriously," Smith added. "Good luck, folks."

"You, too." Tom gave them a half smile and a nod, then called, "Jack, Linda? Grab your packs. We're heading out!"

Reaching for his and Barbara's backpacks, he gripped them by their straps and nodded for Sam to follow. Samantha strode over, stared at Smith and Morales for a lingering moment, then walked off to join her brother and sister. Tom took two paces back, giving the soldiers another nod before turning to where his family waited for him. He started to walk by, but Barbara locked her arm in his and drew him in where the girls had made a circle with Jack and Smooch in the middle. They wrapped their arms around each other, Barbara's grip gentle and loving, Sam's fingers digging into his back almost desperately, painfully, as she cried tears of relief against his shoulder.

"It's over, guys," Tom said. "It's really over."

"And now we can finally begin again," Barbara added with a smile and a kiss on each of their heads.

They broke their embrace, and Tom gave one more nod at the soldiers before striding along the lane through town, followed by Jack and the girls. The street was crowded with locals, all of them quiet and looking on with frightened eyes, whispers that would beget legends of what had happened in Yaviza. Alia and Sophia stood off to the right, their smiles wide as the crowd parted to let the McKnights through as they made their way to the bridge framed in jungle brush and trees, the metal and concrete span stretching across to the Darien wilds, their new home, their new beginning. Tom ushered the kids on first, then Barbara, glancing back one last time before he shouldered his rifle, turned, and followed them.

It was time to begin. Again.

Epilogue

The sun beat down on the valley with golden rays of light that made the air shimmer. It was a relatively dry piece of land, nestled between the swamps and jungle in Central Darien, filled with fields tended by a family with over thirty years of hard labor. The lower fields were marked by cornstalks bursting with ripe ears, ready for harvest and three terraces lay cut into the hillside where sugarcane and coffee beans grew. Outer tracts of soil boasted a few rows of peppers, several banana trees, and an apple tree orchard deeply rooted along the jungle's edge.

At the head of the valley lay a wide, flat homestead, colorful against the green and brown smear of countryside, made of several rooms hammered together with logs, plywood, and sheets of steel taken from cars. The rear section was half of an old school bus, the sunlight glinting off the glass where the kids lived and played, the windows left uncovered so they could watch the rainstorms that often swept through.

The kids' laughter filled the air, two young girls out in a flat field, six and seven years old, running around their older brother who was desperately trying to wrangle them to focus on their work. "Come on, you jerks! Mama said we have to get these potatoes packed up for the market tomorrow, or we don't get a play day!"

His plaintive tone only made the girls giggle harder, and as one sprinted by, he scooped her up, spun her around, and dropped her on her feet, her body vibrating with laughter. Close by in a nearby field, a father sat atop an ancient tractor, its old diesel engine burping up smoke as it struggled to drag their plow through the rough dirt. He waved to a woman standing nearby with a mule's tether in her hand, several more of the pack animals near them with packs of supplies lying across their backs, laden with jugs of oil, jerry cans full of diesel fuel, and their lunch, if they ever got to it.

Tall with slender legs sticking out from a pair of cutoff jeans, she smiled with bright green eyes marked with laugh lines in the corners. She wore her hair loose, a tumble of golden-brown waves over her sunbaked shoulders and an old white T-shirt with the neck cut out. Raising her hand, she made a pulling motion, and her husband responded with a couple of blats on the tractor horn, drawing her smile even wider.

A thumping sound dulled the tractor's noise and the woman looked upward, hand shielding her eyes from the bright sunlight, scanning east toward the vast jungle. As she watched the treetops, a massive, light-gray helicopter burst into view, its thin profile familiar from a day many years prior when she'd ridden with her father to a Navy vessel to witness an event that would change the world. It swooped in, arcing over the fields, sending a windstorm over their crops, the tall cornstalks blowing over like a giant finger was running straight through the middle. Waving as it passed overhead, she turned and glanced at the house. The girls were pointing up and jumping with joy as they scrambled after it toward a grassy landing spot with a big handmade sign written in children's scrawl, a smiley face and the words *Land Here!*

As the helicopter settled, the woman glanced back at her husband where he'd stopped and was waving her to go on, then he raised a finger to tell her he'd be over in a minute. Nodding, smiling, Sam turned and strode across the field, walking between the rows in her ankle-high work boots, watching the Seahawk come to rest on its three wheels, the rotor winds blasting the property in waves, the girls having to stop and hold their arms up, leaning into the wind to avoid being blown over. When she got there, she stopped behind the girls, wrapping her arms around them and squeezing them, chuckling at their infectious laughter as they wiggled and squirmed to get out of her grip. But she held onto them, kissing each of them on the head, waiting for the rotors to spin all the way down.

A man a few years younger than her stepped off the Seahawk and landed in the grass, removing his helmet to reveal a tousle of brown hair and dark eyes above a firm, clean-shaven jaw, a necklace around his neck holding a faded round tag on it along with a scrap of red collar. Turning, he helped a woman closer to Sam's age down, her helmet lifting to release a tumble of wavy chestnut locks that tumbled over her shoulders. Dressed in jeans and a light-brown leather jacket, she took off her sunglasses and walked over while the man helped two others out of the helicopter.

Sam's girls broke away, sprinting, shouting, "Aunt Linda! Uncle Jack! Aunt Linda!"

Linda kneeled and scooped them into her arms, shook them around, and lavished them with kisses. Standing, she held the girls' hands and walked over. "Heya, Sis!"

"Hi, Linda," Sam said, stepping forward to wrap her long arms around Linda's neck, catching the faint scent of her freshly washed hair. "Wow, is that something new? I haven't smelled anything like that in forever."

"Actually, yes," Linda said, reaching up to toss her hair off her shoulders, looking down as she ran her fingers through the cut ends. "It's a new thing out of Guayana City. I love it. And… I brought you some. Not that we came here for that."

"You look great, but…" Sam's eyes held a hint of confusion. "I didn't think you were due in with Mom and Dad for another month."

"Dad will explain." Linda narrowed her eyes, impressed. "As always, you look like a goddess. Nice tan."

"Thanks," Sam laughed, gesturing back toward the field. "It's been crazy hot all summer, and we've been working our butts off. The yield is going to be exceptional this year."

"Hey, where are those little tadpoles of ours?"

It was a gruff voice, the deep, familiar tone drawing the girls' attention. The kids broke around Linda and sprinted toward the helicopter, where two others had climbed down. One was an older man with a slightly bowed walk, wearing blue jeans and a flannel shirt with a white jacket over top, hair turned a dark shade of gray, chin clean-shaven, brown eyes still as sharp as ever. A woman had locked arms with him, the pair leaning together, supporting each other as they strode across the soft grass.

"Emily! Rosa! My granddaughters!" Tom said. "How are you, my sweethearts?"

"Great, Papa!" they shouted in musical glee, swarming their grandparents with open arms, nearly bowling them over if Jack hadn't been there to catch little Rosa.

"Hey, there! Easy on the older folks!" Jack said, snatching the girl up and catching her in his arms. "Whoa! You're way too big to hold!" He let her drop to the grass with mock bluster.

The crowd came over, and Sam lifted her face to Tom and Barbara, giving each a smile. "Dad," Sam said softly, embracing him in a long hug.

"Sam," he whispered back, his voice hoarse with emotion, eyes glassy with a father's pride.

Shifting to her mother, the older woman's once light hair had turned fully gray except for some blonde color streaked through it. "Hi, Mom," she said. "I really missed you."

"We missed you, too, Samantha! Terribly! And we couldn't wait to come."

Turning, Sam grabbed Jack. "Little brother. You look good."

"You, too," he said, breaking the embrace and patting her on the shoulder. "How's Gustav and Michael?"

Turning, Sam gestured back to where her fourteen-year-old was still walking up. "Well, Michael's fine. Gustav and I were getting the field ready for planting late crops…" Hands on her hips, she shook her head and stared at Barbara. "Why are you guys even here? I mean… I'm *glad* you're here, but we weren't supposed to get a visit from you two again until next month. And why are Linda and Jack with you? Where are my nieces and nephews? Is there something wrong?"

Barbara stepped aside and gestured at Tom. "We did come a little early, but there's a perfectly good reason for it. We wanted to surprise you."

Tilting her head to the side, Sam gave him a pensive look. "Surprise me? I have no idea what you guys are talking about."

Tom was already taking something out of his coat, a slim black computer tablet with the United States government Seal. He held the tablet out and turned it on, the device booting up with a soft beep, his fingers sliding over the screen and pushing with light finger strokes, finally holding it out to Sam, who rubbed her chin but didn't take it right away.

"What's this?"

Grinning, he held it closer, turning it so she could see the vivid images displayed there in blue and white topographical formations. "Go ahead, look."

Reluctantly, Sam accepted the tablet and flipped it so that the image was right side up, blinking at what appeared to be a satellite photo of a snowy plain, fields of frost and white drifts that showed as dark shadows around a frozen crust of undulating waves. At first, it was just a bunch of random shapes in the snow, the outline of an ancient ruin from a long-gone time. But then a pensive smile crossed her face, one hand slowly moving to her chest, fingers toying with the sweaty neckline of her shirt as she traced over the objects on the screen, silvery glaze over dilapidated structures, their hard ridges poking through the snow. There were charred edges marking their old homestead, the big red barn with its collapsed walls, the chicken coup's faint contours, and the wind-weathered rabbit hutch that somehow had withstood both time and weather.

Swallowing a lump of emotion, she cleared her throat. "Is this the project you've been working on over the last year?"

A slow smiled crossed his face. "Yes, thanks to some connections I maintained. I've been working overtime to secure the whole family, all of us, one of the first rights of return."

Linda and Jack stepped around them and went to greet Gustav and Michael, exchanging hugs in a haze of pollen and dust, the younger McKnights looking clean and sharp against the work-weary farmers with their smudged faces and dirty clothes. Gustav walked away from the group and approached with a quiet smile, shaking Tom's hand and embracing Barbara briefly before nodding at the tablet, his arm around Samantha's waist.

"What are we looking at?"

"It's the old farmstead," Sam explained, shifting back to Tom with a solemn look. "A… right of return? Are you serious?"

"Dead serious. We've all got the right to reclaim our land, as well as any surrounding unclaimed properties up to the maximum acreage allowed by law. Any disputes will be handled by the government as per their announcements."

"You can't be serious." Smile fading and growing again, Sam looked at Gustav, who wore a bright grin to match hers.

"We've been talking about this for years," he said, resting his hand on her shoulder, "but we never thought the time would come."

"Yes! We can finally go back…" Her words faded just before she said, *home*. With a half step, she turned to face their ramshackle house and its hodgepodge secrets, memories of building it all together over the years to make it their own, a lifetime of reminders captured in those rooms along with all their worldly possessions. She watched Michael and the girls talking and laughing with Linda and Jack, the bonds they'd kept despite the distance they lived apart. With a gasp, she shifted her attention to Gustav and his concerned eyes.

"What's wrong, Sam?" he asked.

With a stiff shake of her head, she handed the tablet back to Tom. "No, I can't. *We* can't. I'm sorry, but this is our home now and—"

Gustav cut her off with a laugh and took the tablet out of Tom's hand, studying the ruins and surrounding countryside with his dark eyes, smiling even wider. "This looks incredible, Tom." Glancing at Jack and Linda, he gave the tablet a shake. "Is everyone else on board with this? Do they all want to go back?"

"They do," Tom said. "Linda and Jack have talked it over with their kids, and their spouses are on board. In fact, they're all excited to be doing it. They're still in Caracas settling matters with their farms and will be along in a few days." He gripped her shoulders and gave them a firm squeeze. "We're going back home, Sam. Can you believe it?"

"I just don't see how you made it work. It seemed like such a long shot when you first told me about it."

"Well, with the weather shifting to warmer temperatures over the past few years, it's really opened up people's minds to going back, and they're taking volunteers. Of course, I've had my name on the list for a long time. Along with that comes a special dispensation from the new planning commission. One guy there knew my old commander, Osaka. And after what Banks did to us, none of the higher ups want that story to *ever* see the light of day. Lieutenant Governor Morales leaned on a few people with some vague threats of exposure so they're pulling out all the stops for us. It's a great opportunity."

Handing the tablet back to Tom, Gustav beamed an even wider smile. "Well, that settles it. We're going. When can we start packing?"

"Gustav, no," Sam said, expression drawn and angsty. "Panama is your home. We've built an entire life here, and this…" With a stiff hand, she gestured toward the terraced hillside with its corn and coffee beans, sweeping to the cornrows and apple orchard on the jungle's edge. "This is our home now."

Gustav gave a bark of laughter, a truly joyful sound. "I'm an orphan, my dear, from a place very far from here. I have no one to root me to this except you and our children."

Sam's expression melted into a frown. "But… what we've built…"

"It doesn't matter," he said, wrapping his arm around her waist, pulling her close, and planting a kiss on her cheek. "What is it you told me, my dear, when we first met? Home isn't a place. It's where your family is. We all…" He nodded to Tom and Barbara, then glanced over at the kids. "We are all family, and we should be together. Think of what we can accomplish if we're all in the same place, working toward the same goals. Because that's what a home is. And I would love to see where my dearest and her family started… I've always wanted to see America."

"Why does that matter when we're so happy here?"

"Happy?" Gustav laughed again. "We live in the middle of the swamp, and it's a struggle to grow even what we can. I have no interest in being here any longer than we have to, especially with the warming temperatures. No, the matter is settled."

Sam's frown lifted, and she embraced Gustav briefly, nodding her acceptance, stepping aside to stand firm. "Okay, Mom and Dad. What are the next steps?"

"Your mother and I are going to fly over to a nearby naval base and fill out some paperwork, and as one of the original residents, you'll need to come with us to do that. In two days, everyone's families will meet up with the convoy heading north." Tom's eyebrows raised. "Remember Lieutenant Smith? Well, he's a colonel now, and he'll be meeting us personally and has arranged for us a nice, comfy ride."

"That sounds great," Gustav said, glancing at Sam.

"Are you sure?" Sam's voice was a whisper, her eyes wide in question. "You don't have to…"

Gustav put a finger to her lips. "Hush, my dear. Let's not think about what we are leaving behind, but where we are going to be."

Her pensive expression held firm for a long moment, and then she agreed. "Okay, Dad. When do we need to be at this meeting?"

Tom glanced at his watch. "Thirty minutes?"

Sam gaped. "Are you serious? We've still got a full day's work left, and—"

"Shush," Gustav ended her complaints with an embrace. "You go ahead with Tom and Barbara, and I'll have the kids start packing to be ready for the convoy in two days."

"What about the farm?" she exclaimed. "What about the harvest?"

"I'll pick someone to take it over, perhaps a nice young couple who needs a fresh start in life." He smiled at her. "Like *our* family once did."

Sam searched his face for any signs of lingering doubt, but when she didn't find any, she smiled. "Thank you, honey. I guess it *is* settled. Let's go, Dad."

After one more embrace and a kiss, Sam said goodbye to the kids and followed Tom, Barbara, Linda, and Jack to the Seahawk, where the pilot was engaging the control panel switches to bring the chopper to life, its turbine winding up, the rotors kicking into a slow spin.

Tom gave her a helmet, and they got buckled in, Sam sitting between Linda and Jack, a familiar nervous tickle in her belly as memories of the events that led them to Panama came flooding back. A quick glance out the window showed Gustav with Michael and the girls all waving, faces bright with hope and delight as the chopper lifted off. Stomach lurching, she gasped and gripped the arms of her seat, gazing downward as they banked gently over the wide, green fields and rose above the vast jungle canopy with its endless, wild expanse.

Jack and Linda slipped their hands over hers, putting her fears to rest, their expressions calm as they each wore a knowing grin. Tom and Barbara had locked arms, relaxed in their seats, staring out the windows at the clear blue skies, and while she couldn't be certain, it seemed her father held a secret gleam in his eye. Sam smiled as they set off together on their next grand adventure.

It was time to begin. Again.

Want More Awesome Books?

Find more fantastic tales right here, at books.to/readmorepa.

* * *

If you're new to reading Mike Kraus, consider visiting his website at www.mikekrausbooks.com and signing up for his free newsletter. You'll receive several free books and a sample of his audiobooks, too, just for signing up, you can unsubscribe at any time and you will receive absolutely *no* spam.

Made in United States
North Haven, CT
30 October 2023

43420566R00439